Anne Thackeray

The Writings of Anne Isabella Thackeray

Anne Thackeray

The Writings of Anne Isabella Thackeray

ISBN/EAN: 9783337275396

Printed in Europe, USA, Canada, Australia, Japan

Cover: Foto ©Andreas Hilbeck / pixelio.de

More available books at **www.hansebooks.com**

THE WRITINGS

OF

ANNE ISABELLA THACKERAY.

WITH ILLUSTRATIONS.

NEW YORK:

HARPER & BROTHERS, PUBLISHERS,

FRANKLIN SQUARE.

1870.

CONTENTS.

THE VILLAGE ON THE CLIFF.

DEDICATED TO HARRIET THACKERAY.

Brighton, January 27, 1867.

PREFACE.

WE have all of us in the course of our life's journeys sometimes lived for a little while in places which were wearisome and monotonous to us at the time ; which had little to attract or to interest ; we may have left them without regret, never even wishing to return. But yet as we have travelled away, we may have found that through some subtle and unconscious attraction, sights, sounds, and peculiarities which we thought we had scarcely noticed, seem to be repeating themselves in our brains ; the atmosphere of the place seems to be haunting us, as though unwilling to let us escape. And this peculiar distinctness and vividness does not appear to wear out with time and distance. The pictures are like those of a magic-lantern, and come suddenly out of the dimness and darkness, starting into life when the lamp is lighted by some chance association ; so clearly and sharply defined and colored, that we can scarcely believe that they are only reflections from old slides which have been lying in our store for years past.

The slides upon which this little history is painted, somewhat rudely and roughly, have come from Petitport in Normandy, a dull little fishing-town upon the coast. It stands almost opposite to Ryde, in the Isle of Wight. The place is quite uninteresting, the district is not beautiful, but broad and fertile and sad and pleasant together. The country folks are high-spirited and sometimes gay, but usually grave, as people are who live by the sea. They are a well-grown, stately race, good-mannered, ready and shrewd in their talk and their dealings ; they are willing to make friends, but they are at the same time reserved and careful of what they say English people are little known at Petitport—one or two had staid at the Château de Tracy "dans le temps," they told me, for Madame herself was of English parentage, and so was Madame Fontaine, who married from there. But the strangers who came to lodge in the place for the sake of the sea-bathing and the fine sands were from Caen and Bayeux for the most part, and only remained during a week or two.

Except just on fête-days and while the bathing-time lasted, every thing was very still at Petitport. Sometimes all the men would go away together in the boats, leaving the women and children alone in the village. I was there after the bathing-season was over, and before the first fishing-fleet left. The fishermen's wives were all busy preparing provisions, making ready, sewing at warm clothes, and helping to mend the nets before their husbands' departure. I could see them hard at work through the open doors as I walked up the steep little village street.

There is a precipitous path at the farther end of the village which leads down to the beach below. One comes to it by some steps which descend along the side of a smart little house built on the very edge of the cliff—a "châlet," they call it. It has many windows and weathercocks, and muslin curtains and wooden balconies ; and there is a sort of embankment or terrace-walk halfway to the sea. This was Madame Fontaine's châlet, the people told me—her husband had left it to her in his last will and testament—but she did not inhabit it. I had never seen any one come out of the place except once a fiercely capped maid-servant with beetle brows, who went climbing up the hill beyond the châlet, and finally disappeared over its crest. It seemed as if the maid and the house were destined to be blown right away in time ; all the winds came rushing across the fields and the country, and beating against the hillside, and it was a battle to reach the steps which led down to the quiet below. A wide sea is heaving and flashing at one's feet, as one descends the steep, the boats lie like specks on the shingle, birds go flying wind-blown below one's feet, and the rushing sound of the tide seems to fill the air When I reached the foot of the cliff at last, I looked about for some place to rest. A young countrywoman was sitting not far off on the side of a boat, —a shabby old boat it was, full of water and sand and sea-weed, with a patch of deal in its old brown coat. I was tired, and I went and sat down too.

The woman did not look round or make any movement, and remained quite still, a quiet figure against the long line of coast, staring at the receding tide. Some sailors not far off were shouting to one another, and busy with a fishing-smack which they had dragged up high and dry, and safe from the water. Presently one of the men came plodding up over the shingle, and I asked him if he wanted his boat.

"Even if I wanted it, I should not think of disturbing you and Mademoiselle Reine," answered the old fellow. He had a kindly puzzled weather-beaten face. "Remain, remain," he said.

"Hé, huh!" shouted his companions, filing off, "come and eat." But he paid no attention to their call, and went on talking. He had been out all night, but he had only caught cuttle-fish, he told me. They were not good to eat—they required so much beating before they could be cooked. They seize the boats with their long straggling legs. . . . . "Did I hear of their clutching hold of poor old Nanon Lefebvre the other day, when she was setting her nets? Mademoiselle Reine could tell the long and short of it, for she was on the spot and called for help."

"And you came and killed the beast, and there was an end of it," said Mademoiselle Reine, shortly, glancing round with a pair of flashing bright eyes, and then turning her back upon us once more.

Hers was a striking and heroic type of physiognomy. She interested me then, as she has done ever since that day. There was something fierce, bright, good-humored about her. There was a heart and strength and sentiment in her face—so I thought, at least, as she flashed round upon us. It is a rare combination, for women are not often both gentle and strong. She had turned her back again, however, and I went on talking to the old sailor. Had he had a good season—had he been fortunate in his fishing?

A strange, doubting look came into his face, and he spoke very slowly. "I have read in the Holy Gospels," he said, turning his cap round in his hands, "that when St. Peter and his companions were commanded to let down their nets, they inclosed such a multitude of fishes that their nets brake. I am sorry that the time for miracles is past. I have often caught fish, but my nets have never yet broken from the quantity they contained."

"You are all preparing to start for Dieppe?" I said, to change the subject.

"We go in a day or two," he answered; "perhaps a hundred boats will be starting. We go here, we go there—may be at a league's distance. It is curious to see. We are drifting about; we ask one another, 'Hast thou found the herring?' and we answer, 'No! there is no sign:' and perhaps at last some one says, 'It is at such and such a place.' We have landmarks. We have one at Asnelles, for instance," and he pointed to the glittering distant village, on the tongue of land which jutted into the sea at the horizon. "And then it happens," said the old fellow, "that all of a sudden we come upon what we are searching for. . . . . We have enough then, for we find them close-packed together, like this;" and he pressed his two brown hands against one another.

"And is not that a miracle to satisfy you, Christophe Lefebvre?" said the woman, speaking in a deep sweet voice, with a strange ringing chord in it, and once more flashing round.

"Ah, mademoiselle," he said, quite seriously, "they are but herrings. Now St. Peter caught trout in his nets. I saw that in the picture which you showed me last Easter, when I went up to Tracy. I am only a rough man," he went on, speaking to me again. "I can't speak like those smart gentlemen from Paris, who make 'calembours,' and who have been to college; you must forgive me if I have offended you, or said any thing wrongly. I have only been to one school in our little village; I learnt what I could there. . . . ."

"And to that other school, Christophe," said the deep voice again; and the young woman pointed to the sea.

Then he brightened up. "There, indeed, I have learnt a great many things, and I defy any of those fine gentlemen to teach me a single fact regarding it."

"And yet there are some of them—of the fine gentlemen, as you call them," she said, looking him full in the face, "who are not out of place on board a boat, as you ought to know well enough."

Lefebvre shrugged his shoulders. "Monsieur Richard," he said, "and M. de Tracy too, they liked being on board, and were not afraid of a wetting. Monsieur Fontaine, pauvre homme, it was not courage he wanted. Vous n'avez pas tort, Mademoiselle Reine. Permit me to ask you if you have had news lately of the widow? She is a good and pretty person" (he said to me), "and we of the country all like her."

"She is good and pretty, as you say," answered the young woman, shortly. "You ask me for news, Christophe. I heard some news of her this morning; they say Madame Fontaine is going to be married again." And then suddenly turning away, Mademoiselle Reine rose abruptly from her seat, and walked across the sands out towards the distant sea.

THE VILLAGE ON THE CLIFF.

PREFACE.

WE have all of us, in the course of our life's journeys, sometimes lived for a little while in places which were wearisome and monotonous to us at the time; which had little to attract or to interest; we may have left them without regret, never even wishing to return. But yet, as we have traveled away, we may have found that, through some subtle and unconscious attraction, sights, sounds, and peculiarities which we thought we had scarcely noticed, seem to be repeating themselves in our brains; the atmosphere of the place seems to be haunting us, as though unwilling to let us escape. And this peculiar distinctness and vividness does not appear to wear out with time and distance. The pictures are like those of a magic-lantern, and come suddenly out of the dimness and darkness, starting into life when the lamp is lighted by some chance association, so clearly and sharply defined and colored that we can scarcely believe that they are only reflections from old slides which have been lying in our store for years past. The slides upon which this little history is painted, somewhat rudely and roughly, have come from Petitport, in Normandy, a dull little fishing town upon the coast. It stands almost opposite to Ryde, in the Isle of Wight. The place is quite uninteresting, the district is not beautiful, but broad, and fertile, and sad, and pleasant together. The country folks are high-spirited and sometimes gay, but usually grave, as people are who live by the sea. They are a well-grown, stately race, good-mannered, ready and shrewd in their talk and their dealings; they are willing to make friends, but they are at the same time reserved and careful of what they say. English people are little known at Petitport—one or two had staid at the Château de Tracy "dans le temps," they told me, for Madame herself was of English parentage, and so was Madame Fontaine who married from there. But the strangers who came to lodge in the place for the sake of the sea-bathing and the fine sands were from Caen and Bayeux for the most part, and only remained during a week or two.

Except just on fête-days and while the bathing-time lasted, every thing was very still at Petitport. Sometimes all the men would go away together in their boats, leaving the women and children alone in the village. I was there after the bathing-season was over, and before the first fishing-fleet left. The fishermen's wives were all busy preparing provisions, making ready, sewing at warm clothes, and helping to mend the nets before their husbands' departure. I could see them hard at work through the open doors as I walked up the steep little village street.

There is a precipitous path at the farther end of the village which leads down to the beach below. One comes to it by some steps which descend along the side of a smart little house built on the very edge of the cliff—a "châlet" they call it. It has many windows and weather-cocks, and muslin curtains and wooden balconies, and there is a sort of embankment or terrace-walk half way to the sea. This was Madame Fontaine's châlet, the people told me —her husband had left it to her in his last will and testament—but she did not inhabit it. I had never seen any one come out of the place except once a fiercely-capped maid-servant with beetle brows, who went climbing up the hill beyond the châlet, and finally disappeared over its crest. It seemed as if the maid and the house were destined to be blown right away in time; all the winds came rushing across the fields and the country, and beating against the hill-side, and it was a battle to reach the steps which led down to the quiet below. A wide sea is heaving and flashing at one's feet, as one descends the steep; the boats lie like specks on the shingle; birds go flying wind-blown below one's feet, and the rushing sound of the tide seems to fill the air. When I reached the foot of the cliff at last, I looked about for some place to rest. A young countrywoman was sitting not far off on the side of a boat—a shabby old boat it was, full of water, and sand, and sea-weed, with a patch of deal in its old brown coat. I was tired, and I went and sat down too.

The woman did not look round or make any movement, and remained quite still, a quiet figure against the long line of coast, staring at the receding tide. Some sailors not far off were shouting to one another, and busy with a fishing-smack which they had dragged up high and dry and safe from the water. Presently one of the men came plodding up over the shingle, and I asked him if he wanted his boat.

"Even if I wanted it, I should not think of disturbing you and Mademoiselle Reine," answered the old fellow. He had a kindly puzzled weather-beaten face. "Remain, remain," he said.

"Hé, huh!" shouted his companions, filing off, "come and eat." But he paid no attention to their call, and went on talking. He had been out all night, but he had only caught cuttle-fish, he told me. They were not good to eat—they required so much beating before they could be cooked. They seize the boats with their long straggling legs . . . "Did I hear of their clutching hold of poor old Nanon Lefebvre the other day, when she was setting her nets? Mademoiselle Reine could tell me the long and the short of it, for she was on the spot and called for help."

"And you came and killed the beast, and there was an end of it," said Mademoiselle Reine, shortly, glancing round with a pair of flashing bright eyes, and then turning her back upon us once more.

Hers was a striking and heroic type of physiognomy. She interested me then, as she has done ever since that day. There was something fierce, bright, good-humored about her. There was heart, and strength, and sentiment in her face—so I thought, at least, as she flashed round upon us. It is a rare combination, for women are not often both gentle and strong. She had turned her back again, however, and I went on talking to the old sailor. Had he had a good season—had he been fortunate in his fishing?

A strange doubting look came into his face, and he spoke very slowly. "I have read in the Holy Gospels," he said, turning his cap round in his hands, "that when St. Peter and his companions were commanded to let down their nets, they inclosed such a multitude of fishes that their nets brake. I am sorry that the time for miracles is past. I have often caught fish, but my nets have never yet broken from the quantity they contained."

"You are all preparing to start for Dieppe?" I said, to change the subject.

"We go in a day or two," he answered; "perhaps a hundred boats will be starting. We go here, we go there—may be at a league's distance. It is curious to see. We are drifting about; we ask one another, 'Hast thou found the herring?' and we answer, 'No! there is no sign;' and perhaps at last some one says, 'It is at such and such a place.' We have landmarks. We have one at Asnelles, for instance," and he pointed to the glittering distant village on the tongue of land which jutted into the sea at the horizon. "And then it happens," said the old fellow, "that all of a sudden we come upon what we are searching for . . . We have enough then, for we find them close-packed together like this;" and he pressed his two brown hands against one another.

"And is not that a miracle to satisfy you, Christopher Lefebvre?" said the woman, speaking in a deep sweet voice, with a strange ringing chord in it, and once more flashing round.

"Ah! mademoiselle," he said, quite seriously, "they are but herrings. Now St. Peter caught trout in his nets. I saw that in the picture which you showed me last Easter, when I went up to Tracy. I am only a rough man," he went on, speaking to me again. "I can't speak like those smart gentlemen from Paris, who make 'calembours,' and who have been to college; you must forgive me if I have offended you, or said any thing wrongly. I have only been to one school at our little village; I learnt what I could there . . ."

"And to that other school, Christophe," said the deep voice again; and the young woman pointed to the sea.

Then he brightened up. "There, indeed, I have learnt a great many things, and I defy any one of those fine gentlemen to teach me a single fact regarding it."

"And yet there are some of them—of the fine gentlemen, as you call them," she said, looking him full in the face, "who are not out of place on board a boat, as you ought to know well enough."

Lefebvre shrugged his shoulders. "Monsieur Richard," he said, "and M. de Tracy too, they liked being on board, and were not afraid of a wetting. Monsieur Fontaine, pauvre homme, it was not courage he wanted. Vous n'avez pas tort, Mademoiselle Reine. Permit me to ask you if you have had news lately of the widow? She is a good and pretty person" (he said to me), "and we of the country all like her."

"She is good and pretty, as you say," answered the young woman, shortly. "You ask me for news, Christophe. I had some news of her this morning; Madame Fontaine is going to be married again." And then suddenly turning away, Mademoiselle Reine rose abruptly from her seat and walked across the sands out toward the distant sea.

CHAPTER I.

ADIEU, CHARMANT PAYS.

FIVE o'clock on a fine Sunday — western light streaming along the shore, low cliffs stretching away on either side, with tufted grasses and thin straggling flowers growing from the loose arid soil—far-away promontories, flashing and distant shores, which the tides have not yet overlapped, all shining in the sun. The waves swell steadily inward, the foam sparkles where the ripples meet the sands.

The horizon is solemn dark blue, but a great streak of light crosses the sea; three white sails gleam, so do the white caps of the peasant-women, and the wings of the sea-gulls as they go swimming through the air.

Holiday people are out in their Sunday clothes. They go strolling along the shore, or bathing and screaming to each other in the waters. The countrymen wear their blue smocks of a darker blue than the sea, and they walk by their wives and sweethearts in their gay-colored Sunday petticoats. A priest goes by; a grand lady in frills, yellow shoes, red jacket, fly-away hat, and a cane. Her husband is also in scarlet and yellow. Then come more women and Normandy caps flapping, gossiping together, and baskets and babies, and huge umbrellas. A figure, harlequin-like, all stripes and long legs, suddenly darts from behind a rock, and frisks into the water, followed by a dog barking furiously. More priests go by from the seminary at Asnelles. Then perhaps a sister of charity, with her large flat shoes, accompanied by two grand-looking bonnets.

I believe M. le Sous-préfet himself had been seen on the sands that afternoon by Marion, by Isabeau, by Madame Potier, and all the village, in short. M. le Maire had also been remarked walking with the English gentlemen from the chateau; one pair of eyes watched the two curiously as they went by. The little Englishman was sauntering in his odd loose clothes; Monsieur Fontaine, the maire, tripping beside him with short, quick military steps, neat gaiters, a cane, thread gloves, and a curly-rimmed Panama hat. M. Fontaine was the taller of the two, but the Englishman seemed to keep ahead somehow, although he only sauntered and dragged one leg lazily after the other. Pélottier, the inn-keeper, had been parading up and down all the afternoon with his rich and hideous bride. She went mincing along, with a parasol, and mittens, and gold earrings, and a great gold ring on her fore finger, and a Paris cap stuck over with pins and orange-flowers. She looked daggers at Reine Chrétien, who had scorned Pélottier, and boxed his great red ears, it was said, earrings and all. As for Reine, she marched past the couple in her Normandy peasant dress, with its beautiful old laces and gold ornaments, looking straight before her, as she took the arm of her grandfather, the old farmer from Tracy.

Besides all these grown-up people there comes occasionally a little flying squadron of boys and girls, rushing along, tumbling down, shouting and screaming at the pitch of their voices, to the scandal of the other children who are better brought up, and who are soberly trotting in their small bourrelets, and bibs and blouses, by the side of their fathers and mothers. The babies are the solemnest and the funniest of all, as they stare at the sea and the company from their tight maillots or cocoons.

The country folks meet, greet one another cheerfully, and part with signs and jokes; the bathers go on shouting and beating the water; the lights dance. In the distance, across the sands, you see the figures walking leisurely homeward before the tide overtakes them; the sky gleams whiter and whiter at the horizon, and bluer and more blue behind the arid grasses that fringe the overhanging edge of the cliffs.

Four or five little boys come running up one by one, handkerchief-flying umbrella-bearer ahead to the martial sound of a penny trumpet. The little captain pursues them breathless and exhausted, brandishing his sword in an agony of command. "Soldats," he says, addressing his refractory troops, "soldats, souvenez-vous qu'il ne faut jamais courrir. Soldats, ne courrez pas, je vous en prrrrie—une, deux, trois," and away they march to the relief of a sand fort which is being attacked by the sea. And so the day goes on, and the children play

Among the waste and lumber of the shore.
Hard coils of cordage, swarthy fishing-nets,
Anchors of rusty fluke, and boats updrawn;

and while they build "their castles of dissolving sand to watch them overflow," the air, and the sounds, and the colors in which all these people are moving seem to grow clearer and clearer; you can see the country people clambering the cliffs behind the village, and hear the voices and the laughter of the groups assembled on the embanked market-place. And meanwhile M. le Maire and the Englishman are walking slowly along the sands toward Tracy, with long grotesque shadows lengthening as the sun begins to set.

"I hope you will revisit our little town before long," M. Fontaine was politely remarking to his companion. "I hear that you start to-morrow, and that Madame de Tracy accompanies you."

"My aunt declares she can not possibly go alone," said the Englishman, shrugging his shoulders, and speaking in very good French for an Englishman, "or I should have been glad to stay another week."

"You have not yet visited the oyster-park at Courseulles," said M. le Maire, looking concerned. "It is a pity that you depart so soon."

"I am very unfortunate to miss such a chance," said the Englishman, smiling.

The Maire of Petitport seemed to think this a most natural regret. "Courseulles is a deeply interesting spot," he said. "Strangers travel from far to visit it. You have nothing of the sort in your country, I believe. You would see the education of the oyster there brought to its highest point of perfection. They are most intelligent animals, I am assured; one would not have imagined it. You would see them sorted out according to size, in commodious tanks. Every variety is there—from enormous patriarchal oysters to little baby ones, *en maillot*, I may say. The returns are enormous, I believe. And then you have such a fine air at Courseulles; magnificent plains—a vast horizon—no trees, nothing to interrupt the coup-d'œil. The effect of the moon shining on the marshes and the establishment is really striking."

"I think old Chrétien has a share in the concern," said the Englishman.

"Mademoiselle Reine and her grandfather are very reserved upon the subject, and I have never been able to ascertain exactly what their yearly percentage amounts to," said Fontaine, confidentially holding up one thin hand. "I know that she drives over once a month in her spring-cart to superintend the affairs. She is a person, as you are aware, of great method and order; and, indeed, in affairs, it is absolutely necessary."

"She seems to manage the farm very fairly," said the other. "Old Chrétien is a stupid old fellow, always drinking cider; he don't seem to do much else."

"Alas! no," replied Fontaine. "I look upon drunkenness as a real misfortune. He has told me in confidence that he can not exist without the stimulant of cider. Even Mademoiselle Reine can not persuade him to abandon it."

"I can not imagine any body having any difficulty in refraining from cider," said the other, smiling again. "She was good to give me some the other day, with soupe aux choux; and I confess—"

"Comment, Monsieur Butler! You do not like our cider?" said the maire, looking quite surprised. "It is because you have the taste of your '*potter*' still in your mouth. Come back to us, and I promise to convert you."

"Very well, that is a bargain," said Butler, looking about him a little distractedly. Madame Pélottier, who happened to be passing, imagined that he was admiring her elegance. She drew herself up, stuck out her fore finger, and bowed. The maire, with a brisk glissade, returned the salute.

"I sometimes ask," Fontaine remarked, as he replaced his curly-rimmed hat, "how that excellent fellow, Pélottier, can have married himself with that monstrous person. She brought him, it is true, an excellent dot and a good connection at Caen, also at Bayeux; but in his place nothing would have persuaded me to unite myself with a young lady so disgracious and ill-brought-up."

"Then you have thought of marrying again?" asked Butler, glancing at the spruce figure beside him.

The maire looked conscious, and buttoned his coat. "I once contemplated some proposals," he said, "to a person who was well off, and

who might have made an amiable mother to my child, but the affair came to nothing. I do not mind telling you it was Mademoiselle Chrétien herself that I had in view. After all, why should I marry? Hein? My good mother takes care of my little son; my father-in-law is much attached to him; I have an excellent cuisinière, entirely devoted to our family—you know Justine? Sometimes," said M. Fontaine, gazing at the sea, "a vague feeling comes over me that if I could find a suitable person, life might appear less monotonous, more interesting. I should feel more gay, in better spirits, with the society of an agreeable companion. These are mere reveries, the emotions of a poetic imagination; for where am I to find the person?"

"Is there much difficulty?" said Butler, amused.

"I do not generally mention it, but I do not mind telling you," said M. le Maire, "that our family, through misfortunes—by the stupidity of some, the ill conduct of others—no longer holds the place in society to which it is entitled. But I do not forget that I belong to an ancient race. I would wish for a certain refinement in my future companion which I can not discover among the ladies of the vicinity. There is nothing to suit me at Bayeux; at Caen I may possibly discover what I require. I shall certainly make inquiries on my next visit."

"And so you did not arrange matters with Mademoiselle Reine?" said the Englishman.

"Steps were taken," M. Fontaine replied, mysteriously nodding his head, "but without any result. I, for one, do not regret it. With all her excellent qualities and her good blood —her mother was of a noble house, we all know —there is a certain abruptness—in a word, Mademoiselle Reine is somewhat bourgeoise in her manner, and I am not sorry that the transaction fell through. Old Père Chrétien required me to produce a sum out of all reason. Neither he nor Mademoiselle Reine were in the least accomodating— Ha, Madame Michaud— Madame!" a bow, a flourish of the Panama to a stout old lady with a clean cap and a parasol. The maire had held Butler fast for the last hour, and might have gone on chattering indefinitely, if the Englishman, seeing him involved with his new friend, had not pulled out his watch and escaped, saying he must go home. The maire took a disconsolate leave. Nemesis, in the shape of Madame Michaud, with some wrongs and a great deal to say about them, had overtaken Monsieur le Maire and held him fast prisoner, while Richard Butler marched off with that odd sauntering walk of his, and made the best of his way to the chateau.

He tramped along the foot of the cliff, crunching over sea-weed, and stones, and mussel-shells. He passed old Nanette Lefebvre trimming her nets, sitting in a heap on the sand, with her bare legs in huge wooden sabots, and her petticoats tucked up. Though it was a fête-day, the old fish-wife could not afford to miss her chance of a *bonne aubaine*. "J'allons mettre mes filets à la basse marée," said Nanon, quite contented. "Je vous souhaite le bonsoir, mon petit monsieur." Mr. Hook might have made a pretty sketch of the old brown face with the shrewd black eyes, and the white coif, of the crisp rocks, the blue sea, and the tattered striped petticoat. A peculiar brightness and clearness of atmosphere is like a varnish to the live pictures one meets with at every turn on the shores yonder. The colors are fainter and brighter than in England, the backgrounds lie flat, undiversified, scantily broken by trees, but the figures stand out in pale relief, with a grace, an unconscious pastoral sentiment which is almost unknown among us. Have we not outgrown the charm of tradition, old songs and saws, and ways and appliances, national dress, and simple country life? Faded, battered wire bonnets; vulgarity, millinery, affectation, parasols, crinolines—it seems strange that such things should so surely supersede in time all the dear and touching relics of the by-going still life of our ancestors. Perhaps a day will come when the old charm will exorcise the land again, bringing back its songs and rural poetry, its grace and vanishing sentiment.

It almost appears as if consciousness destroyed and blighted whatever it laid its fatal hand upon. We have all learned to love and admire art in our daily life, and to look for it here and there; but as we look, somehow, and as we exclaim, Here or there behold it! the fairies vanish, the birds fly away, the tranquil silence is broken, the simple unconsciousness is gone forever, and you suddenly awake from your pleasant dream. A ruin inclosed by a wall and viewed with a ticket; a model old woman in a sham rustic cottage at the park gate; even the red cloaks of the village children which the lady at the hall brought down from Marshall and Snellgrove's, when she was in town last Tuesday—all these only become scenes in a pantomime somehow. In these days, one is so used to sham and imitation, and Brummagem, that when by chance one comes to the real thing, it is hard to believe in it. At least so Butler thought as he trudged along.

Presently he began to climb the cliff, and he reached the top at last with the great fields and the sea on either side, and the fresh breezes blowing. He did not go into the village, but turned straight off and strode up the hill. He passed groups all along the road, resting or plodding through the dust. The west was all aglow with sunset, great ranges of cloud-mountains were coming from a distance and hanging overhead in the sky. He beheld fiery lakes, calm seas, wonderful countries. He could see land, and sky, and sea glowing for miles and miles in wreathing vapors of loveliest tint, and golden sunfloods. Butler tradged along, admiring, wondering, and at the same time with his head full of one thing and another.

He was loth enough to go, but there was no help for it. He had been in scrapes and troubles at home, and had come away for a change,

and now he felt he should get into a scrape if he staid, and they had sent for him home again. His uncle, Charles Butler, had paid his debts once more, and his uncle Hervey had written him a lofty and discursive epistle conveying his forgiveness, desiring him to come back to his work and his studio. His aunt, Madame de Tracy, announced that she would accompany him to England, spend a short time with her two brothers, and make the way smooth for her nephew. Madame de Tracy had but ten fingers, but if she had possessed twenty she would have wished to make use of each one of them in that culinary process to which the old proverb alludes. Her efforts had never been successful as far as Butler was concerned.

Dick, as his friends call him, had been cursed with a facility for getting into scrapes all his lifetime. He had an odd fantastic mind, which had come to him no one knew how or why. He was sensitive, artistic, appreciative. He was vain and diffident; he was generous and selfish; he was warm-hearted, and yet he was too much a man of the world not to have been somewhat tainted by its ways. Like other and better men, Dick's tastes were with the aristocracy, his sympathies with the people. He was not strong enough to carry out his own theories, though he could propound them very eloquently, in a gentle drawling voice, not unpleasant to listen to. He was impressionable enough to be easily talked over and persuaded for a time, but there was with it all a fund of secret obstinacy and determination which would suddenly reassert itself, at inconvenient moments sometimes. In that last scrape of his, Dick having first got deeply into debt, in a moment of aberration had proposed to a very plain but good-natured young lady with a great deal of money. He had made the offer at the instigation of his relations, and to quiet them and deliver himself from their persecutions, and he then behaved shamefully, as it is called, for he was no sooner accepted, to his surprise and consternation, than he wrote a very humble but explicit note to the heiress, telling her that the thing was impossible. That she must forgive him if she could, but he felt that the mercenary motives which had induced him to come forward were so unworthy of her and of himself, that the only course remaining to him was to confess his meanness and to throw himself upon her good-nature. Poor Dick! the storm which broke upon his curly head was a terrible one. He had fled in alarm.

His curly head had stood him in stead of many a better quality; his confidence and good manners had helped him out of many a well-deserved scrape, but he was certainly no sinewy hero, no giant, no Titan, like those who have lately revisited the earth—(and the circulating libraries, to their very great advantage and improvement). So far he was effeminate that he had great quickness of perception, that he was enthusiastic and self-indulgent, and shrunk from pain for himself or for others. He had been petted and spoiled in his youth, and he might have been a mere puppet and walking gentleman to this day, if it had not been for that possession, that odd little craze in his mind which seemed to bring him to life somehow, and force him into independence and self-denial; and Charles Butler, his eldest uncle, used to make jokes at him, or occasionally burst out in a fume when Dick gravely assured him he believed himself possessed, and unaccountable for his actions. But, for all his vexation, the old man could not resist the young fellow's handsome face, and his honest, unaffected ways, and his cleverness, and his droll conceit, and humility, and grateful ingratitude, so to speak. His scrapes, after all, were thoughtless, not wicked ones, and so old Butler paid and paid, and preached a little, and jibed a great deal, and offered him regular employment, but Dick would not be regularly employed, would not be helped, would not be made angry; it seemed all in vain to try to influence him.

"**If** your pictures were **worth the canvas,**" the old man would say, "I should be only too thankful to see you so harmlessly occupied; **but** what is this violet female biting an orange, and standing with her toes turned in and her elbows turned out? P. R. B's. I have no patience with the nonsense. Pray, were Sir Joshua, and Lawrence, and Gainsborough, and Romney before Raphael or after? and could they paint a pretty woman, or could they not?"

"They could paint in their way," Dick would answer, twirling his mustache, "and I, probably, can appreciate them better than you can, sir. You haven't read my article in the *Art Review*, I see." And then the two would talk away at one another for an hour or more. It all ended in Dick going his own way, wasting his time, throwing away opportunities, picking up shreds that he seemed to have thrown away, making friends wherever he went with the children of light or of darkness, as the case might be.

As Dick walked along the high road to Tracy this afternoon, he replied to one greeting and another: good-humored-looking women, stepping out by their men-companions, grinned and nodded to him as they passed on; children trotting along the road cried out "Bon-soïr" in the true Normandy sing-song. Butler occasionally interrupted his somewhat remorseful meditations to reply to them. "What a fool he was!" he was thinking. Alas! this is often what people are thinking as they walk for a little way alone along the high road of life. How he had wasted his youth, his time, his chances. Here he was, at eight-and-twenty, a loiterer in the race. He had tried hard enough at times, but life had gone wrong with him somehow. "Why was he always in trouble?" poor Butler asked himself; "dissatisfied, out of pocket and temper? Why was he unhappy now when matters were beginning to brighten, and one more chance offered itself for him to retrieve the past?" He had a terror lest the future should only be a repetition of times gone by—thoughtless imprudence, idle-

ness, recklessness. He thought if he could turn his back upon it all, and take up a new life under another name, he would be well content—**if he could put on a blouse and dig** in the fields **like these sunburnt fellows, and** forget all cares, and anxieties, and perplexities in hard physical labor and fatigue. A foolish, passionate longing for the simpler forms of life had come over him of late. He was sick of cities, of men, of fine ladies, of unsuccessful efforts, of constant disappointment and failure. He was tired of being **tired,** and of the problems of daily life which haunted and perplexed him. Here, perhaps, he might be at peace, living from day to day, and from hour to hour.

And yet he felt that the best and truest part of him, such as it was, was given to his art, and that he would sacrifice every thing, every hope for better things, if he sacrificed to weariness, to laziness—to a fancy—what he would not give up for expediency and success. He was no genius, he could not look for any brilliant future; he was discouraged and out of heart. He blinked with his short-sighted eyes across the country toward a hollow far away, where a farmstead was nestling; he could see the tall roof gleaming among the trees and the stacks. How loth he was to go. He imagined himself driving cattle to market along the dusty roads; bargaining, hiring laborers, digging drains, tossing hay into carts; training fruit-trees, working in the fields. It was an absurdity, and Butler sighed, for he knew it was absurd. He must go whether he would or not; he had seen the last of the place and the people in it; he had tasted of the fruit of the tree of good and of evil; it was too late; he could not be Adam living with his Eve in the Garden of Eden. It was a garden full of apples, bounteous, fruitful, which was spread out before him, stretching from the lilac hills all down to the sea, but it was not the Garden of Eden. Had Eve bright, quick brown eyes, Butler wondered? did she come and go busily? did she make ciders and salads, and light fires of dried sticks in the evenings? Did she carefully pick up the fruit that fell to the ground and store it away? did she pull flowers to decorate her bower with, and feed the young heifers with leaves out of her hand? Did she scatter grain for the fowls of the air? did she call all the animals by their names, and fondle them with her pretty slim fingers? did she, when they had been turned out of Paradise, weave garments for herself and for Adam with a spinning-wheel, as Butler had seen the women use in these parts? Had she a sweet odd voice, with a sort of chord in it? Dick sighed again, and walked on quickly, watching a great cloud-ship high overhead. And as he walked, writing his cares with his footsteps on the dust, as Carlyle says somewhere, a cart which had been jolting up the hill-side passed him on the road.

It was full of country people: a young man with a flower stuck into his cap was driving, an old man was sitting beside him. Inside the cart were three women and some children. One little fellow was leaning right over, blowing a big trumpet and holding a flag. The other children were waving branches and pulling at a garland of vine-leaves, of which one end was dragging; baskets were slung to the shaft below; two dogs were following and barking; while the people in the cart were chanting a sort of chorus as they went jolting along the road.

They sang while the children waved their branches in accompaniment. It looked like a christening party, with the white ribbons and flowers. One of the young women held a little white baby in her arms; another sat as if she was in a boat, holding fast a pretty little curly-headed girl, while the other arm dropped loosely over the side.

As the cart jogged past him, the children recognized Butler, who was well known to them, and they began to call to him and to wave their toys to attract his attention. The two men took off their caps, the women nodded, and went on singing; all except the young woman who had been leaning back—she looked up, smiled, and made the little girl next her kiss her hand to the wayfarer.

"Good-by, Reine," said Butler, in English, starting forward. "I'm going to-morrow."

Reine, jogging away, did not seem to understand what he said. She stretched out her long neck, half turned to the others, then looked back again at Dick. The other two women did not heed her, but went on shrilly chanting—

Si le chemin nous ennuie
L'un à l'autre nous boirons !

And a second verse—

Voici tous gens de courage
Lesquels s'en vont en voyage
Jusque par-de-là des monts
Faire ce pélerinage.
Tous boire nous ne pouvons.
Que la bouteille on n'oublie.
En regrettant Normandie,
En regrettant . . . .

went the chorus, with the men's voices joining in. There was a sudden decline in the hill, and the horses that had been going slowly before set off at a trot. Reine was still leaning back and looking after Butler. Dick never turned his head as he walked quietly on toward Tracy. It seemed to him as if the sun had set suddenly, and that a cold east wind was coming up from the sea.

The cart jogged off toward the farmstead which Dick had seen nestling among the trees —Dick went on his road through the growing dusk. About half an hour later, Madame Michaud, belated and in a great hurry, drove past him in her little open gig; she pulled up, however, to offer him a lift, which Butler declined with thanks.

The road makes a sudden turn about a mile before you reach the chateau, and Dick could perceive the glow of the windows of the old place already beginning to light up. He could also see a distant speck of light in the plain, shining through darker shadow. Had Reine reached home, he wondered? was that the flare of the Colza blaze through the open door of the dwelling, or the lamp placed in the window as a signal to Dominic and her grandfather that the supper was ready? "It is as well I am going to-morrow," Butler ruefully thought once more.

It was almost dark by the time he reached the iron gate of the Château de Tracy, where his dinner was cooking, and his French relations were awaiting his return. They were sitting out—dusky forms of aunts and cousins—on chairs and benches, upon the terrace in front of the old place, enjoying the evening breeze, fresh though it was. English people would have huddled into cloaks and bonnets, or gathered round close up to the wood-fire in the great bare saloon on a night like this; but French people are less cautious and chilly than we are, and indeed there are no insidious damps lurking in the keen dry atmosphere of Normandy, no hidden dangers to fear as with us. To-night the mansarde windows in the high roof, the little narrow windows in the turret, and many of the shuttered casements down below were lighted up brightly. The old house looked more cheerful than in the daytime, when to English eyes a certain mouldiness and neglect seemed to hang about the place. Persons passing by at night, when the lamps were lighted, travelers in the diligence from Bayeux, and other wayfarers sometimes noticed the old chateau blazing by the roadside, and speculated dimly—as people do when they see signs of an unknown life—as to what sort of people were living, what sort of a history was passing, behind the gray walls. There would be voices on the terrace, music coming from the open windows. The servants clustering round the gates, after their work was over, would greet the drivers of the passing vehicles. As the diligence pulled up, something would be handed down, or some one would get out of the interior, and vanish into this unknown existence—the cheerful voices would exchange good-nights. . . . When Richard Butler first came he arrived by this very Bayeux diligence, and he was interested and amused as he would have been by a scene at the play.

It was by this same Bayeux diligence that he started early the next morning after his walk along the cliff. Madame de Tracy, who always wanted other people to alter their plans suddenly at the last moment, and for no particular reason, had endeavored to persuade her nephew to put off his departure for twenty-four hours. But Dick was uneasy, and anxious to be off. He had made up his mind that it was best to go, and this waiting about and lingering was miserable work. Besides, he had received a letter from a friend, who was looking out for him at a certain shabby little hotel at Caen, well known to them both. Dick told his aunt that he would stay there and wait until she came the next day, but that he should leave Tracy by the first diligence in the morning; and for once he spoke as if he meant what he said.

And so it was settled, and Richard packed up his picture overnight, and went off at seven o'clock, without his breakfast, in the rattling little diligence. An unexpected pleasure was in store for him. He found M. Fontaine already seated within it, tightly wedged between two farmers' wives, who were going to market with their big baskets and umbrellas, and their gold earrings and banded caps. M. le Maire was going into Bayeux, "*pour affaire*," he informed the company. But Richard Butler was silent, and little inclined for the conversation which M. Fontaine tried to keep up as well as he could through the handles of the baskets with his English friend, with the other occupants of the vehicle, and with the ladies on his right and his left. He suited his subjects to his auditory. He asked Madame Nicholas if she was going to the fair at Creully, and if she had reason to believe that there would be as much amusement there this year as the last. He talked to Madame Binaud of the concert in the church the week before, and of the sum which M. le Curé had cleared for the entertainment. To Dick he observed, in allusion to his intended journey, "What a wonderful power is *le steam!* You can, if you choose, dine at Paris to-night, and breakfast in London to-morrow morning. What should we do," asked Fontaine, "without the aid of this useful and surprising invention?"

"Eh bien! moi qui vous parle, Monsieur le Maire," said Madame Binaud; "I have never yet been in one of those machines à vapeur, nor do I ever desire to go. Binaud, he went up to Paris last harvest-time, and he came back, sure enough. But I don't like them," said Madame Binaud, shaking her head, and showing her white teeth.

Madame Binaud was a Conservative. She was very stout, and wore a high cap with big flaps that were somewhat out of date. Madame Nicholas was a bright, lively little woman, with a great store of peaches in her basket, a crinoline, a Paris cap, and all the latest innovations.

They went on slowly climbing the hill for some time, and as they turned a corner, Dick caught one more sight of Petitport, all white against the blue sea, and very distinct in the early morning light. Then the diligence rolled on more quickly, and the great towers of Bayeux Cathedral came rising across the plain. Butler looked back again and again, but he could see the village no more. What was the charm which attracted him so strangely to the poor little place? he asked himself. Did he love the country for its own sake, or only for the sake of the people he left there? But the diligence was banging and rattling over the Bayeux stones by this time, and it was no use asking himself any more questions.

"Monsieur," solemnly said Madame Binaud, as she and her friend prepared to get down, "je vous souhaite un bon voyage."

"Bon jour, messieurs!" said Madame Nicholas, cheerfully, while M. Fontaine carefully handed out the ladies' baskets and umbrellas, and a pair of sabots belonging to Madame Binaud.

The maire himself descended at the banker's. It was an old-fashioned porte-cochère, leading into a sunny, deserted court-yard. M. Fontaine stood in the doorway. He was collecting his mind for one last parting effort. "My dear fren'! good voyage," he said in English, waving his Panama, as Dick drove off to the station.

M. Fontaine accomplished his business, and jogged back to Petitport in the diligence that evening, once more in company with Madame Binaud, and Madame Nicholas, who had disposed of her peaches.

"Il est gentil, le petit Monsieur Anglais," said Madame Nicholas. "Anglais, Allemand: c'est la même chose, n'est-ce pas, Monsieur Fontaine?"

"Not at all, not at all; the nations are entirely distinct," says Fontaine, delighted to have an opportunity of exhibiting his varied information before the passengers.

"I should like to know where he has got to by this time," said Madame Binaud, solemnly nodding her stupid old head.

Dick is only a very little way off, sitting upon a pile, and saying farewell for a time to the country he loves. "Adieu, charmant pays de France," he is whistling somewhat dolefully. There is a river, and some people are sitting on some logs of wood which have been left lying along the embankment, there is a dying sunstreak in the west, and the stars are quietly brightening overhead.

The water reflects the sunstreak and the keels of the ships which are moored to the quai. Beyond the quai the river flows across a plain, through gray and twilight mystery toward Paris with its domes and triumphal arches miles and miles away. Here, against the golden-vaulted background, crowd masts, and spires, and gable-roofs like those of a goblin city, and casements from which the lights of the old town are beginning to shine and to be reflected in the water. The old town whose lights are kindling is Caen, in Normandy. The people who are sitting on the logs are some country folks, and two English travelers who have strolled out with their cigars after dinner.

It seems a favorite hour with the Caennois; many townsfolk are out and about. They have done their day's work, their suppers are getting ready by the gleaming gable lights, and before going in to eat, to rest, to sleep, they come to breathe the cool air, to look at the shipping, to peer down into the dark waters, and to stroll under the trees of the Cours. The avenues gloom damp and dark, and vaporous in the twilight, but one can imagine some natures liking to walk under trees at night and to listen to the dreary chirping of the crickets. For English people who have trees and shady groves at home, there are other things to do at Caen besides strolling along the dark Cours. There are the quais, and the quaint old courts and open squares, and the busy old streets all alight and full of life. They go climbing, descending, ascending with gables and corners, where shrines are and turrets with weather-cocks, and bits of rag hanging from upper windows; carved lintels, heads peeping from the high casements, voices calling, pigeons flying and perching, flowers hanging from topmost stories, and then over all these the upward spires and the ivy-grown towers of the old castle standing on the hill, and down below crumbling Roman walls and green moats all luxuriant with autumn garlands. All day long the bright Norman sky had been shining upon the gardens and hillsides, and between the carved stones, and parapets, and high roofs of the city.

Richard Butler had been wandering about all the afternoon in this pleasant confusion of sight, and sound, and bright color. He had missed the friend he expected to meet, but this did not greatly affect him, for he knew he would turn up that night at the hotel—at the table-d'hôte most likely; and, in the mean time, wandering round and about, stopping at every corner, looking into every church, noting the bright pictures, framed as it were in the arches, staring up at the gables, at the quaint wares in the shops; making mental notes of one kind and another, which might be useful some day—he had spent a tranquil solitary afternoon. He had seen a score of subjects: once, sitting on a bench in one of the churches, a side door had opened, and with a sudden flood of light from a green court-yard outside, an old bent woman came in, carrying great bunches of flowers. She came slowly out of the sunlight, and went with dragging step to the altar of the beautiful white Virgin where the tapers were burning. And then she placed the flowers on the altar and crept away. Here was a subject, Butler thought, and he tried to discover why it affected him? A pretty young girl tripping in, blushing with her offering and her petition, would not have touched him as did the sight of this lonely and aged woman, coming sadly along with her fresh wreaths and nosegays. Poor soul! what can she have to pray for? "Her flowers should be withered immortelles," he thought, but the combinations of real life do not pose for effect, and the simple, natural incongruities of every day are more harmonious than any compositions or allusions, no matter how elaborate. Butler thought of Uhland's chaplet, "Es pflückte blümlein männigfalt," and taking out his note-book he wrote down,

"Old people's petitions, St. G. 4 o'clock. Offering up flowers, old woman blue petticoat, white stripe. Pointed Gothic doorway, light from 1 to r through Red St. glass. Uhland."

The next place into which he strolled was a deserted little court of exchange, silent and tenantless, though the great busy street rolled by only a few score yards away. There were statues in florid niches, windows behind, a wonder of carved stonework, of pillars, of polished stems and brackets. It was a silent little nook, with the deep sky shining overhead, and the great black shadows striking and marking out the love-ly ornaments which patient hands had carved and traced upon the stone. It was all very sympathetic and resting to his mind. It was like the conversation of a friend, who sometimes listens, sometimes discourses, saying all sorts of pleasant things; suggesting, turning your own dull and wearied thoughts into new ideas, brightening as you brighten, interesting you, leading you away from the worn-out old dangerous paths where you were stumbling and struggling, and up and down which you had been wandering as if bewitched.

Dick went back to the table-d'hôte at five o'clock, and desired the waiter to keep a vacant seat beside him. Before the soupe had been handed round, another young man, not unlike Dick in manner, but taller and better looking, came strolling in, and with a nod and a smile, and a shake of the hand, sat down beside him.

"Where have you been?" said Dick.

"Looking for you," said the other. "Brittany—that sort of thing. Have you got on with your picture?"

"Yes," Butler answered, "finished it and begun another. You know I'm on my way home. Better come too, Beamish, and help me to look after all my aunt's boxes."

"Which aunt's boxes?" said Beamish, eagerly.

"Not Mrs. Butler's," Dick answered, smiling. "But Catharine is flourishing—at least she was looking very pretty when I came away, and will, I have no doubt, be very glad to see me again."

And then, when dinner was over, and the odd-looking British couples had retired to their rooms, the two young men lighted their cigars, and strolled out across the Place together, went out and sat upon the log, until quite late at night, talking and smoking together in the quiet and darkness.

CHAPTER II.

THE TWO CATHARINES.

THERE are some things dull, and shabby, and uninteresting to one person, which to another are all shining with a mysterious light and glamour of their own. A dingy London hall, with some hats on pegs, a broad staircase with a faded blue and yellow Turkey carpet, occasionally a gloomy echoing of distant plates, and unseen pots and pans in the kitchens below; a drawing-room up above, the piano which gives out the usual tunes over and over again, like a musical snuff-box; the sofa, the table, the side-table, the paper-cutter, the *Edinburgh*, and the *Cornhill*, and the *Saturday Review*; the usual mamma, with her lace cap, sitting on the sofa, the other lady at the writing-table, the young man just going away standing by the fireplace, the two young ladies sitting in the window with waves of crinoline and their heads dressed. The people outside the window passing, repassing, and driving through Eaton Square, the distant, unnoticed drone of an organ, the steeple of St. Peter's Church. This one spot, so dull, so strange to Madame de Tracy after her own pleasant green pastures, so like a thousand others to a thousand other people, was so unlike to one poor little person I know of; its charm was so strange and so powerful that she could scarcely trust herself to think of it at one time. In after years she turned from the remembrance with a constant pain and effort, until at last by degrees the charm traveled elsewhere, and the sunlight lit up other places.

My little person is only Miss George, a poor little twenty-year-old governess, part worried, part puzzled, part sad, and part happy too, for mere youth and good spirits. You can see it all in her round face, which brightens, changes, smiles, and saddens many times a day. She catches glimpses of the Paradise I have been describing as she runs up and down stairs in pursuit of naughty, refractory Augusta, or dilatory little Sarah, or careless Lydia, who has lost her lesson, and her pinafore, and her pocket-handkerchief, or of Algy, whose life hangs by a leather strap as he slides up and down the precipitous banisters, and suspends himself from the landing by various contrivances of his own. "What a noise those children are making," says the aunt, looking up from her letter to the mamma in the drawing-room. The young man shuts the door as the little person goes past flying after Algy; she captures him and brings him back, a sulky little prisoner, to the school-room on the stairs, where she herself, under the grand-sounding title of "governess," is a prisoner too. In this Domestic Bastile, with its ground-glass windows, from which escape is impossible—for they look into the areas deep down below, and into mews where there are horses and coachmen constantly passing—all the ancient terrors and appliances are kept up. Solitary confinement, the Question by Torture (Pinnock, Mangnall, etc., are the names given by the executioners to the various instruments). The thumb-screw stands in one corner of the room, with a stool which turns round and round, according to the length of the performer's legs; a registry is kept of secret marks where the various crimes and offenses are noted down. Heavy fines are supposed to be levied; utter silence and implicit obedience are requested. But all this is only in theory after all; the prisoners have conspired, mutinied, and carried every thing before them since Miss George's dominion set in. She presides in her official chair by the table, with her work in her hand, looking very bright and pretty, and not in the least like a governess. All the things about her look like a school-room —the walls, and the maps, and the drugget, and the crumpled chintz. There are a few brown-paper books in the cases, and there is a worn-out table-cover on the table, and a blotted ink-stand. There are blots every where, indeed, inside the books, on the chairs, under the table, on the ceiling, where ingenious

Algy, with a squirt, has been able to write his initials and those of Miss Cornelia Bouchon, a former governess; there are blots on the children's fingers and elbows, and on Sarah's nose, and all over Augusta's exercise; only Miss George seems free from the prevailing epidemic.

There she sits, poor little soul! round-faced, dark-eyed; laughing sometimes, and scolding at others; looking quite desperate very often, as her appealing glances are now cast at Algy, now at Augusta or Lydia, as the case may be. Little Sarah is always good and gives no trouble; but the other three are silly children, and tiresome occasionally. The governess is very young and silly, too, for her age, and quite unfitted for her situation. To-day the children are especially lively and difficult to deal with. An aunt arriving in a cab, with a French maid with tall gray boxes; with chocolate in her bag; with frizz curls and French boots, and a funny-looking bonnet; welcomings, embracings, expeditions proposed; Dick with a bag slung across his shoulder; the spare room made ready, a dinner-party to-morrow, the play on Thursday, Augusta and Lydia to appear at breakfast in their afternoon dresses—(so Streatton, their mother's maid, had decreed): all this is quite enough to excite such very excitable young people. Algy nearly dislocates every joint in his body; Augusta reads her history in a loud, drawling voice, without paying attention to the stops, and longs to be grown up like Catharine and Georgie. Lydia ponders on her aunt's attire, and composes rich toilets in the air for herself, such as she should like to wear if she were married, and a French countess like her aunt Matilda. Sarah nibbles her chocolate and learns her poetry distractedly; even Miss George finds it difficult to keep up her interest in the battle of Tewkesbury which happened so many years ago, when all sorts of exciting things are going on at that very instant, perhaps, just outside the school-room door. . . .

There is a sound of rustling, of voices, of discussion. Presently the mother's voice is raised above the rest. "Catharine, make haste; the horses are here," she calls.

Miss George blushes up and says, with a little cough, "Go on, my dear Gussie."

"Kitty," cries another voice, "don't forget to leave the note for Dick."

And Miss George gives another little gulp. It is very foolish; she does not know how foolish and how much she minds it, or I think she would try to struggle against the feeling. She, too, used to be called "Kitty," "Cathy," "Catharine," once upon a time when she was seventeen. But that was three years ago, and no one ever says any thing but "Miss George" now, except Algy, who sometimes cries out, "Hullo, George, you have got another new bonnet!" Even that is better than being a "Miss" always, from one day's end to another, and from morning to night, poor little "George" thinks.

All day long, it seems to her, outside the school-room door she hears voices calling—fathers, mothers, brothers and sisters—

"Catharine, the horses are here! Catharine, we are all waiting for you! Catharine, some flowers have come for you!"

As I have said, the school-room was on the drawing-room stairs, and the children and the governess could hear all that passed. It did seem a little hard sometimes that all the happiness and love, and all the fun and delight of life, and the hope, and the care, and the protection, should be for one Catharine—all the hard work, and the struggles, and loneliness, and friendlessness for the other. Music, bright days, pleasant talk, sympathy, pearls, turquoises, flowers, pretty things, beautiful dresses, for one—only slate-pencils scratching, monotony, silence, rules, rulers, ink-blots, unsatisfied longings, illwritten exercises, copy-books, thumbed-out dictionaries, for the other. There are days when Miss George finds it very hard to listen with lively interest to Augusta's reluctant account of the battle of Tewkesbury. The sun shines, the clock ticks, birds hop up on the window-ledge, pens scratch on the paper, people come and talk outside the door, every thing happens to distract. Thoughts come buzzing and fancies bewilder.

"That is Mr. Beamish's voice," Lydia would say, picking up her ears. "How often he comes."

"No, it is cousin Dick," said Augusta; "he is going to ride out with them. Oh, how I wish they would take me too."

"Go on, my dear, with your reading," says the governess, sternly.

"'She advanced through the counties of Devon, Somerset, and Gloucester, increasing her army on each day's march,'" says the little lectress, in a loud, disgusted voice; "'each day's . . . but was at last overtaken by the rapid—the rapid and expeditious Edward—'"

"It *is* Mr. Beamish, Miss George," said Lydia, complacently.

"And then Mrs. Butler was heard through the keyhole, saying, "We must dine at six o'clock, and mind you bring Richard, M. Beamish. Tell him his aunt, Madame de Tracy, desires him to come."

"Go on, my dear," says Miss George.

"'On the banks of the Severn,'" Augusta continues. And there the armies apparently come to a dead stop, for some one is heard to say something about "the children too."

"Certainly not," replies the mother's voice, and so Gussie begins again in crestfallen tones:

"'The Lancastrians were here totally defeated. The Earl of Devonshire and Lord Wenloc were killed on the field. The Duke of Somerset and about twenty other persons of distinction, having taken shelter in a church, were surrounded, dragged out, and immediately beheaded.'"

"Miss George, have you ever seen an execution?" says Sarah.

"*I* should like to see one," says Algy, in an off-hand way. "I shall get papa to take me, or cousin Dick. I'm sure he will, if I ask him."

"You horrid children!" says Miss George; "how can you talk about such dreadful things. Please, dear Algy, do your sum, and don't draw blocks and heads. Go on, Augusta."

"'Queen Margaret and her son were taken prisoners,'" said Augusta, "'and brought to the king, who asked the prince, after an insulting manner, how he dared to invade his dominions.

"'The young prince, more mindful of his high birth than of his present fortune, replied that he came thither to claim his just inheritance; the ungenerous Edward, insensible to pity, struck him on the face with his gauntlet'"—

"Oh!" says Sarah, reproachfully—"'and the Dukes of Clarence and Glou—'" But here the door opened, and instead of heroic and unfortunate princes, of kings savage and remorseless, of wicked uncles and fierce bearded barons, and heart-broken and desperate queens, a beautiful young lady came into the room in a riding-habit, smiling, with her gold hair in a net. This was poor Catharine's shadow, her namesake, the happy Catharine, who haunted, and vexed, and charmed her all at once, who stood in the open door-way, with all the sunshine behind her, and who was saying it was her birthday, and the little prisoners were to be set free.

"You will be able to go and see your sisters, Miss George," Miss Butler says, smiling, for mamma is going to take the children out to lunch and for all the afternoon."

"And where are you going to? tell me, tell me, Kitty, please tell me," says Augusta, flinging her arms round her.

"I am going to ride in the park with papa, and Georgie, and Mr. Beamish," said Catharine, "and this afternoon aunt Matilda wants us to go to Sydenham with her."

"What fun you do have, to be sure!" said Augusta, with a long groan.

And then one of the voices as usual cries, "Catharine, Catharine," from below, and smiling once more, and nodding to them, the girl runs down stairs into the hall, where her father and the others are waiting, impatient to ride away into the bright summer parks.

The children went off much excited half an hour later, Augusta chattering, Lydia bustling and consequential, and carrying a bag; Algy indulging in various hops, jerks, and other gymnastic signs of content; Sarah saying little, but looking all round eyes and happiness. Lunch with their cousins—shopping with mamma—the Zoological Gardens—buns for the bears—nuts for the monkeys—there seemed to be no end of delights in store for them as they tripped down stairs all ribbon-ends and expectation.

"Good-by, Miss George," cried Lydia.

"Good-by, horrid school-room," said Augusta.

"I do so like going out with mamma! wish I always did," said little Sarah.

The children were not unkind, but they would

have naturally preferred feeding monkeys to do-ing long-division sums with an angel from heaven, and poor Catharine, who was only a mortal after all, wrinkled up her eyebrows and sighed. But her momentary ill-humor was gone in an instant. From her place on the landing she heard the lightful liberty before her. It was all sunny and silent. The pots and pans down below were at rest for once, and hanging quietly upon their pegs. The bedroom doors were open, the study was empty; there was no one in the drawing-room when she looked in, only the sun beating

The two Catharines.

start — the brief squabble with which children invariably set off — the bland maternal inter-ference . . . .

The carriage-wheels rolled away, the door closed, and Catharine found herself all alone in a great empty house, with an afternoon of de-upon the blinds and pouring in through the con-servatory window.

Catharine brought away a Tennyson and a *Saturday Review*, and came back into the school-room again, and sat down upon the little shabby sofa. She was not long in making up her mind as to what she should do with her precious hours of liberty. Her two little sisters filled every spare thought and moment in Catharine's busy life, and her poor little heart yearned toward the grim house in Kensington Square, with the five narrow windows, and the prim-looking wire-blinds, behind which Rosy and Totty's curly heads were bobbing at work and at play, as the case might be.

As Catharine waited, resting in the school-room for a few minutes, she thought, with one more envious sigh, how she wished that she, too, had a large open carriage to drive off in. She longed—it was silly enough—to be the happy, fortunate Catharine, instead of the hard-working, neglected one. She thought how tired she was, and of the long, hot Kensington Road; she thought of the other Catharine riding away through the Park, in her waving gray habit, under the bright green trees, with that kind, red-bearded Mr. Beamish curvetting beside her. It is only an every-day story—one little pig goes to market, another stays at home. One eats bread and butter, another has none, and cries squeak, squeak, squeak. The clock struck one meanwhile. It was no use going off to her sisters until after their dinner; luncheon was not ready yet, and Catharine threw herself down at full length upon the sofa, and opened the paper she had brought off the drawing-room table. In at the window some sweet sultry summer air came blowing through a smutty lilac-tree. There was a clinking of pails and heavy footsteps. She read the review of a novel, of a new book of poetry, and then she turned to an essay. It was something about women and marrying, about feebleness and inaptitude, and missing their vocation; about the just dislike of the world for the persons who could not conduce to its amusement or comfort. Catharine pushed it away impatiently. She did not want to read in black and white what she knew so well already—what she had to read always in the black and white of day and of night—what with unconscious philosophy she tried so hard to ignore.

A poor little thing, just beginning life with all the worlds and dreams of early youth in her heart, chafing, and piteously holding out her soft little hands against the stern laws of existence. No wonder she turned from the hard sentences. Any body seeing the childish face, the gentle little movements, the pretty little hands which had just flung the paper away, would have been sorry for her. Catharine did not look even her twenty years, for she was backward and scarcely full-grown. She looked too young and too childish, one might have thought, to be sent out by fate and respectable references into the world. One might have thought that she should have had older and wiser heads to think for her, kind hands to pull her out of difficulties, kind hearts to cherish her. She should have been alternately scolded and taken for treats, like the children; sent to bed early, set lessons to learn—other than those hard ones which are taught with stripes, and learned only with pain-

B

ful effort. Thus, at least, it would have seemed to us small moralizers looking on from our fancy-ware repositories, where right and wrong, and oughts, and should-have-beens, are taken down from the shelf and measured out so liberally to supply the demand. . . . Half a yard of favor for this person—three quarters of trimming for that one—slashings let into one surtout of which we do not happen to fancy the color—or, instead of slashings, loopholes, perhaps, neatly inserted into another; blue ribbons, gold cords and tassels, and rope-ends—there is no end to our stock, and the things we dispense as we will upon our imaginary men and women: we give them out complacently and without hesitation, and we would fain bestow the same measure in like manner upon the living people we see all about us. But it is in vain we would measure out, dispense, approve, revoke. The fates roll on silent, immutable, carrying us and our various opinions along with them, and the oughts and shoulds, and praises and blamings, and the progress of events.

There was a great deal of talking and discussion about little Catharine at one time—of course the family should have provided for the three girls; her step-mother's relations ought to have adopted Catharine, since she had no relations of her own; Mrs. Buckington was well-off; Lady Farebrother had more money than she knew what to do with; but it all ended in the little step-sisters being put to school, and in Catharine obtaining an excellent situation through an advertisement in *The Times*. She got sixty pounds a year, and as she owned the interest of a thousand pounds besides, she was rich for a governess. But then she helped to pay for her sisters' schooling. She could not bear them to go to the cheap and retired establishment Lady Farebrother had suggested. The aunts did not insist when Catharine offered to pay the difference. People said it was a shame, but only what might have been expected of such worldly, pushing, disagreeable women as Mrs. Buckington and her sister, and so the matter ended. And so little Catharine at nineteen set to work for herself. She came—a blushing, eager little thing—to a certain house in Eaton Square to earn her own living, to help those who were most dear to her, to teach Mrs. Butler's children a great many things she had never learned herself. What a strange new world it was! of stir, of hard work, of thoughts and feelings undreamt of in the quiet old days, before she left her home; running in the garden, playing with her little sister in the old wainscoted hall—only yesterday, so it appeared—adoring her step-mother, being naughty sometimes, being loved and happy always—this was all her experience; so small, so even, so quiet, that it seemed as though it might have lasted for years to come; instead of which now already all was over, and the tranquil memories were haunting poor little Catharine as sadly as though they were of sorrow, of passion, of stirring events.

She had staid in Eaton Place for a year and

more, depending for subsistence on her own exertions, for sympathy on a dream or two, for
love, and home, and family on two little school-
girls, whose pencil-notes she read over and over
again on the many long days when she could
not fly off to Mrs. Martingale's school in Kensington Square to see two little ugly girls, who
would rush into the room and spring into her
arms with as many jumps of delight as Algy himself. Catharine used to tell them every thing,
and depended upon them for advice and assistance in all her difficulties. She had a way of
clinging to every support and outstretched hand
which came in her road. She had lived too
long with her step-mother not to have learned
from her to trust and believe in every one who
made any advance, or who seemed in the least
inclined to be kind and helpful. If she had to
pay for this credulity, it is hard to say what
price would be too great to give for it, it is worth
in itself so much. Time after time, when any
one spoke by chance a few good-natured words,
and seemed to ask with some small interest how
she was, how her sisters were, how she liked her
situation, and so forth, her foolish little heart
would leap with gratitude. "Here is a friend
indeed," she would think to herself; "I see it
in her face, in his manner. Oh, how fortunate
I am—how good people are." And then the
good-natured person would go away and forget
all about the little governess, unconscious of the
bitter pang of longing disappointment he or she
had inflicted.

Meanwhile time went on: Catharine had
worked very hard for many weeks, kept her
temper, made the best of troublesome times,
and struggled bravely in her small little feeble
way, and she began to feel a little tired, as people do sometimes, a little lonely and injured;
she was not quite so simple, cheery, unconscious,
as she had been when she first came, and the
way in which people change and fail under vexation and worry has always seemed to me the
saddest part of pain. The Butlers were very
kind to her, but she lived by herself in the big
busy house, and if she dreamed and longed for
companionship and sympathy that might not be
hers, one can not blame her very harshly. Catharine thought that it was because she was a governess that such things were denied to her; she
did not know then that to no one—neither to
governesses, nor pupils, nor parents—is that full
and entire sympathy given for which so many
people—women especially—go seeking all their
lives long.

For all this discouraging doctrine, a happy
golden hour came to the little weary Catharine
in her school-room this afternoon.

The sympathetic friend who could rouse the
downcast heart and understand its need, the
mighty enchanter whose incantations could be-
witch the wearied little spirit from every-day
life and bondage, and set it free for a time,
was at hand. Catharine opened the book she
had brought, and immediately the spell began to
work. She did not see herself, or her troubles,

or the shabby school-room walls any more, but
suddenly there appeared King Arthur sitting
high in hall, holding his court at Caerleon upon
Usk. It was Prince Geraint who issued from a
world of wood, and, climbing upon a fair and
even ridge, a moment showed himself against
the sky. It was the little town gleaming in the
long valley, and the white fortress and the castle in decay; and presently it was some one
yard it was some one singing as the sweet voice
of a bird—"Turn, fortune, turn thy wheel; our
hoard is little, but our hearts are great." Catharine read on, and Enid rode away all dressed
in faded silk, and then Catharine went following too, through many a woodland pass, by
swamps, and pools, and wilds, through dreamy
castle halls, and out into the country once more,
where phantom figures came and fell upon Geraint. False Doorm, and Edyrn, wild Limours
on his black horse, like the thunder-cloud whose
skirts are loosened by the rising storm . . . The
shadowy arms struck without sound, clashing
in silence. Great fresh winds from a distance
were blowing about the room; the measured
musical tramp of the rhythm was ringing in her
ears; there was a sort of odd dazzle of sunlight
of martial strains very distant; the wheel of
fortune was making a pumping noise in the
court of the castle outside; and in the midst of
it all the door opened, and some one—it might
have been Geraint—walked in. For a moment
Catharine looked up, dreaming still. It only
took an instant for her to be metamorphosed
into a governess once more.

"They are all gone out, Mr. Butler," she
said. "Mr. and Miss Butler are riding to Caerleon, but they will be back to lunch."

Catharine, who had quite recovered her every-
day composure, wondered why young Mr. Butler smiled as he glanced at the little green volume in her hand. He was not so good-looking
a man as Prince Geraint — he was not so broad
or so big; he had fair curly hair, a straight
nose, sleepy gray eyes, and a smart little mustache. He was dressed like a young man of
fashion, with a flower in his coat.

"I am afraid I can't wait till they come
in," Richard said. "Perhaps you would let
them know that it is to-morrow, not Thursday,
I want them to drink tea at my place, and the
children too. Please tell them I shall be excessively disappointed if any body fails me.
Good-morning, Miss James," said Richard, affably, "I see you are reading my book of
Idylls."

Butler ran down stairs, thinking as he went
"Why do people ever choose ugly governesses?
My aunt's Miss James is a little dear. Riding
to Caerleon. She didn't know what she was
saying. I should like to see my uncle Hervey
accoutred as a knight of Arthur's round table.
Poor old Hervey!"

As for "Miss James," as Richard called her,
she looked into the beginning of the book, and
saw R. X. B., in three whirligig letters, all curling up into one corner of the page. She blushed

up now all by herself. "I wish people would not speak to one in that affable, joking voice," she thought; and she did not read any more, but went and put the book back on the drawing-room table, where it had been lying for months past.

At luncheon she duly gave her message. Only Mr. Butler and his two daughters, hungry, blown about, cheerfully excited by their morning's expedition, were present.

Mr. Butler was the usual middle-aged Englishman, with very square-toed boots and grizzly whiskers. He was fond of active pursuits. He talked gossip and statistics. He naturally looked to his older brother Charles, who had never married, to assist him with his large family. Daughters grown up, and growing daily, tempestuous school-boys at Eton, a midshipman, two wild young fellows in India, another very promising stupid son at college, who had gone up for his little go with great *éclat*, Mr. Butler would tell you. There was no end to the young Butlers. But, unfortunately, Charles Butler greatly preferred Dick to any of his brother's sons. The boy was like his mother, and a look in his eyes had pleaded for him often and often when Dick himself wondered at his uncle's forbearance. Now the cousins only resembled their father, who greatly bored Charles Butler with his long stories and his animal spirits.

"We must go without mamma, if it is to be to-morrow," said Catharine Butler.

"We could not possibly go without a chaperone," said Georgina, who was great on etiquette. She was not so pretty as Catharine, and much more self-conscious.

"Capital cold beef this is," said Mr. Butler. "Can't Matilda play chaperone for the occasion? By-the-by, Catharine, I am not sorry to hear a good report of your friend Mr. Beamish. I can't afford any imprudent sons-in-law. Remember that, young ladies."

"Should you like Dick, papa?" said Georgie, with a laugh.

"Humph! that depends," said her father, with his mouth full of cold beef. "I should have thought my brother Charles must be pretty well tired out by this time, but I believe that if he were to drop to-morrow, Dick would come in for Muttondale and Lambswold. Capital land it is, too. I don't believe my poor boys have a chance—not one of them. Down, Sandy, down." Sandy was Catharine's little Scotch terrier, who also was fond of cold beef.

"Dick is such a dear fellow," said Catharine Butler, looking very sweet and cousinly, and peeping round the dish-covers at her father. "Of course, I love my brothers best, papa, but I can understand Uncle Charles being very fond of Richard."

"Oh, Richard is a capital good fellow," said Mr. Butler (not quite so enthusiastically as when he spoke of the beef a minute before). "Let him get hold of any thing he likes, and keep it if he can. I, for one, don't grudge him his good fortune. Only you women make too much of him, and have very nearly spoilt him among you. Painting and music is all very well in its way, but, mark my words, it may be pushed too far." And with this solemn warning the master of the house filled himself a glass of sherry, and left the room.

Miss George, as she tied on her bonnet-strings after luncheon, was somewhat haunted by Dick's sleepy face. The vision of Geraint, and Launcelot, and Enid, and King Arthur's solemn shade, still seemed hovering about her as she went along the dusty road to Kensington, where two little figures were beckoning from behind the iron rail of their school-house yard. Presently the children's arms were tightly clutched round Catharine's neck, as the three went and sat down all in a heap on Mrs. Martingale's gray school-house sofa, and there chattered, and chirped, and chirruped for an hour together, like little birds in a nest.

CHAPTER III.

BY THE RIVER.

CATHARINE had forgotten her morning visions; they had turned into very matter-of-fact speculations about Totty's new hat and Rosa's Sunday frock, as she came home through the park late in the afternoon. A long procession of beautiful ladies was slowly passing, gorgeous young men were walking up and down and along the Row, looking at the carriages and parasols, and recognizing their acquaintances. The trees and the grass were still green and in festive dress; the close of this beautiful day was all sweet, and balmy, and full of delight for those who could linger out in the long daylight. The Serpentine gleamed through the old elm-trees and in the slant sun-rays. Catharine was delighted with the sweet fresh air and childishly amused by the crowd, but she thought she had better get out of it. As she was turning out of the broad pathway by one of the small iron gates of the park, she came face to face with Dick Butler walking with a couple of friends. He took off his hat as he passed, and Miss George again bowed with the air of a meek little princess.

"Who is that?" said Beamish. "I don't know her."

Mr. Beamish was destined to improve his acquaintance, for there came a little note from Mrs. Butler to Dick early next morning.

"MY DEAR RICHARD,—I am very sorry to find that I can not possibly join your party this afternoon, but the girls and your aunt will be delighted to come. The children declare you would be horribly disappointed if they did not make their appearance. I am afraid of their being troublesome. May I send Miss George to keep them in order? They are beyond their sisters' control, I fear.

"Ever affectionately yours,

"S. BUTLER.

"P.S.—Will not you and Mr. Beamish be amiable and look in upon us this evening? you will find some friends."

Dick's studio was in Queen's Walk. He lived in one of those old brown houses facing the river. He could see the barges go by, and the boats and the steamers sliding between the trees which were planted along the water-side. An echo of the roar of London seemed passing by outside the ancient gates of his garden; within every thing was still and silent, and haunted by the past. An old daïs of Queen Anne's time still hung over his doorway, and he was very proud of his wainscoted hall and drawing-room, and of the oaken stairs which led up to his studio. His friend lived with him there. Mr. Beamish was in the Foreign Office, and had good expectations. As he was an only son and had been very rigidly brought up, he naturally inclined to Dick, and to his Bohemian life, and the two young men got on very well together. The house had been a convent school before they came to it, and gentle black-veiled nuns had slid from room to room, rosy ragged children had played about the passages and the oaken hall, and had clattered their mugs and crumbled their bread and butter in the great bow-windowed dining-room at the back. The young men had seen the place by chance one day, were struck by its quaintness and capabilities, and they agreed to take it together and to live there. The children and the nuns went away through the iron gates. Butler put workmen in to repair, and polish, and make ready, and then he came and established himself, with his paint-pots and canvases.

The studio was a great long room, with a cross-light that could be changed and altered at will, for which purpose heavy curtains and shutters had been put up. There was matting on the floor, and some comfortable queer-shaped chairs were standing round the fireplace. The walls were paneled to about four feet from the ground, and from hooks, and nails, and brackets hung a hundred trophies of Butler's fancies and experiences. Pictures begun and never finished, plaster casts, boxing-gloves, foils, Turkish pipes and cimeters, brown jugs of graceful slender form, out of Egyptian tombs. Bits of blue china, and then odd garments hanging from hooks, Venetian brocades of gold and silver, woven with silk, and pale and strange-colored stuffs and gauzes, sea-green, salmon-color, fainting-blue, and saffron and angry orange-browns. English words can not describe the queer, fanciful colors.

There was a comfortable sofa with cushions, and a great soft carpet spread at one end of the room, upon which the tea-table stood, all ready laid with cakes and flowers. Beamish had gone out that morning and bought a wagon-load of flowers for the studio and the balcony. There was a piano in a dark corner of the room, where the curtains cast a gloom, but the windows on the balcony were set wide open, and with a rush, carrying its swift steamers, and boats, and burdens. The distant banks gleamed through the full-leaved branches, a quiet figure stood here and there under the trees, watching the flow of the stream. It was a strange, quaint piece of mediæval life set into the heart of to-day. The young men should have worn powder and periwigs, or a still more ancient garb. In the church near at hand a martyr lies buried, and it is the old by-gone world that every thing tells of—as the river flows past the ancient houses. Presently the clock from the steeple of old St. Mary's Church clanged out, and at that very instant there was a loud ring at the bell. Beamish started up. Dick looked over the balcony. It was only the punctual children, who had insisted upon starting much too soon, and who had been walking up and down the street, waiting until it should be time for them to make their appearance.

"Do you know, we very nearly didn't come at all, Dick?" they instantly began telling him from down below in the hall. "Mamma said she couldn't come, and Miss George didn't want to—did you, Miss George? and they said we should be a bother; and we were afraid we were late, but we weren't." All this was chiefly in Algy's falsetto. Lydia joined in: "Wouldn't you have been disappointed if we had not come, Dick? and why have you hung up all these little things?"

"They are kitchen plates and old clothes," says Algy, splitting with laughter; "and some foils—oh, jolly."

"Algy," said Miss George, very determined and severe, because she was so shy, "remember that I am going to take you away if you are troublesome."

"He won't be troublesome, Miss George. He

never is," said Dick, good-humoredly. "Look here! won't you sit down?" and he pushed forward the enormous tapestried chair in which he had been lounging. Catharine sat down. She looked a very small little person in her white gown, lost in the great arm-chair. She glanced round curiously with her bright eyes, and forgot her rôle of governess for a minute.

"How delightful the river is—what a dear old place!" she said in her plaintive childish voice. "What nice china!"—she happened to have a fancy for bowls and cracked tea-pots, and had kept the key of her step-mother's china-closet. "This is Dutch, isn't it?" she asked. And then she blushed up shyly, and felt very forward all of a sudden.

"Here is a nice old bit," said Beamish, coming up to Dick's assistance with a hideous tureen he had picked up a bargain. "Butler and I are rival collectors, you know."

"Are you?" said Catharine, blushing again.

"Yes," said Beamish. And then there was a pause in the conversation, and they heard the river rushing, and both grew shyer and shyer.

Meanwhile Dick was going about with the children, who had fortunately preserved their composure, and who seemed all over the place in a minute.

"And now show us something else," said Algy. "Miss George!" he shouted, "I mean to be an artist like Dick—when I'm a man."

"What a brilliant career Algy is chalking out for himself, isn't he, Beamish?" said poor Dick.

"He might do worse," Beamish answered, kindly. "You must let Miss George see your picture. He has painted a capital picture this time, Miss George."

Dick had modestly turned it with its face to the wall. "They don't want to see my picture," said Dick; and he went on pulling one thing out after another, to the delight of the three little girls who stood all in a row, absorbed in his wonderful possessions. Algy was inspecting a lay figure, and quite silent and entranced by the charming creature. Poor little Miss George, meanwhile, sat in her big chair, growing shyer and shyer every minute; she was longing for the others to appear. Perhaps Beamish also was looking out for them.

They came at last, with a roll of wheels, a rustle, some gentle laughter and confusion on the stairs, and the two young fellows rushed down to receive their guests. Georgie was in olive, and had her affected manner on; Catharine Butler was all in a light gray cloud from head to foot, and looked like a beautiful apparition as she came under the curtain of the door, following her aunt. Madame de Tracy was bustling in, without any poetic or romantic second thoughts, exclaiming at every thing she saw—delighted with the convenience of the house. She was unlike Mrs. Butler in the sincere and unaffected interest she took in all sorts of other people's schemes, arrangements, money-matters

and love-makings, lodgings, and various concerns.

"But how well off you are here, Dick! I congratulate you! you must feel quite cramped at Tracy after this. Catharine, look at that river and the flowers . . . Is it not charming? You are quite magnificent; my dear Dick, you are receiving us like a prince!"

"Beamish got the flowers," said Richard, smiling; "I only stood the cakes. Now, then, Catharine, you must make tea, please."

They all went and sat round the tea-table in a group. Madame de Tracy and Georgina were upon the sofa. The children were squatting on the floor, while Miss George stood handing them their cakes and their tea, for Dick's chairs were big and comfortable, but not very numerous. Catharine Butler, with deft, gentle fingers, dipped the china into the basin, poured water from the kettle with its little flame, measured, with silver tongs and queer old silver spoons, the cream and sugar into the fragrant cups. She might have been the priestess of the flower-decked altar, offering up steaming sacrifices to Fortune. Beamish secretly pledged her in the cup she handed him with her two hands, and one of her bright sudden smiles. A little person in white, who was standing against some tapestry in the background, cutting bread and jam for the hungry children, caught sight of the two, and thrilled with a feminine kindness, and then smiled, hanging her head over the brown loaf. Dick, who was deeply interested in the issue of the meeting that afternoon, was sitting on the back of the sofa, and by chance he saw one Catharine's face reflected in the other's. He was touched by the governess's gentle sympathy, and noticed, for the first time, that she had been somewhat neglected.

"You want a table, Miss George," said Dick, placing one before her, and a chair . . . "And you have no tea yourself. You have been so busy attending to every body else. Catharine, we want some tea here . . . Beamish, why don't you go and play the piano, and let us feast with music like the Arabian Nights? . . ."

"How pretty the flowers are growing," cried little Sarah, pointing. "Oh, do look, Miss George, dear . . ."

"It's the sun shining through the leaves," said Madame de Tracy, in a matter-of-fact tone.

"The water shines too," said Augusta. "I wish there was a river in Eaton Square; don't you, Catharine?"

"I envy you your drawing-room, Dick," said Madame de Tracy, conclusively. "Mr. Beamish, pray give us an air."

Beamish now got up and went to the piano. "If I play, you must show them your picture," he said, striking a number of chords very quickly, and then he sat down and began to play parts of that wonderful Kreutzer sonata, which few people can listen to unmoved. The piano was near where Catharine Butler had been making the tea, and she turned her head and listened, sitting quite still with her hands in her lap. I think Beamish was only playing to her, although all the others were listening round about. I know he only looked up at her every now and then as he played. Little Catharine George had sunk down on a low chair by the children, and had fallen into one of her dreams again . . . She understood, though no one had ever told her, all that was passing before her. She listened to the music; it seemed warning, beseeching, prophesying by turns. There is one magnificent song without words in the adagio, in which it seems as if one person alone is uttering and telling a story, passionate, pathetic, unutterably touching. Catharine thought it was Beamish telling his own story in those beautiful, passionate notes to Catharine, as she sat there in her gray cloud dress, with her golden hair shining in the sunset. Was she listening? Did she understand him? Ah! yes. Ah! yes, she must. Did every body listen to a story like this once in their lives? Catharine George wondered. People said so. But, ah! was it true? It was true for such as Catharine Butler, perhaps—for beautiful young women, loved, and happy, and cherished; but was it true for a lonely and forlorn little creature, without friends, without beauty (Catharine had only seen herself in her glass darkly as yet), with no wealth of her own to buy the priceless treasure of love and sympathy? The sun was shining outside; the steamers and boats were still sailing by; Catharine Butler's future was being decided. Little Catharine sat in a trance; her dark eyes were glowing. Beamish suddenly changed the measure, and crashed about on the piano, until by degrees it was Mendelssohn's "Wedding March," which went swinging through the room in great vibrations. Then Catharine George seemed to see the mediæval street, the old German town, the figures passing, the bridegroom tramping ahead, the young men marching along in procession. She could almost see the crisp brocades and the strange-cut dresses, and hear the whispering of the maidens following with the crowned bride; while from the gables of the queer old town—(she even gave it a name, and vaguely called it Augsburg or Nuremberg to herself)—people's heads were pushing and staring at the gay procession. It was one of those strange phantasmagorias we all know at times, so vivid for the moment that we can not but believe we have seen it once, or are destined to witness it at some future time in reality.

Beamish left off playing suddenly, and bent over the instrument, and began talking to Catharine Butler in low, eager tones. Madame de Tracy and Georgie, who had had enough music, were standing at the window by this time, watching the scene outside. The children, too, had jumped up, and ran out one by one upon the balcony. Not for the first time, and, alas! not for the last, poor child! a weary, strange, lost feeling came over Catharine George, as she sat on an overturned chest in the great, strange room. It came to her from her very sympathy for the other two, and gladness in their content.

It was a sharp, sudden thorn of aloneness and utter forlornness, which stung her so keenly in her excited and eager state that two great tears came and stood in her eyes; but they were youthful tears, fresh and salt, of clear crystal, unsoiled, undimmed as yet by the stains of life.

Dick, who was himself interested for his friend, and excited beyond his custom, and who had begun to feel a sort of interest in the sensitive little guest, thought she was feeling neglected. He had noticed her from across the room, and he now came up to her, saying very gently and kindly, "Would you care to see my picture, Miss George? my aunt and my cousin say they want to see it. It's little enough to look at."

As he said, it was no very ambitious effort. An interior. A fishwife sitting watching for her husband's return, with her baby asleep on her knee. One has seen a score of such compositions. This one was charmingly painted, with feeling and expression. The colors were warm and transparent; the woman's face was very touching, bright and sad at once; her brown eyes looked out of the picture. There was life in them somehow, although the artist had, according to the fashion of his school, set her head against a window, and painted hard black shadows and deeply marked lines with ruthless fidelity. The kitchen was evidently painted from a real interior. The great carved cupboard, with the two wooden birds pecketing each other's beaks, and the gleaming steel hinges, with two remarkable rays of light issuing from them; the great chimney, with the fire blazing (the shovel was an elaborate triumph of art); the half-open window, looking out across fields to the sea, the distaff, the odd shuttles for making string, hanging from the ceiling; the great brass pan upon the ground with the startling reflections—it was all more than true to nature, and the kitchen—somewhat modified, and less carefully polished—might be seen in any of the cottages and farmsteads round about the Château de Tracy for miles.

"My dear Dick, you have made an immense start," said his aunt. "It's admirable. It's by far the best thing you have done yet. Who is it so like? Catharine, only look at the brass pan and the cupboard. Madame Binaud has got just such a one in her kitchen."

Dick shrugged his shoulders, but he was pleased at the praise. "I have another thing here," he said, smiling, "only it isn't finished." And he rolled out another canvas on an easel.

"It's quite charming! What's the subject?" said Madame de Tracy, looking through her eyeglass.

"Oh, I don't know. Any thing you like. A cart—Normandy peasants going for a drive —coming back from market," said Dick, blushing and looking a little conscious . . . "I have been obliged to paint out the girl's head, Georgie. I wish you'd sit to me." And looking up as he spoke—not to Georgie—he met the glance of two soft dark eyes which were not Georgie's. "I wish YOU would sit to me, Miss

George," cried Dick, suddenly inspired. "You would make a first-rate fishwife; wouldn't she, Aunt Matilda?"

"I think Miss George would look very nice indeed in the costume," Madame de Tracy good-humoredly said. "She is a brunette, like all much occupied, and the children mustn't be neglected, and I hope they are not in trouble now," she added, looking round. "I'm afraid it is time for us to go." The clock of the old church had struck six some time, and, as she said, it was time to go.

Beamish and Catherine

our girls." And Madame de Tracy turned her eyeglass on Miss George, and nodded. She then glanced at Dick.

"I should be very glad to sit to Mr. Butler," said Miss George in her gentle way, "but I am afraid I should not have time. I am very

Madame de Tracy looked at her watch, and gave a little scream. "Yes, indeed," she said, "my brother Charles and half a dozen other people dine in Eaton Square to-night. Are you coming?"

"Beamish and I are coming in to dessert,"

said Dick ; at least he seemed to wish it this morning.

"We have to get home, we have to dress," said Madame de Tracy, preoccupied. "Georgie, where is my parasol? Catharine, are you ready? Have you finished your talk?"

Beamish and Catharine had finished their 'alk by this time, or begun it rather, for it was a life-long talk that they had entered into. The carriage had come back for the elders of the party. The children, who had eaten enormously, went off slightly subdued.

The two young men stood in the iron gateway, watching the carriage as it drove away, and the governess and the little pupils slowly sauntering homeward along the river side.

Beamish looked very tall and very odd as he stood leaning against the iron gate, round which some clematis was clinging.

Dick glanced at him, and then at the river, and then at his friend again. "Well!" he said, at last, pulling a leaf off a twig.

"It is all right," Beamish said, with the light in his face as he put out his hand to Dick; and then the two cordially shook hands, to the surprise of some little ragged children who were squatting in the road.

CHAPTER IV.

EAT, DRINK, AND BE MERRY.

CATHARINE held little Sarah's hand tightly clasped in hers as they went home along the busy streets. She had not met with so much romance in her short hard life, this poor little Catharine, that she could witness it unmoved in others. She had read of such things in books before now, of Lord Orville exclaiming with irresistible fire, "My sweet, my beloved Miss Anville!" of Rochester's energetic love-making; of Mr. Knightley's expressive eyes as he said, "My dearest Emma, for dearest you will be to me, whatever may be the result of this morning's conversation." And she had read of the sweet bunch of fragrant lilac which a young lover had sent to his lady, and now here was a sweet bunch of lilac for Catharine Butler ; so the little governess called it to herself, and the sweetness and scent seemed diffused all round, until they, the by-standers, were all perfumed and made fragrant too.

Catharine had heard Mr. Beamish saying "I shall come this evening and see you," as he put Miss Butler into the carriage. The girl had not answered, but her face looked very sweet and conscious, as she bent over and held out her hand to him. Poor Dick was looking on too, and a little old refrain came into his head. "En regrettant la Normandie," it went, "En regrettant . . ." This sweet dream of love-making made the way short and pleasant, though the children lagged and stopped at every interesting sight along the road. The man pouring beer out of his can, the milk-woman setting down her pails, the cart full of oranges and blue paper, the grocer taking in fagots two by two out of a cart—all was grist that came to their little mills, and delayed the fatal return to evening tasks and bed. For the little governess the sweet summer twilight was all aglow, and she was in a sort of enchanted world, where perfect happiness was waiting at unexpected corners ; where people understood what was in one another's hearts ; where there was a little trouble to begin with, but where at two or three-and-twenty (Miss Butler was little more), or even sooner, the fragrant bunch of lilacs flowered for most people, and then what mattered all the rest? If the flowers were blooming on the branches, a passing storm, or wind, or darkness could not unmake the spring.

One privilege belonging to her position Miss George had not, perhaps, valued so highly as she might have done. It was that of coming down in white muslin with Augusta after dinner whenever she liked. Little sleepy Sarah, and the aggrieved Lydia, would be popped into white calico and disposed of between the sheets, but Miss George and Augusta were at liberty to enjoy the intoxicating scene if they felt so inclined.

Mr. Butler nodding off over the paper—Mrs. Butler at her davenport, writing civil notes, one after another, in her large, even handwriting—Catharine and Georgina strumming on the piano-forte—the back room quite dark, and the tea stagnating on a small table near the doorway : this was when there was nobody there. When there was company the aspect of things was very different. Both the chandeliers would be lighted, the round sofa wheeled out into the middle of the room. Three ladies would be sitting upon it with their backs turned to one another ; Georgina and a friend, in full evening dress, suppressing a yawn, would be looking over a book of photographs.

"Do you like this one of me?" Georgina would say, with a slight increase of animation. "Oh, what a horrid thing!" the young lady would reply ; "if it was me, I should burn it—indeed I should. And is that your sister?—a Silvy, I am sure." Yes ; my cousin Richard can not bear it ; he says she looks as if her neck was being wrung." In the mean time, Catharine Butler, kindly attentive and smiling, would be talking to old Lady Shiverington, and trying to listen to her account of her last influenza, while Mrs. Butler, with her usual tact, was devoting herself to the next grander lady present. Madame de Tracy, after being very animated all dinner-time, would be sitting a little subdued with her fan before her eyes. Coffee would be handed round by the servants. After which the climax of the evening would be attained, and the door would fly open, and the gentlemen come straggling up from dinner, while tea on silver trays was being served to the expectant guests.

Mr. Butler, with a laugh, disappears into the brilliantly-lighted back room with a couple of congenial white neckcloths, while Mr. Bartholomew, the great railway contractor, treads heavily across the room to his hostess, and asks if these are some more of her young ladies? and how was it that they had not had the pleasure of their company at dinner? "My daughter Augusta is only twelve, Mr. Bartholomew, and is not thinking of coming out," Mrs. Butler would say; "and that is Miss George, my children's governess. It amuses her to come down, poor girl. Have you had any tea?"

Miss George, far from being amused by all this brilliancy, generally kept carefully out of the way; but on this particular evening, after the five o'clock tea at the studio, she had been haunted by a vague curiosity and excitement, and she felt as if she must come down—as if it would be horrible to sit all alone and silent in the school-room, out of reach, out of knowledge, out of sight, while below, in the more favored drawing-room, the people were all alive with interest, and expectation, and happiness.

Just before dinner she had met Madame de Tracy on the stairs, fastening her bracelets and running down in a great hurry. Catharine looked up at her and smiled as she made way, and the elder lady, who was brimming over with excitement and discretion, and longing to talk to every one on the subject which absorbed her, said,

"Ah! Miss George, I see you found out our secret this afternoon—not a word to the children. Mr. Beamish is coming to-night after dinner to speak to my brother. Hush! some one is on the stairs."

Miss George was not the only person in the establishment who surmised that something was going on. Madame de Tracy's vehement undertones had roused the butler's curiosity; he had heard the master of the house confessing that he was not totally unprepared; while Mrs. Butler was late for dinner, an unprecedented event, and had been seen embracing her daughter with more than usual effusion in her room up stairs. Mrs. Butler was one of those motherly women entirely devoted to their husbands and children, and who do not care very much for any body else in all the world, except so far as they are conducive to the happiness of their own family. She worked, thought, bustled, wrote notes, arranged and contrived for her husband and children. Her davenport was a sort of handmill, at which she ground down paper, pens, monograms, stamps, regrets, delights, into notes, and turned them out by the dozen. Her standard was not a very high one in this world or in the next, but she acted industriously up to it, such as it was, and although her maternal heart was stirred with sympathy, she was able to attend to her guests and make small talk as usual. I do not think that one of them, from her manner, could have guessed how she longed secretly to be rid of them all.

Catharine George, who was only the little governess and looker-on, felt her heart stirred too as she dressed in her little room up stairs to come down after dinner; unconsciously she took more than usual pains with herself; she peered into her looking-glass, and plumed and smoothed out her feathers like a bird by the side of a pool.

She thought her common gown shabby and crumpled, and she pulled out for the first time one of those which had been lying by ever since she had left her own home. This was a soft India muslin, prettily made up with lace and blue ribbons. Time had yellowed it a little, but it was none the worse for that, and if the colors of the blue ribbons had faded somewhat, they were all the softer and more harmonious. With her rough dark hair piled up in a knot, she looked like a little Sir Joshua lady when she had tied the bead necklace that encircled her round little throat, and then she came down and waited for Augusta in the empty drawing-room. Catharine was one of those people who grow suddenly beautiful at times, as there are others who become amiable all at once, or who have flashes of wit or good spirits; Catharine's odd, sudden loveliness was like an inspiration, and I don't think she knew of it. The little thing was in a strange state of sympathy and excitement. She tried to think of other things, but her thoughts reverted again and again to the sunny studio, the river rushing by, the music, the kind young men, and the beautiful, happy Catharine, leaning back in the old carved chair, with her bright eyes shining as she listened to Beamish's long story. The sun had set since he had told it, and a starlight night was now reigning overhead. The drawing-room windows were open, letting in a glimmer of stars and a faint incense from Catharine Butler's flowers outside on the balcony. Little Miss George took up her place in a quiet corner, and glanced again and again from the dull drawing-room walls to the great dazzling vault without, until the stars were hidden from her by the hand of the butler, who came in to pull down the blinds and light the extra candles, and to place the chairs against the wall. While he was thus engaged in making the room comfortable, he remarked that "the ladies would not be up for ten minutes or more, and if Miss George and Miss Augusta would please to take a little ice there would be plenty of time."

"Yes, certainly," said Augusta; "bring some directly, Freeman." And she and Miss George shared their little feast with one spoon between them.

The ladies came up from dinner, and Augusta was summoned to talk to them, and little Miss George was left alone in her corner. She was quite happy, although she had no one to speak to; she was absorbed in the romance of which she had conned the first chapters, and of which the heroine was before her in her white gauze dress, with the azalias in her hair.

And so one Catharine gazed wondering and speculating, while the other sat there patiently listening to the old ladies' complaining talk—to stories of doctors, and ailments, and old age, and approaching death, coming so soon after the brilliant strains of youth, and music, and romance.

One Catharine's bright cheeks turned very

pale; the other, who was only looking on, blushed up, when, almost immediately after the tea-tray, the door opened, and Dick and Mr. Beamish walked in without being announced. Mrs. Butler looked up and smiled, and held out her hand. Mr. Butler came striding forward from the back room. Madame de Tracy put up her eye-glass; Catharine Butler looked down, but she could say "yes" quite quietly to old Lady Shiverington, who asked, in a loud whisper, if that was Mr. Beamish. "The young men come to dinner, my dear, time after time," said the old lady, nodding her ancient head, "but they are all so much alike I don't know one from another."

And so this was all that Catharine had come out of her school-room to see. Charles Butler had been looking on too from the other end of the room, with little blinking eyes instead of dark fawn-like orbs, and at this stage of the proceedings he moved out of the way, and came across and sank down, much to Miss George's alarm, in a vacant arm-chair beside her. There she sat in her muslin, fair, pretty, soft, with shy, quick, curious glances; and there sat the old fellow with his wrinkled face and thick eyebrows; she need not have been afraid, though he looked somewhat alarming. If Mr. Bartholomew, who was standing by, could have known what was passing in the minds of these two people, he might have been struck, had he been romantically inclined, by the duet they were unconsciously playing.

"Matilda has been in great force to-night," thought Mr. Butler; "but her confidences are overpowering, whispery mystery—hiss, hiss, hiss—how she does delight in a love-affair. If it had been poor unlucky Dick now—but I suppose no woman of sense would have a word to say to him, and he will make a terrible fool of himself sooner or later. Eh, eh, we have all made fools of ourselves . . . It is only about half a century since I first saw his mother under the lime-trees. Poor dear! Poor dear!" and the old fellow began to beat a tune to a dirge with his foot as he thought of what was past. Meanwhile Miss George was playing her treble in the duet. "What can it be like," the little governess was thinking, "to love, to be loved, actually to live the dreams and the stories? Oh, I can not imagine it. Is it like listening to music? is it like that day when we climbed the hill in the sunset, my mother and I, higher and higher, and it was all like heaven in the valley? Is there some secret sympathy which makes quite old and wrinkled people care when they see such things, or does one only cease to feel in time? How calm Catharine looks; she scarcely speaks to Mr. Beamish. I can see Madame de Tracy smiling and nodding her head to her across the room. Can people care really and truly, and with all their hearts, and give no more sign? What should I do if I were Catharine? Ah! what am I thinking?" Here Mr. Butler suddenly gave a grunt and said,

"I am quite convinced the fault of all arm-chairs is that they are not made deep enough in the seat; my legs are quite cramped and stiff from that abominable contrivance in which I have been sitting. I can not imagine how my brother can go to sleep in it night after night in the way he does."

"Isn't Mr. Butler's arm-chair comfortable?" said Catharine, smiling. "The children and I have always looked at it with respect: we never should venture to sit in it, or not to think it deep enough in the seat."

"I see Mr. Beamish is not too shy to occupy the chair of state," said old Mr. Butler, glancing at Catharine from under his thick eyebrows, and unconsciously frightening her into silence.

Catharine was oppressed by circumstance, and somewhat morbid by nature, as people are who have lively imaginations, and are without the power of expansion. She had lived with dull people all her life, and had never learnt to talk or to think. Her step-mother was a tender-hearted and sweet-natured sad woman, who was accustomed to only see the outside of things. Mrs. George had two dozen little sentences in her repertory, which she must have said over many thousand times in the course of her life, and which Catharine had been accustomed hitherto to repeat after her, and to think of as enough for all the exigencies and philosophy of life. But now every thing was changing, and she was beginning to idea thoughts for herself, and to want words to put them into; and with the thoughts and the words, alas! came the longing for some one to listen to her strange new discoveries, and to tell her what they meant. But it was not old Charles Butler to whom she could talk. She looked across the room.

Yes, Beamish was there installed; they were all welcoming him for the sake of their beloved princess. "Ah! what am I thinking?" thought Catharine again; "would there be any one in the world to care if—" She did not finish the sentence, but a vague impossibility, in the shape of a Geraint with sleepy eyes and without a name, passed through her mind. As chance would have it, Dick Butler came sauntering up at this minute, and she started and blushed as usual, and her visions vanished. Catharine almost felt as if he must see them flying away.

It was not Dick, with his short-sighted eyes, who saw the little fancies flying away, but there were others present who were more experienced and more alive to what was passing. Madame de Tracy was a woman of lively imagination, who scarcely knew any of the people present, and had nobody to talk to, and it so happened that at the end of a quarter of an hour she began to think that her nephew had been conversing quite long enough with Miss George.

All the world might have heard what he was saying to her. Dick was only telling Miss George about Normandy, about the beautiful old ruins, the churches turned into barns, talking Murray and little else. For reasons best known to himself, he liked telling of the places he had lately seen, although he said but little of the people he had known there. And Miss George was a good listener; she said not much, but her bright little face brightened as he went on with his stories. They were prosy enough, some people might have thought. His uncle had joined in once and exclaimed, "Spare us the description of the next church you visited, Richard;" but **Catharine** George liked every word, and listened in delighted attention. Catharine listened; **she** had better far have sat up all **alone** in her school-room, poor child, with her candle-ends and fancies of what might have been.

Later in life, when people have outlived the passionate impatience of youth, when the mad wild longings are quieted, and the things their own, perhaps, and no longer valued, for which they would have given their lives once—long ago—when people are sober and matter-of-fact, when **they** have almost forgotten that strange impetuous self of former days, it is easy to **blame** and to phoo-phoo, to crush and brush away the bright beautiful bubbles which the children are making in their play. Madame de Tracy did not feel one moment's remorse, sentimental as she was, when she came across and interrupted little Catharine's happy half hour, and Dick in his eloquent talk.

Dick was asking Catharine what she thought of the five o'clock tea. "We had music, Uncle Charles, hadn't we, Miss George? Beamish played first fiddle, *Ah ti voglio ben assai*, a Neapolitan air, Uncle Charles. Nobody ever sung it to *you*." And Dick, who was excited and in high spirits, began humming and nodding his head in time. He suddenly stopped — old Charles made a warning sign. "Miss George was present and knows all about it; don't be afraid, she is discretion itself, and of course we all are thinking about the same thing. What is the use of pretending?"

"If Miss George is discretion itself, that quite alters the case," said Mr. Butler.

Meanwhile Dick was going on—"Look at Uncle Hervey performing the *père noble*, and making Beamish look foolish. Dear old Beamish, I shouldn't let him marry Catharine if he was not the best fellow in the whole world."

"My niece is fortunate to have secured such a paragon," said Charles, showing his sympathy by a little extra dryness.

"Their faces are something alike, I think," said Miss George, timidly; "they seem very well suited."

"Of course," said Dick; "£5000 a year in prospect—what can be more suitable? If they had no better reason for wanting to get married than because they were in love with one another, then you should hear the hue-and-cry their affectionate relatives can raise."

"Quite right too," said old Mr. Butler.

Catharine glanced from one to the other.

"You don't think it quite right, do you, Miss George?" said Dick, and then his aunt came up and carried him off.

"Young fellows like Dick often talk a great deal of nonsense," said old Butler, kindly, as Catharine sat looking after the two as they walked away arm-in-arm. "Depend upon it, my nephew would no more wish to marry upon an incompetence than I should. Remember, he is not the man to endure privation except for his own amusement."

He spoke so expressively, blinking his little gray eyes, that the girl looked up curiously, wondering whether he could mean any thing. All the evening she had been sitting there in her white gown, feeling like a shade, a thing of no account among all this living people, a blank in the closely written page, a dumb note in the music. A sort of longing had come over her to be alive, to make music too; and now to be warned even, to be acting a part ever so small in this midsummer night's dream, was enough to thrill her sad little childish heart with excitement. Could he be warning her? Then it came like a flash, and her heart began to beat faster and faster. There was something possible, after all, besides governessing and lesson-books in her dull life—something to beware of, to give interest, even the interest of danger to the monotonous road. To be scorned did not seem to her so unutterably sad as to be utterly passed by and ignored. Charles **Butler** never guessed the harm he had **done**.

It was not the Miss George who **had dressed** herself in her yellowed muslin who went up **stairs** to bed that night. It was another **Catharine** George. The little moth had burst out of **its** cocoon, the wings had grown, and it was fluttering and fluttering in the candle's beautiful golden light.

My simile would **have been better** if Catharine, the moth, had not herself **blown out** her candle when she reached her bedroom up stairs. She was hanging out of her window, trying to drink the night calm into her veins. "Is that bright beautiful planet my star, I wonder?" the governess was thinking. "How gayly it sparkles; it seems to be dancing in space. How the night wanes and shines; how the stars blaze beyond the house-tops! Did any one ever tell me that was my star? Why do I think so?" As Catharine gazed at the heavens and thought all this, not in words, but with quick sensitive flashes — down below, just under her feet, the well was being dug into which the poor little philosopher was doomed to tumble. Ah me! was truth at the bottom of it, I wonder, instead of up overhead in the beautiful shining stars of good promise?

It seemed to little Catharine as if a burst of sunshine had come out suddenly into her dull life. She did not know whence or how it came; she did not know very clearly what she was feeling; she did not tell herself that she ought to shut her heart, and ears, and eyes, until some one suitable in fortune and worldly circumstances came across her way. She is only twenty years old, impressionable, soft-hearted. What can her girlish day-dreams have taught her?

Can she have learned from them to mistrust people who are kind—to be careful, and cautious, and reserved—to wall up and bury the natural emotions of youth?

For the first time in her short life, ideas, feelings, sensations hitherto unthought and unfelt, came crowding upon Catharine George. Every thing seemed changed, although she walked the same walks in the square—corrected the same mistakes in the children's exercises—sat in her old place in the school-room. The walls seemed to have opened somehow to let in the unfamiliar crowd of strange new ideas, of feelings impossible to realize or to define. The difference in Catharine was not greater than that which a passing cloud makes in the sky, or a burst of sunshine breaking across the landscape. Out of the vague images and shadows which had hitherto made up her solitary life came a sudden reality. The drifting dreams and fancies of what might be had vanished forever; they were gone, and in their stead it was to-day; and Catharine, as she was—no ideal self to be—who was sitting there, and who had awakened one morning to find herself living her own life in the world of the present. Other discoveries she might make as she traveled farther; and times might come to her, as to most of us, when solemner visions close round about once more, and we realize with terrible distinctness that we are only dreaming in a kingdom of mists and shadows—a kingdom where the sounds die into silence—where the suns set day by day. But at this time every thing was real and keen enough to the poor little thing, of vast meaning and moment—never to finish, she thought—never to seem of import less vital—never, ah! never!

CHAPTER V.

WHAT CATHARINE WISHED FOR.

Fate, which for some time past seemed to have strangely overlooked the thread of Catharine George's existence, now suddenly began to spin it somewhat faster, and to tie a few knots in the loose little string. For one thing, Madame de Tracy's thread flew so fast that it was apt to entangle itself with others alongside, and it would set all those round about flying with the vibrations of its rapid progress.

Dick was a great deal in Eaton Square at this time, more than he had ever been before. The house was not generally so pleasant as it was just then; Madame de Tracy was there bustling about and enjoying herself, and making a great talk, and life, and stir. Charles Butler, too, was in town, and often with his sister, and Dick was unaffectedly fond of his uncle's society. Every body used to scold the young painter when he appeared day by day for leaving his work; but all the same, they would not let him go back to it, when once he was with them.

"I ought to go," Dick would say, as he remained to take his pleasure, and Catharine, coming down demurely at the end of the little procession, never knew who she might find down below. One great triumph Richard had to announce. He had sold his picture, and got a good price for it; although he hesitated, to the dealer's surprise, when it came to parting with his beloved fishwife. He had also received an order for the "Country-cart" as soon as it should be finished, and once again he said at luncheon, "Miss George, I wish you would let me put you into my cart."

Some shy impulse made her refuse—she saw Mrs. Butler looking prim and severe, and Madame de Tracy unconsciously shaking her head. It seemed very hard. Catharine nearly cried afterward when she woke up in the night and wondered whether Richard had thought her ungrateful. What could he think after all his kindness? why had she been so shy and foolishly reserved? . . . "No, Lydia, it was William the Conqueror who came over in 1066, not Julius Cæsar."

Meanwhile Richard the Conqueror, Butler Cæsar, went about his business and his pleasure with feelings quite unwounded by any thing Catharine could do or say; when she saw him again he had forgotten all about her refusal, and, to her delight and surprise, his manner was quite unchanged and as kind as ever. What trifles she pondered over and treasured up! It was like the old German stories of twigs and dried leaves carefully counted and put away in the place of gold pieces—chance encounters—absurdities—she did not know what she was about.

Madame de Tracy, who never let go an idea, or who let it go a hundred times to return to it again and again at stray intervals, shook her head at all these chance meetings. Her departure was approaching—her vigilance would be removed—she could not bear to think of what might not happen in her absence, and she had spoken to Mrs. Butler of a scheme for appealing to Dick's own better feelings.

"My dear Matilda, I entreat you to do nothing of the sort. Dick can bear no remonstrance," Mrs. Butler cried. "I will see that all is right, and, if needs be, Miss George must go. I have a most tempting account of this German governess. Charles told me to bring Miss George to his picnic on Friday, but I think it will be as well that she should not be of the party."

Poor unconscious little Catharine! She would have died of horror, I think, if she had guessed how quietly the secrets of her heart were discussed by unsympathetic by-standers, as she went on her way, singing her song without words. It was a foolish song, perhaps, about silly things, but the voice that sang it was clear, and sweet, and true.

Charles Butler, the giver of the profound entertainment, was one of those instances of waste of good material which are so often to be met with in the world—a tender-hearted man, with few people to love him, living alone, with no nearer ties than other people's children ; a man of ability, who had never done any thing except attend to the commonplaces of life; and these were always better arranged and controlled at Lambswold than any where else, for he knew what should be done and how to make other people to do it, and perhaps gave an attention and effort to small things which should have gone elsewhere. It was a kindly spirit, in a wrinkled, ugly, cranky old body. Charles Butler's hook nose, and protruding teeth, and fierce eyebrows, his contradictoriness and harsh little laugh, were crimes of nature, so to speak, for they frightened away women, and children, and timid people. They had frightened Charles Butler himself into mistrusting his own powers, into believing that there was something about him which must inevitably repel ; they had destroyed his life, his best chance for happiness. He was a diffident man ; for years he had doubted, and hesitated, and waited—waited for this sad, lonely, aching old age which had come upon him now. His little nephews and nieces, however, had learned not to be afraid of him on a certain day in the year when it was his custom to ask them all down for the day to Lambswold in honor of his god-daughter Augusta's birthday. They often staid there at other times, but this one day was the happiest of all, they thought. It came in midsummer, with a thrill of sweetness in the air, with the song of the thrush, when the strawberry-heads were hanging full and crimson, when all the roses were flushing. Little Sarah used to say she thought Lambswold was a pink place.

It was an old-fashioned country house, standing in the hollow of two hills, with a great slope in front, and a wide, plenteous world of wheatfields, farmsteads, and straggling nut-woods to gaze at from the dining-room windows and the terrace. There were rising green meads on either side, and at the back of it kitchen-gardens, fruit-walls, and green-houses, and farm-buildings, all in excellent order and admirably kept.

"Oh, Miss George, how sorry you must be not to come !" Algy would say.

"Yes, I am very sorry," Catharine honestly answered in her child's voice ; for she had not yet outgrown the golden age when all things call and beckon, and the apples, and the loaves, and the cakes cry, Come eat us, come eat us, and the children, wandering in fairy-land, reply, We come, we come. She loved cakes, and apples, and all good things still, and had not reached to the time when it is no penalty to be deprived of them. But she had to pay the price of her youth; and to those who are tied and bound down by circumstance, youth is often, indeed, only a blessing turned into a curse. It consumes with its own fire and tears with its own strength. And so when Catharine, with a sinking heart, heard them all talking over arrangements for spending a day in Paradise with the angels—so it seemed to her—and not one word was spoken to include her in the scheme; when she guessed that she was only to be left in the school-

room, which represented all her enjoyment, all her hopes, her beginning and ending—then a great wave of disappointment, and wishing, and regretting seemed to overflow and to choke the poor little instructress of youth, the superior mind whose business in life it was to direct others and to lead the way to the calm researches of science, instead of longing childishly for the strawberries of life. But there were strawberries ripening for Catharine.

One afternoon she was with the children, crossing the road to the house; they were carrying camp-stools, work, reels, scissors, the *Heir of Redcliffe*, covered in brown paper, for reading aloud; the *Boy's Own Magazine*, *Peter Parley*, a *Squib* ; Sandy, tightly clasped round the neck by Algy ; a rug, and various other means for passing an hour ; when suddenly Catharine's eyes began to brighten as they had a trick of doing, Sandy made a gasping attempt at a bark, and little Sarah, rushing forward, embraced a young gentleman affectionately round the waist. He was standing on the side of the pavement, and laughing and saying, "Do you always walk out with all this luggage ?"

"We have only a very few things," said little Sarah. "Are you coming to our house? Oh, Richard, is it arranged about the picnic ?"

"The carriage has not come back yet—there's nobody at home. Oh, Dick, do wait and have tea with us," cried Lydia.

"I think you might as well," Augusta said, in an aggrieved tone ; "but I suppose you won't, because we are children."

"Oh do, do, do, do, do," said Algy, hopping about with poor Sandy, still choking, for a partner.

"I want to see my aunt and settle about Lambswold," said Richard, walking along with Miss George. "I think we shall have a fine day."

"I hope you will," Catharine answered.

"You are coming, of course ?" said Dick, following them up stairs into the school-room.

"I am going to see my sisters," said Catharine, blushing up. She took off her bonnet as she spoke, and pushed back her black cloud of hair.

Richard thought Catharine looked much prettier when she went up stairs, blushing still and confused, with disheveled locks, than when she came down all neatly smoothed and trimmed a few minutes after, and sat down demurely at the tea-caddy.

Outside she may have looked prim and demure—inside she was happier than any of the children, as she sat there with her radiant downcast eyes reflected on the tea-pot. Never was a guest more welcome, and more made of, than Richard at his little cousins' tea-table. He was to be waited on by them all at once; he was to have the arm-chair ; he was to choose his favorite cup. He chose Algy's little old mug, to the children's screams of laughter.

"I think I shall make this my dinner," said Dick. "A slice and a half of thick bread and butter will be about enough. I don't want to be ungrateful for hospitality, but, pray, why is it cut so very thick?"

"Don't you like it?" said Lydia, anxiously. "I will go and beg Mrs. Bluestring for a small piece of cake for you."

Augusta and Miss George began to laugh. Dick said he was not accustomed to cake, and insisted upon eating his thick bread and butter. The children dispatched theirs, and chattered and enjoyed his jokes, and so did the little governess at her tea-tray. The coachmen were, as usual, pumping in the court.

Again came the sunshine streaming through the window. Dick's hair was all brushed up, and his gray eyes were twinkling. The children's high spirits and delight were infectious; all Miss George's primness, too, seemed to have melted away; pretty little looks of expression of interest, of happiness, were coming and going in her round face. One of the golden half hours which are flying about all over the world had come to them. They had done nothing to deserve it, but it was there.

Catharine was still presiding at her little feast when the carriage came home with Charles Butler and the two elder ladies, who were surprised to hear unusual shouts of laughter coming from the school-room.

"They all seem very merry," said Mrs. Butler, stopping with her hand on the lock.

"I am certain I heard Richard's voice," said Madame de Tracy to Charles, who was toiling up more slowly; and as Mrs. Butler opened the door, to one person within it seemed as if all the fun and the merriment, all the laughter and brightness, escaped with a rush, and left the room quite empty.

"Oh, mamma," said Lydia, sighing from contentment, "we have had such fun; Dick has been having tea with us out of Algy's old mug."

"So I perceive," said Madame de Tracy, with a glance at Catharine.

"Come in, come in," cried the children, hospitably, "do come in too."

"I think you may come up stairs to us," said their mother, after a moment's hesitation, "for our tea is ready in the drawing-room." And then somehow to Catharine—it was like a dream—all the gay little figures disappeared, dancing off, chattering and talking still, with Sandy barking after them. The sunset was still shining in, but the beautiful glowing colors had changed to glare. Dick had risen from his place when the two aunts entered, and seemed to vanish away quite naturally with the rest. It was, indeed, like waking up from a happy little dream of friends' faces and brightness, and with the music of beloved voices still ringing in one's ears, to find one's self alone in the dark.

Catharine remained sitting at the tea-table with the scraps and dregs, the crumbled bits of bread—Algy's half-eaten slice—Lydia's cup overturned before her. She sat quite still; no one had noticed her; even Dick had gone off without saying good-by. As on that day at the

studio, a swift pang came piercing through her. She felt all alone—suddenly quite alone—in a great, cruel, terrible world in which she was of no account, in which she was carried along against her will, feeling—oh, so strangely—helpless and impotent. She did not know what she wanted, she did not know what she feared, but she shrunk from her own self with an aching impatience.

She jumped up and ran to the window to shake her new terror off. She looked down into the yard, where the hard-working coachman was pumping still, and a couple of dogs were turning over and over in play. Every thing was ugly, sad, desolate, that had been so gay and delightful a minute before. Utterly depressed and bewildered, the poor little thing sat down on the window-sill, and leant her weary head against the pane. Richard Butler, coming down a few minutes later, saw her through the half-open door still sitting there, a dark little figure against the light.

"Good-night, Miss George," he said, with a kind inflection in his voice, coming in and shaking her by the hand; "and thank you for your good tea." And then he went away.

He had spoken kindly; he had said something—nothing; but it was more than enough to make her happy again. As for Richard himself, he was vexed, chafed, disquieted. He had had a little talk with his aunts up stairs, which had made him indignant and angry. They had taken him to task gently enough; but all that they said jarred upon him, and stirred up secret springs of which they had no conception. He could hardly conceal his irritation as the two went on, blandly pouring out their advice into either side of the tea-table, when he asked whether Miss George was not to be of the party.

"No; I had not thought of inviting Miss George," said Mrs. Butler, stiffly. "It is always doubtful in these cases . . ."

"Not to speak of the danger of mixin' the different grades of society," said Hervey, who was present, cross-legged, and looking like the Solomon who was to decide all difficulties.

"Danger," said Richard; "what possible danger can there be?"

"You had better bring her," grunted Charles. "She has got a pair of uncommon bright eyes; and I suppose there are strawberries enough for us all?"

"Or we might take down a pottle on purpose for Miss George of an inferior quality," Richard said. "I do think it is hard lines that a nice little pretty thing like that should be shut up from morning to night in a dreary little hole of a sch—"

Mrs. Butler, with a glance at Lydia, who was standing by, absorbed in the conversation, hastened to interpose.

"She is quite admirable and excellent in her own way (children, go into the back drawing-room); but, my dear Richard, there is nothing more undesirable than putting people into false positions . . . The person of whom you speak is not *de notre classe*, and it would be but mistaken kindness."

"Precisely so," said Hervey, much pleased with the expression; "Miss George is not *de notre classe*."

"Confound *notre classe*," said Richard, hastily.

"Don't be blasphemous, Dick," said his uncle Charles.

And then, remembering that this was not the way to speak in such company, the young man stopped short, and begged Mrs. Butler's pardon.

She was pouring out small black-looking cups of tea, and looking offended with a turned-down mouth; and, indeed, the maternal autocrat was not used to such plain talking.

"It seems to me, Richard, that you are scarcely the person to provide amusement for Miss George," she said.

"Ah! Dick," cried Madame de Tracy, giving a little shriek and forgetting her prudence; she could keep silence no longer. "Be careful, my dearest boy; do not let yourself be carried away by your feelings. I guessed—I am rapid to notice things—I have trembled ever since that day at the studio." She looked so anxious and so concerned between her frizzy curls that Dick burst out laughing.

"So this is your fine scheme? No, you have not guessed right, Aunt Matilda. Poor little Miss George is not dangerous for me, but I can not help losing my temper when I hear persons of sense using the wicked old commonplaces which have made so many people miserable, and which condemn a poor child to such a dreary, unsatisfactory mockery of existence. There, she is just as well-mannered and pretty as Georgie or Catharine; and I am not to eat a piece of bread and butter in her company for fear of being contaminated," cried Dick, in a fume.

"Ah! my poor Dick," said Madame de Tracy, "you are unconscious, perhaps, of the sentiment; but I fear it is there."

"I am speaking from no personal feeling," cried Dick, still angry; and to Madame de Tracy at least his words carried conviction at the time. (But was it so, I wonder; and had Miss George's soft, pretty eyes nothing to do with the question?) "It is a mere sense of fairness and justice," Dick went on, "which would make me dislike to see any fellow-creature hardly used; and if I have spoken half a dozen words of kindness to her, it was because . . . It is no use staying any longer; I shall only offend more and more. Good-night." And then he suddenly took up his hat and went away. On his way down stairs, he relieved his mind by being even more kind than usual to a person whom he considered unjustly treated by the world in general and his aunts in particular.

"Women usually respect a man when he is angry, even when he is in the wrong, and Richard was not in the wrong. "I think for once I was mistaken," said Madame de Tracy; "and

yet people are not always conscious of their own feelings. But, under the circumstances, we must take Miss George, or Dick will fancy . . ."

"Oh, certainly, if you all wish it," said Mrs. Butler. "Will you have any more tea, Matilda? Now, children, what are you all about? You may go and ask Miss George to the picnic, and then come up and help me to dress."

Meanwhile Richard was walking away, biting and pulling his mustache. He went along Eaton Square until he came to the public house at the corner of Hobart Place. There he was stopped by a crowd of children and idlers who had taken up their position on the pavement, for Mr. Punch was squeaking at the top of his voice from his pulpit, and they had all gathered round to listen to his morality. The children had already taken up their places in the stalls and were sitting in a row on the curb-stone. "Ookedookedookedoo," said Mr. Punch, "where's the babby? Throw the baby out of window."

"Dook! dere it go," cried another baby, sitting in the gutter clapping its dirty little hands.

Richard stopped for a minute to look at Punch's antics, going on with his reflections meanwhile. It seemed to him as if the world, as it is called, was a great cruel Punch, remorselessly throwing babies and children out of window, and Miss George among the rest, while the people looked on and applauded, and Toby the philosopher sat by quite indifferent in his frill collar.

"That poor little thing," he was thinking, "her wistful, helpless glances move me with pity; was there ever a more innocent little scapegoat? Oh, those women! their talk, and their assumption, and suspicions make me so angry I can scarcely contain myself. *De notre classe*," and he began to laugh again, while Punch, capering and singing his song of "ookedook," was triumphantly beating the policeman about the head. "Would they think Reine *de notre classe*, I wonder?" he said to himself; "will it be her turn some day to be discussed, and snubbed, and patronized? My poor noble Reine"—and Richard seemed to see her pass before him, with her eagle face—"is there one of them to compare to her among the dolls and lay figures *de notre classe?*" He walked on; Punch's shrieks were following him, and ringing in his ears with the children's laughter. As he went along, the thought of Reine returned to him again and again, as it had done that day he walked along the sands to Tracy; again and again he was wondering what she was doing: was she in her farm superintending, was she gone on one of her many journeys along the straight and dusty roads, or was she spinning flax perhaps at the open door, or reading by the dying daylight out of one of her mother's old brown books? . . . A distant echo of Punch's weird "ookedookedoo" reached him like a warning as he walked away.

The day at Lambswold was a great success, the children thought. It was about twelve

o'clock, when the shadows were shortest and the
birds most silent, that the drag and the fly from
the station came driving up the steep and into
the court. Charles Butler received them all at
the door, shaking hands with each as they ascended the steps. Catharine and the children
had come in the fly, and the others preceded
them in the drag. The house had been silent
for months, and now, one instant after the arrival, the voices were echoing in the hall, up
stairs in the bedroom, the children were racing
round and round, Sandy was scampering up
and down. It was like one of Washington Irv-
ing's tales of the Alhambra, and of deserted
halls suddenly repeopled with the life of other
days. There was a great array of muslins, and
smart hats and feathers. Catharine, too, had
unconsciously put out all her simple science to
make herself look harmonious, as it were, and
in keeping with the holiday, with the summer
parks, and the gardens full of flowers, with the
fields through which they had been speeding,
daisy-sprinkled, cool, and deeply shadowed, with
cattle grazing in the sunshine; in keeping with
the sky which was iridescent, azure, and gently fleeced; in keeping with her own youth and
delight in its freshness. As Miss George came
with her pupils, smiling, up the ancient flight
of stone steps leading to the house, Charles Butler was pleased with the bright, happy face he
was looking down upon. It is only older people, after all, who are quite unselfish, and feel
the greatest pleasure in witnessing the happiness of others.

"I am very glad to see you here," he said,
shaking hands with her courteously.

Mrs. Butler, who was in the hall, looked round
surprised at the unusual urbanity. Catharine
George herself was not surprised; she expected
every body to be kind to-day, every thing to be
delightful. The pretty figure came climbing
the steps, with all the landscape for a background. The sun was shining through the flying folds of her muslin draperies, it was again
reflected in the burning feather in her hat.
The lights shone from the dark eyes in antici-
pation of the happiness which was already hers.
What did not she expect?—for the minute any
thing, every thing. Like many of us, she
thought happiness was yet to come, and behold,
the guest was here beside her. Happiness is
but a shy goddess, as we all know; she comes
bashfully into the room, all the hearts suddenly
leap and the eyes begin to brighten, but she is
very apt to fly if we rush forward to embrace
her. "How remarkably well Miss George is
looking," said Beamish to his future mother-
in-law.

"Oh yes," said Mrs. Butler, "remarkably
well."

CHAPTER VI.

MY LOVE IN HER ATTIRE DOTH SHOW HER **WIT**.

THE morning room at Lambswold was a
gray, melancholy, sunshiny room. The light
shone in through two great open windows on
the gray walls and ancient possessions. A
glass drop chandelier, quaint and old-fashioned,
reflected it in bright prisms. A shrouded harp
stood in one corner of the room. There was
an old pink carpet, with a pattern of faded
wreaths; a tall chimney-piece, with marble
garlands, yellowed by time; and fountains and
graceful ornamentations. A picture was hanging over it—a picture of a lady, all blue and
green shadows in a clouded world of paint, with
a sort of white turban or night-cap on. She
had the pretty coquettish grace which belonged
to the women of her time, who still seem to be
smiling archly out of their frames at their **gap**-
ing descendants.

Through the window there was a sight of a
lawn and a great spreading tree, where figures
were busy preparing the tables, and beyond
them again a sweet pastoral valley and misty
morning hills.

"Ah! how pretty!" cried Catharine Butler,
stepping out at once through the window.

Beamish, who had been cross coming down,
and who had fancied she talked too much to
Dick's new friend, Mr. Holland, followed her to
give her a scolding; but Catharine met him
with a smile and a great red rose she had just
pulled off the trellis. And so the two made it
up, and stood picking rose-buds for one another, like a Dresden shepherd and shepherdess.

"What time do we dine?" said Hervey. "**I**
suppose this is only luncheon, Charles?"

"Humph!" said Charles, "I don't know

what this is—earwigs most likely. Dick would have it out there."

"Alas! we are no longer young enough to go without our dinners, my dear brother," cried Madame de Tracy. "Do you remember—"

"I see the croquet ground is in very good order," said Georgie, who had been standing absorbed before one of the windows, and who had not been listening to what they were saying, while Frank Holland (he was a well-known animal painter) walked straight up to the chimney and looked up at the picture.

"Isn't this a Gainsborough?" asked the young man.

"This, ladies and gentlemen," said Dick, who began to play showman, "is the celebrated portrait of my great-aunt, Miss Paventry, the heiress. She brought Lambswold into the family, and two very ugly wine-coolers, which shall be exhibited free of any extra charge. That" —pointing to a picture between the windows— "is Richard Butler, the *first* martyr of the name. He was burned at the stake at Smithfield in Queen Mary's reign, surnamed the—"

"What a charming picture!" said Holland, who had been all this time looking at the portrait of Miss Paventry, while the children stood round, staring at him in turn.

"Charming!" echoed Dick, suddenly astride on his hobby-horse; "I didn't expect this from you, Holland."

"Ta-ta-ta," said Charles Butler. "What have I done with the cellar key? I shall only get out my second-best sherry; it is quite good enough for any of you." And the host trotted off with a candle to a sacred inner vault, where nobody but himself ever penetrated—not even Mundy, the devoted factotum upon whose head it was always found necessary to empty the vials before any thing could be considered as satisfactorily arranged.

Meanwhile Dick was careering round and round at full gallop on his favorite steed, although he was lounging back to all appearance on the sofa by Madame de Tracy. "I see no charm in a lie," he was saying, in his quiet, languid way; "and the picture is a lie from beginning to end." Holland was beginning to interrupt, but Dick went on pointing as he spoke: "Look at that shapeless, impudent substitute for a tree; do you see the grain of the bark? Is there any attempt at drawing in those coarse blotches meant, I suppose, for ivy leaves? Look at those plants in the foreground—do you call that a truthful rendering of fact? Where is the delicate tracery of Nature's lacework?"

"In the first place, I don't quite understand what you mean by a rendering of fact," said Holland; "I can't help thinking you have cribbed that precious phrase out of a celebrated art-critic."

"The phrase isn't English," said Madame de Tracy, who always longed to rush into any discussion, whether she understood or not what it was all about.

"I hate all the jargon," said Holland, draw-

ing himself up (a tall figure in an iron-gray suit, such as young men wear nowadays, with a smart yellow rose in the button-hole). "Art-critic! art-history! word-painting! germ-spoiling of English. Pah! I tell you, my dear fellow, whatever you may choose to criticise, Gainsborough looked at nature in the right way. I tell you he'd got another sort of spectacles on his noble nose than what are worn nowadays by your new-fangled would-be regenerators of art. If you want the sort of truth you are talking about, you had better get a microscope at once to paint with, and the stronger the instrument the more truthful you'll be. I tell you," continued Holland, more and more excited, "if you and your friends are right, then Titian, and Giorgione, and Tintoret are wrong."

"Hang Titian!" interrupted Dick, with quiet superiority, while his hobby-horse gave a sudden plunge and became almost unmanageable. "He was utterly false and conventional—infernally clever, if you like. But we want truth—we want to go back to a more reverential treatment of Nature, and that is only to be done by patience and humble imitation."

The reformer Dick was still lounging among the cushions, but his gray eyes were twinkling as they did when he was excited.

Miss George, who had been listening absorbed all this time, looked up into his face almost frightened at the speech about Titian. Mrs. Butler said, "Fie, fie, you naughty boy!" with lumbering playfulness. The sun was shining so brightly outside that the roses looked like little flames, and the grass was transfigured; the children were tumbling about in it.

Miss George should have remembered that there was youth and inexperience to palliate Richard Butler's irreverence. Youth has a right to be arrogant, or is at least an excuse for presumption, since it can't have experience; and, moreover, Dick's exaggeration had its kernel of truth amid a vast deal of frothy pulp.

The truth, as Dick would write it, was that he and his comrades were reformers, and like reformers they would have broken the time-honored images of the old worship in their new-born zeal. It is healthier to try and paint a blade of grass to the utmost of your ability, than to dash in a bold background and fancy you are a Reynolds or a Gainsborough. But honest Dick will find that to imitate blades of grass, and bits of fern and birds'-nests with bluish eggs, however well and skillfully, is not the end and the object of painting. And, indeed, the right treatment was already visible in his works, fighting against system and theories. What can they produce but dry pieces of mechanism?

The true painter is the man who paints with his soul, and so finds his way to the hearts of his fellow-creatures.

"She was a most delightful person, I believe," said Mrs. Butler, gazing in her turn at Miss Paventry. "She never married."

"It is very curious," said Holland, "but don't you see a decided likeness?" and he looked from the picture to one of the persons present, and then back at the picture again.

"You mean Miss George," said Dick. "I've often noticed it; but she has got a much prettier and more becoming hat on than that affair of poor old Aunt Lydia's. I like your red feather," said he, turning to Catharine. "If I were a woman," Dick went on, still contrary and discursive, "I should like to be a green woman, or a blue woman, or a red one—I shouldn't like to be a particolored woman. I don't know why ladies are so much afraid of wearing their own colors, and are all for semitones and mixtures. Now that feather of yours is a capital bit of color, and gives one pleasure to look at."

"I should think the reason that most ladies prefer quiet colors," said Mrs. Butler, stiffly, "is that they do not generally wish to make themselves conspicuous. No lady wishes to attract attention by overfine clothes," she repeated, glancing at the obnoxious feather, and rustling in all the conscious superiority of two pale mauve daughters, and garments of flowing duncolor and sickly magenta and white.

"I do believe, my dear aunt, there are people who would like to boil down the Union Jack into a sort of neutral tint," said Dick, "and mix up the poor old buff and blue of one's youth into a nondescript green."

"Such things have certainly been tried before now," said Holland, while Butler, turning to Catharine, went on: "Don't let them put you out of conceit with your flame-color, Miss George; it is very pretty indeed, and very becoming." He was vexed with his aunt for the rude, pointed way in which she had spoken; he saw Catharine looking shy and unhappy. But she soon brightened up, and as she blushed with pleasure to hear Dick liked her feather, its flames seemed to mount into her cheeks. In the fair apparel of youth, and innocence, and happiness, no wonder she looked well, and charmed them all by her artless arts. There is no dress more gorgeous and dazzling than Catharine's that day. Not Solomon in all his glory, not Madame Rachel in all her nostrums, not all the hair-pins, and eye-washes, and affectations can equal it. I can not attempt to define how rightly or wrongly Catharine was behaving in looking so pretty and feeling so happy in Dick Butler's company, in having placed an idol upon her most secret shrine, and then fallen down and worshiped it—an idol somewhat languid and nonchalant, with mustaches, with a name, alas! by this time. Poor little worshiper! it was in secret that she brought her offerings, her turtle-dove's eggs, and flowers, and crystal drops, and sudden lights, and flickering tapers. She was a modest and silent little worshiper; she said nothing, did nothing: only to be in this paradise with her idol there before her walking about in a black velvet suit; to be listening to his talk, and to the song of the birds, and to the scythe of the reapers; to witness such beautiful sights, gracious aspects, changing skies—it was too good almost to be true. It seemed to Catharine as if the song in her heart was pouring out; she could not contain it, and all the air seemed full of music. She wondered if the others were listening to it too. But they were busy unpacking the hampers and getting out the sherry, nor had they all of them the ears to hear.

Some gifts are dangerous to those who possess them: this one of Catharine's means much discord in life as well as great harmony; saddest silence, the endless terrors and miseries of an imaginative nature; the disappointment of capacities for happiness too great to be ever satisfied in this world.

But, in the mean time, Mrs. Butler, returning from a short excursion to the hampers, could hardly believe it was her silent and subdued little governess who was standing there chattering and laughing. Her eyes were dancing and her voice thrilling, for was not Dick standing by?

Providence made a great mistake when it put hearts into girls—hearts all ready to love, and to admire, and to be grateful and happy with a word, with a nothing. And if Providence had made a still farther mistake, and made dependents of the same stuff as the rest, and allowed them to forget for one instant their real station in life, Mrs. Butler was determined to supply any such deficiencies, and to remind Miss George if ever she chanced to forget. But poor little Catharine, as I have said, defied her in her brief hour of happiness. She would not remember, and, indeed, she could not prevent her cheeks from blushing and her eyes from shining more brightly than any others present. Her youth, her beauty, her sweet, abrupt girlishness asserted themselves for once, and could not be repressed. Nobody could put them out. Even when she was silent these things were speaking for her in a language no one could fail to understand. If it had been one of Mrs. Butler's own daughters, she would have looked on with gentlest maternal sympathy at so much innocent happiness; but for Miss George she had no feeling save that of uneasiness and disquiet. It was hard upon the poor mother to have to stand by and see her own well-educated, perfectly commonplace Georgie eclipsed—put out—distanced altogether by this stiff, startled, dark-eyed little creature, with the sudden bright blushes coming and going in her cheeks. Mrs. Butler could not help seeing that they all liked talking to her. Charles Butler, Holland (Mr. Holland had quite lost his heart to the pretty little governess), Dick, and Beamish even. But then Georgie did not look up all grateful and delighted if any body noticed her, and flush up like a snow mountain at sunrise!

Of course Catharine would have been behaving much better if she had shown far more strength of character, and never thought of any thing less desirable than Augusta's French or Lydia's history, and if she had overcome any feelings—even before she was conscious of them—except those connected with her interesting profession.

But Catharine had no strength of mind. She was led by any body and any thing that came across her way. She was one of those people who are better liked by men than by women; for it is difficult sometimes for the weary and hardly-tried amazons of life to feel a perfect tolerance and sympathy with other women of weaker mould and nature. These latter are generally shielded and carried along by other strength than their own; they rest all through the heat of the day, leaving others to fight their battles and to defend them, and then, when the battle is over, are resting still. The strongest and fiercest of amazons would be glad to lay down her arms at times, and rest, and be weak, and cared for; but the help comes not for her; she must bear the burden of her strength and courage, and fight on until the night.

Mrs. Butler was one of the amazons of the many tribes of amazons that still exist in the world. They are married as well as unmarried. This woman for years and years had worked, and striven, and battled for her husband and children; she managed them, and her husband, and his affairs; she dictated, and ruled, and commanded; she was very anxious at times, very weary, very dispirited, but she gave no sign, allowed no complaint to escape her, bore her sufferings in silence. Once, and once only, to her eldest daughter she had spoken a little half word, when things were going very wrong—when Francis's debts were most overwhelming—when Robert had got into some new scrape worse than the last — when money was not forthcoming, and every thing was looking dark. "Dear mamma," Catharine Butler had said, with her tender smile, and closed her arms round the poor harassed mother's neck in a yoke that never galled.

As the day wore on, Mrs. Butler seemed to avoid little Catharine, or only to speak to her in a cold, indifferent voice, that made the girl wonder what she had done amiss. Now and again she started at the rude set-downs to which she was little accustomed. What did it all mean? What crime was she guilty of? She could not bring herself to think otherwise than tenderly of any one belonging to the house she had learnt to love. She meekly pursued her persecutrix with beseeching eyes. She might as well have tried to melt a glacier. To people who have taken a prejudice or a dislike, every word is misunderstood, every look offends; and Catharine's wistful glances only annoyed and worried Mrs. Butler, who did not wish to be touched. Had some malicious Puck squeezed some of the juice of Oberon's purple flower upon Catharine's scarlet feather to set them all wandering and at cross purposes all through this midsummer's day? In and out of the house, the garden, the woods, this little Helen went along with the rest, looking prettier, more pathetic, every minute. We all have a gift of second-sight more or less developed, and Catharine knew something was coming now that the first burst of happiness was over. An old saw came into her head about a light heart in the morning bringing tears before night.

The luncheon did credit to Mundy and the hampers. There were no earwigs, only little soft winds to stir the cloth, cross-lights, and a gentle check-work of gray shadow upon the dresses. Charles Butler's second best wine was so good that they all laughed, and asked what his best could be. Sandy frisked about and feasted upon mayonnaise and pressed veal. Sandy had a companion, Mr. Holland's dog Peter, a self-conscious pug, with many affectations, and with all the weaknesses belonging to a sensitive nature. He was nevertheless a faithful and devoted friend, tender-hearted and curly-tailed. Sandy had seen less of the world, and sniffed about in a little rough coat without any pretensions, and was altogether of a less impressionable and artistic nature. He loved good sport, good bones, and a comfortable nap after dinner. His master was of a different calibre to Peter's, and dogs are certainly influenced by the people with whom they live. All day long Peter walked about at Holland's heels, quite regardless of Sandy's unmeaning attacks and invitations to race or to growl. Peter only shook him off, and advanced in that confidential, consequential manner which is peculiar to his race.

Luncheon had come to an end. Catharine looked up, and breathed a great breath as she looked into the keen glimmer overhead; soft little winds, scented with pine-wood and rose-trees, came and blew about. Holland and Dick had got into a new discussion over the famous Gainsborough, and the children, who thought it all very stupid, had jumped up one by one and run away to the croquet-ground. But Catharine forgot to go. There she sat on the grass, with her back against the trunk of the tree, saying nothing, looking every thing, listening and absorbed. Catharine did well to rest in this green bower for a little before starting along the dusty high-road again. People are forever uttering warnings, and telling of the dangers, and deep precipices, and roaring torrents to be passed; but there are every where, thanks be to heaven, green bowers and shady places along the steepest roads. And so, too, when the tempest blows without and the rain is beating—tired, and cold, and weary, you come, perhaps, to a little roadside inn, where lights are burning, and food and rest await you. The storm has not ceased; it is raging still, but a shelter interposes between you and it for a time, and you set off with new strength and new courage to face it.

Mrs. Butler, as usual, recalled Catharine to herself.

"Miss George, be so good as to see what the children are doing." And so poor Catharine was dismissed from her green bower. It was hard to have to go—to be dismissed in disgrace, as it were, with Dick standing by to see it. The children were close at hand, and not thinking of mischief.

"We don't want you, Miss George," cried Lydia; "we are four already; stand there and see me croquet Augusta." Miss George stood where she was told, but she looked beyond the point which was of all-absorbing interest to Lydia at that instant. Her sad eyes strayed to the group under the tree. There was Dick lying at full length on the grass: he was smoking, and had hung up his red cap on a branch. Holland, in his iron-gray suit, was leaning against the trunk; Catharine Butler and Beamish were side by side in the shadow. Georgie was in the sunshine, with her dress all beflecked with trembling lights and shades, while the elders sat at the table talking over by-gone times. Catharine turned away; she could not bear the sight; it made her feel so forlorn and alone to stand apart and watch all these people together.

Catharine was afraid, too, lest some one should come up and see her eyes full of tears as she stood watching the balls roll and listening to the tap of the mallets. It was all so lovely and yet so perverse. The sweetness, the roses, the sunshine, made it *hurt* more, she thought, when other things were unkind. This day's pleasure was like a false friend with a smiling face; like a beautiful sweet rose which she had picked just now, with a great sharp thorn set under the leaf. What had she done? Why did Mrs. Butler look so cold and so displeased when she spoke? Whenever she was happiest something occurred to remind her and warn her that happiness was not for her, Catharine longed to be alone, but it was quite late in the afternoon before she could get away. The children were all called into the drawing-room by their sisters, and then the little governess escaped along the avenue where the rose-leaves which Beamish and Catharine had scattered were lying. She was sick at heart and disappointed. It was something more than mere vanity wounded which stung her as she realized that for some inscrutable reason it is heaven's decree that people should not be alike; that some must be alone and some in company; some sad and some merry; that some should have the knowledge of good and others the knowledge of evil. She must not hope for roses such as Catharine's. She must not be like Georgie, even, and speak out her own mind, and make her own friends, and be her own self. It was hard to be humiliated before Dick. It was no humiliation to be a governess and to earn her own living; but to have forgotten her place, and to be sent down lower like the man in the parable—ah! it was hard.

Catharine wandered on without much caring where she went, until she found herself in a quaint, sunny nook, where all sorts of old-fashioned flowers were blowing—tiger lilies, white lilies, balsam, carnations—in a blaze against the lichen-grown walls. The colors were so bright, the place so silent, and sweet, and perfumed, that Catharine, coming into it, forgot her dull speculations. It had been a flower-garden which Miss Paventry had laid out once upon a time, and it had been kept unchanged ever since. Quaint, bright, strange, it was the almost forgotten perfume of other times that these flowers were exhaling.

Catharine staid there a long time. She could not tear herself away. She was standing by a tall lily, with her nose in the cup, sniffing up the faint sleepy fragrance, when she heard steps upon the gravel-walk, and, turning round, she saw a bright red cap, and beside it a careless figure coming along with the peculiar swinging walk she knew so well. Ever after the scent of lilies conjured up the little scene.

Long afterward, Dick, too, remembered the little figure turning round with startled eyes, and looking as guilty as if it were a crime to be found smelling the lilies. Holland thought she might have been an Italian Madonna in her framework of flowers, such as the old painters loved to paint.

"Have you been hiding yourself away here all the afternoon?" said Dick. "Ain't it a charming little corner?"

The two young men waited for a few minutes, and seemed to take it for granted Catharine was coming back to the house with them.

"Do you dislike our cigars?" said Butler, seeing that she hesitated.

"Oh no! It was—"

She stopped short, blushed, and came hastily forward. What would Mrs. Butler say, she was thinking; and then she was afraid lest they should have guessed what she thought.

What would Mrs. Butler say? What did she say when she saw the three walking quietly toward the house, sauntering across the lawn, stopping, advancing again, and talking as they came?

Catharine's fate, like most people's, was settled by chance, as it were. People seem themselves to give the signal to destiny, Fall axe, strike fatal match. Catharine dropped a rose she was holding, and Dick bent down and picked it up for her, and that was the signal. No one saw the axe, but it fell at that moment, and the poor little thing's doom was fulfilled.

The ladies, tired of the noise indoors, had come out upon the terrace. The children had been dancing—a Spanish dance, they called it—for the last twenty minutes; gracefully sliding about, and waving their legs and arms to Georgie's performance on the piano-forte. The jingle of the music reached the terrace, but it was only loud enough to give a certain zest to the mildness and quiet of the sunset. The long shadows were streaking the hills, a glow shivered, spread, and tranquilly illumined the landscape, as the two figures on the terrace looked out at the three others advancing across the lawn.

"Miss George forgets herself strangely," said Mrs. Butler; "to-morrow shall end all this; but it is really very embarrassing to be obliged to dismiss her. I shall send her to Mrs. Martingale's, from whom I hope to get a German this time."

"Poor child!" said Madame de Tracy, compassionately; "she means no harm. I have a great mind to take her back to Ernestine. I am sure my daughter-in-law would be delighted with her, Ernestine is so fastidious."

"I really can not advise you," said Mrs. Butler. "This is a warning to me never to engage a pretty governess again."

"She can not help being pretty," said Madame de Tracy. "I detest ugly people," remarked this Good Samaritan. "I believe she would be a treasure to Ernestine. Those beloved children are darlings, but they speak English like little cats; their accent is deplorable, and yet their mother will not allow it. I am sure she ought to be eternally grateful to me if I take back Miss George."

"Pray take care, my dear Matilda," said Mrs. Butler. "Interference is always so undesirable. I always try to keep to my own side of the way. I really could not blame Ernestine if she should . . ."

Madame de Tracy could not endure opposition. "I do not agree with you. There is nothing so valuable as judicious interference. I know perfectly what I am about; Ernestine will be quite enchanted." Madame de Tracy was so positive that Mrs. Butler hesitated; she disliked scenes and explanations. Here was an easy way of getting rid of the poor little objection at once, without effort or trouble; she would be provided for, and Mrs. Butler was not without one single grain of kindness in her composition. Miss George had been very useful and conscientious; she had nursed Algy when he was ill. Mrs. Butler was angry with Catharine, but she did not wish her harm; she was, to a certain point, a just woman with her temper under control.

"I think it would be an excellent opportunity," said she, "if Ernestine really wishes for a governess for her children, and you are not afraid of the responsibility."

"Oh, I will answer for that," said Madame de Tracy, waving a welcome to the two young men. "The thing is arranged. Hush-sh-sh!"

Madame de Tracy's warnings usually came after the flash, like the report of a gun. Catharine, coming along and listening a little anxiously for the first greetings, caught the words and the glance of significance. What had they been saying? what did it mean? Her quick apprehensions conjured up a hundred different solutions; reprimands in store, no more holidays, no more merry-making. The reality occurred to her as an impossibility almost. To very young people changes are so impossible. They would like to come and to go, and to see all the world, but to return always to the nest in the same old creaking branch of the tree. Catharine was frightened and uneasy. All the way home in the drag, through the gray and golden evening; in the railway, scudding through a dusky wide country, where lights shone from the farmsteads, and pools still reflected the yellow in the west, she sat silent in her corner, with little Sarah asleep beside her. Catharine sat there half happy, almost satisfied, and yet very sad, and imagining coming evils. Let them come! They only seemed to make the day which was just over shine brighter and brighter by comparison. They could not take

it from her; she should remember it always. And Catharine said grace, as the children do, sitting there in her quiet corner. "Oh, I wish I was always happy," thought the girl; "I do so like being happy! . . ."

"Nothing could have gone off better," said Hervey, at the window, as they all got out at Victoria Station.

"That idiot Mundy very nearly ruined the whole thing," said Charles. "He forgot the soda-water. I had to telegraph to G——"

"Thanks so much," said Mrs. Butler, coming up. "Now, children? Has any one called a cab for them? The carriage has come for us."

"Good-night, Miss George," said Dick, under a lamp-post; and every body else said "Good-night, good-night."

CHAPTER VII.

"À QUOI JE SONGE."

MEANWHILE Catharine's fate was settled, and Mrs. Butler came into the school-room next morning to announce it. A sort of feeling came over her, poor child, that it was her death-warrant which this gracious lady in black silk robes was announcing in a particularly bland, encouraging tone of voice. What had she done? against whom had she conspired? of what treason was she guilty?

"Oh, why am I to go?" said Catharine, looking up very pale from her book with round, dark, startled eyes.

Even Mrs. Butler's much preoccupied heart was touched by the little thing's helpless, woe-begone appeal.

"You have always been quite invaluable to me, my dear Miss George, and I shall miss you excessively, but it is sincerely in your own interest that I am recommending this step to you," Mrs. Butler said, not unkindly.

"Oh no, no," said Catharine, feebly clutching at the table-cover. "This is too far; I can not speak French. I could not bear to be away, to leave my sisters, every body!" And she suddenly burst out crying. "Oh, I am so silly, so sorry," she sobbed, "for of course I must leave, if you wish it."

"Pray, my dear Miss George," said Mrs. Butler, still kind, yet provoked, "do not distress yourself unnecessarily. You are really quite blind, on this occasion, to your own advantage" (and this was a thing that was almost incomprehensible to Mrs. Butler). "Forgive me for saying so, but I do think it is your duty (as it is that of every one of us) to make the best of circumstances, particularly when there is an increase of salary and an excellent opportunity for improving in French. I do seriously recommend you to think my sister-in-law's proposal well over, and to consult your friends."

And the messenger of fate hastened off to her davenport, and poor Catharine sat crying, with the tears dripping over the page.

No, no, no; she could not bear to go tossing about all alone in the world; it was too hard, too hard. What was she to do? who would tell her what she was to do? Once a wild thought came to her of asking Dick to help her; he was kind—he would not let them send her away. Why were they driving her from their door? What had she done?—what indeed? A swift terror jarred through her beyond the other sad complex emotions that were passing in disorder through her mind. Could they think, could they imagine for one minute? The little pale face began to burn, and the eyes to flash, and her hands seemed to grow cold with horror; but no, no, it was impossible. They could not read her heart; and if they did, what was there for them to see? They were worldly, hard people; they did not know what friendship meant, how faithful it could be, how long it could last, how much it was ready to give, how little it required. And then, after a time, a revulsion came, and she felt as if all she wanted was to go—to go away and hide her head from them all. If it were not for Rosy and Totty, she did not care what was to come.

She went to bed that night with a heart aching dully, and she dreamt sad dreams until the morning came; and then, as Mrs. Butler advised, Catharine thought of consulting her friends. She walked down to Kensington to Mrs. Martingale's school, where her two chief advisers were to be found, and she wrote a couple of notes, which she posted on her way—one was to Lady Farebrother, at Tunbridge Wells, who belonged to the religious community there; the other was to Mrs. Buckington, who was staying at Brighton for her health. It was another bright summer day; dinner was over, and the school-girls and governesses seemed to have agreed to a truce, and to have come out together for an hour's peace and refreshment on the green overgrown garden at the back of the house. Jessamines were on the walls, and there were spreading trees, under one of which the French governess was reading a limp *Journal des Demoiselles*, smelling of hair-pins and pomatum from the drawer in which it was kept.

Miss Strumpf, the German governess (she was to leave this quarter, it was darkly whispered), was eating a small piece of cheese which she had saved from her dinner, and a rotten-looking medlar she had picked up off the grass. Some of the girls were dancing a quadrille on the lawn; others were singing and aimlessly rushing about the space inclosed by the four moss-grown walls, against which jessamines, and japonicas, and Virginian creepers were growing. Rosy and Totty, and a few chosen friends, were in a group on the step of the cistern. Totty, who was a quaint and funny little girl of ten, with a red curly wig, and a great deal of imagination, was telling a story: her stories were very popular among the literary portion of the community; but her heroine came to an untimely end when the narrator heard who was up stairs.

Catharine was waiting in the great drawing-room with the many windows and the photograph books, and the fancy-work mats presented by retiring pupils, and the wax water-lily on the piece of looking-glass, a tribute from an accomplished dancing-mistress. She came to meet her sisters, looking very pale, with dark rings round her eyes.

"Cathy, Cathy, why do you look so funny?" said Totty, clutching her round the waist.

"Oh, Totty dear," said Cathy, holding the children tight to her, and trying not to cry, and to speak cheerfully, "I look funny because I am going away from Mrs. Butler's. I don't know what to do. I want you and Rosy to tell me what you think." And then she told them her little history in her plaintive voice, holding the hands tight—tight in hers. She had dreaded so telling them, that, now that it was over, she felt happier and almost relieved; it was not nearly so bad as she had feared.

"It is no use asking our aunts," said Rosy; "they will write great long letters, and be no help at all."

As for little Totty, she was so indignant with Mrs. Butler, so delighted at the promise of a whole six weeks' holiday next year to be spent alone with Catharine and Rosy in a cottage in the air, that she forgot the distance and the separation, and bore the news far more bravely than Catharine herself. Rosy, who was as tall as Catharine nearly, held her hand very tight, and did not say much. She was old for her age—a downright girl, with more courage than poor little Catharine, and a sort of elder sister feeling for her, though she was only thirteen. But some girls have the motherly element strongly developed in them from their veriest babyhood, when they nurse their dolls to sleep upon their soft little arms, and carefully put away the little broken toy because it must be in pain. And Rosy was one of these. She was not clever, but she seemed to understand with her heart what other people felt. She took Cathy's aching head in her arms, and laid it on her shoulder, and kissed her again and again, as a mother might have done.

"My poor old darling," said Rosy, "don't be unhappy at leaving us; I'll take care of Totty, and some day I'll take care of you too."

"But where shall we go to in the holidays?" said Totty, cheering up. "Let there be donkeys, please."

Fraulein Strumpf, who was curious by nature, happened to peep in at the drawing-room door, as she was passing, to see who the little girls' visitor might be. She was rather scandalized to see Rosy sitting in a big arm-chair, with her visitor kneeling on the floor before her, and Totty leaning with straggling legs and drooping curls over the arm. It seemed like a liberty, in this gray grim drawing-room, to be kneeling down on the floor instead of sitting upright and stiff at intervals upon the high-backed chair.

Even the sunshine came in through the tall windows in subdued streaks, playing on the ancient ceiling and the worn-out carpet. The three heads were very close together, and they had settled that it was to be a farm-house in Surrey, where they had once staid before.

"Do you remember the little wood where we picnicked?" said Rosy. "And the farmer's cart?" cried Totty, quite happy by this time. Catharine had all the troubles of youth to bear on her poor little shoulders, but she had also its best consolation. Here she was with the other two children, almost happy again at the thought of a go-cart and a baby-house, and some live toys to play with in the fields.

When she went away the color had come back into her cheeks. Rosy and Totty were leaning over the old-fashioned tall balcony, and kissing their hands. She saw them for many a day after, and carried one more vision away with her of the quaint old square, with its green garden, and ancient panes and doorways, of the dear, dear little faces smiling through their tears, and bidding her good speed.

She did not trust herself to say good-by to them again; and when Madame de Tracy went off in her cab with her maid and her tall gray boxes, little Catharine vanished too out of her accustomed corner in the school-room, and Fräulein Strumpf reigned in her stead. The morning's post brought Catharine two letters, which she read in the railway carriage on her way to Dover.

Mutton's Mansion, Oriental Place, Brighton.

MY DEAR CATHARINE,—Your letter was forwarded to me here from Park Crescent, which I left on Tuesday. For the last three weeks I had been feeling far from well, and scarcely strong enough to bear the exertion of my daily drive round the Regent's Park. My appetite also had fallen off sadly, and I hardly knew what it was to enjoy a meal. My good friend and able physician, Dr. Pattie, urgently recommended me to try sea air; and, notwithstanding my usual reluctance to move from home, I resolved to follow his advice. Dr. Pattie considers that there is nothing equal to sea-bathing for strengthening the nerves and the appetite, and he also has a high opinion of the merits of a fish diet, believing it to be exceedingly light and nutritive. But the difficulty here, and I believe it to be the case in all sea-port towns, is to get a variety of fish. I have only twice ventured to bathe, and found it very trying; but I must say that I am daily gaining strength, and that my appetite has certainly improved, although it is not yet all that I could wish. To return to your letter. I am truly concerned to hear that any thing should have occurred to unsettle your plans, and make you think of leaving your present excellent situation; but I am not indeed in a fit state of health to be able to offer you any advice. Thinking tells so upon my nerves, that Dr. Pattie has forbidden me to make any exertion of the sort. Your aunt Farebrother is far better able than I am to take your af-

fairs into consideration, so you had better write to her at once, and act upon what she says, at the same time using your own judgment in what you think best. Ever your affectionate aunt,   SOPHIA BUCKINGTON.

Tabor Villa, Mount Zion, Tunbridge Wells.

MY DEAREST NIECE,—Surrounded as I am by duties that to every humble Christian spirit stand first and foremost in the path of life, I have but little leisure or inclination to attend to any thing belonging to this world rather than to the next. I am the last person to whom you should apply for counsel, except, indeed, in matters relating to your spiritual welfare, for I have made it a rule never to waste time or thought over the trifling cares of every-day life. My sister, Mrs. Buckington, is better versed in worldly wisdom than I am, and I should recommend you always to ask and follow her advice in your little dilemmas; but you must not think that I am neglectful of you, or that I am not always ready to give my poor help in those subjects which lie within my field of work and thought. Only yesterday I had an opportunity of speaking long and earnestly about you with my dear friend and pastor, Mr. Bland. He and I both agreed that should you decide upon going to France, the one essential point to be considered is whether a young and feeble mind does not run a great risk of falling into the too-tempting snares of Popery. But then again Mr. Bland said, who could tell but that you might be the humble means of bringing some of those lost sheep to light! Surely it would be well to be provided with a few simple tracts, which you could distribute whenever you saw a fitting moment. Before you leave London, do not fail to go to the Religious Tract Society in Piccadilly, and ask for the Rev. Walpole Bland's Tracts for home and foreign use. By presenting a card of Mr. Bland's that I inclose you, you will get them at the reduced rate of half a crown a hundred—a small sum, indeed, for so great a treasure! I should also be glad if you would take with you to France a little parcel of Irish point lace, for which the French ladies (always so fond of dress) would, I dare say, like to raffle thirty tickets, 12s. 6d. each, for the benefit of the Polish Protestant colporteurs.

I shall be glad to hear that you are getting on satisfactorily, and believe me, my dear Catharine, yours affectionately,
                              P. G. FAREBROTHER.

Catharine sighed as she folded up the two letters and put them into her pocket. It was not the first time she had corresponded with her step-mother's sisters, but she was too sad to take things philosophically and to laugh.

All the way Madame de Tracy was in high spirits; she was delighted to get back to her children, to carry off Miss George, to have secured a pure English accent for Nanine, and Henri, and Madelaine. She sat surrounded by bags of which the contents seemed to fly from one to the other, like in some one of those conjuror's tricks. From bag to bag Madame de Tracy and Barbe, her long-suffering attendant, pursued a Bradshaw, a rouleau of sovereigns, a letter which had arrived that morning, a paper-cutter, all of which were captured and replaced in their various homes, only to be dispersed and hunted for again.

"Barbe, I have left my parasol in the cab—and my purse! We must telegraph. I distinctly remember laying it down on the waiting-room table. Ah! what a misfo—"

"Madame, there it is in your lap," said Barbe, calmly, "and your parasol is behind you."

"Ah! what an escape!" sighed Madame de Tracy. "The tickets, and more than thirty pounds, are in this purse, and I could not possibly have lost them; I am utterly ruined, I have bought so many things in London. Miss George, I see your book wants cutting; give it to me, I adore cutting open books. I envy you, you look so calm; you have none of these troublesome concerns to attend to—but some one must do it. Barbe, where is the paper-cutter?"

They had started late in the afternoon, and were to sleep at Calais, and to go on to Tracy the next day. They crossed on a still night with a waning moon. Many and many a sad, confused thought must have come to the little traveler by the light of the creaking lamp in the cabin. Faces, pictures, all the events of the last few weeks, were dancing about in the darkness; voices were sounding, the children's faces were looking at her out of dark corners. The lamp swung on its hinges, the vessel throbbed and shook, Catharine felt as if she was, indeed, a waif upon a great sea tossed hither and thither by wayward winds. How oddly distinct the voices and images fell upon her brain; Kitty, Cathy, she seemed to hear her little sisters calling her through the moans of the sea, by all the names they liked to give her; and another voice sounded in her foolish little ears, and her last few words with Dick seemed to be repeated to her by all the rolling waves.

She had only seen him once after that day at Lambswold. Catharine thought it was a cruel fate which prevented their meeting. It was more likely a sensible precaution. Doors, stairs, conventionalisms, had been piled in a great heap between them, and there is nothing so hard to pass as these simple impediments. The stairs are carpeted and easy to climb; the doors are on the latch, with nice china handles to open them; there is nothing to prevent; and yet prison bars have been burst open, burning deserts crossed, icy passes and steep mountains scaled and surmounted more easily than these simple obstacles.

There was a train to Paris, Madame de Tracy heard on landing, and she determined to go on. Catharine cared not. The night seemed to her like a sort of summary or epilogue to the little slice of a life which had belonged to her hitherto. She sat watching the black ghosts of trees, and walls, and wayside inns flying past the windows, the single lights here and there in the dark plain, and listening to the voices at the little stations, sounding melancholy and sudden as voices always do in the dark.

Her protectress peacefully dreamt through the long hours that Catharine watched and wondered. What would the day be like that had not yet dawned, the new world which awaited her? thought the girl with her wide-open shining eyes. Catharine George somehow expected that the sun would never rise; that the land would be always dark, and strange, and desolate to her; that she would find herself utterly alone, and wandering here and there in the gloom. . . .

She forgot in how great a measure one's future is made up of one's past—how we see and understand things by all those which have preceded them—how it is yesterday which makes to-morrow. The future is never so strange as we picture it to ourselves. A hundred golden threads bind us to it already. It is all one's whole past life which claims the future and draws it into itself. The lesson given long, long ago by the love which foresaw, teaches in after years when the occasion has come. One thing recalls another, as one thing forebodes another, and sometimes the two together make a full chord of happiness, or maybe of sadness, so grateful and so sweet, that it seems as if it must be happiness.

At any rate, when the next day came, Catharine found that instead of creeping slowly along, all gray and black, and dark and terrible, the future had come for her with a cheery clatter, and crack of whips, and blowing of horns, friendly faces looking out, a barking of dogs, some one to help her up the steps, as with cheerful confusion, and noise and jingle, they start through the bright light streets and cross the fertile plains of Normandy.

They had all finished dinner at Tracy, and were sitting about in the great drawing-room. The muffled piano stood in the middle of the room; the lamps were placed here and there; the polished floors were only covered by little square carpets, sprinkled sparsely about. Two rows of pink-striped chairs stood in lines from the fireplace, over which the Tracys had erected a tall and elaborately-carved chimney-piece. The furniture of the castle corresponded in date to the mahogany reign of terror in England, but in France at that period all was harmony and fitness, and you need dread no four-post beds at Tracy, no fierce sideboards, no glowering washstands and looming wardrobes.

The old clock over the chimney was ticking nine o'clock, the windows were open upon a sea of moonlight in the garden. There were glasses and bottles upon a side-table, where Marthe de Coëtlogon, Ernestine's sister, was playing dominoes with the curé, who had been asked to dinner. Monsieur de Tracy and Monsieur Fontaine, who had also had the honor of being invited, were smoking in the moonlit alleys of the garden.

Mademoiselle de Coëtlogon had a sweet, placid face, over which a smile would break now and then—not very often. She sat there in her long white dress, with her soft hair tied up simply with a blue ribbon, and the light of the lamp falling upon her face and the old curé's bald head. It seemed incongruous, somehow, that she should be playing dominoes, with that Madonna-like head—still and tender at once. She had been vowed to the Virgin by her father from the day she was born. Her life had been saved by a miracle, it was said, and Marthe grew up strong and well, but never like other people. She had a vocation from her earliest youth; never changed her mind or faltered for one minute. She was four-and-twenty now. In a year she would be of an age, according to the French law, to decide for herself. No one could influence her: not Jean, who could not bear the subject named before him; not her mother, a widow, who, wistful, half timid, half angry, scolded, entreated, cried, and implored and forbade in vain. Ernestine, her sister, was the only one of them who did not really object; on the contrary, such devotion seemed to reflect a certain credit on the family. But all the same; Madame de Tracy, at her mother's desire, did her best to distract her sister from her intentions by taking Marthe all one year into the world. Madame de Coëtlogon, too, accompanied her daughter. Toilettes, *partis*, music, gayeties of every description, poor Marthe endured in patience; but all these well-meant distractions had a very different effect to that which the poor mother hoped and longed for.

It seems strange to us commonplace, common-sense Protestant people, in these days of commonplace and common sense, living in the rough and ready world of iron, of progress, of matter of fact, to hear of passionate revival, and romance, and abstract speculation, to be told of the different experiences of living beings now existing together. While the still women go gliding along their convent passages to the sound of the prayer-bells, with their long veils hanging between them and the coarse, hard world of every day, the vulgar, careworn toilers, the charwomen and factory hands of life are at their unceasing toil, amid squalor and grime, and oaths, and cruel denseness; the hard-worked mothers of sickly children are slaving, day after day, in common lodging-houses, feeding on hard fare, scraps and ends from the butchers' shops, or refuse and broken victuals from some rich neighbor's kitchen; while others, again, warmed and fed in the body, wearing and starving mentally, are struggling through passionate sorrow and privation. . . .

Are work and suffering the litanies of some lives, one wonders? are patience, and pain, and humiliation, the fasts and the penances of others? No veils hang between the hard, brazen faces and the world; no convent bars inclose them other than the starting, ill-built brick walls of their shabby homes and lodging-places. But who shall say that the struggles, the pangs, the prayers, outcries of all these women, differently expressed and experienced though they are, do not go up together in one common utterance to that place where there is pity for the sorrowful and compassion for the weary?

Dick Butler, who had a tender heart himself, said one day, smoking his pipe, to some one who had cried out that she could **not** understand how the good God who made the little ones so pretty and so touching could bear to hear them weep for pain, "People seem to think themselves in some ways superior to Heaven itself when they complain of the sorrow and want round about them. And yet it is not the Devil for certain who puts pity into their hearts."

It is vain to try to answer such questions, but it is difficult not to wonder and speculate, as every day one sees stranger and subtler contrasts and forms of life. There is the good mother of the family—useful, busy, happy, bright-eyed and light-hearted, approaching her home, of which the shimmer seems to cheer and warm her as she sees it gleaming from a distance. There is the forlorn little traveler from Jerusalem whose wounds have been bound up with wine and oil, coming in her charge to the inn.

On the sofa, like a little lady out of Watteau, eating bonbons, sits young Madame de Tracy, occasionally smiling at the good old curé's compliments. She is a graceful young woman, with bright blue eyes, with a plaintive expression; and as she really has every thing in the world she wishes for, no wonder she is dissatisfied. Her life lies before her quite smooth, flat, uninteresting, all sunshine, and not a bit of shade any where, except what she can make for herself by raising an occasional storm, and, fortunately, her temper is easily upset.

Ernestine dressed charmingly in white, and lilac, and pink; she left blue ribbons to Marthe. She was very graceful in all her movements, even when she was angry. Her husband was a plain, good-natured-looking man, with a ribbon in his button-hole, and a hooked eye-glass. He was very rich, and gave her every thing she liked, and attended very patiently to all her reproaches. Ernestine liked him, and was proud of his abilities and indignant at his want of ambition. She was very proud also of her blue eyes, which she inherited from her mother; and as she did not bury her talents in a napkin, they were very much admired in the world at Paris, where she had an apartment, all full of great vases and cabinets, in which she spent her winters. In the spring and the summer she came down to her mother-in-law's house.

Madame Jean de Tracy was just popping a chocolate bonbon into her mouth when her husband and M. Fontaine came in from the garden.

"Madame, we have just seen a carriage turn into the long avenue," said M. Fontaine, hastening to tell the news; "we surmise that it may be madame votre belle-mère returning."

"It is certain to be her," cried Ernestine; "she told us not to expect her; and it is so late too."

"It is no use going to meet her; she will be here directly," said Jean, walking to the door in his deliberate way.

Almost directly there was a sound of voices, of exclamations—the cook, the valet-de-chambre, Sidonie, Madame Jean's maid, appeared to announce the safe arrival of the travelers. A couple of dogs came in barking—even the children's bonne came rushing down from up stairs ; the game of dominoes was interrupted ; Jean embraced his mother very affectionately as she entered the room ; Fontaine hovered about, deeply interested in the meeting, and hastened to relieve Madame de Tracy of her parasol ; parcels were wildly handed about like buckets at a conflagration ; then came more embraces, explanations, and exclamations. "You never came to meet me. I forgot to post my letter. Casimir brought us up in his little carriage." "Unfortunately we have dined. There is sure to be something. Bon jour, Barbe, here you are returned from England!" "We nearly did not get home at all; old Chrétien ran his cart up against us. He was quite tipsy. Oh, I am sure of it. Give us something to eat, for I am famished." All this in a crescendo, which was brought to a climax by a sudden shriek from Madame Jean.

"Who is that in the window?" she cried, pointing. "Look, there is somebody ;" and she seized her husband's arm.

"I am really too forgetful. Come here, my dear child," cried Madame de Tracy. "Here is my dear young friend, Miss George, Ernestine ; I have persuaded her to come back with me."

At this incantation the little apparition who had been standing clasping her great warm shawl, and childishly absorbed in the scene, wondering who each person could be, advanced blushing, with ruffled hair, and trailing her long draperies. She looked up into their faces with that confiding way she had. Madame Jean made her a little inclination ; Jean came up and good-naturedly shook hands à l'Anglaise ; Monsieur Fontaine, parasol in hand, bowed profoundly Tired as she was, hungry, preoccupied by her return home, an idea flashed through Madame de Tracy's fertile mind at that instant, which, alas! unlike many of her ideas, she was destined to put into execution.

"Monsieur Fontaine, our excellent maire," said she, going on with her introductions ; "Mademoiselle de Coëtlogon, M. l'Abbé Verdier. Ernestine we will give Miss George the yellow room, and some supper. My dear child, I am dying of hunger. I have eaten nothing but little tartlets all day."

The tartlets, the chateau, the moonlight, the ladies, the whole journey, seemed to come out of the *Arabian Nights*, Catharine thought, only the abbé did not belong to them. The quiet little old man, sitting in the corner, caused a thrill to this stern Protestant of which he was happily unconscious.

Catharine and her protectress supped in the great dining-room—a long and lofty room, with a fine ceiling, and many tall windows, barred and shuttered. The one lamp only lighted the table, where cold meat, and cream cheese, and a melon and grapes were spread. Jean accompanied them, and so did Ernestine, who flung a pretty white hood over her head, and sat watching them at their meal.

"And your grandmother, how is she?" asked Madame de Tracy of her son.

"She is as usual," said Jean ; "she has heard of your return, and Baptiste has just come down to ask for a little supper for her from your table. Miss George, you do not eat. You must get a good appetite at Tracy. I hope you are going to stay with us for some time."

Again Catharine blushed up, and looked from her host to the little lady with the bright eyes. "I thought—I hoped," she stammered—

"We have got her safe," interrupted Madame de Tracy, flurriedly, carving away at a cold chicken. "We are not going to part from her." Poor lady, her courage was failing her somewhat. She did not like the looks Madame Jeane was casting at her little *protégée*. She made haste to send Catharine to bed as soon as she had done her supper. Baptiste with a candle, and Barbe, were both deputed to show Miss George the way up the broad stone stairs, with curiously-scrolled iron railings, along a great stone passage, dark with shadows, and with windows at intervals looking on the moonlit court-yard. Their footsteps echoed, and their moon-shadows flitted along with them. Catharine looked out once, and saw a figure crossing the court. The iron gates opened to let it out, and she recognized the tall dark gentleman they had called Monsieur Fontaine. "I imagined he was Monsieur de Tracy when I first came in," Catharine thought. "They were both very kind."

"What is that distant noise?" she asked Barbe, as she followed her up more stairs and passages.

"That is the sound of the sea, mademoiselle," said Barbe. "We hear it very well from here when the wind blows in this direction."

Catharine dreamt of the sea that night, of her journey, of the abbé and Monsieur Fontaine, of Beamish, playing his marches and sonatas in Dick's studio. She dreamt that she heard the music even, and then, somehow, she herself was playing, and they were all listening to her ; but the notes would not strike—in vain she tried—she could bring forth no sound ; and the sea came nearer and nearer all the time, and the waves flowed in tune. It was a horrible dream, though when she awoke there was nothing much in it.

CHAPTER VIII.

REINE.

THE tide which sways between the two great shores of England and of France sometimes beats against our chalk cliffs, which spread in long low lines gleaming tranquilly in the sun, while the great wave-armies roll up with thundering might to attack them; sometimes it rushes over the vast sand-plains and sand-hills, the dunes and the marshes of France, spreading and spreading until its fury of approach is spent, and then perhaps, as the sun begins to set, and the sky to clear, suddenly the water stills and brightens, and the fishing-boats put out to sea with the retiring tide. Some people living on the shores listen to the distant moan of the waters as they roll and roll away; some are so used by long custom that they scarcely heed the sad echoing. But others are never accustomed. One woman has told me that for years after she first came to live in her husband's house by the sea, the consciousness of its moan never left her. She never could grow used to it. It haunted her in her sleep, in her talk, in her daily occupations. She thought at one time she should go mad if the sound did not cease; it would die away into the distance, and then come rolling nearer and louder, with passionate sobs and sudden moans, and the wild, startling, discordant cries of the water-birds. She had a foolish superstition that she should be happy when she ceased to hear the moan of the sea.

What is this strange voice of Nature that says with one utterance so many unlike things? Is it that we only hear the voice of our own hearts in the sound of the waves, in the sad cries of birds as they fly, of animals, the shivering of trees, the creaking and starting of the daily familiar things all about their homes?

This echo of the sea, which to some was a complaint and a reproach, was to Reine Chrétien like the voice of a friend and teacher—of a religion almost. There are images so natural and simple that they become more than mere images and symbols; and to her, when she looked at the gleaming immensity, it was almost actually and in truth to her the great sea, upon the shores of which we say we are as children playing with the pebbles. It was her formula. Her prayers went out unconsciously toward the horizon, as some pray looking toward heaven, in the words which their fathers have used; and some pray by the pains they suffer; and some by the love which is in them; and some, again, without many words, pray in their lives and their daily work, but do not often put into actual phrases and periphrases the story of their labors, and weariness, and effort. The other children on the shore are sometimes at variance with these latter in their play; for while they are all heaping up their stores of pebbles, and stones, and shells, and building strange fantastic piles, and drawing intricate figures upon the sand, and busily digging foundations which the morning tides come and sweep away, suddenly they seem to grow angry, and they wrathfully pick up the pebbles and fling them at one another, wounding, and cutting, and bruising with the sharp edges.

How long ago is it since the children at their play were striking the flints together to make fires to burn the impious ones who dared to point to the advancing tides and say, See, they come to wash away your boundaries. The advancing tides, thanks be to God, have in their turn put out those cruel fires; but sharp stones still go flying through the air, and handfuls of sand, and pebbles, and long, straggling bunches of sea-weed that do no great harm, perhaps, but which sting and draggle where they fall.

Reine, on her sea-shore, picked up her stones with the rest of us, and carefully treasured the relics which she inherited from her mother, the good Catholic, since whose death her life would have been a sad one if it had not been so full of small concerns of unintermitting work. She, too, like the other woman of whom I have been writing, heard the sound of the sea as she went about her daily occupations, but to Reine it seemed like the supplement and encouragement of her lonely life. She listened to it as she went her rounds from the great kitchen to the outer boundaries of the farm, across the orchards and fields to the garden a mile off where her beans were growing, or sometimes sitting, resting by the blazing hearth, where the wood was heaped and the dried colza grass flaring.

Reine's religion was that in which she had been brought up from a child. Her mother professed the same faith as the Marions, and the Sabeans, and the Picards of the place. She had used the same words and outward signs as her husband until his death—as old Pierre Chrétien, the grandfather—but their sense was not the same. The old grandfather, in his blouse, rather avoided contemplating the future. He had a pretty clear idea of a place not unlike the chapel of the Deliverande, only larger, with statuettes at intervals, and Monsieur le Curé triumphant. It was more comfortable, on the whole, to retire to the kitchen of the Golden Sun, where Pélottier dispensed cider and good wine at twopence a bottle, and from whence Pierre's granddaughter, with angry, dogged eyes, had fetched him away on more than one occasion: a terrible apparition in her beauty and her indignation. The children themselves would fly before her on such occasions, and they were generally her best friends.

Reine was one of those people whose inner life works upon their outer life, and battles with it. She had inherited her mother's emotions' nature, and her father's strong and vigorous constitution. She was strong where her mother had been weak. She had thoughts and intuitions undreamt of by those among whom she lived. But things went crossways with her, and she suffered from it. She was hard and rough at times, and had not that gentleness and openness which belong to education and to culture.

Beyond the horizon dawned for her the kingdom of saints and martyrs, for which her mother before her had longed as each weary day
went by ; the kingdom where, for the poor woman, the star-crowned Queen of Heaven reigned
with pitiful eyes. Reine did not want pity or
compassion as yet. She was a woman with love
in her heart, but she was not tender, as some
are, or long-suffering ; she was not unselfish, as,
others who abnegate and submit until nothing
remains but a soulless body, a cataleptic subject
mesmerized by a stronger will. She was not
humble, easily entreated, unsuspicious of evil.
The devil and his angels had sown tares enough
in her heart to spring up in the good soil thick,
and rank, and abundant ; only it was good soil
in which they were growing, and in which the
grain of mustard-seed would spring up too, and
become a great tree in time, with wide-spreading branches, although the thick weeds and poisonous grasses were tangling in a wilderness at
its root.

Reine on her knees, under the great arch of
Bayeux Cathedral, with the triumphant strains
of the anthem resounding in her ears, would
have seemed to some a not unworthy type of
the Peasant Girl of Domremy, in Lorraine. As
the music rang higher and shriller, the vibrations of the organ filled the crowded edifice.
Priests stood at the high altar celebrating their
mysteries ; the incense was rising in streams
from the censers ; people's heads went bending
lower and lower ; to Reine a glory seemed to fill
the place like the glory of the pink cloud in the
Temple, and the heavens of her heart were unfolded. The saints and visions of her dim imaginations had no high commands for their
votary ; they did not bid her deliver her country, but sent her home to her plodding ways and
her daily task, moved, disturbed, with a gentler
fire in her eye, and with the soft chord in her
voice stirred and harmonizing its harsher tone.

Reine's voice was a peculiar one, and must
have struck any one hearing it for the first
time. It rung odd, sudden, harmonious, with a
sort of jar in it, or chord. Voices of this quality are capable of infinite modulation. Sometimes they soften into gay yet melancholy music, like Mozart's, of which they always remind
me ; sometimes they harden into the roughest
and iciest of discordant accents.

She liked going back by herself, after the
service was over, quietly across the plain. She
was strong, and the three miles to Tracy, skirting the road and the corn-fields, were no fatigue
to her, especially in the summer, when the corn
was waving gold, and the blue bright flowers
and the poppies blazed among the tall yellow
stalks. Sometimes Reine would ride back on
her donkey. This was when she stopped at a
low long house with windows opening on the
street at the entrance of the town, at the door
of which she would find poor Annette waiting
patiently, tied to a ring in the wall.

On these occasions Reine would go to the
window and call out in her kindest voice, "Eh

bien, Madame Marteau, am I to have Josette
to-day to come and play with the little chickens?"

Josette was Reine's goddaughter, who had
been christened Josephine Marine Reine des
Cieux, after her "marraine." She was a tiny
little girl, with two round eyes, and a little tight
black cap tied under her chin, and a little black
stuff pinafore and trowsers to match. Reine
was fond of the child, and charming with her.
She was one of those people who are like angels
when they protect and take care of others, and
who are hard, ungrateful, suspicious, unjust, to
those to whom they are obliged to look up.

On this particular Sunday, while the luncheon
trays were steaming into the dining-room in
Eaton Square, with Dick driving up to the door
in a hansom, and Mr. Butler still rustling the
Observer in his study ; while Beamish and Catharine were slowly walking home from church,
and little Catharine, who had preceded them,
was standing all by herself in the school-room,
vacantly plaiting and unplaiting the tassel of
the blind, and pulling the ragged ends, and
thinking of the future looming darkly—it was
her last day in the dismal little bastile ; and,
now that the end was come, she looked back
with a child's passion of persistence and longing
to the threads and straws with which she had
beguiled her time—while all this was going on
in one small corner of the world, in another
Reine was pulling out her strong arms, and
lifting little Josette on to the donkey's back.

Josette's mother—a care-worn woman in
shabby clothes—was standing in the sun, shading her dimmed eyes : the light dazzled poor
Madame Marteau. Her life was spent in a
sort of twilight gloom, nursing the bedridden
husband whose voice even now might be heard
muttering and calling from an inner room.
The poor woman looked on with a glimpse of
pleasure in her sad face, grateful to Reine for
carrying off the little maiden into a wholesome,
bright atmosphere, where there were flowers
growing, and little chickens running about, and
a little boy to play with sometimes, to a place
where Josette expanded with delight in all the
glory of childhood, instead of being dwarfed
into a precocious little woman by Père Marteau's railings and scoldings.

"Well, Josette, what does one say?" said
Madame Marteau.

"Bo zour, marraine," lisped Josette, hanging her head, and pretending to be shy.

"Josette is coming home with me," said
Reine, "to see Belette and Miné, and to ask
Petitpère to give her some brioche," to all of
which propositions Josette nodded her head.
And then she said something which sounded
like J'allonsvoïrletitoto.

"They begin soon enough," said Madame
Marteau, shrugging her weary shoulders. "She
is always talking about le petit Toto. M. Fontaine must take care. . . ."

Here, like a distant roll of musketry, came a
volley of r-r-r's from the inner room. Reine

frowned and turned away. Madame Marteau hastily nodded good-by and passed in, disappearing into the gloom, while Reine and little Josette rode on together through the sunlit fields.

Josette had her wish, and Toto was allowed to come and spend the day with her. Toto's grandmother favored Mademoiselle Chrétien, and never denied her requests. The two children dined with Reine and her father in the great dark farm-kitchen. They had soup with bread in it, and cider, and stewed beef and cabbage, and as much galette as they could eat. Reine took care of them and old Chrétien; she poured out the cider, and went away herself to fetch a particular dish of eggs which her grandfather liked. Dominique dined with them too. The great dog came marching in through the open door; the cocks and hens came and peeped at them. Outside it was all sunny and still; inside there was galette and two pretty little plates and tumblers for the children to use, and all Reine's treasures—brooches, and rosaries, and reliquaries—for them to play with after dinner, and Reine herself bustling about with her gold earrings bobbing as she bent over the table. But she was silent, although she attended to them all, and she looked at the door once and sighed.

Old Chrétien joked her, and asked Dominique what was the matter. Reine answered short and quick. For one thing, the thought of that poor woman's wretchedness oppressed her. "I name no names because of the children," she said, "but it seems to me it must be like a hell upon earth to be chained to wild beasts, as some women are."

"And that is why she don't marry," said old Chrétien to Dominique, filling his glass. "Well, we all please ourselves! I have seen more than one ill-assorted couple in my time. . . . Here in this very room. . . ."

Reine flushed up. "Now, children, make haste," she said, in her harsh, quick voice. "Dominique! you will be here. I shall come back in an hour. Petitpère, here is your pipe already lighted." And then, taking one child by each hand, she dragged them away across the great deserted-looking court, and out at the arched gateway into the road, and into a tall hay-field which skirted it. Paris, the great dog, came too, and Reine pulled a book out of her pocket and sank down in the hay, while the two little things, hand in hand, swam and struggled through the tall grasses. Their heads only overtopped the hay by a very little. Toto made way, and valiantly knocked down a marguérite which stood in Josette's way, and chased away a bluebottle which frightened her with its noises. Josette laughed, and capered, and danced on her little stout boots.

"Oh, the waves, the waves!" cried Toto, as a soft wind came blowing from afar, bending the tall grass and the flower-heads, and shaking a few apples off the branches of the tree where Reine was sitting. "Come and fish for the apples," said she, smiling, as the two little creatures came tumbling and pushing through the deep sea of hay.

Monsieur de Tracy from the chateau happened to be passing along the high-road at that instant, and he, too, smiled good-naturedly and took off his hat.

"Bon jour, Mademoiselle Chrétien," he said. "Are you not afraid of spoiling your hay?"

Reine scarcely acknowledged his greeting: she looked fierce and defiant, and gave a little stiff nod, and went on reading a book.

"Is not that M. Fontaine's little boy?" said Jean, stopping and looking at the trio among the sweet dry grasses and flowers. The children were peeping at him bright-eyed and interested from a safe distance. Reine never lifted her eyes off her book: "Marie, qui avez mené une vie simple et laborieuse, priez pour moi afin que j'apprenne à me contenter de peu de chose et à travailler selon les devoirs de ma condition," she was murmuring to herself, and she did not cease her pious exercise until M. de Tracy had walked on.

"I wonder why that girl always behaves so strangely?" thought Jean, as he walked away. "Can my mother have vexed her in any way? I must ask my wife."

Madame Jean held up her pretty little hands at the question.

"Mon ami, it is not I who would like to answer for what your mother may or may not have said," laughed she.

But Madame de Tracy had said nothing, and indeed she was a favorite with the people all about. They laughed at her flightiness and expansiveness, mistrusted her promise, but they could not help liking her. Reine took to her more kindly than to the rest of the family; all her worst self would come up when she was brought in contact with these people, who came stepping down from their superior grandeur to be intrusively civil to those who did not want them. "What does he mean by his Mademoiselle Chrétiens, and eye-glasses, and politeness?" thought the foolish girl. "I know well enough at what rate he holds us, and I try to tell him so in my way." Reine was not a bad girl, but the sight of all this prosperity turned her sour. "'How do you do? Take care of your hay'—Madame Jean's maddening little nod as she trips in her Paris toilette, and Mademoiselle Martha's great blue eyes—it all offends me," said Reine, cutting the matter short.

This was the class to which her mother belonged. These were the men and the women who had cast her off—never forgiven her—forgotten her utterly. These were the people who would do the same to-morrow again; who would insult her and scorn her, as they had scorned her mother before her, for all her beauty, and good blood, and wealth, if—if she were not firm to a certain resolve she had made. No, she would never marry, never, never. Not if he came back again and again to ask her. Reine had an instinct about the person of whom she was thinking. She believed that no one whom she loved could help loving her ; but she was proud at the same time. She knew her own worth, and a poor, struggling painter, with all his education, did not seem to her any very brilliant match for an heiress like herself, with the blood of the D'Argouges in her veins, and the farms at Tracy, at Petitport, the oyster-parks at Courseulles, the houses at Bayeux, for her dower. "Venez, mes enfants," said Reine, shutting up her prayer-book when the hour was over, and leading them back by the way she had come under the archway across the great court, where Paris was lying stretched out like a lion in the sun, and where Reine looked to find her grandfather on the bench where he was accustomed to smoke his afternoon pipe. There was only Dominique on the bench stretched out on his back at full length.

Reine went up and shook him angrily. "Dominique, are you not ashamed to sleep like a sluggard ? Where is Petitpère ?"

Dominique sat up and rubbed his eyes. "He is asleep in the kitchen," said he, hazarding the statement.

"Ah !" cried Reine, taking one step forward, and looking through the barred window, "he is not in the kitchen. You know as well as I do where he is gone."

While Dominique and the children were having a game in front of the farm-gates, which made the old place echo with Toto's screams of laughter, Reine was marching down the little village street, tall, erect, with her terrible face on. Poor Reine ! poor Petitpère ! He was discoursing very happily and incoherently in one of the little bowers at the back of the Golden Sun. A very little of M. Pélottier's cider was enough to change the aspect of things for poor old Chrétien. He was treating everybody, and offering his granddaughter in marriage to another old gentleman in a blouse, sitting at the same little table.

"Je te l'accorde," said père Chrétien, "avec ses cent cinquante mille livres de rente. Mon ami Barbeau, elle est à toi."

"Merci bien, mon ami," said Barbeau, thumping the little wooden table.

"Et Madame Barbeau, what will she think of the arrangement ?" said a countrywoman, who was sitting at the next table, looking round grinning.

Barbeau looked puzzled. "Ma femme ?" said he. "Le père Chrétien se charge de tout. Buvons à sa santé !"

It was at this instant that the bottle was suddenly wrenched out of poor old Chrétien's trembling hand, and that Reine, pale and with black eyes gleaming, took him by the arm in her unflinching gripe.

"Come," she said, with a glance of indignation at the people who were grinning all round about under Pélottier's little vine bower, and she walked away back toward Tracy with her prisoner. Old Chrétien shambled beside her in silence ; he knew her too well to attempt to make conversation under the circumstances. Only once a sort of groan escaped her. As they were turning the corner by the church, again she came upon the whole community of Tracys — Jean and his wife, and his wife's brother and sister, and the three children running on ahead.

Old Chrétien attempted a low, uncertain bow. Reine thought she saw them smile. She gave one fierce glance and walked on : her heart was beating with indignation, with pride and passionate shame. They scorned her and her grandfather. Their glances, their laughter maddened her. There she was, condemned for life to live with a few tipsy men and vulgar dull women, who saw no shame in their husbands' degradation. There were those people born into an atmosphere of light and refinement. What had they done, what had she done, to deserve such happiness, such misery ? Why was she not like the rest of her class ? Poor grandfather—poor old man, he was only what he had been taught to be from his earliest youth : his servile bow to the grandees from the castle, what was that but a part and parcel of the rest ? She turned to him with a sudden tender impulse of pity and protection, and yet all the time a fierce impatience and anger were tearing at the woman's heart ; as she walked along the dusty road, she stamped her foot in the dust once.

"Comme elle est en colère, cette Reine," whispered Marion Lefebvre, who saw them pass. "Le pauvre père Chrétien, she leads him a rude life."

Poor Reine, she was wrong to be angry, to be impatient, to wish for the things which only time and silent progress can bring about. Like many another before her, she was a little in advance of her days, and of the people among whom she lived ; and the price people are condemned to pay for being somewhat ahead of their neighbors is a heavy one.

CHAPTER IX.

REINE IN HER FARM-YARD.

CATHARINE found herself transported, as if by magic, from the long, dreary, brick-inclosed bowers to a charming world, where vine garlands were wreathing under cloudless skies. There was at once more light, more sound, more sentiment and drowsy peace in it than she had ever known in all her life before. She awakened to a dazzle streaming through the vine round her window, and flickering upon the red brick floor of her little room ; to a glitter, to a cheerful vibration of noises. Some one would bring her a little roll and a cup of steaming coffee, and then, when she was dressed, the children would come tapping and fumbling at her door. Little Henri de Tracy sometimes attempted a réveillée upon his horn, which would be instantly suppressed by a voice outside. Nanine, who was nine years old, and had elegant little manners

like a lady, would wish Catharine good-morning; and Madelaine, who was four and "très raisonnable," Suzanne her nurse said, consented to be kissed through the iron-work balusters of the staircase.

The children would lead the way through the great dining-room, where Baptiste was hopping about on one leg, polishing the shining floor, across the terrace, through green avenues and gardens, looking a little neglected, but fresh with dew, and luxuriant with flowers and fruit-trees. Pumpkins, carnations, and roses were growing between vine-clad walls. There were bees, and there was an old stone well full of deep water, like Jocelyn's well—

Dont la chaîne rouillée a poli la margelle,
Et qu'une vigne étreint de sa verte dentelle.

From the terrace there was a distant view of the sea—of the blue line of the horizon flashing beyond the golden corn-fields.

One morning Nanine said, "We are to go to the Ferme, Miss George, to-day, with a commission from grandmamma. We will go out at the door in the Potager, if you'd not mind, and come back the other way." It was all the same to Catharine, who followed her little conductors through the kitchen-garden door out into the open country, and along the path skirting the corn-fields which spread to the sea. Henri went first, blowing his horn; Nanine loitered to pick the poppies and bleu-bleus, as she called the corn-flowers; Madelaine trotted by Catharine, holding her hand. It was like the nursery rhyme. Miss George thought of the little boy blue, only the sheep were wanting.

From outside the farm at Tracy still looks more like a ruined fortress than a farm where milk is sold in cans, and little pats of butter prepared, and eggs counted out in dozens, and pigs fattened for the market. All over Normandy you come upon these fortified abbayes, built for praying and fighting once, and ruined now, and turned to different uses. It is like Samson's riddle to see the carcass of the lions with honey flowing from them. "Out of the eater came forth meat; out of the strong came forth sweetness." There is a great archway at the farm at Tracy, with heavy wooden doors studded with nails. There is rust in plenty, and part of a moat still remaining. The hay is stacked in what was a chapel once; the yellow trusses are hanging through the crumbling flamboyant east window. There is a tall watch-tower, to which a pigeon-cote has been affixed, and low cloisters that are turned into out-houses and kitchens. The white walls tell a story of penance and fierce battlings, which are over now, as far as they are concerned. The great harvest wagons pass through the archway without unloading; so do the cows at milking-time. Cocks and hens are pecketing the fallen grains, the pigeons circle overhead suddenly white against the sky.

As the children and Miss George pushed open the heavy doors and came into the wide sunny court, a figure descended the stone steps leading from the strong tower where the apples are kept. It was Reine in her white coiffe, who advanced with deliberate footsteps, carrying an earthenware pan under her arm, and who stood waiting in the middle of the great deserted-looking place until they should come up to her.

Catharine wondered whether all Normandy peasant-girls were like this one. It was a princess keeping the cows. There she stood, straight, slender, vigorous; dressed in the Sunday dress of the women of those parts, with this difference, that instead of two plastered loops of hair like a doll's, a tawny ripple flowed under the lace of her cap and low over her arched brows. As for her eyes, they were quick, dancing gray eyes, that looked black when she was angry—clouds and lightning somebody once told her they were, but the lightning became warm sunlight when she smiled upon those she liked. She smiled now, for Reine was a child-lover, and even little De Tracys were welcome, as they came toward her with their bunches of flowers out of the fields, and the pretty strange lady following.

"Who are you bringing me?" Reine asked, "and what do you want, my children? Madelaine, shall I give you some milk and some peaches?"

"Out of Josette's little ménage," said Madelaine, while Henri cried out, "Oh, there is old Paris!" and went and clasped the big dog round the neck.

Nanine, meanwhile advancing very politely and prettily, in a smart little toilette, explained that Miss George was a demoiselle Anglaise who was staying with them, and that they had come to request Mademoiselle Chrétien to supply them with butter for a few days. "Our cows are ill," said Nanine, shrugging her shoulders, "and we are all but reduced to dry bread."

"There are others besides you who eat their

bread dry," said Reine; "but your grandmamma can have as much butter as she likes, Mademoiselle Nanine, at the market price, since she has money to pay for it." She did not say this rudely, but rather sadly, and then she suddenly turned to Catharine, and asked her if she would not like some milk too. "And so you are English?" Reine said, in her odd sweet voice, pushing open a door with both her hands. Reine's hands were not like Madame Binaud's, two red paws which could be seen shining a mile off, but thin and white like a lady's. Catharine glanced at them a little curiously as they lay outspread upon the oak, and she saw that Reine wore a signet-ring on one finger; then she looked up in her face again, and Reine Chrétien caught the glance and melted somehow toward the little thing with the startled look and curious soft eyes that seemed to be taking everything in. The love-making of friendship is not unlike that of sentiment, and friends are friends sometimes in an instant almost, even though they may not have set the feeling to the tune of words and protestations.

I hardly know which of these two women needed the other most, when they met by chance in the silent, sunny court-yard that morning. In after times, doubt, trouble, cruel suspicion, pain, and jealousy came to part them, but they were faithful to one another through it all. There was something to forgive and to forget for each of them, but they loved one another well enough to be able to remember and to need no forgiveness. They suited. Somehow there was a certain affinity between them which is priceless in friendship. It is worth all the virtues, and merits, and accomplishments put together to people who care for one another, or who ought to care.

Catharine, who had never in her life spoken to a Normandy peasant before, listened and looked with all her eyes. There was Reine, dressed like a doll, in flaps, and apron, and ornaments; but Catharine was touched and fascinated by the grave, noble face, the pathetic voice. Alas! she was not the first Reine had charmed.

The girl gave the children their milk out of a great brass pan standing surrounded by little barrels for making butter. "Should you like to see the farm?" she asked them. "This is where we keep our cider;" and, opening a door into an old vaulted cellar, she showed them six huge butts, standing side by side, and reaching to the ceiling. Each one of them was large enough to drown the whole party. Nanine exclaimed at their size. "They are half of them empty already," said Reine, laughing. "Dominique alone could drink one of those for his supper. I don't offer you any," she said to Catharine, leading them away, and locking the door behind her. "I know English people do not like cider," and she sighed as she spoke.

She went before them through many courts, opening arched doors, into store-rooms heaped with the oily colza grain. She showed them a wheat-field inclosed by four walls, against which nectarines and apricots were ripening. The cows were all out in the meadows, but there were a few sheep in a stable; and at last she brought them into the great farm-kitchen. It had been added on to the rest of the buildings; so had Reine's own room, which was over it, and reached by stone steps from outside.

Petitpère was sitting at the table, eating bread and soup. He looked hot and tired, but he got up to make a bow and a little speech. He was a hospitable and courteous old fellow, whatever his other defects may have been. "Ladies, you are welcome to the farm," he said. "Pray excuse my continuing my breakfast. I have been out since five o'clock in the fields, with the soldiers."

"We have not men enough to get in the harvest," Reine explained to Catharine, "and we send for the soldiers to help us."

"And have you, too, been up since sunrise?" Catharine asked.

"I see it every morning of my life," said Reine. "I should like to show it you from our archway. The sea awakens first, all our animals stir as if they knew; it is a most beautiful hour," she said gravely, "and like a prayer before the work."

What was there about Reine Chrétien that attracted and interested her so curiously? Catharine asked herself this, and also how was it and why was it that the place seemed so strangely familiar? Had she been there in some previous existence? She turned and looked round about. The window, the great cupboard, with the gleaming hinges, she had seen them before somewhere—she could not understand it. Petitpère went on composedly drinking his soup; Catharine still stood in a puzzle. She had a silly little fancy there would be a bright brass pot in one of the corners, but it was not there as she expected: she could not understand it at all.

Reine begged them to come and see her again, and stood watching them thoughtfully under the archway as they went home across the fields where the soldiers were reaping with peaceful scythes, and the corn fell against the horizon, and the figures of the gleaners with their golden troven treasures stood out with garments flying against the sky. Then she turned and crossed the court once more, and once she stopped and pulled a letter from her pocket and read it over twice.

Catharine thought as she walked back that morning that if she could have forgotten all that had passed before she came to Tracy, all the people she had known, all the things she had thought, she could breathe on for years happily enough in this fruitful country. But who is there who would forget willingly what has gone before? There are few who would not remember more if they could, if it were even the pangs they have forgotten.

As they reached the court-yard, they met Monsieur de Tracy heavily booted and gaitered, all dressed in white, and finishing his morning rounds. Monsieur Fontaine was with him, also in linen clothes. He acted as a sort of agent or manager in Tracy's absence, and used often to come up to talk over business and bailiffs. They all met just inside the iron gates of the court-yard. Fontaine bowed profoundly to the pretty, fresh-looking little miss, with the great bunch of field-flowers in her hand, and the blue ribbons in her crisp black hair. The children clustered round their father, and Henri held him prisoner while Nanine stuck poppies into all his button-holes, and little Madelaine, who could reach no higher, ornamented his gaiters with flowers.

Meanwhile the following conversation was going on:

"You have quite recovered from the fatigue of your journey, I trust?" said Fontaine. "One need scarcely ask mademoiselle the question."

"Oui, monsieur," said Catharine, looking up shyly.

"And mademoiselle has already surrounded herself with flowers," said Fontaine, alluding to the bouquet.

"Oui, monsieur," said Catharine, who did not know what else to say.

"And I hope that mademoiselle is pleased with our country?" said Fontaine, speaking both in his public and his private capacity.

"Oui, monsieur," said Catharine, with great originality, half laughing at her own stupidity, and moving away toward the house, to put an end to such a silly conversation.

It was like a scene in a play, like a picture on a fan or a bonbon box. It seemed as if nothing could be less serious. The little banality, the bow, the courtesy, it was a nothing, Catharine thought, or she would have thought so had she thought at all. To the children it was an instant of great anxiety: would the flowers tumble off their papa when he moved his legs?—but Catharine tripped away unconscious and unconcerned.

Poor Fontaine's fate, too, was decided in that instant, when he bowed so profoundly, and Catharine turned away with her quick little smile. Not at Bayeux, not at Caen, not including Madame la Sous-Préfette herself, was there any one to be compared to this charming young Englishwoman, thought the maire. As for a *dot*, he would prefer Miss George with a moderate sum, to Reine with all her fortune; and then something told him that the English were so orderly, such excellent housekeepers, caring nothing for follies and expenses. "Toilette is their aversion," thought Fontaine, remembering at the same time some of the bills he had paid for Toto's poor mother. He built a castle in the air, a Tower of Babel it was, poor fellow, reaching to heaven. He perceived himself passing Reine Chrétien, with a lovely and charmingly mannered Madame Fontaine beside him, elegantly but not expensively attired; he pictured her to himself embroidering by his fireside, superintending his ménage. As he thought of Catharine, a sweet, arch, gentle glance came dazzling his eyes, like sunlight through the double eye-glass, and at that minute Jean moved, after patiently standing until his decoration was complete, and, alas for poor little Madelaine, all the flowers fell off him.

"Good-morning, Monsieur le Maire," said Madame de Tracy, suddenly appearing at the hall door. "Won't you stay and breakfast with us?"

"Madame," said the maire, "you are too good. I shall be quite delighted."

Catharine liked the breakfast-hour at Tracy. They all came in cheerful and freshly dressed, and took their places in the long, picturesque-looking salle, with its vaulted roof and many windows. The food was carefully and prettily served and ornamented; the white bright china glittered on the table; the golden and purple fruit was heaped up bountifully. She liked to look at it all from her place by Madame de Tracy, as she liked looking at Marthe's pale, beautiful head opposite to her, or Madame Jean's smart ribbons. Catharine used sometimes to compare the scene at Tracy—the cool green windows, the festive-looking table, the ripple of talk—to the sombre dining-room in Eaton Square, where the smoke had settled in clouds upon the faded stucco walls, where Mr. Butler sliced the eternal legs of mutton while every body sat round and watched the process in silence and anxiety.

Monsieur Fontaine sat next Catharine to-day; Madame de Tracy sent them in together. She could not help thinking, as she followed the couple, what an easy solution there might be to all her difficulties. The little thing would be the very wife for Fontaine—he would make an excellent husband. It would be a home for her—the maire's admiration was evident, and Ernestine had been too provoking that morning. There had been an explanation, ending as explanations generally end, by hopelessly confusing matters. Ernestine declared with the utmost liveliness that she had not room to lodge a fly in her apartments at Paris, and that nothing would induce her to have a governess in the house.

"But it is certain neither I nor your grandmother require one," said poor Madame de Tracy, at her wit's end. "And we go to V—— on the twentieth of next month. What am I to do? How can I tell her?"

It seemed like a second inspiration to this impulsive lady when on her way to the breakfast-room she happened to see the little scene in the court-yard. The bow, the respectful look of admiration, which said nothing to Miss George, were like signals of approaching succor to the distressed hostess. Madame de Tracy thought no more of parceling out the future of two living souls than she did of matching her cap-strings. As she sat there at the head of the table, she talked, schemed, made, looked after them all, carved out destinies and chicken with admirable precision and rapidity. "Baptiste, take this wing to Monsieur de Tracy. Marthe,

D

I know it is no use offering you any. Monsieur le Maire, do you prefer omelette?"

This was the first Friday that Catharine had spent at Tracy, and she saw with a thrill that omelettes were being handed round, and great flowery roast potatoes and fried fish. There were, however, chickens too, and cutlets, of which, as a Protestant, she felt bound to partake. So did Jean and his grandmother. His mother was of an amphibious persuasion, sometimes fish, sometimes flesh, as the fancy took her. She was by way of being a Protestant, but she went to mass with her family, and fasted on Fridays when Marthe and Ernestine were there. Madame de Tracy *mère*, as they called the old lady up stairs, had a dispensation. Catharine was rather disappointed to see them all quietly peppering and salting the nice little dishes before them, and enjoying their breakfasts. She thought of her aunt Farebrother's warnings; the scene did not look very alarming. Monsieur Fontaine, although strictly adhering to the rules laid down, by his church, managed to make an excellent repast, attending at the same time to his companions' wants, and passing salt, and pepper, and sugar with great empressement and gallantry. Catharine herself, before breakfast was over, became conscious of his devotion, and, I am sorry to say, was woman enough to be amused and not displeased by it. Once she caught Madame de Tracy's glance; there were no frozen looks now to chill and terrify. "I am determined I will speak to him on the subject immediately after breakfast," Madame de Tracy was thinking.

"Monsieur le Maire, I want to show you my new plantation. Ernestine, little Madelaine is longing for a bunch of grapes. Baptiste, has Madame de Tracy *mère's* breakfast been taken up?"

"Madame desires a little more chicken," said Baptiste, respectfully. "Mademoiselle Picard has just come down to fetch some; also a little Burgundy wine, and an egg, and some figs."

Catharine used to wonder at the supplies which were daily sent up from every meal to this invisible invalid. She had seen the shutters of her rooms from without, but she never penetrated into the interior of the apartment which Madame de Tracy *mère* inhabited. Once or twice, in passing, she had heard a hoarse voice like a man's calling Picard or Baptiste (they were the old lady's personal attendants); once Catharine had seen a pair of stumpy velvet shoes standing outside her door. That was all. Old Madame de Tracy was a voice, an appetite, a pair of shoes to Catharine, no more.

Every body is something to somebody else. Certain hieroglyphics stand to us in lieu of most of our neighbors. Poor little Catharine herself was a possible storm and discussion to some of the people present—to Marthe, a soul to be saved; to Madame de Tracy, a problem to be solved and comfortably disposed of; to Monsieur Fontaine, carried away by his feelings, the unconscious Catharine appeared as one of the many possible Madame Fontaines in existence, and certainly the most graceful and charming of them all. There was only that unfortunate question of the *dot* to outweigh so much amiability and refinement.

After breakfast every body disappeared in different directions. The children and Miss George went up into Madame de Tracy's bedroom, where she had desired them to sit of a morning. It was a comfortable Napoleonic apartment, with bureaus, and brass inlaid tables, upon which bonbonnières, and liqueur-stands, and arrangements for sugar and water were disposed. A laurel-crowned clock was on the chimneypiece, over which the late M. de Tracy's silhouette legion of honor and lock of hair were hanging neatly framed and glazed. The children sat with their heads together spelling out their tasks. Catharine's bright eyes glanced up and round about the room; and out across the gardens, and the vine-clad roofs of the out-houses, the flies came buzzing. There was silence and a scent of ripe fruit from the garden. Suddenly, with a swift pang, she remembered that it was a week to-day since she had said good-by to Rosy and Totty, and to Dick. The three names used to come together somehow in her thoughts. A week already since she had bade him a hasty farewell at the door of a room with every body standing round . . . She could not bear to think of it, she thought, as she began to recall every expression, every sound, every aspect of that instant, which had been to her like Mohammed's, and which had seemed to last for a thousand years.

The last few days had been so sunny, so easy, so harmonious a medley of sweet summer weather, and gardens and grapes, and lively talk, that Catharine had been too much absorbed to dream. People do not dream when they are happy. For the last few days she had remembered without bitterness. Life seemed to have grown suddenly bearable, and almost easy once more. If she had known how short a time her tranquillity was to last, she might have made more of it perhaps, and counted each minute as it passed. But she did not know, and she wasted many of them as she was doing now, as we all do, in unavailing hankering and regrets—precious little instants flying by only too quickly, and piping to us very sweetly, and we do not dance. Looking back, one laments not so much the unavoidable sorrows of life as its wasted peace and happiness, and then more precious minutes pass in remorse for happiness wasted long ago.

"I wonder what grandmamma is talking to Monsieur Fontaine about?" said Nanine, standing on tiptoe and peeping out. "Look, Miss George, how they go walking up and down the allée verte."

"Monsieur Fontaine seems very much excited," said Catharine, smiling, as Fontaine began gesticulating suddenly, and stopped short in his walk to give more emphasis to what he was saying.

If she could have heard what he was saying!

CHAPTER X.

A BOUQUET OF MARGUERITES.

ABOUT this time one or two people came occasionally to stay in the house for a night or two: the De Vernons, who were neighbors, young Robert de Coëtlogon, Ernestine's brother, and others from time to time. Catharine did not see very much of them; they came and they went without any reference to her. Madame de Tracy was very kind to her always. Even Madame Jean had melted, and got to like the bright-faced little thing, although she never altered her vexatious determination to admit no governess into her house. Madame de Tracy had begged that Catharine might not be told. She did not want the poor child to be unnecessarily distressed, and she looked so happy and comfortably settled, that it seemed a shame to disturb her, when, perhaps, every thing might arrange itself smoothly, and without any explanations. Madame de Tracy used to take Catharine out sometimes. One day they drove to Bayeux, with its cathedral towers, and winding streets, and jewelers' shops all twinkling. Another day they went to Petitpot: the fishwives looked up grinning and nodding as the lady of the manor passed by. "Do you see the pretty little châlet on the cliff overlooking the sea?" said Madame de Tracy, pointing to the little house with the pink curtains, and all its wooden balconies and weather-cocks. "That is where Fontaine lives. Is it not a charming little place? I have to speak to him. We will leave the ponies down here at Pélottier's." And Madame de Tracy put the reins into some idler's hands, and panted up the cliff, too busy, and preoccupied, and breathless to glance at the sapphire sea at her feet.

Fontaine was not at home, but an old gentleman's head was to be seen through one of the windows, and a fat old lady with mustaches was sitting in the garden with her hands on her two knees, and her feet on a footstool, and Toto was galloping round and round the little gravel path.

"My son is out, unfortunately, Madame la Comtesse," said the old lady, bowing from her seat to Madame de Tracy, who remained outside the gate. "He will be in despair when I tell him you passed this way," she added, stiffly.

"I hope you are well, Madame Mérard," said Madame de Tracy, willing to propitiate. "Your son gives me news of you from time to time. What a charming little habitation this is!"

"They offered us five hundred francs a month for it only yesterday," said Madame Mérard, with dignity. "I do all I can to prevail upon Charles to let it. Rents are enormous just now. One should make one's profit when one can. But Charles will not hear reason."

Meanwhile Toto and Catharine were making acquaintance. The little boy had come up to look at the pretty lady his papa had told him about; and Catharine, bending over the low railing and holding out her hand, said, "What nice flowers you have got in your garden! Will you give me one of them?"

"Papa and I water them every evening," said Toto, picking a slug-eaten specimen and holding it up. "I have a little watering-pot of my own."

The sea looked so blue, the shutters so green, the sunlight so yellow, the marguerites so brilliant, that Catharine's eyes were dazzled, and she scarcely noticed the curious, dissatisfied glances old Madame Mérard was casting in her direction. Madame de Tracy, however, saw them, and quickly hurried Catharine away, for fear she should be frightened by this somewhat alarming person.

"Pray tell Monsieur le Maire we asked for him," said Madame de Tracy, as they walked away, bowing, and forcing herself to be civil to the old lady of the châlet.

For Fontaine himself Madame de Tracy began to feel almost a sentimental interest. She looked upon him from an entirely new point of view; a bore no longer, but a hero of romance, an enthusiastic and disinterested lover. Madame de Tracy felt that if she were Catharine, nothing in the world would be more delightful to her than a marriage with Monsieur Fontaine. "Handsome, amiable, warm-hearted, a good man of business, musical, universally respected; it is a piece of good fortune I never dared hope for," said the châtelaine to herself. "I should like the marriage to take place, if possible, before the 15th of next month. It was too absurd of Sarah Butler to alarm me so unnecessarily about Dick. One might be very comfortable in that nice house of Fontaine's," said Madame de Tracy, aloud. "Don't you think so, Catharine?"

"Oh yes," said Catharine, not knowing what she was saying.

Another time Madame de Tracy suddenly asked her how she should like to pass her life among them always. Catharine thought that she was speaking of her as a governess, and said, with grateful effusion, "You are so good to me; I am more happy with you than I could be with any body else. I almost forget I am a governess."

"My dear child, I meant how should you like to settle down among us and marry?" said Madame de Tracy, apparently unconcerned.

"I shall never marry," said Catharine, turning away disappointed, with a wistful, perplexed look in her eyes.

Madame de Tracy did not press the subject, but she went on asking Fontaine to breakfast and dinner, until Ernestine declared it was quite intolerable, and even Marthe gently remonstrated.

Catharine looked happy and contented, but presently, while all was going on as usual, there came a secret change. Outside every thing was the same, inside it was all different. These two existences side by side, "l'âme et la bête," as De Maistre calls them, seem sometimes to lead two lives almost apart, leading in different directions with different results. Do they in their differences supplement one another, one is some-times tempted to ask, and keep the balance even? In one calm and uneventful existence, angels may know of terrible tragedies, of happi-ness, and overwhelming misfortu..e, scarcely ac-knowledged even by the "bête" itself; whereas another life, outwardly hopeless, deserted, un-successful in every thing, may from within have won all the prizes that seemed to have failed it.

When Catharine had been a little time at Tracy, when she began to know her way about the house, and the vine-grown garden, and along the hedgeless paths to the sea, to the farm, to the church; narrow paths skirting the fields, dust-blown, fringed with straggling flowers and scattered with stones—when she had tasted her fill of the grapes that were sweetening upon the walls, when she had gathered handfuls of the flowers that were growing all about the gardens and courts in a sweet yet disordered luxuriance —when all this had grown familiar, she began to turn away from it all, and look back once more toward the past which was already begin-ning to glow with a distant radiance. It was like some one dazzled for a little by a sudden illumination who begins to see clearly again—more clearly, alas! than before.

She had met Reine once or twice in her walks, and had promised to go and see her.

"I shall look out for you every day until you come," said Reine, in her odd, jarring voice, that sometimes began harshly, and ended in a pathetic cadence. "It is not often that any one comes to see me that I care for."

Reine had, like others infinitely wiser and better than herself, to pay a certain penalty of loneliness and misapprehension which seems to be the doom of all those who live upon the mountain tops. Catharine, too, was lonely in her way, and the country girl's cordial sym-pathy was very grateful and sweet to her. But Catharine was lonely from outward influences, and not from inner causes. Poor little soul, it was not for the mountain tops that she longed. Any green valley, any fertile, tranquil plain, would have contented her, if she could only have seen the shadow of one person falling across it and advancing toward her.

One Sunday evening—it was the day after she had called at the chålet—Catharine came down dressed for dinner before any body else. She came into the drawing-room. It was empty, and one lamp only was standing upon a table, and casting its circlet of light upon the cloth. It lit up a card-rack, and Madame de Tracy's paroissien with its golden cross, and some letters which had just arrived by the post, and which had been left there by the servant. Catharine had a book in her hand (it was Eu-génie Grandet, which M. de Tracy had lent her), and she walked quietly across the dark room to the light, and knelt down by the table to read, as she had a trick of doing when she was alone. But she did not open her novel: in an instant she saw one letter lying there with the others, and she started with a sort of shock, and let the

book fall on the table, and the poor little heart gave a great leap, and began throbbing and crying aloud in its own language. If Catharine had seen Dick himself she might have been less moved. A calm belongs to certainty which does not come when there is only a hint, a pos-sible chance, an impossible disappointment in store. "Was he coming? **Oh, was he** coming, perhaps?"

Catharine could not herself have **told you** how it was that she recognized his handwriting **in an** instant among all the others. She had **only** once seen his initials on the fly-leaf of a book—but she knew it—she did not need the English post-mark to tell her whence the letter came: here was his writing, and she might not read it; here was a secret he himself had closed and sealed against her. His thoughts, his words, were there, but they were not for her. **It** seemed to her suddenly as if the thing in the whole world that she most longed for was that letter—even more than to see him again. Did it come straight from the river-side? She re-**membered a table in** the studio, where books, and **loose papers, and envelopes were** lying: was that **where it was written?** She longed to take it up and to read the post-mark, and to look at the stamp upon the seal. With **a sudden** movement like a child's, she put her hands be-hind her to keep them out of temptation, and then, poor little foolish, foolish thing, she bent suddenly forward and touched it **with her lips.**

A minute afterward she would have **given,** oh, how much! not to have done this. **She sat** there in scorn with her own weakness, **angry** with herself, indignant; the red **and white** flames were still coming and going **in her** cheeks when Madame de Tracy came bustling into the room, followed by the inevitable M. Fontaine, who had just arrived.

"This is the only punctual person in the house, Monsieur le Maire," said Madame de Tracy, smiling and nodding at Catharine as she spoke, and then she went straight up to the let-ters, and then she looked up curiously at Catha-rine **a second time,** and caught the girl's **odd,** wistful glance, and saw her suddenly change color. As for Fontaine, he thought he had never seen Miss George in greater beauty. "If she were dressed by one of our first modistes in Caen," thought Monsieur Fontaine, "not Ma-dame la Sous-Préfette herself would present a more distinguished appearance." He took a chair and sat down opposite to her in the lamp-light, and began thanking her for her kindness to his little boy the day before.

"Toto has been talking of you ever since, mademoiselle," said Monsieur le Maire. "His grandmother and I had some difficulty in pre-venting him from quitting his bed to accompany me here to-night. Toto has a great deal of character, poor little fellow," sighed Monsieur, with real kindness and tenderness. "He has no mother, and one is always afraid of not being gentle enough with him. I am afraid we are not quite so decided as we ought to be."

It was impossible not to like Fontaine when he talked about his little son. This man was genuinely and unaffectedly kind-hearted and affectionate. He was absurd, prosy, fussy; he had all sorts of tiresome peculiarities, but he was incapable of a harsh or unkind action.

Madame de Tracy opened her letters, and read them one by one. Catharine answered Fontaine from beyond the sea, as it were; from the river-side, from the quaint old studio; listening to some one else the whole time, to a distant music, playing across all the days that had passed since she heard it.

Every body began to enter the room. "Nothing for me?" said Ernestine, coming in, in a marvelous shimmering toilette. "It is too provoking! people never write—Jean sends me a telegram when he goes away . . . Isn't this from Dick?" she continued, looking over her mother-in-law's shoulder. "What does he say?"

"We will talk it over another time," said Madame de Tracy, in a constrained sort of way —and she handed the letter to Ernestine.

"He asks for fricandeau!" said Ernestine, looking puzzled.

"Poor little prodigal!" said Jean, laughing kindly, and in his turn beginning to read.

Queen's Walk, Sept. 1.

MY DEAR AUNT,—I have been working very hard, or I should have written to you before. There is a bit of the cliff at Petitport which must come into my picture, and I am thinking of running over before the wedding. Will you take me and my canvas for a day or two, and once more prepare the fricandeau for your affectionate R. B.

P.S.—Uncle Charles has been buying some wonderful sherry, he says. Hervey is gone on a walking tour with Francis. The affair is settled for the 9th.

This was the letter Jean de Tracy read in silence. Madame de Tracy for once looked stern, and glanced meaningly at her son as he returned it. She folded it up without a word.

Catharine's troubled manner, Dick's proposal to return so soon again, had filled her with vague alarm once more. Dick might be unconscious, serious, amusing himself with a passing flirtation—it was impossible to say what he was about. He had certainly declared once that Miss George was nothing to him, but it was well to be on the safe side. "We must make some excuse to keep him away a little longer," thought Madame de Tracy. She wanted to be a good genius to all these people. She liked managing, arranging: she meant rather well: it was convenient to dispose of Miss George, and amusing to occupy herself with these sentimental matters. How bitterly she regretted afterward the irreparable work she had accomplished! The good lady disquieted herself a good deal at one time as to whether she had not, perhaps, materially interfered with the plans of Providence.

They seemed to drop the subject by tacit consent. Ernestine asked no more questions. Catharine's heart gave one more flutter, and sank down and down. Ah! why would they not at least talk, and say what they meant. This was all she was to know. This was all the uncertainty: all her life she might expect no more—nothing else. This horrible instinct of what they were thinking was her only certainty. To Catharine, the sight of the letter had brought every thing back with a rush. Poor little thing, she had thought her house was swept and garnished, and here were seven devils worse than the first who had taken possession. It was an absurdity, a childishness, but she longed for that letter. The sudden conviction that for all her life she should have no right even to read what he had written, even to ask a question or to speak his name, was a sort of passing torture. It lasted until dinner was announced, some ten minutes after. It seemed like an hour of agony to Catharine, there in the lamplight, sitting in her muslins as if nothing had happened. It was nonsense; and yet she suffered as keenly as from any of the certainty that came to her later. From his hand it was easy to bear any blow; but to be parted by others . . .

"Permit me, mademoiselle, to have the honor," said Monsieur le Maire, offering his arm.

Catharine suddenly felt as if she hated poor Fontaine, ambling and complimenting beside her, as if it was a cruel mockery of fate to come with this absurd compromise to jeer at her and turn her into ridicule. She had never before felt so sure of poor Fontaine's admiration, and never thought of it so seriously. All dinner-time she was silent; she turned from him—she was almost rude. He had never before seen her so little amiable, so inattentive.

Monsieur Fontaine departed early in the evening, very crestfallen and out of spirits. For the first time in his life he told himself his heart was really touched. He was humble, as most vain people are, and he alternated from absurd complacency to utter despondency. Never until now had he felt like this about any one. His first wife was a small heiress, and the match had been purely one of convenience. For Reine, a terrified fascination induced him reluctantly to come forward at his mother's suggestion; but Catharine's gentleness charmed and touched him at once. Here was a person he could understand and sympathize with. He longed to protect her, to make some great sacrifice for her, to bring her home proudly to his châlet and garden, and to say, "All this is yours; only love me a little and be good to Toto." "My excellent mother will regret her want of fortune," thought Fontaine. "Alas! who knows whether she will ever have the occasion to do so. And yet," said the maire to himself, with a certain simple dignity, "that child might do worse than accept the hand of an honest man." He did not go into his châlet through the kitchen as usual, but walked down the garden to his "cabane," a small wooden sentry-box facing the sea. It had been erected at the bottom of the sloping embankment for the convenience of bathing. A little heap of white stones that Toto had placed upon the seat were gleaming in the darkness. Fontaine pushed them carefully into one corner, and then sat down and smoked one cigar after another until quite late in the night.

Meanwhile the drawing-room of the chateau was still lighted up. Some one had been singing, the others had been dancing, but Catharine would not join them. Poor child, was the music of her life only to be for other people to dance to? Were her dreams of love to be so cruelly realized? Fontaine, with all his devotion, attention, conversation, was not as much alive to Catharine as that one little bit of paper in Madame de Tracy's pocket.

Catharine was standing ready in the hall next morning when the children came running up to her. She had awakened late, refreshed by a long dreamless sleep, and she thought she had shaken off the vivid impressions of the night before. But how relentlessly people are pursued in life by any idea which has once taken possession of them! Every thing seems to suggest and bring it back: the very stones cry out; we open a book, and we read something concerning it; chance people speak of it to us; even the children in their play told Catharine that she was alone, and had neither home nor friend to shield her. The children went into the kitchen-garden, and Miss George followed them there.

Catharine sat down on the side of the old well; the vines were creeping up the iron bars, the grapes were hanging between the leaves. There was one great ripe bunch dropping against the sky, painted purple upon the blue. A few wasps were floating drowsily; a bird flew swiftly by, glancing down for one instant with its bright sleepy eye. There was again that scent of fruit and indescribable sweetness in the air. As she sat there, Catharine began to feel as if she had known it all from the beginning. It was like that strange remembrance in the farm-kitchen, only less vivid. It was all very sweet and lovely; but she thought, with a sudden thrill, that the ugliest London street along which Dick Butler had walked would be more to her than this.

Was she never to see him again? ah! was she never to see him again? And as she thought this, his face seemed to go before her eyes. They had been singing a little song the night before at the chateau,

"Si vous n'avez rien à me dire, pourquoi venir auprès de moi?"

it went. Dreams said nothing to her now. She looked at them in a sort of despair as they went by.

"Why does he come, why does he come?" sighed the little thing, clinging to the iron crank. "Why am I haunted like this?" She felt as if it was cruel—yes, cruel of Fate to mock her and tempt her thus; to have brought the fruit, sweet, and ripe, and tempting to her lips, and to whisper at the same time cruel warnings: "This is for others, not for you. This is for the other Catharine, who does not very much care—this will be for him some day when he chooses. Do you wish? You may wish, and wish, and wish, you will be no nearer; put out your hand, and you will see all these beautiful purple, sweet peaches turn into poisonous berries, bitter and sickening. And yet I did not go after it," thought the girl, with a passionate movement. "Why does this come to me, crossing my path to distract, to vex, to bewilder?" Catharine was but a child still: she leaned over the old moss-grown parapet of the well and let her tears drop deep, deep into it. What a still passage it was down into the cool heart of the earth. She heard a fresh bubble of water rippling at the bottom, and she watched her tears as they fell sparkling into the dark silent depths. "Nobody will find them there," she said to herself, smiling sadly at the poor little conceit. "I will never cry again if I can help it, but if I can not help it I will come here to cry."

And yet this poor little hopeless, sorrowful love of Catharine's was teaching and educating her, although she did not know it. She was only ashamed of it. The thought that they suspected it, that it was no chance which had caused them all to avoid Dick's name so carefully, made her shrink with shame. The poor little wistful, silly thing, with the quick little fancies and warm tender heart, was changing day by day, making discoveries, suddenly understanding things she read, words people spoke. The whole pulse of life seemed to be beating more quickly. Something had come into her face which was not there a year ago. She was thinner, and the moulding of her two arched brows showed as it had not done before. Her little round mouth was longer and more finely drawn; her eyes looked you more straightly in the face through their soft gloom. She got up, hearing voices and footsteps approaching: it was the children, who came running along the pathway.

Henri was holding a great big nosegay, done up in stamped paper. It was chiefly made of marguerites, sorted into wheels, red, white, orange, violet. It was a prim-looking offering, with leaves and little buds at regular intervals, as Nature never intended them to grow.

"This is for you!" cried little Henri, triumphantly. "This beautiful big bouquet. Toto and M. Fontaine have brought it. You will let me smell it, won't you?"

"The flowers are magnificent," said Nanine, following panting and indignant. "M. Fontaine confided them to me; but Henri seized it and ran away. I do not like rude little boys."

"You must tell Monsieur Fontaine I am very much obliged to him," said Catharine. "And you can put it in water if you like, Nanine."

"You must thank him yourself," said the little girl, walking beside her. "I know you like marguerites. You wore some in your hair last night. They look pretty with your white muslin dresses."

Catharine followed the children sadly, walking under the song of birds and the glimmering green branches. She would have escaped, but Madame de Tracy, with Monsieur Fontaine and Toto, came to meet them; the châtelaine was calling out cheerfully and waving her parasol.

Fontaine sprang forward. He looked spruce as usual in his white linen dress; his Panama was in his hand; he wore a double eye-glass like Jean de Tracy. "We are proud, mademoiselle, that you honor us by accepting the produce of our little garden," said Fontaine. "Toto and I cultivate our flowers with some care, and we feel more than repaid . . ."

"Thank you," interrupted Catharine, mechanically. She spoke, looking away over the wall at some poplar-trees that were swaying in the wind. It brought with it a sound of the sea that seemed to fill the air.

"Accustomed as you must be to the magnificent products of your Chatswors and Kieus," said Fontaine, "our poor marguerites must seem very insignificant. Such as they are, we have gathered our best to offer you."

He said it almost pathetically, and Catharine was touched. But how oddly people affect and change one another. This shy, frightened little girl became cold, dignified, absent in Monsieur Fontaine's presence, as she stood enduring rather than accepting his attentions.

"Thank you. They are very pretty," she repeated; "but I am sorry you should have gathered your best for me."

CHAPTER XI.

A PILGRIMAGE.

A CERTAIN expedition had long been arranged for the next day. The ladies wanted to shop, Tracy had business in Caen. They were all to go over and dine at the hotel, and come home in the evening. Catharine begged Madame de Tracy to leave her behind. She was shy and out of spirits, and was glad when the older lady acceded. Nanine and Henri were carried off; only Madelaine, Catharine, and the invisible Madame mère were left at home. In the silence of the house Catharine heard the deep voice resounding more than once.

Miss George went out soon after breakfast, leaving Madelaine with her nurse as usual. She remembered her promise to Reine, and there was something cordial and cheering in the Frenchwoman's kindness. The thought of the farm was always connected with brightness in Catharine's mind, and immediately after breakfast she set off along the fields to see her friend. Something was evidently contemplated at the farm. A cart was waiting in the court-yard as Catharine walked in; Dominique was standing at the old mare's head and affectionately rubbing her

nose. Little Josette and Toto, hand in hand, were wandering up and down. Toto was magnificent in Sunday clothes. "Voyez comme Toto est beau," said Josette, pointing with her little finger and forgetting to be shy in her excitement. Reine was preparing a basketful of provisions in the kitchen—cream in a brass can, roast apples, galette, salad and cold meat, all nicely packed in white napkins, also a terrinée or rice pudding for the children, and a piled-up dish full of ripe figs and green leaves and grapes for dessert. Toto's Sunday clothes looked like a holiday expedition. His grandmother pleased herself by inventing little costumes for him. On this occasion he wore what she called a *turban écossais*. This Scotch turban was ornamented by long streamers, glass buttons, and straw tassels. He also wore a very short jacket and trowsers of the same magnificent plaid. His hair was cropped quite close, so as to make his head look smooth and round like a ball. Toto himself was much pleased with his appearance, and gazed at his reflection approvingly in a tub of dirty water which was standing in a corner of the court.

"They will take me for a soldier, Josette," said he, strutting about.

"Come in, come in," cried Reine from her kitchen to Catharine, who was standing uncertain where to go.

A very odd and unexpected little revelation was awaiting Miss George (at least, so she thought it) as she came, with eyes dazzled by the sunny court, under the old stone porch into the dark kitchen, where Reine was standing, and where Petitpère had been eating his breakfast the time before. The odd-shaped shuttles for making string were hanging from the ceiling and swaying a little in the draught from the open door. There was the brass pan in the corner, which she had looked for; suddenly she recognized it all, the great carved cupboard with the hinges, the vine window looking across the blazing fields! Now she remembered in an instant where, and when, and how it was she had first seen Reine in her farm-kitchen—how could she have ever forgotten? Here was the picture Dick had shown her on his easel, only it was alive. The shuttles swayed, the light flickered on the brazen pan, one of the cupboard doors was swinging on its hinges, and Reine herself, with no hard black lines in her face, only smiles and soft changing shadows, came forward, tall, and bright, and kind, to meet her. So Dick had been here before her, and painted his picture here where she was standing. When this little revelation came to her, Catharine, who had been attracted before, felt as if she loved Reine now for something more than her own sake. This was the explanation—it was all natural enough as she came to think of it, but it struck her like a miracle almost, worked for her benefit. She seized Reine by the arm; all the color came rushing into her cheek. "Now I know where I have seen you," she cried. "Ah! Reine, how strangely things happen!"

"What do you mean?" said Reine, with a quick matter-of-fact glance as she shut down the cover of the basket.

Catharine went on, looking all about the place. "When did Mr. Butler paint you?—used you to sit to him?—was it not a beautiful picture? He showed it to us in his studio."

"It was like the kitchen," said Reine, not seeming much surprised, with another odd, reserved glance at Catharine. "I didn't think it very like me. I wanted him to paint the court-yard and the archway, with Dominique and Petitpère on the bench. A kitchen is always a kitchen. Mademoiselle, how I wish you were coming with us to-day," she said, in another tone. "We are going to the chapel of the Deliverande."

Catharine did not answer; she had not done with her questions. Here at last was some one to whom she could talk without exciting suspicion. Any one may speak of a picture in an unconcerned tone of voice, of Miss Philomel's talent for music, of Strephon's odd-shaped crook, or Chloris's pretty little lambs, but they should choose their confidantes carefully. Let them beware of women of a certain age and sentimental turn; let them, above all, avoid persons also interested in music, and flocks, and shepherds' crooks, or woe betide any one's secret. I think if Catharine had been quite silent, and never mentioned Dick's name, Reine would by degrees have guessed as much as she did the instant the little girl spoke Miss George herself was not deficient in quickness, but she was pre-occupied just now.

"How little I ever thought I should really know you," said Catharine.

"That is how things happen," said Reine. "It has been a great pleasure and happiness to me. Mademoiselle, you have not said No. Will you not honor us by coming to-day? It might amuse you to see the chapel. They say that to-day any thing is accorded that one asks for there. They say so to make people come perhaps," added the skeptic.

"Oh, Reine, what shall I ask for?" said Catharine, who believed every thing.

"An explanation," said Reine, dryly. "I have been expecting one some time. Et vous, mademoiselle?"

Catharine's color rose again and fell. "One would never have the courage to ask for what one wished," she faltered. "Yes, I should like to come with you. I suppose Madame de Tracy will not mind."

"We can send a message by Dominique," said Reine; and so the matter was settled.

Petitpère appeared, brushing his tall beaver hat, and then clambered with strong trembling hands into his place. The two women sat opposite to one another, on straw chairs. Josette and Toto had a little plank to themselves. The children were delighted, and clapped their hands at a wind-mill, an old cow, a flight of crows; so did Catharine, at their request. Something like a reaction had come after her weariness, and then she had had a drop of water, poor little fool, when she did not expect it. Reine smiled to see her so gay, and then sighed as she thought of former expeditions to the Deliverande.

The old farm stood basking in the sun. The cart rolled on, past stubble-fields and wide horizons of corn, and clouds, and meadow-land; the St. Claire was over, and the colza had been reaped. They passed through villages with lovely old church towers and Norman arched windows. They passed acacia-trees, with their bright scarlet berries, hanging low garden walls. They passed more farms, with great archways and brilliant vines wreathing upon the stone. The distance was a great panorama of sky, and corn, and distant sea. The country folks along the road cried out to them as they passed, "Vous voilà en route, père Chrétien," "Amusez-vous bien," and so on. Other carts came up to them as they approached the chapel, and people went walking in the same direction. They passed little roadside inns and buvettes for the convenience of the neighbors, and here and there little altars. Once, on the summit of a hill, they came to a great cross, with a life-size figure nailed upon it. Two women were sitting on the stone step at its foot, and the cloud-drifts were tossing beyond it. It was very awful, Catharine thought.

An hour later she was sitting in the chapel of the Deliverande. In a dark, incense-scented place, full of flames, and priests, and music, and crowding country people, a gorgeously dressed altar was twinkling and glittering in her eyes, where the Virgin of the Deliverande, in stiff embroideries, was standing, with a blaze of tapers burning among the fresh flowers. Voices of boys and girls were loudly chanting the hymn to the Virgin in the darkness behind it. Catharine had groped her way in the dazzling obscurity to some seats, and when she could see she found the children side by side in front of her, and she saw Reine on her knees, and Petitpère's meek gray head bowed. One other thing she saw, which seemed to her sad and almost cruel—poor old Nanon Lefebvre creeping up the centre aisle, and setting her basket on the ground, and then kneeling, and with difficulty kissing the cross let into the marble pavement in front of the altar, and saying a prayer, and slinking quickly away. Poor old Nanon! the penances of poverty and old age were also allotted to her. Just over Catharine's head, on a side altar, stood a placid saint, with outstretched arms, at whose feet numberless little offerings had been placed—orange-flowers and wreaths of immortelles, and a long string of silver hearts. Catharine, who had almost thought it wrong to come into a Popish chapel, found herself presently wondering whether by offering up a silver heart she could ever ease the dull aching in her own. It would have been no hard matter at this time before her marriage to bring this impressionable little sheep into the fold of the ancient Church. But Monsieur le Curé of Petitport, who was of an energetic and decided turn of mind, was away, and the gentle old Abbé Verdier, who had taken his place for a time, did not dream of conversions. Catharine changed very much after her marriage, and the opportunity was lost.

Petitpere having concluded his devotions, presently announced in a loud whisper that he should go and see about the *déjeûner*; he took the children with him. Reine and Catharine staid a little longer. Catharine was fascinated by the odd signs, the barbarous fantastic images, which expressed the faith, and patience, and devotion of these simple people.

"Venez," said Reine at last, laying a kind heavy hand on Catharine's shoulder, and the two went out again through the porch into the white daylight.

The inn was crowded with pilgrims, who, whether or not their petitions were granted, were breakfasting with plenty of wine and very good appetites in the quaint old stone kitchen. The cook was busy at his frizzling saucepans at a fireplace in the centre. The country folks were sitting all about unpacking their baskets, opening cider-bottles. There was a great copper fountain let into the massive wall, from which the people filled their jugs with water; a winding staircase in the thickness of the wall led to the upper story.

"Par ici," said Petitpère, triumphantly leading the way: he had engaged a private room in Catharine's honor, for he had some tact, and had been used to his daughter-in-law's refinements, and he said he thought mademoiselle would not care to dine below with all those noisy people. The private room had a couple of beds in it and various pictures—of the Emperor at Austerlitz, and three shepherdesses in red bodices and colored religious prints alternately; it had also a window opening upon the little *place*, and exactly opposite the chapel where services were constantly going on.

Reine laid the cloth, piling up the fruit in the centre, and pushing the table into the window. Petitpère made the salad very quickly and dexterously, and uncorked the wine and the cider. Reine had no fear of his transgressing before Catharine. "If my aunts were to see me now," thought Catharine, and she smiled to herself as she thought of Mrs. Buckington's face of apoplectic horror at the sight of Petitpère's blouse at the head of the table; of Lady Farebrother trembling in horror of popery upon Mount Ephraim. It was amusing to watch all the tide of white caps and blouses down below; it was odd and exciting to be dining in this quaint old tower, with all the people shouting and laughing underneath.

It was not so great a novelty to Reine as to Catharine; she was a little silent, and once she sighed, but she was full of kind care for them all, and bright and responding. "Petitpere," she said, "give mademoiselle some wine, and Toto and Josette too."

"Let us drink to the health of the absent," said Petitpère, solemnly.

But Catharine gave a sudden exclamation, and put down her glass untouched. "Look! ah! look," she cried, pointing through the window. "Who is that?" **she** cried out. She half feared it was a vision that **would** vanish instantly as it seemed to **have come.** Who was that **standing there in a straw hat,** looking as she had seen him look a hundred times before? It was no dream, no "longing passion unfulfilled" taking form and substance for a time. It was Richard Butler, and no other, who **was** standing there in the middle of the *place*, looking up curiously at their window. Petitpère knew him directly.

"C'est Monsieur Richard," he said, hospitably, and as if it was a matter of course. "Reine, my child, look there. He must come up. C'est monsieur Anglais qui fait de la peinture," he explained hastily to Catharine. "But you recognize him. The English are acquainted among each other."

Recognize him! Dick was so constantly in Catharine's thoughts that, if he had suddenly appeared in the place of the Virgin on the high altar of the chapel, I think she would scarcely have been very much surprised **after** the first instant. That he should be **there** seemed a matter of course; that he should **be absent was** the only thing that she found **it so impossible** to believe. As for Reine, **she sat quite still** with her head turned away; she **did not move** until the door **opened and Dick came in,** stooping under the **low** archway. He was just as usual; they might have been in Mrs. Butler's drawing-room in Eaton Square Catharine thought as he shook hands **first with** one and then with another.

"Did you not know I was coming to Tracy?" he said to Catharine. "I found nobody there and no preparations just now, but they told me you were here, and I got Pélottier to give me a lift, for I thought you would bring me back," he added, turning to Reine. She looked up at last, and seemed trying to speak indifferently.

"You know we are going back in a cart," Reine answered harshly.

"Do you think I am likely to have been dazzled by the splendor of Pélottier's gig?" Dick asked.

Reine did not like being laughed at. "You used to object to many things," she said, vexed, and then melting. "Such as they are, you know you are welcome to any of ours."

"Am I?" Dick answered, looking kindly at her.

Catharine envied Reine at that instant. She had nothing, not even a flower of her own to offer Dick, except, indeed, she thought, with a little smile, that great bouquet out of poor Monsieur Fontaine's garden.

If it was a sort of *Miserere* before, what a triumphal service was not the little evening prayer to Catharine! They went into the chapel after dinner for a minute or two. Sitting there in the darkness, she thought, silly child, that heaven itself would not seem more beautiful with all the radiance of the crystal seas and rolling suns than did this little shrine. To her as to l'etitpère the Deliverande was a little heaven just now, but for Petitpère Dick's presence or absence added but little to its splendor. There was Dick meanwhile, a shadowy living figure should prize it she never expected; that he should return it had never once crossed her mind. All her longing was to see him and hear of him, and some day, perhaps, to do him some service, to be a help, to manifest her love in secret alms of self-devotion, and fidelity, and

"Let us drink to the health of the absent," said Petitpère, solemnly.

in the dimness. Catharine could see him from where she sat by Reine. How happy she was. In all this visionary love of hers, only once had she thought of herself—that day when she sat by the well—at other times she had only thought of Dick, and poured out all the treasure in her kind heart before him. That he charity. She looked up at the string of silver hearts; no longer did they seem to her emblems of sad hearts hung up in bitterness, but tokens of gladness placed there before the shrine.

Petitpère was driving, and proposed to go back another way. The others sat face to face as they had come. The afternoon turned gray and a little chilly. Reine took Josette on her knee; Catharine wrapped Toto in her shawl. Dick had asked Catharine all the questions people ask by this time. He didn't see her doubtful face when he told her he had not waited for an answer to the letter announcing his coming.

"Madame de Tracy isn't like you, Mademoiselle Chrétien," said Dick. "She doesn't snub people when they ask for hospitality."

It struck Catharine a little oddly, afterward, that Dick should speak to Reine in this reproachful tone; that Reine should answer so shortly and yet so softly, so that one could hardly have told whether she was pleased or angry—at the time she only thought that he was there. Yesterday she had longed for a sight of the lines his pen had scratched upon a paper; to-day she was sitting opposite to him with no one to say one word. Petitpère's short cut was longer than it should have been, but Catharine would have gone on forever if she had held the reins. All the gray sky encompassed them—all the fields spread into the dusk—the soft, fresh winds came from a distance. The pale yellow shield of the horizon was turning to silver. The warm lights were coming out in the cottage lattices. As the evening closed in, they were sprinkled like glow-worms here and there in the country. Sometimes the cart passed under trees arching black against the pale sky; once they crossed a bridge with a rush of water below. There was not much color any where, nor form in the twilight, but exquisite tone and sentiment every where.

They passed one or two groups strolling and sitting out in the twilight as they approached Petitport, and the rushing of the sea seemed coming up to meet them at times. They were all very silent. Petitpère had been humming a little tune to himself for the last half hour; Dick had spoken to Reine once or twice, always in that bantering tone; to Catharine he was charming, gay, and kind and courteous, and like himself in short.

"Are you going to stay here, Mr. Butler?" asked Catharine once, suddenly.

"Only a day or two," Dick said abruptly. "I must go back for Beamish's wedding. I came because—because I could not keep away any longer, Miss George. Here we are at the chateau."

"There is M. le Maire," cried Petitpère, pulling up abruptly.

Fontaine had come down to look for Toto, who was asleep and very tired. The *turban écossais* slid off the little nodding head as Dick hauled the child to his father over the side of the cart.

"Good-night, Reine, and thank you," Catharine said. "It has been—oh, such a happy day!"

Fontaine only waited to assist Miss George to jump down, to express his surprise and delight at Mr. Butler's return, and then hurried off with his little sleepy Toto. "I shall come

back in the evening," cried the maire, going off and waving his hat.

"Monsieur Richard, you also get down here," said Petitpère, growing impatient at the horse's head, for Dick delayed and stood talking to Reine.

The two had been alone with Josette in the cart for a minute. Now Richard took Reine's unwilling hand in his, and looked her fixedly in the face, but he only said, "Au revoir, Mademoiselle Reine, is it not so?"

Reine seemed to hesitate. "Au revoir," she faltered at last, in the pathetic voice, and she looked away.

Catharine was safely landed down below, and heard nothing. "He came because he could not help it," she was saying to herself over and over again. For the first time a wild wondering thrill of hope came into her head. It was a certainty while it lasted—she never afterward forgot that minute. She stood outside the iron gate, the moon was rising palely, the evening seemed to thrill with a sudden tremor, the earth shook under her feet. While it lasted the certainty was complete, the moment was perfect. How many such are there even in the most prosperous lives? This one minute lasted until the cart drove away.

As Catharine and Dick were walking slowly across the court together, he stopped short. "I know I can trust you, Miss George," he said. "I—I think you must have guessed how things are with me," and a bright look came into his face. "Pray do not say any thing here. Reine is a thousand times too good for me," he said, with a shake in his voice, "or for them, and they wouldn't understand; and I can't afford to marry yet, but I know I shall win her in time. Dear Miss George, I know you will keep my secret. We have always been friends, have we not?" and he held out his hand.

"Yes," Catharine said, in a dreamy sort of way, as if she was thinking of something else. Friends! If love is the faith, then friendship is the charity of life. Catharine said yes very softly, very gently, and put her hand into his, and then went away into the house. There was no bitterness in her heart, no pang of vanity wounded just then; only an inexpressible sadness had succeeded that instant of foolish, mad certainty. The real depth, and truth, and sweetness of her nature seemed stirred and brought to light by the blow which had shattered the frail fabric she had erected for herself. But when she went up stairs into her room, the first thing she saw was the great nosegay of marguerites which the children had placed upon her table, and then she began to cry.

She was quite calm when she came down again. Dick tried to speak to her again, but he was somehow enveloped by Madame de Tracy, who was all the more glad to see him because she had written to him not to come.

After dinner they all began to dance again, as they had done the night before, and Martha went to the piano and began to play for them.

Ernestine would have liked, if possible, that all the gentlemen should have danced with her, but that could not be so; he was content to let the two little demoiselles de Vernon share in the amusements. Dick came and asked Miss George to dance, but she shook her head, and said she was tired. The little ball lasted some ten minutes perhaps, and ended as suddenly as it had begun. Marthe closed the piano with a sigh: she had very brilliant and supple fingers, and played with grace and sentiment; it was a sort of farewell to which they had all been dancing. Ernestine put one hand into her husband's arm, and one into Dick's. "Come," she said, dragging them out through the open window.

"Jeunesse! jeunesse!" said the countess kindly to Catharine as the young people went scampering and flitting across the grass and disappeared in the winding walks of the garden. Catharine answered with a faint smile. Madame de Tracy took up the newspaper, and drew her chair to the lamp, and then it was that Catharine slid quietly out of the room, and crept along the front of the house, and suddenly began flying down the avenue to the straight terrace walk, from whence she could see the sea gleaming silver under the vast purple-black dome of night. It was full moon again. All the light rippled over the country. The old pots on the parapet were turned to silver. The trees shivered, and seemed to shake the moonlight from their twigs and branches. Once the far-away voices reached her through the silence; but poor little Catharine only shivered when she heard them. She felt so utterly forsaken, and out of tune and harmony in this vast harmony, that she found herself clinging to the old pot with the lichen creeping up the outer edge, and crying and crying as if her heart must break. Poor little moonstruck creature, shedding her silver tears in the moonlight; she was like a little lichen herself, with her soft hands grasping the cold stone, and crying over them, and asking them for sympathy. She shivered, but she did not heed the chill; she seemed ingulfed, as it were, in the great bitter sea of passionate regret and shame, struggling and struggling, with no one to help. The moon traveled on, and now came streaming full upon the terrace, changing every thing fantastically. The gleam of the lamp by which Madame de Tracy was standing pierced through the trees. Sometimes a bird stirred in its sleep; sometimes a dog barked in the valley.

The voices which had sounded so distant presently came nearer and nearer; shadows, figures, sudden bursts of laughter, the shrill exclamations, the deeper tones of the men. Catharine, looking up, saw them all at the end of the walk: she could not face them; she started and fled. The others saw the white figure flitting before them.

"It is a ghost!" some one cried.

"It is Miss George," said Dick.

Catharine had no thought but to avoid them all just then as she went flying along, only as she was turning up the dark pathway leading to the house a figure suddenly emerged into the moonlight. It was no ghost. It was only Fontaine, with his eye-glasses gleaming in the moon rays. But she started and looked back, thinking in vague despair where she should go to escape. Fontaine seemed to guess her thought—

"Will you not remain one instant with me, mademoiselle?" he said. "I was looking for you. Madame de Tracy told me I might find you here."

He spoke oddly. There was a tone in his voice she had never heard before. What had come to him? Suddenly she heard him speaking again, thoroughly in earnest; and when people are in earnest, their words come strongly and simply. All his affectations had left him; his voice sounded almost angry-and fierce.

"I know that to you we country folks seem simple, and perhaps ridiculous at times," he said. "Perhaps you compare us with others, and to our disadvantage. But the day might come when you would not regret having accepted the protection and the name of an honest man," cried Fontaine. "Madame de Tracy has told me of your circumstances—your sisters. You know me, and you know my son. The affection of a child, the devotion of a lifetime, count for something, do they not? And this at least I offer you," said Fontaine, "in all good faith and sincerity. You have no mother to whom I can address myself, and I come to you, mademoiselle; and I think you owe me an answer."

There was a moment's silence; a little wind came rustling through the trees, bringing with it a sound of distant voices and laughter. Catharine shivered again; it sounded so sad and so desolate. She found herself touched, and surprised, and frightened all at once by Fontaine's vehemence. In an hour of weakness he had found her. "Take it, take it," some voice seemed saying to her; "give friendship, since love is not for you!" It seemed like a strange unbelievable dream to be there, making up her mind, while the young people, laughing still and talking, were coming nearer and nearer. Suddenly Fontaine saw a pale, wistful face in the moonlight—two hands put up helplessly. "Take me away, oh, take me away!" she said, with a sudden appealing movement. "I can do nothing for you in return, not even love you."

"Do not say that, my child," said Fontaine. "Do not be afraid; all will be well."

A minute later they were standing before Madame de Tracy. "She consents," said Fontaine; "you were wrong, madame. How shall I ever thank you for making me know her?"

It was Dick who first told Reine the news of the engagement. "I don't half like her to marry that fellow, poor little thing," he said. Reine, who was churning—she always made a point of working harder when Dick was present than at any other time—looked at him over her barrel. "I should not have done it in her place," she said, "but then we are different." Dick thought her less kind at that minute than he had ever known her before.

Love is the faith, and friendship should be the charity of life, and yet Reine in her own happiness could scarcely forgive Catharine for what she had done. Guessing and fearing what she did, she judged her as she would have judged herself. She forgot that she was a strong woman, and Catharine a child still in many things, and lonely and unhappy, while Reine was a happy woman now, at last, for the first time. For her pride had given way, and the struggle was over. Reine, who would not come unwelcome into any family, who still less would consent to a secret engagement, had succumbed suddenly and entirely when she saw Dick standing before her again. She had not answered his letter telling her that he would come and see her once more. She had vowed that she would never think of him again. When he had gone away the first time without speaking, she had protested in her heart; but when he spoke to her at last, the protest died away on her lips, and in her heart too. And so it came about that these two were standing on either side of the churn, talking over their own hopes and future, and poor little Catharine's too. With all her hardness—it came partly from a sort of vague remorse—Reine's heart melted with pity when she thought of her friend, and instinctively guessed at her story.

"Why do you ask me so many questions about Miss George?" Dick said at last. "Poor child, she deserves a better fate."

CHAPTER XII.

PLASTIC CIRCUMSTANCE.

ONCE long afterward, Catharine, speaking of the time before her marriage, said to Reine,

"Ah! Reine, you can not imagine what it is to have been afraid, as I have been. I am ashamed, when I think of my cowardice and want of trust; and yet I do not know that if the time were to come again, I might not be as weak, in my foolish, wicked longing for a fancied security."

"I don't know whether strong people are more or less to be pitied than weak ones, when they are in perplexity," Reine answered, brusquely. "You are much mistaken if you think I have never been afraid. I tell you, there have been days when I have been afraid of jumping over the cliff into the sea, like the swine in the Scriptures, to escape from the torments of the condemned. But we take things more at our ease now," said Reine, with a sigh. "One would soon die of it, if one was always to be young. And yet, for the matter of that," she added, glancing kindly at Catharine, "you look to me very much as you did when I knew you

first." And as she spoke Reine sent her shuttle swiftly whirling, and caught it deftly, while Josette, who had grown up tall and pretty, stood by, scissors in hand, cutting the string into lengths.

But this was long years afterward, when Catharine looked back, as at a dream, to the vague, and strange, and unreal time which had preceded her marriage. There had been a quick confusion, a hurry, a coming and going; it seemed to her like a kaleidoscope turning and blending the old accustomed colors and forms of life into new combinations and patterns. Catharine had watched it all with a bewildered indifference. She had taken the step, she was starting on the journey through the maze of the labyrinth, she had not the heart to go back. There had been long talks and explanations which never explained, and indecisions that all tended one way, and decided her fate as certainly as the strongest resolves. Once she had been on the very point of breaking every thing off; and, looking back, she seemed to see herself again—by the sea-side, watching the waves, and telling them that they should determine; or tête-à-tête with Fontaine, silent and embarrassed, trying to make him understand how little she had to give in return for all his attentive devotion. He would not, perhaps he could not, understand her feeling for him? Why was she troubling herself? He looked conscious, elated, perfectly satisfied; for Fontaine, like a wise man, regarded the outside aspect of things, and did not disturb himself concerning their secret and more difficult complications. She had promised to be his wife. She was a charming person, he required no more; he had even declared that for the present he would not touch a single farthing of the small yearly sum which belonged to her. It was to be expended as heretofore upon the education of her sisters. In the holidays they were to find a home in the châlet. Fontaine felt that he was behaving liberally and handsomely, and it added to his satisfaction. Madame Mérard groaned in agony over her snuff-box at his infatuation. That her son-in-law should marry again she had always expected; "but never, never, Monsieur Mérard, did I think him capable of a folly like this!" cried the old lady. Monsieur Mérard, who was an extremely fat and good-humored old gentleman, tried to look as if the matter was not perfectly indifferent to him. There were but three things in life that really mattered; all the rest must be taken as it came; this was his experience:

I. Your coffee should be hot in the morning.

II. You should have at least five trumps between you and your partner.

III. Your washerwoman should not be allowed to starch your shirt-collars into uncomfortable ridges.

That very day she had sent them home in this horrible condition. Monsieur Mérard could not turn his head without suffering. That Fontaine should marry more or less to please Madame Mérard seemed a trifle in such an emergency.

Dick was the only person who doubted the expediency of the proposed arrangement, or, at least, who said as much to Catharine herself. He found a moment to speak to her alone in the hall.

"Forgive me," he said. "I know I of all people have the least right to speak; but have you thought well over the tremendous importance of the step you are taking. You are young enough to look for something different from . . . If you wanted a home, Reine is always there . . . Fontaine is an excellent fellow; but your tastes are so unlike; your whole education and way of thinking . . ."

"You don't know what it is," said Catharine, controlling herself and speaking very gently; "I shall have a home and some one to look to;" but her heart sank as she spoke.

Butler himself was one of those weak-minded natures that sometimes trouble themselves about other concerns besides their own and those of their own belongings. The stalwart hero who succeeds in life, loves his wife and his children, or the object of his affections, his friends, his dog, but worries himself no farther about the difficulties and sorrows, expressed and unexpressed, by which he is surrounded. He does his day's work, exchanges good-humored greetings with the passers-by, but he lets them pass on. He would never, for instance, dream of being sorry for a lonely, fanciful little woman who chanced to cross his path. He might throw her a sovereign if she were starving, and shut the door, but that would be the extent of his sympathy. The Mr. Grundys of life are sensible, manly fellows, business-like, matter-of-fact, and they would very sensibly condemn the foolish vagaries and compunctions of unpractical visionaries like Dick. And they are safer companions, perhaps, than others of finer nerve and more sympathetic fibre. Catharine might have been heart-whole and laughing still with the children in the garden if Dick Butler had belonged to the tribe of Mr. Grundys. Unluckily for her, he was gentle and kind-hearted, and chivalrous after a fashion. He could not help being touched by helplessness and simplicity. He had said nothing to Catharine more than he had said to any of the young ladies of his acquaintance, but the mere fact of her dependence and inequality—although he would not own it—gave importance to what had no importance. It would have been truer kindness to have left her alone, for it is no longer the business of knights-errant to go about rescuing damsels in distress.

And yet Dick had the gift, which does not belong to all men—a gift of sympathy and an intuitive tenderness. "What chance of happiness was there for that impressionable little creature with the well-meaning but tiresome Fontaine?" So he said to himself and to his aunt one day; but Madame de Tracy only assured him that he was mistaken in his estimate of Fontaine. It was a charming arrangement, and Catharine was perfectly happy.

Catharine's perfect happiness manifested itself by a strange restlessness; she scarcely ate, her dreams were troubled, music would make her eyes fill up with tears. "Voi che sapete," some one was singing one evening; she could not bear it, and jumped up and went out through the open window into the night. She did not go very far, and stood looking in at them all, feeling like a little stray sprite out of the woods peering in at the happy united company assembled in the great saloon.

Madame de Tracy was surprised and somewhat disappointed at the silence and calmness with which Catharine accepted her new lot in life. She took the girl up into her room that night, and talked to her for nearly an hour, congratulated, recapitulated, embraced her affectionately, and then sat holding her hand between her own fat white fingers; but it was all in vain. Her heroine would not perform; the little thing had no confidence to give in return; she seemed suddenly to have frozen up; still, chill, pale, answering only by monosyllables, silent and impenetrable, Catharine seemed transformed into somebody else. She was not ungrateful for the elder lady's kindness, but her eyes looked with a beseeching, fawn-like glance, which seemed to say, "Only leave me—only let me be." This was not in the least amusing or interesting to Madame de Tracy or Catharine. It was a sort of slow torture. Dazed and a little stupefied, and longing for silence, to be expected to talk sentiment when she felt none, to blush, to laugh consciously, to listen to all the countess's raptures and exclamations, was weary work. The child did her best, tried to speak, but the words died away on her lips; tried to say she was happy, but then a sudden pain in her heart seemed to rise and choke her. What was she doing? Dick disapproved. Was it too late to undo the work she had begun?

Fontaine did not come up to the chateau that evening. It was perhaps fortunate for him that he was detained by Madame Mérard. Catharine thought not of the countess's congratulations, but of Dick's two words of warning that night, as she was sitting upon her bed half undressed, with all her hair tumbling about her. She could hear them all dispersing below, and Dick's voice humming *Voi che sapete* as he tramped along the gallery; then a door banged, and all was silent.

She was thinking of his words again in the court-yard next morning, sitting with her work upon a bench under a tree. The De Vernons, and Ernestine, and Dick were at the piano in the little boudoir, of which the windows were open. Little Henri was marching in and out, and beating time with his whip. The young people were singing and screaming with laughter, and banging false notes on the piano sometimes, and laughing again. "Take care, Henri, do not get out of the window," cried his mother from within; but Henri paid no attention. The gay jangle went on, and the laughter and music poured out to where Catharine was sitting with her chin resting on her two folded hands. She could see through the iron gates; beyond the road lay a distance smiling in sunshine. She watched the smoke from a chimney drifting in the breeze. "Clang a rang, clang a rang, Ta ra, ta ta ra," sang the young people; and then came a burst of laughter, and then more voices joined in. Catharine recognized Dick's in the medley of sounds. The sun shone hotter and hotter; a chestnut fell to the ground with a sudden snap, and the brown, bright fruit showed through the green pod. Again the music sounded and her ribbon fluttered gently. How happy they all seemed! What good spirits Butler was in! The languid young Englishman seemed to have caught something of the life and gayety of the people among whom he was staying. But he had looked grave when he spoke to her, Catharine thought. How good of him to think of her! Just then he came out and quickly crossed the yard without seeing her. "Do not be late," cried Ernestine from the window.

Dick nodded, and strode away along the dusty road toward the village. Catharine watched him from under her tree until he disappeared, and Henri and Nanine came up disposed for conversation, and bringing a supply of chestnuts for Miss George's work-basket.

"Mon cousin is very disagreeable," Henri said. "He would not take me with him. I don't care for him any more."

"Mademoiselle, what stuff is this?" said Nanine, taking hold of Catharine's gown. "Something English, is it not? Have you many more toilettes in your box up stairs? Though to be sure," added the child, with instinctive politeness, "one does not require much when one is

traveling, and you did not expect to remain with us long."

"I brought all the prettiest dresses I had, Nanine," Catharine said, sadly, wondering how much the children knew already. "Why do you think I am not going to stay with you?"

Nanine turned red and did not answer; but Henri cried out, "Oh no, Mademoiselle la Curieuse. Miss George has found you out. Miss George, she heard mamma say there was no room for you at Paris the day grandmamma was angry, and mamma had her migraine. It is not pretty to listen, is it?" said Henri, who had not forgiven certain sisterly lectures.

Miss George blushed too, like Nanine, and did not answer. She began slowly throwing the chestnuts one by one into the basket at her side, and then suddenly started up. All the chestnuts which had remained in her lap fell to the ground and rolled away. She left the amazed children to collect their scattered treasures. It was a nothing that the children had inadvertently revealed to her, and yet in her excited state it seemed the last drop in her cup. "What did it all mean?" she said to herself. "Who can I trust? where can I go? Only Mr. Butler and Reine speak the truth to me. Ah! would Reine help me if I went to her? I think—I think she cares for me a little."

Meanwhile Dick, who had not gone to the village after all, was walking along the cliff to the farm. He found Reine sitting in the window of the kitchen, with her head resting upon her hand, as perplexed as Catharine herself, only facing her troubles and looking to no one else for help. What was she afraid of? She scarcely knew. She was afraid for Dick far more than for herself.

Who can account for painful impressions? Reine's was a strong and healthy organization, and of all people she would have seemed the least likely to be subject to vague terrors, to alarms indefinite and without a cause; and yet there were moments of foreboding and depression against which she found it almost impossible to struggle; almost, I say, because therein did her healthy and strengthful nature reassert itself, battling with these invisible foes, and resisting them valiantly.

She, too, sometimes asked herself whether she had done wisely and well? Whether she, a simple country girl, without experience of the world, would ever be able to suffice to a grand seigneur like Dick. Once she had thought herself more than his equal, but that was over now. She was rich and he was poor, he told her; but it was a magnificent sort of poverty, and the word had not the same meaning for him as it had for old Nanon, for example, mumbling her crusts.

"Ah! was he, could he be in earnest?" Reine asked herself. Dick's languid manner might have been that of any young Machiavel of society; it frightened her sometimes, though she laughed at it to him; but his heart was a simple blundering machine, full of kindness and softness. There was a real touch of genius about him for all his crude workmanship. Whatever people may say, genius is gentle and full of tenderness. It is cleverness which belongs perhaps to the children of this world. Some very dull

Reine was not troubling herself about such speculations, but she trembled sometimes for Dick, even more than for herself, and asked herself whether he might not do himself injury by marrying her? and so she told him when he came in now, and took her hand and kissed it,

Dick and Reine.

and sad people have genius, though the world may not count it as such—a genius for love, or for patience, or for prayer, maybe. We know the divine spark is here and there in this world—who shall say under what manifestation or humble disguise?

and asked what she was thinking of, and why she looked so disturbed.

Her answer did not quite please him somehow, though as she spoke she looked more beautiful than he had ever seen her, blushing, with tender deep eyes, as she sat in the light of the window. "Why do you always want to take care of me?" said Butler. "Am I not big enough to take care of myself? Reine, when we are married I shall take care of you too. I shall not let you work any more, and I shall paint you just as you look now, and not one of the fine ladies will be able to hold a candle to you."

"They will despise me," said Reine, "as they did my mother; perhaps for your sake they will just touch me with the end of their fans. You know well enough that it is from no want of love for you that I speak," said Reine, blushing more deeply. "I love you so well that I had rather you left me here now this moment than that you were ever ashamed of me or sorry for what you have done," and suddenly Reine the overbearing, Reine the magnificent, burst into tears.

Dick tried to reassure her, to console her, by every tender word he could think of; but Reine, recovering and ashamed of her weakness, pushed him away. "Go, go," she said, as he bent over her, full of concern and gentleness. He was a little hurt; he loved her, but he could not always understand her—her odd abruptness and independence—her strange moods. He turned away—how well he remembered the scene in after years! The quaint, straggling room, with its odd, picturesque accessories, even the flower-pot in the window, and the faint scent from its blossoms; Reine's noble head bent low, and the light upon it. He turned away, and as he did so he caught sight for one instant of a pale face looking in through the window—a pale, wistful, sad face, that disappeared in a moment. Poor sad eyes! the sight of the two together was more than they could bear. Human nature is very weak as well as very strong. Catharine had come across the sultry fields, looking to the farm for help and consolation. If Reine also advised it, she thought she would break forever with the schemes she had consented to; go back, work hard, and struggle on as best she could. Dear Reine! she at least could be depended upon. Coming to the farm at last, she had found only Paris to welcome her with a lazy wag of his tail. There was no one about; all the doors were shut; even the house-door, with its bars and heavy-headed nails all distinct in the sun. She tapped once or twice without being heard. She turned away at last disappointed, thinking Reine must be out in the fields; and then, as she turned, she glanced in through the window and saw the two. Catharine could think of them together with a certain gentle, loving sympathy; but to come knocking at the door wanting help, and not be heard; to stand by unnoticed, and see them engrossed, utterly oblivious of her existence—oh, it was hard; life was cruel, friendship was an illusion!

"Can any thing be the matter?" Dick said, starting up. "That was little Miss George." And he went to the door and looked out. He was only in time to see the little figure disappearing under the archway.

E

Reine wiped her tears out of her eyes—I don't know that she was the less sad for that—she came to the doorway and stood beside him. "Poor child!" she said; "was she looking in?"

"She looked very strange," said Richard. "It may have been my fancy—" And then, catching Reine's steady gaze, he turned red in his turn. "Don't look like that, dear," said he, trying to laugh, "or I shall think it was a ghost I saw."

A ghost indeed! the ghost of a dead love. Only yesterday some one was saying, with a sigh, "There are other deaths sadder than death itself: friendships die and people live on, and love dies too, and that is the saddest of all." The saddest of all! and sometimes people come and look in through windows and see it.

Petitpère came in a minute after, and found Reine and Richard still standing in the doorway. "What have you been doing to the little demoiselle Anglaise?" said he. "She passed close by the barn just now without speaking to me, and I think she was crying."

Catharine meanwhile was going quickly away from the place, leaving them, "together in their happiness," so she kept telling herself. She hurried along the dusty road; she did not go back to the house, but she took a footway leading to the cliff, and she came to the edge at last and looked over. The small sandy convolvuluses were creeping at her feet, the wind shook the dry, faint-colored, scentless flowers. The wavelets were rolling in, and the light struck and made fire upon each flashing crest. She clambered down the side of the cliff by a narrow little pathway which the fishermen had made there, and she came down upon the beach at last, and went stumbling over the shingle, and sea-weed, and heaps of sea-drift.

Catharine had gone stumbling along under the shadow of the cliff. She did not care or think where she was going. She had come upon the smooth, rippled sands; the sea was swelling inland in a great rushing curve. She had passed the village; she heard the sounds of life overhead as she went by; she had come to the terrace at the end of Fontaine's garden. A little river of sea-water was running in a cleft in the sand. Catharine had to jump to cross it. Ever afterward she remembered the weary effort it was to her to spring. But she crossed the little ford, and came safely to the other side; and it was at this instant that somebody, rushing up, came and clasped her knees with many expressions of delight. It was Toto, who in his little childish squeak gladly exclaimed, "I saw you from the cabane. Papa sent me, and I ran." The child was clinging to her still when Fontaine himself made his appearance, slippered, and newspaper in hand, hastening to welcome her.

"Were you coming to find us, chère demoiselle?" said he. "Come, you are at home, you know."

Was she indeed at home? Catharine felt as if she had been crazy for a few minutes with doubt, mistrust, indecision. She hated herself, and felt herself unworthy of Fontaine's kindness, and yet she was inexpressibly touched and cheered by it. She said to herself that she had found a friend in her sore necessity—that she should never, never forget his kindness, and indeed she kept her vow. This was the last of her indecisions.

A little later Fontaine walked back to the chateau with her. As they were going along she asked him if he knew that they had meant to send her away when they left for Paris?

"Chère demoiselle," said he, "how should I know it? It may or may not be true. I care not, since you remain."

"I felt as if nobody wanted me," Catharine said, as they went in at the gates together.

Butler was alone on the terrace, smoking a cigar, when they came back. When he saw them he got up and came to meet them. He looked a little curious, a little languid, and slightly sentimental.

"Why did you go away?" he said. "I rushed out to call you, Miss George, but you would have nothing to do with us."

"I—I did not want to stop just then," she said, hastily. He had recognized her then! She turned to Fontaine in a confused sort of way, and called him to her.

"Charles," she said, calling him by his Christian name for the first time, "have you . . . Will you . . ." The words died away. But after that first moment she was quite outwardly calm again. Butler had recognized her. She made a great effort. She spoke quietly and indifferently, while to herself she said passionately that at least he could not read her heart. She had taken her resolution, she would abide by it.

Reine, in her place, would have done differently. Catharine was doing wrong, perhaps, but with no evil intent—she was false with a single heart. She thought there was no other solution to her small perplexities than this desperate one she had taken. If she had been older she would have been wiser. Wait. That is the answer to most sorrows, to most troubled consciences. But how can one believe in this when one has not waited for any thing? Some one says, very wisely and touchingly, "To the old, sorrow is sorrow; to the young, sorrow is despair." What other interpretation may there not be hidden beneath the dark veil to those who can see from afar?

CHAPTER XIII.

MENDELSSOHN'S WEDDING-MARCH.

CATHARINE BUTLER was to have been married on the 10th, but old Mr. Beamish was suddenly taken ill, and every thing had to be put off indefinitely. Dick offered himself to remain at Tracy until after Catharine George's wedding.

This wedding was fixed for a very early date.

Madame de Tracy was anxious to have it over before she left for Paris. Lady Farebrother, who was written to, sent back her consent in a strange jumble of religion and worldliness. Mrs. Buckington, to every body's surprise, came out with a fifty-pound note for Catharine's trousseau. The modest little outfit did not take long to make ready. Fontaine undertook the other necessary arrangements at Caen, for from the difference of religion there were some slight complications beyond those which usually attend weddings. The day came very quickly, almost unexpectedly and suddenly at last, like most eventful days.

The Protestant church is a great, gray, vault-like place, with many columns and sad-colored walls. Catharine, who had slept at Caen the night before in a house belonging to the De Vernons, came driving up to the door with Madame de Tracy just as the party arrived from Petitport by the early train. They all passed in together, but Catharine felt a chill as she came into the sombre place. It was so big, so full of echoes; some one brushed against a chair as the little procession passed up the centre aisle, the dismal scraping sound reverberated from column to column. The clergyman was a kind-looking, white-haired old man, who read the service in a plaintive, mumbling voice. He was only passing through the place; he knew none of the people, but he was interested in the little sweet-eyed bride, and long afterward he remembered her when he met her again. Fontaine was uncomfortable, and very glad when this part of the ceremony was over. There was no knowing where these mysterious rites to which he was exposed, defenseless and without redress, might not lead him. He was not anxious for Catharine. She was inured to it, and she was so docile and gentle, too, that nothing would be counted very heavily against her; but for a good Catholic like himself, who knew better, who had been carefully instructed, there was no saying what dangers he might not be incurring.

The service was soon over, but Madame de Tracy had made some mistake in her orders, and when the wedding-party came out into the peristyle of the church, the carriages had both disappeared. It was but a short way to the church where they were going. Most of them had intended to walk, and there was now no other alternative. "Venez, madame," said Jean de Tracy, offering Catharine his arm, while Fontaine followed with Madame de Tracy; then came Marthe, with some children; and last of all, Dick, and a strange lady, who had also arrived from Petitport by the early train. It was not Madame Mérard. She, naturally enough, refused to be present at the ceremony; Madame Ernestine, too, found it quite out of the question to be up at such an impossible hour. The strange lady was handsomely dressed in a gray silk gown and a pale-colored Cashmere shawl. She kept a little apart from the rest, never lifting her eyes off her book during the service. Madame de Tracy could not imagine who she was at first, but Catharine's eyes brightened when she saw her.

The strange lady looked a little ashamed, and shy, and fierce at once. She had fancied people stared at her as she came along; and no wonder, for a more beautiful and noble-looking young creature than Reine Chrétien at that time never existed. Under her bonnet her eyes looked bigger and brighter, and her rippled hair was no longer hidden under the starch of her cap; she came up with a certain grace and stately swing which she had caught from her mother. Secretly, she felt uncomfortable in her long-trained gown; but she came bravely along, as if she had been used to her draperies all her life. Dick was amused and interested to see his peasant maiden so transformed.

"Reine, I never should have dared to fall in love with you if I had first known you like this," said he, watching his opportunity, and taking his place beside her.

"Don't laugh at me," said Reine.

"What a dismal affair this has been! I know my aunt has cooked the whole thing up," Dick went on. "They are not in the least suited to each other."

Reine sighed. "Ill-assorted marriages never answer," she said, in the quick, harsh tones she sometimes used.

"But well-assorted marriages, mademoiselle," said Dick, gayly and kindly, and then he stopped short. A sad glance had crossed his; Catharine looked back with her pale face, and the young man, who always said out what was in his mind, began pitying her to his companion.

Reine, never very talkative, became quite silent by degrees.

Some bells were ringing from some of the steeples, and to Catharine they seemed playing one of the bars of Mendelssohn's wedding-march over and over again. They were passing by some of those old wooden houses which still exist in the quaint old city, piled with carvings, and balconies, and flowers, chiefly balsams, flaming against the blackened walls; heads were peeping through the windows, casements were gleaming. It was like the realization of a fancy Catharine once had long ago, when she was listening to Beamish in the studio.

"How loudly those bells are ringing! they will break their necks," said Jean de Tracy, by way of something to say, for conversation was a little difficult under the circumstances, and silence was difficult too.

All round the church of St. Pierre there is a flower-garden. The church stands at the end of the quai, and at the meeting of many streets. The market-people were in groups all about when the wedding-party arrived. There seemed to be an unusual stir in the place. It is always gay and alive; to-day it was more than usually crowded with white caps, and flowers, and blouses, and baskets of vegetables. Jean de Tracy, who was used to the place, led the way across to a side door, which he opened and held back for Catharine to pass in, but she waited until the others came up. Fontaine and Madame de Tracy first entered, the others following after, and then there was a sudden stop, and no one advanced any farther. If the Protestant temple seemed melancholy, this was terrible to them as they came in out of the cheerful clatter and sunshine, into a gloom and darkness which startled them all. The high altar was hung completely in black; the lights burnt dimly; by degrees, when they could distinguish more clearly, they saw that figures in mourning were passing up the long aisle, while voices at the altar were chanting a requiem for the dead. Catharine gave a little cry, and seized hold of some one who was standing near her.

"Ah! how terrible!" cried Madame de Tracy, involuntarily.

"There must be some mistake," said Dick. "Have we come to the wrong church?"

"It often happens so in our churches," Reine said, quietly taking Catharine's hand. "I do not think there is any mistake."

Fontaine and Jean de Tracy went hastily forward to speak to an official who was advancing up a side aisle. As Reine said, there was no mistake—they were expected; a little side-altar had been made ready for them, where l'Abbé Verdier's well-known face somewhat reassured them, but not entirely. We all know that the marriage service goes on though there are mourners in the world. Why not face the truth? and yet it was sad and very depressing. The ceremony was hurried through, but Catharine was sobbing long before it came to an end. Marthe was the person who was least moved. It put her in mind of her own profession, now soon approaching, when neither marriage nor burial-service, but something between the two, would be read over her. Reine was trying to cheer and reassure the children. Toto said he wanted to go; he was frightened, and began to whimper, and at last Reine took him out into the porch.

Butler, who always seemed to know where she was, followed her a minute after, and stood with her under the noble old porch, with its ornamentations and gurgoyles carved against the blue of the sky; stony saints and flowers, fantastic patterns, wreaths, birds flying, arch built upon arch, delightful bounty and intricate loveliness, toned and tinted by the years which had passed since these noble gates were put up to the house of the Lord, and the towers overhead were piled. Dick thought he should be well content to stand there with Reine like the abbots and saints all about, and see the centuries go by, and the great tides of the generations of people.

Reine was busy meanwhile answering Toto's impatient little questions; her shawl was half slipping off as she leant against a niche in the wall; with one hand (it was a trick she had) she was shading her eyes from the sun, with the other she was holding Toto's little stout fist.

"I am trying to give you a name," said Dick at last, smiling. "I do not know what noble lady was martyred in Cashmere, for whom you might stand, in your niche, just as you are."

As he spoke, some more of the mourners passed in. It was the funeral of a high dignitary in the place, and numbers of people were attending it. "What a sad wedding for poor Catharine," Reine said, looking after them.

"Poor little thing! It must be almost over now," Dick answered.

"I shall not be sorry for one, if it were, only to get rid of all this," said Reine, tugging at her great Indian shawl, "and to go back to Petitport quietly in my own every-day clothes."

"I think, after all, I like you best in your cap and apron," said Butler, looking at her critically.

"I knew it — I knew it!" Reine cried, suddenly flashing up; "I am not used or fit for any thing else but what I am accustomed to. I often feel, if I ever put off my poor peasant dress, it may turn out an evil day for you and me. You might change and be ashamed of me perhaps, and . . . "

"Hush, Reine," said Butler; "it isn't worthy of you to have so little trust in me. Why wouldn't you believe me the other day, as now, when I tell you . . ."

"Shall I tell you what makes me mistrust you?" the girl answered, and her eyes seemed to dilate, and then she suddenly broke off and went on angrily: "Ah! I am no angel from heaven; I have told you that often enough. We in our class are not like you others. We don't pretend to take things as they come, and to care, as you do, for nothing, nor do we women trick our husbands, and speak prettily to them as if they were children to be coaxed and humored. I have good blood in my veins, but I am a woman of the people for all that, and I love frankness above all things; and there are things belonging to this dress — belonging to rich people I hate, and I always shall hate; never will I condescend to deceive you, to pretend to be what I am not. I can not dissemble, do you see?" she cried; "and if there is any thing in my mind, it comes out in time — hatred, or jealousy, or whatever it may be."

"You are pretending to be what you are not when you make yourself out worse than you are," Dick said gravely, chipping off a little piece of the cathedral with his penknife. The little bit of soft stone fell to the ground like dust. Reine looked up, hesitated, and suddenly calmed down. Forgive me," she said at last, with a thrilling low voice; "I was wrong to doubt you;" and she tore off her glove and put her honest hand in his. Butler was touched, and stooped and kissed it; but he wished, and in his turn hated himself for wishing, that she had not pulled off her glove.

And so the martyr came out of her niche, and it was time to go; but before the wedding-party left the church some one whispered to M. Fontaine to come out by the side door, for the funeral carriages were drawn up at the great front entrance.

Fontaine took his wife away to Rouen for a fortnight's distraction after the ceremony. While the two were going off in a nervous tête-à-tête in the coupé of a railway carriage, the others were returning to Tracy, silent and depressed, for the most part, like people after an unsuccessful expedition.

"I am going to smoke a cigar," said Dick, looking in at the door of the carriage where Madame de Tracy, and Marthe, and the children were installed. De Tracy, hearing this, started up from his seat and said he would come too, and Dick walked along the second-class carriages until he had made his selection.

In one corner of a crowded department sat a peasant-girl with two great baskets at her knees. De Tracy got in without even observing her, sat down at the other end of the bench, and let down the window and puffed his smoke out into the open air. Dick did not light his cigar after all, but sat turning one thing and another in his head. Once looking up, he caught the glance of Reine's two kind eyes fixed upon him, and he could not help saying, "What has become of the grand lady, Mademoiselle Chrétien?" Reine pointed to her baskets and looked down, trying to be grave. Butler did not speak to her any more; the compartment was full of blouses; he had only wanted to see her safe to her journey's end.

Dominique was at the station with the cart he had brought for Reine, and the Tracy carriage was waiting too. Madame de Tracy, nodding greetings right and left, got in, followed by Marthe, and the children, and little Toto, who was to spend a couple of days at the chateau before he went to his grandmother. Madame de Tracy knew every body by name, and graciously inquired after numbers of Christian names.

"Jean, there is that excellent Casimir," pointing to a repulsive-looking man with one eye. "Bring him here to me. How do you do? How is your poor wife? Ah! I forgot you are not married. How are you yourself? Not coming, Jean? Then drive on, Jourdain. Baptiste, put Monsieur Toto on my great fur cloak; yes, my child, you must, indeed; I should never forgive myself if you were to catch cold now your papa is away. Never mind being a little too warm." And so the carriage load drove off in slight confusion, poor Toto choking, and trying in vain to get his mouth out of the fur.

Meanwhile Dick went and helped Reine into her cart with as much courtesy as if she was a duchess getting into a magnificent chariot. She blushed, nodded good-night, and drove off immediately; and then Butler came back and joined his cousin, who was standing by, looking rather surprised.

"Come along, my Don Quixote," said Jean, turning off the little platform and striking out toward the fields. It was a quiet twilight walk. They both went on in silence for a time. There was a sound of grasshoppers quizzing at their feet from every grass tuft and distant coppice and hedgerow. One or two villagers passed them, tramping home to their cottages.

"I hope my mother is satisfied," said Jean de Tracy at last, "and easy in her mind. I must confess, Dick, that I myself had some misgivings. That poor little thing! I could see very well that it was not Fontaine she was thinking of all the time. He! It is not the first wedding I have been at."

Dick could not answer; he felt horribly guilty and uncomfortable. "Heaven knows," he was thinking to himself, "I am unconscious of ever having said a word or done any thing to make that poor child fancy I cared for her!" . . . . He was haunted by the remembrance of that pale face looking in through the window, and yet it might have been a mere chance after all. His course was plain enough now; to Reine he had spoken words of love; to her he was bound by every tie of honor and sincere affection, and yet his head was full of all sorts of regrets and remorses. Reine's sudden outbreak had left a discomfort in his mind which he tried in vain to shake off—a discomfort which concerned Reine herself as well as poor little Catharine. He began to hate concealment, to tell himself that the sooner he had done with mysteries the better. Should he tell them all now, directly; should he speak to his cousin here walking beside him, and tell him of his plans, or wait a little longer until he had spoken to his uncle Charles first before declaring himself to the others? On the whole, he decided this last plan would be best. But he vowed to himself that Reine at least should have no cause to reproach him. "At all events, she is rich; they ought to approve of that," thought Dick, bitterly. "I shall have a terrible time of it, but that can not be helped." He would work hard and make himself independent, and brave the coming storm. It was true that she had enough for them both, even now; but to accept her money was an impossibility, and she had acknowledged it herself when she had once told him how rich she was.

Now that Reine knew him better, that a certain education in the way of the world had come to her, she began to understand better than she had done before their relative positions. It was no longer the poor and struggling artist aspiring to the hand of the rich *fermière* who had been so courted and much made of by the small dignitaries and needy *propriétaires* of the place. She understood better the differences between them; she began to see the gulf which she must cross if she did not wish to shock him and repulse him unconsciously at almost every step. He could not come to her as she had imagined once: she must go to him. Her heart failed her sometimes. That sham, idle, frittering, fidgety, trammeled, uneasy life had no attractions for her. Reine imagined herself playing the piano and nodding her head in time, and occasionally fanning herself with a scented pocket-handkerchief, and burst out laughing at the idea. Her notions of society were rather vague,

and Dick hardly knew how to explain to her the things he was so used to.

"I hope you will never fan yourself with your pocket-handkerchief," he said, when Reine described her visions for the future. He owned to himself sometimes that she was right in what she said. He liked her best when he thought of her as herself, at home in her farm, with her servants and her animals round her. There she was, simple, and gentle, and thoughtful in all her ministrations, occupied always, unselfish, and only careful for others. After that last outbreak she met him with a sweet humility and womanliness which charmed him and touched him utterly. The night he said good-by to her she came out with him under the great arch, and stood looking at him with her noble tender face.

"Fate has done its best to separate us, has it not?" said Reine, smiling; "putting us like this, on different sides of the sea. But you will come back—is it not so?" she said, "and I have no fear any more. I shall wait for you here."

The sunset was illuminating the old farm and the crumbling barns, and Petipère's blue smock and white locks, as he sat on his bench smoking his evening pipe; some cows were crossing the road from one field to another, with tinkling bells sounding far into the distance; the great dog came up and rubbed his head at his mistress's knee. "He will know you again," Reine said, holding out both her hands, "when you come back to me," and so they parted.

The next day the whole family of Tracys started together for Paris. Madame *mère* in a huge bonnet, which almost completely concealed her face, was assisted from her apartment by her grandson to a close carriage. She was anxious to consult some Paris doctors on the state of her health.

CHAPTER XIV.

MADAME FONTAINE AT HOME IN THE CHALET.

WHEN Catharine and her husband returned from their trip a fortnight later and looked out through the diligence windows at the chateau, the blinds were drawn, the shutters shut, the garden chairs were turned up on their seats, the great iron gates were closed fast. Catharine never had realized so completely that she was not coming back there any more, but to the little chalet with the balconies and weathercocks which Madame de Tracy had shown her. It was like the story of *Rip Van Winkle*; she had been away among the elves and gnomes a hundred years. Every body was gone that she was used to: Dick was gone, the others dispersed here and there; most of the strangers lodging in the village had left; even Catharine George had vanished; Monsieur and Madame Mérard had retired to their *campagne*. It was a mouldy little villa on the high road to Bayeux; but Fontaine assured her from experience that they would doubtless return before long. Perhaps in his heart of hearts the worthy *maire* regretted that his *tête-à-tête* should be so soon interrupted, but he blamed himself severely for the inconsiderate feeling. "After all that I owe to these excellent parents," he explained, "the magnificent *dot* which their daughter brought me, I feel that they must always look upon the châlet as their home whenever they feel inclined to do so. You, *ma très-chère amie*, are gifted with a happy and equable temper: I know you will not hesitate to bestow upon them those filial attentions which are so graceful when accorded by youth to old age. Believe me, I shall not be ungrateful."

Catharine smiled at the solemn little address: she was glad that there was any thing she could do for her husband. For already his kindness, his happiness, his entire contentment, had made her ashamed. "Ah! it was cruel to have taken so much, to have so little to give in return," she had thought once or twice. At least she would do her duty by him, she told herself, and it was with a very humble and yet hopeful heart that she passed the threshold of her new home. Toto was there to welcome them, and to trample upon all the folds of Catharine's muslin dress with his happy little feet, and Justine, the excellent cook, came out to stare at the new inmate of the châlet.

" *Soyez la bienvenue*," said Fontaine, embracing his wife affectionately; and they all three sat down very happily, to dine by the light of the lamp. The entertainment began with a melon.

"Grandmamma is coming on Saturday week," said Toto. "Mr. Pélottier will call for them on his way back from Caen."

"Ah! so much the better," said Justine, who was carrying away the empty dishes. Justine did not approve of second marriages.

Madame Fontaine soon found that she would have little or nothing to do with the domestic arrangements in the châlet. She was much too greatly in awe of Justine, the excellent cook, who had fried Fontaine's cutlets for fifteen years, to venture to interfere in the kitchen. Fontaine himself had been accustomed, during his long bachelor life and after his first wife's death, to interest himself in the cares of the ménage. He superintended the purchase of fish, the marketing, the proper concocting of the pot-au-feu. He broke sugar, and made himself supremely useful in the house. He might be discovered sometimes of a fine morning busily employed in the court-yard, sawing up pieces of wood for the stove. He cut pegs with his penknife to hang up the clothes in the field; he had even assisted on occasion to get them in before a shower came down. He knocked nails, gardened, mended windows, signed papers for the villagers, contracts of marriage, agreements, disagreements. The people of Petitport were constantly coming to their maire for redress and advice.

Fontaine used to do his best to dissuade them from going to law, but the neighbors were tena-

cious of their rights, and enjoyed nothing so much as a good lawsuit. Even old Nanon Lefebvre once insisted on spending her wretched earnings in summoning her cousin Leroi at Bayeux, who had unjustly grasped a sum of two pounds, she declared, to which she was entitled. She lost her trial, and received back a few shillings from Fontaine's own pocket, with a lecture which she took in very ill part. She never would believe he had not made some secret profit by the transaction.

The very first morning after her arrival, Catharine, who was outside upon the terrace, heard the stormy voices of some of Monsieur le Maire's clients coming shrill and excited from the kitchen, where Fontaine often administered justice. From the little embankment Catharine could see the sea and the village street descending, and the *lavatoire*, where the village women in their black stockings, and white coiffs, and cotton nightcaps were congregated, scrubbing, and flapping, and chattering together. The busy sounds came in gusts to Catharine in her garden, the fresh sea-breezes reached her scented by rose-trees. On fine days she could make out in the far distance the faint shimmer of the rocks of the Calvados out at sea, where the Spanish galleon struck. It struck and went down, and all on board perished, the legend runs, and the terrible rocks were called by its name for a warning. But nowadays all the country round is christened Calvados, and the name is so common that it has lost its terror.

Fontaine sometimes administered justice in the kitchen, sometimes in a little dark draughty office, where he kept odd pieces of string, some ink, some sealing-wax, and some carpenter's tools. The châlet was more picturesque than comfortable as a habitation. The winds came thundering against the thin walls, and through the chinks and crevices; the weathercocks would go twirling madly round and round, with a sound like distant drums. In the spring tides, Justine had said, the water would come up over the embankment and spread over the marguerite beds and the rose-trees, and the rain falling from the cliff would make pools in front of the dining-room door. The drawing-room was up stairs. It was a room of which the shutters were always closed, the covers tied down tightly over the furniture, the table-cloths and rugs rolled up, and the piano locked. The room was never used. When Monsieur Mérard was there they were in the habit of sitting in his bedroom of an evening, Fontaine told his wife. "C'est plus *snog*, comme vous dites," he said. Catharine demurred at this, and begged to be allowed to open the drawing-room, and make use of it and of the piano. Fontaine agreed—to what would he not have agreed that she wished?—but it was evidently a pang to him, and he seemed afraid of what Madame Mérard might say.

The second day seemed a little longer to Catharine than the first at the châlet, and the third a little longer than the second. Not to Fontaine, who settled down to his accustomed occupations, came, went, always taking care that Catharine should not be left for any time alone. Now and then, as days went on, she wished that she could be by herself a little more; she was used to solitude, and this constant society and attention was a little fatiguing. All that was expected from her was, "Yes, mon ami," "Non, mon ami." At the end of a month it became just a little wearisome; for, counting the fortnight at Rouen, Catharine had now been married a month. Petitport had begun to put on its nightcap; scarcely any one remained; shutters were put up, and there was silence in the street. She walked up to the farm, but Reine had been away at Caen for some time, Dominique told her. One day was like another. Nobody came. Fontaine talked on, and Catharine almost looked forward to the arrival of Toto's grandparents to break the monotony.

"Ce qui coûte le plus pour plaire, c'est de cacher que l'on s'ennuie." Catharine had read this somewhere in a book of French maxims, and the words used to jangle in her ears long afterward, as words do. Sometimes she used to think of them involuntarily in those early days in the beginning of her married life, when she would be sitting by her own fireside alone with Fontaine. Monsieur le Maire was generally bolt upright on a stiff-backed chair by the table, delightedly contemplating the realization of his dreams; while Madame Fontaine, on a low little seat by the fire, with her work falling upon her lap, was wondering, perhaps, whether this could be her own self and the end of all her vague ideals. The little gold ring upon her finger seemed to assure her it was so indeed. This was her home at last. There sat her husband, attentive, devoted, irreproachable, discursive—how discursive! Conversation was Fontaine's forte, his weakness, his passion, his necessity. The most utterly uninteresting and unlikely subjects would suggest words to this fertile brain; his talk was a wonder of ingenuity and unintermittingness. Now, for the first time for many years, he had secured a patient and a silent listener, and the torrent which had long been partially pent up had found a vent. Poor Fontaine was happy and in high spirits; and, under the circumstances, could any repetition, retrospection, interrogation, asseveration, be sufficient? Must not every possible form of speech be employed to tell Catharine how sensible he was to the happiness which had befallen him? "And you too are happy," he used to say, triumphantly; and if his wife smiled gratefully, and answered "Yes," no one, I think, could blame her.

She was happy after a fashion. It was so strange to be wanted, to be loved and of importance, and looked for and welcomed. She found this as difficult to believe in as all the rest. Fontaine was always thinking of what would give her pleasure. Her sisters were to come to her for their holidays always—whenever she liked, he said; and Catharine's heart beat with delight at the thought of welcoming them to her own roof. The pretty room up stairs, looking down the street, should be theirs, she thought; she would buy two little beds, some flower-pots for the window. Every day she looked in on her way up and down, planning small preparations for them, and one little scheme and another to please them. How happy they would be! This thought was almost perfect delight to her. She loved to picture them there, with their little beloved ugly heads. She took Toto into her confidence, and one day he came rushing in with a plaster statuette of Napoleon at St. Helena he had bought in the street. "C'est pour tes petites sœurs," said he, and his stepmother caught him in her arms and covered his round face with kisses. Fontaine happened to be passing by the door at the moment. His double eyeglasses were quite dim, for his eyes had filled with tears of happiness as he witnessed the little scene.

"Je me trouve tout attendri!" said he, coming in. "Ah! mon amie, you have made two people very happy by coming here. I am shedding tears of joy. They relieve the heart."

It was a pathetic jumble. When Fontaine was unconscious he was affecting in his kindliness and tenderness of heart, and then the next moment he would by an afterthought become suddenly absurd.

In the first excitement of his return Fontaine had forgotten many little harmless precisions and peculiarities which gradually revived as time went by. On the morning that Monsieur and Madame Mérard were expected he appeared in a neat baize apron, dusting with a feather brush, arranging furniture, bustling in and out of the kitchen, and personally superintending all the preparations made to receive them.

"Can't I do something?" Catharine timidly asked.

"Va-t'en, mon enfant," said Fontaine, embracing her. "I am busy."

Catharine knew it was silly, but she could not bear to see him so occupied. She took her work, went and sat in the dining-room window waiting, and as she sat there she thought of the day she had come with Madame de Tracy, a stranger, to the gate of her future home.

Toto came running in at last to announce the arrival of his grandmother and grandfather. Fontaine took off his apron and rushed into the garden, and Catharine went and stood at the door to welcome them, a little shy, but glad, on the whole, to do her best to please her husband and his relations.

Monsieur and Madame Mérard were heavy people. They had to be carefully helped down from the little high carriage in which they had arrived by Justine and Fontaine, who together carried in their moderate boxes and packages. Although her trunk was small, Madame Mérard was neatly and brilliantly dressed. Monsieur Mérard, who was a very, very stout old gentleman, wore slippers, a velvet cap, and short checked trowsers. He took off his coat immediately on arriving, as a matter of course, and sat down, breathless, in a chair near the window.

"Venez, mon amie," said Fontaine, much excited, leading Catharine up by the hand. "Mon père, ma mere" (the maire had a turn for oratory and situation), "I bring you a daughter," he said; "accord to her a portion of that affection you have for many years bestowed on me."

A snuffy kiss from Madame Mérard on her forehead, something between a sniff and a shake of the head, was the portion evidently reserved for Catharine. Monsieur Mérard signed to her to advance, and also embraced her slowly, on account of his great size. After that they seemed to take no more notice of her, only every now and then Catharine felt the old lady's sharp eyes fixed upon her like the prick of two pins.

"Eh bien, Justine," said Madame Mérard, addressing the cuisinière. "Has every thing been going on well? You have taken good care of Monsieur and of Toto? What are you going to give us for our breakfast to-day?"

"Monsieur is responsible for the breakfast," said Justine, irascible now that she was sure of an ally. "If he thinks it is possible for a cook to attend to her business when the masters are perpetually in and out of the kitchen, he is much mistaken."

"You are right, ma fille," said Madame Mérard, soothingly. "I have told him so a hundred times. Eh bien, dites-moi! Where have you been taking your butter since I left?"

"I have taken it from Madame Binaud, as madame desired," said Justine.

"That is right," said Madame Mérard; "and yet there is no trusting any one. Imagine, Charles, that I have been paying thirty-eight sous a pound! It was for good Isyngny butter, that is true, but thirty-eight sous! Ah! it is abominable. How much do you pay for butter in England, madame?" said the old lady, suddenly turning round upon Catharine, and evidently expecting a direct answer to a plain question.

"Half a cr—I don't know," said Catharine, looking to Fontaine to help her. Fontaine turned away much disappointed: he wanted his wife to shine, and he guessed the painful impression her ignorance would produce.

"Ho! ho!" said old Mérard, in a droll little squeaking voice, "Madame Mérard must give you some lessons, my young lady." He was good-naturedly trying to avert disagreeables.

"Lessons!" said Madame Mérard, hoarsely. "It is no longer the fashion for young women to interest themselves in the management of their domestic expenses. It is perhaps because they contribute nothing to them."

"Catharine felt very angry at this unprovoked attack. She made an effort. "I shall be very glad to learn any thing you will teach me," she said. But already she was beginning to wonder whether she had not been wrong to wish for the tête-à-tête to be interrupted. If it is hard to seem amused when one is wearied, it is also difficult to conceal one's pain when one is wounded. They all sat down to breakfast. Monsieur Mérard asked for a pin, and carefully fastened his napkin across his shirt-front. Madame Mérard freely used her knife to cut bread, to eat dainty morsels off her plate. Every thing went on pretty smoothly until Toto, who had been perfectly good for a whole fortnight, incited by the reappearance of his grandparents, and perhaps excited by some wine the old lady had administered, became as one possessed. He put his hands into the dishes, helped himself in this fashion to a nice little sole he had taken a fancy to, beat the rappel with his spoon upon the table-cloth, and held up his plate for more, so that the gravy dropped down upon Catharine's dress. She put her gentle hands upon his shoulder, and whispered gravely to him. This was a terrible offense. Madame Mérard took snuff, and wiped both eyes and nose in her handkerchief, shaking her head.

"Ah!" she said, "Charles, do you remember how patient his poor mother used to be with him? She never reproved him—never."

"I don't think poor Léonie herself could be more gentle with her son than his stepmother is," Fontaine answered, with great courage, holding out his hand to Catharine with a smile.

But this scarcely made matters better. Catharine had found no favor in Madame Mérard's little ferret eyes. She looked afraid of her for one thing, and there is nothing more provoking to people with difficult tempers and good hearts than to see others afraid. All day long Catharine did her best. She walked out a little way with the old couple; she even took a hand at whist. They began at one and played till five. Then Monsieur le Curé came in to see his old friend Madame Mérard, and Catharine escaped into the garden to breathe a little air upon the terrace, and to try and forget the humiliations and weariness of the day. So this was the life she had deliberately chosen; these were to be the companions with whom she was to journey henceforth. What an old ménagère! what economies! what mustaches! what fierce little eyes! what a living tariff of prices! A cool, delicious evening breeze came blowing through her rose-trees, consoling her somewhat, and a minute afterward Catharine saw her husband coming toward her. He looked beaming, as if he had just heard good news; he waved his hand in the air, and sprang lightly forward to where she was standing.

"All the morning I have not been without anxiety; I was afraid that something was wrong," he confided frankly to Catharine. "But now I am greatly relieved. My mother is telling Monsieur le Curé that she and my stepfather fully intend to pass the winter with us." Catharine tried to say something, but could not succeed—her husband noticed nothing.

Fontaine, from the very good-nature and affectionate fidelity of his disposition, seemed to cling very much to his early associates, and to the peculiar prejudices which he had learned from them. The odd ways were familiar to him, the talk did not seem strange. It was of people and places he had known all his life.

Their habits did not offend any very fine sense of taste. The translations which English minds make to themselves of foreign ways and customs are necessarily incorrect and prejudiced. Things which to Catharine seemed childish, partly humorous, partly wearisome, were to Fontaine only the simple and natural arrangements of every day. He could sit contentedly talking for hours in his cabane, with the little flag flying from the roof. He could play away the bright long afternoons with a greasy pack of cards or a box of dominoes. He could assume different costumes with perfect complacency—the sport costume, when he went to the shooting-gallery some enterprising speculator had opened at Bayeux—the black gaiters *pour affaire*—the red flannel shirt for the sea-side stroll . . . Fontaine asked her one day if she would come down to the chateau with him. He had some business with the bailiff, who was to meet him there. Leaving the Mérards installed upon the terrace, Catharine went for her hood and her cloak, and walked down the steep little ascent, and through the street, rm in arm with Monsieur le Maire. She had not been at the place since she left on the eve of her marriage. She began to think of it all; she remembered her doubts, her despair. They came to the gates at last, where only a few weeks ago Dick had told her of his love for Reine; the whole thing seemed running through her head like the unwinding of a skein. While Fontaine was talking to the bailiff she went and rang at the bell, and told Baptiste, who opened the door, that she wanted to go up to her room.

"Mais certainement, madame! Vous allez bien? Vous voyez il n'y a plus personne." Catharine crossed the hall and looked into the deserted drawing-room—how different it looked—how silent! The voices and music had drifted elsewhere, and Catharine George, she no longer existed. Only a little smoke was left curling from the charred embers and relics of the past. Thinking thus, she went up to her own old little room, which was dismantled and looked quite empty, and as if it had belonged to a dead person.

Catharine's heart was very full; she looked round and about; the sunset was streaming in through the curtainless window; she heard the faint old sound of the sea; she went to the little secrétaire presently, and opened one of the drawers and looked in.

That last night when she had been packing her clothes, she had come upon one little relic which she had not had the heart to destroy. She had thrust it into a drawer in the bureau where she had already thrown some dead marguerites, and locked it in. No one finding it there would have been any the wiser. It was only a dead crumpled brown rose which Dick had picked up off the grass one day, but that had not prevented it from withering like other roses. It was still lying in the drawer among a handful of dry marguerites. Who would have guessed that the whole story of her life was written upon these withered stalks and leaves? She felt as if the story and life all had belonged to some one else. She opened the drawer—no one else had been there. As she took up the rose a thorn pricked her finger. "Neither scent, nor color, nor smell, only a thorn left to prick," Catharine sadly sighed: "these other poor limp flowers at least have no thorns." So she thought. Then she went and sat down upon the bed, and began to tell herself how good Fontaine had been to her, and to say to herself that it was too late now to wonder whether she had done rightly or wrongly in marrying him. But, at least, she would try to be good, and contented, and not ungrateful. Perhaps, if she was very good, and patient, and contented, she might see Dick again some day, and be his friend and Reine's, and the thorn would be gone out of the dead rose. Fontaine's voice calling her name disturbed her resolutions.

She found her husband waiting for her at the foot of the stairs.

"Shall we revisit together the spot where we first read in each other's hearts," said he, sentimentally.

"Not this evening," said Catharine, gently. "I should like to go down to the sea before it grows quite dark."

Everybody had not left Petitport, for one or two families were still sitting in their little wooden boxes along the edge of the sands, and a hum of conversation seemed sounding in the air with the monotonous wash of the sea. The ladies wore bright-colored hoods; the waves were gray, fresh, and buoyant, rising in crisp crests against a faint yellow sky. A great line of soft clouds, curled and tossed by high currents of wind, was crossing the sea. One or two pale brown stars were coming out one by one, pulsating like little living hearts in the vast universe. Catharine went down close to the water's edge, and then threw something she held in her hand as far as she could throw.

"What is that?" Fontaine asked, adjusting his eyeglass.

"Only some dead flowers I found in a drawer," said Catharine.

"My dear child, why give yourself such needless trouble?" asked the practical husband. "You might have left them where they were or in the court-yard, if you did not wish to litter the room, or . . ."

"It was a little piece of sentiment," said Catharine, humbly trying to make a confession. "Some one gave me a rose once in England, long ago, and . . ."

"Some one who—who—who loved you," Fontaine interrupted, in a sudden fume, stammering and turning round upon her.

"Oh no," Catharine answered; "you are the only person who has ever loved me."

She said it so gently and sweetly that Fontaine was touched beyond measure. And yet, though she spoke gently, his sudden anger had terrified her. She felt guilty that she could not bring herself to tell him more. She could not have made him understand her; why disquiet him with stories of the past, and destroy his happiness and her own too? Alas! already this had come to her.

CHAPTER XV.

IN THE TWILIGHT AT LAMBSWOLD.

It seemed that there were many things of which Fontaine was unconscious. Catharine never dared to trust him with the secret of Dick's engagement to Reine Chrétien. This was too valuable a piece of gossip to be confided to the worthy maire's indiscretion. The country people talked a little; but they were all used to Mademoiselle Chrétien's odd, independent ways, and after Dick had been gone some weeks they appeared for a time to trouble their heads no more about him.

But Richard Butler reached home more than ever determined to make a clean breast of it, as the saying goes. Reine's good-by and last bright look seemed to give him courage. What would he not do for her sake?

Her knight in ancient times would have gone out valiantly, prepared to conquer dragons, fierce giants, monsters of land and sea. The only fierce dragon in Butler's way was the kind old man at Lambswold; and yet, somehow, he thought he would rather encounter many dragons, poisonous darts, fiery tails and all. But then he thought again of Reine standing in the sunset glory, in all her sweet nobility, and a gentle look came into Dick's own face. Women who have the rare gift of great beauty may well cherish it, and be grateful to Heaven. With the unconscious breath of a moment, they can utter all that is in them. They have said it at once, for-

ever, while others are struggling for words, toiling with effort, trying in vain to break the bonds which fetter them so cruelly. What sermon, what text, is like that of a tender heart, speaking silently in its own beauty and purity, and conscious only of the meaning of its own sincerity? What words can speak so eloquently as the clear sweet eyes looking to all good, all love, all trust, encouraging with their tender smile?

Queen's Walk did not look so deserted as the other more fashionable parts of London. The dirty little children had not left town. The barges were sailing by; the garden door was set wide open. The housekeeper let him in, smiling, in her best cap. Mr. Beamish was away, she told him, in Durham with his father, who was recovering, poor gentleman. There were a great many letters waiting on the 'all table, she said. Dick pulled a long face at the piles of cheap-looking envelopes directed very low down, with single initial-letters upon the seals. Mrs. Busby had cleaned down and rubbed up the old staircase to shining pitch. The studio, too, looked very clean, and cool, and comfortable. Every body was away. Mr. and Mrs. Hervey Butler were at Brighton, and Mr. Charles Butler had not been up in town for some time; Mr. Beamish had desired all his letters to be forwarded to Durham; he was coming back as soon as he could leave his father.

Every body knows the grateful, restful feeling of coming home after a holiday; crowded hotels, fierce landladies' extortions, excursions, all disappear up the chimney; every thing looks clean and comfortable; the confusion of daily life is put to rights for a time, and one seems to start afresh. Mrs. Busby had had the carpets beat, she said, and dinner would be quite ready at six. Dick, who was not sorry to have an excuse to stay where he was and to put off the announcement he had in his mind, wrote a few words to Lambswold, saying that he would come down in a week or two, as soon as he had finished a picture he had brought back with him from Tracy.

For some weeks Dick worked very hard — harder than he had ever done in his life before. "I suppose the figures upon my canvas have come there somehow out of my brain," he wrote to Reine, "but they seem to have an odd, distinct life of their own, so that I am sometimes almost frightened at my own performance." The picture he was painting was a melancholy one: a wash of brown transparent sea, a mist of gray sky, and some black-looking figures coming across the shingle, carrying a drowned man. A woman and a child were plodding dully alongside. It was unlike any of the pictures Butler had ever painted before. There was no attempt at detail; every thing was vague and undetermined; but the waves came springing in, and it seemed as if there was a sunlight behind the mist . . . Sometimes he fell into utter despondency over his work, plodding on at it as he did, day after day, with no one to speak to or encourage him; but he struggled on, and at last said to himself one day that, with all its faults and incompleteness, there was more true stuff in it than in any thing he had yet produced.

One day Dick received a short note in his uncle Charles's careful handwriting : "When are you coming down here?" the old man wrote. "I have not been well, or I should have been up to town. I suppose you could paint here as well as in your studio or under Matilda's auspices? but this place is dismal, and silent, and empty, and has no such attractions as those which, from all accounts, Tracy seems to hold out, so I shall not be surprised if I do not see you. Mundy takes very good care of me. If I really want you I will send for you. Yours, C. B."

"What has he heard?" thought Dick, when he read the note. "Who can have told him any thing? Is he vexed or only out of spirits?" Butler felt he must go, of course. It was tiresome, now that he was just getting into the swing, and doing the first piece of work which was worth the canvas upon which it was painted. As for taking his picture there, Dick was more afraid of his uncle's sarcastic little compliments than of any amount of criticism ; and, besides, there was no knowing what might be the result of their meeting. He would go down and pay him a visit, and tell him his story, and then, if he were not turned out forever, it would be time enough to see about transporting the canvas.

Dick took his ticket in a somewhat injured frame of mind. All the way down in the railway carriage he was rehearsing the scene that was to take place; he took a perverse pleasure in going over it again and again. Sometimes he turned himself out of doors, sometimes he conjured up Charles Butler's harsh little sarcastic laugh, sneering and disowning him. Once he saw himself a traitor abandoning Reine for the sake of the bribe; but no, that was impossible; that was the only thing which could not happen. When he got to the station he had to hire the fly, as he was not expected, and to drive along the lanes. They were damp and rotting with leaves : gray mists came rolling along the furrows; a few belated birds were singing an autumnal song.

"They say the old gentleman's a-breaking up fast," said the flyman, cheerfully, as he dismounted at the foot of one of the muddy hills. "He's not an old man, by no means yet, but my missis she see him go by last Sunday for'night, and says she to me just so, 'Why,' says she, 'old Mr. Butler ain't half the man he wer' in the spring-time.'"

Dick could not help feeling uncomfortable; he was not in the best of spirits; the still, close afternoon, with the rotting vegetation all about, and the clouds bearing heavily down, predisposed him to a gloomy view of things. They drove in at the well-known gates.

"I hope I shall find my uncle better," he said, trying to speak hopefully as he got down at the hall door and ran up the old-fashioned steps. Mundy opened the door.

"Oh, Mr. Richard," he said, "I have just been writing to you. My master is very poorly. I am sorry to say—very poorly indeed."

Old Mr. Butler was alone in the morning-room when his nephew came in. He had had a fire lighted, and he was sitting, wrapped in an old-fashioned palm dressing-gown, in a big chair drawn close up to the fender. The tall windows were unshuttered still, and a great cloud of mist was hanging like a veil over the landscape.

"Well, my dear boy," said a strange yet familiar voice, "I didn't expect you so soon."

It was like some very old man speaking and holding out an eager, trembling hand. As old Butler spoke, he shut up and put into his pocket a little old brown prayer-book in which he had been reading. Dick, who had been picturing imaginary pangs to himself all the way coming down, now found how different a real aching pain is to the visionary emotions we all inflict upon ourselves occasionally. It was with a real foreboding that he saw that some terrible change for the worse had come over the old man. His face was altered, his voice faint and sharp, and his hand was burning.

"Why didn't you send for me, my dear Uncle Charles? I never knew . . . I only got your letter this morning. If I had thought for one instant . . ."

"My note was written last week," said Charles. "I kept it back on purpose. You were hard at work, weren't you?" Dick said nothing. He had got tight hold of the trembling, burning hand. "I'm very bad," said old Charles, looking up at the young fellow. "You won't have long to wait for my old slippers."

"Don't, my dear, dear old boy," cried Dick.

"Pah!" said old Butler; "your own turn will come sooner or later. You won't find it difficult to go. I think you won't," said the old broken man, patting Dick's hand gently.

Dick was so shocked by the suddenness of the blow he was scarcely able to believe it.

"Have you seen any one?" the young man asked.

"I've seen Hickson, and this morning Dr. de M—— came down to me," Charles Butler answered, as if it was a matter of every-day occurrence. "He says it's serious, so I told Mundy to write to you."

Old Charles seemed quite cheerful and in good spirits; he described his symptoms, and seemed to like talking of what might be—he even made little jokes.

"You ungrateful boy," he said, smiling, "there is many a young man who would be thankful for his good luck, instead of putting on a scared face like yours. Well, what have you been about?"

It was horrible. Dick tried to answer and to speak as usual, but he turned sick once, and bit his lip, and looked away when his uncle, after a question or two, began telling him about some scheme he wanted carried out upon the estate.

"Won't you send for Uncle Hervey," Dick said gravely, "or for my aunt?"

"Time enough—time enough," the other answered. "They make such a talking. I want to put matters straight first. I've got Baxter coming here this afternoon."

Mr. Baxter was the family attorney. Dick had for the minute forgotten all about what he had come intending to say. Now he looked in the fire, and suddenly told himself that if he had to tell his uncle what had been on his mind all these last months, the sooner it was done the better. But now, at such a crisis—it was an impossibility.

So the two sat by the fire in the waning light of the short autumn day. The night was near at hand, Dick thought. There was a ring at the bell, and some one came in from the hall. It was not the lawyer, but Dr. Hickson again, and it seemed like a reprieve to the young man to have a few minutes longer to make up his mind. He followed the doctor out into the hall. His grave face was not reassuring. Dick could see it by the light of the old lattice-window.

"Tell me honestly," he said, "what you think of my uncle's state. I never even heard he was ill till this morning."

"My dear Mr. Richard," said Dr. Hickson, "we must hope for the best. Dr. de M—— agreed with me in considering the case very serious. I can not take upon myself to disguise this from you. Your uncle himself has but little idea of recovering; his mind is as yet wonderfully clear and collected . . . and there may be little change for weeks, but I should advise you to see that any arrangements . . . Dear me! dear me!"

The little overworked doctor hurried down the steps and rode away, all out of spirits, and leaving scant comfort behind him. He was thinking of all that there was to make life easy and prosperous in that big, well-ordered house, and of his own little struggling home, with his poor Polly and her six babies, who would have scarcely enough to put bread in their mouths if he were to be taken. He was thinking that it was a lonely ending to a lonely life, with only interested people watchers, waiting by the old man's death-bed. Dr. Hickson scarcely did justice to Dick, who had spoken in his usual quiet manner, who had made no professions, but who was pacing up and down the gravel sweep, backward and forward, and round and round, bare-headed, in the chill dark, not thinking of inheritance or money, but only of the kind, forbearing benefactor to whom he owed so much, and toward whom he felt like a traitor in his heart.

He went back into the morning-room, where Mundy had lighted some candles, and he forced himself to look hopeful, but he nearly broke down when Charles began saying in his faint, cheerful voice, "I've made a most unjust will. Baxter is bringing it for me to sign this evening. I have left almost every thing to a scapegrace nephew of mine, who will, I'm afraid, never make a fortune for himself. Shall I throw in the Gainsborough?" he added, nodding at the lady who was smiling as usual out of her frame. "You will appreciate her some day." There

was a moment's silence. Dick flushed up, and the veins of his temples began to throb, and a sort of cloud came before his eyes. He must speak. He could not let his uncle do this, when, if he knew all, he would for certain feel and act so differently. He tried to thank him, but the words were too hard to speak. He would have given much to keep silence, but he could not somehow. Charles wondered at his agitation, and watched him moving uneasily. Suddenly he burst out.

"Uncle Charles," said Dick at last, with a sort of choke for breath, "don't ask why; leave me nothing—except—except the Gainsborough, if you will. I mustn't take your money . . ."

"What the devil do you mean?" said the old man, frightened, and yet trying to laugh. "What have you been doing?"

"I've done no wrong," Dick said, looking up, with the truth in his honest eyes, and speaking very quick. "I don't want to bother you now. I want to do something you might not approve. I had come down to tell you, and I couldn't let you make your will without warning ."

The young fellow had turned quite pale, but the horrible moment was past, the temptation to silence was overcome. In all Dick's life this was one of the hardest straits he ever encountered. It was not the money; covetousness was not one of his faults, but he said to himself that he should have sacrificed faith, honor, any thing, every thing, sooner than have had the cruelty to inflict one pang at such a time. But the next instant something told him he had done right; he saw that a very gentle, tender look had come into the old man's eyes as he leant back in his chair.

"I suppose you are going to get married," Charles said, faintly, "and that is the meaning of all this? Well," he went on, recovering peevishly, "why the deuce don't you go on, sir?"

This little return of the old manner made it easier for the young man to speak. "I've promised to marry a woman; I love her, and that is my secret," he said, still speaking very quickly. "I'm not quite crazy; she is educated and good, and very beautiful, but she is only a farmer's daughter at Tracy. Her mother was a lady, and her name is Reine Chrétien."

Dick, having spoken, sat staring at the fire.

"And—and you mean to establish that—this farmer's daughter here as soon as . . ." Charles, trembling very much, tried to get up from his chair, and sank down again.

"You know I don't," said Dick, with a sad voice, "or I should not have told you."

Then there was another silence.

"I—I can't bear much agitation," Charles said at last, while a faint color came into his cheeks. "Let us talk of something else. Is the paper come yet? Ring the bell and ask."

The paper had come, and Dick read out column after column, scarcely attending to the meaning of one word before him. And yet all the strange every-day life rushing into the sick-room jarred horribly upon his nerves. Records of speeches, and meetings, and crime, and advertisements—all the busy stir and roar of the world seemed stamped upon the great sheet before him. His own love, and interest, and future seemed part of this unquiet tide of life, while the old man sat waiting in his big chair, away from it all; and the fire burnt quietly, lighting up the room, and outside the white mist was lying upon the trees and the gardens.

At last Dick saw, to his great relief, that his uncle had fallen asleep, and then he gently got up from his chair, and went and looked out at the twilight lawn. He thought of the picnic, and all the figures under the trees; he could not face the present; his mind turned and shifted, as people's minds do in the presence of great realities.

"Dick!" cried the old man, waking anxiously, "are you there? Don't leave me. I shall be more comfortable in bed. Call Mundy and help me up."

They had to carry him almost up the old-fashioned wooden flight.

Richard Butler dined alone in the great dismal dining-room, and while he was at dinner Mundy told him the lawyer had come. "Mr. Butler desired me to open a bottle of his best claret for you, sir," said Mundy; "he wishes to see you again after dinner. Mr. Baxter is with him now."

The lawyer had not left when Dick came into the room. He was tying red tape round long folded slips of paper and parchment. Old Charles was in his old-fashioned four-post bed, with the ancient chintz hangings, upon which wonderful patterns of dragons and phœnix's had been stamped. Dick had often wondered at these awful scrolled figures when he was a child; he used to think they were horrible dreams which had got fixed upon the curtains somehow. Charles was sitting upright in the middle of it all; he had shrunk away and looked very small.

"I'm more comfortable up here," the old man said. "I've been talking to Mr. Baxter about this business of yours, Dick. It's lucky for you, sir, it didn't happen a year ago—isn't it, Baxter?"

"Your uncle shows great trust in you, Mr. Butler," the attorney said. "There are not many like him who . . ."

"You see, Dick, one thing now is very much the same as another to me," interrupted the master of Lambswold. "It seems a risk to run, but that is your look-out, as you say, and I should have known nothing about it if you had not told me. If in another year's time you have not changed your mind . . . Mr. Baxter has provided, as you will find. I have experienced a great many blessings in my life," he said, in an altered tone—"a very great many. I don't think I have been as thankful as I might have been for them, and—and—. I should like you, too, to have some one you care for by your bedside when Lambswold changes masters again," Charles Butler said, holding out his kind old hand once more. "I was very fond of your mother, Dick."

Dick's answer was very incoherent, but his uncle understood him. Only the old man felt a doubt as to the young man's stability of purpose, and once more spoke of the twelve months which he desired should elapse before the marriage was publicly announced; he asked him to say nothing for the present. He owned with a faint smile that he did not want discussion.

Of course Dick promised; and then he wrote to Reine, and told her of the condition, and of the kind old uncle's consent.

Twelve months seemed but a very little while to Dick, faithful and busy with a prosperous lifetime opening before him. As days went on his uncle rallied a little; but he knew that this improvement could not continue, and of course he was not able to get away. He often wrote to Reine, and in a few simple words he would tell her of his gratitude to his uncle, and of his happiness in the thought of sharing his future, whatever it might be, with her. "Although heaven knows," he said, "how sincerely I pray that this succession may be put off for years; for you, my Reine, do not care for these things, and will take me, I think, without a farthing."

But a year to Reine was a long, weary time of suspense to look forward to. She found the strain very great; the doubts, which returned for all her efforts against them, the terror of what might be in store. She loved Dick as she hated his surroundings, and sometimes she almost feared that her love was not worthy of his, and sometimes the foolish, impatient woman would cry out to herself that it was he who wanted to be set free.

CHAPTER XVI.

MUSIC HATH CHARMS.

It had required all Fontaine's persuasion, backed by the prestige of his municipal authority, to persuade Justine to open the drawing-room shutters, and to allow Catharine to use that long-abandoned territory. With many mumbles, and grumblings, and rumblings of furniture, the innovation had been achieved a few days before Madame Mérard's return; Monsieur Fontaine himself assisting in most of the work, or it never would have been accomplished. He was not the man to do things by halves. Catharine wished for a drawing-room and a piano; poor Léonie's instrument was standing there, it is true, but cracked and jarred, and with a faded front. Soon a piece of bright new red silk replaced the sickly green, the rosewood complexion was polished to a brilliant brown by the indefatigable master of the house; he would have tuned it if he could, but this was beyond his powers, and the organist was mysteriously brought in by a back door, while Toto was desired to detain Catharine on the terrace until a preconcerted signal should announce that all was ready for her to be brought in, in triumph. Monsieur le Maire was delighted. He led her in with both hands, and then stepped back to contemplate the result of his labors. "Now we shall make music," he said. "Come, Catharine, place yourself at the piano. Another day, perhaps I myself . . ." Catharine looked which he had disinterred from its green-baize sarcophagus, and rubbed up during office hours. He had practiced upon it in his early youth, and he now amused himself by accompanying the movements of Catharine's gentle little fingers

A "VACARME."

up with her dark grateful eyes, and began to play as she was bid.

Monsieur Fontaine contented himself at first by beating time to his wife's performance with great spirit and accuracy; but one evening, somewhat to her dismay, he produced a cornet, with sudden sounds, somewhat uncertain perhaps, but often very loud. Justine sulkily called it a "vacarme" as she banged the kitchen door. Passers-by, driving their cows or plodding home with their fish-baskets, stopped outside, astonished, to ask what it could be. The old cidertibbers at Pelottier's could hear the rich notes when the wind blew in that direction. Poor Madame Fontaine herself burst out laughing, and put her hands up to her ears the first time she heard her husband's music ; but Monsieur le Maire instantly stopped short, and looked so pained and disappointed that she begged him to go on, and immediately began to play again. Only she took care afterward to select the calmest, and the most pastoral and least impassioned music in her repertory. When she came to passages marked con *expressione* or with *arpeggios*, or when she saw *fff*'s looming appallingly in the distance, she would set her teeth and brace up her courage for the onslaught. By degrees, however, Fontaine's first ardor toned down, or Catharine's nerves grew stronger. Toto thought it great fun, only he wished they would play polkas and waltzes, as he stood leaning against the piano with his round eyes fixed upon Catharine's face. People almost always look their best when they are making music ; how often one sees quite plain and uninteresting faces kindle with sweet sound into an unconscious harmony of expression. Catharine was no great performer, but she played with feeling and precision. There always was a charm about her, which it would be difficult to define, and now especially, with her dark head bent a little forward to where the light fell upon her music-book, she would have made a lovely little study—for Dick Butler, let us say. "A Woman set to Music" it might have been called ; she felt nothing but a harmony of sound at such a time, except, indeed, when the cornet burst in with a wrong note. Monsieur Fontaine, between the intervals of his own performance, liked to look at her proudly and admiringly. Any stranger coming in would have thought it a pretty picture of a happy family group, and carried away the pleasant image.

Justine was not so easily taken in. Having banged her door, she would shrug her shoulders down in her kitchen below ; she could bide her time. Madame Mérard was coming. She was not fond of music any more than Justine.

Fontaine felt as if some guilty secret was buried in his bosom, when, for the first two nights after the old people's arrival, he tried to make excuses for remaining down stairs in the dining-room, and was glad that Catharine retired early with a headache. Justine said nothing. She left every body to make their own discoveries. These would not be long about, she knew ; for Madame Mérard's fierce little eyes went poking here and there with a leisurely yet unceasing scrutiny.

It was Madame Mérard who had educated Justine, placed her in Fontaine's kitchen, and desired her to remain there ; and the invaluable servant had accordingly, for years past, done her best to make his life miserable, his soup and his coffee clear, strong, and well-flavored. She did many other things—washed, scrubbed, marketed, waited at table, put Toto to bed—no easy matter. She would go about with the air of a sulky martyr, working miracles against her will. Madame de Tracy, with all her household, was not so well served as Fontaine, with this terrible ewe-lamb of his.

Madame Mérard was the only person who ventured to drive this alarming creature ; but then, to judge from the old lady's conversation, she seemed gifted with a sort of second sight. She could see through cupboard doors into the inside of barrels ; she could overhear conversations five miles off, or the day after to-morrow. Madame Nicholas must have been nearly demented when she tried to palm off her Tuesday's eggs upon her last Friday. Justine herself never attempted to impose upon this mistress-mind, and would take from her, in plain language, what the maire, with all his official dignity, would never have ventured to hint.

At Madame Mérard's own suggestion and Justine's, a girl from the village had been lately added on to the establishment. A girl? a succession of girls rather. They would come up in their Sunday clothes, smiling and cheerful, bobbing courtesies to the Mérards, to Toto, to Monsieur, to Madame, to the all-powerful Justine, anxious for employment, and willing to do their best. And then they would immediately begin to perish away, little by little : smiles would fade, the color go out of their cheeks, and one day, at last, they would disappear, and never be heard of any more. Justine the Terrible had claws, and a long tongue, and a heavy hand : she did not drive them over the cliff, but she sent them home in tears to their mothers. Fontaine used to try to interfere in the behalf of these victims, but it was in vain. Catharine made a desperate sally once into the kitchen ; she was routed ignominiously by Madame Mérard, who would be superintending the punishment.

"Why don't you send Justine away ?" Catharine said to her husband one morning after one of these scenes.

"My dear, you do not think of what you are saying ! It is not from you, my dear Catharine, that I should have expected such a proposition." And Fontaine, who had interrupted his hammering for an instant, shocked at the bold proposal, resumed his occupation.

Madame Mérard had observed one or two motes calling for remark in the last arrival's goggle blue eyes, and she went stumping down stairs early one morning for a little consultation in the kitchen before breakfast. The old lady, in her morning costume, and short jacket or camisole, and stiff starched cap, and slippers, managed to look quite as formidable as she did later in the day. Her mustaches seemed to curl more fiercely, unrelieved by the contrast of a varied and brilliant toilette ; her little, even white teeth, with which she could crack a whole plateful of nuts, seemed to gleam beneath the mustaches. Madame Mérard was surprised to see that the drawing-room door was open as she passed ; still more aghast was she when she looked in and perceived the shutters unclosed, the little bits of rug spread out here and there upon the floor, the furniture standing on its legs instead of being piled up in a heap, the piano dragged out from its dark recess in a convenient angle for playing. . . What was the meaning of all this? What madness did it denote? Were they going to give an evening party? Had they given one without her knowledge? The old lady trotted up to the piano—her own daughter's piano—magnificently done up, with music piled upon the top! She looked round and saw a window open, a cup with flowers in the window, and a work-basket and writing materials upon the table. . . . The light began to dawn upon her. What! did they make a common sitting-room of Léonie's state drawing-room, which was never made use of in her lifetime except on the occasion of Toto's christening, and once when a ball was given which Madame Mérard herself had opened? Oh, it could not be; it was impossible! But as she was still staring, bewildered, the door opened, and Catharine came in, looking quite at home, bringing some more leaves and berries from her winter-garden, and looking as if she was quite used to the place, and sat in it every hour of the day.

"Good-morning," said Madame Fontaine, in her gentle, cheerful way, unconscious of the sword hanging over her head. "I think breakfast is on the table."

"Indeed!" said Madame Mérard. "I am looking in surprise, madame. I was not aware of the changes which had taken place during my absence."

"Monsieur Fontaine was kind enough to get the piano tuned for me," said Catharine, "and I asked him to let me use this room. It has such a pleasant look-out." And still provokingly unconcerned she put her leaves into the flower-cup, and began putting her writing things together.

"And you are not afraid, madame, of the damage which may befall this handsome furniture, for which my daughter paid so large a sum?" cried the old lady, in a voice of suppressed thunder, "She took care of it, but you, no doubt, not having contributed any thing, can afford . . ."

Catharine looked up frightened, and was shocked by the angry gleam she encountered; Madame Mérard looked stiff with indignation.

"You have, without doubt, madame, engaged servants in abundance to attend to your various wants?" she went on quivering. "We quiet people must seem to you very contemptible as you sit in your elegant drawing-room. Pray, do you intend to receive your fine friends here, in the apartment upon which my poor Léonie bestowed so much care and expense? Ah! there are only English capable of such baseness."

Madame Mérard stopped, much satisfied, for Catharine had turned pale, and then looking round, and seeing Fontaine standing in the doorway, the silly little thing ran up to him and burst out crying.

"Poor child!" he said, very tenderly. "Go, go. I will explain to my good mother; she does not understand; perhaps a little eau sucrée . . . Try it, mon amie. We will follow immediately."

This was the first encounter between these very unequal opponents. Fontaine was so humble and affectionate that he presently brought the old lady down to breakfast almost mollified. She was really fond of him, and when he made a personal request, and talked of the rest after his mental occupations, the diversion and repose the pursuit of music gave him, she reluctantly consented, with a pinch of snuff, to the innovation. It was not the only one.

At one time Madame Mérard suddenly became quite affectionate in her manners. This was soon after her arrival, when M. le Curé was a great deal at the house. He also treated Catharine with great kindness, and called her mon enfant. Old Mérard would dispose himself for sleep during these visits, and Monsieur le Curé and Madame Mérard would enter into long and pointed conversations upon the subject of their common faith. Monsieur le Curé would produce little brown books from his ample pockets, with the pictures of bishops, and fathers and mothers, and agonizing saints upon their narrow pallets; and from one sign and another Madame Fontaine guessed that the time had come when it was considered fitting for her to prepare to go over to the religion of the strangers among whom she lived. She would look at the two sitting in the window, Madame Mérard taking snuff as she listened, the curé, with his long brown nose, and all the little buttons down his shabby frock, and his heavy black legs crossed, and his thick fingers distended as he talked. The Abbé Verdier was a gentleman, and once Catharine might have been willing to be gently converted by him to a faith which had at all times a great attraction for this little heretic; but now to be dragged over by main force, by the muscular curé, to the religion of Madame Mérard—never, never. Fontaine used to look in sometimes, and retire immediately on tiptoe when the curé was there. The maire had promised before his marriage not to interfere with his wife's religious opinions; but, all the same, he did not wish to disturb the good work by any inopportune creaking noises. When Catharine was younger, before she had gone through a certain experience which comes to most people, her conversion might have been possible, and even likely; but now it was too late. From inner causes working silently, and from outer adverse influence, a change had come over her; she could no longer accept new beliefs and creeds, and vivid emotions which she could not even realize, they seemed so distant. She could only cling with a loving persistence to the things of the past, which were still her own and part of her own old life.

The curé was a clever man, although bigoted, and unlike the abbé in his gentle charity and sympathy even for heretics; after a time he ceased importuning, and only snubbed Madame Fontaine; Madame Mérard scowled afresh; Justine, who had also temporarily suspended hostilities, banged her door in disgust, and took care for many weeks to iron Madame Fontaine's fine things all crooked and on the wrong side. Monsieur le Maire was grievously disappointed, but he said nothing, and only seemed, if possible, more tender, more gentle and anxious to make his wife happy.

It was on this occasion that Madame Mérard was at least relieved from another special grief which she cherished against Catharine. One Protestant impoverished Englishwoman in the family was bad enough; but the contemplated arrival of two more at Christmas, their admission into the châlet built with Léonie's money, furnished with her taste—oh, it was not to be endured. The very thought had to be chased away with much snuff, and many wavings of the big checked handkerchief. The poor little girls, however, escaped the exorcisings to which they would doubtless have been subject if they had arrived, for Lady Farebrother, taking alarm at some chance expressions in Catharine's letters, wrote in her flowing capitals to tell her that she felt she would not be justified in exposing Rosa and Totty to the insidious and poisoned influences of Jesuitism, and that, acting upon Mr. Bland's suggestion, she had determined to make other arrangements for the children during the holidays. And poor Catharine's eyes filled up with bitter tears as she read the heart-broken little scrawls inclosed in her aunt's more elaborate epistle. And yet she could scarcely have borne to see them unkindly treated. For herself she did not care. She looked upon it as an expiation in some sort. Often and often she felt ashamed and guilty as she caught the maire's kind and admiring glance. So much affection and devotion deserved some better return than the grateful toleration which was all she had to give. A little patience, a few small services—this was all she could pay toward that vast debt she owed him. As she began to love her husband a little, she found out how little it was. She ought never to have married him. She knew it now, although at the time, in her agitation and excitement, she had fancied that she could at will forget where she would, love where she should; and that, by flinging away a poor faded rose, she could cast from her all memory of the time when it was sweet and red. Alas! the wrong was done, and could not be undone. She could only do her best now, and repair as much as it lay in her power, by patient effort, the harm one moment's weakness had brought about.

Catharine's gentleness maddened the old lady, who was afraid her victim would escape her by sheer obedience and sweetness. Why didn't she laugh and make jokes? Why didn't she get angry? Why was she so indifferent? Even when she gained four tricks running the night before, she did not seem to care. The elegant veil Fontaine presented to her might have been

imitation for all the pains she took, wearing it out in the garden, with no one to see. If Catharine had only scolded, and worried, and complained of migraine, and lived with her husband in a way Madame Mérard could understand, she might in time have got to like her, but all this good temper was insupportable.

The time passed on. The people at Petitport heard but little from without. The Tracys were still at Paris; Charles Butler lingered still, although the poison in his system had already attacked some vital organ. It was a long sad watch for Dick. In the beginning of the winter, at Charles Butler's own request, Catharine Butler had been married quite quietly to Beamish. The news of the marriage came across the sea to Catharine Fontaine, but it all seemed very distant and hard to realize.

As the winter went on the people in the cottages lit larger fires in the deep chimneys, and huddled round the blaze. The winds seemed to shake the very foundations of the wooden house, and the maire anxiously inspected his embankment against the expected onslaught of the early spring-tides. Outside the châlet there was cold, and drift, and storm, and low mists came rolling over the fields and along the edges of the cliffs; inside, fires of wood and charcoal were burning, stew-pots simmering on the hob, and the daily pendulum of life swung on monotonously. Old Mérard's taper burnt with a quiet flicker as he warmed himself in his chimney corner. Madame Mérard's light blazed, and hissed, and spluttered; it was not set under a bushel; nor was Justine's, as she sat below darning away the long winter evenings, while Fontaine busily rapped, tapped, conversed, practiced his cornet, settled his accounts, came and went, cheerfully humming little snatches from operas, or with alacrity joined the inevitable partie. That horrible, greasy pack of cards which was brought out every afternoon inspired poor Catharine with a morbid feeling of disgust that would have been absurd if she had not struggled so hard against it. When they all noisily insisted that she must join them, she would put down her book in silence and come to the table. No one noticed the weary look in her dark eyes, or would have understood it any more than did the knaves of clubs and spades, with the thumb-marks across their legs, staring at her with their goggle eyes. Sometimes, thinking of other things as the hours went on, she would forget and hold the cards so loosely that old Mérard, in his odd little piping voice, would cry out, "Take care! take care! What are you about?" and then Catharine would start and blush, and try to be more careful. Little Madame Fontaine's lamp, although she was somewhat dazzled by the light as she tried, with a trembling, unaccustomed hand, to trim the wick, was burning more brightly now perhaps than it had ever done in all her life before; and yet she might have told you (only that she found it difficult to speak) she had never thought so hardly of herself, never felt so ashamed, so

F

sorry for all that she had done amiss. Fontaine must have sometimes had a dim suspicion that his wife was tired, as she drooped over the cards, for he would send her to the piano while he dealt the cards to the elders, and to himself, and the dummy that replaced her, to the sound of Catharine's music. The shabby kings and queens, performing their nightly dance, circled round and round, and in and out, in the country dance which mortals call whist, and kept unconscious time to the measure. The lamp would spread its green light, the blue flames of the wood fire would sparkle and crackle, old Mérard, in his velvet cap with the long hanging tassel, would unconsciously whistle a little accompaniment to the music as he pondered over his trumps, and Fontaine would beat time with his foot under the table; as for Madame Mérard, erect and preoccupied, she avoided as much as possible listening to the sounds which distracted her, for the flick of her cards falling upon the table was the music she loved best to hear.

One night Madame Fontaine suddenly ceased playing, and went and looked out through the unshuttered window. Handfuls of stars were scattered in the sky. There was the sound of the distant sea washing against the bastions of the terrace. The moon had not yet risen; the narrow garden-paths glimmered in the darkness; except where two long rays of light from the window lit up every pebble and blade of grass, elsewhere shadows were heaping, and the great cliff rose black purple before the sky. Catharine, looking out, saw some one coming through the gloom, and stop at the gate and open it, and she recognized Reine by the quick movement.

"Knave of trumps," said Madame Mérard, triumphantly, as Madame Fontaine stepped gently out of the room, and went out to meet her friend. The two women stood in the doorway talking in low tones, which seemed to suit the silence; they could scarcely see each other's faces, only Reine's white flaps streamed in the shadow; her voice shook a little as she spoke, and her hand was trembling in Catharine's soft, warm fingers. Poor Reine, she had come to Catharine in a sad and troubled mood. She had received a sad, hurried word from Dick to tell her all was over at last; that there was confusion and stir now in the house of which he was virtually the master. Mr. Baxter had untied his red tapes, and read the will by which it was left to him. Dick was not to take actual possession for a year, during which the income was to be applied to keeping up the estate as usual, and to succession expenses. Only a small sum was apportioned to Dick himself until he came into the property. And for the present their engagement was still to be secret. And poor Reine, in her perplexity, had written back to offer to set him free. "He ought to marry a great lady now," she said. It was not fitting that she should be his wife. His prospect of succession gave her no pleasure; on the contrary, it seemed to put them more widely asun-

der. A great house! she liked her brick-floored room better than any splendid apartment in a palace. Her cotton curtains and quilt, with the stamped blue pictures from the life of Joan of Arc, were more familiar to her than down, and damask, and quilting. Better than any carpeted flight to her was the old stone staircase leading to her bedroom, built without shelter against the outside wall of the house; she went up to bed in the rain, sometimes with the roar of the sea booming on the wind from a distance; sometimes she sat down on the steps on still nights when the stars were shining over the horizon, and thought of Richard Butler, and looked, and wondered, and felt at peace. But in the daylight she was unquiet and restless; she came and went, and worked harder than ever before Petitpère remonstrated with her and told her she could afford to spare herself. He did not know how things were going, but he had a shrewd suspicion. Reine said no, she could not spare herself; she must go on working for the present. And now she came half crying to Catharine. "I hate the secrecy," she said; "it is not fair upon me. If I were one of them they would not treat me so."

Only yesterday Madame Pélottier had spoken to her in a way she could not misunderstand about people who set their caps so high that they tumbled off; some one else had laughed, and asked her what she thought of Mr. Butler's great fortune; Petitpère, too, who so rarely interfered, had rubbed his old chin, and told her that he heard from Barbeau, Monsieur Richard's visits at the farm had been remarked upon. Petitpère warned Reine to be careful if she saw him again—people might chatter.

"It is my grandfather himself and Père Barbeau who chatter," said Reine. "They do not know what harm they do me. This morning only I met M. de Tracy and his wife. Did you not know they were come back? Catharine, they looked at me so strangely."

Catharine laughed. "Dear Reine, you fancy things."

"I am ridiculous, and I know it—ridiculous as well as unhappy. Oh, if he loved me he would not make me so unhappy."

Catharine felt a little frightened when she heard Reine say this. As a little drift upon the darkness, she seemed to see her own story—that poor little humble, hopeless love flitting before her; and then she thought of Dick, kind, and gay, and loyal, and unsuspecting: of his fidelity there was no doubt.

"Ah! Reine," she said, almost involuntarily, "he is too kind to do any thing willingly to make you unhappy. I sometimes think," she said, speaking quickly, and frightened at her own temerity, "that you scarcely know what a prize you have gained. Mr. Butler makes no professions, but he is true as steel; he never speaks a harsh word, nor thinks an ungenerous thought." How could he help this promise if his dying uncle asked for it? "It seems so hard," she went on, with suppressed emotion, "to see those who have for their very own the things others would have once given their whole lives to possess, doubting, unhappy . . ."

She stopped short: there was a sound, a window opening overhead, and Fontaine's voice cried out, "Catharine! where are you? imprudent child."

Catharine only answered quickly, "Yes, mon ami, I am coming . . ." Long afterward she used to hear the voice calling, although sometimes at the moment she scarcely heeded it. "Reine, you are not angry," she said.

"Angry! no, indeed," said Reine, her soft, pathetic tones thrilling through the darkness. "One other thing I came to tell you. I shall go into retreat on Wednesday. Will you go up and visit Petitpère one day during my absence?"

"Oh, Reine, are you really going," said Catharine, to whom it seemed a terrible determination.

Reine thought little of it. She had been before with her mother to the convent of the Augustines at Caen. Impatient, sick at heart, vexed with herself, the girl longed for a few days of rest and prayer in a place where the rumors and anxieties of the world would only reach her as if from a far distance. In Reine Chrétien's class the proceeding is not common, but grand ladies not unfrequently escape in this fashion from the toil and penalty of the world. Madame Jean de Tracy herself had once retired for a few days, without much result. The nuns put up a muslin toilet-table in her cell, and made her welcome, but she left sooner than had been expected. The air disagreed with her, she said.

Marthe was now in this very convent commencing her novitiate. She had entered soon after Catharine's marriage. Jean, who had seen her, said she was looking well, and more beautiful than ever. The air did not disagree with her. Before long, Madame de Tracy and Madame Mère returned to the chateau, with Barbe and all the servants in deep mourning: the last sad news had reached them at Paris of Charles Butler's death. Madame de Tracy bustled down to see Catharine in her new home; she was very kind, and cried a good deal when she spoke of her brother, and asked many questions, and embraced Catharine very often. She did not pay a long visit, and having fluttered off and on her many wraps, departed, desiring madame to be sure to come constantly to see her. Catharine was glad to go; it made a break in the monotony of her life.

CHAPTER XVII.

M. AND N.

ALL the autumn blaze of dahlias and marguerites in front of the little châlet had been put out by the wintry rains and winds; only the shutters looked as brilliantly green as ever, and the little weathercocks were twirling cheerfully upon the tall iron spikes, when Dick came walking up to the châlet one February morning about twelve o'clock. He rang the bell. Madame Mérard saw him through the dining-room window, and called to Justine to let the gentleman in.

"Monsieur was not at home," Justine said. "Madame Fontaine was on the terrace. Would he like to see Madame Mérard?"

Dick hastily replied that he would try and find Madame Fontaine, and he strode off in the direction Justine indicated.

"You can not lose your way," she said, as she went back to her kitchen, well pleased to escape so easily, and the dining-room door opened to invite the gentleman in just as he had disappeared round the corner of the house.

As Dick went walking down the little slopes which led from terrace to terrace, he took in at a glance the look of Catharine's life and the sound of it, the many-voiced sea with its flashing lights, the distant village on the jutting promontory, Petitport close at hand with its cheerful sounds, its market-place and echoes, the hammer of the forge, the dogs barking on the cliff, the distant crow of cocks. The sun was shining in his eyes, so that it was Toto who saw Dick first, and came running up hastily from the cabane, calling to his step-mother. Then Catharine appeared with a glow upon her cheeks, for the morning air was fresh and delightful.

The two met very quietly. A gentleman in mourning took off his hat, a lady in a scarlet hood came up and held out her hand. As she did so Catharine thought she was holding out her hand across a great gulf. Heaven had been merciful to her, and she was safe, standing on the other side. Now that she saw him again she knew that she was safe. This was the moment she had secretly dreaded and trembled to contemplate, and it was not very terrible after all.

"I am sorry my husband is out," said Catharine, after she had asked him when he had come, and heard that the Beamishes had crossed with him the day before and wanted to see her again. We all talk a sort of algebra now and then, as Catharine talked just now. The history of the past, the faith of the future, the pain, the hope, the efforts of her poor little life, its tremulous unknown quantities, were all expressed in these few common platitudes—"How do you do? I am glad to see you. My husband is not at home."

To all of which, indeed, Dick paid but little heed, though he returned suitable answers. He was sorry to miss Fontaine, and yet he was glad to find her alone, he said. Something had vexed him, and, like Reine, he had come to Catharine for sympathy and advice, only before he began upon his own concerns he looked at her. Now that the flush had faded he saw that Madame Fontaine was a little thin and worn; her eyes were bright as ever, but there was a touching tired look under the dropping eyelids which made him fear all was not well. And yet her manner was very sweet, cordial, and placid, like that of a happy woman. She seemed unaffectedly glad to see him, as indeed she was; and it was with an innocent womanly triumph that she felt she could welcome him in her own home for the first time. The time had come, she told herself, when she could hold out her hand and be of help to him, and show him how truly and sincerely she was his friend. It was all she had ever dared to hope for, and the time had come at last. Perhaps, if she had been less humble, less single-minded and inexperienced in the ways of the world, she might have been more conscious, more careful, more afraid; but the fresh, crisp winter sun was illuminating her world; every thing seemed to speak to her of hope, promise, courage, and the dead thorn had ceased to wound.

"I was told to come here to find you," Dick said, after the first few words. "Madame Fontaine, I want you to tell me about Reine. I can not understand it. I have just come from the farm; they tell me she has gone into a convent; she will not be home for a week. What folly is this?"

Catharine saw he was vexed, and she tried to describe to him the state of depression and anxiety in which Reine had come to her to tell her of her resolution. . . . "She had no idea you were coming," said Madame Fontaine.

"But what else could she expect?" said Dick. "She writes a miserable letter, poor dear! She proposes to give me up; she says I am cruel, and leave her here alone to bear all sorts of injurious suspicion and insult. Of course she must have known that this would bring me, and when I come I find her gone—vanished in this absurd way. Indeed, I wrote and told her to expect me; but I see the letter unopened at the farm." Dick, whose faults were those of overeasiness, was now vexed and almost unreasonable. For one thing, he was angry with Reine for being unhappy. "Why will she always doubt and torture herself in this needless way? Why should she mind the gossip of a few idiots? I want to see her, and hear from her that she does not mean all she says about throwing me over."

"Oh, indeed," said Madame Fontaine, "she does not mean it."

"It is a very little time to wait, and I could not help promising. My good old uncle has done every thing for us," Butler went on; "she ought not to have been so over-sensitive when she knew it would all be set right."

Catharine wished he could have seen the girl; one look of her proud sweet eyes would have been more to the purpose than all her own gentle expostulations. They were walking slowly toward the house all this time, when at a turn of the path, and coming from behind a bush, they met a short stumpy figure in a sun-bonnet. "I have not even told my husband your secret," Catharine was saying, and she stopped short, although she remembered afterward that Madame Mérard spoke no English.

But Madame Mérard's little eyes could see, penetrate, transfix. Oh, it was not easy to blind Madame Mérard; she could see Catharine looking and talking earnestly to this unknown young man; she could see his expression as he replied to her appeal. Secret—surely Madame Fontaine had said secret. Oh! it was horrible. Madame Mérard knew enough English for that. Secret! could she have heard aright?

"I do not know this gentleman," said Madame Mérard, standing in the middle of the pathway on her two feet, and staring blankly.

"Let me present Mr. Butler," said Catharine, gently, in French.

"Monsieur Fontaine is not at home," said Madame Mérard, still scowling and sniffing the sea breeze.

"Mr. Butler is coming again to-morrow to see him," said Catharine.

"Indeed!" said the old lady.

If Madame Mérard could have had her way, Dick would never have entered the châlet again. What infatuation was it that prompted Madame Fontaine to ask him to dinner—to invite him—to press refreshment on him? Even old Mérard came out with some proposition. Eau sucrée? One would think it flowed ready made from the sea. Happily she herself was there. No doubt her presence would prevent this young man from coming as often as he would otherwise have done. There was a secret flattery in this reflection.

But Dick was hardly out of the house when Madame Mérard began to speak her mind. Perhaps it was an English custom for young women to invite strange gentlemen to dinner in their husband's absence. Oh, she required no explanation. She could see quite plainly for herself, only she confessed that it was what she herself would not have done—not now, at her present age. In her time a wife could devote herself to the domestic hearth. Her husband's approbation was all that she desired. Now it seemed that excitement, dissipation, admiration, were indispensable. "Dinners in town," said the old lady, darkly, "music at home, expeditions, literature, correspondence, visits! . . ."

"Dear Madame Mérard," said Catharine, "I only go to Tracy."

"Hon! and is not that enough?" said Madame Mérard, angrily stirring something in a saucepan (it was the tisane the devoted wife liked to administer to poor Monsieur Mérard, who secretly loathed the decoction. He was now sitting in the office to avoid the fumes). "Tracy! that abode of vanity and frivolity! Where else would you go?"

Tracy, in truth, was the secret mainspring of all Madame Mérard's indignation and jealousy. The chateau had never called upon the châlet in Léonie's reign—never once. Madame Mérard herself was not invited, even now. But now, since the family had returned, notes and messages were forever coming for this English-woman. Madame de Tracy had caught cold; Catharine must go down to see her in her bedroom. Madame de Tracy had bought a new bonnet; Catharine must give her opinion. Madame de Tracy could not disagree with any member of her household that Madame Fontaine was not sent for to listen to the story. And, in truth, Catharine was so discreet, so silent and sympathetic, that she seemed created to play the rôle of confidante. The countess really loved the little woman. Poor Catharine! she sometimes thought that she would be glad to go no more to a place where she was so much made of and so kindly treated. It seemed hard to come home and to compare the two. One place full of welcoming words of kindness and liberality; the other, narrow, chill, confined. And yet here she had met with truest kindness, thought the little creature, remembering all Fontaine's devotion and patient kindness. She was thinking of this now as she met the onslaught of the old lady, who went on with her attack, bombs flying, shells exploding, cannon going off, while the horrible steam of the saucepan seemed to choke and sicken the poor little enemy.

"Yes," cried the furious old lady. "If you loved your husband, I could forgive you all! but you do not love him, and he knows it, and his life is destroyed. You have come into this peaceful circle with a heart elsewhere. You look upon us with contempt. You scorn our simple ways. Your fine friends come and insult me, and you secretly compare us with them and their powdered lackeys. Ah! do you imagine that we do not know it, though you are so silent? Do you imagine that Charles is not aware of all that passes in your mind? He knows it, for I have told him. But he is loyal, and good, and tender, and he does not reproach you for having brought sorrow and disturbance into the châlet, formerly so peaceful." And old Mérard banged the lid of the saucepan, and took a great flourish of snuff. Poor Catharine turned as pale as she had done once before, and gave a little cry and ran to the door. Fontaine was not standing there to make things smoother.

It was horrible, and, what was most hard to bear was, there was some truth in the angry old woman's reproach — how much truth Madame Mérard herself did not know. Catharine could not bear the house; it seemed to stifle her; the fumes of that choking stew seemed pursuing her. She pulled a cloak over her shoulders, and took up her hood, and went out. Another time she might have been less moved. But to-day, when she had met Dick again, when all her heart had been softened and stirred by memories of past emotions, these reproaches seemed to her to have a meaning they might not have had another time. Old Mérard nodded, and called to her through the office window, but Catharine shook her head with a gentle little movement and hurried out. This was what the sight of her old love had done for her. She had been glad at the time to see him once more, but now, when she thought of Fontaine, her heart seemed to die within her. Was he unhappy, and by her fault? What a weary maze

the last few years had been! In and out, and round and about she had wandered, hoping to go right, and coming out again and again at the same blank passage. And yet she had tried, Heaven knows she had tried, and prayed to be helped, and hoped for peace in time, and this was the end!—a good man's life embittered and destroyed — had not his mother said so? — her own life saddened and wasted in hopeless endurance, when elsewhere, perhaps, a worthier fate might have been hers. What had she done, she thought, to be so tortured? She had got up on the cliff by this time. She was plucking the long stems of the poppies as she went along. She felt as if she, too, had been torn up by some strong hand only to be flung away. She had been mad, or she would never have taken this fatal step. And yet she had hoped for a peaceful home, and she had thought that her poor little sisters at least might have found a safe refuge, and now, by her own act, they were parted from her forever perhaps.

With small strength of her own to bear with wrongs or to assert her rights, she was apt to cling to those about her, to rely on them, to leave her fate in their hands. She wished no harm to any mortal being; she could not say a hard word, but she could fear, and shrink away, and wince and shrink with pain. The sensitive little frame could thrill with a terror and anguish unconceived by stronger and tougher organizations. It was not of Dick she was thinking, but of Fontaine all this time, and her remorse was all the greater because her heart was so true and so full of gratitude to him. She had left her fate in the hands of others, and this was what had come of it; a poor little heart crushed and half broken, another person dragged by her fault into sorrow and remorse, a deed done which could never, never be undone. A crime! ah! was it indeed a crime which she had committed that could never be repented of? Was there no atonement possible—no pardon— no relenting of fate?

The colors were all aglow still, for the sun was scarcely set; the red, and blue, and striped petticoats, and the white caps of the fish-wives down in Petitport, jumbled up into bright, pretty combinations. The creeping grays and shades gave tone and softness to the pretty scene. Indoors the fires were flaring and crackling, and presently the church bell came ringing up the street in very sweet tinkling tones, calling the villagers to the *salut*, or evening service. The peaceful twilight prayers, coming at the close of the day's work, seem to sanctify to silence the busy cares of the long noisy hours — to absolve, to tranquilize before the darkness of the night.

The bell tolled on — the curé left his house and walked through his wild overgrown wilderness to the *vestiary*. Poor little Catharine, who had been flitting along the hedge of the great field, heard it too. She had walked till she was weary, then she had rested till her heart grew so sad that she could not sit still, and she jumped up again and walked to Arcy without stopping, and without purpose, and then came back along the cliffs and across into the fields. She was weary of pain; she felt as if she had no strength left to bear, or even to suffer or to repent; she dragged on, utterly worn and dispirited, holding one or two poppies in her hand still with the white drapery of her dress. Catharine was a delicate and orderly person, and she held up her dress with unconscious care, even when she was struggling in the Slough of Despond. It was indeed the Slough of Despond for her. A vision of the future came before her so utterly unendurable, with a struggle between right, and duty, and wrong, for which she felt herself so unfitted that she longed to lie down in the hard brown furrows of the field and die, and own herself vanquished, and give up the fight, and struggle no longer.

I think it was just then the bell began to toll. It seemed like a sudden sympathy, and companionship, and comfort to the poor thing. It turned her thoughts, it gave her some present object, for she began to walk in the direction of the church. She crossed the brook, along which the figures were coming, with the great glowing west at their backs. She turned up the quiet end of the village, and followed M. le Curé at a distance as he led the way through the back court of the church into which the vestry opened; and the side door near the altar of St. Joseph was where the poor little heart-petition was offered up for strength, and help, and peace.

Catharine saw the people prostrate all about. She knew what passionate prayers some of them were praying. There was poor Thérèse Fournier, whose little girl was dying. There was Joseph Leroux, who had cruel trouble in his home; and then presently Madame Fontaine caught sight of some one kneeling on a low straw chair, and she recognized her husband, although his face was buried in his hands.

It was very quiet and solemn. Very few of us can come in to an evening service untouched or unsoftened. To many it is but the contrast of the daylight and the candles which makes the scene impressive. But some of us must be content to be dazzled by a candle in this world, to measure the sun's light by a taper's flame. In this man's church and that man's, candles are shining at the high altar, which seem bright enough for a time: only when the service is over and the prayers are ended shall we come out into the open air, and shall our eyes behold the fathomless waves of the mighty light of heaven.

Catharine, who was worn out and exhausted, sank into a chair in her dim corner, grateful for ease after her pain. She was no longer feeling much: a sort of calm had come after the storm. The priest's voice ceased uttering, the choristers were silent, the service was ended, and people rose from their knees, took up their baskets and umbrellas—one old woman slung on her *hotte* again—and they all went away. Catharine mechanically tried to escape by the side door through which she had entered. Her chief troubles in life had come from the timidity and want of courage and trust in herself. She did not know why she was flying from her husband now—from poor Fontaine, who also had been offering up his petitions. He prayed for his mother's rheumatism; he prayed for a blessing upon his wife and child; for Catharine's conversion and happiness; for a little more calm and repose at home in the châlet; for a little gayety even, if possible. Fontaine did not like to ask for too much at once; and though one smiles at such a simple creed, it does not seem as if a humble petition for a calm and cheerful spirit was the worse means of attaining so good a thing. The maire jumped up quickly from his knees when the service was over, and unconsciously made for the same side door through which his wife was escaping, and so it happened that the two came face to face.

"At last I find you!" he cried, as they both stepped out almost together on to the worn stone flight which led down by a few steps to the ground. Fontaine was almost inclined to believe in a miracle after all as he looked at his wife. They were a handsome couple, Mère Nanon thought, hobbling away with her great basket on her back. They stood looking at one another in the glow of the gloaming; the breeze came salt and fresh from the sea; the twilight was warm still, with brown and fading golden tints; the silver stars were coming out overhead. "Imagine my anxiety," said Fontaine. "I have been looking for you every where. I went home. Ma mère told me you were gone. You were not at the farm. I did not know what to do or where to search."

"I walked to Arcy," said Catharine, looking up with her dark, wistful eyes. "Oh, Charles, I am very unhappy."

"Unhappy, dear?" said Fontaine.

"I am unhappy to think that through me you are unhappy," said the poor little woman. "Indeed and indeed I have tried to do my duty."

"Don't talk like this," said Fontaine. "You are a little angel, my Catharine. What has any one been saying to you?"

Poor little Catharine! Half in sobs, half in words, the explanation came, and with the explanation half her terrors vanished. Fontaine was a little puzzled. She did not love him enough! Why not? She would gladly love him more. Only now that he was so kind did she know how much he deserved to be loved. She had broken his heart. Madame Mérard said so. It was a bewildering story. But he began to understand by degrees.

"Dear Catharine," Fontaine said at last, very sensibly, "I am many years older than you. I do not require a romantic affection: I want a good, kind little wife to take a little care of me, and to like me a little. I am satisfied —more than satisfied. In my eyes there is no one to compare to you. Madame Mérard is a most excellent person, but impressionable; she does not mean always what she says. Do not be unhappy, my very dear friend; believe I am happy if you are; I ask for nothing else."

But before they reached home Catharine had told him why it was that Madame Mérard's reproaches had stung her so sharply.

"Do you remember one night when you asked me why I threw some dead flowers into the sea?" said Catharine. "I wanted to throw away the memory of my silly girlish fancies. Indeed it is true what I told you then—no one ever loved me but you; I have never spoken to any one of what I am speaking now. You are the only person in all the world who cared enough for me to give me a resting-place."

Fontaine begged her to leave off. He believed her, and understood her perfectly. But Catharine could not stop; and as she poured forth her story, in her agitation and emotion poor Dick's secret escaped her somehow. "To-day Mr. Butler came to speak to me of something I have known ever since—ever since the summer. He and Reine are going to marry one another. Sometimes they have come to me to help them. Oh, Charles, I can not help being glad to be his friend, and to help him when I can, even though I am your wife. But oh! what have I done? I ought not to have told you."

As they walked along many of the villagers wondered what Monsieur Fontaine and his wife were talking of so earnestly. They spoke of it afterward, and Catharine, too, remembered that walk. They went along the dusky street—the little woman with dark eyes glowing beneath her scarlet hood. Fontaine looked very pale, for he was much affected by her confidence.

"I am profoundly touched," he said, "by the trust you repose in me. You shall see that I have entire confidence in you. The news you give me is surprising, but not utterly unexpected. At this moment I am too much preoccupied to realize its great importance."

Candles were alight in the châlet, the dinner-table was laid, and something was simmering on the hob. It was a tisane-de-thé, without any milk, which Madame Mérard was preparing as a conciliation treat for her daughter-in-law. The old lady had been alarmed by her long absence; she thought she had gone too far, perhaps, and was sincerely glad to see her come in safely with her husband.

"Coffee is good, and so is wine, and a little eau de carmes occasionally to fortify the stomach," said old Mérard, in his little piping voice, after dinner; "but tea is worth nothing at all."

"Englishwomen like to destroy themselves with tea, Monsieur Mérard," said his wife, almost graciously for her.

While the little party at the châlet discussed the merits of tea and eau de carmes—while Fontaine, always kind and gentle, seemed to try in a thousand ways to show his wife how happy he was, and how he loved her, and how unfounded her terrors had been—Dick waited impatiently at the chateau for Reine's return. Catharine Beamish smiled, and chattered, and brightened them all up with her sweet spirits and happiness. She enjoyed every thing, insisted upon going every where, charmed every one. Ernestine was furious at being made to play a second. The very morning after all this agitation Mrs. Beamish sent a little note by the maire, who had been up there, to implore Catharine to join them immediately. They were all going sight-seeing to Bayeux, first to the museum, and then to Caen, to pay Marthe a visit in her convent; would Catharine please come too? She was longing to see her.

"I promised for you," said Fontaine. "I thought it would do you good to be with your friends. Madame de Tracy says you are looking ill," he added, looking anxiously at her.

"How kind you are to me, Charles," cried Catharine, delighted, and looking well on an instant, as she jumped up and upset all her bobbins and reels.

Fortunately for her, Monsieur and Madame Mérard were not present. When they came in from a short stroll to the fish-market, Fontaine and Catharine had started. Toto told them that maman was going with the countess, and that she had got on her Indian shawl and her pretty rose-colored bonnet.

"Grandmamma, do you like rose-color?" asked Toto.

"No, no, no, my child," said Madame Mérard with a shudder.

CHAPTER XVIII.

THE ABBAYE AUX DAMES.

MEANWHILE Catharine, in good spirits and in better heart than she had felt for many a day, was picking her way between the stones, and walking up the little village street with her husband. Fontaine, nimbly advancing with neatly-gaitered feet, bowed right and left to his acquaintance, stopping every now and then to inquire more particularly after this person's health, or that one's interest, as was his custom. The children were at play in the little gardens in front of the cottages, the women were sitting in groups dancing their bobbins, spinning, whirring, twisting, stitching. Their tongues were wagging to the flying of their fingers and the bobbing of their white caps. Some of the men were winding string upon nails fixed to the walls, some were mending their nets, others were talking to the women, who answered, never ceasing their work for an instant. Between the houses a faint, hazy sea showed glittering against the lime walls. Dominique, from the farm, came down the middle of the street with some horses clattering down to the water; Marion and others called out a greeting to him as he passed. "And when does Mademoiselle Chrétien return?" said Madame Potier from the door of her shop.

"Who can tell?" said Dominique, clattering away. "To-morrow perhaps." He took off his hat to Monsieur Fontaine, and Madame Potier beamed a recognition as they passed.

Catharine asked her husband why so many of the men were at home. She had not been long enough by the sea to read the signs of the times in the southwest wind now blowing gently in their faces—in the haze which hid the dark rocks of the Calvados.

Fontaine adjusted his glasses and looked up at the sky, and then at the faint blue horizontal line. "These fine mornings are often deceptive," said he, "although it is hard to believe in bad weather on such a day as this." Every thing was so bright and so still, the wind so gentle, that it seemed as if gales could never blow again, or storms rise. The sun poured down upon the dusty road. Now and then the threads of the women at work stirred in the soft little breeze; the voices sounded unusually distinct—a cheerful echo of life from every doorway. Presently two men and a boy, tramping down toward the sea, passed by, carrying oars and rope-ends. These were Lefebvres, who evidently thought, like Catharine, that no storm need be apprehended when the sun shone so steadily and the sea lay so calm. The boy looked up and grinned, and his bright blue eyes gave a gleam of recognition, for he knew Madame Fontaine; one of the men, Christophe Lefebvre, touched his cap; the other, who was his cousin, tramped on doggedly. Joseph Lefebvre was the most obstinate man in the village, and no one dared remonstrate with him. Christophe and he had words that morning, it was said, about their coming expedition, but it ended in Christophe going too at Isabeau's prayer. He never refused Isabeau any thing she asked, poor fellow—that was known to them all. The men went their way, and at some distance, watching them, and muttering to herself, old Nanon followed: her brown old legs trembled as she staggered along under her load of seaweed. "Christophe was a fool," she said. "What did he mean by giving in to that dolt of a Joseph?" So she passed in her turn, muttering and grumbling. Catharine would have stopped and spoken to her, but the old woman shook her head and trudged on. "What is it to you?" she was saying. "You have your man dry and safe upon shore, always at your side; he is not driven to go out at the peril of his life to find bread to put into your mouth."

The old woman's words meant nothing perhaps, but they struck Catharine with a feeling of vivid reality, for which she could hardly account. Poor souls, what a life was theirs—a life of which the sweetest and wholesomest food must be imbittered by the thought of the price which they might be called upon to pay for it some day. Yes, she had her "man," as Nanon called Monsieur Fontaine, and she looked at him as he walked beside her, active and brisk, and full of life and good-humor. He talked away cheerfully, of storms, and fish, and fishermen, of the *Ecole de Natation* at Bayeux, which he had attended with much interest, and where he meant Toto to go before long; he talked of the good and bad weather, storms, and of the great piles of sea-weed with which the coast was sometimes covered when the tide went down after a boisterous night. "That is a sight you must see, my very dear Catharine," said the maire. "People rise at the earliest dawn, and come down with carts and spades, and barrows and baskets. It would amuse you to see the various expedients for carrying away the *varech* before the evening tide."

"But what do they do with it?" said Catharine

"It forms a most valuable manure," said the maire, in his instructive voice. "The odor is not agreeable, but its beneficial properties can not be too highly commended. I remember, last spring, in the early dawn, some one tapping at my window, saying, 'Get up, get up, Monsieur le Maire, the *varech* is arrived.' I hastily dressed, and found all the company assembled upon the beach, although it was but three o'clock in the morning." They had come to the church at the end of the village by this time, and Monsieur le Curé was descending the well-worn steps. He pulled off his three-cornered hat, and Fontaine, hastily stepping forward, panama in hand, returned the salutation, and asked M. le Curé whether he would be at home in the course of half an hour? "I have certain *paperasses* to sign," said the maire, with a beaming and important face, "and I venture to ask if you would kindly witness them? I will return after escorting my wife to the chateau," said the maire, with some slight complaisance at the thought of such good company. "She joins the niece of Madame de Tracy and others in an expedition to Bayeux."

"We shall have rain soon," said the curé, looking at the horizon from the church. "We must make the most of this fine sunshine while it lasts." And as he spoke the whole place seemed to grow bright.

"Joseph Lefebvre is putting out," said the maire. "It seems hazardous; but these people are fish, not men." And he adjusted his eye-glass, and looked at a long low bank of clouds beyond the rocks of the Calvados.

"There will be a storm to-night," said the curé, dryly. "Madame, however, has time to divert herself before it comes. I'm afraid Joseph will scarcely return à sec."

"Monsieur le Curé," cried Fontaine, walking off, "I shall drop in at the presbytery on my way home."

Catharine looked after the curé as he trudged away toward a cottage, where she, too, sometimes paid visits of charity. The black figure with its heavy skirts passed through the brilliant waves of light. This light seemed to make every thing new and beautiful, the fields, the distant lanes, the very grass along the roadside. The two, walking toward Tracy, presently reached a place where the field-path joined the road, and where one of those wayside crosses which are so common in Normandy had been erected. Some faded garlands were still hanging to it, and the grass was growing between the stone steps. Here Fontaine stopped.

"Is not that the carriage from Tracy coming to meet us?"

"Yes, I think so," Catharine answered.

"Then I will leave you with your friends, for I have several things to do," Fontaine said, hastily. "Good-by, dear Catharine; they will see you home; they promised me they would, if I spared you to them."

"Good-by, Charles," said Catharine. "Thank you for coming with me when you were so busy."

Fontaine smiled and kissed her forehead. "Good-by, my little Catharine," said he, a second time, so kindly that it seemed to her that the sound of his voice echoed long after he had spoken. When the carriage drove up, Catharine was standing quite still by the cross, watching Fontaine as he walked away. Once he turned and looked back, and then the slope of the field hid him from her eyes.

"It was not like Monsieur Fontaine to run away from us," said Mrs. Beamish, cheerfully, driving up in her furs and smiles. "We came to meet you. My aunt changed her mind at the last moment, and wouldn't come. Ernestine declares we are going to see old rags and bones, and that it is a fast-day, and they won't let us into the convent. But we mean to try, don't we? Jump in, dear."

The convent of the Augustines at Caen stands upon a hill next to the great Cathedral of the Holy Trinity, which the people call l'Abbaye aux Dames. The convent walls inclose shady lime-walks, and quadrangles, and galleries, and flights of steps, along which the white nuns go drifting. The galleries lead to sick wards and dispensaries, to refuges and nurseries. The care of the soldier's hospital is given to the nuns, and it is almost a city which you come to within the great outer gates. Life and prayer, and work, and faith, the despairs of this world, and the emblems of the next, meet you at every step in the halls, and courts, and quiet gardens, in the sunshine and shadow, peopled by this pathetic multitude—men, and women, and children, who have fled hither for refuge. They come up from the great battle-fields of the world, and from the narrow streets and dark tenements below. Some go to the hospital, some to the convent, and some to the little grave-yard upon the hill-side, from whence you may see the city lying in the plain, and the river shining and flowing, and the distant curve of encompassing hills painted with the faint and delicate colors of the north.

De Tracy led the two Catharines, Dick and Beamish toiling up the steep streets with their rugged stones. They crossed a lonely "Place" at last, where the sun beat upon the grass-grown pavements, and no one was to be seen but some masons chipping at the great blocks of marble which were being prepared for the restoration of the cathedral. There it stood before them, high up above the town, silent, and gleaming white, and beyond it the two great gates, closed and barred, with the words HÔTEL DIEU emblazoned upon them. Reine had passed through those gates. Butler was thinking as he stood waiting with the others for the porteress to come with the key and admit them into the precincts. To Butler there was an inde-scribable sadness about the place. The monotonous sound of the blows from the workmen's mallets seemed to fill the air. He looked at the closed way, at the great silent cathedral, at the distant valley; some presentiment saddened and oppressed him: none of the others felt as he did. Catharine was in high spirits—gay in the passing excitement, thankful for relief after her pain, happy in the consciousness of her husband's trust and Butler's friendship.

As for Mrs. Beamish, every thing was grist that came to her mill; she was one of those princesses who know how to grind gold out of straw. Beamish used to laugh at her energy and enthusiasm, but he loved her for it. Fossils, doubtful relics, Bishop Odo's staff, jolting omnibuses, long half-hours in waiting-rooms—Mrs. Beamish laughed, and enjoyed every thing untiringly. She stood now leaning against the iron gate, and holding one great bar in her hand, as she chattered on in her pleasant way, while Catharine, who had perched herself upon a block of stone, sat listening to the talk of the others. It was only woman's talk after all—of needle-work, and of samplers, and of stitches, but the stitches had been set eight hundred years ago, and the seamstress was an empress, and the pattern was the pattern of her times. They had just come from the Bayeux tapestry. "I should as soon have thought of seeing the Gordian knot," cried Mrs. Beamish, flippantly.

"Or Penelope's web," said Dick.

"Hush," said Beamish. "Here comes the abbess."

A little, bright-eyed, white-robed sister, followed by an attendant in a blue cotton gown, now came to the gate and unlocked it. "Mademoiselle will conduct you over the hospital," she said, in answer to their various requests and inquiries. "You wish to see Mademoiselle Chrétien, madame? The ladies here who are in retreat admit no visits. I am sorry to refuse you, but the convent is closed to the public." Then they asked for Marthe. It was a fast-day, and as Ernestine had predicted, no strangers could be allowed to see the ladies. Any vague hopes which might have brought Dick all the way from Petitport were quickly extinguished by the gentle little nun who glided away from them along the arched cloister, in and out of the shade and the light, with silent steps, like a ghost.

Then the lay sister took up the story in a cheerful, sing-song voice, and began to recite the statistics of this House Beautiful. So many loaves, so many fishes, so many doctors, so many caldrons of soup, of physic, so many people cured, so many buried. She led them into the kitchen, where two nuns were busy cooking vegetables, while a third was sitting at a table chanting out canticles from the Psalms, to which the others responded loudly. She led them into the long wards where the sick were lying, with their nurses coming and going from bedside to bedside; one pale man, with great dark eyes, raised himself wearily to see them go by, and then fell back again upon his pillow. The curtains of the bed next to his were drawn close, and Catharine bent her head as she hurried past it. The nursery was the prettiest and most cheerful sight of all. It was on the ground floor, where two or three rooms opened out upon one of the cloisters, and in these rooms were small cradles and babies asleep, with their little fat hands warm and soft upon the pillows, and some little children playing quietly, and some old nuns keeping watch. The shadows made a shifting pattern on their woolen gowns, and the lights through the open door painted the unconscious little groups. They sat there busy, peaceful, beatified, with the children all about them, and saintly halos round about their worn old heads. They were not saints, only old women as yet. Though, indeed, it is not more difficult to imagine them as saints and angels one day yet to come, than to think of them like the children round about—young, golden-haired, round-eyed. One of the children, a little boy called Henri, took a great fancy to Dick, and trotted up to him with a sticky piece of sugar, which he silently thrust into his hand. A baby, who was sitting upon the floor, began to make a cooing noise as if to call attention, but when Mrs. Beamish stooped to take her up into her arms she saw that the poor little thing was blind.

"Blind from her birth," the nurse cried, "but a little angel of goodness."

"I think if I had not married I should have liked this life," said Mrs. Beamish thoughtfully. "And you, Madame Fontaine?"

Little Catharine flushed up, and shook her head gently.

"Our sisters are very happy," said their conductress. "We have three who are over eighty years of age. They never come out of the convent, where they remain with the novices."

"Do any of them ever go back into the world?" asked Beamish in a John Bull sort of tone.

"Last year a novice came," said the conductress; "there was a grand ceremony at her reception. She came, dressed as a bride, in a great carriage with two horses, and many gentlemen and ladies were present to take leave of her. Then her mother came and cried, and threw herself at her feet. The unfortunate girl's courage failed; apparently hers was no real vocation. She left in a common hackney-coach next morning, disgraced and pitied by us all. . . . This is the Abbaye, which is, as you see, in reparation."

Matilda and her successors have raised the church upon tall upspringing arches, so light, so beautiful, that they strike one like the vibrations of music as one enters. If our faith of late years had been shown by such works as these, what strange creeds and beliefs would have seemed represented by the Egyptian mausoleums, the stucco, the Grecian temples, in which we have been content to assemble. "Here, through a side-door in the massive wall, they entered in among the springing forest of arches, first passing through a small outer chapel which seemed echoing with a distant chant, and where a coffin was lying on the marble pavement. The lay sister quietly pointed to it, saying, "The bearers will be presently here to take it away. It is a young man who died in the hospital two days ago. We do not know his name." And then she opened a grating and led them into the church. They were all silent as they moved about; the whiteness and cheerfulness of the place seemed at once lovely and sad to Catharine: she was glad to be there. "The tomb of the empress is in the choir," their conductress continued, "behind that black curtain. You have seen her *tapisserie*, no doubt. I can not take you in, for, as I told you, the service is going on, but, if you like, I may raise the curtain for an instant."

She was quite at home and matter-of-fact. Catharine Beamish was silent and impressed; Catharine Fontaine felt as if it was a sort of allegorical vision passing before her; she could hardly believe in the reality of this calm oasis in the midst of the roaring work-a-day world: the coffin, the children, the sick people, all seemed like a dream somehow. She was thinking this when the sister called them to the grating which separated the choir from the nave, and raised the curtain, and as she did so a flood of yellow light from the west window came pouring through the bars, and then the most unreal sight of all met Catharine's eyes. It was like some vision of a saint in ecstasy. In the midst of the choir stood the great black tomb; all round about the praying nuns knelt motionless in their white garments. The priests at the altar were intoning in a low sing-song voice. All the faces were toward them; closed eyes, some hands clasped, some crossed devoutly, some outstretched in supplication. Catharine suddenly seized Dick's arm: "Look!" she whispered.

"Do you see her?" he asked, eagerly, in a low voice, turning to Madame Fontaine; but the curtain fell almost at that instant, and it was too late.

"No, madame," said the lay sister, decidedly, "I must not do it again; it is impossible."

She was deaf to all their entreaties, and stood before the pully to prevent any one attempting to look again.

"She saw you," said Catharine to Butler, as they walked away at once, touched, impressed, and curious, with the sound of the chanting in their ears. Presently the unconscious Beamish began asking them all if they had seen that beautiful young woman to the right? "She was not so well trained as the others, and opened her eyes," said he.

The last thing to see was the garden, where the sick people were strolling in the sunshine, and then by a great alley of lime-trees they came to the hill beyond the grave-yard, from whence they could look for miles and miles at plains and hills all bathed in misty sunshine. A little wind was blowing, and smoke drifting over the gables of the town, and an odd bank of clouds seemed piled against the west. Coming back under the bare branches of the avenue they met the little funeral procession, and stood still to let it pass. Two choristers were trudging ahead, chanting as they hurried along; an old white-headed priest was hurrying beside the coffin. Some birds were faintly chirruping overhead, the wind came rushing through the bare branches, shaking the shadows upon the dry turf.

"It does one good to come to this place. I shall ask my husband to bring me here again," said Catharine.

No one answered her. Butler was a little ahead, walking with his hands deep in his pockets. Catharine Beamish had got hold of her husband's arm and was talking to him. For the first time that day a strange chill presentiment came to Madame Fontaine; she remembered it afterward. As she came out through the gates again it seemed to her as if she was leaving behind her more of peace and of prayer than were to be found outside, and yet she was glad to escape and to be carried away by the tide of life.

Who shall say where peace is to be found? George Eliot has nobly written that the kingdom of heaven is within us, and not to be found here or there by those who vainly search for it.

Reine Chrétien thought once that she had discovered it to the sound of the chanted prayers in the companionship of sacred, indifferent women. She had been torn by mistrust. Catharine's poor little warning had roused the sleeping jealousy of this strange and difficult nature. She had hated herself—struggled against it, forgotten it in a passionate enthusiasm of devotion, of gratitude; and by some strange chance, praying in the choir, within the gates of the convent, she had opened her eyes to see the curtain raised, and, like a terrible revelation, the secret visions of her heart standing realized before her. There were Dick and Catharine standing outside at the grating, side by side; and within it, the nuns at their prayers, and Reine still on her knees, with a sudden tempest raging in her heart.

Another time the chance might have meant nothing, but now she was in a demoralized state of mind, and, as it often happens, the very efforts which she had made to overcome the evil seemed to increase its strength, like water poured upon the flames.

Certain combinations, which at one time, to some people, seem utterly shifting and unmeaning, to others are, as it were, stamped and arrested forever in their minds. A certain set of emotions have led up to them; a certain result follows. The real events of life happen silently, and in our hearts the outward images are but signs and faint reflections of its hopes, longings, failings, victories.

* * *

CHAPTER XIX.

FONTAINE TO THE RESCUE.

In the absence of his wife, poor Fontaine had been making mischief at home; he had let out Dick's secret to Madame de Tracy, who happened to meet him as he was coming out of the curé's house with his *paperasses*, as he called them, in his hands. She had been transacting some business with the lace-makers at the end of the village, and had walked home with him, talking of one thing and another, little thinking as she went along that this was the last of their many gossips. Madame de Tracy listened with interest to Fontaine, who was speaking of his wife, and saying how happy he was, how good she was, how charmingly she bore with the small peculiarities of a tender and excellent, but over-anxious and particular mother.

"My nephew told me that he was afraid Madame Mérard had taken a great dislike to him," said the countess, laughing. "I know she is a little difficult at times."

"She is a person of great experience," said Fontaine, "and one can not blame her, madame, for feeling that in a usual way the acquaintance of an elegant young man of the world is not desirable for a young wife in Catharine's position. She might be tempted to draw comparisons—but of course, under the circumstances—Monsieur Butler is engaged," and here poor Fontaine suddenly stopped short and looked Madame de Tracy in the face . . . . "You did not know it," he said; "I have forgotten myself—madame, I entreat you to ask no more—let my words be buried in oblivion."

He might have known that Madame de Tracy, of all the people in the world, was the last person to comply with such a request. She asked a hundred questions, she plied him in every way. She never rested for one instant until she finally extracted poor Reine's name from her victim. Her next proceeding was to rush off to the farm in a state of indescribable agitation. Petitpère was plodding about in company with his friend Barbeau, the wisps of straw hanging from their wooden sabots. Together they poked the pigs, inspected their barns, examined the white horse's lame foot. The apparition of the countess took them by surprise; but old Chrétien courteously replied to all Madame de Tracy's agitated questions. Reine was absent; she would return next day —offered her refreshment, a little bread and butter after her walk, a little milk—would she not rest? She was tired, would she not permit him to send her home on Annette, who should be instantly saddled? for the weather was threatening, and as he spoke the storm which Fontaine had predicted broke. So Madame de Tracy had to wait for shelter at the farm, and meanwhile the little party of excursionists had not yet reached home. The carriage was waiting at the station, and as they passed through the streets Bayeux looked black, and then again suddenly lighted by gleams from the setting sun, the window-panes blazed here and there, drops of rain began to fall, and presently clouds came spreading and hid in the pale gold, and the rain began to pour upon the roads and hedges, by the stunted fruit-trees, upon the wide fields which spread to the sea; and soon the mists came creeping up, and hid the distant glimpses of the sea and the hills.

They were all tired and silent, and spoke little on the way back. Baptiste was standing at the door of the chateau when the carriage drove up through the gusts of rain. "Madame has not yet returned from the village," he said. "She has sent a message; she wishes the carriage to go for her to Lefebvre's cottage. The poor wife is in great trouble; he has not yet returned. They say the boat has been seen making for the port."

"Ah! poor woman!" said Madame Fontaine, with an ache in her heart. A sudden gust of wind and rain came blowing in her face, and Baptiste staggered under the great umbrella which he was holding over Mrs. Beamish as she alighted.

Dick had got down too, but he sprang into the carriage again when he found that De Tracy did not get off the box, but was buttoning up his coat and preparing to go on. "Good-by," said Catharine Beamish, and then the carriage set off again. The horses went with a sudden

swiftness, and presently they came in sight of a brown sea tossing fiercely in the twilight. Tracy stood up upon the box, and tried to make out something of the boat, but the wind blew his hat off into the carriage, and he could see nothing. The wind had changed since the morning, and was now blowing in fierce gusts from the northwest. They passed the wayside cross, upon which the wet garlands were swinging to and fro; the wet was dripping upon the stony steps, the mists were thickening behind it. Catharine could hardly believe that this was the sunshine place where she had parted from her husband in the morning. Then they passed the church, and the dark-looking gates of the presbytery, over which the bushy branches were swinging and creaking; and then they came at last to Lefebvre's cottage, which stood by itself at some little distance from the street. Here Jean pulled up, but no one seemed to be there. There was the sound of an infant's voice screaming within, and at last two or three little frightened children came crowding round the door, and peeped out and ran away. "Ils sont allé voire," one little girl said at last; and the countess was gone too, she told them, in reply to Catharine's questions.

The rain fell with soaking force. The child inside the cottage went on crying in piercing sad tones, forlorn, helpless, deserted. Jean looked in. "It is on the floor, poor little wretch," he said.

"Please let me out," Catharine cried suddenly; "that poor little baby! I know it. I will wait here for Madame de Tracy, if you will tell my husband where I am, and ask him to come for me presently."

"Had we not better take you home," said Jean; "how will you get back?"

"Oh, Charles does not mind the rain; it is a very little way," Catharine said. "I must stay with these children."

The two young men turned and walked away, with the empty carriage following, as Catharine disappeared into the cottage. She took the wailing child into her arms, and throwing a few branches of colza upon the fire, she sat down upon a low stool, and tried to warm it and comfort it by the blaze. It was a long, dark room, with the usual oaken cupboard and the deep chimney of those parts, like the chimneys in our own cottages. The wind shook the window-panes, and the slant rain struck against it as it fell; the fire seemed to make a melancholy and fitful glare, every now and then lighting up a little plaster statuette of the Virgin, ornamented with a tiny garland of artificial flowers. The kitchen was in confusion: chairs pushed about, the spinning-shuttle lying on the floor. Catharine noticed it all when her eyes grew accustomed to the darkness; for little light came from the window, and she had asked the children to close the door. They were standing round her now, staring in amazement. One of them who had not seen her before thought it was, perhaps, a lady from heaven who had come to quiet the baby. As she hushed the wailing baby, she had taken off her bonnet, and her sweet little dark head was bent thoughtfully as one thing after another very far away from the cottage came into her mind. Every now and then the baby gave a little appealing moan; but after a time it dropped off to sleep in the folds of the Cashmere shawl. Now and then Catharine would think she heard a step, and imagined it might be Fontaine coming to fetch her; but no one came for a very long time—so at least it seemed to her.

When the door did open at last it was old Nanon who appeared, slowly hobbling in from the storm outside, and staring and blinking with her odd, bloodshot eyes. A little rush of sleet seemed to burst in with her, and the baby set up a fresh moaning. The old woman did not seem surprised to see Catharine there.

"I came back to look to the children," she said. "If I had known you were here I should have staid down below. They can't get the boat round the point. Isabeau has gone to the Chapel of our Lady to pray for their safety. That child wants food." And, going to a cupboard, she poured some milk into a cup, and gave it to the baby. The other children clamored round her, but Nanon pushed them away. Then she pulled the wheel with trembling haste up to the fire, and began to spin as if from habit, mumbling and looking at the door. "They will bring us news," she said. "M. le Maire is on the *plage*, and M. de Tracy and the countess. Ah! it is not the first time they have gone down. . . . Look at my wheel; there it is, forty years old. Many things have happened since it first began to turn."

"How many thousand times it must have turned!" Catharine said.

"Ah! madame, many a time I have sat up till two o'clock in the morning to get bread to put into my children's mouths, after my poor defunct man's death. They used to cry sometimes because I had no food to give them. But M. le Curé was very good to me. 'Courage, my poor girl,' he said; and he made a *quête* of four francs for me. That was one day when I had nothing in the house."

Catharine shivered as she listened to the sad old voice complaining of the troubles of by-gone years. She began to long to get away—to be at home. The place seemed unutterably sad. The baby was asleep by this time. She listened to the sound of the rain pattering without, of the fire blazing fitfully, of the wheel turning. The elder children had begun a little game with a broom in a corner, and were laughing over it. Old Nanon span on. "Ah! what trouble I have had!" she was mumbling. "My 'petiot,' he was only ten—so gentle, so obedient. Listen, that I may tell you. He went out with his father and his elder brother, and about the time I was expecting them I went into a neighbor's house, and she said, 'My poor Nanon, will you spin two pounds of flax?' But I said, 'No, I had to repair the "camiche" of my husband. He

would want a dry one when he came home; and I was arranging a pretty little pair of sabots for my petiot.' This is what Marion said to me: 'Perhaps he may never want them, my poor Nanon.' And then I looked up, and I saw that more people had come in. 'Qui se mouchaient,' said the old woman, in her Norman patois. And I said, 'Listen to me, Marion; I like best to know the worst. I have lost my husband?' Ah! madame, it was not my husband then; my husband had come safe to shore: the men of St. Laurent had saved him. But my petiot; he was holding on to his father in the water, and the cravate give way. Ah! I have had misfortune in my time." . . . And old Nanon went on spinning.

It was just then that the door opened, and the curé of the village came in. Catharine started up, holding the baby to her, and gave a little cry. She seemed to guess instinctively that sorrow was at hand. The curé advanced to meet her with a face full of compassion.

"My poor child," he said, "come home. I have come to fetch you home. There has been an accident."

Catharine said nothing; she put the child quickly down and pulled the shawl over her head as they hurried through the wet street in the storm of sleet and wind. It seemed to Madame Fontaine that one or two people came to their doors and looked at them, but she was not sure; she did not dare to ask what had happened; she knew without being told, somehow. The curé was holding her hand and hurrying her along through the rain. As they came out upon the ascent leading to the châlet, Catharine saw a crowd of people down below upon the shingle, and some people standing in the little garden in front. "They have got him home," the curé said. "Let us hurry, my poor child; there is no time to lose."

Catharine gave a cry, and put her hand to her head, and began running through the rain. The people at her door made way for her; but no haste she could have made would have been of any avail.

The two young men had come upon the beach just as the other boats had been hauled up safe and dry; the men were waiting to give a helping hand to the poor Lefebvres, whose boat—*La Belle Marion*—had just appeared through the mist. It was endeavoring to round a little promontory which jutted out into the sea beyond the terrace of the châlet, and which, with the rocks at the other extremity of the village, helped to form a small harbor for the fishing-boats. The name of the place came from this little natural port. There were some sunk rocks round the promontory against which the water dashed fiercely at all times. To-day the whole horizon was upheaving and tossing in the twilight. There was one faint gleam in the west where the black waves were tumbling, and where clouds seemed to be shifting and tearing behind the mist, while below the terrible flushing sea was sobbing in passionate fury. Each time the boat attempted to weather the point round which it had to pass before making for the shore, the shrieking wind and the great throbbing flood tide drove it back again and again; once a great wave came rolling from afar, gathering strength as it approached, and completely covered the poor little laboring bark.

There was a cry of terror from the poor women looking on, but the water rolled away, and the three sailors were still there, fighting for their lives upon this terrible battle-field. Two or three of the people upon the beach hurried to the little promontory of which mention has been made. There was only standing-place for two or three. Dick and Fontaine were among the number. Fontaine was very much excited; he gesticulated vehemently, and with the others shouted to the men; but the wind carried their voices away. The storm was at its height. The white horses were dashing against the embankment at the extremity of the maire's little garden, and the spray came washing over the promontory. The wind shrieked like a human voice. The poor little boat seemed doomed; in its efforts to get under shelter it came too near the wind, and once again entirely disappeared. It was like a miracle to the lookers-on, standing helpless on the beach, to see that when it emerged a second time, bottom upward, from the water, the three men were clinging to it still; but it only rose to be drifted rapidly past into the mist by the furious tide from the shore. It passed only some twenty yards from the sand-bank upon which they were standing—Fontaine and Dick, and the two other men.

"Good heavens! one of them is gone," said Dick, beginning, by a sort of instinct, to fasten a rope round his waist.

Fontaine pointing to an object floating upon a wave. "Look," said he, "what is that?" and as he spoke, in his excitement, he seized a rope, and dashed into the water before any one could prevent him. Poor fellow, it was only a barrel, and as he caught at it it slipped from his grasp. There came a shriek from the wind, and a sudden squall of rain, and the rope came slack into the hand of the man who held it. "He has let go the rope," said one of the men, horrified, and then, somehow, it was Dick, in his turn, who was struggling in the sea.

It was a strange and awful moment as he rose upon the great roaring wave which caught him off his feet. The sky seemed to fall to meet him, his heart stood still, chill mountains were rising and falling. At first he was quite conscious; he could even notice a long string of black sea-weed pass before his face. Suddenly, sooner than he had expected, he seemed flung with a dash against some floating substance, which he clutched; the water closed over his head; and then they began to pull the rope in from the shore. He scarcely knew what he was grasping; his senses seemed to fail; stunned and bewildered, he struggled through the terrible valley of the shadow of death. When he came

to himself he was lying on the shingle, some one was pouring brandy down his throat, and some one else was rubbing his hands.

Richard sat up, bewildered. They had carried him far away to a sheltered place, where they were less exposed to the storm; the sea was roaring still, but the fury of the wind had abated. As he looked, he saw that some people were carrying away the lifeless form of a man upon their shoulders; a women with fluttering garments, and a child, sobbing in piteous tones, were trudging alongside.

"Thank God!" said Madame de Tracy, flinging her arms round Dick's neck, while Jean nodded and put up his brandy-flask.

"You must take him home in the carriage, mamma," said Tracy; "and now I will go and see how it fares with my poor Fontaine."

How it fared! He lay quite still upon his bed, with Toto still sobbing and holding his hand, and the old Mérards coming and going with scared white faces, and with remedies that were not wanted now, for he would suffer no more. Some terrible blow in the water had stunned him to death. It was no living man that poor Dick had brought to shore. Poor Fontaine had been dashed by the storm against the barrel or some sunken rock.

Dear simple heart! So foolish, so absurd, so confident, so tender and thoughtful for others! "He could swim like a fish," he had said, to some one. "It was not for him to remain behind when others were going to their deaths." Ridicule is hushed, the humble are crowned with good things when the solemn wave which cast Fontaine upon the unknown shore comes for each in turn. Some of those who had laughed at his odd, kindly ways were waiting outside in the rain with eyes full of tears; some who had prayed more fervently, felt more deeply, perhaps realized the solemn mysteries of life and death more vividly, than this simple soul, were awe-stricken and silent as they thought of him now, for he was wiser than they. Love thy neighbor as thyself is the divine law of life, and if ever man fulfilled it cheerfully, unpretendingly, it was Fontaine. He had done his task gayly, kindly, ungrudgingly; he had gone his way, and died in harness.

Madame de Tracy awoke from troubled sleep in great agitation and depression on the morning after the storm. She could not rest: her nerves had been greatly shaken by the terrible calamity of the day before, by the sight of the poor little widow's terror and anguish. The good châtelaine longed to be of use to her, but Catharine had begged her to go, to leave her alone.

Poor lady! all night long she had wondered, reproached herself, sorrowed for her friend, trembled, and reproached herself again. Madame de Tracy rose at last from her uneasy bed, where the little sharp points of conscience were piercing the down and the elastic mattresses; she went to one of the windows, and opened it, and looked out. From this window she could see the châlet far away, and a bit of the sea and of the beach, upon which a light was burning, and she saw that the shingle was quite black with the sea-weed which the night's storm had cast up. The châlet looked very still; no one seemed moving; but pres-

white cap-strings flying, as if it had been five o'clock in the afternoon instead of in the morning. "Barbe, go to Mr. Richard's door and ask him how he feels."

"Madame, he is asleep," said Barbe; "his door was open as I passed."

"Out of the Valley of the Shadow of Death."

ently from one of its upper windows there came a light.

Madame de Tracy looked at it with a pain aching and tugging at her kind old heart; she waited for a while, and then rang for Barbe, who appeared presently, bright and smiling, with

"Asleep! ah! perhaps it is the best thing for him. Tell me, is any one stirring in the house?"

"I think, madame, that M. Le Comte is rising."

"Barbe! go and knock gently at his door. Ah! no; prepare my dressing things and a small cup of coffee, and one also for yourself. I want you to come with me to the châlet. I must go and see after that poor child. Ah! what a terrible scene! I little thought when they sent for me . . ."

When Barbe and her mistress reached the village it was all alive with early voices. The morning after the storm had broken with brilliant sunshine, although great mountains of clouds still hung mid-air. The doors were open, the people busily coming and going, the children half-dressed were peeping, the early plants in the gardens were bathed in brightness. Even Madame Potier was at her unopened shop. She stared at Madame de Tracy, who, for the first time for many years, appeared in public without her frizzy curls.

"You have heard the news, madame?" she cried. "They came back in the night. They managed to get on shore at St. Laurent! It is a miracle." From the steep ascent to the châlet Madame de Tracy could see the figures crowding down below like ants, to clear away the great piles of black sea-weed, and gather the harvest which the storm had cast up upon the shore. Nanon had her *hotte* full of the long hanging fringes: carts heaped with the fluttering ribbons slowly rolled away. Poor Catharine, too, saw the sight, looking out at early dawn, and languidly wondering what the bright lights moving here and there upon the beach could mean. Were they watching as she was? It seemed to her like a great pall cast up out of the sea, and she turned away with a sickening pang and a groan. She was afraid she had awakened Toto, who was lying asleep in a great chair, but the poor child only stirred uneasily, and breathed gently to sleep again.

About midday the storm came on again with so much fury that they were obliged to close the shutters of the châlet, and burn candles all day long.

On the third day it abated, and poor Fontaine was laid in his grave.

Once after the funeral Catharine saw the little feather brush which had vexed her so often lying on a table. She caught it up, the poor little widow, in her long black dress, and covered it with kisses and tears. Tears of such tender love, and longing, and remorse; no hero of romance, no knight dying in tournament, could have inspired truer and more tender sorrow.

On the third day after the storm Reine came walking quietly across the fields from the station, wrapping her cloak round about her, for the evening was chill. Every thing looked dusky, silent; low pale lights were shining through the broken heaps of cloud that were, at last, dispersing in the west. The salt pool under the dark bushes at the end of the road was gleaming with these pale lights. The horses in the fields were moving here and there, scarcely distinguishable in the darkness. Just over the farm, where the clouds had not yet risen, a little bit of red moon was hanging. The lights were pale chilly gold; but some deep shadows were heaping against the faint background. The windows of the farm were lighted up warmly, and looked home-like and welcoming to the young mistress of the house as she reached the great arch and went in.

She thought her own home had never looked so home-like, with its friendly seamed face, and quaint yet familiar aspect. She had a feeling as of a living friend or spirit of the hearth welcoming her, and inclosing her within open arms. She was glad to come back to liberty, to daily work—glad to meet her grandfather—glad to meet Dick once more. But something—a presentiment, perhaps, growing out of the feelings of the last few days—seemed to mix with the happiness which she felt. It was like a little bitter taste, a little passing fear—like a small cloud no bigger than a man's hand rising out of the horizon.

We all know how strangely, as we travel on in life, we suddenly reach new countries, states of mind, and of being, undreamt of, or at least unrealized by us. Those terrible phantoms of our youth—the selves to be of the future—come silently upon us before we are aware. They come vigorously at first, impatiently, with quick blood flowing. Then more indifferent. Then middle-aged, careworn, lean and slippered figures, advancing quietly out of the unknown, whispering secrets to us which we have not suspected, telling us truths that we sometimes hate to hear, sometimes thank heaven with unspeakable relief for knowing at last. There had been a strange revelation to Reine in that sudden withdrawing of the curtain of the chapel. She had seen, as it were, the thoughts, the unexpressed anxieties of her secret heart, in flesh and blood, there actually represented before her. The sight might have meant nothing if it had not been for the feelings which had preceded it: Dick at his ease among those rustling silks and furs; Catharine there, and, as it were, one of them. What had Reine in common with it all? Nothing—ah! nothing but her great love. So great it was that she sometimes felt alone in it: her love, which was as a pain and a burden to her, for she could not express it. It was scarcely a part of herself, she thought sometimes. It seemed to her like something from without, bearing down upon her from a great distance. She could only offer it up with terror and awe, in solemn sacrifice to an unknown God. Alas! poor woman, these great silent emotions are not the offerings which are accepted most willingly in this good-humored world. Thousands of little affectionate fires are burning on our neatly-blackened hearths, in our kitchens, in our hospitals and refuges. We deal out our fuel in scuttlefuls, and put in a few sticks of sentiment if the flame is very low; but I think Reine would have lighted a great pile, if she could have heaped upon it all the most worthy and valuable things; flung into it all the rich flowers, sweet fruit, and a few bitter herbs and incense, set fire to it all, and walked herself into the flames had she seen the occasion. Reine, with all her defects and her tenderness, her jealousy, her fidelity, her passionate emotions, her angry, rough words, could speak of the small passing feelings of an instant; but it was so hard to her to put words to the great harmonious discords of her secret heart that she rarely tried to do so. It was in the look of her eyes, the flush of her face, its sometimes tender brilliance of anger and sweetness, that Richard Butler could read her heart.

Although Reine was old for her years in feeling, she was young in the knowledge of the world, and many a child of thirteen is wiser than she was then. It is only as women grow older and know more of life that they escape from the Rhadamanthine adoration which haunts their inexperience. They find out later how fallible all human judgments are—how unsatisfactory and incomplete—and they discover, when it is too late sometimes, that the tall superior beings who are to take the calm direction of their poor little flustered souls are myths and impossibilities.

Poor Reine's ideal had appeared to her through the bars in company with two rustling ladies of another country, and class, and religion to her own. Little combinations which at one time and to some people seem utterly shifting and unmeaning, to others are arrested forever in their minds. A certain set of emotions have been silently leading up to this particular instant, and date from it ever after. The girl walked across the court with the heavy, deliberate footstep of the Chrétiens. The ladies of the d'Argonges family, her mother's ancestors, had not been in the habit of wearing such heavy leather shoes; but one of them, Jeanne d'Argonges, had once been painted in a peasant dress with the same old golden crucifix hanging round her neck that Reine now wore. She used to be called "La Fée," and the girl had often heard her mother tell the story of her sad end, and how she died of a cruel word. Reine was like the picture, poor Madame Chrétien thought, and she had been used to laugh and say that perhaps her daughter's beauty came to her from the drop of fairy blood in her veins.

As she came in, Petitpère, who was sitting by the fire, looked up and smiled at her, and knocked the ashes out of his pipe.

CHAPTER XX.

NEVER, NEVER.

PETITPÈRE looked up and smiled, and shook his head a moment after, as he began the recital of all that had befallen them since Reine had been away. It was too true that sad and terrible things had happened, and yet tobacco and gossip were not the less sweet because storms had raged and misfortunes thickened; and the old fellow puffed his pipe, and leisurely recounted his story. "Hé! poor boy, who would have thought it?" said old Chrétien, as he finished

G

the little tragedy. "He ought to be alive at this moment, and there he was in the cimetière, while two old fellows were still in their sabots." Strangely enough, poor Fontaine had signed his will that very morning, in the presence of M. le Curé and his gardener, so Barbeau reported. It was not known for certain, but it was said that he had left every thing to his widow for her life, and appointed her sole guardian to his boy. Poor little woman! it was a rude shock for her. People talked of her return to England. Then Père Chrétien went on to other things: The white cow was ill: it had been hurt in the nostril; Barbean had examined the wound; he thought badly of it; and, by the way, what was the matter with Madame la Comtesse? She had been up at the farm asking all manner of questions, ferreting here and every where. "She didn't discover much," said old Chrétien, with a chuckle; "but take care, my girl: she looked malicious; I could see it plain enough." Barbeau, too, had commented upon the circumstance. "They don't like the Englishman to come too often, that is not hard to divine. Only this morning I had to send him off very short," said Petitpère, complacently. "That sort of person it comes, and goes, and amuses itself, and thinks itself of consequence. He might have broken his head in the sea in the place of poor Fontaine for all he cared. "Voilà," the old fellow concluded philosophically, "Barbeau says there is no depending—"

"Oh, don't, don't, Petitpère," cried poor Reine, flinging herself down upon the oak bench against the wall, and beginning to cry. "Poor Fontaine, poor friend, poor, poor Catharine! Oh, what a sad world! Oh, how bitter was life!" she cried, in her pathetic voice, hiding her face in her hands, while the sobs came faster and faster. "Fontaine dead; that kind creature, so alive, so full of gentleness and goodness."

Poor soul, was it only for Fontaine that she was mourning, and did her tears flow for all sad hearts, all future troubles, all possible separation?

She was sitting there still; the old man had put down his pipe, and was patting her on the shoulder with his horny old fingers, and doing his best to console her.

"Now then, now then," said he, "you are not his widow to give way to desolation like this. Hush! there is some one coming. It is perhaps Barbeau . . ."

But even the hated name of Barbeau did not rouse poor Reine as did the step upon the tiled floor of the kitchen, and the voice which gladly exclaimed and called her by her name, and then the sweet tear-stained face looked up, and the pathetic eyes met Dick's proud glad glance. For a minute Reine forgot all her doubts, jealousy, hard resolves—forgot every thing but Dick for a minute, as he stood before her, holding both her hands in his, and then he spoke.

"You have been badly wanted, dear Reine. I have come for you. I promised that poor little woman to bring you back to her. I knew I should find you this time . . . ."

Why did he speak? Ah! why, if this was all he had to say? The tender heart seemed suddenly to grow hard and rough, the light died out of the wistful eyes. Why did he speak, if his first words were to be of Catharine? It was in vain that the girl tried to hush the devilish voice, the hateful thought away. Reine stood, with dry eyes and a pale face, glancing from Dick to Petitpère, who was once again sitting doubled up over the fire, shaking his head doubtfully to himself every now and then.

"Could you come now?" Dick persisted.

"Not to-night, sir," interrupted old Chrétien, without looking round. "Reine is tired, and has come from far. To-morrow she will visit the poor lady."

"Where is she?" Reine asked, in an odd, indifferent voice, beginning to tie on her cloak. Petitpère shrugged his shoulders. In a minute more Reine and Butler were crossing the dark court-yard together.

"I shall send Dominique after you with the cart," cried Petitpère, coming to the door. "Reine, you would have done better to stay."

They came out into the wide open plain. There were rolling mists, clouds, sudden winds; darkness was descending like a veil. The two went side by side through wreathing vapors; they scarcely broke the silence. For a minute Petitpère watched their dusky figures, which were hardly perceptible as they crossed the road and struck across the fields. Reine, walking along beside her lover, tried to put away all thought that was not of the present—of a present that to others might seem dark, and doubtful, and chill, and yet which to them both was vibrating with an unconscious and unspeakable delight, for were they not walking together through the darkness, and yet, at the same time, they were both doubting whether it was a reality that made them happy, or only a semblance of what might have been true once.

Alas! Reine was not strong enough to forbid sad thoughts of the future to come between them. She was so strange, so reserved, at once so agitated and so unmoved, that Butler, who had been looking forward all through his long sick watch to this happy meeting, was disappointed, wounded, and pained. When Catharine had sent for him, and begged him to bring her friend, it was not of this Reine he had been thinking, but of another, tender and full of sympathy. This was so sad and so cold that she seemed to freeze him over and sadden him, and all the while the poor soul was aching and sickening for the loving words, the tender reassurances she had waited and hoped to hear. It was in vain Dick tried to extort the sympathy from her he wanted. She would not, could not respond. Reine was for the moment wondering who might be most to be pitied if—if—— She interrupted him once when he was speaking of Catharine.

"Do you know that Madame de Tracy was up at the farm yesterday? She asked my grandfather a great many questions. Can she suspect the truth? Can Madame Fontaine have told her . . . ."

"I am sure she guesses the real state of the case," Dick said; "but Catharine Fontaine has not told her. Poor little woman! she has other things to think of just now."

"Is she very unhappy?"

"How can you ask? Should not you be unhappy if I had been drowned instead of Fontaine?"

The girl shivered, and then suddenly, with a passionate movement, drew her hand from his arm, and almost pushed him away.

"I am not married to you," she said, bitterly and furiously; "perhaps if I were only your widow, I could bear to part from you. Widows recover and marry again . . . ."

"Hush, Reine!" said Dick, angrily.

"Why do you mind my saying this?" persisted the girl, in her rough, grating voice.

"Because it is not like you to show no sympathy for some one in great sorrow. I think you must be already sorry for what you have said," the young man answered, gravely.

The girl did not speak, except, indeed, by a strange and wistful look, and walked on by his side in silence.

I have no excuse to make for Reine Chrétien, nor do I want to make one for her. With all her faults, her pride, her waywardness, there was a noble truth and devotion in her nature that spoke for itself, and forced you to forgive, even while you were vexed still and angry. The two walked on for a long way. For once evil and good were urging her in the same direction. Her jealousy was helping her to fulfill what she had grown to look upon as a duty.

Ah me! how often it happens in life that the generous self, the passionate great heart, unconscious, or perhaps ashamed of its own tenderness and nobility, takes, in self-defense, small means to accomplish great ends. Reine was one of those who would swallow a camel and strain at a gnat. We have all of us been blinded and ungrateful in our life, at one time or another, unconsciously accepting together the great sacrifice and the small one, grudgingly granted; we have all complained, perhaps, of the vexing word, the passing caprice of a moment, unconscious, ah! forever unconscious of the whole world, of love, of sacrifice, of utter devotion, which was ours just then to forget, to ignore, to accept without thanks, to abandon, if we could.

They had reached the gate of the châlet by this time; the moonlight seemed to be streaming every where.

"Oh, Richard, Richard, do you mean to tell me you do not know that she has always loved you?" cried Reine, with a sudden burst, and then with a scared sort of look, and she broke away from him, and pushed at the door of the house, and went in.

The poor little châlet, with all its absurd ornamentations, and whirling flags and weathercocks, looked so sad and forlorn, so black and hearse-like in the darkness. The blinds of some of the windows were down; a pale light shone in Catharine's window. Dick, pacing up and down outside in the moonlight, looked up at it more than once, and laughed a little bitterly to himself over the perversity of women. He did not like Reine the better for her jealousy. It was not worthy of her, he thought. The house was very dark and silent within and without. Monsieur and Madame Mérard had gone away for a few days; Madame Binaud had come for them, and Catharine had piteously begged them to go—to leave her with Toto. She was only longing for silence and rest.

Poor old Mérard's little piping voice quavered when he came to say good-by, and his jolly face seemed circled with dark round wrinkles which had not been there before. "Pauvre petite," said he, kissing the two little cold clinging hands which he held in his. Madame Mérard, too, seemed changed and greatly shaken. She said little, but trotted about, overturning drawers, and keeping vigilant watch over the goings-on in the house. Just before starting she carried up a cup of strong broth to Catharine, which she had made with her own hands. "Drink it down hot," said she. "There is a good pound of meat in it, for I arranged it myself."

Dick would not have thought Reine hard or perverse could he have seen into the room from where the faint ray of light was streaming, and where poor little Catharine was sitting on a low chair by the smouldering fire, while Reine knelt beside her, holding her hand in a tender clasp. Reine had that strange gift of healing and comfort which some people possess; there was strength and peace in the touch of her strong gentle hands, and in the wise, wistful look of her eyes. Catharine spoke a few broken words telling her how it had happened, speaking of Dick's courage and devotion. Reine listened, gazing into the fire, keeping time with her heart to Richard's footsteps outside. It was long before she listened to them again; the clock ticked monotonously, and time went on.

And then they heard a voice speaking down below. "Justine, do not let Mademoiselle Chrétien go without seeing me," said somebody.

"It is Madame de Tracy," said Catharine, languidly. "She has been here all day."

It was Madame de Tracy's voice; it was Madame de Tracy herself who stood waiting in ambush in the kitchen, waiting in agitation, palpitation, and excitement, expecting her prey, not without some alarm, poor lady; for her own claws were not very fierce, nor her bites very fatal, and, dragon though she was, she would have liked to run away. Justine the cynical saw that something was going on. It did not concern her; she only shrugged her shoulders as she plodded about the house from one creaking wooden room to another. She was putting away the linen in the maire's little office, which was now, at last, disponible. It was convenient and near the kitchen; she had always wanted a place for her table-cloths. Coming down stairs with an arm full of linen, she met Reine leaving Catharine's room. "You are wanted in the kitchen," said she. "Madame de Tracy certainly will not let you go without seeing her." And as she spoke, Madame de Tracy, with her bonnet all on one side, came out at the sound of the voices, and held open the door with much difficulty.

"I have to speak to you; come in here, if you please. My nephew is outside, but it is to you, mademoiselle, I address myself. He is waiting for you—do not deny it; I know all—every thing." And the countess blazed round upon the peasant girl, who, however, seemed but little discomposed by the attack. "Ah! mademoiselle," continued Madame de Tracy, suddenly changing from ferocity to supplication, "if you do really care for that foolish, impetuous boy, you will forgive me and sympathize with me when I implore you to reflect upon the sacrifice he is making—a sacrifice that will disgrace him, and drag him down in the eyes of the world. It is so hard in its judgments. Is that door securely closed? I would not for the world that Justine should overhear, that Dick should suspect me of influencing you. He was furious once not long ago, when I foolishly dreaded another attraction, but this would be still less . . . still more — Catharine at least was . . ." The poor lady stopped short, embarrassed, unable to finish her sentence; well she might be, for she caught sight of Reine's indignant cheeks burning, and of the much-dreaded Dick himself coming in through the glass door. A chill night-wind surged in as he opened the door, of which the shutters had not yet been closed. He had been quietly walking outside up and down, biding his time. It had come now; and now Dick guessed in an instant what had happened; he went straight up to Reine, and put his arm round her, as if to defend her, and yet Reine was strong enough to defy the poor trembling, agitated lady without his assistance.

"You mustn't say any thing to Reine, Aunt Matilda, that you wouldn't say to me," said Dick, haughtily.

"Dear boy," cried Madame de Tracy, more and more fluttered and anxious, "indeed, and indeed, I only speak for your good and hers. Of course you have passed your word, but you do not know the world as I do, nor to what you are exposing . . . you—you . . ."

"Hush!" said Dick, speaking savagely, almost for the first time in his life. "Reine and I understand one another very well, and are quite willing to put up with any inconvenience," and his voice softened: he looked at the girl with a smile. But she did not answer; she was quite pale, and her eyes were on fire; she drew herself up to her full length, and stood there in the moonlight in her country dress, looking like a wraith; even her words sounded faint and toneless.

"Heaven knows," she said, quietly, "that I am ready to die for you, Richard, but I will never marry you—never, never. It is not for the first time that I hear these things, that I reflect upon the sacrifice you make, upon the danger of marriage ill assorted and unhappy. Nothing will ever change my affection; you are part of my life, of my prayers, ever since I first knew you . . ." The passionate cadence of her voice broke into a sob. Reine spoke with emotion, feeling that she was safe in Madame de Tracy's agitated presence; she imagined Richard would say nothing, do nothing, but somehow she was mistaken, and she found herself folded in the young man's arms.

"My Reine," he said, "I want no words—I understand." But the girl put herself quickly away out of his embrace. What strange love-parting was this in the sad house of mourning.

"You do not understand me," cried Reine; "and you, madame, need not be so much afraid of the harm I shall do him," she said, passionately, turning to Madame de Tracy. "I shall not drag him down; I shall not force him to keep his word; I shall not disgrace him!"

The girl's anger and sorrow had gradually reached a hysterical and almost uncontrollable point. The things Madame de Tracy had glibly explained, meaning no harm, poor lady! had nearly maddened her. Her allusion to Catharine was the last drop in the brimming cup. In vain Dick tried to calm and to soothe her. She did not listen; she would not look at him even; for a minute she stared through the glass door into the moonlight without, and then at Madame de Tracy, agitated and fleckered by the blaze of the fire.

"Catharine, of whom you spoke just now," cried the girl, "would have been a thousand thousand times more suited than I should ever be. Ah! do not interfere again, madame. You do not know what you are doing!" and with a scared sort of look Reine broke away from Dick, and pushed at the glass door, and ran out into the night. She had forgotten all about it, but she found Dominique, with the cart, waiting at the garden gate. Dick, following an instant after only, came in time to see her drive away.

I think, if he had caught her then, if he had scolded, and then forgiven her, all would have been right between them then; but the horse set off at a trot down the hill; the cart rolled away with a dull jolt of wheels over the sodden earth; mists came between them, and distance greater and greater. Butler was too angry and hurt to follow her at the time—more angry, I think, because she went off in the cart than for all she had said to vex him.

"Never—never." Did some one whisper it in his ear? What a strange creature—lovely, womanly, tender, and pathetic, and furious; how hard to satisfy, how difficult to love, how impossible not to love.

Dick spent a sulky evening at the chateau, smoking by himself in the smoking-room, while Madame de Tracy retired with fluttering dignity to her own apartment. Jean thought it a bad business; but it was his maxim not to interfere. It was no affair of his. Dick was old enough to attend to his own concerns; and though Mrs. Beamish and Ernestine went down upon their knees to him, they could not undo the past, or prevent him from thinking that there was but one woman in the world, and her name was Reine Chrétien.

Dick made up his mind very quietly without asking any one's leave. He was a little touched, and very much provoked, by the allusions to poor Madame Fontaine; but he hoped there was some mistake, and rather avoided dwelling upon that part of the subject. Reine had been jealous, as women are sometimes. He walked up to the farm before breakfast. The fine weather had come at last; fields and furrows were twinkling with early dew; a thousand lights, and crystals, and refractions were shining out of the earth; a cheerful sound of labor echoed under the dazzling morning vault. Old Chrétien was sitting on the bench sunning himself outside the great archway in his blue smock; the queer old pinnacles, and chimney-stacks, and pigeon-cotes were all distinct against the clear heaven, and the two tall poplar-trees on the roadside showed every twig and spray full with the coming leaves. Paris came to meet Dick, shaking his lazy long body and wagging his tail. Petitpère sat staring at the field where his men were busy digging up vegetables and loading a cart.

"Good-morning," cried Dick, cheerfully. "Monsieur Chrétien, where shall I find your granddaughter?"

"That is more than I can tell you," said the old fellow, looking utterly vacant and stupid. "Reine is gone, and I am busy enough in her absence. As monsieur sees, I am getting in my turnips;" and he pointed to the field where they were growing, and where the laborers were busy digging up the earth. It was the field which the lovers had crossed in the darkness the night before.

"Gone," said Dick, looking at the turnips, without seeing any thing before him.

"She is gone back to the convent," the old man said. "I should not like it for myself, but she finds her pleasure there."

"Did she leave no letter—no message for me?" Richard asked, trying to light a cigar, though his fingers were trembling as he did so. Petitpère gazed stupidly at the young man.

"I was to let her know as soon as you were gone, that she might come back and see to the fatting of the pigs," said he; "that was what she said."

With a sudden movement, Dick threw the unlighted cigar away over the hedge.

"She need not delay her return on my account," said Butler, flushing up, and turning his back to Petitpère. "I shall leave the place to-day for good. Pray tell her so when she comes back to—to her pigs."

Old Petitpère shrugged his shoulders for the last time in this little history, and rubbed his old knees, pleased with the effect of that parting shaft; and yet he was a little sorry, too, for the young fellow, as he went swinging angrily along the road, and disappeared at the turn by the willow-trees.

Dick was far away, safe among the green pastures and cool waters of Lambswold, and Reine might have come back from her convent without fear of meeting him; but many and many a day went by before the girl returned to the farm-kitchen, to her accustomed ways and works, and when she came, it was a wan, and weak, and weary woman recovering from an illness through which the good nuns had nursed her. Poor Reine! she came back to Petitpère, and the pigs, and the cows for companionship and sympathy. She could not think of the past, it filled her with such doubt and remorse; she did not dare to contemplate the future, it seemed so endless, so gray, so unbearable; she would not have been sorry to die in the convent in the sunny ward among the tranquil nuns, and so to solve the difficulty and riddle of her life. But it was only a low nervous fever from which she had suffered, and she knew that there was no chance of any end to it but that prosaic end of getting well and going home to her dull and neglected duties. If Catharine had been at Petitport she would have found comfort and happiness with the tender little woman; but a chance had happened, which would have been stranger if it had happened sooner, and Catharine was away in England with her sisters, looking after some property which had come to her and to them. What did she want with it now? Fontaine had provided for her, and she liked better to owe ease and comfort to him, to his care and his tender thought for her, than to a chance by which Lady Farebrother had died before she could sign her name to a will. Mr. Bland would have been a good many thousand pounds the richer if the poor lady had lived a few hours longer. He never had even the satisfaction of knowing it; for, though both the doctor and lawyer were sent for, they both came too late. As it was, Catharine's two little sisters came in for no inconsiderable portion of their aunt's possession, and a certain sum was left to Catharine, their guardian, by their mother' will.

It was in autumn, this year, after poor Fontaine's death, that I staid at Petitport, and first made Reine Chrétien's acquaintance on the sea-shore, as I described in the beginning of my little history. These were not prosperous times. There was a great deal of sickness in the village, the harvest had failed, and wherever I went I heard complaints, and witnessed pain and suffering. Reine seemed to be every where, helping and tending her poorer neighbors. It is impossible not to believe that some people have an unexplained power, which must be magnetic of its kind, for healing and soothing pain. Reine possessed this odd influence over the sick, and was conscious of it, although she could not account for it; she unfortunately had full opportunity for exercising her gift. Fever and famine were common enough in the poor little village; these two grim visitors were almost as certain to come in their season as the bathers and holiday-makers with the summer and sunshine. This year fell unusually heavy upon the little population; there was hardly a family that had not some member stricken with the fever. Reine herself lost her grandfather soon before I came to the village. For some time she was living by herself in a great empty farm-house on a hill. When I knew her first she seemed to take to me, perhaps because I was English, perhaps because I happened to know something of the people she most cared for, partly because I was fascinated by her. After that day on the sands I went up to see her once or twice at the farm. A widow woman was living with her, a certain Madame Marteau, to whose little daughter she was greatly attached.

Poor Reine! these were hard times for her. On the very day I first made her acquaintance she had heard a report from Justine at the châlet concerning Catharine, which had stirred up many a feeling still fresh and vivid, though she scarcely believed the report. Sometimes she spoke of the past, but with evident pain and shrinking, and doubt and remorse. Had she done right? Had she done wrong? She seemed to be sure of nothing but of the love which was in her.

Once, only once, she sat down to write to him. She never meant to send the letter, but it was a relief to her to put down upon paper all that was in her heart—all her loving remembrance; to write the words of benediction, although he might never need her blessing now. When she had written the tender little scrawl, she burnt it; but the words were somewhere, every where, she thought, as she saw the cinders float away. She said to herself that no fire could burn them out, nothing could destroy them; in some distant world, if not in this one, they would find him.

CHAPTER LAST.

"TURN, FORTUNE, TURN THY WHEEL."

ONE day, Reine, walking down the village street, met Madame Mérard coming from the châlet, where she had been superintending some packing and re-ordering. The old lady was trotting heavily along, with a large packet on her arm. She was panting fiercely, in a state of fume and excitement. No wonder. "She had heard an announcement," she said, "which she had always predicted—always. What else was to be expected of a young woman so entirely engrossed by society and amusement as Madame Fontaine had always shown herself?" Madame Mérard declined to give her authority for the news she had heard. "Non! time would prove the truth of her assertions. Well-informed and dispassionate persons had assured her that Catharine Fontaine was on the eve of contracting a second and highly advantageous alliance with Mr. Butler. In that event, the châlet and all the elegant fittings would return to Toto. Most providentially a clause to that effect had been inserted in the will, at the curé's suggestion; for the poor infatuated Charles would never have shown this necessary provision. Poor man, already forgotten! Ah! how differently she, Madame Mérard, had acted under similar circumstances. Although assiduously pressed, within six months of her widowhood, to make up her mind, by no less than three different gentlemen, in no wise connected with one another, she had refused to give any answer whatever for a space of two whole years, during which their attentions had been unremitting. At the end of that time, having made Monsieur Mérard's acquaintance, she had dismissed the other aspirants with every mark of esteem and consideration. Nowadays things were different. Do not seek for disinterested affection. Oh, no," said Madame Mérard, " for it would be no use." And the old lady stumped away at her quickest pace up the road and across the field; she had business at the chateau, she vaguely intimated, snorting and shaking her head. In truth, her authority was only that of Justine at the châlet, who had heard the news from Baptiste at the chateau, who had it in a letter from Barbe, now in England with her mistress; and Madame Mérard was anxious to gather every particular.

Poor Reine did not take so much pains to verify the news. She had heard some such report before, that seemed corroborated now. It was natural, and only what she had expected all along. The blow had fallen at last. Amen. She knotted her two hands together, and walked along erect and abstracted, with eyes that seemed looking at a far-off distance, silent, with a passionate cry in her heart. She walked on to the little village grave-yard on the roadside, behind the iron railing where her mother was lying, and Petitpère resting under the poplar-tree, and where, in a sunny corner, Fontaine's name was carved upon the stone cross which Catharine had put up to his memory, and over which the ivy was creeping.

The struggle which came to Reine then was that sore one which comes to each one of us at one time or another; when passionate hopes die away, and longings, how eager none can know, except each one for himself; when the last hope fails, and when the aching void and emptiness of the future seem bearing down like the inevitable dusk at the end of a busy day. Darkness, and oblivion, and death would seem welcome at such times, rather than the dim shadow and gray silence of these sad twilight hours—dark gray, though the sun is shining, perhaps, and the summer lights flooding the land. Then the fight begins, a lonely one with no witness, for who can see or understand another's mood? And the fight is this. " I

wanted that, I tried for this, I would have been the person that I am not, I would have liked the happiness which is denied me. Give, give, O Lord, unto thy servant. Is not happiness my right? Is not content my right, and success, and love, and prosperity?" And even amid the fierce pangs of pain and disappointment the mad question is answered. " Why should not sorrow and disappointment be thy right? Why should not the experience of grief be thine; the knowledge of evil as well as of good? Submit, oh, submit, poor heart!" And the spirit seems to speak to the weary body, and one last desperate effort comes for resignation, for obedience to the terrible teaching, for acquiescence.

We bow to Heaven that willed it so.

In this frame of mind every thing all round about seems to have an answering voice to urge, to help, to comfort. When all seems lost, there comes a new courage, a new peace dawning overhead, life bursting from the dry branches, light from the clouds, the very stones cry out and testify in the world all round about. Reine, walking homeward along the cliff, read a thousand meanings in the sights along her way—peace, resignation, regret, remembrances more or less aching, but singing a song all the while, which echoed with hitherto undreamt-of meaning: there was comfort in the sound of the sea, in its flowing music, its minor notes, in the cries for help, in the rush of wind blowing here and there, in the very moods of her heart, changing from one emotion to another. Even the trembling shadow of the poplar-tree upon the turf seemed to whisper peace to her and tranquillity; and so, by degrees, her sad excitement abated. She did not reproach herself; she did not know now whether she had been most to blame for that which she should regret all her life; but when she reached home, she felt somehow that the worst was over. Little Josette ran up to her, and pulled her by the hand into the every-day world again, telling her to come and see the galette she and her mother had cooked for dinner; Paris rubbed his head against his mistress's black gown; Madame Marteau came smiling to the door to greet her.

Reine, coming and going about her business with a pale face and a sad heart, all that day kept telling herself that it was too late to regret, but not too late to love still, and then she determined to write to Dick once again; and this time the letter was sent. It was addressed to Catharine, though it was intended for Dick. Only a few words, in the Frenchwoman's quaint, stiff handwriting: " I have heard news of you," she wrote. " With my whole heart I pray heaven for your happiness —that heart which is full of love for you, of hope for the future, and of faith in your tender friendship. You will come here some day —will you not?—both of you, and give me the greatest happiness which I can hope for on earth—the happiness of seeing you happy?"

And then Reine, holding Josette by the hand,

went and slipped the letter herself into the box in the village wall, where it lay until old Pierre, the postman, with his clumsy key and his old worn pouch, carried it away to Bayéux, across the plain.

Dick was sitting with Catharine when this letter was put into her hand. She flushed up, poor little widow, and began to tremble when she read it, and with a sudden movement half held it out to Butler, and then changed her mind and took it back once more; and so sat, without speaking for a minute, with her dark eyes fixed gravely upon his face. She looked like a child trying to remember some half-forgotten lesson, and Dick wondered what words she was trying to fashion. It was a long, low, old-fashioned room in which they were sitting,—the drawing-room of a house on the terrace at Rich-mond, with three deep windows looking out upon the loveliest haze and distance upon the river—wandering at its own sweet will—upon the showers of autumnal gold sparkling beneath the mists that were spreading to the silver hills. Toto and Totty were in one of the windows, whispering and exploding into sudden shrieks of laughter at one another's witticisms. Rosy was curled up over a novel on the floor; and Catharine, sitting in her little bowery corner, with some work and some flowers on her table, was looking prettier and more gentle than ever in her black dress, with her plaintive childish face crowned with the sad dignity of a widow's cap. So she sat talking to the melancholy and ill-humored young man in the arm-chair beside her. "You must find me a great bore," Dick was saying; "I come and grumble, and abuse every body and every thing. I tried to go back to my painting this morning—confound it, I can do nothing with it; I can do nothing but grum-ble." Dick often rode over to see the little wid-ow; he would come in the worst of spirits, and go away cheered and touched by Madame Fon-taine's constant kindness and sympathy. The little woman had learned out of the depths of her own morbid experiences to be tender, and gen-tle, and forbearing with others wandering in the same dreary labyrinth in which she had been utterly lost only a very little while ago; so it seemed to her, looking back. Things were dif-ferent now, and Catharine could not help won-dering why, sometimes, and feeling that to the dearest friend, the tenderest, the most loyal sim-ple heart that ever beat, she owed more than she could ever pay with a lifetime of love and fidel-ity. She did not feel any particular gratitude to Lady Farebrother, whose money had contrib-uted to the pleasant home and its various luxu-ries, and was doing more good now than it had ever done in the old lady's lifetime; but the helping hand, the kindness, the protecting love which first rescued her was Fontaine's, and Catharine did not forget it: one was a chance, the other a blessing. Catharine, sitting there with Reine's letter in her hand, wondered over the many changes and chances of this mortal

life. She knew well enough by this time that poor Madame de Tracy was only eager to re-pair the breach between her and her nephew; that Mrs. Butler and Catharine Beamish were longing to prevent the possible and horrible mis-alliance that was always hanging over the fam-ily; and that they would all have gladly and eagerly consented to a marriage between Ma-dame Fontaine and this terrible Richard. She sadly wonders why she, a widow woman, is deemed a fitter wife for Dick now than two years ago, when all her heart's best devotion was his. Catharine felt she loved him still, as some wom-en must love the ideal of their youth—loved him with a gentle, true-hearted friendship and faith-ful sympathy that would be always his; but not as Reine loved him. Ah! that love was alive, and did not die at its birth. As for Dick him-self, he made no profession of affection—he was sincerely fond of Catharine. He was touched—how could he help it?—by the knowledge of her old affection for him. He came, with a long-ing for sympathy, for a kind soul to talk to, from his empty, lonely house, to Catharine's tranquil, bright home. He came with a sad scorn for himself in his heart, but there he was sitting be-side her day after day. She suited him better than his own relations. Reine, who he thought was true as steel, had deceived him and jilted him. Catharine had but to put out her hand, he was not unwilling; and Catharine, still look-ing him full in the face, put out her hand, but Reine's little letter was in it.

"Oh, Richard," Madame Fontaine said, un-consciously calling him by his Christian name, "I want you to read this—to forgive me for what I am going to say—"

Her eyes were brimming, her voice was fail-ing, but she made a great effort and spoke. Just now every thing seemed of very little con-sequence to her in comparison with the great sadness which had long filled her heart. There was a pathos in her tones of which she was un-conscious, as she tried, by talking as straight and direct to the point as Reine herself might have done, to put away at once, forever, all mis-conception. At another time, perhaps, she could not have spoken as she did just then. But her sorrow still encompassed her like a shield; she was invulnerable; a new strength had come to her from her very weakness and remorse for the past.

"I did not love my husband as I ought to have loved him when I married him," she said. "I deserve any thing—every thing. Even this explanation is a punishment for my folly. But if I had to live my life again now, and if I might choose, with open eyes, between the man who loved me and —and—I would not have things otherwise. Oh, Richard, you do not think me ungrateful for speaking? I know all that pass-ed. Poor Reine—dear Reine," said the true-hearted little woman, "there is no one so noble, so faithful. She left you because she loved you. Do you know how ill she has been? Miss Wil-liamson (it was of the present writer that Catharine was speaking then) has written to me about her. She thinks she will die some day if you leave her much longer alone. Oh, Richard, dear friend, won't you forgive her and me, and go back to her again? No one has ever loved you as she does."

Those of my good friends who already despise Dick Butler, and who think him a poor creature at best, and no better than his paintings, will, I fear, despise him still more, for his eyes were full of tears when he looked up at last from the paper on which Reine's few words of sad congratulation were standing in black and white before him.

"God bless you, dear lady," he said, taking Madame Fontaine's outstretched hand, and starting up. "You have saved me from committing a great wrong. I will write to you to-morrow when I have seen her."

And then he went away quickly, without noticing the children, and a minute afterward they heard his horse's feet clattering down the road. Then the three children, who had been listening with all their ears, and perfectly understanding every thing, and thrilling with sympathy as children do, came and flung themselves upon the little widow, almost crushing her down upon the sofa.

"No, no, no," said Toto, in his broken English, "I shall not 'ave you marry. I want you, and when I'm a man . . ." "Oh, Cathy, you won't leave us again, will you? Promise, please promise," cried Totty, and Rosa said nothing, but threw away her novel, griped one of Cathy's poor little hands tight in hers, crushing it with all her might, until her sister, half laughing, half crying, had to call out for mercy. And so, with one last bright appealing look, Catharine happily disappears, in the children's adoring but somewhat tyrannical embrace.

Good-by, little Catharine. Yours is no hard fate, after all. Toto is your defender; Rosy and Totty your faithful companions; friends, and plenty, and peaceful leisure are yours now.

Courseulles, where the oysters are preserved, and where the establishment is situated of which poor Fontaine spoke with so much enthusiasm, is a dreary little tumble-down village of odds and ends; of broken barrels, torn garments, oyster-heaps, and swinging shutters, standing upon the border of a great mud marsh, which at low water reaches out for a mile or more to meet a gray and turbid sea. The oysters are sorted out in long tanks, according to size, and fatten undisturbed, and in their places, round a little counting-house which stands in the middle of these calm and melancholy waters. The shutters swing, in the village a child or two turns over the oyster-heaps, the ragged garments flutter in the wind. It is not a place likely to attract mere pleasure-seekers, and yet, as Dominique, the day after that little conversation at Richmond, comes leading the horse out of the stable of the inn at Courseulles, he meets a gentleman who has ridden over from Petitport upon M. de Tracy's bay mare, and who quietly asks him to see to the horse, and to tell him where Mademoiselle Chrétien is to be found.

"Mademoiselle is in the counting-house," says Dominique, staring and grinning, and showing his great red gums; and Richard, for it is Richard of course, makes his way across the desolate waste between the inn and the oyster-tanks, and opens a gate for himself, and walks along a narrow raised pathway leading to the little counting-house.

Before Butler could reach the door it opened, and Reine came out and stood for an instant looking at the great waste where the dredgers were at work, and where a dirty red gleam of sunset was glaring upon the mud. She sighed, and then she turned suddenly, feeling, as people do, that some one was watching her. Some one! She turned and looked with a quick, sudden motion, and then, although she stood quite still, all her heart seemed to go out to welcome the one person in the whole world she most wearied for, and least thought she should see ever again. She did not speak, but somehow she was in his arms, and her wondering, tender, passionate eyes were recounting silently all the story of the long sad months through which she had wasted; and as Dick looked at her when he saw her sweet face once more, the dreary marshes, the falling houses, seemed to be touched with some brightest and most sudden brilliance. Every thing was plain to them both. I don't think they either of them ever knew how or in what words the story was told—the best and most perfect story which belongs to this complaining world—to the world in which there are sad histories and wicked ones, in which some stories are well forgotten, and others, alas! never uttered, but in which the sacred inspiration of love comes now and again to kindle cold hearts, to brighten sad lives, to bless and to cheer the failing and doubtful, and to tell them that a living and sacred power is moving upon the troubled waters of life.

We most of us have seen at one time or another great rocks piled upon rocks, landslips, and devastations, blasted trunks of trees sliding down the fierce sides of the mountains, the overflow of angry waters, vapor floating mid air in the solitude. And Nature, working by some great law unknown, and only vaguely apprehended by us insects crawling a little way up the sides of her vast chasms, heaps and orders in some mighty fashion, and brings about noblest harmonies out of chaos. And so, too, out of the dire dismays and confusions of the secret world come results both mighty and gentle; great rocks stand shading daisies from the midday heat; trees uptorn by some avalanche lie soft upon lichen and little clinging mosses; there are fissures where the snow lies dazzling; and huge stones sliding down the sides of the mountain seem arrested by the soft sprays of gentle little creeping plants, whose green leaves sparkle against the granite.

FROM AN ISLAND.

FROM AN ISLAND.

I.

THE long room was full of people sitting quietly in the twilight. Only one lamp was burning at the far end. The verandah outside was dim with shadow; between each leafy arch there glimmered a line of sea and of down. It was a gray still evening, sad, with distant storms. St. Julian, the master of the house, was sitting under the verandah, smoking, with William, the eldest son. The mother and Mrs. William were on a sofa together, talking in a low voice over one thing and another. Hester was sitting at the piano with her hands in her lap, looking music, though she was not playing, with her white dress quivering in the gloom. Lord Ulleskelf, who had come over to see us, was talking to Emilia, the married daughter, and to Aileen, the youngest of the three; while I and my own little Mona and the little ones were playing at the other end of the room at a sort of twilight game of beating hands and singing sing-song nursery rhymes—haymaking, the children called it.

"Are there any letters?" said St. Julian, looking in at them all from his verandah. "Has Emmy got hers?"

"I have sent Rogers into Tarmouth to meet the post," said the mother; and as she spoke the door opened, and the post came in.

Poor Emmy's face, which had lighted up eagerly, fell in an instant: she saw that there was no foreign letter for her.

It was a small mail, not worth sending for, Mrs. St. Julian evidently thought as she looked at her daughter with her kind, anxious eyes. "Here is something for you, Emmy," she said; "for you," Queenie (to me). "My letter is from Mr. Hexham; he is coming to-morrow."

My letter was from the grocer :—

MRS. CAMPBELL is respectfully informed by Mr. Tiggs that he has sent different samples of tea and coffee for her approbation, for the use of Mr. St. Julian's household and family: also a choice assortment of sperms. Mr. Tiggs regrets extremely that any delay should have arisen in the delivery of the preserved cherries and apricots. He forwards the order this day, as per invoice. Mr. T. trusts that his unremitting exertions may meet with Mrs. C.'s approval and continued recommendation and patronage.

ALBERT EDWARD HOUSE.

September 21.

This was not very interesting, except to the housekeeper: Mrs. St. Julian had set me to keep house for her down here in the country. The children, however, who generally insisted upon reading all my correspondence, were much excited by the paragraph in which Mr. Tiggs mentioned cherries and dried apricots. "Why did Mr. Tiggs forget them?" said little Susan the granddaughter, solemnly. "Oh, I wish they would come!" said Nelly. "Greedy, greedy!" sung George, the youngest boy. Meanwhile the elders were discussing their correspondence, and the mother had been reading out Mr. Hexham's note :—

Lyndhurst, September 21.

HAVE you room for me, my dear Mrs. St. Julian, and may I come to-morrow for a few days with my van? I find it is a most delightful mode of conveyance, and I have been successful enough to take some most lovely photographic views in the New Forest. I now hope to explore your island, beginning with the "Lodges," if you are still in the same hospitable mind you were when I last saw you.

With best remembrances to your husband and the young ladies, your devoted

G. HEXHAM.

"I like Mr. Hexham. I am glad he is coming," said Mrs. St. Julian.

"This is an official-looking missive," said Lord Ulleskelf, holding out the large square envelope, with a great red seal, which had come for Emmy.

"What a handwriting!" cried Aileen. She was only fifteen, but she was taller already than her married sister, and stood reading over her shoulder. "What a letter! Oh Emmy, what a—"

But Mrs. St. Julian, seeing Emmy flush up, interposed again :—

"Aileen, take these papers to your father. What is it, my dear?" to Emilia.

"It is from my sister-in-law," Emilia said, blushing in the light of the lamp. "Mamma, what a trouble I am to you . . . . ! She says she is—may she come to stay . . . . ? And—and—you see she is dear Bevis's sister, and—"

"Of course, my dear," said her mother, almost reproachfully. "How can you ask?"

Emilia looked a little relieved, but wistful still. "Have you room? To-morrow?" she faltered.

Mrs. St. Julian gave her a kiss, and smiled and said, "Plenty of room, you goose." And then she read :—

To the Hon. MRS. BEVIS BEVERLEY, *The Island, Tarmouth, Broadshire.*

Scudamore Castle, September 21.

MY DEAR EMILIA,—Bevis told me to be sure and pay you a **visit in** his absence, if I had an opportunity, **and so I** shall come, if convenient to you, with **my** maid and a man, on Saturday, across country **from Scudamore** Castle. I hear I must cross from **Helmington.** I can not imagine how people can live on an island when there is the main-land for them to choose. Yours is not even an island on the map. Things have been very pleasant here till two days ago, when it began to pour with rain, and my stepmother arrived unexpectedly with Clem, and Clem lost her temper, and Pritchard spoilt my new dress, and several pleasant people went away, and I, too, determined to take myself off. I shall only stay a couple of days with you, so pray tell Mrs. St. Julian that I shall not, I hope, be much in her way. Do not let her make any changes for me; I shall be quite willing to live exactly as you are all in the habit of doing. Any room will do for my man. The maid need only have a little room next to mine. You won't mind, I know, if I go my own gait while I stay with you, for I am an odd creature, as I dare say you may have often heard from Bevis. I expect to feel dreadfully small with all of you clever artistic people, but I shall be safe from my lady and Clem, who would never venture to come near you.

My father is all alone at home, and I want to get back to him if I can steal a march on my lady. She is so jealous that she will not let me be alone with him for one hour if she can help it, in her absence. Before she left Castlerookham she sent for that odious sister of hers to play piquet with him, and there was a general scene when I objected. My father took part against me, so I started off in a huff, but he has managed to shake off the old wretch, I hear, and so I do not mind going back. I must say it is very pleasant to have a few half-pence that one can call one's own, and to be able to come and go one's own **way.** I assure you that the said half-pence do not last forever, however. Clem took £50 **to pay** her milliner's bill, and Bevis borrowed £100 before he **left, but I dare** say he will pay me back.

So good-bye, my dear Emilia, for the present.

Yours **ever.**   JANE BEVERLEY.

Mrs. St. Julian did not offer to show Lady Jane's letter to St. Julian, but folded it up with a faint **little** suppressed smile. "I think she **must** be a character, Emmy," she said. "I dare say she will be very happy with **us.** Queenie" (**to** me), "will you see what can be done to make Lady Jane comfortable?" and there was an end of the matter. Lord Ulleskelf went and sat out in the verandah, with the others until the storm burst which had been gathering, through which he insisted on hurrying home, notwithstanding all **they** could say to detain him.

We had **expected** Lady Jane by the boat which **brought our other guest** the next day, but only **Mr. Hexham's** dark close-cropped head appeared out of the carriage which had been sent to meet them. The coachman declared there was no lady alone **on** board. Emilia wondered why her **sister-in-law had** failed: the others took Lady **Jane's** absence very calmly, and after some five-o'clock tea St. Julian proposed a walk.

"Perhaps I had better stay," Mrs. Beverley said to her mother.

"No, my dear, your father will be disappointed. She can not come now," said Mrs. St. Julian, decidedly; "and if she does, I am here to receive her. Mr. Hexham, you did not see her on board? A lady alone. . . . ?"

No. Hexham had not seen any lone lady on board. There was a good-looking person who might have answered the description, but she had a gentleman with her. He lost sight of them at Tarmouth, as he was looking after his man, and his van, and his photographic apparatus. It was settled Lady Jane could not possibly come till next **day.**

II.

LADY JANE BEVERLEY had always declared that she hated three things—islands, clever people, and interference. She knew she was clever, but she did not encourage this disposition. It made people bores and radical in their own class of life, and forward if they were low. She was not pretty. No ; she didn't care for beauty, though she confessed she should be very sorry if she was not able to afford to dress in the last fashion. It was all very well for artists and such people to say the contrary, but she knew that a plain woman well dressed would look better than the loveliest dowdy that ever tied her bonnet-strings crooked. It was true her brother Bevis had thought otherwise. He had married Emilia, who was not in his own rank of life ; but Lady Jane supposed he had taught her to dress properly after her marriage. She had done her very best to dissuade him from that crazy step : once it was over she made the best of it, though none of them would listen to her ; and indeed she had twice had to lend him sums of money when his father stopped his allowance. It is true he paid her back, otherwise she really did not know how she could have paid her bills that quarter. If she had not had her own independence she scarcely could have got on at all or borne with all Lady Mountmore's whims. However, thanks to old aunt Adelaide, she need not think of any body but herself, and that was a very great comfort to her in her many vexations. As it was, Clem was forever riding Bazook, and laming her ponies, and borrowing money. Beverley and Bevis, of course, being her own brothers, had a right to expect she would be ready to lend them a little now and then ; but really Clem was only her step-sister, and considering the terms she and Lady Mountmore were on. . . . Lady Jane had a way of rambling on, though she was a young woman still, not more than six or seven and twenty. It was quite true that she had had to fight her own battles at home, or else she would have been utterly fleeced and set aside. Beverley, her eldest brother, never quite forgave her for being the old aunt's heiress, and did not help her as he should have done. Bevis was always away on his missions or in disgrace. Old Lord Mountmore was feeble and almost childish. Lady Mountmore was not a pleasant person to deal with, and such heart as she possessed was naturally given to Lady Clem, her own child.

Lady Jane was fortunately not of a sensitive disposition. She took life calmly, and did not yearn for the affection that was not there to get, but she made the best of things, and when Bevis was sent to South America on a mission, she it was who brought about a sort of general reconciliation. She was very much pleased with herself on this occasion. Every body looked to her and consulted her. "You will go and see Emmy sometimes, won't you, Jane ?" said poor Bevis, who was a kind and handsome young fellow. Lady Jane said, "Most likely," and congratulated herself on her own tact and success on this occasion, as well as on her general ways, looks, style, and position in life. She thought poor Emmy was not certainly worth all this fuss, but determined to look after her. Lady Jane was rather Low Church, slightly suspicious, but good-natured and not unamenable to reason. She cultivated an abrupt frankness and independence of manner. Her frankness was almost bewildering at times, as Lady Jane expected her dictums to be received in silence and humility by the unlucky victims of her penetration. But still, as I have said, being a true-hearted woman, if she was once convinced that she was in the wrong, she would always own to it. Marriage was rather a sore subject with this lady. She had once notified to a young evangelical rector that although his prospects were not brilliant, yet she was not indisposed to share them, if he liked to come forward. To her utter amazement, the young man got up in a confused manner, walked across the room, talked to Lady Clem for the rest of his visit, and never called again. Lady Jane was much surprised ; but, as her heart was not deeply concerned in the matter, she forgave him on deliberation. The one softness in this strange woman's nature lay in her love for children. Little Bevis, her brother's baby, would coo at her, and beat her high cheek-bones with his soft little fat hand ; she let him pull her hair, the curls, and frill, and plaits of an hour's erection, poke his fingers into her eyes, swing her watch violently

round and round. She was still too young to have crystallized into a regular old maid. She had never known any love in her life except from Bevis, but Bevis had been a little afraid of her. Beverley was utterly indifferent to any body but himself.

Lady Jane had fifteen hundred a year of her own. She was not at all bad-looking. Her thick reddish hair was of the fashionable color. She was a better woman than some people gave her credit for being, seeing this tall, over-dressed, and overbearing young person going about the world with her two startled attendants and her hunters. Lady Jane had not the smallest sense of humor or feeling for art : at least, this latter faculty had never been cultivated, though she had furnished her boudoir with bran new damask and sprawling gilt legs, and dressed herself in the same style ; and had had her picture taken by some travelling artist — a pastel all frame and rose-colored chalk — which hung up over her chimney, smirking at a rose, to the amusement of some of her visitors. Lady Jane's notion of artists and art were mainly formed upon this trophy, and by what she had seen of the artist who had produced it. Lady Clem used to say that Jane was a born old maid, and would never marry ; but every body was not of that opinion. Lady Jane had been made a great deal of at Scudamore Castle, especially by a certain Captain Sigourney, who had been staying there, a nephew of Lady Scudamore's—tall, dark, interesting, in want of money, notwithstanding his many accomplishments. Poor Tom Sigourney had been for many years a hanger-on at Scudamore. They were extremely tired of him, knew his words, looks, tones, by heart. Handsome as he undoubtedly was, there was something indescribably wearisome about him after the first introduction—a certain gentle drawl and prose that irritated some people. But Lady Jane was immensely taken by him. His deference pleased her. She was not insensible to the respectful flattery with which he listened to every word she spoke. Tom Sigourney said she was a fine spirited girl, and Lady Scudamore seized the happy occasion— urged Tom forward, made much of Lady Jane. "Poor girl! she needs a protector," said Lady Scudamore gravely to her daughters. At which the young ladies burst out laughing. "Can you fancy Tom Sigourney taking care of any body ?" they cried.

Lady Mountmore arrived unexpectedly, and the whole little fabric was destroyed. Sigourney, who had not much impudence, was simply driven off the field by the elder lady's impertinences. Lady Jane was indignant, and declared she should not stay any longer under the same roof as her mother-in-law. Lady Scudamore did not press her to remain. She had not time to attend to her any longer or to family dissensions ; but she did write a few words to Tom, telling him of Lady Jane's movements, and then made it up with Lady Mountmore all the more cordially that she felt she had not been quite loyal to her in sending off this little missive.

The little steamer starts for Tarmouth in a little crowd and excitement of rolling barrels and oxen driven and plunging sheep in barges. The people come and look over the side of the wooden pier and talk to the captain at his wheel. Afternoon rays stream slant, and the island glistens across the straits, and the rocks stand out in the water; limpid waters beat against the rocks, and toss the buoys and splash against the busy little tug; one or two coal-barges make way. Idlers and a child or two in the way of the half-dozen passengers are called upon by name to stand aside on this occasion. There are two country dames returning from market; friend Hexham in an excitement about his van, which is to follow in a barge; and there is a languid, dark, handsome gentleman talking to a grandly dressed lady, whose attendants have been piling up wraps and *Times* and dressing-cases and umbrellas.

"Let me hold this for you, it will tire you," said the gentleman, tenderly taking *The Times* out of her hand; "are you resting? I thought I would try and meet you, and see if I could save you from fatigue. My aunt Scudamore told me you were coming this way. There, that is where my people live: that white house among the trees."

"It is a nice place," said Lady Jane.

The rocks were coming nearer, and the island was brightening to life and color, and the quaint old bricks and terraces of Tarmouth were beginning to show. There was a great ship in the distance sliding out to sea, and a couple of gulls flew overhead.

"Before I retired from the service," said Sigourney, "I was quartered at Portsmouth. I know this coast well; that is Tarmouth opposite, and that is—ah, 'm—a pretty place, and an uncommon pretty girl at the hotel."

"How am I to get to these people if they have not sent to meet me, I wonder?" interrupted Lady Jane, rather absently.

"Leave that to me," said Captain Sigourney; "I am perfectly at home here and I will order a fly. They all know me, and if they are not engaged will always come for *me*. You go to the inn. I order you a cup of tea, and one for your maid. I see a fast horse put up into a trap, and start you straight off."

"Oh, Captain Sigourney, I am very much obliged," said Lady Jane; and so the artless conversation went on.

At Tarmouth the ingenious captain would not let her ask whose was a carriage she saw standing there, nor take one of the two usual flys in waiting, but he made her turn into the inn until a special fast horse, with whose paces he was well acquainted, could be harnessed. This took a long time; but Lady Jane, excited by the novelty of the adventure, calmly enjoyed her afternoon tea and devotion, and sat on the horse-hair sofa of the little inn, admiring the

stuffed carp and cuttle-fish on the walls, and listening with a charmed ear to Tom's reminiscences of the time when he was quartered at Portsmouth.

The fast horse did not go much quicker than his predecessors, and Lady Jane arrived at the Lodges about an hour after Hexham, and at the same time as his great photographic van.

III.

THEY were all strolling along the cliffs towards the beacon. It stood upon the summit of High Down, a long way off as yet, though it seemed close at hand, so clearly did it stand out in the still atmosphere of the sunset. It stood there stiff and black upon its knoll, an old weather-beaten stick with a creaking coop for a crown, the pivot round which most of this little story turns. For when these holiday people travelled away out of its reach, they also passed out of my ken. We could see the beacon from most of our windows, through all the autumnal clematis and ivy sprays falling and drifting about. The children loved the beacon, and their little lives were one perpetual struggle to reach it in despite of winds, of time of meals, of tutors and lessons. The elders, too, loved it after their fashion. Had they not come and established themselves under the shadow of High Down, where it had stood as long as the oldest inhabitant could remember! Lord Ulleskelf, in his yacht out at sea, was always glad to see the familiar old stubby finger rising up out of the mist. My cousin, St. Julian the R. A., had made a strange, rough sketch of it, and of his wife and her eldest daughter sitting beneath it; and a sea, and a cloud horizon, gray, green, mysterious beyond. He had painted a drapery over their heads, and young Emilia's arms round the stem. It was an awful little picture, Emilia the mother thought when she saw it, and she begged her husband to turn its face to the wall in his studio.

"Don't you see how limpid the water is, and how the mist is transparent and drifting before the wind?" St. Julian said. "Why do you object, you perverse woman?"

The wife didn't answer, but her soft cheeks flushed. Emilia the daughter spoke, a little frightened.

"They are like mourners, papa," she whispered.

St. Julian shrugged his shoulders at them. "And this is a painter's wife!" he cried; "and a painter's daughter!" But he put the picture away, for he was too tender to pain them, and it lay now forgotten in a closet. This was two years ago, before Emilia was married, or had come home with her little son during her husband's absence. She was carrying the child in her arms as she toiled up the hill in company with the others, a tender bright flush in her face. Her little Bevis thinks it is he who is

carrying "Mozzer," as he clutches her **tight**
round the neck with his two little arms.

I suppose nobody ever reached the top of a
high cliff without some momentary feeling of
elation—so much left behind, so much achieved.
There you stand at peace, glowing with exertion, raised far above the din of the world. They
were gazing as they came along (for it is only
of an island that I am writing) at the great sight
of shining waters, of smiling **fertile** fields and
country; and of distant waters again, that separated them from the pale glimmering coast of
the main-land. The straits, which lie between
the island and Broadshire, are not deserted like
the horizon on the other side (it lies calm, and
tossing, and self-sufficing, for the coast is a dangerous one, and little frequented); but are
crowded and alive with boats and white sails:
ships go sliding past, yachts drift, and great
brigs slowly travel in tow of the tiny steamer
that crosses and recrosses the water with letters
and provisions, and comers and goers and guests
to Ulles Hall and to the Lodge, where St. Julian
and his family live all through the summer-
time; and where some of us indeed remain the
whole year round.

The little procession comes winding up the
down, Lord Ulleskelf and the painter walking
first, in broad-brimmed hats and coats fashion-
ed in the island, of a somewhat looser and more
comfortable cut than London coats. The tutor
is with them. Mr. Hexham, too, is with them;
as I can see, a little puzzled and interested by
the ways of us islanders.

As St. Julian talks his eyes flash, and he puts
out one hand to emphasize what he is saying.
He is not calm and self-contained as one might
imagine so great a painter, but a man of strong
convictions, alive to every life about him and to
every event. His cordial heart and bright artistic nature are quickly touched and moved.
He believes in his own genius, grasps at life as
it passes, and translates it into a strange, quaint
revelation of his own, and brings others into his
way of seeing things almost by magic. But his
charm is almost irresistible, and he knows it,
and likes to know it. The time that he is best
himself is when he is at his painting; his brown
eyes are alight in his pale face, his thick gray
hair stands on end; he is a middle-aged man,
broad, firmly knit, with a curly gray **beard**, active, mighty in his kingdom. He **lets people in**
to his sacred temple; but he makes them put
their shoes off, so to speak, and will allow no
word of criticism except from one or two. In a
moment his thick brows knit, and the master
turns upon the unlucky victim.

The old tutor had a special and unlucky knack
of exciting St. Julian's ire. He teaches the
boys as he taught St. Julian in bygone days, but
he can not forget that he is not always St. Julian's tutor, and constantly stings and irritates
him with his caustic, disappointed old wits. **But**
St. Julian bears it all with admirable impatience
for the sake of old **days** and of age and misfortune.

As they all climb the hill together on this
special day, the fathers go walking first, then
comes a pretty rout of maidens and children,
and Hexham's tall dark head among them.
Little Mona goes wandering by the edge of the
cliff, with her long gleaming locks hanging in
ripples not unlike those of the sea. The two
elder girls had come out with some bright-colored scarfs tied round their necks; but finding
them oppressive, they had pulled them off, and
given them to the boys to carry. These scarfs
were now banners streaming in the air as the
boys attacked a tumulus where the peaceful
bones of the bygone Danish invaders were lying
buried. The gay young voices echo across the
heather calling to each other.

Hester comes last with Mrs. William—Hester
with the mysterious sweet eyes and crown of
soft hair. It is not very thick, but like a dark
yet gleaming cloud about her pretty head. She
is quite pale, but her lips are bright carnation
red, and when she smiles she blushes. Hester is
tall, as are all the sisters, Emilia Beverley, and
Aileen, who is only fifteen, but the tallest of the
three. Aileen is walking a little ahead with
Mrs. William's children, and driving them away
from the edge of the cliff, towards which these
little moths seem perpetually buzzing.

The sun begins to set in a strange wild glory,
and the light to flow along the heights; all these
people look to one another like beatified men
and women. Ulleskelf and St. Julian cease their
discussion at last, and stand looking seaward.

"Look at that band of fire on the sea," said
Lord Ulleskelf.

"What an evening vesper!" said St. Julian.
"Hester, are you there?"

Hester was there, with sweet, wondering sunset eyes. Her father put his hand fondly **on**
her shoulder. There was a sympathy between
the two which was very touching; they liked to
admire together, to praise together. In sorrow
or trouble St. Julian looked for his wife, in happiness he instinctively seemed to turn to his favorite daughter.

Hester's charm did not always strike people at
first sight. She was like some of those sweet
simple tunes which haunt you after you have
heard them, or like some of those flowers of
which the faint delicate scent only comes to you
when you have waited for an instant.

Hexham, for instance, until now had admired
Mrs. Beverley infinitely more than he did her
sister. He thought Miss St. Julian handsome
certainly, but charmless; whereas the sweet,
gentle young mother, whose wistful eyes seemed
looking beyond the sunset, and trying in vain to
reach the distant world where her husband would
presently see it rise, appealed to every manly
feeling in his nature. But as the father and
daughter turned to each other, something in the
girl's face—a dim reflex light from the pure
bright soul within—seemed to touch him, to
disclose a something, I can not tell you what.
It seemed to Hexham as if the scales had fallen
suddenly from his eyes, and as if in that instant

Hester was revealed to him. She moved on a little way with two of the children who had joined her. The young man followed her with his eyes, and almost started when some one spoke to him. . . .

As St. Julian walked on, he began mechanically to turn over possible effects and combinations in his mind. The great colorist understood better than any other how to lay his colors, luminous, harmonious, shining with the real light of nature, for they were in conformity to her laws; and suddenly he spoke, turning to Hexham, who was a photographer, as I have said, and who indeed was now travelling in a gypsy fashion, in search of subjects for his camera.

"In many things," he said; "my art can equal yours, but how helpless we both are when we look at such scenes as these. It makes me sometimes mad to think that I am only a man with oil-pots attempting to reproduce such wonders."

"Fortunately they will reproduce themselves whether you succeed or not," said the tutor. St. Julian looked at him with his bright eyes. The old man had spoken quite simply. He did not mean to be rude—and the painter was silent.

"My art is 'a game half of skill, half of chance,'" said Hexham. "When both these divinities favor me I shall begin to think myself repaid for the time and the money and the chemicals I have wasted."

"Have you ever tried to photograph figures in a full blaze of light?" Lord Ulleskelf asked, looking at Mona and his own little girl standing with Hester, and shading their eyes from a bright stream that was playing like a halo about their heads. There was something unconscious and lovely in the little group, with their white draperies and flowing locks. A bunch of illumined berries and trailing creepers hung from little lady Millicent's hair: the light of youth and of life, the sweet wondering eyes, all went to make a more beautiful picture than graces or models could ever attain to. St. Julian looked and smiled with Lord Ulleskelf.

Hexham answered, a little distractedly, that he should like to show Lord Ulleskelf the attempt he had once made. "Nature is a very uncertain sort of assistant," he added; "and I, too, might exclaim, 'Oh that I am but a man, with a bit of yellow paper across my window, and a row of bottles on my shelf, trying to evoke life from the film upon my glasses . . . .!'"

"I think you are all of you talking very profanely," said Lord Ulleskelf; "before all these children, and in such a sight as this. But I shall be very glad to come down and look at your photographs, Mr. Hexham, to-morrow morning," he added, fearing the young man might be hurt by his tone.

The firebrand in the still rippled sea turned from flame to silver as the light changed and ebbed. The light on the sea seemed dimmer, but then the land caught fire in turn, and trees and downs and distant roof-tops blazed in this great illumination, and the shadows fell black upon the turf.

Here Mrs. William began saying in a plaintive tone of voice that she was tired, and I offered to go back with her. Every body indeed was on the move, but we two took a shorter cut, while the others went home with the Ulleskelfs, turning down by a turning of the down towards a lane that leads to Ulles Hall.

And so, having climbed up with some toil and effort to that beautiful height, we all began to descend once more into the every-day of life, and turn from glowing seas and calm-sailing clouds to the thought of cutlets and chickens. The girls had taken back their scarfs and were running down hill. Aileen was carrying one of Margaret's children, Emilia Beverly had her little Bevis in her arms, Hester was holding by her father's arm, as they came back rather silent, but satisfied and happy. The sounds from the village below began to reach us, and the lights in the cottages and houses to twinkle; the cliffs rose higher and higher as we descended our different ways. The old beacon stood out black against the ruddy sky: a moon began to hang in the high faint heaven, and a bright star to pierce through the daylight.

Ulles Hall stands on the way from Tarmouth to the Lodges: it is a lovely old house standing among woods in a hollow, and blown by sea-breezes that come through pine-stems and sweet green glades, starred with primroses in spring, and sprinkled with russet leaves in autumn. The Lodges where St. Julian lives are built a mile nearer to the sea. Houses built on the roadside, but inclosed by tall banks and hedges, and with long green gardens running to the down. They have been built piece by piece. It would be difficult to describe them: a gable here, a wooden gallery thatched, a window twinkling in a bed of ivy, hanging creepers, clematis and loveliest Virginian sprays reddening and drinking in the western light, and reflecting it undimmed in their beautiful scarlet veins—scarlet gold melting into green: one of the rooms streams with light like light through stained windows of a church.[*]

IV.

As I reached the door with Mrs. William, I saw a bustle of some sort, a fly, some boxes, a man, a maid, a tall lady of about seven or eight

---

[*] A little child passing by in the road looked up one day at the Lodges, and said: "Oh, what pretty leaf-houses! Oh, mother, do let us live there! I think the robins must have made them." "I think that is where we are going to, Mona," said the mother. She was a poor young widowed cousin of St. Julian's. She came for a time, but they took her in and never let her go again out of the leaf-house. She staid and became a sort of friend, chaperone, governess, and house-keeper; and to these kind and tender friends and relations, if she were to attempt to set down here all that she owes to them, to their warm, cordial hearts, and bright, sweet natures, it would make a story apart from the one she has in her mind to write to-day.

and twenty, dressed in the very height of fashion, with a very tall hat and feather, whom I guessed at once to be Lady Jane. Mrs. William, who has not the good manners of the rest of the family, shrank back a little, saying —"I really can not face her: it's that Lady Jane;" but at that moment Lady Jane, who was talking in a loud querulous tone, suddenly ceased, and turned round.

"Here is Mrs. St. Julian," said the flyman, and my dear mistress came out into the garden to receive her guest.

"I am so glad you have come," I heard her say, quietly; "we had given you up—are you tired? Come in. Let the servant see to your luggage." She put out her white gentle hand, and I was amused to see Lady Jane's undisguised look of surprise: she had expected to meet with some bustling, good-humored housekeeper. Bevis had always praised his mother-in-law to her, but Lady Jane had a way of not always listening to what people said, as she rambled on in her own fashion; and now, having fully made up her mind as to the sort of person Mrs. St. Julian would be, Lady Jane felt slightly aggrieved at her utter dissimilarity to her preconceptions. She followed her into the house, with her high hat stuck upon the top of her tall head, walking in a slightly defiant manner.

"I thought Emilia would have been here to receive me," said Lady Jane, not over-pleased.

"I sent her out," the mother said. "I thought you would let me be your hostess for an hour. Will you come up into my room?"

Mrs. St. Julian led the way into the drawing-room, where Lady Jane sank down into a chair, crossing her top-boots and shaking out her skirts.

"I am afraid there was a mistake about meeting you," said the hostess; "the carriage went, but only brought back Mr. Hexham and a message that you were not there."

"I fortunately met a friend on board," said Lady Jane, hurriedly. "He got me a fly; thank you, it did not signify."

Lady Jane was not anxious to enter into particulars, and when Mrs. St. Julian went on to ask how it was she had had to wait so long, the young lady abruptly said something about afternoon tea, asked to see her room and to speak to her maid.

"Will you come back to me when you have given your orders?" said Mrs. St. Julian. "My cousin, Mrs. Campbell, will show you the way."

Lady Jane, with a haughty nod to poor Mrs. Campbell, followed with her high head up the quaint wooden stairs along the gallery with its odd windows and slits, and china, and ornaments.

"This is your room; I hope you will find it comfortable," said the housekeeper, opening a door, through which came a flood of light.

"Is that for my maid?" asked Lady Jane, pointing to a large and very comfortably furnished room just opposite to her own door.

"That room is Mr. Hexham's," said Queenie;

"your maid's room leads out of your dressing-room." The arrangement seemed obvious, but Lady Jane was not quite in a temper to be pleased.

"Is it comfortable, Pritchard? Shall you be able to work there? I must speak about it if you are not comfortable."

Pritchard was a person who did not like to commit herself. Not that she wished to complain, but she should prefer her ladyship to judge; it was not for her to say. She looked so mysterious that Lady Jane ran up the little winding stair that led to the turret, and found a little white-curtained chamber, with a pleasant bright look-out over land and sea.

"Why, this is a delightful room, Pritchard," said Lady Jane. "I should like it myself; it is most comfortable."

"Yes, my lady, I thought it was highly comfortable," said Pritchard; "but it was not for me to venture to say so."

Lady Jane was a little afraid of Mrs. St. Julian's questionings. To tell the truth, she felt that she had been somewhat imprudent; and though she was a person of mature age and independence, yet she was not willing to resign entirely all pretensions to youthful dependence, and she was determined, if possible, not to mention Sigourney's name to her entertainers. Having frizzed up her curling red locks, with Mrs. Pritchard's assistance, shaken out her short skirts, added a few more bracelets, tied on a coroneted locket, and girded in her tight silver waistband, she prepared to return to her hostess and her tea. She felt excessively ill used by Emilia's absence, but, as I have said, dared not complain for fear of more questions as to the cause of her delay.

All along the passage were more odds and ends, paintings, pictures, sketches framed, a cabinet or two full of china. Lady Jane was too much used to the ways of the world to mistake the real merit of this heterogeneous collection; but she supposed that the artists made the things up, or perhaps sold them again to advantage, and that there was some meaning which would be presently explained for it all. What most impressed Lady Jane with a feeling of respect for the inhabitants of the house was a huge Scotch sheep-dog, who came slowly down the gallery to meet her, and then passed on with a snuff and a wag of his tail.

The door of the mistress's room, as it was called, was open; and as Lady Jane followed her conductress in, she found a second five o'clock tea and a table spread with rolls and country butter and home-made cake. A stream of western light was flowing through the room and out into the gallery beyond, where the old majolica plates flashed in the glitter of its sparkle. The mistress herself was standing with her back turned, looking out through the window across the sea, and trying to compose herself before she asked a question she had very near at heart.

Lady Jane remained waiting, feeling for once a little shy, and not knowing exactly what to do next, for Mrs. Campbell, who was not without a certain amount of feminine malice, stood meekly until Lady Jane should take the lead. The young lady was not accustomed to deal with inferiors who did not exactly behave as such, and though inwardly indignant, she did not quite know how to resent the indifference with which she considered she was treated. She tossed her head, and at last said, not in the most conciliatory voice, "I suppose I may take some tea, Mrs. St. Julian?" The sight of the sweet pale face turning round at her question softened her tone. Mrs. St. Julian came slowly forward, and began to push a chair with her white feeble hands, evidently so unfit for such work, that Jane, who was kind-hearted, sprang forward, lockets, top-boots, and all, to prevent her. "You had much better sit down yourself," said she, good-naturedly. "I thought you looked ill just now, though I had never seen you in my life before. Let me pour out the tea."

Mrs. St. Julian softened, too, in the other's unexpected heartiness and kindness. "I had something to say to you. I think it upset me a little. I heard—I feared"—she said, nervously hesitating. "Lady Jane, did you hear from your brother—from Bevis—by the last mail . . . . ? Emmy does not know the mail is in. . . . . I have been a little anxious for her," and Mrs. St. Julian changed color.

"Certainly I heard," said Lady Jane; "or at least my father did. Bevis wanted some money raised. Why were you so anxious, Mrs. St. Julian?" asked Lady Jane, with a slightly amused look in her face. It was really too absurd to have these people making scenes and alarms when she was perfectly at her ease.

"I am thankful you have heard," said Mrs. St. Julian, with a sudden flush and brightness in her wan face, which made Lady Jane open her eyes in wonder.

"Do you care so much?" said she, a little puzzled. "I am glad that I do not belong to an anxious family. I am very like Bevis, they say; and I know there is nothing that he dislikes so much as a fuss about nothing."

"I know it," said Mrs. St. Julian. "He is very good and kind to bear with my foolish alarms, and I wonder—could you—would you too—forgive me for my foolishness, Lady Jane, if I were to ask you a great favor? Do you think I might see that letter to your father? I can not tell you what a relief it would be to me. I told you Emilia does not know that the mail is in; and if—if she might learn it by seeing in his own handwriting that Bevis was well, I think it would make all the difference to her, poor child."

There was something in the elder lady's gentle persistence which struck the young one as odd, and yet touching; and although she was much inclined to refuse, from a usual habit of contradiction, she did not know how to do so when it came to the point.

"I'll write to my father," said Lady Jane,

with a little laugh. "I have no doubt he will let you see the letter since you wish it so much."

"Thank you, my dear," said Mrs. St. Julian, "and for the good news you have given me; and I will now confess to you," she added, smiling, "that I sent Emmy out on purpose that I might have this little talk. Are you rested? Will you come into the garden with me for a little?"

Lady Jane was touched by the sweet maternal manner of the elder woman, and followed quite meekly and kindly. As the two ladies were pacing the garden-walk they were joined by the housekeeper and by Mrs. William, with her little dribble of small-talk.

Many of the windows of the Lodges were alight. The light from without still painted the creepers, the lights from within were coming and going, and the gleams were falling upon the ivy-leaves here and there. One-half of the place was in shadow, and the western side in daylight still. There was a sweet rush of scent from the sweetbriers and clematis. It seemed to hang in the still evening air. Underneath the hedges, bright-colored flowers seemed suddenly starting out of the twilight, while above, in the lingering daylight, the red berries sparkled and caught the stray limpid rays. There was a sound of sea waves washing the not distant beach; a fisherman or two, and soldiers from the little fort, were strolling along the road, and peering in as they passed the bright little homes. The doors were wide open, and now and then a figure passed—a servant, Mrs. Campbell—who was always coming and going: William, the eldest son, coming out of the house: he had been at work all day.

The walking party came up so silently that they were there in the garden almost before the others had heard them: a beloved crowd, exclaiming, dispersing again. It was a pretty sight to see the meetings; little Susan running straight to her father, William St. Julian. He adored his little round-eyed daughter, and immediately carried her off in his arms. Little Mona, too, had got hold of her mother's hand, while Lady Jane was admiring Bevis, and being greeted by the rest of the party, and introduced to those whom she did not already know.

"We had quite given you up, dear Jane," said little Emilia, wistfully gazing and trying to see some look of big Bevis in his sister's face. "How I wish I had staid, but you had mamma."

"We gave you up," said Hester, "when Mr. Hexham came without you. . . . ."

"I now find I had the honor of travelling with Lady Jane," said Hexham, looking amused, and making a little bow.

Lady Jane turned her back upon Mr. Hexham. She had taken a great dislike to him on board the boat; she had noticed him looking at her once or twice, and at Captain Sigourney. She found it a very good plan, and always turned her back upon people she did not like. It checked any familiarity. It was much better to do so at once, and let them see what their proper place was. If people of a certain position in the world did not keep others in their proper places, there was no knowing what familiarity might not ensue. And then she ran back to little Bevis again, and lifted him up, struggling. For the child had forgotten her, and seemed not much attracted by her appearance.

"Lady Jane Beverley has something military about her," said Hexham to Mrs. Campbell.

As he spoke a great loud bell began to ring, and with a little chorus of exclamations, the ladies began to disperse to dress for dinner.

"You know your way, Mr. Hexham," said Mrs. Campbell, pointing. "Go through that side door, and straight up and along the gallery."

Mrs. St. Julian had put her arm into her husband's, and walked a little way with him towards the house.

"Henry," she said, "thank Heaven, all is well. Lord Mountmore heard from Bevis by this mail. Lady Jane has promised to show me the letter: she had heard nothing of that dreadful report."

"It was not likely," St. Julian said ; "Ulleskelf only saw the paper by chance. I am glad you were so discreet, my dear."

"I should like to paint a picture of them," said Hexham to the housekeeper, looking at them once more before he hurried into the house.

The two were standing at the threshold of their home, Mrs. St. Julian leaning upon her husband's arm: the strong keen-faced man with his bright gallant bearing, and the wife with her soft and feminine looks fixed upon him as she bent anxiously to catch his glance. She was as tall as he was: for St. Julian was a middle-sized man, and Mrs. St. Julian was tall for a woman.

Meanwhile Hexham, who was not familiar with the ways of the house, and who took time at his toilet, ran up stairs, hastily passed his own door, went along a passage, up a staircase, down a staircase. . . . . He found himself in the dusky garden again, where the lights were almost put out by this time, though all the flowers were glimmering, and scenting, and awake still. There was a red streak in the sky ; all the people had vanished, but turning round he saw—he blinked his eyes at the sight—a white figure standing, visionary, mystical, in the very centre of a bed of tall lilies, in a soft gloom of evening light. Was it a vision ? For the first time in his life Hexham felt a little strangely, and as if he could believe in the super-nature which he sometimes had scoffed at ; the young man made one step forward and stopped again.

"It is I, Mr. Hexham," said a shy, clear voice. "I came to find some flowers for Emilia." It was Hester's voice. Surely some kindly providence sets true lovers' way in pleasant places ; and all they do and say has a grace of its own which they impart to all inanimate things.

The evening, the sweet stillness, the trembling garden hedges, the fields beyond, the sweet girlish *tinkle* of Hester's voice, made Hexham feel for the first time in his life as if he was standing in a living shrine, and as if he ought to fall down on his knees and worship.

"Can I help you ?" he said. "Miss Hester, may I have a flower for my button-hole ?"

"There are nothing but big lilies," said the voice.

V.

In writing this little episode I have tried to put together one thing and another—to describe some scenes that I saw myself and some that were described to me. My window looks out upon the garden, and is just over the great bed of lilies. I shut it down, and began to dress for dinner, with an odd dim feeling already of what the future might have in store. It was a half-conscious consciousness of what was passing in the minds of those all about. For some days past Mrs. St. Julian's anxious face seemed to follow me about the room. Poor little Emilia's forced patience and cheerfulness were more sad to me than any impatience or fretfulness. Hexham, Hester, even Lady Jane, each seemed to strike a note in my present excited and receptive state of mind. It is one for which there is no name, but which few people have not experienced. I dressed quickly, the dark corners of my room seemed looming at me, and it was with an odd, anxious conviction of disturbance at hand that I hurried down along the gallery to the drawing-room, where we assembled before dinner. On my way I met Emilia on the stairs, in her white dinner-dress, with a soft white knitted shawl drawn closely round her. She slid her little chill hand through my arm, and asked me why I looked so pale. Dear soft little woman, she seemed of us all the most tender and disarming. Even sorrow and desolation, I thought, should be vanquished by her sweetness. And perhaps I was right when I thought so.

We were not the last. Hester followed us. She was dressed in a floating gauze dress, and she had one great white lily in her dark hair. "It is a great deal too big, Hester," cried Mrs. William ; but I thought I had never seen her more charming.

"How much better mamma is looking !" Hester said that evening at dinner, and as she spoke she glanced at her mother sitting at the head of the long table in the tall carved chair.

When the party was large, and the sons of the house at home, we dined in an old disused studio of St. Julian's : a great wooden room, unpapered and raftered, with a tressle table of the painter's designing, and half-finished frescoes and sketches hanging upon the walls. There was a high wooden chimney, and an old-fashioned glass reflecting the scene, the table, the people, the crimson drugget, of which a

square covered the boards. In every thing St.
Julian touched there was a broad quaint stamp
of his own, and this room had been inhabited
and altered by him. Two rough hanging
lamps from the rafter lit up the long white table, and the cups of red berries and green leaves
with which I had attempted to dress it. There
was something almost patriarchal in this little
assembly : the father at the end of the table,
the sons and daughters all around, William and
his wife by Mrs. St. Julian, and pretty Hester
sitting by her father. On the other side Lady
Jane was established. St. Julian had taken
her in. He had asked her a few questions at
first, specially about the letter she had received
from Bevis, but carefully, so that Emilia should
not overhear them.

"He seemed to be enjoying himself," said
Lady Jane. "He was talking of going on a
shooting-party a little way up the river, if he
could get through his work in time."

She did not notice St. Julian's grave look as
she spoke, and went on in her usual fashion.
I remember she was giving him one person's
views on art and another's, and her own, and
describing the pastel she had had done. St.
Julian looked graver and graver, and more impatient as she went on. Patience was not his
strong point.

"How long does it take you to paint a picture, Mr. St. Julian?" Lady Jane asked. "I
wish I could paint, and I'm sure I wish Beverley could, for he can not manage upon his allowance at all. How nice it must be to take
up a brush and—paint checks, in fact, as you
do. Clem can sketch wonderfully quickly ; she
took off Lord Scudamore capitally. Of course
she would not choose to sketch for money, but
artists have said they would gladly offer large
sums for her paintings. Do your daughters help
you?" inquired poor Lady Jane affably, feeling
that she was suiting her conversation to her
company. "Do you ever do caricatures?"

"We will talk about painting, Lady Jane,
when you have been here some days longer,"
said St. Julian. "You had better ask the girls
any questions you may wish to have answered,
and get them, if possible, to give you some idea
of the world we live in."

To poor Lady Jane's utter amazement St.
Julian then began talking to Hexham across the
table, and signed to his wife to move immediately after dinner was over. We all went
back walking across the garden to the drawing-
room, for the night was fine, and the little covered way was for bad weather.

Some of us sat in the verandah. It was a
bright starry evening. A great bright planet
was rising from behind the sweeping down.
The lights from the wooden room were shining
too. Lady Jane presently seemed to get tired of
listening to poor Mrs. William's nursery retro-
spections,—Mary Annes, and Susans, and tea
and sugar, and what Mrs. Mickleman had said
when she parted from her nursery-maid ; and
what Mrs. William herself meant to say to the

girl when she got home on Monday ; not that
Mrs. William was disposed to rely entirely upon
Mrs. Mickleman, who was certainly given to ex-
aggerate, etc. The girls were in the garden.
Emilia had gone up to little Bevis. Lady Jane
jumped up with the usual rattle of bracelets and
necklaces, and said she should take a turn too
and join the young ladies.

Mrs. William confessed, **as Lady Jane** left the
verandah, that she was glad she was not *her* sister-in-law.

"She has such a strange abrupt manner,"
said the poor lady. "Don't you find it **very**
awkward, Queenie? I never know whether she
likes me to talk to her or not—do you?"

"I have no doubt about it," I said, laughing.

The evening was irresistible : starlit, moonlit, soft-winded.

A few minutes later I, too, went out into the
garden, and walked along the dark alley towards
the knoll, from whence there is a pretty view of
the sea by night, and over the hedge and along
the lane. From where I stood I saw that the
garden-gate was open, for the moon was shining
in a broad silver stream along the lane that led
to the farm. The farm was not really ours, but
all our supplies came from there, and we felt as
if it belonged to us. Mona knew the cows and
the horses, and the very sheep inclosed in their
pen for the night. As I was standing peaceful
and resting under the starlit dome, something a
little strange and inexplicable now happened,
which I could not at all understand at the time.
I saw some one moving in the lane beyond the
hedge. I certainly recognized Lady Jane walking away in the shadow that lay along the banks
of that moonlit stream ; but what was curious
to me was this: it seemed to me that she was
not alone, that a dark tall figure of a man was
beside her. It was not one of our men, though
I could not see the face—of this I felt quite
sure. The two went on a little way, then she
turned ; and I could have declared that I saw
the gleam of his face in the distance through
the shadow. Lady Jane's hand was hanging in
the moonlight, and her trinkets glistening. Of
her identity I had no doubt. There is a big
tree which hangs over the road, and when they,
or when she, reached it, she stopped for a moment, as if to look about her, and then, only
Lady Jane appeared from its shadow—the other figure had vanished. I could not understand
it at all. I have confessed that I am a foolish
person and superstitious at times. I had never
seen poor Bevis. Had any thing happened?
Could it be a vision of him that I had seen? I
got a little frightened, and my heart began to
beat. It was only for an instant that I was so
absurd. I walked hastily towards the garden
door, and met Lady Jane only a few steps off,
coming up very coolly.

"How lovely this moonlight is, Mrs. Campbell!" she cried, more affably than usual.

"Who was that with you? Didn't I see some
one with you, Lady Jane?" I asked, hurriedly.

Lady Jane looked me full in the face. "What do you mean?" said she. "I went out for a stroll by myself. I am quite alone, as you see."

Something in her tone reassured me. I felt sure she was not speaking the truth. It was no apparition I had seen, but a real tangible person. It was no affair of mine, though it struck me as a singular proceeding. We both walked back to the house together. The girls' white dresses were gleaming here and there upon the lawn. Hexham passed us hastily and went on and joined them. William was taking a turn with his cigar. As we passed the dining-room window I happened to look in. St. Julian was sitting at the table, with his head resting on his hands, and beside him Mrs. St. Julian, who must have gone back to the room after dinner. A paper was before them, over which the two were bending.

We found no one in the drawing-room, and only a lamp spluttering and a tea-table simmering in one corner, and Mrs. William, who was half asleep on the sofa. "I shall go back to the others," said my companion; and I followed, nothing loath.

What a night it was! Still, dark, sweet, fragrant shadows, quivering upon the moon-stream; a sudden, glowing summer's night, coming like a gem set in the midst of gray days, of storms, swift gales, of falling autumnal leaves and seasons.

The clear three-quarter moon was hanging over the gables and roofs of the Lodges; the high stars streamed light; a distant sea burnt with pale radiance; the young folks chattered in the trembling gleams.

"Look at that great planet rising over the down," said Hexham. "Should you like that to be your star, Miss St. Julian?"

"I should like a fixed star," Hester answered, gravely. "I should like it to be quite still and unchanging, and to shine with an even light!"

"That is not a bit like you, Hester," said William, who had come up, and who still had a school-boy trick of teasing his sisters; "it is much more like Emilia, or my wife. You describe them and take all the credit to yourself."

"Oh William! Emilia is any thing but a fixed star," cried Aileen. "She would like to jump out of her orbit to-morrow, and go off to Bevis, if she could. Margaret is certainly more like."

"You shall have the whole earth for your planet, Miss Hester," said Hexham. Then he added less seriously, "They say it looks very bright a little way off."

Moonlight gives a strange, intensified meaning to voices as well as to shadows. No one spoke for a minute, until Lady Jane, who was easily bored, jumped up and said that people ought to be ashamed to talk about stars nowadays, so much had been said already; and that, after all, she should go back for some tea.

I left her stirring her cup, with Mrs. William still half asleep in her corner, and I myself went up to my room. Mrs. St. Julian was sitting with her husband in the studio, the parlor-maid told me. Outside was the great burning night, inside a silent house, dark, with empty chambers and doors wide open on the dim staircase and passages. I would gladly have staid out with the others, but I had a week's accounts to overlook on this Saturday night. The odd anxiety I had felt before dinner came back to me again now that I was alone. I tried to shake off the feeling which oppressed me, and I went in and stood for a moment by my little Mona's bedside. Her sweet face, her quiet breath, and peaceful dreams seemed to me to belong to the stars outside. As I looked at the child, I found myself once more thinking over my odd little adventure with Lady Jane, and wondering whether it would be well 'to speak of it, and to whom? I had lived long enough to feel some of the troubles and complications both of speech and of silence. Once more my heart sank, as it used to do when difficulties seemed to grow on every side before I had come to this kind house of refuge; and yet, difficult as life was undoubtedly to me, as well as to others, it seemed to me, looking back, that, seen from a distance, a light shone from the hearts and doings of the children of men, as clear as the light of which Hexham had spoken, reflected from this sin-weighted and sorrow-driven world. I pulled my table and my lamp to the window: the figures were still wandering in the garden; I saw Hester's white dress flit by more than once. Such nights count in the sum of one's life.

VI.

Mona was standing ready dressed in her Sunday frills and ribbons by my bedside when I awoke next morning.

"It is raining, mamma," she said. "We had wanted to go up to the beacon before breakfast."

It seemed difficult to believe that this was the same world that I had closed my eyes upon. The silent, brilliant, mysterious world of stars and sentiment was now gray, and mist-wreathed and rain-drenched. The practical result of my observations was to say, "Mona, go and tell them to light a fire in the dining-room."

St. Julian, who is possessed by a horrible stray demon of punctuality, likes all his family to assemble to the sound of a certain clanging bell that is poor Emilia's special aversion. Mrs. St. Julian never comes down to breakfast. I was only just in time this morning to fulfill my duties and make the tea and the coffee. Hester came out of her room as I passed the door. She, too, had come back to every-day life again, and had put away her white robes and lilies for a stuff dress—a quaint blue dress, with puffed sleeves, and a pretty fanciful trimming of her mother's devising, gold braid and velvet round the wrists and neck. Her pretty gloom of dark hair was pinned up with golden pins. As I looked at her admiringly, I began to think to myself that, after all, rainy mornings were perhaps as compatible with sentiment as purple starry skies. I could not help thinking that there was something a little shy and conscious in her manner: she seemed to tread gently, as if she were afraid of waking some one, as if she were thinking of other things. She waited for me, and would not go into the dining-room until she had made sure that I was following. Only Hexham was there, reading his letters by the burning fire of wood, when we first came in. He turned round and smiled:—had the stars left their imprint upon him too? He carried his selection of eggs and cutlets and toasted bread from the side-table, and put himself quietly down by Hester's side: all the others dropped in by degrees.

"Here is another French newspaper for you, papa," said Emilia, turning over her letters with a sigh. St. Julian took it from her quickly, and put it in his pocket.

Breakfast was over. The rain was still pouring in a fitful, gusty way, green ivy-leaves were dripping, creepers hanging dully glistening about the windows, against which the great fresh drops came tumbling. The children stood curiously watching, and making a play of the falling drops. There was Susy's rain-drop, and George's on the window-ledge, and Mr. Hexham's.

"Oh, Mr. Hexham's has won!" cried Susy, clasping her little fat hands in an agony of interest.

I looked out and saw the great gusts of rain beating and drifting against the hedgerows, wind-blown mists crossing the fields and the downs. It was a stormy Sunday, coming after that night of wonders. But the wind was high; the clouds might break. The church was two miles off, and we could not get there then; later we hoped we might have a calmer hour to walk to it.

The afternoon brightened as we had expected, and most of us went to afternoon service snugly wrapped in cloaks, and stoutly shod, walking up hill and down hill between the bright and dripping hedges to the little white-washed building where we Islanders are exhorted, buried, christened, married by turns. It is always to me a touching sight to see the country folks gathering to the sound of the old jangling village bells, as they ring their pleasant calls from among the ivy and bird's-nests in the steeple, and summon—what a strange, toil-worn, weather-beaten company!—to prayer and praise. Furrowed faces bent, hymn-books grasped in hard crooked fingers, the honest red smiling cheeks of the lads and lasses trudging along side by side, the ancient garments from lavender drawers, the brown old women from their kitchen corners, the babies toddling hand in hand. Does one not know the kindly Sunday throng, as it assembles, across fields and downs, from nestling farm and village byways? Mrs. William's children came trotting behind her, exchanging cautious glances with the Sunday-school, and trying to imitate a certain business-like, church-going air which their mother affected. Hexham and the others were following at some little distance. Emilia never spoke much, and to-day she was very silent; but though she was silent I could feel her depression, and knew, as well as if she had put it all into words, what was passing in her mind. Once during the service, I heard a low shivering sigh by my side, but when I glanced at her, her face looked placid, and as we came away the light of the setting sun came shining full upon it. A row of boys were sitting on the low churchyard wall in this western light, which lit up the fields and streamed across the homeward paths of the little congregation. I must not forget to say that, as we passed out, it seemed to me that, in the crowd waiting about the door, I recognized a tall and bending figure that I had seen somewhere before. Somewhere—by moonlight. I remembered presently when and where it was.

"Who was that?" asked Emilia, seeing me glance curiously.

"That is what I should like to know," said I. "Shall we wait for Lady Jane? I have a notion she could tell us."

We waited, but no Lady Jane appeared.

"She must have gone on," said Emilia. "It is getting cold; let us follow them, dear Queenie."

I was still undecided as to what I had better do. It seemed that it would be better to speak to Lady Jane herself than to relate my vague suspicions to any body else. Little Emilia, of all people, was so innocent and unsuspecting that I hesitated before I told her what I had seen. I was hesitating still, when Emmy took my arm again.

"Come!" she said; and so we went on together through the darkening village street; past the cottages where the pans were shining against the walls as the kitchen fires flamed. The people began to disperse once more: some were at home, stooping as they crossed their low cottage thresholds; others were walking away along the paths and the hills that slope from the village church to cottages by the sea. We saw Hester and Aileen and Hexham going off by the long way over the downs; but no Lady Jane was with them. We were not far from home when Emilia stopped before a little rising mound by the roadside, on which a tufted holly-tree was standing, already reddened against the winter.

"That is the tree my husband likes," said she. "It was bright red with holly-berries the morning we were married. Little Bevvy watches the berries beginning to burn, as he calls it. I often bring him here."

Some people can not put themselves into

words, and they say, not the actual thing they are feeling, but something quite unlike, and yet which means all they would say. Some other people, it is true, have words enough, but no selves to put to them. Emilia never said a striking thing, rarely a pathetic one; but her commonplaces came often more near to me than the most passionate expressions of love or devotion. Something in the way she looked, in the tone with which she spoke of the holly-tree, touched me more than there seemed any occasion for. I can not tell what it was; but this I do know, that silence, dullness, every thing, utters at times, the very stones cry out, and, in one way or another, love finds a language that we all can understand.

We stood for a few minutes under the holly-tree, and then walked quickly home. I let Emilia go in. I waited outside in the dim gray garden, pacing up and down in the twilight. Lady Jane, as I expected, arrived some ten minutes after we did; but I missed the opportunity I had wished for, for Hexham and the two girls appeared almost at the same minute, with bright eyes and fresh rosy faces, from their walk, and we all went up to tea in the mistress's room.

This was the Williams' last evening. Only one little incident somewhat spoiled its harmony.

"Who was that Captain Sigourney, who called just after we had gone to church?" Mrs. William asked innocently, during a pause in the talk at dinner.

This simple question caused some of us to look up curiously.

"Captain Sigourney," said Lady Jane, in a loud trumpet-like tone, "is a friend of mine. I asked him to call upon me."

St. Julian gave one of his flashes, a look half amused, half angry. He glanced at his wife, and then at Lady Jane, who was cutting up her mutton into long strips, calmly excited and prepared for battle. St. Julian was silent, however, and the engagement, if engagement there was to be, did not take place until later in the evening. I felt very glad that the matter was taking this turn and that the absurd mystery, whatever it might be, should come to an end without my being implicated in it. It was no affair of mine if Lady Jane liked to have a dozen captains in attendance upon her, but it seemed to me a foolish proceeding. I had reason to conclude that St. Julian had said something to Lady Jane that evening. I was not in the drawing-room after dinner. One of the servants was ill, and I was obliged to attend to her; but as I was coming down to say good-night to them all I met Lady Jane—I met a whirlwind in the passage. She gave me one look. Her whole aspect was terrible: her chains and many trinkets seemed rattling with indignation. She looked quite handsome in her fury; her red hair and false plaits seemed to stand on end, her eyes to pierce me through and through, and if I had been guilty I think I must have run away from this irate apparition.

Do I dream it, or did I hear the two words, "impertinent interference," as she turned round with the air of an empress, and shut her door loud in my face? Mrs. St. Julian happened to be in her room, and the noise brought her kind head out into the passage, and, not I am afraid very calmly or coherently, I told her what had happened.

"I must try and appease her, I suppose my husband has spoken to her," said Mrs. St. Julian; and she boldly went and knocked at the door of Lady Jane's room, and, after an instant's hesitation, walked quietly in. I do not know what charm she used, but, somewhat to my dismay, a messenger came to me in the drawing-room presently to beg that I would speak to Lady Jane. I saw malicious Aileen with a gleam of fun in her eyes at my unfeigned alarm. I found Lady Jane standing in the middle of the room, in a majestic sort of dressing-gown, with all her long tawny locks about her shoulders. Mrs. St. Julian was sitting in an arm-chair near the toilet-table, which was all glittering with little bottles and ivory handles. This scarlet apparition came straight up to me as I entered, with three brisk strides. "I find I did you an injustice," she said, loftily relenting, though indignant still. "Mrs. St. Julian has explained matters to me. I thought you would be glad to know at once that I was aware of the mistake I had made. I beg your pardon. Good-evening, Mrs. Campbell," said Lady Jane dismissing me all of a breath. I found myself outside in the dark passage again, with a curious dazzle of the brilliantly lighted room, with its odd perfume of ottar of roses, of that weird apparition with its flaming robe and red hair and burning cheeks.

I was too busy next morning helping Mrs. William and her children and boxes to get off by the early boat, to have much time to think of apparitions or my own wounded feelings. Dear little Georgy and Susey peeped out of the carriage-window with many farewell kisses. The three girls stood waving their hands as the carriage drove past the garden. The usual breakfast-bell rang and we all assembled, and Lady Jane, whose anger was never long-lived, came down in pretty good humor. To me she was most friendly. There was a shade of displeasure in her manner to St. Julian. To Hexham she said that she had quite determined upon an expedition to Warren Bay that afternoon, and to the castle next day, and she hoped he would come too. Lady Jane bustled off after breakfast to order a carriage.

VII.

From "the mistress's room," with its corner windows looking out every way, we could see downs, and sea, and fields, and the busy road down to the shore. Mrs. St. Julian was able to be out so little that she liked life at second-hand, and the sight of people passing, and of her children swinging at the gate, and of St. Julian as he came and went from his studio sometimes, with his pipe and his broad-brimmed hat—all this was a never-failing delight to her. Hester sat writing for her mother this morning. It was the Monday after Lady Jane's arrival, and I established myself with my work in the window. Suddenly the mother asked, "Where is Emilia?"

"Emilia is in the garden with Bevis," said Hester; "they were picking red berries off the hedge when I came up."

"And where is Lady Jane?" said Mrs. St. Julian.

"She is gone to look at a pony-carriage, with her maid," said Hester.

"Poor Lady Jane was very indignant last night. You will be amused to hear that I am supposed to be encouraging a young man at this moment, for purposes of my own, to carry her off," said Mrs. St. Julian. "I am afraid Henry is vexed about it. Look here." As she spoke she gave me a satiny, flowingly written note to read.

Castle Scudamore, Saturday.

DEAR MRS. ST. JULIAN—I have been made aware that my step-daughter has been followed to your house by a person with whom I and her father are most anxious that she should have no communication *whatever*. Whether this has happened with your cognizance I can not tell, but I shall naturally consider you responsible while she is under your roof, and I must beg you will be so good as not to continue to admit Captain Sigourney's visits. He is a person totally unsuitable in *every* respect to my step-daughter, and it is a marriage her father could not sanction.

I hope Emilia is well, and that she has had satisfactory accounts by this last mail. We received a few lines only, on business, from Bevis.

Believe me, yours truly,
E. MOUNTMORE.

"The whole thing is almost too absurd to be vexed about," said Mrs. St. Julian, smiling.

"Why was Lady Jane so angry with you, Queenie?" Hester asked; and then it was I confessed what I had seen that evening on the Knoll.

"Lady Jane told me all about it," my mistress continued. "She says Captain Sigourney's only object in life is to see her pass by. To tell you the truth, I do not think she cares in the least for him. She found him at the gate that evening, she says." Mrs. St. Julian hesitated, and then went on. "She must be very attractive. She tells me that she believes Mr. Hexham admires her very much, and that, on the whole, she thinks he is more the sort of person to suit her." Mrs. St. Julian spoke with a little gentle malice; and yet I could see she half believed, and that there was prudence, too, in what she was saying.

There was a pause. Hester looked straight

before her, and I stitched on. At last the mother spoke again :—

"I wish you would go to Emilia, my Hester," she said, a little anxiously. "I am afraid she is fretting sometimes when she is by herself."

"You poor mamma," cried Hester, jumping up and running to her, and kissing her again and again; "you have all our pain and none of our fun."

"Don't you think so, my dear," said the mother; "I think I have both." Then she called Hester back to her, held her hand, and looked into her face tenderly for a minute. "Go, darling!—but—but take care," she said, as she let her go.

"Take care of what, mamma?" the girl asked, a little consciously; and then Hester ran off, as all young girls will do, nothing loath to get out into the sunshine.

I stitched on at my work, but presently looking up I saw that Hester and Emilia were not alone; Mr. Hexham, who had, I suppose, been smoking his cigar in the garden, had joined them. He was lifting Bevis high up overhead, to pick the berries that were shining in the hedge. The Lodges seemed built for pretty live pictures; and the mistress's room, most specially of all the rooms in the house, is a peepshow to see them from. Through this window, with its illuminated border of clematis and ivy and Virginian creeper, I could see the bit of garden lawn, green still and sunlit; the two pretty sisters, in their flowing dresses, straight and slim, smiling at little Bevis; the high sweetbrier hedge, branching like a bower over their heads; and the swallows skimming across the distant down. This was the most romantic window of the three which lighted her room, and I asked my cousin to come and see a pretty group. She smiled, and then sighed as she looked. Poor troubled mother!

"I can not feel one moment's ease about Bevis," she said. "My poor Emmy! And yet Lady Jane was very positive."

"We shall know to-morrow. You are too anxious, I think," I answered cheerfully; and then I could not help asking her if she thought she should ever be as anxious about George Hexham.

She did not answer except by a soft little smile. Then she sighed again.

Lady Jane's expected letter had not come that Monday evening, but Mrs. St. Julian hoped on. Emilia was daily growing more anxious; she said very little, but every opening door startled her, every word seemed to her to have a meaning. She began to have a clear, ill-defined feeling that they were hiding something from her, and yet, poor little thing, she did not dare ask, for fear of getting bad news. Her soft, wan, appealing looks went to the very hearts of the people looking on. Lady Jane was the only person who could resist her. She was, or seemed to be, ruffled and annoyed that any one should be anxious when she had said there was no occasion for fear. Mrs. St. Julian would have quietly put off a certain expedition which had been arranged some time before for the next day; but Lady Jane, out of very opposition, was most eager and decided that it should take place. An invitation came for the girls to a ball; this the parents decidedly refused, though Hexham, and Hester too, looked sorely disappointed. Of course Lady Jane knew no reason for any special anxiety, any more than Emilia, and perhaps her confidence and cheerfulness were the best medicine for the poor young wife; who, seeing the sister so bright, began to think that she had over-estimated dangers which she only dimly felt and guessed at. So the carriages were ordered after luncheon; but the sun was shining bright in the morning, and Hexham asked Hester and Aileen (shyly, and hesitating as he spoke) if they would mind being photographed directly.

"Why should you not try a group?" said St. Julian. "Here are Hester, Lady Jane, Mona, Aileen, and Emilia, all wanting to be done at once."

Emilia shrank back, and said she only wanted baby done, not herself.

"I was longing to try a group," said Hexham, "and only waiting for leave. How will you sit?" And he began placing them in a sort of row, two up and one down, with a property-table in the middle. He then began focusing, and presently emerged, pale and breathless and excited, from the little black hood into which he had dived. "Will you look?" said he to St. Julian.

"I think it might be improved upon," said St. Julian, getting interested. "Look up, Mona, —up, up. That is better. And can not you take the ribbon out of your hair?"

"Yes, Uncle St. Julian," said Mona; "but it will all tumble down."

"Never mind that," said he; and with one hand Mona pulled away the snood, and then the beautiful stream came flowing and rippling and falling all about her shoulders.

"That is excellent," said the painter. "You, too, Aileen, shake out your locks." Then he began sending one for one thing and one for another. I was dispatched for some lilies into the garden, and Lady Jane came too, carrying little Bevis in her arms. When we got back we found one of the prettiest sights I have ever yet seen—a dream of fair ladies against an ivy wall, flowers and flowing locks, and sweeping garments. It is impossible to describe the peculiar charm of this living, breathing picture. Emilia, after all, had been made to come into it; little Bevis clapped his hands, and said, "Pooty mamma!" when he saw her.

"I don't mind being done in the group," said Lady Jane, "if you will promise not to put any of those absurd white pinafores on me."

Neither of the gentlemen answered, they were both too busy. As for me, I shall never forget the sweet child-wonder in my little Mona's face, Hester's bright deep eyes, or my poor Emilia's patient and most affecting expression, as they all stood there motionless; while Hexham held his watch, and St. Julian looked on almost as excited as the photographer. As Hexham rushed away into his van, with the glass under his arm, we all began talking again.

"It takes one's breath away," said St. Julian, quite excited, "to have the picture there, breathing on the glass, and to feel every instant that it may vanish or dissolve with a word, with a breath. I should never have nerve for photography."

"I believe the great objection is that it blackens one's fingers so," said Lady Jane. "I should have tried it myself, but I did not care to spoil my hands."

As for the picture, Hexham came out wildly exclaiming from his little dark room; never had he done any thing so strangely beautiful—he could not believe it—it was magical. The self-controlled young man was quite wild with delight and excitement. Lord Ulleskelf walked up, just as we were all clustering round, and he, too, admired immensely.

Hexham rushed up to St. Julian. "It is your doing," he said. "It is wonderful. My fortune is made." He all but embraced his precious glass.

St. Julian was to be the next subject. What a noble wild head it was! There was something human and yet almost mysterious to me in the flash of those pale circling eyes with the black brows and shaggy gray hair. But Hexham's luck failed him, perhaps from over-excitement and inexperience in success. Three or four attempts failed, and we were still at it when the luncheon-bell rang. Hexham was for going on all day; but St. Julian laughed and said it should be another time. This sentiment was particularly approved by Lady Jane, who had a childish liking for expeditions and picnickings, and who had set her heart upon carrying out her drive that afternoon.

VIII.

Hexham had known scarcely any thing before this of home life or home peace. He had carefully treasured his liberty, and vowed to himself that he would keep that liberty always. But now that he had seen Hester, fair, and maidenly, and serene, he could not tell what mysterious sympathy had attracted him. To speak to her, to hear her shy tender voice, affected him strangely. George Hexham did not care to give way to sentimental emotion; he felt that his hour had come. He had shared the common lot of men. It was a pity, perhaps, to give up independence and freedom and peace of mind, but no sacrifice was too great to win so dear a prize. So said George to himself as he looked at the glass upon which her image was printed, the image with the wondering eyes. He must get one more picture, he thought, eating his luncheon thoughtfully, but with a good appetite undisturbed by these reflections—one more of Hester alone. He determined to try and keep her at home that afternoon.

He followed her as she left the room.

"**You** are not going? Do stay," said Hexham, imploringly; "I want you; I want a picture of you all to myself. I told my man we should come back after luncheon."

Hester colored up. Her mother's warning was still in her ears.

"I—I am afraid I must go," she said shyly.

"What nonsense!" cried Hexham, who was perfectly unused to contradiction, and excited by his success. "I shall go and tell your mother that it is horrible tyranny to send you off with that *corvée* of children and women, and that you want to stay behind. Lady Jane would stay if I asked her."

Hester did not quite approve of this familiar way of speaking. She drew herself up more and more shyly and coldly.

"No, thank you," she said, "mamma lets me do just as I like. I had rather go with the others."

"In that case," said Hexham, offended, "I shall not presume to interfere." And he turned and walked away.

What is a difference? A word that means nothing—a look a little to the right or to the left of an appealing glance. I think that people who quarrel are often as fond of one another as people who embrace. They speak a different language, that is all. Affection and agreement are things quite apart. To agree with the people you love is a blessing unspeakable. But people who differ may also be travelling along the same road on opposite sides. And there are two sides to every road that both lead the same way.

Hexham was so unused to being opposed that his indignation knew no bounds. He first thought of remaining behind, and showing his displeasure by a haughty seclusion. But Lady Jane happened to drive up with Aileen in the pony-carriage she had hired, feathers flying, gauntleted, all prepared to go to conquer.

"Won't you come with us, Mr. Hexham?" she said, in her most gracious tone.

After a moment's hesitation, Hexham jumped in, for he saw Hester standing not far off, and he began immediately to make himself as agreeable as he possibly could to his companion. It was not much that happened this afternoon, but trifles show which way the wind is blowing. Lady Jane and her cavalier went first, the rest of us followed in Mrs. St. Julian's carriage. We were bound for a certain pretty bay some two miles off. The way there led across a wide and desolate warren, where sand and gorse spread on either side to meet a sky whose reflections always seemed to me saddened by the dark growth of this arid place. A broad stony military road led to a building on the edge of the cliff—a hotel, where the carriages put up. Then we began clambering down the side of the cliff, out of this somewhat dreary region, into a world brighter and more lovely than

I have words to put to it—a smiling plain of glassy blue sea, a vast firmament of heaven ; and close at hand bright sandy banks, shining with streams of color reflected from the crystals and strata upheaved in shining strands ; and farther off the boats drifting towards the opal Broadshire Hills.

I do not suppose that any body seeing us strolling along these lovely cliffs would have guessed the odd and depressing influence that was at work upon most of us. As far as Lady Jane and Hexham and Aileen were concerned, the expedition seemed successful enough ; they laughed and chattered, and laughed again. Emilia and her sister followed, listening to their shrieks, in silence, with little Bevis between them. Mona and I brought up the rear. Lady Jane seemed quite well pleased with her companion, and evidently accepted his homage all to herself. I could have shaken her for being so stupid. Could she not see that not one single word he spoke was intended for her. Every one of Hexham's arrows flew straight to the gentle heart for which they were intended. It was not a very long walk—perhaps half an hour in duration—but half an hour is long enough to change a lifetime, to put a new meaning to all that has passed, and to all that is yet to come. People may laugh at such a thing as *désillusionnement*, but it is a very real and very bitter thing, for all that people may say. To some constant natures certainty and unchangeableness are the great charm, the whole meaning of love. Hester, suddenly bewildered and made to doubt, would freeze, and change, and fly at a shadow ; where Hester, once certain, would endure all things, bear, and hope, and forgive. I could see that Hexham did not dislike a little excitement ; *l'imprévu* had an immense charm for him. He was rapid, determined ; so sure of himself that he could afford not to be sure of others. Hexham's tactics were very simple. He loved Hester. Of this he had no doubt, but he had no idea of loving a woman as Shakspeare, for instance, was content to love, or at least to write of it—"Being your slave, what should I do but wait?" This was not in Hexham's philosophy. Hester had offended him, and he had been snubbed ; he would show her his indifference, and punish her for his punishment.

We were all on our way back to the carriages when Hester stopped suddenly at a little zigzag path leading down to the sands, down which Mona and I had been scrambling. "Do you think Bevy could get down here?" she asked. "Do let us go down, Emilia. I think we have time ; the carriages are not yet ready."

Emilia, although frightened out of her wits, instantly assented, and Mona and I watched Hester springing from rock to rock and from step to step. She lifted Bevis safe down the steep side ; little falling stones and shells and sands went showering on to the shingle below ; a sea-gull came out of a hole in the sand, and flew out to sea. Bevy screamed with delight. Hester's quick light step seemed every where ;

she put him safe down below, and then sprang up again to her sister's help. The little excitement acted like a tonic. "How pretty it is here!" she said.

We had sat for some ten minutes under the wing of the great cliff, in an arch or hollow, lined with a slender tracery of granite lines close following one another. The arching ridge of the cliff cut the high line of blue sea sharply into a curve.

"It was like a desert island," Hester said, looking at the little cove inclosed in its mighty walls, with the smooth unfurrowed crescent of shingle gleaming and shining, and the white, light little waves rushing against the stones; "an island upon which we had been wrecked."

"An island," I thought to myself, "no Hexham had as yet discovered." I wondered how long it would be desert?

Mona, tired of sitting, soon wandered off, and disappeared at the side of the cliff. I do not know how long we should have staid there if little Bevis, who had never yet heard of a desert island, and who thought people always all lived together, and that it was naughty to be shy, and that he was getting very hungry, and that he had better cry a little, had not suddenly set up a shrill and imperious demand for his dinner, his "'ome," as he called it, Toosan his nurse, and his rocking-horse. Emilia jumped up, and Hester too.

"It must be time for us to go," said Mrs. Beverley.

It is generally easier to climb up than to descend, and so it would have been now for Hester alone. I do not know why the sun-beaten path seemed so hard, the blocks of stone so loose and crumbling. Hester went first, with Bevis in her arms, and at first got on pretty well; but for some reason or other—perhaps that in coming down we had disturbed the stones—certainly as she went on her footsteps seemed less rapid and lucky than they usually were. She stumbled, righted herself, took another step, Bevis clinging tight to her neck. Emilia cried out, frightened. Hester, a little nervous, put Bevvy on a big stone, and stood breathless for an instant. "Come up, Emmy," she said; "this way—there, to that next big step." Emmy did her best, but before she could catch at Hester's extended hand her foot slipped again, and she gave another little scream.

"Hester, help me!"

I was at some little distance. I had tried a little independent track of my own, which proved more impracticable than I had expected. It was in vain I tried to get to Emilia's assistance. There was no real danger for Emilia, clinging to a big granite boulder fixed in the sand, but it was absurd and not pleasant. The sun baked upon the sandy paths. Hester told Bevvy to sit still while she went to help mamma. "No, no, no," cried little Bevis when his aunt attempted to leave him, clutching at her with a sudden spring, which nearly overset her. It

was at this instant that I saw, to my inexpressible relief, two keen eyes peering over the edge of the cliff, and Hexham coming down the little path to our relief.

"I could not think where you had got to," he said; "I came back to see. Will you take hold of my stick, Mrs. Beverley? I will come back for the boy, Miss St. Julian." Hexham would have returned a third time for Hester, but she was close behind him, and silently rejected his proffered help. George Hexham turned away in silence. Hester was already scarcely grateful to him for coming back at all. He had spoken to her, but her manner had been so cold, his voice so hard, that it seemed as if indeed all was over between them. Hester was no gentle Griselda, but a tender and yet imperious princess, accustomed to confer favors and to receive gratitude from her subjects. Here was one who had revolted from her allegiance.

*   *   *   *   *   *

(Fragment of a letter found in Mr. Hexham's room after his departure:)

. . . . A little bit of the island is shining through my open glass-pane. I see a green field with a low hedge, a thatched farm, woods, flecks of shade, a line of down rising from the frill of the muslin blind to the straggling branch of clematis that has been put to grow round my window. It is all a nothing compared to really beautiful scenery, and yet it is every thing when one has once been conquered by the charm of the place—the still, sweet influence of its tender lights, its charming *humility* and unpretension, if one can so speak of any thing inanimate. It is six o'clock; the sky is patched and streaked with gray and yellowish clouds upon a faint sunset aquamarine; a wind from the sea is moving through the clematis and making the light tendrils dance and swing; a sudden unexpected gleam of light has worked enchantment with the field and the farmstead, the straw is aflame, the thatch is golden, the dry stubble is gleaming. A sense of peace and evening and rest comes over me as I write and look from my window. This sort of family life suits me. I do not find time heavy on my hands. St. Julian is a lucky fellow to be the ruler of such a pleasant dominion. I never saw any thing more charmingly pretty than its boundaries studded with scarlet berries, and twisted twigs, with birds starting and flying across the road, almost under our horses' feet, as we came along. I am glad I came. Old St. Julian is as ever capital company, and the most hospitable of hosts. Mrs. St. Julian is an old love of mine: she is a sweet and gracious creature. This is more than I can say of my fellow-guest, Lady Jane Beverley, who is the most overpowering of women. I carefully keep out of her way, but I can not always escape her. Hester St. Julian is very like her mother, but with something of St. Julian's strength of character—she has almost too much. She was angry with me to-day. Perhaps I deserved it. I hope she has forgiven me by this time, for I, to tell the truth, can not afford to quarrel with her.

Lord Ulleskelf is here a good deal; his long white hair is more silvery than ever; he came up this morning to see my photography; I wish you had been standing by to see our general eagerness and excitement; the fact is, that here in this island the simplest emotions seem intensified and magnified. Its very stillness and isolation keep us and our energies from overpassing its boundaries. I have been here two days—I feel as if I had spent a lifetime in the place, and were never going away any more, and as if the world all about was as visionary as the gray Broadshire Hills that we see from High Down. As for certain old loves and interests that you may have known of, I do not believe they ever existed, except upon paper. If I mistake not, I have found an interest here more deep than any passing fancy.

＊　　＊　　＊　　＊　　＊　　＊

IX.

The day had begun well and brightly, but there was a jar in the music that evening which was evident enough to most of us. We had all been highly wrought from one cause and another, and this may have accounted for some natural reaction. For one thing, we missed William and his family; tiresome as Mrs. William undoubtedly was, her placid monotone harmonized with the rest of the performance, for though she was prosy, she was certainly sweet-tempered, and the children were charming. It had seemed like the beginning of the summer's end to see them drive off; little hands waving and rosy faces smiling good-bye. Poor Mona was in despair, and went to bed early. Lady Jane sat looking still black and offended with her host in her corner; something had occasioned a renewed access of indignation. Mrs. St. Julian did her very best to propitiate her indignant guest, but the poor lady gave up trying at last, and leaned back in her chair wearily, and closed her eyes. I myself was haunted by the ill-defined feeling of something amiss—of trouble present or at hand. Hester, too, was out of spirits. It was evident that she and Mr. Hexham had not quite forgiven each other for the morning's discussion. Altogether, it was a dismal disjointed evening, during which a new phase of Hexham's character was revealed to us, and it was not the best or the kindest. There was a hard look in his handsome face and skeptical tone in his voice. He seemed possessed by what the French call l'esprit moqueur. Hester, pained and silenced at last, would scarcely answer him when he spoke. Her father with an effort got up and took a book and began to read something out of one of Wordsworth's sonnets. It is always delightful to me to hear St. Julian read. His voice rolled and thrilled through the room, and we were all silent for a moment:—

Thy soul was like a star, and dwelt apart,
Thou hadst a voice whose sound was like the sea.

"I hate Wordsworth. He is always preaching to one," said Hexham, not very politely, as St. Julian ceased reading. "I never feel so wicked as when I am being preached to."

"I am sorry for you," said St. Julian dryly. "I have never been able to read this passage of Wordsworth without emotion since I was a boy, and first found it in my school-books."

Hester had jumped up and slipped out of the room while this discussion was going on; I followed presently, for I remembered a little bit of work which St. Julian had asked us to see to that evening.

He used sometimes to give me work to do for him, although I was not so clever as Hester in fashioning and fitting the things he wanted for his models; but I did my best, and between us we had produced some very respectable coiffes, wimples, slashed bodices, and other bygone elegances. We had also concocted an Italian peasant, and a mediæval princess, and a dear little Dutch girl—our triumph. I found I had not my materials at hand, and I went to the studio to look for them. I was looking for a certain piece of silken stuff which I thought I had seen in the outer studio, and which my cousin had asked me to stitch together so as to make a cloak. I turned the things over and over, but I could not discover what I was in quest of among the piles and heaped-up properties that were kept there. I supposed it must be in the inner room, and I lifted the curtain and went in. I had expected to find the place dark, and silent, and empty. But the room was not dark. The wood-fire was burning; the tall candles were lighted; the pictures on the walls were reflecting the light, and looking almost alive, crowding there, and gazing with those strange living eyes that St. Julian knew so well how to paint; a statesman in his robe; a musician leaning against the wall, drawing his bow across the strings of his violin. As I looked at him in the stream of the fire-flame, I almost expected to hear the conquering sound of the wailing melody. But he did not play; he seemed to me to be waiting, and looking out, and listening to other music than his own. All these pictures were so familiar to us all as we came and went, that we often scarcely paused to look at them. But to-night, in the firelight, they impressed me anew with a sense of admiration for the wonderful power of the man who had produced them. Over the chimney hung a poet, noble and simple and kingly, as St. Julian had painted him. Next to the poet was the head of a calm and beautiful woman, bending in a stream of light. It was either Emilia or her mother in her youth. . . . . An evangelist, with a grand, quiet brow and a white flood of silver beard, came next; and then warriors, and nobles, and maidens with flowing hair. They seemed almost touched to life to-night. Hester was standing underneath the picture of the evangelist, a real living picture. Her head was leaning wearily against the wall. She had come in before me, and seemed standing in a dreary way, with hanging hands. The silk stuffs she had collected were on the ground at her feet, and the pattern cloak was hanging from a chair; but she had thrown her work away. I don't know why, unless it was that her eyes were full of great tired tears that she was trying vainly to keep back.

"My dear," I said, frightened; "my dear, what is it? What has happened? Has he vexed you?" I hated myself the next instant. I had spoken hastily and without reflection. My question upset her; she struggled for a minute, and then burst out crying, though she was a brave girl—courageous, and not given to useless complaints. Then she looked up, flushing crimson reproach at me. "It is not what you seem to think," she said. "Don't you know me better? It is something—I don't know what. How foolish I am!" And this time, with an effort, she conquered her tears. "Oh Queenie!" she said, "I know there is something wrong; some terrible news. I don't dare ask, for they have not told me; and I don't, don't dare ask," she repeated. I was silent, for she was speaking the thought which had been in my own heart of late. At last I said, "One has foolish, nervous frights at times. What makes you so afraid, Hester?"

Hester smiled faintly, with her tear-dimmed face.

"There has been another absurd and provoking scene," she said, "with Lady Jane. Something she said of anxiety, and a letter, and—and—I don't know what frightened me," said Hester, faltering. "She said she would go immediately, that she should marry, meet, write, invite any body she chose, and that if it were not for this anxiety for Emilia—some letter she expected—she would leave us that instant; and then my mother stopped her, and that is all I know," said Hester, with a great sigh. "It is not worth crying for, is it, Queenie?"

As she spoke the door opened and St. Julian and Hexham came in to smoke their evening pipes. Hester drew herself up with bright flushed cheeks and said a haughty good-night to Hexham as she passed him. But in my heart I thought more than one doubt had caused Hester's tears to flow that night.

Hexham seemed unconscious enough. "I shall be quite ready for sitters to-morrow morning, Miss Hester," said the provoking young man, cheerfully. "You won't disappoint me again?"

Hester did not answer, and walked out of the room.

Hexham tried to persuade himself next day that he had made it all right with Hester overnight. He had come down late and had missed her at breakfast, but he made sure she would not fail him, and he got ready his chemicals and kept telling himself that she would come. The glasses were polished bright, and in their places.

Every thing was as it should be, he thought; the sun was shining as photographers wish it to shine. Once, hearing steps, Hexham turned hastily, but it was only St. Julian on his way to his studio; Lady Jane went by presently; then it was Lord Ulleskelf who passed by; and each time Hexham felt more aggrieved and disappointed. Hexham came to me twice as I sat at work in the drawing-room window, but I did not know where Hester had gone, or if she meant to sit to him. Little Mona went by last of all. The child had her hands full of grasses that I had sent her to gather. She went wandering on between the garden beds with a little busy brain full of pretty fancies, strange fairy-dreams and stories of a world in which she was living apart from us all. It was an enchanted world, a court where lords and ladies were doing stately obeisance to a fairy Queen in the lily-bed. The tall pampas grasses waved over my little maiden's head and bowed their yellow flowers in the wind. The myrtles glimmered mysteriously, the tamarisks drooped their fringed stems, wind-blown shrubs shivered and shook, while a woodpecker from the outer world who had ventured into fairy realms was laboriously climbing the stem of a slender elm-tree. Hexham asked Mona if she knew where Hester was, and the child, waking up, pointed to the house: "She was there, at work for Uncle Henry, in the housekeeper's room, as I passed," said Mona.

Hexham was, as I have said, a young man of an impatient humor. He was a little hard, as young men are apt to be. But there was something reassuring in his very hardness and faith in himself and his own doings—reassuring because it was a genuine expression of youthful strength and power. No bad man could have had that perfect confidence which marked most of George Hexham's sayings and doings. His was, after all, the complacency of good intentions.

He had taken it as a matter of course, not only that Hester would come, but that she would come with a feeling not unlike the feeling with which he was expecting her. He could not understand her absence, her continued coldness. What did it mean? did it, could it mean that she was unconscious of his admiration? It had suddenly become a matter of utter consequence to the young man that he should find her now, reproach her, read her face, and discover why she had thwarted him. He might see her all day and at any hour, and yet this was the hour he had set apart as his own—when he wanted her—the hour he had looked forward to and counted on and longed for. He came to me a third time, and asked me if I would take a message for him. I was a little sorry for him, although I thought he deserved this gentle punishment.

"If you will come with me we will go and look for her," I said.

"You are doing me an immense kindness," cried Hexham, gratefully.

The housekeeper's room could be entered by the court-yard: it was next to the outer studio, into which it led by a door. It was used for models and had been taken from the servants. As Mona had said, Hester was sitting in the window at work when we came in; the door into the studio was open, and I heard voices of people talking within.

Hester's needle flew along in a sort of rhythmic measure. She knew Hexham had come in with me, but she did not look up, only worked on. Poor Hester! her heart was too heavy for blushes or passing agitations. Hexham had wounded her and disappointed her, but, young as she was, the girl had a sense of the fitness of things which kept her from betraying all she felt; and, indeed, this great unaccountable feeling of anxiety now occupied most thoughts and feelings, except those to which she would not own. George Hexham stood with a curious face, full of anger and sympathy and compunction, watching her stitches as they flew. One, two, three, he counted, and the quaint little garment turned and twisted in her pale hands. Once she looked up at him. It would have been better if she had looked reproachful; but no, it was a grave cold glance she gave, and then her head bent down once more over her work. I left them to their own explanations, and went back to my drawing-room window.

Afterward Hester told me how angry she was with me for bringing him.

"Have you nearly done? May I talk to you when you have finished that stitching?" he said to her presently.

"I can listen while I work," said Hester, still sewing, and if she paused it was only to measure the seams upon the little model for whom they were intended.

That needle flying seemed to poor Hexham an impassable barrier—a weapon wielded by this Amazon that he could not overcome. It kept him at arms' length; it absorbed her attention; she scarcely listened to what he said, as she stuck and threaded and travelled along the strange little garment. He found himself counting the stitches—one, two, three, four, five, six, seven, eight—it was absurd; it was like an enchantment.

"Hester," cried Hexham, "you won't understand me!" Hester worked on and did not answer. His voice was quick, passionate, and agitated. "You are so calm," he cried. "I do not believe the common weaknesses of life touch you in the least, or that you ever know how to make any allowance for others."

"I can make allowance," faltered Hester, as with trembling hands she stooped and began tying on the child's little garment.

To Hexham's annoyance, at that moment St. Julian appeared.

"You here, Hexham? Come and see Lord Ulleskelf. Is the child ready?" he asked. "That is right;" and he led off the little girl, in her funny Velasquez dress, trotting along to his long quick strides. Hexham followed them to the door, and then turned back slowly.

Hester had sunk wearily in the chair in which she had been sitting, leaning her head upon her hand. She thought it was all over; Hexham was gone. "She did not care," she said to herself; as people say they do not care, when they know in their heart of hearts that they **have** but to speak to call a welcome answering voice, to put out their hand for another hand to grasp. They do not say so when all is really gone, and there is no answer any where. Sometimes she softened, but Hester was indignant to think of the possibility of having been laughed at and made a play of when she herself had come with a heart trusting and true and tender. He could not care for Lady Jane, but he had ventured to say more than he really felt to Hester herself. Now it seemed to her that the whole aim and object of her care should be to prevent Hexham from guessing what she had foolishly fancied—Hexham, who had come back, and who was standing looking with keen doubtful glances into her face. She turned her two clear inscrutable eyes upon him once more, and tried to meet his gaze quietly, but her eyes fell beneath his.

"Hester," he said once again, and stopped short, hearing a step at the door. Poor Hester blushed up crimson with blushes that she blushed for again. Had she betrayed herself? Ah, no, no! She started up. "I must go," she said. Ah! she would go to her father. There was love, tender and generous love, to shield, to protect, to help her; not love like this, that was but a play, false, cruel, ready to wound.

"Dear Hester, don't go! Stay!" Hexham entreated, as she began to move toward the door leading to her father's studio. He had not chosen his time well, poor fellow, for Lady Jane, who was still in the outer studio, hearing his voice, came to the door, looked in for one instant, and turned away with an odd expression in her face and a brisk shrug of the shoulders. They both saw her. Hester looked up once again, with doubtful, questioning eyes, and then there was a minute's silence. Hexham understood her: a minute ago he had been gentle, now her doubts angered him.

"Why are you so hard to me?" he burst out at last, a little indignantly, and thoroughly in earnest. "How can you suppose I have ever fancied that odious woman? Will you believe me, or not, when I tell you how truly and devotedly I love and admire you? You are the only woman I have ever seen whom I would make my wife. If you send me away, you will crush all that is best and truest in my nature, and destroy my only chance of salvation."

"This is not the way to speak," said Hester, gravely, with a beating heart. His hardness frightened her, as her coldness and self-control angered him; and yet he could not quite forget her sudden emotion of a moment before. It was a curious reluctant attraction that seemed to unite these two people, who loved each other, and yet were cold ; and who, like a pair of children as they were, were playing with their best chance of happiness, and willfully putting it away. They stood looking at each other, doubtful still, excited, at once angry and gentle.

"How can I trust you," said proud Hester, coldly still, "after yesterday?—after—no, you do not really care for me, or—"

It was, I think, at that moment that they heard a sort of low stifled scream from outside, and then hasty footsteps. Hester started. "Was that Lady Jane?" she said. "Oh, what is it? Oh, has it come?" Unnerved, excited, she put up her two hands nervously, and instinctively turning to Hexham for help.

"My dearest," said Hexham, melting, utterly forgetting all her coldness, thinking only of her—"what is it—what do you fear?" and as he spoke he kept her back for one instant by the two trembling hands, grasping them firmly in his own. . . . .

No other word was spoken, but from that moment they felt that they belonged to each other.

"I don't know what I fear," she said. "Oh, come, come!"

X.

LADY JANE had walked angrily out through the studio door into the garden. Her temper had'not been improved by a disagreeable scolding letter from Lady Mountmore which had just been put into her hand. It contained the long-looked-for scrap from Bevis, which his father had forwarded. Lady Jane was venting a certain inward indignation in a brisk walk up and down the front of the house, when Lord Ulleskelf came toward her.

"Are you coming this afternoon to explore the castle with us?" she asked. "I believe we are all going—that is, most of us. Aileen and Mona have gone off with my maid in the coach."

He shook his head. "No," he said. "And I think if it were not for the children's sake you none of you would much care to go. But I suppose it is better to live on as usual and make no change to express the hidden anxieties which must trouble us all at times."

"Well, I must say I think it is very ridiculous," said Lady Jane, who was thoroughly out of temper. "These young wives seem to think that they and their husbands are of so much consequence, that every convulsion of life and nature must combine to injure them and keep them apart."

Lord Ulleskelf had spoken forgetting that Lady Jane was quite ignorant of their present cause for alarm. He was half indignant at what he thought utter want of feeling, half convinced by Lady Jane's logic. He had first known St. Julian at Rome, years before, and had been his friend all his life. He admired his genius, loved the girls, and was devoted to

the mother: any trouble which befell them came home to him almost as a personal matter. . . . .

"It is perfectly absurd," the young lady went on. "We have heard at home all was well; and I can not sympathize with this mawkish sentimentality. I hate humbug. I'm a peculiar character, and I always dislike much ado about nothing. I am something of a stoic."

"You heard by this mail?" said Lord Ulleskelf, anxiously.

"Of course we did," said Lady Jane. "I had written to my father to send me the letter. Here it is." And she put it into his hand. They had walked on side by side, and come almost in front of the house, with its open windows. Lady Jane was utterly vexed and put out. Hexham's look of annoyance when she had come in upon them a minute before was the last drop in her cup, and she now went on, in her jerky way :—

"Emilia is all very well ; but really I do pity poor Bevis if this is the future in store for him—an anxious wife taking fright at every shadow. Mrs. St. Julian only encourages her in her want of self-control. It is absurd."

Lord Ulleskelf, who had been examining the letter with some anxiety, folded it up. He was shocked and overcome. He confessed to me afterward that he thought there was no necessity for sparing the feelings of a young lady so well able as Lady Jane to bear anxiety and to blame the over-sensitiveness of others. The letter was short, and about money affairs. In a postscript to the letter, Bevis said : "Da Costa and Dubois want me to join a shooting expedition ; but I shall not be able to get away." This was some slight comfort, though to Lord Ulleskelf it only seemed a confirmation of his worst fears.

"It is not a shadow," he said, gravely. "If you like to look at this"—and he took a folded newspaper out of his pocket—"you will see why we have been so anxious for poor Emmy. Some one sent me a French paper, in which a paragraph had been copied from the Rio paper, containing an account of an accident to some young Englishman there. I have now, with some difficulty, obtained the original paper itself, with fuller particulars. You will see that this translation is added. I need not ask you to spare Mrs. Bevis a little longer, while the news is uncertain. The accident happened on the 2d, four days before the steamer left. This letter is dated the 30th August, and must have been written before the accident happened."

He turned away as he spoke, and left her standing there, poor woman, in the blaze of sunshine. Lady Jane never forgot that minute. The sea washed in the distance, a flight of birds flew overhead, the sun poured down. She stamped upon the crumbling gravel, and then, with an odd choked sort of cry—hearing some of them coming—fairly ran into the house and up stairs and along the passage into the mistress's room, of which the door happened to be open.

This was the cry which brought Hester and

Hexham out into the yard. I was in the drawing-room, when Lord Ulleskelf came in hurriedly, looking very much disturbed.

"Mrs. Campbell, for Heaven's sake go to
Lady Jane!" he cried. "Do not let her alarm
Emilia. I have been most indiscreet—much
to blame. Pray go."

I put down my work and hurried up stairs as
he told me. As I went I could hear poor Lady
Jane's sobs. I had reached the end of the
gallery when I saw a door open, and a figure
running toward the mistress's room. Then I
knew I was too late, for it was Emmy, who from
her mother's bedroom had also heard the cry.

"Mamma, something is wrong," said Emilia,
"hold Bevvy for me!" And before her mother
could prevent her, she had put the child in her
arms and run along the passage to see what
was the matter.

How shall I tell the cruel pang which was
waiting for her, running up unconscious to meet
the stab! Lady Jane was sitting crying on Mrs.
St. Julian's little sofa. When she saw Emmy
she lost all presence of mind: she cried out,
"Don't, don't come, Emmy!—not you—not
you!" Then jumping up she seized the newspaper and ran out of the room; but the translation Lord Ulleskelf had written out fell on the
floor as she left, and poor frightened Emilia, fearing every thing, took it up eagerly.

I did not see this—at least I only remembered it afterward, for poor Lady Jane, meeting me at the door, seized hold of my arm, saying, "Go back, go back! Oh, take me to St.
Julian!" The poor thing was quite distraught
for some minutes. I took her to her room and
tried to quiet her, and then I went, as she asked
me, to look for my cousin. I ran down by the
back way and the little staircase to the studio.
It was empty, except that the little model and
her mother were getting ready to go. The gentleman was gone, the child said: he had told
her to come back next day. She was putting
off her little quaint cloak, with her mother's
help, in a corner of the big room. I hurried
back to the house. On the stairs I found Hester, with her companion, and my mistress at the
head of the stairs. Hester and Hexham both
turned to me, and my mistress eagerly asked
whether I had found St. Julian. I do not know
how it was—certainly at the time I could not
have described what was happening before my
eyes; but afterward, thinking things over, I
seemed to see a phantasmagoria of the events
of the day passing before my eyes. I seemed
to see the look of motherly sympathy and benediction with which, in all her pain for Emilia,
Mrs. St. Julian turned to her Hester. I don't
know if the two young folks had spoken to her.
They were standing side by side, as people who
had a right to one another's help; and afterward, when I was alone, Hester's face came
before me, sad, troubled, and yet illumined by
the radiance of a new-found light.

I suppose excitement is a mood which stamps
events clearly marked and well defined upon our

minds. I think for the most part our lives are
more wonderful, sadder, and brighter, more
beautiful and picturesque, than we have eyes to
see or ears to understand, except at certain moments when a crisis comes to stir slow hearts,
to brighten dim eyes to sight, and dull ears to
the sounds that vibrate all about. So it is with
happy people, and lookers-on at the history of
others: for those who are in pain a merciful
shadow falls at first, hiding, and covering, and
tempering the cruel pangs of fear and passionate regret.

XI.

EMMY read the paper quite quietly, in a sort
of dream: this old crumpled paper, lying on the
table, in which she saw her husband's name printed. Her first thought was, why had they kept
it from her? Here was news, and they had not
given it. Bevis Beverley! She even stopped
for an instant to think what a pretty, strange
name it was; stopped willfully, with that sort
of instinct we all have when we will not realize
to ourselves that something of ill to those we
love is at hand. Then she began to read, and
at first she did not quite understand. A shooting-party had gone up the Paraná River; the
boat was supposed to have overturned. The
names, as well as they could gather, were as
follows:—Don Manuel da Costa, Mr. P. Dubois,
Mr. Bevis Beverley of the English Embassy, Mr.
Stanmore, and Señor Antonio de Caita—of
whom not one had been saved. Emilia read it
once quietly, only her heart suddenly began to
beat, and the room to swim round and round;
but even in the bewildering circles she clutched
the paper and forced herself to read the dizzy
words again. At first she did not feel very
much, and even for an instant her mind glanced
off to something else—to her mother waiting
down below with little Bevis in her lap—then a
great dark cloud began to descend quietly and
settle upon the poor little woman, blotting out
sunlight and landscape and color. Emilia lost
mental consciousness as the darkness closed in
upon her, not bodily consciousness. She had a
dim feeling as if some one had drawn a curtain
across the window, so she told me afterward.
She was sitting in her mother's room, this she
knew; but a terrible, terrible trouble was all
about her, all around, every where, echoing in
the darkness, and cold at her heart. Bevis,
she wanted Bevis or her mother: they could
send it away; and with a great effort she cried
out, "Mamma! mamma!" And at that instant somebody who had been talking to her,
but whom she had not heeded, seemed to say,
"Here she is," and in a minute more her mother's tender arms were round her, and Emilia,
coming to herself again, looked up into that tender, familiar face.

"My darling," said the mother, "you must
hope, and trust, and be brave. Nothing is confirmed; we must pray and love one another,

and have faith in a heavenly mercy. If it had been certain, do you think I should have kept it from you all this time?"

"How long?" said the parched lips; and Emilia turned in a dazed way from Mrs. St. Julian to Lady Jane, who had come back, and who was standing by with an odd, startled face, looking as pale almost as Emmy herself.

"Oh, Emmy, dear, dear Emmy, don't believe it: we have had a letter since. I shall never forgive myself as long as I live—never! I left it out; that hateful paper. Oh dear! Oh dear! Oh dear!" sobbed poor Lady Jane, once more completely overcome, as she sank into a chair and hid her face in her hands.

Little Emilia made a great effort. She got up from her seat with a piteous look; she went up to her sister-in-law and put her hand on her shoulder. "Don't cry, Jane," she said, trembling very much. "Mamma says there is hope; and Bevis said I was to try and make the best of things. I had rather know," said poor Emilia, turning sick and pale again. "May I see your letter?"

Lady Jane was almost overawed by the gentle sweetness of these two women.

"How can you think of me just now? Oh Emilia! I—I don't deserve it!" And she got up and a second time rushed out of the room.

Emmy's wonderful gentleness and self-control touched me more than I can express. She did not say much more, but went back to her mother, and knelt down and buried her face in her knees in a childish attitude, kneeling there still and motionless, while all the bright light came trembling and shining upon the two bent heads, and the sound of birds and of bleating sheep and shouting children came in at the open windows. I thought they were best alone, and left them, shutting the door. The house was silent and empty of the life which belonged to it, only it seemed to me crowded to suffocation by this great trouble and anxiety. This uncertainty was horrible. How would the time pass until the next mail came due? I was thankful from my heart to think that half the time had passed. Only I felt now at this moment that I must breathe, get out upon the downs, shake off the overpowering sense of sorrow. I could not but feel when those so dear and so near to me were in so much pain; but on my way, as I passed Lady Jane's door, some compunction made me pause for a moment, and knock and go in. Poor Lady Jane! She was standing at the toilet-table. She had opened her dressing-case to get out the letter which she had hidden away there only a few minutes before, and in so doing she seemed to have caught sight of her own face in the glass, frightened and strange, and unlike any thing she had ever seen before. And so she stood looking in a curious stupid way at the tears slowly coursing down her cheeks. She started as I came in, and turned round.

"I—I am not used to this sort of thing," said she. "I have been feeling as if I was somebody else, Mrs. Campbell. I don't know what I ought to do. What do you think? Shall I take this in? Will it be of any comfort?"

"It will be of no comfort, I fear. It was written before—before that happened. But I fear it is of no use trying to keep any thing from her now," I said, and then together we went back to the door of the mistress's little room. Mrs. St. Julian put out her hand for the letter, and signed to us to go. Only as we walked away along the passage I heard a great burst of sobbing, and I guessed that it was occasioned by the sight of Bevis's well-known handwriting. Poor Lady Jane began to cry too, and then jerked her tears impatiently away, beginning to look like herself again.

"It's too absurd," she said. "All about nothing. Dear old Bevis! I am sure he will come back all safe. I have no patience with such silly frights. I am frightened too now; but there is no more danger than there was yesterday."

I could not help thinking there was some sense in Lady Jane's cheerful view of things: after all it was the barest uncertainty and hint of evil, when all around, on every side, dangers of every sort were about each one of those whom we loved, from which no loving cares or prayers could shield them: a foot slips, a stone falls, and a heart breaks or a life is ended, and what then . . .? A horrible vision of my own child —close, close to the edge of the dreadful cliff—came before me. I was nervous and infected, too, with sad terrors and presentiments which the sight of the poor sweet young wife's misery had suggested.

In her odd, decided way, she said she must come out too. She could not bear the house, she could not bear to see the others.

Lady Jane walked beside me with firm, even footsteps, occasionally telling me one thing and another of her favorite brother. Her flow of talk was interrupted: the real true heart within her seemed stirred by an unaffected sympathy for the trouble of the people with whom she was living. Her face seemed kindled, the hard look had gone out of it; for the first time I could imagine a likeness between her and her brother, and I began to feel a certain trust and reliance in this strange wayward woman. After a little she was quite silent. We had a dreary little walk, pacing on together along the lane: how long the way seemed, how dull the hedges looked, how dreary the road! It seemed as if our walk had lasted for hours, but we had been out only a very little time. When we came in there was a three-cornered note addressed to Lady Jane lying on the hall table. "A gentleman brought it," said the parlor-maid; and I left Lady Jane to her correspondence, while I ran up to see how my two dear women were going on.

The day lagged on slowly: Emmy had got her little Bevis with her, and was lying down in her own room while he played about. Mrs. St. Julian came and went, doing too much for

I

her own strength, but I could not prevent her. She put me in mind of some bird hovering about her nest, as I met her again and again standing wistful and tender by her daughter's door, listening, and thinking what she could do more to ease her pain.

In course of the afternoon St. Julian, who had been out when all this happened—having suddenly dismissed his model, and gone off for one of the long solitary tramps to which he was sometimes accustomed—came home to find the house in sad confusion. I think his presence was better medicine for Emmy than her mother's tender, wistful sympathy.

"I don't wonder at your being very uncomfortable," he said; but I myself think there is a strong probability that your fears are unfounded. Bevis says most distinctly that he has refused to join the expedition. His name has been talked of: that is enough to give rise to a report that he is one of the party. . . . . I would give you more sympathy if I did not think that it won't be wanted, my dear." He pulled her little hand through his arm as he spoke, and patted it gently. He looked so tender, so encouraging, so well able to take care of the poor little thing, she clung to him closer and closer.

"Oh, my dearest papa," she said, "I will try, indeed I will!" And she hid her face, and tried to choke down her sobs.

I had prepared a bountiful tea for them, to which St. Julian came; but neither Mrs. St. Julian nor Emilia appeared. Lady Jane came down, somewhat subdued, but trying to keep up a desultory conversation, as if nothing had happened, which vexed me at the moment. Even little Bevis soon found out that something was wrong, and his little voice seemed hushed in the big wooden room.

And then the next day dawned, and another long day lagged on. St. Julian would allow no change to be made in the ways of the house. He was right, for any change would but have impressed us all more strongly with the certainty of misfortune. On Thursday we should hear our fate. It was but one day more to wait, and one long, dark, interminable night. Hexham did not mean to leave us: on the contrary, when St. Julian made some proposal of the sort, he said, in true heart-tones, "Let me stay; do not send me away. Oh! St. Julian, don't I belong to you? I don't think I need tell you now that the one great interest of my life is here among you all." The words touched St. Julian very much, and there could be no doubt of their loyalty. "Let him stay, papa," said Hester gently. In his emotion the young man spoke out quite openly before us all. It was a time which constrained us all to be simple, from the very strength of our sympathy for the dear, and gentle, and stricken young wife above.

Little Bevis came down before dinner, and played about as usual. I was touched to see the tenderness which they all showed to him. His grandfather let him run into his studio, upset his color-pots, turn over his canvases—one of them came down with a great sound upon the floor. It was the picture of the two women at the foot of the beacon waiting together in suspense. Little Bevis went to bed as usual, and we dined as usual, but I shall never forget that evening, how endless and interminable it seemed. After dinner St. Julian, who had been up to see Emmy in her room, paced up and down the drawing-room, quite unnerved for once. "My poor child," he kept repeating; "my poor child!"

The wind had risen: we could hear the low roar of the sea moaning against the shingle; the rain suddenly began to pour in the darkness outside, and the fire burnt low, for the great drops came down the chimney. Hexham did his best to cheer us. He was charming in his kindness and thoughtfulness. His manner to Hester was so tender, so gentle, at once humble and protecting, that I could only wonder that she held out as she did against its charm. She scarcely answered him, scarcely looked at him. She sat growing paler and paler. Was it that it seemed to her wrong, when her sister was in such sorrow and anxiety, to think of her own happiness or concerns? It was something of this, for once in the course of the evening I heard her say to him:—

"I can not talk to you yet. Will you wait?"

"A lifetime," said Hexham, in a low moved voice.

Hexham went away to smoke with St. Julian. I crossed the room and sat down by Hester, and put my arms round her. The poor child leaned her head upon my shoulder. Lady Jane was with Emilia, who had sent for her. Long after they had all gone up sad and wearily to their rooms, I sat by the fire watching the embers burn out one by one, listening to the sudden gusts of wind against the window-pane, to the dull rush of the sea breaking with loud cries and sobs.

All the events of the day were passing before me, over and over again: first one troubled face, then another; voice after voice echoing in my ears. Was there any hope any where in Hester's eyes? I thought; and they seemed looking up out of the fire into my own, as I sat there drowsily and sadly.

It was about two o'clock, I think, when I started: for I heard a sound of footsteps coming. A tall white-robed woman, carrying a lamp, came into the room, and advanced and sat down beside me. It was poor Lady Jane. All her cheerfulness was gone, and I saw now what injustice I had done her, and how she must have struggled to maintain it; she looked old and haggard suddenly.

"I could not rest," she said. "I came down, —I thought you might be here. I couldn't stay in my room listening to that dreadful wind." Poor thing, I felt for her. I made up the fire once more, and we two kept a dreary watch for an hour and more, till the wind went down and the sea calmed, and Lady Jane began to nod in her arm-chair.

XII.

I AWOKE on the Thursday **morning more** hopeful than I had gone to bed. I don't know why, for there was no more reason to hope either more or less than there had been the night before. On Thursday or on Friday the French mail would come with news: that was our one thought. We still tried to go on as usual, as if nothing was the matter. The bells rang, the servants came and went with stolid faces. It is horrible to say, but already at the end of these few interminable hours it seemed as if we were getting used to this new state of things. Emilia still kept up stairs. Lady Jane paced about in her restless way; from one room to another, from one person to another, she went. Sometimes she would burst out into indignation against Lady Mountmore, who had driven poor Bevis to go. She had influenced his father, Lady Jane declared, and prevented him from advancing a certain sum which he had distinctly promised to Bevis before his marriage. "A promise is a promise," said Lady Jane. "The poor boy was too proud to ask for his rights. He only went, I do believe, to escape that horrid Ephraim. We behaved like brutes, every one of us. I am just as bad as the rest," said the poor lady.

It was as she said. One day in June, when the Minister had sent to Mr. F., of the Foreign Office, to ask who was next on the list of Queen's messengers, it was found that the gentleman first in order had been taken ill only the day before; the second after him was making up his book for the Derby next year.

Poor Bevis—who was sitting disconsolately wondering how it would be possible to him to take up that bill of Ephraim's, which was daily appearing more terrible and impossible to meet —had heard St. Gervois and De Barty, the two other men in his room, discussing the matter, and announcing in very decided language their intention of remaining in London for the rest of the season, instead of starting off at a moment's notice with dispatches to some unknown President in some unknown part of South America.

Bevis said nothing, but got up and left the room. A few minutes after he came back looking very pale. "You fellows," he said, "I shall want you to do a few things for me. I start for Rio to-morrow."

"Mr. St. Gervois told me all about it," poor Lady Jane said, with a grunt, as she told me the story.

This sudden determination took the Mountmores and Mr. Ephraim by surprise, and, as I have said, it was on this occasion that Lady Jane spoke up on her brother's behalf, and that Emilia, after his departure, was formally recognized by his family. "If he—when he comes back," cried Lady Jane in a fume, "my father, in common decency, must increase his allowance." A sudden light came into her face as she spoke. The thought of any thing to do or say for Bevis was a gleam of comfort to the poor sister.

All that day was a feverish looking for news.

St. Julian had already started off to London that morning in search of it. Once I saw the telegraph-boy from Tarmouth coming along the lane. I ran down eagerly, but Lady Jane was beforehand, and had pocketed the dispatch which the servant had brought her. "It is nothing," she said, "and only concerns me." A certain conscious look seemed to indicate Sigourney. But I asked no questions. I went on in my usual plodding way, putting by candles and soap, serving out sugar. Sometimes now when I stand in the store-closet I remember the odd double feeling with which I stood there that Thursday afternoon, with my heart full of sympathy, and then would come a sudden hardness of long use to me, looking back at the storms of life through which I had passed. A hard, cruel feeling of the inevitable laws of fate came over me. What great matter was it: one more life struck down, one more innocent happiness blasted, one more parting; were we not all of us used to it? was any one spared ever? . . . . One by one we are sent forth into the storm, alone to struggle through its fierce battlings till we find another shelter, another home, where we may rest for a little while, until the hour comes when once more we are driven out. It was an evil frame of mind, and a thankless one, for one who had found friends, a shelter, and help when most in need of them. As I was still standing among my stores that afternoon, Aileen came to the door, looking a little scared. "Queenie," she said, "Emilia is not in her room. Lady Jane, too, has been out for ever so long. Her maid tells me that she had a telegraphic message from that Captain Sigourney. Is it not odious of her now, at such a time? Oh, she can't have—can't have—"

"Eloped?" I said, smiling. "No, Aileen, I do not think there is much fear."

As time went on, however, and neither of them reappeared, I became a little uneasy. Lady Jane's maid when questioned knew nothing of her mistress's intentions. Bevis was alone with his nurse, contentedly stocking a shop in his nursery out of her workbox. But it was not for Lady Jane that I was anxious— she could take care of herself; it was Emilia I was looking for. I put on my bonnet, and set off to try and find her. Hester and Hexham said they would go towards Ulles Hall, and see if she was there.

I walked up the down, looking on every side. I thought each clump of furze was Emilia; but at last, high up by the beacon, I saw a dark figure against the sky.

Yes, it was Emilia up there, with beaten garments and with wind-blown hair. She had unconsciously crouched down to escape the fierce blast. She was looking out seaward, at the dull tossing horizon. It seemed to me such an image of desolation that it went to my heart to see her so. I called her by her name, and ran up and put my hand upon her shoulder.

"My dear," I said, "we have been looking for you every where."

Emilia gave a little start. She had not heard me call.

"I could not rest at home," she said. "I don't know what brought me here. I think I ran almost all the way."

She spoke with a trembling desperateness that frightened me. Two nights of sleeplessness and these long maddening hours were enough to daze the poor child. If she were to break down? But gentle things like Emilia bend and rise again.

"Come home now, dear Emilia," I said; "it is growing dark. Your mother will be frightened about you."

"Ah! people are often frightened when there is nothing to fear," said Emilia, a little strangely.

I could see that she was in a fever. Her cheeks were burning, while I was shivering: for the cold winds came eddying from the valley, and sweeping round and round us, making the beacon creak as they passed. The wind was so chill, the sky so gray, and the green murky sea so dull at our feet, that I longed to get her away. It seemed to me much later than it really was. The solitude oppressed me. There was no life any where—no boats about. Perhaps they were lost in the mist that was writhing along from the land, and spreading out to sea. I can not say why it was so great a relief to me at last to see one little dark speck coming across the straits where the mist was not drifting. The sight of life—for boats are life to people looking out with lonely eyes—this little dark gray speck upon the waters, seemed to me to make the blast less dreary, and the lonely heights less lonesome.

We began our walk in silence. Emilia's long blue cloak flapped in the wind, but I pulled it close about her. She let me do as I liked. She didn't speak. Once I said to her, "Emilia, do you know, when I came up just now, I thought you looked like the picture your father painted. Do you remember it?"

"I—I forget," said poor Emilia, turning her face away suddenly. All her strength seemed to have left her; her limbs seemed scarcely able to drag along; her poor little feet slipped and stumbled on the turf and against the white chalk-stones. I put my arm round her waist and helped her along as best I could, as we crept down the side of the hill.

"I think I can not walk because my heart is so heavy," said Emilia once in her childish way, and her head dropped on my shoulder. I hardly can tell what I feared for her, or what I hoped. Sleeplessness and anxiety were enemies too mighty for this helpless little frame to encounter.

I was confused and frightened, and I took a wrong turning. It brought us to the end of a field where a gate had once stood, which was now done away with. We could not force through the hedges and the palings: there was nothing to do but to turn back. It seems childish to record, but when I found that we must retrace so many of our weary steps, stumbling back all the way, in one of those biting gusts of wind, I burst out crying from fatigue, and sympathy, and excitement. It seemed all so dreary and so hopeless. Emilia roused herself, seeing me give way. Poor child, her sweet natural instincts did not desert her, even in her own bewildered pain. She took hope suddenly, trying to find strength to help me.

"Oh Queenie!" she said. "Think if we find, to-morrow, that all is well, and that all this anxiety has been for nothing. But it could not be for nothing, could it?" she said.

It is only another name for something greater and holier than anxiety, I thought; but I could not speak, for I was choking, and I had not yet regained command of my own voice. Our walk was nearly over; we got out on to the lane, and so approached our home. At the turn of the road I saw a figure standing looking for us —a little figure, with hair flying on the gale, who, as we appeared, stumbling and weary, sprang forward to meet us; then suddenly stopped, turned, and fled, with fluttering skirts and arms outstretched, like a spirit of the wind. I could not understand it, nor why my little Mona (for it was she) should have run away. Even this moment's sight of her, in the twilight, did me good and cheered me. How well I remember it all! The dark rustling hedges, a pale streak of yellow light in the west shining beyond the hedge, and beyond the stem of the hawthorn-tree. It gleamed sadly and weirdly in the sky, among clouds of darkness and vaporous shadows; the earth reflected the light faintly at our feet, more brightly in the garden, which was higher than the road. Emilia put out her hand, and pulled herself wearily up the steps which led to the garden. It was very dark, but in the light from the stormy gleam she saw something which made her cry out. I pulled Emilia back, with some exclamation, being still confused and not knowing what dark figure it was standing before me in the gloaming; but Emilia burst away from me with a cry, with a low passionate sob. She flew from me straight into two arms that caught her. My heart was beating, my eyes were full of tears, so that I could scarcely see what had happened.

But I heard a low "Bevis! Oh Bevis!" For a moment I stood looking at the two standing clinging together. The cold wind still came in shrill gusts, the gray clouds still drifted, the sun-streak was dying: but peace, light, love unspeakable were theirs, and the radiance from their grateful hearts seemed to overflow into ours.

XIII.

"WHERE is Lady Jane?" interrupted Hexham, coming home in the twilight, from a fruitless search with Hester, to hear the great news. It was so great, so complete, so unexpected, that we none of us quite realized it yet. We were strangely silent ; we looked at each other : some sat still ; the younger ones went vaguely rushing about the house, from one end to the other. Aileen and Mona were like a pair of mad kittens, dancing and springing from side to side. It was pretty to see Hester rush in, tremulous, tender, almost frightened by the very depth of her sympathy. The mistress was holding Emilia's hand, and turning from her to Bevis.

"Oh Bevis, if you knew what three days we have spent !" said Hester, flinging her arms round him.

"Don't let us talk about it any more," said he, kissing her blooming cheek, and then he bent over the soft mother's hand that trembled out to meet his own.

It was not at first that we any of us heard very clearly what had happened, for Emilia turned so pale at first when her husband began speaking of that fatal expedition in the boat up the Paraná River, that Bevis abruptly changed the subject, and began describing the road from London to Tarmouth, instead of dwelling on his escape from the accident, or the wonders of that dream-world from whence he had come—an unknown land to us all of mighty streams and waving verdure ; of great flowers, and constellations, and mysterious splashings and stirrings along the waters. Emmy—her nerves were still unstrung—turned pale, and Bevis suddenly began to describe his journey from Waterloo to Tarmouth, and his companion from London.

One of the first questions Bevis had asked was for news of his sister. Not knowing where any body was to be found, he had gone straight to the Foreign Office on his arrival, for he was anxious to start again by the midday train for Broadshire. It was so early that none of his friends were come ; only the porter welcomed him, and told him that there had been many inquiries after him—a gentleman only that morning, who had left his card for Mr. St. Gervois, with a request for news to be immediately forwarded to him at his lodgings. Bevis glanced at the name on the card—Captain Sigourney : it was unknown to him, and, to tell the truth, the poor fellow did not care to meet strangers of any sort until he had seen or heard from his own people, and received some answer to that last appeal to his father. "The gentleman was to come again," said the porter ; "he seemed very particular." Mr. St. Julian, too, had been there the evening before : he had come up from Broadshire on purpose to make inquiries. Bevis impatiently looked at his watch : he had not time to find St. Julian out—he had only time to catch the train. He wanted to get to his little Emmy—to put her heart at rest, since all this anxiety had been going on about him. "I shall be back again on Saturday," he wrote on his card, and desired the porter specially to give it to St. Gervois, and to refer all references to him, and to no one else.

"And if the captain should come ?" asked the porter.

"Oh, hang the captain !" said Bevis ; "I don't know what he can want. Tell him any thing you like, so long as he does not come after me."

"There is the gentleman," said the porter, pointing to a languid figure that was crossing the street.

Bevis looked doubtfully at the stranger. He hastily turned away, called a passing Hansom, and, driving round by the hotel where he had left his luggage, reached the station only in time to catch the quick train to Helmington. He thought of telegraphing, but it was scarcely necessary when he was to see them all so soon. He had posted a note to his father ; he also wrote a line to St. Julian, which he left at the "Athenæum" as he passed . . . .

As Bevis settled himself comfortably in the corner of his carriage, he was much annoyed when the door opened just as the train was starting, and a tall, languid person whom he recognized as Captain Sigourney was jerked in. What did he want ? Was he following him on purpose ? Was it a mere accident, or was this an emissary of that Ephraim's, already on his track ? It seemed scarcely possible, and yet . . . Bevis opened his *Times* wide, knitted his handsome brows, and glanced at his companion suspiciously. He had come already to the old anxieties, but the thought of seeing his little Emilia was so delightful to him that it prevented him from troubling himself very seriously about any possible chances or mischances that might be across their path. . . . . The young fellow dropped his *Times* gradually, forgetting bills overdue, money troubles, debtors to forgive, and debts to be forgiven. He sat looking out at the rapid landscape, village spires, farms, and broad pleasant fields, dreaming of happy meetings, of Emilia's glad looks of recognition, the boys, of Aileen, and his favorite Hester hopping about in an excitement of welcome gladness. "Will you let me look at your *Times?*" said a voice—this was from Captain Sigourney, in his opposite corner. "I had to send off a telegraph at the last moment, and had no time to get a paper," explained that gentleman. Bevis stared, and gave him the paper without speaking ; but the undaunted captain, who loved a listener, went on to state that he was anxious about the arrival of the South American mail. "I believe the French steamer comes in about this time ?" he said, in an inquiring tone of voice. "Ah !" said Bevis, growing more and more reserved. Poor Sigourney's odd insinuating manner was certainly against him. "I shall probably have to telegraph again on the way," continued Sigourney, unabashed, as they neared Winchester. One thing struck Bevis oddly, which was this : when the guard at Winchester came to look at their tickets, his companion's was a return ticket ; and the poor young fellow, having got a suspicious idea in his head, began to ask himself what possible object a man could have in travelling all this way down and back again in one day, and whether it would not be as well, under the circumstances, to change carriages, and get out of his way. "Here, let me out," he cried to the guard; and, to his great relief, Sigourney made no opposition to this move on his part.

"A fellow gets suspicious," said honest Bevis. "It was too bad. But I can't understand the fellow now. He seemed dodging me about. He had a return-ticket, too, and I only got away from him by a chance. I don't mind so much, now that I have seen you, little woman. Ephraim may have a dozen writs out against me, for all I know. I thought there was something uncomfortable about the man the moment I saw him; and I asked the porter at the Foreign Office not to tell him any thing about me." As Bevis went on with the account of his morning, my mistress and I had looked at one another and dimly begun to connect one thing and another in our minds. "I suppose I was mistaken," Bevis ended, shrugging his shoulders; "since here I am. But if not to-day, he will have me to-morrow. I only put off the evil day by running away. Well, I've brought back Jane's hundred pounds, and I have seen my little woman again, and the boy, and all of you, and now I don't care what happens."

"Hush," said Mrs. St. Julian; "my husband must help you. Your father has written to him. You should have come to us."

"I believe I acted like a fool," said Beverley, penitently. "Perhaps, after all, I fancied things worse than they were. I couldn't bear to come sponging on St. Julian, and I was indignant at something which my stepmother said, and—is Jane here, do you say?"

We were all getting seriously uneasy. Lady Jane's maid brought in the telegram she had found in her room, which seemed to throw some vague light upon her movements.

CAPTAIN SIGOURNEY, *Waterloo Station, to* LADY JANE BEVERLEY, *Tarmouth, Broadshire.*

I implore you to meet me at Tarmouth. I come by the four-o'clock boat. I have news of your brother.

　　　(Signed)　　　　　　　SIGOURNEY.

"Sigourney!" cried Bevis.

There was a dead silence, and nobody knew exactly what to say next. All our anxiety and speculation were allayed before dinner by the return of the pony-carriage with a hasty note from Lady Jane herself:—

DEAREST MRS. ST. JULIAN,—Kind Captain Sigourney has been to London inquiring for us. He has heard confidentially, from a person at the Foreign Office, that my brother *has been heard of* by this mail. He thought it best to come to me straight, and I have decided to go off to London immediately. I shall probably find my father at home in Bruton Street. I will write to-morrow. Fond love to dearest Emilia. Your affectionate, anxious

　　　　　　　　　　JANE BEVERLEY.

"But what does it all mean?" cried Bevis,

in a fume. "What business has Captain Sigourney with my safety?" And it was only by degrees that he could be appeased at all.

"This fire won't burn!" cried Mona.

There is a little pine-wood growing not far from the Lodges, where Aileen and Mona sometimes boil a kettle and light a fire of dry sticks, twigs, and fir-cones. The pine-wood runs up the side of a steep hill that leads to the down. In the hollow below lie bright pools glistening among wet mosses and fallen leaves and pine-twigs; but the abrupt sides of the little wood are dry and sandy, and laced and overrun by a network of slender roots that go spreading in every direction. In between the clefts and jagged fissures of the ground the sea shines, blue and gleaming, while the white ships, like birds, seem to slide in between the branches. The tea-party was in honor of Bevis's return, the little maidens said. They had transported cups and cloths, pats of butter and brown loaves, all of which good things were set on a narrow ledge; while a little higher the flames were sparkling, and a kettle hanging in the pretty thread of blue faint smoke. Mona, on her knees, was piling sticks and cones upon the fire; Aileen was busy spreading her table; and little Bevis was trotting about, picking up various little shreds and stones that took his fancy, and bringing them to poke into the bright little flame that was crackling and sparkling and growing every moment more bright.

Bevis and Emilia were the hero and heroine of the entertainment. Hexham was fine, Aileen said, and would not take an interest, and so he was left with Hester pasting photographs in the dining-room, while the rest of us came off this bright autumnal afternoon to camp in the copse. The sun still poured unwearied over the country, and the long delightful summer seemed ending in light and brilliancy. It was during this picnic tea-drinking that I heard more than I had hitherto done of Mr. Beverley's adventures.

"This kettle *won't* boil!" said Mona.

And while Bevis was good-naturedly poking and stirring the flames, Emilia began in a low, frightened voice: "Oh, Queenie, even now I can hardly believe it. He has been telling me all about it. He finished his work sooner than he had expected. I think the poor General was shot with whom he was negotiating: at all events he found that there was nothing more for him to do, and that he might as well take his passage by the very next ship. And then, to pass the time, he went off with those other poor men for a couple of days' shooting, and then they met a drove of angry cattle swimming across the stream, and they could not get out of the way in time, and two were drowned," faltered Emilia; "but when dear Bevis came to himself, he had floated a long way down the stream. He had been unconscious, but bravely clinging to an oar all the time . . . . and then he scrambled on shore and wandered on till he got to a wooden house, belonging to two young men, who took him in—but he had had a blow on the head, and he was very ill for three days, and the steamer was gone when he got back to Rio—and that was how it was."

As she ceased she caught hold of little Bevis, who was trotting past her, and suddenly clutched him to her heart. How happy she was! a little frightened still, even in her great joy, but with smiles and lights in her radiant face—her very hair seemed shining as she sat under the pine-trees, sometimes looking up at her husband, or with proud eyes following Bevy's little dumpling figure as he busily came and went.

"Here is Hexham, after all," cried Bevis from the heights, looking down as he spoke, and Hexham's head appeared from behind a bank of moss and twigs.

"Why, what a capital gypsy photograph you would all make!" cried the enthusiastic Hexham as he came up. "I have brought you some letters. Hester is coming directly with William St. Julian, who has just arrived."

"I really don't think we can give you all cups," said Aileen, busily pouring from her boiling kettle into her teapot. "You know I didn't expect you."

Bevis took all the letters and began to read them out :—

LORD MOUNTMORE *to the* HON. BEVIS BEVERLEY.

Friday.

MY DEAR BOY,—The news of your safe return from Rio has relieved us all from a most anxious state of mind. You have had a providential escape, upon which we most warmly and heartily congratulate you. With regard to the subject of your letter, I am willing to accede to your request, and to allow you once more the same sum that you have always had hitherto. I will also assist you to take up the bill, if you will give me your solemn promise never to have any thing more to do with the Jews. Jane has pleaded your cause so well that I can not refuse her. My lady desires her love.

Your affectionate father, M——.

Jane is writing, so I send no message from her. She arrived, poor girl, on Thursday, in a most distressed state of mind. I hope we shall see you here with your wife before long.

II.

UNKNOWN FRIEND, *Ch. Coll., Cambridge, to* GEO. HEXHAM, ESQ., *The Island, Tarmouth.*

MY DEAR GEORGE,—I have been expecting this letter ever since I received your last, from which, by-the-by, one page was missing. Farewell, O friend of my bachelorhood. Seriously, I long to see you, and to hear all about it. I must also beg to congratulate the future Mrs. Hexham upon having secured the affections of one of the best and truest-hearted of men. I have no doubt she fully deserves her good fortune.

Ever, my dear fellow, affectionately yours,
——— ——.

III.

MRS. WILLIAM ST. JULIAN, *Kensington Square, to* MRS. ST. JULIAN, *Tarmouth.*

MY DEAREST MRS. ST. JULIAN,—I send this by William, who can not rest until he has seen you all and told you how heartfelt are our sympathies and congratulations. How little we thought, as we drove off on Monday morning, of all that was at hand! It seems very *unfeeling* as I look back now. I shall feel quite nervous until William comes back, but he has promised to take a return ticket to reassure me. I am quite surprised by the news you send me this morning of Hester's engagement. I always had my own ideas, though I did not speak of them (we quiet people often see a good deal more than people imagine), and I quite expected that Lady Jane would have been the lady. However, it is much better as it is, and Mr. Hexham is, I have no doubt, all you could wish for dear Hester. Do give my best and kindest congratulations to dear Emilia. How delighted she must have been to get the good news of her husband's safety! I hope it was not too much for her—excitement is very apt to knock one up. The children send a hundred loves and kisses,

Believe me
Your affectionate daughter,
MARGARET ST. JULIAN.

P.S.—I have had a visit from a very delightful Captain Sigourney. He called upon me to ask for news of you all. It seems he escorted Lady Jane to town, and that in consequence of information he had received at the Foreign Office he was able to be of great service to her, although the information afterwards turned out incorrect. A person there had assured him that Mr. Beverley had been in town some time, and had returned to South America for good. What strange reports get about! One should be very careful never to believe any body.

FIVE OLD FRIENDS,

DEDICATED TO

FIVE YOUNG PRINCESSES.

A. C. R.
A. G.
M. C. S.
A. M.
M. A. B.

THE SLEEPING BEAUTY IN THE WOOD.

A KIND enchantress one day put into my hand a mystic volume prettily lettered and bound in green, saying, "I am so fond of this book! It has all the dear old fairy tales in it; one never tires of them. Do take it."

I carried the little book away with me, and spent a very pleasant quiet evening at home by the fire, with H. at the opposite corner, and other old friends, whom I felt I had somewhat neglected of late. Jack and the Beanstalk, Puss in Boots, the gallant and quixotic Giant-killer, the dearest Cinderella, whom we every one of us must have loved, I should think, ever since we first knew her in her little brown pinafore: I wondered, as I shut them all up for the night between their green boards, what it was that made these stories so fresh and so vivid. Why did not they fall to pieces, vanish, explode, disappear, like so many of their contemporaries and descendants? And yet far from being forgotten and passing away, it would seem as if each generation in turn as it came into the world looks to be delighted still by the brilliant pageant, and never tires nor wearies of it. And on their side the princes and princesses never seem to grow any older; the castles and the lovely gardens flourish without need of repair or whitewash, or plumbers or glaziers. The princesses' gowns, too — sun, moon, and star color — do not wear out, or pass out of fashion, or require altering. Even the seven-leagued boots do not appear to be the worse for wear. Numbers of realistic stories for children have passed away. Little Henry and his Bearer, and Poor Harry and Lucy, have very nearly given up their little artless ghosts and prattle, and ceased making their own beds for the instruction of less excellently brought-up little boys and girls, and notwithstanding a very interesting article in the *Saturday Review*, it must be owned that Harry Sandford and Tommy Merton are not familiar playfellows in our nurseries and school-rooms, and have passed somewhat out of date. But not so all these centenarians, Prince Riquet, Carabas, Little Red Riding Hood, Bluebeard, and others. They seem as if they would never grow old. They play with the children, they amuse the elders, there seems no end to their fund of spirits and perennial youth.

H., to whom I made this remark, said from the opposite chimney-corner: "No wonder; the stories are only histories of real living persons turned into fairy princes and princesses. Fairy stories are every where and every day. We are all princes and princesses in disguise, or ogres or wicked dwarfs. All these histories are the histories of human nature, which does not seem to change very much in a thousand years or so, and we don't get tired of the fairies because they are so true to it."

After this little speech of H.'s, we spent an unprofitable half-hour reviewing our acquaintance, and classing them under their real characters and qualities. We had dined with Lord Carabas only the day before and met Puss in Boots—Beauty and the Beast were also there; we uncharitably counted up, I am ashamed to say, no less than six Bluebeards. Jack and the Beanstalk we had met just starting on his climb. A Red Riding Hood; a girl with toads dropping from her mouth: we knew three or four of each. Cinderellas—alas! who does not know more than one dear, poor, pretty Cinderella! and as for sleeping Princesses in the Woods, how many one can reckon up! Young, old, ugly, pretty, awakening, sleeping still.

"Do you remember Cecilia Lulworth," said H., "and Dorlicote? Poor Cecilia!" Some lives are *couleur de rose*, people say; others seem to be, if not *couleur de rose* all through, yet full of bright beautiful tints, blues, pinks, little bits of harmonious cheerfulness. Other lives, not so brilliant, and seeming more or less gray at times, are very sweet and gentle in tone, with faint gleams of gold or lilac to brighten them. And then again others are black and hopeless from the beginning. Besides all these, there are some which have always appeared to me as if they were of a dark, dull hue; a dingy, heavy brown, which no happiness, or interest, or bright color could ever enliven. Blues turn sickly, roses seem faded, and yellow lilacs look red and ugly upon these heavy backgrounds. "Poor Cecilia," as H. called her, — hers had always seemed to me one of these latter existences, unutterably dull, commonplace, respectable, stinted, ugly, and useless.

Lulworth Hall, with the great dark park bounded by limestone walls, with iron gates here and there, looked like a blot upon the bright and lovely landscape. The place from a distance, compared with the surrounding country, was a blur and a blemish, as it were, sad, silent, solitary.

Travellers passing by sometimes asked if the place was uninhabited, and were told, "No, shure,—the fam'ly lives thear all the yeaurr round." Some charitable souls might wonder what life could be like behind those dull gates. One day a young fellow riding by saw rather a sweet woman's face gazing for an instant through the bars, and he went on his way with a momentary thrill of pity. Need I say that it was poor Cecilia, who looked out vacantly to see who was passing along the high-road. She was surrounded by hideous moreen, oil-cloth, punctuality, narrow-mindedness, horse-hair, and mahogany. Loud bells rang at intervals, regular, monotonous. Surly but devoted attendants waited upon her. She was rarely alone; her mother did not think it right that a girl in Cecilia's position should "race" about the grounds unattended; as for going outside the walls, it was not to be thought of. When Cecilia went out, with her gloves on, and her galoches, her mother's companion, Miss Bowley, walked beside her up and down the dark laurel walk at the back of the house—up and down, down and up, up and down. "I think I am getting tired, Maria," Miss Lulworth would say at last. "If so, we had better return to the hall," Maria would reply, "although it is before our time." And then they would walk home in silence, between the iron railings and laurel-bushes.

As Cecilia walked erectly by Miss Bowley's side, the rooks went whirling over their heads, the slugs crept sleepily along the path under the shadow of the grass and the weeds; they heard no sounds except the cawing of the birds, and the distant monotonous hacking noise of the gardener and his boy digging in the kitchen-garden.

Cecilia, peeping into the long drab drawing-room on her return, might perhaps see her mother, erect and dignfied, at her open desk, composing, writing, crossing, re-writing, an endless letter to an indifferent cousin in Ireland, with a single candle and a small piece of blotting paper, and a pen-wiper made of ravellings, all spread out before her.

"You have come home early, Cecil," says the lady, without looking up. "You had better make the most of your time, and practise till the dressing-bell rings. Maria will kindly take up your things."

And then in the chill twilight Cecilia sits down to the jangling instrument with the worn silk flutings. A faded rack it is upon which her fingers have been distended ever since she can remember. A great many people think there is nothing in the world so good for children as scoldings, whippings, dark cupboards, and dry bread and water, upon which they expect them to grow up into tall, fat, cheerful, amiable men and women; and a great many people think that for grown-up young people the silence, the chillness, the monotony, and sadness of their own fading twilight days is all that is required. Mrs. Lulworth and Maria Bowley her companion, Cecilia's late governess, were quite of this opinion. They themselves, when they were little girls, had been slapped, snubbed, locked up

in closets, thrust into bed at all sorts of hours, flattened out on backboards, set on high stools to play the piano for days together, made to hem frills five or six weeks long, and to learn immense pieces of poetry, so that they had to stop at home all the afternoon. And though Mrs. Lulworth had grown up stupid, suspicious, narrow-minded, soured, and overbearing, and had married for an establishment, and Miss Bowley, her governess's daughter, had turned out nervous, undecided, melancholy, and anxious, and had never married at all, yet they determined to bring up Cecilia as they themselves had been brought up, and sincerely thought they could not do better.

When Mrs. Lulworth married, she said to Maria: "You must come and live with me, and help to educate my children some day, Maria. For the present I shall not have a home of my own; we are going to reside with my husband's aunt, Mrs. Dormer. She is a very wealthy person, far advanced in years. She is greatly annoyed with Mr. and Mrs. John Lulworth's vagaries, and she has asked me and my husband to take their places at Dorlicote Hall." At the end of ten years Mrs. Lulworth wrote again: "We are now permanently established in our aunt's house. I hear you are in want of a situation; pray come and superintend the education of my only child Cecilia (she is named after her godmother, Mrs. Dormer). She is now nearly three years old, and I feel that she begins to require some discipline."

This letter had been written at that same desk twenty-two years before Cecilia began her practising this autumn evening. She was twenty-five years old now, but like a child in experience, in ignorance, in placidity; a fortunate stolidity and slowness of temperament had saved her from being crushed and nipped in the bud, as it were. She was not bored, because she had never known any other life. It seemed to her only natural that all days should be alike, rung in and out by the jangling breakfast, lunch, dinner, and prayer bells. Mr. Dormer—a little chip of a man—read prayers suitable for every day in the week; the servants filed in, maids first, then the men. Once Cecilia saw one of the maids blush and look down smiling as she marched out after the others. Miss Lulworth wondered a little, and thought she would ask Susan why she looked so strangely; but Susan married the groom soon after, and went away, and Cecilia never had an opportunity of speaking to her.

Night after night Mr. Dormer replaced his spectacles with a click, and pulled up his shirt-collar when the service was ended. Night after night old Mrs. Dormer coughed a little moaning cough. If she spoke, it was generally to make some little bitter remark. Every night she shook hands with her nephew and niece, kissed Cecilia's blooming cheek, and patted out of the room. She was a little woman with starling eyes. She had never got over her husband's death. She did not always know when she moaned. She dressed in black, and lived alone in her turret, where she had various old-fashioned occupations, tatting, camphor-boxes to sort, a real old spinning-wheel and dis-taff among other things, at which Cecilia, when she was a child, had pricked her fingers trying to make it whir as her aunt did. Spinning-wheels have quite gone out, but I know of one or two old ladies who still use them. Mrs. Dor-mer would go nowhere, and would see no one. So at least her niece, the master-spirit, declared, and the old lady got to believe it at last. I don't know how much the fear of the obnox-ious John and his wife and children may have had to do with this arrangement.

When her great-aunt was gone it was Ceci-lia's turn to gather her work together at a warn-ing sign from her mother, and walk away through the long chilly passages to her slumbers in the great green four-post bed. And so time passed. Cecilia grew up. She had neither friends nor lovers. She was not happy nor un-happy. She could read, but she never cared to open a book. She was quite contented; for she thought Lulworth Hall the finest place, and its inmates the most important people, in the world. She worked a great deal, embroider-ing interminable quilts and braided toilet-cov-ers and fish-napkins. She never thought of any thing but the uttermost commonplaces and platitudes. She considered that being respect-able and decorous, and a little pompous and overbearing, was the duty of every well-brought-up lady and gentleman. To-night she banged away very placidly at Rhodes's air, for the twentieth time breaking down in the same pas-sage and making the same mistake, until the dressing-bell rang, and Cecilia, feeling she had done her duty, then extinguished her candle, and went up stairs across the great chill hall, up the bare oil-cloth gallery, to her room.

Most young women have some pleasure, whatever their troubles may be, in dressing, and pretty trinkets, and beads and ribbons and neck-laces. An unconscious love of art and intuition leads some of them, even plain ones, to adorn themselves. The colors and ribbon-ends bright-en bright faces, enliven dull ones, deck what is already lovable, or, at all events, make the most of what materials there are. Even a May-pole, crowned and flowered and tastily ribbon-ed, is a pleasing object. And, indeed, the art of decoration seems to me a charming natural instinct, and one which is not nearly enough en-couraged, and a gift which every woman should try to acquire. Some girls, like birds, know how to weave, out of ends of rags, of threads and morsels and straws, a beautiful whole, a work of real genius for their habitation. Friv-olities, say some; waste of time, say others—expense, vanity. The strong-minded dowagers shake their heads at it all—Mrs. Lulworth among them; only why had Nature painted Cecilia's cheeks of brightest pink, instead of bilious orange, like poor Maria Bowley's? why was her hair all crisp and curly? and were her

white even teeth and her clear gray eyes vanity and frivolity too? Cecilia was rather too stout for her age; she had not much expression in her face. And no wonder. There was not much to be expressive about in her poor little stinted life. She could not go into raptures over the mahogany sideboard, the camphene lamp in the drawing-room, the four-post beds in-doors, the laurel-bushes without, the Moor-ish temple with yellow glass windows, or the wigwam summer-house, which were the alter-nate boundaries of her daily walks.

Cecilia was not allowed a fire to dress herself by; a grim maid, however, attended, and I sup-pose she was surrounded, as people say, by every comfort. There was a horse-hair sofa, with a creaking writing-table before it, a metal ink-stand, a pair of plated candlesticks: every thing was large, solid, brown, as I have said, grim, and in its place. The rooms at Lulworth Hall did not take the impress of their inmate, the inmate was moulded by the room. There were in Cecilia's no young-lady-like trifles lying here and there; upon the chest of drawers there stood a mahogany work-box, square, with a key, and a faded needle-book and darning-cotton in-side—a little dusty chenille, I believe, was to be seen round the clock on the chimney-piece, and a black and white check dressing-gown and an ugly little pair of slippers were set out before the toilet-table. On the bed, Cecilia's dinner costume was lying—a sickly green dress, trim-med with black—and a white flower for her hair. On the toilet-table an old-fashioned jasper ser-pent-necklace and a set of amethysts were dis-played for her to choose from, also mittens and a couple of hair-bracelets. The girl was quite content, and she would go down gravely to din-ner, smoothing out her hideous toggery.

Mrs. Dormer never came down before dinner. All day long she staid up in her room, dozing and trying remedies, and occasionally looking over old journals and letters until it was time to come down stairs. She liked to see Cecilia's pretty face at one side of the table, while her nephew carved, and Mrs. Lulworth recounted any of the stirring events of the day. Mrs. Dor-mer was used to the life—she was sixty when they came to her, she was long past eighty now—the last twenty years had been like a long sleep, with the dream of what happened when she was alive and in the world continually pass-ing before her.

When the Lulworths first came to her she had been in a low and nervous state, only stipu-lated for quiet and peace, and that no one was to come to her house of mourning. The John Lulworths, a cheery couple, broke down at the end of a month or two, and preferred giving up all chance of their aunt's great inheritance to living in such utter silence and seclusion. Upon Charles, the younger brother and his wife, the habit had grown, until now any thing else would have been toil and misery to them. Except the old rector from the village, the doctor now and then, no other human creature ever crossed the threshold. "For Cecilia's sake," Miss Bowley once ventured to hint—"would it not be desirable to see a little more society . . . . ?"

"Cecilia with her expectations has the whole world before her, Maria!" said Mrs. Lulworth, severely; and indeed to this foolish woman it seemed as if money would add more to her daughter's happiness than the delights, the wonders, the interests, the glamours of youth. Charles Lulworth, shriveled, selfish, dull, worn out, did not trouble his head about Cecilia's happiness, and let his wife do as she liked with the girl.

This especial night when Cecilia came down in her ugly green dress, it seemed to her as if something unusual had been going on. The old lady's eyes looked bright and glittering, her father seemed more animated than usual, her mother looked mysterious and put out. It might have been fancy, but Cecilia thought they all stopped talking as she came into the room; but then dinner was announced, and her father offered Mrs. Dormer his arm immediately, and they went into the dining-room.

It must have been fancy. Every thing was as usual. "They have put up a few hurdles in Dalron's field, I see," said Mrs. Lulworth. "Charles, you ought to give orders for repairing the lock of the harness-room."

"Have they seen to the pump-handle?" said Mr. Lulworth.

"I think not." And there was a dead silence.

"Potatoes," said Cecilia to the footman. "Mamma, we saw ever so many slugs in the laurel walk, Maria and I—didn't we, Maria? I think there are a great many slugs in our place."

Old Mrs. Dormer looked up while Cecilia was speaking, and suddenly interrupted her in the middle of her sentence. "How old are you, child?" she said; "are you seventeen or eighteen?"

"Eighteen! Aunt Cecilia. I am five-and-twenty," said Cecilia, staring.

"Good gracious! is it possible?" said her father, surprised.

"Cecil is a woman now," said her mother.

"Five-and-twenty," said the old lady, quite crossly. "I had no idea time went so fast. She ought to have been married long ago; that is, if she means to marry at all."

"Pray, my dear aunt, do not put such ideas—" Mrs. Lulworth began.

"I don't intend to marry," said Cecilia, peeling an orange, and quite unmoved, and she slowly curled the rind of her orange in the air. "I think people are very stupid to marry. Look at poor Jane Simmonds—her husband beats her; Jones saw her."

"So you don't intend to marry?" said the old lady, with an odd inflection in her voice. "Young ladies were not so wisely brought up in my early days," and she gave a great sigh. "I was reading an old letter this morning from my brother John, your poor father, Charles—

all about happiness, and love in a cot, and two little curly-headed boys—Jack, you know, and yourself. I should rather like to see Jack again."

"What, my dear aunt, after his unparalleled audacity? I declare the thought of his impudent letter makes my blood boil," exclaimed Mrs. Lulworth.

"Does it?" said the old lady. "Cecilia, my dear, you must know that your uncle has discovered that the entail was not cut off from a certain property which my father left me, and which I brought to my husband. He has therefore written me a very business-like letter, in which he wishes for no alteration at present, but begs that, in the event of my making my will, I should remember this, and not complicate matters by leaving it to yourself, as had been my intention. I see nothing to offend in the request. Your mother thinks differently."

Cecilia was so amazed at being told any thing that she only stared again, and, opening a wide mouth, popped into it such a great piece of orange that she could not speak for some minutes.

"Cecilia has certainly attained years of discretion," said her great-aunt; "she does not compromise herself by giving any opinion on matters she does not understand." Then the old lady got up and slowly led the way back to the drawing-room again, across the great empty hall.

Notwithstanding her outward imperturbability, Cecilia was a little stirred and interested by this history, and by the short conversation which had preceded it, and after an hour's silence she ceased working, and looked up from the embroidered shaving-cloth she was making. Her mother was sitting upright in her chair as usual, netting with vigorous action. Her large foot outstretched, her stiff bony hands working and jerking monotonously. Her father was dozing in his arm-chair; old Mrs. Dormer, too, was nodding in her corner. The monotonous Maria was stitching in the lamplight. Gray and black shadows loomed all round her. The far end of the room was quite dark; the great curtains swept from their ancient cornices. Cecilia, for the first time in all her life, wondered whether she should live all her life in this spot—ever go away? It seemed impossible, unnatural, that she should ever do so. Silent, dull as it was, she was used to it, and did not know what was amiss. . . . . Was any thing amiss? Mrs. Charles Lulworth certainly seemed to think so. She made the tea in frowns and silence, and closed the lid of the teapot with a clink which re-echoed through the room.

Young Frank Lulworth, the lawyer of the family — John Lulworth's eldest son — it was who had found it all out. His father wrote that with Mrs. Dormer's permission he proposed coming down in a day or two to show her the papers, and to explain to her personally how the matter stood. "My son and I," said John Lulworth, "both feel that this would be far more agreeable to our feelings, and perhaps to yours, than having recourse to the usual professional intervention, for we have no desire to press our claims for the present, and we only wish that in the ultimate disposal of your property you should be aware how the matter really stands. We have always been led to suppose that the estate actually in question has been long destined by you for your grand-niece, Cecilia Lulworth. I hear from our old friend Dr. Hicks, that she is remarkably pretty and very amiable. Perhaps such vague possibilities are best unmentioned, but it has occurred to me that in the event of a mutual understanding springing up between the young folks—my son and your grand-niece—the connection might be agreeable to us all, and lead to a renewal of that family intercourse which has been, to my great regret, suspended for some time past."

Old Mrs. Dormer, in her shaky Italian handwriting, answered her nephew's letter by return of post:—

"MY DEAR NEPHEW,—I must acknowledge the receipt of your epistle of the 13th instant. By all means invite your son to pay us his proposed visit. We can then talk over business matters at our leisure, and young Francis can be introduced to his relatives. Although a long time has elapsed since we last met, believe me, my dear nephew, not unmindful of bygone associations, and yours very truly always,

"C. DORMER."

The letter was in the postman's bag when old Mrs. Dormer informed Mrs. Charles of what she had done.

Frank Lulworth thought that in all his life he had never seen any thing so dismal, so silent, so neglected, as Dorlcote Park, when he drove up a few days after, through the iron gates and along the black laurel wilderness which led to the house. The laurel branches, all unpruned, untrained, were twisting savagely in and out, wreathing and interlacing one another, clutching tender shootings, wrestling with the young oak-trees and the limes. He passed by black and sombre avenues leading to mouldy temples, to crumbling summer-houses; he saw what had once been a flower-garden now all run to seed—wild, straggling, forlorn; a broken-down bench, a heap of hurdles lying on the ground, a field-mouse darting across the road, a desolate autumn sun shining upon all this mouldering ornament and confusion. It seemed more forlorn and melancholy by contrast, somehow, coming as he did out of the loveliest country and natural sweetness into the dark and tangled wilderness within these limestone walls of Dorlicote.

The parish of Dorlicote-cum-Rockington looks prettier in the autumn than at any other time. A hundred crisp tints, jeweled rays—grays, browns, purples, glinting golds, and silvers, rustle and sparkle upon the branches of the nut-trees, of the bushes and thickets. Soft blue mists and purple tints rest upon the distant hills; scarlet berries glow among the brown leaves of the hedges; lovely mists fall and vanish suddenly, revealing bright and sweet autumnal sights; blackberries, stacks of corn, brown leaves, crisping upon the turf, great pears hanging sweetening in the sun over the cottage lintels, cows grazing and whisking their tails, blue smoke curling from the tall farm chimneys: all is peaceful, prosperous, golden. You can see the sea on clear days from certain knolls and hillocks. . . . .

Out of all these pleasant sights young Lulworth came into this dreary splendor. He heard no sounds of life—he saw no one. His coachman had opened the iron gate. "They doan't keep no one to moind the gate," said the driver; "only tradesmen cooms to th' 'ouse." Even the gardener and his boy were out of the way; and when they got sight of the house at last, many of the blinds were down and shutters shut, and only two chimneys were smoking. There was some one living in the place, however, for a watch-dog who was lying asleep in his kennel woke up and gave a heart-rending howl when Frank got out and rang at the bell.

He had to wait an immense time before any body answered, although a little page in buttons came and stared at him in blank amazement from one of the basement windows, and never moved. Through the same window Frank could see into the kitchen, and he was amused when a sleepy fat cook came up behind the little page and languidly boxed his ears, and ordered him off the premises.

The butler, who at last answered the door, seemed utterly taken aback—nobody had called for months past, and here was a perfect stranger taking out his card, and asking for Mrs. Dormer as if it was the most natural thing in the world. The under-butler was half asleep in his pantry, and had not heard the door-bell. The page—the very same whose ears had been boxed—came wondering to the door, and went to ascertain whether Mrs. Dormer would see the gentleman or not.

"What a vault, what a catacomb, what an ugly old place!" thought Frank, as he waited. He heard steps far, far away: then came a long silence, and then a heavy tread slowly approaching, and the old butler beckoned to him to follow—through a cobweb-color room, through a brown room, through a gray room, into a great dim drab drawing-room, where the old lady was sitting alone. She had come down her back stairs to receive him; it was years since she had left her room before dinner.

Even old ladies look kindly upon a tall, well-built, good-looking, good-humored young man. Frank's nose was a little too long, his mouth a little too straight; but he was a handsome young fellow with a charming manner. Only as he came up he was somewhat shy and undecided—he did not know exactly how to address the old lady. This was his great-aunt. He knew nothing whatever about her, but she was very rich; she had invited him to come, and she had a kind face, he thought: should he—ought he to embrace her—perhaps he ought, and he made the slightest possible movement in this direction. Mrs. Dormer, divining his object, pushed him weakly away. "How do you do? No embraces, thank you. I don't care for kissing at my age. Sit down—there, in that chair opposite—and now tell me about your father, and all the family, and about this ridiculous discovery of yours. I don't believe a word of it."

The interview between them was long and satisfactory, on the whole. The unconscious Cecilia and Miss Bowley returned that afternoon from their usual airing, and, as it happened, Cecilia said, "Oh, Maria! I left my mittens in the drawing-room last night. I will go and fetch them." And little thinking of what was awaiting her, she flung open the door and marched in through the anteroom—mushroom hat and brown veil, galoches and dowdy gown, as usual. "What is this?" thought young Lulworth; "why, who would have supposed it was such a pretty girl;" for suddenly the figure stopped short, and a lovely fresh face looked up in utter amazement out of the hideous disguise.

"There, don't stare, child," said the old lady. "This is Francis Lulworth, a very intelligent young man, who has got hold of your fortune and ruined all your chances, my dear. He wanted to embrace me just now. Francis, you may as well salute your cousin instead: she is much more of an age for such compliments," said Mrs. Dormer, waving her hand.

The impassive Cecilia, perfectly bewildered and not in the least understanding, only turned her great sleepy astonished eyes upon her cousin, and stood perfectly still, as if she was one of those beautiful wax-dolls one sees stuck up to be stared at. And, indeed, a stronger-minded person than Cecilia might have been taken aback, who had come into the drawing-room to fetch her mittens, to be met in such an astounding fashion. If she had been surprised before, utter consternation can scarcely convey her state of mind when young Lulworth stepped forward and obeyed her aunt's behest. Frank, half laughing, half kindly, seeing that Cecilia stood quite still and stared at him, supposed it was expected, and did as he was told.

The poor girl gave one gasp of horror, and blushed for the first time, I believe, in the course of her whole existence. Bowley, fixed and open-mouthed from the inner room, suddenly fled with a scream, which recalled Cecilia to a sense of outraged propriety; for, blushing and blinking more deeply, she at last gave three little sobs, and then, oh horror! burst into tears!

"Highty-tighty; what a much ado about nothing!" said the old lady, losing her temper and feeling not a little guilty, and much alarmed as to what her niece Mrs. Lulworth might say were she to come on the scene.

"I beg your pardon. I am so very, very sorry," said the young man, quite confused and puzzled. "I ought to have known better. I frightened you. I am your cousin, you know, and really—pray, pray excuse my stupidity," he said, looking anxiously into the fair placid face along which the tears were coursing in two streams, like a child's.

"Such a thing never happened in all my life before," said Cecilia. "I know it is wrong to cry, but really—really—"

"Leave off crying directly, miss," said her aunt, testily, "and let us have no more of this nonsense." The old lady dreaded the mother's arrival every instant. Frank, half laughing, but quite unhappy at the poor girl's distress, had taken up his hat to go that minute, not knowing what else to do.

"Ah! you're going," says old Mrs. Dormer; "no wonder. Cecilia, you have driven your cousin away by your rudeness."

"I am not rude," sobbed Cecilia. "I can't help crying."

"The girl is a greater idiot than I took her for," cried the old lady. "She has been kept here locked up, until she has not a single idea left in her silly noddle. No man of sense could endure her for five minutes. You wish to leave the place, I see, and no wonder?"

"I really think," said Frank, "that under the circumstances it is the best thing I can do. Miss Lulworth, I am sure, would wish me to go."

"Certainly," said Cecilia. "**Go away, pray** go away. Oh, how silly I am!"

Here was a catastrophe!

The poor old fairy was all puzzled and bewildered: her arts were powerless in this emergency. The princess had awakened, but in tears. Although he had said he was going, the prince still stood by, distressed and concerned, feeling horribly guilty, and yet scarcely able to help laughing; and at that instant, to bring matters to a climax, Mrs. Lulworth's gaunt figure appeared at the drawing-room door.

"I wash my hands of the whole concern," said Mrs. Dormer, limping off to her corner in a great hurry and flutter. "Your daughter is only a few degrees removed from an idiot, ma'am."

Poor Cecilia! her aunt's reproaches only scared her more and more; and for the first time in her life she was bewildered, discomposed, forgetful of hours. It was the hour of calisthenics; but Miss Lulworth forgot every thing that might have been expected from a young lady of her admirable bringing up.

"Oh mamma, I didn't mean to be rude," repeated Cecilia, crying still, and the sweet, wet, vacant face, looked imploringly and despairingly up into Frank's. "I'm so sorry, please forgive me," she said.

He looked so kind, so amused, so gentle and handsome, that Cecilia actually felt less afraid of him at this moment than she did of her mother, who, with tight lips and sharp eyes, was surveying the two.

"Go and take off your galoches and your walking-dress, Cecilia," said Mrs. Lulworth, exactly in her usual voice, "and do not come down without your apron."

In a few minutes, when Cecilia returned, blushing and more lovely than ever, in her great apron and dark stuff dress, it was to find her cousin comfortably installed in a big easy-chair, and actually talking above his breath to Miss owley. He sprang up and came to meet the girl, and held out his hand, "In token that you forgive me," he said.

"I thought it was I who had been rude and unkind," Cecilia falteringly said. "How good of you not to be vexed!"

"Cecilia," said Mrs. Lulworth and Miss Bowley both at once, in different tones of warning; but the princess was awake now, and her simplicity and beauty touched the young prince, who never, I think, really intended to go, even when he took up his hat. Fairy tales are never very long, and this one ought to come to an end.

Certainly the story would not have been worth the telling if they had not been married soon after, and lived happily all the rest of their lives.

* * * * * *

It is not in fairy tales only that things fall out as one could wish, and indeed, as H. and I agreed the other night that fairies, although invisible, have not entirely vanished out of the land.

It is certainly like a fairy transformation to see Cecilia nowadays in her own home with her children and husband about her. Bright, merry, full of sympathy and interest, she seems to grow prettier every minute.

When Frank fell in love with her and proposed, old Mrs. Dormer insisted upon instantly giving up the Dorlicote Farm for the young people to live in. Mr. and Mrs. Frank Lulworth are obliged to live in London, but they go there every summer with their children; and for some years after her marriage, Cecilia's godmother, who took the opportunity of the wedding to break through many of her recluse habits, used to come and see her every day in a magnificent yellow chariot.

CINDERELLA.

It is, happily, not only in fairy tales that things sometimes fall out as one could wish, that anxieties are allayed, mistakes explained away, friends reconciled; that people inherit large fortunes, or are found out in their nefarious schemes; that long-lost children are discovered disguised in soot, that vessels come safely sailing into port after the storm; and that young folks who have been faithful to one another are married off at last. Some of these young couples are not only happily married, but they also begin life in pleasant palaces tastefully decorated, and with all the latest improvements; with convenient cupboards, bath-rooms, back staircases, speaking-tubes, lifts from one story to another, hot and cold water laid on; while outside lie well-kept parks, and gardens, and flower-beds; and from the muslin-veiled windows they can see the sheep browsing, the long shadowy grass, deer starting across the sunny glades, swans floating on the rivers, and sailing through the lilies and tall lithe reeds. There are fruit-gardens, too, where great purple plums are sunning on the walls, and cucumbers lying asleep among their cool dark leaves. There are glasshouses where heavy dropping bunches of grapes are hanging, so that one need only open one's mouth for them to fall into it all ready cooked and sweetened. Sometimes, in addition to all these good things, the young couple possess all the gracious gifts of youth, beauty, gay and amiable dispositions. Some one said, the other day, that it seemed as if Fate scarcely knew what she was doing, when she lavished with such profusion every gift and delight upon one pair of heads, while others were left bald, shorn, unheeded, disheveled, forgotten, dishonored. And yet the world would be almost too sad to bear, if one did not sometimes see happiness somewhere. One would scarcely believe in its possible existence, if there was nobody young, fortunate, prosperous, delighted; nobody to think of with satisfaction, and to envy a little. The sight of great happiness and prosperity is like listening to harmonious music, or looking at beautiful pictures, at certain times of one's life. It seems to suggest possibilities, it sets sad folks longing; but while they are wishing, still, maybe, a little reproachfully, they realize the existence of what perhaps they had doubted before. Fate has been hard to them, but there is compensation even in this life, they tell themselves. Which of us knows when his turn may come? Happiness is a fact: it does lie within some people's grasp. To this or that young fairy couple, age, trial, and trouble may be in store; but now at least the present is golden; the innocent delights and triumphs of youth and nature are theirs.

I could not help moralizing a little in this way, when we were staying with young Lulworth and his wife the other day, coming direct from the struggling dull atmosphere of home to the golden placidity of Lulworth farm. They drove us over to Cliffe Court—another oasis, so it seemed to me, in the arid plains of life. Cliffe Court is a charming, cheerful Italian-looking house, standing on a hill in the midst of a fiery furnace of geraniums and flower-beds. "It belongs to young Sir Charles Richardson. He is

K

six-and-twenty, and the handsomest man in the county," said Frank.

"Oh no, Frank; you are joking, surely," said Cecilia; and then she stared, and then blushed in her odd way. She still stared sometimes when she was shy, as she used to do before she married.

So much of her former habits Cecilia had also retained, that as the clock struck eight every morning a great punctual breakfast-bell used to ring in the outer hall. The dining-room casement was wide open upon the beds of roses, the tea was made, Cecilia in her crisp white morning dress, and with all her wavy bronze hair curling about her face, was waiting to pour it out, the eggs were boiled, the bacon was frizzling hot upon the plate to a moment; there was no law allowed, not a minute's grace for any body, no matter how lazy. They had been married a little more than two years, and were quite established in their country home. I wish I could perform some incantation like those of my friends the fairies, and conjure up the old farm bodily with a magic wave of my pen, or by drawing a triangle with a circle through it upon the paper, as the enchanters do. The most remarkable things about the farm were its curious and beautiful old chimneys—indeed the whole county of Sussex is celebrated for them, and the meanest little cottages have noble-looking stacks all ornamented, carved, and weather-beaten. There were gables, also, and stony mullioned windows, and ancient steps with rusty rings hanging to them, affixed there to fasten the bridles of horses that would have run away several hundred years ago, if this precaution had not been taken. And then there were storehouses and ricks and barns, all piled with the abundance of the harvest. The farm-yard was alive with young fowls and cocks and hens; and guinea-hens, those gentle little dowagers, went about glistening in silver and gray, and Cecilia's geese came clamoring to meet her. I can see it all as I think about it. The old walls are all carved and ornamented, sometimes by art and work of man's hand, sometimes by time and lovely little natural mosses. House-leeks grow in clumps upon the thatch, a pretty girl is peeping through a lattice window, a door is open, while a rush of sweet morning scent comes through the shining oaken passage from the herb-garden and orchard behind. Cows with their soft brown eyes and cautious tread are passing on their way to a field across the road. A white horse waiting by his stable door shakes his head and whinnies.

Frank and Cecilia took us for a walk after breakfast the first morning we came. We were taken to the stables first and the cow-houses, and then we passed out through a gate into a field, and crossing the field we got into a copse which skirted it, and so by many a lovely little winding path into the woods. Young Lulworth took our delight and admiration as a personal compliment. It was all Lulworth property as far as we could see. I thought it must be strangely delightful to be the possessor of such beautiful hills, mist, sunshine and shadow, violet tones, song of birds, and shimmer of foliage; but Frank, I believe, looked at his future prospects from a material point of view. "You see it ain't the poetic part of it which pays," he said. But he appreciated it nevertheless, for Cecilia came out of the woods that morning, all decked out with great convolvulus leaves, changed to gold, which Frank had gathered as we went along and given to her. This year all the leaves were turning to such beautiful colors that people remarked upon it, and said they never remembered such a glowing autumn; even the year when Frank came to Dorlicote was not to compare to it. Browns and russet, and bright amber and gold flecks, berries, red leaves, a lovely blaze and glitter in the woods along the lanes and beyond the fields and copses. All the hills were melting with lovely color in the clear warm autumn air, and the little nut-wood paths seemed like Aladdin's wonderful gardens, where precious stones hung to the trees; there was a twinkle and crisp shimmer, yellow leaves and golden light, yellow light and golden leaves, red hawthorn, convolvulus-berries, holly-berries beginning to glow, and heaped-up clustering purple blackberries. The sloe-berries, or snowy blackthorn fruit, with their soft gloom of color, were over, and this was the last feast of the year. On the trees the apples hung red and bright, the pears seemed ready to drop from their branches and walls, the wheat was stacked, the sky looked violet behind the yellow ricks. A blackbird was singing like a ripple of water, somebody said. It is hard to refrain from writing of all these lovely things, though it almost is an impertinence to attempt to set them down on paper in long lists, like one of Messrs. Rippon and Burton's circulars. As we were walking along the high-road on our way back to the farm, we passed a long pale melancholy-looking man riding a big horse, with a little sweet-faced creature about sixteen who was cantering beside him.

He took off his hat, the little girl kissed her hand as they passed, nodding a gay triumphant nod, and then we watched them down the hill, and disappearing at the end of the lane.

"I am quite glad to see Ella Ashford out riding with her father again," said Lulworth, holding the garden gate open for us to pass in.

"Mrs. Ashford called here a day or two ago with her daughter," said Cecilia. "They're going to stay at the Ravenhill, she told me. I thought Colonel Ashford was gone too. I suppose he is come back."

"Of course he is," said Frank, "since we have just seen him with Ella, and of course his wife is away for the same reason."

"The child has grown very thin," said H.

"She has a difficult temper," said Cecilia—who, once she got an idea into her soft, silly head, did not easily get rid of it again. "She is a great anxiety to poor Mrs. Ashford. She is very different, she tells me, to Julia and Lisette Garnier, her own daughters."

"I knew them when they were children," said H. "We used to see a great deal of Mrs. Ashford when she was first a widow, and I went to her second wedding."

We were at Paris one year—ten years before the time I am writing of—and Mrs. Garnier lived over us, in a tiny little apartment. She was very poor, and very grandly dressed, and she used to come rustling in to see us. Rustling is hardly the word, she was much too graceful and womanly a person to rustle; her long silk gowns used to ripple, and wave, and flow away as she came and went; and her beautiful eyes used to fill with tears as she drank her tea and confided her troubles to us. H. never liked her; but I must confess to a very kindly feeling for the poor, gentle, beautiful, forlorn young creature, so passionately lamenting the loss she had sustained in Major-General Garnier. He had left her very badly off, although she was well connected, and Lady Jane Peppercorne, her cousin, had offered her and her two little girls a home at Ravenhill, she used to tell us in her eploré manner. I do not know why she never availed herself of the offer. She said once that she would not be doing justice to her precious little ones, to whom she devoted herself with the assistance of an experienced attendant. My impression is, that the little ones used to scrub one another's little ugly faces, and plait one another's little light Chinese-looking tails, while the experienced attendant laced and dressed and adorned, and scented and powdered their mamma. She really was a beautiful young woman, and would have looked quite charming if she had left herself alone for a single instant, but she was always posing. She had dark bright eyes; she had a lovely little arched mouth; and hands so white, so soft, so covered with rings, that one felt that it was indeed a privilege when she said, "Oh, how do you do?" and extended two or three gentle confiding fingers. At first she went nowhere except to church, and to walk in the retired paths of the Park de Monçeau, although she took in Galignani and used to read the lists of arrivals. But by degrees she began to—chiefly to please me, she said—go out a little, to make a few acquaintances. One day I was walking with her down the Champs Elysées, when she suddenly started and looked up at a tall, melancholy-looking gentleman who was passing, and who stared at her very hard; and soon after that it was that she began telling me she had determined to make an effort for her children's sake, and to go a little more into society. She wanted me to take her to Madame de Girouette's, where she heard I was going one evening, and where she believed she should meet an old friend of hers, whom she particularly wished to see again. Would I help her? Would I be so very good? Of course I was ready to do any thing I could. She came punctual to her time, all gray moire and black lace; a remise was sent for, and we set off, jogging along the crowded streets, with our two lamps lighted, and

a surly man, in a red waistcoat and an oilskin hat, to drive us to the Rue de Lille. All the way there, Mrs. Garnier was strange, silent, nervous, excited. Her eyes were like two shining craters, I thought, when we arrived, and as we climbed up the interminable flights of stairs. I guessed which was the old friend in a minute: a tall, well-looking, sick-looking man with a gray mustache, standing by himself in a corner.

I spent a curious evening, distracted between Madame de Girouette's small-talk, to which I was supposed to be listening, and Mrs. Garnier's murmured conversation with her old friend in the corner, to which I was vainly endeavoring not to attend.

"My dear, imagine a bouillon surmounted with little tiny flutings all round the bottom, and then three ruches, alternating with three little volants, with great choux at regular intervals; over this a tunic, caught up at the side by a jardinière, a ceinture à la Bébé."

"When you left us I was a child, weak, foolish, easily frightened and influenced. It nearly broke my heart. Look me in the face if you can, and tell me you do not believe me," I heard Mrs. Garnier murmuring in a low thrilling whisper. She did not mean me to hear it, but she was too absorbed in what she was saying to think of all the people round about her.

"Ah, Lydia, what does it matter now?" the friend answered in a sad voice which touched me somehow. "We have both been wrecked in our ventures, and life has not much left for either of us now."

"It is cut en biais," Madame de Girouette went on; "the pieces which are taken out at one end are let in at the other: the effect is quite charming, and the economy is immense."

"For you, you married the person you loved," Lydia Garnier was answering; "for me, out of the wreck I have at least my children, and a remembrance and a friend—is it so? Ah, Henry, have I not at least a friend?"

"Every body wants one," said Madame de Girouette, concluding her conversation, "and they can not be made fast enough to supply the demand. I am promised mine to wear to-morrow at the opening of the salon, but I am afraid that you have no chance. How the poor thing is over-worked—her magazine is crowded—I believe she will leave it all in charge of her première demoiselle, and retire to her campagne as soon as the season is over."

"And you will come and see me, will you not?" said the widow, as we went away, looking up at her friend. I do not know to this day if she was acting. I believe, to do her justice, that she was only acting what she really felt, as many of us do at times.

I took Mrs. Garnier home, as I agreed. I did not ask any questions. I met Colonel Ashford on the stairs next day, and I was not surprised when, about a week after, Mrs. Garnier flitted into the drawing-room early one morning, and, sinking down at my feet in a careless attitude, seized my hand, and said that she had come for counsel, for advice. . . . .

She had had an offer from a person whom she respected, Colonel Ashford, whom I might have remarked that night at Madame de Girouette's; would I—would I give her my candid opinion; for her children's sake, did I not think it would be well to think seriously? . . . .

"And for your own, too, my dear," said I. "Colonel Ashford is in Parliament, he is very well off. I believe you will be making an excellent marriage. Accept him, by all means."

"Dear friend, since this is your real heartfelt opinion, I value your judgment too highly not to act by its dictates. Once, years ago, there was thought of this between me and Henry. I will now confide to you, my heart has never failed from its early devotion. A cruel fate separated us. I married. He married. We are brought together as by a miracle, but our three children will never know the loss of their parents' love," etc. etc. Glance, hand, pressure, etc.— tears, etc., Then a long, soft, irritating kiss. I felt for the first time in my life inclined to box her ears.

The little Garniers certainly gained by the bargain, and the Colonel sat down to write home to his little daughter, and tell her the news.

Poor little Ella, I wonder what sort of anxieties Mrs. Ashford had caused to her before she had been Ella's father's wife a year. Miss Ashford made the best of it. She was a cheery, happy little creature, looking at every thing from the sunny side, adoring her father, running wild out of doors, but with an odd turn for housekeeping, and order and method at home. Indeed, for the last two years, ever since she was twelve years old, she had kept her father's house. Languid, gentle, easily impressed, Colonel Ashford was quite curiously influenced by this little daughter. She could make him come and go, and like and dislike. I think it was Ella who sent him into Parliament; she could not bear Sir Rainham Richardson, their next neighbor, to be an M.P., and an oracle, while her father was only a retired colonel. Her ways and her sayings were a strange and pretty mixture of childishness and precociousness. She would be ordering dinner, seeing that the fires were alight in the study and dining-room, writing notes to save her father trouble (Colonel Ashford hated trouble) in her cramped, crooked, girlish hand; the next minute she was perhaps flying, agile-footed, round and round the old hall, skipping up and down the oak stairs, laughing out like a child as she played with her puppy, and dangled a little ball of string under his black nose. Puff, with a youthful bark, would seize the ball and go scuttling down the corridors with his prize, while Ella pursued him with her quick flying feet. She could sing charmingly, with a clear true piping voice, like a bird's, and she used to dance to her own singing in the prettiest way imaginable. Her dancing was really remarkable: she had the most beautiful feet and hands,

and as she seesawed in time, still singing and moving in rhythm, any one seeing her could not fail to have been struck by the weird-like little accomplishment. Some girls have a passion for dancing—boys have a hundred other ways and means of giving vent to their activity and exercising their youthful limbs, and putting out their eager young strength; but girls have no such chances; they are condemned to walk through life, for the most part, quietly, soberly, putting a curb on the life and vitality which is in them. They long to throw it out, they would like to have wings to fly like a bird, and so they dance sometimes with all their hearts and might and energy. People rarely talk of the poetry of dancing, but there is something in it of the real inspiration of art. The music plays, the heart beats time, the movements flow as naturally as the branches of a tree go waving in the wind. . . . .

One day a naughty boy, who had run away, for a lark, from his tutor and his school-room at Cliffe, hard by, and who was hiding in a ditch, happened to see Ella alone in a field. She was looking up at the sky and down at the pretty scarlet and white pimpernels, and listening to the birds; suddenly she felt so strong and so light, and as if she *must* jump about a little, she was so happy; and so she did, shaking her pretty golden mane, waving her poppies high overhead, and singing higher and higher, like one of the larks that were floating in mid air. The naughty boy was much frightened, and firmly believed that he had seen a fairy.

"She was all in white," he said afterwards, in an aggrieved tone of voice. "She'd no hat, or any thing; she bounded six foot into the air. You never saw any thing like it."

Master Richardson's guilty conscience had something to do with his alarm. When his friends made a few facetious inquiries he answered quite sulkily: "Black pudden? He offered me no pudden or any thing else. I only wish you had been there, that's all, then you'd believe a fellow when he says a thing, instead of always chaffing."

Ella gave up her dancing after the new wife came to Ash Place. It was all so different; she was not allowed any more to run out into the fields alone. She supposed it was very nice having two young companions like Lisette and Julia, and at first, in her kindly way, the child did the honors of her own home, showed them the way which led to her rabbits, her most secret bird's-nest, the old ivy-grown smugglers' hole in the hollow. Lisette and Julia went trotting about in their frill trowsers and Chinese tails of hair, examining every thing, making their calculations, saying nothing, taking it all in (poor little Ella was rather puzzled, and could not make them out). Meantime her new mother was gracefully wandering over the house on her husband's arm, and standing in attitudes, admiring the view from the windows, and asking gentle little indifferent questions, to all of which Colonel Ashford replied unsuspectingly enough.

"And so you give the child an allowance? Is she not very young for one? And is this Ella's room? how prettily it is furnished!"

"She did it all herself," said her father, smiling. "Look at her rocking-horse, and her dolls' house, and her tidy little arrangements."

The housekeeping books were in a little pile on the table; a very suspicious-looking doll was lying on the bed, so were a pile of towels, half marked, but neatly folded; there was a bird singing in a cage, a squirrel, a little aged dog—Puff's grandmother—asleep on a cushion, some sea-anemones in a glass, gaping with their horrid mouths, strings of birds' eggs were suspended, and whips were hanging up on the walls. There was a great bunch of flowers in the window, and a long daisy-chain fastened up in festoons round the glass; and then on the toilet-table there were one or two valuable trinkets set out in their little cases

"Dear me," said Mrs. Ashford, "is it not a pity to leave such temptation in the way of the servants? Little careless thing—had I not better keep them for her, Henry? they are very beautiful." And Mrs. Ashford softly collected Ella's treasures in her long white hands.

"Ella has some very valuable things," Colonel Ashford said. "She keeps them locked up in a strong box, I believe; yes, there it is in the corner."

"It had much better come into my closet," Mrs. Ashford said. "Oh, how heavy! Come here, strong-arm, and help me." Colonel Ashford obediently took up the box as he was bid.

"And I think I may as well finish marking the dusters," said Mrs. Ashford, looking around the room as she collected them all in her apron. "The books, of course, are now my duty. I think Ella will not be sorry to be relieved of her cares. Do you know, dear, I think I am glad, for her sake, that you married me, as well as for my own. I think she has had too much put upon her, is a little too decided, too *prononcée*, for one so young. One would not wish to see her grow up before the time. Let them remain young and careless while they can, Henry."

So when Ella came back to mark the dusters that she had been hemming, because Mrs. Milton was in a hurry for them and the housemaid had hurt her eye, they were gone, and so were her neat little books that she had taken such pride in, and had been winding up before she gave them to Mrs. Ashford to keep in future; so was her pretty coral necklace that she wore of an evening; and her pearls with the diamond clasp; and her beautiful clear carbuncle brooch that she was so fond of, and her little gold clasp bracelet. Although Eliza and Susan had lived with them all her life long, *they* had never taken her things, poor Ella thought, a little bitterly. "Quite unsuitable at your age," dearest," Mrs. Ashford murmured, kissing her fondly.

And Ella never got them back any more. Many and many other things there were she

never got back, poor child. Ah me! treasures dearer to her than the pretty coral necklace and the gold clasp bracelet—liberty, confidence—the tender atmosphere of admiring love in which she had always lived, the first place in her father's heart. That should never be hers again, some one had determined.

The only excuse for Mrs. Ashford is that she was very much in love with her husband, and so selfishly attached to him that she grudged the very care and devotion which little Ella had spent upon her father all these years past. Every fresh proof of thought and depth of feeling in such a childish little creature hurt and vexed the other woman. Ella must be taught her place, this lady determined, not in so many words. Alas! if we could always set our evil thoughts and schemes to words, it would perhaps be well with us, and better far than drifting, unconscious, and unwarned, into nameless evil, unowned to one's self, scarcely recognized.

And so the years went by. Julia and Lisette grew up into two great tall fashionable bouncing young ladies; they pierced their ears, turned up their pigtails, and dressed very elegantly. Lisette used to wear a coral necklace, Julia was partial to a clear carbuncle brooch her mother gave her. Little Ella, too, grew up like a little green plant springing up through the mild spring rains and the summer sunshine, taller and prettier and sadder every year. And yet perhaps it was as well after all that early in life she had to learn to be content with a very little share of its bounties; she might have been spoiled and over-indulged if things had gone on as they began, if nothing had ever thwarted her, and if all her life she had had her own way. She was a bright smiling little thing for all her worries, with a sweet little face; indeed her beauty was so remarkable, and her manner so simple and charming, that Julia and Lisette, who were a year or two her elders, used to complain to their mother nobody ever noticed them when Ella was by. Lady Jane Peppercorne, their own cousin, was always noticing her, and actually gave her a potato off her own plate the other day.

"I fear she is a very forward, designing girl. I shall not think of taking her out in London this year," Mrs. Ashford said, with some asperity; "nor shall I allow her to appear at our croquet-party next week. She is far too young to be brought out."

So Ella was desired to remain in her own room on this occasion. She nearly cried, poor little thing, but what could she do? her father was away, and when he came back Mrs. Ashford would be sure to explain every thing to him. Mrs. Ashford had explained life to him in so strangely ingenious a manner that he had got to see it in a very topsy-turvy fashion. Some things she had explained away altogether, some she had distorted and twisted, poor little Ella had been explained and explained, until there was scarcely any thing of her left at all. Poor child, she sometimes used to think she had not a single friend in the world, but she would chide herself for such fancies: it must be fancy. Her father loved her as much as ever, but he was engrossed by business, and it was not to be expected he should show what he felt before Julia and Lisette, who might be hurt. And then Ella would put all her drawers in order, or sew a seam, or go out and pull up a bedful of weeds, to chase such morbid fancies out of her mind.

Lady Jane Peppercorne, of whom mention has been already made, had two houses, one in Onslow Square, another at Hampstead. She was very rich, she had never married, and was consequently far more sentimental than ladies of her standing usually are. She was a flighty old lady, and lived sometimes at one house, sometimes at the other, sometimes at hotels here and there, as the fancy seized her. She was very kind as well as flighty, and was constantly doing generous things, and trying to help any one who seemed to be in trouble or who appeared to wish for any thing she had it in her power to grant.

So when Mrs. Ashford said, "Oh, Lady Jane, pity me! My husband says he can not afford to take me to town this year. I should so like to go, for the dear girls' sake, of course—" Lady Jane gave a little grunt, and said, "I will lend you my house in Onslow Square, if you like —that is, if you keep my room ready for me in case I want to come up at any time. But I dare say you won't care for such an unfashionable quarter of the world."

"Oh Lady Jane, how exceedingly kind, how very delightful and unexpected!" cried Mrs. Ashford, who had been hoping for it all the time, and who hastened to communicate the news to Lisette and Julia.

"I shall want a regular outfit, mamma," said Julia, who was fond of dress. "Perhaps we shall meet young Mr. Richardson in town."

"I shall be snapped up directly by some one, I expect," said Lisette, who was very vain, and thought herself irresistible.

"Am I to come too?" asked Ella, timidly, from the other end of the room, looking up from her sewing.

"I do not know," replied her stepmother, curtly, and Ella sighed a little wistfully, and went on stitching.

"At what age shall you let me come out?" she presently asked, shyly.

"When you are fit to be trusted in the world, and have cured your unruly temper," said Mrs. Ashford. Ella's eyes filled with tears, and she blushed up; but her father came into the room, and she smiled through her tears, and thought to herself that since her temper was so bad, she had better begin to rule it that very instant. . . When Mrs. Ashford began to explain to her husband, however, how much better it would be for Ella to remain in the country, the child's wistful glance met his, and for once he insisted that she should not be left behind.

It is a bright May morning after a night of rain, and although this is London and not the country any more, Onslow Square looks bright and clean. Lady Jane has had the house smartly done up; clean chintz, striped blinds, a balcony full of mignonnette. She has kept two little rooms for herself and her maid, but all the rest of the house is at the Ashfords' disposal. Every body is satisfied, and Ella is enchanted with her little room up stairs. Mrs. Ashford is making lists of visits and dinner-parties and milliners' addresses; Lisette is looking out of the window at some carriages which are passing; the children and nurses are sitting under the trees in the square; Julia is looking at herself in the glass and practising her court courtesies; and Ella is in the back room arranging a great heap of books in a bookcase. "I should so like to go to the Palace, mamma," she says, looking up with a smudgy face, for the books were all dirty and covered with dust. "Do you think there will be room for me?"

Ella had no proper pride, as it is called, and always used to take it for granted she was wanted, and that some accident prevented her from going with the others. "I am sorry there is no room for you, Ella," said Mrs. Ashford, in her deep voice; "I have asked Mr. Richardson to come with us, and if he fails, I promised to call for the Countess Bricabrac. Pray, if you do not care for walking in the square this afternoon, see that my maid puts my things properly away in the cupboards, as well as Julia's and Lisette's, and help her to fold the dresses, because it is impossible for one person to manage these long trains unassisted."

"Very well," said Ella, cheerfully. "I hope you will have a pleasant day. How nice it must be to be going!"

"I wish you would learn not to wish for every thing and any thing that you happen to hear about, Ella," said Mrs. Ashford. "And by the way, if you find any visitors coming, go away, for I can not allow you to be seen in this dirty state."

"There's a ring," said Ella, gathering some of the books together. "Good-bye."

Young Mr. Richardson, who was announced immediately after, passed a pretty maid-servant, carrying a great pile of folios, upon the stairs. She looked so little fitted for the task that he involuntarily stopped and said, "Can I assist you?" The little maid smiled and shook her head, without speaking. "What a charming little creature!" thought Mr. Richardson. He came to say that he and his friend, Jack Prettyman, were going to ride down together, and would join the ladies at the Palace.

"We are to pick Colonel Ashford up at his club," Mrs. Ashford said, "and Madame de Bricabrac. I shall count upon you, then." And the young ladies waved him gracious *au revoir* from the balcony.

"Oh! don't you like white waistcoats, Julia?" said Lisette, as she watched him down the street.

They are gone. Ella went up to help with the dresses, but presently the maid said in her rude way that she must go down to dinner, and she could not have any body messing the things about while she was away. Carter hated having a "spy" set over her, as she called Miss Ashford. The poor little spy went back to the drawing-room. She was too melancholy and out of spirits to dress herself and go out. Her face was still smudgy, and she had cried a little over Lisette's pink tarlatan. Her heart sank down, down, down. She did so long for a little fun and delight, and laughter and happiness. She knew her father would say, "Where is Ella?" and her mother would answer, "Oh, I really can not account for Ella's fancies. She was sulky this morning again. I can not manage her strange tempers."

The poor child chanced to see her shabby face and frock and tear-stained cheeks in one of the tall glasses over the gilt tables. It was very silly, but the woe-begone little face touched her so; she was so sorry for it that all of a sudden she burst out sob, sob, sob, crying. "Oh, how nice it must be to be loved and cherished, and very happy!" she thought. "Oh, I could be so good if they would only love me!" She could not bear to think more directly of her father's change of feeling. She sat down on the floor, as she had a way of doing, all in a little heap, staring at the empty grate. The fire had burnt out, and no one had thought of re-lighting it. For a few minutes her tears overflowed, and she cried and cried in two rivulets down her black little face. She thought how forlorn she was, what a dull life she led, how alone she lived—such a rush of regret and misery overpowered her, that she hid her face in her hands, unconscious of any thing else but her own sadness. . . . .

She did not hear the bell ring, nor a carriage stop, nor Lady Jane's footsteps. That lady came across the room and stood looking at her. "Why, my dear little creature, what is the matter?" said Lady Jane at last. "Crying? don't you know it is very naughty to cry, no matter how bad things are? Are they all gone—are you all alone?"

Ella jumped up quite startled, blushed, wiped her tears in a smudge. "I thought nobody would see me cry," she said, "for they are all gone to the Crystal Palace."

"And did they leave you behind quite by yourself?" the old lady asked.

"They were so sorry they had no room for me," said good-natured little Ella. She could not bear to hear people blamed. "They had promised Madame de Bricabrac."

"Is that all?" said Lady Jane, in her kind imperious way. "Why, I have driven in from Hampstead on purpose to go there too. There's a great flower-show to-day, and you know I am a first-rate gardener. I've brought up a great hamper of things. Put on your bonnet, wash your face, and come along directly. I've plenty of room. Who is that talking in that rude way?" for at that instant Carter called out with a sniff from the drawing-room door, without looking in :—

"Now then, Miss Ella, you can come and help me fold them dresses. I'm in a hurry."

Carter was much discomposed when, instead of her victim, Lady Jane appeared, irate, dignified.

"Go up stairs directly, and do not forget yourself again," said the old lady.

"Oh, I think I ought to go and fold up the dresses," said Ella, hesitating, flushing, blushing, and looking more than grateful. "How very kind, very kind of you to think of me! I'm afraid they wouldn't—I'm afraid I've no bonnet. Oh, thank you, I—but—"

"Nonsense, child," said Lady Jane; "my maid shall help that woman. Here," ringing the bell violently (to the footman), "what have you done with the hamper I brought up? let me see it unpacked here immediately. Can't trust those people, my dear—always see to every thing myself."

All sorts of delicious things, scents, colors, spring-flowers and vegetables, came out of the hamper in delightful confusion. It was a hamper full of treasures—sweet, bright, delicious-tasted—asparagus, daffodillies, bluebells, salads, cauliflowers, hothouse flowers, cowslips from the fields, azalias. Ella's natty little fingers arranged them all about the room in plates and in vases so perfectly and so quickly that old Lady Jane cried out in admiration :—

"Why, you would be a first-rate girl, if you didn't cry. Here, you John, get some bowls and trays for the vegetables, green peas, strawberries; and oh, here's a cucumber and a nice little early pumpkin. I had it forced, my dear. Your stepmother tells me she is passionately fond of pumpkins. Here, John, take all this down to the cook; tell her to put it in a cool larder, and order the carriage and horses round directly. Now then," to Ella, briskly, "go and put your things on, and come along with me. I'll make matters straight. I always do. There, go directly. I can't have the horses kept. Raton, my coachman, is terrible if he is kept waiting—frightens me to death by his driving when he is put out."

Ella did not hesitate a moment longer; she rushed up stairs: her little feet flew as they used to do formerly. She came down in a minute, panting, rapturous, with shining hair and a bright face, in her very best Sunday frock, cloak, and hat. Shabby enough they were, but she was too happy, too excited, to think about the deficiencies in her toilet.

"Dear me, this never will do, I see," said the old lady, looking at her disapprovingly; but she smiled so kindly, as she spoke, that Ella was not a bit frightened.

"Indeed, I have no other," she said.

"John," cried the old lady, "where is my maid? Desire her to come and speak to me directly. Now then, sir!"

All her servants knew her ways much too well not to fly at her commands. A maid appeared as if by magic.

"Now, Batter, be quick; get that blue and

silver bournous of mine from the box up stairs, —it will look very nice; and a pair of gray kid gloves, Batter; and let me see, my dear, you wouldn't look well in a brocade. No, that gray satin skirt, Batter; her own white bodice will do, and we can buy a bonnet as we go along. Now, quick; am I to be kept waiting all day?"

Ella in a moment found herself transformed somehow into the most magnificent lady she had seen for many a day. It was like a dream, she could hardly believe it; she saw herself move majestically, sweeping in silken robes across the very same pier-glass where a few minutes before she had looked at the wretched little melancholy creature crying with a dirty face, and watched the sad tears flowing. . . .

"Now then—now then," cried Lady Jane, who was always saying "Now then," and urging people on — "where's my page — are the outriders there? They are all workhouse boys, my dear; they come to me as thin and starved as church-mice, and then I fatten them up and get 'em situations. I always go with outriders. One's obliged to keep up a certain dignity in these Chartist days—universal reform—suffrage —vote by ballot. I've no patience with Mr. Gladstone, and it all rests with us to keep ourselves well aloof. Get in, get in! Drive to Sydenham, if you please."

Lady Jane's manners entirely changed when she spoke to Raton. And it is a fact that coachmen from their tall boxes rule with a very high hand, and most ladies tremble before them. Raton looked very alarming in his wig, with his shoe-buckles and great red face.

What a fairy tale it was! There was little Ella sitting in this lovely chariot, galloping down the Brompton Road, with all the little boys cheering and hurrahing; and the little outriders clattering on ahead, and the old lady sitting bolt upright as pleased as Punch. She really had been going to Sydenham; but I think, if she had not, she would have set off instantly, if she thought she would make anybody happy by so doing. They stopped at a shop in the Brompton Road — the wondering shopwoman came out.

"A white bonnet, if you please," said Lady Jane. "That will do very well. Here, child, put it on, and mind you don't crease the strings." And then away and away they went once more through the town, the squares, over the bridges. They saw the ships and steamers coming down the silver Thames, but the carriage never stopped: the outriders paid the toll and clattered on ahead. They rolled along pleasant country lanes and fields, villas and country-houses, roadside inns, and pedestrians and crawling carts and carriages. At the end of three quarters of an hour, during which it seemed to Ella as if the whole gay cortége had been flying through the air, they suddenly stopped at last at the great gates of a Crystal Palace blazing in the sun, and standing on a hill. A crowd was looking on. All sorts of grand people were driving up in their carriages; splen-

did ladies were passing in. Two gentlemen in white waistcoats were dismounting from their horses just as Ella and Lady Jane were arriving. They rushed up to the carriage door, and helped them to the ground.

"And pray, sir, who are you?" said Lady Jane, as soon as she was safely deposited on her two little flat feet with the funny old-fashioned shoes.

The young man colored up and bowed. "You don't remember me, Lady Jane," he said. "Charles Richardson. I have had the honor of meeting you at Ash Place, and at Cliffe, my uncle's house. This is my friend Mr. Prettyman."

"This is Mr. Richardson, my dear Ella, and that is Mr. Prettyman. Tell them to come back in a couple of hours" (to the page), "and desire Raton to see that the horses have a feed. Now then—yes—give her your arm, and you are going to take me?—very well," to the other white waistcoat; and so they went into the Palace.

What are young princes like nowadays? Do they wear diamond aigrettes, swords at their sides, top-boots, and little short cloaks over one shoulder? The only approach to romance that I can see, is the flower in their button-hole, and the nice little mustaches and curly beards in which they delight. But all the same besides the flower in the button, there is also, I think, a possible flower of sentiment still growing in the soft hearts of princes in these days, as in the old days long, long ago,

Charles Richardson was a short ugly little man, very gentlemanlike, and well dressed. He was the next heir to a baronetcy; he had a pale face and a snub nose, and such a fine estate in prospect—Cliffe Court its name was— that I do not wonder at Miss Lisette's admiration for him. As for Ella, she thought how kind he had been on the stairs that morning; she thought what a bright genial smile he had. How charming he looked, she said to herself; no, never, never had she dreamt of any one so nice. She was quite—more than satisfied; no prince in romance would have seemed to her what this one was, there actually walking beside her. As for Richardson himself, it was a case of love at first sight. He had seen many thousand young ladies in the last few years, but not one of them to compare with this sweet-faced, ingenuous, tender, bright little creature. He offered her his arm, and led her along.

Ella observed that he said a few words to his friend; she little guessed their purport. "You go first," he whispered, "and, if you see the Ashfords, get out of the way. I should have to walk with those girls, and my heart is here transfixed forever." . . . . . "Where have I seen you before?" he went on, talking to Ella, as they roamed through the beautiful courts and gardens, among fountains and flowers, and rare objects of art. "Forgive me for asking you, but I must have met you somewhere long ago, and have never forgotten you. I am haunted by your face." Ella was too much ashamed to tell him where and how it was they had met that very morning. She remembered him perfectly, but she thought he would rush away **and** leave her, if she told him that the untidy little scrub upon the stairs had been herself. And she was so happy; music playing, flowers blooming, the great wonderful fairy Palace flashing overhead; the kind, clever, delightful young man to escort her; the gay company, the glitter, the perfume, the statues, the interesting figures of Indians, the dear, dear, kind Lady Jane to look to for sympathy and for good-humored little nods of encouragement. She had *never* been so happy; she had never known what a wonder the Palace might be. Her heart was so full. It was all so lovely, so inconceivably beautiful and delightful, that she was nearly tipsy with delight; her head turned for an instant, and she clung to young Richardson's protecting arm.

"Are you faint? are you ill?" he said anxiously.

"Oh no!" said Ella, "it's only that every thing is so beautiful; it is almost more than I can bear. I—I am not often so happy; oh, it is so charming! I do not think any thing could be so delightful in all the world." She looked herself so charming and unconscious as she spoke, looking up with her beautiful face out of her white bonnet, that the young fellow felt as if he *must* propose to her, then and there, offhand on the very spot; and at the instant he looked up passionately—oh, horror!—he caught sight of the Ashfords, mother, daughters, Madame de Bricabrac, all in a row, coming right down upon them.

"Prettyman, this way, to the right," cried little Richardson, desperately; and Prettyman, who was a good-natured fellow, said: "This way, please, Lady Jane; there's some people we want to avoid over there."

*   *   *   *   *

"I'm *sure* it was," Lisette said. "I knew the color of his waistcoat. Who could he have been walking with, I wonder?"

"Some lady of rank, evidently," said Julia. "I think they went up into the gallery in search of us."

"Let us go into the gallery, dears," said Mrs. Ashford, and away they trudged.

*   *   *   *   *

The young men and their companions had gone into the Tropics, and meanwhile were sitting under a spreading palm-tree, eating pink ices; while the music played and played more delightfully, and all the air was full of flowers and waltzes, of delight, of sentiment. To young Richardson the whole Palace was Ella in every thing, in every sound and flower and fountain; to Ella young Richardson seemed an enormous giant, and his kind little twinkling eyes were shining all round her.

Poor dear! she was so little used to being happy, her happiness almost overpowered her.

"Are you going to the ball at Guildhall to-morrow?" Mr. Richardson was saying to his unknown princess. "How shall I ever meet you again? Will you not tell me your name? But—"

"I wonder what o'clock it is, and where your mother can be, Ella," said Lady Jane; "it's very odd we have not met."

*   *   *   *   *

"I *can't* imagine where they can have hid themselves," said Julia, very crossly, from the gallery overhead.

"I'm so tired, and I'm ready to drop," said Miss Lisette.

"Oh, let us sit," groaned Madame de Bricabrac. "I can walk no more; what does it matter if we do not find your friends?"

"If we take our places at the door," said Lisette, "we shall be sure to catch them as they pass."

*   *   *   *   *

"Perhaps I may be able to go to the ball," said the princess, doubtfully. "I—I don't know." Lady Jane made believe not to be listening. The voices in the gallery passed on. Lady Jane, having finished her ice, pulled out her little watch, and gave a scream of terror. "Heavens! my time is up," she said. "Raton will frighten me out of my wits, driving home. Come, child, come—come—come. Make haste—thank these gentlemen for their escort," and she went skurrying along, a funny little active figure, followed by the breathless young people. They got to the door at last, where Raton was waiting, looking very ferocious. "Oh, good-bye," said Ella. "Thank you so much," as Richardson helped her into the chariot.

"And you will not forget me?" he said, in a low voice. "I shall not need any name to remember you by."

"My name is Ella," she answered, blushing, and driving off; and then Ella flung her arms round Lady Jane, and began to cry again, and said: "Oh, I have been so happy! so happy! How good, good of you to make me so happy! Oh, thank you, dear Lady Jane!"

The others came back an hour after them, looking extremely cross, and were much surprised to find Lady Jane in the drawing-room. "I am not going back till Wednesday," said the old lady. "I've several things to do in town. . . . . Well, have you had a pleasant day?"

"Not at all," said Mrs. Ashford, plaintively. "The colonel deserted us; we didn't find our young men till just as we were coming away. We are all very tired, and want some supper—some of your delicious fruit, Lady Jane."

"Oh dear, how tired I am!" said Julia.

"Poor Richardson was in very bad spirits," said Lisette.

"What a place it is for losing one another!" said old Lady Jane. "I took Ella there this afternoon, and though I looked about I couldn't see you any where."

"*Ella!*" cried the other girls, astonished; "was *she* there?" . . . . But they were too much afraid of Lady Jane to object more openly.

That evening, after the others left the room, as Ella was pouring out the tea, she summoned up courage to ask whether she might go the ball at Guildhall, with the others, next evening. "Pray, pray, please take me," she implored. Mrs. Ashford looked up amazed at her audacity.

Poor little Ella! refused, scorned, snubbed, wounded, pained, and disappointed. She finished pouring out the tea in silence, while a few bitter scalding tears dropped from her eyes into the teacups. Colonel Ashford drank some of them, and asked for more sugar to put into his cup.

"There, never mind," he said, kindly. He felt vexed with his wife, and sorry for the child; but he was, as usual, too weak to interfere. "You know you are too young to go into the world, Ella. When your sisters are married, then your turn will come."

Alas! would it ever come? The day's delight had given her a longing for more; and now she felt the beautiful glittering vision was only a vision, and over already: the cloud-capped towers, the gorgeous palace; and the charming prince himself—was he a vision too? Ah! it was too sad to think of. Presently Lisette and Julia came back: they had been up stairs to see about their dresses.

"I shall wear my bird-of-paradise, and my yellow tarlatane," said Lisette; "gold and purple is such a lovely contrast."

"Gobert has sent me a lovely thing," said Julia; "tri-color flounces all the way up—she has so much taste."

Good old Lady Jane asked her maid next morning if any dress was being got ready for Miss Ella. Hearing that she was not going, and that no preparations were being made, she dispatched Batter on a secret mission, and ordered her carriage at nine o'clock that evening. She went out herself soon after breakfast in a hired brougham, dispensing with the outriders for once. Ella was hard at work all day for her sisters; her little fingers quilled, fluted, frilled, pleated, pinned, tacked the trimmings on their dresses more dexterously than any dressmaker or maid-servant could do. She looked so pretty, so kind, and so tired, so wistful, as she came to help them to dress, that Lisette was quite touched, and said: "Well, Ella, I shouldn't wonder if, after I am snapped up, you were to get hold of a husband some day. I dare say some people might think you nice-looking."

"Oh, do you think so really, Lisette?" said Ella, quite pleased; and then faltering, "Do you think. . . . . Shall you see Mr. Richardson?"

"Of course I shall," said Lisette. "He was talking great nonsense yesterday after we found him; saying that he had met with perfection at last—very devoted altogether; scarcely spoke to me at all; but that is the greatest proof of devotion, you know. I know what he meant very well. I shouldn't be at all surprised if he was to propose to-night. I don't know whether I shall have him. I'm always afraid of being thrown away," said Lisette looking over her shoulder at her train.

Ella longed to send a message, a greeting of some sort, to Lisette's adorer. Oh, how she envied her! what would she not have given to be going too? . . . .

"What! are not you dressing, child?" said Lady Jane, coming into the room. "Are they again obliged to call for Madame de Bricabrac? I had looked up a pair of shoe-buckles for you in case you went; but keep them all the same, they only want a little rubbing up."

"Oh, thank you; how pretty they are; how kind you are to me!" said Ella, sadly. "I—I—am not going." And she gulped down a great sob.

It was just dreadful not to go; the poor child had had a great draught of delight the day before, and she was aching and sickening for more, and longing with a passion of longing which is only known to very young people—she looked quite worn and pale, though she was struggling with her tears.

"Rub up your shoe-buckles, that will distract you," said the old lady, kindly. "They are worth a great deal of money, though they are only paste; and if you peep in my room you will find a little pair of slippers to wear them with. I hope they will fit. I could hardly get any small enough for you." They were the loveliest little white satin slippers, with satin heels, all embroidered with glass beads; but, small as they were, they were a little loose, only Ella took care not to say so, as she tried them on.

We all know what is coming, though little Ella had no idea of it. The ball was at Guildhall, one of the grandest and gayest that ever was given in the city of London. It was in honor of the beautiful young Princess, who had just landed on our shores. Princes, ambassadors, nobles, stars, orders and garters, and decorations, were to be present; all the grandest, gayest, richest, happiest people in the country, all the most beautiful ladies and jewels and flowers, were to be there to do homage to the peerless young bride. The Ashfords had no sooner started, than Lady Jane, who had been very mysterious all day, and never told any one that she had been to the city to procure two enormous golden tickets which were up in her bedroom, now came, smiling very benevolently, into the drawing-room. Little Ella was standing out in the balcony with her pale face, and all her hair tumbling down her back. She had been too busy to put it up, and now she was only thinking of the ball, and picturing the dear little ugly disappointed face of Prince Richardson, when he should look about every where for her in vain—while she was standing hopelessly gazing after the receding carriage.

"Well, my dear, have you rubbed up the shoe-buckles? That is right," said the old lady.

"Now come quick into my room and see some of my conjuring."

Conjuring! It was the most beautiful white net dress, frothed and frothed up to the waist, and looped up with long grasses. The conjuring was her own dear old pearl necklace with the diamond clasp, and a diamond star for her hair. It was a bunch of grasses and delicate white azalias for a head-dress, and over all the froth a great veil of flowing white net. The child opened her violet eyes, gasped, screamed, and began dancing about the room like a mad thing, jumping, bounding, clapping her hands, all so softly and gayly, and yet so lightly, in such an ecstasy of delight, that Lady Jane felt she was more than rewarded.

* * * * *

"Ah! there she is at last!" cried Mr. Richardson, who was turning carefully round and round with the energetic Lisette.

"What do you mean?" said Lisette.

Can you fancy her amazement when she looked round and saw Ella appearing in her snow and sunlight dress, looking so beautiful that every body turned to wonder at her, and to admire? As for Ella, she saw no one, nothing; she was looking up and down, and right and left, for the kind little pale plain face which she wanted.

"Excuse me one minute, Miss Lisette," said Mr. Richardson, leaving poor Lisette planted in the middle of the room, and rushing forward.

"Are you engaged," Ella heard a breathless voice saying in her ear, "for the next three, six, twenty dances? I am so delighted you have come! I thought you were never coming."

Julia had no partner at all, and was standing close by the entrance with her mother. They were both astounded at the apparition. Mrs. Ashford came forward to make sure that her eyes were not deceiving her. Could it be? yes—no—yes, it was Ella! She flicked her fan indignantly into an alderman's eye, and looked so fierce that the child began to tremble.

"Please forgive me, mamma," said Ella, piteously.

"Forgive you! never," said Mrs. Ashford, indignant. "What does all this mean, pray?" she continued. "Lady Jane, I really must—" and then she stopped, partly because she was so angry she could scarcely speak, and partly because she could not afford to quarrel with Lady Jane until the season was over.

"You really must forgive me, dear Lydia," said Lady Jane. "She wanted to come so much, I could not resist bringing her."

Weber's inspiriting Last Waltz was being played; the people and music went waving to and fro like the waves of the sea, sudden sharp notes of exceeding sweetness sounded, and at the sound the figures all swayed in harmony. The feet kept unseen measure to the music; the harmonious rhythm thrilled and controlled them all. The music was like an enchantment, which kept them moving and swaying in circles and in delightful subjection. Lassitude, sad-ness, disappointment, Ella's alarm, all melted away for the time; pulses beat, and the dancers see-sawed to the measure.

All that evening young Richardson danced with Ella and with no one else: they scarcely knew how the time went. It was a fairy world: they were flying and swimming in melody—the fairy hours went by to music, in light, in delightful companionship. Ella did not care for Mrs. Ashford's darkening looks, for any thing that might happen: she was so happy in the moment, she almost forgot to look for Lady Jane's sympathetic glance.

"You must meet me in the ladies' cloak-room punctually at half past eleven," her patroness had whispered to her. "I can not keep Raton, with his bad cough, out after twelve o'clock. Mind you are punctual, for I have promised not to keep him waiting."

"Yes, yes, dear Lady Jane," said Ella, and away she danced again to the music. And time went on, and Julia had no partners; and Colonel Ashford came up to his wife, saying—"I'm so glad you arranged for Ella too," he said. "How nice she is looking! What is the matter with Julia; why don't she dance?" Tumty, tumty, tumty, went the instruments. And meanwhile Mr. Richardson was saying, "Your dancing puts me in mind of a fairy I once saw in a field at Cliffe long ago. Nobody would ever believe me, but I did see one."

"A fairy—what was she like?" asked Ella.

"She was very like you," said Mr. Richardson, laughing. "I do believe it was you, and that was the time when I saw you before."

"No, it was not," said Ella, blushing, and feeling she ought to confess. "I will tell you," she said, "if you will promise to dance one more dance with me, after you know.—Only one."

"Then you, too, remember," he cried, eagerly. "One more dance?—twenty—forever and ever. Ah, you must know, you must guess, the feeling in my heart. . . . ."

"Listen first," said Ella, trembling very much and waltzing on very slowly. "It was only the other day—" The clock struck three quarters.

"Ella, I am going," said Lady Jane, tapping her on the shoulder. "Come along, my dear—"

"One word!" cried Richardson, eagerly.

"You can stay with your mother if you like," the old lady went on, preoccupied—she was thinking of her coachman's ire—"but I advise you to come with me."

"Oh, pray, pray stay!" said young Richardson; "where is your mother? Let me go and ask her?"

"You had better go yourself, Ella," said old Lady Jane. "Will you give me your arm to the door, Mr. Richardson?"

Ella went up to Mrs. Ashford—she was bold with happiness to-night—and made her request. "Stay with me? certainly not, it is quite out of the question. You do me great honor," said the lady, laughing sarcastically. "Lady

Jane brought you, Lady Jane must take you back," said the stepmother. "Follow your chaperone, if you please, I have no room for you in my brougham. Go directly, miss !" said Mrs. Ashford, so savagely that the poor child was quite frightened, and set off running after the other two. She would have caught them up, but at that instant Lisette—who had at last secured a partner—came waltzing up in such a violent, angry way, that she bumped right up against the little flying maiden and nearly knocked her down. Ella gave a low cry of pain, they had trodden on her foot roughly —they had wounded her; her little satin slipper had come off. Poor Ella stooped and tried to pull at the slipper, but other couples came surging up, and she was alone, and frightened, and obliged to shuffle a little way out of the crowd before she could get it on. The poor little frightened thing thought she never should get through the crowd. She made the best of her way to the cloak-room : it seemed to her as if she had been hours getting there. At last she reached it, only to see, to her dismay, as she went in at one door, the other two going out of another a long way off! She called, but they did not hear her, and at the same moment St. Paul's great clock began slowly to strike twelve. "My cloak, my cloak, my thing, please," she cried in great agitation and anxiety ; and a stupid, bewildered maid hastily threw a shabby old shawl over her shoulders—it belonged to some assistant in the place. Little Ella, more and more frightened, pulled it up as she hurried along the blocked passages and corridors all lined with red and thronged with people. They all stared at her in surprise as she flew along. Presently her net tunic caught in the door-way and tore into a long ragged shred which trailed after her. In her agitation her comb fell out of her hair—she looked all scared and frightened —nobody would have recognized the beautiful triumphal princess of half an hour before. She heard the link - men calling, " Peppercorne's carriage stops the way !" and she hurried faster and faster down the endless passages and steps, and at last, just as she got to the door-way— oh, horror ! she saw the carriage and outriders going gleaming off in the moonlight while every thing else looked black, dark, and terrible.

"Stop, stop, please stop !" cried little Ella, rushing out into the street through the amazed footmen and link-men. "Stop ! stop !" she cried, flying past Richardson himself, who could hardly believe his eyes. Raton only whipped his horses, and Ella saw them disappearing into gloom in the distance in a sort of agony of despair. She was excited beyond measure, and exaggerated all her feelings. What was to be done ? Go back ?—that was impossible ; walk home ?—she did not know her way. Was it fancy ?—was not somebody following her ? She felt quite desperate in the moonlight and dark-

ness. At that instant it seemed to her like a fairy chariot coming to her rescue, when a cabman, who was slowly passing, stopped and said, " Cab, mum ?"

"Yes ! Oh yes ! To Onslow Square," cried Ella, jumping in and shutting the door in delight and relief. She drove off just as the bewildered little Richardson, who had followed her, reached the spot. He came up in time only to see the cab drive off, and to pick up something which was lying shining on the pavement. It was one of the diamond buckles which had fallen from her shoe as she jumped in. This little diamond buckle might perhaps have led to her identification if young Richardson had not taken the precaution of ascertaining from old Lady Jane Ella's name and address.

He sent a servant next morning with a little parcel and a note to inquire whether one of the ladies had lost what was inclosed, and whether Colonel Ashford would see him at one o'clock on business.

"Dear me, what a pretty little buckle !" said Lisette, trying it on her large flat foot. " It looks very nice, don't it, Julia ? I think I guess—don't you ?—what he is coming for. I shall say ' No.' "

"It's too small for you. It would do better for me," said Julia, contemplating her own long slipper, embellished with the diamonds. "It is not ours. We must send it back, I suppose."

"A shoe - buckle ?" said Ella, coming in from the kitchen, where she had been superintending preserves in her little brown frock. "Let me see it. Oh, how glad I am ! it is mine. - Look here!" and she pulled the fellow out of her pocket. " Lady Jane gave them to me."

And so the prince arrived before luncheon, and was closeted with Colonel Ashford, who gladly gave his consent to what he wanted. And when Mrs. Ashford began to explain things to him, as was her way, he did not listen to a single word she said. He was so absorbed wondering when Ella was coming into the room. He thought once he heard a little rustle on the stairs outside, and he jumped up and rushed to the door. It was Ella, sure enough, in her shabby little gown. Then he knew where and when he had seen her before.

" Ella, why did you run away from me last night ?" he said. "You see I have followed you, after all."

They were so good, so happy, so devoted to one another, that even Lisette and Julia relented. Dear little couple ; good luck go with them, happiness, content, and plenty. There was something quite touching in their youth, tenderness, and simplicity ; and as they drove off in their carriage for the honeymoon, Lady Jane flung the very identical satin slipper after them which Ella should have lost at the ball.

BEAUTY AND THE BEAST.

I.

Fairy times, gifts, music, and dances, are said to be over, or, as it has been said, they come to us so disguised and made familiar by habit that they do not seem to us strange. H. and I, on either side of the hearth, these long past winter evenings could sit without fear of fiery dwarfs skipping out of the ashes, of black puddings coming down the chimney to molest us. The clock ticked, the window-pane rattled. It was only the wind. The hearth-brush remained motionless on its hook. Pussy dozing on the hearth, with her claws quietly opening to the warmth of the blaze, purred on, and never once startled us out of our usual placidity by addressing us in human tones. The children sleeping peacefully up stairs were not suddenly whisked away and changelings deposited in their cribs. If H. or I opened our mouths pearls and diamonds did not drop out of them, but neither did frogs and tadpoles fall from between our lips. The looking-glass tranquilly reflecting the comfortable little sitting-room, and the stiff ends of H.'s cap-ribbons, spared us visions of wreathing clouds parting to reveal distant scenes of horror and treachery. Poor H.! I am not sure but that she would gladly looked in a mirror in which she could have sometimes seen the images of those she loved; but our chimney-glass, with its gilt moulding and bright polished surface, reflects only such homely scenes as two old women at work by the fire, some little Indian children at play upon the rug, the door opening and Susan bringing in the tea-things. As for wishing-cloths and little boiling-pots, and such like, we have but to ring an invisible bell (which is even less trouble), and a smiling genius in a white cap and apron brings in any thing we happen to fancy. When the clock strikes twelve, H. puts up her work and lights her candle; she has not yet been transformed into a beautiful princess all twinkling with jewels, neither does a scullion ever stand before me in rags; she does not murmur farewell forever and melt through the key-hole, but "Good-night," as she closes the door. One night at twelve o'clock, just after she had left me, there was indeed a loud orthodox ring at the bell, which started us both a little; H. came running down again without her cap, Susan appeared in great alarm from the kitchen. "It is the back-door bell, ma'am," said the girl, who had been sitting up over her new Sunday gown, but who was too frightened to see who was ringing.

I may as well explain that our little house is in a street, but that our back windows have the advantage of overlooking the grounds of the villa belonging to our good neighbor and friend Mr. Griffiths in Castle Gardens, and that a door opens out of our little back garden into his big one, of which we are allowed to keep the key. This door had been a postern-gate once upon a time, for a bit of the old wall of the park is still standing, against which our succeeding bricks have been piled. It was a fortunate chance for us when our old ivy-tree died and we found the quaint little door-way behind it. Old Mr. Griffiths was alive then, and when I told him of my discovery, he good-naturedly cleared the way on his side, and so the oak turned once more upon its rusty hinges to let the children pass through, and the nurse-maid, instead of pages and secret emissaries and men-at-arms; and about three times a year young Mr. Griffiths stoops under the arch on his way to call upon us. I say young Mr. Griffiths, but I suppose he is over thirty now, for it is more than ten years since his father died.

When I opened the door, in a burst of wind and wet, I found that it was Guy Griffiths who stood outside bare-headed in the rain, ringing the bell that winter night. "Are you up?" he said. "For Heaven's sake come to my mother, she's fainted; her maid is away; the doctor doesn't come. I thought you might know what to do." And then he led the way through the dark garden, hurrying along before me.

Poor lady, when I saw her I knew that it was no fainting-fit, but a paralytic stroke, from which she might perhaps recover in time; I could not tell. For the present there was little to be done: the maids were young and frightened; poor Guy wanted some word of sympathy and encouragement. So far I was able to be of use. We got her to bed and took off her finery—she had been out at a dinner-party, and had been stricken on her return home—Guy had discovered her speechless in the library. The poor fellow, frightened and overcome, waited about, trying to be of help, but he was so nervous that he tumbled over us all, and knocked over the chairs and bottles in his anxiety, and was of worse than no use. His kind old shaggy face looked pale, and his brown eyes *ringed* with anxiousness. I was touched by the young fellow's concern, for Mrs. Griffiths had not been a tender mother to him. How she had snapped and laughed at him, and frightened him, with her quick sarcastic tongue and hard, unmotherlike ways! I wondered if she thought of this as she lay there cold, rigid, watching us with glassy, senseless eyes.

The payments and debts and returns of affection are at all times hard to reckon. Some people pay a whole treasury of love in return for a stone, others deal out their affection at interest, others again take every thing, to the uttermost farthing, and cast it into the ditch and go their way and leave their benefactor penniless and a beggar. Guy himself, hard-headed as he was, and keen over his ledgers in Moorgate Street, could not have calculated such sums as these. All that she had had to give, all the best part of her shallow store, poor Julia Griffiths had paid to her husband, who did not love her: to her second son, whose whole life was a sorrow to his parents. When he died she could never forgive poor Guy for living still, for being his father's friend and right hand, and sole successor. She had been a real mother to Hugh, who was gone; to Guy, who was alive still and patiently waiting to do her bidding, she had shown herself only a stepdame; and yet I am sure no life-devoted parent could have been more anxiously watched and tended by her son. Perhaps—how shall I say what I mean?—if he had loved her more and been more entirely one with her now, his dismay would have been less, his power greater to bear her pain, to look on at her struggling agony of impotence. Even pain does not come between the love of people who really love.

The doctor came and went, leaving some comfort behind him. Guy sat up all that night, burning logs on the fire in the dressing-room, out of the bedroom in which Mrs. Griffiths was lying. Every now and then I went in to him, and found him sitting over the hearth shaking his great shaggy head, as he had a way of doing, and biting his fingers, and muttering, "Poor soul, poor mother." Sometimes he would come in creaking on tiptoe; but his presence seemed to agitate the poor woman, and I was obliged to motion him back again. Once when I went in and sat down for a few minutes in an armchair beside him, he suddenly began to tell me that there had been trouble between them that morning. "It made it very hard to bear," he said. I asked him what the trouble had been. "I told her I thought I should like to marry," Guy confessed with a rueful face. (Even then I could hardly help smiling.) "Selfish beast that I am. I upset her, poor soul. I behaved like a brute." His distress was so great that it was almost impossible to console him, and it was in vain to assure him that the attack had been produced by physical causes. "Do you want to marry any one in particular?" I asked at last, to divert his thoughts, if I could, from the present. "No," said he; "at least—of

course she is out of the question—only I thought perhaps some day I should have liked to have a wife and children and a home of my own. Why, the counting-house is not so dreary as this place sometimes seems to me." And then, though it was indeed no time for love-confidences, I could not help asking him who it was that was out of the question.

Guy Griffiths shrugged his great round shoulders impatiently, and gave something between a groan and sigh and smile (dark and sulky as he looked at times, a smile brightened up his grim face very pleasantly).

"She don't even know my name," he said. "I saw her one night at the play, and then in a lane in the country a little time after. I found out who she was. She's a daughter of old Barly the stockbroker. Belinda they call her—Miss Belinda. It's rather a silly name, isn't it?" (This, of course, I politely denied.) "I'm sure I don't know what there is about her," he went on in a gentle voice; "all the fellows down there were head over ears in love with her. I asked—in fact I went down to Farmborough in hopes of meeting her again. I never saw such a sweet young creature—never. I never spoke to her in my life." "But you know her father?" I asked. "Old Barly?—Yes," said Guy. "His wife was my father's cousin, and he and I are each other's trustees for some money which was divided between me and Mrs. Barly. My parents never kept up with them much, but I was named trustee in my father's place when he died. I didn't like to refuse. I had never seen Belinda then. Do you like sweet sleepy eyes that wake up now and then? Was that my mother calling?" For a minute he had forgotten the dreary present. It all came rushing back again. The bed creaked, the patient had moved a little on her pillow, and there was a gleam of some intelligence in her pinched face. The clock struck four in quick tinkling tones; the rain seemed to have ceased, and the clouds to be parting; the rooms turned suddenly chill, though the fires were burning.

When I went home, about five o'clock, all the stars had come out and were shooting brilliantly overhead. The garden seemed full of a sudden freshness and of secret life stirring in the darkness; the sick woman's light was burning faintly, and in my own window the little bright lamp was flickering which H.'s kind fingers had trimmed and put there ready for me when I should return. When we reached the little gate, Guy opened it and let me pass under some dripping green creeper which had been blown loose from the wall. He took my old hand in both his big ones, and began to say something that ended in a sort of inarticulate sound as he turned away and trudged back to his post again. I thought of the many meetings and partings at this little postern gate, and last words and protestations. Some may have been more sentimental perhaps than this one, but Guy's grunt of gratitude was more affecting to me than many a long string of words. I felt very sorry for him, poor old fellow, as I barred the door and climbed up stairs to my room. He sat up watching till the morning. But I was tired, and soon went to sleep.

II.

SOME people do very well for a time. Chances are propitious, the way lies straight before them up a gentle inclined plane, with a pleasant prospect on either side. They go rolling straight on, they don't exactly know how, and take it for granted that it is their own prudence and good driving and deserts which have brought them prosperously so far upon their journey. And then one day they come to a turnpike, and Destiny pops out of its little box and demands a toll, or Prudence trips, or Good Sense shies at a scarecrow put up by the wayside—or nobody knows why, but the whole machine breaks down on the road and can't be set going again. And then other vehicles go past it, hand-trucks, perambulators, cabs, omnibuses, and great prosperous barouches, and the people who were sitting in the broken-down equipage get out and walk away on foot.

On that celebrated and melancholy Black Monday of which we have all heard, poor John Barly and his three daughters came down the carpeted steps of their comfortable sociable for the last time, and disappeared at the wicket of a little suburban cottage—disappeared out of the prosperous, pompous, highly respectable circle in which they had gyrated, dragged about by two fat bay horses, in the greatest decorum and respectability; dining out, receiving their friends, returning their civilities. Miss Barlys had left large cards with their names engraved upon them, in return for other large cards upon which were inscribed equally respectable names, and the addresses of other equally commodious family mansions. A mansion—so the house-agents tell us—is a house like another with the addition of a back staircase. The Barlys and all their friends had back staircases to their houses and to their daily life as well. They only wished to contemplate the broad, swept, carpeted drawing-room flights. Indeed to Anna and Fanny Barly this making the best of things, card-leaving and visiting, seemed a business of vital importance. The youngest of the girls, who had been christened by the pretty silly name of Belinda, had only lately come home from school, and did not value these splendors and proprieties so highly as her sisters did. She had no great love for the life they led. Sometimes, looking over the balusters of their great house in Capulet Square, she had yawned out loud from very weariness, and then she would hear the sound echoing all the way up to the skylight, and reverberating down from baluster to baluster. If she went into the drawing-room, instead of the yawning echoes the shrill voices of Anna and of Fanny were vibrating monotonously as they complimented Lady Ogden upon her new barouche, until Be-

linda could bear it no longer, and would jump up and run away to her bedroom to escape it all. She had a handsome bedroom, draped in green damask, becarpeted, four-posted, with an enormous mahogany wardrobe of which poor Belle was dreadfully afraid, for the doors would fly open of their own accord in the dead of night, revealing dark abysses and depths unknown, with black ghosts hovering suspended or motionless and biding their time. There were other horrors ; shrouds waving in the blackness, feet stirring, and low creakings of garroters, which she did not dare to dwell upon as she hastily locked the doors and pushed the writing-table against them.

It must therefore be confessed, that to Belinda the days had been long and oppressive sometimes in this handsomely appointed Tyburnean palace. Anna, the eldest sister, was queen-regnant ; she had both ability and inclination to take the lead. She was short, broad, and dignified, and some years older than either of her sisters. Her father respected her business-like mind, admired her ambition, regretted sometimes secretly that she had never been able to make up her mind to accept any of the eligible young junior partners, the doctor, the curate, who had severally proposed to her. But then of course, as Anna often said, they could not possibly have got on without her at home. She had been in no hurry to leave the comfortable kingdom where she reigned in undisputed authority, ratifying the decisions of the ministry down stairs, appealed to by the butler, respectfully dreaded by both the house-maids. Who was there to go against her ? Mr. Barly was in town all day and left every thing to her; Fanny, the second sister, was her faithful ally. Fanny was sprightly, twenty-one, with black eyes, and a curl that was much admired. She was fond of fashion, flirting, and finery, inquisitive, talkative, feeble-minded, and entirely devoted to Anna. As for Belle, she had only come back from school the other day. Anna could not quite understand her at home. Fanny was of age and content to do as she was bid ; here was Belle at eighteen asserting herself very strangely. Anna and Fanny seemed to pair off somehow, and Belle always had to hold her own without any assistance, unless, indeed, her father was present. He had a great tenderness and affection for his youngest child, and the happiest hour of the day to Belinda was when she heard him come home and call for her in his cheerful quavering voice. By degrees it seemed to her, as she listened, that the cheerfulness seemed to be dying away out of his voice, and only the quaver remained ; but that may have been fancy, and because she had taken a childish dislike to the echoes in the house.

At dinner-time, Anna used to ask her father how things were going in the City, and whether shirtings had risen any higher, and at what premium the Tre Rosas shares were held in the market. These were some shares in a Cornish mine company of which Mr. Barly was a director. Anna thought so highly of the whole concern that she had been anxious to invest a portion of her own and her sister Fanny's money in it. They had some small inheritance from their mother, of part of which they had the control when they came of age; the rest was invested in the Funds in Mr. Griffith's name, and could not be touched. Poor Belle, being a minor, had to be content with sixty pounds a year for her pin-money, which was all she could get for her two thousand pounds.

When Anna talked business, Mr. Barly used to be quite dazzled by her practical clear-headedness, her calm foresight, and powers of rapid calculation. Fanny used to prick up her ears and ask, shaking her curl playfully, how much girls must have to be heiresses, and did Anna think they should ever be heiresses? Anna would smile and nod her head, in a calm and chastened sort of way, at this childish impatience. "You should be very thankful, Frances, for all you have to look to, and for your excellent prospects. Emily Ogden, with all her fine airs, would not be sorry to be in your place." At which Fanny blushed up bright red, and Belinda jumped impatiently upon her chair, blinking her white eyelids impatiently over her clear gray eyes, as she had a way of doing. "I can't bear talking about money," she said; "any thing is better. . . ." Then she too stopped short and blushed.

"Papa," interrupted Fanny, playfully, "when will you escort us to the pantomime again? The Ogdens are all going next Tuesday, and you have been most naughty and not taken us any where for such a long time."

Mr. Barly, who rarely refused any thing any body asked him, pushed his chair away from the table and answered with strange impatience for him, "My dear, I have had no time lately for plays and amusements of any sort. After working from morning to night for you all, I am tired, and want a little peace of an evening. I have neither spirits nor—"

"Dear papa," said Belinda, eagerly, "come up into the drawing-room and sit in the easy-chair, and let me play you to sleep." As she spoke Belinda smiled a delightful fresh, sweet, tender smile, like sunshine falling on a fair landscape. No wonder the little stock-broker was fond of his youngest daughter. Frances was pouting, Anna frowned slightly as she locked up the wine, and turned over in her mind whether she might not write to the Ogdens and ask them to let Frances join their party; as for Belinda, playing Mozart to her father in the dim drawing-room up stairs, she was struck by the worn and harassed look in his face as he slept, snoring gently in accompaniment to her music. It was the last time Belle ever played upon the old piano. Three or four days after, the crash came. The great Tre Rosas Mining Company (Limited) had failed, and the old established house of Barly and Co. unexpectedly stopped payment.

If poor Mr. Barly had done it on purpose, his ruin could not have been more complete and ingenious. When his affairs came to be looked into, and his liabilities had been met, it was found that an immense fortune had been muddled away, and that scarcely any thing would be left but a small furnished cottage, which had been given for her life to an old aunt just deceased, and which reverted to Fanny her godchild, and the small sum which still remained in the Three per Cents, of which mention has been made, and which could not be touched until Belle the youngest of three daughters, should come of age.

After two or three miserable days of confusion—during which the machine which had been set going with so much trouble still revolved once or twice with the force of its own impetus, the butler answering the bell, the footman bringing up the coals, the cook sending up the dinner as usual—suddenly every thing collapsed, and the great mass of furniture, servants, human creatures, animals, carriages, business and pleasure engagements, seemed overthrown together in a great struggling mass, panting and bewildered, and trying to get free from the confusion of particles that no longer belonged to one another.

First, the cook packed up her things and some nice damask table-cloths and napkins, a pair of sheets, and Miss Barly's umbrella, which happened to be hanging in the hall; then the three ladies drove off with their father to the cottage, where it was decided they should go to be out of the way of any unpleasantness. He had no heart to begin again, and was determined to give up the battle. Belle sat with her father on the back seat of the carriage, looking up into his haggard face a little wistfully, and trying to be as miserable as the others. She could not help it—a cottage in the country, ruin, roses, novelty, clean chintzes instead of damask, a little room with mignonnette, cocks crowing, had a wicked morbid attraction for her which she could not overcome. She had longed for such a life when she had gone down to stay with the Ogdens at Farnborough last month, and had seen several haystacks and lovely little thatched cottages, where she had felt she would have liked to spend the rest of her days; one in particular had taken her fancy, with dear little latticed windows and a pigeon-cote and two rosy little babies, with a kitten toddling out from the ivy porch; but a great rough-looking man had come up in a slouched wide-awake and frightened Emily Ogden so much that she had pulled Belinda away in a hurry . . . .; but here a sob from Fanny brought Belle back to her place in the barouche.

Anna felt she must bear up, and nerved herself to the effort. Upon her the blow fell more heavily than upon any of the others. Indignant, injured, angry with her father, furious with the managers, the directors, the shareholders, the secretary, the unfortunate company, with the Bankruptcy Court, the Ogdens, the laws of fate, the world in general, with Fanny for sobbing, and with Belle for looking placid, she sat blankly staring out of the window as they drove past the houses where they had visited, and where she had been entertained an honored guest; and now—she put the hateful thought away—bankrupt, disgraced! Her bonnet was crushed in, she did not say a word, but her face looked quite fierce and old, and frightened Fanny into fresh lamentations. These hysterics had been first brought on by the sight of Emily Ogden driving by in the new barouche. This was quite too much for her poor friend's fortitude. "Emily will drop us, I know she will," sobbed Fanny. "Oh Anna, will they ever come and ask us to their Thursday luncheon - parties any more?"

"My children," said Mr. Barly, with a placid groan, pulling up the window, "we are disgraced; we can only hide our heads away from the world. Do not expect that any one will ever come near us again." At which announcement Fanny went off into new tears and bewailings. As for the kind, bewildered, weak-headed, soft-hearted little man, he had been so utterly worn out, harassed, worried, and wearied of late, that it was almost a relief to him to think that this was indeed the case. He sat holding Belle's hand in his, stroking and patting it, and wondering that people so near London did not keep the roads in better repair. "We must be getting near our new abode," said he at last almost cheerfully.

"You speak as if you were glad of our shame, papa," said Anna, suddenly, turning round upon him.

"Oh, hush!" cried Belle, indignantly. Fortunately the coachman stopped at this moment on a spot a very long way off from Capulet Square; and leaning from his box, asked if it was that there little box across the common.

"Oh, what a sweet little place!" cried Belinda. But her heart rather sank as she told this dreadful story.

Myrtle Cottage was a melancholy little tumble-down place, looking over Dumbleton Common, which they had been crossing all this time. It was covered with stucco, cracked and stained and mouldy. There was a stained - glass window, which was broken. The verandah wanted painting. From outside it was evident that the white muslin curtains were not so fresh as they might have been. There was a little garden in front, planted with durable materials. Even out of doors, in the gardens in the suburbs, the box-edges, the laurel-bushes, and the fusty old jessamines are apt to look shabby in time if they are never renewed. A certain amount of time and money might, perhaps, have made Myrtle Cottage into a pleasant little habitation; but (judging from appearances) its last inhabitants seemed to have been in some want of both these commodities. Its helpless new occupants were not likely to have much of either to spare. A little dining-room, with glass drop candlesticks and a rickety table, and a print of a church and a Dissenting minister on the

wall. A little drawing-room, with a great horse-hair sofa, a huge round table in the middle of the room, and more glass drop candlesticks, also a small work-table of glass over faded worsted embroidery. Four little bedrooms, mousy, musty, snuffy, with four posts as terrific as any they had left behind, and a small black dungeon for a maid-servant. This was the little paradise which Belle had been picturing to herself all along the road, and at which she looked round half sighing, half dismayed. Their bundles, baskets, blankets, were handed in, and a cart full of boxes had arrived. Fanny's parrot was shrieking at the top of its voice on the narrow landing.

"What fun!" cried Belinda, sturdily, instantly setting to work to get things into some order, while Fanny lay exhausted upon the horse-hair sofa; and Anna, in her haughtiest tones, desired the coachman to drive home, and stood watching the receding carriage until it had dwindled away into the distance—coachman, hammer-cloth, bay horses, respectability, and all. When she re-entered the house, the parrot was screeching still, and Martha, the under-housemaid—now transformed into a sort of extract of butler, footman, ladies' maid, and cook, was frying some sausages, of which the vulgar smell pervaded the place.

III.

BELLE exclaimed, but it required all her courage and natural brightness of spirit to go on looking at the bright side of things, praising the cottage, working in the garden, giving secret assistance to the two bewildered maids who waited on the reduced little family, cheering her father, smiling, and putting the best face on things, as her sisters used to do at home. If it had been all front stairs in Capulet Square, it was all back staircase at the cottage. Rural roses, calm sunsets, long shadows across the common, are all very well; but when puffs of smoke come out of the chimney and fill the little place; when if the window is opened a rush of wind and dust—worse almost than the smoke—comes eddying into the room, and careers round the four narrow walls; when poor little Fanny coughs and shudders, and wraps her shawl more closely round her with a groan; when the smell of the kitchen frying-pan perfumes the house, and a mouse scampers out of the cupboard, and black beetles lie straggling in the milk-jugs, and the pump runs dry, and spiders crawl out of the tea-caddy, and so forth —then, indeed, Belle deserves some credit for being cheerful under difficulties. She could not pretend to very high spirits, but she was brisk and willing, and ready to smile at her father's little occasional puns and feeble attempts at jocularity. Anna, who had been so admirable as a general, broke down under the fatigue of the actual labor in the trenches which belonged to their new life. A great many people can order others about very brilliantly and satisfactorily, who fail when they have to do the work themselves.

Some of the neighbors called upon them, but the Ogdens never appeared. Poor little Fanny used to take her lace-work and sit stitching and looping her thread at the window which overlooked the common, with its broad roads crossing and recrossing the plain; carriages came rolling by, people came walking, children ran past the windows of the little cottage, but the Ogdens never. Once Fanny thought she recognized the barouche—Lady Ogden and Emily sitting in front, Matthew Ogden on the back seat; surely, yes, surely it was he. But the carriage rolled off in a cloud of dust, and disappeared behind the wall of the neighboring park; and Frances finished the loop, and passed her needle in and out of the muslin, feeling as if it was through her poor little heart that she was piercing and sticking; she pulled out a long thread, and it seemed to her as if the sunset stained it red like blood.

In the mean while Bell's voice had been singing away overhead, and Fanny, going up stairs presently, found her, with one of the maids, clearing out one of the upper rooms. The window was open, the furniture was piled up in the middle. Belle, with her sleeves tacked up and her dress carefully pinned out of the dust, was standing on a chair, hammer in hand, and fixing up some dimity curtains against the window. Table-cloths, brooms, pails, and brushes were lying about, and every thing looked in perfect confusion. As Fanny stood looking and exclaiming, Anna also came to the door from her own room, where she had been taking a melancholy nap.

"What a mess you are making here!" cried the elder sister, very angrily. "How can you take up Martha's time, Belinda? And oh! how can you forget yourself to this degree? You seem to *exult* in your father's disgrace." Belinda flushed up.

"Really, Anna, I do not know what you mean," said she, turning round, vexed for a minute, and clasping a long curtain in both arms. "I could not bear to see my father's room looking so shabby and neglected; there is no disgrace in attending to his comfort. See, we have taken down those dusty curtains, and we are going to put up some others," said the girl, springing down from the chair and exhibiting her treasures.

"And pray where is the money to come from," said Anna, "to pay for these wonderful changes?"

"They cost no money," said Belinda, laughing. "I made them myself, with my own two hands. Don't you remember my old white dress that you never liked, Anna? Look how I have pricked my finger. Now, go down," said the girl, in her pretty imperative way, "and don't come up again till I call you."

Go down at Belle's bidding. . . . .

Anna went off fuming, and immediately set to work also, but in a different fashion. She unfortunately found that her father had returned, and was sitting in the little sitting-room down below by himself, with a limp paper of the day before open upon his knees. He was not reading. He seemed out of spirits, and was gazing in a melancholy way at the smouldering fire, and rubbing his bald head in a perplexed and troubled manner. Seeing this, the silly woman, by way of cheering and comforting the poor old man, began to exclaim at Belinda's behavior, to irritate him, and overwhelm him with allusions and reproaches.

"Scrubbing and slaving with her own hands," said Anna. "Forgetting herself; bringing us down lower indeed than we are already sunk. Papa, she will not listen to me. You should tell her that you forbid her to put us all to shame by her behavior."

When Belle, panting, weary, triumphant, and with a blackened nose and rosy cheek, opened the door of the room presently and called her father exultingly, she did not notice, as she ran up stairs before him, how wearily he followed her. A flood of light came from the dreary little room overhead. It had been transformed into a bower of white dimity, bright windows, clean muslin blinds. The fusty old carpet was gone, and a clean crumb-cloth had been put down, with a comfortable rug before the fireplace. A nosegay of jessamine stood on the chimney, and at each corner of the four-post bed the absurd young decorator had stuck a smart bow, made out of some of her own blue ribbons, in place of the terrible plumes and tassels which had waved there in dust and darkness before. One of the two arm-chairs which blocked up the wall of the dining-room had been also covered out of some of Belinda's stores, and stood comfortably near the open window. The sun was setting over the great common outside, behind the mill and the distant fringe of elm-trees. Martha, standing all illuminated by the sunshine, with her mop in her hand, was grinning from ear to ear, and Belle turned and rushed into her father's arms. But Mr. Barly was quite overcome. "My child," he said, "why do you trouble yourself so much for me? Your sister has told me all. I don't deserve it. I can not bear that you should be brought to this. My Belle working and slaving with your own hands through my fault—through my fault." The old man sat down on the side of the bed by which he had been standing, and laid his face in his hands, in a perfect agony of remorse and regret. Belinda was dismayed by the result of her labors. In vain she tried to cheer him and comfort him. The sweeter she seemed in his eyes, the more miserable the poor father grew at the condition to which he had brought her.

For many days after he went about in a sort of despair, thinking what he could do to retrieve his ruined fortunes; and if Belinda still rose betimes to see to his comfort and the better ordering of the confused little household, she took care not to let it be known. Anna came down at nine, Fanny at ten. Anna would then spend several hours regretting her former dignities, reading the newspaper and the fashionable intelligence, while the dismal strains of Fanny's piano (there was a jangling piano in the little drawing-room) streamed across the common. To a stormy spring, with wind flying and dust dashing against the window-panes, and gray clouds swiftly bearing across the wide open country, had succeeded a warm and brilliant summer, with sunshine flooding and spreading over the country. Anna and Fanny were able to get out a little now, but they were soon tired, and would sit down under a tree and remark to one another how greatly they missed their accustomed drives. Belinda, who had sometimes at first disappeared now and then to cry mysteriously a little bit by herself over her troubles, now discovered that at eighteen, with good health and plenty to do, happiness is possible, even without a carriage.

One day Mr. Barly, who still went into the city from habit, came home with some news which had greatly excited him. Wheal Tre Rosas, of which he still held a great many shares which he had never been able to dispose of, had been giving some signs of life. A fresh call was to be made; some capitalist, with more money than he evidently knew what to do with, had been buying up a great deal of the stock. The works were to be resumed. Mr. Barly had always been satisfied that the concern was a good one. He would give every thing he had, he told Anna that evening, to be able to raise enough money now to buy up more of the shares. His fortune was made if he could do so; his children replaced in their proper position, and his name restored. Anna was in a state of greater flutter, if possible, than her father himself. Belle sighed; she could not help feeling doubtful, but she did not like to say much on the subject.

"Papa, this Wheal has proved a very treacherous wheel of fortune to us," she hazarded, blushing and bending over her sewing; "we are very, very happy as we are."

"Happy?" said Anna, with a sneer.

"Really, Belinda, you are too romantic," said Fanny with a titter; while Mr. Barly cried out, in an excited way, "that she should be happier yet, and all her goodness and dutifulness should be rewarded in time." A sort of presentiment of evil came over Belinda, and her eyes filled up with tears; but she stitched them away and said no more.

Unfortunately the only money Mr. Barly could think of to lay his hands upon was that sum in the Three per Cents upon which they were now living; and even if he chose he could not touch any of it until Belinda came of age; unless, indeed, young Mr. Griffiths would give him permission to do so.

"Go to him, papa," cried Anna, enthusiastically. "Go to him; entreat, insist upon it, if necessary."

All that evening Anna and Frances talked over their brilliant prospects. "I should like to see the Ogdens again," said poor little Fanny. "Perhaps we shall if we go back to Capulet Square." "Certainly, certainly," said Anna. "I have heard that this Mr. Griffiths is a most uncouth and uncivilized person to deal with," continued Miss Barly, with her finger on her chin. "Papa, wouldn't it be better for me to go to Mr. Griffiths instead of you?" This, however, Mr. Barly would not consent to.

Anna could hardly contain her vexation and spite when he came back next day dispirited, crestfallen, and utterly wretched and disappointed. Mr. Griffiths would have nothing to say to it.

"What's the good of a trustee," said he to Mr. Barly, "if he were to let you invest your money in such a speculative chance as that? Take my advice, and sell out your shares now, if you can, for any thing you can get."

"A surly, disagreeable fellow," said poor old Mr. Barly. "I heartily wish he had nothing to do with our affairs."

Anna fairly stamped with rage. "What insolence, when it is our own! Papa, you have no spirit to allow such interference."

Mr. Barly looked at her gravely, and said he should not allow it. Anna did not know what he meant.

Belinda was not easy about her father all this time. He came and went in an odd excited sort of way, stopping short sometimes as he was walking across the room, and standing absorbed in thought! One day he went into the city unexpectedly about the middle of the day, and came back looking quite odd, pale, with curious eyes; something was wrong, she could not tell what. In the mean time Wheal Tre Rosas seemed, spite of Mr. Griffiths's prophecies, to be steadily rising in the world. More business had been done, the shares were a trifle higher. A meeting of directors was convened, and actually a small dividend was declared at midsummer. It really seemed as if there was some chance after all that Anna should be reinstated in the barouche, in Capulet Square, and her place in society. She and Fanny were half wild with delight. "When we leave—" was the beginning of every sentence they uttered. Fanny wrote the good news to her friend Miss Ogden, and, under these circumstances, to Fanny's unfeigned delight, Emily Ogden thought herself justified in driving over to the village one fine afternoon and affably partaking of a cracked cupful of five o'clock tea. It was slightly smoked, and the milk was turned. Belinda had gone out for a walk and was not there to see to it at all; I am afraid she did not quite forgive Emily the part she had played, and could not make up her mind to meet her.

One morning Anna was much excited by the arrival of a letter directed to Mr. Barly in great round handwriting, and with a huge seal, all over bears and griffins. Her father was forever expecting news of his beloved Tre Rosas, and he broke the seal with some curiosity. But this was only an invitation to dine and sleep at Castle Gardens from Mr. Griffiths, who said he had an offer to make Mr. Barly, and concluded by saying that he hoped Mr. Barly forgave him for the ungracious part he had been obliged to play the other day, and that, in like circumstances, he would do the same by him.

"I sha'n't go," said Mr. Barly, a little doggedly, putting the letter down.

"Not go, papa? Why, you may be able to talk him over if you get him quietly to yourself. Certainly you must go, papa," said Anna. "Oh, I'm sure he means to relent—how nice!" said Fanny. Even Belinda thought it was a pity he should not accept the invitation, and Mr. Barly gave way as usual. He asked them if they had any commands for him in town.

"Oh, thank you, papa," said Frances. "If you are going shopping, I wish you would bring me back a blue alapaca, and a white grenadine, and a pink sou-poult, and a—"

"My dear Fanny, that will be quite sufficient for the short time you remain here," interrupted Anna, who went on to give her father several commissions of her own—some writing-paper stamped with Barly Lodge and their crest in one corner; a jacket with buttons for the knife-boy they had lately engaged upon the strength of their coming good fortune; a new umbrella, a house-agent's list of mansions in the neighborhood of Capulet Square, the *Journal des Modes*, and the *New Court Guide*. "Let me see, there was something else," said Anna, thoughtfully.

"Bella," said Mr. Barly, "how comes it you ask for nothing? What can I bring you, my child?"

Belle looked up with one of her bright melancholy smiles and replied, "If you should see any roses, papa, I think I should like a bunch of roses. We have none in the garden."

"Roses!" cried Fanny, laughing. "I didn't know you cared for any thing but what was useful, Bella."

"I quite expected you would ask for a saucepan, or a mustard-pot," said Anna, with a sneer.

Belle sighed again, and then the three went and stood at the garden-gate to see their father off. It made a pretty little group for the geese on the common to contemplate—the two young sisters at the wicket, the elder under the shade of the veranda, Belle upright, smiling, waving her slim hand; she was above the middle height, she had fair hair and dark eye-brows and gray eyes, over which she had a peculiar way of blinking her smooth white eyelids; and all about, the birds, the soft winds, the great green common with its gorgeous furze-blossoms blazing against the low bank of clouds in the horizon. Close at hand a white pony was tranquilly cropping the grass, and two little village children were standing outside the railings, gazing up open-mouthed at the pretty ladies who lived at the cottage.

IV.

THE clouds which had been gathering all the afternoon broke shortly before Mr. Barly reached his entertainer's house. He had tried to get there through Kensington Gardens, but could not make out the way, and went wandering round and round in some perplexity under the great trees with their creaking branches. The storm did not last long and the clouds dispersed at sunset. When Mr. Barly rang at the gate of the villa in Castle Gardens at last that evening, he was weary, wet through, and far less triumphant than he had been when he left home in the morning. The butler who let him in gave the bag which he had been carrying to the footman, and showed him the way up stairs immediately to the comfortable room which had been made ready for him. . Upholsterers had done the work on the whole better than Belle with all her loving labor. The chairs were softer than her print-covered horse-hair cushions. The wax-lights were burning, although it was broad daylight. Mr. Barly went to the bay-window. The garden outside was a sight to see; smooth lawns, arches, roses in profusion and abundance, hanging and climbing and clustering every where, a distant gleam of a fountain, of a golden sky, a chirruping and rustling in the bushes and trellises after the storm. The sunset which was lighting up the fern on the rain-sprinkled common was twinkling through the rose-petals here, bringing out odors and aromas and whiffs of delicious scent. Mr. Barly thought of Belle, and how he should like to see her flitting about in the garden and picking roses to her heart's content. As he stood there he thought, too, with a pang, of his wife whom he had lost, and sighed in a sort of despair at the troubles which had fallen upon him of late; what would he not give to undo the work of the last few months, he thought—nay, of the last few days? He had once come to this very house with his wife in their early days of marriage. He remembered it now, although he had not thought of it before.

Sometimes it happens to us all that things which happened ever so long ago seem to make a start out of their proper places in the course of time, and come after us, until they catch us up, as it were, and surround us, so that one can hear the voices, and see the faces and colors, and feel the old sensations and thrills as keenly as at the time they occurred—all so curiously and strangely vivid that one can scarcely conceive it possible that years and years perhaps have passed since it all happened, and that the present shock proceeds from an ancient and almost forgotten impulse. And so as Mr. Barly looked and remembered and thought of the past, a sudden remorse and shame came over him. He seemed to see his wife standing in the garden, holding the roses up over her head, looking like Belle; like, yet unlike. Why it should have been so, at the thought of his wife among the flowers, I can not tell; but as he remem-

bered her he began to think of what he had done
—that he was there in the house of the man
he had defrauded—he began to ask himself how
could he face him? how could he sit down beside him at table, and break his bread? The
poor old fellow fell back with a groan in one of
the comfortable arm-chairs. Should he confess? Oh no—no, that would be the most terrible of all.

What he had done is simply told. When
Guy Griffiths refused to let Mr. Barly lay hands
on any of the money which he had in trust for
his daughters, the foolish and angry old man
had sold out a portion of the sum belonging to
Mr. Griffiths which still remained in his own
name. It had not seemed like dishonesty at
the time, but now he would have gladly—oh,
how gladly! awakened to find it all a dream.
He dressed mechanically, turning over every
possible chance in his own mind. Let Wheal
Tre Rosas go on and prosper, the first money
should go to repay his loan, and no one would
be the wiser. He went down into the library again when he was ready. It was empty
still, and, to his relief, the master of the house
had not yet come back. He waited a very long
time, looking at the clock, at the reviews on
the table, at the picture of Mrs. Griffiths, whom
he could remember in her youth, upon the wall.
The butler came in again to say that his master had not yet returned. Some message had
come by a boy, which was not very intelligible,
he had been detained in the city. Mrs. Griffiths was not well enough to leave her room, but
she hoped Mr. Barly would order dinner—any
thing he required—and that her son would
shortly return.

It was very late. There was nothing else to
be done. Mr. Barly found a fire lighted in the
great dining-room, dinner laid, one plate and
one knife and fork, at the end of the long table.
The dinner was excellent, so was the wine.
The butler uncorked a bottle of champagne, the
cook sent up chickens and all sorts of good
things. Mr. Barly almost felt as if he, by some
strange metempsychosis, had been converted into
the owner of this handsome dwelling and all
that belonged to it. At twelve o'clock Mr.
Griffiths had not yet returned, and his guest,
after a somewhat perplexed and solitary meal,
retired to rest.

Mr. Barly breakfasted by himself again next
morning. Mr. Griffiths had not returned all
night. In his secret heart Mr. Griffiths's guest
was almost relieved by the absence of his entertainer: it seemed like a respite. Perhaps, after
all, every thing would go well, and the confession
which he had contemplated with such terror the
night before need never be made. For the present it was clearly no use to wait any longer at
the house. Mr. Barly asked for a cab to take
him to the station, left his compliments and regrets, and a small sum of money behind him,
and then, as the cab delayed, strolled out into
the front garden to wait for it.

Even in the front court the roses were all

abloom; a great snow cluster was growing over
the door-way, a pretty tea-rose was hanging its
head over the scraper; against the outer railing
which separated the house from the road, rose-
trees had been planted. The beautiful pink
fragrant heads were pushing through the iron
railings, and a delicious little rose-wind came
blowing in the poor old fellow's face. He began to think again—no wonder—of Belle and
her fancy for roses, and mechanically, without
much reflecting upon what he was about, he
stopped and inhaled the ravishing sweet smell
of the great dewy flowers, and then put out his
hand and gathered a spray from which three
roses were hanging . . . .; as he gathered it, a
sharp thorn ran into his finger, and a heavy
grasp was laid upon his arm. . . . .

"So it is you, is it, who sneak in and steal
my roses?" said an angry voice. "Now that
I know who it is, I shall give you in charge."

Mr. Barly looked round greatly startled. He
met the fierce glare of two dark brown eyes
under shaggy brows, that were frowning very
fiercely. A broad, thick-set, round-shouldered
young man of forbidding aspect had laid hold
of him. The young man let go his grasp when
he saw the mistake he had made, but did not
cease frowning.

"Oh! it is you, Mr. Barly," he said.

"I was just going," said the stockbroker,
meekly. "I am glad you have returned in
time for me to see you, Mr. Griffiths. I am
sorry I took your rose. My youngest daughter
is fond of them, and I thought I might, out of
all this garden-full, you would not—she had
asked—"

There was something so stern and unforgiving in Mr. Griffiths's face that the merchant
stumbled in his words, and stopped short, surprised, in the midst of his explanations.

"The roses were not yours, not if there were
ten gardens full. I won't have my roses broken
off," said Griffiths; "they should be cut with a
knife. Come back with me; I want to have a
little talk with you, Mr. Barly."

Somehow the old fellow's heart began to beat,
and he felt himself turn rather sick.

"I was detained last night by some trouble
in my office. One of my clerks, in whom I
thought I could have trusted, absconded yesterday afternoon. I have been all the way to
Liverpool in pursuit of him. What do you
think should be done with him?" And Mr.
Griffiths, from under his thick eyebrows, gave
a quick glance at his present victim, and seemed
to expect some sort of answer.

"You prosperous men can not realize what
it is to be greatly tempted," said Mr. Barly,
with a faint smile.

"Do you know that Wheal Tre Rosas has
come to grief a second time?" said young Mr.
Griffiths, abruptly, holding out the morning's
Times, as they walked along. "I am *not* a
prosperous man; I had a great many shares in
that unlucky concern."

Poor Barly stopped short and turned quite

pale, and began to shake, so that he had to put his hand out and lean against the wall.

Failed! Was he doomed to misfortune? Then there was never any chance for him—never. No hope! No hope of paying back the debt which weighed upon his conscience. He could not realize it. Failed! The rose had fallen to the ground; the poor unlucky man stood still, staring blankly in the other's grim, unrelenting face.

"I am ruined," he said.

"You are ruined! Is that the worst you have to tell me?" said Mr. Griffiths, still looking piercingly at him. Then the other felt that he knew all.

"I have been very unfortunate—and very much to blame," said Mr. Barly, still trembling; —"terribly to blame—Mr. Griffiths. I can only throw myself upon your clemency."

"My clemency! my mercy! I am no philanthropist," said Guy, savagely. "I am a man of business, and you have defrauded me!"

"Sir," said the stockbroker, finding some odd comfort in braving the worst, "you refused to let me take what was my own; I have sold out some of your money to invest in this fatal concern. Heaven knows it was not for myself, but for the sake of—of—others; and I thought to repay you ere long. You can repay yourself now. You need not reproach me any more. You can send me to prison if you like. I—I don't much care what happens. My Belle, my poor Belle—my poor girls!"

All this time Guy said never a word. He motioned Mr. Barly to follow him into the library. Mr. Barly obeyed, and stood meekly waiting for the coming onslaught. He stood in the full glare of the morning sun, which was pouring through the unblinded window. His poor old head was bent, and his scanty hair stood on end in the sunshine.

His eyes, avoiding the glare, went vacantly traveling along the scroll-work on the fender, and so to the coal-scuttle and to the skirting on the wall, and back again. Dishonored—yes. Bankrupt—yes. Three-score years had brought him to this—to shame, to trouble. It was a hard world for unlucky people, but Mr. Barly was too much broken, too weary and indifferent, to feel very bitterly even against the world. Meanwhile Guy was going on with his reflections, and, like those among us who are still young and strong, he could put more life and energy into his condemnation and judgment of actions done, than the unlucky perpetrators had to give to the very deeds themselves. Some folks do wrong as well as right, with scarcely more than half a mind to it.

"How could you do such a thing?" cried the young man, indignantly, beginning to rush up and down the room in his hasty, clumsy way, knocking against tables and chairs as he went along. "How could you do it?" he repeated. "I learned it yesterday by chance. What can I say to you that your own conscience should not have told you already? How could you do

it?" Guy had reached the great end window, and stamped with vexation and a mixture of anger and sorrow. For all his fierceness and gruffness, he was sorry for the poor feeble old man whose fate he held in his hand. There was the garden outside, and its treasure and glory of roses; there was the rose-spray, lying on the ground, that old Barly had taken. It was lying broken and shining upon the gravel —one rose out of the hundreds that were bursting and blooming, and fainting and falling on their spreading stems. It was like the wrong old Barly had done his kinsman—one little wrong, Guy thought, one little handful out of all his abundance. He looked back, and by chance caught sight of their two figures reflected in the glass at the other end of the room—his own image, the strong, round-backed, broad-shouldered young man, with gleaming white teeth and black bristling hair; the feeble and uncertain culprit, with his broken wandering looks, waiting his sentence. It was not Guy who delivered it. It came—no very terrible one after all, prompted by some unaccountable secret voice and impulse. Have we not all of us sometimes suddenly felt ashamed in our lives in the face of misfortune and sorrow? Are we Pharisees, standing in the market-place, with our phylacteries displayed to the world? we ask ourselves, in dismay—does this man go home justified rather than we? Guy was not the less worthy of his Belinda, poor fellow, because a thought of her crossed his mind, and because he blushed up, and a gentle look came into his eyes, and a shame into his heart—a shame of his strength and prosperousness, of his probity and high honor. When had he been tempted? What was it but a chance that he had been born what he was? And yet old Barly, in all his troubles, had a treasure in his possession for which Guy felt he would give all his good fortune and good repute, his roses—red, white, and golden—his best heart's devotion, which he secretly felt to be worth all the rest. Now was the time, the young man thought, to make that proposition which he had in his mind.

"Look here," said Guy, hanging his great shaggy head, and speaking quickly and thickly, as if he was the culprit instead of the accuser. "You imply it was for your daughter's sake that you cheated me. I can not consent to act as you would have me do and take your daughter's money to pay myself back. But if one of them—Miss Belinda, since she likes roses—chooses to come here and work the debt off, she can do so. My mother is in bad health and wants a companion; she will engage her at—let me see, a hundred guineas a year, and in this way, by degrees, the debt will be cleared off."

"In twenty years," said Mr. Barly, bewildered, relieved, astonished.

"Yes, in twenty years," said Guy, as if that was the most natural thing in the world. "Go home and consult her, and come back and give me the answer."

And as he spoke, the butler came in to say that the hansom was at the door.

Poor old Barly bent his worn meek head and went out. He was shaken and utterly puzzled. If Guy had told him to climb up the chimney, he would have obeyed. He could only do as he was bid. As it was, he clambered with difficulty into the hansom, told the man to go to the station for Dumbleton, and he was driving off gladly when some one called after the cab. The old man peered out anxiously. Had Griffiths changed his mind? Was his heart hardened like Pharaoh's at the eleventh hour?

It was certainly Guy who came hastily after the cab, looking more awkward and sulky than ever. "Hoy! Stop! You have forgotten the roses for your daughter," said he, thrusting in a great bunch of sweet foam and freshness. As the cab drove along, people passing by looked up and envied the man who was carrying such loveliness through the black and dreary London streets. Could they have seen the face looking out behind the roses they might have ceased to envy.

Belle was on the watch for her father at the garden gate, and exclaimed with delight, as she saw him toiling up the hill from the station with his huge bunch of flowers. She came running to meet him with fluttering skirts and outstretched hands, and sweet smiles gladdening her face. "Oh, papa, how lovely! Have you had a pleasant time?" Her father hardly responded. "Take the roses, Belle," he said. "I have paid for them dearly enough." He went into the house wearily, and sat down in the shabby arm-chair. And then he turned and called Belinda to him wistfully, and put his trembling arm round about her. Poor old Barly was no mighty Jephthah; but his feeble old head bent with some such pathetic longing and remorse over his Belle as he drew her to him, and told her, in a few simple broken words, all the story of what had befallen him in those few hours since he went away. He could not part from her. "I can't, I can't," he said, as the girl put her tender arms round her neck. . . . .

Guy came to see me a few days after his interview with old Mr. Barly, and told me that his mother had surprised him by her willing acquiescence in the scheme. I could have explained matters to him a little, but I thought it best to say nothing. Mrs. Griffiths had overheard, and understood a word or two of what he had said to me that night, when she was taken ill. Was it some sudden remorse for the past? Was it a new-born mother's tenderness stirring in her cold heart, which made her question and cross-question me the next time that I was alone with her? There had often been a talk of some companion or better sort of attendant. After the news came of poor old Barly's failure, it was Mrs. Griffiths herself who first vaguely alluded again to this scheme.

"I might engage one of those girls—the—the—Belinda, I think you called her?"

I was touched and took her cold hand and kissed it.

"I am sure she would be an immense comfort to you," I said. "You would never regret your kindness."

The sick woman sighed and turned away impatiently, and the result was the invitation to dinner, which turned out so disastrously.

V.

When Mr. Barly came down to breakfast the morning after his return, he found another of those great square official-looking letters upon the table. There was a check in it for £100. "You will have to meet heavy expenses," the young man wrote. "I am not sorry to have an opportunity of proving to you that it was not the money which you have taken from me I grudged, but the manner in which you took it. The only reparation you can make me is by keeping the inclosed for your present necessity."

In truth the family prospects were not very brilliant. Myrtle Cottage was resplendent with clean windows and well-scrubbed door-steps, but the furniture wanted repairing, the larder refilling. Belle could not darn up the broken flap of the dining-room table, nor conjure legs of mutton out of bare bones, though she got up ever so early; sweeping would not mend the hole in the carpet, nor could she dust the mildew stains off the walls, the cracks out of the looking-glass.

Anna was morose, helpless, and jealous of the younger girl's influence over her father. Fanny was delicate; one gleam of happiness, however, streaked her horizon: Emily Ogden had written to invite her to spend a few days there. When Mr. Barly and his daughter had talked over Mr. Griffiths's proposition, Belle's own good sense told her that it would be folly to throw away this good chance. Let Mrs. Griffiths be ever so trying and difficult to deal with, and her son a thousand times sterner and ruder than he had already shown himself, she was determined to bear it all. Belinda knew her own powers, and felt as if she could endure any thing, and that she should never forget the generosity and forbearance he had shown her poor father. Anna was delighted that her sister should go; she threw off the shawl in which she had muffled herself up ever since their reverses, brightened up wonderfully, talked mysteriously of Fanny's prospects as she helped both the girls to pack, made believe to shed a few tears as Belinda set off with her father, and bustled back into the house with renewed importance. Belinda looked back and waved her hand, but Anna's back was already turned upon her, and she was giving directions to the page.

Poor Belinda! For all her courage and cheerfulness her heart sank a little as they reached the great bronze gates in Castle Gardens. She would have been more unhappy still if she had not had to keep up her father's spirits. It was almost dinner-time, and Mrs. Griffiths's maid came down with a message. Her mistress was tired, and just going to bed, and would see her in the morning; Mr. Griffiths was dining in town; Miss Williamson would call upon Miss Barly that evening.

Dinner had been laid as usual in the great dining-room, with its marble columns and draperies, and Dutch pictures of game and of birds and flowers. Three servants were in waiting, a great silver chandelier lighted the dismal meal, huge dish-covers were upheaved, decanters of wine were handed round, all the *entrées* and delicacies came over again. Belle tried to eat to keep her father in company. She even made little jokes, and whispered to him that they evidently meant to fatten her up. The poor old fellow cheered up by degrees; the good claret warmed his feeble pulse, the good fare comforted and strengthened him. "I wish Martha would make us ice-puddings," said Belle, helping him to a glittering mass of pale-colored cream, with nutmeg and vanilla, and all sorts of delicious spices. He had just finished the last mouthful when the butler started and rushed out of the room, a door banged, a bell rang violently, a loud scraping was heard in the hall, and an echoing voice said: "Are they come? Are they in the dining-room?" And the crimson curtain was lifted up, and the master of the house entered the room carrying a bag and a great-coat over his arm. As he passed the sideboard the button of the coat caught in the fringe of a cloth which was spread upon it, and in a minute the cloth and all the glasses and plates which had been left there came to the ground with a wild crash, which would have made Belle laugh, if she had not been too nervous even to smile.

Guy merely told the servants to pick it all up, and put down the things he was carrying and walked straight across the room to the two frightened people at the far end of the table. Poor fellow! After shaking hands with old Barly and giving Belle an abrupt little nod, all he could find to say was:

"I hope you came of your own free-will, Miss Barly?" and as he spoke he gave a shy scowl and eyed her all over.

"Yes," Belle answered, blinking her soft eyes to see him more clearly.

"Then I'm very much obliged to you," said Guy.

This was such an astonishingly civil answer that Belinda's courage rose.

Poor Belinda's heart failed her again, however, when Griffiths, still in an agony of shyness, then turned to her father, and in his roughest voice said:

"You leave early in the morning, but I hope we shall keep your daughter for a very long time."

Poor fellow! he meant no harm, and only intended this by way of conversation. Belle in her secret heart said to herself that he was a cruel brute; and poor Guy, having made this impression, broken a dozen wine-glasses, and gone through untold struggles of shyness, now wished them both good-night.

"Good-night, Mr. Barly; good-night, Miss Belle," said he. Something in his voice caused Belle to relent a little.

"Good-night, Mr. Griffiths," said the girl, standing up, a slight graceful figure, simple and nymph-like, amidst all this pomp of circumstance. As Griffiths shuffled out of the room he saw her still; all night he saw her in his dreams. That bright winsome young creature, dressed in white soft folds, with all the gorgeous gildings and draperies, and the lights burning, and the pictures and gold cups glimmering round about her. They were his, and as many more of them as he chose: the inanimate, costly, sickening pomps and possessions; but a pure spirit like that, to be a bright living companion for him? Ah, no! that was not to be—not for him, not for such as him. Guy, for the first time in his life, as he went up stairs that evening, stopped and looked at himself attentively in the great glass on the staircase. He saw a great loutish, round-backed fellow, with a shaggy head and brown glittering eyes, and little strong white teeth like a dog's; he gave an uncouth sudden caper of rage and regret at his own appearance. "To think that happiness and life itself and love eternal depend upon tailors and hair-oil," groaned poor Guy, as he went into his room to write letters.

Mrs. Griffiths did not see Belle that evening; she was always nervously averse to seeing strangers, but she had sent for me to speak to her, and as I was leaving she had asked me to go down and speak to Miss Barly before I went. Belinda was already in her room, but I ventured to knock at the door. She came to meet me with a bright puzzled face and all her pretty hair falling loose about her face. She had not a notion who I was, but begged me to come in. When I had explained things a little, she pulled out a chair for me to sit down.

"This house seems to me so mysterious and unlike any thing else I have ever known," said she, "that I'm very grateful to any one who will tell me what I'm to do here—please sit down a little while."

I told her that she would have to write notes, to add up bills, to read to Mrs. Griffiths, and to come to me whenever she wanted any help or comfort. "You were quite right to come," said I. "They are excellent people. Guy is the kindest, best fellow in the whole world, and I have long heard of you, Miss Barly, and I'm sure such a good daughter as you have been will be rewarded some day."

Belle looked puzzled, grateful, a little proud, and very charming. She told me afterwards that it had been a great comfort to her father to hear of my little visit to her, and that she had succeeded in getting him away without any very painful scene.

Poor Belle! I wonder how many tears she shed that day after her father was gone? While she was waiting to be admitted to Mrs. Griffiths she amused herself by wandering about the house, dropping a little tear here and there as she went along, and trying to think that it amused her to see so many yards of damask and stair-carpeting, all exactly alike, so many acres of chintz of the same pattern.

"Mr. Griffiths desired me to say that this tower room was to be made ready for you to sit in, ma'am," said the respectful butler, meeting her and opening a door. "It has not been used before." And he gave her the key, to which a label was affixed, with "MISS BARLY'S ROOM" written upon it, in the housekeeper's scrawling handwriting.

Belle gave a little shriek of admiration. It was a square room, with four windows, overlooking the gardens, the distant park, and the broad cheerful road which ran past the house. An ivy screen had been trained over one of the windows, roses were clustering in garlands round the deep sill casements. There was an Indian carpet, and pretty silk curtains, and comfortable chintz chairs and sofas, upon which beautiful birds were flying and lilies wreathing. There was an old-fashioned-looking piano, too, and a great bookcase filled with books and music. "They certainly treat me in the most magnificent way," thought Belle, sinking down upon the sofa in the window which overlooked the rose-garden, and inhaling a delicious breath of fragrant air. "They can't mean to be very unkind." Belle, who was a little curious, it must be confessed, looked at every thing, made secret notes in her mind, read the titles of the books, examined the china, discovered a balcony to her turret. There was a little writing-table, too, with paper and pens and inks of various colors, which especially pleased her. A glass cup of cut roses had been placed upon it, and two dear little green books, in one of which some one had left a paper-cutter.

The first was a book of fairy tales, from which I hope the good fairy editress will forgive me for stealing a sentence or two.

The other little green book was called the *Golden Treasury;* and when Belle took it up, it opened where the paper-cutter had been left, at the seventh page, and some one had scored the sonnet there. Belle read it, and somehow, as she read, the tears in her eyes started afresh.

> Being your slave, what should I do but tend
> Upon the hours and times of your desire?

it began. "To ———" had been scrawled underneath; and then the letter following the "To" erased. Belle blinked her eyes over it, but could make nothing out. A little farther on she found another scoring—

> Oh, my love's like a red, red rose
> That's newly sprung in June!
> **Oh,** my love's like the melody
> That's sweetly played in tune!

and this was signed with a G.

"Love! That is not for me; but I wish I had a slave," thought poor Belle, hanging her head over the book as it lay open in her lap, "and that he was clever enough to tell me what my father is doing at this minute." She could imagine it for herself, alas! without any magic interference. She could see the dreary little cottage, her poor old father wearily returning alone. She nearly broke down at the thought, but some one knocked at the door at that instant, and she forced herself to be calm as one of the servants came in with a telegram. Belinda tore open her telegram in some alarm and trembling terror of bad news from home; and then smiled a sweet loving smile of relief. The telegram came from Guy. It was dated from his office. "Your father desires me to send word that he is safe home. He sends his love. I have been to D. on business, and traveled down with him."

Belinda could not help saying to herself that Mr. Griffiths was very kind to have thought of her. His kindness gave her courage to meet his mother.

It was not very much that Belle had to do for Mrs. Griffiths; but whatever it was she accomplished well and thoroughly, as was her way. Whatever the girl put her hand to, she put her whole heart to at the same time. Her energy, sweetness, and good spirits cheered the sick woman and did her infinite good. Mrs. Griffiths took a great fancy to her, and liked to have her about her. Belle lunched with her the first day. She had better dine down below, Mrs. Griffiths said; and when dinner-time came the girl dressed herself, smoothed her yellow curls, and went shyly down the great staircase into the dining-room. It must be confessed that she glanced a little curiously at the table, wondering whether she was to dine alone or in company. This problem was soon solved; a side-door burst open, and Guy made his appearance, looking shy and ashamed of it as he came up and shook hands with her.

"Miss Belinda," said he, "will you allow me to dine with you?"

"You must do as you like," said Belinda, quickly, starting back.

"Not at all," said Mr. Griffiths. "It is entirely as you shall decide. If you don't like my company, you need only say so. I shall not be offended. Well, shall we dine together?"

"Oh, certainly," laughed Belinda, confused in her turn.

So the two sat down to dine together. For the first time in his life Guy thought the great room light enough and bright and comfortable. The gold and silver plate didn't seem to crush him, nor the draperies to suffocate, nor the great columns ready to fall upon him. There was Belinda picking her grapes and playing with the sugar-plums. He could hardly believe it possible. His poor old heart gave great wistful thumps (if such a thing is possible) at the sound of her voice. She had lost much of her shyness, and they were talking of any thing that came into their heads. She had been telling him about Myrtle Cottage, and the spiders there, and looking up, laughing, she was surprised to see him staring at her very sadly and kindly. He turned away abruptly, and began to help himself to all sorts of things out of the silver dishes.

"It's very good of you," Guy said, looking away, "to come and brighten this dismal house, and to stay with a poor suffering woman and a great uncouth fellow like myself."

"But you are both so very kind," said Belinda, simply. "I shall never forget—"

"Kind!" cried Guy, very roughly. "I behaved like a brute to you and your father yesterday. I am not used to ladies' society. I am stupid and shy and awkward."

"If you were very stupid," said Belle, smiling, "you would not have said that, Mr. Griffiths. Stupid people always think themselves charming."

When Guy said good-night immediately after dinner as usual, he sighed, and looked at her again with such kind and melancholy eyes that Belle felt an odd affection and compassion for him. "I never should have thought it possible to like him so much," thought the girl, as she slowly went along the passage to Mrs. Griffiths's door.

It was an odd life this young creature led in the great silent stifling house, with uncouth Guy for her playfellow, the sick woman's complaints and fancies for her duty in life. The silence of it all, its very comfort and splendidness, oppressed Belinda more at times than a simpler and more busy life. But the garden was an endless pleasure and refreshment, and she used to stroll about, skim over the terraces and walks, smell the roses, feed the birds and the gold-fishes. Sometimes I have stood at my window watching the active figure flitting by in and out under the trellis, fifteen times round the pond, thirty-two times along the terrace walk. Belle was obliged to set herself tasks, or she would have got tired sometimes of wandering about by herself. All this time she never thought of Guy except as a curious sort of companion; any thought of sentiment had never once occurred to her.

VI.

ONE day that Belle had been in the garden longer than usual, she remembered a note for Mrs. Griffiths that she had forgotten to write, and springing up the steps into the hall, on the way, with some roses in her apron, she suddenly almost ran up against Guy, who had come home earlier than usual. The girl stood blushing and looking more charming than ever. The young fellow stood quite still too, looking with such expressive and admiring glances that Belinda blushed deeper still, and made haste to escape to her room. Presently the gong sounded, and there was no help for it, and she had to go down again. Guy was in the dining-room as polite and as shy as usual, and Belinda gradually forgot the passing impression. The butler put the dessert on the table and left them, and when she had finished her fruit, Belinda got up to say good-bye. As she was leaving the room she heard Guy's footsteps following. She stop-

ped short. He came up to her. He looked very pale, and said suddenly, in a quick, husky voice, "Belle, will you marry me?" Poor Belinda opened her gray eyes full in his face. She could hardly believe she had heard aright. She was startled, taken aback, but she followed her impulse of the moment and answered gravely, "No, Guy."

He wasn't angry or surprised. He had known it all along, poor fellow, and expected nothing else. He only sighed, looked at her once again, and then went away out of the room.

Poor Belle! she stood there where he had left her—the lights burnt, the great table glittered, the curtains waved. It was like a strange dream. She clasped her hands together, and then suddenly ran and fled away up to her own room—frightened, utterly puzzled, bewildered, not knowing what to do or to whom to speak. It was a comfort to be summoned as usual to read to Mrs. Griffiths. She longed to pour out her story to the poor lady, but she dreaded agitating her. She read as she was bid. Once she stopped short, but her mistress impatiently motioned her to go on. She obeyed, stumbling and tumbling over the words before her, until there came a knock at the door, and, contrary to his custom, Guy entered the room. He looked very pale, poor fellow, and sad and subdued. "I wanted to see you, Miss Belinda," he said aloud, "and to tell you that I hope this will make no difference, and that you will remain with us as if nothing had happened. You warned me, mamma, but I could not help myself. It's my own fault. Good-night. That is all I had to say."

Belle turned wistfully to Mrs. Griffiths. The thin hand was impatiently twisting the coverlet. "Of course—who would have any thing to say to him?—Foolish fellow!" she muttered in her indistinct way. "Go on, Miss Barly."

"Oh, but tell me first, ought I remain here?" Belle asked imploringly.

"Certainly, unless you are unhappy with us," the sick woman answered, peevishly. Mrs. Griffiths never made any other allusion to what had happened. I think the truth was that she did not care very much for any thing outside the doors of her sick-room. Perhaps she thought her son had been over hasty, and that in time Belinda might change her mind. To people lying on their last sick-beds, the terrors, anxieties, longings of life seem very curious and strange. They seem to forget that they were once anxious, hopeful, eager themselves, as they lie gazing at the awful veil which will so soon be withdrawn from before their fading eyes.

A sort of constraint came between Guy and Belinda at first, but it wore away by degrees. He often alluded to his proposal, but in so hopeless and gentle a way that she could not be angry; still she was disquieted and unhappy. She felt that it was a false and awkward position. She could not bear to see him looking ill and sad, as he did at times, with great black rings under his dark eyes. It was worse still when she saw him brightened up with happiness at some chance word she let fall now and then—speaking inadvertently of his house as "home," or of the roses next year. He must not mistake her. She could not bear to pain him by hard words, and yet sometimes she felt it was her duty to speak them. One day she met him in the street, on her way back to the house. The roll of the passing carriage-wheels gave Guy confidence, and, walking by her side, he began to say, "Now I never know what delightful surprise may not be waiting for me at every street corner. Ah, Miss Belle, my whole life might be one long dream of wonder and happiness, if . . . ." "Don't speak like this ever again, or I shall have to go away," said Belle, interrupting, and crossing the road, in her agitation, under the very noses of two omnibus horses. "I wish I could like you enough to marry you. I shall always love you enough to be your friend; please don't talk of any thing else." Belle said this in a bright brisk imploring decided tone, and hoped to have put an end to the matter. That day she came to me and told her little story. There were almost as many reasons for her staying as for her leaving, the poor child thought. I could not advise her to go, for the assistance that she was able to send home was very valuable. (Guy laughed, and utterly refused to accept a sixpence of her salary.) Mrs. Griffiths evidently wanted her; Guy, poor fellow, would have given all he had to keep her, as we all knew too well.

Circumstance orders events sometimes, and people themselves, with all their powers and knowledge of good and of evil, are but passive instruments in the hands of fate. News came that Mr. Barly was ill; and little Belinda, with an anxious face, and a note in her trembling hand, came into Mrs. Griffiths's room one day to say she must go to him directly. "Your father is ill," wrote Anna. "Les convenances demand your immediate return to him." Guy happened to be present, and when Belle left the room he followed her out into the passage.

"You are going?" he said.

"I don't know what Anna means by 'les convenances,' but papa is ill, and wants me," said Belinda, almost crying.

"And I want you," said Guy; "but that don't matter, of course. Go—go, since you wish it."

After all, perhaps it was well she was going, thought Belle, as she went to pack up her boxes. Poor Guy's sad face haunted her. She seemed to carry it away in her box with her other possessions.

It would be difficult to describe what he felt, poor fellow, when he came upon the luggage standing ready corded in the hall, and he found that Belle had taken him at his word. He was so silent a man, so self-contained, so diffident of his own strength to win her love in time, so unused to the ways of the world and of women,

that he could be judged by no ordinary rule. His utter despair and bewilderment would have been laughable almost, if they had not been so genuine. He paced about the garden with hasty uncertain footsteps, muttering to himself as he went along, and angrily cutting at the rose-hedges. "Of course she must go, since she wished it; of course she must—of course, of course. What would the house be like when she was gone?" For an instant a vision of a great dull vault without warmth, or light, or color, or possible comfort any where, rose before him. He tried to imagine what his life would be if she never came back into it; but as he stood still trying to seize the picture, it seemed to him that it was a thing not to be imagined or thought of. Wherever he looked he saw her, every where and in every thing. He had imagined himself unhappy; now he discovered that for the last few weeks, since little Belinda had come, he had basked in the summer she had brought, and found new life in the sunshine of her presence. Of an evening he had come home eagerly from his daily toil looking to find her. When he left early in the morning he would look up with kind eyes at her windows as he drove away. Once, early one morning, he had passed her near the lodge-gate, standing in the shadow of the great aspen-tree, and making way for the horses to go by. Belle was holding back the clean stiff folds of her pink muslin dress; she looked up with that peculiar blink of her gray eyes, smiled, and nodded her bright head, and shrunk away from the horses. Every morning Guy used to look under the tree after that to see if she were there by chance, even if he had parted from her but a minute before. Good stupid old fellow! he used to smile to himself at his own foolishness. One of his fancies about her was that Belinda was a bird that would fly away some day, and perch up in the branches of one of the great trees, far, far beyond his reach. And now was this fancy coming true? was she going—leaving him—flying away where he could not follow her? He gave an inarticulate sound of mingled anger and sorrow and tenderness, which relieved his heart, but which puzzled Belle herself, who was coming down the garden-walk to meet him.

"I was looking for you, Mr. Griffiths," said Belle. "Your mother wants to speak to you. I, too, wanted to ask you something," the girl went on, blushing. "She is kind enough to wish me to come back. . . . . But—"

Belle stopped short, blushed up, and began pulling at the leaves sprouting on either side of the narrow alley. When she looked up after a minute, with one of her quick short-sighted glances, she found that Guy's two little brown eyes were fixed upon her steadily.

"Don't be afraid that I shall trouble you," he said, reddening. "If you knew—if you had the smallest conception what your presence is to me, you would come back. I think you would."

Miss Barly didn't answer, but blushed up

again and walked on in silence, hanging her head to conceal the two bright tears which had come into her eyes. She was so sorry, so very sorry. But what could she do? Guy had walked on to the end of the rose-garden, and Belle had followed. Now, instead of turning towards the house, he had come out into the bright-looking kitchen-garden, with its red brick walls hung with their various draperies of lichen and mosses, and garlands of clambering fruit. Four little paths led up to the turf carpet which had been laid down in the centre of the garden : here a fountain plashed with a tranquil fall of waters upon water : all sorts of sweet kitchen herbs, mint and thyme and parsley, were growing along the straight-cut beds. Birds were pecking at the nets along the walls; one little sparrow that had been drinking at the fountain flew away as they approached. The few bright-colored straggling flowers caught the sunlight and reflected it in sparks like the water.

The master of this pleasant place put out his great clumsy hand, and took hold of Belle's soft reluctant fingers. "Ah, Belle," he said, "is there no hope for me? Will there never be any chance?"

"I wish with all my heart there was a chance," said poor Belle, pulling away her hand impatiently. "Why do you wound and pain me by speaking again and again of what is far best forgotten? Dear Mr. Griffiths, I will marry you to-morrow, if you desire it," said the girl, with a sudden impulse, turning pale and remembering all that she owed to his forbearance and gentleness; "but please, please don't ask it." She looked so frightened and desperate that poor Guy felt that this was worse than any thing, and sadly shook his head.

"Don't be afraid," he said. "I don't want to marry you against your will, or keep you here. Yes, you shall go home, and I will stop here alone, and cut my throat if I find I can not bear the place without you. I am only joking. I dare say I shall do very well," said Griffiths with a sigh; and he turned away and began stamping off in his clumsy way. Then he suddenly stopped and looked back. Belle was standing in the sunshine with her face hidden in her hands. She was so puzzled, and sorry, and hopeless, and mournful. The only thing she could do was to cry, poor child!—and by some instinct Griffiths guessed that she was crying; he knew it—his heart melted with pity. The poor fellow came back trembling. "My dearest," he said, "don't cry. What a brute I am to make you cry! Tell me any thing in the whole world I can do to make you happy."

"If I could only do any thing for you," said Belle, "that would make me happier."

"Then come back, my dear," said Guy, "and don't fly away yet forever, as you threatened just now. Come back and cheer up my mother, and make tea and a little sunshine for me, until—until some confounded fellow comes and carries you off," said poor Griffiths.

"Oh, that will never be. Yes; I'll come," said Belle, earnestly. "I'll go home for a week and come back; indeed I will."

"Only let me know," said Mr. Griffiths, "and my mother will send the carriage for you. Shall we say a week?" he added, anxious to drive a hard bargain.

"Yes," said Belinda, smiling; "I'll write and tell you the day."

Nothing would induce Griffiths to order the carriage until after dinner, and it was quite late at night when Belle got home.

VII.

Poor little Myrtle Cottage looked very small and shabby as she drove up in the darkness to the door. A brilliant illumination streamed from all the windows. Martha rubbed her elbows at the sight of the gorgeous equipage. Fanny came to the door surprised, laughing, giggling, mysterious. Every thing looked much as usual, except that a large and pompous-looking gentleman was sitting on the drawing-room sofa, and beside him Anna, with a huge ring on her fourth finger, attempting to blush as Belle came into the room. Belle saw that she was not wanted, and ran up stairs to her father, who was better, and sitting in the arm-chair by his bedside. The poor old man nearly cried with delight and surprise, held out both his shaking hands to her, and clung tenderly to the bright young daughter. Belle sat beside him, holding his hand, asking him a hundred questions, kissing his wrinkled face and cheeks, and telling him all that had happened. Mr. Barly, too, had news to give. The fat gentleman down stairs, he told Belle, was no other than Anna's old admirer, the doctor, of whom mention has been made. He had re-proposed the day before, and was now sitting on the sofa on probation. Fanny's prospects, too, seemed satisfactory. "She assures me," said Mr. Barly, "that young Ogden is on the point of coming forward. An old man like me, my dear, is naturally anxious to see his children settled in life and comfortably provided for. I don't know who would be good enough for my Belinda. Not that awkward lout of a Griffiths. No, no; we must look out for better than that."

"Oh, papa, if you knew how good and how kind he is!" said Belle, with a sudden revulsion of feeling; but she broke off abruptly, and spoke of something else.

The other maid, who had already gone to bed the night before when Belle arrived at the cottage, gave a loud shriek when she went into the room next morning and found some one asleep in the bed. Belle awoke, laughed and explained, and asked her to bring up her things.

"Bring 'em hup?" said the girl. "What! all them 'ampers that's come by the cart? No, miss, that's more than me and Martha have the strength for. I should crick my back if I were to attempt for to do such a thing."

"Hampers—what hampers?" Belle asked; but when she went down she found the little passage piled with cases, flowers and game, and preserves, and some fine old port for Mr. Barly, and some roses for Belle. As Belinda came down stairs, in her fresh morning-dress, Anna, who had been poking about and examining the various packages, looked up with offended dignity.

"I think, considering that I am mistress here," said she, "these hampers should have been directed to me, instead of to you, Belinda. Mr. Griffiths strangely forgets. Indeed, I fear that you too are wanting in any great sense of ladylike propriety."

"Prunes, prism, propriety," said Belle, gayly. "Never mind, dear Anna; he's sent the things for all of us. Mr. Griffiths certainly never meant me to drink two dozen bottles of port wine in a week."

"You are evading the question," said Anna. "I have been wishing to talk to you for some time past—come into the dining-room, if you please."

It seems almost impossible to believe, and yet I can not help fearing that out of sheer spite and envy Anna Barly had even then determined that, if she could prevent it, Belinda should never go back to the Castle Gardens again, but remain in the cottage. The sight of the pretty things which had been given her there, all the evidences which told of the esteem and love in which she was held, maddened the foolish woman. I can give no other reason for the way in which she opposed Belinda's return to Mrs. Griffiths. "Her duty is at home," said Anna. "I myself shall be greatly engaged with Thomas"—so she had already learnt to call Dr. Robinson. "Fanny also is preoccupied; Belinda must remain."

When Belle demurred, and said that for the next few weeks she would like to return as she had promised, and stay until Mrs. Griffiths was suited with another companion, Anna's indignation rose and overpowered her dignity. Was it her sister who was so oblivious of the laws of society, propriety, modesty? Anna feared that Belinda had not reflected upon the strange appearance her conduct must have to others, to the Ogdens, to them all. What was the secret attraction which took her back? Anna said she had rather not inquire, and went on with her oration. "Unmaidenly—not to be thought of—the advice of those whose experience might be trusted"—does one not know the rigmarole by heart? When even the father, who had been previously talked to, sided with his eldest daughter; when Thomas, who was also called into the family conclave, nodded his head in an ominous manner, poor little Belinda, frightened, shaken, undecided, almost promised that she would do as they desired; and as she promised, the thought of poor Guy's grief and wistful haggard face came before her, and her poor little heart ached and sank at the thought. But not even Belinda, with all her courage, could resist

the decision of so much experience, or Anna's hints and innuendoes, or, more insurmountable than all the rest, a sudden shyness and consciousness which had come over the poor little maiden, who turned crimson with shame and annoyance.

Belinda had decided as she was told—had done as her conscience bade her—and yet there was but little satisfaction in this duty accomplished. For about half an hour she went about feeling like a heroine, and then, without any reason or occasion, it seemed to her that the mask had come off her face, that she had discovered herself to be a traitress, that she had betrayed and abandoned her kindest friends; she called herself a selfish, ungrateful wretch, she wondered what Guy would think of her; she was out of temper, out of spirits, out of patience with herself, and the click of the blind swinging in the draught was unendurable. The complacent expression of Anna's handsome face put her teeth on edge. When Fanny tumbled over the footstool with a playful shriek, to everybody's surprise Belinda burst out crying.

Those few days were endless, slow, dull, unbearable—every second brought its pang of regret and discomfort and remorse. It seemed to Belinda that her ears listened, her mouth talked, her eyes looked at the four walls of the cottage, at the furze on the common, at the faces of her sisters, with a sort of mechanical effort. As if she were acting her daily life, not living it naturally and without effort. Only when she was with her father did she feel unconstrained; but even then there was an unexpressed reproach in her heart like a dull pain that she could not quiet. And so the long days lagged. Although Dr. Robinson enlivened them with his presence, and the Ogdens drove up to carry Fanny off to the happy regions of Capulet Square (E. for Elysium Anna, I think, would have docketed the district), to Belinda those days seemed slow, and dark, and dim, and almost hopeless at times.

On the day on which Belinda was to have returned, there came a letter to me telling her story plainly enough: "I must not come back, my dearest Miss Williamson," she wrote. "I am going to write to Mrs. Griffiths and dear kind Mr. Guy to-morrow to tell them so. Anna does not think it is right. Papa clings to me and wants me, now that both my sisters are going to leave him. How often I shall think of you all—of all your goodness to me, of the beautiful roses, and my dear little room! Do you think Mr. Guy would let me take one or two books as a remembrance—Hume's *History of England*, Porteous's *Sermons* and *Essays on Reform?* I should like to have something to remind me of you all, and to look at sometimes, since they say I am not to see you all again. Good-bye, and thank you and Mrs. H. a thousand thousand times.—Your ever, ever affectionate BELINDA. P.S.—Might I also ask for that little green volume of the *Golden Treasury* which is up in the tower-room?"

This was what Guy had feared all along. Once she was gone, he knew by instinct she would never come back. I hardly know how it fared with the poor fellow all this time. He kept out of our way, and would try to escape me, but once by chance I met him, and I was shocked by the change which had come over him. I had my own opinion, as we all have at times. H. and I had talked it over—for old women are good for something, after all, and can sometimes play a sentimental part in life as well as young ones. It seemed to us impossible that Belinda should not relent to so much goodness and unselfishness, and come back again some day never to go any more. We knew enough of Anna Barly to guess the part *she* had played, nor did we despair of seeing Belinda among us once more. But some one must help her, she could not reach us unassisted; and so I told Mrs. Griffiths, who had remarked upon her son's distress and altered looks.

"If you will lend us the carriage," I said, "either H. or I will go over to Dumbleton to-morrow, and I doubt not that we shall bring her." H. went. She told me about it afterwards. Anna was fortunately absent. Mr. Barly was down stairs, and H. was able to talk to him a little bit before Belinda came down. The poor old man always thought as he was told to think, and since his illness he was more uncertain and broken than ever. He was dismayed when H. told him in her decided way that he was probably sacrificing two people's happiness for life by his ill-timed interference. When at last Belinda came down, she looked almost as ill as Griffiths himself. She rushed into H.'s arms with a scream of delight, and eagerly asked a hundred questions. "How were they all—what were they all doing?"

H. was very decided. Every body was very ill and wanted Belinda back. "Your father says he can spare you very well," said she. "Why not come back with me this afternoon, if only for a time? It is your duty," H. continued, in her dry way. "You should not leave them in this uncertainty." "Go, my child—pray go," urged Mr. Barly. And at last Belinda consented shyly, nothing loath.

H. began to question her when she had got her safe in the carriage. Belinda said she had not been well. She could not sleep, she said. She had had bad dreams. She blushed, and confessed that she had dreamt of Guy lying dead in the kitchen-garden. She had gone about the house trying, indeed she had tried, to be cheer-ful and busy as usual, but she felt unhappy, ungrateful. "Oh, what a foolish girl I am!" she said. All the lights were burning in the little town, the west was glowing and reflected in the river, the boats trembled and shot through the shiny waters, and the people were out upon the banks, as they crossed the bridge again on their way from Dumbleton. Belle was happier, certainly, but crying from agitation.

"Have I made him miserable, poor fellow? Oh, I think I shall blame myself all my life," said she, covering her face with her hands. "Oh, H.! H.! what shall I do?"

H. dryly replied that she must be guided by circumstances, and when they reached Castle Gardens kissed her and set her down at the great gate, while she herself went home in the carriage.

It was all twilight by this time among the roses. Belinda met the gate-keeper, who touched his hat and told her his master was in the garden; and so instead of going into the house she flitted away towards the garden, crossed the lawns, and went in and out among the bowers and trellises looking for him—frightened by her own temerity at first, gaining courage by degrees. It was so still, so sweet, so dark; the stars were coming out in the evening sky, a meteor went flashing from east to west, a bat flew across her path; all the scent hung heavy in the air. Twice Belinda called out timidly, "Mr. Griffiths, Mr. Griffiths!" but no one answered. Then she remembered her dream in sudden terror, and hurried into the kitchen-garden to the fountain where they had parted.

What had happened? Some one was lying on the grass. Was this her dream? was it Guy? was he dead? had she killed him? Belinda ran up to him, seized his hand, and called him Guy—dear Guy; and Guy, who had fallen asleep from very weariness and sadness of heart, opened his eyes to hear himself called by the voice he loved best in the world; while the sweetest eyes, full of tender tears, were gazing anxiously into his ugly face. Ugly? Fairy tales have told us this at least, that ugliness and dullness do not exist for those who truly love. Had she ever thought him rough, uncouth, unlovable? Ah! she had been blind in those days; she knew better now. As they walked back through the twilight garden that night, Guy said, humbly: "I sha'n't do you any credit, Belinda; I can only love you."

"*Only!*" said Belinda.

She didn't finish her sentence; but he understood very well what she meant.

LITTLE RED RIDING HOOD.

I.

THERE is something sad in most pretty stories, in most lovely strains, in the tenderest affections and friendships; but tragedy is a different thing from the indefinable feeling which lifts us beyond to-day into that dear and happy region where our dearest loves, and plays, and dreams, are to be found even in childish times. Poor little Red Riding Hood, with bright eyes glancing from her scarlet caplet, has been mourned by generations of children; but though they pity her, and lament her sad fate, she is no familiar playmate and companion. That terrible wolf with the fiery eyes, glaring through the brushwood, haunts them from the very beginning of the story; it is too sad, too horrible, and they hastily turn the leaves and fly to other and better-loved companions, with whose troubles they sympathize, for they are but passing woes, and they know that brighter times are in store. For the poor little maiden at the well, for dear Cinderella, for Roebrother and little sister, wandering through the glades of the forest, and Snowwhite and her sylvan court of kindly woodland dwarfs—all these belong to the sweet and gentle region where beautiful calm suns shine after the storm, amid fair landscapes, and gardens, and palaces. Even we elders sympathize with the children in this feeling, although we are more or less hardened by time, and have ourselves, wandering in the midway of life, met with wolves roving through the forest—wolves from whose cruel claws, alas! no father's or mother's love can protect us, and against whose wiles all warnings except those of our own experience are vain. And these wolves devour little boys as well as little girls and pats of butter.

This is no place to write of some stories, so sad and so hopeless that they can scarcely be spoken; although good old Perrault, in his simple way, to some poor Red Riding Hoods straying from the path utters a word of warning rhyme at the end of the old French edition: some stories are too sad, others too trifling. The sketch which I have in my mind is no terrible tragedy, but a silly little tale, so foolish and trivial that if it were not that it comes in its place with the others, I should scarcely attempt to repeat it. I met all the personages by chance at Fontainebleau only the other day.

The wolf was playing the fiddle under Little Red Riding Hood's window. Little Red Riding Hood was peeping from behind her cotton curtains. Rémy (that was the wolf's Christian name) could see the little balls bobbing, and guessed that she was there. He played on louder than ever, dragging his bow with long sobbing chords across his fiddle-strings, and as he played, a fairy palace arose at his bidding, more beautiful than the real old palace across the Place that we had come to see. The fairy palace arose story upon story, lovely to look upon, enchanted; a palace of art, with galleries, and terraces, and belvederes, and orange-flowers scenting the air, and fragrant blossoms falling in snow-showers, and fountains of life murmuring and turning marble into gold as they flowed. Red Riding Hood from behind her cotton curtains, and Rémy, her cousin, outside in the court-yard, were the only two inhabitants of this wonderful building. They were alone in it together, far away in that world of which I have been speaking, at a long, long distance from the every-day all round about them, though the cook of the hotel was standing at his kitchen door, and the stable-boy was grinning at Rémy's elbow, and H. and I, who had arrived only that evening, were sitting resting on the bench in front of the hotel, among the autumnal profusion of nasturtiums and marigolds with which the court-yard was planted. H. and I had come to see the palace, and to walk about in the stately old gardens, and to breathe a little quiet and silence after the noise of the machines thundering all day in the Great Exhibition of the Champ de Mars, the din of the cannons firing, of the carriages and multitudes rolling along the streets.

The Maynards, Red Riding Hood's parents, were not passers-by like ourselves, they were comfortably installed at the hotel for a month at a time, and came over once a year to see Mrs. Maynard's mother, an old lady who had lived at Fontainebleau as long as her two daughters could remember. This old lady's name was Madame Capuchon; but her first husband had been an Englishman, like Mr. Maynard, her son-in-law, who was also her nephew by this first marriage. Both Madame Capuchon's daughters were married—Marthe, the eldest, to Henry Maynard, an English country gentleman; Félicie, the youngest, to the Baron de la Louvière, who resided at Poictiers, and who was sous-préfet there.

It is now forty years since Madame Capuchon first went to live at Fontainebleau, in the old house at the corner of the Rue de la Lampe. It has long been doomed to destruction, with its picturesque high roof, its narrow windows and balconies, and sunny old brick passages and staircases, with the round ivy œil-de-bœuf windows. Staircases were piled up of brick in the time of the Louises, broad and wide, and easy to climb, and not of polished wood, like the slippery flights of to-day. However, the old house is in the way of a row of shops and a projected café and newspaper office, so are the ivy-grown garden-walls, the acacia trees, the sun-dial, and the old stone seat. It is a pity that newer buildings can not sometimes be selected for destruction; they might be rebuilt and redestroyed again and again, and people who care for such things might be left in peace a little longer to hold the dear old homes and traditions of their youth.

Madame Capuchon, however, is a kind and despotic old lady; she has great influence and authority in the town, and during her life the old house is safe. It is now, as I have said, forty years since she first came to live there—a young widow for the second time, with two little daughters and a faithful old maid to be her only companions in her flight from the world where she had known great troubles and changes. Madame Capuchon and her children inhabited two upper stories of the old house. The rez de chaussée was partly a porter's lodge, partly a warehouse, and partly a little apartment which the proprietor reserved for his use. He died twice during Madame Capuchon's tenancy; once he ventured to propose to her—but this was the former owner of the place, not the present proprietor, an old bachelor who preferred his Paris café and his boulevard to the stately silence and basking life of Fontainebleau.

This life suited Madame Capuchon, who, from sorrow at first and then from habit, continued the same silent cloistered existence for years—years which went by and separated her quietly but completely from her old habits and friends and connections and long-past troubles, while the little girls grew up and the mother's beauty changed, faded quietly away in the twilight life she was leading.

The proprietor who had ventured to propose to the widow, and who had been refused with so much grace and decision that his admiration remained unaltered, was no more; but shortly before his death he had a second time accosted her with negotiations of marriage: not for himself this time, but for a nephew of his, the Baron de la Louvière, who had seen the young ladies by chance, heard much good of them from his uncle and their attached attendant Simonne, and learnt that their dot was ample and their connections respectable. Marthe, the eldest daughter, was the least good-looking of the two, but to most people's mind far more charming than Félicie, the second. M. de la Louvière had at first a slight preference for Marthe, but learning through his uncle that an alliance was contemplated between her and an English connection of her mother's, he announced himself equally anxious to obtain the hand of Félicie, the younger sister. After some hesitation, much addition of figures, subtraction, division,

rule of three worked out, consultations and talk between Simonne and her mistress, and long discussions with Henry Maynard himself, who was staying with a friend at Fontainebleau at the time, this favor was accorded to the baron.

The young baroness went off nothing loath: she was bored at home, she did not like the habit of severity and silence into which her mother had fallen. She was a slim, active, decided person, of calm affections, but passionately fond of her own way, as indeed was Madame Capuchon herself, for all her regrets for that past in which it must be confessed she had always done exactly as she liked, and completely ruled her two husbands. For all Madame Capuchon's blacks and drabs and seclusion, and shut shutters, and confessors, and shakes of the head, she had greatly cheered up by this time: she had discovered in her health a delightful source of interest and amusement; Félicie's marriage was as good as a play, as the saying goes; and then came a catastrophe, still more exciting than Félicie's brilliant prospects, which occupied all the spare moments of the two years which succeeded the youngest girl's departure from home.

Madame Capuchon's nephew, Henry Maynard, was, as I have said, staying at Fontainebleau, with a friend, who was unfortunately a very good-looking young man of very good family, who had come to Fontainebleau to be out of harm's way, and to read French for some diplomatic appointment. Maynard used to talk to him about his devotion for his pretty cousin Marthe with the soft trill in her voice and the sweet quick eyes. Young Lord John, alas! was easily converted to this creed—he also took a desperate fancy to the pretty young lady; and Madame Capuchon, whose repeated losses had not destroyed a certain ambition which had always been in her nature, greatly encouraged the young man. And so one day poor Maynard was told that he must resign himself to his hard fate. He had never hoped much, for he knew well enough that his cousin, as he called her, did not care for him; Marthe had always discouraged him, although her mother would have scouted the notion that one of her daughters should resist any decree she might lay down, or venture to think for herself on such matters.

When Lord John proposed in the English fashion to Marthe one evening in the deep embrasure of the drawing-room window, Madame Capuchon was enchanted, although disapproving of the irregularity of the proceeding. She announced her intention of settling upon her eldest daughter a sum so large and so much out of the proportion to the dot which she had accorded to Madame de la Louvière, that the baron hearing of it by chance through Monsieur Micotton, the family solicitor, was furious, and an angry correspondence then commenced between him and his mother-in-law which lasted many years, and in which Madame Capuchon found another fresh interest to attach her to life, and an unfailing vent for much of her spare energy and excitement.

Henry Maynard went back to his father's house at Littleton on Thames, to console himself as best he could among the punts and water-lilies. Lord John went back to England to pass his examination, and to gain his family's consent, without which he said he could not marry; and Marthe waited in the old house with Simonne and her mother, and that was the end of her story.

Lord John didn't pass his examination, but interest was made for him, and he was given another chance, and he got the diplomatic appointment all the same, and he went to Russia and was heard of no more at Fontainebleau. Madame Capuchon was naturally surprised at his silence; while Marthe wondered and wearied, but spoke no word of the pain which consumed her. Her mother sat down and wrote to the duke, presented her compliments, begged to remind him of his son's engagement, and requested information of the young man's whereabouts and intentions. In the course of a week she received a few polite lines from the duchess, regretting that she could give Madame Capuchon no information as to Lord John's whereabouts or intentions, informing her that she had made some mistake as to his engagement, and begging to decline any further correspondence on the subject, on paper so thick that Simonne had to pay double postage for the epistle, and it would scarcely burn when Madame Capuchon flung it into the fire. The widow stamped her little foot, flashed her eyes, bit her lips, darted off her compliments to the duchess a second time, and begged to inform her that her son was a coward and a false gentleman, and that it was the Capuchon family that now begged to decline any further communication with people who held their word so cheaply. Naturally enough, no answer came to this, although Madame Capuchon expected one, and fumed and flashed and scolded for weeks after, during which poor Marthe still wondered and knew nothing.

"Don't let us tell her any thing about it," Simonne had said when the first letter came. "Let her forget 'tout doucement;'" and Madame Capuchon agreed.

And so Marthe waited and forgot tout doucement, as Simonne proposed, for fifteen years, and the swans came sailing past her when she took her daily walk, and the leaves fell and grew again, and every night the shadow of the old lamp swinging in the street outside cast its quaint lines and glimmer across her dark leaf-shaded room, and the trees rustled when the wind blew, and her dreams were quieter and less vivid.

Once Henry Maynard wrote, soon after Lord John's desertion, renewing his proposals, to Marthe herself, and not to his aunt; but the letter came too soon. And, indeed, it was by Henry Maynard's letter that Marthe first realized for certain what had happened.

But it came too soon. She could not yet bear to hear her faithless lover blamed. Lord John was a villain and unworthy of a regret, Henry said. Would she not consent to accept an honest man instead of a false one?

"No, no, no, a hundred times no," cried Marthe to herself, with something of her mother's spirit, and she nervously wrote her answer and slid out by herself and posted it. She never dared tell Madame Capuchon what she had done.

As time went on, one or two other "offers" were made to her; but Marthe was so reluctant that, as they were not very good ones, Madame Capuchon let them go by; and then Marthe had a long illness, and then more time passed by.

"What have we been about?" said Madame Capuchon to her confidante one day as her daughter left the room. "Here she is an old maid, and it is all her own obstinacy."

At thirty-three Marthe was still unmarried: a gracious, faded woman, who had caught the trick of being sad; although she had no real trouble, and had almost forgotten Lord John. But she had caught the trick of being sad, as I say, of flitting aimlessly across the room, of remembering and remembering instead of living for to-day.

Madame Capuchon was quite cheerful by this time; besides her health, her angry correspondence, her confessor, her game of dominos, and her talks with Simonne, she had many little interests to fill up spare gaps and distract her when M. de la Louvière's demands were too much for her temper. There was her comfortable hot and well-served little dinner to look forward to, her paper to read of a night, her chocolate in bed every morning, on a nice little tray with a pat of fresh butter and her nice little new roll from the English baker's. Madame was friande, and Simonne's delight was to cater for her. But none of these distractions quite sufficed to give an interest to poor Marthe's sad life. She was too old for the fun and excitement of youth, and too young for the little comforts, the resignations, and satisfactions of age. Simonne, the good old fat woman, used to think of her as a little girl, and try to devise new treats for her as she had done when Félicie and Marthe were children. Marthe would kiss her old nurse gratefully, and think, with a regretful sigh, how it was that she could no longer be made happy by a bunch of flowers, a hot buttered cake, a new trimming to her apron; she would give the little cake away to the porter's grandchildren, put the flowers into water and leave them, fold up the apron, and, to Simonne, most terrible sign of all, forget it in the drawer. It was not natural, something must be wrong, thought the old woman.

The old woman thought and thought, and poked about, and one day with her spectacles on her nose, deciphered a letter which was lying on Madame Capuchon's table; it was signed Henry Maynard, and announced the writer's arrival at Paris. Next day, when Simonne was frizzling her mistress's white curls (they had come out of their seclusion for some years past), she suddenly asked what had become of Monsieur Maynard, madame's English nephew, who used to come so often before Mademoiselle Félicie was married.

"What is that to you?" said the old lady. "He is at Paris. I heard from him yesterday."

"And why don't you ask him to come down and see you?" said Simonne, frizzling away at the crisp silver locks. "It would cheer up mademoiselle to have some one to talk to. We don't want any one; we have had our day, you and I; but mademoiselle, I confess I don't like to see her going on as she does."

"Nor I!" said the old lady sharply. "She is no credit to me. One would almost think that she reproaches me for her existence, after all the sacrifices I have made."

Simonne went on frizzling without stopping to inquire what these sacrifices might be. "I will order a fricandeau for to-morrow," she said; "madame had better invite Monsieur to spend the day."

"Simonne, you are an old fool," said her mistress. "I have already written to my nephew to invite him to my house."

Maynard came and partook of the fricandeau, and went for a little walk with Marthe, and he had a long talk with his aunt and old Simonne in the evening, and went away quite late—past ten o'clock it was. Maynard did not go back to Paris that night, but slept at the hotel, and early next morning there came a note addressed to Marthe, in which the writer stated that he was still of the same mind in which he had been fifteen years before, and if she was of a different way of thinking, would she consent to accept him as her husband?

And so it came about that long after the first best hopes of her youth were over, Marthe consented to leave her own silent home for her husband's, a melancholy middle-aged bride, sad and frightened at the thought of the tempestuous world into which she was being cast adrift, and less able, at thirty-three than at twenty, to hold her own against the kindly domineering old mother, who was much taken with the idea of this marriage, and vowed that Marthe should go, and that no daughter of hers should die an old maid if she could help it. She had been married twice herself; once at least, if possible, she was determined that both her daughters should follow her example. Félicie's choice was not all that Madame Capuchon could have wished as far as liberality and amiability of character were concerned; but Félicie herself was happy, and indeed—so Madame Capuchon had much reason to suspect—abetted her husband in his grasping and extortionate demands. "And now Marthe's turn had come," said Madame Capuchon complacently, sitting up among her pillows, sipping her chocolate; "she was the eldest, she should have married first; she had been a good and devoted daughter, she would make an excellent wife," cried the valiant old lady.

When Marthe demurred: "Go, my child, go in peace, only go, go, go! Simonne is quite able to take care of me: do you think I want the sacrifice of your life? For what should I keep you? Can you curl me, can you play at dominos? You are much more necessary to your cousin than you are to me. He will be here directly—what a figure you have made of yourself! Simonne, come here, give a coup de peigne to mademoiselle. There I hear the bell, Henry will be waiting."

"He does not mind waiting, mamma," said Marthe, smiling sadly. "He has waited fifteen years already."

"So much the worse for you both," cried the old lady, angrily. "If I had only had my health, if my spirits had not been completely crushed in those days, I never would have given in to such ridiculous ideas."

Ridiculous ideas! This was all the epitaph that was uttered by any one of them over the grave where poor Marthe had buried with much pain and many tears the trouble of her early life. She herself had no other text for the wasted love of her youth. How angry she had been with her cousin Henry when he warned her once, how she had hated him when he asked her to marry him before, tacitly forcing upon her the fact of his friend's infidelity, and now it was to Maynard, after all, that she was going to be married! After all that had passed, all the varying fates, and loves, and hopes, and expectations of her life. A sudden alarm came over the poor woman—was she to leave it, this still life, and the old house, and the tranquil shade and silence—and for what? Ah, she could not go, she could not—she would stay where she was. Ah! why would they not leave her alone?

Marthe went up to her room and cried, and bathed her eyes and cried again, and dabbed more water to dry her tears; then she came quietly down the old brick stairs. She passed along the tiled gallery, her slim figure reflecting in the dim old looking-glass in the alcove at the end, with the cupids engraved upon its mouldy surface. She hesitated a moment, and then took courage and opened the dining-room door. There was nobody there. It was all empty, dim-pannelled, orderly, and its narrow tall windows reflecting the green without, and the gables and chimney-stacks piling under the blue. He was in the drawing-room then; she had hoped to find him here. Marthe sighed and then walked on across the polished floor, and so into the drawing-room. It was dimmer, more chill than the room in which their meals were served. Some one was standing waiting for her in one of the windows. Marthe remembered at that instant that it was Lord John's window, but she had little time for such reminiscences. A burly figure turned at her entrance, and Henry Maynard came to meet her, with one big hand out, and his broad good-natured face beaming.

"Well, Minnie," said Henry Maynard, calling her by his old name for her, "you see I'm here again already."

"Yes," she answered, standing before him, and then they were both silent: these two middle-aged people waiting for the other to speak.

"How is your mother?" Maynard asked. "I thought her very little changed, but you are not looking over well. However, time touches us all."

Marthe drew herself up, with her eyes gleaming in her pale face, and then there was another silence. At last Marthe faltered out, gaining courage as she went on:—

"I have been agitated, and a little disturbed. My mother is quite well, Cousin Henry," she said, and as she spoke her sad looks encountered Maynard's good-natured twinkling glance. She blushed suddenly like a girl of fifteen. "You seem amused," she said, with some annoyance.

"Yes, dear," spoke Maynard, in his kind, manly tones. "I am amused that you and I, at our time of life, should be shilly-shallying and sentimentalizing, like a couple of chits who have all their life before them, and don't care whether they know or not what is coming next. I want to know very much—for I have little time to lose—what do you and your mother think of my letter this morning?"

This was coming to the point very abruptly, Mademoiselle Capuchon thought.

"I am so taken by surprise," Marthe faltered, retreating a step or two, and nervously twisting her apron round about her fingers. "She wishes it. I—I hardly know. I have had so little time to . . . ."

"My dear Marthe," said Maynard, impatiently, "I am not a romantic young man. I can make no professions and speeches. You must take me as I am, if I suit you. I won't say that after you sent me away I have never thought of any body but you during these past fifteen years. But we might have been very happy together all this long time, and yesterday when I saw how hipped you were looking, I determined to try and bring you away with me from this dismal place into the fresh air of Littleton, that is, if you liked to come with me of your own free will, and not only because my aunt desires it." And Henry Maynard drew a long breath, and put his hands in his pockets.

This honest little speech was like a revelation to Marthe. She had come down feeling like a victim, meaning graciously, perhaps, in the end, to reward Maynard's constancy, taking it for granted that all this time he had never ceased being in love. She found that it was from old friendship and kindness alone that he had come to her again, not from sentiment, and yet this kindness and protection touched her more than any protestations of romantic affection.

"But—but—should you really like it?" she stammered, forgetting all her dreams, and coming to life as it were, at that instant.

"Like it," he said with a smile. "You don't know how fond I mean to be of you, if you will

come with me, dear Marthe. You shall make me as happy as you like, and yourself into the bargain. I don't think you will be sorry for it, and indeed you don't seem to have been doing much good here, all by yourself. Well, is it to be yes or no?" And once more Maynard held out the broad brown hand.

And Marthe said, "Yes," quite cheerfully, and put her hand into his.

Marthe got to know her future husband better in these five minutes than in all the thirty years which had gone before.

The Maynards are an old Catholic family, so there were no difficulties on the score of religion. The little chapel in the big church was lighted up, the confessor performed the service. Madame Capuchon did not go, but Simonne was there, in robes of splendor, and so were the De la Louvières. The baron and his mother-in-law had agreed to a temporary truce on this auspicious occasion. After the ceremony the new-married pair went back to a refection which the English baker and Simonne had concocted between them. The baron and baroness had brought their little son Rémy, to whom they were devoted, and he presented Marthe with a wedding present—a large porcelain vase, upon which was a painting of his mother's performance —in both his parents' name. Madame Capuchon brought out a lovely pearl and emerald necklace, which Félicie had coveted for years past.

"I must get it done up," the old lady said; "you won't want it immediately, Marthe; you shall have it the first time you come to see me. Do not delay too long," added Madame Capuchon, with a confidential shake of her head, to her son-in-law Maynard, as Marthe went away to change her dress. "You see my health is miserable. I am a perfect martyr. My doctor tells me my case is serious; not in so many words, but he assures me that he can not find out what ails me; and when doctors say that we all know what it means."

Henry Maynard attempted to reassure Madame Capuchon, and to induce her to take a more hopeful view of her state; but she grew quite angry, and snapped him up so short with her immediate prospect of dissolution, that he desisted in his well-meant endeavors, and the old lady continued more complacently:—

"Do not be uneasy; if any thing happens to me, Simonne will write directly to your address. Do not forget to leave it with her. And now go and fetch your wife, and let me have the pleasure of seeing her in her travelling-dress."

It was a kind old lady, but there was a want in her love—so it seemed to her son-in-law as he obeyed her behest.

Marthe had never quite known what real love was, she thought. Sentiment, yes, and too much of it, but not that best home-love—familiar, tender, unchanging. Her mother had not got it in her to give. Félicie de la Louvière was a hard and clear-headed woman; all her affection was for Rémy, her little boy. Maynard disliked her and the baron too, but they were all apparently very good friends.

Marthe came back to the salle to say good-bye, looking like herself again, Maynard thought, as his bride, in her rippling trailing gray silks, entered the room, with Simonne's big bouquet of roses in her hand, and a pretty pink glow in her cheeks.

She was duly embraced by Félicie and her husband, and then she knelt down to ask for her mother's blessing. "Bless you! bless you!" cried Madame Capuchon, affectionately pushing her away. "There, you will disarrange yourself; take care, take care." Simonne sprang to the rescue, and Marthe found herself all at once embraced, stuck with pins, shaken out, tucked in, flattened, folded, embraced again; the handkerchief with which she had ventured to wipe her tears was torn out of her hand, folded, smoothed, and replaced. "Voilà!" said Simonne, with two last loud kisses, "bon voyage; good luck go with you." And Maynard following after, somewhat to his confusion, received a couple of like salutations.

Simonne's benediction followed Mrs. Maynard to England, where she went and took possession of her new home. The neighbors called; the drawing-room chintzes were renewed; Marthe Capuchon existed no longer; no one would have recognized the listless ghost flitting here and there, and gazing from the windows of the old house in the Rue de la Lampe, in the busy and practical mistress of Henry Maynard's home. She had gained in composure and spirits and happiness since she came to England. Her house was admirably administered; she wore handsome shining silk dresses and old lace; and she rustled and commanded as efficiently as if she had been married for years. Simonne threw up her hands with delight at the transformation, the first time she saw Marthe after her marriage. "But you are a hundred times better-looking than Madame la Baronne," said the old woman. "This is how I like to see you."

II.

MORE years went by, and Simonne's benediction did not lose its virtue.

The chief new blessing and happiness of all those blessings and happinesses which Simonne had wished to Marthe Maynard was a blessing called Marthe Maynard, too; a little girl adored by her mother. Marthe is considered a pretty name in French, and Maynard loved it for his wife's sake, and, as time went on, for her daughter's as well. He called her Patty, however, to distinguish the two. Far more than the happiness some people find in the early spring, in the voices of birds, the delight of the morning hours, the presence of this little thing brought to her mother, this bright, honest, black and brown and white and coral maiden, with her sweet and willful ways and gay shrill warble. Every year the gay voice became more clear and decided,

the ways more pretty and more willful. Mrs. Maynard used to devise pretty fanciful dresses for her Patty, and to tie bright ribbons in the child's crisp brown locks, and watch over her and pray for her from morning to night. Squire Maynard, who was a sensible man, used to be afraid lest so much affection should be bad for his little girl; he tried to be stern now and then, and certainly succeeded in frightening Patty on such occasions. The truth was he loved his wife tenderly, and thought that Patty made a slave of her mother at times. It was a happy bondage for them both. Marthe dreamt no more dreams now, and only entered that serene country of her youth by proxy, as it were, and to make plans for her Patty. The child grew up as the years went by, but if Marthe made plans for her they were very distant ones, and to the mother as impossible still as when Patty had been a little baby tumbling in her cradle. Even then Marthe had settled that Patty was not to wait for years as she had waited. What hero there was in the big world worthy of her darling, Mrs. Maynard did not know. The mother's heart sickened the first time she ever thought seriously of a vague possibility of which the very notion filled her with alarm. She had a presentiment the first time that she ever saw him.

She was sitting alone in her bed-room, drowsily stitching in the sun-light of the pleasant bow-window, listening to the sound of the clippers at work upon the ivy-hedge close by, and to the distant chime from the clock-tower of the town across the river. Just below her window spread the lawn where her husband's beloved flower-beds were flushing—scarlet and twinkling violet, white and brilliant amber. In the field beyond the sloping lawn some children were pulling at the sweet wild summer garlands hanging in the hedges, and the Alderneys were crunching through the long damp grasses. Two pretty creatures had straggled down hill to the water-side, and were looking at their own brown eyes reflected in a chance clear pool in the margin of the river. For the carpet of green and meadow verdure was falling over and lapping and draggling in the water in a fringe of glistening leaves and insects and weeds. There were white creamy meadow-sweets, great beds of purple flowers, bronzed water-docks arching and crisping their stately heads, weeds upspringing, golden slimy water-lilies floating upon their shining leaves. A water rat was starting out of his hole, a dragon-fly floating along the bank. All this was at the foot of the sloping mead down by the bridge. It crossed the river to the little town of spires and red brick gables which had been built about two centuries ago, and all round about spread hills and lawns and summer cornfields. Marthe Maynard had seen the cornfields ripen year after year: she loved the place for its own sake and for the sake of those who were very dear to her then; but to-day, as she looked, she suddenly realized, poor soul, that a time might come when the heart and the sweetest life of this little home-Eden might go from it. And as she looked through her window something like a chill came over her: she dropped her work into her lap, and sat watching two figures climbing up the field side by side; coming through the buttercups, disappearing behind the hedge, reappearing at the bottom of the lawn, and then one figure darted forward, while the other lingered a little among the flower-beds; and Mrs. Maynard got up resolutely, with a pain and odd apprehension in her heart, and went down to meet her daughter. The steeples of the little town which strike the hours, half-hours, and the very minutes as they pass, were striking four quarters, and then five again, as Mrs. Maynard came out upon her lawn, and at each stroke the poor mother's heart sank, and she turned a little sick at the possibility which had first occurred to her just now in her own room. It seemed to thrust itself again upon her as she stood waiting for the two young people—her own Patty and the strange young man coming through the flower-beds.

There was a certain likeness to herself, odd, touching, bewildering, in the utter stranger, which said more plainly than any words, I belong to you and yours; I am no stranger though strange to you. Patty had no need to explain, all breathless and excited and blushing, "Mamma, do you know who this is? This is Rémy de la Louvière. Papa and I found him at the hotel;" for the poor mother had already guessed that this was her sister's son.

She could not help it. Her greeting was so stiff, her grasp so timid and fluttering, her words so guarded, that M. Rémy, who was used to be cordially welcomed and made much of, was surprised and disappointed, though he said nothing to show it. His manner froze, his mustaches seemed to curl more stiffly. He had expected to like his aunt from her letters and from what he had seen of her daughter, and here she was just the same as any body else, after all!

Rémy introduced himself all the same. He had come to make acquaintance with his English relations, he told Mrs. Maynard. His mother "sent her love, and would they be kind to him?" and Marthe, for all her presentiments, could not but relent towards the handsome young fellow; she did not, however, ask him to stay, but this precaution was needless, for her husband had done so already. "We heard him asking for us at the inn," explained Patty. "Mamma, was not it fortunate? Papa was talking about the old brown mare, and I was just walking with Don in the court-yard, and then I heard my cousin saying, 'Where is Sunnymede?' and I said. 'Oh, how delightful!'"

"Hush, darling," said her mother. "Go and tell them to bring us some tea on the lawn."

There was a shady corner not too far from the geraniums, where the table was set, and Rémy liked his aunt a little better, as she attended to his wants, making a gentle clatter among the white cups, and serving out cream strawberries with liberal hand, unlike any thing he was used to at home. Mr. Maynard came in, hot, grizzled, and tired, and sank into a garden-chair; his wife's face brightened as he nodded to her; the distant river was flashing and dazzling. Rémy, with his long nose and bright eyes, sat watching the little home scene, and envying them somewhat the harmony and plenty. There was love in his home, it is true, and food too, but niggardly dealt out and only produced on occasions. If this was English life, Rémy thought it was very pleasant, and as he thought so, he saw the bright and splendid little figure of his cousin Patty advancing radiant across the lawn. For once Mrs. Maynard was almost angry with her daughter for looking so lovely; her shrill sweet voice clamored for attention; her bright head went bobbing over the cake and the strawberries; her bright cheeks were glowing; her eyes seemed to dance, shine, speak, go to sleep, and wake again with a flash. Mrs. Maynard had tied a bright ribbon in her daughter's hair that morning. She wore a white dress like her mother, but all fancifully and prettily cut. As he looked at her, the young man thought at first—unworthy simile—of coffee and cream and strawberries, in a dazzle of sunlight; then he thought of a gypsy, and then of a nymph, shining, transfigured: a wood-nymph escaped from her tree in the forest, for a time consorting with mortals, and eating and joining in their sports, before she fled back to the ivy-grown trunk, which was her home, perhaps.

Rémy had not lived all these years in the narrow home-school in which he had been bred without learning something of the lesson which was taught there: taught in the whole manner and being of the household, of its incomings and outgoings, of its interests and selfish preoccupations. We are all sensible, coming from outside into strange homes, of the different spirit or lares penates pervading each household. As surely as every tree in the forest has its sylph, so every house in the city must own its domestic deity—different in aspect and character, but ruling with irresistible decision—orderly and decorous, disorderly; patient, impatient; some stint and mean in contrivances and economies, others profuse and neglectful; others, again, poor, plain of necessity, but kindly and liberal. Some spirits keep the doors of their homes wide open, others ajar, others under lock and key, bolted, barred, with a little cautious peep-hole to reconnoitre from. As a rule, the very wide-open door often invites you to an indifferent entertainment going on within; and people who are particular generally prefer those houses where the door is left, let us say, on the latch.

The household god that Rémy had been brought up to worship was a mean, self-seeking, cautious, and economical spirit. Madame de la Louvière's object and ambition in life had been to bring her servants down to the well-known straw a day; to persuade her husband (no difficult matter) to grasp at every chance and shadow of advantage along his path; to educate her son to believe in the creed which she professed. Rémy must make a good marriage; must keep up with desirable acquaintances: must not neglect his well-to-do uncle, the La Louvières in Burgundy; must occasionally visit his grandmother, Madame Capuchon, whose savings ought to be something considerable by this time. Madame de la Louvière had no idea how considerable these savings were until one day about a week before Rémy made his appearance at Littleton, when the family lawyer, Monsieur Micotton, had come over to see her on business. This grasping clear-headed woman exercised a strange authority and fascination over the stupid little attorney—he did her business cheaper than for any other client; he told her all sorts of secrets he had no right to communicate—and now he let out to her that her mother had been making her will, and had left every thing that she had laid by in trust for little Marthe Maynard, her eldest daughter's only child.

Madame de la Louvière's face pinched and wrinkled up into a sort of struggling knot of horror, severity, and indignation.

"My good Monsieur Micotton, what news you give me! What a culpable partiality! What an injustice; what a horror! Ah, that little intriguing English girl! Did you not remonstrate with, implore my unfortunate mother? But it must not be allowed. We must interfere."

"Madame," said Micotton, respectfully, "your mother is, as you well know, a person of singular decision and promptness of character. She explained to me that when your sister married, her husband (who apparently is rich) refused to accept more than a portion of the dot which came by right to madame your sister. M. de la Louvière unfortunately at that moment requested some advance, which apparently vexed madame your mother, and—"

"Ah, I understand. It was a plot; it was a conspiracy. I see it all," hissed the angry lady. "Ah, Monsieur Micotton, what a life of anxiety is that of a mother, devoted as I have been, wounded cruelly to the heart; at every hour insulted, trampled on!"

Madame de la Louvière was getting quite wild in her retrospect; and M. Micotton, fearing a nervous attack, hastily gathered his papers together, stuffed them into his shabby bag, and making a great many little parting bows, that were intended to soothe and calm down his angry client, retreated towards the door. As he left he ran up against a tall, broad-shouldered, good-looking young man, with a long nose, quick dark eyes, and a close-cropped dark beard, thick and soft and bright. Rémy had a look of his mother, who was a tall, straight, well-built woman; but his forehead was broader, his face softer, and his smile was charming. It was like the smile of his unknown aunt, far away in England, the enemy who had, according to his mother's account, defrauded and robbed him of his rights.

"My son, my poor child!" said the baroness, excitedly, "be calm, and come and help me to unravel this plot."

"What is the matter?" Rémy asked, in a cheerful voice. He, however, shrugged his shoulders rather dolefully when he heard the news, for to tell the truth he was in debt, and had been counting upon his grandmother's legacy to help him out. "Hadn't we better make sure of her intentions before we remonstrate?" he suggested, and the baron was accordingly sent for and desired to copy out another of those long letters of his wife's devising, which he signed with a flourish at the end.

Madame Capuchon, appealed to, refused to give any information as to the final disposition of her property. She should leave it to any body she liked. She thought, considering her state of health, that the baron might have waited in patience until she was gone, to satisfy his curiosity. She sent her love to her grandson, but was much displeased with both his parents.

This was a terrible climax. Madame de la Louvière lay awake all one night. Next morning she sent for Rémy and unfolded her plans to him.

"You must go over to England and marry your cousin," she said, decisively; "that is the only thing to be done."

When Micotton came next day for further orders, Madame de la Louvière told him that Rémy was already gone.

All his life long Rémy remembered this evening upon the river, sweeter, more balmy and wonderful than almost any evening he had ever spent in his life before. He had come with a set purpose, this wolf in sheep's clothing, to perform his part in a bargain, without thought of any thing but his own advantage. The idea of any objection being made never occurred to him. He was used to be made much of, as I have said; he could please where he chose. This project accorded so entirely with his French ideas, and seemed so natural and simple an arrangement, that he never thought of doubting its success. For the first time now a possibility occurred to him of something higher, wiser, holier, than money-getting and grasping, in his schemes for the future and for his married life. He scarcely owned it to himself, but now that he had seen his cousin, he unconsciously realized that if he had not already come with the set purpose of marrying her, he should undoubtedly have lost his heart to this winsome and brilliant little creature. All that evening, as they slid through the water, paddling between the twilight fields, pushing through the beds of water-lilies, sometimes spurting swiftly through the rustling reeds, with the gorgeous banks on either side, and the sunset beyond the hills, and the figures strolling tranquilly along the meadows, De la Louvière only felt himself drifting and drifting into a new and wonderful world. This time-wise young fellow felt as if he was being washed white and happy and peaceful in the lovely purple river. Every thing was at once twilit, moonlit, and sunlit. The water flowed deep and clear. Patty, with a bulrush wand, sat at the stern, bending forward and talking happily; the people on the shore heard her sweet chatter.

Once Patty uttered a cry of alarm. "Don! Where was Don?" He had been very contentedly following them, trotting along the bank; but now in the twilight they could not make him out. Patty called and her father hallooed, and Rémy pulled out a little silver whistle he happened to have in his pocket and whistled shrilly. Old Don, who had been a little ahead, hearing all this hullabaloo, quietly plashed from the banks into the water, and came swimming up to the side of the boat, with his honest old nose in the air, and his ears floating on the little ripples. Having satisfied them of his safety, and tried to wag his tail in the water, he swam back to shore again, and the boat sped on its way home through the twilight.

"What a nice little whistle!" said Patty.

"Do take it," said Rémy. "It is what I call my dogs at home with. Please take it. It will give me pleasure to think that any thing of mine is used by you."

"Oh thank you," said Patty, as she put out her soft warm hand through the cool twilight, and took it from him. Maynard was looking out for the lock and paying no attention. Rémy felt as glad as if some great good-fortune had happened to him.

The light was burning in the drawing-room when they got back. Mrs. Maynard had ordered some coffee to be ready for them, and was waiting with a somewhat anxious face for their return.

"Oh, mamma, it has been so heavenly!" said Patty, once more sinking into her own corner by the window.

And then the moon came brightly hanging in the sky, and a nightingale began to sing. Rémy had never been so happy in his life before. He had forgotten all about his speculation, and was only thinking that his English cousin was more charming than all his grandmother's money-bags piled in a heap. For that night he forgot his part of wolf altogether.

In the morning Patty took her cousin to the green-house, to the stable to see her pony; she did the honors of Sunnymede with so much gayety and frankness that her mother had not the heart to put conscious thoughts into the child's head, and let her go her own way. The two came back late to the early dinner; Mr. Maynard frowned, he disliked unpunctuality. Rémy was too happy to see darkness anywhere, or frowns in any body's face; but then his eyes were dazzled. It was too good to last, he thought, and in truth a storm was rising even then.

During dinner the post came in. Mrs. Maynard glanced at her correspondence, and then at her husband, as she put it into her pocket. "It is from my mother," she said. Rémy look-

ed a little interested, but asked no questions, and went on talking and laughing with his cousin; and after dinner, when Mrs. Maynard took her letter away to read in the study, the two young people went and sat upon the little terrace in front of the house.

The letter was from Madame Capuchon, and Mrs. Maynard, having read it, put it into her husband's hands with a little exclamation of bewildered dismay.

"What is the matter, my dear?" said Maynard, looking up from his paper, which had come by the same afternoon post.

"Only read this," she said; "you will know best what to do. Oh Henry, he must go; he should never have come."

My heroine's mother was never very remarkable for spirit: her nearest approach to it was this first obstinate adherence to any thing which Henry might decree. Like other weak people she knew that if she once changed her mind she was lost, and accordingly she clung to it in the smallest decisions of life with an imploring persistence: poor Marthe, her decision was a straw in a great sea of unknown possibilities. Madame Capuchon was a strong-minded woman, and not afraid to change her mind.

"I have heard from Félicie," the old lady wrote; "but she says nothing of a certain fine scheme which I hasten to acquaint you with. I learned it by chance the other day when Micotton was with me consulting on the subject of my will, which it seems has given great offense to the De la Louvières. Considering the precarious state of my health, they might surely have taken patience; but I am now determined that they shall not benefit by one farthing that I possess. Micotton, at my desire, confessed that Rémy has gone over to England for the express purpose of making advances to Marthe, your daughter, in hopes of eventually benefiting through me. He is a young man of indifferent character, and he inherits, no doubt, the covetous and grasping spirit of his father." Mr. Maynard read no farther; he flushed up and began to hiss out certain harmless oaths between his teeth. "Does that confounded young puppy think my Patty is to be disposed of like a bundle of hay? Does he come here scheming after that poor old woman's money? Be hanged to the fellow! he must be told to go about his business, Marthe, or the child may be taking a fancy to him. Confound the impertinent jackanapes!"

"But who is to tell him?" poor Marthe faltered, with one more dismal presentiment.

"You, to be sure," said Maynard, clapping on his felt hat and marching right away off the premises.

In the mean time Rémy and his cousin had been very busy making Don jump backward and forward over the low parapet. They had a little disjointed conversation between the jumping.

"What is your home like?" Patty asked once.

"I wish it was more like yours," said Rémy, with some expression; "it would make me very happy to think that, some day, it might become more so."

The girl seemed almost to understand his meaning, for she blushed and laughed, and tossed her gloves up in the air and caught them again.—"I love my home dearly," said she.

At that moment the garden door opened, and Mr. Maynard appeared, but instead of coming towards them, he no sooner saw the two young folks than he began walking straight away in the direction of the outer gate, never turning his head or paying any attention to his daughter's call.

"Papa, papa!" cried Patty, springing up; but her father walked on, never heeding, and yet she was sure he must have heard. What could it mean? She looked at Rémy, who was quite unconscious, twirling his mustache, and stirring up Don with the toe of his boot; from Rémy she looked round to the library window, which was open wide, and where her mother was standing.

"Do you want me?" Patty cried, running up.

"Ask your cousin to come and speak to me," said Mrs. Maynard, very gravely —"here, in papa's room."

Patty was certain that something was wrong. She gave Rémy her mother's message with a wistful glance, to see whether he did not suspect any trouble. The young man started up obediently, and Patty waited outside in the sun, listening to the voices droning away within, watching the sparkle of the distant river, lazily following the flight of a big bumble-bee—wondering when their talk would be over and Rémy would come out to her again. From where she sat Patty could see the reflection of the two talkers in the big sloping looking-glass over the library table. Her mother was standing very dignified and stately, the young man had drawn himself straight up —so straight, so grim and fierce-looking, that Patty, as she looked, was surer and more sure that all was not right; and she saw her mother give him a letter, and he seemed to push it away. And then it was not Rémy but Mrs. Maynard who came out, looking very pale, and who said, "Patty, darling, I have been very much pained. Your cousin has behaved so strangely and unkindly to you and me and to your father, that we can never forget or forgive it. Your father says so."

Mrs. Maynard had tried to perform her task as gently as she could. She told Rémy that English people had different views on many subjects from the French; that she had learned his intentions from her mother, and thought it best to tell him plainly at once that she and Mr. Maynard could never consent to any such arrangement; and under the circumstances—that —that—that—

"You can never consent," repeated the young man, stepping forward and looking through her and round about her, seeing all her doubts, all her presentiments, reading the letter, overhearing her conversation with her husband all in one instant—so it seemed to poor Marthe. "And why not, pray?"

"We can not argue the question," his aunt said, with some dignity. "You must not attempt to see my daughter any more."

"You mean to say that you are turning me, your sister's son, out of your house," the indignant Rémy said. "I own to all that you accuse me of. I hoped to marry your daughter, I still hope it; and I shall do so still," cried the young man.

Rémy's real genuine admiration for Patty stood him in little stead; he was angry and lost his temper in his great disappointment and surprise. He behaved badly and foolishly.

"I had not meant to turn you out of my house," said his aunt, gravely; "but for the present I think you had certainly better go. I can not expose my daughter to any agitation."

"You have said more than enough," said Rémy. "I am going this instant." And as he spoke he went striding out of the room.

And so Rémy came back no more to sit with Patty under the ash-tree; but her mother, with her grave face, stood before her, and began telling her this impossible, unbelievable fact—that he was young, that he had been to blame.

"He unkind! he to blame! Oh mamma!" the girl said, in a voice of reproach.

"He has been unkind and scheming, and he was rude to me, darling. I am sorry, but it is a fact." And Marthe, as she spoke, glanced a little anxiously at Patty, who had changed color, and then at De la Louvière himself, who was marching up, fierce still and pale, with bristling hair—his nose looking hooked and his lips parting in a sort of scornful way. He was carrying his cloak on his arm.

"I have come to wish you good-bye, and to thank you for your English hospitality, madame," said he, with a grand sweeping bow. "My cousin, have you not got a word for me?"

But Mrs. Maynard's eyes were upon her, and Patty, with a sudden shy stiffness for which she hated herself then and for many and many a day and night after, said good-bye, looking down with a sinking heart, and Rémy marched away with rage and scorn in his. "They are all alike; not one bit better than myself. That little girl has neither kindness, nor feeling, nor fidelity in her. The money: they want to keep it for themselves—that is the meaning of all these fine speeches. I should like to get hold of her all the same, little stony-hearted flirt, just to spite them; yes, and throw her over at the last moment, money and all—impertinent, ill-bred folks." And it happened that just at this minute Mr. Maynard was coming back thoughtfully the way he had gone, and the two men stopped face to face, one red, the other pale. Mrs. Maynard, seeing the meeting, came hastily up.

"You will be glad to hear that I am going," said Rémy, defiantly looking at his uncle as he had done at his aunt.

"I am very glad to hear it," said Mr. Maynard. "I have no words to express the indignation which fills me at the thought of your making a speculation of my daughter's affections, and the sooner you are gone the better."

"Hush, dear," said Mrs. Maynard, laying her hand on her husband's arm, and looking at Patty, who had followed her at a little distance. She had had her own say, and was beginning to think poor Rémy hardly dealt with.

"Let him say what he likes, madame, I don't care," De la Louvière said. "I am certainly going. You have failed, both of you, in kindness and hospitality; as for my cousin—" but, looking at Patty, he saw that her eyes were full of tears, and he stopped short. "I am all that you think," Rémy went on. "I am in debt, I have lost money at gambling, I am a good-for-nothing fellow. You might have made something of me, all of you, but you are a sordid nation and don't understand the feelings of a French gentleman."

With this bravado Rémy finally stalked off.

"I think, perhaps, we were a little hasty," said the injudicious Marthe, while Patty suddenly burst out crying and ran away.

Poor little Patty came down to tea that evening looking very pale, with pouting red lips, prettier than ever, her mother thought, as she silently gave the child her cupful of tea and cut her bread-and-butter, and put liberal helpings of jam and fruit before her, dainties that were served in the old cut-glass dishes that had sparkled on Maynard's grandmother's tea-table before. The old Queen Anne teapot, too, was an heirloom, and the urn and the pretty straight spoons, and the hideous old china tea-set with the red and yellow flowers. There were other heirlooms in the family, and even Patty's bright eyes had been her great-grandmother's a century ago, as any body might see who looked at the picture on the wall. Mr. Maynard was silent; he had been angry with his wife for her gentle remonstrance, furious with the young man for the high hand in which he had carried matters, displeased with Patty for crying, and with himself for not having foreseen the turn things were taking; and he now sat sulkily stirring his tea—sulky but relenting, and not indisposed for peace. After all, he had had his own way, and that is a wonderful calming process. Rémy was gone; nothing left of him but a silver whistle that Patty had put away in her work-table drawer. He was gone; the echo of his last angry words were dinning in Maynard's ears, while a psalm of relief was sounding in the mother's heart. Patty sulked like her father, and ate her bread and jam without speaking a word. There was no great harm done, Mrs. Maynard thought, as she kept her daughter supplied. She herself had been so disturbed and overcome by the stormy events of the day that she could not eat. She made the mistake that many elders have made before her: they mistake physical for mental disturbance; poor well-hacked bodies that have been jolted, shaken, patched and mended, and strained in half a dozen places, are easily affected by the passing jars of the moment: they suffer and lose their appetite, and get aches directly which take away much sense of the mental inquietude which brought the disturbance about. Young healthy creatures like Patty can eat a good dinner and feel a keen pang and hide it, and chatter on scarcely conscious of their own heroism.

But as the days went by Mrs. Maynard suspected that all was not well with the child; there seemed to be a little effort and strain in the life which had seemed so easy and smooth before. More than once Mrs. Maynard noticed her daughter's eyes fixed upon her curiously and wistfully. One day the mother asked her why she looked at her so. Patty blushed, but did not answer. The truth was, it was the likeness to her cousin which she was studying. These blushes and silence made Marthe Maynard a little uneasy.

But more days passed and the mother's anxious heart was relieved, Patty had brightened up again, and looked like herself, coming and going in her Undine-like way, bringing home long wreaths of ivy, birds'-eggs, sylvan treasures. She was out in all weathers. Her locks only curled the crisper for the falling rain, and her cheeks only brightened when the damp rose up from the river. The time came for their annual visit to Madame de Capuchon. Patty, out in her woods and meadows, wondered and wondered what might come of it; but Poictiers is a long way from Fontainebleau, "fortunately," "alas!" thought the mother—in her room, packing Patty's treasures—and the daughter out in the open field in the same breath. They were so used to one another, these two, that some sort of magnetic current passed between them at times, and certainly Marthe never thought of Rémy de la Louvière that Patty did not think of him too.

III.

OLD Madame de Capuchon was delighted with her granddaughter, and the improvement she found in her since the year before. She made more of her than she had ever done of Marthe her daughter. All manner of relics were produced out of the old lady's ancient stores to adorn Miss Patty's crisp locks and little round white throat and wrists; small medallions were hung round her neck, brooches and laces pinned on, ribbons tied and muslins measured, while Simonne tried her hand once again at cake-making. Patty, in return, brought a great rush of youth, and liberty, and sunshine into the old closed house, where she was spoiled, worshipped, petted, to her heart's content. Her mother's tender speechless love seemed dimmed and put out by this chorus of compliments and admiration. "Take care of your complexion; whatever you do, take care of your complexion," her grandmother was always saying. Madame Capuchon actually sent for the first modiste in the town, explained what she wanted, and ordered a scarlet "capeline,"—such as ladies wear by the seaside—a pretty frilled, quilted, laced, and braided scarlet hood, close round the cheeks and tied up to the chin, to protect her granddaughter's youthful bloom from the scorching rays of the sun. She need not have been so anxious. Patty's roses were of a damask that does not fade in the sun's rays.

Squire Maynard, who was a sensible man, did not approve of all this to-do, and thought it was all very bad for Miss Patty, "whose little head was quite full enough of nonsense already," he said. One day Patty came home with the celebrated pearls round her neck that Madame de la Louvière had tried so hard to get. Madame Capuchon forgot that she had already given them to her eldest daughter, but Mrs. Maynard herself was the last to have remembered this, and it was her husband who said to her, with a shrug of the shoulders:—

"It is all very well, but they are yours, my dear, and your mother has no more right to them than Patty has."

Patty pouted, flashed, tossed her little head, flung her arms round her mother's neck, all in an instant. She was a tender-hearted little person, heedless, impulsive, both for the best and the worst, as her poor mother knew to her cost. The squire thought his wife spoiled her daughter, and occasionally tried a course of judicious severity, and, as I have already said, he had only succeeded in frightening the child more than he had any idea of.

"Take them, dear mamma," said Patty, pulling off her necklace. "I didn't know anything about them. Grandmamma tied them on."

"Darling," said her mother, "you are my jewel. I don't want these pearls: and if they are mine I give them to you."

Two pearl drops were in Mrs. Maynard's eyes as she spoke. She was thinking of her long lonely days, and of the treasures which were now hers. Looking at this bright face in its scarlet hood — this gay, youthful presence standing before them all undimmed, in the splendor of its confidence and brightness—it seemed to Mrs. Maynard as if now, in her old age, now that she had even forgotten her longings for them, all the good things were granted to her, the want of which had made her early life so sad. It was like a miracle, that at fifty all this should come to her. Her meek glad eyes sought her husband's. He was frowning, and eying his little girl uneasily.

"I don't like that red bonnet of yours," said he. "It is too conspicuous. You can't walk about Paris in that."

"Paris!" shrieked Patty. "Am I going to Paris, papa?"

"You must take great care of your father, Patty," said her mother. "I shall stay here with my mother until you come back."

I am not going to describe Patty's delights and surprise. Every body has seen through her eyes, at one time or another, and knows what it is to be sixteen, and transported into a dazzling ringing world of sounds, and sights, and tastes, and revelations. The good father took his daughter to dine off delicious little dishes with sauces, with white bread and butter to eat between the courses; he hired little carriages, in which they sped through the blazing streets, and were set down at the doors of museums and palaces, and the gates of cool gardens where fountains murmured and music played; he had some friends in Paris—a good-natured old couple, who volunteered to take charge of his girl; but for that whole, happy, unspeakable week he rarely left her. One night he took her to the play—a grand fairy piece—where a fustian peasant maiden was turned into a satin princess in a flash of music and electric light. Patty took her father's arm, and came away with the crowd, with the vision of those waving halos of bliss opening and shining with golden rain and silver-garbed nymphs, and shrieks of music and admiration, all singing and turning before her. The satin princess was already retransformed, but that was no affair of Patty's. Some one in the crowd, better used to plays and fairy pieces, coming along behind the father and daughter, thought that by far the prettiest sight he had seen that night was this lovely eager little face before him, and that those two dark eyes—now flashing, now silent—were the most beautiful illuminations he had witnessed for many a day. The bright eyes never discovered who it was behind her. Need I say that it was Rémy? who, after looking for them for a couple of days in all the most likely places, took a ticket for Fontainebleau on the third evening after he had seen them. What fascination was it that attracted him? He was hurt and angry with her, he loved and he longed to see her. And then again vague thoughts of revenge crossed his mind; he would see her and win her affections, and then turn away and leave her, and pay back the affront which had been put upon him. M. Rémy, curling his mustaches in the railway-carriage, and meditating this admirable scheme, was no very pleasant object to contemplate.

"That gentleman in the corner looks ready to eat us all up," whispered a little bride to her husband.

Meanwhile Patty had been going on her way very placidly all these three days, running hither and thither, driving in the forest, dining with her grandmother, coming home at night under the stars. The little red hood was well known in the place. Sometimes escorted by Betty, an English maid who had come over with the family; oftener Mr. Maynard himself walked with his daughter. Fontainebleau was not Littleton, and he did not like her going about alone, although Patty used to pout and rebel at these precautions. Mrs. Maynard herself rarely walked; she used to drive over to her mother's of an afternoon, and her husband and daughter would follow her later; and Simonne, radiant, would then superintend the preparation of fricandeaus and galettes, such as she loved to set before them, and cream-tarts and chicken and *vol au vent*. There was no end to her resources. And yet, to hear Madame Capuchon, one would think that she led the life of an invalid ascetic starving on a desert island. "These railways carry away every thing," the old lady would say; "they leave one nothing. When I say that I have dined, it is for the sake of saying so. You know I am not particular, but they leave us nothing, absolutely nothing, to eat." On this especial occasion the old lady was in a state of pathetic indignation over M. Bougu, her butterman, who had been taken up for false practices. Simonne joined in—"I went in for the tray," she said. "Oh, I saw at once, by the expression of madame's face, that there was something wrong. It was lard that he had mixed with his butter. As it is, I do not know where to go to find her any thing fit to eat. They keep cows at the hotel," she added, turning to Marthe as she set down a great dish full of cream-cakes upon the table. "Perhaps they would supply us, if you asked them."

Mrs. Maynard undertook the negotiation; and next day she called Patty to her into the little drawing-room, and gave the child a piece of honeycomb and a little pat in a vine-leaf, to take to Madame Capuchon, as a sample. "Give her my love, and tell her she can have as much more as she likes; and call Betty to go with you," said Mrs. Maynard. "Betty, Betty, Betty, come directly," cried Patty, outside the door, dancing off delighted with her commission. Betty came directly; but there are two roads to Madame Capuchon's, one by the street and one by the park. Patty certainly waited for three minutes at the park gate, but Betty was trudging down the town, and gaping into all the shops as she went along, while her young mistress, who had soon lost patience, was hurrying along the avenues, delighted to be free —hurrying and then stopping, as the fancy took her. The sun shone, the golden water quivered, the swans came sailing by. It was all Patty could do not to sing right out and dance to her own singing. By degrees her spirits quieted down a little. . . . .

* * * * * *

Patty was standing leaning over the stone parapet at the end of the terrace, and looking deep down into the water which laps against it A shoal of carp was passing through the clear cool depths. Solemn patriarchs, bald, dim with age, bleared and faded and overgrown with strange mosses and lichens, terrible with their chill life of centuries, solemnly sliding, followed by their court through the clear cool waters where they had floated for ages past. Unconscious, living, indifferent while the generations were succeeding one another, and angry multitudes surging and yelling while kingdoms changed hands; while the gay court ladies, scattering crumbs with their dainty fingers, were hooted by the hags and furies of the Revolution, shrieking for blood, and for bread for their children;—the carps may have dived for safety into the cool depths of the basins, while these awful ghosts of want and madness clamored round the doors of the palace—ghosts that have not passed away forever, alas! with the powders and patches, and the stately well-bred follies of the court of Dives. After these times a new order of things was established, and the carps may have seen a new race of spirits in the quaint garb and odd affectation of a bygone age, of senates and consuls and a dead Roman people; and then an Emperor, broken-hearted, signed away an empire, and a Waterloo was fought; and to-day began to dawn, and the sun shone for a while upon the kingly dignity of Orleans; and then upon a second empire, with flags and many eagles and bees to decorate the whole, and trumpets blowing, and looms at work, and a temple raised to the new goddess of industry.

What did it all matter to the old gray carp? They had been fed by kings and by emperors; and now they were snatching as eagerly at the crumbs which Patty Maynard was dropping one by one into the water, and which floated pleasantly into their great open maws. The little bits of bread tasted much alike, from wherever they came. If Patty had been used to put such vague speculations into words, she might have wondered sometimes whether we human carps, snatching at the crumbs which fall upon the waters of life, are not also greedy and unconscious of the wonders and changes that may be going on close at hand in another element to which we do not belong, but at which we guess now and then.

A crumb fell to little Patty herself, just then gazing down deep into the water. The sun began to shine hot and yet more hot, and the child put up her big white umbrella, for her hood did not shade her eyes. A great magnificent stream of light illumined the grand old place, and the waving tree-tops, and the still, currentless lake. The fish floated on basking, the birds in the trees seemed suddenly silenced by the intense beautiful radiance, the old palace courts gleamed bravely, the shadows shrank and blackened; hot, sweet, and silent the light streamed upon the great green arches and courts and colonnades of the palace of garden without, upon the arches and courts and colonnades of the palace of marble within, with its quaint eaves and mullions, its lilies of France and D's and H's still intwined, though D and H had been parted for three centuries and more. It was so sweet and so serene that Patty began to think of her cousin. She could not have told you why fine days put her in mind of him, and of that happy hour in the boat. She pulled the little silver whistle out of her pocket, and to-day she could not help it; instead of pushing the thought of Rémy away, as she had done valiantly of late, the silly child turned the whistle in her hands round and round again. It gleamed in the sun like a whistle of fire; and then slowly she put it to her lips. Should she frighten the carp? Patty wondered; and as she blew a very sweet long note upon the shrill gleaming toy, it echoed oddly in the stillness, and across the water. The carp did not seem to hear it; but Patty stopped short, frightened, ashamed, with burning blushes, for, looking up at the sound of a footstep striking across the stone terrace, she saw her cousin coming towards her.

To people who are in love each meeting is a new miracle. This was an odd chance certainly, a quaint freak of fortune. The child thought it was some incantation that she had unconsciously performed; she sprang back, her dark eyes flashed, the silver whistle fell to the ground and went rolling and rolling and bobbing across the stones to the young man's feet.

He picked it up and came forward with an amused and lover-like smile, holding it out in his hand. "I have only just heard you were here," he said; "I came to see my grandmother last night, from Paris. My dear cousin, what a delightful chance! Are not you a little bit glad to see me?" said the young man, romantically. It was a shame to play off his airs and graces upon such a simple downright soul as Marthe Maynard. Some one should have boxed his ears as he stood there, smiling, handsome, irresistible, trying to make a sentimental scene out of a chance meeting. Poor little Patty, with all her courage and simpleness, was no match for him at first; she looked up at his face wistfully and then turned away, for one burning blush succeeded to another, and then she took courage again. "Of course I am glad to see you, Cousin Rémy," said she, brightly, and she held out her little brown hand and put it frankly into his, "It is the greatest pleasure and delight to me, above all now, when I had given up all hopes forever; but it's no use," said Patty, with a sigh, "for I know I mustn't talk to you, they wouldn't like it. I must never whistle again upon the little whistle, for fear you should appear," she said, with a sigh.

This was no cold-hearted maiden. Rémy forgot his vague schemes of revenge and desertion the moment he heard the sound of her dear little voice. "They wouldn't like it," said Rémy, reddening, "and I have been longing and wearying to see you again, Patty. What do you suppose I have come here for?—Patty, Patty, confess that you were thinking of me when you whistled," and as he said this, the wolf's whole heart melted. "Do you know how often I have thought of you since I was cruelly driven away from your house?"

Two great, ashamed, vexed, sorrowful tears started into Marthe's eyes as she turned away her head and pulled away her hand.

"Oh Rémy, indeed, indeed there must have been some reason, some mistake : dear papa, if you knew how he loves me and mamma, and, oh, how miserable it made me."

"I dare say there was some mistake, since you say so," said the wily wolf. "Patty, only say you love me a little, and I will forgive every thing and any thing."

"I mustn't let any one talk about forgiving

them," said the girl. "I would love you a great deal, if I might," she added, with another sigh. "I do love you, only I try not to, and I think—I am sure I shall get over it in time, if I can only be brave."

This was such an astounding confession that De la Louvière hardly knew how to take it; touched and amused and amazed, he stood there, looking at the honest little sweet face. Patty's confession was a very honest one. The girl knew that it was not to be; she was loyal to her father, and, above all, to that tender wistful mother. Filial devotion seemed, like the bright eyes and silver teapot, to be an inheritance in her family. She did not deceive herself; she knew that she loved her cousin with something more than cousinly affection, but she also believed that it was a fancy which could be conquered. And she set her teeth and looked quite fierce at Rémy; and then she melted again, and said in her childish way: "You never told me you would come if I blew upon the whistle."

Do her harm—wound her—punish her parents by stabbing her tender little heart! Rémy said to himself that he had rather cut off his mustaches.

There was something loyal, honest, and tender in the little thing, that touched him inexpressibly. He suddenly began to tell himself that he agreed with his uncle, that to try to marry Patty for money's sake had been a shame and a sin. He had been a fool and a madman, and blind and deaf. Rémy de la Louvière was only half a wolf, after all—a sheep in wolf's clothing. He had worn the skin so long that he had begun to think it was his very own, and he was perfectly amazed and surprised to find such a soft, tender place beneath it.

It was with quite a different look and tone from the romantic, impassioned, corsair manner in which he had begun, that he said very gently : "Dear Patty, don't try too hard not to like me. I can not help hoping that all will be well. You will hope, too, will you not?"

"Yes, indeed, I will," said Patty; "and now, Rémy, you must go : I have talked to you long enough. See, this is the back gate and the way to the Rue de la Lampe." For they had been walking on all this time and following the course of the avenue. One or two people passing by looked kindly at the handsome young couple strolling in the sunshine; a man in a blouse, wheeling a hand-truck, looked over his shoulder a second time as he turned down the turning to the Rue de la Lampe. Patty did not see him, she was absorbed in one great resolution. She must go now, and say good-bye to her cousin.

"Come a little way farther with me," said Rémy, "just a little way under the trees. Patty, I have a confession to make to you. You will hate me, perhaps, and yet I can not help telling you."

"Oh, indeed I must not come now," Patty said. "Good-bye, good-bye."

"You won't listen to me, then?" said the young man, so sadly that she had not the courage to leave him, and she turned at last, and walked a few steps.

"Will you let me carry your basket?" said her cousin. "Who are you taking this to?"

"It is for my grandmother," said the girl, resisting. "Rémy, have you really any thing to say?"

They had come to the end of the park, where its gates lead into the forest; one road led to the Rue de la Lampe, the other into the great waving world of trees. It was a lovely summer's afternoon. There was a host in the air, delighting and basking in the golden comfort; butterflies, midges, flights of birds from the forest were passing. It was pleasant to exist in such a place and hour, to walk by Rémy on the soft springing turf, and to listen to the sound of his voice under the shade of the overarching boughs.

"Patty, do you know I did want to marry you for your money?" Rémy said at last. "I love you truly; but I have not loved you always as I ought to have done—as I do now. You scorn me, you can not forgive me?" he added, as the girl stopped short. "You will never trust me again."

"Oh, Rémy, how could you . . . . Oh, yes, indeed, indeed I do forgive you. I do trust you," she added quickly, saying any thing to comfort and cheer him when he looked so unhappy. Every moment took them farther and farther on. The little person with the pretty red hood and bright eyes and the little basket had almost forgotten her commission, her conscience, her grandmother, and all the other duties of life. Rémy, too, had forgotten every thing but the bright sweet little face, the red hood, and the little hand holding the basket, when they came to a dark, inclosed halting-place at the end of the avenue, from whence a few rocky steps led out upon a sudden hillside, which looked out into the open world. It was a lovely surprising sight, a burst of open country, a great purple amphitheatre of rocks shining and hills spreading to meet the skies, clefts and sudden gleams, and a wide distant horizon of waving forest fringing the valley. Clouds were drifting and tints changing, the heather springing between the rocks at their feet, and the thousands of tree-tops swaying like a ripple on a sea.

Something in the great wide freshness of the place brought Patty to herself again.

"How lovely it is!" she said. "Oh, Rémy, why did you let me come? Oh, I oughtn't to have come."

Rémy tried to comfort her. "We have not been very long," he said. "We will take the short cut through the trees, and you shall tell your mother all about it. There's no more reason why we shouldn't walk together now than when we were at Littleton."

As he was speaking he was leading the way through the brushwood, and they got into a cross avenue leading back to the carriage-road.

"I shall come to Madame Capuchon's, too, since you are going," said Rémy, making a grand resolution. "I think perhaps she will help us. She is bound to, since she did all the mischief;" and then he went on a few steps, holding back the trees that grew in Patty's way. A little field-mouse peeped at them and ran away, a lightning sheet of light flashed through the green and changing leaves, little blue flowers were twinkling on the mosses under the trees, dried blossoms were falling, and cones and dead leaves and aromatic twigs and shoots.

"Is this the way?" said Patty, suddenly stopping short, and looking about her. "Rémy, look at those arrows cut in the trees; they are not pointing to the road we have come. Oh Rémy, do not lose the way," cried Patty, in a sudden fright.

"Don't be afraid," Rémy answered, laughing, and hurrying on before her; and then he stopped short, and began to pull at his mustache, looking first in one direction and then in another. "Do you think they would be anxious if you were a little late?" he said.

"Anxious," cried Patty. "Mamma would die; she could not bear it. Oh Rémy, Rémy, what shall I do?" She flushed up, and almost began to cry. "Oh, find the way, please. Do you see any more arrows? Here is one; come, come."

Patty turned, and began to retrace her steps, hurrying along in a fever of terror and remorse. The wood-pigeons cooed overhead, the long lines of distant trees were mingling and twisting in a sort of dance, as she flew along.

"Wait for me, Patty," cried Rémy. "Here is some one to ask." And as he spoke he pointed to an old woman coming along one of the narrow cross pathways, carrying a tray of sweet-meats and a great jar of lemonade.

"Fontainebleau, my little gentleman?" said the old woman. "You are turning your back upon it. The arrows point away from Fontainebleau and not toward the town. Do you know the big cross near the gate? Well, it is just at the end of that long avenue. Wait, wait, my little gentleman. Won't you buy a sweet sugar-stick for the pretty little lady in the red hood? Believe me, she is fond of sugar-sticks. It is not the first time that she has bought some of mine."

But Rémy knew that Patty was in no mood for barley-sugar, and he went off to cheer up his cousin with the good news. The old woman hobbled off, grumbling.

It was getting later by this time. The shadows were changing, and a western light was beginning to glow upon the many stems and quivering branches of the great waving forest. Every thing glowed in unwearied change and beauty, but they had admired enough. A bird was singing high above over their heads, they walked on quickly in silence for half an hour, a long, interminable half-hour, and at the end of

the avenue—as the old woman had told them—
they found a wide stony ascending road, with
the dark murmuring fringe of the woods on either side, and a great cross at the summit of the
ascent. Here Patty sank down for a minute,
almost falling upon the step, and feeling safe.
This gate was close to the Rue de la Lampe.

"Now go," she said to her cousin. "Go on
first, and I will follow, dear Rémy. I don't
want to be seen with you any more. People
know me and my red hood."

De la Louvière could only hope that Patty
had not already been recognized.

All the same he utterly refused to leave her
until they reached the gates of the forest; then
he took the short way to the Rue de la Lampe,
and Patty followed slowly. She had had a
shock, she wanted to be calm before she saw
her grandmother. Her heart was beating still,
she was tired and sorry. Patty's conscience
was not easy—she felt she had done wrong, and
yet—and yet—with the world of love in her
heart it seemed as if nothing could be wrong
and nobody angry or anxious.

Mrs. Maynard herself had felt something of
the sort that afternoon after the little girl had
left her. The mother watched her across the
courtyard, and then sat down as usual to her
work. Her eyes filled up with grateful tears as
she bent over her sewing; they often did when
Henry spoke a kind word or Patty looked specially happy. Yes, it was a miracle that at fifty
all this should come to her, thought Marthe
Maynard — brilliant beauty and courage and
happiness, and the delight of youth and of early
hopes unrepressed. It was like a miracle that
all this had come to her in a dearer and happier form than if it had been given to herself.
Marthe wondered whether all her share had been
reserved for her darling in some mysterious fashion, and so she went on stitching her thoughts
to her canvas, as people do: peaceful, tranquil,
happy thoughts they were, as she sat waiting for
her husband's return. An hour or two went
by, people came and went in the court-yard below, the little diligence rattled off to the railway; at last, thinking she heard Henry's voice,
Marthe leaned out of the window and saw him
speaking to an old woman with a basket of
sweetmeats, and then she heard the sitting-room
door open, and she looked round to see who it
was coming in. It was Simonne, who came
bustling in with a troubled look, like ripples in
a placid smooth pool. The good old creature
had put on a shawl and gloves, and a clean cap
with huge frills, and stood silent, umbrella in
hand, and staring at the calm-looking lady at
her work-table.

"What is it?" said Marthe, looking up.
"Simonne, is my mother unwell?"

"Madame is quite well; do not be uneasy,"
said Simonne, with a quick, uncertain glance in
Mrs. Maynard's face.

"Have you brought me back Patty?" said
Mrs. Maynard. "Has Betty come with you?"

"Betty? I don't know where she is," said
Simonne. "She is a craze-pated girl, and you
should not allow her to take charge of Patty."

Mrs. Maynard smiled. She knew Simonne's
ways of old. All cooks, housekeepers, ladies'
maids, etc., under fifty, were crazy-pated girls
with Simonne, whose sympathies certainly did
not rest among her own class. Mrs. Maynard's
smile, however, changed away when she looked
at Simonne a second time.

"I am sure something is the matter," Marthe cried, starting up. "Where's Patty?"
The poor mother, suddenly conjecturing evil, had
turned quite pale, and all the soft contentment
and calm were gone in one instant. She seized
Simonne's arm with an imploring nervous clutch,
as if praying that it might be nothing dreadful.

"Don't be uneasy, madame," said Simonne.
"Girls are girls, and that Betty is too scatter-
brained to be trusted another time: she missed
Patty and came alone to our house. Oh, I sent
her off quickly enough to meet mademoiselle.
But you see, madame," Simonne was hurrying
on nervously over her words, "our Patty is so
young, she thinks of no harm, she runs here and
there just as fancy takes her; but a young girl
must not be talked of, and—and it does not do
for her to be seen alone in company with any
body but her mother or father. There's no
harm done, but—"

"What are you talking of — why do you
frighten me for nothing, Simonne?" said Mrs.
Maynard, recovering crossly with a faint gasp
of relief, and thinking all was well. She had
expected a broken limb at least in her sudden
alarm.

"There, Marthe," said Simonne, taking her
hand, "you must not be angry with me. It
was the concierge de chez nous, who made a remark which displeased me, and I thought I had
best come straight to you."

"My Patty! my Patty! What have you been
doing, Simonne? How dare you talk of my
child to common people!" said the anxious
mother.

"I was anxious, madame," said poor Simonne, humbly. "I looked for her up the street
and along the great avenue, and our concierge
met me and said: 'Don't trouble yourself. I
met your young lady going towards the forest in
company with a young man.' She is a naughty
child, and I was vexed, madame, that is all,"
said Simonne.

But Mrs. Maynard hardly heard her to the
end—she put up her two hands with a little cry
of anxious horror. "And is she not back?
What have you been doing? why did you not
come before? My Patty! my Patty! what absurd mistake is this? Oh, where is my husband? Papa, papa!" cried poor Mrs. Maynard,
distracted, running out upon the landing. Mr.
Maynard was coming up stairs at that instant,
followed by the blowsy and breathless Betty.

Mr. Maynard had evidently heard the whole
story: he looked black and white, as people do
who are terribly disturbed and annoyed. Had

they been at home in England, Patty's disappearance would have seemed nothing to them; there were half a dozen young cousins and neighbors to whose care she might have been trusted, but here where they knew no one, it was inexplicable, and no wonder they were disquieted and shocked. Mr. Maynard tried to reassure his wife, and vented his anxiety in wrath upon the luckless Betty.

Marthe sickened as she listened to Betty's sobs and excuses. "I can't help it," said the stupid girl, with a scared face. "Miss Patty didn't wait for me. The old woman says she saw a red hood in the forest, going along with a young man—master heard her . . ."

"The concierge says he thinks it is missis's nephew!"

"Ah!" screamed poor Mrs. Maynard; "I see it all."

"Hold your tongue, you fool! How dare you all come to me with such lies?" shouted Maynard to the maid. He was now thoroughly frightened. After all, it might be a plot; who could tell what villainy that young man might be capable of—carrying her off, marrying her; all for the sake of her money. And, full of this new alarm, he rushed down into the court again. The old woman was gone, but a carriage was standing there waiting to be engaged.

"We may as well go and fetch Patty at your mother's," Maynard called out to his wife, with some appearance of calmness. "I dare say she is there by this time." Mrs. Maynard ran down stairs and got in, Simonne bundled in too, and sat with her back to the horses. But that ten minutes' drive was so horrible that not one of them ever spoke of it again.

They need not have been so miserable, poor people, if they had only known Patty had safely reached her grandmother's door by that time. When the concierge, who was sitting on his barrow at the door, let her in and looked at her with an odd expression in his face, "Simonne was in a great anxiety about you, mademoiselle," said he; "she is not yet come in. Your grandmamma is up stairs, as usual. Have you had a pleasant walk?"

Patty made no answer; she ran up stairs quickly. "I must not stay long," she said to herself. "I wonder if Rémy is there." The front door was open, and she went in, and then along the passage, and with a beating heart she stopped and knocked at her grandmother's door. "Come in, child," the old lady called out from the inside; and as Patty nervously fumbled at the handle, the voice inside added, "Lift up the latch, and the hasp will fall. Come in," and Patty went in as she was told.

It was getting to be a little dark in-doors by this time, and the room seemed to Patty full of an odd dazzle of light—perhaps because the glass door of the dressing-closet, in which many of Madame Capuchon's stores were kept, was open.

"Come here, child," said her grandmother, hoarsely, "and let me look at you."

"How hoarsely you speak!" said Patty; "I'm afraid your cold is very bad, grandmamma."

The old lady grunted and shook her head. "My health is miserable at all times," she said. "What is that you have got in your basket, butter, is it not, by the smell?"

"What a good nose you have, grandmamma!" said Patty, laughing faintly, and opening her basket. "I have brought you a little pat of butter, and some honeycomb, with mamma's love," said Patty. "They will supply you from the hotel, if you like, at the same price you pay now."

"Thank you, child," said Madame Capuchon. "Come a little closer, and let me look at you. Why, what is the matter? You are all sorts of colors—blue, green, red. What have you been doing, miss? See if you can find my spectacles on that table."

"What do you want them for, grandmamma?" Patty asked, fumbling about among all the various little odds and ends.

"The better to see you, my dear, and anybody else who may call upon me," said the grandmamma, in her odd broken English. Patty was nervous still and confused, longing to ask whether Rémy had made his appearance, and not daring to speak his name first. "Come down here," said her grandmother, deliberately putting on her spectacles. "What is this I hear from your cousin, mademoiselle? Do you know that no well-bred young woman gives her heart without permission; and so I told him, and sent him about his business," said the old lady, looking fixedly through her glasses. "Ah, little girls like you are fortunate to have grannies to sever them from importunate admirers, and to keep such histories from their parents' ear."

"What do you mean, grandmamma? I don't want to hide any thing," cried Patty, clasping her hands piteously, and bursting into tears. "Only I do care for him dearly, dearly, dearly, grandmamma," and turning passionately, in her confusion she knocked over a little odd-shaped box that was upon the table, and it opened and something fell out.

"Be careful, child! What have you done?" said the old lady, sharply. "Here, give the things to me."

"It's—it's something made of ivory, grandmamma," said stupid Patty, looking up bewildered. "What is it for?"

"Take care; take care. Those are my teeth, child. I can not eat comfortably without them," said the old lady, pettishly. "Here, give them to me," and as Patty put out her hand the old woman seized it in her own withered old fingers, and, holding the child by a firm grip, said again, "And so you love him?"

"What is the use—who cares?" answered poor Patty, desperately, "when you all want to send him away from me."

"We know better," Madame Capuchon was beginning, or going to begin, when there was a sudden crack at the door of the glass cupboard. It seemed to Patty as if her grandmother, changing her mind, cried out passionately, "No, they shall not send me away." In a moment, a figure coming, Patty knew not from whence, had sprung upon her, and caught the little thing in two strong arms, and held her close to a heart that was beating wildly. "You are my wife—you shall not escape me," cried Rémy, who had been silent all this while, but who could keep silence no longer, while Patty, blushing deeper and more deeply, then pale, then trembling, angry, and frowning all at once, tried in vain to escape.

Madame de Capuchon, against all historical facts, began to scream and ring her bell, and at that instant, as it happened, came voices in the passage, a confusion outside, the door of the room burst open, and Mrs. Maynard, rushing in, burst into a flood of tears, tore Patty away from Rémy, and clasped her to her heart.

"I tell you she is here, monsieur," Simonne was saying to Maynard himself, who was following his wife. As soon as he saw her there, with Patty in her arms, "Now, Marthe," he said, "you will at last believe what a goose you are at times;" and he began to laugh in a superior sort of fashion, and then he choked oddly and sat down with his face hidden in his hands. He had not even seen Rémy as yet, who thought it best to leave them all to themselves for a while, and went away through the glass cupboard to the dining-room again.

"But what is it all about?" asked Madame Capuchon from her bed.

"My child, I thought your cousin had robbed us of you," her mother sobbed.

It was all over now, and Patty, also in penitent tears, was confessing what had detained her. They could not be angry at such a time, they could only clasp her in their loving arms. All the little miniatures were looking on from their hooks on the wall, the old grandmother was shaking her frills in excitement, and nodding and blinking encouragement from her alcove.

"Look here, Henry," said she to her son-in-law; "I have seen the young man, and I think he is a very fine young fellow. In fact, he is now waiting in the dining-room, for I sent him away when I heard la petite coming. I wanted to talk to her alone. Félicie has written to me on the subject of their union; he wishes it, I wish it, Patty wishes it; oh, I can read little girls' faces: he has been called to the bar; my property will remain undivided; why do you oppose their marriage? I can not conceive what objection you can ever have had to it."

"What objection!" said the squire, astounded. "Why, you yourself warned me. Félicie writes as usual with an eye to her own interest —a grasping, covetous—"

"Hush, hush, dear; since Rémy has brought Patty safe back we have no reason to be angry," interceded Mrs. Maynard, gently pushing her husband towards the door.

The remembrance of her own youth had come back to her here in the place where she had suffered so long. Ah! she had acted a hard mother's part when she ever forgot it; and was not Patty her own child? and could she condemn her to a like trial? The old lady's hands and frills were trembling more and more by this time; she was not used to being thwarted; the squire also was accustomed to have his own way.

"My Félicie, my poor child, I can not suffer her to be spoken of in this way," cried Madame Capuchon, who at another time would have been the first to complain.

"Patty is only sixteen," hazarded Mrs. Maynard.

"I was sixteen when I married," said Madame Capuchon.

"Patty shall wait till she is sixty-six before I give her to a penniless adventurer," cried the squire, in great wrath.

"Very well," said the old lady, spitefully. "Now I will tell you what I have told him. As I tell you, he came to see me just now, and is at this moment, I believe, devouring the remains of the pie Simonne prepared for your luncheon. I have told him that he shall be my heir whether you give him Patty or not. I am not joking, Henry, I mean it. I like the young man exceedingly. He is an extremely well-bred young fellow, and will do us all credit, and a girl does not want money like a man."

Maynard shrugged his shoulders and looked at his wife.

"But, child, do you really care for him?" Patty's mother said reproachfully. "What can you know of him?" and she took both the little hands in hers.

Little Patty hung her head for a minute. "Oh mamma, he has told me every thing; he told me he did think of the money at first, but only before he knew me. Dear papa, if you talked to him you would believe him, indeed you would—indeed, indeed you would." Patty's imploring wistful glance touched the squire, and, as she said, Maynard could not help believing in Rémy when he came to talk things over quietly with him, and without losing his temper.

He found him in the dining-room, with a bottle of wine and the empty pie-dish before him; the young man had finished off every thing but the bones and the cork and the bottle. "I had no breakfast, sir," said Rémy, starting up, half laughing, half ashamed. "My grandmother told me to look in the cupboard, but, hearing your daughter's voice, I could not help going back just now."

"Such a good appetite should imply a good conscience," Maynard thought; and at last he relented, and eventually grew to be very fond of his son-in-law.

Patty and Rémy were married on her seventeenth birthday. I first saw them in the courtyard of the hotel, but afterwards at Sunnymede, where they spent last summer.

Madame Capuchon is not yet satisfied with the butter. It is a very difficult thing to get anywhere good. Simonne is as devoted as ever, and tries hard to satisfy her mistress.

JACK THE GIANT-KILLER.

CHAPTER I.

ON MONSTERS, ETC.

Most of us have read at one time or another in our lives the article entitled *Gigantes*, which is to be found in a certain well-known dictionary. It tells of that terrible warfare in which gods and giants, fighting in fury, hurled burning woods and rocks through the air, piled mountains upon mountains, brought seas from their boundaries, thundering, to overwhelm their adversaries ;—it tells how the gods fled in their terror into Egypt, and hid themselves in the shapes of animals, until Hercules, the giant-killer of those strange times, sprang up to rescue and deliver the world from the dire storm and confusion into which it had fallen. Hercules laid about him with his club. Others since then, our Jack among the rest, have fought with gallant courage and devotion, and given their might and their strength and their lives to the battle. That battle which has no end, alas ! and which rages from sunrise to sundown—although hero after hero comes forward, full of hope, of courage, of divine fire and indignation.

Who shall gainsay us, if nowadays some of us may perhaps be tempted to think that the tides of victory flow, not with the heroes, but with the giants ; that the gods of our own land are hiding in strange disguises ; that the heroes battling against such unequal odds are weary and sad at heart ; while the giants, unconquered still, go roaming about the country, oppressing the poor, devouring the children, laying homes bare and desolate ?

Here is *The Times* of to-day,* full of a strange medley and record of the things which are in the world together—Jacks and giants, and champion-belts and testimonials ; kings and queens, knights and castles and ladies, screams of horror, and shouts of laughter, and of encouragement or anger. Feelings and prejudices and events—all vibrating, urging, retarding, influencing one another.

And we read that some emperors are feasting in company at their splendid revels, while another is torn from his throne and carried away by a furious and angry foe, by a giant of the race which has filled the world with such terror in its time. Of late a young giant of that very tribe has marched through our own streets ; a

giant at play, it is true, and feeding his morbid appetite with purses, chains and watches, and iron park-railings ; but who shall say that he may not perhaps grow impatient as time goes on, and cry for other food.

And meanwhile people are lying dying in hospitals, victims of one or more of the cruel monsters, whose ill deeds we all have witnessed. In St. Bartholomew's wards, for instance, are recorded twenty-three cases of victims dying from what doctors call *delirium tremens*. Which Jack is there among us strong enough to overcome this giant with his cruel, fierce fangs, and force him to abandon his prey ? Here is the history of two men suffocated in a vat at Bristol by the deadly gas from spent hops. One of them, Ambrose, is hurrying to the other one's help, and gives up his life for his companion. It seems hard that such **men** should be sent unarmed into the clutch of such pitiable monsters as this ; and one grudges these two lives, and the tears of the widows and children. I might go on for many pages fitting the parable to the commonest facts of life. The great parochial Blunderbore still holds his own ; some of his castles have been seized, but others are impregnable ;—their doors are kept closed, their secrets are undiscovered.

Other giants, of the race of Cormoran, that " dwell in gloomy caverns, and wade over to the main-land to steal cattle," are at this instant beginning to creep from their foul dens, by sewers and stagnant waters, spreading death and dismay along their path. In the autumn their raids are widest and most deadly. Last spring I heard two women telling one another of a giant of the tribe of Cormoran camping down at Dorking in Surrey. A giant with a poisoned breath and hungry jaws, attacking not only cattle, but the harmless country people all about : children, and men, and women, whom he seized with his deadly gripe, and choked and devoured. Giant Blunderbore, it must be confessed, has had many a hard blow dealt him of late from one Jack and another. There is one gallant giant-killer at Fulham hard by, waging war with many monsters, the great blind giant Ignorance among the rest. Some valiant women, too, there are, who have armed themselves and gone forth with weak hands and tender strong hearts to do their best. I have seen some lately who are living in the very midst of the dreary labyrinth where one of the great Minotaurs of the city is lurking. They stand at the dark mouth of the poisonous caverns, warning and entreating those who, in their blindness and infatuation, are rushing thither, to beware. "I took a house and came," said one of them simply to my friend Mrs. K——, when she asked her how it happened that she was established there in the black heart of the city. All round her feet a little ragged tribe was squatting on the floor, and chirping, and spelling and learning a lesson which, pray Heaven, will last them their lives; and across the road, with pretty little crumpled mob-caps all awry on their brown heads, other children were sewing and at work under the quiet rule of their good teachers. The great business of the city was going on outside. The swarming docks were piled with bales, and crowded with workmen; the main thoroughfares streaming and teeming with a struggling life; the side streets silent, deserted, and strangely still. A bleak north-east wind was blowing down some of these gray streets. I have a vision before me now of one of them: a black deserted alley or passage, hung with some of those rags that seem to be like the banners of this reign of sorrow and sin. The wind swooped up over the stones, the rags waved and fell, and a colorless figure, passing up the middle of the dirty gutter pulled at its grimy shawl and crouched as it slid along. We may well say, we Londoners, See how far the east is from the west. I myself, coming home at night to the crowded cheerful station, and travelling back to the light of love, of warmth, of comfort, find myself dimly wondering whether those are not indeed our sins out yonder set away from us, in that dreary East of London district: our sins alive and standing along the roadside in rags, and crying out to us as we pass.

Here in our country cottage the long summer is coming to an end, in falling leaves and setting suns, and gold and russet, where green shoots were twinkling a little time ago. The banks of the river have shifted their colors, and the water, too, has changed. The song of the birds is over; but there are great flights in the air, rapid, mysterious. For weeks past we have been living in a gracious glamour and dazzle of light and warmth; and now, as we see it go, H. and I make plans, not unwillingly, for a winter to be passed between the comfortable walls of our winter home. The children, hearing our talk, begin to prattle of the treasures they will find in the nursery at London, as they call it. Dolly's head, which was unfortunately forgotten when we came away, and the panniers off the wooden donkey's back, and little neighbor Joan, who will come to ten again, in the doll's tea-things. Yesterday, when I came home from the railway-station across the bridge, little Anne, who had never in her short life seen the lamps of the distant town alight, came toddling up chattering about "de pooty tandles," and pulling my dress to make me turn and see them too.

To-night other lights have been blazing. The west has been shining along the hills with a gorgeous autumnal fire. From our terrace we have watched the lights and the mists as they succeed one another, streaming mysteriously before yonder great high altar. It has been blazing as if for a solemn ceremonial and burnt sacrifice. As we watch it, other people look on in the fields, on the hills, and from the windows of the town. Evening incense rises from the valley, and mounts up through the stillness. The waters catch the light and repeat it; the illumination falls upon us, too, as we look and see how high the heavens are in comparison with the earth; and suddenly, as we are waiting still, and looking and admiring, it is over—the glory has changed into peaceful twilight.

And so we come away, closing shutters and doors and curtains, and settling down to our common occupations and thoughts again; but outside another high service is beginning, and the lights of the great northern altar are burning faintly in their turn.

————————

CHAPTER II.

CORMORAN.

In the same way that fancy worlds and dreams do not seem meant for the dreary stone streets and smoky highways of life, neither do they belong to summer and holiday time, when reality is so vivid, so sweet, and so near. It is but a waste to dream of fairies dancing in rings, or peeping from the woods, when the singing and shining is in all the air, and the living sunshiny children are running on the lawn, and pulling at the flowers with their determined little fingers; and when there are butterflies and cuckoos and flowing streams, and the sounds of flocks and the vibrations of summer everywhere. Little Anne comes trotting up with a rose-head tight-crushed in her hand; little Margery has got a fern-leaf stuck into her hat; Puck, Peas-blossom, Cobweb, Moth, Mustard-seed, themselves, are all invisible in this great day-shine. The gracious fancy kingdom vanishes at cock-crow, we know. It is not among realities so wonderful and beautiful that we can scarce realize them that we must look for it. Its greatest triumphs are where no other light shines to brighten—by weary sick-beds: when distance and loneliness oppress. Who can not remember days and hours when a foolish conceit has come now and again, like a "flower growing on the edge of a precipice," to distract the dizzy thoughts from the dark depths below?

Certainly it was through no fancy world that poor John Trevithic's path led him wandering in life, but amid realities so stern and so pitiful at times that even his courage failed him now and then. He was no celebrated hero, though I have ventured to christen him after the great type of our childhood; he was an honest outspoken young fellow, with a stubborn temper and a tender heart, impressionable to outer things, although from within it was not often that any thing seemed to affect his even moods and cheerful temper. He was a bright-faced, broad-set young fellow, about six-and-twenty, with thick light hair and eagleish eyes, and lips and white teeth like a girl. His hands were like himself, broad and strong, with wide competent fingers that could fight and hold fast, if need be; and yet they were so clever and gentle withal that children felt safe in his grasp and did not think of crying, and people in trouble would clutch at them when he put them out. Perhaps Jack did not always understand the extent of the griefs for which his cheerful sympathy was better medicine, after all, than any mere morbid investigation into their depths could have proved to most of us.

The first time I ever heard of the Rev. John Trevithic was at Sandsea one morning, when my maid brought in two cards, upon which were inscribed the respective names of Miss Moineaux and Miss Triquett. I had taken a small furnished house at the seaside (for H. was ailing in those days and had been ordered salt air by the doctors); we knew nobody and nothing of the people of the place, so that I was at first a little bewildered by the visit; but I gathered from a few indescribable indications that the small fluttering lady who came in sideways was Miss Moineaux, and the bony, curly, scanty personage with the big hook-nose who accompanied her, Miss Triquett. They both sat down very politely, as people do who are utter strangers to you and about to ask you for money. Miss Moineaux fixed a little pair of clear meek imploring eyes upon me. Miss Triquett took in the apartment with a quick uncomfortable swoop or ball-like glance. Then she closed her eyes for an instant as she cleared her throat.

She need not have been at any great pains in her investigations; the story told itself. Two middle-aged women, with their desks and work-baskets open before them, and *The Times* and some Indian letters just come in, on the table, the lodging-house mats, screens, Windsor chairs, and druggets, a fire burning for H.'s benefit, an open window for mine, the pleasant morning wash and rush of the sea against the terrace upon which the windows opened, and the voices of H.'s grandchildren playing outside. I can see all the cheerful glitter now as I write. I loved the little place that strikes me so quaintly and kindly as I think of it. The sun shone all the time we were there; day by day I saw health and strength coming into my H.'s pale face. The house was comfortable, the walks were pleasant, good news came to us of those we loved. In short, I was happy there, and one can not always give a reason for being happy. In the mean time, Miss Triquett had made her observations with her wandering ball eyes.

"We called," she said in a melancholy, clerical voice, "thinking that you ladies might possibly be glad to avail yourselves of an opportunity for subscribing to a testimonial which we are about to present to our friend and pastor, the Reverend John Trevithic, M.A., and for which my friend Miss Moineaux and myself are fully prepared to receive subscriptions. You are perhaps not aware that we lose him on Tuesday week?"

"No, indeed," said I, and I am afraid my cap-strings began to rustle as they have a way of doing when I am annoyed.

"I'm sure I'm afraid you must think it a great liberty of us to call," burst in little Miss Moineaux, flurriedly, in short disconnected sentences. "I trust you will pardon us. They say it is *quite* certain he is going. We *have* had a suspicion — perhaps . . . ." Poor Miss Moineaux stopped short, and turned very red, for Triquett's eye was upon her. She continued falteringly, "Miss Triquett kindly suggested collecting a teapot and strainer, if possible — it depends, of course, upon friends and admirers. You know how one *longs* to show one's gratitude; and I'm sure in our hopeless state of apathy . . . . we had so neglected the commonest precautions—"

Here Miss Triquett interposed. "The authorities were greatly to blame. Mr. Trevithic did his part, no more; but it is peculiarly as a pastor and teacher that we shall miss him. It is a pity that you have not been aware of his ministry." (A roll of the eyes.) A little rustle and chirrup from Miss Moineaux.

"If the ladies had only heard him last Sunday afternoon—no, I mean the morning lecture."

"The **evening** appeal was still more impressive," said Miss Triquett. "I am looking forward anxiously to his farewell next Sunday."

It was really too bad. Were these two strange women who had come to take forcible possession of our morning-room about to discuss at any length the various merits of Mr. Trevithic's last sermon but two, but three, next but one, taking up my time, my room, asking for my money? I was fairly out of temper when, to my horror, H., in her flute voice from the sofa, where she had been lying under her soft silk quilt, said, "Mary, will you give these ladies a sovereign for me towards the teapot? Mr. Trevithic was at school with my Frank, and this is not, I think, the first sovereign he has had from me."

Miss Triquett's eyes roved over to the sofa. It must have seemed almost sacrilege to her to speak of Mr. Trevithic as a school-boy, or even to have known him in jackets. "It is as a tribute to the pastor that these subscriptions are collected," said she, with some dignity, "not on any lower—"

But it was too late, for little Miss Moineaux had already sprung forward with a grateful "Oh, thank you!" and clasped H.'s thin hand.

And so at last we got rid of the poor little women. They fluttered off with their prize, their thin silk dresses catching the wind as they skimmed along the sands, their little faded mantes and veils and curls and petticoats flapping feebly after them, their poor little well-worn feet patting off in search of fresh tribute to Trevithic.

"I declare they were both in love with him, ridiculous old gooses," said I. "How could you give them that sovereign?"

"He was a delightful boy," said H. (She melts to all school-boys still, though her own are grown men and out in the world.) "I used to be very angry with him; he and Frank were always getting into scrapes together," said H., with a smiling sigh, for Major Frank was on his way home from India, and the poor mother could trust herself to speak of him in her happiness. "I hope it is the right man," H. went on, laughing. "You must go and hear the farewell oration, Mary, and tell me how many of these little ladies are carried out of church."

They behaved like heroines. They never faltered or fainted, they gave no outward sign (except, indeed, a stifled sob here and there). I think the prospect of the teapot buoyed them up; for after the service two or three of them assembled in the churchyard, and eagerly discussed some measure of extreme emphasis. They were joined by the gentleman who had held the plate at the door, and then their voices died away into whispers, as the rector and Mr. Trevithic himself came out of the little side-door, where Miss Bellingham, the rector's daughter, had been standing waiting. The rector was a smug old gentleman in a nice Sunday tie. He gave his arm to his daughter, and trotted along, saying, "How do? how do?" to the various personages he passed.

The curate followed: a straight and active young fellow, with a bright face—a face that looked right and left as he came along. He didn't seem embarrassed by the notice he excited. The four little girls from Coote Court (so somebody called them) rushed forward to meet him, saying, "Good-bye, dear Mr. Trevithic, good-bye." Mrs. Myles herself, sliding off to her pony carriage, carrying her satin train all over her arms, stopped to smile, and to put out a slender hand, letting the satin stuff fall into the dust. Young Lord and Lady Wargrave were hurrying away with their various guests, but they turned and came back to say a friendly word to this popular young curate; and Colonel Hambledon, Lord Wargrave's brother, gave him a friendly nod, and said, "I shall look in one day before you go." I happened to know the names of all these people, because I had sat in Mrs. Myles's pew at church, and I had seen the Wargraves in London.

The subscribers to the teapot were invited to visit it at Mr. Philip's, in Cockspur Street, to whom the design had been intrusted. It was a very handsome teapot, as ugly as other teapots of the florid order, and the chief peculiarity was that a snake grasped by a clenched hand formed the handle, and a figure with bandages on its head was sitting on the melon on the lid. This was intended to represent an invalid recovering from illness. Upon one side was the following inscription:—

TO

THE REV. JOHN TREVITHIC, M.A.,

FROM HIS PARISHIONERS, AT SANDSEA,
IN GRATEFUL REMEMBRANCE OF HIS EXERTIONS DURING
THE CHOLERA SEASON OF 18—,
AND HIS SUCCESSFUL AND ENTERPRISING EFFORTS FOR THE IMPROVED
DRAINAGE OF HIGH STREET AND THE NEIGHBORING ALLEYS,
ESPECIALLY THOSE
KNOWN AS "ST. MICHAEL'S BUILDINGS."

Upon the other—

TO THE REV. JOHN TREVITHIC, M.A.

Both these inscriptions were composed by Major Coote, of Coote Court, a J. P. for the county. Several other magistrates had subscribed, and the presentation-paper was signed by most of the ladies of the town. I recognized the bold autograph of Louisa Triquett, and the lady-like quill of Sarah Moineaux, among the rest. H. figured as "Anon." down at the bottom.

Jack had honestly earned his teapot, the pride of his mother's old heart. He had worked hard during that unfortunate outbreak of cholera, and when the summer came round again, the young man had written quires, ridden miles, talked himself hoarse, about this neglected sewer in St. Michael's Buildings. The Town Council, finding that the whole of High Street would have to be taken up, and what a very se-

rious undertaking it was likely to be, were anxious to compromise matters, and they might have succeeded in doing so if it had not been for the young man's determination. Old Mr. Bellingham, who had survived some seventy cholera seasons, was not likely to be very active in the matter. Every body was away, as it happened, at that time, except Major Coote, who was easily talked over by any body; and Jobsen, the mayor, had got hold of him, and Trevithic had to fight the battle alone. One person sympathized with him from the beginning, and talked to her father, and insisted, very persistently, that he should see the necessity of the measure. This was Anne Bellingham, who, with her soft pink eyes fixed on Trevithic's face, listened to every word he said with interest—an interest which quite touched and gratified the young man, breathless and weary of persuading fish-mongers, of trying to influence the sleek obstinate butcher, and the careworn baker with his ten dusty children, and the stolid oil-and-color man, who happened to be the mayor that year. It seemed, indeed, a hopeless case to induce these worthy people to increase the rates, to dig up the High Street under their very windows, to poison themselves and their families, and drive away custom just as the season was beginning. John confessed humbly that he had been wrong, that he should have pressed the matter more urgently upon them in the spring, but he had been ill and away, if they remembered, and others had promised to see to it. It would be all over in a week, before their regular customers arrived.

Jack's eloquence succeeded in the end. How it came about I can scarcely tell—he himself scarcely knew. He had raised the funds, written to Lord Wargrave, and brought Colonel Hambledon himself down from town; between them they arranged with the contractors, and it was all settled almost, without any body's leave or authority. One morning, Trevithic, hearing a distant rumbling of wheels, jumped up from his breakfast and ran to the window. A file of carts and workmen were passing the end of the street; men with pickaxes and shovels; carts laden with strange-looking pipes and iron bars. Mr. Moffat, the indignant butcher, found a pit of ten feet deep at his shop-door that evening; and Smutt, the baker, in a fury, had to send his wife and children to her mother, to be out of the way of the mess. In a week, however, the whole thing was done, the pit was covered over, the foul stream they dreaded was buried down deep in the earth, and then in a little while the tide of opinion began to turn. When all the coast was in a terror and confusion, when cholera had broken out in one place and in another, and the lodging-houses were empty, the shop-keepers loud in complaints—at Sandsea, thanks to these "well-timed exertions," as people call draining, not a single case was reported, and though the season was not a good one for ordinary times, compared to other neighboring places, Sandsea was triumphant. Smutt was apologetic, Moffat was radiant, and so was Anne Bellingham in her quiet way. As for Miss Triquett, that devoted adherent, she nearly jumped for joy, hearing that the mayor of the adjoining watering-place was ill of the prevailing epidemic and not expected to live.

And then the winter went by, and this time of excitement passed over and the spring-time came, and John began to look about and ask questions about other men's doings and ways of life. It did not come upon him all in one day that he wanted a change, but little by little he realized that something was amiss. He himself could hardly tell what it was when Colonel Hambledon asked him one day. For one thing, I think his own popularity oppressed him. He was too good-humored and good-natured not to respond to the advances which met him

from one side and another, but there were but few of the people, except Miss Bellingham, with whom he felt any very real sympathy, beyond that of gratitude and good-fellowship. Colonel Hambledon was his friend, but he was almost constantly away, and the Wargraves, too, only came down from time to time. Jack would have liked to see more of Mrs. Myles, the pretty widow, but she was the only person in the place who seemed to avoid him. Colonel Coote was a silly good-natured old man; Miss Triquett and Miss Moineaux were scarcely companions. Talking to these ladies, who agreed with every word he said, was something like looking at his own face reflected in a spoon.

Poor Trevithic used to long to fly when they began to quote his own sermons to him; but his practice was better than his preaching, and, too kind-hearted to wound their feelings by any expression of impatience, he would wait patiently while Miss Moineaux nervously tried to remember what it was that had made such an impression upon her the last time she heard him; or Miss Triquett expressed her views on the management of the poor-kitchen, and read out portions of her correspondence, such as :—

"MY DEAREST MARIA,—I have delayed answering your very kind letter until the return of the warmer weather. Deeply as I sympathize with your well-meant efforts for the welfare of your poorer neighbors, I am sorry that I can not subscribe to the fund you are raising for the benefit of your curate."

"My aunt is blunt, very blunt," said Miss Triquett, explaining away any little awkwardness; "but she is very good, Mr. Trevithic, and you have sometimes said that we must not expect too much from our relations; I try to remember that."

It was impossible to be seriously angry Jack looked at her oddly, as she stood there by the pump in the market-place where she had caught him. How familiar the whole scene was to him; the village street, the gable of the rectory on the hill up above, Miss Triquett's immovable glare; —a stern vision of her used to rise before him long after, and make him almost laugh, looking back from a different place and world, with strange eyes that had seen so many things that did not exist for him in those dear tiresome old days.

On this occasion Jack and Miss Triquett were on their way to the soup-kitchen, where the district meeting was held once a month. Seeing Colonel Hambledon across the street, Trevithic escaped for a minute to speak to him, while Triquett went on. The ladies came dropping in one by one. It was a low room with a box-window on the street, and through an open door came a smell of roast-mutton from the kitchen, where a fire was burning; and a glimpse of a poultry-yard beyond the kitchen itself. There were little mottoes hung up all about in antique spelling, such as "Caste thy bridde upon ye watteres," the fancy and design of Mrs. Vickers, the present manager. She was very languid, and High Church, and opposed to Miss Triquett and her friend Miss Hutchetts, who had reigned there before Mrs. Vickers's accession. This housekeeping was a serious business. It was a labor of love, and of jealousy too: each district lady took the appointment in turn, while the others looked on and ratified her measures. There was a sort of house of commons composed of Miss Simmonds, who enjoyed a certain consideration because she was so very fat; good old Mrs. Fox, with her white hair; and Mrs. Champion, a sort of lord chancellor in petticoats; and when every body made objections the housekeeper sometimes resigned. Mrs. Vickers had held firm for some months, and here she is sorting out little tickets, writing little bills into a book, and comparing notes with the paper lists which the ladies have brought in.

"Two-and-sixpence a week for her lodging, three children, two deformed; owes fifteen shillings, deserted wife, can get no relief from the parent," Miss Moineaux reads out from her slip.

"That is a hopeless case," says Mrs. Champion; "let her go into the work-house."

"They have been there for months," says Miss Moineaux, perhaps.

"It is no use trying to help such people," says Miss Triquett, decidedly.

"Here is a pretty doctrine," cried Miss Simmonds: "the worse off folks are, the less help they may expect."

"When people are hopelessly lazy, dirty, and diseased," said Miss Triquett, with some asperity, "the money is only wasted which might be invaluable to the deserving. As long as I am intrusted with funds from this charity, I shall take care they are well bestowed."

"I—I have promised Gummers some assistance," faltered Miss Moineaux.

Miss Simmonds. "And she ought to have it, my dear."

Miss T. "I think you forget that is for Mr. Trevithic to decide."

Miss S. "I think you are forgetting your duty as a Christian woman."

Miss T. "I choose to overlook this insult. I will appeal to Mr. Trevithic."

Miss S. "Pray do not take the trouble to forgive me, Miss Triquett, or to appeal to any one. Never since Miss Hutchetts went away—"

Miss T. "Miss Hutchetts is my friend, and I will not allow her name to be—"

Exit Miss Moineaux in alarm to call for assistance. Miss Hutchetts, as they all know by experience, is the string of the shower-bath, the war-cry of the Amazons.

The battle was raging furiously when Miss Moineaux came back and flung herself devotedly into the *mêlée*. Miss Triquett was charging right and left, shells were flying, artillery rattling. It was a wonder the windows were not broken. Mrs. Champion was engaged with a hand-to-

hand fight with Miss Simmonds. Mrs. Vickers was laughing, Miss Moineaux was trembling; out of the window poured such a clamorous mob of words and swell of voices that John and the Colonel stopped to listen instead of going in. A dog and a puppy, attracted by the noise, stood wagging their tails in the sun.

"Hutchetts—Christian duty—dirty children — statistics — gammon," that was Miss Simmonds's voice, there was no mistaking. "Ladies, I beg," from Mrs. Vickers; and here the alarm-bell began to ring ten minutes before the children's dinner, and the sun shone, and the heads bobbed at the window, and all of a sudden there was a lull.

Trevithic, who like a coward had stopped outside while the battle was raging, ran up the low flight of steps to see what had been going on, now that the danger was over, the guns silent, and the field, perhaps, strewed with the dead and the dying. No harm was done, he found, when he walked into the room; only Miss Triquett was hurt, her feelings had been wounded in the engagement, and she was murmuring that her friend Miss Hutchetts's character as a gentlewoman had been attacked, but no one was listening to her. Mrs. Vickers was talking to a smiling and pleasant-looking lady, who was standing in the middle of the room. I don't know by what natural art Mary Myles had quieted all the turmoil which had been raging a minute before, but her pretty winsome ways had an interest and fascination for them all; for old Miss Triquett herself, who had not very much that was pleasant or pretty to look at, and who by degrees seemed to be won over, too, to forget Miss Hutchetts, in her interest in what this pretty widow was saying— it was only something about a school-treat in her garden. She stopped short and blushed as Trevithic came in. "Oh, here is Mr. Trevithic," she said; "I will wait till he has finished his business."

Jack would rather not have entered into it in her presence, but he began as usual, and plodded on methodically, and entered into the mysteries of soup-meat, and flannelling, and rheumatics, and the various ills and remedies of life, but he could not help feeling a certain scorn for himself, and embarrassment and contempt for the shame he was feeling; and as he caught Mary Myles's bright still eyes curiously fixed upon him, Jack wondered whether anywhere else in the world, away from these curious glances, he might not find work to do more congenial and worthy of the name. It was not Mrs. Myles's presence which affected him so greatly, but it seemed like the last grain in the balance against this chirruping tea-drinking life he had been leading so long. It was an impossibility any longer. He was tired of it. There was not one of these old women who was not doing her part more completely than he was, with more heart and good spirit than himself.

Some one had spoken to him of a work-house chaplaincy going begging at Hammersley, a great inland town on the borders of Wales.

Jack was like a clock which begins to strike as soon as the hands point to the hour. That very night he determined to go over and see the place; and he wrote to a friend of his at Hammersley to get him permission, and to tell the authorities of the intention with which he came.

CHAPTER III.

AN OGRESS.

WHEN John Trevithic, with his radiant, cheerful face, marched for the first time through the wards of St. Magdalene's, the old creatures propped up on their pillows to see him pass, both the master and mistress went with him, duly impressed with his possible importance, and pointed out one person and another; and as the mighty trio advanced, the poor souls cringed, and sighed, and greeted them with strange nods, and gasps, and contortions. John trudged along, saying little, but glancing right and left with his bright eyes. He was very much struck, and somewhat overcome by the sight of so much that was sad, and in orderly rows, and a blue cotton uniform. Was this to be his charge? all these hundreds of weary years, all these aching limbs and desolate waifs from stranded homes, this afflicted multitude of past sufferings? He said nothing, but walked along with his hands in his pockets, looking in vain to see some face brighten at the master's approach. The faces worked, twitched, woke up eagerly, but not one caught the light which is reflected from the heart. What endless wards, what a labyrinth of woes inclosed in the white-washed walls! A few poor prints of royal personages, and of hop-gathering, and Christmas, out of the *London News*, were hanging on them. Whitewash and blue cotton, and weary faces in the women's wards; whitewash and brown fustian, and sullen, stupid looks in the men's: this was all Trevithic carried away in his brain that first day; — misery and whitewash, and a dull choking atmosphere, from which he was ashamed almost to escape out into the street, into the square, into the open fields outside the town, across which his way led back to the station.

Man proposes, and if ever a man honestly proposed and determined to do his duty, it was John Trevithic, stretched out in his railway corner, young and stout of heart and of limb, eager for change and for work. He was not very particular; troubles did not oppose him morbidly. He had not been bred up in so refined a school that poverty and suffering frightened him; but the sight of all this hopelessness, age, failure, all neatly stowed away, and whitewashed over in those stony wards, haunted him all the way home. They haunted him all the way up to the rectory, where he was to dine that evening, and between the intervals of talk, which were pretty frequent after Miss Bellingham had left the room and the two gentlemen to their claret.

Jack had almost made up his mind, and indeed he felt like a traitor as he came into the drawing-room, and he could not help seeing how Anne brightened up as she beckoned him across the room and made him sit down beside her. A great full harvest-moon was shining in at the window, a late autumnal bird was singing its melancholy song, a little wind blew in and rustled round the room, and Anne, in her muslins and laces, looked like a beautiful pale pensive dream-lady by his side. Perhaps he might not see her again, he thought, rather sentimentally, and that henceforth their ways would lie asunder. But how kind she had been to him! How pretty she was! What graceful womanly ways she had! How sorry he should be to part from her! He came away and said good-bye quite sadly, looking in her face with a sort of apology, as if to beg her pardon for what he was going to do. He had a feeling that she would be sorry that he should leave her—a little sorry, although she was far removed from him. The birds sang to him all the way home along the lane, and Jack slept very sound, and awoke in the morning quite determined in his mind to go. As his landlady brought in his breakfast-tray he said to himself that there was nothing more to keep him at Sandsea, and then he sat down and wrote to Mr. Bellingham that instant, and sent up the note by Mrs. Bazley's boy.

A little later in the day, Trevithic went over to the rectory himself. He wanted to get the matter quite settled, for he could not help feeling sorry as he came along, and wondering whether he had been right, after all. He asked for the rector, and the man showed him into the study, and in a minute more the door opened, but it was Miss Bellingham, not her father, who came in.

She looked very strange and pale, and put out two trembling hands, in one of which she was holding John's letter.

"Oh, Mr. Trevithic, what is this? what does this mean?" she said.

What indeed? he need never have written the words, for in another minute suddenly Miss Bellingham burst into tears.

They were very ill-timed tears as far as her own happiness was concerned, as well as that of poor John Trevithic, who stood by full of compassion, of secret terror at his own weakness, of which for the first time he began to suspect the extent. He was touched and greatly affected. He walked away to the fireplace and came back and stood before her, an honest, single-hearted young fellow, with an immense compassion for weak things, such as women and children, and a great confidence in himself; and as he stood there he flushed in a struggle of compassion, attraction, revulsion, pity, and cruel disappointment. Those tears coming just then relieved Anne Bellingham's heavy heart as they flowed in a passionate stream, and at the same time they quenched many a youthful fire, destroyed in their track many a dream of battle and victory, of persevering struggle and courageous efforts for the rights of the wronged upon earth. They changed the course of Trevithic's life at the time, though in the end, perhaps, who shall say that it was greatly altered by the complainings and foolish fondness of this poor soul whom he was now trying to quiet and comfort? I, for my part, don't believe that people are so much affected by circumstance in the long run as some people would have it. We think it a great matter that we turned to the right or the left; but both paths go over the hill. Jack, as his friends called him, had determined to leave a certain little beaten track of which he was getting weary, and he had come up to say good-bye to a friend of his, and to tell her that he was going, and this was the result.

She went on crying—she could not help herself now. She was a fragile-looking little thing, a year or so younger than Jack, her spiritual curate and future husband, whom she had now known for two years.

"You see there is nothing particular for me to do here," he stammered, blushing. "A great strong fellow like myself ought to be putting his shoulder to the wheel."

"I—I had so hoped that you had been happy here with us," said Miss Bellingham.

"Of course I have been happy—happier than I have ever been in my life," said Jack, with some feeling; "and I shall never forget your kindness; but the fact is, I have been too happy. This is a little haven where some worn-out old veteran might recruit and grow young again in your kind keeping. It's no place for a raw recruit like myself."

"Oh, think—oh, think of it again," faltered Anne. "Please change your mind. We would try and make it less—less worldly—more like what you wish."

"No, dear lady," said Trevithic, half smiling, half sighing. "You are goodness and kindness itself, but I must be consistent, I'm afraid. Nobody wants me here; I may be of use elsewhere, and . . . . Oh Miss Bellingham, don't—don't—pray don't—".

"You know—you know you are wanted here," cried Miss Bellingham; and the momentous tears began to flow again down her cheeks all unchecked, though she put up her fingers to hide them. She was standing by a table, a slim creature, in a white dress. "Oh, forgive me!" she sobbed, and she put out one tear-washed hand to him, and then she pushed him away with her weak violence, and went and flung herself down into her father's big chair, and leaned against the old red cushion in an agony of grief and shame and despair. Her little dog began barking furiously at John, and her bird began to sing, and all the afternoon sun was streaming and blinding into the room.

"Oh, don't, don't despise me!" moaned the poor thing, putting up her weary hand to her head. The action was so helpless, the voice so pathetic, that Trevithic resisted no longer.

"Despise you, my poor darling," said John,

utterly melted and overcome, and he stooped over, and took the poor little soul into his arms. "I see," he said, "that we two must never be parted again, and if I go, you must come with me. . . . ."

It was done. It was over. When Jack dashed back to his lodging, it was in a state of excitement so great that he had hardly time to ask himself whether it was for the best or the worst. The tears of the trembling appealing little quivering figure had so unnerved him, so touched and affected him, that he had hardly known what he said or what he did not say, his pity and innate tenderness of heart had carried him away; it was more like a mother than a lover that he took this poor little fluttering bird into his keeping, and vowed and prayed to keep it safe. But every thing was vague and new and unlifelike as yet. The future seemed floating with shadows and vibrations, and waving and settling into the present. He had left home a free man, with a career before him, without ties to check him or to hold him back (except, indeed, the poor old mother in her little house at Barfleet, but that clasp was so slight, so gentle, so unselfish, that it could scarcely be counted one now). And now "Chained and bound by the ties of our sins," something kept dinning in his bewildered brain.

Mrs. Bazley opened the door with her usual grin of welcome, and asked him if he had lunched, or if she should bring up the tray. Trevithic shook his head, and brushed past her up the stairs, leaping three or four at a time, and he dashed into his own room and banged the door, and went and leaned against the wall, with his hand to his head, in a dizzy, sickened, miserable bewilderment, at which he himself was shocked and frightened. What had he done, what would this lead to? He paced up and down his room until he could bear it no longer, and then he went back to the rectory. Anne had been watching for him, and came out to meet him, and slid her jealous hand in his arm.

"Come away," she whispered. "There are some people in the house. Mary Myles is there talking to papa. I have not told him yet. I can't believe it enough to tell any one."

John could hardly believe it either, or that this was the Miss Bellingham he had known hitherto. She seemed so dear, so changed, this indolent county beauty, this calm young mistress of the house, now bright, quick, excited, moved to laughter: a hundred sweet tints and colors seemed awakened and brought to light which he had never noticed or suspected before.

"I have a reason," Anne went on. "I want you to speak of this to no one but me and papa. I will tell you very soon, perhaps to-morrow. Here, come and sit under the lilac-tree, and then they can not see us from the drawing-room."

Anne's reason was this, that the rector of a living in her father's gift was dying, but she was not sure that Jack would be content to wait for a dead man's shoes, and she gave him no hint of a scheme she had made.

The news of John's departure spread very quickly, but that of his engagement was only suspected; and no allusion to his approaching marriage was made when the teapot was presented to him in state.

I have ventured to christen my hero Jack, after a celebrated champion of that name; but we all know how the giant-killer himself fell asleep in the forest soon after he received the badge of honor and distinction to which he was so fairly entitled. Did poor John Trevithic, now the possessor of the teapot of honor, fall asleep thus early on his travels and forget all his hopes and his schemes? At first, in the natural excitement of his engagement, he put off one plan and another, and wrote to delay his application for the chaplaincy of the work-house. He had made a great sacrifice for Anne; for he was not in love with her, as he knew from the very beginning; but he soon fell into the habit of caring for her and petting her, and, little by little, her devotion and blind partiality seemed to draw him nearer and nearer to the new ways he had accepted. The engagement gave great satisfaction. Hambledon shook him warmly by the hand, and said something about a better vocation than Bumbledom and work-houses. Jack bit his lips. It was a sore point with him, and he could not bear to think of it.

How Anne had begged and prayed and insisted, and put up her gentle hands in entreaty, when he had proposed to take her to live at Hammersley.

"It would kill me," she said. "Oh John, there is something much better, much more useful for you coming in a very little while. I wanted people to hear of our marriage and of our new home together. Poor old Mr. Jorken is dead. Papa is going to give us his Lincolnshire living; it is his very own. Are you too proud to take any thing from me, to whom you have given your life?" And her wistful entreaties were not without their effect, as she clung to him with her strange jealous eagerness. The determined young fellow gave in again and again. He had fallen into one of those moods of weakness and irresolution of which one has heard even among the fiercest and boldest of heroes. It was so great a sacrifice to him to give up his dreams that it never occurred to him for a moment that he was deserting his flag. It was a strange transformation which had come over this young fellow, of which the least part was being married.

I don't know whether the old ladies were disappointed or not that he did not actually go away as soon as was expected. The announcement of his marriage, however, made up for every thing else, and they all attended the ceremony. Mr. and Mrs. Trevithic went away for their honey-moon, and to see old Mrs. Trevithic at Bardeet, and then they came back to the rectory until the house in Lincolnshire should be ready to receive them.

For some time after his marriage Jack could hardly believe that so great an event had come about so easily. Nothing was much changed; the port-wine twinkled in the same decanters, the old rector dozed off in his chair after dinner, the sunset streamed into the dining-room from the same gap in the trees which skirted the churchyard. Anne, in the drawing-room in her muslins and lilac ribbons, sewed her worsted work in the corner by the window, or strummed her variations on the piano-forte. Tumty tinkle tumty—no—tinkle tumty tumty, as she corrected herself at the same place in the same song. "Do you know the songs without words?" she used to say to him when he first came. Know them! At the end of six weeks poor Jack could have told you every note of the half-dozen songs which Anne had twittered out so often, only she put neither song nor words to the notes, nor time, nor any thing but pedals and fingers. One of these she was specially fond of playing. It begins with a few tramping chords, and climbs on to a solemn blast that might be sounded in a cathedral or at the triumphant funeral of a warrior dying in victory. Anne had taken it into her head to play this with expression, and to drag out the crisp chords—some of them she thought sounded prettier in a higher octave—and then she would look up with an archly affectionate smile as she finished. Jack used to respond with a kind little nod of the head at first, but he could not admire his wife's playing, and he wished she would mind her music and not be thinking of herself and nodding at him all the time. Had he promised to stuff up his ears with cotton-wool and to act fibs at the altar? He didn't know; he rather thought he had—he—psha! Where was that number of the *North British Review?* and the young man went off into his study to look for it and to escape from himself.

Poor Jack! He dimly felt now and then that all his life he should have to listen to tunes such as these, and be expected to beat time to them. Like others before and since, he began to feel that what one expects and what is expected of one are among the many impossible conditions of life. You don't get it and you don't give it, and you never will as long as you live, except, indeed, when Heaven's sacred fire of love comes to inspire and teach you to do unconsciously and gladly what is clearer and nearer and more grateful than the result of hours of straining effort and self-denial.

But these hours were a long way off as yet, and Jack was still asking himself how much longer it would all last, and how could it be that he was here settled for life and a married man, and that that pale little woman with the straight smooth light hair was his wife, and that fat old gentleman fast asleep, who had been his rector a few weeks ago, was his father-in-law now, while all the world went on as usual, and nothing had changed except the relations of these three people to each other?

Poor Jack! He had got a treasure of a wife, I suppose. Anne Bellingham had ruled at the rectory for twenty-four years with a calm, despotic sway that old Mr. Bellingham never attempted to dispute. Gentle, obstinate, ladylike, graceful, with a clear complexion, and one of those thin transparent noses which some people admire, she glided about in her full flitting skirts, feeling herself the prop and elegant comforter of her father's declining years. She used to put rosebuds into his study; and though old Mr. Bellingham didn't care for flowers, and disliked any thing upon his table, he never thought of removing the slender glass fabric his daughter's white fingers had so carefully ornamented. She took care that clean muslin covers, with neat little bows at each corner, should duly succeed one another over the back of the big study-chair. It is true the muslin scratched Mr. Bellingham's bald head, and he once ventured to remove the objectionable pinafore with his careful, clumsy old fingers; but next day he found it was firmly and neatly stretched down in its place again, and it was beyond his skill to unpick the threads. Anne also took care that her father's dressing-things should be put out for dinner; and if the poor old gentleman delayed or tried to evade the ceremony, the startled man who cleaned the plate and waited upon the family was instructed to tell his master that the dressing-bell had rung: housemaids came in to tidy the room; windows were opened to renew the air: the poor rector could only retire and do as he was bid. How Anne had managed all her life to get her own way in every thing is more than I can explain. It was a very calm, persistent, commonplace way, but every one gave in to it. And so it happened that as soon as Jack was her husband, Anne expected that he was to change altogether; see with her pink, watery eyes; care for the things she cared for; and be content henceforth with her mild aspirations after county society in this world, and a good position in the next. Anne imagined, in some vague manner, that these were both good things to be worked out together by punctuality on Sundays, family prayer, a certain amount of attention to the neighbors (varying, of course, with the position of the persons in question), and due regard for the decencies of life. To see her rustling into church in her long silk dress and French bonnet, with her smooth bands of hair, the slender hands neatly gloved, and the prayer-book, hymn-book, pocket-handkerchief, and smelling-bottle, all her little phylacteries in their places, was an example to the neighborhood—to the vulgar Christians straggling in from the lodging-houses and the town, and displaying their flyaway hats or highly pomatumed heads of hair; to the little charity children, gaping at her over the wooden gallery; to St. Mary Magdalene up in the window, with her tangled locks; to Mrs. Coote herself, who always came in late, with her four little girls tumbling over her dress and shuffling after her; not to mention Trevithic himself, up in his reading-desk, leaning back in his chair. For the last six months, in the excitement of his presence, in the disturbance of her usual equa-

ble frame of mind, it was scarcely the real Anne Bellingham he had known, or maybe, perhaps, it was the real woman stirred out of her Philistinism by the great tender hand of nature and the wonderful inspiration of love. Now, day by day her old ways began to grow upon her. Jack had not been married three weeks before a sort of terror began quietly to overwhelm him, a terror of his wife's genteel infallibility. As for Anne, she had got what she wanted; she had cried for the moon, and it was hers; and she, too, began almost immediately to feel that now she had got it she did not know what to do with it exactly. She wanted it to turn the other way, and it wouldn't go—always to rise at the same hour, and it seemed to change day by day on purpose to vex her.

And then she cried again, poor woman; but her tears were of little avail. I suppose Jack was very much to blame, and certainly at this time his popularity declined a little, and people shrugged their shoulders and said he was a lucky young fellow to get a pretty girl and a good living and fifteen thousand pounds in one morning, and that he had feathered his nest well. And so he had, poor fellow, only too well, for to be sunk in a moral feather-bed is not the most enviable of fates to an active-minded man of six or seven and twenty.

The second morning after their return, Anne had dragged him out to her favorite lilac-tree bench upon the height in the garden, from whence you can see all the freshness of the morning brightening from bay to bay, green close at hand, salt wave and more green down below, busy life on land, and a flitting, drifting, white-sailed life upon the water. As Trevithic looked at it all with a momentary admiration, his wife said:—

"Isn't it much nicer to be up here with me, John, than down in those horrid lodgings in the town?"

And John laughed, and said, "Yes, the air was very delicious."

"You needn't have worked so hard at that draining if you had been living up here," Anne went on, quite unconsciously. "I do believe one might live forever in this place and never get any harm from those miserable dens. I hear there is small-pox in Mark's Alley. Promise me, dear, that you will not go near them."

"I am afraid I must go if they want me," said John.

"No, dearest," Anne said, gently. "You have to think of me first now. It would be wrong of you to go. Papa and I have never had the small-pox."

Trevithic didn't answer. As his wife spoke, something else spoke too. The little boats glittered and scudded on; the whole sight was as sweet and prosperous as it had been a minute before; but he was not looking at it any more; a strange new feeling had seized hold of him, a devil of sudden growth, and Trevithic was so little used to self-contemplation and inner experience, that it shocked him and frightened him to find himself standing there calmly talking to his wife—without any quarrel, angry in his heart; without any separation, parted from her.

"Anne and I could not be farther apart at this instant," thought John, "if I were at the other side of that sea, and she standing here all alone."

"What is the matter?" said poor Anne, affectionately brushing a little thread off his coat.

"Can't you understand?" said he, drawing away.

"Understand?" Anne repeated. "I know that you are naughty, and want to do what you must not think of."

"I thought that when I married you, you cared for the things that I care about," cried poor John, exasperated by her playfulness, "and that you understood that a man must do his business in life, and that marriage does not absolve him from every other duty. I thought you cared —you said you did—for the poor people in trouble down there." Then, melting, "Don't make it difficult for me to go to them, dear."

"No, dear John. I could not possibly allow it," said his wife, decidedly. "You are not a doctor; it is not your business to nurse small-pox patients. Papa never thinks of going where there is infection."

"My dear Anne," said John, fairly out of temper, "nobody ever thought your father had done his duty by the place, and you must allow your husband to go his own way, and not interfere any more."

"It is very, very wrong of you, John, to say such things," said Anne, flushing, and speaking very slowly and gently. "You forget yourself and me too, I think, when you speak so coarsely. You should begin your reforms at home, and learn to control your temper before you go and preach to people with dreadful illnesses. They can not possibly want you, or be in a fit state to be visited."

If Anne had only lost her temper, flared up at him, talked nonsense, he could have borne it better; but there she stood, quiet, composed, infinitely his superior in her perfect self-possession. Jack left her, all ashamed of himself, in a fume and a fury, as he strode down into the town.

The small-pox turned out to be a false alarm, spread by some ingenious parishioners who wished for relief and who greatly disliked the visits of the excellent district ladies, and the matter was compromised. But that afternoon Miss Triquett, meeting John in the street, gave a penetrating and searching glance into his face. He looked out of spirits. Miss Triquett noticed it directly, and her heart, which had been somewhat hardened against him, melted at once.

Jack and his wife made it up. Anne relented, and something of her better self brought her to meet him half-way. Once more the strange accustomed feeling came to him, on Sundays especially. Old Billy Hunsden came cloppeting into church just as usual. There was the clerk, with his toothless old warble joining in with the chirp of the charity-school children. The three rows of grinning little faces were peering at him from the organ-loft. There was the empty bench at the top, where the mistress sat throned in state; the marble rolled down in the middle of the second lesson, with all the children looking preternaturally innocent and as if they did not hear the noise; the old patches of color were darting upon the pulpit cushion from St. Mary Magdalene's red scarf in the east window. These are all small things, but they have taken possession of my hero, who is preaching away, hardly knowing what he says, but conscious of Anne's wistful gaze from the rectory pew, and of the curious eyes of all the old women in the free seats, who dearly love a timely word, and who have made up their minds to be stirred up that Sunday. It is not a bad sermon, but it is of things neither the preacher nor his congregation care very much to hear.

CHAPTER IV.

JACK GOES TO SLEEP IN THE WOOD.

FEATHERSTON VICARAGE was a quaint, dreary, silent old baked block of bricks and stucco, standing on one of those low Lincolnshire hillocks—I do not know the name for them. They are not hills, but mounds; they have no shape or individuality, but they roll in on every side; they inclose the horizon; they stop the currents of fresh air; they give no feature to the foreground. There was no reason why the vicarage should have been built upon this one, more than upon any other of the monotonous waves of the dry ocean of land which spreads and spreads about Featherston, unchanging in its monotonous line. To look from the upper windows of the vicarage is like looking out at sea, with nothing but the horizon to watch—a dull sand-and-dust horizon, with monotonous waves and lines that do not even change or blend like the waves of the sea.

Anne was delighted with the place when she first came. Of course it was not to compare with Sandsea for pleasantness and freshness, but the society was infinitely better. Not all the lodging-houses at Sandsea could supply such an eligible circle of acquaintances as that which came driving up day after day to the vicarage door. The carriages, after depositing their owners, would go champing up the road to the little tavern of "The Five Horseshoes," at the entrance of the village, in search of hay and beer for the horses and men. Anne in one afternoon entertained two honorables, a countess, and two Lady Louisas. The countess was Lady Kidderminster and one of the Lady Louisas was her daughter. The other was a nice old maid, a cousin of Mrs. Myles, and she told Mrs. Trevithie something more of poor Mary Myle's married life than Anne had ever known before.

"It is very distressing," said Anne, with a ladylike volubility, as she walked across the lawn with her guest to the carriage, "when married

people do not get on comfortably together. Depend upon it, there are generally faults on both
sides. I dare say it is very uncharitable of me,
but I generally think the woman is to blame when
things go wrong," said Anne, with a little conscious smirk. "Of course, we must be content
to give up some things when we marry. Sandsea was far pleasanter than this as a residence;
but where my husband's interests were concerned, Lady Louisa, I did not hesitate. I hope
to get this into some order in time, as soon as I
can persuade Mr. Trevithic . . . ."

"You are quite right, quite right," said Lady
Louisa, looking round approvingly at the grass-
grown walks and straggling hedges. "Although
Mary is my own cousin, I always felt that she
did not understand poor Tom. Of course, he
had his little fidgety ways like the rest of us."

(Mary had never described her husband's little fidgety ways to any body at much length, and
if brandy and blows and oaths were among them,
these trifles were forgotten now that Tom was
respectably interred in the family vault and beyond reproaches.)

Lady Louisa went away favorably impressed
by young Mrs. Trevithic's good sense and high-
mindedness. Anne, too, was very much pleased
with her afternoon. She went and took a complacent turn in her garden after the old lady's
departure. She hardly knew where the little
paths led to as yet, nor the look of the fruit-walls
and of the twigs against the sky, as people do
who have well paced their garden-walks in rain,
wind, and sunshine, in spirits and disquiet, at
odd times and sad times and happy ones. It
was all new to Mrs. Trevithic, and she glanced
about as she went, planning a rose-tree here, a
creeper there, a clearance among the laurels.
"I must let in a peep of the church through
that elm-clump, and plant some fuchsias along
that bank," she thought. (Anne was fond of
fuchsias.) "And John must give me a hen-house.
The cook can tend to that. The place looks
melancholy and neglected without any animals
about; we must certainly buy a pig. What a
very delightful person Lady Kidderminster is;
she asked me what sort of carriage we meant to
to keep—I should think with economy we *might*
manage a pair. I shall get John to leave every
thing of that sort to me. I shall give him so
much for his pocket-money and charities, and do
the very best I can with the rest." And Anne
sincerely meant it when she made this determination, and walked along better pleased than ever,
feeling that with her hand to pilot it along the
tortuous way their ship could not run aground,
but would come straight and swift into the haven
of country society, for which they were making,
drawn by a couple of prancing horses, and a
riding-horse possibly for John. And seeing her
husband coming through the gate and crossing
the sloping lawn, Anne hurried to meet him
with glowing pink cheeks and tips to her eyelids
and nose, eager to tell him her schemes and adventures.

Trevithic himself had come home tired and

dispirited, and he could scarcely listen to his
wife's chirrups with very great sympathy or encouragement.

"Lady Kidderminster wishes us to set up a
carriage and a pair of horses!" poor Trevithic
cried out aghast. "Why, my dear Anne, you
must be—must be . . . . What do you imagine
our income to be?"

"I know very well what it is," Anne said,
with a nod; "better than you do, sir. With
care and economy a very great deal is to be done.
Leave every thing to me, and don't trouble your
foolish old head."

"But, my dear, you must listen for one minute," Trevithic said. "One thousand a year is
not limitless. There are calls and drains upon
our incomings—"

"That is exactly what I wanted to speak to
you about, John," said his wife, gravely. "For
one thing, I have been thinking that your mother has a very comfortable income of her own,"
Anne said, "and I am sure she would gladly . . ."

"I have no doubt she would," Trevithic interrupted, looking full in his wife's face; "and
that is the reason that I desire the subject may
never be alluded to again, either to her or to
me." He looked so decided and stern, and his
gray eagle eyes opened wide in a way his wife
knew that meant no denial. Vexed as she was,
she could not help a momentary womanly feeling of admiration for the undaunted and decided rule of the governor of this small kingdom in
which she was vicegerent; she felt a certain
pride in her husband, not in what was best in his
temper and heart, but in the outward signs that
any one might read. His good looks, his manly
bearing, his determination before which she had
to give way again and again, impressed her oddly; she followed him with her eyes as he walked away into the house, and went on with her
calculations as she still paced the gravel path, de-
termining to come back secretly to the charge, as
was her way, from another direction, perhaps failing and again only to ponder upon a fresh attack.

And meanwhile Anne was tolerably happy
trimming her rose-trees, and arranging and re-
arranging the furniture, visiting at the big houses,
and corresponding with her friends, and playing
on the piano, and with her baby, in time, when
it came to live with them in the vicarage. Trevithic was tolerably miserable, fuming and con-
suming his days in a restless, impatient search
for the treasures which did not exist in the arid
fields and lanes round about the vicarage. He
certainly discovered a few well-to-do farmers riding about their inclosures on their rough horses,
and responding with surly nods to his good-
humored advances; a few old women selling
lollipops in their tidy front kitchens; with shining pots and pans, and starch caps, the very pictures of respectability; little tidy children trotting to school along the lanes, hand in hand,
with all the strings on their pinafores, and hard-
working mothers scrubbing their parlors, or
hanging out their linen to dry. The cottages
were few and far between, for the farmers farm-

ed immense territories; the laborers were out in the fields at sunrise, and toiled all day, and staggered home worn out and stupefied at night; the little pinafores released from school at midday would trot along the furrows with their fathers' and brothers' dinners tied up in bundles, and drop little frightened courtesies along the hedges when they met the vicar on his rounds. Dreary, dusty rounds they were—illimitable circles. The country folks did not want his sermons, they were too stupid to understand what he said, they were too aimless and dispirited. Jack the Giant-Killer's sleep lasted exactly three years in Trevithic's case, during which the time did not pass, it only ceased to be. Once old Mr. Bellingham paid them a visit, and once Mrs. Trevithic, senior, arrived, with her cap-boxes, and then every thing again went on as usual until Dulcie came to live with her father and mother in the old sun-baked, wasp-haunted place.

Dulcie was a little portable almanac to mark the time for both of them, and the seasons and the hour of the day, something in this fashion:—

Six months and Dulcie began to crawl across the drugged floor of her father's study; nine months to crow and hold out her arms; a year must have gone by, for Dulcie was making sweet inarticulate chatterings and warblings, which changed into words by degrees—wonderful words of love and content and recognition, after her tiny lifelong silence. Dulcie's clock marked the time of day something in this fashion:—

Dulcie's breakfast o'clock.

Dulcie's walk in the garden o'clock.

Dulcie's dinner o'clock.

Dulcie's bedtime o'clock, etc.

All the tenderness of Jack's heart was Dulcie's. Her little fat fingers would come tapping and scratching at his study door long before she could walk. She was not in the least afraid of him, as her mother was sometimes. She did not care for his sad moods, nor sympathize with his ambitions, nor understand the pangs and pains he suffered, the regrets and wounded vanities and aspirations. Was time passing, was he wasting his youth and strength, in that forlorn stagnant Lincolnshire fen? What was it to her? Little Dulcie thought that, when he crossed his legs and danced her on his foot, her papa was fulfilling all the highest duties of life; and when she let him kiss her soft cheek, it did not occur to her that every wish of his heart was not gratified. Hard-hearted, unsympathetic, trustful, and appealing little comforter and companion! Whatever it might be to Anne, not even Lady Kidderminster's society soothed and comforted Jack as Dulcie's did. This small Egyptian was a hard task-mistress, for she gave him bricks to make without any straw, and kept him a prisoner in a land of bondage; but for her he would have thrown up the work that was so insufficient for him, and crossed the Red Sea, and chanced the fortunes of life; but with Dulcie and her mother hanging to the skirts of his long black clerical coat, how could he go! Ought he to go? £400 a year is a large sum to get together,

but a small one to provide for three people—so long as a leg of mutton costs seven shillings, and there are but twenty shillings in the pound and 365 days in the year.

It was a hot, sultry afternoon, the dust was lying thick upon the lanes, on the country roads, that went creeping away white in the glare to this and that distant sleepy hollow. The leaves in the hedges were hanging upon their stalks; the convolvuluses and blackberries drooped their heads beneath the clouds that rose from the wreaths and piles of dust along the way. Four o'clock was striking from the steeple, and echoing through the hot still air; nobody was to be seen, except one distant figure crossing a stubble-field; the vicarage windows were close-shuttered, but the gate was on the latch, and the big dog had just sauntered lazily through. Anne heard the clock strike from her darkened bedroom, where she was lying upon the sofa resting. Dulcie, playing in her nursery, counted the strokes. "Tebben, two, one; nonner one," that was how she counted. John heard the clock strike as he was crossing the dismal stubble-field; every thing else was silent. Two butterflies went flitting before him in the desolate glare. It was all so still, so dreary, and feverish, that he tried to escape into a shadier field, and to force his way through a gap in the parched hedge, regardless of farmer Burr's fences and restrictions.

On the other side of the hedge there was a smaller field, a hollow with long grasses and nut-hedges and a little shade, and a ditch over which Trevithic sprang with some remnant of youthful spirit. He sprang, breaking through the briers and countless twigs and limp-wreathed leaves, making a foot-standing for himself among the lank grasses and dull autumn flowers on the other side, and as he sprang he caught a sight of something lying in the ditch, something with half-open lips and dim glazed eyes turned upward under the crossing diamond network of the shadow and light of the briers.

What was this that was quite still, quite inanimate, lying in the sultry glow of the autumn day? Jack turned a little sick, and leaped back down among the dead leaves, and stooped over a wan helpless figure lying there motionless and ghastly, with its head sunk back in the dust and tangled weeds. It was only a worn and miserable-looking old man, whose meek, starved, weary face was upturned to the sky, whose wan lips were drawn apart, and whose thin hands were clutching at the weeds. Jack gently tried to loosen the clutch, and the poor fingers gave way in an instant and fell helplessly among the grasses, frightening a field-mouse back into its hole. But this helpless, loose fall first gave Trevithic some idea of life in the hopeless figure, for all its wan rigid lines. He put his hand under the rags which covered the breast. There was no pulse at first, but presently the heart just fluttered, and a little color came into the pale face, and there was a long sigh, and then the glazed eyes closed.

John set to work to rub the cold hands and the stiff body. It was all he could do, for people don't walk about with bottles of brandy and blankets in their pockets; but he rubbed and rubbed, and some of the magnetism of his own vigorous existence seemed to enter into the poor soul at his knees, and another faint flush of life came into the face, and the eyes opened this time naturally and bright, and the figure pointed faintly to its lips. Jack understood, and he nodded; gave a tug to the man's shoulders, and propped him up a little higher against the bank. Then he tied his handkerchief round the poor old bald head to protect it from the sun, and sprang up the side of the ditch. He had remembered a turnpike upon the highway, two or three hundred yards beyond the boundary of the next field.

Lady Kidderminster, who happened to be driving along that afternoon on her way to the Potlington flower-show, and who was leaning back comfortably under the hood of her great yellow barouche, was surprised to see from under the fringe of her parasol the figure of a man suddenly bursting through a hedge on the roadside, and waving a hat and shouting, red, heated, disordered, frantically signing to the coachman to stop.

"It's a Fenian!" screamed her ladyship.

"I think—yes, it's Mr. Trevithic," said her companion.

The coachman, too, had recognized Jack, and began to draw up; but the young man, who had now reached the side of the carriage, signed to him to go on.

"Will you give me a lift?" he said, gasping and springing on to the step. "How d'ye do, Lady Kidderminster? I heard your wheels and made an effort," and Jack turned rather pale. "There is a poor fellow dying in a ditch. I want some brandy for him and some help; stop at the turnpike," he shouted to the coachman, and then he turned with very good grace to Lady Kidderminster, aghast and not over pleased. "Pray forgive me," he said. "It was such a chance catching you. I never thought I should have done it. I was two fields off. Why, how d'ye do, Mrs. Miles?" And still holding on to the yellow barouche by one hand, he put out the other to his old acquaintance, Mary Miles, with the still kind eyes, who was sitting in state by the countess.

"You will take me back, and the brandy, I know?" said Trevithic.

"Is it any body one knows?" said the countess.

"Only some tramp," said Jack; "but it's a mercy I met you." And before they reached the turnpike, he had jumped down, and was explaining his wants to the bewildered old chip of a woman who collected the tolls.

"Your husband not here? a pity," said John. "Give me his brandy-bottle; it will be of some good for once." And he disappeared into the lodge, saying, "Would you please have the horses' heads turned, Lady Kidderminster?" In

a minute he was out again. "Here, put this in" (to the powdered footman), and John thrust a blanket off the bed, an old three-legged chair, a wash-jug full of water, and one or two more miscellaneous objects into the man's arms. "Now back again," he said, "as quick as you can." And he jumped in with his brandy; and the great barouche groaned, and at his command actually sped off once more along the road. "Make haste," said Trevithic; "the man is dying for want of a dram."

The sun blazed hot in their faces. The footman sat puzzled and disgusted on his perch, clasping the blanket and the water-jug. Lady Kidderminster was not sure that she was not offended by all the orders Mr. Trevithic was giving her servants; Mrs. Miles held the three-legged chair up on the seat opposite with her slender wrist, and looked kind and sympathetic; John hardly spoke—he was thinking what would be best to do next.

"I am so sorry," he said, "but I am afraid you must wait for us, Lady Kidderminster. I'll bring him up as soon as I can, and we will drop him at the first cottage. You see nobody else may pass for hours."

"We shall be very late for our fl—" Lady Kidderminster began, faintly, and then stopped ashamed at the look in Trevithic's honest face which she saw reflected in Mrs. Myles's eyes.

"Oh my dear Lady Kidderminster," cried Mrs. Myles, bending forward from her nest of white muslins. "We must wait."

"Of course we will wait," said Lady Kidderminster, hastily, as the coachman stopped at the gap through which Jack had first made his appearance. Trevithic was out in an instant.

"Bring those things quick," said Jack to the magnificent powder-and-plush man; and he set off running himself as hard as he could go, with his brandy-flask in one hand and the water-jug in the other.

For an instant the man hesitated and looked at his mistress, but Lady Kidderminster had now caught something of Mr. Trevithic's energy: she imperiously pointed to the three-legged chair, and Tomlins, who was good-natured in the main, seeing Jack's figure rapidly disappearing in the distance, began to run too, with his silken legs plunging wildly, for pumps and stubble are not the most comfortable of combinations. When Tomlins reached the ditch at last, Jack was pouring old Glossop's treacle-like brandy down the poor gasping tramp's throat, dashing water into his face and gradually bringing him to life again; the sun was streaming upon the two, the insects buzzing, and the church clock striking the half-hour.

There are combinations in life more extraordinary than pumps and ploughed fields. When Trevithic and Tomlins staggered up to the carriage carrying the poor old ragged, half-lifeless creature on the chair between them, the two besatined and be-feathered ladies made way and helped them to put poor helpless old Davy Hopkins with all his rags into the soft-cushioned corner, and drove off with him in triumph to the little public at the entrance of Featherston, where they left him.

"You have saved that man's life," said Jack, as he said good-bye to the two ladies. They left him standing glad and excited, in the middle of the road, with bright eyes and more animation and interest in his face than there had been for many a day.

"My dear Jack, what is this I hear?" said Anne, when he got home. "Have you been to the flower-show with Lady Kidderminster? Who was that in the carriage with her? What a state you are in!"

Jack told her his story, but Mrs. Trevithic scarcely listened. "Oh!" said she, "I thought you had been doing something pleasant. Mrs. Myles was very kind. It seems to me rather a fuss about nothing, but, of course, you know best."

Little Dulcie saw her father looking vexed; she climbed up his leg and got on his knee, and put her round soft cheek against his. "Sall I luboo?" said she.

CHAPTER V.

BLUNDERBORE AND HIS TWO HEADS.

WHEN Jack went to see his *protégé* next day, he found the old man sitting up in the bar warming his toes, and finishing off a basin of gruel and a tumbler of porter with which the landlady had supplied him. Mrs. Penfold was a frozen sort of woman, difficult to deal with, but kind-hearted when the thaw once set in, and though at first she had all but refused to receive poor old Davy into her house, having relented and opened her door to him, she had warmed and comforted him, and brought him to life in triumph, and now looked upon him with a certain self-contained pride and satisfaction as a favorable specimen of her art.

"He's right eno'," said Mrs. Penfold, with a jerk of the head. "Ye can go in and see him in the bar." And Jack went in.

The bar was a comfortable little oaken refuge and haven for Miles and Hodge, where they stretched their stiff legs safe from the scoldings of their wives and the shrill cries of their children. The shadows of the sunny-latticed window struck upon the wooden floor, the fire burnt most part of the year on the stone hearth, where the dry branches and logs were crackling cheerfully, with a huge black kettle hissing upon the bars. Some one had christened it "Tom," and from its crooked old spout at any hour of the day a hot and sparkling stream went flowing into the smoking grog-glasses, and into Penfold's punch-pots and Mrs. Penfold's tea-cups and soup-pans.

Davy's story was a common one enough—a travelling umbrella-mender—hard times—fine weather, umbrellas to mend, and "parasols ain't no good; so cheap they are," he said, with a

shake of the head; "they ain't worth the mendin'." Then an illness, and then the work-house, and that was all his history.

"I ain't sorry I come out of the 'ouse; the ditch was the best place of the two," said Davy. "You picked me out of the ditch; you'd have left me in the 'ouse, sir, all along with the ruck. I don't blame ye," Davy said; "I see'd ye there for the first time when I was wuss off than I ever hope to be in this life again; ye looked me full in the face, and talked on with them two after ye—devil take them, and he will."

"I don't remember you," said John. "Where was it?"

"Hammersley Workus," said Davy. "Don't you remember Hammersley Union? I was in the bed under the winder, and I says to my pardner (there were two on us), says I—'That chap looks as if he might do us a turn.' 'Not he,' says my pardner. 'They are werry charitable, and come and stare at us; that's all,' says he, and he was right you see, sir. He'd been in five years come Christmas, and knew more about it than I did then."

"And you have left it now?" said Trevithic, with a strange expression of pity in his face.

"So I 'ave, sir, I'm bound to say," said Davy, finishing off his porter, "and I'd rather die in the ditch any day than go back to that d—— place."

"It looked clean and comfortable enough," said Trevithic.

"Clean, comfirable!" said Davy. "Do you think *I* minds a little dirt, sir? Did you look under the quilts? Why, the vermin was a running all over the place like flies, so it were. It come dropping from the ceiling; and my pardner he were paralytic, and he used to get me to wipe the bugs off his face with a piece of paper. Shall I tell ye what it was like?" And old Davy, in his ire, began a history so horrible, so sickening, that Trevithic flushed up as he listened—an honest flush and fire of shame and indignation.

"I tell you fairly I don't believe half you say," said Jack, at last. "It is too horrible and unnatural."

"True there," said Davy, comforted by his porter and his gruel. "It ain't no great matter to me if you believes 'arf or not, sir. I'm out of that hole, and I ain't agoin' back. Maybe your good lady has an umbrella wants seeing to; shall I call round and ask this afternoon, sir?"

Jack nodded and said he might come if he liked, and went home, thinking over the history he had heard. It was one of all the histories daily told in the sunshine, of deeds done in darkness. It was one grain of seed falling into the ground and taking root. Jack felt a dull feeling of shame and sadness; an uncomfortable pricking as of a conscience which has been benumbed; a sudden pain of remorse, as he walked along the dusty lane which led to the vicarage. He found his wife in the drawing-room, writing scented notes to some of her new friends, and accepting proffered dinners and teas and county hospitalities. Little Dulcie was lying on her back on a rug, and crooning and chattering; the shutters were closed; there was a whiff of roses and scented water. Coming in from the baking lanes, it was a pleasant contrast, a pretty home picture, all painted in cool whites and grays and shadows, and yet it had by degrees grown intolerable to him. Jack looked round, and up and down, and then with a sudden impulse he went up and took his wife's hand, and looked her full in the face. "Anne," he said, "could you give up something for me—something, every thing, except what is yours as a right? Dear, it is all so nice, but I am very unhappy here. May I give up this pretty home, and will you come and live with me where we can be of more use than we are here?" He looked so kind and so imploring that for an instant Anne almost gave way and agreed to any thing. There was a bright constraining power in Jack's blue eye which had to deal with magnetism, I believe, and which his wife was one of the few people to resist. She recovered herself almost immediately.

"How ridiculous you are, John!" she said, pettishly. "Of course I will do any thing in reason; but it seems to me very wrong and unnatural and ungrateful of you," said Mrs. Trevithic, encouraging herself as she went on, "not to be happy when you have so much to be thankful for; and though, of course, I should be the last to allude to it, yet I do think when I have persuaded papa to appoint you to this excellent living, considering how young you are and how much you owe to him, it is not *graceful*, to say the least, on your part . . . ."

John turned away and caught up little Dulcie, and began tossing her in the air. "Well," said he, "we won't discuss this now. I have made up my mind to take a week's holiday," he added, with a sort of laugh. "I am going to stay with Frank Austin till Saturday. Will you tell them to pack up my things?"

"But, my dear, we are engaged to the Kidd . . . ."

"You must write and make my excuses," Jack said, wearily. "I must go, I have some business at Hammersley." And he left the room.

Chances turn out so strangely at times that some people—women especially, who live quietly at home and speculate upon small matters—look on from afar and wonder among themselves as they mark the extraordinary chainwork of minute stitches by which the mighty machinery of the world works on. Men who are busy and about, here and there in life, are more apt to take things as they find them, and do not stop to speculate how this or that comes to be. It struck Jack oddly when he heard from his friend Frank Austin that the chaplain who had been elected instead of him at the work-house was ill and obliged to go away for a time. "He is trying to find some one to take

his place, and to get off for a holiday," said Mr. Austin. "He is a poor sort of creature, and I don't think he has got on very well with the guardians."

"I wonder," said Trevithic, "whether I could take the thing for a time? We might exchange, you know; I am tired of play, Heaven knows. There is little enough to do at Featherston, and he might easily look after my flock while I take the work here off his hands."

"I know you always had a hankering after those unsavory flesh-pots," Austin said with a laugh. "I should think Skipper would jump at your offer, and from all I hear there is plenty to be done here, if it is work you are in want of. Poor little Skipper did his best at one time; I believe he tried to collect a fund for some of the poor creatures who couldn't be taken in, but what is one small fish like him among so many guardians?" said Mr. Austin, indulging in one of those clerical jokes to which Mr. Trollope has alluded in his delightful Chronicles.

Jack wrote off to his bishop and to his wife by that day's post. Two different answers reached him; his wife's came next day, his bishop's three days later.

Poor Anne was frantic, as well she might be. "Come to Hammersley for two months in the heat of the summer; bring little Dulcie; break up her home!—Never. Throw over Lady Kidderminster's Saturdays; admit a stranger to the vicarage!—Never! Was her husband out of his senses?" She was deeply, deeply hurt. He must come back immediately, or more serious consequences than he imagined might ensue.

Trevithic's eyes filled up with tears as he crumpled the note up in his hand and flung it across the room. It was for this he had sacrificed the hope of his youth, of his life—for this. It was too late now to regret, to think of what another fate might have been. Marriage had done him this cruel service: It had taught him what happiness might be, what some love might be, but it had withheld the sweetness of the fruit of the tree. If it had indeed disclosed the knowledge of good, it was through the very bitterness of the fruit that came to his share, that this unhappy Adam, outside the gates of the garden, realized what its ripe sweetness might have been.

Old Mr. Bellingham did not mend matters by writing a trembling and long-winded remonstrance. Lady Kidderminster, to whom Anne had complained, pronounced Trevithic mad; she had had some idea of the kind, she said, that day when he behaved in that extraordinary manner in the lane.

"It's a benevolent mania," said Lord Axminster, her eldest son.

Mrs. Myles shook her head, and began, "He is not mad, most noble lady . . . ." Mrs. Trevithic, who was present, flushed up with resentment at Mrs. Myles venturing to interpose in Jack's behalf. She did not look over-pleased when Mrs. Myles added that she should meet Mr. Trevithic probably when she went from thence to stay at Hammersley with her cousin, Mrs. Garnier.

Jack, who was in a strange determined mood, meanwhile wrote back to his wife to say that he felt that it was all very hard upon her; that he asked it from her goodness to him and her wifely love; that he would make her very happy if she would only consent to come, and if not she must go to her father's for a few weeks until he had got this work done. "Indeed it is no sudden freak, dear," he wrote. "I had it in my mind before" (John hesitated here for a minute and took his pen off the paper)—"that eventful day when I walked up to the rectory, and saw you and learnt to know you." So he finished his sentence. But his heart sank as he posted the letter. Ah me! he had dreamed a different dream.

If his correspondence with his wife did not prosper as it should have done, poor Trevithic was greatly cheered by the bishop's letter, which not only gave consent to this present scheme, but offered him, if he wished for more active duty, the incumbency of St. Bigot's in the North, which would shortly be vacant in Hammersley, and which, although less valuable than his present living, as far as the income was concerned, was much more so as regards the souls to be saved, which were included in the bargain.

New brooms sweep clean, says the good old adage. After he took up his residence at St. Magdalene's, Jack's broomstick did not begin to sweep for seven whole days. He did not go back to Featherston; Anne had left for Sandsea; and Mr. Skipper was in possession of the rectory, and Trevithic was left in that of 500 paupers in various stages of misery and decrepitude, and of a two-headed creature called Bulcox, otherwise termed the master and the matron of the place. Jack waited; he felt that if he began too soon he might ruin every thing, get into trouble, stir up the dust which had been lying so thickly, and make matters worse than before; he waited, watched, looked about him, asked endless questions, to not one of which the poor folks dared give a truthful answer. "Nurse was werry kind, that she was, and most kinsiderate, up any time o' night and day," gasped poor wretches, whose last pinch of tea had just been violently appropriated by "nurse" with the fierce eyebrows sitting over the fire, and who would lie for hours in an agony of pain before they dared awaken her from her weary sleep. For nurse, whatever her hard rapacious heart might be, was only made of the same aching bones and feeble flesh as the rest of them. "Every body was kind and good, and the mistress came round reg'lar and ast them what they wanted. The tea was not so nice, perhaps, as it might be, but they was not wishin' to complain." So they moaned on for the first three days. On the fourth, one or two cleverer and more truthful than the rest

began to whisper that "nurse" sometimes indulged in a drop too much; that she had been very unmanageable the night before, had boxed poor Tilly's ears—poor simpleton. They all loved Tilly, and didn't like to see her hurt. See, there was the bruise on her cheek; and Tilly, a woman of thirty, but a child in her ways, came shyly up in a pinafore, with a doll in one arm and a finger in her mouth. All the old hags, sitting on their beds, smiled at her as she went along. This poor witless Tilly was the pet of the ward, and they did not like to have her beaten. Trevithic was affected, he brought Tilly some sugar-plums in his pocket, and the old toothless crones brightened up and thanked him, nodding their white nightcaps encouragingly from every bed.

At the end of two days John sickened; the sights, the smells, the depression of spirits produced by this vast suffering mass of his unlucky brothers and sisters, was too much for him, and for a couple of days he took to his bed. The matron came to see him twice; she took an interest in this cheerful new element, sparkling still with full reflection of the world outside. She glanced admiringly at his neatly appointed dressing-table, the silver top to his shaving-gear, and the ivory brushes.

John was feverish and thirsty, and was draining a bottle of murky-looking water, when Mrs. Bulcox came into the room on the second day.

"What is that you are drinking there, sir?" said she. "My goodness, it's the water from the tap—we never touch it! I'll send you some of ours; the tap-water comes through the cesspool and is as nasty as nasty can be."

"Is it what they habitually drink here?" Trevithic asked, languidly.

"They're used to it," said Mrs. Bulcox; "nothing hurts them."

Jack turned away with an impatient movement, and Mrs. Bulcox went off indignant at his want of courtesy. The fact was, that Jack already knew more of the Bulcox's doings than they had any conception of, poor wretches, as they lay snoring the comfortable sleep of callousness on their snug pillows. "I don't 'alf like that chap," Mr. Bulcox had remarked to his wife, and Mrs. Bulcox had heartily echoed the misgiving. "I go to see him when he is ill," said she, "and he cuts me off as sharp as any thing. What business has he comin' prying and spying about the place?"

What, indeed! The place oppressed poor Jack, tossing on his bed; it seemed to close in upon him, the atmosphere appeared to be full of horrible moans and suggestions. In his normal condition Jack would have gone to sleep like a top, done his best, troubled his head no more on the subject of troubles he could not relieve; but just now he was out of health, out of spirits—although his darling desire was his—and more susceptible to nervous influences and suggestions than he had ever been in his life before. This night especially he was haunted and overpowered by the closeness and stillness of his room. It looked out through bars into a narrow street, and a nervous feeling of imprisonment and helplessness came over him so strongly that, to shake it off, he jumped up at last and partly dressed himself, and began to pace up and down the room. The popular history of Jack the Giant-Killer gives a ghastly account of the abode of Blunderbore; it describes "an immense room where lay the limbs of the people lately seized and devoured," and Blunderbore, "with a horrid grin," telling Jack "that men's hearts eaten with pepper and vinegar were his nicest food. The giant then locked Jack up," says the history, "and went to fetch a friend."

Poor Trevithic felt something in Jack's position when the gates were closed for the night, and he found himself shut in with his miserable companions. He could from his room hear the bolts and the bars and the grinding of the lock, and immediately a longing would seize him to get out.

To-night, after pacing up and down, he at last took up his hat and a light in his hand, and opened his door and walked down stairs to assure himself of his liberty and get rid of this oppressive feeling of confinement. He passed the master's door and heard his snores, and then he came to the lower door opening into the inner court. The keys were in it—it was only locked on the inside. As Jack came out into the court-yard he gave a great breath of relief: the stars were shining thickly overhead, very still, very bright; the place seemed less God-forgotten than when he was up there in his bedroom; the fresh night-air blew in his face and extinguished his light. He did not care, he put it down in a corner by the door, and went on into the middle of the yard and looked all round about him. Here and there from some of the windows a faint light was burning and painting the bars in gigantic shadows upon the walls; and at the end of the court, from what seemed like a grating to a cellar, some dim rays were streaming upward. Trevithic was surprised to see a light in such a place, and he walked up to see, and then he turned quickly away, and if like Uncle Toby he swore a great oath at the horrible sight he saw, it was but an expression of honest pity and most Christian charity. The grating was a double grating, and looked into two cellars which were used as casual wards when the regular ward was full. The sight Trevithic saw is not one that I can describe here. People have read of such things as they are and were only a little while ago when the *Pall Mall Gazette* first published that terrible account which set people talking and asking whether such things should be and could be still.

Old Davy had told him a great many sad and horrible things, but they were not so sad or so horrible as the truth, as Jack now saw it. Truth, naked, alas! covered with dirt and vermin, shuddering with cold, moaning with disease, and heaped and tossed in miserable uneasy sleep at the bottom of her foul well. Every now and then a voice broke the darkness, or a cough or

a moan reached him from the sleepers above. Jack did not improve his night's rest by his midnight wandering.

Trevithic got well, however, next day, dressed himself, and went down into the little office which had been assigned to him. His bedroom was over the gateway of the work-house and looked into the street. From his office he had only a sight of the men's court, the wooden bench, the stone steps, the grating. Inside was a stove and green drugget, a little library of books covered with greasy brown paper for the use of those who could read. There was not much to comfort or cheer him, and as he sat there he began to think a little disconsolately of his pleasant home, with its clean comfortable appointments, the flowers round the window, the fresh chintzes, and, above all, the dear little round face upturned to meet him at every coming home.

It would not do to think of such things, and Jack put them away, but he wished that Anne had consented to come to him. It seemed hard to be there alone—him a father and a husband, with belongings of his own. Trevithic, who was still weak and out of sorts, found himself making a little languid castle in the air, of crooked places made straight, of whited sepulchres made clean, of Dulcie, grown tall and sensible, coming tapping at his door to cheer him when he was sad, and encourage him when he was weary.

Had the fever come back, and could it be that he was wandering? It seemed to him that all the heads of the old men he could see through the grating were turning, and that an apparition was passing by—an apparition, gracious, smiling, looking in through the bars of his window, and coming gently knocking at his door; and then it opened, and a low voice said —"It's me, Mr. Trevithic—Mrs. Myles: may I come in?" and a cool, gray phantom stepped into the dark little room.

Jack gladly welcomed his visitor, and brought out his shabby old leather chair for her; but Mrs. Myles would not sit down, she had only come for a minute.

"How ill you are looking!" Mary said, compassionately. "I came to ask you to come back and dine with us; I am only here for a day or two with my cousin Fanny Garnier. She visits this place, and brought me, and I thought of asking for you; and do come, Mr. Trevithic. These — these persons showed me the way to your study." And she looked back at the grinning old heads that were peeping in at the door. Mary Myles looked like the lady in *Comus*—so sweet, and pure, and fair, with the grotesque faces peering and whispering all about her. They vanished when Trevithic turned, and stood behind the door watching and chattering like apes, for the pretty lady to come out again. "I can not tell you how glad we are that you have come here, Mr. Trevithic?" said Mrs. Myles. "Poor Fanny has half broken her heart over the place, and Mr. Skipper was so hopeless that it was no use urging him to appeal. You will do more good in a week than he has done in a year. I must not wait now," Mrs. Myles added. "You will come, won't you?—at seven; we have so much to say to you. Here is the address."

As soon as Jack had promised to come, she left him, disappearing with her strange little court hobbling after her to the very gate of the dreary place.

Jack was destined to have more than one visitor that afternoon. As he still sat writing busily at his desk in the little office, a tap came at the door. It was a different apparition this time, for an old woman's head peeped in, and an old nutcracker-looking body, in her charity-girl's livery, staggered feebly into his office and stood grinning slyly at him. "She came to borrow a book," she said. "She couldn't read, not she, but, law bless him, that was no matter." Then she hesitated. "He had been speaking to Mike Rogers that morning. You wouldn't go and get us into trouble," said the old crone, with a wistful, doubtful, scanning interrogation of the eyes; "but I am his good lady, and 'ave been these thirty years, and it do seem hard upon the gals, and if you could speak the word, sir, and get them out . . . . ."

"Out?" said Jack.

"From the black kitchen—so they name it," said the old crone, mysteriously: "the cellar under the master's stairs. Kate Hill has been in and out a week come yesterday. I knowed her grandmother, poor soul. She shouldn't have spoke tighty to the missis; but she is young and don't know no better, and my good man and me was thinking if maybe you could say a word, sir—as if from yourself. Maybe you heard her as you went up stairs, sir; for we know our cries is 'eard."

So this was it. The moans in the air were not fancy, the complainings had been the real complaints of some one in suffering and pain.

"Here is the book," said Jack, suddenly; "and I'm afraid you can have no more snuff, ma'am." And with a start poor old Betty Rogers nearly stumbled over the matron, who was standing at his door.

"Well, what is it you're wanting now?" said Mrs. Bulcox. "You mustn't allow them to come troubling you, Mr. Trevithic."

"I am not here for long, Mrs. Bulcox," said Jack, shrugging his shoulders. "While I stay I may as well do all I can for these poor creatures."

A gleam of satisfaction came into Mrs. Bulcox's face at the notion of his approaching departure. He had been writing all the morning, covering sheets and sheets of paper. He had been doing no harm, and she felt she could go out for an hour with her Bulcox, with an easy mind.

As Mr. and Mrs. Bulcox came home together, Jack, who was looking from his bedroom window, saw them walking up the street. He had put up his sheets of paper in an envelope,

and stamped it, and addressed it. He had not wasted his time during their absence, and he had visited a part of the work-house unknown to him before, having bribed one pauper and frightened another into showing him the way. Mr. Bulcox coming under the window heard Jack calling to him affably. "Would you be so kind as to post this packet for me?" cried Jack. The post-box was next door to the work-house. "Thank you," he said, as Mr. Bulcox picked up the thick letter which came falling to the ground at his feet. It was addressed to Colonel the Hon. Charles Hamble-don, Lowndes Square, London. "Keeps very 'igh company," said Bulcox to his wife, and he felt quite pleased to post a letter addressed to so distinguished a personage.

"Thank you," said Jack again, looking very savagely pleased and amused; "it was of importance." He did not add that it was a letter to the editor of the *Jupiter*, who was a friend of his friend's. Trevithic liked the notion of having got Bulcox to fix the noose round his own neck. He felt ashamed of the part he was playing, but he did not hurry himself for that. It was necessary to know all, in order to sweep clean once he began. Poor Kate Hill, still in durance, received a mysterious and encouraging message, and one or two comforts were smuggled in to her by her jailer. On the Wednesday morning his letter would appear in the *Jupiter*—nothing more could be done until then. Next day was Tuesday: he would go over to Sandsea and talk Anne into reason, and get back in time for the Board; and in the mean time Jack dressed himself and went to dine with the widows.

CHAPTER VI.

THE PARCÆ CUT A THREAD OF MRS. TREVITHIC'S KNITTING.

MRS. MYLES'S cousin, Mrs. Garnier, lived in a quaint, comfortable-looking low house on the Chester high-road, with one or two bow-windows and gables standing out for no apparent reason, and a gallery up stairs, with four or five windows, which led to the drawing-room.

The two widows were very fond of one another and often together; there was a similarity in tastes and age and circumstance. The chief difference in their fate had been this—that Fanny Garnier had loved her husband, although she could not agree with him—for loving and gareeing do not go together always—and Mary Myles's married life had been at best a struggle for indifference and forgiveness: she was not a very easily moulded woman; she could do no more than forgive, and repent her own ill-doing in marrying as she did.

The trace of their two lives was set upon the cousins. A certain coldness and self-reliance, a power of living for to-day and forgetting, was the chief gift that had come to Mary Myles out of the past experience of her life. **Fanny Garnier** was softer, more impressionable, **more easily** touched and assimilated by the people **with** whom she came in contact: she was less crisp **and** bright than Mary, and older, **though she** was **the same age.** She **had loved more and** sorrowed more, **and people remember their sorrows** in after years **when their angers are** forgotten and have **left only a blank in their** minds.

George **Garnier,** Fanny Garnier's **husband,** had belonged to that sect of people who **have an** odd fancy in their world for making **themselves** and other folks as miserable as they possibly can—for worrying and wearying and torturing, for doubting and trembling, for believing far more eagerly in justice (or retribution, which is their idea of justice) than in mercy. Terror has a strange morbid attraction for these folks; mistrust, for all they say, seems to be the **motive power of their** lives: they gladly offer pain **and tears and** penitence as a ghastly propitiation. **They are of all** religions **and creeds;** they are **found with** black skins **and woolly** heads, building up their altars and offering **their** human sacrifices in the unknown African deserts; they are chipping and chopping **themselves** before their emerald-nosed idols **who sit** squatting in unclean temples; they are living in the streets and houses all round about us, in George Garnier's pleasant old cottage outside the great Hammersley city, or at number five, and six, and seven in our street, as the case may be; in the convent at Bayswater, in the manses and presbyteries. You or I may belong to the fraternity, so did many a better man, as the children say—St. Simon Stylites, Athanasius, John Calvin, Milton, Ignatius Loyola, Savonarola, not to speak of Saints A, B, C, D, and E.

Mary poured Jack out a big cup of strong tea, and brought it across the lamp-lit room to him with her own white hands. Mrs. Garnier shivered as she heard his story. The tea smoked, the lamps burnt among the flower-stands, the wood-fire blazed cheerfully, for Mrs. Myles was a chilly and weak-minded person, and lit her fire all the year round, more or less. Trevithic, comfortably sunk back in a big arm-chair, felt a grateful sense of ease and rest and consolation. The atmosphere of the little house was so congenial and fragrant, the two women were such sympathizing listeners; Mary Myles's bright eyes lighted with such kindly interest; while Mrs. Garnier, silent, available, sat with her knitting under the shade of the lamp. The poor fellow was not insensible to these soothing influences. As he talked on, it seemed to him that for the first time in his life he had realized what companionship and sympathy might mean. Something invisible, harmonious, delicate, seemed to drive away from him all thought of sin or misery and turmoil when in company with these two kind women. This was what a home might have been—a warm, flower-scented, lamp-twinkling haven with sweet still eyes to respond and

brighten at his success and to cheer his failing efforts. This was what it never, never would be, and Trevithic put the thought away. It was dangerous ground for **the** poor heart-weary fellow, longing for peace and home, comfort and love; whereas Anne, **to whom he** was bound to look for these good **things, was** at Sandsea, fulfilling every duty **of civilized life,** and not greatly troubled for **her husband, but** miserable on her own account, hard **and vexed and** deeply offended.

Mrs. Trevithic was tripping along the south cliff on the afternoon of the next day, when the sound of footsteps behind her made her stop and look round. As she saw that it was her husband coming towards her, her pale face turned a shade more pale.

"Oh, how d'ye do?" Anne said. "I did not expect you. Have you come for long?" And she scarcely waited for him to come up to her, but began to walk on immediately.

Poor John; what a coming home! He arrived with his various interests, his reforms, his forthcoming letter in the *Jupiter;* there was the offer of the bishop's in his pocket—the momentary gladness and elation of return—and this was all he had come back to!

"Have you come on business?" Mrs. Trevithic asked.

"I wanted to see you and Dulcie," John answered; "that was my business. Time seems very long without you both. All this long time I have only had Mrs. Myles to befriend me. I wish—I wish you would try to like the place, too, Anne. Those two ladies seem very happy there."

"Mrs. Myles, I have no doubt," said Anne, bitterly. "No," she cried, "you need not talk so to me. I know too much, too much, too much," she said, with something like real pathos in her voice.

"My dearest Anne, what do you mean?" Trevithic said kindly, hurrying after her, for she was walking very fast.

"It is too late. I can not forgive you. I am not one of those people who can forget easily and forgive. Do you think I do not know that your love is not mine—never was—never will be mine? Do you think gossip never reaches me here, far away, though I try to live in peace and away from it all? And you dare mention Mary Myles's name to me, you dare—you dare!" cried Anne, in her quick, fierce manner.

"Of course I dare," said Trevithic. "Enough of this, Anne," and he looked as hard as Anne herself for a minute; then he melted. "Dear Anne, if something has failed in our home hitherto, let us forgive one another and make a new start in life. Listen," and he pulled out the bishop's letter, with the offer of St. Bigot's, and read it to her. "I need not tell you how much I wish for this."

His wife did not answer. At first he thought she was relenting. She went a little way down the side of the cliff and waited for him, and then suddenly turned upon him. The wash of the sea seemed to flow in time with her words.

"You are cruel—yes, cruel!" said Anne, trembling very much, and moved for once out of her calm. "You think I can bear any thing, I can not bear your insults any longer! I must go—leave you. Yes, listen to me, I *will* go, I tell you. My father will keep me here, me and little Dulcie, and you can have your own way, John, and go where you like. You love your own way better than any thing else in the world, and it will make up to you for the home which, as you say, has been a failure on the whole." And Mrs. Trevithic tried to choke down a gulp of bitter angry tears.

As she spoke John remembered a time not so very long ago, when Anne had first sobbed out she loved him, and when the tears which she should have gulped away had been allowed to overflow into those bitter waters of strife—alas! neither of them could have imagined possible until now.

They had been walking side by side along the beach, the parson trudging angrily a little ahead, with his long black coat flapping and swinging against his legs; Anne skimming along skillfully after him, with her quick slender footsteps; but as she went along she blamed him in her heart for every roughness and inequality of the shore, and once when she struck her foot against a stone her ire rose sore against him. Little Dulcie from the rectory garden spied them out afar off, and pointed and capered to attract their attention; but the father and mother were too much absorbed in their own troubles to heed her, even if they could have descried her small person among the grasses and trees.

"You mean to say," said Jack, stopping short suddenly, and turning round and speaking with a faint discordant jar in his voice, "that you want to leave me, Anne?"

"Yes," said Anne, quite calm and composed, with two glowing cheeks that alone showed that a fire of some sort was smouldering within. "Yes, John, I mean it. I have not been happy, I have not succeeded in making you happy. I think we should both be better people apart than together. I never, never felt so—so ashamed of myself in all my life as since I have been married to you. I will stay here with papa. You have given up your living; you can now go and fulfill those duties which are more to you than wife or children or home." Anne—who was herself again by this time—calmly rolled up her parasol as she spoke, and stood waiting for an answer. I think she expected a tender burst of remonstrance from her husband, a pathetic appeal, an abandonment possibly of the mad scheme which filled her with such unspeakable indignation. She had not counted on his silence. John stopped short a second time, and stood staring at the sea. He was cut to the heart; cruelly stunned and shocked and wounded by the pain, so that he had almost forgotten his wife's presence, or what he should say, or any thing but the actual suffering that he was enduring

It seemed like a revelation of a horrible secret to which he had been blind all along. It was like a curse falling upon his home—undreamt of for a time, and suddenly realized. A great swift hatred flamed up in his heart against the calm and passive creature who had wrought it—who was there before him waiting for his assent to her excellent arrangements; a hatred, indeed, of which she was unworthy and unconscious; for Anne was a woman of slow perception. It took a long time for her to realize the effect of her words, or to understand what was passing in other people's minds. She was not more annoyed now with Trevithic than she had been for a long time past. She had no conception of the furies of scorn and hatred which were battling and tearing at the poor fellow's kind heart; she had not herself begun to respond even to her own emotions; and so she stood quite quietly, expecting, like some stupid bird by the water's edge, waiting for the wave to overwhelm her. "Do you not agree with me?" she said at last. Trevithic was roused by his wife's question, and answered it. "Yes; just as you wish," he said, in an odd, cracked voice, with a melancholy jar in it. "Just as you like, Anne." And without looking at her again, he began once more to tramp along the shingle, crushing the pebbles under his feet as he went. The little stones started and rolled away under his impatient tread. Anne from habit followed him, without much thinking where she was going, or what aim she had in so doing; but she could not keep up with his strong progress—the distance widened and widened between them. John walked farther away, while Mrs. Trevithic, following after, trying in vain to hasten her lagging steps, grew sad and frightened all at once as she saw him disappearing in the distance. And then it was her turn to realize what she had done. Seeing her husband go, this poor woman began to understand at last that her foolish longing was granted.

Her feet failed, her heart sank, her courage died away all suddenly. Like a flame blown out, all the fire of her vexation and impatience was gone, and only a dreary nothing remained. And more hard to bear even than the troubles, the pains, the aches, the longings of life, are its blanks and its wants. Outer darkness, with the tormenting fires and the companion devils, is not the outer darkness that has overwhelmed most hearts with terror and apprehension. No words, no response, silence, abandonment—to us weak, loving, longing human creatures, that is the worst fate of all.

Anne became very tired, struggling after Trevithic. Little by little she began to realize that she had sent him away and he was going. A gull flapped across her path, and frightened her. She could see him still; he had not yet turned up the steps from the cliff to the rectory garden, but he was gone as certainly as if she could no longer see him. And then she began to learn in a void of incredulous amaze, poor sluggish soul, that life was hard, very hard, and terribly remorseless; that when you strike, the blow falls; that what you wish is not always what you want; that it is easy to call people to you once perhaps, and to send them away once, but that when they come they stay, and when they go they are gone and all is over. Why was he so headstrong, so ungrateful, so unreasonable? Was she not right to blame him? and had he not owned himself to be in the wrong? Ah, poor wife, poor wife! Something choking and blinding seemed to smite the unhappy woman in her turn. She reached the steps at last that lead up the cliff to the rectory garden where little Dulcie had been playing when her mother left her. Anne longed to find her there—to clutch her in her poor aching arms, and cover her sweet little rosy face with kisses. "Dulcie," she called, "Dulcie, Dulcie!" her voice echoing so sadly that it struck herself, but Dulcie's cheery little scream of gladness did not answer, and Anne—who took this silence as a bad omen—felt her heart sink lower. In a vague way she thought that if she could have met Dulcie all would have been well.

She was calling still, when some one answered; figures came to the hall-door, half a dozen officious hands were outstretched, and friendly greetings met her. There was Miss Triquett who was calling with Miss Moineaux, and Miss Simmonds who had driven up in her basket-carriage, and old Mr. Bellingham trying in a helpless way to entertain his visitresses, and to make himself agreeable to them all. The old gentleman, much relieved at the sight of his daughter, called her to him with a cheerful, "Ah, my dear, here you are. I shall now leave these ladies in better hands than mine. I am sorry to say I have a sermon to write." And Mr. Bellingham immediately and benevolently trotted away.

With the curious courage of women, and long habitude, Mrs. Trevithic took off her hat and smoothed her straight hair, and sat down, and mechanically began to make conversation for the three old ladies who established themselves comfortably in the pleasant bow-windowed drawing-room, and prepared for a good chat. Miss Simmonds took the sofa as her right (as I have said before, size has a certain precedence of its own). Miss Triquett, as usual, rapidly glanced round the apartment, took in the importation of work-boxes, baskets, toy-boxes, etc., which Anne's arrival had scattered about, the trimming on Mrs. Trevithic's dress, the worn lines under her eyes. Mrs. Trevithic took her knitting from one of the baskets, and rang the bell and desired the man to find Miss Dulcie and send her; and meanwhile the stream of conversation flowed on uninterruptedly. Mr. Trevithic was well. Only come for a day! And the little girl? Thanks—yes. Little Dulcie's cold had been severe—linseed poultices, squills, ipecacuanha wine;—thanks, yes. Mrs. Trevithic was already aware of their valuable medicinal properties. Mr. Pettigrew, the present curate, had sprained his thumb in the pulpit door—wet bandages, etc., etc. Here Miss Simmonds, whose eyes had been fixed upon the window all this time, suddenly exclaimed:—

"How fond your husband is of that dear child Dulcie, Mrs. Trevithic! There she is with her papa in the garden."

"Dear me!" said Triquett, stretching her long neck and lighting up with excitement. "Mr. Trevithic must be going away; you never told us. He is carrying a carpet-bag."

As she spoke, Anne, who had been sitting with her back to the window, started up, and her knitting fell off her lap. She was irresolute for an instant. He could not be going—going like that, without a word. No, she would not follow him.

"Oh dear me!" said Miss Simmonds, who had been trying to hook up the little rolling ball of worsted with the end of her parasol, "just see what I have done." And she held the parasol up spindle-fashion with the long entangled thread twisted round it.

"I think I can undo it," said Miss Moineaux.

"I beg your pardon, I—I want to speak to my husband," said Mrs. Trevithic, all of a sudden starting up and running to the door.

"He is going," said Miss Triquett to the others, looking once more out through the big pleasant window, as Anne left the room. "Dear Miss Moineaux, into what a mess you have got that knitting; here are some scissors —let me cut the thread."

"Poor thing! she is too late," said Miss Moineaux, letting the two ends of the thread fall to the ground.

CHAPTER VII.

IN BLUNDERBORE'S CASTLE.

When Jack first made the acquaintance of the Board on the Wednesday after he first came to the work-house, the seven or eight gentlemen sitting round the green table greeted him quite as one of themselves as he came into the room. This was a dull September morning; the mist seemed to have oozed in through the high window and continually opening door. When Jack passed through the outer or entrance room, he saw a heap of wistful faces and rags already waiting for admittance, some women and some children, a man with an arm in a sling, one or two work-house habitues—there was no mistaking the hard coarse faces. Two old paupers were keeping watch at the door, and officially flung it open for him to pass in. The guardians had greeted him very affably on the previous occasion—a man of the world, a prosperous but eccentric vicar, was not to be treated like an every-day curate and chaplain. "Ah, how d'ye do, Mr. Trevithic?" said the half-pay Captain, the chairman. The gas-fitter cleared his throat and made a sort of an attempt at a bow. The wholesale grocer rubbed his two hands together

—Pitchley his name was, I think—for some reason or other, he exercised great influence over the rest. But on this second Wednesday morning the *Jupiter* had come out with an astounding letter—about themselves, their workhouse, their master, their private paupers. It was a day they never forgot, and the natural indignation of the Board overflowed.

Perhaps Jack would have done better had he first represented matters to them, but he knew that at least two of the guardians were implicated. He was afraid of being silenced and of having the affair hushed up. He cared not for the vials of their wrath being emptied upon him, so long as they cleansed the horrible place in their outpour. He walked in quite brisk and placid to meet the storm. The guardians had not all seen the *Jupiter* as they came dropping in. Oker, the gas-man, was late, and so was Pitchley as it happened, and when they arrived Jack was already standing in his pillory and facing the indignant chairman.

"My friend Colonel Hambledon wrote the letter from notes which I gave him," said Jack. "I considered publicity best;—under the circumstances, I could not be courteous," he said, "if I hoped to get through this disagreeable business at all effectually. I could not have selected any one of you gentlemen as confidants, in common fairness to the others. I wish the inquiry to be complete and searching. I was obliged to brave the consequences."

"Upon my word I think you have acted right," said one of the guardians, a doctor, a bluff old fellow who liked frank speaking. But an indignant murmur expressed the dissent of the other members of the Board.

"I have been here a fortnight," said Jack. "I had not intended speaking so soon of what I now wish to bring before your notice, but the circumstances seem to me so urgent and so undoubted that I can see no necessity for deferring my complaint any longer."

"Dear me, sir," said the gas-fitter, coming in, "I 'ope there's nothink wrong?"

"Everything, more or less," said Trevithic, quietly. "In the first place, I wish to bring before you several cases of great neglect on the part of Mr. and Mrs. Bulcox."

Here the chairman colored up. "I think, Mr. Trevithic, we had better have the master present if you have any complaint to lodge against him."

"By all means," said Trevithic, impassively; and he turned over his notes while one of the trembling old messengers went off for the master.

The master arrived and the matron too. "How d'ye do, Bulcox?" said the chairman. Mrs. Bulcox dropped a respectful sort of courtesy, and Trevithic immediately began without giving time for the others to speak. He turned upon the master.

"I have a complaint to lodge against you and Mrs. Bulcox, and at the chairman's suggestion I waited for you to be present."

"Against me, sir?" said Bulcox, indignantly.

"Against me and Mr. Bulcox?" said the woman, with a bewildered, injured, saint-like sort of swoop.

"Yes," Jack answered, curtly.

"Have you seen the letter in the *Jupiter?*" said the chairman, gravely, to Mr. Bulcox.

"Mr. Bulcox was good enough to post the letter himself," Jack interposed briskly. "It was to state, what I honestly believe to be the fact, that I consider that you, Mr. Bulcox, are totally unfit for your present situation as master. I am aware that you have good friends among these gentlemen, and that, as far as they can tell, your conduct has always been a model of deference and exemplariness. Now," said Jack, "with the Board's permission. I will lodge my complaints against you in form." And here Trevithic pulled out his little book, and read out as follows:—

"1. That the management and economy of this work-house are altogether disgraceful.

"2. That you have been guilty of cruelty to two or three of the inmates.

"3. That you have embezzled or misapplied certain sums of money allowed to you for the relief of the sick paupers under your care."

But here the chairman, guardians, master and mistress, would have no more; all interrupted Trevithic at once.

"Really, sir, you must substantiate such charges as these. Leave the room" (to the messengers at the door).

"I can not listen to such imputations," from the master.

"What have we done to you that you should say such cruel, false things?" from the mistress. "Oh sir" (to the chairman), "turn him away; say you don't believe him."

"If you will come with me now," Jack continued, addressing the guardians, "I think I can prove some of my statements. Do you know that the little children here are crying with hunger? Do you know that the wine allowed for the use of the sick had been regularly appropriated by these two wretches?" cried Trevithic, in an honest fury. "Do you know that people here are lying in their beds in misery, at this instant, who have not been moved or touched for weeks and weeks; that the nurses follow the example of those who are put over them, and drink, and ill-use their patients; that the food is stinted, the tea is undrinkable, the meat is bad and scarcely to be touched; that the very water flows from a foul cesspool; that at this instant, in a cellar in the house, there are three girls shut up, without beds or any conceivable comfort—one has been there four days and nights, another has been shut up twice in one week in darkness and unspeakable misery? Shall I tell you the crime of this culprit? She spoke saucily to the matron, and this is her punishment. Will you come with me now, and see whether or not I have been speaking the truth?"

There was not one word he could not substantiate. He had not been idle all this time,
he had been collecting his proofs—ghastly proofs
they were.

**The sight of the three girls brought blinded
and staggering out of the cellar had more effect
than all the statements** and assertions which
Mr. Trevithic had been at such great pains to
get together. The Bulcoxes were doomed; **of**
this there could be no doubt. They felt it themselves as they plodded across the yard with the
little mob of excited **and** curious guardians.
Oker, the gas-fitter, took their part, indeed, so
did the grocer. The old doctor nearly fell upon
the culprits then and there. The rest of the
guardians seemed to be divided in their indignation against Jack for telling, against Bulcox
for being found out, against the paupers for being ill-used, for being paupers; against the re-
porter for publishing such atrocious libels. It
was no bed of roses that Trevithic had made for
himself.

A special meeting was convened for **the** end
of the week.

———————

CHAPTER VIII.

MARY.

As years go by, and we see more of life and
of our fellow-creatures, the by-play of existence
is curiously unfolded to us, and we may, if we
choose, watch its threads twisting and untwist-
ing, flying apart and coming together. People
rise from their sick-beds, come driving up in
carriages, come walking along the street into
each other's lives. As A. trips along by the
garden-wall, Z. at the other end of the world,
perhaps, is thinking that he is tired of this solitary bushman's life; he was meant for something better than sheep-shearing and driving
convicts, and he says to himself that he will
throw it all up and go back to England, and
see if there is not bread enough left in the old
country to support one more of her sons. Here,
perhaps A. stoops to pick a rose, and places it in
her girdle, and wonders whether that is C. on
the rough pony riding along the road from market. As for Z., A. has never even conceived
the possibility of his existence. But by this
time Z. at the other end of the world has made
up his mind, being a man of quick and determined action, and poor C.'s last chance is over,
and pretty A., with the rose in her girdle, will
never be his. Or it may be that Z., after due
reflection, likes the looks of his tallows, X. and
Y. come to the station, which had hitherto only
been visited by certain very wild-looking letters
of the alphabet, with feathers in their heads,
and faces streaked with white paint, and A.
gives her rose to C., who puts it in his button-
hole with awkward country gallantry, quite unconscious of the chance they have both run that
morning, and that their fate has been settled for
them at the other end of the world.

When my poor A. bursts into tears at the be-

ginning of this story, another woman, who
should have been Trevithic's wife, as far as one
can judge speaking of such matters, a person
who could have sympathized with his ambitions
and understood the direction of his impulses, a
woman with enough enthusiasm and vigor in
her nature to carry her bravely through the
tangles and difficulties which only choked and
scratched and tired out poor Anne—this person,
who was not very far off at the time, and no
other than Mary Myles, said to some one **who**
was with her—and she gave a pretty sad **smile**
and quick shake of the head as she spoke:—

"No, it is no use. I have nothing but
friendliness, a horrible, universal feeling of
friendliness, left for any of my fellow-creatures.
I will confess honestly" (and here she lost her
color a little) "I did wrong once. I married
my husband for a home—most people know how
I was punished, and what a miserable home it
was. I don't mind telling you, Colonel Hambledon, for you well understand how it is that I
must make the best of my life in this arid and
lonely waste to which my own fault has brought
me."

Mrs. Myles's voice faltered as she spoke,
and she hung her head to hide the tears which
had come into her eyes. And Colonel Hambledon took this as an answer to a question he had
almost asked her, and went away.

"If ever you should change your mind," he
said, "you would find me the same a dozen
years hence." And Mary only sighed and
shook her head.

But all this was years ago—three years nearly by the Dulcie almanac—and if Mary Myles
sometimes thought she had done foolishly when
she sent Charles Hambledon away, there was
no one to whom she could own it—not even
to her cousin Fanny, who had no thoughts of
marrying or giving in marriage, or wishes for
happiness beyond the ordering her garden-beds
and the welfare of her poor people.

Fanny one day asked her cousin what had
become of her old friend the Colonel. Mary
blushed up brightly, and said she did not know;
she believed he was in Hammersley. Fanny,
who was cutting out little flannel vests for her
school-children, was immediately lost in the intricacies of a gore, and did not notice the blush
or the bright amused glance in the quiet gray
eyes that were watching her at her benevolent
toil. Snip, snip, sni-i-i-i-i-ip went the scissors
with that triumphant screeching sound which all
good housewives love to hear. Mary was leaning back in her chair, perfectly lazy and unoccupied, with her little white hands crossed upon
her knees, and her pretty head resting against
the chair. She would not have been sorry to
have talked a little more upon a subject that
was not uninteresting to her, and she tried to
make Fanny speak.

"What do you think of him? Have you
heard that he has come?" she asked a little shyly.

"Oh, I don't know. No, I have not seen
any of them for a long time," said Fanny, ab-

sently. "Mary, are you not ashamed of being so lazy? Come and hold these strips."

Mary did as she was bid, and held out gray flannel strips at arms' length, and watching the scissors flashing, the pins twinkling, and the neat little heaps rising all about on the floor and the chairs and the tables. Then Mrs. Myles tried again. "Mr. Trevithic tells me that Colonel Hambledon is coming down to help him with this work-house business. You will have to ask them both to dinner, Fanny."

Fanny did not answer for a minute. She hesitated, looked Mary full in the face, and then said very thoughtfully: "Don't you think unbleached calico will be best to line the jackets with? It will keep the children warm, poor little things." The children's little backs might be warmed by this heap of snips and linings; but Mary suddenly felt as if all the wraps and flannels and calicos were piled upon her head, and choking and oppressing her, while all the while her heart was cold and shivering, poor thing! There are no flannel jackets that I know of to warm sad hearts such as hers.

Fanny Garnier was folding up the last of her jackets; Mary, after getting through more work in half an hour than Fanny the methodical could manage in two, had returned to her big arm-chair, and was leaning back in the old listless attitude, dreaming dreams of her own, as her eyes wandered to the window and followed the line of the trees showing against the sky—when the door opened, and a stupid country manservant suddenly introduced Jack, and the Colonel of Mrs. Myles's visionary recollections in actual person, walking into the very midst of the snippings and parings which were scattered about on the floor. Fanny was in no wise disconcerted. She rather gloried in her occupation. I can not say so much for Mary, who nervously hated any show of affectation of philanthropy, and who now jumped up hastily, with an exclamation, an outstretched hand, and a blush.

"There seems to be something going on," the Colonel said, standing over a heap of straggling "backs" and "arms."

"Do come up stairs out of this labyrinth of good intentions," cried Mary, hastily. "Fanny, please put down your scissors, and let us go up."

"I'll follow," said Fanny, placidly, and Mary had to lead the way alone to the long low bow-windowed drawing-room which Trevithic knew so well. She had regained her composure and spirits by the time they reached the landing at the top of the low flight of oak steps; and, indeed, both Hambledon and Mrs. Myles were far too much used to the world and its ways to betray to each other the smallest indication of the real state of their minds. Three years had passed since they parted. If Mary's courage had failed then, it was the Colonel's now that was wanting; and so it happens with people late in life—the fatal gift of experience is theirs. They mistrust, they hesitate, they bargain to the uttermost farthing; the jewel is there, but it is

locked up so securely in strong boxes and wrappers, that it is beyond the power of the possessors to reach it. Their youth and simplicity is as much a part of them still as their placid middle age; but it is hidden away under the years which are heaped upon the past, and its glory is not shining as of old upon their brows. Mrs. Myles and the Colonel each were acting a part, and perfectly at ease as they discussed all manner of things that had been since they met, and might be before they met again. Fanny, having folded away the last of her flannels, came up placid and smiling too; and after half an hour the two gentlemen went away. Fanny forgot to ask them to dinner, and wondered why her cousin was so cross all the rest of the afternoon.

No, Mary would not go out. No, she had no headache, thank you. As soon as she had got rid of Fanny and her questionings, Mary Myles ran up to her room and pulled out some old, old papers and diaries, and read the old tear-stained records till new tears fell to wash away the old ones. Ah, yes, she had done rightly when she sent Hambledon away. Three years ago—it had seemed to her then that a lifetime of expiation would not be too long to repent of the wrong she had done when she married—loveless, thriftful, longing (and that, poor soul, had been her one excuse), for the possible love that had never come to her. Life is so long, the time is so slow that passes wearily: she had been married three years, she had worn sackcloth three years, and now—now if it were not too late, how gladly, how gratefully, she would grasp a hope of some life more complete than the sad one she had led ever since she could remember almost. Would it not be a sign that she had been forgiven if the happiness she had so longed for came to her at last? Mary wondered that her troubles had left no deeper lines upon her face; wondered that she looked so young still, so fair and smiling, while her heart felt so old; and smiled sadly at her own face in the glass.

And then, as people do to whom a faint dawn of rising hope shows the darkness in which they have been living, Mrs. Myles began to think of some of her duties that she had neglected of late, and of others still in darkness for whom no dawn was nigh: and all the while, still feeling as people feel whose hearts are full, she was longing for some one to speak to, some one wiser than herself to whom she could say, What is an expiation? can it, does it exist? is it the same as repentance? are we called upon to crush our hearts, to put away our natural emotions? Fanny would say yes, and would scorn her for her weakness, and cry out with horror at a second marriage. "And so would I have done," poor Mary thought, "if—if poor Tom had only been fond of me." And then the thought of Trevithic came to her as a person to speak to, a helper and adviser. He would speak the truth; he would not be afraid, Mary thought; and the secret remembrance that he was Hambledon's friend did not make her feel less confidence in his decisions.

Mrs. Myles had been away some little time from her house at Sandsea, and from the self-imposed duties which were waiting undone until her return. Before Fanny came home that evening, she sat down and wrote to her old friend, Miss Triquett, begging her to be so good as to go to Mrs. Gummers, and one or two more whose names, ages, troubles, and families were down upon her list, and distribute a small sum of money inclosed. "I am not afraid of troubling you, dear Miss Triquett," wrote Mary Myles, in her big, picturesque hand-writing. "I know your kind heart, and that you never grudge time nor fatigue when you can help any one out of the smallest trouble or the greatest. I have been seeing a good deal lately of Mr. Trevithic, who is of your way of thinking, and who has been giving himself an infinity of pains about some abuses in the work-house here. He is, I do believe, one of the few people who could have come to the help of the poor creatures. He has so much courage and temper, such a bright and generous way of sympathizing and entering into other people's troubles, and I do not despair of his accomplishing this good work. My cousin and I feel very much with and for him. He looked ill and worn one day when I called upon him; but I am glad to think that coming to us has been some little change and comfort to him. He is quite alone, and we want him to look upon this place as his home while he is here. Your old acquaintance, Colonel Hambledon, has come down about this business. It is most horrifying. Can you imagine the poor sick people left with tipsy nurses, and, more dreadful still, girls locked up in cellars by the cruel matron for days at a time? but this fact has only just been made public.

"Goodness and enthusiasm like Mr. Trevithic's seem all the more beautiful when one hears such terrible histories of wickedness and neglect: one needs an example like his in this life to raise one from the unprofitable and miserable concerns of every day, and to teach one to believe in nobler efforts than one's own selfish and aimless wanderings could ever lead to unassisted.

"Pray remember me very kindly to Miss Moineaux and to Mrs. Trevithic, and believe me, dear Miss Triquett, very sincerely yours,
                                        "MARY MYLES."

"Is Mrs. Trevithic again suffering from neuralgia? Why is not she able to be with her husband?"

"Why, indeed?" said Miss Moineaux, hearing this last sentence read out by Miss Triquett. This excellent spinster gave no answer. She read this letter twice through deliberately; then she tied her bonnet securely on, and trotted off to Gummers and Co. Then, having dispensed the bounties and accepted the thanks of the poor creatures, she determined to run the chance of finding Mrs. Trevithic at home. "It is my painful dooty," said Triquett to herself, shaking her head—"my painful dooty. Anne

Trevithic should go to her husband; and I will tell her so. If I were Mr. Trevithic's wife, should I leave him to toil alone? No, I should not. Should I permit him to seek sympathy and consolation with another, more fascinating, perhaps? No, certainly not. And deeply grateful should I have felt to her who warned me on my fatal career; and surely my young friend Anne will be grateful to her old friend whose finger arrests her on the very edge of the dark precipice." Miss Triquett's reflections had risen to eloquence by the time she reached the rectory door. A vision of Anne clinging to her in tears, imploring her advice, of John shaking her warmly by the hand and murmuring that to Miss Triquett they owed the renewed happiness of their home, beguiled the way. "Where is Mrs. Trevithic?" she asked the butler, in her deepest voice. "Leave us," said Miss Triquett to the bewildered menial, as he opened the drawing-room door and she marched into the room; and then encountering Mrs. Trevithic, she suddenly clasped her in her well-meaning old arms.

"I have that to say to you," said Miss Triquett, in answer to Anne's amazed exclamation, "which I fear will give you pain; but were I in your place, I should wish to hear the truth." The good old soul was in earnest; her voice trembled, and her little black curls shook with agitation.

"Pray do not hesitate to mention any thing," said Mrs. Trevithic, surprised but calm, and sitting down and preparing to listen attentively. "I am sure any thing you would like to have attended to—"

Miss Triquett, at the invocation, pulled out the letter from her pocket. "Remember, only remember this," she said, "this comes from a young and attractive woman." And then in a clear and ringing voice she read out poor Mary's letter, with occasional unspeakable and penetrating looks at Anne's calm features.

Poor little letter! It had been written in the sincerity and innocence of Mary's heart. Any one more deeply read in such things might have wondered why Colonel Hambledon's name should have been brought into it; but as it was, it caused one poor jealous heart to beat with a force, a secret throb of sudden jealousy, that nearly choked Anne for an instant as she listened, and a faint pink tinge came rising up and coloring her face.

"Remember, she is very attractive," Miss Triquett re-echoed, folding up the page. "Ah! be warned, my dear young friend! Go to him; throw yourself into his arms; say, 'Dearest, darling husband, your little wife is by your side once more; I will be your comforter!' Do not hesitate." Poor old Triquett, completely carried away by the excitement of the moment, had started from her seat, and with extended arms had clasped an imaginary figure in the air. It was ludicrous, it was pathetic, to see this poor old silly meddlesome creature quivering, as her heart beat and bled for the fate of others. She had no tear or emotions of her own. It was absurd—was it not?—that she should care so deeply for things which could not affect her in the least degree. There was Anne, with her usual self-possession, calmly subduing her irritation. She did not smile; she did not frown; she did not seem to notice this momentary ebullition. To me it seems that, of the two, my sympathy is with Miss Triquett. Let us be absurd, by all means, if that is the price which must be paid for something which is well worth its price.

Miss Triquett's eyes were full of tears. "I am impetuous, Mrs. Trevithie," she said. "My aunt has often found fault with me for it. Pray excuse me if I have interfered unwarrantably."

"Interference between married people rarely does any good, Miss Triquett," said Anne, standing up with an icy platitude, and unmistakably showing that she considered the visit at an end.

"Good-bye," said poor Miss Triquett, wistfully. "Remember me most kindly to your papa."

"Certainly," said Mrs. Trevithie. "I am afraid you will have a disagreeable walk back in the rain, Miss Triquett. Good-evening. Pray give my compliments to Miss Moineaux."

The old maid trudged off alone into the mud and the rain, with a mortified sense of having behaved absurdly, disappointed and tired, and vaguely ashamed and crestfallen. The sound of the dinner-bell ringing at the rectory as she trudged down the hill in the dark and dirt did not add to her cheerfulness.

Anne, with flushed red cheeks and trembling hands, as Triquett left the room, sank down into her chair for a moment, and then, suddenly starting up, busied herself exactly as usual with her daily task of putting the drawing-room in order before she went up to dress. Miss Triquett's seat she pushed right away out of sight. She collected her father's writing-materials and newspapers, and put them straight. She then re-read her husband's last few lines. There was nothing to be gleaned from them. She replenished the flower-stands, and suddenly remembering that it was Mrs. Myles who had given them to her, she seized one tall glass fabric and all but flung it angrily on the ground. But reflecting that if it were broken it would spoil the pair, she put it back again into its corner, and contented herself with stuffing in all the ugliest scraps of twigs, dead leaves and flowers from the refuse of her basket.

The rector and his daughter dined at five; it was a whim of the old man's. Anne clutched Dulcie in her arms before she went down after dressing. The child had never seen her mamma so excited, and never remembered being kissed like that before by her. "D'oo lub me vely mush to-day, mamma?" said Dulcie, pathetically. "Is it toz I have my new fock?"

Old Mr. Bellingham came in at the sound of the second bell, smiling as usual, and rubbing his comfortable little fat hands together; he did not remark that any thing was amiss with his daughter, though he observed that there was not enough cayenne in the gravy of the veal cutlets, and that the cook had forgotten the necessary tea-spoonful of sugar in the soup. For the first time since he could remember, Anne failed to sympathize with his natural vexation, and seemed scarcely as annoyed as usual at the neglect which had been shown. Mr. Bellingham was vexed with her for her indifference: he always left the scolding to her; he liked every thing to go smooth and comfortable, and he did not like to be called upon personally to lose his temper. "For what we have received"—and the butler retires with the crumbs and the cloths, and the little old gentleman—who has had a fire lighted, for the evenings are getting chilly—draws comfortably in to his chimney-corner; while Anne, getting up from her place at the head of the table, says abruptly that she must go up stairs and see what Dulcie is about. A restless mood had come over her; something unlike any thing she had ever felt before. Little Triquett's eloquence, which had not even seemed to disturb Anne at the time, had had full time to sink into this somewhat torpid apprehension, and excite Mrs. Trevithie's indignation. It was not the less fierce because it had smouldered so long.

"Insolent creature!" Anne said to herself, working herself up into a passion; "how dare she interfere? Insolent, ridiculous creature! 'Remember that that woman is attractive'— How dare she speak so to me? Oh, they are all in league—in league against me!" cried poor Anne, with a moan, wringing her hands with all the twinkle of stones upon her slim white fingers. "John does not love me, he never loved me! He will not do as I wish, though he promised and swore at the altar he would. And she—she is spreading her wicked toils round him, and keeping him there, while I am here alone—all alone; and he leaves me exposed to the insolence of those horrible old maids. Papa eats his dinner and only thinks of the flavor of the dishes, and Dulcie chatters to her doll and don't care, and no one comes when I ring," sobbed Mrs. Trevithie, in a burst of tears, violently tugging at the bell-rope. "Oh, it is a shame, a shame!"

Only as she wiped away the tears a gleam of determination came into Mrs. Trevithie's blue eyes, and the flush on her pale cheeks deepened. She had taken a resolution. This is what she would do—this was her resolution: she would go and confront him there on the spot and remind him of his duty—he who was preaching to others. It was her right; and then—and then she would leave him forever, and never return to Sandsea to be scoffed at and jeered at by those horrible women, said Anne vaguely to herself as the door opened and the maid appeared. "Bring me a Bradshaw, Judson," said Mrs. Trevithie, very much in her usual tone of voice, and with a great effort recovering her equanimity. The storm had passed over, stirring the waters of this overgrown pool, breaking away the weeds which were growing so thickly on the stagnant surface, and rippling the slow shallows underneath. It seems a contradiction to write of this dull and unimpressionable woman now and then waking and experiencing some vague emotion and realization of experiences which had been slowly gathering, and apparently unnoticed, for a long time before: but who does not count more than one contradiction among their experiences? It was not Anne's fault that she could not understand, feel quickly and keenly, respond to the calls which stronger and more generous natures might make upon her; her tears fell dull and slow long after the cause, unlike the quick bright drops that would spring to Mary Miles's clear eyes—Mary whom the other woman hated with a natural, stupid, persistent hatred that nothing ever could change.

Judson, the maid, who was not deeply read in human nature and who respected her mistress immensely as a model of decision, precision, deliberate determination, was intensely amazed to hear that she was to pack up that **night**, and that Mrs. Trevithic would go to London that evening by the nine-o'clock train.

"Send for a fly directly, Judson, and dress Miss Dulcie."

"Dress Miss Dulcie?" Judson asked bewildered.

"Yes, Miss Dulcie will come too," said Anne, in a way that left no remonstrance.

She did not own it to herself: but by a strange and wayward turn of human nature, this woman—who was going to reproach her husband, to leave him forever, to cast herself adrift from him—took Dulcie with her: Dulcie, a secret defense, a bond and a strong link between them, that she knew no storm or tempest would ever break.

Mr. Bellingham was too much astounded to make a single objection. He thought his daughter had taken leave of her senses when she came in and said good-bye.

Poor thing, she, too, felt at moments as if her senses were deserting her; the storm raging in her heart was a fierce one. Gusts of passion and jealousy were straining and beating and tearing; "sails ripped, seams opening wide, and compass lost." Poor Anne, whose emotions were all the more ungovernable when they occasionally broke from the habitual restraint in which she held them, sat in her corner of the carriage, torturing herself, and picturing to herself Trevithic enslaved, enchanted. If she could have seen the poor fellow adding up long lists of figures in his dreary little office, by the light of a smoking lamp, I think her jealousy might have been appeased.

All the way to town Anne sat silent in her corner; but if she deserved punishment, poor thing, she inflicted it then upon herself, and with an art and an unrelenting determination for which no other executioner would have found the courage.

They reached the station at last, with its lights and transient life and bustle. A porter called a cab. Dulcie, and the maid, and Mrs. Trevithic got in. They were to sleep at the house of

an old lady, a sister of Mr. Bellingham's, who was away, as Anne knew, but whose housekeeper would admit them.

And then the journey began once more across dark cuts, winding thoroughfares, interminable in their lights and darknesses, across dark places that may have been squares. The darkness changed and lengthened the endless road: they had left Oxford Street, with its blazing shops; they had crossed the Park's blackness; the roll of the wheels was like the tune of some dismal night-march. The maid sat with Dulcie asleep in her arms, but presently Dulcie woke up with a shrill piteous outcry. "I'se so ti'ed," she sobbed in the darkness, the coldness, the dull trip of the rain, the monotonous sound of the horse's feet striking on the mud. "I wan' my tea; I'se so ti'ed, wan' my little bed"—this was her piteous litany.

Anne was very gentle and decided with her, only once she burst out, "Oh, don't, don't, I can not bear it, Dulcie."

CHAPTER IX.

OUR lives often seem to answer strangely to our wishes. Is there some hidden power by which our spirits work upon the substance of which our fate is built? Jack wished to fight. Assault him now, dire spirit of ill-will, of despondency, and that most cruel spirit of all, called calumny. This tribe of giants are like the bottle-monsters of the Arabian Nights, intangible, fierce, sly, remorseless, springing up suddenly, mighty shadows coming in the night and striking their deadly blows. They raise their clubs (and these clubs are not trees torn from the forest, but are made from the forms of human beings massed together), and the clubs fall upon the victim and he is crushed.

There was a brandy-and-water weekly meeting at Hammersley called "Ours," every Thursday evening, to which many of the tradespeople were in the habit of resorting and there discussing the politics of the place. Mr. Bulcox had long been a member, so was Pitchley the grocer, and Oker himself did not disdain to join the party; and as John was not there to contradict them, you may be sure these people told their own story. How it spread I can not tell, but it is easy to imagine: one rumor after another to the hurt and disadvantage of poor Trevithic began to get about. Reformers are necessarily unpopular among a certain class. The blind and the maimed and the halt worshipped the ground Trevithic stood upon at first. "He was a man as would see to their rights," they said; "and if he had his way, would let them have their snuff and a drop of something comfortable. He had his cranks. These open windows gave 'em the rheumatics, and this sloppin' and washin' was all along of it, and for all the talk there were some things but what they wouldn't deny was more snug in Bulcox's time than now; but he were a good creature for all that, Mr. Trevithic, and meant well he did," etc., etc. Only when the snuff and the comfortable drop did not come as they expected, and the horrors of the past dynasty began to be a little forgotten—at the end of a month or so of whitewashing and cleansing and reforming, the old folks began to grumble again much as usual. Trevithic could not take away their years and aches and pains and wearinesses, and make the workhouse into a bower of roses, and the old people into lovely young lasses and gallant lads again.

He had done his best, but he could not work miracles.

It happened that a Lincolnshire doctor writing from Downham to the *Jupiter* not long after, eloquently describing the symptoms, the treatment, the means of prevention for this new sort of cholera, spoke of the devotion of some and the curious indifference of others. "Will it be believed," he said, "that in some places the clergyman has been known to abandon his flock at the first threat of danger—a threat which in one especial case at F. not far from here was not fulfilled, although the writer can testify from his own experience to the truth of the above statement?"

As far as poor Jack's interests were concerned it would have been better for him if the cholera had broken out at Featherston; it would have brought him back to his own home. But Penfold recovered, Mrs. Hodge—the only other patient—died, Hodge married again immediately, and that was the end of it. "Ours" took in the *Jupiter*; somebody remembered that Downham and Featherston were both in the same neighborhood; some one else applied the story, and Bulcox and the gas-fitter between them concocted a paragraph for the *Anvil*, the great Hammersley organ; and so ill-will and rumor did their work, while Jack went his rounds in the wards of St. Magdalene's, looking sadder than the first day he had come, although the place was cleaner, the food warmer and better, the sick people better tended than ever before; for the guardians had been persuaded to let in certain deaconesses of the town—good women, who nursed for love and did not steal the tea. But in the mean time this odd cabal which had set in had risen and grown, and from every side Jack began to meet with cold looks and rebuffs. He had ill used his wife, deserted her, they said; abandoned his parish from fear of infection. He had forged, he had been expelled from his living. There was nothing that poor Jack was not accused of by one person or another. One day when his friend Austin came in with the last number of the *Anvil*, and showed him a very spiteful paragraph about himself, Jack only shrugged his shoulders. "We understand that the gentleman whose extraordinary revelations respecting the management of our work-house have been met by some with more credence than might have been expected, considering the short time which had passed since he first came

among us, is the rector alluded to in a recent letter to the *Jupiter* from a medical man, who deserted his parish at the first alarm of cholera." "Can this be true?" said Austin, gravely.

"Mrs. Hodge certainly died of the cholera," Jack answered, "and Penfold was taken ill and recovered. Those are the only two cases in my parish."

"I am afraid that Skipper did not behave very well; in fact, I had to write to him to go back."

A little later in the day, as the two young men were walking along the street, they met Mr. Oker puffing along the pavement. He stopped as usual to rub his hands when he saw Trevithic.

"'As your attention been called, sir," he said, "to a paragraft in the *Hanvil*, that your friends should contradict, if possible, sir? It's mos' distressin' when such things gets into the papers. They say at the club that some of the guardians is about to ask for an account of the sick-fund money, sir, which, I believe, Mr. Skipper put into your 'ands, sir. For the present this paragraft should be contradicted, if possible, sir."

Oker was an odious creature, insolent and civil; and as he spoke he gave a sly, spiteful glance into Jack's face. Trevithic was perfectly unmoved, and burst out laughing. "My good Mr. Oker," he said, "you will be sorry to hear that there is no foundation whatever in the paragraph. It is some silly tittle-tattling tale, which does not affect me in the least. If any one is to blame, it is Mr. Skipper, the work-house chaplain, who was at Featherston in my place. You can tell your friends at the club that they have hit the wrong man. Good-day." And the young fellow marched on his way with Mr. Austin, leaving Oker to recover as best he could.

"I'm afraid they will give you trouble yet," Austin said, "King Stork though you are."

When Jack appeared before the board on the next Wednesday, after the vote had been passed for dismissing the Bulcoxes, it seemed to him that one-half of the room greeted his entrance with a scowl of ill-will and disgust, the other half with alarm and suspicion. No wonder. It was Jack's belief that some of the guardians were seriously implicated in the charges which had been brought against Bulcox; others were certainly so far concerned that the *Jupiter* had accused them of unaccountable neglect; and nobody likes to be shown up in a leader even for merely neglecting his duties.

All this while the work-house had been in a commotion; the master and mistress were only temporarily fulfilling their duties until a new couple should have been appointed. The Board, chiefly at the instance of Oker the gas-fitter, and Pitchley the retail grocer, did not press the charges brought against Mr. Bulcox; but they contented themselves with dismissing him and his wife. It was not over pleasant for Trevithic to meet them about the place, as he could not help doing occasionally; but there was no help for it, and he bore the disagreeables of the place as best he could, until Mr. and Mrs. Evans, the newly appointed master and matron, made their appearance. The Board was very civil, but it was any thing but cordial to Trevithic. Jack, among other things, suspected that Pitchley himself supplied the bad tea and groceries which had been so much complained of, and had exchanged various bottles of port from the infirmary for others of a better quality, which were served at the master's own table. So the paupers told him.

Meanwhile the opposition had not been idle. It was Balcox himself, I think, who had discovered that Jack, in administering the very limited funds at his disposal, had greatly neglected the precaution of tickets. One or two ill-conditioned people, whom Trevithic had refused to assist, had applied to the late master, and assured him that Trevithic was not properly dispensing the money at his command. One tipsy old woman in particular was very indignant; and, judging by her own experience, did not hesitate to accuse the chaplain of keeping what was not his own.

This credible witness in rags and battered wires stood before the chairman when Jack came in. It seems impossible that any body should have seriously listened to a complaint so absurd and unlikely. But it must be remembered that many of the people present were already ill-disposed, that some of them were weak, and others stupid, and they would not have been sorry to get out of their scrape by discovering Jack to be of their own flesh and blood.

Trevithic heard them without a word, mechanically buttoning up his coat, as he had a trick of doing, and then in a sudden indignation he tore it open, and from his breast-pocket drew the small book in which he had made all his notes. "Here," said he, "are my accounts. They were made hastily at the time, but they are accurate, and you will see that I have paid every farthing away that was handed over to me by Mr. Skipper, and about twice the amount besides, out of my own pocket. You can send for the people to whom I have paid the money, if you like." The little book went travelling about from one hand to another, while the remorseless Trevithic continued, "I now in my turn demand that the ledgers of these gentlemen"—blazing round upon the retail grocer and Oker the gas-fitter—"be produced here immediately upon the spot, without any previous inspection, and that I, too, may have the satisfaction of clearing up my doubts as to their conduct." "That is fair enough," said one or two of the people present. "It's quite impossible, unheard of," said some of the others; but the majority of the guardians present were honest men, who were roused at last, and the ledgers were actually sent for.

I have no time here to explain the long course of fraud which these books disclosed. The grocer was found to have been supplying the house at an enormous percentage, with quantities differing in his book and in that of the master, who must again have levied a profit. The gas-fitter, too, turned out to be the contractor from a branch establishment, and to have also helped himself. This giant of peculation certainly fell dead upon the floor when he laid open his accounts before the Board, for Hammersley Work-house is now one of the best managed in the whole kingdom.

CHAPTER X

JACK HELPS TO DISENCHANT THE BEAUTIFUL
LADY.

FANNY GARNIER bustled home one afternoon, brimming over, good soul, with rheumatisms, chicken-poxes, and other horrors that were not horrors to her, or interjections, or lamentations; but new reasons for exertions which were almost beyond her strength at times—as now, when she said wearily, "that she must go back to her ward; some one was waiting for things that she had promised." She was tired, and Mary, half ashamed, could not help offering to go in her cousin's place. It seemed foolish to refrain from what she would have done yesterday in all simplicity, because there was a chance that Hambledon was there to-day, or Trevithic, who was Hambledon's friend, if not quite Hambledon himself, who talked to him and knew his mind, and could repeat his talk.

When Mary reached the infirm-ward, where she was taking her jellies, and bird's-eye and liquorice, her heart gave a little flutter, for she saw that two figures were standing by one of the beds. One was Jack, who turned round to greet her as she came up with her basket on her arm. The other was Hambledon, who looked at her and then turned away. As for all the old women in their starched nightcaps, it was a moment of all-absorbing excitement to them—sitting bolt upright on their beds, and bowing affably, as was the fashion in the infirm-ward. It was quite worth while to be civil to the gentry, let alone manners; you never knew but what they might have a quarter of a pound of tea or a screw of snuff in their pockets. "Law bless you, it was not such as them as denies themselves anythink they may fancy." Such was the Hammersley creed.

As she came up, Mary made an effort, and in her most self-possessed and woman-of-the-worldest manner put out her hand again and laughed, and exclaimed at this meeting. Her shyness, and the very effort she made to conceal it, gave her an artificial manner that chilled and repelled poor Hambledon as no shyness or hesitation would have done. "She's no heart," said the poor Colonel to himself. "She don't remember. She would only laugh at me." He forgot that Mary was not a child, not even a very young woman; that this armor of expediency had grown up naturally with years and with the strain of a solitary life. It is a sort of defense to which the poor little hedgehogs of women, such as Mary Myles, resort sometimes. It meant very little, but it frightened the Colonel away. Mrs. Myles heard him go as she bent over poor old Mrs. Crosspoint, and her heart gave a little ache, which was not entirely of sympathy for the poor old thing's troubles.

However, Mary had a little talk with Trevithic in the dark as she crossed the courts and passages, and he walked beside her, which did her good, though she said nothing that any one who did not know would have construed into more than it seemed to mean.

She told him a little about her past life. She did not tell him that Colonel Hambledon had once asked her to come into his life ; but Trevithic knew all that she wanted to say as he listened to the voice speaking in the dark—the sweet low voice with the music in it—a revelation came to him there in the archway of that narrow work-house stone passage.

A revelation came to him, and that instant, as was his way, he acted upon it. "I think some people—" he began, and then he stopped. "I think you should secure a friend," he said quickly, in an odd voice. "You should marry," and he faltered, as he made way for two poor women who limped past on their way to their corners in the great pigeon-holes case of human suffering. That little shake in his voice frightened Trevithic. What was it to him? How did Mary Myles's fate concern him? He let her out at the great gate. He did not offer to walk back with her. The great iron bars closed with a clang, as she went away out into the dim world that was surging round about these prison walls. He would go back to Anne, Trevithic said to himself ; even while the last grateful words were uttering in his ears, and the sweet quick eyes still lighting up for him the dullness of the stony place. Mary Myles went back alone ; and all that night Jack lay awake thinking, turning some things in his mind and avoiding others, wondering what he should say to Hambledon, what he should leave unsaid ; for some nameless power had taught him to understand now, as he never had understood before, what was passing in other minds and hearts. A power too mighty for my poor Jack to encounter or hope to overcome in fight, a giant from whom the bravest can only turn away—so gentle is he, so beautiful, so humble in his irresistible might, that though many might conquer him if they would, they will not, and that is the battle.

And I think this giant must have been that nameless one we read of in the story, whom Jack did not care to fight, but he locked him up and barred him in the castle, and bolted gates and kept him safe behind them : the giant who in return for this strange treatment gave Jack the sword of sharpness and the cap of knowledge. The sword pricked fiercely enough, the cap of knowledge weighed, ah, too heavily, but Jack, as we know, did not shrink from pain.

The imprisoned giant touched some kindly chord in Jack's kind heart. Was he not Hambledon's friend ? was he not a link between two people, very near, and yet very far apart ? Had Mary Myles's kindness been quite disinterested ? he asked himself, a little bitterly, before he spoke ;—spoke a few words which made Charles Hambledon flush up and begin to tug at his mustache, and which decided Mary Myles's fate as much as Anne Bellingham's tears had decided Jack's three years ago.

"Why don't you try again ?" Trevithic said. "I think there might be a chance for you."

The Colonel did not answer, but went on pulling at his mustache. Trevithic was silent, too, and sighed. "I never saw any one like her," he said at last. "I think she carries a blessing wherever she goes. I, who am an old married man, may say so much, mayn't I? I have seen some men go on their knees for gratitude for what others are scarcely willing to put out their hands to take."

Poor Jack! The cap of knowledge was heavy on his brow as he spoke. He did not look to see the effect of his words. What would he not have said to serve her ? He walked away to the desk where he kept his notes and account-books, and took pen and paper, and began to write.

"It is a lucky thing for me that you are a married man," the Colonel said, with an uneasy laugh. "It's one's fate. They won't like the connection at home. She don't care about it one way or another, for all you say ; and yet I find myself here again and again. I have a great mind to go this very evening."

"I am writing to her now," Trevithic answered, rather incoherently, after a minute. "The ladies have promised to come with me to-morrow to see the rectory-house at St. Bigot's. I shall call for them about twelve o'clock ; and it will take us a quarter of an hour to walk there."

It was a bright autumn morning, glittering and brilliant. Jack stood waiting for Mrs. Myles and her cousin in the little wood at the foot of the garden slope, just behind the lodge. A bird with outstretched wings, fluttered from the ivy-bed at his feet, and went and perched upon the branch of a tree. All the noises of life came to him from the town, glistening between the gleam of the trees : the fall of the hammer from the wood-yard where the men were at work, and the call of the church-bell to prayer, and the distant crow of the farm-yard upon the far-off hill, and the whistle of the engine, starting and speeding through the quiet country valley to the junction in the town, where the great world's gangways met and diverged.

All this daily life was going on, and John Trevithic struck with his stick at a dead branch of a tree. Why was work, so simple and straightforward a business to some honest folks, so tangled and troubled and unsatisfactory to others ? In daily life hard labor is simple enough. Old Peascod, down below in the kitchen-garden, turns over mother earth, throbbing with life and all its mysteries, with what he calls a "purty shovel," and pats it down, and complacently thinks it is his own doing that the ivy-slips cut off the branch which he has stuck into the ground are growing and striking out fresh roots.

Peascod is only a sort of shovel himself, destined to keep this one small acre out of the square **acres** which cover the surface of the earth in tolerable order, and he does it with a certain amount of spurring and pushing, and when his day's work is over hangs up comfortably on a nail and rests with an easy mind ; but Jack, who feels himself a shovel too, has no laws to guide him. Some of the grain he has sown has come up above the ground, it is true, but it is unsatisfactory, after all; he does not know whether or not his slips are taking root—one or two of them he has pulled up, like the children do, to see whether they are growing.

As Jack stands moralizing, crow cocks, ring bells, strike hammers. It was a fitting chorus, distant and cheerful, and suggestive to the sweet and brilliant life of the lady for whom he waits. Not silence, but the pleasant echoes of life should accompany her steps, the cheerful strains of summer, and the bright colors of spring. Trevithic saw every thing brightened and lighted up by her presence, and thought that it was so in fact, poor fellow. Sometimes in a foul ward, when the dull sights and sounds oppressed him almost beyond bearing, with a sudden breath of relief and happiness the image of this charming and beautiful woman would pass before him, sweet and pure, and lovely and unsoiled amidst lovely things, far away from these ghastly precincts. What had such as she to do with such as these ? Heaven forbid that so fair a bird, with its tender song and glancing white plumage, should come to be choked and soiled and caged in the foul dungeons to which he felt called. John Trevithic, like many others, exaggerated, I think, to himself the beauty and the ugliness of the things he looked upon as they appeared to others; not that things are not ten thousand times more beautiful, and more hideous too perhaps, than we have eyes to see or hearts to realize, but they are not so as far as the eyes with which others see them are concerned. To this sweet and beautiful and graceful woman the world was not so fair a place as to this careworn man with his haggard eyes and sad knowledge of life. He thought Mrs. Myles so far above him and beyond him in all things, that he imagined that the pains of others must pain her and strike her soft heart more cruelly even than himself, that the loveliness of life was more necessary to her a thousand times than it could be to him.

Meanwhile all the little dried pine-twigs were rustling and rippling, for she was coming down the little steep path, holding up her muslin skirts as she came, and stepping with her rapid slender footsteps, stooping and then looking up to smile. Mrs. Myles was always well dressed—there was a certain completeness and perfection of dainty smoothness and freshness about all her ways which belonged to her dress and her life, and her very loves and dislikes. The soft flutter of

her ribbons belongs to her as completely as the pointed ends of old Peascod's Sunday shirt-collars and the broad stiff tapes of his best waist-coat do to him, or as John Trevithic's fancies as he stands in the fir-wood. Another minute and she is there beside him, holding out her hand and smiling with her sweet still eyes, and the bird flutters away from **its branch**. " Fanny can not come," she said. " **We must go** without her, Mr. Trevithic."

A something—I can not **tell you** what—told Jack as she spoke that this was the **last** walk they would ever take together. It was **one of** those feelings we all know and all believe in at the bottom of our hearts. This something, coming I know not from whence, going I know not where, suddenly began to speak in the silent and empty chambers of poor Trevithic's heart, echoing mournfully, but with a warning in its echoes that he had never understood before. This something seemed to say, No, No, No. It was like a bell tolling as they walked along the road. Jack led the way, and they turned off the high-road across a waste, through sudden streets springing up around them, across a bridge over a branch of the railway, into a broad black thoroughfare, which opened into the quiet street leading into Bolton Fields. The fields had long since turned to stones and iron-railings inclosing a church-yard, in the midst of which a church had been built. The houses all round the square were quaint red brick dwellings, with here and there a carved lintel to a doorway, and old stone steps whitened and scrubbed by three or four generations of patient house-maids. The trees were bare behind the iron-railing; there was silence, though the streets beyond Bolton Fields were busy like London streets. Trevithic stopped at the door of one of the largest of these dwellings. It had straight windows like the others, and broken stone steps upon which the sun was shining, and tall iron railings casting slant shadows on the pavement. It looked quaint and narrow, with its high rooms and blackened bricks, but it stood in sunshine. A child was peeping from one of the many-paned windows, and some birds were fluttering under the deep eaves of the roof.

Jack led the way into the dark-panelled entrance, and opened doors and windows, and ran up stairs. Mrs. Myles flitted here and there, suggested, approved of the quaint old house, with the sunny landings for Dulcie to play on, and the convenient cupboards for her elders, and quaint recesses, and the pleasant hints of an old world, more prosy and deliberate and less prosaic than to-day. There was a pretty little niche on the stairs, where Jack fancied Dulcie perching, and a window looking into the garden down below ; there was a little wooden dining-room, and a study with faded wire book-cases let into the walls. It was all in good order, for Trevithic had had it cleaned and scrubbed. The house was more cheerful than the garden at the back, where stone and weeds seemed to be flourishing unmolested.

"It is almost time to go," Mrs. Myles said at last, seeing Trevithic looking at his watch.

"Not yet—you have not half seen the garden," answered Trevithic, hastily. "Come this way." And Mary followed, wrapping her velvet cloak more closely round her slender shoulders.

They were standing in the little deserted garden of the house, for the garden was all damp, as gardens are which are rarely visited. The back of the house, less cheerful than the front, was close-shuttered, except for the windows Trevithic had opened. Some dreary aloe-trees were sprouting their melancholy spikes, a clump of fir-trees and laurel-bushes was shuddering in one corner; a long grass-grown lawn, with rank weeds and shabby flower-beds, reached from the black windows to the stony paths, in which, in some unaccountable manner, as is usual in deserted places, the sand and gravel had grown into stones and lumps of earth and clay. Jack was strangely silent and distracted, and paced round and round the place in an unmeaning way.

"This is very dreary," said Mrs. Myles, pulling her cloak still closer round her. "I like the house, but no one could be happy walking in this garden."

Trevithic smiled a little sadly. "I don't know," he said. "I don't think happiness depends upon locality."

Poor fellow, his outward circumstances were so prosperous, his inner life so sad and untoward. No wonder that he undervalued external matters, and counted all lost that was not from within.

Mary Myles blushed, as she had a way of blushing when she was moved, and her voice failed into a low measured music of its own. "I envy you," she said. "You do not care, like me, for small things, and are above the influences of comfort and discomfort, of mere personal gratifications. It has been the curse of my life that I have never risen above any thing, but have fallen shamefully before such easy temptations that I am ashamed even to recall them. I wonder what it is like," she said, with her bright, half-laughing, half-admiring smile, "to be, as you are, above small distractions, and able to fight real and great battles—and win them, too?" she added, kindly and heartily.

A very faint mist came before Trevithic's eyes as Mary spoke, unconsciously encouraging him, unknowingly cheering him with words and appreciation—how precious she did not know, nor did he dare to tell himself.

"I am afraid what you describe is a sensation very few people know," said Trevithic. "We are all, I suspect, trying to make the best of our defeats; triumphant, if we are not utterly routed."

"And have you been routed at Featherston?" Mrs. Myles asked.

"Completely," said Trevithic. "Anne will retreat with flying colors, but I am ignobly defeated, and only too thankful to run away and come and live here—in this very house perhaps—if she will consent to it."

"Anne is a happy woman to have any one to want her," said Mrs. Myles, coming back to her own thoughts with a sigh; "people love me, but nobody wants me."

"Here is a friend of yours, I think," said Jack, very quickly, in an odd sort of voice; for as he spoke he saw Hambledon coming in from the passage-door. Mrs. Myles saw him too, and guessed in an instant why Trevithic had detained her. Now in her turn she tried to hold him back.

"Do you believe in expiations, Mr. Trevithic?" said Mary, still strangely excited and beginning to tremble.

"I believe in a grateful heart, and in love and humility, and in happiness when it comes across our way," said Jack, with kind sad eyes, looking admiringly at the sweet and appealing face.

Mary was transformed. She had laid aside all her gentle pride and self-contained sadness: she looked as she must have looked long ago, when she was a girl, humble, imploring, confused; and though her looks seemed to pray him to remain, Trevithic turned away abruptly, and he went to meet Hambledon, who was coming shyly along the weedy path, a tall and prosperous-looking figure in the sunshine and desolation. "You are late," Trevithic said, with a kind, odd smile; "I had given you up." And then he left them and went into the house.

As Jack waited, talking to the housekeeper meanwhile, he had no great courage to ask himself many questions; to look behind; to realize very plainly what had happened; to picture to himself what might have been had fate willed it otherwise. He prayed an honest prayer. "Heaven bless them," he said in his heart, as he turned his steps away and left them together. He waited now patiently, walking in and out of the bare rooms, where people had once lived and waited too, who were gone with their anxious hearts, and their hopes, and their hopeless loves, and their defeats, to live in other houses and mansions which are built elsewhere. Was it all defeat for him?—not all. Had he not unconsciously wronged poor Anne, and given her just cause for resentment; and was any thing too late while hope and life remained? If he could not give to his wife a heart's best love and devotion—if she herself had forbidden this—he could give her friendship, and in time the gentle ties of long use and common interest and Dulcie's dear little arms might draw them closer together—so Jack thought in this softened mood.

John had waited a long time, pacing up and down the empty rooms with the faded wire bookcases for furniture, and the melancholy pegs and hooks and wooden slabs which people leave behind them in the houses they abandon: nearly an hour had passed and the two there out in the garden were talking still by the laurel-bushes. What was he waiting for? he ask-

P

ed himself presently. Had they not forgotten his very existence? There was work to be done—he had better go. What had he waited for so long? What indeed, poor fellow! He had been longing for a word; one sign. He only wanted to be remembered: with that strange selfish longing which pities the poor familiar self, he longed for some word of kindness and sign of recognition from the two who had forgotten that any where besides in all the world there were hearts that loved or longed or forgot. John trudged away patiently as soon as he had suddenly made clear to himself that it was time to go. He knew the road well enough by this time, and cut off side turnings and came into the town—black and faded—even in this brilliant sunshine that was calling the people out of their houses, opening wide windows, drying the rags of clothes, brightening the weary faces. The children clustered round the lamp-posts, chattering and playing. One or two people said good-morning to him as he passed, who would have stared sulkily in a fog; the horses in the road seemed to prick their ears, and the fly from the station, instead of crawling wearily along, actually passed him at a trot. Jack turned to look after it: a foolish likeness had struck him.' It was but for an instant, and he forgot it as he reached the heavy door of the work-house.

The porter was out, and the old pauper who let Jack in began some story to which he scarcely listened. He was full of the thought of those two there in the garden—happy! ah, how happy in each other's companionship; while he, deserted, lonely, discontented, might scarcely own to himself, without sin, that his home was a desolate one; that his wife was no wife, as he felt it; that life had no such prospects of love, solace, and sympathy for him, as for some of the most forlorn of the creatures under his care. It was an ill frame of mind coming so quickly after a good one—good work done, and peace-making, and a good fight won; but the very giant he had conquered with pain and struggle had given him the cap of knowledge, and it pressed and ached upon his brow, and set its mark there. Trevithic put up his hand to his forehead wearily, as he walked along the dull paved courts and passed through one barred iron door after another. Most of the old folks were sunning themselves upon the benches, and the women were standing gossiping in the galleries of the house. There are stone galleries at Hammersley, from which the clothes are hung. So he came in, opening one last iron gate to his office on the ground-floor, at the further extremity of the great building. It was not very far from the children's wards, and on these fine mornings the little creatures, with their quaint mobcaps, and straight bonnets, came scrambling down the flight of steps into the yards. The very young ones would play about a little bo-peep behind an iron grating, or clinging to the skirts of the limp figures that were wearily lagging about the place. But the children did not very long keep up their little baby frolics. Sad-faced little paupers in striped blue dresses would sometimes stand staring at Trevithic—with dark eyes gleaming in such world-weighed little faces, that his kind heart ached for them. His favorite dream for them was a children's holiday. It would almost seem that they had guessed his good intentions towards them to-day: a little stream was setting in in the direction of his office, a small group stood watching not far off. It made way before him and disappeared, and then, as he came near, he saw that the door was open. A little baby pauper was sitting on the flags and staring in, two other little children had crept up to the very threshold, a third had slipped its fingers into the hinge and was peeping through the chink, and then at the sound of his tired footsteps falling wearily on the pavement, there came a little cry of "Daddy, daddy!" The sweet little voice he loved best in the whole world seemed to fill the room, and Dulcie, his own little Dulcie, came to the door in the sunlight, and clasped him round the knees.

Trevithic, with these little arms to hold him safe, felt as if his complaints had been almost impious. In one minute, indeed, he had forgotten them altogether, and life still had something for him to love and to cling to. The nurse explained matters a little to the bewildered chaplain. Nothing had happened that she knew of. Mrs. Trevithic was gone to look for him. She had driven to Mrs. Myles's straight in the fly from the railway. She had left Miss Dulcie and her there to wait. She had left no message. Mrs. Trevithic had seemed put out like, said the nurse, and had made up her mind all of a sudden. They had slept in London at missis's aunt's. Trevithic was utterly bewildered.

In the mean time it was clear that something must be done for Dulcie, who was getting hungry, now that her first little rapture was over (for raptures are hungry work). After some little demur, Trevithic told the girl to put on Miss Dulcie's cloak again.

While John is talking to Dulcie in his little office, Anne had driven up to Mrs. Garnier's door, and been directed from hence to the rectory in Bolton Fields. It was thus she first crossed the threshold of her husband's house. "I want to speak to the lady and gentleman," she said to the woman who let her in. And the housekeeper pointed to the garden and told her she would find them there. Anne, the stupid commonplace woman, was shivering with passion and emotion as she passed through the empty rooms; a few letters were lying on the chimney that John had torn open; the window-shutter was flapping, the wood creaked under her fierce angry footsteps. There, at the end of the path, under a little holly-tree, stood Mary Myles, and suddenly Anne, hurrying along in her passion, clutched her arm with an angry fevered hand, and with a fierce flushed face confronted her. "Where is my husband?" hissed Anne. "You did not think that I should come .... How dare you take him from me?"

Colonel Hambledon, who had only gone away for a step or two, came back, holding a voice, with Mary's glove, which she had left on the broken seat where they had been sitting. "What is this?" said he.

"Where is he?" cried the foolish stupid woman, bursting into tears. "I knew I should find him here with her. Where is my husband?"

"He has been gone some time, poor fellow," said the Colonel, with a look of repugnance and dislike that Anne saw and never forgot. "Mrs. Trevithic, why do you think such bad thoughts?"

While Mary Myles, indignant in her turn, cried, "Oh, for shame, for shame, Anne Trevithic! You are cold-hearted yourself, and do you dare to be jealous of others? You, who have the best and kindest husband any woman ever had in all the world." Mary, as she spoke clung with both hands to Hambledon's arm, trembling, too, and almost crying. The Colonel, in his happiness, could hardly understand that any one else should be unhappy on such a day. While he was comforting Mary, and entreating her not to mind what that woman had said, Anne, overpowered with shame, conscience-smitten, fled away down the path and through the house—"deadly pale, like a ghost," said the housekeeper afterwards—and drove straight to the work-house, where she had left her child. As she came to the great door, it opened with a dull sound, even before the driver had pulled at the big bell.

Anne, who had got out of the carriage, stood in a bewildered sort of dream, stupidly staring at a little procession that was coming under the archway—a couple of paupers, the nursemaid, and, last of all, her husband, carrying little Dulcie in his arms, who were all advancing towards her.

"Oh John! I have been looking for you everywhere," she said, with a little cry, as with a revulsion of feeling she ran up to him, with outstretched hands. "Where have you been? Mrs. Myles did not know, and I came back for Dulcie. We shall miss the train. Oh, where am I to go?"

Mrs. Trevithic, nervous, fluttered, bewildered, for perhaps the second time in her life, seemed scarcely to know what she was saying—she held up her cheek to be kissed; she looked about quite scared, and shrunk away again. "It's no use, you will be too angry to forgive me," she said; "but about these trains . . . ."

"What do you mean by the trains, Anne?" her husband said. "Dulcie wants something to eat. Get into the carriage again."

It is difficult to believe—Trevithic himself could not understand it—Anne obeyed without a word. He asked no questions when she burst out with an incoherent, "Oh John, they were so strange and unkind!" and then began to cry and cry and tremble from head to foot.

It was not till they got to the hotel that Mrs. Trevithic regained her usual composure, and ordered some rooms and lunch off the carte for the whole party. Trevithic never asked what had

happened, though he guessed well enough, and when Hambledon told him afterwards that Mrs. Trevithic had burst in upon them in the garden, it was no news to poor John.

They had finished their dinner on the ground-floor room of the quiet old inn. Little Dulcie was perched at the window watching the people as they crossed and recrossed the wire-blind. A distant church-clock struck some quarters, the sound came down the street, and Trevithic smiled, saying, "I think you will be too late for your train, Anne, to-day." Anne's heart gave a throb as he spoke. She always thought people in earnest, and she looked up wistfully and tried to speak; but the words somehow stuck in her throat. Meanwhile Trevithic looked at his watch, and jumped up in a sudden fluster. It was later than he imagined. He had his afternoon service at the work-house to attend to. It was Friday, and he must go. He had not a moment to lose, so he told his wife in a word as he seized his hat, and set off as hard as he could. He had not even a moment to respond to little Dulcie's signals of affection, and waves and capers behind the wire-blind.

Anne, who had been in a curious maze all this time, sitting in her place at the table and watching him, and scarcely realizing the relief of his presence as he busied himself in the old way for her comfort and Dulcie's, carving the chicken and waiting on them both, understood all at once how great the comfort of his presence had been. In her dull, sleepy way she had been basking in sunshine for the last two hours, after the storm of the day before. She had untied her bonnet, and thrown it down upon a chair, and forgotten to smooth her sleek hair; her collar and ribbons were awry; her very face had lost its usual placidity—it was altered and disturbed, and yet Jack thought he had never liked her looks so well, though he had never seen her so, ruffled and self-forgetful in all the course of his married life.

For the moment Mrs. Trevithic was strangely happy in this odd re-union. She had almost forgotten at the instant the morning's jealousy and mad expedition — Colonel Hambledon's look of scorn and Mary Myles's words—in this new unknown happiness. It seemed to her that she had never in her life before realized what the comfort might be of some one to love, to hold, to live for. She watched the quick clever hands dispensing the food for which, to tell the truth, she had no very great appetite, though she took all that her husband gave her. Had some scales fallen from her pale wondering eyes? As he left the room she asked herself, in her stupid way, what he had meant. Was this one little glimpse of home the last that she would ever know? was it all over, all over? Anne tied her bonnet on again, and telling the maid to take care of little Dulcie, went out into the street again and walked off in the direction of the chapel. She had a vague wish to be there. She did not know that they would admit her; but no difficulties were made, and she passed for the second time under the big arch. Some one pointed out the way, and she pushed open a green-baize door and went in; and so Anne knelt in the bare little temple where the paupers' prayers were offered up — humble prayers and white-wash, that answer their purpose as well perhaps as Gothic, and iron castings, and flamboyant windows, as the beautiful clear notes of the choristers answering each other and bursting into triumphal utterance. The paupers were praying for their daily bread, hard, and dry, and butterless; for forgiveness for trespasses grosser and blacker perhaps than ours; for deliverance from evil of which Annie and others perhaps have never realized; and ending with words of praise and adoration which we all use in truth, but which mean far, far more when uttered from that darkness upon which the divine light beams most splendidly. Anne for the first time in her life was kneeling a pauper in spirit, ashamed and touched, and repentant.

There was no sermon, and Mrs. Trevithic got up from her knees and came away with her fellow-petitioners and waited in the court-yard for John. The afternoon sun of this long eventful day was shining on the stones and casting the shadows of the bars and bolts, and brightening sad faces of the old men and women, and the happy faces of two people who had also attended the service, and who now advanced arm in arm to where Anne was standing. She started back as she first saw them: they had been behind her in the chapel, and she had not known that they were there.

The sight of the two had brought back with it all the old feeling of hatred, and shame, and mistrust; all the good that was in her seemed to shrink and shrivel away for an instant at their approach, and at the same time came a pang of envious longing. They seemed so happy together; so one, as, with a glance at one another, they both came forward. Was she all alone when others were happy? had she not of her own doing put her husband away from her, and only come to him to reproach and leave him again? For a woman of such obstinacy and limited perception as Mrs. Trevithic to have settled that a thing was to be, was reason enough for it to happen; only a longing, passionate longing, came, that it might be otherwise than she had settled; that she might be allowed to stay—and a rush of the better feelings that had overcome her of late kept her there waiting to speak to these two who had scorned her. It was they who made the first advance.

"I want to ask you to forgive me," said Mary, blushing, "any thing I may have said. Your husband has done us both such service, that I can't help asking you for his sake to forget my hastiness."

"You see we were taken aback," said the Colonel, not unkindly. "Shake hands, please, Mrs. Trevithic, in token that you forgive us, and wish us joy. I assure you we are heartily

sorry if we pained you." Anne flushed and flushed and didn't speak, but put out her hand —not without an effort. "Are you going back directly, or are you going to stay with your husband?" said the colonel, shaking her heartily by the hand.

Poor Anne looked up, scared, and shrank back once more—she could not bear to tell them that she did not know. She turned away all hurt and frightened, looking about for some means of escape, and then at that moment she saw that John was coming up to them across the yard from the office where he had gone to leave his surplice.

"Oh John," she said, still bewildered, and going to meet him, and with a piteous face, "here are Colonel Hambledon and Mary."

"We have come to ask for your congratulations," the Colonel said, laughing and looking very happy; "and to tell you that your match-making has been successful."

Mary Myles did not speak, but put out her hand to Trevithic.

Mrs. Trevithic meanwhile stood waiting her sentence. How new the old accustomed situations seem as they occur again and again in the course of our lives. Waters of sorrow overwhelm in their depths, as do the clear streams of tranquil happiness, both rising from distant sources, and flowing on either side of our paths. As I have said, the sight of these two, in their confidence and sympathy, filled poor Anne's heart with a longing that she had never known before. Mary Myles, I think, guessed what was passing in the other's mind—women feel one another's passing emotions—but the good Colonel was utterly unconscious.

"We have been asking your wife if she remains with you, or if she is going back directly," said he. "I thought perhaps you would both come to dine with us before we go."

There was a mist before Anne's eyes, an unspeakable peace in her heart, as Jack drew her hand through his arm, and said, in his kind voice, "Of course she stays; I am not going to let my belongings go away again, now that I have got them here."

As they were walking back to the inn together, Anne told her husband of her morning's work, and John sighed as he listened.

"We have both something to forgive," he said once more, looking at her with his kind speaking eyes.

Anne winced and looked away, and then her heart turned again, and she spoke and said, with real sensibility:—

"I have nothing to forgive, John. I thought you were in the wrong, but it was I from the beginning."

After a little time Trevithic and Anne and Dulcie went to live together in the old house in Bolton Fields. The woman was humbled, and did her best to make her husband's home happy, and John too remembered the past, and loved his wife, with all her faults, and did not ask too much of her, and kept clear, as best he could, of possible struggles and difficulties. His life was hard, but blows and fatigue he did not grudge, so long as he could help to deliver the land. Foul caverns were cleansed, ignorant monsters were routed, dark things were made light. He was not content in his parish to drive away evil; he tried his best and strove to change it, and make it into good. These tangible dragons and giants were hard to fight, but once attacked they generally succumbed in the end, and lost perhaps one head or a claw in each successive encounter, and then other champions rose up, and by degrees the monster began to fall and dwindle away. But poor Trevithic's work is not over. Another giant is coming to meet him through the darkness. He is no hideous monster of evil like the rest: his face is pitiless, but his eyes are clear and calm. His still voice says "Hold," and then it swells by degrees, and deafens all other sound. "I am a spirit of truth, men call me evil because I come out of the darkness," the giant cries; "but see, my works are good as well as bad! See what bigotry, what narrow prejudice, what cruelty and wickedness and intolerance I have attacked and put to rout!" In the story-book it is Jack who is the conqueror; he saws through the bridge by which the giant approaches, and the giant falls into the moat and is drowned. But, as far as I can see, the Jacks of this day would rather make a way for him than shut him out; some of the heroes who have tried to saw away the bridge have fallen into the moat with their enemy, and others are making but a weak defense, and in their hearts would be glad to admit him into the palace of the King.

Mrs. Trevithic rarely goes into the garden at the back of her house. The other day, being vexed with her husband about some trifling matter, she followed him out to remonstrate. He was standing with Dulcie by the prickly holly-tree that she remembered so well, and, seeing her coming, he put out his hand with a smile. The words of reproach died away on Anne's lips, and two bright spots came into her cheeks, as with a very rare display of feeling she suddenly stooped and kissed the hand that held hers.

As I finish the story of Jack Trevithic, which, from the play in which it began, has turned to earnest, H. looks up from her knitting, and says that it is very unsatisfactory, and that she is getting tired of calling every thing by different names; and she thinks she would like to go back to the realities of life again. In my dream-world they have been forgotten, for the fire is nearly out and the gray mist is spreading along the streets. It is too dark to write any more—an organ is playing a dismal tune, a carriage is rolling over the stones; so I ring the bell for the lamp and the coals, and Susan comes in to shut the shutters.

THE STORY OF ELIZABETH.

TO

J. M. C.

THE STORY OF ELIZABETH.

CHAPTER I.

*   *   *   *   *

If singing breath, or echoing chord,
To every hidden pang were given,
What endless melodies were poured
As sad as earth, as sweet as heaven!

THIS is the story of a foolish woman, who, through her own folly, learned wisdom at last; whose troubles—they were not very great, they might have made the happiness of some less eager spirit—were more than she knew how to bear. The lesson of life was a hard lesson to her. She would not learn, she revolted against the wholesome doctrine. And while she was crying out that she would not learn, and turning away and railing and complaining against her fate, days, hours, fate, went on their course. And they passed unmoved; and it was she who gave way, she who was altered, she who was touched and torn by her own complaints and regrets.

Elizabeth had great soft eyes and pretty yellow hair, and a sweet flitting smile, which came out like sunlight over her face, and lit up yours and mine, and any other it might chance to fall upon. She used to smile at herself in the glass, as many a girl has done before her; she used to dance about the room, and think: "Come life, come life, mine is going to be a happy one. Here I am awaiting, and I was made handsome to be admired, and to be loved, and to be hated by a few, and worshipped by a few, and envied by all. I am handsomer than Lætitia a thousand times. I am glad I have no money as she has, and that I shall be loved for myself, for my *beaux yeux*. One person turns pale when they look at him. Tra la la, tra la la!" and she danced along the room singing. There was no carpet, only a smooth polished floor. Three tall windows looked out into a busy Paris street paved with stones, over which carriages and cabs and hand-trucks were jolting. There was a clock, and artificial flowers in china vases on the chimney, a red velvet sofa, a sort of *étagère* with ornaments, and a great double-door wide open, through which you could see a dining-room, also bare, polished, with a round table and an oil-cloth cover, and a white china stove, and some waxwork fruit on the sideboard, and a maid in a white cap at work in the window.

Presently there came a ring at the bell. Elizabeth stopped short in her dance, and the maid rose, put down her work, and went to open the door; and then a voice, which made Elizabeth smile and look handsomer than ever, asked if Mrs. and Miss Gilmour were at home?

Elizabeth stood listening, with her fair head a little bent, while the maid said, "No, *sare*," and then Miss Gilmour flushed up quite angrily in the inner room, and would have run out. She hesitated only for a minute, and then it was too late; the door was shut, and Clementine sat down again to her work.

"Clementine, how dare you say I was not at home?" cried Elizabeth, suddenly standing before her.

"Madame desired me to let no one in in her absence," said Clementine, primly. "I only obeyed my orders. There is the gentleman's card."

"Sir John Dampier" was on the card, and then, in pencil, "I hope you will be at home in Chester Street next week. Can I be your *avant-courier* in any way? I cross to-night."

Elizabeth smiled again, shrugged her shoulders, and said to herself: "Next week; I can afford to wait better than he can, perhaps. Poor man! After all, *il y en a bien d'autres;*" and she went to the window, and, by leaning out, she just caught a glimpse of the Madeleine, and of Sir John Dampier walking away; and then presently she saw her mother on the opposite side of the street, passing the stall of the old apple-woman, turning in under the archway of the house.

Elizabeth's mother was like her daughter, only she had black eyes and black hair, and where her daughter was wayward and yielding, the elder woman was wayward and determined. They did not care much for one another, these two. They had not lived together all their lives, or learned to love one another, as a matter of course; they were too much alike, too much of an age: Elizabeth was eighteen, and her mother thirty-six. If Elizabeth looked twenty, the mother looked thirty, and she was as vain, as foolish, as fond of admiration as her daughter. Mrs. Gilmour did not own it to herself, but she had been used to it all her life—to be first, to be much made of; and here was a little girl who had sprung up somehow, and learned of herself to be charming—more charming than she had ever been in her best days; and now that they had slid away, those best days, the elder woman had a dull, unconscious discontent in her heart. People whom she had known, and who had admired her but a year or two ago, seemed to neglect her now and to pass her by, in order to pay a certain homage to her daughter's youth and brilliance: John Dampier, among others, whom she had known as a boy, when she was a young woman. Good mothers, tender-hearted women, brighten again and grow young over their children's happiness and success. Caroline Gilmour suddenly became old, somehow, when she first witnessed her daughter's triumphs, and she felt that the wrinkles were growing under her wistful eyes, and that the color was fading from her cheeks, and she gasped a little sigh and thought: "Ah! how I suffer! What is it? what can have come to me?" As time passed on, the widow's brows grew darker, her lips set ominously. One day she suddenly declared that she was weary of London and London ways, and that she should go abroad; and Elizabeth, who liked everything that was change, that was more life and more experience—she had not taken into account that there was any other than the experience of pleasure in store for her—Elizabeth clapped her hands and cried: "Yes, yes, mamma; I am quite tired of London and all this excitement. Let us go to Paris for the winter, and lead a quiet life."

"Paris is just the place to go to for quiet," said Mrs. Gilmour, who was smoothing her shining locks in the glass, and looking intently into her own dark gloomful eyes.

"The Dampiers are going to Paris," Elizabeth went on; "Lady Dampier and Sir John, and old Miss Dampier and Lætitia. He was saying how he wished you would go. We could have such fun! *Do* go, dear, pretty mamma!"

As Elizabeth spoke, Mrs. Gilmour's dark eyes brightened, and suddenly her hard face melted; and, still looking at herself in the glass, she said: "We will go if you wish it, Elly. I thought you had had enough of balls."

But the end of the Paris winter came, and even then Elly had not had enough; not enough admiration, not enough happiness, not enough new dresses, not enough of herself, not enough time to suffice her eager, longing desires, not enough delights to fill up the swift-flying days. I can not tell you—she could not have told you herself—what she wanted, what perfection of happiness, what wonderful thing. She danced, she wore beautiful dresses, she flirted, she chattered nonsense and sentiment, she listened to music; her pretty little head was in a whirl. John Dampier followed her from place to place; and so, indeed, did one or two others. Though she was in love with them all, I believe she would have married this Dampier if he had asked her, but he never did. He saw that she did not really care for him; opportunity did not befriend him. His mother was against it; and then, her mother was there, looking at him with her dark, reproachful eyes—those eyes which had once fascinated and then repelled him, and that he mistrusted so and almost hated now.

And this is the secret of my story; but for this it would never have been written. He hated, and she did not hate, poor woman! It would have been better, a thousand times, for herself and for her daughter, had she done so. Ah me! what cruel perversion was it, that the best of all good gifts should have turned to trouble, to jealousy, and wicked rancor; that this sacred power of faithful devotion, by which she might have saved herself and ennobled a mean and earthly spirit, should have turned to a curse, instead of a blessing!

There was a placid, pretty niece of Lady Dampier, called Lætitia who had been long destined for Sir John. Lætitia and Elizabeth had been at school together for a good many dreary years, and were very old friends. Elizabeth all her life used to triumph over her friend, and to bewilder her with her careless, gleeful ways, and yet win her over to her own side, for she was irresistible, and she knew it. Perhaps it was because she knew it so well that she was so confident and so charming. Lætitia, although she was sincerely fond of her cousin, used to wonder that her aunt could be against such a wife for her son.

"She is a sort of princess," the girl used to say; "and John *ought* to have a beautiful wife for the credit of the family."

"Your fifty thousand pounds would go a great deal further to promote the credit of the family, my dear," said old Miss Dampier, who was a fat, plain-spoken, kindly old lady. "I like the girl, though my sister-in-law does not; and I hope that some day she will find a very good husband. I confess that I had rather it were not John."

And so one day John was informed by his mother, who was getting alarmed, that she was going home, and that she could not think of crossing without him. And Dampier, who was careful, as men are mostly, and wanted to think about his decision, and who was anxious to do the very best for himself in every respect—as is the way with just and good and respectable gentlemen—was not at all loath to obey her summons.

Here was Lætitia, who was very fond of him—there was no doubt of that—with a house in the country and money at her bankers'; there was a wayward, charming, beautiful girl, who didn't care for him very much, who had little or no money, but whom he certainly cared for. He talked it all over dispassionately with his aunt—so dispassionately that the old woman got angry.

"You are a model young man, John. It quite affects me, and makes me forget my years to see the admirable way in which you young people conduct yourselves. You have got such well-regulated hearts, it's quite a marvel. You are quite right; Tishy has got £50,000, which will all go into your pocket, and respectable connections, who will come to your wedding, and Elly Gilmour has not a penny except what her mother will leave her—a mother with a bad temper, and who is sure to marry again; and though the girl is the prettiest young creature I ever set eyes on, and though you cared for her as you never cared for any other woman before, men don't marry wives for such absurd reasons as that. You are quite right to have nothing to do with her; and I respect you for your noble self-denial." And the old lady began to knit away at a great long red comforter she had always on hand for her other nephew the clergyman.

"But, my dear aunt Jean, what is it you want me to do?" cried John.

"Drop one, knit two together," said the old lady, cliquetting her needles.

She really wanted John to marry his cousin, but she was a spinster still and sentimental; and she could not help being sorry for pretty Elizabeth; and now she was afraid that she had said too much, for her nephew frowned, put his hands in his pockets, and walked out of the room.

He walked down stairs, and out of the door into the Rue Royale, the street where they were lodging; then he strolled across the Place de la Concorde, and in at the gates of the Tuileries, where the soldiers were pacing, and so along the broad path, to where he heard a sound of music, and saw a glitter of people. Tum to tum, bom, bom, bom, went the military music; twittering busy little birds were chirping up in the branches; buds were bursting; colors glimmering; tinted sunshine flooding the garden, and music, and the people; old gentlemen were reading the newspapers on the benches; children were playing at hide-and-seek behind the statues; nurses gossiping, and nodding their white caps, and dandling their white babies; and there on chairs, listening to the music, the mammas were sitting in grand bonnets and parasols, working, and gossiping too, and ladies and gentlemen went walking up and down before them. All the windows of the Tuileries were ablaze with the sun; the terraces were beginning to gleam with crocuses and spring flowers.

As John Dampier was walking along, scarcely noting all this, he heard his name softly called, and turning round he saw two ladies sitting under a budding horse-chestnut tree. One of them he thought looked like a fresh spring flower herself smiling pleasantly, all dressed in crisp light gray, with a white bonnet, and a quantity of bright yellow crocus hair. She held out a little gray hand and said:—

"Won't you come and talk to us? Mamma and I are tired of listening to music. We want to hear somebody talk."

And then mamma, who was Mrs. Gilmour, held out a straw-colored hand, and said, "Do you think sensible people have nothing better to do than to listen to your chatter, Elly? Here is your particular friend, M. de Vaux, coming to us. You can talk to him."

Elizabeth looked up quickly at her mother, then glanced at Dampier, then greeted M. de Vaux as pleasantly almost as she had greeted him.

"I am afraid I can not stay now," said Sir John to Elizabeth. "I have several things to do. Do you know that we are going away immediately?"

Mrs. Gilmour's black eyes seemed to flash into his face as he spoke. He felt them, though he was looking at Elizabeth, and he could not help turning away with an impatient movement of dislike.

"Going away! oh, how sorry I am," said Elly. "But, mamma, I forgot—you said we were going home, too, in a few days; so I don't mind so much. You will come and say good-bye, won't you?" Elizabeth went on, while M. de Vaux, who had been waiting to be spoken to, turned away rather provoked, and made some remark to Mrs. Gilmour. And then Elizabeth seeing her opportunity, and looking up, frank, fair, and smiling, said quickly: "To-morrow at three, mind—and give my love to Lætitia," she went on, much more deliberately, "and my best love to Miss Dampier! and oh, dear! why does one ever have to say good-bye to one's friends? Are you sure you are all really going?"

"Alas!" said Dampier, looking down at the kind young face with strange emotion and tenderness, and holding out his hand. He had not meant it as good-bye yet, but so Elly and her mother understood it.

"Good-bye, Sir John; we shall meet again in London," said Mrs. Gilmour.

"Good-bye," said Elly, wistfully raising her sweet eyes.

As he walked away, he carried with him a bright picture of the woman he loved looking at him kindly, happy, surrounded with sunshine and budding green leaves, smiling and holding out her hand; and so he saw her in his dreams sometimes; and so she would appear to him now and then in the course of his life; so he sometimes sees her now, in spring-time, generally when the trees are coming out, and some little chirp of a sparrow or some little glistening green bud conjures up all these old bygone days again.

Mrs. Gilmore did not sleep very sound all that night. While Elizabeth lay dreaming in her dark room, her mother, with wild-falling black hair, and wrapped in a long red dressing-gown, was wandering restlessly up and down, or flinging herself on the bed or the sofa, and trying at her bedside desperately to sleep, or falling on her knees with clasped outstretched hands. Was she asking for her own happiness at the expense of poor Elly's? I don't like to think so—it seems so cruel, so wicked, so unnatural. But remember, here was a passionate selfish woman, who for long years had had one dream, one idea; who knew that she loved this man twenty times—twenty years—more than did Elizabeth, who was but a little child when this mad fancy began.

"She does not care for him a bit," the poor

wretch said to herself over and over again. "He likes her, and he would marry her if—if I chose to give him the chance. She will be as happy with any body else. I could not bear this—it would kill me. I never suffered such horrible torture in all my life. He hates me. It is hopeless; and I—I do not know whether I hate him or I love him most. How dare she tell him to come to-morrow, when she knew I would be out. She shall not see him. We will neither of us see him again; never—oh! never. But I shall suffer, and she will forget. Oh! if I could forget!" And then she would fall down on her knees again; and because she prayed, she blinded herself to her own wrong-doings, and thought that Heaven was on her side.

And so the night went on. John Dampier was haunted with strange dreams, and saw Caroline Gilmour more than once coming and going in a red gown and talking to him, though he could not understand what she was saying; sometimes she was in his house at Guilford; sometimes in Paris; sometimes sitting with Elly up in a chestnut-tree, and chattering like a monkey; sometimes gliding down interminable rooms and opening door after door. He disliked her worse than ever when he woke in the morning. Is this strange? It would have seemed to me stranger had it not been so. We are not blocks of wax and putty with glass eyes, like the people at Madame Tussaud's; we have souls, and we feel and we guess at more than we see round about us, and we influence one another for good or for evil from the moment we come into the world. Let us be humbly thankful if the day comes for us to leave it before we have done any great harm to those who live their lives alongside with ours. And so the next morning Caroline asked her daughter if she would come with her to M. le Pasteur Tourneur's at two. "I am sure you would be the better for listening to a good man's exhortation," said Mrs. Gilmour.

"I don't want to go, mamma. I hate exhortations," said Elizabeth, pettishly; "and you know how ill it made me last Tuesday. How can you like it—such dreary, sleepy talk? It gave me the most dreadful headache."

"Poor child!" said Mrs. Gilmour, "perhaps the day may come when you will find out that a headache is not the most terrible calamity. But you understand that if you do not choose to come with me, you must stay at home. I will not have you going about by yourself, or with any chance friends—it is not respectable."

Elly shrugged her shoulders, but resigned herself with wonderful good grace. Mrs. Gilmour prepared herself for her expedition: she put on a black silk gown, a plain bonnet, a black cloak. I can not exactly tell you what change came over her. It was not the lady of the Tuileries the day before; it was not the woman in the red dressing-gown. It was a respectable, quiet personage enough, who went off primly with her prayer-book in her hand, and who desired Clementine on no account to let any body in until her return.

"Miss Elizabeth is so little to be trusted," so she explained quite unnecessarily to the maid, "that I can not allow her to receive visits when I am from home."

And Clementine, who was a stiff, ill-humored woman, pinched her lips and said, "Bien, madame."

And so when Elizabeth's best chance for happiness came to the door, Clementine closed it again with great alacrity, and shut out the good fortune, and sent it away. I am sure that if Dampier had come in that day and seen Elly once more, he could not have helped speaking to her and making her and making himself happy in so doing. I am sure that Elly, with all her vanities and faults, would have made him a good wife, and brightened his dismal old house; but I am not sure that happiness is the best portion after all, and that there is not something better to be found in life than mere worldly prosperity.

Dampier walked away, almost relieved, and yet disappointed too. "Well, they will be back in town in ten days," he thought, "and we will see then. But why the deuce did the girl tell me three o'clock, and then not be at home to see me?" And as ill-luck would have it, at this moment up came Mrs. Gilmour. "I have just been to see you, to say good-bye," said Dampier. "I was very sorry to miss you and your daughter."

"I have been attending a meeting at the house of my friend the Pasteur Tourneur," said Mrs. Gilmour; "but Elizabeth was at home—would not she see you?" She blushed up very red as she spoke, and so did John Dampier; her face glowed with shame, and his with vexation.

"No; she would not see me," cried he. "Good-bye, Mrs. Gilmour."

"Good-bye," she said, and looked up with her black eyes; but he was staring vacantly beyond her, busy with his own reflections, and then she felt it was good-bye forever.

He turned down a wide street, and she crossed mechanically and came along the other side of the road, as I have said; past the stall of the old apple-woman; advancing demurely, turning in under the archway of the house.

She had no time for remorse. "He does not care for me," was all she could think; "he scorns me—he has behaved as no gentleman would behave." (Poor John!—in justice to him I must say that this was quite an assumption on her part.) And at the same time John Dampier, at the other end of the street, was walking away in a huff, and saying to himself that "Elly is a little heartless flirt; she cares for no one but herself. I will have no more to do with her. Lætitia would not have served me so."

Elly met her mother at the door. "Mamma, how could you be so horrid and disagreeable?—why did you tell Clementine to let no one in?" She shook back her curly locks, and stamped her little foot, as she spoke, in her childish anger.

"You should not give people appointments when I am out of the way," said Mrs. Gilmour, primly. "Why did you not come with me? Dear M. Tourneur's exposition was quite beautiful."

"I hate Monsieur Tourneur!" cried Elizabeth; "and I should not do such things if you were kind, mamma, and liked me to amuse myself and to be happy; but you sit there, prim and frowning, and thinking every thing wrong that is harmless; and you spoil all my pleasure; and it is a shame—and a shame—and you will make me hate you too;" and she ran into her own room, banged the door, and locked it.

I suppose it was by way of compensation to Elly that Mrs. Gilmour sat down and wrote a little note, asking Monsieur de Vaux to tea that evening to meet M. le Pasteur Tourneur and his son.

Elizabeth sat sulking in her room all the afternoon, the door shut; the hum of a busy city came in at her open window; then the glass panes blazed with light, and she remembered how the windows of the Tuileries had shone at that time the day before, and she thought how kind and how handsome Dampier looked, as he came walking along, and how he was worth ten Messieurs de Vaux and twenty foolish boys like Anthony Tourneur. The dusky shadows came creeping around the room, dimming a pretty picture.

It was a commonplace little *tableau de genre* enough—that of a girl sitting at a window, with clasped hands, dreaming dreams more or less silly, with the light falling on her hair, and on the folds of her dress, and on the blazing petals of the flowers on the balcony outside, and then overhead a quivering green summer sky. But it is a little picture that nature is never tired of reproducing; and, besides nature, every year, in the Royal Academy, I see half a dozen such representations.

In a quiet, unconscious sort of way, Elly made up her mind, this summer afternoon—made up her mind, knowing not that perhaps it was too late, that the future she was accepting, half glad, half reluctant, was, maybe, already hers no more, to take or to leave. Only a little stream, apparently easy to cross, lay, as yet, between her and the figure she seemed to see advancing towards her. She did not know that every day this little stream would widen and widen, until in time it would be a great ocean lying between them. Ah! take care, my poor Elizabeth, that you don't tumble into the waters, and go sinking down, down, down, while the waves close over your curly yellow locks.

"Will you come to dinner, mademoiselle?" said Clementine, rapping at the door with the finger of fate which had shut out Sir John Dampier only a few hours ago.

"Go away!" cries Elizabeth.

"Elizabeth! dinner is ready," says her mother, from outside, with unusual gentleness.

"I don't want any dinner," says Elly; and then feels very sorry and very hungry the minute she has spoken. The door was locked, but she had forgotten the window, and Mrs. Gilmour, in a minute, came along the balcony, with her silk dress rustling against the iron bars.

"You silly girl! come and eat," said her mother, still strangely kind and forbearing. "The Vicomte de Vaux is coming to tea, and Monsieur Tourneur and Anthony; you must come and have your dinner, and then let Clementine dress you; you will catch cold if you sit here any longer;" and she took the girl's hand gently and led her away.

For the first time in her life, Elizabeth almost felt as if she really loved her mother; and, touched by her kindness, and with a sudden impulse, and melting, and blushing, and all ashamed of herself, she said, almost before she knew what she had spoken: "Mamma, I am very silly, and I've behaved very badly, but I did so want to see him again."

Mrs. Gilmour just dropped the girl's hand. "Nonsense, Elizabeth; your head is full of silly school-girl notions. I wish I had had you brought up at home instead of at Mrs. Straightboard's."

"I wish you had, mamma," said Elly, speaking coldly and quietly; "Lætitia and I were both very miserable there." And then she sat down at the round table to break bread with her mother, hurt, wounded, and angry. Her face looked hard and stern, like Mrs. Gilmour's; her bread choked her; she drank a glass of water, and it tasted bitter, somehow. Was Caroline more happy? did she eat with better appetite? She ate more, she looked much as usual, she talked a good deal. Clementine was secretly thinking what a good-for-nothing, ill-tempered girl mademoiselle was; what a good woman, what a good mother, was madame. Clementine revenged some of madame's wrongs upon Elizabeth, by pulling her hair after dinner, as she was plaiting and pinning it up. Elly lost her temper, and violently pushed Clementine away, and gave her warning to leave.

Clementine, furious, and knowing that some of the company had already arrived, rushed into the drawing-room with her wrongs. "Mademoiselle m'a poussée, madame; mademoiselle m'a dit des injures; mademoiselle m'a congédiée—" But in the middle of her harangue, the door flew open, and Elizabeth, looking like an empress, bright cheeks flushed, eyes sparkling, hair crisply curling, and all dressed in shining pink silk, stood before them.

CHAPTER II.

But for his funeral train which the bridegroom sees in the
  distance,
Would he so joyfully, think you, fall in with the marriage
  procession?
But for that final discharge, *would he* dare to enlist in
  that service?
But for that certain release, ever sign to that perilous
  contract?

I DON'T think they had ever seen any body
like her before, those two MM. Tourneurs, who
had just arrived; they both rose, a little **man**
and a tall one, father and son; and besides
these gentlemen, there was an old lady in a
poke-bonnet sitting there too, who opened her
shrewd eyes and held out her hand. Clementine was crushed, eclipsed, forgotten. Elizabeth advanced, tall, slim, stately, with wide-
spread petticoats; but she began to blush very
much when she saw Miss Dampier. For a
few minutes there was a little confusion of
greeting, and voices, and chairs moved about,
and then :—

"I came to say good-bye to you," said the
old lady, "in case we should not meet again.
I am going to Scotland in a month or two—perhaps I may be gone by the time you get back
to town."

"Oh no, no! I hope not," said Elizabeth.
She was very much excited, the tears almost
came into her eyes.

"We shall most likely follow you in a week
or ten days," said Mrs. Gilmour, with a sort of
laugh; "there is no necessity for any sentimental leave-taking."

"Does that woman mean what she says?"
thought the old lady, looking at her; and then
turning to Elizabeth again, she continued:
"There is no knowing what may happen to
any one of us, my dear. There is no harm in
saying good-bye, is there? Have you any message for Lætitia or Catherine?"

"Give Lætitia my very best love," said Elly,
grateful for the old lady's kindness; "and—and
I was very, very sorry that I could not see Sir
John when he came to-day so good-naturedly."

"He must come and see you in London,"
said Miss Dampier, very kindly still. (She
was thinking. "She does care for him, poor
child.")

"Oh yes! in London," repeated Mrs. Gilmour; so that Elly looked quite pleased, and
Miss Dampier again said to herself: "She is
decidedly not coming to London. What can
she mean? Can there be any thing with that
Frenchman, De Vaux? Impossible!" And
then she got up, and said aloud: "Well, good-
bye. I have all my old gowns to pack up, and
my knitting, Elly. Write to me, child, sometimes!"

"Oh yes, yes!" cried Elizabeth, flinging her
arms round the old lady's neck, kissing her, and
whispering, "Good-bye, dear, dear Miss Dampier."

At the door of the apartment Clementine was
waiting, hoping for a possible five-franc piece.
"Bon soir, madame," said she.

"Oh indeed," said Miss Dampier, staring at
her, and she passed out with a sort of sniff, and
then she walked home quietly through the dark
back-streets, only, as she went along, she said to
herself every now and then, she hardly knew
why, "Poor Elly—poor child!"

Meanwhile, M. Tourneur was taking Elizabeth gently to task. Elizabeth was pouting her
red lips and sulking, and looking at him defiantly from under her drooped eyelids; and all
the time Anthony Tourneur sat admiring her,
with his eyes wide open, and his great mouth
open too. He was a big young man, with immense hands and feet, without any manners to
speak of, and with thick hair growing violently
upon end. There was a certain distinction
about his father which he had not inherited.
Young Frenchmen of this class are often singularly rough and unpolished in their early youth;
they tone down with time, however, as they see
more of men and of women. Anthony had never known much of either till now; for his young
companions at the Protestant college were rough
cubs like himself; and as for women his mother was dead (she had been an Englishwoman,
and died when he was ten years old), and old
Françoise, the *cuisinière*, at home, was almost the
only woman he knew. His father was more
used to the world and its ways: he fancied he
scorned them all, and yet the pomps and vanities and the pride of life had a horrible attraction for this quiet pasteur. He was humble
and ambitious; he was tender-hearted, and
hard-headed, and narrow-minded. Though
stern to himself, he was weak to others, and yet
feebly resolute when he met with opposition.
He was not a great man; his qualities neutral-
ized one another, but he had a great reputation.
The Oratoire was crowded on the days when he
was expected to preach, his classes were thronged, his pamphlets went through three or four
editions. Popularity delighted him. His manner had a great charm, his voice was sweet, his
words well chosen; his head was a fine melancholy head, his dark eyes flashed when he was
excited. Women especially admired and respected Stephen Tourneur.

Mrs. Gilmour was like another person when
she was in his presence. Look at her to-night,
with her smooth black hair, and her gray silk
gown, and her white hands busied pouring out
his tea. See how she is appealing to him, def-
erentially listening to his talk. I can not write
his talk down here. Certain allusions can have
no place in a little story like this one, and yet
they were allusions so frequently in his thoughts
and in his mouth that it was almost unconsciously that he used them. He and his brethren like him have learned to look at this life
from a loftier point of view than Elly Gilmour
and worldlings like her, who feel that to-day
they are in the world and of it, not of their own
will, indeed—though they are glad that they are
here—but waiting a further dispensation. Tourneur, and those like him, look at this life only
in comparison with the next, as though they had

already passed beyond, and had but little concern with the things of to-day. They speak
chiefly of sacred subjects; they have put aside
our common talk, and thought, and career.
They have put them away, and yet they are
men and women, after all. And Stephen Tourneur, among the rest, was a soft-hearted man.
To-night, as indeed often before, he was full of
sympathy for the poor mother who had so often
spoken of her grief and care for her daughter,
of her loneliness. He understood her need;
her want of an adviser, of a friend whom she
could reverence and defer to. How meekly she
listened to his words, with what kindling interest she heard him speak of what was in his heart
always, with what gentleness she attended to his
wants. How womanly she was, how much more
pleasant than any of the English, Scotch, Irish
old maids who were in the habit of coming to
consult him in their various needs and troubles!
He had never known her so tender, so gentle, as
to-night. Even Elly, sulking and beating the
tattoo with her satin shoes, thought that her
mother's manner was very strange. How could
any one of the people sitting round that little tea-
table guess at the passion of hopelessness, of rage,
of despair, of envy, that was gnawing at the elder woman's heart? at the mad, desperate determination she was making? And yet every now
and then she said odd, imploring things—she
seemed to be crying wildly for sympathy—she
spoke of other people's troubles with a startling
earnestness.

De Vaux, who arrived about nine o'clock, and
asked for a *soupçon de thé*, and put in six lumps
of sugar, and so managed to swallow the mixture, went away at ten, without one idea of the
tragedy with which he had been spending his
evening—a tragical farce, a comedy—I know
not what to call it.

Elly was full of her own fancies; Monsieur
Tourneur was making up his mind; Anthony's
whole head was rustling with pink silk, or dizzy with those downcast, bright, bewildering blue
eyes of Elly's, and he sat stupidly counting the
little bows on her skirt, or watching the glitter
of the rings on her finger, and wishing that she
would not look so cross when he spoke to her.
She had brightened up considerably while De
Vaux was there; but now, in truth, her mind
was travelling away, and she was picturing to
herself the Dampiers at their tea-table—Tishy,
pale and listless, over her feeble cups; Lady
Dampier, with her fair hair and her hook nose,
lying on the sofa; and John in the arm-chair
by the fire, cutting dry jokes at his aunt. Elly's
spirits had travelled away like a ghost, and it
was only her body that was left sitting in the
little gaudy drawing-room; and though she did
not know it, there was another ghost flitting
alongside with hers. Strangely enough the
people of whom she was thinking were assembled
together very much as she imagined them to be.
Did they guess at the two pale phantoms that
were hovering about them? Somehow or other, Miss Dampier, over her knitting, was still

muttering, "Poor child!" to the click of her
needles; and John Dampier was haunted by
the woman in red, and by a certain look in Elly's
eyes, which he had seen yesterday when he found
her under the tree.

Meanwhile, at the other side of Paris, the
other little company was assembled round the
fire: and Mrs. Gilmour, with her two hands
folded tightly together, was looking at M. Tourneur with her great soft eyes, and saying:
"The woman was never yet born who could
stand alone, who did not look for some earthly
counsellor and friend to point out the road to
better things—to help her along the narrow
thorny way. Wounded, and bruised, and weary,
it is hard, hard for us to follow our lonely
path." She spoke with a pathetic passion, so
that Elizabeth could not think what had come
to her. Mrs. Gilmour was generally quite capable of standing, and going, and coming, without any assistance whatever. In her father's
time, Elly could remember that there was not
the slightest need for his interference in any of
their arrangements. But the mother was evidently in earnest to-night, and the daughter
quite bewildered. Later in the evening, after
Monsieur de Vaux was gone, Mrs. Gilmour
got up from her chair and flung open the window of the balcony. All the stars of heaven
shone splendidly over the city. A great, silent,
wonderful night had gathered round about them
unawares; a great calm had come after the
noise and business of the careful day. Caroline Gilmour stepped out with a gasping sigh,
and stood looking upward; they could see her
gray figure dimly against the darkness. Monsieur Tourneur remained sitting by the fire, with
his eyes cast down and his hands folded.
Presently he too rose and walked slowly across
the room, and stepped out upon the balcony;
and Elizabeth and Anthony remained behind,
staring vacantly at one another. Elizabeth
was yawning and wondering when they would
go.

"You are sleepy, miss," said young Tourneur, in his French-English.

Elly yawned in a very unmistakable language, and showed all her even white teeth.
"I always get sleepy when I have been cross,
Mr. Anthony. I have been cross ever since
three o'clock to-day, and now it is long past ten,
and time for us all to go to bed: don't you think
so?"

"I am waiting for my father," said the young
man. "He watches late at night, but we are
all sent off at ten."

"'We!'—you and old Françoise?"

"I and the young Christians who live in our
house, and study with my father and read under his direction. There are five, all from the
south, who are, like me, preparing to be ministers of the gospel."

Another great wide yawn from Elly.

"Do you think your father will stop much
longer? if so, I shall go to bed. Oh dear me!"
and with a sigh she let her head fall back upon

the soft-cushioned chair, and then, somehow, her eyes shut very softly, and her hands fell loosely, and a little quiet dream came, something of a garden and peace, and green trees, and Miss Dampier knitting in the sunshine. Click, click, click, she heard the needles, but it was only the clock ticking on the mantelpiece. Anthony was almost afraid to breathe, for fear he should wake her. It seemed to him very strange to be sitting by this smouldering fire, with the stars burning outside, while through the open window the voices of the two people talking on the balcony came to him in a low murmuring sound. And there opposite him Elly asleep, breathing so softly and looking so wonderfully pretty in her slumbers. Do you not know the peculiar, peaceful feeling which comes to any one sitting alone by a sleeping person? I can not tell which of the two was for a few minutes the most tranquil and happy.

Elly was still dreaming her quiet, peaceful dreams, still sitting with Miss Dampier in her garden, under a chestnut-tree, with Dampier coming towards her, when suddenly some voice whispered "Elizabeth" in her ear, and she awoke with a start of chill surprise. It was not Anthony who had called her, it was only fancy; but as she woke he said:

"Ah! I was just going to wake you."

What had come to him? He seemed to have awakened too—to have come to himself suddenly. One word which had reached him—he had very big sharp ears—one word distinctly uttered amid the confused murmur on the balcony, brought another word of old Françoise's to his mind. And then in a minute—he could not tell how it was—it was all clear to him. Already he was beginning to learn the ways of the world. Elly saw him blush up, saw his eyes light with intelligence, and his ears grow very red; and then he sat up straight in his chair, and looked at her in a quick, uncertain sort of way.

"You would not allow it," said he, suddenly, staring at her fixedly with his great flashing eyes. "I never thought of such a thing till this minute. Who ever would?"

"Thought of what? What are you talking about?" said Elly, startled.

"Ah! that is it." And then he turned his head impatiently: "How stupid you must have been. What can have put such a thing into his head and hers. Ah! it is so strange, I don't know what to think or to say;" and he sank back in his chair. But, somehow or other, the idea which had occurred to him was not nearly so disagreeable as he would have expected it to be. The notion of some other companionship besides that of the five young men from the south, instead of shocking him, filled him with a vague, delightful excitement. "Ah! then she would come and live with us in that pink dress," he thought. And meanwhile Elizabeth turned very pale, and she too began dimly to see what he was thinking of, only she could not be quite sure. "Is it that I am to marry him?" she thought; "they can not be plotting that."

"What is it, M. Anthony?" said she, very fierce. "Is it—they do not think that I would ever—ever dream or think of marrying you?" She was quite pale now, and her eyes were glowing.

Anthony shook his head again. "I know that," said he; "it is not you or me."

"What do you dare to imply?" she cried, more and more fiercely. "You can't mean—you would never endure, never suffer that—that—" The words failed on her lips.

"I should like to have you for a sister, Miss Elizabeth," said he, looking down; "it is so triste at home."

Elly half started from her chair, put up her white hands, scarce knowing what she did, and then suddenly cried out, "Mother! mother!" in a loud, shrill, thrilling voice, which brought Mrs. Gilmour back into the room. And Monsieur Tourneur came too. Not one of them spoke for a minute. Elizabeth's horror-stricken face frightened the pasteur, who felt as if he was in a dream, who had let himself drift along with the feeling of the moment, who did not know even now if he had done right or wrong, if he had been carried away by mere earthly impulse and regard for his own happiness, or if he had been led and directed to a worthy helpmeet, to a Christian companion, to one who had the means and the power to help him in his labors. Ah, surely, surely he had done well, he thought for himself, and for those who depended on him. It was not without a certain dignity at last, and nobleness of manner, that he took Mrs. Gilmour's hand, and said:

"You called your mother just now, Elizabeth: here she is. Dear woman, she has consented to be my best earthly friend and companion, to share my hard labors; to share a life poor and arduous, and full of care, and despised perhaps by the world; but rich in eternal hope, blessed by prayer, and consecrated by a Christian's faith." He was a little man, but he seemed to grow tall as he spoke. His eyes kindled, his face lightened with enthusiasm. Elizabeth could not help seeing this, even while she stood shivering with indignation and sick at heart. As for Anthony, he got up, and came to his father and took both his hands, and then suddenly flung his arms around his neck. Elizabeth found words at last:

"You can suffer this?" she said to Anthony. "You have no feelings, then, of decency, of fitness, of memory for the dead. You, mamma, can degrade yourself by a second marriage? Oh! for shame, for shame!" and she burst into passionate tears, and flung herself down on a chair. Monsieur Tourneur was not used to be thwarted, to be reproved; he got very pale, he pushed Anthony gently aside, and went up to her. "Elizabeth," said he, "is this the conduct of a devoted daughter; are these the words of good-will and of peace, with which your mother should be greeted by her children?

I had hoped that you would look upon me as a friend. If you could see my heart, you would know how ready I am; how gladly I would love you as my own child," and he held out his hand. Elly Gilmour dashed it away.

"Go," she said; "you have made me wretched; I hate your life, and your ways, and your sermons, and we shall all be miserable, every one of us; I know well enough it is for her money you marry her. Oh, go away out of my sight." Tourneur had felt doubts. Elizabeth's taunts and opposition reassured him and strengthened him in his purpose. This is only human nature, as well as pasteur nature in particular. If every thing had gone smoothly, very likely he would have found out a snare of the Devil in it, and broken it off, not caring what grief and suffering he caused to himself in so doing. Now that the girl's words brought a flush into his pale face and made him to wince with pain, he felt justified, nay, impelled to go on—to be firm. And now he stood up like a gentleman, and spoke :—

"And if I want your mother's money, is it hers, is it mine, was it given to me or to her to spend for our own use? Was it not lent, will not an account be demanded hereafter? Unhappy child! where have you found already such sordid thoughts, such unworthy suspicions? Where is your Christian charity?"

"I never made any pretense of having any," cried Elizabeth, stamping her foot and tossing her fair mane. "You talk and talk about it and about the will of Heaven, and suit yourselves, and break my heart, and look up quite scandalized, and forgive me for my wickedness. But I had rather be as wicked as I am than as good as you."

"Allons, taisez-vous, Mademoiselle Elizabeth!" said Anthony, who had taken his part; "or my father will not marry your mother, and then you will be in the wrong, and have made every body unhappy. It is very, very sad and melancholy in our house; be kind and come and make us happy. If I am not angry, why should you mind? but see here, I will not give my consent unless you do, and I know my father will do nothing against my wishes and yours."

Poor Elizabeth looked up, and then she saw that her mother was crying too; Caroline had had a hard day's work. No wonder she was fairly harassed and worn out. Elizabeth herself began to be as bewildered, as puzzled as the rest. She put her hand wearily to her head. She did not feel angry any more, but very tired and sad. "How can I say I think it right when I think it wrong? It is not me you want to marry, M. Tourneur; mamma is old enough to decide. What need you care for what a silly girl like me says and thinks? Good-night, mamma; I am tired and must go to bed. Good-night, Monsieur Tourneur. Good-night, M. Anthony. Oh dear!" sighed Elizabeth, as she went out of the room with her head hanging, and with pale cheeks and dim eyes.

You could hardly have believed it was the triumphant young beauty of an hour ago. But it had always been so with this impetuous, sensitive Elizabeth; she suffered, as she enjoyed, more keenly than any body else I ever knew; she put her whole heart into her life without any reserve, and then, when failure and disappointment came, she had no more heart left to endure with.

I am sure it was with a humble spirit that Tourneur that night, before he left, implored a benediction on himself and on those who were about to belong to him. He went away at eleven o'clock with Anthony, walking home through the dark, long streets to his house, which was near one of the gates of the city. And Caroline sat till the candles went out, till the fire had smouldered away, till the chill night-breezes swept round the room, and then went stupefied to bed, saying to herself: "Now he will learn that others do not despise me, and I—I will lead a good life."

CHAPTER III.

Le temps emporte sur son aile
Et le printemps et l'hirondelle,
Et la vie et les jours perdus ;
Tout s'en va comme la fumée,
L'espérance et la renommée,
Et moi qui vous ai tant aimée,
Et toi qui ne t'en souviens plus !

A LOW, one-storied house standing opposite a hospital, built on a hilly street, with a great white porte-cochère closed and barred, and then a garden wall: nine or ten windows only a foot from the ground, all blinded and shuttered in a row; a brass plate on the door, with Stephen Tourneur engraved thereon, and grass and chickweed growing between the stones and against the white walls of the house. Passing under the archway, you come into a grass-grown courtyard; through an iron grating you see a little desolate garden with wallflowers and stocks and tall yellow weeds all flowering together, and fruit-trees running wild against the wall. On one side there are some empty stables, with chickens pecketting in the sun. The house is built in two long low wings; it has a dreary moated-grange sort of look; and see, standing at one of the upper windows, is not that Elizabeth looking out? An old woman in a blue gown and a white coif is pumping water at the pump, some miserable canaries are piping shrilly out of green cages, the old woman clacks away with her sabots echoing over the stones, the canaries cease their piping, and then nobody else comes. There are two or three tall poplar-trees growing along the wall, which shiver plaintively; a few clouds drift by, and a very distant faint sound of military music comes borne on the wind.

"Ah, how dull it is to be here! Ah! how I hate it, how I hate them all!" Elizabeth is saying to herself: "There is some music, all the Champs Elysées are crowded with people, the

Q

soldiers are marching along with glistening bayonets and flags flying. Not one of them thinks that in a dismal house not very far away there is any body so unhappy as I am. This day year—it breaks my heart to think of it—I was nineteen; to-day I am twenty, and I feel a hundred. Oh, what a sin and shame it is to condemn me to this hateful life! Oh, what wicked people these good people are! Oh, how dull! Oh, how stupid! Oh, how prosy! Oh, how I wish I was dead, and they were dead, and it was all over!"

How many weary yawns, I wonder, had poor Elizabeth yawned since that first night when M. Tourneur came to tea? With what distaste she set herself to live her new life I can not attempt to tell you. It bored her, and wearied and displeased her, and she made no secret of her displeasure, you may be certain. But what annoyed her most of all, what seemed to her so inconceivable that she could never understand or credit it, was the extraordinary change which had come over her mother. Mme. Tourneur was like Mrs. Gilmour in many things, but so different in others that Elly could hardly believe her to be the same woman. The secret of it all was a love of power and admiration, purchased no matter at what sacrifice, which had always been the hidden motive of Caroline's life. Now she found that by dressing in black, by looking stiff, by attending endless charitable meetings, prayer-meetings, religious meetings, by influencing M. Tourneur, who was himself a man in authority, she could eat of the food her soul longed for. "There was a man once who did not care for me, he despised me," she used to think sometimes; "he liked that silly child of mine better; he shall hear of me one day."

Lady Dampier was a very strong partisan of the French Protestant Church. Mme. Tourneur used to hope that she would come to Paris again and carry home with her the fame of her virtues, and her influence, and her conversion; and in the mean while the weary round of poor Elly's daily existence went on. To-day, for two lonesome hours, she stood leaning at that window with the refrain of the distant music echoing in her ears long after it had died away. It was like the remembrance of the past pleasures of her short life. Such a longing for sympathy, for congenial spirits, for the pleasures she loved so dearly, came over her, that the great hot tears welled into her eyes, and the bitterest tears are those which do not fall. The gate-bell rang at last, and Clementine walked across the yard to unbolt, to unbar, and to let in Monsieur Tourneur, with books under his arm, and a big stick. Then the bell rang again, and Madame Tourneur followed, dressed in prim scant clothes, accompanied by another person even primmer and scantier than herself; this was a widowed step-sister of M. Tourneur's, who, unluckily, had no home of her own, so the good man received her and her children into his. Lastly, Elizabeth, from her window, saw Anthony arrive with four of the young Protestants, all swinging their legs and arms. (The fifth was detained at home with a bad swelled face.) All the others were now coming back to dinner, after attending a class at the Pasteur Boulot's. They clattered past the door of Elly's room—a bare little chamber, with one white curtain she had nailed up herself, and a straight bed and a chair. A clock struck five. A melancholy bell presently sounded through the house, and a strong smell of cabbage came in at the open window. Elly looked in the glass; her rough hair was all standing on end curling, her hands were streaked with chalk and brick from the window, her washed-out blue cotton gown was creased and tumbled. What did it matter? she shook her head, as she had a way of doing, and went down stairs as she was. On the way she met two untidy-looking little girls, and then clatter, clatter, along the uncarpeted passage, came the great big-nailed boots of the pupils; and then at the dining-room door there was Clementine in a yellow gown—much smarter and trimmer than Elizabeth's blue cotton—carrying a great long loaf of sour bread.

Madame Tourneur was already at her post, standing at the head of the table, ladling out the cabbage-soup with the pieces of bread floating in every plate. M. Tourneur was eating his dinner quickly; he had to examine a class for confirmation at six, and there was a prayer-meeting at seven. The other prim lady sat opposite to him with her portion before her. There was a small table-cloth, streaked with blue, and not over clean; hunches of bread by every plate, and iron knives and forks. Each person said grace to himself as he came and took his place. Only Elizabeth flung herself down in a chair, looked at the soup, made a face, and sent it away untasted.

"Elizabeth, ma fille, vous ne mangez pas," said M. Tourneur, kindly.

"I can't swallow it!" said Elizabeth.

"When there are so many poor people starving in the streets, you do not, I suppose, expect us to sympathize with such pampered fancies?" said the prim lady.

Although the sisters-in-law were apparently very good friends, there was a sort of race of virtue always being run between them, and just now Elly's shortcomings were a thorn in her mother's side, so skillfully were they wielded by Mrs. Jacob. Lou-Lou and Tou-Tou, otherwise Louise and Thérèse, her daughters, were such good, stupid, obedient, uninteresting little girls, that there was really not a word to say against them in retort; and all that Elly's mother could do, was to be even more severe, more uncompromising than Madame Jacob herself. And now she said:—

"Nonsense, Elizabeth; you must really eat your dinner. Clementine, bring back Miss Elizabeth's plate."

M. Tourneur looked up—he thought the soup very good himself, but he could not bear to see any body distressed. "Go and fetch the bouillie quickly, Clementine. Why should Elizabeth take what she does not like? Rose," said he to his sister, "do you remember how our poor mother used to make us breakfast off—*porridge*, I think she called it—and what a bad taste it had, and how we used to cry?"

"We never ungratefully objected to good soup," said Rose. "I make a point of never giving in to Lou-Lou and Tou-Tou when they have their fancies. I care more for the welfare of their souls than for pampering their bodies."

"And I only care for my body," Elly cried. "Mamma, I like porridge, will you have some for me?"

"Ah! hush! hush! Elizabeth. You do not think what you say, my poor child," said Tourneur. "What is mere eating and drinking, what is food, what is raiment, but dust and rottenness? You only care for your body!—for that mass of corruption. Ah, do not say such things, even in jest. Remember that for every idle word—"

"And is there to be no account for spiteful words?" interrupted Elizabeth, looking at Mrs. Jacob.

Monsieur Tourneur put down the glass of wine he was raising to his lips, and with sad, reproachful glances, looked at the unruly stepdaughter. Madame Jacob, shaking with indignation, cast her eyes up and opened her mouth, and Elizabeth began to pout her red lips. One minute and the storm would have burst, when Anthony upset a jug of water at his elbow, and the stream trickled down and down the table-cloth. These troubled waters restored peace for the moment. Poor Tourneur was able to finish his meal, in a puddle truly, but also in silence. Mrs. Jacob, who had received a large portion of the water in her lap, retired to change her dress, the young Christians sniggered over their plates, and Anthony went on eating his dinner.

I don't offer any excuse for Elizabeth. She was worried, and vexed, and tried beyond her powers of endurance, and she grew more wayward, more provoking every day. It is very easy to be good-natured, good-tempered, thankful and happy, when you are in the country you love, among your own people, living your own life. But if you are suddenly transplanted, made to live some one else's life, expected to see with another man's eyes, to forget your own identity almost, all that happens is, that you do not do as you were expected. Sometimes it is a sheer impossibility. What is that rare proverb about the shoe? Cinderella slipped it on in an instant; but you know her poor sisters cut off their toes and heels, and could not screw their feet in, though they tried ever so. Well, they did their best; but Elly did not try at all, and that is why she was to blame. She was a spoiled child, both by good and ill fortune. Sometimes, when she sat sulking, her mother used to look wondering at her with her black eyes, without saying a word. Did it ever occur to her that this was *her* work? that Elizabeth might have been happy now, honored, prosperous, well loved, but for a little lie which had been told—but for

a little barrier which had been thrown, one summer's day, between her and John Dampier? Caroline had long ceased to feel remorse—she used to say to herself that it would be much better for Elizabeth to marry Anthony, she would make any body else miserable with her wayward temper. Anthony was so obtuse that Elizabeth's fancies would not try him in the least. Mrs. Gilmour chose to term obtuseness a certain chivalrous devotion which the young man felt for her daughter. She thought him dull and slow, and so he was; but at the same time there were gleams of shrewdness which came quite unexpectedly, you knew not whence; there was a certain reticence and good sense of which people had no idea. Anthony knew much more about her and about his father than they knew about him. Every day he was learning to read the world. Elly had taught him a great deal, and he in return was her friend always.

Elly went out into the court-yard after dinner, and Anthony followed her—one little cousin had hold of each of his hands. If the little girls had not been little French Protestant girls, Elizabeth would have been very fond of them, for she loved children; but when they ran up to her, she motioned them away impatiently, and Anthony told them to go and run round the garden. Elizabeth was sitting on a tub which had been overturned, and resting her pretty dishevelled head wearily against the wall. Anthony looked at her for a minute.

"Why do you never wear nice dresses now," said he at last, "but this ugly old one always?"

"Is it not all vanity and corruption?" said Elizabeth, with a sneer; "how can you ask such a question? Every thing that is pretty is vanity. Your aunt and my mother only like ugly things. They would like to put out my eyes because they don't squint; to cut off my hair because it is pretty."

"Your hair! It is not at all pretty like that," said Anthony; "it is all rough, like mine."

Elizabeth laughed and blushed very sweetly. "What is the use, who cares?"

"There are a good many people coming to-night," said Anthony. "It is our turn to receive the prayer-meeting. Why should you not smooth your curls and change your dress?"

"And do you remember what happened once, when I did dress, and make myself look nice?" said Elizabeth, flashing up, and then beginning to laugh.

Anthony looked grave and puzzled; for Elizabeth had caused quite a scandal in the community on that occasion. No wonder the old ladies in their old dowdy bonnets, the young ones in their ill-made woollen dresses, the preacher preaching against the vanities of the world, had all been shocked and outraged, when after the sermon had begun, the door opened, and Elizabeth appeared in the celebrated pink silk dress, with flowers in her hair, white lace falling from her shoulders, a bouquet, a gold fan, and glittering bracelets. Mme. Jacob's head nearly shook off with horror. The word was with the Pasteur

Boulot, who did not conceal his opinion, and whose strictures introduced into the sermon were enough to make a less hardened sinner quake in her shoes. Many of the great leaders of the Protestant world in Paris had been present on that occasion. Some would not speak to her, some did speak very plainly. Elizabeth took it all as a sort of triumph, bent her head, smiled, fanned herself, and when ordered out of the room at last by her mother, left it with a splendid courtesy to the Rev. M. Boulot, and thanked him for his beautiful and improving discourse. And then, when she was up stairs in her own room again, where she had been decking herself for the last hour—the tallow candle was still sputtering on the table—her clothes all lying about the room—she locked the door, tore off her ornaments, her shining dress, and flung herself down on the floor, crying and sobbing as if her heart would break. "Oh, I want to go! I want to go! Oh, take me away!" she prayed and sobbed. "Oh, what harm is there in a pink gown more than a black one! Oh, why does not John Dampier come and fetch me? Oh, what dolts, what idiots, those people are! What a heart-broken girl I am! Poor Elly, poor Elly, poor, poor girl!" said she, pitying herself, and stroking her tear-stained cheeks. And so she went on, until she had nearly worn herself out, poor child. She really was almost heart-broken. This uncongenial atmosphere seemed to freeze and chill her best impulses. I can not help being sorry for her, and sympathizing with her against that rigid community down below, and yet, after all, there was scarcely one of the people whom she so scorned who was not a better Christian than poor Elizabeth, more self-denying, more scrupulous, more patient in effort, more diligent—not one of them that did not lead a more useful life than hers. It was in vain that her mother had offered her classes in the schools, humble neighbors to visit, sick people to tend. "Leave me alone," the girl would say. "You know how I hate all that cant!" Mme. Tourneur herself spent her whole days doing good, patronizing the poor, lecturing the wicked, dosing the sick, superintending countless charitable communities. Her name was on all the committees, her decisions were deferred to, her wishes consulted. She did not once regret the step she had taken; she was a clever, ambitious, active-minded woman; she found herself busy, virtuous, and respected; what more could she desire? Her daughter's unhappiness did not give her any very great concern. "It would go off in time," she said. But days went by, and Elly was only more hopeless, more heart-broken; black lines came under the blue eyes; from being a stout hearty girl, she grew thin and languid. Seeing her day by day, they none of them noticed that she was looking ill, except Anthony, who often imagined a change would do her good; only how was this to be managed? He could only think of one way. He was thinking of it, as he followed her out into the court-yard to-day. The sun was low in the west, the long shadows of the trees flickered across the stones. Say what he would, the blue gown, the wall, the yellow hair, made up a pretty little piece of coloring. With all her faults, Anthony loved Elly better than any other human being, and would have given his life to make her happy.

"I can not bear to see you so unhappy," said he, in French, speaking very simply, in his usual voice. "Elizabeth, why don't you do as your mother has done, and marry a French pastuer, who has loved you ever since the day he first saw you? You should do as you liked, and leave this house, where you are so miserable, and get away from Aunt Rose, who is so ill-natured. I would not propose such a scheme if I saw a chance for something better; but any thing would be an improvement on the life you are leading here. It is wicked and profitless, and you are killing yourself and wasting your best days. You are not taking up your cross with joy and with courage, dear Elizabeth. Perhaps by starting afresh—" His voice failed him, but his eyes spoke and finished the sentence.

This was Anthony's scheme. Elly opened her round eyes, and looked at him all amazed and wondering. A year ago it would have been very different, and so she thought as she scanned him. A year ago she would have scorned the poor fellow, laughed at him, tossed her head, and turned away. But was this the Elly of a year ago? This unhappy, broken-spirited girl, with dimmed beauty, dulled spirits, in all her ways so softened, saddened, silenced. It was almost another person than the Elizabeth Gilmour of former times, who spoke, and said, still looking at him steadfastly: "Thank you, Anthony; I will think about it, and tell you to-morrow what—what I think."

Anthony blushed, and faltered a few unintelligible words, and turned away abruptly, as he saw Madame Jacob coming towards them. As for Elly, she stood quite still, and perfectly cool, and rather bewildered, only somewhat surprised at herself. "Can this be me?" she was thinking. "Can that kind fellow be the boy I used to laugh at so often? Shall I take him at his word? Why not—?"

But Madame Jacob's long nose came and put an end to her wonderings. This lady did not at all approve of gossiping; she stepped up with an inquiring sniff, turned round to look after Anthony, and then said, rather viciously: "Our Christian brothers and sisters will assemble shortly for their pious Wednesday meetings. It is not by exchanging idle words with my nephew that you will best prepare your mind for the exercises of this evening. Retire into your own room, and see if it is possible to compose yourself to a fitter frame of mind. Tou-Tou, Lou-Lou, my children, what are you about?"

"I am gathering pretty flowers, mamma," shouted Lou-Lou.

"I am picking up stones for my little basket," said Tou-Tou, coming to the railing.

"I will allow four minutes," said their mother, looking at her watch. "Then you will come to me, both of you, in my room, and apply yourselves to something more profitable than filling your little baskets. Elizabeth, do you mean to obey me?"

Very much to Madame Jacob's surprise, Elizabeth walked quietly before her into the house without saying one word. The truth was, she was preoccupied with other things, and forgot to be rebellious. She was not even rebellious in her heart when she was up stairs sitting by the bedside, and puzzling her brains over Anthony's scheme. It seemed a relief certainly to turn from the horrible monotony of her daily life, and to think of his kindness. He was very rough, very uncouth, very young; but he was shrewd, and kind, and faithful, more tolerant than his father — perhaps because he felt less keenly;—not sensitive, like him, but more patient, dull over things which are learnt by books, but quick at learning other not less useful things which belong to the experience of daily life. When Elly came down into the réfectoire where they were all assembled, her mother was surprised to see that she had dressed herself, not in the objectionable pink silk, but in a soft gray stuff gown, all her yellow hair was smooth and shining, and a little locket hung round her neck tied with a blue ribbon. The little bit of color seemed reflected somehow in her eyes. They looked blue to-night, as they used to look once when she was happy. Madame Tourneur was quite delighted, and came up and kissed her, and said, "Elly, this is how I like to see you."

Madame Jacob tossed her head, and gave a rough pull at the ends of the ribbon. "This was quite unnecessary," said she.

"Ah!" cried Elly, "you have hurt me!"

"Is not that the locket Miss Dampier gave you?" said Madame Tourneur. "You had best put such things away in your drawer another time. But it is time for you to take your place."

CHAPTER IV.

Unhappier are they to whom a higher instinct has been given, who struggle to be persons, not machines; to whom the universe is not a warehouse, or at best a fancy bazar, but a mystic temple and a hall of doom.

A NUMBER of straw chairs were ranged along the room, with a row of seats behind, for the pasteurs who were to address the meeting.

The people began to arrive very punctually: One or two grand-looking French ladies in cashmeres, a good many limp ones, a stray man or two, two English clergymen in white neckcloths, and five or six Englishwomen in old bonnets. A little whispering and chattering went on among the young French girls, who arrived guarded by their mothers. The way in which French mothers look after their daughters, tie their bonnet-strings, pin their collars, carry their books and shawls, etc., and sit beside them, and always answer for them if they are spoken to, is very curious. Now and then, however, they relax a little, and allow a little whispering with young companions. There was a low murmur and a slight bustle as four pasteurs of unequal heights walked in and placed themselves in the reserved seats. M. Stephen Tourneur followed and took his place. With what kind steadfast glances he greeted his audience! Even Elizabeth could not resist the charm of his manner, and she admired and respected him, much as she disliked the exercise of the evening.

His face lit up with Christian fervor, his eyes shone and gleamed with kindness, his voice, when he began to speak, thrilled with earnestness and sincerity. There was at times a wonderful power about the frail little man, the power which is won in many a desperate secret struggle, the power which comes from a whole life of deep feeling and honest endeavor. No wonder that Stephen Tourneur, who had so often wrestled with the angel and overcome his own passionate spirit, should have influence over others' less strong, less impetuous than his own. Elly could not but admire him and love him, many of his followers worshipped him with the most affecting devotion; Anthony, his son, loved him too, and would have died for him in a quiet way, but he did not blindly believe in his father.

But listen! What a host of eloquent words, of tender thoughts, come alive from his lips to-night! What reverent faith, what charity, what fervor! The people's eyes were fixed upon his kind, eloquent face, and their hearts all beat in sympathy with his own.

One or two of the Englishwomen began to cry. One French lady was swaying herself backward and forward in rapt attention; the two clergymen sat wondering in their white neckcloths. What would they give to preach such sermons! And the voice went on uttering, entreating, encouraging, rising and sinking, ringing with passionate cadence. It ceased at last, and the only sounds in the room were a few sighs, and the suppressed sobs of one or two women. Elizabeth sighed, among others, and sat very still with her hands clasped in her lap. For the first time in her life she was wondering whether she had not perhaps been in the wrong hitherto, and Tourneur, and Madame Jacob, and all the rest in the right—and whether happiness was not the last thing to search for, and those things of which he had spoken the first and best and only necessities. Alas! what strange chance was it that at that moment she raised her head and looked up with her great blue eyes, and saw a strange familiar face under one of the dowdy English bonnets—a face, thin, pinched, with a hooked nose, and sandy hair—that sent a little thrill to her heart, and made her cry out to herself eagerly, as a rush of old memories and hopes came over her, that happiness was sent into the world for a gracious purpose, and that love meant goodness and happiness too sometimes. And, yes—no—yes—that was Lady Dampier! and was John in Paris, perhaps? and Miss Dampier? and were the dear, dear old days come back? . . . .

After a few minutes the congregation began to sing a hymn, the English ladies joining in audibly with their queer accents. The melody swayed on, horribly out of tune and out of time, in a wild sort of minor key. Tou-Tou and Lou-Lou sang, one on each side of their mother, exceedingly loud and shrill, and one of the clergymen attempted a second, after which the discordance reached its climax. Elly had laughed on one or two occasions, and indeed I do not wonder. To-day she scarcely heard the sound of the voices. Her heart was beating with hope, delight, wonder; her head was in a whirl, her whole frame trembling with excitement, that increased every instant. Would M. Boulot's sermon never come to an end? Monsieur Bontemps's exposition, Monsieur de Marveille's reports, go on forever and ever?

But at last it was over; a little rustling, a little pause, and all the voices beginning to murmur, and the chairs scraping; people rising, a little group forming round each favorite pasteur, hands outstretched, thanks uttered, people coming and going. With one bound Elly found herself standing by Lady Dampier, holding both her hands, almost crying with delight. The apathetic English lady was quite puzzled by the girl's exaggerated expressions. She cared very little for Elly Gilmour herself; she liked her very well, but she could not understand her extraordinary warmth of greeting. However, she was carried away by her feelings to the extent of saying: "You must come and see us to-morrow. We are only passing through Paris on our way to Schlangenbad for Lætitia; she has been sadly out of health and spirits lately, poor dear! We are at the Hôtel du Louvre. You must come and lunch with us. Ah! here is your mother. How d'ye do, dear Madame Tourneur? What a privilege it has been! What a treat Mossu Tourneur has given us to-night. I have been quite delighted, I assure you," said her ladyship, bent on being gracious.

Mme. Tourneur made the most courteous of salutations. "I am glad you came, since it was so," said she.

"I want you to let Elly come and see me," continued Lady Dampier; "she must come to lunch; I should be so glad if you would accompany her. I would offer to take her to the play, but I suppose you do not approve of such things any more."

"My life is so taken up with other more serious duties," said Mme. Tourneur, with a faint superior smile, "that I have little time for mere worldly amusements. I can not say that I desire them for my daughter."

"Oh, of course," said Lady Dampier. "I myself—but it is only en passant, as we are all going on to Schlangenbad in two days. It is really quite delightful to find you settled here so nicely. What a privilege it must be to be so constantly in Mossu Tourneur's society!"

Madame Tourneur gave a bland assenting smile, and turned to speak to several people who were standing near. "Monsieur de Marveille, are you going? Thanks, I will be at the committee on Thursday without fail. Monsieur Boulot, you must remain a few minutes; I want to consult you about that case in which la Comtesse de Glaris takes so deep an interest. Lady Macduff has also written to me to ask my husband's interest for her. Ah, Lady Sophia! how glad I am you have returned! is Lady Matilda better?"

"Well, I'll wish you good-bye, Madame Tourneur," said Lady Dampier, rather impressed, and not much caring to stand by quite unnoticed while all these greetings were going on. "You will let Elly come to-morrow?"

"Certainly," said Mme. Tourneur. "You will understand how it is that I do not call. My days are much occupied. I have little time for mere visits of pleasure and ceremony. Monsieur Bontemps, one word—"

"Elly, which is the way out?" said Lady Dampier, abruptly, less and less pleased, but more and more impressed.

"I will show you," said Elly, who had been standing by all this time, and she led the way bare-headed into the court, over which the stars were shining tranquilly. The trees looked dark and rustled mysteriously along the wall, but all heaven was alight. Elly looked up for an instant, and then turned to her companion and asked her, with a voice that faltered a little, if they were all together in Paris?

"No; Miss Dampier is in Scotland still," said my lady.

It was not Miss Dampier's name of which Elizabeth Gilmour was longing to hear, she did not dare ask any more; but it seemed as if a great weight had suddenly fallen upon her heart, as she thought that perhaps, after all, he was not come; she should not hear of him, see him—who knows?—perhaps, never again.

Elly tried to unbar the great front door to let out her friend; but she could not do it, and called to old Françoise, who was passing across to the kitchen, to come and help her. And suddenly the bolt, which had stuck in some manner, gave way, the gate opened wide, and as it opened Elly saw that there was somebody standing just outside under the lamp-post. The foolish child did not guess who it was, but said "Good-night," with a sigh, and held out her soft hand to Lady Dampier. And then, all of a sudden the great load went away, and in its place came a sort of undreamed-of peace, happiness, and gratitude. All the stars seemed suddenly to blaze more brightly; all the summer's night to shine more wonderfully; all trouble, all anxiousness, to melt away; and John Dampier turned round and said: "Is that you, Elizabeth?"

"And you?" cried Elly, springing forward, with both her hands outstretched. "Ah, I did not think who was outside the door."

"How did you come here, John?" said my lady, very much flustered.

"I came to fetch you," said her son. "I wanted a walk, and Letty told me where you were gone." Lady Dampier did not pay much attention to his explanations; she was watching Elly with a dissatisfied face; and glancing round too, the young man saw that Elly was standing quite still under the archway, with her hands folded, and with a look of dazzled delight in her blue eyes that there was no mistaking.

"You don't forget your old friends, Elly?" said he.

"I! never, never," cried Elizabeth.

"And I, too, do not forget," said he, very kindly, and held out his hand once more, and took hers, and did not let it go. "I will come and see you, and bring Lætitia," he added, as his mother looked up rather severely. "Good-night, dear Elly? I am glad you are unchanged."

People, however slow they may be naturally, are generally quick in discovering admiration, or affection, or respectful devotion to themselves. Lady Dampier only suspected, her son was quite sure of poor Elly's feelings, as he said good-night under the archway. Indeed he knew a great deal more about them than did Elizabeth herself. All she knew was that the great load was gone; and she danced across the stones of the yard, clapping her hands in her old happy way. The windows of the salle were lighted up. She could see the people within coming and going, but she did not notice Anthony, who was standing in one of them. He, for his part, was watching the little dim figure dancing and flitting about in the starlight. Had he, then, anything to do with her happiness? Was he indeed so blessed? His heart was overflowing with humble gratitude, with kindness, with wonder. He was happy at the moment, and was right to be grateful. She was happy, too—as thoroughly happy now, and carried away by her pleasure, as she had been crushed and broken by her troubles. "Ah! to think that the day has come at last, after watching all this long, long, cruel time! I always knew it would come. Every body gets what they wish for sooner or later. I don't think any body was ever so miserable as I have been all this year, but at last—at last—" No one saw the bright, happy look that came into her face, for she was standing in the dark outside the door of the house. She wanted to dream, she did not want to talk to any body; she wanted to tell herself over and over again how happy she was; how she had seen him again; how he had looked; how kindly he had spoken to her. Ah! yes, he had cared for her all the time; and now he had come to fetch her away. She did not think much of poor Anthony; if she did, it was to say to herself that somehow it would all come right, and every body would be as well contented as she was. The door of the house opened while she still stood looking up at the stars. This time it was not John Dampier, but the Pasteur Tourneur, who came from behind it. He put out his hand and took hold of hers.

"You there, Elizabeth! Come in, my child, you will be cold." And he drew her into the hall, where the Pasteurs Boulot and De Marveille were pulling on their cloaks and bidding every body good-night.

The whole night Elizabeth lay starting and waking—so happy that she could not bear to go to sleep, to cease to exist for one instant. Often it had been the other way, and she had been thankful to lay her weary head on her pillow, and close her aching eyes, and forget her troubles. But all this night she lay wondering what the coming day was to bring forth. She had better have gone to sleep. The coming day brought forth nothing at all, except, indeed, a little note from Lætitia, written on a half-sheet of paper, which was put into her hand about eleven o'clock, just as she was sitting down to the déjeûner à la fourchette.

"Hôtel du Rhin, Place Vendôme,
Wednesday evening.

"MY DEAR ELIZABETH,—I am so disappointed to think that I shall not perhaps see you, after all. Some friends of ours have just arrived, who are going on to Schlangenbad to-morrow, and Aunt Catherine thinks it will be better to set off a little sooner than we had intended, so as to travel with them. I wish you might be able to come and breakfast with us about nine to-morrow; but I am afraid this is asking almost too much, though I should greatly enjoy seeing you again. Good-bye. If we do not meet now, I trust that on our return in a couple of months we may be more fortunate, and see much of each other. We start at ten, and shall reach Strasbourg about eight. Ever, dear Elizabeth, affectionately yours, LÆTITIA MALCOLM."

"What has happened?" said Madame Tourneur, quite frightened, for she saw the girl's face change and her eyes suddenly filling with tears.

"Nothing has happened," said Elizabeth. "I was only disappointed to think I should not see them again." And she put out her hand and gave her mother the note.

"But why care so much for people who do not care for you?" said her mother. "Lady Dampier is one of the coldest women I ever knew; and as for Lætitia, if she loved you in the least, would she write you such a note as this?"

"Mamma! it is a very kind note," said Elizabeth. "I know she loves me."

"Do you think she cried over it, as you did?" said her mother. "'So disappointed'—'more fortunate on our return through Paris?'"

"Do not let us judge our neighbors so hastily, my wife," said M. Tourneur. "Let Elizabeth love her friend. What can she do better?"

Caroline looked up with an odd expression, shrugged her shoulders, and did not answer.

Until breakfast was over, Elly kept up pretty well; but when M. Tourneur rose and went away into his writing-room, when Anthony and the young men filed off by an opposite door, and

Mme. Tourneur disappeared to look to her household duties—then, when the room was quiet again, and only Madame Jacob remained sewing in a window, and Lou-Lou and Tou-Tou whispering over their lessons, suddenly the canary burst out into a shrill piping jubilant song, and the sunshine poured in, and Elly's heart began to sink. **And then suddenly the horrible reality seemed realized to her.** . . . .

They were gone—those who had come, as she thought, to rescue her. Could it be true—could it be really true? She had stood lonely on the arid shore waving her signals of distress, and they who should have seen them never heeded, but went sailing away to happier lands, disappearing in the horizon, and leaving her to her fate. That fate which—it was more than she could bear. It seemed more terrible than ever to her to-day. . . . . Ah! silly girl, was her life as hard as the lives of thousands struggling along with her in the world, tossed and broken against the rocks, while she, at least, was safely landed on the beach? She had no heart to think of others. She sat sickening with disappointment, and once more her eyes filled up with stinging tears.

"Lou-Lou, Tou-Tou, come up to your lessons," said Mrs. Jacob. "I do not wish you to see such a wicked example of discontent." The little girls went off on tiptoe; and when these people were gone, Elizabeth was left quite alone.

"I dare say I am very wicked," she was saying to herself. "I was made wicked. But this is more than I can bear—to live all day with the people I hate, and then when I do love with my whole heart, to be treated with such cruel indifference—such coldness. He *ought* to know, he must know, that he has broken my heart. Why does he look so kindly, and then forget so heartlessly? . . . ."

She hid her face in her hands, and bent her head over the wooden table. She did not care who knew her to be unhappy—what pain her unhappiness might give. The person who was likely to be most wounded by her poignant grief came into the room at the end of half an hour, and found her sitting still in the same attitude, with her head hanging, and her tears dribbling on the deal table. This was enough answer for poor Anthony.

"Elizabeth," he faltered, "I see you can not make up your mind."

"Ah! no, no, Anthony, not yet," said Elizabeth; "but you are the only person in the world who cares for me; and indeed, indeed, I am grateful."

And then the poor little head sank down again, overwhelmed with its load of grief.

"Tell me, Elizabeth, is there any thing in the world I **can** do to make you more happy?" said Anthony. "My prayers, my best wishes, are yours. Is there nothing else?"

"Only not to notice me," said Elly; "only to leave me alone."

And so Anthony, seeing that he **could** do

nothing, went away very sad at heart. He had been so happy and confident the night before, and now he began to fear that what he longed for was never to be his. Poor boy, he buried his trouble in his own heart, and did not say one word of it to father, or mother, or young companions.

Five or six weeks went by, and Elly heard no more of the Dampiers. Every day she looked more ill, more haggard; her temper did not mend, her spirits did not improve. **In June the** five young men went home to their families. M. and Madame Tourneur went down to Fontainebleau for a week. Anthony set off for the South of France to visit an uncle. He was to be ordained in the autumn, and was anxious to pay this visit before his time should be quite taken up by his duties. Clementine asked for a holiday, and went off to her friends in Passy; and Elly remained at home. It was her own fault: Monsieur Tourneur had begged her to come with them; her mother had scolded and remonstrated, all in vain. The wayward girl declared that she wanted no change, no company, that she was best where she was. Only for a week? she would stay, and there was an end of it. I think the secret was, that she could not bear to quit Paris, and waited and waited, hoping against hope.

"I am afraid you will quarrel with Madame Jacob," said her mother, as she was setting off.

"I shall not speak to her," said Elly; and for two days she was as good as her word. But on the third day this salutary silence was broken. Madame Jacob, coming in with her bonnet on, informed Elizabeth that she was going out for the afternoon.

"I confess it is not without great apprehensions lest you should get into mischief," says the lady.

"And pray," says Elly, "am I more likely to get into mischief than you are? I am going out."

"You will do nothing of the sort," says Madame Jacob.

"I will do exactly as I choose," says Elizabeth.

In a few minutes a battle royal was raging; Tou-Tou and Lou-Lou look on, all eyes and ears; old Françoise comes up from the kitchen, and puts her head in at the door.

Madame Jacob was desiring her, on no account, to let Elizabeth out that afternoon, when Lou-Lou said, "There, that was the street-door shutting;" and Tou-Tou said, "She is gone." And so it was.

The willful Elizabeth had brushed past old Françoise, rushed up to her own room, pulled out a shawl, tied on her bonnet, defiantly, run down stairs and across the yard, and, in a minute, was walking rapidly away without once looking behind her. Down the hill, past the hospital—they were carrying a wounded man in at the door as she passed, and she just caught a glimpse of his pale face, and turned shrinking away. Then she got into the Faubourg St. Honoré, with its shops and its cabstands, and busy people coming and going; and then she turned up the Rue d'Angoulême. In the Champs Elysées the afternoon sun was streaming; there was a crowd, and, as it happened, soldiers were marching along to the sound of martial music. She saw an empty bench, and sat down for a minute to regain breath and equanimity. The music put her in mind of the day when she had listened at her window—of the day when her heart was so heavy and then so light—of the day when Anthony had told her his scheme, when John Dampier had waited at the door: the day, the only one—she was not likely to forget it when she had been so happy, just for a little. And now—? The bitter remembrance came rushing over her; and she jumped up, and walked faster and faster, trying to escape from it.

She got into the Tuileries, and on into the Rue de Rivoli, but she thought that people looked at her strangely, and she turned homewards at last. It was lonely, wandering about this busy city by herself. As she passed by the columns of St. Philip's Church, somebody came out, and the curtain swang back, and Elly, looking up, saw a dim, quiet interior, full of silent rays of light falling from the yellow windows and checkering the marble. She stopped, and went in with a sudden impulse. One old woman was kneeling on the threshold, and Elly felt as if she, too, wanted to fall upon her knees. What tranquil gloom, and silence, and repose! Her own church was only open at certain hours. Did it always happen that precisely at eleven o'clock on Sunday mornings she was in the exact frame of mind in which she most longed for spiritual communion and consolation? To be tightly wedged in between two other devotees, plied with *chaufferettes* by the pew-opener, forced to follow the extempore supplications of the preacher—did all this suffice to her wants? Here was silence, coolness, a faint, half-forgotten smell of incense, there were long, empty rows of chairs, one or two people kneeling at the little altars, five or six little pious candles burning in compliment to the various saints and deities to whom they were dedicated. The rays of the little candles glimmered in the darkness, and the foot-falls fell quietly along the aisle. I, for my part, do not blame this poor foolish heart, if it offered up an humble supplication here in the shrine of the stranger. Poor Elly was not very eloquent; she only prayed to be made a good girl and to be happy. But, after all, eloquence and long words do not mean any more.

She walked home, looking up at the sunset lines which were streaking the sky freshly and delicately; she thought she saw Madame Jacob's red nose up in a little pink cloud, and began to speculate how she would be received. And she had nearly reached her own door, and was toiling wearily up the last hilly piece of road, when she heard some quick steps behind; somebody passed, turned round, said, "Why, Elly! I was going to see you."

In an instant Elly's blue eyes were all alight, and her ready hand outstretched to John Dampier—for it was he.

CHAPTER V.

In looking backward, they may find that several things which were not the charm have more reality to this groping memory than the charm itself which embalmed them.

HE had time to think, as he greeted her, how worn she looked, how shabbily she was dressed. And yet what a charming, talking, brightening face it was. When Elly smiled, her bonnet and dress became quite new and becoming, somehow. In two minutes he thought her handsomer than ever. They walked on, side by side, up the hilly street. She, trying to hide her agitation, asked him about Lætitia, about his mother, and dear Miss Dampier.

"I think she does care for me still," said Elly; "but you have all left off."

"My dear child," said he, "how can you think any thing so foolish?"

"I have nothing else to do," said Elly, plaintively; "all day long I think about those happy times which are gone. I thought you had forgotten me when you did not come."

Dampier laughed a little uneasily. "I have had to take them to their watering-place," said he; "I could not help it. But tell me about yourself. Are you not comfortable?" he asked.

"I am rather unhappy," said Elizabeth. "I am not good, like they are, and oh! I get so tired;" and then she went on and told him what miserable days she spent, and how she hated them, and she longed for a little pleasure and ease and happiness.

He was very much touched, and very, very sorry. "You don't look well," he said. "You should have some amusement—some change. I would take you anywhere you liked. Why not come now for a drive? See, here is a little open carriage passing. Surely, with an old friend like me, there can be no harm." And he signed to the driver to stop.

Elizabeth was quite frightened at the idea, and said, "Oh no, no! indeed." Whereas, Dampier only said: "Oh yes! indeed, you must. Why, I knew you when you were a baby—and your father and your grandmother—and I am a respectable middle-aged man, and it will do you good, and it will soon be a great deal too dark for any of your pasteurs to recognize you and report. We have been out riding together before now—why not come for a little drive in the Bois? Why not?"

So said Elly to herself, doubtfully; and she got in, still hesitating, and in a minute they were rolling away swiftly out at the gates of Paris, out towards the sunset—so it seemed to Elizabeth—and she forgot all her fears. The heavens glowed overhead; her heart beat with intensest enjoyment. Presently, the twilight came falling with a green glow, with stars, with evening perfumes, with lights twinkling from the carriages reflected on the lakes as they rolled past. **And so at** last she was happy, **sometimes silent from** delight, sometimes talking **in her simple, foolish way, and telling him all about herself, her regrets, her troubles—about Anthony.** She could **not help it—indeed, she could not.** Dampier, for his part, cried out at the notion **of** her marrying Anthony, made fun of him, laughed at him, pitied him. The poor fellow, now that she compared him to John Dampier, did indeed seem dull, and strangely uncouth, and commonplace.

"Marry that cub!" said Sir John; "you mustn't do it, my dear. You would be like the princess in the fairy tale, who went off with the bear. It's downright wicked to think of such a thing. Elizabeth, *promise* me you won't. Does he ever climb up and down a pole? is he fond of **buns?** is he tame? If your father were alive, would he suffer such a thing? Promise me, Elly, that you will never become Mrs. Bruin."

"Yes; I promise," said Elly, with a sigh. "But he is so kind. Nobody is as—" And then she stopped, and thought: "Yes; here was some one who was a great deal kinder." Talking to Dampier was so easy, so pleasant, that she scarcely recognized her own words and sentences; it was like music in tune after music out of tune; it was like running on smooth rails after rolling along a stony road: it was like breathing fresh air after a heated stifling atmosphere. Somehow, he met her half-way; he need not explain, recapitulate, stumble for words, as she was forced to do with those practical, impractical people at home. He understood what she wanted to say before she had half finished her sentence; he laughed at her fine little jokes; he encouraged, he cheered, he delighted her. If she had cared for him before, it was now a mad adoration which she felt for this man. He suited her; she felt now that he was part of her life—the better, nobler, wiser part; and if he was the other half of her life, surely, somehow, she must be as necessary to him as he was to her. Why had he come to see her else? Why had he cared for her, and brought her here? Why was his voice so gentle, his manner so kind and sympathetic? He had cared for her once, she knew he had; and he cared for her still, she knew he did. If the whole world were to deceive her and fail her, she would still trust him. And her instinct was not wrong: he was sincerely and heartily her friend. The carriage put them down a few doors from M. Tourneur's house, and then Elly went boldly up to the door and rang at the bell.

"I shall come at four o'clock to-morrow, and take you for a drive," said John; "you look like another woman already."

"It is no use asking Madame Jacob," said Elly; "she would lock me up into my room. I will come somehow. How shall I thank you?"

"By looking well and happy again. I shall be so glad to have cured you!"

"And it is so pleasant to meet with such a kind doctor," said Elly, looking up and smiling.

"Good-bye, Elly," repeated Sir John, quite affected by her gentle looks.

Old Françoise opened **the door.** Elly turned a little pale.

"Ah, ha! vous voilà," says the old woman; "méchante fille, you are going to get **a** pretty scolding. Where have you been?"

"Ah, Françoise!" said Elly, "I have been so happy. I met Sir John Dampier: he is an old, old friend. He took me for a drive in the Bois. Is Madame Jacob very, very angry?"

"Well, you are in luck," says the old woman, who could never resist Elizabeth's pretty pleading ways; "she came home an hour ago and fetched the children, and went out to dine in town, and I told her you were in your room."

"Ah, you dear kind old woman!" said Elly, flinging her arms round her neck, and giving her a kiss.

"There, there!" said the unblushing Françoise; "I will put your couvert in the salle."

"Ah! I am very glad. I am so hungry, Françoise," said Elly, pulling off her bonnet, and shaking her loose hair as she followed the old woman across the court-yard.

So Elizabeth sat down to dine off dry bread and cold mutton. But though she said she was hungry, she was too happy to eat much. The tallow candle flickered on the table. She thought of the candles in St. Philip's Church; then she went over every word, every minute which she had spent since she was kneeling there. Old Françoise came in with a little cake she had made her, and found Elizabeth sitting, smiling, with her elbows on the table. "Allons, allons!" thought the old cook. "Here, eat, mamzelle," said she; "faut plus sortir sans permission—hein?"

"Thank you, Françoise. How nice! how kind of you!" said Elizabeth, in her bad French—she never would learn to talk properly; and then she ate her cake by the light of the candle, and this little dim tallow wick seemed to cast light and brilliance over the whole world, over her whole life, which seemed to her as if it would go on for ever and ever. Now and then, a torturing doubt, a misgiving, came over her, but these she put quickly aside.

Madame Jacob was pouring out the coffee when Elly came down to breakfast next morning, conscious and ashamed, and almost disposed to confess. "I am surprised," said Madame Jacob, "that you have the impudence to sit down at table with me;" and she said it in such an acid tone that all Elly's sweetness and ashamedness and penitence turned to bitterness.

"I find it very disagreeable," says Elly; "**but** I try and resign myself."

"I shall write to my brother about you," continued Madame Jacob.

"Indeed!" says Elizabeth. "Here is a letter which he has written to me. What fun if it should be about you!" It was like Tourneur's handwriting, but it did not come from him. Elly opened it carelessly enough, but Tou-Tou and Lou-Lou exchanged looks of intelligence. Their mother had examined the little missive, and made her comments upon it:—

"Avignon, Rue de la Clochette,
Chez le Pasteur Ch. Tourneur.

"MY DEAR ELLY,—I think of you so much and so constantly that I can not help wishing to make you think of me, if only for one minute, while you read these few words. I have been telling my uncle about you ; it is he who asks me why I do not write. But there are some things which are not to be spoken or to be written—it is only by one's life that one can try to tell them ; and you, alas! do not care to hear the story of my life. I wonder will the day ever come when you will listen to it ?

"I have been most kindly received by all my old friends down in these parts. Yesterday I attended the service in the Temple, and heard a most soul-stirring and eloquent oration from the mouth of M. le Pasteur David. I receive cheering accounts on every side. A new temple has been opened at Beziers, thanks to the munificence of one of our coréligionnaires. The temple was solemnly opened on the Monday of the Pentecost. The discourse of dedication was pronounced by M. le Pasteur Borrel, of Nismes. Seven pasteurs en robe attended the ceremony. They tell me that the interdiction which had weighed for some years upon the temple at Fouqueure (Charente) has been taken off, and that the faithful were able to reopen their temple on the first Sunday in June. Need I say what vivid actions of grace were uttered on this happy occasion ? A Protestant school has also been established at Montauban, which seems to be well attended. I am now going to visit two of my uncle's confrères, MM. Bertoul and Joseph Aubré. Of M. Bertoul I have heard much good.

"Why do I tell you all this ? Do you care for what I care ? Could you ever bring yourself to lead the life which I propose to lead ? Time only will show, dear Elizabeth. It will also show to you the faithfulness and depth of my affection. A. T."

Elly put the letter down with a sigh, and went on drinking her coffee and eating her bread. Madame Jacob hemmed and tried to ask her a question or two on the subject, but Elly would not answer. Elly sometimes wondered at Anthony's fancy for her, knowing how little suited she was to the way of life she was leading ; she was surprised that his rigid notions should allow him to entertain such an idea for an instant. But the truth was that Anthony was head over ears in love with her, and thought her perfection at the bottom of his heart.

Poor Anthony! This is what he got in return for his letter:—

"MY DEAR ANTHONY,—It can not be—never—never. But I do care for you, and I mean

to always. For you are my brother in a sort of way. I am your affectionate, grateful
ELLY."

"P.S.—Your father and my mother are away at Fontainebleau. Madame Jacob is here, and more disagreeable than any thing you can imagine."

And so it was settled ; and Elly never once asked herself if she had been foolish or wise ; but, after thinking compassionately about Anthony for a minute or two, she began to think about Dampier, and said to herself that she had followed his advice, and he must know best ; and Dampier himself, comfortably breakfasting in the coffee-room of the hotel, was thinking of her, and, as he thought, put away all unpleasant doubts or suggestions. "Poor little thing! dear little thing!" he was saying to himself. "I will not leave her to the tender mercies of those fanatics. She will die—I see it in her eyes—if she stays there ! My mother or Aunt Jean must come to her help ; we must not desert her. Poor, poor little Elly, with her wistful face! Why did not she make me marry her a year ago ? I was very near it."

He was faithful next day to his appointment, and Elly arrived breathless. "Madame Jacob had locked her up in her room," she said, only she got out of the window and clambered down by the vine, and here she was. "But it is the last time," she added. "Ah! let us make haste ; is not that Françoise ?" He helped her in, and in a minute they were driving along the Faubourg. Elly let down the veil. John saw that her hand was trembling, and asked if she was afraid?

"I am afraid, because I know I am doing wrong," said Elly; "only I think I should have died for want of fresh air in that hateful prison, if I had not come."

"You used to like your little apartment near the Madeleine better," said Dampier; "that was not a prison."

"I grow sick with regret when I think of those days," Elly said. "Do you know that day you spoke to us in the Tuileries was the last happy day of my life, except—"

"Except?" said Dampier.

"Except yesterday," said Elly. "It is so delightful to do something wrong again."

"Why should you think this is doing wrong ?" said Dampier. "You know me, and can trust me—can't you, Elly ?"

"Have I shown much mistrust ?" said Elly, laughing ; and then she added more seriously, "I have been writing to Anthony this morning —I have done as you told me. So you see whether I trust you or not."

"You have refused him ?" said Dampier.

"Yes ; are you satisfied ?" said Elly, looking with her bright blue-eyed glance.

"He was unworthy of you," cried Dampier, secretly rather dismayed to find his advice so quickly acted upon. What had he done ? would not that marriage, after all, have been the very best thing for Elly perhaps? He was glad and sorry, but I think he would rather have been more sorry and less glad, and have heard that Elly had found a solution to all her troubles. He thought it necessary to be sentimental; it was the least he could do, after what she had done for him.

"Why wouldn't you let me in when I came to see you one day long ago, just before I left Paris?" he asked, suddenly. "Do you know what I wanted to say to you?"

Elly blushed up under her veil. "Mamma had desired Clementine to let no one in. Did you not know I would have seen you if I could?"

"I knew nothing of the sort," said Dampier, rather sadly. "I wish—I wish—I had known it." He forgot that, after all, that was not the real reason of his going away without speaking. He chose to imagine that this was the reason —that he would have married Elly but for this. He forgot his own careful scruples and hesitations; his doubts and indecision; and now to-day he forgot every thing, except that he was very sorry for Elly, and glad to give her a little pleasure. He did not trouble himself as to what people would say of her—of a girl who was going about with a man who was neither her brother nor her husband. Nobody would know her. The only people to fear were the people at home, who should never hear any thing about it. He would give her and give himself a little happiness, if he could; and he said to himself that he was doing a good action in so doing; he would write to his aunt about her, he would be her friend and her doctor, and if he could bring a little color in those wasted cheeks and happiness into those sad eyes, it would be wicked and cruel not to do so.

And so, like a quack doctor, as he was, he administered his drug, which soothed and dulled her pain for the moment, only to increase and hasten the progress of the cruel malady which was destroying her. They drove along past the Madeleine, along the broad glittering Boulevards, with their crowds, their wares, people thronging the pavements, horses and carriages travelling alongside with them; the world, the flesh, and the devil jostling and pressing past.

"There is a theatre," cried Elly, as they came to a sudden stop. "I wonder, shall I ever go again? What fun it used to be!"

"Will you come to-night?" asked Dampier, smiling. "I will take care of you."

Elly, who had found her good spirits again, laughed and clasped her hands. "How I should like it! Oh! how I wish it was possible! but it would be quite, quite impossible."

"Have you come to think such vanities wrong?" said Dampier.

"Not wrong. Where is the harm? Only unattainable. Imagine Madame Jacob; think of the dragons, who would tear me to pieces if they found me out—of Anthony—of my stepfather."

"You need not show them the play-bill,"

said Dampier, laughing. "You will be quite sure of not meeting any of the pasteurs there. Could not you open one of those barred windows and jump out? I would come with a ladder of ropes, if you will let me."

"I should not want a ladder of ropes," said Elly; "the windows are quite close to the ground. What fun it would be! but it is quite, quite impossible, of course."

Dampier said no more. He told the driver to turn back, and to stop at the Louvre; and he made her get out, and took her up stairs into the great golden hall with the tall windows, through which you can see the Seine as it rushes under the bridges, and the light as it falls on the ancient stately quays and houses, on the cathedral, on the towers of Paris. It was like enchantment to Elly; all about the atmosphere was golden, was bewitched. She was eagerly drinking her cup of happiness to the dregs, she was in a sort of glamour. She hardly could believe that this was herself.

They went and sat down on the great round sofa in the first room, opposite the "Marriage of Cana," with "St. Michael killing the Dragon" on one side, and the green pale wicked woman staring at them from behind: the pale woman with the unfathomable face. Elly kept turning round every now and then, fascinated by her cold eyes. Dampier was a connoisseur, and fond of pictures, and he told Elizabeth all about those which he liked best; told her about the painters—about their histories. She was very ignorant, and scarcely knew the commonest stories. How she listened, how she treasured up his words, how she remembered, in after days, every tone as he spoke, every look in his kind eyes! He talked when he should have been silent, looked kind when he should have turned his eyes away. What cruel kindness! what fatal friendship! He imagined she liked him; he knew it, indeed: but he fancied that she liked him and loved him in the same quiet way in which he loved her—hopelessly, regretfully, resignedly. As he walked by her side along those wonderful galleries, now and then it occurred to him that, perhaps, after all, it was scarcely wise; but he put the thought quickly away, as I have said already, and blinded himself, and said, surely it was right. They were standing before a kneeling abbess in white flannel, painted by good old Philip of Champagne, and laughing at her droll looks and her long nose, when Sir John, happening to turn round, saw his old acquaintance De Vaux coming directly towards them, with his eye-glasses stuck over his nose, and his nose in the air. He came up quite close, stared at the abbess, and walked on without apparently seeing or recognizing them. Elly had not turned her head, but Dampier drew a long breath when he was gone. Elly wondered to see him looking so grave when she turned around with a smile and made some little joke. "I think we ought to go, Elly," said he. "Come, this place will soon be shut."

They drove home through the busy street, once more, through the golden sunset. They stopped at the corner by the hospital, and Elly said "Good-bye," and jumped out. As Elly was reluctantly turning to go away, Dampier felt that he *must* see her once more: that he *couldn't* part from her now. "Elly," he said, "I shall be here at six o'clock on Friday. This is Tuesday, isn't it? and we must go to the play just once together. Won't you come? Do, please, come."

"Shall I come? I will think about it all to-morrow," said Elly, "and make up my mind." And then Dampier watched the slim little figure disappear under the doorway.

Fortune was befriending Elly to-day. Old Françoise had left the great door open, and now she slipped in and ran up to her own room, where she found the key in the lock. She came down quite demurely to dinner when Lou-Lou came to summon her to the frugal repast.

All dinner-time she thought about her scheme, and hesitated and determined, and hesitated and wished wistfully, and then suddenly said to herself that she would be happy her own way, come what might. "We will eat, drink, and be merry," said Elly to herself, with a little wry face at the cabbage, "for to-morrow we die."

And so the silly girl almost enjoyed the notion of running wild in this reckless way. Her whole life, which had been so dull and wearisome before, glittered with strange happiness and bewildering hope. She moved about the house like a person in a dream. She was very silent, but that of late had been her habit. Madame Jacob looked surprised sometimes at her gentleness, but thought it was all right, and did not trouble herself about much else besides Tou-Tou's and Lou-Lou's hymns and lessons. She had no suspicion. She thought that Elizabeth's first escapade had been a mere girlish freak; of the second she knew nothing; of the third not one dim imagination entered her head. She noticed that Elly did not eat, but she looked well and came dancing into the room, and she (Mme. Jacob) supposed it was all right. Was it all right? The whole summer nights Elly used to lie awake with wide-open eyes, or spring from her bed and stand for long hours leaning from her window, staring at the stars and telling them all her story. The life she was leading was one of morbid excitement and feverish dreams.

CHAPTER VI.

What are we sent on earth for? Say to toil,
Nor seek to leave the tending of the vines,
For all the host of day till it declines,
And death's mild curfew shall from work assoil.

MADAME JACOB had a friend at Asnières, an old maiden lady, Tou-Tou's godmother, who was well-to-do in the world, with her £200 a year, it was said, and who lived in a little Chinese pagoda by the railway. Now and then this old lady used to write and invite Tou-Tou and Lou-Lou and their mother to come to see her, and you may be sure her invitations were never disregarded.

Mme. Jacob did look at Elizabeth rather doubtfully when she found on Wednesday morning the usual ill-spelt, ill-written little letter. But, after all, Tou-Tou's prospects were not to be endangered for the sake of looking after a young woman like Elizabeth, were she ten times more wayward and ill-behaved, and so the little girls were desired to make up their paquets. It was a great event in Mme. Jacob's eyes; the house echoed with her directions; Françoise went out to request assistance, and came back with a friend, who helped her down with the box. The little girls stood at the door to stop the omnibus, which was to take them to the station. They were off at last. The house-door closed upon them with a satisfactory bang, and Elly breathed freely and ran through the deserted rooms, clapping and waving her hands, and dancing her steps, and feeling at last that she was free. And so the morning hours went by. Old Françoise was not sorry either to see everybody go. She was sitting in the kitchen in the afternoon, peeling onions and potatoes, when Elly came wandering in in her restless way, with her blue eyes shining and her curly hair pushed back. What a tranquil little kitchen it was, with a glimpse of the court-yard outside, and the cocks and the hens, and the poplar-trees waving in the sunshine, and the old woman sitting in her white cap busy at her homely work. Elly did not think how tranquil it was, but said to herself, as she looked at Françoise, how old she was, and what a strange fate hers, that she should be there quietly peeling onions at the end of her life. What a horrible fate, thought Elizabeth, to be sitting by one's grave, as it were, paring vegetables and cooking broth to the last day of one's existence. Poor Françoise! And then she said out loud, "Françoise, tell me, are cooks like ladies? do they get to hate their lives sometimes? Are you not tired to death of cooking *pot-au-feu?*"

"I am thankful to have *pot-au-feu* to cook," said Françoise. "Mademoiselle, I should like to see you *éplucher* vegetables sometimes, as I do, instead of running about all day. It would be much better for you."

"Ecoutez, Françoise," said Elly, imploringly; "when I am old like you I will sit still by the fire; now that I am young I want to run about. I am the only young person in this house. They are all old here, and like dead people, for they only think of heaven."

"That is because they are on the road," said Françoise. "Ah! they are good folks—they are."

"I see no merit in being good," Elizabeth said, crossly, sitting down on the table, and dabbling her fingers in a bowl of water which stood there; "they are good because they like it. It amuses them, it is their way of thinking—they like to be better than their neighbors."

"*Fi donc*, Elizabeth!" said Françoise. "You do not amuse them; but they are good to you. Is it Anthony's way of thinking when he bears with all your caprices? When my master comes home quite worn out and exhausted, and trudges off again without so much as waiting for his soup, if he hears he is wanted by some poor person or other, does he go because it pleases him, or because he is serving the Lord in this world, as he hopes to serve him in the next?"

Elly was a little ashamed, and said, looking down: "Have you always lived here with him, Françoise?"

"Not I," said Françoise; "ten years, that is all. But that is long enough to tell a good man from a bad one. Good people live for others, and don't care about themselves. I hope when I have known you ten years, that you too will be a good woman, mademoiselle."

"Like Madame Jacob?" said Elly.

Françoise shrugged her shoulders rather doubtfully, and Elly sat quite still watching her. Was it not strange to be sitting there in this quiet every-day kitchen, with a great unknown world throbbing in her heart. "How little Françoise guesses!" thought Elly. "Françoise, who is only thinking of her marmite and her potatoes." Elly did not know it, but Françoise had a very shrewd suspicion of what was going on in the poor little passionate heart. "The girl is not suited here," thought the old woman. "If she has found some one, so much the better; Clementine has told me something about it. If madame were to drive him off again, that would be a pity. But I saw them quite plainly that day I went to Martin, the chemist's, driving away in that little carriole, and I saw him that night when he was waiting for his mother."

So old Françoise peels potatoes, and Elly sits wondering and saying over to herself, "Good people live for others." Who had she ever lived for but herself? Ah! there was one person whom she would live and die for, now. Ah! at last she would be good. "And about the play?" thought Elly; "shall I go—shall I send him word that I will not? There is no harm in a play; why should I not please him and accept his kindness? it is not the first time that we have been there together. I know that plays are not wrong, whatever these stupid people say. Ah! surely if happiness is sent to me, it would be wicked to turn away, instead of being always—always grateful all my life." And so, though she told herself that it could not be wrong to go, she forgot to tell herself that it was wrong to go with him; her scruples died away one by one; once or twice she thought of being brave and staying away, and sending a message by old Françoise, but she only thought of it.

All day long, on Friday, she wandered about the empty house, coming and going, like a girl bewitched. She went into the garden; she picked flowers and pulled them to pieces, trying to spell out her fate; she tried to make a wreath of vine-leaves, but got tired, and flung it away. Old Françoise, from her kitchen window, watched her standing at the grating and pulling at the vine; but the old woman's spectacles were somewhat dim, and she did not see Elly's two bright feverish eyes and her burning cheeks from the kitchen window. As the evening drew near, Elly's cheeks became pale and her courage nearly failed her, but she had been three days at home. Monsieur and Madame Tourneur were expected the next morning; she had not seen Dampier for a long, long time—so it seemed to her. Yes, she would go; she did not care. Wrong? Right? It was neither wrong nor right—it was simply impossible to keep away. She could not think of one reason in the world why she should stop. She felt a thousand in her heart urging, ordering, compelling her to go. She went up to her own room after dinner, and began to dress, to plait, and to smooth her pretty curly hair. She put on a white dress, a black lace shawl, and then she found that she had no gloves. Some of her ancient belongings she kept in a drawer, but they were not replaced as they wore out. And Elly possessed diamond rings and bracelets in abundance; but neither gloves nor money to buy them. What did it matter? She did not think about it twice; she put on her shabby bonnet and ran down stairs. She was just going out, when she remembered that Françoise would wonder what had become of her, and so she went to the kitchen door, opened it a little way, and said, "Good-night, Françoise. Don't disturb me to-night, I want to get up early to-morrow."

Françoise, who had invited a friend to spend the evening, said, "Bon soir, mamzelle!" rather crossly—she did not like her kitchen invaded at all times and hours—and then Elly was free to go.

She did not get out by the window—there was no need for that, but she unfastened it, and unbarred the shutter on the inside, so that, though every thing looked much as usual on the outside, she had only to push and it would fly open.

As she got to the door her heart began to beat, and she stopped for an instant to think. Inside, here, where she was standing, was dullness, weariness, security, death; outside, wonderful happiness, dangerous happiness, and life —so it seemed to her. Inside were cocks and hens, and sermons, weary exhortations, old Françoise peeling her onions. Outside, John Dampier waiting, the life she was created for, fresh air, congenial spirits, light and brightness—and heaven there as well as here, thought Elly, clasping her hands; heaven spreading across the house-tops as well as over this narrow courtyard. "What shall I do? Oh, shall I be forgiven? Oh! it will be forgiven me, surely, surely!" the girl sighed, and, with trembling hands, she undid the latch and went out into the dusky street. The little carriole, as Françoise called it, was waiting, a short way down, at the corner of the hospital; and Dampier came to meet her, looking very tall and straight through the twilight. She wondered at his grave, anxious face; but, in truth, he too was exceedingly nervous, though he would not let her know it; he was beginning to be afraid for her, and had resolved that he would not take her out again; it might, after all, be unpleasant for them both; he had seen De Vaux, and found out, to his annoyance, that he had recognized them in the Louvre the day before, and had passed them by on purpose. There was no knowing what trouble he might not get poor Elly into. And besides, his aunt Jean was on her way to Paris. She had been keeping house for Will Dampier, she wrote, and she was coming. Will was on his way to Switzerland, and she should cross with him.

That very day John had received a letter from her, in answer to the one he had written about Elly. He had written it three days ago; but he was not the same man he had been three days ago. He was puzzled, and restless, and thoroughly wretched—that was the truth; and he was not used to be unhappy, and he did not like it. Elly's face haunted him day and night; he thought of her continually; he tried, in vain, to forget her, to put her out of his mind. Well, on the whole, he was glad that his aunt was coming, and very glad that his mother and Lætitia were still away, and unconscious of what he was thinking about.

"So you did not lose courage?" he said, as they were driving off. "How did you escape Madame Jacob?"

"I have been all alone," said Elly, "these two days. How I found courage to come I can not tell you. I don't quite believe that it is I myself who am here. It seems impossible. I don't feel like myself—I have not for some days past. All I know is, that I am certain those horrible long days have come to an end." John Dampier was frightened—he hardly knew why—when he heard her say this.

"I hope so, most sincerely," said he. "But, after all, Elly, we men and women are rarely contented; and there are plenty of days, more or less tiresome, in store for me and for you, I hope. We must pluck up our courage and go through with them. You are such a sensitive, weak-minded little girl that you will go on breaking your heart a dozen times a day to the end of your life."

Dampier looked very grave as he spoke, but it was too dark for her to see him. He was angry and provoked with himself, and an insane impulse came over him to knock his head violently against the sides of the cab. Insane, do I say? It would have been the very best thing he could have done. But they drove on all the same: Elly in rapture. She was not a bit afraid now. Her spirits were so high and so daring that they would carry her through anything; and when she was with Dampier she was content to be happy, and not to trouble herself with vague apprehensions. And she was happy now; her eyes danced with delight, her heart beat with expectation, she seemed to have become a child again, she was not like a woman any more.

"Have you not a veil?" said Dampier, as they stopped before the theatre. There was a great light, a crowd of people passing and repassing; other carriages driving up.

"No," said Elly. "What does it matter? Who will know me?"

"Well, make haste. Here, take my arm," said Sir John, hurriedly; and he hastily sprang down and helped her out.

"Look at the new moon," said Elly, looking up smiling.

"Never mind the new moon. Come, Elly," said Dampier. And so they passed on into the theatre.

Dampier was dreading recognition. He had a feeling that they would be sure to come against some one. Elly feared no one. When the play began she sat entranced, thrilling with interest, carried away. Faust was the piece which they were representing; and as each scene was played before her, as one change after another came over the piece, she was lost more and more in wonder. If she looked up for an instant it was to see John Dampier's familiar face opposite; and then outside the box, with its little curtain, great glittering theatre-lights, crystals reflecting the glitter, gilding, and silken drapery; everywhere hundreds of people, silent, and breathless too, with interest, with excitement. The music plays, the scene shifts and changes, melting into fresh combinations. Here is Faust. Listen to him as he laments his wasted life. Of what use is wisdom? What does he care for knowledge? A lonely man without one heart to love, one creature to cherish him. Has he not willfully wasted the best years of his life? he cries, in a passion of rage and indignation—wasted them in the pursuit of arid science, of fruitless learning? Will these tend him in his old age, soothe his last hours, be to him wife, and children, and household, and holy home ties? Will these stand by his bedside, and close his weary, aching eyes, and follow him to his grave in the churchyard?

Faust's sad complaint went straight to the heart of his hearers. The church-bell was ringing up the street. Fathers, mothers, and children were wending their way obedient to its call. And the poor desolate old man burst into passionate and hopeless lamentation.

It was all so real to Elly that she almost began to cry herself. She was so carried away by the play, by this history of Faust and of Margaret, that it was in vain Dampier begged her to be careful, to sit back in the shade of the curtain, and not to lean forward too eagerly. She would draw back for a minute or two, and then by degrees advance her pretty breathless head, turning to him every now and then. It was like a dream to her. Like a face in a dream, too, did she presently recognize the face of De Vaux, her former admirer, opposite, in one of the boxes. But Margaret was coming into the chapel with her young companions, and Elly was too much interested to think of what he would think of her. Just at that moment it was Margaret who seemed to her to be the important person in the world.

De Vaux was of a different opinion: he looked towards them once or twice, and at the end of the second act Dampier saw him get up and leave his seat. Sir John was provoked and annoyed beyond measure. He did not want him, De Vaux, least of all people in the world. Every moment he felt as he had never felt before—how wrong it was to have brought Elly, whom he was so fond of, into such a situation. For a moment he was undecided, and then he rose, biting his lips, and opened the door of the box, hoping to intercept him; but there was his Mephistopheles, as ill-luck would have it, standing at the door ready to come in.

"I thought I could not be mistaken," De Vaux began, with a smirk, bowing, and looking significantly from one to the other. "Did you see me in the gallery of the Louvre the other day?"

Elly blushed up very red, and Dampier muttered an oath as he caught sight of the other man's face. He was smiling very disagreeably. John glanced a second time, hesitated, and then said, suddenly and abruptly: "No, you are not mistaken. This is Miss Gilmour, my *fiancée*, M. de Vaux. I dare say you are surprised that I should have brought her to the play. It is the custom in our country." He did not dare look at Elly as he spoke. Had he known what else to say he would have said it.

De Vaux was quite satisfied, and instantly assumed a serious and important manner. The English miss was to him the most extraordinary being in creation, and he would believe any thing you liked to tell him of her. He was prepared to sit down in the vacant chair by Elizabeth, and make himself agreeable to her.

The English miss was scarcely aware of his existence. Faust, Margaret, had been the whole world to her a minute ago. Where was she now? . . . . where were they? . . . . Was she the actress? and were they the spectators looking on? . . . . Was that the Truth which he had spoken? Did he mean it? Was there such wonderful, wonderful happiness in store for a poor little wretch like herself? Ah! could it be — could it be true? Her whole soul shone in her trembling eyes, as she looked up for one instant, and upturned her flashing, speaking, beaming face. Dampier was very pale, and was looking vacantly at the stage. Margaret was weeping, for her troubles had begun. Mephistopheles was laughing, and De Vaux chatting on in an agreeable manner with his hat between his knees. After some time, he discovered that they were not paying attention to one single word he was saying; upon which he rose in an *empressé* manner, wished them good-bye politely, and went away very well pleased with his own good-breeding. And then, when he was gone, when the door was shut, when they were alone together, there was

a silence, and Elly leaned her head against the side of the box; she was trembling so that she could not sit up. And Dampier, looking white and gray in the face somehow, said, in an odd, harsh voice :—

"Elly, you must not mind what I was obliged to say just now. You see, my dear child, that it doesn't do. I ought never to have brought you, and I could think of no better way to get out of my scrape than to tell him that lie."

"It was—it was a lie?" repeated Elly, slowly raising herself upright.

"What could I do?" Sir John continued, very nervously and exceedingly agitated. "Elly, my dear little girl, I could not let him think you were out upon an unauthorized escapade. We all know how it is, but he does not. You must, you do forgive me—only say you do."

"And it is not true?" said Elly, once more, in a bewildered piteous way.

"I—I belong to Lætitia. It was settled before we came abroad," faltered Dampier; and he just looked at her once, and then he turned away. And the light was gone out of her face; all the sparkle, the glitter, the amazement of happiness — just as this shining theatre, now full of life, of light, of excitement, would be in a few hours black, ghastly, and void. John Dampier did not dare to look at her again—he hesitated, he was picking and choosing the words which should be least cruel, least insulting; and while he was still choking and fumbling, he heard a noise outside, a whispering, as the door flew open. Elly looked up and gave a little low plaintive cry, and two darkling, frowning men in black coats came into the box.

They were the Pasteurs Boulot and Tourneur.

Who cares to witness, who cares to read, who cares to describe, scenes such as these? Reproach, condemnation, righteous wrath and indignation, and then one crushed, bewildered, almost desperate little heart.

She was hurried out into the night air. She had time to say good-bye, not one other word. He had not stretched out a hand to save her. The play was going on, all the people were sitting in their places, one or two looked up as she passed by the open doors. Then they came out into the street; the stars were all gone, the night was black with clouds, and a heavy rain was pouring down upon the earth. The drops fell wet upon her bare, uncovered head. "Go under shelter," said the Pasteur Boulot; but she paid no heed, and in a minute a cab came up, the two men clasped each other's hands in the peculiar silent way to which they were used. Boulot walked away. And Elly found herself alone, inside the damp vehicle, driving over the stones. Her stepfather had got upon the box: he was in a fury of indignation, so that he could not trust himself to be with her.

His indignation was not what she most feared. Another torturing doubt filled her whole heart. Her agony of hopelessness was almost unendurable: she was chilled through and through, but she did not heed it—and faint, and sick, and wearied, but too unhappy to care. Unhappy is hardly the word—bewilderment, a sort of crushed dull misery, would better describe her state. She felt little remorse: she had done wrong, but not very wrong, she thought. She sat motionless in the corner of the jolting cab, with the rain beating in at the open window, as they travelled through the black night and the splashing streets.

By what unlucky chance had M. Boulot been returning home along the Boulevards about half-past seven, at the very moment when Elly, jumping from the carriage, stopped to look up at the little new moon? He, poor man, could hardly believe his eyes. He did not believe them, and went home wondering, and puzzling, and asking himself if that audacious girl could be so utterly lost as to set her foot in that horrible den of iniquity. Ah! it was impossible; it was some one strangely like her. She could not be so lost, so perverted. But the chances were still against Elly; for when he reached the modest little apartment where he lived, his maidservant told him that M. Tourneur had been there some time, and was waiting to see him. And there in the study, reading by the light of the green lamp, sat Tourneur, with his low-crowned hat lying on the table. He had come up on some business connected with an appointment he wanted to obtain for Anthony. His wife was to follow him next day, he said, and then he and Boulot fell to talking over their affairs and Anthony's prospects and chances.

"Poor Anthony, he has been sorely tried and proved of late," said his father. "Elizabeth will never make him happy."

"Never—never!" cried Boulot. "Elizabeth! —she!—the last person in the world a pastor ought to think of as a wife!"

"If she were more like her mother," said Tourneur.

"Ah! that would be different," said Boulot; "but the girl causes me deep anxiety, my friend. Hers is, I fear, an unconverted spirit. Her heart is of this world; she requires much earnest teaching. Did you take her to Fontainebleau with you?"

"She would not come," said Tourneur; "she is at home with my sister, Madame Jacob; or rather by herself, for my sister went away a day or two ago."

"Tourneur, you do not do wisely to leave that girl alone; she is not to be trusted," said the other, suddenly remembering all his former doubts. And so, when Tourneur asked what he meant, he told him what he had seen. The mere suspicion was a blow for our simple-minded pasteur. He loved Elly; with all her waywardness, there was a look in her eyes which nobody could resist. In his heart of hearts he liked her better for a daughter-in-law than any one of the decorous young women who were in the habit of coming to be catechised by him. But to think that she had deceived him, to think that she had forgotten herself so far, forgotten his teaching, his wishes, his firm convictions, sinned so outrageously! Ah, it was too much; it was impossible, it was unpardonable. He fired up, and in an agitated voice said it could not be; that he knew her to be incapable of such horrible conduct, and then, seizing his hat, he rushed down stairs and called a carriage which happened to be passing by.

"Where are you going?" asked Boulot, who had followed him, somewhat alarmed.

"I am going home, to see that she is there. Safe in her room, and sheltered under her parents' roof, I humbly pray. Far away from the snares and dangers and temptations of the world."

Alas! poor Elly was not at home, peacefully resting or reading by the lamplight. Françoise, to be sure, told them she was in bed, and Tourneur went hopefully to her door and knocked:

"Elly," he cried, "mon enfant! êtes-vous là, ma fille? Répondez, Elizabeth!" and he shook the door in his agitation.

Old Françoise was standing by, holding the candle, Boulot was leaning against the wall. But there came no answer. The silence struck chill. Tourneur's face was very pale, his lips were drawn, and his eyes gleamed as he raised his head. He went away for a minute and came back with a little tool; it did not take long to force back the lock—the door flew open, and there was the empty room all in disorder! In silence truly, but emptiness is not peace always, silence is not tranquillity; a horrible dread and terror came over poor Tourneur; Françoise's hand, holding the light, began to tremble guiltily. Boulot was dreadfully shocked:

"My poor friend! my poor friend!" he began.

Tourneur put his hand to his head:

"How has this come to pass—am I to blame?" said he. "Oh! unhappy girl, what has she done?—how has she brought this disgrace upon us?" and he fell on his knees by the bedside, and buried his head in the clothes—kneeling there praying for Elly where she had so often knelt and poured out all her sad heart. . . . .

Elly, at that minute—sitting in the little box, wondering, delighted, thrilling with interest, with pleasure—did not guess what a strange scene was taking place in her own room at home; she did not once think of what trouble, what grief, she was causing to others, and to herself, poor child, most of all. Only a few minutes more—all the music would cease abruptly for her; all the lights go out; all the sweetness turn to gall and to bitterness. Nearer and nearer comes the sad hour, the cruel awakening; dream on still for a few happy minutes, poor Elly!—nearer and nearer come these two angry silent men, in their black, sombre clothes—nearer and nearer the cruel spoken word which will chill, crush, and destroy. Elizabeth's dreams lasted a little longer, and then she awoke at last.

R

CHAPTER VII.

Not a flower, not a flower sweet,
    On my black coffin let there be strown;
Not a friend, not a friend greet
    My poor corpse where my bones shall be thrown.
A thousand, thousand sighs to save,
    Lay me, oh! where
Sad true lover never find my grave,
    To weep there.

It was on the evening of the Monday after that Miss Dampier arrived in Paris, with her bonnet-box, her knitting, her carpet-bag. She drove to Meurice's, and hired a room, and then she asked the servants there who knew him whether Sir John Dampier was still staying in the house. They said he had left the place some time before, but that he had called twice that day to ask if she had arrived. And then Miss Dampier, who always liked to make herself comfortable and at home, went up to her room, had the window opened, light brought, and ordered some tea. She was sitting at the table in her cap, in her comfortable black gown, with her knitting, her writing-desk, her books, all set out about the room. She was pouring out tea for herself, and looking as much at home as if she had lived there for months, when the door opened, and her nephew walked in. She was delighted to see him.

"My dear Jack, how good of you to come!" said the old lady, looking up at him, and holding out her hand. "But you don't look well. You have been sitting up late and racketing. Will you have some tea to refresh you? I will treat you to any thing you like."

"Ah, don't make jokes," said Dampier. "I am very unhappy. Look here, I have got into the most horrible scrape; and not myself only." And the room shook, and the tea-table rattled, as he went pacing up and down the room with heavy footsteps. "I want to behave like a gentleman, and I wake up one morning to find myself a scoundrel. Do you see?"

"Tell me about it, my dear," said Miss Dampier, quietly.

And then poor John burst out and told all his story, confounding himself, and stamping, flinging himself about into one chair after another. "I meant no harm," he said. "I wanted to give her a little pleasure, and this is the end. I think I have broken her heart, and those pasteurs have murdered her by this time. They won't let me see her; Tourneur almost ordered me out of the house. Aunt Jean, do say something; do have an opinion."

"I wish your cousin was here," said Miss Dampier; "he is the parson of the family, and bound to give us all good advice; let me write to him, Jack. I have a certain reliance on Will's good sense."

"I won't have Will interfering with my affairs," cried the other testily. "And you—you will not help me, I see?"

"I will go and see Elizabeth," said Miss Dampier, "to-night, if you like. I am very, very sorry for her, and for you too, John. What more can I say? Come again in an hour, and I will tell you what I think."

So Miss Dampier was as good as her word, and set off on her pilgrimage, and drove along the lighted streets, and then past the cab-stand and the hospital to the house with the shuttered windows. Her own heart was very sad as she got out of the carriage and rang at the bell. But looking up by chance, she just saw a gleam of light which came from one of the upper windows and played upon the wall. She took this as a good omen, and said to herself that all would be well. Do you believe in omens? The light came from a room where Elly was lying asleep, and dreaming gently—calm, satisfied, happy for once, heedless of the troubles and turmoils and anxieties of the waking people all round about her. She looked very pale, her hands were loosely clasped, the light was in the window, flickering; and meanwhile, beneath the window, in the street, Miss Dampier stood waiting under the stars. She did not know that Elly saw her in her dim dreams, and somehow fancied that she was near.

The door opened at last. How black the court-yard looked behind it! "What do you want?" said Clementine, in a hiss. "Who is it?"

"I want to know how Miss Gilmour is," said Miss Dampier, quite humbly, "and to see Monsieur or Madame Tourneur."

"Vous êtes Madame Dampierre," said Clementine. "Madame est occupée. Elle ne reçoit pas."

"When will she be disengaged?" said the old lady.

"Ma foi!" said Clementine, shrugging her shoulders, "that I can not tell you. She has desired me to say that she does not wish to see any body." And the door was shut with a bang. Elly woke up, startled from her sleep; and old Françoise happening to come into the room, carried the candle away.

Miss Dampier went home very sad and alarmed, she scarcely knew why. She wrote a tender little letter to Elly next day. It was:—

"Dear Child,—You must let me come and see you. We are very unhappy, John and I, to think that his imprudence has caused you such trouble. He does not know how to beg you to forgive him—you and M. Tourneur and your mother. He should have known better; he has been unpardonably thoughtless, but he is nearly broken-hearted about it. He has been engaged to Lætitia for three or four months, and you know how long she has loved him. Dearest Elly, you must let me come and see you, and perhaps one day you may be trusted to the care of an old woman, and you will come home with me for a time, and brighten my lonely little house. Your affectionate old friend,
                        "Jean Dampier."

But to this there came no answer. Miss Dampier went again and could not get in. She wrote to Madame Tourneur, who sent back the letter unopened. John Dampier walked about, pale and haggard and remorseful.

One evening he and his aunt were dining in the public room of the hotel, and talking over this affair, when the waiter came and told them that a gentleman wanted to speak to Miss Dampier, and the old lady got up and went out of the room. She came back in an instant, looking very agitated. "John!" she said—"Oh John!" and then began to cry. She could not speak for a minute, while he, quite frightened for his part, hastily went to the door. A tall young man was standing there, wrapped in a loose coat, who looked into his face and said:—

"Are you Sir John Dampier? My sister Elizabeth would like to see you again. I have come for you."

"Your sister Elizabeth!" said Dampier, looking surprised.

The other man's face changed as he spoke again. "I am Anthony Tourneur; I have come to fetch you, because it is her wish, and she is dying, we fear."

The two men stood looking at one another for one horrible moment, then Dampier slowly turned his face round to the wall. In that one instant all that cruel weight which had almost crushed poor Elly to death came and fell upon his broad shoulders, better able, in truth, to bear it, than she had ever been.

He looked up at last. "Have I done this?" said he to Tourneur, in a sort of hoarse whisper. "I meant for the best."

"I don't know what you have done," said the other, very sadly. "Life and death are not in your hands or mine. Let us pray that our mistakes may be forgiven us. Are you ready now?"

Elly's visions had come to an end. The hour seemed to be very near when she should awake from the dream of life. Dim figures of her mother, her stepfather, of old Françoise, came and stood by her bedside. But how far off they appeared! how distant their voices sounded! Old Françoise came into her room the morning after Elly had been brought home, with some message from Tourneur, desiring her to come down stairs and speak to him: he had been lying awake all night, thinking what he should say to her, praying for her, imploring grace, so that he should be allowed to touch the rebellious spirit, to point out all its errors, to bring it to the light. And meanwhile, Elly, the rebellious spirit, sat by her bedside in a sort of bewildered misery. She scarcely told herself why she was so unhappy. She wondered a little that there was agony so great to be endured; she had never conceived its existence before. Was he gone forever—was it Lætitia whom he cared for? "You know that I belong to Lætitia," he had said. How could it be? all heaven and earth would cry out against it. Lætitia—Lætitia, who cared so little, who was so pale, and so cold, and so indifferent? How could he speak such cruel words? Oh shame, shame!

that she should be so made to suffer. "A poor little thing like me," said Elly, "lonely and friendless and heart-broken." The pang was so sharp that it seemed to her like physical pain, and she moaned, and winced, and shivered under it—was it she herself or another person that was here in the darkness? She was cold, too, and yet burning with thirst; she groped her way to the jug, and poured out a little water, and drank with eager gulps. Then she began to take off her damp clothes; but it tired her, and she forgot to go on; she dropped her cloak upon the floor and flung herself upon the bed, with a passionate outcry. Her mouth was dry and parched, her throat was burning, her hands were burning too. In the darkness she seemed to see his face and Lætitia's glaring at her, and she turned sick and giddy at the sight; presently, not theirs only, but a hundred others—Tourneur's, Boulot's, Faust's, and Mephistopheles's—crowding upon her and glaring furiously. She fell into a short, uneasy sleep once, and woke up with a moan as the hospital clock struck three. The moon was shining into her room, ineffably gray, chill, and silent, and as she woke, a horror, a terror, came over her—her heart scarcely beat; she seemed to be sinking and dying away. She thought with a thrill that her last hour was come; the terror seemed to bear down upon her, nearer and closer and irresistible—and then she must have fallen back senseless upon her bed. And so when Françoise came with a message in the morning, which was intended to frighten the rebellious spirit into submission, she found it gone, safe, far away from reproach, from angry chiding, and the poor little body lying lifeless, burnt with fierce fever, and racked with dull pain. All that day Elly was scarcely sensible, lying in a sort of stupor. Françoise, with tender hands, undressed her and laid her within the sheets; Tourneur came and stood by the poor child's bedside. He had brought a doctor, who was bending over her.

"It is a sort of nervous fever," said the doctor, "and I fear that there is some inward inflammation as well; she is very ill. This must have been impending for some time past."

Tourneur stood with clasped hands and a heavy heart, watching the changes as they passed over the poor little face. Who was to blame in this? He had not spoken one word to her the night before. Was it grief? was it repentance? Ah me! Elly was dumb now, and could not answer. All his wrath was turned against Dampier; for Elly he only felt the tenderest concern. But he was too unhappy just now to think of his anger. He went for Madame Tourneur, who came back and set to work to nurse her daughter; but she was frightened and agitated, and seemed scarcely to know what she was about. On the morning of the second day, contrary to the doctor's expectations, Elly recovered her consciousness; on the third day she was better. And when Tourneur came into the room, she said to him with one of her old pretty, sad smiles: "You are very angry with me, are you not? You think I ought not to have gone to the play with John Dampier?"

"Ah, my child," said Tourneur, with a long-drawn, shivering sigh, "I am too anxious to be angry."

"Did he promise to marry you, Elly?" said Madame Tourneur, who was sitting by her bedside. She was looking so eagerly for an answer that she did not see her husband's look of reproach.

"How could he?" said Elly, simply. "He is going to marry Lætitia."

"Tell me, my child," said Tourneur, gently taking her hand, "how often did you go with him?"

"Three times," Elly answered, faintly. "Once to the Bois, and once to the Louvre, and then that last time," and she gasped for breath. Tourneur did not answer, but bent down gently and kissed her forehead.

It was on that very day that Dampier called. Elly seemed somehow to know that he was in the house. She got excited, and began to wander, and to call him by his name. Tourneur heard her, and turned pale, and set his teeth as he went down to speak to Sir John. In the evening the girl was better, and Anthony arrived from the south. And I think it was on the fifth day that Elly told Anthony that she wanted to see Dampier once again.

"You can guess how it has been," she said, "and I love him still, but not as I did. Anthony, is it not strange? Perhaps one is selfish when one is dying. But I want to see him—just once again. Every thing is so changed. I can not understand why I have been so unhappy all this time. Anthony, I have wasted all my life; I have made nobody happy—not even you."

"You have made me love you, and that has been my happiness," said Anthony. "I have been very unhappy too; but I thank Heaven for having known you, Elly."

Elly thought that she had but a little time left. What was there in the solemn nearness of death that had changed her so greatly? She had no terror: she was ready to lie down and go to sleep like a tired child in its mother's arms. Worldly! we call some folks worldly, and truly they have lived for to-day and cared for to-day; but for them, as for us, the great to-morrow comes, and then they cease to be worldly—is it not so? Who shall say that such and such a life is wasted, is purposeless? that such and such minds are narrow, are mean, are earthly? The day comes, dawning freshly and stilly, like any other day in all the year, when the secret of their life is ended, and the great sanctification of Death is theirs.

Boulot came to see Tourneur, over whom he had great influence, and insisted upon being shown to Elizabeth's bedside. She put out her hand and said, "How d'ye do, Monsieur Boulot?" very sweetly, but when he had talked to

her for some little time, she stopped him and said: "You can not know how near these things seem, and how much more great and awful and real they are, when you are lying here like me, than when you are standing by another person's sick-bed. Nobody can speak of them to me as they themselves speak to me." She said it so simply, with so little intention of offense, that Boulot stopped in the midst of his little sermon, and said farewell quite kindly and gently. And then, not long after he was gone, Anthony came back with the Dampiers.

They walked up the wooden stairs with hearts that ached sorely enough. Miss Dampier was calm and composed again; she had stood by many a death-bed—she was expecting to go herself before very long—but John was quite unnerved. Little Elly, whom he had pitied and looked down upon and patronized, was she to be to him from this minute a terror, a lifelong regret and remorse?—he could hardly summon courage to walk into the room when the door was opened and Anthony silently motioned him to pass through it.

And yet there was nothing very dreadful. A pale, sweet face lying on the little white bed; the gentle eyes, whose look he knew so well, turned expectantly towards him; a cup with some flowers; a little water in a glass by the bedside; an open window; the sun setting behind the poplar-trees.

Old Françoise was sitting in the window, sewing; the birds were twittering outside. John Dampier thought it strange that death should come in this familiar guise—tranquilly, with the sunset, the rustling leaves of the trees, the scent of the geraniums in the court below, the cackle of the hens, the stitching of a needle—he almost envied Elly, lying resting at the end of her journey: Elly, no longer the silly little girl he had laughed at, chided, and played with—she was wise now, in his eyes.

She could not talk much, but what she said was in her own voice and in her old manner—"You kind people, to come and see me," she said, and beckoned to them to approach nearer.

Miss Dampier gave her nephew a warning touch; she saw how agitated he was, and was afraid that he would disturb Elizabeth. But what would he not have done for her? He controlled himself, and spoke quietly, in a low voice:—

"I am very grateful to you, dear Elly, for sending for me. I was longing to hear about you. I want to ask you to forgive me for the ill I have done you. I want to tell you just once that I meant no harm, only it was such a pleasure to myself that I persuaded myself it was right. I know you will forgive me. All my life I will bless you." And his head fell as he spoke.

"What have I to forgive?" faltered Elly. "It seems so long ago!—Faust and Margaret, and those pleasant drives. Am I to forgive you because I loved you? That was a sort of madness; but it is gone. I love you still, dear John, but differently. I am not mad now, but in my senses. If I get well, how changed it will be! if I die—"

If she died? Dampier, hating himself all the while, thought, with a chill pang, that here would be a horrible solution to all his perplexities. Perhaps Elly guessed something of what was passing in his mind, for she gave him her hand once more, and faltered:—

"My love to Lætitia," and, as she spoke, she raised her eyes, with the old familiar look in them.

It was more than he could bear; he stooped and kissed her frail, burning fingers, and then, with scorched, quivering lips, turned aside and went softly out of the room. Anthony and Madame Tourneur were standing outside, and as Dampier passed she looked at him piteously, and her lips trembled too, but she did not speak. It seemed to him somehow—only he was thinking of other things—as if Elly's good and bad angels were waiting there. He himself passed on with a hanging head; what could he say to justify himself?—his sorrow was too real to be measured out into words, his penitence greater almost than the offense had been. Even Tourneur, whom he met in the court-yard, almost forgave him as he glanced at the stricken face that was passing out of his house into the street.

After he was gone, Elly began to wander. Françoise, who had never taken such a bad view of Elly's condition as the others, and who strongly disapproved of all this leave-taking, told Miss Dampier that if they wanted to kill her outright, they need only let in all Paris to stare at her, as they had been doing for the last two days; and Miss Dampier, meekly taking the hint, rose in her turn to go. But Elly, from her bed, knew that she was about to leave her, and cried out piteously, and stretched out her hands, and clutched at her gown.

"Faut rester," whispered Françoise.

"I mean to stay," said Miss Dampier, after a moment's deliberation, sitting down at the bedside and untying her bonnet.

Under her bonnet she wore a little prim cap, with loops of gray ribbon; out of her pocket she pulled her knitting and a pair of mittens. She folded up her mantlet and put it away; she signed to Françoise to leave her in charge. When Tourneur came in he found her installed, and as much at home as if she were there by rights. Elly wished it, she told him, and she would stay were ten pasteurs opposed to it.

Tourneur reluctantly consented at last, much against his will. It seemed to him that her mother ought to be Elly's best nurse, but Madame Tourneur eagerly implored him to let Miss Dampier remain; she seemed strangely scared and helpless, and changed and odd. "Oh, if you will only make her well!" said she to the old Scotchwoman.

"How can I make her well?" Miss Dampier answered. "I will try and keep her quiet, that is the chief thing; and if M. Tourneur will let me, I should like to send for my old friend, Dr. Bertin."

And her persistency overcame Tourneur's bewildered objections; her quiet good sense and determination carried the day. Doctor Bertin came, and the first doctor went off in a huff, and Elly lay tossing on her bed. What a weary rack it was to her, that little white bed! There she lay scorched and burning—consumed by a fierce fire. There she lay through the long days and the nights, as they followed one by one, waiting to know the end. Not one of them dared think what that end might be. Doctor Bertin himself could not tell how this queer illness might turn; such fevers were sometimes caused by mental disquietude, he said. Of infection there was no fear; he came day after day, and stood pitifully by the bedside. He had seen her once before in her brilliance and health; he had never cared for her as he did now that she was lying prostrate and helpless in their hands.

Madame Jacob had carried off her children at the first alarm of fever; the house was kept darkened and cool and quiet; and patient Miss Dampier sat waiting in the big chair for good or for ill fortune. Sometimes of an evening she would creep down stairs and meet her nephew in the street outside and bring him news.

And besides John, there was poor Anthony wandering about the house, wretched, anxious, and yet resigned. Often, as a boy, he had feared death; the stern tenets to which he belonged made him subject to its terrors, but now it seemed to him so simple a thing to die, that he wondered at his own past fears. Elly thought it a simple thing to die, but of this fever she was weary—of this cruel pain and thirst and misery; she would moan a little, utter a few complaining words, and wander off into delirium again. She had been worse than usual one evening, the fever higher. It was a bad account that Miss Dampier had to give the doctor when he came, to the anxious people waiting for news. All night long Elly's kind nurse sat patiently in the big arm-chair, knitting, as was her way, or sometimes letting the needles fall into her lap, and sitting still with clasped hands and a wistful heart. The clocks of the city struck the dark hours as they passed—were these Elly's last upon earth? Jean Dampier sadly wondered. The stars set behind the poplar-trees, a night-breeze came shivering now and then through the open window. The night did not appear so very long: it seemed hastening by, dark and silent, relentless to the wearied nurse; for presently, before she knew it almost, it seemed as if the dawn had begun; and somehow, as she was watching still, she fell asleep for a little. While she slept the shadows began to tremble and fade, and fly hither and thither in the death-like silence of the early morning, and when she woke it was with a start and a chill terror, coming she knew not whence. She saw that the room was gray, and black no longer. Her heart began to beat, and with a terrified glance

she looked round at the bed where Elly was
lying.

She looked once, and then again, and then
suddenly her trembling hands were clasped in
humblest thanksgiving, and the gray head bent
lower and lower.

There was nothing to fear any more. Elly
was sleeping quietly on her pillow, the fiery
spots had faded out of her cheeks, her skin looked fresh and moist, the fever had left her.
Death had not yet laid his cold hand on the
poor little prey, he had not come while the nurse
was sleeping—he had not called her as yet. I
speak in this way from long habit and foolishness. For, in truth, had he come, would it have
been so sad, would it have been so hard a fate—
would it have been Death with his skeleton's
head, and his theatrical grave-clothes, and his
scythe, and his hour-glass? Would it have
been this, or simply the great law of Nature
working peacefully in its course—only the seed
falling into the ground, only the decree of that
same merciful Power which sent us into the
world?—us men and women, who are glad to
exist, and grateful for our own creation, into a
world where we love to tarry for a while?

Jean Dampier, sitting there in the dawning,
thought something of all this, and yet how could
she help acknowledging the mercy which spared
her and hers the pang of having fatally injured
this poor little Elly, whom she had learned to
love with all her tender old heart? It seemed
a deliverance, a blessing a hundred times beyond
their deserts.

She had been prepared for the worst, and yet
she had shrunk with terror from the chastise-
ment. Now, in this first moment of relief—now
that, after all, Elly was, perhaps, given back to
them, to youth, to life—she felt as if she could
have borne the blow better than she had ever
dared to hope. The sun rose, the birds chirped
freshly among the branches, the chill morning
spread over the city. Sleepers began to stir,
and to awake to their daily cares, to their busy
life. Elizabeth's life, too, began anew from this
hour.

Some one said to me just now that we can
best make others happy by the mere fact of our
own existence; as she got well day by day, Elly
found that it was so. How had she deserved so
much of those about her? she often wondered
to herself. A hindrance, a trouble, a vexation
to them was all she had ever been; and yet as
one by one they came to greet her, she felt that
they were glad. Anthony's eyes were full of
tears; Tourneur closed his for an instant, as he
uttered a silent thanksgiving—she herself did
not know how to thank them all.

And here, perhaps, my story ought to end,
but in truth it is not finished, though I should
cease to write it down, and it goes on and on as
the years go by.

CHAPTER VIII.

Move eastward, happy earth, and leave
    Yon orange sunset, waning slow
From fringes of the faded eve.
    O happy planet, eastward go,
    Till over thy dark shoulder glow
Thy silver sister-world, and rise
To glass herself in dewy eyes,
    That watch me from the glen below.

AND so she had left all behind, Elizabeth
thought. Paris, the old house, mother, stepfather, and pasteur, the court-yard, the familiar
wearisome life, the dull days breaking one by
one, John Dampier, her hopeless hopes, and her
foolish fancies—she had left them all on the
other side of the sea for a time, and come away
with kind Miss Dampier.

Here, in England, whither her good friend
had brought her to get well, the air is damp
with sea-breezes; the atmosphere is not keen
and exciting as it is abroad; the sky is more
often gray than blue; it rarely dazzles and
bewilders you with its brilliance; there is hu-
midity and vegetation, a certain placidity and
denseness and moisture of which some people
complain. To Elizabeth—nervous, eager, excitable—this quiet green country, these autumn
mists were new life. Day by day she gained
strength, and flesh, and tone, and health, and
good spirits.

But it was only by slow degrees that this good
change was effected; weaknesses, faintnesses, re-
lapses—who does not know the wearisome course
of a long convalescence?

To-night, though she is by way of being a
strong woman again, she feels as if she was a
very, very old one, somehow, as she sits at the
window of a great hotel looking out at the sunset. It seems to her as if it was never to rise
again. There it goes sinking, glorying over
the sea, blazing yellow in the west. The place
grows dark; in the next room through the open
door her white bed gleams chilly; she shudders
as she looks at it, and thinks of the death-bed
from which she has scarce risen. There are
hours, especially when people are still weak and
exhausted by sickness, when life seems unbearable, when death appears terrible, and when
the spirit is so weary that it seems as if no sleep
could be deep enough to give it rest. "When
I am dead," thought Elizabeth; "ah me! my
body will be at rest, but I myself, shall I have
forgotten—do I want to forget . . . . ?"

Meanwhile Miss Dampier, wrapped in her
gray cloak, is taking a brisk solitary little walk
upon the wooden pier which Elly sees reflected
black against the sea. Aunt Jean is serenely
happy about her charge; delighted to have carried her off against all opposition; determined
that somehow or other she shall never go back;
that she shall be made happy one day.

It is late in the autumn. Tourists are flock-
ing home; a little procession of battered ladies
and gentlemen carrying all sorts of bundles and
bags and parcels disembarks every day; and
then another procession of ladies and gentlemen
goes to see them land. Any moment you may

chance to encounter some wan sea-sick friend staggering along with the rest of the sufferers, who are more or less other people's friends. The waves wash up and down, painted yellow by the sunset. There is no wind, but it has been blowing hard for a day or two, and the sea is not yet calm. How pleasant it is, Miss Dampier thinks; chill, fresh, wholesome. This good air is the very thing for Elly. Along the cliffs the old lady can see the people walking against the sky like little specks. There are plenty of fishing-boats out and about. There is the west still blazing yellow, and then a long gray bank of clouds; and with a hiss and a shrill clamor here comes the tossing, dark-shadowed steamer across the black and golden water. All the passengers are crowding on deck and feebly gathering their belongings together; here the *Frederic William* comes close alongside, and as every body else rushes along the pier to inspect the new-comers, good old Jean trots off too, to see what is what. In a few minutes the passengers appear, slowly rising through a trap like the ghost in the *Corsican Brothers*.

First, a lilac gentleman, then a mouldy green gentleman (evidently a foreigner), then an orange lady.

Then a ghostly blue gentleman, then a deadly white lady, then a pale lemon-colored gentleman with a red nose.

Then a stout lady, black in the face, then a faltering lady's-maid, with a bandbox.

Then a gentleman with an umbrella.

Jean Dampier is in luck to-night, as, indeed, she deserves to be : a more kindly, tender-hearted, unselfish old woman does not exist—if that is a reason for being lucky—however, she has been my good friend for many a long year, and it is not to-day that I am going to begin to pay her compliments.

I was saying she is in luck, and she finds a nephew among the passengers—it is the gentleman with the umbrella; and there they are, greeting one another in the most affectionate manner.

The Nephew.—"Let me get my portmanteau, and then I will come and talk to you as much as you like."

The Aunt.—"Never mind your portmanteau, the porter will look after it. Where have you been, Will? Where do you come from? I am at the 'Flag Hotel,' close by."

The Nephew.—"So I hear."

The Aunt.—"Who told you that?"

The Nephew.—"A sour-faced woman at Paris. I asked for you at Meurice's, and they sent me to this Madame Tourneur. She told me all about you. What business is it of yours to go about nursing mad girls?"

Aunt Jean.—"Elly is not mad. You have heard me talk of her a hundred times. I do believe I saved her life, Will; it was my business, if any body's, to care for her. Her heart was nearly broken."

The Nephew.—"John nearly broke her heart, did he? I don't believe a word of it " (*smiling very sweetly*). "You are always running away with one idea after another, you silly old woman. Young ladies' hearts are made of india-rubber, and Lady Dampier says this one is an artful—designing—horrible—abominable—"

Aunt Jean (*sadly*).—"Elly nearly died, that is all. You are like all men, Will—"

The Nephew (*interrupting*).—"Don't! Consider, I'm just out of the hands of the steward. Let me have something to eat before we enter into any sentimental discussion. Here (*to a porter*), bring my portmanteau to the hotel.—Nonsense (*to a flyman*), what should I do with your carriage?"

Will Dampier was a member of the Alpine Club, and went year by year to scramble his holiday away up and down mountain-sides. He was a clergyman, comfortably installed in a family living. He was something like his cousin in appearance, but, to my mind, better looking, browner, broader, with bright blue eyes and a charming smile. He looked like a gentleman. He wore a clerical waistcoat. He had been very much complimented upon his good sense; and he liked giving advice, and took pains about it, as he was anxious not to lose his reputation. Now and then, however, he did foolish things, but he did them sensibly, which is a very different thing from doing sensible things foolishly. It seems to me that is just the difference between men and women.

Will was Miss Dampier's ideal of what a nephew should be. They walked back to the hotel together, chattering away very comfortably. He went into the coffee-room and ordered his dinner, and then he came back to his aunt, who was walking on the lawn outside. Meanwhile the sun went on setting, the windows lighted up one by one. It was that comfortable hour when people sit down in little friendly groups and break bread, and take their ease, the business of the day being over. Will Dampier and his aunt took one or two turns along the gravel path facing the sea ; he had twenty minutes to wait, and he thought they might be well employed in giving good counsel.

"It seems to me a very wild scheme of yours, carrying off this unruly young woman," he began; "she will have to go home sooner or later. What good will you have done?"

"I don't know, I'm sure," says Miss Dampier, meekly; "a holiday is good for us at all times. Haven't you enjoyed yours, Will?"

"I should rather think I had. You never saw any thing so pretty as Berne the other morning as I was coming away. I came home by the Rhine, you know. I saw Aunt Dampier and Tishy for an hour or two."

"And did you see John at Paris?"

"No; he was down at V——, staying with the M——s. And now tell me about the young lady with the heart. Is she up stairs tearing her hair? Aunt Dampier was furious."

"So she had heard of it?" said Miss Dampier, thoughtfully. And then she added rather sharply, "You can tell her that the young lady is quite getting over her fancy. In fact, John doesn't deserve that she should remember him. Now, listen, Will, I am going to tell you a story." And then, in her quiet, pleasant, old-fashioned way, she told him her version of all that had been happening.

Will listened and laughed, and said, "You will think me a brute, but I agree with Aunt Dampier. Your young woman has behaved as badly as possible; she has made a dead set at poor John, who is so vain that any woman can get him into her clutches."

"What do you mean?" cries the aunt, quite angry.

"If she had really cared for him, would she have forgotten all about him already? I warn you, Aunt Jenny; I don't approve of your heroine."

"I must go and look after my heroine," says Miss Dampier, dryly. "I dare say your dinner is ready."

But Will Dampier, whose curiosity at all events was excited, followed his aunt up stairs and along the passage, and went in after her as she opened a door; went into a dim chill room, with two wide-set windows, through which the last yellow streaks of the sunset were fading, and the fresh evening blast blew in with a gust as they entered. It was dark, and nothing could be seen distinctly, only something white seemed crouching in a chair, and as the door opened they heard a low sobbing sigh, which seemed to come out of the gloom; and then it was all very silent.

"Elly, my dear child," said Miss Dampier, "what is the matter?"

There was no answer.

"Why don't you speak?" said the kind old lady, groping about, and running up against chairs and tables.

"Because I can't speak without crying," gasps Elly, beginning to cry. "And it's so ungrateful—"

"You are tired, dear," says Aunt Jean, "and cold"—taking her hand; and then turning round and seeing that her nephew had come in with her, she said: "Ring the bell Will, and go to your dinner. If you will tell them down stairs to send up some tea directly I shall be obliged to you." William Dampier did as he was bid, and walked away considerably mollified towards poor Elly. "One is so apt to find fault with people," he was thinking. "And there she was crying up stairs all the time, poor wretch."

He could never bear to see a woman cry. His parishioners—the women, I mean—had found this out, and used to shed a great many tears when he came to see them. He had found them out—he knew that they had found him out, and yet as sure as the apron-corner went up, the half-crown came out of the pocket.

9.30.—*Reading Room, Flag Hotel, Boats-town.*—Mr. William Dampier writing at a side-table to a married sister in India. Three old gentlemen come creaking in; select limp newspapers and take their places. A young man who is going to town by the 10.30 train lies down on the sofa and falls asleep and snores gently. A soothing silence. Mr. Dampier's blunt pen travels along the thin paper. . . . .
"What a dear old woman Aunt Jenny is! How well she tells a story! Lady Dampier was telling me the same story the other day. I was very much bored. I thought each one person more selfish and disagreeable than the other Now Aunt Jenny takes up the tale. The personages all brighten under her friendly old spectacles, and become good, gentle-hearted, romantic, and heroic all at once—as she is herself. I was a good deal struck by her report of poor John's sentimental imbroglio. I drank tea with the imbroglio this evening, and I can't help rather liking her. She has a sweet pretty face, and her voice, when she talks, pipes and thrills like a musical snuff-box. Aunt Jenny wants her for a niece, that is certain, and says that a man ought to marry the wife he likes best. You are sure to agree to that; I wonder what Miles says? But she's torn with sympathy, poor old dear, and first cries over one girl, and then over the other. She says John came to her one day at Paris in a great state of mind, declared he was quite determined to finish with all his uncertainty, and that he had made up his mind to break with Lætitia, and to marry Elizabeth, if she was still in her old way of thinking. Aunt Jean got frightened, refused to interfere, carried off the young lady, and has not spoken to her on the subject. John, who is really behaving very foolishly, is still at Paris, and has not followed them, as I know my aunt hoped he would have done. I can't help being very sorry for him. Lady Dampier has heard of his goings-on. A Frenchman told some people, who told some people, who—you know how things get about. Some day when I don't wish it, you will hear all about me, and write me a thundering letter all the way from Lucknow. There is no doubt about the matter. It would be a thousand pities if John were to break off with Lætitia, to speak nothing of the cruelty and the insult to the poor child.

"And so Rosey and Posey are coming home. I am right sorry for their poor papa and mamma. I hope you have sometimes talked to my nieces about their respectable Uncle Will. They are sure to be looked after and happy with Aunt Jenny, but how you will be breaking your hearts after them! A priest ought perhaps to talk to you of one consolation very certain and efficacious. But I have always found my dear Prue a better Christian than myself, and I have no need to preach to her."

Will Dampier wrote a close straight little handwriting; only one side of his paper was full, but he did not care to write any more that night: he put up his letter in his case, and walked out into the garden.

It was a great starlight night. The sea gloomed vast and black on the horizon. A few other people were walking in the garden, and they talked in hushed yet distinct voices. Many of the windows were open and alight. Will looked up at the window of the room where he had been to see his aunt. That was alight and open too, and some one was sitting with clasped hands looking at the sky. Dampier lit a cigar, and he, too, walked along gazing at the stars, and thinking of Prue's kind face as he went along. Other constellations clustered above her head, he thought; between them lay miles of land and sea, great countries, oceans rushing, plains arid and unknown; vast jungles, deserted cities, crumbling in a broiling sun; it gave him a little vertigo to try and realize what hundreds of miles of distance stretched between their two beating hearts. Distance so great, and yet so little; for he could love his sister, and think of her, and see her, and talk to her, as if she was in the next room. What was that distance which could be measured by miles, compared to the immeasurable gulf that separates each one of us from the nearest and dearest whose hands we may hold in our own?

Will walked on, his mind full of dim thoughts, such as come to most people on starlight nights; when constellations are blazing, and the living soul gazes with awe-stricken wonder at the great living universe, in the midst of which it waits and trembles and adores. "The world all about has faded away," he thought; "and lies dark and dim and instinct. People are lying like dead people stretched out, unconscious on their beds, heedless, unknowing. Here and there in the houses, a few dead people are lying like the sleepers. Are they as unconscious as the living?" He goes to the end of the garden, and stands looking upward, until he can not think longer of things so far above him. It seems to him that his brain is like the string of an instrument, which will break under the passionate vibration of harmonies so far beyond his powers to render. He goes back into the house. Every thing suddenly grows strangely real and familiar, and yet it seemed, but a moment ago, as if to-day and its cares had passed away forever.

CHAPTER IX.

To humbler functions, awful Power,
    I call thee: I myself commend
Unto thy guidance from this hour.
    Oh, let my weakness have an end.
Give unto me, made lowly wise,
The spirit of self-sacrifice—
The confidence of reason give,
And in the light of truth *thy bondman* let me live.
                        Ode to Duty.

Elly had a little Indian box that her father had once given to her. It served her for a work-box and a treasure-casket. She kept her scissors in it and her ruby ring; some lavender, a gold thimble, and her father's picture. And then in a lower tray were some cottons and tapes, one or two letters, a pencil, and a broken silver chain. She had a childish habit of play-

ing with it still, sometimes, and setting it to rights. It was lying on the breakfast-table next morning when Will Dampier came in to see his aunt. Miss Dampier, who liked order, begged Elly to take it off, and Dampier politely, to save her the trouble, set it down somewhere else, and then came to the table and asked for some tea. The fishes had had no luck that morning, he told them; he had been out in a boat since seven o'clock, and brought back a basketful. The sea air made them hungry, no doubt, for they came by dozens—little feeble whiting—and nibbled at their bait. "I wish you would come," he said to his aunt; "the boat bobs up and down in the sunshine, and the breeze is delightfully fresh, and the people come down on the beach and stare at you through telescopes." As he talked to his aunt he glanced at Elly, who was pouring out his tea; he said to himself that she was certainly an uncommonly pretty girl; and then he began to speculate about an odd soft look in her eyes. "When I see people with that expression," he wrote to his sister, "I always ask myself what it means? I have seen it in the glass, sometimes, when I have been shaving. Miss Gilmour was not looking at me, but at the muffins and teacups. She was nicely dressed in blue calico; she was smiling; her hair trim and shiny. I could hardly believe it was my wailing banshee of the previous night." (What follows is to the purpose, so I may as well transcribe a little more of Will's letter.) "When she had poured out my tea, she took up her hat and said she should go down to the station and get *The Times* for my aunt. I should have offered my services, but Aunt Jean made me a sign to stay. What for, do you think? To show me a letter she had received in the morning from that absurd John, who can not make up his mind. 'I do not,' he says, 'want you to talk poor Elly into a *grande passion*. But if her feelings are unchanged, I will marry her to-morrow, if she chooses; and I dare say Tishy will not break her heart. Perhaps you will think me a fool for my pains; but I shall not be alone in the world. What was poor little Elly herself when she cried for the moon?' This is all rodomontade; John is not acting fairly by Lætitia, to whom he is bound by every possible promise.

"My aunt said just now that it would be hard for Tishy if he married her, liking Elizabeth best: and there is truth in that. But he mustn't like her best; Miss Gilmour will get over her fancy for him, and he must get over his for her. If he had only behaved like a man and married her right off two years ago, and never hankered after the flesh-pots of Egypt, or if he had only left her alone to settle down with her French pasteur—

"'If—if,' cried my aunt, impatiently, when I said as much (you know her way)—'he has done wrong and been sorry for it, Will, which of us can do more? I doubt whether you would have behaved a bit better in his place.'"

This portion of Mr. Will's letter was written at his aunt's writing-book immediately after their little talk. Elly came in rosy from her walk, and Will went on diligently, looking up every now and then with the sense of *bien-être* which a bachelor experiences when he suddenly finds himself domesticated and at home with kind women.

Miss Dampier was sitting in the window. She had got *The Times* in her hand, and was trying to read. Every now and then she looked up at her nephew, with his curly head bent over his writing, at Elly leaning lazily back in her chair, sewing idly at a little shred of work. Her hair was clipped, the color had faded out of her cheeks, her eyes gleamed. Pretty as she was, still she was changed—how changed from the Elizabeth of eighteen months ago whom Miss Dampier could remember! The old lady went on with her paper, trying to read. She turned to the French correspondent, and saw something about the Chamber, the Emperor, about Italy; about M. X——, the rich banker, having resolved to terminate his existence, when fortunately his servant enters the room at the precise moment when he was preparing to precipitate himself.... "The servant to precipitate .... the window .... the ... poor Tishy! At my age I did think I should have done with sentimental troubles. Heigho! heigh-ho!" sighs Miss Dampier.

Elly wanted some thread, and rose with a soft rustle, and got her box, and came back to her easy-chair. Out of the window they could see all the pleasant idle business of the little seaport going on, the people strolling in the garden, or sitting in all sorts of queer corners, the boats, the mariners (I do believe they are hired to stand about in blue shirts, and shake their battered old noses as they prose for hours together). The waiter came and took away the breakfast, William went on with his letter, and Miss Dampier, with John's little note in her pocket, was, as I say, reading the most extraordinary things in *The Times* all about her own private concerns. Nobody spoke for some ten minutes, when suddenly came a little gasp, a little sigh from Elly's low chair, and the girl said, "Aunt Jean! look here," almost crying, and held out something in her thin hand.

"What is it, my dear?" said Miss Dampier, looking up hastily, and pulling off her spectacles: they were dim somehow, and wanted wiping.

"Poor dear, dearest Tishy," cried Elly, in her odd impetuous way. "Why does he not go to her? Aunt Jean, look here, I found it in my box—only look here;" and she put a little note into Miss Dampier's hand.

Will looked up curiously from his writing. Elly had forgotten all about him. Miss Dampier took the letter, and when she had read what was written, and then turned over the page, she took off her glasses again with a click, and said, "What nonsense!"

And so it was nonsense, and yet the nonsense touched Elizabeth and brought tears into her eyes. They came faster and faster, and then suddenly remembering that she was not alone, and ashamed that Dampier should see her cry again, she jumped up with a shining, blushing tear-dimmed tender face, and ran away out of the room. Aunt Jean looked at Will doubtfully, then hesitated, and gave him the little shabby letter that had brought these bright tears into the girl's eyes. Dear old soul! she made a sort of confessor of her nephew.

The confessor saw a few foolish words which Lætitia must have written days ago, never thinking that her poor little words were to be scanned by stranger eyes—written perhaps unconsciously on a stray sheet of paper. There was "John. Dear John! Dear, dearest! I am so hap.... John and Lætitia. John my jo. Goose and gander." And then, by some odd chance, she must have folded the blotted sheet together and forgotten what she had written and sent it off to Elly Gilmour, with a little careless note about Schlangenbad, and "more fortunate next time," on the other side.

"Poor little Letty!" thought Dampier, and he doubled the paper up and put it back into the lavender box as the door opened, and Miss Gilmour came back into the room. She had dried her eyes, she had fastened on her gray shawl. She picked up her hat, which was lying on the floor, and began pulling on two very formidable looking gauntlets over her slim white hands. "I am going for a little walk," she said to Miss Dampier. "Will you"—hesitating and blushing—"direct that little note of Lætitia's to Sir John? I am going along the cliff towards the pretty little bay."

Will was quite melted and touched. Was this the scheming young woman against whom he had been warned? the woman who had entangled his cousin with her wiles?

"Aunt Jenny," he says, with a sudden glance, "are you going to tell her why John Dampier does not go to Lætitia?"

"Why does he not go?" Elly repeats, losing her color a little.

"He says that if you would like him to stay, he thinks he ought not to go," says Jean Dampier, hesitating, and tearing corners off *The Times* newspaper.

Will Dampier turned his broad back and looked out of the window. There was a moment's silence. They could hear the tinkling of bells, the whistling of the sea, the voices of the men calling to each other in the port: the sunshine streamed in: Elly was standing in it, and seemed gilt with a golden background. She ought to have held a palm in her hand, poor little martyr!

It seemed a long time, it was only a minute, and then she spoke; a sweet honest blush came deepening into Elizabeth's pale cheeks: "I don't want to marry him because I care for him," she said, in a thrilling, pathetic voice. "Why should Lætitia, who is so fond of him, suffer because I behaved so badly?" The tears once more came welling up into her eyes.

"I shall think I ought to have died instead of getting well," she said. "Aunt Jean, send him the little note; make him go, dear Aunt Jean."

Miss Dampier gave Elly a kiss; she did not know what to say; she could not influence her one way or another.

She wrote to John that morning, taking good care to look at the back of her paper first.

"Flag Hotel, Boatstown,
November 15th.

"MY DEAR JACK,—I had great doubts about communicating your letter to Elizabeth. It seemed to me that the path you had determined upon was one full of thorns and difficulties, for her, for you, and for my niece Lætitia. But although Elly is of far too affectionate a nature ever to give up caring for any of her friends, let me assure you that her feelings are now only those of friendly regard and deep interest in your welfare. When I mentioned to her the contents of your letter (I think it best to speak plainly), she said, with her eyes full of tears, that she did not want to marry you—that she felt you were bound to return to Lætitia. She had been much affected by discovering the inclosed little note from your cousin. I must say that the part which concerns you interested me much, more so than her letter to her old friend. But she was evidently preoccupied at the time, and Elly, far from feeling neglected, actually began to cry, she was so touched by this somewhat singular discovery. Girls' tears are easily dried. If it lies in my power, she shall yet be made happy.

"There is nothing now, as you see, that need prevent your fulfilling your engagements. You are all very good children, on the whole, and I trust that your troubles are but fleeting clouds that will soon pass away. That you and Lætitia may enjoy all prosperity is the sincere hope and desire of your affectionate old aunt,

"J. M. DAMPIER."

Miss Dampier, having determined that she had written a perfectly impartial letter, put it up in an envelope, rang the bell, and desired a waiter to post it.

Number twenty-three's bell rang at the same moment; so did number fifteen; immediately after a quantity of people poured in by the eleven o'clock train; the waiter flung the letter down on his pantry table, and rushed off to attend to half a dozen things at once, of which posting the note was not one.

About three o'clock that afternoon Miss Dampier in her close bonnet was standing in the passage talking to a tall young man with a black waistcoat and wide-awake.

"What are you going to do?" he said. "Couldn't we go for a drive somewhere?"

"I have ordered a carriage at three," said Miss Dampier, smiling. "We are going up on the hills. You might come, too, if you liked it." And when the carriage drove up to the door there he was, waiting to hand her in.

He had always, until he saw her, imagined Elly a little flirting person, quite different from the tall young lady in the broad hat, with the long cloak falling from her shoulders, who was prepared to accompany them. She had gone away a little, and his aunt sent him to fetch her. She was standing against the railing, looking out at the sea with her sad eyes. There was the lawn, there was the sea, there was Elly. A pretty young lady always makes a pretty picture; but out-of-doors in the sunshine she looks a prettier young lady than anywhere else, thought Mr. Will, as Elizabeth walked across the grass. He was not alone in his opinion; more than one person looked up as she passed. He began to think that, far from doing a foolish thing, his aunt had shown her usual good sense in taking such good care of this sad, charming, beautiful young woman. It was no use trying to think ill of her. With such a face as hers, she has a right to fall in love with any body she pleases, he thought; and so, as they were walking towards the carriage, Will Dampier, thinking that this was a good opportunity for a little confidential communication, said, somewhat in his professional manner: "You seem out of spirits, Miss Gilmour. I hope that you do not regret your decision of this morning."

"Yes, I do regret it," said poor Elly, and two great tears came dribbling down her cheeks. "Do you think that when a girl gives up what she likes best in the world she is not sorry? I am horribly sorry."

Will was very much puzzled how to answer this unexpected confidence. He said, looking rather foolish:—

"One is so apt to ask unnecessary questions. But, take my word for it, you have done quite right, and some day you will be more glad than you are now."

I must confess that my heroine here got exceedingly cross.

"Ah, that is what people say who do not know of what they are talking. What business of yours is my poor, unlucky, bruised and broken fancy?" she said. "Ah! Why were you ever told? What am I? What is it to you?"

All the way she sat silent and dull, staring out at the landscape as they went along; suffering, in truth, poor child, more than either of her companions could tell: saying good-bye to the dearest hope of her youth, tearing herself away from the familiar and the well-loved dreams. Dreams, do I say? They had been the Realities to her, poor child! for many a day. And the realities had seemed to be the dreams.

They drove along a straight road, and came at last to some delightful fresh downs, with the sea sparkling in the distance, and a sort of autumnal glow on the hills all about. The breeze came in fresh gusts, the carriage jogged on, still uphill, and Will Dampier walked alongside, well pleased with the entertainment, and making endless jokes at his aunt. She rather liked being laughed at; but Elly never looked up once, or heeded what they said. They were going towards a brown church, that was standing on the top of a hill. It must have been built by the Danes a thousand years ago. There it stood, looking out at the sea, brown, grim, solitary, with its grave-yard on the hill-side. Trees were clustering down in a valley below; but here, up above, it was all bleak, bare, and solitary, only tinted and painted by the brown and purple sunshine.

They stopped the carriage a little way off, and got out and passed through a gate, and walked up the hill-top. Elly went first, Will followed, and Miss Dampier came slowly after. As Elly reached the top of the hill she turned round, and stood against the landscape, like a picture with a background, and looked back and said:—

"Do you hear?"

The organ inside the church was playing a chant, and presently some voices began chanting to the playing of the organ. Elly went across the grave-yard, and leaned against the porch, listening. Five minutes went by; her anger was melting away. It was exquisitely clear, peaceful, and tranquil here, up on this hill where the dead people were lying among the grass and daisies. All the bitterness went away out of her heart, somehow, in the golden glow. She said to herself that she felt now, suddenly, for the first time, as if she could bury her fancy and leave it behind her in this quiet place. As the chant went on, her whole heart uttered in harmony with it, though her lips were silent. She did not say to herself, what a small thing it was that had troubled her: what vast combinations were here to make her happy; hills, vales, light, with its wondrous refractions, harmony, color; the great ocean, the great world, rolling on amid the greater worlds beyond!

But she felt it somehow. The voices ceased, and all was very silent.

"Oh, give thanks," the Psalm began again; and Elly felt that she could indeed give thanks for mercies that were more than she had ever deserved. When she was at home with her mother she thought—just now the thought of returning there scarce gave her a pang—she should remember to-day, all the good hopes, good prayers, and aspirations which had come to her in this peaceful grave-yard up among the hills. She had been selfish, discontented, and ungrateful all her life, angry and chafed but an hour ago, and here was peace, hers for the moment; here was tranquil happiness. The mad, rash delight she had felt when she had been with John Dampier was nothing compared to this great natural peace and calm. A sort of veil seemed lifted from her eyes, and she felt for the first time that she could be happy, though what she had wished for most was never to be hers—that there was other happiness than that

which she had once fancied part of life itself. Did she ever regret the decision she had made? Did she ever see occasion to think differently from this? If, in after times she may have felt a little sad, a little lonely now and then—if she may have thought with a moment's regret of those days that were now already past and over forever—still she knew she had done rightly when she determined to bury the past, with all kindness, with reverent hands. Somehow, in some strange and mysterious manner, the bitterness of her silly troubles had left her—left her a better girl than she had been ever before. She was more good, more happy, more old, more wise, now, and, in truth, there was kindness in store for her, there were suns yet to shine, friendly words to be spoken, troubles yet to be endured, other than those sentimental griefs which had racked her youth so fiercely.

While they were all on the hill-top the steamer came into the port earlier than on the day when Will Dampier arrived. One of the passengers walked up to the hotel and desired a waiter to show him to Miss Dampier's room. It was empty, of course; chairs pushed about, windows open, work and books on the table. The paper was lying on the floor—the passenger noticed that a corner had been torn off; a little box was open on the table, a ruby ring glittering in the tray. "How careless!" he thought; and then went and flung himself into a great arm-chair.

So! she had been here a minute ago. There was a glove lying on a chair; there were writing-materials on a side-table—a blotting-book open, pens with the ink scarcely dry; and in this room, in this place, he was going to decide his fate—rightly or wrongly he could not tell. Lætitia is a cold-blooded little creature, he kept saying to himself; this girl with all her faults, with all her impulses, has a heart to break or to mend. My mother will learn too late that I can not submit to such dictation. By Jove! what a letter it is! He pulled it out of his pocket, read it once more, and crumpled it up and threw it into the fireplace. It was certainly not a very wise composition—long, vicious, wiry tails and flourishes. "John, words can not," etc., etc. "What Lady Tomsey," etc., etc. "How horror-struck Major Potterton," etc., etc.; and finally concluded with a command that he should instantly return to Schlangenbad; or, failing this, an announcement that she should immediately join him, *wherever* he might be!

So Sir John, in a rage, packed up and came off to Boatstown—his mother can follow him or not, as she chooses; and here is walking up and down the room, while Elly, driving over the hills, is saying farewell, farewell, good-bye to her old love forever.

Could he have really cared for any body? By some strange contradiction, now that the die is cast, now that, after all these long doubts and mistrusts, he has made up his mind, somehow new doubts arise. He wonders whether he and Elly will be happy together? He pictures stormy scenes; he intuitively shrinks from the idea of her unconventionalities, her eagerness, her enthusiasm. He is a man who likes a quiet life, who would appreciate a sober, happy home—a gentle, equable companion, to greet him quietly, to care for his tastes and his ways, to sympathize, to befriend him. Whereas now it is he who will have to study his companion all the rest of his life; if he thwart her she will fall ill of sorrow; if he satisfy her she will ask more and more; if he neglect her—being busy, or weary, or what not—she will die of grief; if he want sympathy and common sense she will only adore him. Poor Elly! it is hard upon her that he should make such a bugbear of her poor little love. His courage is oozing out at his finger-ends. He is in a rage with her, and with himself, and with his mother, and with his aunt. He and every body else are in a league to behave as badly as possible. He will try and do his duty, he thinks, for all that, for my hero is an honest-hearted man, though a weak one. It is not Lady Dampier's letter that shall influence him one way or another; if Elly is breaking her heart to have him, and if Letty doesn't care one way or the other, as is likely enough, well then he will marry Elizabeth, he cries, with a stout desperation, and he dashes up and down the room in a fury.

And just at this minute the waiter comes in, and says Miss Dampier has gone out for a drive, and will not be back for some time. Mr. Dampier is staying in the house, but he has gone out with her, and who shall he say? And Sir John, looking up, gives his name and says he will wait.

Upon which the waiter suddenly remembers the letter he left in his pantry, and, feeling rather guilty, proposes to fetch it. And by this time Elly, and Will, and Miss Dampier have got into the carriage again and are driving homeward.

There was a certain humility about Elly, with all her ill-humors and varieties, which seemed to sweeten her whole nature. Will Dampier, who was rather angry with her for her peevishness, could not help forgiving her, when, as he helped her out of the carriage in the court-yard, she said :—

"I don't quite know how to say it—but I was very rude just now. I was very unhappy, and I hope you will forgive me," and she looked up. The light from the hills was still in her face.

"It was I who was rude," says Will, good-naturedly holding out his hand; and of course he forgave her.

The band was playing, the garden was full of people; but Aunt Jenny was cold, and glad to get home. The ladies went up stairs: Will remained down below, strolling up and down in the garden with the rest of the people; but at five o'clock the indefatigable bell began to ring once more; the afternoon boat was getting up its steam, and making its preparations to cross over to the other side.

Will met a friend of his, who was going over in it, and he walked down with him to see him off. He went on board with him, shook hands, and turned to come away. At that minute some one happened to look round, and Will, to his immense surprise, recognized his cousin. That was John; those were his whiskers; there was no doubt about it.

He sprang forward and called him by name. "John," he said, "you here?"

"Well!" said John, smiling a little, "why not me, as well as you? Are you coming across?"

"Are you going across?" said Will, doubtfully.

"Yes," the other answered; "I came over on business; don't say any thing of my having been here. Pray remember this. I have a particular reason."

"I shall say nothing," said Will. "I am glad you are going, John," he added, stupidly. "I think I know your reason—a very nice, pretty reason too."

"So those women have been telling you all about my private affairs?" said Sir John, speaking quick, and looking very black.

"Your mother told me first," Will said. "I saw her the other day. For all sakes, I am glad you are giving up all thoughts of Elly Gilmour."

"Are you?" said John, dryly. They waited for a minute in awkward silence, but as they were shaking hands and saying "Good-bye," suddenly John melted and said: "Look here, Will, I should like to see her once more. Could you manage this for me? I don't want her to know, you know; but could you bring her to the end of the pier? I am going back to Letty, as you see, so I don't think she need object."

Will nodded, and went up the ladder and turned towards the house without a word, walking quickly and hurrying along. The band in the garden burst out into a pretty melancholy dance tune. The sun went down peg by peg into the sea; the steamer still whistled and puffed as it got up its steam.

Elly was sitting alone. She had lighted a candle, and was writing home. Her hat was lying on a chair beside her. The music had set her dreaming; her thoughts were far away, in the dismal old home again, with Françoise, and Anthony, and the rest of them. She was beginning to live the new life she had been picturing to herself; trying to imagine herself good and contented in the hateful old home; it seemed almost endurable just at this minute, when suddenly the door burst open, and Will Dampier came in with his hat on.

"I want you to come out a little way with me," he said. "I want you to come and see the boat off. There's no time to lose."

"Thank you," said Elly, "but I'm busy."

"It won't take you five minutes," he said.

She laughed. "I'm lazy and rather tired."

Will could not give up. He persisted: he

knew he had a knack of persuading his old women at home; he tried it on Miss Gilmour.

"I see you have not forgiven me," he said; "you won't trust yourself with me."

"Yes, indeed," said Elly; "I am only lazy."

The time was going. He looked at his watch; there were but five minutes—but five minutes for John to take leave of his love of many a year; but five minutes and it would be too late. He grew impatient.

"Pray, come," he said. "I shall look upon it as a sign that you have forgiven me. Will you do me this favor—will you come? I assure you I shall not be ungrateful."

Elly thought it odd, and still hesitated; but it seemed unkind to refuse. She got up, fetched her hat and cloak, and in a minute he was hurrying her along across the lawn, along the side of the dock, out to the pier's end.

They were only just in time. "You are very mysterious," said Elly. "Why do you care so much to see the boat go out? How chilly it is! Are you not glad to be here on this side of the water? Ah! how soon it will be time for me to go back!"

Will did not answer, he was so busy watching the people moving about on board. Puff! puff! Can not you imagine the great boat passing close at their feet, going out in the night into the open sea; the streaks of light in the west; Elly, with flushed, rosy-red cheeks, like the sunset, standing under the light-house, and talking in her gentle voice, and looking out, saying it would be fine to-morrow?

Can't you fancy poor Sir John leaning against a pile of baggage, smoking a cigar, and looking up wistfully? As he slid past he actually caught the tone of her voice. Like a drowning man who can see in one instant years of his past life flashing before him, Sir John saw Elly—a woman with lines of care in her face—there, standing in the light of the lamp, with the red streams of sunset beyond, and the night closing in all round about; and then he saw her as he had seen her once—a happy, unconscious girl, brightening, smiling at his coming: and as the picture travelled on, a sad girl, meeting him in the street by chance—a desperate, almost broken-hearted woman, looking up gravely into his face in the theatre. Puff! puff!—it was all over, she was still smiling before his eyes. One last glimpse of the two, and they had disappeared. He slipped away right out of her existence, and she did not even guess that he had been near. She stood unwitting for an instant, watching the boat as it tossed out to sea, and then said, "Now we will go home." A sudden gloom and depression seemed to have come over her. She walked along quite silently, and did not seem to heed the presence of her companion.

CHAPTER X.

. . . . Poor forsaken Flos!
Not all her brightness, sportfulness, and bloom,
Her sweetness and her wildness, and her wit,
Could save her from desertion. No; their loves
Were off the poise. Love competent
Makes better bargains than love affluent.

BEFORE he went to bed that night, Dampier wrote the end of his letter to Prue. He described, rather amusingly, the snubbing which Elly had given him, the dry way in which Sir John had received his advances, the glances of disfavor with which Aunt Jean listened to his advice. "So this is all the gratitude one gets for interfering in the most sensible manner. If you are as ungrateful, Prue, for this immense long letter, I shall, indeed, have labored in vain. It is one o'clock. Bong! there it went from the tower. Good-night, dear; your beloved brother is going to bed. Love to Myles. Kiss the children all round for their and your affectionate W. D."

Will Dampier was not in the least like his letter. I know two or three men who are manly enough, who write gentle, gossiping letters like women. He was a big, commonplace young man, straight-minded and tender-hearted, with immense energy, and great good spirits. He believed in himself; indeed, he tried so heartily and conscientiously to do what was right, that he could not help knowing more or less that he was a good fellow. And then he had a happy knack of seeing one side of a question, and having once determined that so and so was the thing to be done, he could do so and so without one doubt or compunction. He belonged to the school of athletic Christianity. I heard some one once say that there are some of that sect who would almost make out cock-fighting to be a religious ceremony. William Dampier did not go so far as this; but he heartily believed that nothing was wrong that was done with a Christian and manly spirit. He rode across country, he smoked pipes, he went out shooting, he played billiards and cricket, he rowed up and down the river in his boat, and he was charming with all the grumbling old men and women in his parish, he preached capital sermons—short, brisk, well considered. He enjoyed life and all its good things with a grateful temper, and made most people happy about him.

One day, Elly began to think what a different creed Will Dampier's was from her stepfather's, only she did not put her thoughts into words. It was not her way.

Tourneur, with a great heart, set on the greatest truth, feeling the constant presence of those mightier dispensations, cared but little for the affairs of to-day: they seemed to him subordinate, immaterial; they lost all importance from comparison to that awful reality that this man had so vividly realized to himself. To Dampier, it was through the simple language of his daily life that he could best express what good was in him. He saw wisdom and mercy, he saw order and progression, he saw infinite variety and wonder in all natural things, in all life, at all places and hours. By looking at this world, he could best understand and adore the next.

And yet Tourneur's was the loftier spirit; to him had come a certain knowledge and understanding, of which Dampier had scarce a conception. Dampier, who felt less keenly, could well be more liberal, more forbearing. One of these two told Elly that we were put into the world to live in it, and to be thankful for our creation; to do our duty, and to labor until the night should come when no man can work. The other said, sadly, you are born only to overcome the flesh, to crush it under foot, to turn away from all that you like most, innocent or not. What do I care? Are you an immortal spirit, or are you a clod of earth? Will you suffer that this all-wondrous, all-precious gift should be clogged, and stifled, and choked, and destroyed, maybe, by despicable daily concerns? Tourneur himself set an example of what he preached by his devoted, humble, holy, self-denying life. And yet Elly turned with a sense of infinite relief to the other creed: she could understand it, sympathize with it, try to do good, though to be good was beyond her frail powers. Already she was learning to be thankful, to be cheerful, to be unselfish, to be keenly penitent for her many shortcomings.

As the time drew near when an answer to her note might be expected, Miss Dampier grew anxious and fidgety, dropped her stitches, looked out for the post, and wondered why no letter came. Elly was only a little silent, a little thoughtful. She used to go out by herself and take long walks. One day Will, returning from one of his own peregrinations, came upon her sitting on the edge of a cliff staring at the distant coast of France. It lay blue, pale, like a dream-country, and glimmered in the horizon. Who would believe that there was reality, busy life in all earnest, going on beyond those calm, heavenly-looking hills! Another time his aunt sent him out to look for her, and he found her at the end of the pier, leaning against the chain, and still gazing towards France.

In his rough friendly manner he said, "I wish you would look another way sometimes, Miss Gilmour, up or down, or in the glass even. You make me feel very guilty, for to tell the truth I—I advised John—"

"I thought so," Elly cried, interrupting him. "And you were quite right. I advised him too," she said, with a smile. "Don't you think he has taken your advice?"

Will looked down uncomfortably. "I think so," he said, in a low tone.

And, meanwhile, Miss Dampier was sitting in the window and the sunshine, knitting castles in the air.

"Suppose he does not take this as an answer? Suppose Lætitia has found somebody else, suppose the door opens and he comes in, and the sun shines into the room, and then he seizes Elly's hand, and says, 'Though you give me up, I will not give up the hope of calling you mine,'

and Elly glances up bright, blushing, happy. . . . Suppose Lady Dampier is furious, and dear Tishy makes peace? I should like to see Elizabeth mistress of the dear old house. I think my mother was like her. I don't approve of cousins' marriages. . . . How charming she would look coming along the old oak gallery!" Look at the old maid in the window building castles in the air through her spectacles. But it is a ridiculous sight; she is only a fat, foolish old woman. All her fancies are but follies flying away with caps and jingling bells—they vanish through the windows as the door opens and the young people come in.

"Here is a letter for you the porter gave me in the hall," said Will, as carelessly as he could; Jean saw Elly's eyes busy glancing at the writing.

"MY DEAR AUNT JEAN,—Many thanks for your note, and the inclosure. My mother and Lætitia are with me, and we shall all go back to Friar's Bush on Thursday. Elly's decision is the wisest under the circumstances, and we had better abide by it. Give her my love. Lætitia knows nothing, as my mother has had the grace to be silent. Yours affectionately,
                        "J. C. D.
"P.S.—You will be good to her, won't you?"

Miss Dampier read the note imperturbably, but while she read there seemed to run through her a cold thrill of disappointment, which was so unendurable that after a minute she got up and left the room.

When she came back, Elly said with a sigh, "Where is he?"

"At Paris," said Miss Dampier. "They have saved him all trouble and come to him. He sends you his love, Elly, which is very handsome of him, considering how much it is worth."

"It has been worth a great deal to me," said Elly, in her sweet voice. "It is all over; but I am grateful still and always shall be. I was very rash; he was very kind. Let me be grateful, dear Aunt Jean, to those who are good to me." And she kissed the old woman's shrivelled hand.

Miss Gilmour cheered up wonderfully from that time. I am sure that if she had been angry with him, if she had thought herself hardly used, if she had had more of what people call self-respect, less of that sweet humility of nature, it would not have been so.

As the short, happy, delightful six weeks which she was to spend with Miss Dampier came to an end, she began to use all her philosophy and good resolves to reconcile herself to going home. Will Dampier was gone. He had only been able to stay a week. They missed him. But still they managed to be very comfortable together. Tea-talk, long walks, long hours on the sands, novels and story-books, idleness and contentment—why couldn't it go on forever? Elly said. Aunt Jean laughed and said they might as well be a couple of jelly-fish at once. And so the time went by, but one day, just before she went away, Mr. Will appeared again unexpectedly.

Elly was sitting in the sun on the beach, throwing idle stones into the sea. She had put down her novel on the shingle beside her. It was *Deerbrook*, I think—an old favorite of Jean Dampier's. Every body knows what twelve o'clock is like on a fine day at the seaside. It means little children, nurses in clean cotton gowns, groups of young ladies scattered here and there; it means a great cheerfulness and tranquillity, a delightful glitter, and life, and light: happy folks plashing in the water, bathing-dresses drying in the sun, all sorts of aches, pains, troubles, vanishing like mist in its friendly beams. Elly was thinking: "Yes, how pleasant and nice it is, and how good, how dear, Aunt Jean is! Only six months, and she says I am to come to her in her cottage again." (Splash a stone goes into the water.) "Only six months! I will try and spend them better than I ever spent six months before. Eugh! If it was not for Mme. Jacob . . . . I really do love my stepfather, and could live happily enough with him." (Splash.) Suddenly an idea came to Elly—the Pasteur Boulot was the idea. "Why should not he marry Mme. Jacob? He admires her immensely. Ah! what fun that would be!" (Splash, splash, a couple of stones.) And then, tramp, tramp, on the shingle behind her, and a cheery man's voice says, "Here you are!"

Elly stares up in some surprise, and looks pleased, and attempts to get up, but Will Dampier—he was the man—sits down beside her, opens his umbrella, and looks very odd. "I only came down for the day," he said, after a little preliminary talk. "I have been with Aunt Jean; she tells me you are going home to-morrow."

"Yes," says Elly, with a sigh; "but I'm to come back again and see her in a little time."

"I'm glad of that," says the clergyman. "What sort of a place do you live in at Paris?"

"It is rather a dull place," says Elly. "I'm very fond of my stepfather; besides him, there is Anthony, and five young pupils, there is an old French cook, and a cross maid, and my mother, and a horri—a sister of Monsieur Tourneur's, and Tou-Tou and Lou-Lou, and me."

"Why that is quite a little colony," said Dampier. "And what will you do there when you get back?"

"I must see," said the girl, smiling. "Till now I have done nothing at all; but that is stupid work. I shall teach Tou-Tou and Lou-Lou a little, and mind the house if my mother will let me, and learn to cook from Françoise. I have a notion that it may be useful some day or other."

"Do, by all means," said Will; "it is a capital idea. But as years go on, what do you mean to do? Tou-Tou and Lou-Lou will grow up, and you will have mastered the art of French cookery—"

"How can you ask such things?" Elly said,

looking out at the sea. "I can not tell, or make schemes for the future."

"Pray forgive me," said Will, "for asking such a question, but have you any idea of marrying M. Anthony eventually?"

"He is a dear old fellow," said Elly, flushing up. "I am not going to answer any such questions. I am not half good enough for him, —that is my answer."

"But suppose—?"

"Pray don't suppose. I am not going to marry any body, or to think much about such things ever again. Do you imagine that I am not the wiser for all my experience?"

"Are you wise now?" said Will, still in his odd manner.

"Look at that pretty little fishing-smack," Elly interrupted.

"Show it," he went on, never heeding, "by curing yourself of your fancy for my cousin John; by curing yourself, and becoming some day a really useful personage and member of society."

Elly stared at him, as well she might.

"Come back to England some day," he continued, still looking away, "to your home, to your best vocation in life, to be happy, and useful, and well loved," he said, with a sweet inflection in his voice; "that is no very hard fate."

"What are you talking about?" said Elly. "How can I cure myself? How can I ever forget what is past? I am not going to be discontented, or to be particularly happy at home. I am going *to try*—to try and do my best."

"Well, then, do your best to get cured of this hopeless nonsense," said Mr. William Dampier, "and turn your thoughts to real good sense, to the real business of life, and to making yourself and others happy, instead of wasting and maudling away the next few best years of your life, regretting and hankering after what is past and unattainable. For some strong minds, who can defy the world and stand alone without the need of sympathy and sustainment, it is a fine thing to be faithful to a chimera," he said, with a pathetic ring in his voice. "But I assure you infidelity is better still sometimes, more human, more natural, particularly for a confiding and uncertain person like yourself." Was he thinking of to-day as he spoke? Was he only thinking of Elly, and preaching only to her?

"You mean I had better marry him?" said Elly, while her eyes filled up with tears, and she knocked one stone against another. "And yet Aunt Jean says, 'No!'—that I need not think of it. It seems to me as if I—I had rather jump into the sea at once," said the girl, dashing the stones away, "though I love him dearly, dear old fellow!"

"I did not exactly mean M. Anthony," said Will, looking round for the first time and smiling at her tears and his own talk.

Elizabeth was puzzled still. For, in truth,

her sad experience had taught her to put but little faith in kindness and implications of kindness—to attach little meaning to the good-nature and admiration a beautiful young woman was certain to meet with on every side. It had not occurred to her that Will, who had done so little, seen her so few times, could be in love with her; when John, for whom she would have died, who said and looked so much, had only been playing with her, and pitying her as if she had been a child; and she said, still with tears, but not caring much :—

"I shall never give a different answer. I believe you are right, but I have not the courage to try. I think I could try and be good if I stay as I am; but to be bound and chained to Anthony all the rest of my life—once I thought it possible; but now—— You who advise it do not know what it is."

"But I never advised it," Will said; "you won't understand me. Dear Elizabeth, why won't you see that it is of myself that I am speaking?"

Elly felt for a moment as if the sea had rushed up suddenly, and caught her away on its billows, and then the next moment she found that she was only sitting crying in the sun, on the sands.

"Look here: every day I live, I get worse and worse," she sobbed. "I flirt with one person after another—I don't deserve that you should ever speak to me again—I can't try and talk about myself—I do like you, and—and yet I know that the only person I care for really is the one who does not care for me; and if I married you to-morrow, and I saw John coming along the street, I should rush away to meet him. I don't want to marry him, and I don't know what I want. But, indeed, I have tried to be good. You are stronger than me, don't be hard upon me."

"My dear little girl," said Will, loyally and kindly, "don't be unhappy, you have not flirted with me. I couldn't be hard upon you if I tried: you are a faithful little soul. Shall I tell you about myself? Once not so very long ago I liked Tishy almost as well as you like John. There, now, you see that you have done no great harm, and only helped to cheer me up again, and I am sure that you and I will be just as good friends as ever. As for John," he added, in quite a different tone, "the sooner you forget all about him the better."

Will took her hand, which was lying limp on the shingle, said "Good-bye," took up his umbrella, and walked away.

And so, by some strange arrangement, Elly put away from her a second time the love of a good and honorable man, and turned back impotently to the memory—it was no more—of a dead and buried passion. Was this madness or wisdom? Was this the decree of fate or of folly?

She sat all in a maze, staring at the sea and the wavelets, and in half an hour rushed into the sitting-room, flung her arms round Miss Dampier's neck, and told her all that happened.

8

CHAPTER XI.

Of all the gifts of Heaven to us below, that felicity is the sum and the chief. I tremble as I hold it, lest I should lose it, and be left alone in the blank world without it. Again, I feel humiliated to think that I possess it; as hastening home to a warm fireside, and a plentiful table, I feel ashamed sometimes before the poor outcast beggar shivering in the street.

ELLY expected, she did not know why, that there would be some great difference when she got back to the old house at Paris. Her heart sank as Clementine, looking just as usual, opened the great door, and stepped forward to help with the box. She went into the court-yard. Those cocks and hens were pecketing between the stones, the poplar-trees shivering, Françoise in her blue gown came out of the kitchen; it was like one of the dreams which used to haunt her pillow. This sameness and monotony was terrible. Already in one minute it seemed to her that she had never been away. Her mother and father were out. Mme. Jacob came down stairs with the children to greet her and see her. Ah! they had got new frocks, and were grown—that was some relief. Tou-Tou and Lou-Lou were not more delighted with their little check black-and-white alpacas than Elly was.

Anthony was away—she was glad. After the first shock the girl took heart and courage, and set herself to practise the good resolutions she had made when she was away. It was not so hard as she had fancied to be a little less ill-tempered and discontented, because you see she had really behaved so very badly before. But it was not so easy to lead the cheerful devoted life she had pictured to herself. Her mother was very kind, very indifferent, very unhappy, Elizabeth feared. She was ill too, and out of health, but she bore great suffering with wonderful patience and constancy. Tourneur looked haggard and worn. Had he begun to discover that he could not understand his wife? that he had not married the woman he fancied he knew so well, but some quite different person? Ill-temper, discontent, he could have endured and dealt with, but a terrible mistrust and doubt had come into his heart, he did not know how or when, and had nearly broken it.

A gloom seemed hanging over this sad house; a sort of hopeless dreariness. Do you remember how cheerful and contented Caroline had been at first? By degrees she began to get a little tired now and then—a little weary. All these things grew just a little insipid and distasteful. Do you know that torture to which some poor slaves have been subjected? I believe it is only a drop of water falling at regular intervals upon their heads. At first they scarcely heed it, and talk and laugh; then they become silent; and still the drop falls and drips. And then they moan and beg for mercy, and still it falls; and then scream out with horror, and cry out for death, for this is more than they can bear—but still it goes on falling. I have read this somewhere, and it seems to me that this applies to Caroline Tourneur, and to the terrible life which had begun for her.

Her health failed, and she daily lost strength and interest in the things by which she was surrounded; then they became wearisome. Her tired frame was not equal to the constant exertions she had imposed upon herself; from being wearisome, they grew hateful to her; and, one by one, she gave them up. Then the terrible sameness of a life in which her heart was no longer set, seemed to crush her down day by day; a life never lived from high and honorable motives, but for mean and despicable ends; a life lofty and noble to those who, with great hearts and good courage, know how to look beyond it, and not to care for the things of the world, but dull and terrible beyond expression to a woman whose whole soul was set amidst the thorns and thistles, and who had only rushed by chance into this narrow path blindfold with passion and despair.

Now she has torn the bandage off her eyes; now she is struggling to get out of it, and beating against the thorns, and wearily trying to trace back her steps. Elly used to cry out in her childish way. Caroline, who is a woman, is silent, and utters not one word of complaint; only her cheeks fall away and her eyes glare out of great black rings.

Elly came home blooming and well, and was shocked and frightened at first to see the change which had come over her mother. She did not ask the reason of it, but, as we all do sometimes, accepted without much speculation the course of events. Things come about so simply and naturally that people are often in the midst of strangest histories without having once thought so, or wondered that it should be. Very soon all the gloomy house, though she did not know it, seemed brightened and cheered by her coming home. Even Mme. Jacob relented a little when she heard Tou-Tou and Lou-Lou's shouts of laughter one day coming through the open window. The three girls were at work in the garden. I do not know that they were doing much good except to themselves. It was a keen, clear, brilliant winter morning, and the sun out of doors put out the smouldering fires within.

The little girls were laughing and working with all their hearts. Elly was laughing too, and tearing up dried old plants, and heaping broken flower-pots together. Almost happy, almost contented, almost good. . . . . And there is many a worse state of mind than this. She was sighing as she laughed, for she was thinking of herself, pacing round and round the neglected garden once not so long ago; then she thought of the church on the hill-top, then of Will Dampier, and then of John, and then she came upon a long wriggling worm, and she jumped away and forgot to be sentimental. Besides working in the garden, she set to teaching the children in her mother's school. What this girl turned her hand to, she always did well and thoroughly. She even went to visit some of the sick people, and though she never took kindly to these exercises, the children liked to say their lessons to her, and the sick people

were glad when she came in. She was very popular with them all; perhaps the reason was, that she did not do these things from a sense of duty, and did not look upon the poor and the sick as so many of us do, as a selfish means for self-advancement; she went to them because it was more convenient for her to go than for anybody else—she only thought of their needs, grumbled at the trouble she was taking, and it never occurred to her that this unconsciousness was as good as a good conscience.

My dear little Elizabeth! I am glad that at last she is behaving pretty well. Tourneur strokes her head sometimes, and holds out his kind hand to her when she comes into his room. His eyes follow her fondly as if he were her father. One day she told him about William Dampier. He sighed as he heard the story. It was all ordained for the best, he said to himself. But he would have been glad to know her happy, and he patted her cheek and went into his study.

Miss Dampier's letters were Elly's best treasures: how eagerly she took them from Clementine's hands! how she tore them open and read them once, twice, thrice! No novels interest people so much as their own—a story in which you have ever so little a part to enact thrills, and excites, and amuses to the very last. You don't skip the reflections; the descriptions do not weary. I can fancy Elly sitting in a heap on the floor, and spelling out Miss Dampier's; Tou-Tou and Lou-Lou looking on with respectful wonder.

But suddenly the letters seemed to her to change. They became short and reserved; they were not interesting any more. Looked for so anxiously, they only brought disappointment when they came, and no word of the people about whom she longed to hear, no mention of their doings. Even Lady Dampier's name would have been welcome. But there was nothing. It was in vain she read and re-read so eagerly, longing and thirsting for news.

Things were best as they were, she told herself a hundred times; and so, though poor Elly sighed and wearied, and though her heart sank, she did not speak to any one of her trouble: it was a wholesome one, she told herself, one that must be surmounted and overcome by patience. Sometimes her work seemed almost greater than her strength, and then she would go up stairs and cry a little bit and pity herself, and sop up all her tears, and then run round and round the garden once or twice, and come back, with bright eyes and glowing cheeks, to chatter with Françoise, to look after her mother and Stephen Tourneur, to scold the pupils and make jokes at them, to romp with the little girls.

One day she found her letter waiting on the hall-table, and tore it open with a trembling hope. . . . . Aunt Jean described the weather, the pig-sty, made valuable remarks on the news contained in the daily papers, signed herself ever her affectionate old friend. And that was all. Was not that enough? Elly asked herself, with such a sigh. She was reading it over in the door-way of the salle-à-manger, bonneted and cloaked, with all the remains of the midday meal congealing and disordered on the table.

"Es-tu prête, Elizabeth?" said Tou-Tou, coming in with a little basket—there were no stones in it this time. "Tiens, voilà ce que ma tante envoie à cette pauvre Madame Jonnes."

Madame Jonnes was only Mrs. Jones, only an old woman dying in a melancholy room hard by—in a melancholy room in a deserted street, where there were few houses, but long walls, where the mould was feeding, and yellow placards were pasted and defaced and flapping in shreds, and where Elly, picking her little steps over the stones, saw blades of grass growing between them. There was a chantier—a great wood-yard—on one side; now and then a dark door-way leading into a black and filthy court, out of which a gutter would come with evil smells, flowing murkily into the street; in the distance, two figures passing; a child in a night-cap, thumping a doll upon a curbstone; a dog snuffing at a heap; at the end of the street the placarded backs of tall houses built upon a rising ground; a man in a blouse wheeling a truck, and singing out dismally; and meanwhile, good old Mrs. Jones was dying close at hand, under this black and crumbling door-way, in a room opening with cracked glass-doors upon the yard.

She was lying alone upon her bed; the nurse they had sent to her was gossiping with the porter in his lodge. Kindly and dimly her eyes opened and smiled somehow at the girl, out of the faded bed, out of a mystery of pain, of grief, and solitude.

It was a mystery indeed, which Elizabeth, standing beside it, could not understand, though she herself had lain so lately and so resignedly upon a couch of sickness. Age, abandonment, seventy years of life — how many of grief and trouble? As she looked at the dying, indifferent face, she saw that they were almost ended. And in the midst of her pity and shrinking compassion Elly thought to herself that she would change all with the sick woman, at that minute, to have endured, to have surmounted so much.

She sat with her till the dim twilight came through the dirty and patched panes of the windows. Even as she waited there her thoughts went wandering, and she was trying to picture to herself faces and scenes that she could not see. She knew that the shadows were creeping round about those whom she loved, as quietly as they were rising here in this sordid room. It was their evening as it was hers; and then she said to herself that they who made up so large a part of her life must, perforce, think of her sometimes: she was part of their lives, even though they should utterly neglect and forget and abandon her; even though they should never meet again from this day; though she should never hear their names so much as mentioned; though their paths should separate for-

ever. For a time they had travelled the same road—ah! she was thankful even for so much; and she unconsciously pressed the wasted hand she was holding; and then her heart thrilled with tender, unselfish gladness as the feeble fingers tried to clasp hers, and the faltering whisper tried to bless.

She came home sad and tired from her sick woman's bedside, thinking of the last kind gleam of the eyes as she left the room. She went straight up stairs and took off her shabby dress, and found another, and poured out water and bathed her face. Her heart was beating, her hands trembling. She was remembering and regretting; she was despairing and longing, and yet resigned, as she had learned to be of late. She leaned against the wall for a minute before she went down; she was dressed in the blue dress, with her favorite little locket hanging round her neck. She put her hand tiredly to her head; and so she stood, as she used to stand when she was a child, in a sort of dream, and almost out of the world. And as she was waiting a knock came at the door. It was Clementine who knocked, and who said, in the sing-song way in which Frenchwomen speak—"Mademoiselle, voilà pour vous."

It was too dark to see any thing except that it was another familiar-looking letter. Elly made up her mind not to be disappointed any more, and went down stairs leisurely to the study, where she knew she should find Tourneur's lamp alight. And she crossed the hall and turned the handle of the door, and opened it and went in.

The lamp with its green shade on the table lit up one part of the room, but in the dimness, standing by the stove and talking eagerly, were two people whom she could not distinguish very plainly. One of them was Tourneur, who looked round and came to meet her, and took her hand; and the other . . . .

Suddenly her heart began to beat so that her breath was taken away. What was this? Who was this?—What chance had she come upon? Such mad hopes as hers were they ever fulfilled? Was this moment, so sudden, so unlooked for, the one for which she had despaired and longed, for which she had waited and lived through an eternity of grief? Was it John Dampier into whose hand Tourneur put hers? Was she still asleep and dreaming one of those delighting but terrible dreams from which, ah me! she must awake? In this dream she heard the pasteur saying, "Il a bien des choses à vous dire, Elizabeth," and then he seemed to go away and to leave them.

In this dream, bewildered and trembling, with a desperate effort, she pulled her hand away, and said: "What does it mean? Where is Tishy? Why do you come, John? Why don't you leave me in peace?"

And then it was a dream no longer, but a truth and a reality, when John began to speak in his familiar way, and she heard his voice, and saw him before her, and—yes, it was he; and he said : "Tishy and I have had a quarrel, Elly. We are nothing to one another any more, and so I have come to you—to—to—tell you that I have behaved like a fool all this time." And he turned very red as he spoke, and then he was silent, and then he took both her hands and spoke again : "Tell me, dear," he said, looking up into her sweet eyes—"Elly, tell me, would you—won't you—be content with a fool for a husband?" And Elizabeth Gilmour only answered, "Oh John, John!" and burst into a great flood of happy tears : tears which fell raining peace and calm after this long drought and misery; tears which seemed to speak to him, and made him sad, and yet happier than he had ever dreamt of or imagined ; tears which quieted her, soothed her, and healed all her troubles.

Before John went away that night, Elly read Miss Dampier's letter, which explained his explanations. The old lady wrote in a state of incoherent excitement. It was some speech of Will's which had brought the whole thing about.

"What did he say?" Elly asked, looking up from the letter with her shining eyes.

Sir John said : "He asked me if I did not remember that church on the hill, at Boatstown? We were all out in the garden, by the old statue of the nymph. Tishy suddenly stopped, and turned upon me, and cried out, When was I last at Boatstown? And then I was obliged to confess, and we had a disagreeable scene enough, and she appealed to William—gave me my congé, and I was not sorry, Elly."

"But had you never told her about—?"

"It was from sheer honesty that I was silent," said Sir John ; "a man who sincerely wishes to keep his word doesn't say, 'Madam, I like some one else, but I will marry you if you insist upon it;' only the worst of it is, that we were both uncomfortable, and I now find she suspected me the whole time. She sent me a note in the evening. Look here."

The note said :—

"I have been thinking about what I said just now in the garden. I am more than ever decided that it is best we two should part. But I do not choose to say good-bye to you in an angry spirit, and so this is to tell you that I forgive you all the injustice of your conduct to me. Every body seems to have been in a league to deceive me, and I have not found out one true friend among you all. How could you for one moment imagine that I should wish to marry a man who preferred another woman? You may have been influenced and worked upon : but for all that I should never be able to place confidence in you again, and I feel it is best and happiest for us both that all should be at an end between us.

"You will not wonder that, though I try to forgive you, I can not help feeling indignant at the way in which I have been used. I could never understand exactly what was going on in your mind. You were silent, you equiv-ocated ; and not you only, every body seems to have been thinking of themselves, and never once for me. Even William, who professes to care for me still, only spoke by chance, and revealed the whole history. When he talked to you about Boatstown, some former suspicions of mine were confirmed, and by the most fortunate chance two people have been saved from a whole lifetime of regret.

"I will not trust myself to think of the way in which I should have been bartered had I only discovered the truth when it was too late. If I speak plainly, it is in justice to myself, and from no unkindness to you; for though I bid you farewell, I can still sincerely sign myself, yours affectionately, LÆTITIA."

Elly read the letter, and gave it back to him, and sighed, then smiled, then sighed again, and then went on with Miss Dampier's epistle.

For some time past, Jean Dampier wrote, she had noticed a growing suspicion and estrangement between the engaged couple. John was brusque and morose at times, Tishy cross and defiant. He used to come over on his brown mare and stop at the cottage gate, and ask about Elly, and then interrupt her before she could answer and change the talk. He used to give her messages to send and then retract them. He was always philosophizing and discoursing about first affections. Lætitia, too, used to come and ask about Elly.

Miss Dampier hoped that John himself would put an end to this false situation. She did not know how to write about either of them to Elly. Her perplexities had seemed unending.

"But I also never heard that you came to Boatstown," Elly said.

"And yet I saw you there," said John, "standing at the end of the pier." And then he went on to tell her a great deal more, and to confess all that he had thought while he was waiting for her.

Elly passed her hand across her eyes with the old familiar action.

"And you came to Boatstown, and you went away when you read Tishy's writing, and you had the heart to be angry with me?" she said.

"I was worried, and out of temper," said John. "I felt I was doing wrong when I ran away from Tishy. I blamed you because I was in a rage with myself. I can't bear to think of it. But I was punished, Elly. Were you ever jealous?" She laughed and nodded her head. "I dare say not," he went on ; "when I sailed away and saw you standing so confidentially with Will Dampier, I won't try and tell you what I suffered. I could bear to give you up—but to see you another man's wife—Elly, I know you never were jealous, or you would understand what I felt at that moment."

When their tête-à-tête was over they went into the next room. All the family congratulated them, Madame Tourneur among the rest ; she was ill and tired that evening, and lying on the yellow Utrecht velvet sofa. But it was awkward for them and uncomfortable, and John went home early to his inn. As Elly went up to bed that night, Françoise brought her one other piece of news—Madame Jonnes was dead. They had sent to acquaint the police. But Elly was so happy, that, though she tried, she could not be less happy because of this. All the night she lay awake, giving thanks and praise, and saying over to herself, a hundred times, "At last—at last!"

At last! after all this long rigmarole. At last! after all these despairing adjectives and adverbs. At last! after all these thousands of hours of grief and despair. Did not that one minute almost repay her for them all? She went on telling herself, as I have said, that this was a dream—from which she need never awake. And I, who am writing her story, wonder if it is so—wonder if even to such dreams as these there may not be a waking one day, when all the visions that surround us shall vanish and disappear forever into eternal silence and oblivion. Dear faces—voices whose tones speak to us even more familiarly than the tender words which they utter! It would, in truth, seem almost too hard to bear, if we did not guess—if we were not told—how the love which makes such things so dear to us endures in the eternity out of which they have passed.

Happiness like Elly's is so vague and so great that it is impossible to try to describe it. To a nature like hers, full of tenderness, faithful and eager, it came like a sea, ebbing and flowing with waves, and with the sun shining and sparkling on the water, and lighting the fathoms below. I do not mean to say that my poor little heroine was such a tremendous creature that she could compass the depths and wide extent of a sea in her heart. Love is not a thing which belongs to any one of us individually; it is everywhere, here and all round about, and sometimes people's hearts are opened, and they guess at it, and realize that it is theirs.

Dampier came early next morning, looking kind and happy and bright, to fetch her for a walk; Elly was all blue ribbons and blue eyes; her feet seemed dancing against her will, she could hardly walk quietly along. Old Françoise looked after them as they walked off towards the Bois de Boulogne; Tou-Tou and Lou-Lou peeped from their bed-room window. The sun was shining, the sky had mounted Elly's favorite colors.

CHAPTER XII.

Oh blessed rest, oh royal night!
   Wherefore seemeth the time so long
Till I see yon stars in their fullest light,
   And list to their loudest song?

WHEN I first saw Lady Dampier, she had only been married a day or two. I had been staying at Guildford, and I drove over one day to see my old friend Jean Dampier. I came across the hills and by Coombe Bottom and

along the lanes, and through the little village street, and when I reached the cottage I saw Elly, of whom I had heard so much, standing at the gate. She was a very beautiful young woman, tall and straight, with the most charming blue eyes, a sweet frank voice, and a taking manner, and an expression on her face that I can not describe. She had a blue ribbon in her hair, which was curling in a crop. She held her hat full of flowers: behind her the lattices of the cottage were gleaming in the sun; the creepers were climbing and flowering about the porch.

All about rose a spring incense of light, of color, of perfume. The country folks were at work in the fields and on the hills. The light shone beyond the church spire, beyond the cottages and glowing trees. Inside the cottage, through the lattice, I could see Aunt Jean nodding over her knitting.

She threw down her needles to welcome me. Of course I was going to stay to tea—and I said that was my intention in coming. As the sun set, the clouds began to gather, coming quickly we knew not from whence: but we were safe and dry, sitting by the lattice and gossiping, and meanwhile Miss Dampier went on with her work.

Elly had been spending the day with her, she told me. Sir John was to come for her, and presently he arrived, dripping wet, through the April shower which was now pouring over the fields.

The door of the porch opens into the little dining-room, where the tea was laid: a wood-fire was crackling in the tall cottage chimney. Elizabeth was smiling by the hearth, toasting cakes with one hand and holding a book in the other, when the young man walked in.

He came into the room where we were sitting and shook hands with us both, and then he laughed and said he must go and dry himself by the fire, and he went back.

So Jean Dampier and I sat mumbling confidences in the inner room, and John and Elly were chattering to one another by the burning wood logs.

The door was open which led, with a step, into the dining-room, where the wood-fire was burning. Darkness was setting in. The rain was over, the clouds swiftly breaking and coursing away, and such a bright, mild-eyed little star peeped in through the lattice at us two old maids in the window. It was a shame to hear, but how could we help it? Out of the fire-lit room the voices came to us, and when we ceased chattering for an instant, we heard them so plainly :—

"I saw Will to-day," said a voice. "He was talking about Lætitia. I think there will be some news of them before long. Should you be glad?"

"Ah! so glad. I don't want to be the only happy woman in the world."

"My dearest Elly!" said the kind voice. "And you will never regret—and are you happy?"

"Can you ask?" said Elly. "Come into the porch, and I will tell you." And then there was a gust of fresh rain-scented air, and a soft rustle, and the closing click of a door. And then we saw them pass the window, and Jean clasped my hand very tightly, and flung her arms round my neck, and gave me a delighted kiss.

"You dear, silly woman," said I, "how glad I am they are so happy together!"

"I hope she won't catch cold," said Jean, looking at the damp walks. "Could not you take out a shawl?"

"Let her catch cold!" said I; "and in the mean time give me some tea, if you please. Remember, I have got to drive home in the dark."

So we went into the next room. Jean rang for the candles. The old silver candlesticks were brought in by Kitty on a tray.

"Don't shut the curtains," said Miss Dampier; "and come here, Mary, and sit by the fire."

While Elizabeth and John Dampier were wandering up and down in the dark damp garden, Jenny and I were comfortably installed by the fire, drinking hot, sweet tea, and eating toasted cakes, and preserves, and cream. I say we, but that is out of modesty, for she had no appetite, whereas I was very hungry.

"Heigh-ho!" said Jean, looking at the fire. "It's a good thing to be young, Mary. Tell me honestly: what would you give—"

"To be walking in the garden with young Dampier," said I (and I burst out laughing), "without a cloak, or an umbrella, or india-rubbers? My dear Jenny, where are your five wits?"

"Where indeed?" said Jean, with another sigh. "Yet I can remember when you used to cry instead of laughing over such things, Mary."

Her sadness had made me sad. Whilst the young folks were whispering outside, it seemed as if we two old women were sitting by the fire and croaking the elegy of all youth, and love, and happiness. "The night is coming for you and me, Jenny," I said. "Dear me, how quickly!"

"The night is at hand," echoed she, softly, and she passed her fingers across her eyes, and then sighed, and got up slowly and went to the door which opened into the porch. And then I heard her call me. "Come here!" she said, "Mary!" And then I, too, rose stiffly from my chair, and went to her. The clouds had cleared away. From the little porch, where the sweet-brier was climbing, we could see all the myriad worlds of heaven, alight and blazing, and circling in their infinite tracks. An awful, silent harmony, power and peace, and light and life eternal—a shining benediction seemed to be there hanging above our heads. "This is the night," she whispered, and took my hand in hers.

And so this is the end of the story of Eliza-beth Gilmour, whose troubles, as I have said, were not very great; who is a better woman, I fancy, than if her life had been the happy life she prophesied to herself. Deeper tones and understandings must have come to her out of the profoundness of her griefs, such as they were. For when other troubles came, as they come to all as years go by, she had learned to endure and to care for others, and to be valiant and to be brave. And I do not like her the less because I have spoken the truth about her, and written to her as the woman she is.

I went to Paris a little time ago. I saw the old grass-grown court; I saw Françoise and Anthony, and Tou-Tou and Lou-Lou, who had grown up two pretty and modest and smiling young girls. The old lady at Asnières had done what was expected, and died and left her fortune to Tou-Tou, her goddaughter. (The little Chinese pagoda is still to let.) Poor Madame Jacob did not, however, enjoy this good luck, for she died suddenly one day, some months before it came to them. But you may be sure that the little girls had still a father in Tournenr, and Caroline too was very kind to them in her uncertain way. She loved them because they were so unlike herself—so gentle, and dull, and guileless. Anthony asked me a great many questions about Elizabeth and her home, and told me that he meant to marry Lou-Lou eventually. He is thin and pale, with a fine head like his father, and a quiet manner. He works very hard, he earns very little—he is one of the best men I ever knew in my life. As I talked to him, I could not but compare him to Will Dampier and to John, who are also good men. But then they are prosperous and well-to-do, with well-stored granaries, with vineyards and fig-trees, with children growing up round them. I was wondering if Elizabeth, who chose her husband because she loved him, and for no better reason, might not have been as wise if she could have appreciated the gifts better than happiness, than well-stored granaries, than vineyards, than fig-trees, which Anthony held in his hand to offer? Who shall say? Self-denial and holy living are better than ease and prosperity? But for that reason some people willfully turn away from the mercies of Heaven, and call the angels devils, and its gracious bounties temptation.

Anthony has answered this question to himself, as we all must do. His father looks old and worn. I fear there is trouble still under his roof—trouble, whatever it may be, which is borne with Christian and courageous resignation by the master of the house: he seems, somehow, in these later years to have risen beyond it. A noble reliance and peace are his; holy thoughts keep him company. The affection between him and his son is very touching.

Madame Tournenr looks haggard and weary: and one day, when I happened to tell her I was going away, she gasped out suddenly—"Ah! what would I not give—" and then was silent and turned aside. But she remains with her husband, which is more that I should have given her credit for.

And so, when the appointed hour came, I drove off, and all the personages of my story came out to bid me farewell. I looked back for the last time at the court-yard with the hens pecketting round about the kitchen door; at the garden with the weeds and flowers tangling together in the sun; at the shadows falling across the stones of the yard. I could fancy Elizabeth a prisoner within those walls, beating like a bird against the bars of the cage, and revolting and struggling to be free.

The old house is done away with and exists no longer. It was pulled down by order of the Government, and a grand new boulevard runs right across the place where it stood.

TO ESTHER.

TO

𝕮. 𝖉𝖊 𝕽.   𝕰. 𝕸. 𝕾.

𝕬. 𝖉𝖊 𝕽.   and 𝕬. 𝕷.

A REMEMBRANCE.

March, 1869.

TO ESTHER.

1859—'60.

"'Tis Rome-work, made to match."

THE first time that I ever knew you was at Rome, one winter's evening. I had walked through the silent streets—I see them now—dark with black shadows, lighted by the blazing stars overhead and by the lamps dimly flickering before the shrines at street corners. After crossing the Spanish-place I remember turning into a narrow alley and coming presently to a great black archway, which led to a glimmering court. A figure of the Virgin stood with outstretched arms above the door of your house, and the light burning at her feet dimly played upon the stone, worn and stained, of which the walls were built. Through the archway came a glimpse of the night sky above the court-yard, shining wonderfully with splendid stars; and I also caught the plashing sound of a fountain flowing in the darkness. I groped my way up the broad stone staircase, only lighted by the friendly star-shine, stumbling and knocking my shins against those ancient steps, up which two centuries of men and women had clambered; and at last, ringing at a curtained door, I found myself in a hall, and presently ushered through a dining-room, where the cloth was laid, and announced at the drawing-room door as Smith.

It was a long room with many windows, and cabinets and tables along the walls, with a tall carved mantel-piece, at which you were standing, and a Pompeian lamp burning on a table near you. Would you care to hear what manner of woman I saw; what impression I got from you as we met for the first time together? In after days, light, mood, circumstance, may modify this first image more or less, but the germ of life is in it—the identical presence—and I fancy it is rarely improved by keeping, by painting up, with love, or dislike, or long use, or weariness, as the case may be. Be this as it may, I think I knew you as well after the first five minutes' acquaintance as I do now. I saw an ugly woman, whose looks I liked somehow; thick brows, sallow face, a tall and straight-made figure, honest eyes that had no particular merit besides, dark hair, and a pleasant, cordial smile. And somehow, as I looked at you and heard you talk, I seemed to be aware of a frank spirit, uncertain, blind, wayward, tender, under this somewhat stern exterior; and so, I repeat, I liked you, and, making a bow, I said I was afraid I was before my time.

"I'm afraid it is my father who is after his," you said. "Mr. Halbert is coming, and he, too, is often late;" and so we went on talking for about ten minutes.

Yours is a kindly manner, a sad-toned voice; I know not if your life has been a happy one; you are well disposed towards every soul you come across; you love to be loved, and try with a sweet artless art to win and charm over each man or woman that you meet. I saw that you liked me, that you felt at your ease with me, that you held me not quite your equal, and might perhaps laugh at, as well as with me. But I did not care. My aim in life, heaven knows, has not been to domineer, to lay down the law, and triumph over others, least of all over those I like.

The Colonel arrived presently, with his white hair trimly brushed and his white neckcloth neatly tied. He greeted me with great friendliness and cordiality. You have got his charm of manner; but with you, my dear, it is not manner only, for there is loyalty and heartiness shining in your face, and sincerity ringing in every tone of your voice. As for the Colonel, your father, if I mistake not, he is a little shrivelled-up old gentleman, with a machine inside to keep him going, and outside a well-cut coat and a well-bred air and a certain knowledge of the world, to get on through life with. However, this is not the way to speak to a young lady about her father; and besides it is you, and not he, in whom I take the interest which prompts these maudlin pages.

Mr. Halbert and little Latham, the artist, were the only other guests. You did not look round when Halbert was announced, but went on speaking to Latham, with a strange flush in your face; until Halbert had, with great *empressement*, made his way through the chairs and tables, and had greeted, rather than been greeted by, you.

So thinks I to myself, concerning certain vague

notions I had already begun to entertain, I am rather late in the field, and the city is taken and has already hoisted the conqueror's colors. Perhaps those red flags might have been mine had I come a little sooner; who knows? "*De tout laurier un poison est l'essence,*" says the Frenchman; and my brows may be as well unwreathed.

"I came up stairs with the dinner," Mr. Halbert was saying. "It reassured me as to my punctuality. I rather pique myself on my punctuality, Colonel."

"And I'm afraid I have been accusing you of being always late," you said, as if it were a confession.

"Have you thought so, Miss Olliver?" cried Halbert.

"Dinner, sir," said Baker, opening the door.

All dinner-time Halbert, who has very high spirits, talked and laughed without ceasing. You, too, laughed, listened, looked very happy, and got up with a smile at last, leaving us to drink our wine. The Colonel presently proposed cigars.

"In that case I shall go and talk to your daughter in the drawing-room," Halbert said. "I'm promised to Lady Parker's to-night; it would never do to go there smelling all over of smoke. I must be off in half-an-hour," he added, looking at his watch.

I, too, had been asked to the tea-party, and I was rather surprised that Halbert should be in such a desperate hurry to get there. Talking to Miss Olliver in the next room I could very well understand; but leaving her to rush off to Lady Parker's immediately, did not accord with the little theories I had been laying down. Could I have been mistaken? In this case it seemed to me this would be the very woman to suit me—(you see I am speaking without any reserve, and simply describing the abrupt little events as they occurred)—and I thought, who knows that there may not be a chance for me yet? But, by the time my cigar had crumbled into smoke and ashes, it struck me that my little castle had also wreathed away and vanished. Going into the drawing-room, where the lamps were swinging in the dimness, and the night without streaming in through the uncurtained windows, we found you in your white dress, sitting alone at one of them. Mr. Halbert was gone, you said; he went out by the other door. And then you were silent again, staring out at the stars with dreamy eyes. The Colonel rang for tea, and chirped away very pleasantly to Latham by the fire. I looked at you now and then, and could not help surprising your thoughts somehow, and knowing that I had not been mistaken after all. There you sat, making simple schemes of future happiness; you could not, would not, look beyond the present. You were very calm, happy, full of peaceful reliance. Your world was alight with shining stars, great big shining meteors, all flaring up as they usually do before going out with a splutter at the end of the entertainment. People who are in love I have always found very much alike; and now,

having settled that you belonged to that crack-brained community, it was not difficult to guess at what was going on in your mind.

I, too, as I have said, had been favored with a card for Lady Parker's rout; and as you were so absent and ill-inclined to talk, and the Colonel was anxious to go off and play whist at his club, I thought I might as well follow in Halbert's traces, and gratify any little curiosity I might feel as to his behavior and way of going on in your absence. I found that Latham was also going to her ladyship's. As we went down stairs together Latham said, "It was too bad of Halbert to break up the party and go off at that absurd hour. I didn't say I was going, because I thought his rudeness might strike them."

"But surely," said I, "Mr. Halbert seems at home there, and may come and go as he likes?" Latham shrugged his shoulders. "I like the girl; I hope she is not taken in by him. He has been very thick all the winter in other quarters. Lady Parker's niece, Lady Fanny Fareham, was going to marry him, they said; but I know very little of him. He is much too great a swell to be on intimate terms with a disreputable little painter like myself. What a night it is!" As he spoke we came out into the street again, our shadows falling on the stones; the Virgin overhead still watching, the lamp burning faithfully, the solemn night waning on. Lady Parker had lodgings in the Corso. I felt almost ashamed of stepping from the great entertainment without into the close racketing little tea-party that was clattering on within. We came in, in the middle of a jangling tune, the company spinning round and round. Halbert, twirling like a Dervish, was almost the first person I saw; he was flushed, and looked exceedingly handsome, and his tall shoulders overtopped most of the other heads. As I watched him I thought with great complacency that if any woman cared for me, it would not be for my looks. No! no! what are mere good looks compared to those mental qualities which, etc., etc. Presently, not feeling quite easy in my mind about these said mental qualities, I again observed that it was still better to be liked for one's self than for one's mental qualities; by which time I turned my attention once more to Mr. Halbert. The youth was devoting himself most assiduously to a very beautiful, oldish young lady, in a green gauzy dress; and I now, with a mixture of satisfaction and vexation, recognized the very same looks and tones which had misled me at dinner.

I left him still at it and walked home, wondering at the great law of natural equality which seems to level all mankind to one standard, notwithstanding all those artificial ones which we ourselves have raised. Here was a successful youth, with good looks and good wits and position and fortune; and here was I, certainly no wonder, insignificant, and plain and poor, and of commonplace intelligence, and as well satisfied with my own possessions, such as they were, as he, Halbert, could be with the treasures a prodigal fortune had showered upon him. Here was I, judging him, and taking his measure as accurately as he could take mine, were it worth his while to do so. Here was I, walking home under the stars, while he was flirting and whispering with Lady Fanny, and both our nights sped on. Constellations sinking slowly, the day approaching through the awful realms of space, hours waning, life going by for us both alike: both of us men waiting together amidst these awful surroundings.

You and I met often after this first meeting—in churches where tapers were lighting and heavy censers swinging—on the Pincio, in the narrow, deep-colored streets: it was not always chance only which brought me so constantly into your presence. You yourself were the chance, at least, and I the blind follower of fortune.

All around about Rome there are ancient gardens lying basking in the sun. Gardens and villas built long since by dead cardinals and popes; terraces, with glinting shadows, with honeysuckle clambering in desolate luxuriance; roses flowering and fading and falling in showers on the pathways; and terraces and marble steps yellow with age. Lonely fountain splash in their basins, statues of fauns and slender nymphs stand out against the solemn horizon of blue hills and crimson-streaked sky; of cypress-trees and cedars, with the sunset showing through their stems. At home I lead a very busy, anxious life: the beauty and peace of these Italian villas fill me with inexpressible satisfaction and gratitude towards those mouldering pontiffs, whose magnificent liberality has secured such placid resting-places for generations of weary men. Taking a long walk out of Rome one day in the early spring, I came to the gates of one of these gardens. I remember seeing a carriage waiting in the shade of some cedar-trees; hard by horses with drooping heads, and servants smoking as they waited. This was no uncommon sight; the English are forever on their rounds; but somehow, on this occasion, I thought I recognized one of the men, and instead of passing by, as had been my intention, I turned in at the half-opened gate, which the angels with the flaming swords had left unguarded and unlocked for once, and, after a few minutes' walk, I came upon the Eve I looked for.

You were sitting on some time-worn steps; you wore a green silk dress, and your brown hair, with the red tints in it, was all ablaze with the light. You looked very unhappy, I thought got up with an effort, and smiled a pitiful smile.

"Are you come here for a little quiet?" I asked. "I am not going to disturb you."

"I came here for pleasure, not quiet," you said, "with papa and some friends. I was tired, so they walked on and left me."

"That is the way with one's friends," said I. "Who are the culprits, Miss Olliver?"

"I am the only culprit," you said, grimly. "Lady Fanny and Mr. Halbert came with us to-day. Look, there they are at the end of that alley."

And as you spoke, you raised one hand and pointed, and I made up my mind. It was a very long alley. The figures in the distance were advancing very slowly. When they reach that little temple, thought I, I will tell her what I think.

This was by no means so sudden a determination as it may appear to you, reading over these pages. It seems a singular reason to give; but I really think it was your hopeless fancy for that rosy youth which touched me and interested me so. I know I used to carry home sad words, spoken not to me, and glances that thrilled me with love, pity, and sympathy. What I said was, as you know, very simple and to the purpose. I knew quite well your fancy was elsewhere; mine was with you, perhaps as hopelessly placed. I didn't exactly see what good this confession was to do either of us, only there I was, ready to spend my life at your service.

When I had spoken there was a silent moment, and then you glowed up—your eyes melted, your mouth quivered. "Oh, what can I say? Oh, I am so lonely. Oh, I have not one friend in the world; and now, suddenly, a helping hand is held out, and I can't—I can't push it away. Oh, don't despise. Oh, forgive me."

Despise! scorn! . . . Poor child! I only liked you the more for your plaintive appeal; though I wondered at it.

"Take your time," I said; "I can wait, and I shall not fly away. Call me when you want me; send me away when I weary you. Here is your father; shall I speak to him? But no. Remember there is no single link between us, except what you yourself hold in your own hands."

Here your father and Halbert and Lady Fanny came up. "Well, Esther, are you rested?" says the Colonel cheerfully. "Why, how do you do?" (to me). "What have you been talking about so busily?"

You did not answer, but fixed your eyes on your father's face. I said something; I forget what. Halbert, looking interested, turned from one to the other. Lady Fanny, who held a fragrant heap of roses, shook a few petals to the ground, where they lay scattered after we had all walked away.

If you remember, I did not go near you for a day or two after this. But I wrote you a letter, in which I repeated that you were entirely free to use me as you liked: marry me—make a friend of me—I was in your hands. One day, at last, I called; and I shall never forget the sweetness and friendly gratefulness with which you received me. A solitary man, dying of lonely thirst, you meet me smiling with a cup of sparkling water: a weary watcher through the night—suddenly I see the dawn streaking the bright horizon. Those were very pleasant times. I remember now, one afternoon in early spring, open windows, sounds coming in from the city, the drone of the *pifferari* buzzing drowsily in the sultry streets. You sat at your window in some light-colored dress, laughing now and then, and talking your tender little talk. The Colonel, from behind *The Times*, joined in now and again: the pleasant half-hours slid by. We were still basking there, when Halbert was announced, and came in, looking very tall and handsome. The bagpipes droned on, the flies sailed in and out on the sunshine: you still sat tranquilly at the open casement; but somehow the golden atmosphere of the hour was gone. Your smiles were gone; your words were silenced; and that happy little hour was over forever.

When I got up to come away Halbert rose too: he came down stairs with me, and suddenly looking me full in the face said, "When is it to be?"

"You know much more about it than I do," I answered.

"You don't mean to say that you are not very much smitten with our hostess?" said he.

"Certainly I am," said I; "I should be ready enough to marry her, if that is what you mean. I dare say I shan't get her. She is to me the most sympathetic woman I have ever known. You are too young, Mr. Halbert, to understand and feel her worth. Don't be offended," I added, seeing him flush up. "You young fellows can't be expected to see with the same eyes as we old ones. You will think as I do in another ten years."

"How do you mean?" he asked.

"Isn't it the way with all of us?" said I; "we begin by liking universally; as we go on we pick and choose, and weary of things which had only the charm of novelty to recommend them; only as our life narrows we cling more and more to the good things which remain, and feel their value ten times more keenly. And surely a sweet, honest-hearted young woman like Esther Olliver is a good thing."

"She is very nice," Halbert said. "She has such good manners. I have had more experience than you give me credit for, and I am very much of your way of thinking. They say that old courtly Colonel is dreadfully harsh to her—wants to marry her off his hands. I assure you you have a very good chance."

"I mistrust that old Colonel," said I, dictatorially; "as I trust his daughter. Somehow she and I chime in tune together;" and, as I spoke, I began to understand why you once said wofully, that you had not one friend in the world; and my thoughts wandered away to the garden where I had found you waiting on the steps of the terrace.

"What do you say to the serenade Lady Fanny and I have been performing lately?" Halbert was saying meanwhile, very confidentially. "Sometimes I can not help fancying that the Colonel wants to take a part in the performance, and a cracked old tenor part, too. In that case I shall cry off, and give up my engagements." And then, nodding good-bye, he left me.

I remember the evening of that day, a sudden wind had risen, driving the clouds across the city; the soft, wild gust came with a wail and a splashing of rain dashing against my uncurtained window. The city lights were flaring and extinguished. The woman of the house had piled up a wood fire on the stone hearth, and the logs were smouldering in a bed of white ashes. I had not gone out as usual, but I had staid at home reading a book which had been sent out to me from England. It was the *Idylls of the King*, I remember, which had lately come out. About nine o'clock some one came ringing at the door, and old Octavia brought me a note in a writing I recognized. "The Signorina's cook had left it on his way home," said Octavia. "He lodges close by."

Poor little note! it was wet with rain-drops. I have it now.

"Via della Croce, Friday.

"DEAR MR. SMITH" (I read),—"I have just seen my father and heard some news which has surprised and bewildered me. He is engaged to be married to Lady Fanny Fareham. Will you come and see me to-morrow? Good-night, dear kind friend.   ESTHER."

That was all. Poor little Esther!

I met Halbert in the Babuino the very next day. He came straight up to me, saying, "Going to the Ollivers', eh? Will you take a message for me, and tell the Colonel I mean to look in there this evening? That old fox the Colonel—you have heard that he *is* actually going to marry Lady Fanny. She told me so herself, yesterday."

"I think her choice is a prudent one," I answered. "I suppose Colonel Olliver is three times as rich as yourself? You must expect a woman of thirty to be prudent. I'm not fond of that virtue in very young people, but it is not unbecoming with years."

Halbert flushed up. "I suppose from that you mean she was very near marrying me? I'm not sorry she has taken up with the Colonel, after all. You see, my mother was always writing, and my sisters at home; and they used to tell me . . . and I myself thought she—you know what I mean. But, of course, they have been reassured on that point."

"Do you mean to say," I asked, in a great panic, "that you would marry any woman who happened to fall in love with you?"

"I don't know what I might have done a year ago," said he, laughing; "but just now, you see, I have had a warning, and, besides, it is my turn to make the advances."

I was immensely relieved at this, for I didn't know what I was not going to say.

Here, as we turned a street-corner, we came upon a black-robed monk, standing, veiled and motionless, with a skull in one bony hand. This cheerful object changed the current of our talk, and we parted presently at a fountain. Women with black twists of hair were standing round about, waiting in careless attitudes, while the limpid **water** flowed.

When I reached your door, I found the carriage waiting, and you and your **father** under **the** archway. "Come with us," said he, and I gladly accepted. And so **we drove** out at one of the gates of the city, out **into the** Campagna, over which melting waves of **color** were rolling. Here and there we passed **ancient ruins** crumbling in **the sun; the roadsides** streamed with color and fragrance **from violets** and wild hyacinths **and sweet-smelling flowers.** After some time **we came suddenly to some green** hills, and leaving the carriage climbed **up the slopes. Then** we found ourselves looking down **into a green glowing** valley, with an intense heaven above, all melting into light. You, with **a** little **transient** gasp of happiness, fell down kneeling **in the** grass. I shall always see the picture I had before me then—the light figure against the bright green, the black hat, and long falling feather; the eager face looking out at the world. May it be forever green and pleasant to you as it was then, oh eager face!

As we were parting in the twilight, I at last remembered to give Halbert's message. It did not greatly affect your father; but how was it? Was it because I knew you so well that I instinctively guessed you were moved by it? When I shook hands with you and said goodnight, your hand trembled in mine.

"Won't you look in too?" said the Colonel. But I shook my head. "Not to-night—no, thank you." And so we parted.

My lodgings were in the Gregoriana; the windows looked out over gardens and cupolas; from one of them I could see the Pincio. From that window, next morning, as I sat drinking my coffee, I suddenly saw you, walking slowly along by the parapet, with your dog running by your side. You went to one of those outlying terraces which flank the road, and, leaning over the stone-work, looked out at the great panorama lying at your feet:—Rome with her purple mantle of mist, regally spreading, her towers, her domes, and great St. Peter's rising over the house-tops, her seven hills changing and deepening with noblest color, her golden crown of **sunlight** streaming and melting with the mist. **Somehow** I, too, saw all this presently when I **reached the** place where you were still standing.

And now **I** have almost come to the end of my story—that is, of those few days of my life of which you, Esther, were the story. You stood there waiting, **and I** hastened towards you, and fate (I fancied **you** were my Fate) went on its course quite **unmoved** by my hopes or your fears. I thought **that** you looked almost handsome for once. **You** certainly seemed more happy. Your face flushed and faded, your eyes brightened and darkened. As you turned and **saw** me, a radiant quiver, a piteous smile came

to greet me somewhat strangely. You seemed trying to speak, but the words died away on your lips—to keep silence, at least, but the faltering accents broke forth.

"What is it, my dear?" said I at last, with a queer **sinking** of the heart, **and I** held out my hand.

You **caught** it softly between both yours. "Oh!" **you** said, with sparkling eyes, "I am a mean, wretched girl—oh! don't think too ill of me. He, Mr. Halbert, came to see me last night, and—and he says . . . Oh! I don't deserve it. Oh! forgive me, for I am so happy ;" and you burst into tears. "You have been **so** good to me," you whispered on. "I hardly know how good. He says he only thought of me when you spoke of me to him, when—when he saw you did not dislike me. I am behaving shamefully—yes, shamefully, but it is because I know you are too kind not to forgive—not to forgive. What can I do? You know how it has always been. You don't know what it would be to marry one person, caring for another. Ah! you don't know what it would be to have it otherwise than as it is" (this clasping your hands). "But you don't ask it. Ah! forgive me, and say you don't ask it." Then standing straight and looking down with a certain sweet dignity, you went on—"Heaven **has sent me a great and unexpected happiness, but there** is, indeed, a bitter, bitter **cup to** drink as well. **Though** I throw you over, though I behave so selfishly, don't think that I am utterly conscienceless, that I do not suffer a cruel pang indeed. When I think how you must look at me, when I remember what return I am making for all your forbearance and generosity, when I think of myself, I am ashamed and humiliated; when I think of him—" Here you suddenly broke off, and turned away your face.

Ah me! turned away your face forever from me. The morning mists faded away; the midday sun streamed over hills and towers and valley. The bell of the Trinità hard by began to toll.

I said, "Good-bye, and Heaven keep you, my dear. I would not have had you do otherwise." And so I went back to my lodging.

1866.

(After seven years.)

> "I leaned a little and overlooked my prize,
> By the low railing round the fountain-source
> Close to the statue, where a step descends."

Bosset, August 20.

"Do you remember the story I wrote you in 1860, when I came back from Rome? To complain was a consolation, when it was to you I complained. I was lonely enough and disappointed, and yet I have been more unhappy since. Then I thought that at least you were happy, but later they said it was not so, and bitterness and regret overpowered me for a time. But this was after I had written to you.

"I scarcely remember what I said now, it is so long ago, but I know every word had a meaning since you were to see it, and the Esther I wrote to, the Esther whose image was forever before me, seemed mine sometimes though we were forever parted. I have often thought that the Esther I loved loved me though the other one married Halbert. Perhaps you were only her semblance, and she was waiting for me elsewhere in a different form. But the familiar face with the sallow cheeks and dark brows, and all the sudden light in it, comes before me as I write even now. I have seen it a thousand thousand times since we parted by the Trinità; do you remember when the bell was ringing for matins? Only as years have gone by the lines have faded a little, the eyes look deep and tender, but they have lost their color; though I know how the lights and the smiles still come and still go, I can not see them so plainly. The woman herself I can conjure across the years and the distance, but the face does not start clear-set before me as in those days when I only lived to follow your footsteps, to loiter among the shadows in your way, and in the sunshine through which you seemed to move; to drink up the sweet tones of your voice, to watch you when you sat at your window, when you lingered in the silent Italian gardens, or moved with a gentle footfall along echoing galleries, with dim golden pictures, and harmonies of glowing color all about you.

"What sea-miles and land-miles, what flying years and lagging hours, what sorrows and joys lie between us—and joys separate more surely than sorrows do. People scale prison-walls, they wade through rivers, they climb over arid mountains, to rejoin those whom they love, but the great barriers of happiness and content, who has surmounted them?

"I say this, and yet success has been mine since I saw you. Many good things have come to me for which I did not greatly care, but though the spring tides and bright summers and the bitter winter winds and autumnal mists were fated to part us year after year, yet it also seemed destined that I should love you faithfully through all—that even forgetfulness should not prevent it, that disappointment should not embitter, that indifference should not chill. What I have borne from you I could not have endured from any other. Once, long before I knew you, a woman spoke to me hastily, and I left her, and could not forgive her for years, and sometimes I ask myself is my ill-luck a judgment upon me?

"I, who was so impatient once and hard of heart, make no merit of my long affection for you, Esther: it was simply fate, and I could not resist it. Changing, unchanging, faithful, unfaithful, who can account for his experiences? Does mistrust bring about of itself that which it imagines? is *every thing* there that we fancy we see in people? Often I think that fallen as we are, and weary and soiled by the wayside dust and mud, and the many cares of life, some gleam of the divine radiance is ours still, and to those who love us best it is given to see it. That the sweetness and goodness and brightness we had fancied are no fancies, but truth. True though clouds and darkness come between us, and the mortal parts can not always apprehend the divine.

"Love is blind; indifference sees more clearly, people say, and I wonder if this can be true; for my part I think it is the other way. I have sometimes asked about you from one and from another, and people have spoken of you as if you were to me only what they are, what I am to them, or they to you. I seem to be writing riddles and ringing the changes upon the words which you will not see. Whether you see them or not, what does it matter? you would not understand their meaning, their sorrowful fidelity, nor do I wish that you should.

"For, as I have said, years have passed, other thoughts and ties and interests have come to me; I am sometimes even vexed and wearied by my own unchanging nature, and I am tired of the very things from which I can not tear myself away. I don't think I care for you now, though I still love the woman who jilted me years ago upon the Pincio. It might be that, seeing you again, all the old tender emotion of feeling would revive towards you. It might be that you would wound me a second time by destroying my dreams, my ideal remembrance. Very sad, very sweet, very womanly and trustful my remembrance is. I should imagine you must have hardened—improved as people call it —since then, and been moulded into some different person. Six years spent with Halbert must have altered you, I think, and marred the sweet imperfections of your nature. At any rate you are as far removed from me as if poor Halbert were alive still to torment you.

"This morning at Luchon my courier brought me a letter which interested me oddly enough, and brought back all the old fancies and associations. It came from my cousin's wife, Lady Mary. There were but a few lines, but your name was written thrice in it; and like an old half-remembered tune, all the way riding along the rough road I have been haunted by a refrain —'Meet Esther again, shall it be, can it be?' —fitting to a sort of rhythm, which is sing-songing in my head at this instant.

"For want of a companion to speak to, I have written this nonsense at length. I can not talk to my courier except to swear at the roads. They narrowed and roughened as we got into Spain, after we had crossed a bridge with a black river rushing beneath it. High up in the mountains the villages perched like eagles' nests; the streams were dashing over the rocks in the clefts below. This is not a golden and sun-painted land like the country we have been used to. Italy seems like summer as I think of it, and this is like autumn to me. The colors have sombre tints; there are strange browns and yellows, faded greens with deep blue shades in them. Stones roll from the pathway and fall crashing into the ravines below. No roads lead to the villages where the people live for a lifetime, tilling their land, weaving their clothes, tending their cattle; many of them never coming down into the valley all their lives long, sufficing to themselves and ignoring the world at their feet. So my guides have told me, at least, and it was their business to know...."

* * * *

All this had been written on the rail of a balcony to the jangling of a church-bell and the sympathetic droning of a guitar with one note. It was played by a doleful-looking soldier in tight regimentals, sitting upright on a chair on the landing-place, and never moving a muscle, while the flies buzzed about his head. A motionless companion sat near, listening to the melody. Presently, in the midst of his writing, Geoffry Smith, who had scarcely heeded the guitar or the bell, suddenly heard a great chattering and commotion in the street below, and looking over the rail, he saw a crowd of little gipsy children swarming in front of the house. They were trying to climb up into the balcony, getting on one another's backs, clapping their hands, screaming and beckoning to him:—"Mossoo! Mossoo!—tit sou—allons donc!" with an encouraging gesture. "Tit sou—'lons donc—vite, *Mossoo !*" and the brown faces grinned beneath their little Moorish-looking turbans—yellow green, scarlet handkerchiefs; and all the brown bare legs went capering. The narrow street was crowded with people hurrying to the call of the church-bell. Women came out of the low doorways of their houses, adjusting their mantillas. Rosina tripped by with the duenna. Don Basilio strode past with flapping skirts, pantomime-like cocked hat, cotton umbrella, and all. Smith looked at them all from over his balcony, like from a box at the opera. At the other end of the Place—Plaza de la Constitucion its name was—the French Consul, leaning over his eagle, was sleepily smoking a cigar and watching the church-goers pass by. Strumtumty, strum-tumty — tumty-strum, went the guitar, and presently—still like a scene at the play—the light darkened, the people looked up at the sky, and there came an artificial clap of thunder from the hill-top over the town, with a sudden storm of hail and lightning. Rosina set off scampering with her duenna. So did the priests; the young men with their bright red caps lounging at the corner of the street; the old man with his donkey; and the little grinning beggar-children.

Smith thought he, too, should like to see the inside of the church, which seemed to be looked upon as a safe refuge: every body was rushing in the same direction. He had not very far to go: up a short street, and along the Plaza, and then, after crossing a little wooden drawbridge, Smith found himself at the church door. He stooped and went in through a low Moorish-looking arch, and descended a short flight of black marble steps which led down into the aisle.

It seemed quite dark at first, except that the

tapers were flaring at the altar, where three unprepossessing-looking priests were officiating. By degrees Smith found that he was standing in a beautiful old Templar church, with arches, with red silk hangings, and a chequered marble floor, and a dark carved gallery from which some heads were peeping. The women were sitting and squatting on the floor with their shoes neatly ranged at their sides, and their babies dandling in their arms. The men were behind, nearer the door; and in the front row of all, grinning, showing their teeth, and plucking at his legs as he went by, Smith discovered the little company of persecuting boys and girls, pretending to bury their faces in their hands when he looked at them, and peeping at him through their wiry little fingers with shining malicious eyes.

The service came to an end; the storm passed away. Smith left the church with the children swarming at his heels, and found his guide waiting with the horses ready harnessed. They had no time to lose, the man said—the bill was paid. Smith sprang into the saddle, flung a handful of halfpence to the Moorish little bandits, and rode off as hard as he could go along the rough bridle-path.

It was very late before he got back. He dined by himself about ten o'clock, with a tired, shirt-sleeved waiter to attend upon him, and then he went and sat under the trees on the Cours, listening to the music and trying to make up his mind. Should he go to Bigorre? Yes; no; *un peu; beaucoup; pas du tout.* He changed his plans over and over again. About midnight, when the music and the lights were still alive, the people still drinking their coffee and lemonade in the soft starlit night, and chatting and humming all round about, Smith determined at last that he would stay for a day or two longer, and then go to Tarbes and on to Marseilles and to Italy. Having made out this scheme, he called a voiturier with a whip and jack-boots who happened to be passing, and asked him if he was engaged and what was his fare to St. Bertrand. Smith had a fancy to see the old place, which lies on the road to Tarbes. It also lies on the road to Bigorre, but Smith thought that he did not remember this. The guide was a Bigorre man and anxious to get there. He was willing enough to go to St. Bertrand. After that he should like to get home, he said. His horses wanted a rest. Smith came to a compromise with him at last. The tired horses were to take him to St. Bertrand, and then they were to make further arrangements.

Two roads cross the country which divides Luchon from Bigorre. One runs direct in noble undulations over hill-tops and mountain ranges. It goes bursting over the great Col d'Aspin, from whence you may see the world, like a sea, tossing and heaving at your feet, and trembling with the light upon a thousand hills; and then the highway plunges down into deep valleys, where the air is scented with pine-wood.

The other road winds by the plain and follows

T

the course of a flowing river, past villages sun-decked and vine-wreathed, but silent and deserted in their whiteness. A sad-faced woman looks from her cottage-door; a dark-headed boy comes skimming over the stones with his naked feet, and holds up his hand for alms; a traveller, resting on a heap by the dusty roadside, nods his head in token of weary fellowship. At last, as you still follow the road in the valley, with the low range on either side, you suddenly reach a great hill with the towers of a strong city rising from its summit. It dominates the landwaves, which seem flowing down from the mountains, and the great flat marshes which stretch away to the sea.

Smith chose the plain to return by, wishing, as I have said, to see St. Bertrand: he had crossed the mountain before, in the course of his travels. He went rolling along through the fresh morning air, with his head full of old sights and thoughts—very far away, hankerings and fancies which he had imagined safely buried in the Campagna or mouldering with the relics of his old Italian sight-seeing times. Along the banks of the river, crossing and recrossing many times from one side to another, through plains and sunny villages, they had come at last to St. Bertrand, the city on the hill. The driver, a surly fellow, hissed and cursed as the horses went stumbling up the steep ascent, straining and slipping in the blazing sun over bleached white stones. There were four bony horses, ornamented with bells and loaded with heavy harness. Smith reclined at his ease among the fusty cushions of the carriage; his courier clung nervously to the narrow railing on the box; Pierre, the driver, cracked his long whip, muttered horrible oaths between his teeth, gulped, choked, shrieked, with hideous jerks and sounds. They slowly climb the hill of St. Bertrand. Every thing seems to grow whiter and brighter as they mount. They reach the town at last there is an utter silence and look of abandonment; flowers are hanging over the walls and gables and postern-gates. They pass fountains of marble, stone casements, and turrets and balconies, all white, blazing, deserted, with geraniums hanging and flowering. They pass under an archway with carvings and emblazonments throwing deep shadows, by strange gables and corners and turrets, up a fantastic street. It was like a goblin city, so dreary, silent, deserted, with such strange conceits and ornaments at every corner.

The hotel was empty, too; one demure, sour visage came to the door to receive them. Yes, there was food prepared; the horses could be put up in the stables. A human voice seemed to break the enchantment, for I think until then Smith had almost expected to find a sleeping princess upon a bed, a king, a queen, a court, all dreaming and dozing inside this ancient palace: for the inn had been a palace, at some time or other perhaps inhabited by the ancient Bishops of St. Bertrand, or by some of the nobles whose escutcheons still hang on the gates of the city. There were two tables, both laid and spread in readiness, in the solemn old dining-room, with its white painted panels and carved chimney. Smith was amused to see a Murray lying on the white cloth nearest the window. Even here, in this forgotten end of the world, the wandering tribes of Britain had hoisted the national standard and hastened to secure the best place at the feast. There were three plates, three forks, three knives. Smith, dimly pursuing his morning fancy, and bewitched by the unreality and silence of all about him, thought that this was the place in which he should like to meet Esther again—if he was ever to meet her. Here, in this white, blinding silence, she might come like an apparition out of his dreams—come up the steep mediæval street, past the fountain, with her long dress—how well he remembered it—rippling over the stones, her slim straight figure standing in relief against the blazing sky. . . . "Cutlets—yes; and a chicken; and a bottle of St. Julien. . . ." This was to the waiting-woman, who asked him what he would like.

Geoffry walked out into the garden to wait until his cutlets should be ready, and he found an unkept wilderness, tangled and sweet with autumnal roses, and a carved stone terrace or loggia, facing a great beautiful landscape. As he leaned against the marble parapet, Smith, who still thought he was only admiring the view, imagined Esther walking up the street, coming nearer and nearer, approaching along the tangled walk through the rose-trees, and standing beside him at last on the terrace. It was a fancy, nothing more; it was not even a presentiment; all the beautiful world below shimmered and melted into greater and greater loveliness; an insect went flying and buzzing over the parapet and out into the clear atmosphere; a rose fell to pieces, and as the leaves tumbled to the ground one or two floated on to the yellow time-worn ledge against which Smith was leaning. No, he would not go to Bigorre; he said to himself he would turn his horses' heads, or travel beyond Bigorre, to some one of the other mountains—to Luz or St. Sauveur, or farther still, to Eaux Bonnes, in the heart of the Pyrenees. He pulled out his letter and read it again; this was all it said, in Lady Mary's cramped little hand:—

"B. de Bigorre.

"DEAR GEOFFRY—Some one has seen you somewhere in the Pyrenees; will you not take Bigorre on your way, and come and spend a few days with us? It would cheer my husband up to see you; his cough is troublesome still, though he is greatly better than when we left the rectory. There are one or two nice people in the place. I am sure you would spend a few pleasant days. We have the three Vulliameys, Mr. and Mrs. Penton, and Olga Halbert; that poor Mrs. Halbert, too, is with them; her children make great friends with ours. Mrs. Halbert tells us she knows you. She is very much

altered and shaken by her husband's death,
though one can not but feel that it must be more
a shock than a sorrow to her, poor woman. The
Pentons and Mrs. Halbert are at the hotel.
She says they find it comfortable. I know you
like being independent best, otherwise we have
a nice little room for you, and should much
prefer having you with us while you stay. The
children are flourishing, and I expect my sister
Lucy to join us in a few days. *Do* try and
come, and give us all a great deal of pleasure.

"Affectionately yours, MARY SMITH.

"P. S.—I shall send this to St. James's
Place on the chance that it may be forwarded
back again to you with your other letters."

Smith read the letter and tore it up absently,
and threw it on the ground. He would not go
to Bigorre; he was past the age of sentiment;
he would never marry; he did not want to see
Esther again and destroy his remembrance of
her, or make a fool of himself perhaps, and be
bound to a woman hardened by misfortune, by
long contact with worldly minds, by devotion
to an unworthy object. "How could she prefer Halbert to me?" Smith thought, with an
amused self-consciousness. Esther was a clever
woman—she had thought for herself: she needed a certain intellectual calibre of companionship. Halbert cultivated his whiskers; his best
aspirations were after Lady X and Y and Z and
their tea-parties; and then Smith wandered
away from poor Halbert, who was gone now, to
the lovely sight before him.

It was not so much the view as the beautiful
fires which were lighting it up. If color were
like music—if one could write it down, and
possess for good, the gleams of sudden sweetness, the modulation, the great bursting sym-
phonies of light thrilling from a million notes
at once into one great triumphal harmony: if
the passion of loveliness—I know no better
word—which seems all about us at times, could
be written down, one would need words that
should change and deepen and sweeten with
the reader's mood, and shift forever into combinations lovely and yet more lovely.

Smith was looking still with a heart full of
gratitude and admiration, when he heard a step
upon the gravel walk. He turned round to see
who was coming. Was this an enchanted city
he had come to? A tall slim figure of a woman in black robes was advancing along the gravel walk and coming to the overhanging terrace
where he was standing. Alas! it was no enchantment. The genii had not brought his
princess on their wings. It was no one he had
ever seen before—no sallow face with the sweet
bright look in it; it was only a handsome-look-
ing young woman, one of the thousands there
are in the world, with peach-red cheeks and
bright keen eyes, who glanced at him suspiciously. Two great black feathers were hanging
from her hat; her long silk gown rippled in
the sunshine, and her black silk cloak was fastened round her neck by a silver clasp.

It was a very charming apparition, Smith
thought, though it was not the one he had
hoped for—there was nothing gracious about
this well-grown young lady. This was no Esther—this was not a woman who would change
her mind a dozen times a day, who would be
weak and foolish and trustful always. Geoffry
was half repelled, half attracted by the keen determined face, the firm-moulded lines. He
might not have thought twice about her at
another time; but in this golden solitude and
Garden of Eden it almost seemed as if a companion was wanted. He had been contented
enough until now with a shadowy friend of his
own exorcising. The lady in black, after looking at the view for a second, turned round and
walked away again as deliberately as she had
come, and he presently followed her example
for want of something better to do. The hills
were still melting, roses were flushing and
scenting the air, insects floating as before; but
Smith, whose train of thought had been disturbed, turned his back upon all their loveliness and strolled into the house to ask if his
breakfast was ready.

Prim-face, who was busy at a great carved
cupboard, seemed amazed at the question.
"You have not seen the cathedral yet: travellers always go over the cathedral before the *déjeu-
ner*. We have had to catch and kill the fowl,"
in an aggrieved tone. "Encore vingt minutes—
n'est-ce pas, Auguste!" shrieks the woman suddenly, without budging from her place.

"Vingt minutes," repeats a deep voice from
somewhere or other behind the great cupboard,
and there was no more to be said on the subject.

Smith spent the twenty minutes during which
his chicken was grilling and his potatoes frizzling, in a great lofty cathedral. It stands on
the very summit of the hill, high above the town
and the surrounding plains: wide flights lead
to the great entrance, the walls and roof are
bare, but of beautiful and generous propor-
tions: lofty arches vault high overhead. The
sunshine, which seems weird and goblin in the
city, falls here with a more solemn light: slant
gleams flit across the marble pavement as the
great door swings on its hinges, and footfalls
echo in the distance. Smith seemed to recognize the place somehow—it looked familiar:
the rough beautiful arches, the vastness, the
desertion; no priests, no one praying, no glimmer of shrines and candles; only space, silence,
light from the large window, only a solemn figure of an abbot lying upon his marble bed with
a date of three hundred years ago.

Smith remembered dreaming of such a place
in his old home years and years before, when
he was a boy, and had never even heard Esther's
name. The abbot on his marble bed seemed
familiar, the placid face, the patient hands, the
dog crouching at his feet. A great gleam of
sun from a window overhead streaked and
lighted the marble. Smith sat down on the
step of the tomb and looked up at the great

window. A white pigeon with a beautiful breast shining in the sun was sitting upon the mullion. It sat for a time, and then it flew away with a sudden rush across the violet-blue sky. Smith did not move, but waited in a tranquil, gentle frame of mind, like that of a person who is dreaming beautiful dreams, nor had waited very long when he seemed to be conscious of people approaching, voices and footsteps coming nearer and nearer, until at last they were somewhere close at hand, and he overheard the following uninteresting conversation between two voices:

"Why don't they do it up with chintz if they are so poor? chintz costs next to nothing. I am sure that lily of the valley and ribbon pattern in my dressing-room seems as if it never would wear out. I was saying to Hudson only the other day, 'Really, Hudson, I think while we are away you must get some new covers for my dressing-room.'"

Here a second voice interrupted with— "Charles, do you remember any allusion to St. Bertrand in *Jamieson's Lives of the Saints?* I read the book very carefully, but I can not feel quite certain."

To which the first voice rejoined—"Why, Olga, I do wonder you don't remember. I think Charles has a very bad memory indeed. And so have I ; but *you* read so much."

Charles now spoke. "Here, Mira, look at this a-hm—a-interesting monument.—To the right, Mira, to the right. You are walking away from it."

"Dear me, Charles! what a droll creature. He puts me in mind of uncle John."

"I can not help thinking," Charles said impressively, "that this is the place Lady Kidderminster was describing at Axminster House. I am almost convinced of it."

Then Smith heard Charles saying rapidly and speaking his words all in a string as it were—

" Lady-Kidderminster-a-été-beaucoup-frappée-par-une-Cathédrale-dans-les-Pyrénées. Est-ce-qu'elle-a-passé-par-ici ? .... I am sure—I—a-beg your pardon.—I had not perceived—" and a stout consequential-looking gentleman, who was in the middle of his sentence, stumbled over Smith's umbrella, while Smith, half amused, half provoked, rose from his seat and seemed to the speaker to emerge suddenly, red beard and all, from the tomb. Mira gave a little scream, Olga looked amused.

"I trust I have not seriously injured—a-hm! any thing," said the gentleman ; "we were examining this—a—relic, and had not observed—" Smith made a little bow, and another to the beautiful apparition on the terrace, whom he recognized. Next to her stood another very handsome youngish lady, stout, fair, and grandly dressed, who graciously acknowledged his greeting, while Olga slightly tossed her head, as was her way when she thought herself particularly irresistible. Behind them the curé was waiting—a sad, heavy-featured man, in thick country shoes, whose shabby gown flapped against his legs as he walked with his head wearily bent. He only shrugged his shoulders at the many questions which were put to him. Such as, Why didn't they put in stained-glass windows? wasn't it very cold in winter? was he sure he didn't remember Lady Kidderminster? Leading the way, he opened a side-door, through which Smith saw a beautiful old cloister, with a range of violet hills gleaming through the arches. It was unexpected, and gave him a sudden thrill of pleasure.

"What a delightful place you have here," he said to the guide. "I think I should like to stay altogether."

"Not many people care to pass by this way now," said the curé. "It is out of the road ; they do not like to bring their horses up the steep ascent. Yes, it is a pretty *point de vue.* I come here of an evening sometimes."

"Extremely so," said Mira. "Olga, do you know I am so tired ? I am convinced that I want bracing. I wish we had gone to Brighton instead of coming to this hot place.—Charles, do you think the 'déjeûner' is ready ? I am quite exhausted," she went on, in the same breath.

"Would *ces dames* care to see the vestments ?" the curate asked, a little wistfully, seeing them prepare to go.

"Oh-a-merci, we are rather pressed for time," Charles was beginning, when Smith saw that the man looked disappointed, and said he should like to see them. Olga, as they called her, shook out her draperies, and told Charles they might as well go through with the farce, and Mira meekly towered after her husband and sister. These are odious people, poor Smith thought. The ladies are handsome enough, but they are like About's description of his two heroines: "L'une était une statue, l'autre une poupée." This statue seemed always complacently contemplating its own pedestal. In the *sacristie* there were only one or two relics and vestments to be seen, and a large book open upon a desk.

"People sometimes," said the curé, humbly shuffling and looking shyly up, "inscribe their names in this book, with some slight donation towards the repairs of the church."

"I thought as much," said Olga, while Charles pompously produced his purse and began fumbling about. Smith was touched by the wistful looks of the guide. This church was his child, his companion, and it was starving for want of food. He wrote his name— "Mr. Geoffry Smith"—and put down a couple of napoleons on the book, where the last entry was three months old, of two francs which some one had contributed. The others opened their eyes as they saw what had happened. The curé's gratitude and delight amply repaid Geoffry, who had more napoleons to spend than he could well get through. The pompous gentleman now advanced, and in a large, aristocratic hand inscribed—"Mr. and Mrs. Penton, of Penton ;" "Miss Halbert." And at the same time Mr. Penton glanced at the name over his own, and suddenly gleamed into life, in that

way which is peculiar to people who unexpectedly recognize a desirable acquaintance.

"Mr. Smith! I have often heard your
name. You—a—knew my poor brother-in-
law, Frank Halbert, I believe.—Mrs. Penton—
Miss Halbert.—A most curious and fortunate
chance—hm-a!—falling in with one another in
this out-of-the-way portion of the globe. Perhaps we may be travelling in the same direction? we are on our way to Bigorre, where we
rejoin our sister-in-law, Mrs. Frank Halbert."

Geoffry felt as if it was the finger of Fate interfering. He followed them mechanically out
into the street.

"How hot the sun strikes upon one's head.
Do you dislike it?—I do," said Mrs. Penton,
graciously, as they walked back to the hotel together. . . .

People say that as they live on, they find answers in life to the problems and secrets which
have haunted and vexed their youth. Is it so?
It seems as if some questions were never to be
answered, some doubts never to be solved.
Right and wrong seem to change and blend as
life goes on, as do the alternate hours of light
and darkness. Perhaps some folks know right
from wrong always and at all times. But there
are others weak and inconsistent, who seem to
live only to regret. They ask themselves with
dismay, looking back at the past—Was that me
myself? Could that have been me? That person going about with the hard and angry heart;
that person uttering cruel and unforgiving words;
that person thinking thoughts that my soul ab-
hors? Poor Esther! Often and often of late
her own ghost had come to haunt her, as it had
haunted Smith—sometimes in a girlish guise,
tender, impetuous, unworn and unsoiled by the
wayside wear, the thorns and the dust of life.
At other times—so she could remember herself
at one time of her life—foolish, infatuated, mad,
and blind—oh, how blind! Her dream had not
lasted very long; she awoke from it soon. It
was not much of a story. She was a woman
now. She was a girl when she first knew her
husband, and another who she once thought
would have been her husband. She had but
to choose between them. That was all her
story; and she took in her hand and then put
away the leaden casket with the treasure inside,
while she kept the glittering silver and gold for
her portion.

> "Some there be that shadows kiss;
> Some have but a shadow's bliss."

Poor Esther! her shadows soon fled, parted,
deepened into night; and long sad years succeeded one another: trouble and pain and hardness of heart, and bitter, bitter pangs of regret;
remorse of passionate effort after right, after
peace, and cruel failures and humiliations. No
one ever knew the life that Esther Halbert led
for the six years after she married. Once in
an agony of grief and humiliation she escaped to
her stepmother with her little girl. Lady Fanny pitied her, gave her some luncheon, talked

good sense. Old Colonel Olliver sneered, as
was his way, and told his daughter to go home
in a cab. He could not advise her remaining
with him, and, in short, it was impossible.

"You married Frank with your eyes open,"
he said. "You knew well enough what you
were about when you threw over that poor fellow
Smith, as if he had been an old shoe; and now
you must make the best of what you have. I am
not going to have a scandal in the family, and a
daughter without a husband constantly about the
house. I'll talk to Halbert and see if matters
can't be mended; but you will be disgraced if
you leave him, and you are in a very good position as you are. Injured wife, patient endurance
—that sort of thing—nothing could be better."

Esther, with steady eyes and quivering lips,
slowly turned away as her father spoke. Lady
Fanny, her stepmother, was the kindest of the
two, and talked to her about her children's welfare, and said she would drive her back in her
brougham. Poor Esther dazed, sick at heart;
she thought that if it were not for her Jack and
her Prissa she would go away and never come
back again. Ah! what a life it was; what a
weary delusion, even for the happiest—even for
those who obtained their heart's desire! She
had a great burst of crying, and then she was
better, and said meekly, Yes, she would go
home, and devote herself to her little ones, and
try to bear with Frank. And she made a vow
that she would complain no more, since this way
all that came to her when she told her troubles
to those who might have been a little sorry. Esther kept her vow. Was it her good angel that
prompted her to make it? Halbert fell, out
hunting, and was brought home senseless only
a few days after, and Esther nursed him tenderly and faithfully: when he moaned, she forgave and forgot every pain he had ever inflicted
upon her, every cruel word or doubt or suspicion. He never rallied; and the doctors looked graver and graver, until at last Frank Halbert died, holding his wife's hand in his.

The few first weeks of their married life,
these last sad days of pain and sufferings,
seemed to her all that she had left to her; all
the terrible time between she blotted out and
forgot as best she could, for she would clutch
her children suddenly in her arms when sickening memories overpowered her, and so forget
and forgive at once. For some time Esther
was shocked, shaken, nervous, starting at every
word and every sound, but by degrees she gained
strength and new courage. When she came to
Bigorre she was looking better than she had done
for years; and no wonder: her life was peaceful
now, and silent; cruel sneers and utterances had
passed out of it. The indignities, all the miseries
of her past years were over for ever; only their
best blessings, Jack and Prissa, remained to
her; and she prayed with all her tender mother's
heart that they might grow up different from
either of their parents, good and strong and wise
and upright—unlike her, unlike their father.

The Pentons, who were good-natured people

in their way, had asked her to come; and Esther, who was too lazy to say no, had agreed, and was grateful to them for persuading her to accompany them. She liked the place. The bells sounding at all the hours with their sudden musical cadence, the cheery stir, the cavalcades arriving from the mountains, the harnesses jingling, the country-folks passing and repassing, the convents tinkling, Carmes close at hand, Carmelites a little farther down the street —the streams, the pretty shady walks among the hills, the pastoral valley where the goats and the cattle were browsing—it was all bright and sunshine and charming. Little Prissa in her big sun-bonnet, and Jack helping to push the perambulator, went up every morning to the Salut, along a road with shady trees growing on either side, which led to some baths in the mountain. One day the children came home in much excitement, to say they had seen a horse in a chequed cotton dressing-gown, and with two pair of trowsers on. But their greatest delight of all was the Spaniard of Bigorre with his pack. Esther soon grew very tired of seeing him parading about in a dress something between a brigand and a circus-rider; but Prissa and Jack never wearied, and the dream of their outgoing and incoming was to meet him. Prissa's other dream of perfect happiness was drinking tea on the terrace at the Châlet with little Geoffry and Lucy and Lena Smith, where they all worshipped the Spaniard together, and told one another stories about the funny horse and the little pig that tried to eat out of Lena's hand. Their one trouble was that Mademoiselle Bouchon made them tell their adventures in French. At all events, they could *laugh* in English, and she never found it out. Lady Mary would come out smiling while the tea was going on, and nod her kind cap-ribbons at them all. She was a portly and good-humored person, who did foolish things sometimes, and was fond of interfering and trying to make people happy her own way. She had taken a fancy to Esther, and one day —ingenious Lady Mary—she said to herself, "I am sure this would do for poor Geoffry: he ought to marry. This is the very thing. Dear me, I wish he would come here for a day or two," and she went back into her room and actually wrote to him to come.

The two ladies went to the service of the Carmes that evening. It was the fashion to go and listen for the voice of one of the monks. There was a bustle of company rustling in; smart people were coming up through the darkening streets; old French ladies protected by their little maids, arriving with their "Heures" in their hands; lights gleamed in the windows here and there, and in the chapel of the convent a blaze of wax and wick, and artificial flowers, and triumphant music. It was a lovely voice, thrilling beyond the others, pathetic with beautiful tones of subdued passionate expression. The Carme who sang to them was a handsome young man, very pale, with a black crisp beard; his head overlooked the others as they came and

went with their flaming tapers in mystic processions. Was it something in the man's voice, some pathetic cadence which recalled other tones to which Esther had listened once in her life, and that of late years she had scarcely dared to remember? Was it chance, was it fate, was it some strange presentiment of his approach, which made Esther begin to think of Rome, and of Geoffry, and of the days when she first knew him, and of the time before she married? As she thought of old days she seemed to see Smith's kind blue eyes looking at her, and to hear his voice sounding through the music. How often she had longed to see him—how well she remembered him—the true heart, the good friend of her youth.

Esther's heart stirred with remembrances of things far far away from the convent and its prayers and fastings and penances. Penance and fastings and vigils—such things should be her portion, she thought, by rights; and it was with a pang of shame, of remorse, of bitter regret, and of fresh remorse for the pang itself, that she rose from her knees—the service over, the music silent, and wax-lights extinguished— and came out into the night with her friend. As they were walking up the street Lady Mary said quietly and unconsciously enough, though Esther started guiltily, and asked herself if she had been speaking her thoughts aloud—

"Mrs. Halbert, did you ever meet my husband's cousin, Jeff Smith? I hear he is in the Pyrenees; I am writing to him to come and stay with us, he is such a good fellow."

Esther, if she had learnt nothing else since the old Roman days, had learnt at least to control herself and to speak quietly and indifferently, though her eyes suddenly filled with tears and there came a strange choking in her throat. Her companions noticed nothing as Mrs. Halbert said, "Yes, she had known him at Rome, but that she had not seen him for years."

"Ah, then, you must renew your acquaintance," Lady Mary said; adding, abruptly, "Do you know, I hear a Carmelite is going to make her profession next week?—we must go. These things are horrible, and yet they fascinate me somehow."

"What a touching voice that was," said Esther. "It affected me quite curiously." To which Lady Mary replied,

"I remember that man last year; he has not had time to emaciate himself to a mummy. He sat next me at the table-d'hôte, and we all remarked him for being so handsome and pleasant, and for the quantities of champagne he drank. There was a little quiet dark man, his companion. They used to go out riding together, and sit listening to the music at the Thermes. There was a ball there one night, and I remember seeing the young fellow dancing with a beautiful Russian princess."

"Well?" said Esther, listening and not listening.

"Well, one day he didn't come to dinner, and the little dark man sat next me alone. I asked after my neighbor; heard he had left the place, but Marguerite—you know the handsome chambermaid—told me, under breath, that Jean had been desired to take the handsome gentleman's portmanteau down on a truck to the convent of the Carmes; a monk had received it at the garden-door, and that was all she knew. I am sure I recognized my friend to-night. He looked as if he knew me when he came round with the purse."

"Poor thing," said Mrs. Halbert, sighing. Esther came home to the hotel, flushed, with shining eyes, looking like she used to look ten years ago. She found Mrs. Penton asleep in the sitting-room, resting her portly person upon the sofa. Olga was nodding solemnly over a dubious French novel. Mr. Penton was taking a nap behind his *Galignani*—the lamp was low. It all looked inexpressibly dull and commonplace after the glimpses of other lives which she had had that night. She seemed lifted above herself somehow by the strains of solemn music, by memories of tenderest love and hopeless separation, by dreams of what might have been, what had been before now, of the devotion which had triumphed over all the natural longings and aspirations of life. Could it be that these placid sleepy people were of the same race and make as herself and others of whom she had heard? Esther crept away to the room where her children were sleeping in their little cots with faithful old Spicer stitching by the light of a candle. As the mother knelt down by the girl's little bed, a great burst of silent tears seemed to relieve her heart, and she cried and cried, she scarcely dared tell herself why.

Have you ever seen a picture painted in black and in gold? Black-robed saints, St. Dominic and others, on a golden glory, are the only instances I can call to mind, except an Italian painter's fancy of a golden-haired woman in her yellow damask robe, with a mysterious black background behind her. She had a look of my heroine, though Esther Halbert is an ugly woman, and the picture is the likeness of one of those beautiful fair-haired Venetians whose beauty (while people are still saying that beauty fades away and perishes) is ours after all the centuries, and has been the munificent gift of Titian and his compeers, who first discerned it, to the unknown generations that were yet to be born and to admire. As one looks at the tender face, it seems alive, even now, and one wonders if there is light anywhere for the yellow lady. Can she see into that gloom of paint more clearly than into the long gallery where the people are pacing and the painters are working at their easels?—or is she as blind as the rest of us? Does she gaze unconscious of all that surrounds her? Does she fancy herself only minute particles of oil and yellow ochre and coloring matter, never guessing that she is a whole, beautiful with sentiment, alive with feeling and harmony?

I dare say she is blind like the rest of us, as Esther was that Friday in July when she came hurrying through the midday sunshine, with her little son scampering beside her, hiding his head from the burning rays among the long folds of her black widow's dress.

At Bigorre, in the Pyrenees, there is one little spot where the sun's rays seem to burn with intenser heat—a yellow blaze of light amid black and sudden shade. It is a little *Place* leading to the Thermes. In it a black marble fountain flows, with a clear limpid stream, and a Roman inscription still renders grace for benefits received to the nymph of the healing waters. Arched gates with marble corner-stones, windows closed and shuttered, form three sides of the little square; on the fourth there is a garden behind an iron railing, where tall hollyhocks nod their heads, catalpas flower and scent the air, and great beds of marguérites and sad autumnal flowers lead to the flight of black marble steps in front of the house.

Esther, hurrying along, did not stop to look or to notice. She was too busy shielding and helping little blinded Jack to skurry across the burning desert, as he called it. They reached the shady street at last. Jack emerged from his mother's skirts, and Esther stopped, hesitated, and looked back across the place from which they had just come. The sun was blinding and burning, great dazzling patches were in her eyes, and yet— It was absurd; but she could not help thinking that she had seen some one as she crossed: a figure that she now seemed to *remember* seeing coming down the black marble steps of the house in the garden—a figure under an umbrella, which put her in mind of some one she had known. It was absurd: it was a fancy, an imagination; it came to her from the foolish thoughts she had indulged in of late. And yet she looked to make sure that such was the case; and, turning her head, she perceived in the distance a man dressed in white, as people dress in the Pyrenees, walking under a big umbrella down the opposite street, which leads to the Baths. Esther smiled at her own fancies. An umbrella! why should not an umbrella awaken associations?

"Come along, mamma," said Jack, who had seen nothing but the folds of his mother's dress, and who was not haunted by associations as yet. "Come along, mamma; don't stop and think."

Esther took Jack's little outstretched paw into her long slim fingers, but as she walked along the shady side of the street—past the Moorish shop-fronts arched with black marble, with old women gossiping in the interiors, and while Jack stared at the passers-by, at a monk plodding by with sandalled feet, at a bath-woman balancing an enormous machine on her head, or longed as he gazed at the beautiful peaches and knitted wool-work piled on the shop-ledges, Esther went dreaming back to ten years before, wishing, as grown-up people wish, not for the good things spread before them, but for those of years long gone by—for the fruit long since eaten, or rotten, or planted in the ground.

"Mammy, there's the Spaniard. Oh! look at his legs," said Jack, "they are all over ribbons." And Esther, to please him, smiled and glanced at a bandy-legged mountebank disposing of bargains to two credulous Britons.

"Why, there's uncle Penton come back," Jack cried in great excitement; "he is buying muffetees. Mammy, come and see what he has got," cried Jack, trying to tug away his hand.

"Not now, dear," said Esther. The slim fingers closed upon Jack's little hand with too firm a grasp for him to escape, and he trudges on perforce.

They had almost reached the hotel where they lived by this time. The great clock-tower round which it is built serves as a landmark and beacon. The place was all alive—jangling and jingling; voices were calling to one another, people passing and repassing along the wooden galleries, horses clamping in the courtyard. A riding-party had just arrived; yellow, pink, red-capped serving-women were hurrying about, showing guests to their chambers or escorting them across the road to the dependencies of the house.

As Esther and her little boy were walking along the wooden gallery which led to her rooms, they met Hudson, Mrs. Penton's maid, who told them with a sniff that her mistress was in the drawing-room.

"Was Mrs. Penton tired after her journey last night?" Esther asked. "I was sorry not to be at home to receive her, but I did not expect you till to-day."

"No wonder she's exhausted," said Hudson; "not a cup of tea have we 'ad since we left on Tuesday-week. They wanted me to take some of their sloppy things. I shan't be sorry to see Heaton Place again."

Hudson was evidently much put out, and Esther hurried to the sitting-room, where she found Mrs. Penton lying down as usual, and Olga, in a state of excitement, altering the feathers in her hat.

"How d'ye do, dear?" said Mrs. Penton. "We are come back again."

"We have had a most interesting excursion," said Olga, coming up to kiss her sister-in-law. "I wish you had cared to leave the children, Esther. You might have visited the Lac d'Oo, and that most remarkable ruin, St. Bertrand de Comminges. In *Jamieson's Lives of*—"

"We met such a nice person," interrupted Mrs. Penton. "He came to Bigorre with us in another carriage, but by the same road. He knows you, Esther, and he and Olga made great friends. They got on capitally over the cathedral, and he kindly fetched the Murray for us. We had left it on the table in the *salle-à-manger*, and were really afraid we had lost it." And Mrs. Penton rambled on for a whole half hour, unconscious that no one was listening to her.

Esther had turned quickly to Olga, and asked who this was who knew her.

"Oh, I dare say you don't remember the name," said Olga, rather consciously. "Smith—Mr. Smith of Garstein. He told me he had known you at Rome, before he came into his property."

"Did he say that?" said Esther, flushing a little.

"Or before you married, I really don't remember," said Olga. "We had a great deal of conversation, and persuaded him to come back to Bigorre."

"It's so hot at twelve o'clock," Mrs. Penton was going on; "and parasols are quite insufficient. Are you fond of extreme heat, Esther? Charles says that Lady Kidderminster, summer and winter, always carries a fan in her pocket. They are very convenient when they double up, and take less—"

"What sort of looking person is Mr. Smith?" Esther asked, with a little effort.

"Distinguished-looking, certainly: a long red beard, not very tall, but broadly built, and a very pleasant gentlemanlike manner. You shall see him at the table-d'hôte to-day; he promised to join us. In fact," said Olga, "he proposed it himself."

"I heard him," said Mrs. Penton, placidly. "Olga, I think you have made another conquest. I remember," etc.

Poor Esther could not wait any longer to hear Mrs. Penton's reminiscences, or Olga's self-congratulations; she went away quickly with Jack to her own room, and got her little Prissa into her lap, and made her put her two soft arms round her neck and love her. "Mamma, why are you crying?" said Jack; "we are both quite well, and we have been very good indeed, lately. Madame Bouchon says I am her *petty marry*. I shan't marry her, though. I shall marry Lena when I am a man."

Esther dressed for dinner in her black gauze gown, and followed the others to her usual place at the long crowded table. Her hands were cold, and she clasped them together, reminding herself by a gentle pressure that she must be quiet and composed, and give no sign that she remembered the past. She no longer wore her widow's cap, only a little piece of lace in her hair, in which good old Spicer took a pride as she pinned up the thick braids. Esther's gray eyes were looking up and down a little frightened and anxiously: but there was no one she had ever seen before, and she sat down with a sigh of relief; only in another minute, somehow, there was a little stir, and Olga said—"Esther, would you make room?" and popped down beside her; and then Mrs. Halbert saw that her sister-in-law was signing to some one to come into the seat next beyond her.

Esther had been nervous and excited, but she was suddenly quite herself again. And as Smith took his place, he bent forward, and their eyes met, and then he put out his hand. "Is it my old Esther?" he thought, with a thrill of secret delight; while Esther, as she gave him her slim fingers, said to herself—"Is this my old friend?"—and she looked wistfully to see whether she could read his kind, loyal heart, stamped in his face as of yore. They were both quite young people again for five minutes; Olga attributed the laughter and high spirits of her neighbor to the charms of her own conversation. Esther said not one word, did not eat, did not drink, but was in a sort of dream.

After dinner they all got up, and went and stood in one of the wooden galleries, watching the lilac and gold as it rippled over the mountains, the Bedat, the Pic du Midi.

And so this was all, and the long-looked-for meeting was over. Esther thought it was so simple, so natural, she could hardly believe that this was what she had hoped for and dreaded so long. There was Smith, scarcely changed—a little altered in manner perhaps, with a beard which improved him, but that was all. All the little tricks of voice and of manner, so familiar once, were there; it was himself. She was glad, and yet it was not all gladness. Why did he not come up to his old friend? Why did he not notice or speak to her? Why did he seem so indifferent? Why did he talk so much to the others, so little to her? Mrs. Halbert was confused, disappointed, and grieved. And yet it was no wonder. She thought that of all people she had least right to expect much from him. She was leaning over the side of the gallery, Olga stood next to her in her white dress, with the light of the sunset in her raven black hair, and Smith was leaning against one of the wooden pillars and talking to Olga. He glanced from the raven black hair to the gentle bent head beyond. But he went on talking to Olga. Esther felt a little lonely, a little deserted. She was used to the feeling, but she sighed, and turned away with a suppressed yet impatient movement from the beautiful lilac glow. A noisy, welcome comfort was in store for her. With a burst of childish noise and laughter, Prissa and Jacky came rushing up the gallery, and jumped upon her with their little eager arms wide open.

"Come for a walk, a little, little short walk, please mammy," said Jack. And Esther kissed him, and said yes, if he would fetch her hat and her gloves and her shawl.

As she was going, Smith came up hesitating, and said, not looking her full in the face—

"I had a message from my cousin, to beg you to look in there this evening. Miss Halbert has kindly promised to come." And Esther, looking up with a reproachful glance (so he thought), answered very quietly she would try to come after her walk. He watched her as she walked away down the long gallery with her children clinging to her side; with all the sunset lights and shadows falling upon them as they went. "What a pretty picture it makes," he said to Miss Halbert.

"I'm so glad you think Esther nice-looking," said Olga. "It is not every body who does. Shall we take a stroll towards the music, Mr. Smith? . . . ."

Esther had no heart for the music and company, and wandered away into a country road. All the fields of broad Indian-corn leaves were glowing as the three passed along: low bright streaks lay beyond the western plains, and a still evening breeze came blowing and gently stirring the flat green leaves. Jacky and Prissa were chattering to one another. Esther could not speak very much; her heart was too full. Was she glad—was she sad? What had she expected? Was this the meeting she had looked for so long? "He might have spoken one word of kindness, he might have said something more than that mere How do you do? Of course he was indifferent—how could it be otherwise? but he might have shammed a little interest," poor Esther thought; "only a very little would have satisfied me."

It was quite dark when she reached Lady Mary's, after seeing her children to bed. Olga, and Mr. Penton, and Smith were there already, and Lady Lucy was singing, when Esther came into the great, bare, dark room. The young lady was singing a little French song in the dimness, with a pathetic, pleasant tune— "Si tu savais," its name was. She gave it with charming expression, and when she had finished, they were all silent for a moment or two, until Lady Mary began to bustle about and to pour out the tea.

"Take this to Mrs. Halbert, Geoffry," she said, "and tell her about my scheme for to-morrow, and persuade her to come."

Smith brought the tea as he was bid.

"We all want to go over to Grippe, if you will come too," he said.

He looked down kindly at her as he spoke, and the poor foolish woman flushed up with pleasure as she agreed to join them. She was sorry afterwards when she, and Olga, and Mr. Penton walked home together through the dark streets.

"I wonder whether Mr. Smith means to join all our excursions," said Miss Halbert. "I just mentioned my wish to see Grippe, and he jumped at it directly."

Esther felt a chill somehow as Mr. Penton answered—

"Certainly, I—a—remarked it, Olga; you-a-are not—perhaps aware that you have attractions—to a—no common degree. Mr. Smith has certainly—a—discovered them."

Poor Esther! it seemed hard to meet her old friend at last, only to see how little he remembered her; and yet she thought, "All is as it should be; and with my Jacky and my Prissa to love, I am not to be pitied." Only, there was a strange new ache in her heart next morning, when they all assembled after the early breakfast; she could not feel cheery and unconscious like Lady Mary, or conscious and flattered like Olga. The children in their clean cotton frocks were in raptures, and so far Esther was happy.

The road to Grippe is along a beautiful mossy valley, with a dashing stream foaming over the pebbles, and with little farms and homesteads dotting the smooth green slopes. Olga and Smith were on horseback; Penton was also bumping majestically along upon a huge bay mare ; Esther and Lady Mary, and the Smith children and her own, were packed away into a big carriage with Mdlle. Bouchon, and little Geoffry Smith on the box. The children were in a state of friskiness which seriously alarmed the two mammas. They seemed to have at least a dozen little legs apiece. Their screams of laughter reached the equestrians, who were keeping up a somewhat solemn conversation upon the beauties of nature, and the cultivation of Indian corn : Geoffry wondered what all the fun might be, and Olga remarked that the children were very noisy, and that Esther certainly spoilt little Jack.

"Lady Kidderminster strongly advises his being sent to a preparatory school," said Penton, with a jog between each word ; while Smith looked up at the blue sky, then down into the green valley, and forgot all about his two companions, trying to catch the tones of the woman he had loved.

The châlet was a little rough unfinished place at the foot of the Pie, where people come to drink milk out of clean wooden bowls : the excursionists got down, and the horses were put up. The whole party crowded round the wood fire, and peeped at the rough workmen and shepherds who were playing cards in the next compartment—room it could not be called, for the walls were only made of bars of wood at a certain distance from each other. The children's delight at seeing all over the house at once was unbounded. Jacky slipped his hand between the wooden bars, and insisted on shaking hands with a great rough road-maker in a sheepskin, who smiled kindly at the little fellow's advances.

Lady Mary was very much disappointed and perplexed to see the small result of her kindly schemes. It was unbelievable that Geoffry should prefer that great, uninteresting, self-conscious Miss Halbert, to her gentle and tender little widow ; and yet it was only too evident. What could be the reason of it? She looked from one to the other. Esther was sitting by the fire on a low wooden stool. She seemed a little sad, a little drooping. The children were laughing about her as usual ; and she was holding a big wooden bowl full of milk, from which they sipped when they felt inclined. The firelight just caught the golden tints in her brown thick hair ; her hat was on the floor at her feet ; little Prissa—like her, and not like her—was peeping over her shoulder. It was a pretty picture : the flame, the rough and quaint simplicity of the place, seemed to give it a sort of idyllic grace. As for Smith, he was standing at the paneless window looking out at the view ; all the light was streaming through his red beard. It was a straight and well-set figure, Lady Mary thought ; he looked well able to take care of himself, and of her poor gentle Esther too. He was abstracted—evidently thinking of something besides the green valleys and pastures—could it, could it

be that odious affected woman stuck up in an attitude in the middle of the room who was the object of his dreams ?

An odd jumble of past, present, and future was running through Geoffry's mind, as he looked out of the hole in the wall, and speculated upon what was going to happen to him here in this green pasture-land by the side of the cool waters. Were they waters of comfort—was happiness his own at last ? somewhat sadly he thought to himself that it was not now what it would have been ten years ago. He could look at the happiest future with calmness. It did not dazzle and transport him as it would have done in former times—he was older, more indifferent : he had seen so many things cease and finish, so many fancies change, he had awakened from so many vivid dreams, that now perhaps he was still dreaming ; life had only become a light sleep, as it were, from which he often started and seemed to awaken. Even Esther . . . . what did it all mean ? did he love her less now that he had seen her, and found her unchanged, sweeter, if possible—and he could not help thinking it—not indifferent ? Would the charm vanish with the difficulties, as the beauty of a landscape ends where the flat and prosperous plains begin ? He did not think so —he thought so—he loved her—he mistrusted her ; he talked to Olga, and yet he could not keep his eyes from following Esther as she came and went. All she said, all she did, seemed to him like some sort of music which modulates and changes from one harmonious thing to another. A solemn serenity, a sentiment of wordless emotion was hers, and withal, the tender waywardness and gentle womanliness which had always seemed to be part of her. She was not handsome now, any more than she had ever been—the plain lines—the heavy hair—the deepset eyes were the same—the same as those eyes Smith could remember in Roman gardens, in palaces with long echoing galleries, looking at him through imploring tears on the Pincian Hill. They had haunted him for seven years since he first caught the trick of watching to see them brighten. Now, they brightened when the two little dark-headed children came running to her knee. Raphael could find no subject that pleased him better. Smith was no Raphael, but he, too, thought that among all the beautiful pictures of daily life there is no combination so simple, so touching as that of children who are clinging about their mother. And these pictures are to be seen everywhere and in every clime and place ; no galleries are needed, no price need be paid ; the background is of endless variety, the sun shines, and the mother's face brightens, and all over the world, perhaps, the children come running into her arms. White arms or dusky, bangled or braceleted, or scarred with labor, they open, and the little ones, clasped within loving walls, feel they are safe.

Quite oblivious of some observation of Miss Halbert's, Smith suddenly left his window and walked across to the fire, and warmed his hands, and said some little words to Esther, who was still sitting on her low seat. She was hurt and annoyed by his strange constraint and distance of manner. She answered coldly, and got up by a sudden impulse, and walked away to where Lady Mary was standing cutting bread-and-butter for the children. "Decidedly," thought the elder lady, "things are going wrong. I will ask Geoffry to-night what he thinks of my widow." "I am a fool for my pains," Geoffry thought, standing by the fire, "and she is only a hard-hearted flirt after all."

He was sulky and out of temper all the way back. In vain did Olga ransack her brain, and produce all her choicest platitudes for his entertainment. In vain Penton recalled his genteelest reminiscences. Smith answered civilly, it is true, but briefly and constrainedly. He was a fool to have come, to have fancied that such devotion as his could be appreciated or understood by a woman who had shown herself once already faithless, fickle, unworthy. Smith forgot, in his odd humility and mistrust of himself, that he too had held back, made no advance, kept aloof, and waited to be summoned.

Geoffry had the good habit of rising early, and setting out for long walks across the hills before the great heat came to scorch up all activity. The water seemed to sparkle more brightly than later in the day. The flowers glistened with fresh dew. Opal morning lights, with refractions of loveliest color, painted the hills and brooks, the water-plants, the fields where the women were working already, and the slippery mountain-sides where the pine-trees grew, and the flocks and goats with their tinkling bells were grazing. It was a charming medley of pastoral sights and scent and fresh air; shadows trembling and quivering, birds fluttering among the green, clear-cut ridges of the hills, the water bubbling among reeds and creeping plants and hanging ferns, among which beautiful dragon-flies were darting. Smith had been up to the top of the Bedat, and was coming down into civilized life again, when he stopped for an instant to look at the bubbling brook which was rushing along its self-made ravine, some four or five feet below the winding path; a field lay beyond it, and farther still, skirting the side of a hill, the pretty lime-tree walk which leads to the baths in the mountain. Smith, who had been thinking matters over as he stumbled down the steep pathway, and settling that it was too late—she did not care for him—he had ceased caring for her—best go, and leave things as they were—suddenly came upon a group which touched and interested him, and made him wonder whether, after all, prudence and good sense were always the wisest and the most prudent of things. In the middle of the stream, some thousand years ago, a great rock had rolled down from the heights above, and sunk into the bed of the stream, with the water rushing and bubbling all round it, and the water-lilies floating among the ripples. . . . Perched on the rock, like the naiad of the stream, was

Esther, with Jacky and Prissa clinging close to her, and sticking long reeds and water-leaves into her hair. The riverkin rushed away, twisting and twirling and disappearing into green. The leaves and water-plants swayed with the ripples, the children wriggled on their narrow perch, while Esther, with a book in her hand, and a great green umbrella, looked bright, and kind, and happy.

"Cousin Jeff, cousin Jeff!" cried little Jack, in imitation of the little Smiths, "come into the steamer, there's lots of room."

"How d'ye do?" said his mother, still laughing.

"How d'ye do, Mrs. Undine?" said Smith, brightening and coming to the water's edge.

As Smith walked back to his breakfast, he thought to himself—"If she would but give me one little sign that she liked me, I think—I think I could not help speaking."

And Lady Mary, who had her little talk out with her cousin after breakfast, discovered, to her great surprise, that what she had thought of as a vague possibility some day, very far off, was not impossible, and might be near at hand after all. She did not say much to Smith, and he did not guess how much she knew of all that was passing in his mind. "He will go away, he will never come forward unless Esther meets him half-way," the elder lady thought to herself, as he left the room; and she longed to speak to Esther, but she could not summon courage, though opportunity was not wanting.

They were all standing in the balcony of the chälet that very afternoon, watching the people go by: but first one child went away, then another, and at last Lady Mary and Esther were left alone. "Look at that team of oxen dragging the great trunks of the trees," said Lady Mary; "how picturesque the peasant people are in their mountain dress!"

"The men look so well in their *bérets*," Esther said; "that is a fine-looking young fellow who is leading the cart. There is Mr. Smith crossing the street—he would look very well in a *béret*, with his long red beard."

"Certainly he would," said Lady Mary; and then she suddenly added, "Esther, would you do me a favor? You have been talking of going to the fair at Tarbes to-morrow. I shall be obliged to stay at home with my husband and Lucy. Would you bring Geoffry a *béret*, and give it to him, and make him wear it? I know you will if I ask you."

"A red, or a blue one?" said Esther, smiling.

"The nicest you can get," said Lady Mary. "Thank you very much indeed."

Lady Kidderminster, who must have employed her time well while she was in the Pyrenees, "had been very much struck by Tarbes," Mr. Penton declared. "It is pleasantly situated," Murray says, "on the clear Adour, in the midst of a fertile plain in full view of the Pyrenees. Public walks contribute to the public health and recreation. The market-people, in their various costumes, are worth seeing."

Geoffry Smith received a short note from Mrs. Penton two mornings after the Grippe expedition. It ran as follows:—

"DEAR MR. SMITH—Mr. Penton is planning an excursion to Tarbes to-day. We start at two, so that we may not miss our lunch, as it is not safe to trust to chance for it, and we should be much pleased for you to join us after, but in case of rain we should give it up. Unfortunately, there appears no chance of any thing so refreshing. Sincerely yours,

"MIRA PENTON."

To which Smith, who was rather bewildered, briefly answered that he should be delighted to join them at the station at two. The station was all alive with country-folks, in their quaint pretty dresses, *bérets*, red caps and blue-brown hoods, and snooded gay-colored kerchiefs, and red cloaks like ladies' opera-cloaks. The faces underneath all these bright trappings were sad enough, with brown wistful eyes, and pinched worn cheeks. Ruskin has written of mountain gloom and mountain glory, and in truth the dwellers among the hills seem to us, who live upon the plain, sad and somewhat oppressed.

Smith looked here and there for his party, and discovered, rather to his dismay, only Olga, her sister and her brother-in-law, sitting on a bench together. Then Esther had not come, after all? He felt inclined to escape and go back to the town, but Olga caught sight of him, and graciously beckoned.

"Mrs. Halbert is not coming, I am afraid," said Smith, shaking hands.

"Esther, do you mean?" asked Mrs. Penton. "She was here a minute ago. Jacky took her to look at a pig.—Was it a pig or a goat, Olga? I didn't notice."

Mrs. Penton's naïve remarks gave Smith a little trouble sometimes, and he could not always suppress a faint amusement. Fortunately Esther came up at this moment, and he could smile without giving offense.

Esther at one time had not meant to come, but she could not resist the children's entreaties, or trust them to the Pentons alone. She was weary and dispirited; she had passed a wakeful, feverish night. How or when or where it began, she did not know, but she was conscious now that in her heart of hearts she had looked to meet Geoffry again some day, and hoped and believed that he would be unchanged. But she now saw that it was not so—he liked her only as he liked other people, with that kindly heart of his—no thought of what had been, occurred to him. He might be a friend, a pleasant acquaintance, but the friend of old, never, never again. How foolish she had been, how unwomanly, how forward. Even at seven-and-twenty Esther could blush like a girl to think how she had thought of Geoffry. She whose heart should be her children's only; she who had rejected his affection when it might have been hers; she who had been faithless and

selfish and remorseful so long—she was glad almost to suffer now, in her self-anger and vexation. In future she thought she would try to be brave and more simple; she would love her darlings and live for them only; and perhaps some day it might be in her power to do something for him—to do him some service—and when they were very old people she might tell him one day how truly she had been his friend all her life.

The sun was blazing and burning up every thing. The train stopped at a bridge, and they all got down from their carriages, and set off walking towards the market. Squeak, chatter, jingle of bells, screaming of babies, pigs and pigs and pigs; pretty gray oxen, with carts yoked to their horns, priests, a crowd assembled round an old woman with a sort of tripod, upon which you placed your foot for her to blacken and smarten your shoes; mantillas, green and red umbrellas, rows of patient-looking women, with sad eyes, holding their wares in their hands—scraggy fowls, small little pears, a cabbage, perhaps brought from over the mountain, a few potatoes in a shabby basket;—the scarcity and barrenness struck Smith very sadly. Esther was quite affected; she was emptying her purse and putting little pieces right and left into the small thin hands of the children. They passed one stall where a more prosperous-looking couple—commerçants from Toulouse—were disposing of piles of blue and red Pyrenean caps. Esther stopped and called Jack to her, and tried a small red *béret* on his dark curly head, and kissed her little son as she did so. She had not seen Smith, who was close behind her with Olga, and who smiled as he watched her performance. Miss Halbert, after leaving the railway-carriage, had complained of fatigue, and taken poor Geoffry firmly but gently by the arm, with a grasp that it was impossible to elude. Esther scarcely noticed them: she walked on with her children as usual, and her motherly heart was melting over the little wan babies, whose own mothers found it so hard a struggle to support them. They were lying in the vegetable-baskets on the ground, or slung on to their mothers' backs, and staring with their dark round eyes. Some of the most flourishing among them had little smart caps, with artificial flowers, tied under their chins. After buying Jack's *béret*, Mrs. Halbert seemed to hesitate, and then making up her mind she asked for another somewhat larger, which she paid for, and she turned to Smith with one of her old bright looks and gave it him, saying—

"I think you would look very well in a *béret*, Mr. Smith—don't you like a blue one best?"

Smith wore his *béret* all day; but Olga the inevitable held him, and would not let him go. Esther thought it a little hard, only she was determined *not* to think about it. They wandered for hours through the bare burning streets. There seemed to be no shade: the brooks sparkled, bright blazing flowers grew in gardens, the houses were close shuttered, scarcely any one was to be seen; little bright-plumaged birds came and drank at the streams, and flew away stirring the dust. The children got tired and cross and weary; the elders' spirits sank. Some one, standing at a doorway, told them of a park, which sounded shady and refreshing, and where they thought they would wait for their train. The road lay along a white lane with a white wall on either side, and dusty poplars planted at regular intervals. Esther tried to cheer the children, and to tell them stories as well as she could in the clouds of dust. Mrs. Penton clung to her husband, Olga hung heavily upon Geoffry's aching arm. . . . They reached the gates of the park at last. It was an utter desolation inclosed behind iron railings—so it seemed, at least, to the poor mother: ragged shrubs, burning sun, weeds and rank grass growing along the neglected gravel walks. There was a great white museum or observatory in the middle to which all these gravel paths converged; and there was—yes, at last! there was a gloomy-looking clump of laurel and fir-trees, where she thought she might perhaps find some shade for Jack and for Prissa. As she reached the place, it was all she could do not to burst out crying, she was so tired, so troubled, and every minute the dull aching at her heart seemed to grow worse and worse. Poor Esther! The others came up and asked her if she would not like to see the view from the observatory; but she shook her head, and said she was tired, and should stay where she was with Prissa, and they all went away and left her. One French lady went by in her slippers, with a faded Indian scarf and an old Leghorn hat, discoursing as she went to some neglected-looking children—

"Savez-vous, ma fille, que vous faites des grimaces; ce n'est pas joli, mon enfant, il faut vous surveiller, mon Hélène. Les grimaces ne se font pas dans la bonne société. . . . Le parc est vaste," she continued, changing the subject; her voice dwindled away into the arid, burning distance, and the desolation seemed greater than ever. . . . It seemed to Esther as if hours and hours had passed since the others had left her. . . . Prissa was languidly listening to the story poor Esther was still trying to tell.

"Why don't you make it more funny, mamma? You say the same things over and over. I don't like this story at all," said Prissa.

"I have some good news for you," said Smith, cheerfully, appearing from behind the laurels. "Mrs. Halbert, we have only just time to catch the train. Come, Jack, I'm going to be your horse; get up on my back," and Geoffry set off running with the delighted Jack, just as Olga appeared in search of him.

Esther and Prissa set off running too, and the Pentons followed as best they could.

The little station was again all alive and crowded by peasants and countrywomen, Spanish bandits with their packs, three English tourists in knickerbockers. Smith met them with Jack capering at his side, and swinging by his new friend's hand—

"I have taken the tickets," he said. "Thank goodness, we have done with Tarbes. What a horrible hole it is."

"I am surprised," Penton remarked, "that Lady Kidderminster should have had such a high opinion of this—a—position. She particularly mentioned an amphitheatre of which I can gain no information."

"Oh, dear! we shall never get in in time for the table-d'hôte," faintly gasped Mrs. Penton, sinking into a seat, "and the dinner will be over."

The benches were full, and they were all obliged to disperse here and there as they could find places. Esther perched herself upon a packing-case once more, with little Prissa half asleep on her knee. What a dreary day she had spent—she gave a sigh of relief to think it was over.

"Have you room here for Jack?" said Geoffry, coming up. "He won't own he is tired."

"Come, my son," said Esther, putting her arm round the boy, and pulling him up beside her. "You have been very good to Jack, Mr. Smith," she said, with an upward look of her clear eyes.

Smith looked at her.

"It seems very strange," he said, with a sudden emotion, "to meet you again like this. I sometimes wonder whether we are indeed you and me, or quite different people."

"I thought," said Esther, "you had forgotten that we had ever been friends, Mr. Smith."

"I thought you had forgotten it," said Smith, very crossly. There was a jar in his voice—there was a mist before her eyes. She was tired, vexed, overdone. Poor Esther suddenly burst into tears.

"My dear, my dear, don't cry," said Smith. "What can I say to beg your pardon? you should have known me better—you . . ."

"I can not understand about that amphitheatre," said Mr. Penton, coming up. "Murray, you see, does not allude to it."

"Why don't you go and ask the man at the ticket-office?" said Smith authoritatively, and Penton, rather bewildered, obeyed.

"I was a little afraid of you," said Smith, when I first saw you. I tried to keep away, but I could not help myself and came. I should have gone to the end of the world if you had been there. I have never changed—never forgotten. I love you as I have always loved you. Dear Esther, say something to me; put me out of this horrible suspense—"

"What a fearful crowd; how it does crush one," said Mrs. Penton, suddenly appearing. "Can you tell me where Charles has hidden himself? He put my eau-de-Cologne in his pocket, and really in this crowd. . . ."

Esther could not answer. She was bending over Prissa, and trying to hide her tears. Smith politely pointed out the ticket-office to Mrs. Penton, and then, with great gravity, turned his back upon the lady, and took Esther's hand, and said with his kind voice, "Dear Esther, once you used not be afraid of telling me what you thought. Won't you speak to me now? Indeed I am the same as I was then."

"And I am not the same?" said Esther, smiling, with her sweet face still wet with tears; and with a tender Esther-like impulse she took her children's two little hands and put them into Geoffry's broad palm.

Geoffry understood her, though he did not know all she meant. The Pentons joined them again, and the train came up, and the others wearily sank into their places, but Mrs. Halbert's fatigue was gone. All the way back neither Smith nor Esther spoke one word to each other. The sun was setting; all the land was streaming with light; the stars were beginning to shine behind the hills when they got back to Bigorre.

"Shall you be too tired to come for a walk after dinner?" said Smith, as he left Esther at the door of the inn; and in the evening he came for her; and, though Olga looked puzzled and not over-pleased, Esther put on her hat, and said,

"I am ready, Mr. Smith." And they went out together without any explanation.

They went up the pretty lime-tree walk which leads to the baths of the Salut. People were sitting in the dark on the benches talking in low evening whispers. Priests were taking their recreation, and pacing up and down in groups. From the valley below came an occasional tinkle of goats' bells, a fresh smell of wild thyme, a quizzing of crickets. The wain was moving over the hillside, the lights twinkled from the houses in the town; and Smith and Esther talked and talked, counting over the fears, the doubts, and the perplexities of the last few days. Now, for the first time, Esther felt a comfort and security which had never been hers before, —not even in the first early days of her marriage; not since the time when she bade Smith farewell on the Pincio. It seemed to her now as if all care for the future, all bewilderment and uncertainty, were over. It was all real to her—vivid, overwhelming. Here was the faithful friend once more ready to do battle for her with the difficulties of life: ready to shield, and to serve, and encourage to decide—to tell her what was right; and poor Esther had long felt that to her decision was like a great pain and impossibility. But here was Smith to advise, and it seemed to her as if troubles and difficulties became like strong places now that he was there. His manner of looking at life was unlike that of the people among whom she had been living: he seemed to see things from a different level, and yet she felt as if he only saw clearly, and that every thing he said was right and true. Some people, as I have said, seem by intuition to see only truth and right; others must needs work out their faith by failing and sorrow. They realize truth by the pain of what is false, honor through dishonor, right by wrongs repented of with bitter pangs. And Esther had long felt that this was her fate. She did not realize all that she understood later—only she felt it somehow; she drifted into a peaceful calm; she seemed suddenly and unawares to be gliding through still waters after the tempest, and a thankful song of praise went up from her heart.

When she awoke in the morning she knew that he was near at hand; she heard his kind voice, and the children's prattle down in the courtyard below. Later in the day he would come up to see her, and they talked over old days, and the new days seemed to shine with a sudden gleam now that he had come into them; the dull hours went more swiftly, the sky seemed brighter; evening came full of sweet tones, mysterious lights, and peace and perfume; people passing by seemed strolling, too, in a golden beatitude. They too, Esther fancied, surely must feel the sweetness and depth of the twilight. The morning came with a bright flash, not dawning with a great weight of pain and listlessness as before. In the hot blaze of the mid-day sun Geoffry would enter the shaded room where the women were sitting at work by the window.

To Esther it was very real—to Geoffry it was still like a memory of old times, to be sitting with Esther at an open window, with the shadows of the orange-trees lying on the floor where the shade of the awning did not reach. Jack liked playing with the shadows, putting his little leg out into the sunshine, and pulling it back, to try and cheat the light and carry some away; but Prissa (her grown-up name was to be Priscilla) liked best sitting quietly on her mother's knee, and, as it were, staring at the stories she told her with great round eyes. The story broke off abruptly when Smith came in, and another tale began. It seemed like a dream to Geoffry to find himself sitting there, with Esther, at an open window, with the sounds and the sunshine without, sounds of horses at the water, of the water rushing, of voices calling to each other, of sudden bursts of bells from the steeples of Bagnères de Bigorre. It was as if all the years were not, and he was his old self again. Can you fancy what it was to him after his long waiting, long resignation, long hopelessness, to find himself with his heart's desire there before him and within his grasp? Can you wonder that for a little while he almost doubted his own happiness, and lived on in the past instead of the present? Death, indifference, distance, other men and women, years, forgetfulness, chance, and human frailty, had all come between them and divided them, and now, all these things surmounted, like a miracle these two seemed to be brought together again, only divided by a remembrance.

Some things are so familiar, so natural, that while they last they seem almost eternal, and as if they had been and would be forever. They suit us, and harmonize and form part of ourselves and of our nature, and so far in truth they are eternal if we ourselves are eternal, with our wondering and hopes and faithful love.

OUT OF THE WORLD.

OUT OF THE WORLD.

"Why should we faint and fear to live alone,
 Since all alone so Heaven has willed we die?
 Not e'en the tenderest heart and next our own
 Knows half the reasons why we smile and sigh."

I.

ONE afternoon Dr. Rich rode up as usual to the door of Dumbleton House; he passed in through the iron gates, came up the sweep along which the lilac-trees were beginning to scatter their leaves, and then he dismounted at the stone steps under the portico (it was a red brick house with a Grecian portico), rang the bell, and asked if Miss Berners was at home.

He was shown into the drawing-room—a pleasant, long, ground-floor room, full of comfortable chairs and sofas, with windows through which you saw the garden, the autumn flowers all aglow, the sun setting behind the trees. One or two tall pictures of Dumbletons who had once lived in the long drawing-room, and walked in the garden, hung upon the walls. There was a pleasant perfume of hot-house flowers and burning wood. The room was hot, be-chintzed, be-perfumed; Horatia, dressed in a black velvet gown, was sitting by the fire.

She got up to welcome the doctor. He thought that this black-velvet lady, with the glowing window behind her, was like a picture he had seen somewhere; or had he read about it? or had he dreamt it? Somehow, he knew she was going to say, "We are going away; good-bye!" And Horatia gave him her hand, and said—

"Oh, Doctor Rich!—I am so sorry—my aunt **tells** me we are going away!"

"Well," he said, wondering a little at this odd realization, "I am sorry to lose my patient. Though, in truth, I had meant to tell you to-day that **yon** yourself can best cure yourself. All you want is regular exercise and living, and occupation. And this is physic I can not tell the chemist to put up in a bottle and send you."

"What makes you think I want occupation?" said Horatia, a little angry, and not over-pleased.

"Don't most women?" said the doctor, smiling. "Don't I find you all like prisoners locked up between four walls, with all sorts of wretched make-shift employments, to pass away time? Why, this room is a very pretty prison, but a great deal too hot to be a wholesome one."

"You are right; I am a prisoner," said Horatia, in her velvet gown; "but I assure you I work very hard." The doctor looked doubtful. "Shall I tell you what I do?" she went on. "This is not the first time you speak in this way."

"It is an old observation of mine," Doctor Rich said, "and I can not help repeating, that women in your class of life have not enough to do."

"That is because you do not know: take my life, for instance; I never have a moment to myself. I have to keep up, correspond, make appointments, dine, drive, drink tea, with three or four hundred people all as busy and over-tired as I am. I go out to dinner, to a party, to a ball almost every night in the season. All the morning I shop and write letters; all the afternoon I drive about here and there, and drink five-o'clock tea. I am never alone; I must for ever be talking, doing, attending, coming, going. Is not this work for ten women, instead of one poor, unhappy, tired-out creature like myself?" cried she, strangely excited.

Dr. Rich was a soft-hearted man, especially so when he thought of Horatia, and he said kindly, "That does, indeed, seem a dreadful life to me. Can't I help you? Can't I prescribe some more rational scheme of existence?"

"No, no; nobody, nothing can save me," said Miss Berners. "I am utterly jaded, battered, wearied out. I owe every thing to my aunt. I must go her ways and lead her life; there is no help for me."

"But you might, perhaps," said the doctor, hesitating—"perhaps—"

"No!" cried Horatia, with some emotion, "I shall never marry! if that is what you mean. Ten or fifteen years ago it might have been; but now—now I am ashamed to look people in the face when she tries. . . . What dreadful things I am saying!—but, all the same, I must go on, and on, and on. There is no rest for me except where the weary go in time. Where —where—" She finished her sentence by bursting out crying.

U

Dr. Rich thought there was some excuse for her. He went up to one of the windows, and, pushing aside the flower-stand, opened it wide, and looked out into the garden. Then he walked up and down the room once or twice, and then he came back to the fire. It was a tall old chimney-piece, round which the Dumbletons (the masters of the house) had assembled for two centuries and more. A lady let into the wall, with a pearl necklace and powdered hair, seemed to look him full in the face, and nod her head once or twice.

Horatia had sunk down on a low sort of couch, and was wiping her tears away. The fresh gust of air which had blown in through the open window cheered and revived her more than any consoling remarks or talking. When she had wiped her tears, she looked up, and he saw all the lines that care had written under those dark eyes, and he was suddenly filled with immense sympathy, pity, liking. For a moment he was silent, and then he made a great resolve, and he said, in a low voice,

"I think I could help you, if you would let me. Instead of being a straw in a whirlpool, how would you like to come and stagnate in a pond? How would you like to be a country doctor's wife?"

Horatia blushed up, started with amazement, and then leant back among her cushions to hide her agitation, while Dr. Rich went on to say, with extra deliberation, that social differences had never impressed him greatly—that he could not see why a fine lady should not take a turn at every-day life; "for it is at best only a very commonplace, every-day life that I have to offer you," he said smiling.

He was apt to be a little didactic; but he had soon finished his speech, and he waited for Horatia to begin hers.

"I am so surprised," she said, trying to speak steadily. "I—I don't—you don't know me, Dr. Rich."

The doctor answered, still at his ease, that he had wished to marry for some time past, that he did not expect his sister, who had been his housekeeper, to remain with him always, that he had never fancied any body in the neighborhood, and it seemed to him that this arrangement might make them both more happy than they had either of them been hitherto. He spoke so quietly and deliberately (it was his way when he was excited) that Horatia never guessed that this was an ardent, loving heart, full of chivalrous impulse, of passionate feeling; a treasure which he was offering her—that this homely country doctor was as much her superior in every tender, feminine quality as in manly strength, and power, and vigor.

She was looking at him intently with flushed cheeks. She saw a middle-sized, thick-set man, with a kind face, with what seemed to her trustworthy and keen eyes, instead of sleepy ones like her own, with a very sweet voice, whose tones she seemed to hear after he had ceased speaking.

She pictured to herself his ivy-grown house. She had once driven past it with her cousin, Mrs. Dumbleton. She tried to imagine the daily round of life, the quiet little haven, the silence after all these years of noise and racket, the stillness after all this coming and going—one good friend instead of a hundred more or less indifferent. A man with every worldly advantage would not have tempted her so greatly just at that moment. She thought to herself that she wished she had the courage to say "yes."

When she found courage at last to speak at all, she said—not the "no" she imagined she was going to say—but, "I can't—I can't give you any answer now. I will send—I will write. I will talk to them. *Please* go, before they come in."

So Dr. Rich made her a little grave bow, and walked away. His plebeian breeding stood him in good service. He was quite composed and quiet, and at his ease, and here she was trembling, and agitated, and scarcely able to control herself. When he was gone she went up stairs, slowly crossing the hall, and passing along the gallery which led to her room. There was nobody else coming or going, there were only gathering shadows and shut oaken doors, and more Dumbletons hanging from the walls, and windows set with carved panels, looking out over the country and the tree-tops, and the sunset.

She stopped and looked out. She saw the high-road gleaming white between the dark woods on either side; she saw a horseman riding away; past the gate, and the haycock, and the little row of cottages; past the break in the trees, and then the road turned, and she could see him no longer. She looked out for some ten minutes, without much heeding all that was going on. Great purple clouds heaving out of the horizon, blending and breaking; winds rising; leaves fluttering in the evening breeze; birds wheeling in the air, and rooks cawing from their nests; the great Day removing in glory, and speeding in solemn state to other countries; the Night arriving, with her pompous, shining train—all these great changes of dynasties and states of living did not affect her; only as she watched the sun disappear behind the trees, Horatia found, to her great surprise, that she had almost made up her mind—that what had seemed at first so impossible, and so little to be thought of; that what had appeared to her only a day ago unattainable, and far beyond her reach, was hers now, if she had but the resolution to open her hand and to take it—to accept that tranquil existence, that calm happiness, which she had told herself a thousand thousand times was never to be hers. Suddenly the poor battered barque had drifted into a calm little haven: the ocean was roaring still; the winds and the waves beating and tossing all about; but here, sheltered, protected, safely anchored, she might stay if she would. And yes, she would stay. If she had scarcely the courage to remain, she had still less to face the ocean again. She would stay, come what might. Perhaps Horatia exaggerated to herself the past storms and troubles of her life, but it is certain (and so she kept saying to herself) that at two-and-thirty she was old enough to be her own mistress. She was not ungrateful to her aunt for years of kindness, but she could surely best judge for herself. And so, telling herself that she was not ungrateful, she began to wonder how she could send a note to the doctor; how she could best break the dreadful news to Lady Whiston, who was her aunt, to Mrs. Dumbleton, who was her cousin, and Lady Whiston's daughter. It is a way that people have: they tell themselves that they are not ungrateful, and they go and do the very thing which does not prove their gratitude.

II.

THE ladies came in very late, and went to their rooms at once to make ready for dinner. Horatia, who had dressed with nervous haste, and who was too much excited to be still, went wandering up and down the drawing-room in her white dinner-dress, trying to find words and courage to tell them of what had occurred.

The housemaids came in to put the room to rights, to straighten cushions and chairs, to sweep the hearth, and make up the fire. The Dumbletons were chilly people, and fires burned on their hearth almost all the year round. The housemaids departed, leaving a cheerful blaze behind them, comfortable furniture in orderly array, lights with green shades, evening papers folded on the table. The place might have looked tranquil and homelike enough but for the restless Horatia pacing backward and forward. She hardly noticed Mr. Dumbleton, the master of the house, who came in quietly and sank down in a big chair, and watched her as she flitted to and fro. This constant coming and going worried him. He was a good-looking, kindly, shrewd, reserved young man. He was usually silent, but he would answer if he was spoken to. Sometimes he spoke of his own accord.

To-night he spoke and said, " What is the matter, Horatia? What are you going into training for?" and Horatia stopped suddenly, and turned round, and looked at him for a minute without speaking. An hour ago her mind had been made up, and now again she was hesitating, shrinking, and thinking that she had almost rather change her mind than tell it, it seemed so terrible a task. But here was an opening. Henry Dumbleton was good-natured, perhaps he might help her; at all events, he would give her good advice. She stopped short in her walk, stood straight and still in her white dress, with a drooping head. " You can help me," she said, at last looking up; " I am trying to decide for myself for once, and I do not know how to do it."

" You surprise me—and so you actually don't

know your own mind?" said Dumbleton, smiling.

" Tell me," said Horatia suddenly, " would you think a woman foolish who—suppose you were a woman over thirty, Henry?"—

" I shouldn't own to it," says Mr. Dumbleton.

" Henry, listen to me," said Horatia. " Suppose the case of some one whose life is passing on, who has no settled home, who has not known for years and years the blessing and privilege of being much considered, or much loved. Don't think me heartless—aunt Car has been kindness itself— I shall always, always be grateful; but—"

" All the gratitude in the world would not induce me to live with her, if that is what you mean," said Dumbleton.

" Oh, Henry!" said Horatia, coming and standing in front of him: " should you think very badly of me if, if—can *any thing* be a *mésalliance* for a woman in my position?" The tears came into her eyes as she spoke, and Dumbleton saw that her hands were trembling. I think it was for this foolish reason, as much as for any she could give him, that he determined to help her through the ordeal if he could.

" Who is it?" he asked, a little alarmed as to what the answer might be.

The answer came, and Horatia, blushing, and looking twenty again, said—" Dr. Rich."

" So that is what he came for?" says Henry, opening his eyes.

" Don't you like him?" implored Horatia.

" I think Rich is a capital good fellow," said Dumbleton, hesitating. " I don't think he is doing a very wise thing. You will have to turn over a new leaf, Ratia, and tuck up your sleeves, and all that sort of thing; but I suppose you are prepared?"

" You do like him?" said Horatia. " Oh, Henry, I think you are very, very kind! I did not expect to find one single person to listen to me so patiently." And Horatia was, in truth, a little surprised that Henry did not insist more upon the inequality of the match. To her, brought up as she had been, in the semi-fashionable world, the difference seemed greater than it really was. She seemed to be performing some heroic feat; she had a sort of feeling that she was a princess stepping down from her throne; that her resolution did her extraordinary credit; that the favor she was conferring was immense; that Dr. Rich's gratitude must be at least equal to her condescension. . . .

And now I must confess that the doctor only spoke a truth when he had said that social differences did not greatly impress him. For Horatia herself he had the tenderest regard and admiration; for her position as the niece of a baroness, and the cousin of one or two Honorables, he did not greatly care; he might have thought more of it if he had been more in the world. As it was, the subject scarcely occurred to him. He was at that moment close at home, riding along a dark lane, hedged with black-looking trees, with the stars coming out overhead in a sky swept by drifting clouds. The wind was rising and shaking the branches, but the doctor was absorbed as he rode along, and as he thought with tenderest affection of the gracious and beautiful woman whom he had enshrined in the temple of his honest heart. It was for herself that he loved her, and not for her surroundings. He would have married her out of a hovel, if she had happened to be born there; whereas she, I fear, took him more for what he had to give her than for what he was. She wanted to marry him, not because he was upright and tender and wise; not because she could hope to make him happy and be a good wife to him—but because she told herself he could make *her* happy. She was by way of giving up every thing for him, but in truth, if she gave any thing up, it was for her own sake, and because she was tired of it.

Lady Whiston and her daughter came down as the dinner was announced. Mr. Dumbleton offered his arm to his mother-in-law, the other two followed across the hall. The dinner-table dazzled them for a moment with its lights and shining silver and flowers, but their eyes soon became accustomed, and they sat down and took their places. Lady Whiston was a shrivelled and rather flighty old lady; Mrs. Dumbleton, a kind little fat woman, who chirped and chattered and responded to her mother's constant flow of talk. Mr. Dumbleton, as usual, carved, and did not mix much in the conversation. Horatia could hardly rouse herself to attend to what was going on. Why are people always expected to rouse themselves and to talk of the things they are not thinking about?

"I am quite worn out," Lady Whiston was saying. "Henry, you know how far from strong I am. I drove to town this morning. I was shopping for two hours. I lunched at the De Beauvilles'. There I met Jane Beverley, who insisted upon taking me all over the South Kensington Museum, and from there to Marochetti's studio. We then went back to Chapel Street, and paid a number of visits. We got to Lady Ferrars's about half-past five, and had only time to drink a cup of tea. I found the carriage with Augusta in it waiting at the door. Henry, you ought to get Lady Jane to come down and stay with you. There is no one like her."

Mr. Dumbleton smiled rather grimly, and Mrs. Dumbleton hastily changed the conversation, and said—

"Well, dear Ratia, what have you been about all day?"

Horatia looked at her plate, Mr. Dumbleton looked at Horatia.

"Did Dr. Rich call again?" said Lady Whiston.

"Yes," Horatia said.

"Those people are really unconscionable," cried the old lady. "Horatia, I hope you made him understand that we are going away, and all that, and shall not require his attend-

ance any more. I don't know what he will not charge. He is not an M.D. though he calls himself a doctor. Now, Mr. Bonsey, a married man with a large family, never asked more than 3s. 6d. a visit. Those sort of people must be kept down."

Horatia was blushing pinker and pinker, Henry Dumbleton was more and more amused, and so the desultory conversation went on, all at cross purposes. There seemed to be some fatality in the way in which doctors kept popping up with every course, and from under every dishcover. Dr. Rich, and Mr. Caton his partner, went round with the *entrées*; with the roast Mr. Bonsey was served over again, and all the London physicians. And then, with the dessert, arrived a series of horrible illnesses, which had attacked various ladies of high rank, symptoms following each other in alarming succession. Horatia heard nothing. She was sitting in a sort of dream, only she listened when they spoke of Dr. Rich. Was it indeed fated? Was this new distant country awaiting her? Was she an alien already doomed to go away and leave them all, and live the unknown life he had offered her? It seemed unreal and shadowy, like the night all round about. When the ladies got up from the table, Horatia followed. But Dumbleton got up, too, contrary to his usual custom, and said, "*I* will tell my lady," in an undertone, as she passed him.

So Horatia, with a beating heart, staid in the hall, and went and gazed out through the glass door at the black landscape, at the murky, wind-blown sky. It had been raining, but the clouds were breaking; the crescent moon rose palely and faintly from behind the black trees, the veils of vapor wreathed and curled in the sky, the wind blew in soft sudden gusts over the country, and across the grass and the fields. A lamp was burning, hanging from the pillars in the hall. It looked like a sort of temple, and Horatia in her white robes might have passed for a priestess, looking out at the heavens and trying to read her fate—her fate, which other people after all were settling and arranging at their fancy: for Lady Whiston, discomposed, astonished, indignant, on the drawing-room sofa, was condemning her to live her present life to the very end of her days. Mr. Dumbleton, in the arm-chair, was mildly but firmly marrying her to the doctor. Mrs. Dumbleton was sympathizing with her mother and husband alternately, and Horatia herself, who had most at stake, waiting outside, was watching the clouds and the moon. At last Mr. Dumbleton got up with a yawn, and sauntered out of the room. He came out into the hall with the lamp and the flowers and the white-robed lady staring out at the sky. She started as he called her.

"I am going to send down to the station," he said. "The man can take a note if you like to put poor Rich out of suspense. There is a pen and ink in my room." He lit a cigar as he spoke, and went out and stood on the wet steps under the portico. And Horatia, doing as he told her, went into the study. It was all lighted up, for Dumbleton often sat there of an evening. She sat down at his table, and slowly took up a pen, and then hid her face in her hands for a moment, and then wrote, hardly seeing the words as she formed them :—

"You must help me to bear my aunt's displeasure. I have determined to come to you—I know I can rely upon you. HORATIA."

She folded up the piece of paper and sealed it, and came out again, carrying it in her hand. Dumbleton, who was still waiting outside talking to one of his grooms, took it without asking any questions. He merely nodded "Thank you," and gave it to the man, saying, "You can leave this at the doctor's on your way, and call and see if there is any answer coming back."

And then Horatia knew that the die was cast, and with her own hand she had signed and sealed her fate.

III.

It is very puzzling to define the extraordinary difference, so small and yet so great, which exists between a number of people living in the same place, talking the same tongue, feeling the same emotions. There are, let us say, first, the great people, a number of whom make up what is called the great world. Then, people of the world ; then, people out of the world ; and, lastly, the people — *le peuple*, properly speaking. Dr. Rich and his sister Roberta, and Mr. Caton, his partner, were people out of the world, who had been very happy notwithstanding. Horatia was a small person of the world, who had been very unhappy in it, and yet who had learned unconsciously certain ways and habits there which made her unlike Roberta Rich, and superior to her as far as mere outward manner was concerned. As for the doctor, he was forty years old and more. He had been a surgeon on board ship, he had been to India and back, he had knocked about for fifteen years, he had been at death's door once or twice (the last time was when he nearly died of small-pox, before Roberta came to live with him—some one, to whom she was not as grateful as she might have been, had nursed him through it all). If years and experience ; if rubbing up against people of every degree, from savages without any clothes at all, to lords and ladies in silken gear ; if a good heart, if good wit, and good education, do not make a gentleman after two-score years, it is hard to say what will. Poor Mr. Caton had not enjoyed all these advantages—only the good heart was his. That very morning the doctor and his sister had had a little discussion out in the garden about the young surgeon's merits. Roberta liked him and she didn't like him ; she almost loved him when he was sad, silent, subdued ; she almost hated him if, finding her perchance more kind, he became gay,

confident, talkative, and funny. Even George owned sometimes it was a pity that Caton had so noisy a scorn for social observance.

If Berta had declared that she fancied him, very likely her brother might have regretted her fancy, and thought she was throwing herself away ; as she seemed to care little for him—shook her head, laughed, blushed, would have nothing to say when she saw him—George, out of some strange contradiction, had all the more sympathy for Caton because his sister showed so little ; asked him to the house, praised him continually, and told Berta at last that she was fine and foolish not to be able to appreciate a kind and honorable man when he came in her way.

"I may be foolish, George ; you know I am not fine—I hate fine ladies," said Berta, with whom it was a sore subject.

They had just done breakfast on the morning of this eventful day, the doctor had come out for a stroll with *The Times* and his cigar, Berta walked beside him with a basketful of roses. The garden was on a slope—a long, narrow, and somewhat neglected strip, with grass, with rose-beds, with elm-trees, with all London and its domes and spires for a background. There lay the city in the valley stretching farther and farther away beyond the morning mist. Long lines of railway viaducts and arches, lonely church towers, domiciles nestling amidst trees, chinking workshops, fields, roads, and gardens, children's voices shouting, cattle lowing, sheep, and the sound of cocks and hens—all this life lay between the doctor's quiet garden and the great misty city. A great silent city it seemed to be as it glistened in the gentle morning rays ; for its roar could scarcely reach the two standing on their distant hill-top. Every now and then came the shrill whistle of a train dashing across the landscape and gone in a moment, only a little smoke remained curling, drifting, breaking, shining with sunlight, vanishing away. All the late summer roses were smelling sweet and were heavy with drops of dew, all the birds in the trees were chirping and fluttering, and Berta, in her pink cotton dress, fresh, slim, and and smiling, looked up into her brother's face and said—

"You know I am not fine—I hate fine ladies."

Dr. George winced, and puffed his cigar.

"They have never done you any harm. Why should you hate people you know nothing about ?" said her brother.

Roberta looked up a little surprised, a little hurt ; she could not understand how it was possible that George should speak in such a tone. "They have never done me any *real* harm," she said, in a voice not quite her own. "They have made me feel very uncomfortable."

"Nonsense, my dear Berta," said George, hastily turning away ; "that was your fault, not theirs. I can't talk to you now ; order a good dinner, at all events, for poor Caton is coming, and don't starve him and snub him too."

And he walked across the lawn, at the glass door, and Berta heard the hall-door shut with a bang as he rode off to his fate.

Roberta was a born housewife, a domestic woman—she was gentle and deliberate—she was placid and happy—she was contented with small interests. A calm summer's evening, a kind word from George, a novel sometimes, a friend to talk to, an occasional jaunt to London—these were her chiefest pleasures. Her troubles lay in her store-room, her kitchen, in the meshes of her needlework, in the cottages of the poor people round about, and now and then, it must be confessed, in occasional and frightful ordeals gone through at her brother's desire, when she called at Dumbleton House, and such like ogres' castles, once in six months. Berta's thoughts were all of objects, of things almost always the most pleasant and the most simple. She had no mental experience in particular: crises of morbid dissatisfaction were undreamt of by her; hankerings after what she could not get, aspirations after other duties than the simple one which fell to her share, passionate self-reproach and abasement, fervent resolutions, presently to be forgotten—all these things were unknown, unrealized, unimagined by the girl as she came and went about her little busy domain, while Horatia was fuming, fussing, railing at herself and her cruel fate elsewhere.

Berta was not clever. She had not half Miss Berners's powers; she performed her simple duties simply, and without an effort. Horatia did not always do her duty, but sometimes she went through prodigies of self-reproach, control, denial, culture, inspection, condemnation, or whatever it might happen to be.

Roberta's life was a tranquil progress from one day to another. Her steps paced across the grass-plot, tarried at every rose-tree in turn, led her along the walks to her favorite seat in the arbor, into the house again, moving from one room to another, arranging, straightening, ordering.

And so at six o'clock Berta had put out some of her roses upon the dinner-table, dressed herself in her muslin dress, looked into the kitchen to see that all was satisfactory. At five minutes past six Mr. Caton arrived, and found Berta sitting in the window at work.

As the time went by they both began to think that George would never come back. Caton did not like to say what was in his mind when she told him that the doctor was at Dumbleton House, she was so perfectly unconscious. What was the use of setting her against the inevitable fate? Her brother could best tell her if any thing was to be told.

Only that morning, with the strange knowledge of another person's feelings which we all possess, Caton had known more than Berta, or Dr. Rich, or Horatia; but meanwhile the day had sped on its course, causes had produced effects, one destiny had evolved out of another, the world rolled into the appointed space in the firmament, and, after ceaselessly travelling hither and thither upon its face for forty years and more, Dr. Rich rode up that afternoon as usual to the door of Dumbleton House, came up the sweep along which the lilacs were beginning to scatter their leaves, and asked if Miss Berners was at home? . . . .

When the tramp of a horse's hoofs came, some two hours later, thudding along the quiet glimmering lane which led back to the doctor's own house, the doctor's sister, who had grown very weary of a long tête-à-tête, ran out to the door to meet her brother, and Mr. Caton followed more leisurely. As George dismounted, agitated, wearied, excited, the kindly welcome seemed inexpressibly soothing and pleasant.

For home opened its wide door to him, he thought, and seemed to say, "Come in; here you have a right to enter, a right to be loved; whatever befalls you without, come in; forget your anxiety, your suspense, put away your fears for to-night. Welcome, welcome!" Home said all this as Berta kissed him, and Caton his partner cried—

"I say, George Rich, you ask me to dinner at six, and it is near eight before you come in."

"I—I couldn't come; I was detained," said Dr. Rich; "order dinner, Berta."

And in a few minutes they also were sitting down to dinner, at a table with roses, with candles, and over-roasted mutton; with Betty in desultory attendance: it was a silent repast, chill, belated, and yet pleasant and friendly enough.

After the sun had set, as I have said, the purple clouds turned to gray, and to black, and the wreathing mist began to fall down in occasional showers pattering against the window. Berta could not go out into the garden for her evening stroll, and she had to return into the darkling little sitting-room after dinner, while the gentlemen sat over their wine.

She got out one of her long seams to sew, and as she stitched she faintly wondered what was to be the end of these silent tête-à-têtes and long seams. She heard the voices rising and mumbling in the dining-room; she could distinguish George's soft tones from Caton's harsh treble; she asked herself whether it was possible that she could one day like the harsh voice as well as she loved the other; she broke her thread, and stitched—no, never, never; nobody could be to her what her brother was—whom else did she want? she would live for him always.

And now while Berta is still sewing at her seam some one passes the window through the rain; there is a ring at the bell, a brief colloquy, and Betty comes in with a letter which she puts upon the table. Berta, busy speculating, wondering to find herself so silly—she always counted silliness and sentiment together—with an effort turns her well-regulated little mind from a dim involuntary mystic dream, and wakes up to every day.

It was time to make the tea, to fold up her work. Should she be able to find her way in the dark to the cupboard upon the landing?

Poor little Roberta, she did not guess what was at hand, and in what manner she would find her way there. For she looked up with a smile when the door opened, and George and Caton came in.

Caton glanced at the table and the letter lying there, and then walked across and sat down beside Berta, and began to tell her that he and her brother had been having a discussion; and meanwhile George took up the letter, a candle, and walked away out of the room.

About five minutes passed, and then Berta heard his voice calling—"Roberta!" She ran out to him.

He was standing in the study, with the letter still in his hand; he looked bright, round-eyed, strange, unlike himself. "Berta," he said, "something has made me very happy," and he put out his hand.

She looked up, with her sweet anxious face wondering, as she took it. "Some one has promised to be your sister, whom you must love for my sake," he went on, smiling. He did not see that Berta was trembling and quaking, as she gasped, "Who is it, George?"

"You know her, dear. You have seen her at Mrs. Dumbleton's," the doctor went on. "You must love her, and help me to make her happy."

Berta's grasp loosened, and her heart sank with dismay. She had seen a beautiful fashionable lady at Mrs. Dumbleton's, who had made her feel all elbows when she talked to her; a fine lady—did not she hate fine ladies? —a terrible alarming London beauty. What had he done—what foolish thing had he done? She was clinging to her brother again, with her arms round his neck.

"Oh, how I hope you will be happy! oh, how I hope she will make you happy! Why didn't you tell me? Why have you never said a word?"

"I only made up my mind and spoke to her this afternoon," said her brother, pulling her gently away. "I have only had her answer this moment."

Berta looked at him once again, with her fond doubting eyes. She felt somehow as if it was the last time, and as if Horatia's husband would not be the same man as her brother George. And then she went gently out of the room, still carrying her work, for she felt that tears were coming into her eyes, and she did not want him to see them. She turned and went up stairs, and then, walking along the familiar dark passage, she felt for the key, and opened the great cupboard door, and put down her work upon the shelf with the lavender. Only as she did so, suddenly a great sorrowful pang came over her, and, with a choking sob, she laid her head upon the shelf, feeling all alone in the dark, with her bitter bitter grief. She had not thought, as she sat below sewing her seam, in what a sad fashion it was fated she should put it away. After this night, Roberta could never smell lavender without thinking of darkness and trou-

ble. The rain had ceased by this time, and, as the clouds broke, a faint pale moonlight came creeping coldly along the passage.

IV.

While Berta was crying in the cupboard, Horatia was sitting with her cousin, Mrs. Dumbleton, and saying, "Augusta, you must stand by me and help me. I assure you I shall be happy. You know I have always wished for a quiet country life, and hoped to marry a clergyman."

"But you have not always wished to marry a country doctor," said Mrs. Dumbleton.

"He will do quite as well," said Horatia, eagerly. "I shall occupy myself with the poor people, with the schools. I shall escape from the hateful monotonous round of dismal gayety."

"But this will be still more dull in a little while," said Mrs. Dumbleton.

"No," said Miss Berners, decisively; "because it is a natural and wholesome existence: the other is unnatural, and morbid, and exhausting. Augusta, you must help me, and persuade aunt Car to forgive me. For it is too late to prevent it any more, and—and—Henry sent off a note when the groom went to the station."

"Is it all settled?" cried Mrs. Dumbleton, very much relieved. She was always delighted when people decided things without her. "Then, of course, mamma must forgive you;" and the good-natured little woman went off, and knocked at Lady Whiston's door, and there was a great long long conference, and at last Horatia was summoned. And when she came out she was pale and exhausted, but triumphant. She and Mrs. Dumbleton had talked over the old lady between them. "Of course, you are going to do exactly as you like," says Lady Whiston, "but I suppose you know you have forfeited your place in society. I shall come and see you now and then, when I am not too busy. My consent is all nonsense. I must say I had hoped differently."

"But you will forgive her in time, mamma?" pleaded Augusta.

"I can not discharge Mr. Bonsey, if that is what she wants. Horatia! what could you want when you made this ridiculous arrangement?"

"Good-night, dearest, kindest aunt Car," said Horatia, suddenly clasping the little old woman in her arms. "I can't tell you what I wanted, but I must keep to my decision. Good-night, Augusta."

What had she desired? Happiness, rest, quiet, a tranquil home, sympathy: and now all this was hers at last. She caught a glimpse of her glowing cheeks in the glass. She could hardly believe that bright and brilliant face was her own—her own old face, whose wan glances had met her for so many years. . . .

One day, not long after the day I have been describing, Mrs. Dumbleton's little carriage was travelling along the road which leads from Dumbleton to Wandsworth; Augusta was driving the ponies, and Horatia was going in state to visit her new dominions. They roll on across the country roads, and lanes, and commons; through the western sunshine, through the warm sweet September air, with a great dazzling vault overhead, a shining world all round about them. Horatia leans back too languid, too happy, too excited to talk. She lazily watches the crisp shadows that advance alongside—the nodding heads of the ponies, the trees and houses in the distance, the children and wayfarers who look up to see them pass. It is like a fairy-tale, Horatia thinks—a princess driving along the road. And what will be the end of the story? They come to a cross-road at last, and then Augusta turns the ponies' heads, and they trot up a lane full of flickering shadow and sunshine. They stop suddenly at an iron gate in front of a Queen Anne brick house, with all the windows open, and growing ivy-wreaths. And Horatia, with a start, says to herself, "So this is my home?" while Augusta points and says, "Here we are; doesn't it look nice?"

Behind the iron gate is a little garden, full of red and blue, margarites and geraniums; then three worn steps lead to the door with the old-fashioned cornice, over which a rose-tree is nailed. When Betty opened the door, they could see into the passage, and into the garden beyond, green and sunlight there as here in the lane.

Dr. Rich was not at home; Miss Rich was in the garden: Betty proposed to go and tell her; but Horatia quickly said, "No, we will go to her."

So the ladies got down. As Horatia crossed the threshold, she suddenly thought, with a thrill, how this was her new life, her future into which she was stepping. It had all lain concealed behind the door but a moment ago, and now it was revealed to her. It had begun from that minute when Betty admitted the strangers. The ladies swept through the little hall in their silk gowns, glanced with interest at the doctor's hats hanging upon their hooks, peeped into the little sitting-rooms on either side: the drawing-room with the horsehair sofa and mahogany chairs, the cottage piano, the worsted works of art, the three choristers hanging up on the wall, the funny old china cups and bowls on the chimney, the check tablecloth, some flowers in a vulgar little vase on the table, a folding-door half open into an inner room.

"Is that another drawing-room?" Horatia asked.

"It ain't used much," says Betty. "It 'ave been Miss Rich's play-room. She does the lining there now, and keeps the preserves and groceries."

Horatia peeped in. There was no carpet; there was a wooden press, there was a glass door leading into the garden. It was not much of a place; but she thought how she would have chintz curtains, tripod tables, gilt gimcracks;

and how pretty she could make it! Mrs. Dumbleton was quite enthusiastic.

"These are very nice rooms, Horatia, all except the furniture; with a few alterations they might be made quite pretty."

But she was so used to her own trim lawns and hothouses that she could find no praise for the garden. However, there was all Fulham beyond for her to expatiate on. "The view is too lovely," said Augusta; "it would be too, too beautiful, if you could only help looking at the railways and the houses. . . . I should advise you to build a high wall, Ratia."

"It will do very well when the garden is put in order," said Horatia, drawing a deep breath.

"It is a pity the garden is so neglected," Augusta went on, looking up and down, and round about. Cabbages and roses were growing in friendly confusion, honeysuckle straggled up the old brick walls; parsley, mint, saffron, herbs of every sort, grew along the beds, Joe, the odd man, kept it in a certain trim; and the doctor sometimes ordered in a barrowful of flowers. It was not much of a place. Three straight walks led up to the low ivy wall at the end, where a little arbor had been put up, and where the ivy, and spiders'-webs, and honeysuckle, and various pretty creeping plants, tangled, and sprouted, and hung luxuriantly, as you see them at the end of a long summer. The entertainment is nearly over, and they lavishly fling out all their treasures, their garlands, their sweetness.

Under this pleasant, triumphal, autumnal arch, Berta, in a broad hat and blue ribbons, was sitting with a novel; and looking up as she heard steps, she saw a tall woman coming towards her with a long silk trailing gown which swept the mint and parsley borders; and then she guessed in a moment that this was the future mistress of the little domain. What a beautiful lady! the heroine of the novel she had just been reading was not to be compared to her. What dark eyes! what bright glowing cheeks! What a charming smile!

Roberta, who had only seen her once before and who had thought her very alarming, and said to herself that she hated fine ladies, was vanquished utterly for a moment. No wonder George was in love with this gracious creature, who was ready to give up all her state for him. She jumped up to meet her.

"I have come to see my new home," said Horatia, holding out her hand in a royal sort of way.

And Berta, blushing, took it timidly, and said—

"George told me. How I hope you will both be happy. Isn't it a dear old house?"

The old cistern at the back, the familiar chimney-stacks, the odd windows, the waterspout with the bird's nest, the worn steps where she had played when she was a child, the mouldy little arbor, had all dear old charms for Roberta, which naturally enough Horatia could not appreciate.

"I am afraid it is more for the sake of your brother, than for the merits of the house, that I mean to come and live here," said Horatia, smiling. "I want you to show me over the house, and to give us some tea. We came on purpose, when we thought he would be out. I think you know Mrs. Dumbleton."

"We peeped into your store-room as we came along," said Mrs. Dumbleton, shaking hands, "and we want to see some more. I see you do not care much for your garden."

"I am so glad to have found you," continued Horatia; "but we meant to come, anyhow."

Roberta was rather bewildered by all this conversation, but most of all by the demand for tea. Betty was apt to be ill-tempered if any thing was expected that did not come naturally in the course of every twenty-four hours. She began to feel as if her future sister-in-law was a fine lady again. Her heart sank within her. What had George done? What foolish thing had he done? However, she put the doubt away, and said, smiling, that she would be delighted to show them every thing. There was not much to see. She pointed out St. Paul's, and the Abbey, and the Tower, and the new railway bridge close at hand; and then tripped back into the house before them, opened doors, showed them the surgery, the study, the drawing-room over again, the dining-room (there were some old carved chairs in the dining-room the ladies were pleased to approve of); she pointed out the convenient cupboards, but she felt a little awkward and sad as she led them here and there; she could not help feeling that their praises and dispraises were alike distasteful to her.

"What an old-fashioned paper!" said Mrs. Dumbleton. "Horatia, you ought to have white and gold, and matting on the floor, with Persian rugs. Yes; and we must do up this room."

"What a funny, dismal little room," said Horatia, stepping in, and indeed almost entirely filling it with her voluminous skirts.

They had turned poor Roberta's store-room into a boudoir; they had built a bow-window, they had sacrificed all the dear old chairs and tables, and now this was George's study that they were invading. It was very hard to bear. Berta only came in on great occasions—when she wanted money, when she said good-bye, and when she dusted his books. It seemed almost sacred to her, and Betty the clumsy was never allowed to dust or to touch George's possessions. There was a little inner closet with a window, where her brother used to let her sit when she was a child, as a great great treat, while he was at work. In the looking-glass over the chimney, she had, in former years, standing on tiptoe, looked at herself with a sort of guilty feeling of profanation; and now, instead of Roberta's demure, respectful peeping face, it reflected two flounced ladies poking about, staring at the shabby old furniture, turning over the books, talking and laughing.

"What a bachelor's house it is!" said Hora-

tia to Berta, without a notion of the wounds she and good-natured little Mrs. Dumbleton, who would not willfully have pained any living creature, were inflicting; but women of thirty and upwards have a knack of snubbing and ruffling very young girls, and Berta was very young for twenty summers. She slipped away to the kitchen to order the tea, and to recover her temper.

"Please, Betty, put it out in the dining-room; Dr. Rich would particularly wish it if he were at home," Berta said.

"Well, this is the fust time I ever heard of tea before dinner!" says Betty, with a bang of the tray upon the table; and Berta fled at the sound, and came back to find her guests up stairs on the bed-room landing, opening doors, and talking and laughing still.

"That is my brother's room—that is the spare room," Berta said.

"This one would make a nice boudoir," chirped Mrs. Dumbleton, thoughtlessly, looking into a pleasant chamber full of western sun-rays, with a window full of flowers.

"That is my room," said Berta, shortly, blushing up; "it has always been mine ever since I came to live with George."

"How pretty you have made it," said Horatia, who saw that she was vexed. "Shall we go down again?"

Berta made way for them to pass, and they sallied down into the drawing-room again.

But no tea was to be seen; so, at Berta's request, they went across the passage once more into the dining-room, and sure enough there it was. Betty had not vouchsafed a cloth, but had put out three cups on the red table-cover, three very small old-fashioned willow-patterned plates, knives and forks, a dish of thick bread and scraped butter, a plate of hard biscuits, a teapot, and a glass milk-jug. Three chairs were set, at which they took their places; and while Berta was busy pouring out the tea, Betty arrived with a huge black kitchen kettle to fill up the pot.

"Shall you want any more bread and butter cut, Miss Roberta?" she said; and poor Berta could not help seeing that Mrs. Dumbleton and Horatia glanced at each other somewhat amused. They did not hear Berta's sigh as she sent Betty away. Berta sighed indeed, but then she forced herself to smile; and when George Rich rode up, a minute or two later, he came in to find a dream of old days realized at last—a little happy family group in the old house, a beautiful woman looking up with bright gladness to greet him; Berta, evidently happy too, already adopted as a sister. He had not thought as he came slowly along the lane that it was to this that he was coming. He was touched to be able at last to welcome Horatia under his roof; and as he glanced at her beautiful face, as he realized the charm of her refinement, her soft breeding, he asked himself more than once if that was indeed his wife? His welcome was charming, his tender kindness melted and delighted Horatia, who had not experienced overmuch in her life. She was grateful, gentle, and happy, and cordial. When they drove off, the doctor was standing at the gate, as happy and as certain of coming happiness as she was herself.

I wonder would it have been different if Dr. Rich could have known that evening what was to come as days went by? It was yet time. If he could have been told the story of the next two years, would he have hesitated—have held back? I think not. He was a man so brave and so incautious that I imagine he would not have heeded the warning. I am sure he could have borne to know the end of it all—and could have heard of trouble to come, with that same courage with which he endured it when it fell upon him.

<hr/>

V.

HORATIA had determined to marry her husband against all warnings: except Mr. and Mrs. Dumbleton there was no one in favor of the match. But she would not listen to any objections. Her aunt's laments, angry retractions, exclamations of horror, shakes of the head, nods, groans, sighs, grand and agitated relations who drove up from town to put a stop to the match, and to crush the presumptuous doctor under their horses' hoofs, if need be—nothing could prevent her from doing as she liked.

"I am beginning to see that this is not at all a good match for you," the doctor said one day. "Horatia, do you understand that you will have to be really a woman of the working classes? You will have to do as Berta does—for instance, sew and stitch, and make a pudding on occasions, and I don't know what else."

"I am older than Berta, and have been brought up differently," said Horatia, smiling. "I assure you it is a popular fallacy to think that households do not go on very well with a little judicious supervision. The mistress is not necessarily always in and out of the kitchen.— Where are you going to?"—she went on, glad to change the subject, which was one she hated.

"I am going to see a very sick man, who lives three miles off. Caton is attending him, and he has sent for me."

"I do not much fancy that Mr. Caton," said Horatia. "I wish you would beg your friends not to congratulate me without knowing me."

"Caton is a very good young fellow—he is a rough diamond," said the doctor. "He saved my life once when I had the small-pox, so you must forgive him for that and other reasons, Horatia." And he nodded, and went away more in love than ever.

When Mr. Caton, whom he met presently, began talking over the marriage, with as many misgivings as the grandest of Horatia's great aunts, George Rich stopped him almost angrily.

"What do you mean about keeping in one's own class of life? I suppose a gentleman is the equal of any lady; and if she does not object to marry me, I can not see what concern it is of yours. Men or women are none the worse in any station of life for a good education, and for having some idea of what is happening out of one particular narrow sphere."

"Look at your sister," began Mr. Caton.

"My sister will be all the better for learning a little more of the world," said Dr. Rich; "she is too fond of housekeeping." But he knew very well what Mr. Caton thought of Roberta.

Six weeks went by—very happily for George and Horatia, very slowly for poor Berta, who all the while fought a heroic little battle which nobody suspected: she was fighting with herself, poor child! and got all the blows.

Andrew Caton, indeed, may have guessed that she was not happy; and one day he came up to condole with her, but he had put on such a very long sympathetic face for the occasion that Berta burst out laughing, and would not say a word on the subject. Much less would she understand when he tried to speak of what was much nearer his heart. The little maiden gently parried and avoided all sentiment. At the very bottom of *her* heart I think she liked him, and meant some day to make him happy; but at twenty life is long, the horizon stretches away far, far into the distance. There is plenty of time to love, to live, to hate, to come, to go. Older people are more impatient, and hurry things on. Young folks don't mind waiting; at least, so it has seemed to me. Roberta did not mind much, only sometimes, when a sort of jealous loneliness came wearily weighing upon her. She could not help feeling that she was changed somehow, that life was not the placid progress she had always imagined; wishes, terrors, fancies, were crowding round her more and more thickly every day. She began to see what was going on all about her, to understand what was passing in other people's minds, as she had never done in her life before.

As the day approached which was settled for George's marriage, Berta became more sad. Her wistful eyes constantly crossed his, she took to following him about; she would come out to meet him on his return, and creep gently into his room when he was smoking, or at work. The night before his marriage she whispered a little sobbing blessing in his ear.

"My dearest Berta," he said, "let us pray that we may all be happy—don't cry, you silly child—you do not think that any one or any thing can ever change my love for you."

George was not demonstrative; he had never said so much before, and Berta slept sounder than she had slept for weeks.

Dr. Rich and Miss Berners were married at Putney Church early one wintry morning. Mr. and Mrs. Dumbleton went to the wedding, and Roberta, in a pretty white bonnet. There was scarcely any one else. After it was all over, Roberta walked home, packed up her things, and went back by the train to the country village where her stepfather was vicar, and where her mother, who was not George's mother, but his late father's wife, was busy from morning to night with little boys and girls at home and abroad; with soup-kitchens, training-schools; with a very tiresome, fidgety second husband, who could do nothing himself, but was very particular about everybody else's doings. He loved his own children, but was not over fond of his stepdaughter; and I think that is why Mrs. Baron was glad that Berta, her dearest and favorite child, should be almost constantly away. But, all the same, it was a delight to have her at home, and Roberta came to the garden-gate to be clasped in kind motherly arms, while all the stepbrothers and sisters streamed out in a little procession to welcome her. It was Christmas holiday time—the boys were at home. Ricarda (Mrs. Baron had a fancy for inventing names) was grown up quite a young woman; Tina had broken her front tooth; Stephana was naughty, but she should come down from her room after tea; Will, and Nick, and Harry, were hovering about, long-legged, kindly, and glad. It seemed impossible to Berta that she was only an hour or two away from the struggle of love and jealousy, of tenderness and anxiety, she had been going through for the last few weeks — only two hours distant from the last tears she had dropped, as with Betty's assistance she packed up her boxes and came away; only an hour away from George's last kind words and thoughtful care. And so she settled down quietly in this other home.

She cut out frocks for the children, set to work 'at the choir, and for three whole days she and her sisters were busy dressing up the old church with ivy, and holly, and red berries.

Months went by. She heard from George; she had one or two letters from Horatia, in the beautiful handwriting. They were back long ago, and settled down quite comfortably, Darby and Joan-wise. They hoped she would come soon, and stay as long as she liked one day. George added, "Caton says he would like to come down and pay you a visit. I dare say you may see him before long." Poor Mrs. Baron was very much excited, but also rather alarmed by this piece of intelligence. She did not know how her husband might take this attention of the young doctor's. I think, as a rule, women are more hospitable than men, and more glad to see their friends at more hours of the day, but I must confess that it was not only hospitality which made her so anxious on this occasion to play hostess. Mr. Caton was ten years younger than George, was very well to do, and certainly was not coming all this way to see her and the ungracious vicar only. She was right. When Mr. Caton arrived, he asked for Berta eagerly, and Berta appeared. But so unwilling, so little glad to see him, so silent, so anxious to get out of his way, that he determined to go back again without saying any thing of what he had meant to say, and had come all this long way to tell her.

"How is George getting on?" Mrs. Baron asked, by way of making some sort of talk.

Mr. Caton shrugged his broad shoulders. "I hardly ever go there now. Mrs. Rich gives herself no end of airs, but I can not drop him altogether; he looks ill enough, poor fellow, and I think he begins already to repent of his bargain."

"These unsuitable marriages rarely answer," said Mrs. Baron, with a sigh.

"That is just what he was so angry with me for saying," said the young man. "*I* like a woman who is not above her station, who minds her house, and takes care of her husband, **and** that is what Mrs. R. *doesn't do*. Why, it was as different in Miss Berta's time. . . . Now, the house is all topsy-turvy. She's got a lady's maid, they tell me, but the dinner is disgraceful. I assure you, I am not particular—you know I'm not, Miss Berta—but I couldn't eat what was on my plate. I give you my honor I couldn't."

Berta hoped that this might be a prejudiced report, but she could not help feeling sad and anxious as the time came near for her to go back to them again.

Alas! the prejudiced report happened to be the true one.

If Horatia had married younger it might have been different, but it is almost impossible suddenly, in middle life, to become a new woman altogether; and from being lazy, nervous, languid, and unhandy, suddenly to grow brisk, orderly, thoughtful, and hard-working.

Berta paid them one very short visit, during which all went smoothly, and yet she went home for another six months, very doubtful as to how things might turn. Her brother was not repenting, as Mr. Caton had told them, but it seemed to her that Horatia might begin to get tired of this new life, as she had wearied of the old one.

When George and Horatia married, they both pictured to themselves the lives they were going to lead; and the two pictures were not in the least like one another, or like the reality even. George's picture was of Horatia, a happy woman, a good wife, beautiful, sympathetic, interested in his schemes, contented with her destiny, cheerful, and devoted. He saw her busy in a thousand ways, working among the poor with more energy than Roberta had ever shown, understanding his plans far better, better able to advise, helping him, encouraging him in all good, the best friend, the most faithful companion. "These instincts are unfailing," he said to himself; "I know her as well as I know myself; by what strange, happy intuition is one led to these discoveries?"

Horatia's picture was also of herself. Elegantly but simply dressed, gracefully entertaining her relations, leading a sort of Petit Trianon existence. Giving delicious but inexpensive little dinners, with croquet on the lawn, perhaps; afterwards returning among her old companions; gracious, unpresuming, independent, much made of; she was, especially at first, well satisfied with herself and with what she had done, and with her husband. He might be a little rough and abrupt, but *that* she should be able to change. He was kind and clever and

full of consideration ; and, with her connections, it would indeed be strange if he did not
get on, and become—who knows?—a prosperous man in time. Then, of course, he would
have to make some radical change in his way
of life. I do not know when it began, but by
degrees she began to think the calm haven was
perhaps a little too calm after all—if it was to
continue only broken by the vagaries of Betty
and the cook. Horatia had now and then lost
all patience with them, as well as with other
peculiarities of her husband's house. She de-
tested a racket, but she was not accustomed to
this utter seclusion, or, what was even worse,
this strange company :—young ladies who called
her dear, and who were surprised at every thing ;
homely matrons, with funny husbands ; and
that intolerable young man, Mr. Caton, who
was worst of all. Fortunately she had still her
own relations to go to.

And meanwhile George went on prosing to
himself—nearly a year since he married! Long
happy evenings, Horatia playing on the piano
while he sat and smoked (as he was doing now)
on the lawn. The whole house brightened by
her coming—a stir of life, pleasant talk where
there had only been silence before, or poor Roberta's gentle commonplaces. Dear Berta!
It would be as happy a change for her as for himself. He could hardly believe that all this
treasure of happiness was his, that he had a
wife in the drawing-room, and that wife Horatia ; and he put down his cigar, and went and
looked in at the window to assure himself that
it was not all a fancy brought about by the
smoke, the faint perfume of roses, the sweet bewildering air of a summer's day. And in a
minute he came back, and began to puff tobacco,
not castles in the air any more. For Horatia
was there certainly, but so was Lady Whiston ;
so was Mrs. Dumbleton. Voices, flounces, big
carriage at the garden-gate. It was no fancy ;
and as he did not want to face them all, he went
back to his seat in the arbor.

"George!" Horatia calls, opening the window and looking out.

George looks round and shakes his head.

Horatia, surprised, comes out across the grass.
"Won't you come and see aunt Car?"

"I am busy," says the doctor.

"They want us to dine there," says Horatia,
putting her hand on his shoulder. "They expect Lord Holloway."

"We dined there yesterday—there is that
breakfast next week ; make some excuse."

"But in your profession it is of great consequence that you should improve your acquaintance," says Horatia, blushing up. "They
were just saying so. Lord Holloway has dreadful attacks of the gout."

"That is what I shall have if I dine there
any more. You can go, you know. You can
make up to Lord Holloway all the better if I am
not there."

"How can you say such disagreeable things?
Of course I must go without you, if you will not

come. It will look very odd ; I don't like it at
all."

"Then why don't you stay?" says the doctor in his kind voice, smiling as she frowns.

"Aunt Car will be hurt as it is," says Horatia, looking round. "I suppose I had better
go back and tell her. It is most unpleasant."

George glanced a quick, doubtful look as she
walked away unconscious, slim, tall, graceful,
with her violet dress trailing over the grass and
the daisies. She stoops her head at the window, and passes in under the clustering roses.
After all, why should not she like to go? George
asks himself, and though he might have answered the question, perhaps he took care not to do
so. How many such questions are there which
are best unasked and unanswered? Truth, indeed, is greater than silence, and if we could
always tell what was true, it would be well to
speak always. But silence is often better than
the half-truths we utter ; silence to ourselves
and of ourselves, as well as to others.

Horatia came home about one o'clock in the
morning, and found her husband still up, sitting in the little study, and Mr. Caton with him.
The window was open, a candle was flaring on
the table, and she thought there was a strange
aromatic smell in the room. But it was hard
to find Mr. Caton always there, even at that
hour of the night. She was not safe and she
looked her displeasure.

He got up with such a grave face as he made
her a little stiff bow, that she was still more indignant. George too was grave, though he
smiled and put out his hand.

Horatia wrapped her white cloak round her,
and turned her back upon Caton.

"What have you been concocting, George?
why do you sit with the window open? I wish
you had been with me. Lord Holloway is perfectly charming, and—"

"Well, good-night," said Caton suddenly.
"Good-evening, Mrs. Rich," and he walked
off. As the door shut Horatia began indignantly, "That man is insup—" but her husband stopped her languidly, and said he was
not up to fighting his friend's battles that night.
He was tired. "Is this the way he speaks to
me?" Horatia thought.

The next day the doctor went up to town and
came back to dinner very silent and much out
of spirits. And Mr. Caton, as usual, looked in
in the evening, and they were closeted together
for some time. Horatia had taken a nervous
dislike to the poor young man ; his presence was
almost unendurable to her. Rich looked hurt
and vexed when she said so one day.

"Why have you taken this aversion to my
old companion?" he asked.

"Because he is familiar and interfering,"
cries Horatia.

"What do you say to Lady Whiston, then?"
says the doctor, provoked.

Horatia was still more provoked, and the little discussion ended in her going off alone, as
usual, to the Dumbleton fête.

But she looked so bright and so handsome in her white dress, as she wished him good-bye, that George secretly relented, and thought he should like to see her admired, and determined if he could, to come for her, after all.

VI.

HORATIA was not sorry to go by herself. She felt more at her ease when her husband was not there. Old friends came up to greet her. Two old adorers asked her to dance. Mr. Dumbleton gave her his arm, and took her into the conservatory for an ice. Here they all were, making much of her, welcoming her. Horatia could not help contrasting all this with her husband's grave looks and unconcerned manner.

"How does the housekeeping go on?" said Mr. Dumbleton.

"Don't talk about it," cried Horatia. "Every thing is so different. My genius does not lie in that direction; and yet—would you believe it? my doctor grumbles at times. What a pretty effect!"

They were in a long conservatory, full of trees and shrubs and flowers and Chinese lanterns. The sound of distant music, the perfume of the plants, the soft glimmer of the lights, filled the whole place, and the stars came twinkling through the glass domes. Horatia was enchanted instead of being bored as in old times. It was an Arabian Night's Entertainment. One of her cousins, who had been an old admirer of hers, came up and scarcely recognized her, she looked so wonderfully handsome and happy; he asked her to dance, and Horatia consented, and went off laughing and radiant, but Henry Dumbleton looked after her a little doubtful as to the entire success of his match-making.

Horatia, meanwhile, twirled and twisted, the musicians played one of those charming waltzes that seem to be singing and sighing with one breath. The music surged and sank again; it was like the sea flowing upon a shore; breathless, excited, Horatia danced on in cadence to the tune, and thought this moment ought to last forever; she and her partner went to one of the windows to refresh themselves, and stood out upon a low balcony, close to the ground, and began to talk of old days, as people do when they suddenly grow confidential with time and place, and then they talked down to later days, and the cousin, whose name was Charles Whiston, reproached her for having left them as she had done: "Did she never regret it? Had she quite given up old friends for new?"

"No, no, no!" cried Horatia; "unequal marriages are foolish things, Charles. It is not until you find yourself lonely and misunderstood in the midst of people who have been brought up to see things *en-dessous*, instead of *en-dessus*, that you begin to discover how real and how insurmountable certain differences are. Things with which I have been familiar all my life seem strange and unfamiliar to them. There is a sort of suspicious defiance I can not describe—a sort of meanness, of familiarity, of low jocularity."

"But how could you ever marry him?" cried Charles Whiston, much concerned. "This is terrible. You must come away; you must come to us, we are always—"

Some one who had been sitting under the window started up at that moment, and got up and walked away.

"I am not speaking of my husband," said Horatia, blushing, and starting, and a little ashamed of herself. "I was thinking of—of friends—persons who come to the house whom I can not be rid of. There is his stepmother, for instance—who came a short time ago, and interfered in the most unwarrantable manner. There is a certain dreadful Dr. Caton whom George is forever asking. Can you fancy that man daring to call me Mrs. Gallipots?—don't laugh—such vulgar insults are no laughing matter."

"Poor Horatia," said her companion, sentimentally. "I assure you I do not feel inclined to laugh."

The musicians began to play a new measure, and the dancers set off with fresh spirit. The people outside were still pacing and talking in low voices, the trees were hung with brilliant jewels of fire, no breath stirred the branches, the white dresses gleamed mysteriously through the darkness, the light steps loitered, the low voices sank. Horatia stood immovable, with her head against her hand: her companion was sitting on the low stone parapet, and leaning lazily over the side of the balcony, when suddenly he started up, and stood listening.

"Did you hear that?" he said. And once more distinctly sounding through the still night came a plaintive cry out of the wood.

"Oh! go and see," said Horatia; "what can it be?"

In a moment all the silent enchantment of the hour seemed broken and dispelled. That forlorn cry had shaken and dispersed the dreams, the illusions, the harmonies of the summer's night. It was like a pebble falling into still waters. But it was only for a moment: by degrees the silence, the music, the starlight, reassured the startled people; they forgot once more that pain existed in the world, that trouble could approach them. Horatia had almost forgotten her alarm when her cousin rejoined her.

"It was nothing," he said. "Some one fainted—a woman was frightened and screamed. Dr. Rich was there, and another doctor."

"My husband!" said Horatia, surprised.

"Some one told me he had gone home with the patient," said Charles Whiston. "Shall we have another waltz?" Tum—tum-te-tum, te-tum—the music plays, and off they go.

When Horatia got home she found a little note hurriedly scrawled. "Don't expect me to-night, I am detained.—Yours, G. R."

He came home next day, looking pale and exhausted, as if he had been up all night.

"Who was ill?" Horatia asked. "Who fainted?"

"I can not tell you who it was," said the doctor. "Caton attended him. I have been very busy, and I am not well myself, Horatia. I shall go and lie down."

"You went up to the hall last night, then?" persisted Horatia.

George did not answer, but looked at her once in an odd sort of way, and then went out of the room.

Horatia never knew exactly what had happened that night. It seemed to her somehow that her husband was never quite the same again after this unlucky fête. She actually began to wish for Berta to come back again.

Roberta's mother had brought her the first time, and left her and gone away, after managing to give great offense to George, as well as to his wife, by one or two awkward speeches. And when Berta came back to the old trouble once more—the old battle and disappointment—she determined to be warned by her mother's example. She would gladly have staid on at home, but George kept writing for her to come, and the bugbear of a stepfather growled out, "Why didn't she go, since they were so anxious to have her?" and besides, there was a natural yearning after George in her heart, which would have brought her from the end of the world, if he wished it.

So now that Horatia was mistress of his house, Berta did not like to interfere in the household disarrangements—for it was nothing else: she found Horatia evidently discontented and unsatisfied—George looking worn and out of spirits—the dinner unsatisfactory, the furniture dim and neglected, maids careless and unpunctual. Horatia had theories about every thing, but did not possess the gift of putting them in practice. Every human being had its rights, she used to say, and those of servants were constantly infringed. The consequence was, that though Betty had time to read the paper and a course of history judiciously selected by her mistress, she had not time to dust and scrub and scour, as in days of yore, when the poor doctor's rights only were considered.

Roberta found that it was almost more than she could do, not to speak, not to interfere. She was ready to cry sometimes when her brother came in, tired and exhausted, and had to wait an hour for his dinner. She thought him looking ill, indeed, and changed. By degrees she almost got to hate Horatia, and did not do her justice for those good qualities she certainly possessed. Horatia's temper was perfect; she bore Berta's irrepressible glances and loud reproaches admirably. She saw that her husband loved his sister; she would not pain him by blaming her. She often wondered that he should seem more at home with Roberta than with herself. She thought herself infinitely superior, cleverer, handsomer, better bred; but

she had not Berta's rare gift of home-making, her sweet repose of manner, her unselfish devotion to those for whom she cared. Horatia rarely forgot herself. Berta was like her brother, and almost lived in the people she loved.

And so Horatia's beautiful black eyes did not see all the many things that were amiss; her soft white hands did not work for her husband's comfort; days went by; little estrangements went by; the geese cackled on the common: sick people died or got well; well people fell sick; George Rich went his rounds, and sighed sometimes as he looked at his beautiful wife. It had not answered, somehow.

Every day little stories are told: sometimes about great things, sometimes about nothing at all. This one was about nothing at all, and yet the story was there to read, and I am trying to write it down.

The people who tell the stories are generally too interested and unhappy, or happy, or anxious, or vexed, to look at their daily lives from another person's point of view; and sometimes even other people standing by have not the gift of seeing what is passing before their eyes. Horatia, who was quick about other people, was blind to her own faults. Dr. Rich was the person in that household who could best read the disappointing little history that was telling out, day by day, under his roof, and the struggle of his daily life was to be blind, and not to read the open page. Horatia had no such scruples, and always said what she thought, and thought what she liked, and spoke openly to George, to the Dambletons, of her fancies, disappointments, dislikes, particularly of her dislike to Mr. Caton. Now that Berta was there, he was always coming, and Horatia did not at all fancy such a brother-in-law; and so she told the girl, who laughed, and blushed, and acquiesced. Horatia said as much to George one day: he answered, somewhat absently, "Caton is a very clever, good fellow. I am afraid Roberta will have nothing to say to him; but he comes to see me, Horatia." And that evening, after dinner, coming out into the garden, she saw, much to her disgust, Mr. Caton's red whiskers and a cloud of tobacco under the arbor, where her husband was also sitting, apparently deep in conversation with his friend.

Another grievance she had, which was this: she inherited a few hundred pounds unexpectedly about this time, which she wanted to lay out in doing up the house and the garden, and in more Persian mats, and a brougham. Dr. Rich insisted on her leaving the whole sum untouched at the banker's. "You shall have it in due time," he said. "Horatia, can't you believe that I have some good reason for not spending money just now?" She could not understand this strange fancy for saving. He would go nowhere; he would insist on economizing in every way; he would not willingly ask even her cousins to dinner. Wearied, disappointed, provoked, she began to tell herself that her marriage had been a mistake—she began to long to get away, to sigh for and to dream of liberty. She did not know how far these dreams had carried her, once she had given way to them. She had wished for Berta, but when Berta came she grew jealous of her. Life was a miserable delusion, Horatia often thought.

Berta could not help seeing there was something wrong, and put it all to poor Horatia's score. It seemed to her that Mr. Caton knew more than he chose to tell; for sometimes she would catch a half-pitying, hesitating glance; and once, when she met him on the common, he stopped short and said, "Miss Roberta, I want to speak to you;" but she walked on rapidly and pretended not to hear, and then he changed his mind and turned away abruptly. She did not dare to ask what it was, for she thought that after all it might only be the old story that she did not want to listen to. It had been settled that she was to go home that day for a Sunday to see her mother. She was glad to go, for she felt as if she could keep silence no longer, and might say something to George or to Horatia which she would afterwards regret. She felt that her mother's sympathy could help her to silence and toleration. She had but an hour more to be silent. Who can tell what an hour may do?

VII.

She had made her preparations and she was sitting that afternoon sewing in the window, until it should be time to go. Horatia was lying on the sofa, the sun was pouring in. It looked a peaceful little scene enough—flowers and young women, novels, needlework, silence, sunlight—when presently Horatia put down her novel, and began to talk; and as she talked, Berta began to sew very fiercely, and to blush up angrily.

"It is a shame," Horatia was saying, "that I may not choose my own company: that I am to be forced to receive a person so distasteful to me as Mr. Caton. His familiarity is really unbearable. Until your return, Roberta, I hope we shall see less of him. To-day he came up to me, and told me that I ought to take more care of George. You and your brother can not understand how distasteful this sort of thing is—what a real want this want of congenial society is to me."

"You have George," said Berta, stitching away.

"George is a dear, good George," said Horatia, passing her hand wearily over her eyes; "but he has not been brought up to many things that I have been accustomed to. I feel a little want of sympathy, a little lonely sometimes."

A cleverer person than Roberta might have understood her better; but the girl was thoroughly provoked and offended. All her pent-up passion burst out: after all her days of silence she spoke, scarcely knowing what she said:

"Do you dare to complain—you who have made George sad and lonely by coming to live with him—you who don't appreciate him, who can't understand his goodness? He is the best, wisest, and dearest of men; his gentleness and forbearance are wonderful. You neglect him as no wife ever neglected her husband. You do nothing to help him. When he is worn out you complain to him about yourself—you are so used to think of yourself, Horatia. I must speak. I may never come into your house again; but it breaks my heart to see it all. And when he comes home sad and out of spirits, you don't look up—you scarcely heed him; you say, 'George, shut the door,' or 'poke the fire,' or whatever it may be. I always used to think George's wife would be the happiest, proudest woman in the whole world, until you came to undeceive me."

Even Horatia could not bear this: she, too, got angry and started up upon her sofa.

"You certainly shall never come here again, Roberta, unless I am away. You speak of things which are not your concern; and you should have been silent. I am quite able to appreciate my husband without any body to point out his merits. But sometimes I think, Roberta, that either you or I had better go. Stay," she said: "I am not at all certain that it is I who should remain." And she gathered up her papers and books, and drew herself up to her full height, and sailed out of the room.

And so poor tired George, coming home earlier than usual to see his sister before she left, found only Roberta crying and sobbing in the drawing-room. Horatia was up stairs with a nervous attack. A strong smell of burning and a black smoke came in whiffs out of the kitchen. The maids were in her room sympathizing with the mistress; and the dinner was spoiling unheeded. The penitent Roberta tried in vain to stop crying.

"I am going away," she said; "and oh, George, I don't know when I may come back again. It is too disagreeable for Horatia to have me in the house. I have behaved so dreadfully. I only wonder she did not turn me out on the common. I am very sorry, dear George. I will do any thing. I will beg her pardon, if she will be only kind enough to forgive what has passed, and let me come and see you again. Because I do love you almost more than any body in the world. Please don't hate me for behaving so badly."

Then he had to go up stairs to Horatia. When he came down he was looking very pale and biting his lips. His wife had gasped out things about "your relations;" about the way in which he preferred them and their ways to hers; about his being more happy before she came; about her loneliness; about— But there is no use in recapitulating all her nervous griefs. "Are you packed up, Roberta?" said the doctor, with one more sigh. "I will drive you down to the station. I must see you off. It is only four o'clock now; if we catch the five-o'clock train it will still be light by the time you get home. I think your sister will get over it sooner if you are not here. Don't cry, dearest; it will be all right in a little. I can quite understand her annoyance. Don't cry any more, Berta; that won't mend matters," he said, cheerfully. Then he went into his study, and shut the door, and fell down into his big chair, and let his head fall heavily on his breast. His pulses were throbbing with grief; it was all he could do to subdue his agitation. His wife's passionate indignation and reproaches had upset him; and that Berta, whom he looked upon almost as a daughter, should be estranged, and that he should be left quite alone—more lonely than he had ever been—was a cruel stab to this tender and sensitive heart. When it was time for Berta to go, he came out of his room, looking exactly as usual. He went to his wife's bedside, and said good-bye, but she would not answer him; and then he came down again, and helped his sister into the little carriage, and **took** his place leisurely beside her, and they drove away.

The trees seemed to fly past them, the birds went wheeling over the fields, a blue-gray mist hung over the distant hedgerows and the hay-stacks, over the farmsteads and cottages nestling in the little hollows.

The landscape was painted in black and gray, with clouds and rain-water. Now and then a rain-laden wind would come blowing freshly into Roberta's face.

As they were nearing the station, somebody came up alongside upon a tired horse. It was Mr. Caton.

"I was going to look for you," said Dr. Rich, pulling up. "Will you come in this evening, about nine o'clock? We can't wait now, we shall miss the train." And then he bent forward and said a few words, in a low voice. Berta wondered what it was all about, as she nodded a grave good-bye. Mr. Caton looked up with a strange expression. She wondered whether it was because she was going away; and then she wondered whether she should ever forgive herself, and thought what a comfort it would be to tell her mother every thing, and to be well scolded as she deserved, and then kissed and forgiven like a child. She gave such a tremendous sigh once, that her brother began to laugh. "You silly child!" he said; forget all about it. I will undertake that Horatia shall bear no malice. A little change will make all smooth again, and you must come back directly." Then he drove on silently for a minute, **and** then he said, "Berta, do you think you could ever fancy Caton?—he is a little rough, but he is a thorough good fellow, and very fond of you."

"I am very fond of him," said Berta, smiling, "but I don't want to marry him. Perhaps, if you praise him very much, George, in time— Ah, here we are!" And presently Berta had kissed him, and said good-bye, and

watched him until the train had carried her away, and he disappeared. By leaning out she just saw him for one instant more, looking after her with his kind, smiling face; and then the train went suddenly on through the quiet country, carrying away Roberta, with her troubles and puzzles. The doctor travels homeward, strangely abstracted; and Horatia has risen from her bed, where she had been lying, and is making desperate and angry resolutions.

"Was he indeed more happy before I came? He did not deny it. When I gave up every thing for him, I thought, at least, that he would love me." She smoothed her tumbled hair, put on a shawl, and went down stairs and out into the open air. "It will do me good," she thought, as she opened the garden door, and walked along the gravel walk towards her arbor. A book was lying on the seat; George or Roberta must have left it. He sometimes smoked under the honeysuckles after dinner. Roberta used to take her work there of a morning. Horatia hated the place, and never went near it. The faded summer green looked almost fresh again in the gray, damp atmosphere; the birds flew over her head; and across the common the dahlias were beginning to come out.

It was chilly and dismal enough, and Horatia went back presently into the house. She was **shocked** and hurt and wounded. She was not angry, exactly; she did not **like** her husband less, but she was astonished to find she had not made him happy. He had not denied it when she accused him of unhappiness. She was telling herself, with some quiet scorn, that he wanted a housekeeper, like Roberta, and not a wife; that if he had been really happier before she came to him, it would be perhaps as well that she should leave him now. She was in a hard and cruel frame of mind. She began to ask herself the old question, if it had not been better for them both if they had never married? She began to wonder how she had ever been so infatuated as to give up every thing for this commonplace man. She was sitting on the sofa, with her head against her hand when he came in.

"You saw her off?" said Horatia, by way of saying something.

"Yes, we just caught the train," her husband answered, "or I should have had to bring her back."

"I am glad you were in time," said Horatia, coldly. "George, you must make Roberta understand that she is never to speak to me in such a way again."

"She was over-excited: she is very sorry for what has happened; she told me to tell you so."

"She may well be sorry," said the wife. "I am very sorry that all this has happened; it has made me know—made me understand—" and she burst into tears.

Poor George sank back wearily into his chair. "Go on," he said. "Tell me all your troubles, you poor woman. What has it made you understand?"

"That we have failed to make one another happy," said Horatia, in her willfulness. "I could have borne to be miserable myself, but I confess I can not bear to hear that you—that you were happier before I came."

"But it is not so. I have been more happy since you came, Horatia," said the doctor, with kind and wonderful forbearance. "I have been more happy and more unhappy. I have had you as well as myself to care for."

"Ah, no!" cried the woman, foolishly and madly; "it isn't so. I see it in your face, George; I have made up my mind. We shall be friends always, whatever happens, but I will go back to my aunt. Roberta, who is a drudge at heart, can come and keep your house, and satisfy you better than your wife could ever hope to do. Do you hear me?" she said, shrilly, for he did not answer. "It is because I wish to be your friend, and not your housekeeper, that I am going; it is because people who do not agree are best apart."

"I don't think so," the doctor said, slowly, and looking at her in a strange, odd sort of way. "Long habit brings folks together at last; forbearance is a wholesome discipline for one and for the other; a man and a woman who are both sincerely trying to do their duty can't fail one day to find their best happiness in it, and together. Suppose we part—it may be forever : the ways of Providence are inscrutable—what do we gain ? —a lifelong, maybe an eternal, loneliness and estrangement and indifference ; or suppose we struggle on together for a little time, Horatia, and learn at last to love one another, at any rate to forgive, to sympathize, to endure ? Can you hesitate one moment ?" he said, in his sad voice.

"I should not hesitate," said Horatia, sobbing still, "if it were not for Roberta. If she comes here, I can not and will not stay ; my duty does not extend to her. George, we might love one another, even if we did not live together—I might still be your best friend."

The poor doctor, hurt, wounded beyond expression, could listen no longer, and he got up with a great sigh and walked away out of the room. Horatia flung herself down on the floor, and buried her face in her hands. "He doesn't mean it," she kept saying to herself. "I know he would be more happy without me. He is too good for me. I own he is too good for me. I can't love him; I can't understand him ; I make him miserable. He looks wretched, and ill, and unhappy, and it is all my doing ; and it is his doing that I am wretched. Why did he bring me here ? I must go ; it will be better for each of us. Yes, I must—I will go."

George was walking up and down outside in the garden. He once looked up through the uncurtained window, and saw her prostrate in her trouble. How could he make her more happy?—it was indeed a strange puzzle and bewilderment. He felt that she scarcely deserved kindness, and then he said to himself, kindness deserved was no kindness. "What merit have ye ?" he muttered, and something more about publicans and sinners, and so once more he went back into the warm little fire-lighted room. He went up to her, but she did not heed him ; he stooped over her ; he picked her up off the floor. "Horatia," he said, "don't you care for me in the least ? do you want to make me very lonely, very wretched ? Go, if you like, but I tell you you will be more miserable than you are now. Look at me, and tell me what you mean to do."

How sad he looked, how kind, how enduring. Horatia could not help it. She was forced to give in. She still wanted to go, to turn back to her old easy life ; but she had not the heart or the courage to say so. She was silent ; and she left her hand in his. He accepted her silence.

"We will never talk about it again," he said. "And you must try and be more happy, my poor woman."

Then he took a cigar, and went and lit it at the fire, and took up his hat, and said he would be in directly.

"I should like a cup of tea," he said. "I am only going to smoke my cigar in the garden. Call me when it is ready."

Horatia watched him as he passed the window ; and she then rang the bell and ordered some tea ; and then once more sat down by the fire, staring at the embers. It was useless trying to get away. He would not let her go. By this fireside she must remain to the end. How inconceivably forbearing he was, how kind, how patient, how forgiving. Was it indeed impossible to love him ? She heard his steps pacing the gravel outside. Why would he not let her go ? What could make him wish that she should remain? What, indeed ! Then, at last, she began suddenly to blame herself.

"I don't think I know how to appreciate his goodness," she said. "Heigho! I wish he had married a model wife, who would have known how to make him happy, and at home."

VIII.

BETSY brought in the tea and the candles. Horatia started from her low chair, where she had been sitting in a sort of dream of remorse, reproach, regret, indecision, and proceeded to make it ; and then she poked the fire, and straightened her somewhat untidy locks, and then she went and tapped at the window for George to come in.

When she looked out at the end of five minutes, she was surprised to see that a shower of rain was falling. She opened the casement, and all the wet drops came plashing into her face. She said to herself that he must have come in at the garden-door, and gone up to his room. She went out into the passage, his hat was not there ; she ran up the narrow staircase, and went and knocked at his door. Then she looked in. The room was dark and empty. No, he was not there; for she spoke his name and no one answered. Horatia went down into the drawing-room to wait once more. The kettle was boiling over on the hearth, the candles were flaring, for she had forgotten to shut the window. As she went to close it, a great gust of wet-laden wind surged into the room, and one of the candles went out, and the door banged.

It was dismal and cheerless enough. She began to wish that George would come in. Had he gone across the common? No; she would have seen him pass. She went to the window once more; the trees were waving a little in the darkness. The rain was falling still when she went to the garden-door and called out, "George! come to tea!" Do you not know the dreary sound of a voice calling in the darkness? She came back into the sitting-room, took up a book, and tried to read, glancing at the window every instant. Once she almost thought she saw her husband looking in, but it was only fancy. The book she had taken was the second volume of some novel. She looked on the table for the first, and then remembered that she had seen it lying, not on the table, but on the seat in the arbor at the end of the garden. And then suddenly she said to herself, "That is where George has taken shelter from the rain; how foolish of him not to come home! I think I will go and fetch him."

She went into the hall and tied on a waterproof; she pulled the hood over her head; she went to the garden-door a second time, hesitated a moment, and then passed out. It was darker and wetter than she had expected, and she thought of turning back; but while she was thinking of it she was going quickly along the gravel-walk towards the arbor, brushing the wet gooseberry-bushes and box borders, a little afraid of the blackness, a little provoked with herself for her foolishness in coming. She could just make out the arbor looking very black in the night; as she came nearer, a sort of terror thrilled over her, for she thought she saw something within the darkness. "George!" she said, in a sort of frightened way, springing forward. "Why are you there, George?" she almost screamed as she came close up. She saw—yes, surely she saw—his white face gleaming through the blackness. She began to tremble with terror, for he did not move or seem to notice her, though she came quite close up, and stood before him, gasping. With a desperate fear, she put out her hand and touched the white face. And still George did not move or speak.

A few minutes ago he had been a man with a tender heart sorely tried; with a voice to speak, with eyes to watch her reproachfully as she thrust him away, with a kindly, forgiving hand always ready, and willingly outstretched. And now, what was he?—who was he? What distance lay between them! Could he hear her feeble wails and outcries across the awful gulf? "George—George!—Oh! George!"

the poor woman screamed out, hardly conscious. She did not faint; she did not quite realize the awful truth—she could not.

In a minute, with hurried voices and footsteps, the maids came up the garden, and with them the boy, who had brought a lantern. And suddenly flashing through the darkness the light fell upon the dead man's face. It lit up the arbor, the dripping creepers, the wooden walls, the awful figure that was sitting there unmoved; and then Horatia fell with a sort of choking cry to the ground, prostrate in the wet, crushing the borders, the green plants that were drinking in the rain which still fell heavily.

The day had begun to dawn when Horatia came to herself, and opened her eyes in a dazed, wide, strange way. For a minute she hardly understood where she was, and then somehow she knew that she was lying on the sofa in the disordered drawing-room. A maid was kneeling beside her, the garden-door was open, the keen morning air was blowing in in gusts—so gray, so chill, so silent was it, that for a moment Horatia almost fancied that it was she who had died in the night; not George, surely not George. A man's low voice at her head, saying, "She is coming to herself," thrilled through her as she thought for a moment that it might be her husband. What she seemed to remember was too horrible to be thought of—too horrible to be true. It was not true. The wild hope brought the blood into her cheeks. She moved a little in an agony of suspense, and faltered his name. Only as she spoke, somehow there was no response. The half-uttered words died away, the hands that were bathing her head ceased their toil. By the silence—by the sudden quiet—she knew that she had spoken to the empty air; that though he might hear her, he would never, never answer any more, never come, never heed her call again; and then, suddenly, with a swift pang of despair, hopeless, desperate, she realized it all.

Caton, who had almost hated her, who had said to himself that he would be her judge—she had killed her husband, she had wearied and embittered the last few hours of his life, and he, Caton, would tell her the truth, if there was no one else to speak it—Caton, who, in his indignation, had thought all this, could not find it in his heart now to utter one harsh word. He came round, and stood looking compassionately at her white wan face lying back, with all the black rippling hair pushed away; and as he stood there, she put up her hands and covered her eyes, and shivered. How could he judge one so forlorn? Instead of the hard words he had meant to use, he only said, "He had feared it all along, Mrs. Rich. He was not afraid for himself, but for those he loved. It was a heart disease. It was hopeless from the first; he knew it, but he would not let me tell you. He was the best, the dearest—" the young man's voice broke as he spoke; he turned away, and went and stood at the window.

There was a long silence. At last, Horatia, speaking faintly, said, "I want you to send for Roberta. Can you send now, at once?"

"I telegraphed last night," Caton answered, "when I thought there might be hope. She will be here in the morning. I will meet her and bring her to you."

Once more Horatia moved; she got up from the couch where she had been lying, and she tottered forward a few steps towards the door.

Caton sprang after her. "Are you going up stairs to lie down? Where are you going?"

"Where, oh, where, indeed, am I going?" cried poor Horatia. "Oh, my George, my George!" and with a sort of cry, she flung herself back into a great arm-chair, which was near. "Go—pray, go away," she sobbed to them; "only tell me when Roberta comes." And so, sacred, reluctant, they went away and left her.

Caton never forgot that terrible dawning. The black garden, the white mist creeping along the ground, the chill light spreading, the widow's sobs and sorrowful outcries breaking the silence of the night.

It was Roberta who roused poor Horatia from a sort of swoon of grief and remorse—Roberta, white, trembling, silent, who led her into the next room, where all was so peaceful that their sobs were hushed; so sacred, that it seemed to them as if it was a profanity to even complain. Only once more Horatia burst out. "Forgive me, George!" she suddenly cried, falling on her knees, and then she wildly and imploringly looked up at Roberta's set white face. The girl changed, melted, faintly smiled, and stooped and kissed her sister.

"Oh, Horatia, what has he to do with trouble and injury and sorrow now? Forgiveness belongs to this world; only peace, only love to the next."

Horatia was very ill for a long time after this. Roberta was able to stay with George's wife, and to nurse her very faithfully and tenderly in her sorrows. In time Horatia got well, and prepared to live her old life again. It was the old life, but the woman was not the same woman. And George was carried away from his sister, from his wife, from his home, from his daily work. He was still alive somehow when Roberta thought of him. She could see his face, hear his voice, love him more tenderly even than in his life.

One day Caton told Berta, as he had told Horatia, that George had thought himself seriously ill for some short time, and though he did not consider the danger imminent, he had taken pains to put his affairs in order, and to leave enough behind for the provision of those he loved.

"When did he first know—"

Roberta hesitated, and her eyes filled with tears, and Caton said that his first attack was one night when they were sitting together in the study. Mrs. Rich had gone off to her grand relations. "I remember she came back and talked about her partners," he said.

"She did not know?" Berta said.

"Perhaps you never heard that he fainted away at that party at Mrs. Dumbleton's?" Caton went on, sighing. "He went up to town next day to see a doctor. I am not sure that he was right to keep it secret. He would not let me speak. I very nearly told you once, only you stopped me."

And Berta remembered the day she had met Caton on the road, and when she would not stop to speak to him. Things were changed now, for they had met in the lane by chance, and were walking on side by side towards the common. The common rippled westward, scattered with stones, and clumps of furze, and dells and hollows; geese cackled; sunset streamed across it; roads branched here and there leading to other green lanes, or to distant villages, or to London, whose neighboring noise and rush seemed to make this quiet country suburb seem more quiet. The river runs between these furze-grown commons and London. People coming from the city, as they cross the bridge, seem to leave their cares and busy concerns behind them, and to breathe more freely as they come out upon the fresh, wind-blown plains.

Caton and Roberta walked along one of these straight roads, talking sadly enough; her eyes were full of tears. Caton's voice was broken as he spoke of what was past: to walk along with Roberta, even in this sorrowful companionship, was a sort of happiness: but even this was not to last for long; she was going; Horatia was going; and Caton was to succeed to the old place, with all its sad memories, and he thought to himself that he had lost his friend, and that Roberta would never care for him, and that life was a dismal thing, and he almost wished it was over. And he said almost as much. They had come to the place where their two roads parted; Roberta said good-bye, and looked up shy and gentle, blushing under her black hat. Caton put out his hand, and said: "This has been our last walk. You will go that way by the gate, and I shall walk straight on across the common, and we may perhaps never even meet again." His voice sounded sad and reproachful, though he did not know it; and Berta's blushes suddenly faded, and she looked away, and did not speak.

A number of birds flew over their heads as they stood there, parting. There was nobody near to heed them, only an old gray horse browsing the turf, a little flock of geese clustering round a pool hard by. Berta saw it all in a strange vivid way. She stood there, reluctant to wait, and yet still more reluctant to go. The roads gleamed farther and farther asunder; she hesitated, wondered, waited still; but she did not know all that she had tacitly decided until she looked up at last, and met Caton's honest bright eyes with her gentle glance. And so at last he was made happy, and the woman he had loved so well had learnt to care for him, touched by his faithful friendship for her brother, his faithful devotion to herself.

MAKING MERRY.

MAKING MERRY.

"Such as the jocund flute or gamesome pipe."

WE were all upon the terrace one morning, in front of the old château. The *déjeûner* was just over, the sunshine had not reached us yet, and we were sitting under the old gray towers, watching a river, and some wooded slopes, all changing in the morning light. This September sunshine had turned the whole country to gold and lovely red and russet. The rising grounds upon which the old towers stand, the valley, the far-away hill, were painted and checkered and shaded with bright crisp autumnal color. The trees were like the trees in Aladdin's gardens, with gold pieces and jewels hanging from the branches, or sparkling in the brown turf.

The morning seemed to come to us across fields and villages, over the river which went shining and wending away beyond the arches of the bridge at Meulan into that dim and unknown country which seems to bound all that is most beautiful. M. de V. had lighted his cigar, the ladies were working, the gentlemen were making their plans for the day, and the **turkey-cocks** came ambling down the hill, to be **fed** by little Mary. *"Tiens, voilà ta St. Côme,"* said she, giving one of them a big piece of bread, with which it instantly scrambled off in a fluster, shaking all its red bags and tassels as it went. Winifred asked what was a "St. Côme." Madame de V. smiled, and said it was something that she must see. It was a *fête* at Meulan, beyond the bridge on the little island in the river, and they called the fairings "St. Cômes" in that part of the world. In the mean time the kind host was making arrangements for every one of us to be driven there and back in various open carriages, which were to be in waiting at **the** very moment at which each of us wished to **go** and to return. Some begged to go twice, **others, less** enthusiastic, said once would content them.

St. **Côme was** a martyr: it is his memory which is **held** sacred, and to which all these small altars **are** erected, with their offerings of gingerbread, **sugar** - stick toys and crockery, bobbins, cotton laces, and nightcaps. Popguns are fired off, a dentist with a drum comes all the way from Paris, the celebrated two-headed child arrives in its bottle of spirits-of-wine, pleasures succeed one another, and **all** this

cheerful clatter, all the little flags, all the games and lotteries which are going on, are to do the saint honor. He was, while in the flesh, a wise Arabian physician, who seems to have given his advice gratis, and to have practised in partnership with his brother, St. Damien. They were afterwards both martyred towards the close of the thirteenth century; but the 27th of September ever since has been consecrated to the memory of the good St. Côme, and the inhabitants of Meulan and its surrounding villages have elected themselves his especial votaries.

All the carts from all the neighborhood seemed to be jogging along the white dusty road which leads from V., with its white walls and vines and trellises, and glimpses of the river, to Meulan. The country carts were heaped up with delightful primitive-looking people, with kind smiling faces, and caps and satin-bows, and bran-new blouses. In one jolting conveyance I noticed seven happy - looking girls, packed closely away, all in smart white caps, with satin ribbons, and loops and ruffles quite crisp and standing on end. They jogged on laughing, while the young men of the party walked along the road by their side. Other vehicles there were, with nice nutcracker old women in the old-fashioned cap and red cotton dress of the last century. They looked like the figures out of Noah's arks, like chimney ornaments, or water-color sketches, or descriptions in books of travels. They danced fat white doll-babies; they held little girls upon their knees, tied up into pinafores, and with funny frill caps fitting close to their round little bullet-heads. There were expectant little boys in pinafores, too, and old fellows in snuff-brown coats and wonderful waistcoats, with patterns like maps and leopard-skins. There were also donkeys, with tall wooden erections upon their backs, containing their mistresses, whose feet dangled into baskets.

All the people along the road came to their doors to see us go by, and presently we drove into the old-fashioned market-place, with the bridge spanning the river, and with the great town-hall, whose spire dominates the town, and strikes the hours. It was an abbey once, and stands on the hill: the town clusters round it: the narrow streets climb the hillside, and wind corners and disappear. The river flows down below between glittering banks. Broad white roads lead to Vaux, to Poissy, and along them the carts come rolling through the dust.

We already begin to hear the distant booming of the fair, to the accompaniment of the screaming of a thousand pigs. If the old men had put one in mind of Mr. and Mrs. Noah and Shem and Ham (or Cham as he is called in France), it would seem as if all these animals had been emptied out of a gigantic Noah's ark into the market-place. They are lying about, on their backs, on their heads, on their fat sides, grunting, squalling, squeaking in the most distracting manner: whereas the little donkeys are quiet and well-behaved, and stand in rows under the cathedral walls, waiting to be bought. There is such a noise and chatter and confusion that one scarcely knows at last which are pigs and which are old women; for they are all talking together, remonstrating violently, and tumbling about over one another in the straw. The little children stand at safe distances absorbed in the bargains which are going on. The poor little pigs are poked and pinched, and caught up by the leg and the ear, and flung anywhere and anyhow. They are small and lively, not horrible contemplative obesities like those one sees in England. Of all the interesting animals I remarked on this occasion, I will only particularize one little tortoise-shell pig with brown and red spots, for I was struck by the wistful glances a pretty peasant-woman was directing towards it. "That is the one I should have liked!" she said with a sigh to a sympathizing friend; and, indeed, who has not a little tortoise-shell pig somewhere or other out of reach—unattainable? If the pretty peasant-woman were to obtain her little pig, she would pop it into one of those great earthenware pots that are being sold by the bridge—they are something the shape of the Roman amphoræ, very gracefully designed and prettily ornamented—the pretty peasant-woman would then salt down the object of her desires, and eat it up by degrees during the winter.

But all this squeaking and moralizing is only a flourish of trumpets at the opening of the entertainment. We hurry across the bridge to the little island where the fair is held: country blouses, babies, amiable papas in white linen with their families, elegant mammas in the last Meulan fashions. Here is one street of stalls for the sale of gingerbread and gimcracks, with a cross-street for entertaining games and shows. The great time for the shows is at night; in the day-time we content ourselves with munching gingerbread and playing at *rouge et noir*. The fortunate may win seven dozen of macaroons stuck at equal distances upon dubious sheets of white paper, with very little trouble, or exchange them for elegant chimney-ornaments, or water-color sketches of dragoons, and ladies, and roses. It is a pretty sight, blue sky overhead, shining and twinkling through the branches of the avenue; people singing, talking, and staring at the gingerbread, of which perhaps the most delicious sort is called *semelle*, from its appetizing likeness

to the sole of a shoe. The grand ladies from the town are walking up and down between the stalls, gracefully courtesying and dipping to each other. One élégante affects a blue Scotch cap, with a tuft of blue ostrich feathers; all the ladies are neatly finished off with beautiful little frills, and many of them lean on the arms of gaitered husbands with broad-brimmed hats, evidently prepared to initiate their families into all the amusements of the show.

THE CELEBRATED TWO-HEADED CHILD invites us to enter and examine. He is represented alive and crowned with roses, and surrounded by an admiring throng. We are satisfied with the picture outside, for M. de V., who good-naturedly goes in to reconnoitre, assured us that the sight is not only revolting, but in a bottle. Next door, MADEMOISELLE RACHEL gives her interesting exhibition. Mademoiselle Rachel is a bright-eyed little bird, who hops out of a cage, and presents you with the card you selected at hazard from her master's well-worn pack. Her discrimination would be more extraordinary still if the cards in the pack were not *all* kings of spades; but Mademoiselle Rachel is unconscious of the deception: she hops from her little perch with a clear conscience, neatly digs up the card with her bill, and takes a single grain of millet from her keeper's hand, as a reward, before she goes back into her prison. She has a rival; it is like Andersen's fairy tale of the "Princess and the Potsherd." Mademoiselle Rachel is all very well in her way, but not to be compared to the wonderful singing-bird out of the snuff-box, who is to be seen next door for twenty centimes, together with the port of Niagara, the sultan of Turkey and his favorite sultana, and Robert Houdin at home *en famille*. Here at least is no deception. The singing-bird comes out of its snuff-box and squeaks and wags its tail, and wrings its own neck in the most alarming fashion. The sultan of Turkey carefully rolls his eyes with a repugnant stare, which now rests upon his favorite sultana, now upon the alarmed spectators. All the ladies of the harem squat muslin-legged upon cushions round about him. The favorite fans herself spasmodically; while in the next compartment Robert Houdin, in majestic robes of black velvet and a sugar-cone hat, is playing thimblerig, surrounded by his numerous family. One spectatrix of about six years old, who is not afraid of turkey-cocks, is yet not quite certain that she derives pleasure from the entertainment; for, besides the glance of the sultan's eye, and the magic flow of Houdin's mystic robes, the terrific waves of green calico in the port of Niagara have to be encountered. There are but three, but then they appear to be of enormous size and fury. A ship rests upon the crest of each one of them, and remains in that precarious position notwithstanding the stress of weather and the imminent dangers to which navigation must be exposed in that little-known part of the world. The raging of the storm had not abated when we left the tent. As we escaped, we heard the exhibitor loudly calling upon the crowds outside to seize the auspicious moment, and not to forego their chance of admission. The mechanician has a rival opposite, who exhibits attractive sketches of all the celebrated crimes of the last fifty years. To judge from a hasty glance, murderers are invariably dressed in tights, topboots, velvet caps, and elegantly floating feathers. This is a thing to be remembered, that such persons may be avoided in future. All this time the merry-go-rounds are twirling round and round, and we tear ourselves away from the dark exciting scenes of bloodshed to watch a little fat baby sitting quite happy and alone in its little flying carriage, a small ragged boy clinging to a horse, and some young amazons, who cast triumphant glances in our direction; the organ strikes up a military tune, and away they all go flying, men, women, children, one after another in the race.

There is something very cheering and inspiriting in all this. The people are lively, but not too loud; there is more vivacity, but more gentleness too, than there would be among our people at home. One's heart aches a little as one thinks of one's own fellow-countrymen, patient and dull, and strong and clumsy, and weary, not able to rest content with light passing interests, with half-happiness with small things, but hurrying up in wistful crowds with a violence of effort, an earnestness in their amusements even, that seems to carry them almost beyond bounds when they are once let free. One is always being told that nations are like individuals, and we all have to learn in our lives how to be happy with trifles, how to put away care in the passing sunshine of the moment, and to find pleasure even in the bright colors of a bubble.

If the sight was pretty in the day-time, it was prettier still at night. Madame de V. and her husband M. de V., Winifred and I, left the old castle about nine o'clock. It was all lighted up, turret windows and arched gate-ways; and from outside we could see the elders of the party sitting in the gallery in their quiet lamp-shine. It was pleasant to hurry down through the rustling woods and dark avenues, with the crisp leaves under foot, and the great stars blazing over the wide country. At the foot of the steep ascent and the avenue are great iron gates where the carriage was standing. All along the road we passed dusky forms hastening in one direction. The moon looked as if it was going to fall into the river and be extinguished with a great splutter; the wain travelled over the hills, the familiar triangles and figures blazed and hung in the sky. When we reached the island we found other illuminations: bright little arcades of fire were shining among the dark trees, and reflected in the water; and all the little gambling booths were lighted up in a simple fashion with candle-ends.

These games of skill are not very complicated. One energetic little man's whole stock-in-trade was an india-rubber tube, a halfpenny, and a soup-plate. The object of the game was to try and knock the tube and the sou together out of the soup-plate. He could do it, because he passed his life in practising his art; but none of the by-standers succeeded, and the professor always pocketed the halfpenny. Another exciting game was throwing a ball through a round hole lighted up by a candle.

The lady to whom the establishment belonged counted up the failures and payments with great rapidity: "Un et deux et quatre font onze; et trois et deux font vingt-deux, et six et trois, trente-cinq," and so on with surprising aplomb and inaccuracy. Instead of scolding her, M. de V. good-naturedly nodded his head and said, "Allez toujours, madame, ne vous gênez pas;" at which madame herself begins to scold, and gets very red in the face, and vehement and angry. So we leave her to her arithmetic, and go on past the little brawling shops where customers are chaffering—(we saw one priest buying quantities of gingerbread)—and people with white caps and bright dark eyes keeping watch over their wares. Crockery twinkles, little gilt ornaments shine and flicker in abundance, lotteries whizz and whirl, some of the prizes are of the most remarkable description, but the trumpet-calls and the rappel is sounded, and we all hasten with the crowd to the central Place, where some one is alternately discoursing and playing on the drum.

"Venez, venez, messieurs et dames, venez voir la JEUNE SAUVAGE, qui mange de la viande TOUTE CRUE," roars the proprietor of the booth. She is a native of those distant countries where the inhabitants nourish themselves upon the unfortunate crews of the vessels which are wrecked upon their coast. This woman is in noways related to the man you beheld last year. He was dangerous and was destroyed by order of the Government. She can only speak her own language. Walk in, walk in, "et vous serez-z r-r-récompensé de votre peine."

So we walk in, much interested by the description, and behold the appalling spectacle of a being whose name appears to be Juana, gambading behind the bars of a dark cage, grinning at us, and gnashing its teeth. Its face is painted of the approved cannibal brown; it occasionally shakes a great black woolly wig, which fills us with horror.

"Abawaba!" Juana bounds with delight, recognizes the melodious language of her native isles; suddenly she stops, stares, with both hands eagerly outstretched. An extremely small and dirty-looking piece of meat is now produced out of the exhibitor's pocket. He carefully cuts off a minute portion with a pair of scissors. Juana glares at the delicious morsel, and then suddenly seizes it through the bars, and thrusts it into her mouth. "Ah, see how savage she is," says the man in the blouse. "Nous allons maintenant lui préparer de la salade à la mode de son pays." Some black stuff is then set fire to with a candle, which also goes into Juana's mouth. It seems that in her country the savages instantly expectorate their nourishment; and Juana accordingly deposits hers in a corner of the cage, dancing with rapture the whole time.

A *demoiselle de vingt-deux ans* now comes forward. The "administration," as the exhibitor calls himself, selects M. de V. and requests him to weigh the little dwarf, and to observe that she does not exceed two feet in stature nor ten pounds avoirdupois in weight. He then announces that the young lady will dance a little waltz *sans musique*, upon which she instantly twirls rapidly round two or three times. Her friend then begs to remark that she depends entirely upon the generosity of the public, "*n'étant nullement payée par l'administration!*"

Poor little dwarf! There was something affecting in the small, melancholy company. The administration looked very pale and hungry. Juana's life in the cage must have been somewhat monotonous. It seemed a weary way of gaining a livelihood. We hoped that their daily bread was not raw meat only, nor such very uninviting salad.

A great booth had been erected next door. All the simple country-folks had been gazing with delight at the glare and the tinsel on the coats of the pages and actors. We went up with the crowd. "Quand on est marié on finit toujours par céder," one man cried, appealing to us, when his wife insisted upon taking a place he had objected to. A melancholy, well-bred actor, in red silk, with a quiet humorous manner, now came on before the curtain, and said things which made the audience laugh, but which it was impossible for our stranger ears to follow. Every thing he said was witty, M. de V. told me; and all he did was well done. He had a quiet nonchalant way: he put one in mind of Marielle, in George Sand's charming *Théâtre de Nohant*, of Wilhelm Meister among the players. The entertainment turned out to be *tableaux-vivants*, behind a gauze curtain, on a revolving stage. It put one in mind of the "Pilgrim's Progress" and the sights that Christian saw. There was the story of Cain and Abel; there was the history of Joan of Arc; and besides these there were things which seemed so terrible to English eyes that I can not write of them at length. And yet it is not so long ago since miracle-plays were performed. Every day we look unmoved upon pictures and paintings of sacred subjects; we listen to descriptions and allusions which seem to approach with far less effort, with far more familiarity, towards awful mysteries. To me there did not even seem any great want of reverence, though I was frightened and taken by surprise. They had chosen two of Rubens's well-known pictures for imitation; there was not a sound in the crowded booth when the curtain drew up for an instant, and then fell again almost immediately. The figures in this miracle-play were quite motionless. I have rarely seen nobler-looking people than the two chief performers. They en-

acted their parts with perfect gravity and harmony of sentiment. Both the man and the woman were tall, majestic, fair-haired, with a noble outline of form and feature, and a simpleness which was really grand and remarkable.

As Joan of Arc, this tall, straight, sorrowful-looking young woman, with all her fair hair falling about her shoulders, and her beautiful up-turned face, seemed the very personification of sweetness and valiance and misfortune.

It is only in Brittany that such noble types are found, our friends told us; but they also added, that though nothing could have been better and more decorous than the performance of these principal actors, yet before the curtain drew up, allusions were made which would have been far better avoided. Baroness Tautphœus has admirably described these miracle-plays in the Tyrol, which are looked upon in the light of religious ceremonies almost, and which must be less objectionable than these representations so near home. And yet, where no harm is intended, where none is understood, where, like children, the troops of simple country-folks come pouring in, quiet their laughter in a moment, say it is *la religion*, sit silent and hushed for a minute, until the curtain falls, and then pour out into the night, where the stars are shining, and the lamps flaring, and where, like children, they begin to laugh and talk again in the sudden glare and glitter—one can not say how far all this is wrong or right. It does not strike one as it would in England, where feelings are more complex, faith less simple and unreasoning, and the natures of men more intricate and rough and dangerous to deal with.

The ball was a very pretty sight. There were quantities of lamps and festoons hanging round, a great boarded dancing-place, with an arched colonnade outside it for the spectators who walked about upon the dried turf. Then came an inner row of benches for the chaperons, who sat round like real ones at a London ball, only they were little old peasant-women in their tight white caps, with their little shawls pinned across their shoulders, and they were holding other little shawls for their daughters when they should return to them. The middle part was crowded with dancers. The musicians were scraping away from a flowery bower. It was a pretty, pleasant, funny sight: glissades, galopades, gambades, like Juana's. Sometimes a good old couple would stand up and foot it with great intrepidity. One little wiry brown old woman with her husband in his high-shouldered coat, were hopping opposite to one another like a pair of lively old sparrows. As the night wears on, the excitement grows: the music plays faster and more gayly, the steps increase in rapidity, and they begin to skip and to bound, with immense sprightliness and variety. The ladies grin reprovingly at their partners, but at their smiles the gentlemen's spirits only seem to leap like fire when a little water is thrown upon it. There is one delightful little man with an immense tall partner, and a very tall hat with a curly rim; either of them would have seemed quite sufficient to weigh him down, but he is equal to the occasion. His evolutions and revolutions, his inflections and ascensions, and flights and inspirations, are something quite wonderful. Retreats, advances, salutations, clapping of hands—one does not know which to admire most. His lady joins in with great spirit. Their vis-à-vis try in vain to surpass them. The gay refrain of the waltz echoes, and the dancers seem to sway with the tune; the chaperons nod their heads, and look on with smiling approbation. At last the dance comes to an end, the young ladies return to their mammas, but carefully lift up their dresses before they sit down.

We see the little man with the tall hat walking off with his partner to treat her to gingerbread outside; they seem conscious of a triumph, and some of the lookers-on shake their heads, laughing as they march past. One or two ladies who have the gift of the dance jerk with peculiar adeptness; but these are far less interesting and more sophisticated than the simple peasant-women delightedly jumping, and bobbing, and flouncing, or rolling like the

friendly teetotums of one's youth. There is scarcely a pretty face in the whole room. They are "gentilles," that is the most that can be said for them. Their hair is smartly dressed, parted, and twisted up tight and spruce. Most of them have their petticoats neatly looped up over tidy brodequins, quite different from the splay, web-shaped chaussure of the inhabitants of our native isles.

The lamps were beginning to go out and to splutter when we came away, only the stars seemed brighter than ever in the dark sky, and almost starting from their places. The moon had not set, and we climbed the hill and came out from the avenue of lime-trees and nut-trees into a great calm sea of moonshine rippling over the old towers and pointed roofs. It was late, and every one was gone to bed. Only one red lamp was left burning for us when we returned. But until the early morning I heard the carts rolling homeward with their weary, happy burdens, and the distant voices chanting cheerily through the silence of the night. They rolled through the darkness to their peaceful villages all round in the valleys and among the hills; and this distant, odd, pleasant music only ceased with the dawn.

SOLA.

SOLA.

"Where are the great whom thou wouldst wish to praise thee?
Where are the pure whom thou wouldst choose to love thee?
Where are the brave to stand supreme above thee,
Whose high commands would cheer, whose chiding raise thee?
Seek, seeker, in thyself, submit to find
In the stones bread, and life in the blank mind."

I.

ONCE two hundred years ago, or more, in an old Italian city where the workers still knead their clay in the sun and set it drying along the walls of the deserted streets, some workman designed an open dish. It may have been meant as a gift for a betrothed maiden; it may have been ordered by a fanciful customer. There was a rough garland of citrons and green leaves all round about the edge, and then came a circlet of oranges, and then, in the centre of the platter, two clasped right hands and a scroll upon which "Sola" was written. The dish was old and chipped, the varnish was covered with a fine network of hair-like cracks; but neither time, nor cracks, nor infidelity could unclasp the two hands in the centre, firmly grasping each other through the long ages. Strangers speaking a different tongue still guessed that "Sola" meant the only one—a life's fidelity; for there is a silent language belonging to no particular time, or age, or place, which all sorts of people can understand.

I do not know how the plate had come to be one of the ornaments of the china cupboard in the morning-room at Harpington Hall. There it stood on the faded old shelf in the old gray room, looking eastward; with the spindle-legged chairs standing against the panels, the faded Turkey rug before the fireplace, the two deep window-sills where Felicia used to sit a blooming little girl in the midst of these ancient appurtenances. One almost wondered where the child found her youth, her bright colors, her gay spirits; she was like a little Phœnix rising out of the ashes at Harpington. The old Hall was haunted by ashes and dust and rats; by all sorts of ghosts, and sad memories of the past. The poor old owner's dead children's pictures hung in the mother's dressing-room; Mr. Marlow's gun was slung up in the dining-room; the stables were empty; the state-rooms were closed. Sometimes if people asked her to show them over the house, Mrs. Marlow would take them quickly round from one great wooden room to another, and perhaps stop for an instant at the china cupboard, and point out the plate as a quaint old piece of Italian ware, and then shut the glass doors quickly. She had a nervous, hasty manner, and never seemed to be quite in the same mind as other people; but in a world of her own and her husband's. And Mr. Marlow did not certainly care either for cracked china or sentiment; it was only Felicia, the granddaughter, who had sometimes wondered what it all meant as she looked at the lemon wreath and the grasping fingers. "Sola," clasped hands—it all seemed very meaningless to her until one day, when her eyes were opened, and she understood once for all.

When Felicia was fifteen she was told by her grand-parents that she was engaged to her cousin, James Marlow, a gentle, good-humored little fellow, who was to be master after the old Squire's death. The old Squire made some broad jokes on the occasion; Mrs. Marlow treated the business in a very dry, off-hand way. James took it as a matter of course, and went back to college, and Felicia remained at the Hall.

The way of life in the old house was a close and narrow way, not leading to salvation, though year by year Mr. Marlow added more and more to his store, and counted up with satisfaction various items of moth and dust.

These were largely eked out by his own and his household's discomfort; Felicia's little shoes were rubbed out at the toes. Mrs. Marlow's Sunday dress was shining with age, but the five guineas a new one might cost were safe in the bank. Loneliness, stinginess, self-denial, and denials of every sort, had added to a moderate fortune until it was now a large one. That trembling, bandy-legged old fellow, with his gaiters and his felt hat, did not look much like a speculator, but such he had been, in fact. He was sly, he was dull, he had been lucky. His wife had sympathized in his ventures, and the narrow economies of the household had been begun by her years ago. Now Mr. Marlow was old and timid, and afraid of loss. He speculated no more, but still, from habit, the two ground down life to its narrowest compass. Such people would like to prevent the sun from rising so early for fear of wasting its heat; they would only have leaves on the alternate branches of the trees, or keep the autumnal sprays over for another year. But they could not prevent nature from being bountiful, and lovely, and wasteful, and from flooding Felicia's life with youth and wild girlish spirits, with sunshine, with full fresh country winds and sweet rural sights, to all of which she turned more readily than to the house-stinting and keeping her grandmother tried to teach her. All the summer-time she was happy, wandering about the deserted gardens, where the straggling flower-beds travelled over the ill-kept lawns; and the great trees gave shade upon the grasses and the laurels. The little chestnut-trees in the wood, where the birds hid their nests, rustled and trembled; now and then dividing their close branches to give a sight of the tranquil furrows in the spreading fields beyond, where the great elms were sailing like ships at sea. . . .

The house, with its high sloping roof, stood on a hill, and might be seen for miles. From the front blistered door, with its broken steps, an avenue ran down to the road. There was an old gateway, of which the iron doors stood always open. The ivy had crept up in slender sprays, covering the hinges, and hiding the brickwork, and wreathing over the stone balls at either side of the entrance. One day, Felicia, picking periwinkles in the avenue, tried to imagine a vision of herself at some future day, as a bride, passing through the gate, on her way to the little church close by. Somehow, in this fancy of Felicia's, she was the bride, scarcely changed, except that her stuff gown was altered to shining satin; but poor James was strangely transformed and metamorphosed. He was a great deal older, taller; he had broad shoulders, and a set straight figure in this representation; he had a fiery, quick, scornful sort of way, quite unlike his usual gentle manner. The fiery manner softened in the vision when the bridegroom turned to his bride. He was holding her hand close in his. What was it he whispered? something out of the marriage service: "To thee only," "Sola!" Was it James's voice? It was certainly James's voice that Felicia heard in the avenue calling her, "Felicia! Felicia!"

Felicia was seventeen by this time. She had been engaged two years. She started and blushed. She knew she ought not to wish James to be different from what he was. She jumped up hastily from the pile of stones and periwinkles upon which she had been kneeling, dreaming her little love-dream, with her head bent over the flowers. She heard voices. A great dog came running down the avenue, and jumped upon her faded gown; and James, no taller, no more mysterious or romantic-looking than usual, followed with his grandmother, looking for her down the

avenue, to say good-bye. "Felicia," said the young fellow, "why did you run away? It is time for me to be off. Good-bye, dear; take care of yourself."

"Good-bye, dear James," said Felicia, kissing his cheek. "It is you who must take care of yourself; and mind you wear the comforter I knitted you."

"James"—this was the old grandfather on the house-step—"you will miss the train."

"Here I am," cried James, kissing both his grandmother and Felicia, and hurrying off. Only he stopped at the foot of the steps to look a good-bye and to take breath. "London—10th —don't forget," he cried.

Some people said that James, who was of a delicate stock, was ailing for want of care and of necessary comforts beyond the bare allowance his grandfather made him. He never complained, and I am sure it never occurred to Felicia to complain for him. She believed her grandmother, who assured her that the doctor was mistaken in ordering another climate—what air was so good as Harpington? Felicia had thriven upon it, and James could come home from college whenever he felt inclined. He was making but a poor thing of his career there. The old lady spoke a little bitterly. Felicia was sorry. She herself sometimes felt angry with her cousin for the way in which he submitted to the tyrannical rule of the old people. Felicia had been so little away from home that she had no standard by which to measure its ways. She did not care about a brilliant career in the world. She scarcely knew what it meant; but she could not but feel a secret vexation when she saw how poor Jim was a cypher in the determined old hands that ruled both their destinies. Felicia, who was wayward and impetuous, sometimes revolted against the discipline in which she was kept; the young fellow never did. It did not much matter whether the children revolted or not, for the grim old couple were not to be stirred from their strange fixed ways by all Felicia's reproaches and girlish demands. The old lady was not even angry; she had taken her as a child, and brought her up with a vigorous rule, and it was not a quick passionate creature like Felicia who could move that rugged rock.

In summer Felicia laid up her store of youth and brightness; but the winters were long and dreary. Poor Felicia! How the cold blasts used to pinch and bite her. Her somewhat languid circulation seemed stopped and frozen by the wooden echoes of those long bare passages at Harpington. There was a window looking into a court past which she used to run, giving a wistful glance at the warm-lighted kitchen-window, looking out upon moonlight in winter. The kitchen was the only really comfortable corner in the house—long wooden passages, stone stairs, up which winds blew shrilly. Some old people do not feel the cold, and Mrs. Marlow was one of them. "Shivering again, Fay?" It was absurd that Felicia should shiver when there was a fire in the dining-room.

This old house seemed, like its owners, in some fashion dreary, yet capable of better things —of warmth, and comfort, and brightness, too; a stately old place, with all that was wanting for a generous life, and yet, through some curious whim of chance, all shabby, and closed, and narrow. Jim and Felicia in some measure belonged to the sad past and were expected to keep up its traditions. He was a son's son, and she a younger daughter's daughter. The pictures of the dead children were hanging carefully guarded in an inner closet; no new interests were admitted. The doors opened not to the living joys or interests of others, but to calculations of interest, and money-getting, and money-saving, and to the remembrances of a few dead people. It was for this reason Felicia was to marry Jim; for this, and also because old Marlow hated strangers, and liked his own way. One of the young people was indifferent on the subject. This was Felicia, who told James what her grandmother had told her. James, who had seen more of the world, looked at her earnestly and curiously for a minute.

"You must think of it, dear," he said.

II.

FELICIA, being now solemnly engaged to be married, had settled that it was time they should give up keeping rabbits. It seemed a pursuit scarcely consistent with the dignity of a young betrothed couple; and yet from day to day she put off the execution of this stern decree. It was not to be any very tragical transaction, for rabbit-pie, which the Squire affectioned, was a horror and an abomination in Felicia's eyes. Jim had made a private arrangement with a little gardener's boy, who consented, after some bargaining, to accept the unconscious creatures, upon payment of twopence apiece from James. The gardener's boy did not make an unfair bargain: it is the usual charge for giving away rabbits. But besides the twopences, there was also the pang of separation. It must be confessed that Felicia had the most to be pitied on this occasion. The rabbits went on nibbling their salad-leaves to the last moment, nibbling and relishing up to the very edge of the stalk.

"Why don't you keep them?" said James, seeing the girl's eyes full of tears.

"No, I don't want them any more," says Felicia. "Good-bye, Puck; good-bye, Cobweb; good-bye, Mustard; and she stroked the stupid sleek ears, and laid her soft cheek upon them, and kissed them with an affection that was scarcely requited.

It was some joke of her grandfather's which had determined Felicia to part from her favorites. She had a morbid horror of being laughed at. I think she was deficient in humor, and people who are wanting in fun, as a rule, are those who can least bear being laughed at. James's was a different nature. He used to smile at life. It had been a hard one for him on the whole. Weak health, small powers of application, failure, a generous and tender heart, and a narrow meed of love in return. All this did not go to make his fate a very bright one. Little Jim Marlow was a fatalist in his way: he resigned himself to his narrow destiny. As for Felicia, that was a hope too bright for him to reckon on; he never expected to win his cousin's affections, though he did not say no when Felicia came to him that day, saying, "Jim, is it true we are to be engaged?" He loved her so truly that he would have almost consented to give her up if he had felt convinced it would be for her welfare. His nature was so gentle and peaceful, that no thought of himself or of his rights ever seemed to trouble him. Some people worry over their own interests, but he let them alone. Perhaps he had a secret presentiment that there were not many more for him. Reproofs which would have been an indignity almost if they had carried any bitterness with them, he scarcely noticed. He went his own way: he dreamt over his books: Felicia was the one person he loved best in the world, and in her service he would wake up from his dream of peace to face the troubled realities of life; or perhaps I should say from his realities of peace to face the troubled dreams of life; but that is the problem.

"I don't know what you will do without your rabbits, Felicia," said Jim, feeling that this moment had now come for a little good advice. "You will have to take to reading, or music."

"Jim," said Felicia, suddenly turning round, and opening her gray penetrating eyes, "do you know any other young ladies besides me?"

Her cousin blushed up. "I know one or two," he said.

"What are they like?" says Felicia, looking quickly at him, and then again stroking her rabbit. "I suppose they all talk French and play the piano?"

"Some of them do," said Jim. "Felicia, I wish you knew something of music."

"I am very glad I don't," says Felicia, changing color. "It's too much trouble."

"I know a Miss Flower who plays all sorts of charming old tunes," said James. "I should like you to know her; she does not live very far from this: though, after all, perhaps you would not like her."

"I hate young ladies," said Felicia. "They are all so silly."

"Only now and then," said James, smiling. "Is Miss Flower silly?" says Felicia. "I think you are very unkind;" and her gray eyes circled deeper, and she drew herself up slight, white, against the old stable-door.

"Miss Flower may be silly for all I know," said James. "I hope not, for I think some day she will marry a friend of mine—Baxter—you know. She is his cousin, she lives with his aunt and his little girl, and he seems very—"

"Shut the door," says Felicia, still very cross.

Y

"I hear grandpapa's voice; he will be laughing at my rabbits again."

So James shut the door as he was bid, and the two stood waiting silent in the stable darkness, with the great lines of brightness shining through the joints of the planking, and red lights where the knots were in the rough boards against the windows, while the rabbits went on nibbling and crunching. The empty stalls gloomed dark and mysterious. The two stood silent, waiting for the voices to pass.

"There, you can see the boundary from here," old Marlow was saying, outside. "You can think we offer over, Captain, and let me hear from you in a day or two. It will make a pretty addition to the farm, whoever buys it."

"I have almost determined upon buying the farm," said the other.

"It's Baxter," whispered James.

"Hush!" said Felicia.

The voice went on. "This is rather a fancy price for the field, Mr. Marlow, and I am afraid I must give up thinking of it. I will speak to my lawyer, and—"

"Why did you come to me if you didn't know your own mind?" growled old Marlow. "I thought you wanted the field as a favor. Who told you I wanted to sell it?"

"I was told you were thinking of selling it," said Baxter; "and I asked your grandson if you would give a neighbor the refusal."

"I thought so," says the old man, more and more angry. "James is a meddlesome blockhead, and it is all along of such chattering fools as him people think my land is going about begging, d—— him; I believe he does it on purpose."

James turned away, as this growl reached the two young folks in the stable. There was a sort of low angry sound from Felicia, then a silence, then—"Why, why don't you go and contradict him?" cried the girl, giving her cousin a push. "Go."

James hung back. "What is the good?" he said with a sigh. "He is an old man. I hate a scene."

But if James hated a scene, it was not so with Felicia. There was something new stirring in her nature that seemed to cry out for a vent for action, for spectators. Baxter should not hear James insulted. "I am not afraid," said Miss Marlow magnificently; and before James could stop her, she had sprung to the great stable-door, flung it wide open, and was standing outside in a blaze of sunshine, confronting the two—the old grandfather and Captain Baxter, whose dark face didn't show much of the surprise he felt. For that the old stable-door should fly open before them, and an avenging goddess should appear sudden, overwhelming, breathing vengeance and retribution, was certainly the last thing the angry old schemer, or the disappointed neighbor, had in their minds. Felicia's eyes were radiating, her lips pouting, her cheeks brilliantly flushed. She had never looked more beautiful—certainly never so angry. "How

dare you say such things of poor Jim, grandpapa? It is cruel of you and unjust; yes, and you know it. I told Captain Baxter about the field."

"Oh, listening!" says grandpapa, quite unmoved; "and James too. Come out of your hiding, James, and you" (to Felicia) "go back to your grandmamma."

"You know it is not James who chatters," persists Felicia, stamping; but her courage begins to fail a little at the two steady shaggy old eyes fixed upon her. As for the stranger, she indefinitely feels that there is protection in that straight, dark-looking figure now greeting her cousin. But she scarcely realizes this. Some sudden storm had been stirred; some sudden flame had burnt up fiercely, only to go out as such flames do after a minute's flashing and flaring.

"Do you hear me, Fay?" says Mr. Marlow; "go up to your grandmother. I'm busy with the Captain, and don't want you here."

"But you have been unjust," cries Felicia, worked up, more and more passionately. "I will not have James spoken of as you have done."

"Do you hear me or not?" roars old Marlow; and then James came forward and pulled Felicia's arm through his and led her off without a look or a word at the angry old man. Baxter looked after the two as they walked away. At first Felicia clung to her cousin, trembling and sobbing; then in a moment she pushed him violently away, then she set off running; and when she ran poor James could not follow her, for his breath failed, his heart beat so that he could not hear or see; he sat down upon the steps of the house, and there Baxter found him a few minutes after, almost fainting and utterly exhausted by the morning's work.

III.

Felicia, having pulled her arm away from her cousin, ran back to the house in a troubled, furious, tearful mood. She was indignant with her grandfather, angry with herself; for James she was feeling something almost like scornful pity. Why had he been so silent?—why did he allow that intemperate old man to speak of him in such a way? She had seen Captain Baxter give one glance at James and then at her grandfather. Why did not Jim do something, instead of putting down a basket of lettuces and offering her his arm? He was more like a rabbit himself than a man. Oh, why was she not a man herself? as she stamped in a fury.

"Where is James?" said her grandmother, meeting the girl in the hall.

"I don't know; how should I?" said Felicia, and she passed on, flitting from room to room, till she found herself at the end of the house in a certain play-room which she considered her own. Here she began to cry afresh;

then she dried her tears; then Felicia, defiant, ran to an old piano, and began strumming noisily on the keys. "Miss Flower, Miss Flower," she sang, banging with all her might, and thumping.

And meanwhile, outside in the hot garden, poor Jim was still straggling and panting for breath. When he heard a quick foot upon the gravel, the sound turned him faint and sick with apprehension. He thought it was his grandfather, and, in his present state, every thing seemed to him terrible. But it was only Baxter who, black as his face was, and fierce of aspect, sympathized with any thing that was in want of help, or that was weak, or in pain. He stopped short, sat down on the stone step beside his friend, and asked him if he was ill?

"Ill!" gasped Jim, "no—that is—I—I'm used to it. Is Felicia—"

"Felicia!—is your cousin coming back?" said Baxter, guessing more than poor Jim meant to reveal.

"If she would come—she would know—" said the young man, panting still.

"I will fetch some one," said Baxter, really frightened; and he hurried up the steps and along the stone terraces, and hearing a sound of noisy music coming through an open window, he stooped under the creepers that were hanging over it and went in. He only came into an empty little passage-room; but from a door he heard loudly now the jangle of some old cracked piano, and he knocked impatiently, and entered without waiting for an answer.

Felicia was still playing; for, notwithstanding her protest, she could play a little, and she was strumming at some old-fashioned jig, I think she called it, which had grown out of the noise. She was standing, and playing, and bending over the music. The room was not a sitting-room, but some sort of lumber-place such as people, who live in big old houses, can afford to spare to old boxes and scraps and odds and ends of furniture, and the discarded piano had been put away there among the lumber. The room was dark: great green wreaths were hanging before the windows. There were no other blinds, and none others were wanted. There was nothing to shade except old boxes and fishing-rods, some broken chairs; a great cracked looking-glass, leaning against the wall, reflected the checkered light and the whole slim length of the musician. She stood in her green faded dress among the rakes and geranium-pots, where feeble sprigs were sprouting; and, close by, was an old chest, upon which stood a ship full sail, and three bald-headed goggling dolls. Any other time Aurelius might have paid some martial compliment, and admired the pretty girl making merry among the rubbish; but he scarcely noticed her. It was only after he got home, in reply to the questions they asked him, that he seemed to see it all again, and remembered how she had looked, and where he had found her. Tum-tum-te-tumty! clattered Felicia, stopping short as the door opened. She was somewhat taken aback

when the dark lean figure came marching up to her straight and grim-looking.

"Will you come to your cousin?" said the Captain, without any preamble. Her feelings did not require much tender handling in his estimation. "He seems to me very ill. Perhaps you may know what to do for him."

"Ill!" exclaimed Felicia, starting away from the piano, with a slight crash among the geranium-pots. "Have you seen grandmamma? she always nurses him when he is ill." And she stooped to pick up the flower-pots, and to stick back the sprigs and cuttings that had fallen out of them. Felicia did not appear to think much of James's illness.

Baxter was more and more indignant.

"Poor fellow," said Aurelius; "he does not seem to get much nursing from any body." The Captain was downright angry, and did not care who he offended. At home, if his little finger ached, aunt and cousin and attendant maids were in tears almost, his little daughter would turn pale. It was foolish, and Aurelius made fun of their solicitude, but how infinitely better than this cold-bloodedness.

"He must have some wine," cried Felicia, carelessly. She did not choose to let Baxter see she had noticed his taunt, and she went on before him, leading the way with a little careless dancing step. "Oh dear me, who has got the keys? Scruby, Scruby," sang the girl, and at her call a dilapidated-looking man put his bald head out of the dining-room door. "Scruby, Master James isn't well; have you got any wine out?"

The three-o'clock dinner-table was set, and a bottle with a little wine in it was put ready by the old Squire's seat.

"Not that," said Scruby, feebly proceeding to explore various drawers and cupboards. But Baxter impatiently seized the bottle and poured its contents into a tumbler.

"That's grandpapa's wine!" said Felicia, a little awe-stricken, and Scruby made a toothless exclamation.

Baxter did not say a word in reply, but walked off quickly. As he hurried along Felicia followed him. "I thought you cared for your cousin," said the Captain to the girl as she came up a little timidly to the place where poor James was lying. He was better; the color had come back into his cheeks, and he was drinking the wine which Baxter had brought him. He looked up, smiled, and held out his hand to Felicia, and she, without speaking, held it between her own two soft palms as she knelt leaning against the stone banister of the terrace.

So the Captain left them. He met Mrs. Marlow coming out of the house with a reproof on her lips.

"He should not excite himself over trifles," said the old lady, briskly. "I have never had a day's illness in my life." Mrs. Marlow seemed to think that it was her own good sense which had kept her well all these years. She did not mean to be unkind, but she never pretended to any thing she did not feel. It was her way; she had no morbid terrors, no hidden pains and shrinking nerves, wherewith to sympathize with others. All this had died out in her; nowadays no impressions reached her, though the old ones of fifty years before sometimes came to life again. She loved her husband and she loved Felicia. She tolerated James. When her children had died, in her despair she had almost blamed them for their weakness—she had mourned them after her own fashion. The whole generation of sons and daughters and sons and daughters-in-law had passed away, but the tough old folks lived on, tending the two little orphan grandchildren.

Here is one of them dragging himself up the steps with the help of the other. Felicia at least bears no sign of illness or premature decay. How blooming she looks as she drags Jim up with her arms. Mrs. Marlow thinks in her heart there never was a sweeter, brighter face, and half pities the girl linked to poor little Jim for life.

As Aurelius rode off he thanked heaven that all women were not like those two. He had found it very sweet to have come back after years of hard work and loneliness to the tender solicitude of a gentle old aunt, and Lucy his little daughter. They were of a different type and order to those two women he had just left. Good and tender and unselfish, and living for others instead of existing scarce alive in that strange silence and exhausted atmosphere which oppressed him and every one else at Harpington.

Baxter had often heard James Marlow speak of Felicia; this was only the second time he had ever seen her. His first impression was of something that he never forgot—a wild, bright, sudden gleam. In later days he sometimes thought of the beautiful angry face that had flashed out upon them from the darkness. When he thought of this he melted and softened, and by some contradiction he told himself that it was a pity that such a bright brilliant flame of youth and unreserve should be dimmed and chilled down by rough cold blasts, and by time, and by indifference. But that is the story of many and many a beautiful flame. Just now, however, it was Felicia's indifference and not her beauty that was paramount in Baxter's mind; her indifference shocked him. He thought of her more than once that day.

"Is she pretty?" asked his aunt, and Aurelius paused for a minute before he answered.

"I forget—yes, she is wonderfully pretty. Those may admire her who like." Poor James had got a bad bargain, for all her brilliant loveliness. Sometimes the Captain relented a little, and then he thought of Felicia as a thoughtless child; but again he would tell himself that she was at best but a hard-hearted little siren playing jigs in her beautiful golden hair, while her victims drowned round about her. That hateful tune he had heard her play kept nagging in his ears: he found himself humming it at night as he paced the quiet lane in front of the house, smoking his midnight pipe before going to bed, long after the other members of the peaceful little household retired.

IV.

THE poor siren was also sitting up in the dark in her little room at that minute. The great hall clock had struck one, but the child had not gone to bed; and yet midnight was a much more terrible affair at Harpington than in the cottage where Captain Baxter was staying, and where you could hear the cat purring in the kitchen all over the house. At Harpington far-off rats raced down the long passages. Far-off creaks and starts sounded in the ears of startled watchers. Felicia was frightened, but she was used to being frightened. If any thing terrible came out of the barred door which led to the empty rooms she could run down the passage screaming, and her grandmother, who rarely slept, would hear her. Room after room, dark and gloomy and ghostlike, dim passages, staircases winding into blackness—all this was round about. Jim was under the roof at the other end of the wing, and the old people were sleeping in state in the great front rooms. Felicia had opened her window. She had heard a dog bay somewhere across the dark fields, and seen a star or two shine out through the dim veil of clouds overhead. She could not see, though she peered out ever so far with her two bright gray eyes, where the line of the fields met the heavens. It was all dark, and sweet, and dim, and fresh with that indescribable calm of sleeping night. The air was touched by the scent of the fresh green blades, and of the pinks in the kitchen-garden. Some young owls began to hoot and whistle, but only for a little. Then every thing was silent again. And when every thing was quite silent, Felicia once more sat listening to a voice that began telling her the events of the day over and over again. These voices are apt to speak in the silence of the night, and to keep people awake.

"I thought you might have cared a little more," the voice said to Felicia.

"He thought me hard, cold, cruel," said Felicia to herself; and she began to remember how Baxter had looked at her—just as he had looked at her grandfather—with a curious, hard, indifferent look, such as no one had ever given her before. Then she went over it all again and saw James lying straight out on the stone-step, and the broad shoulders of Aurelius bending over him. She saw the orange-trees on the terrace, and her grandfather crossing by the side-walk to avoid them, and her grandmother coming out of the house. There was the little scene bright painted on the darkness before her. She was sick of it, but there it was.

"Poor fellow, he does not seem to get much

nursing from any one," said the voice again; and then again, "I thought *you* might have cared for your cousin."

This time the voice sounded more forgiving; but no, there was the vision of the tall unrelenting figure walking away without another word. Why was she not angry? Oh, he was right—he was right—that was why. She should have been more gentle with her cousin. She should not have pushed him from her. How kind he had been: yes, he was right to take her away when her grandfather stormed. He (Jim) had no strength for scenes and fights, and she had no strength. She only stormed and failed. She had never loved Jim so well as at that moment. Even though she had been so angry with him, she never before understood his goodness and gentleness as she did now. And then no one had ever told her before what was right: what she ought to feel and to do. Oh, if she had but one friend in the world whom she could trust, who would help her a little; then she would know how to be good, and how to take care of Jim, and how to make him happy. Captain Baxter should see that she did care—that she was not utterly heartless. . . . So Felicia, sitting there, dreamt her waking dreams through the night.

Poor little Jim, tossing on his bed in the garret under the roof, did not know of Felicia's remorse and love, as she sat wakeful at the foot of her little iron couch, and yet—this is a theory which people may scout if they will—the unconscious magnetism of her good-will reached him in some mysterious fashion, and by degrees the fever left him, and he was soothed and quieted and fell asleep. Felicia longed for the morning to come that she might go to him, comfort him, make him forgive her. Jim was peacefully dreaming: he thought he was eating his dinner off the old china plate in the morning-room, and that Felicia came in and tossed it up in the air.

He came down late, and breakfast was over. The old couple were already on their rounds; but Felicia, who was sitting on the window-sill waiting, jumped up and ran to meet him. As she came up, Jim, looking into her face, saw a sweet troubled tender look that he had never seen before; gray eyes half tearful, a trembling color, a quivering mouth.

"Dearest Jim," she said, with both hands put out to meet his; "forgive me, I was so cruel yesterday; I have been so unhappy about it;" and she held up her sweet face to be kissed. Never in all his life before had he seen her look like this. It was almost more than he could bear.

"Forgive, dearest Fay! Don't talk of forgive," he said, putting his arm round about her, and leaning his head for a moment on her shoulder.

"You are still quite tired and weak; here is your tea and your egg," she said jumping away. And all breakfast-time Felicia waited on him, bringing him at last a bunch of ripe grapes she

had stolen (though she did not tell him so), by breaking a pane of the grape-house.

"If Captain Baxter could see us now," thought Felicia, "he would see I am sorry to have been heartless."

Poor Jim! How delicious the grapes tasted, how happy it made him to be a little comforted and loved! He could hardly realize his own happiness, or believe that this was in truth his own Felicia.

When Aurelius rode over that afternoon to see his friend he found him quite restored, reading in the window of the old lumber-room. Felicia, in her green dress, was still strumming on the piano, *La ci darem:* she was playing, with a great many false notes, out of an old music-book she had discovered in a corner. She shut up the piano with a bang, however, when Aurelius came into the room, and soon after disappeared, leaving the two young men together.

Baxter sat on for some time talking to Jim. He tried to give him good advice, and tell him to hold his own. James, as usual, shrugged his shoulders, and smiled, and sighed: so long as he had Felicia he did not care what others said or did or thought of him, and so he said. Baxter did not answer, but soon after got up and went away.

He was very sorry for his friend. It did not seem to him, for all James told him, that Felicia cared for him in the least. Once more he told himself that she was a hard-hearted, ill-tempered little creature; and so thinking, he walked away, and down the old stone steps along the periwinkle walk leading to the road. And then he looked up, and saw that there was a figure at the gate sitting waiting on the grass-grown step. The figure jumped up quickly, and came to meet him. A wild, nymph-like little figure, in her quaint green dress, with her hair flying. It was Felicia who had taken a great resolution.

"I was waiting for you," she said, opening her gray eyes wider and wider. "I have something to say to you. I want you to listen." And she stood before him so that he could not pass. "You think me heartless," she said. "You think I do not care for James. You think I am not good enough for him. Oh, Captain Baxter, you are right; that is what I wanted to say to you; but, indeed, indeed I know how good he is, and I do love him, and do try to take care of him, and I can't bear that you should think me quite wicked and heartless." And the tears stood in her eyes.

"Wicked! heartless!" said Aurelius, feeling in his turn ashamed. "It is I who am wicked and heartless, ever to think any thing of the sort, and I thank you for making me know you as you are." And he held out his hand, and went away touched and melted by the girl's confidence.

James, who had seen the two from his window, came down the walk a minute later, and found Felicia standing quite still in the middle of the path where Aurelius had left her.

"What have you two been talking about?" Jim said.

"Never mind," said Felicia. "Do you want **to know?** He told me I was heartless that day you **were** so ill, and I wanted to say to him that I do love my friends, and am not quite without **a heart.**" She said it so prettily, so shyly, so **quickly,** that Jim's vague jealousy melted away, and he looked down admiringly at the sweet bright face beside him.

This was only a very little while before Jim went back to college for his last term. Baxter came once or twice to see him, and then, when he was gone, the Captain's visits ceased. Mrs. Marlow **gave** him very plainly to understand she did not care for him to come, and there was nothing at the Hall that Baxter cared to come for; not even Felicia, although he often thought of her in her slim green dress.

Once or twice he met her in the lanes; once, the very day he left for town, in a buttercup field with a great golden ball of flowers in her hand. That day little Lacy was with him, and Felicia gave the child the flowers. Little Lacy, who had read of princesses in fairy tales, firmly believed Felicia to be one of them, and talked of her all the way home. Felicia was a very silent princess, and never spoke, but always ran away.

V.

MY story, as I am telling it, seems to be a sad one, of which the actors themselves scarcely know the meaning. What does it take to make a tragedy? Youth, summer days, beauty, kind hearts, a garden to stroll in; on one side an impulsive word, perhaps a look, in which an unconscious truth shines out of steadfast eyes, perhaps a pang of jealousy; and then a pause or two, a word, a rose off a tree—that is material enough for Tragedy. She lays her cold hand upon the best, the fairest, and sweetest, and most innocent. For my own part, Tragedy seems less terrible, with her dark veil and cold, stern face, than Comedy in her tinsel and mask. Tragedy is terrible; and as she passes, tears flow and cries of pain are uttered; but along with these are heroic endurance, faithfulness, self-denial, and tender, unflinching love, that her dark veil can not hide nor her terrors dismay, and she passes by, leaving a benediction behind her. Flowers spring up along the road, her arid wastes are repeopled, the plough travels over the battle-fields, and the living stand faithful by the sacred memories of the past.

But Comedy seems to scorn her victims. How can they rise again from her jibes and jeers? For Comedy take middle age, take false sentiment, and weakness, and infidelity; take small passions, unworthy objects, affectations, rouge-pots, calculations, the blunting influence of time. It makes one's heart ache to think of the cruel, cruel comedies of life, into which good people are drawn, and gentle natures, only to be cast out again, sullied and mortified, and broken-spirited and defiled. When the crisis comes, Comedy grinds her mad teeth and tears her false hair and cries and writhes, and the spectators laugh and shrug their shoulders; but they love and pity Tragedy, as she passes along despairing, but simple and beautiful even in her woe. We pass through all these phases, youth and tragedy and the comedy of middle life, and then, I suppose, if we are sensible and honest-minded people, comes the peace of age, and, at all events, the silence that follows all youth and life and age; when at last Comedy shrinks away abashed and powerless.

This silence was hanging over the old house at Harpington; its unconscious inmates came and went as usual, sitting out in the lovely summer sunshine, living the same still life. For the last time—it was all for the last time—and yet it seemed like any of the other summers that had flooded through the old place, across the fields, into the remotest nooks and corners of the neglected gardens, shining on the high tiled roofs and the ancient elms and rooks. Even old Marlow would come out and bask in the lovely summer weather, conning his account books, and making his calculations under the trees to the singing of the birds. One day two butterflies came flitting and bobbing about his head. Felicia burst out laughing at the sight.

Jim had gone off, telling them to remember the 10th. He was to come back from Oxford in the beginning of July, and it had long been settled that Felicia and her grandmother were to accept an invitation they had received, and meet him in London, and spend ten days there, and buy Felicia's wedding-clothes. Mrs. Marlow was to see her doctor and the lawyer at the same time; old Marlow had desired this arrangement—I don't know in what fit of generosity—it was a whim: a sort of remembrance of the week he had spent in London before his marriage. The clothes were unnecessary, but he would not have to pay for them; so he chose to do the thing handsomely for once; and all this being accomplished, there would be no further reason for delay. Jim and Fay should come back and be married out of hand. It was also a sort of intended encouragement to Felicia, who certainly showed no eagerness to enter into matrimonial bonds; but, if going to London depended upon being married, here was Felicia as eager as any one to be married, for London was her dream, her heaven upon earth, her soul's aspiration. Why she should have sighed and longed after all these millions of brown half-baked bricks, piled one on the top of the other, I can not tell. Jim had sometimes told her stories of London streets and parks, and promised that he would take her to see the sights. They were to stay with an opportune old sister of Mr. Marlow's, from whom a letter had come one morning to every body's surprise:

"Queen Square, June 27.

"MY DEAR BROTHER," wrote the old lady—"When I think how many years we have both lived, and how many have passed since we last met, and how very few more we can expect to be together in the world, it occurs to me to write to you and ask you if it is not time to let past things be past. This is our mother's birthday, and I have been thinking over old times, and I feel that I should much like to see you once more. Are you coming to town? and if so, will you give me the great pleasure of receiving you, and come to me with your wife and your granddaughter? I hear Felicia's marriage is to take place before very long: and she must be doubtless thinking about her trousseau. I should like to contribute a hundred pounds towards it, in token of the good-will of an old maiden aunt who has not quite forgotten her earlier days. She can expend it to the best advantage during her stay with me.

"I am thinking of going abroad, so that I would only beg that I may soon have the pleasure of welcoming you in my house. With love to your wife, your affectionate sister,

"MARY ANNE MARLOW."

"Well," said Mrs. Marlow, as she finished, "Mary Anne seems to be flourishing—going abroad."

"I shall answer that letter," said the Squire, in a determined voice. "You had better go, and take Fay with you."

"Me!" cried Mrs. Marlow. "I am not going to leave home, Robert. I am just making my jam."

"Jam!" said the Squire, "who wants jam? But I tell you what, Mary Anne seems disposed to be liberal, and I don't see why we shouldn't get the benefit of our own as well as any body else. That house in Queen Square ought to have been mine at this minute."

"Nothing will induce me to set foot in it," cried Mrs. Marlow, "after all that has passed. You can take Felicia yourself, Robert, if you choose to go."

"Go! It is out of the question," said old Marlow. "I must look after my crops. What should I do in London?" said the Squire.

As usual, the old fellow had his way in the end. He frowned and insisted, being determined not to lose that chance £100.

"Harpington, June 29.

"MY DEAR SISTER,—I thank you for your letter, inviting us to your house, and alluding to old times. Although I am unfortunately prevented from accepting your invitation, my wife and granddaughter will avail themselves of your kindness, and Felicia will be glad to do her shopping under your auspices.

"It is many years, as you say, since we met, and we are both, doubtless, very much changed. Believe me, your affectionate brother,

"R. MARLOW."

Felicia felt as if they were really going when she went into her grandmother's room one morning to find doors and cupboards wide open, and strange garments and relics piled on the floor, and on the bed, and on the window-sill, and Hannah Morton, the housekeeper, dragging in a great hair-trunk and a rope. The old lady was selecting from a curious store of wimples, and pockets, and mittens, and furbelows, and out of numbers of faded reticules and bags, the articles which she thought necessary for her journey. Felicia's experience was small; but she asked her grandmother if she thought so many things would be wanted for a ten-days' excursion.

"Who is this, grandmamma?" cried the girl, holding up a black plaster silhouette.

"Put it down, child," said Mrs. Marlow.

She could not bear her treasures to be inspected. Few old ladies like it. They store their keepsakes and mementos away in drawers and dark cupboards—cupboards fifty years old, drawers a lifetime deep.

And so even these slow, still, wall-inclosed days at Harpington came to an end at last. They ended as the old trap, with its leather straps and chains, drove up to the door with George, the gardener, on the box, and the drag swinging. The carriage was at the door; the sandwiches were cut; the old hair-box was corded. Felicia, who even now, within ten minutes of her going, expected that an earthquake would come to engulf London before she should see it, that her grandfather would change his mind, or, at least, that the white horse would take to his heels and run away down hill, began at last to believe in their going.

The thought of it all had been so delightful that the delight was almost an agony, as very vivid feelings must be. Felicia had been wide-awake all night, starting and jumping in her little bed, and watching the dawn spread dull beyond the trees (as it was spreading behind the chimney-pots in the dream-city to which she was going). Now she stood, with her little brown hat tied over her hair, watching the proceedings with incredulous eyes. The old gig, with its bony horse, was no miraculous apparition; but miracles take homely shapes at times, and we don't always recognize them when we see them. The gray hair-trunk was hoisted up by Hannah and George, the bags were brought down, and then Mrs. Marlow, walking brisk and decided, equipped for the journey, with strange loopings and pinnings, with a bag and a country bonnet, appeared arm in arm with her husband. The grandfather had sometimes driven off for a day or two, but the grandmother's departure was a much more seldom and special occurrence. So Felicia felt, as well as Mrs. Marlow, as she stood on the threshold, with her arm still in the old Squire's. It is affecting to see some leave-takings: outstretched hands that have lost strength in each other's service; eyes meeting that have seen each other's brightness fade. I don't know if the end of love is a triumph or a requiem: the young man and woman are gone, but their two souls are there still in their changed garments; the throb of the full flooding current is over, but it has carried them on so far on their way. Here were two whose aims had not been very great, nor could you see in their faces the trace of past aspirations and high endeavor. Two mean worn faces looking at each other for the last time with faithful eyes.[*]

"Good-bye, Robert," said Mrs. Marlow, wistfully. "Take care of yourself. You will find the cellar-key on the hook in my cupboard."

"Good-bye, my dear. Give my love to Mary Anne," says the Squire, signing to the **man to** help his mistress up. When the old lady was safe hoisted on the seat of the little carriage, once more she put out her thin hand, and he took it in his. "There," said he, "be off; don't stay beyond your time."

"You will have to come for me," said Mrs. Marlow, smiling; and then Felicia jumped up and they drove away. Then the Squire tramped back into the house again. How dull and lonely it seemed, all of a sudden. Empty rooms; silence. Why did he let them go? Confound Mary Anne and her money! It was all his own doing, and he loved his own way, but it was dismal all the same. What was this? his wife come back **for something.** For an instant he had fancied her **in the room.** Marlow pulled down the blind noisily, making his study still darker than it was before; then he pulled on his wide-awake, and trudged out through the stable-yard into the fields, where he staid till dinner-time, finding fault with the men for company's sake. Mrs. Marlow had not yet left home in spirit, though she was driving away through the lanes; she was roaming through the house, and pondering on this plan and that for the Squire's comfort: and Felicia was flying ahead of gigs and railways, through a sort of dream landscape, all living and indistinct, like one of Turner's pictures. That was London—that dim, harmonious city; **and Jim was** there; and Captain Baxter, would he come and see them, she wondered? **Perhaps** they might meet one day suddenly; **and then** her London heart, as she called it, began to throb.

VI.

The old house in Queen Square stood hospitably waiting for the travellers. An old butler came to the door; an old lady, looking something like the Squire in a bonnet, beamed down to meet them. Two old four-post beds were prepared for Felicia and her grandmother. There was some indescribable family likeness to Harpington in the quiet old house, with its potpourri pots, and Chinese junks, and faded carpets, and narrow slit windows. But the welcome was warmer; for Miss Marlow nodded, and brightened, and twinkled more often in five minutes than the Squire in his **whole lifetime.**

"How do you do? Welcome, **my dear.** Well!"—taking both her hands—"are you very much in love? Pretty thing, isn't she? Eliza, I wish you had brought my brother **with** you. Come up, come up. There, this is the drawing-room, and this is the balcony, with a nice little iron table for lovers to sit at. Now come up stairs. There is some one to dinner. Matthew, send my maid. We must make the bride look prettier still for dinner; mustn't we, Jim?"

Miss Marlow enjoyed nothing so much as a romance, for she had been in love many many times herself.

"And so you say Robert is not a bit changed since he was last here? why, that is a century ago at least; we are a good wearing family, and as for Felicia, I hope she will look just as she does now for twenty years to come."

They all had some tea very sociably together. Miss Marlow poured it out, with her bonnet very much on one side. Mrs. Marlow imagined it to be London fashion, and mentally railed at new-fangled **London** ways; as for Felicia—breathless, excited, with radiating gray eyes—she took in all that was round about her—the aunt, the old servants, the potpourri, the fusty cushions and gilt tables, the winding Westminster streets outside, the Park, the distant roar of the town, the tops of statues, and turrets, the Horse Guards—and ah! the Prince of Wales actually in person, riding down Birdcage Wall. She went up stairs to dress for dinner, and presently Mrs. Marlow came in with some ancient amethyst ornaments.

"Here, Felicia, I shall not wear them myself. You may have them," she said.

Felicia, who had been looking disconsolately in the glass at a pretty face and shining hair, was charmed, and instantly fastened the bygone elegance round her slim white neck, and felt herself beautiful.

"Oh, *thank* you, grandmamma. Shall you wear your jaspers?" Felicia asked.

But Mrs. Marlow answered abruptly, she was tired, and she should not come down at all. She looked black and rigid, and it was in vain Felicia implored her to relent in her determination.

"Your great-grandfather's will was iniquitous," said Mrs. Marlow, absently. "Mary Anne has no possible right to this house. Yes, I shall remain in my room. You may stay with me, Felicia, if you feel as I do on the subject."

"Oh, grandmamma!" gasped poor Fay. "It happened such a *very* long time ago. I think I will go down."

"You can do as you like in the matter, and judge for yourself," said Mrs. Marlow, coldly. "Send me that volume I gave you to read on the way."

* "Tous les hommes sont menteurs, inconstants, faux, bavards, hypocrites, orgueilleux ou lâches, méprisables et sensuels; toutes les femmes sont perfides, artificieuses, vaniteuses; le monde n'est qu'un égout sans fond où les plaqués les plus informes rampent et se tordent sur des montagnes de fange; mais il y a au monde une chose sainte et sublime; c'est l'union de deux de ces êtres si imparfaits et si affreux."

And so Felicia left her grandmother reading a volume of Porteous's sermons, and escaped much relieved, and went and knocked at her aunt's door to tell her of the change. Miss Marlow popped her head, still in her bonnet, out of her bedroom.

"Not coming! Dear me, what a pity. Ready? —that is right, my dear: make yourself pretty, for Captain Baxter is come."

* * * * *

A kind fate sometimes gives people what they wish for long long before they have ventured even to expect it; Felicia had hoped to see Baxter once perhaps, or twice—meeting in a street just before she left—and now, the very first evening of her arrival, she was told he was come—down stairs, actually in the house! Make herself pretty! Her cheeks brightened up of their own accord, her lips began to smile, and such sweet, gay, childish happiness beamed from her gray eyes, that Miss Marlow was obliged to come out of her room and embrace her on the spot then and there.

Felicia lingered a little as she went, and as she lingered it was with an odd feeling that she recognized the living of some of the old home things, some chairs like those at Harpington, and some old Italian china, and a plate not unlike the Sola plate at home, with arabesques and ornaments, but no clasped hands were there. Felicia came to the drawing-room door, at last, hesitated and went in very slowly. James had not come down. Felicia in her amethysts turned pale, as Baxter, who was standing alone in the room, came up to greet the young lady.

At a first glance Aurelius thought Felicia very much changed. She looked older, graver; perhaps the dusky damask, and gorgeous picture-frames, and gilt tables made a less becoming background than the ivy walls and periwinkles at Harpington.

"I am so glad to see you again," he said. "It was very kind of Miss Marlow to let me come and meet you."

As Aurelius finished this little speech, he looked at her again. What had he been dreaming of? she was prettier, far far prettier than he remembered her even. A sort of curious bright look, half conscious, half doubting, was in her eyes; she blushed and smiled.

"I am so glad you have come. I was afraid I should only see you by chance," said she.

"We have not had a talk since that last time we parted," said Aurelius, stupidly; "but little Lucy treasured up her flowers."

"And you believe me?" Felicia cried earnestly, blushing as she spoke.

"I never doubted you," said Aurelius; and he believed he was speaking the truth. Beauty is the most positive of all convictions.

The others presently came into the room, Miss Marlow resplendent and ushered in by gongs.

"James, take your bride in to dinner," she cried, with a nod and an intelligent look at Baxter, who glanced at the two and then stiffly

offered his arm to the old lady. The Captain was a favorite with Miss Marlow, who liked good looks, and had not yet got over an early penchant for the army. She had asked him first at James's suggestion, and now counted on him as an agreeable escort on the many occasions she had already devised for taking herself and Felicia to see sights, theatres, parties, toilettes. There was no end to the things Miss Marlow wanted to take Felicia to see.

Mrs. Marlow let her sister-in-law go her own way. She could not forgive her, and would not join many of the schemes and expeditions. She was envious, lonely, and home-sick: after that first day she would come down and sit dismally in a corner; but, in her way, she was touched by Felicia's delight, and, perhaps, she wondered if she had always done enough for the happiness of the two children she had reared. Felicia and her betrothed behaved exactly as usual. Jim tried to find a proof of Fay's affection for him in the long hours she spent among the ribbons and gauzes of her trousseau. The girl brightened, chattered, ruled her kind and patient little lover with an iron rod, and then rewarded him by one word of happiness. If she was happy it was all he asked. Poor Jim! his was but a small share of all this excitement and pleasure. Fay wounded him one day by saying before Baxter, "You don't look at all like a husband, Jim; you are much more like an uncle." This was the first time she had ever talked about their approaching marriage. In vain Jim spoke of coming times, and tried to find out what was in her mind. She shifted, parried, doubled, and finally would run away altogether; she was too happy in the present to face the future, and all Felicia's present, like a dissolving view, had opened and revealed delights more endless, even, than any she had imagined for herself.

Many people, seeing her sitting in the Park one morning between Jim and Captain Baxter, looked a second time and smiled at the dazzling young creature. There was a great flower-bed of red rhododendrons just behind her chair. She had put on one of her pretty new trousseau dresses; she was gay, glad, happy, beyond any happiness she had ever conceived before. As for her approaching marriage, I do not honestly believe she had ever given it a single thought; all she knew was that she was sitting there with Jim to take care of her, and to wait as long as ever she liked, with Baxter—who was kind now, and who no longer thought her heartless—with a sight so glittering and cheerful that that alone would have been enough for her. The horses went by with their beautiful shining necks and smooth clean-cut limbs; the amazons rode along, laughing and talking as they passed; the young men, magnificent and self-conscious, were squaring their elbows and swooping by on their big horses; the grand dresses and ladies went rustling along the footpath; the pleasant green park spread and gleamed; a sort of song, of talk, and footsteps and sunshine was in the air. High over head the little pinkish gray London clouds were sailing across the blue sky, and the long distant lines of white houses were twinkling with light. And yet nothing is quite perfect; why did Aurelius ask her just then when the marriage was to take place?

"Marriage!" said Felicia, "what marriage? Ours do you mean? Oh, any time."

"My grandfather talks of August," said James gravely.

"August! when is August?" said Felicia, looking a little strangely. For the first time a swift quick pang of certainty seemed to come over her. It was like nothing that she had ever felt before. But she was brave, young, and confident; she wanted to be happy, and so in a moment her dancing gray eyes were raised to Baxter's.

"You must never talk about our wedding again," she said; "we don't like it. We mean to be happy while we can, without troubling ourselves about the future; don't we, Jim?"

"I hope we shall be happy any way, dear," said Jim, gravely.

Aurelius looked from one to the other and thought this was the strangest love-making he had ever witnessed. The next time he came he brought a little parcel in his hand, which he asked her, in an ashamed sort of voice, to accept as a token of sympathy on an occasion he was not permitted to name. Felicia had heard of wedding-presents, but had not thought they would come to her. She screamed with delight, seeing a beautiful little gold-glittering ring for her arm, from which a crystal locket was hanging.

"Oh, how pretty!" she cried. "Is it for me —really for me? Oh, thank you. Look, Jim; look, grandmamma."

Mrs. Marlow looked, and dryly said it must have cost a good deal of money. As for Felicia, she was radiant. The loan of her grandmother's amethysts had charmed her; how much more this lovely thing, glittering, twinkling, her very own. It was a link, poor little soul, in her future destiny.

*   *   *   *   *   *

Days went on, and the time was drawing near for their return. Felicia's pretty gowns were bought, and Miss Marlow's hundred pounds expended. The old Squire wrote to his wife bidding her come home and bring the girl. Our poor little Proserpine, whose creed it was to live in the present, and to pick the flowers, and not to trouble herself with what she did not see, woke one day to find that the present was nearly over, and the past was beginning again. The past! was she to go back to it; to leave life and light for that tomb in which she had been bred; to see Aurelius no more, London no more, living men and women no more; live with only sheep, only silence, only shadows, and the drone of insects to fill up the rest of her life; only Jim, Jim whose every thought and word and look she knew by heart? "Oh! it was hor-

rible; it was a shame. It shouldn't be. She couldn't go," said Felicia to herself. "She would stay on with her aunt. She would ask her. She would not go." She began walking up and down her little bedroom, like a young tigress pacing a narrow cage. Her grandmother looked in hearing a hasty rush of footsteps, and Felicia stopped short in her walk.

"Is any thing the matter?" said Mrs. Marlow.

"Nothing, grandmamma," said Felicia. And then when the door was shut again, once more she began her fierce gymnastics. A few minutes before James had said, "We must come again when we are married, Felicia, and see all the sights we leave unseen now."

"There is plenty of time," says Felicia.

"Three days," says James.

"Three days!" cries the girl; "but I don't mean to go, I don't want to go, I shall stay, James, do you hear? Aunt Mary Anne will ask me. How unkind you are!"

"I am afraid Aunt Mary Anne is packing up to go, too," said poor stupid James. "Dear, some day when I have the right to bring you, you shall come for as long as you like."

"Some day! I want it now," cries Felicia. "I haven't seen the waxworks or the lions. I —I *will stay*," she flashed at him in a passion. And then, as usual, she ran away, realizing that she was talking nonsense, that she was powerless, that she was only a girl, and that here was happiness, delight, interest, a world where every hour meant its own special delight, sympathy, friendship; and friendship was more than love, thought Felicia, a thousand times, and she might not taste it. To be her own self, that was what Felicia longed for. Here in London life seemed made for her; there at Harpington it seemed to her, looking back, that she was like one of the periwinkles growing round the garden-gate.

VII.

Baxter was, as I have said, a widower; he looked back to his early married days now from the heights of thirty-five. Life was not to him the wonderful strange new thing it seemed to Felicia, coming from her periwinkle haunts, from the still lichen-grown walls of brick, which so effectually keep out many spiritual things, and within which all her existence had been inclosed. When Baxter found himself gratefully accepting Miss Marlow's invitations to dinner, coming day after day to the old dark house, patiently waiting among the needlework chairs and cushions in the gorgeous drawing-room; planning one scheme and another to give pleasure to little Felicia, who was so happy, and in such delight at his coming—when he found himself thinking of her constantly, and living perpetually in her company, he said to himself —for he was a loyal gentleman—that this must not be. It was a pity, but it must not be. He had respected his wife, but she had never charmed him. People generally destined him for her cousin, Miss Flower; but now he began to tell himself that this also was impossible. There had been one real story in his life, of which people knew nothing, which was told now, and to which (for it was there written and finished) there were no new chapters to add, for the dictating spirit was gone forever. As for Emily Flower, she and Aurelius understood each other very well: they were sincere friends, nothing more, and they let people talk as they perhaps talked of others in turn, without caring or knowing very much of concerns that were not their own.

If Felicia had not been going back so soon, and her fate decided, and if James himself had not asked him again and again to come home, to join them in one excursion and another, Baxter might have kept to his good resolves, and avoided the bright sweet young sylph who had beguiled him. But it was for such a little while, surely there was no harm in it, he told himself. She would not guess her secret, poor little thing—sacrificed to the old people's convenience and cupidity. Suddenly, thinking of it all, of Felicia's unconsciousness, a sort of indignation seized the young man at the thought of this marriage. Some one should save her; some one should hold her back—say a warning word before it was too late. He would interfere; he would go to Mrs. Marlow and protest. But then came a thought of Jim, generous, gentle, unselfish, full of heart and affection—worth a dozen Felicias, thought Baxter, who was not blind to her faults—only he loved her all the same—and Jim also loved her, and Felicia was indifferent; that was the cruel part of the bargain.

Who are we, to judge for others? In after days, Baxter remembered his indignation, remembered it in shame and in remorse. It was too late then to change the past; but not too late to regret it.

Felicia cried herself to sleep that night, and again Mrs. Marlow came into the child's room, and stood by the great four-post bed, where the little creature was writhing and starting.

"Fay, my dear," said the old lady, "you forget yourself. Wake up. What is it?"

Felicia woke up, with her great sleepy eyes full of tears, stared about her vaguely, and then fell asleep again, as girls do.

I think, if she had spoken then, the old lady would have helped her; but she slept quietly, and Mrs. Marlow, who had been frightened, left her. Felicia was so little used to talk to her grandmother, that she did not know how to do it. She would as soon have thought of telling the marble washstand that she was unhappy.

But, nevertheless, Jim had spoken, and Felicia's looks had implored, and Mrs. Marlow, with heroic self-sacrifice, had written to ask for leave to stay another week. Felicia, hearing the great news, never for an instant doubted that all was right, and once more she embarked in her golden seas of contentment.

There was a little expedition she looked forward to with some excitement. It should be the last, Baxter had mentally decided. There was to be a river, a row, a tea-making in the woods. Little Lucy and her cousin, Miss Flower, were to come to it, and James, and Fay, and Miss Marlow, who was always ready to enjoy herself. Mrs. Marlow, according to her wont, said she should not be able to go.

Felicia came down early that morning to breakfast, and flung open a window to let in a fresh gust of early London soot. Some distant cries reached her ears. A morning sight of busy park and passing people spread before her. Some far-away bells were ringing. All was wide, bright, and misty. She tried to realize her own happiness for a minute; but couldn't. A whole day's pleasuring—a whole week's respite. Her grandmother had written, and all was well. Another week! Another week was another lifetime; and she need not trouble herself about what would come after.

"Oh, Jim, I am so happy," she said, going up to him, as he came into the room.

And then came post, tea-urns, old ladies, and funny old mahogany tea-caddies; and then came, once more, swift, and sharp, and overwhelming, a pang of disappointment more cruel than any that had gone before.

"I have heard from your grandfather," said Mrs. Marlow, quite cheerfully (as if it did not seem a matter of life and death to poor Fay), "and he says, my dear, that we have been away quite long enough, and that we must start to-morrow, as we first arranged."

"To-morrow?" gasped the girl, in a strange numb horror.

"I suppose you have got your finery, and I hope James has bought the gold ring" (reading). "There is nothing to wait for now, and the wedding may as well take place on your return. The banns shall be put up next Sunday, and there need be no more talk about the matter. As for Parsons, the way he has behaved about that horse was only what might have been expected. I shall have him up at the next assizes, and let the county see that I am not the man to be put upon. Remember me to Mary Anne . . . ." So read the old lady.

Felicia heard no more: she listened, turning white and red over her teacup: she looked up once imploringly at James, and met a shy adoring glance that made her hate him. Mrs. Marlow nodded relief. Miss Marlow was beaming and kissing her hand; the old butler, who had come in with some boiling water, seemed to guess what was passing, and he too smiled. And Felicia was cold, pale, furious, in a strange desperate state of mind—desperate, and yet determined, and sure even in her despair of some secret help somewhere—she did not tell herself whence it was to come. She could bear it no longer, and jumping up, white as a ghost, she ran out of the room.

Felicia never forgot that day in its strange jumble of happiness and misery. Baxter was right when he called her cold-hearted. She no more cared for Jim, no more thought of his possible pain, than she thought of the feelings of the footman who opened the door, or the stoker who drove the engine.

The sun shone, the engine was whistling; Aurelius, holding little Lucy by the hand, and accompanied by a smiling young lady in a hat and long blue veil, met them at the station. Jim, still unconscious of his companion's silence and preoccupation, pulled her arm through his and carried her along the long line of carriages, leaving his aunt to Aurelius's care. All the way Jim had talked and asked questions in his unusual elation; every word he said worried and jarred upon the girl. Now, in his happiness, he went on talking and chirping, but Felicia was in a cloud, and did not listen; sometimes, waking up, she thought of appealing to him then and there, in the carriage, with all the others to take her part, and of imploring him to help her—to what? to escape from him. Sometimes she felt that her one chance would be to run away, and never be heard of again; sometimes, with a start, she asked herself what was this new terrible thing hanging over her—this close-at-hand horrible fate—made for her, such as no one before had ever experienced. Then for some minutes, as was her nature, she put it all away, and began to play cat's-cradle with little Lucy Baxter, who was sitting beside her.

They reached Henley at last, scudding through broad sunny meadows, with a sight of blue summer woods, and of the hills overhanging the flooding river; they lunched at the old red brick house, with the great lilac westerias hanging and flowering, and then they took a boat and rowed against the stream to Wargrave. Sliding, gliding along, against the rush of the clear water, past the swirls of the wavelets, and the rat-holes, and the pools; among the red reeds and white flowers, along damp, sweet banks of tangle and grass. It soothed and quieted poor Felicia's fever; by degrees a feeling came to her of a whole world passing away in remorseless motion and of a fate against which it was vain to struggle. This was life and fate to be travelling along between green banks, with summer sights, and flying birds, and woods and wreathing green things all about, while the stream of life and feeling flowed away quick in a contrary direction, with a rapid rush carrying the sticks and leaves and mementos, and passing lights along with it. And so at last she was soothed and calmed a little as the boat swung on. Perhaps there is happiness even in travelling against one's fate, thought poor Felicia, despairing. The happiest person in that boat - load was little Lucy, who had not yet reached her life, and next to her the old lady, who was well nigh over it, who sat talking and chirping to Miss Flower. James was silent, for he had at last discovered Felicia's abstraction, and he had seen that she did not hear him when he spoke to her. But when Aurelius once made a little joke, Felicia brightened up again, and suddenly seemed to throw off the cloud which oppressed her.

As the boats touched the shore they saw a fire burning in the little wood; the smoke was rising blue and curling, and the flames sparkling among the sticks. All the summer - green slopes of the wood were bright with leaves, twigs, buds, fragrant points; faint showers of light and blossom and perfume seemed falling upon the branches; it may have been the effect of the sunbeams shining on the woods lighting the waters. The lodge-keeper's wife had lighted the fire, which smoked and sparkled, and Emily Flower made tea. Aurelius laughed and shook his head when she offered him some—tea was not much in his line, he said; nor was Felicia yet of an age much given to tea-drinking: that is a consolation which is reserved for her elders, who are more in need of such mild stimulation; but she stirred her cup, and set it down upon the grass, and waved away the flies with the stem of a wild rose that James had picked for her.

Every now and then Felicia stole a glance at Miss Flower. She could not understand that demure young lady, who looked so little, spoke so rarely. She seemed so unlike any of Felicia's experiences (experiences, by the way, which were chiefly confined to herself, for she had never had a companion), that Felicia could not understand her. Emily Flower, however, understood Felicia very well, and the two did not somehow seem to amalgamate. Felicia wished that she could be sure Miss Flower and Aurelius were nothing to each other. She looked from one to the other more than once.

"Are you still happy, Felicia?" said Jim, sadly, coming up to her as she stood there waving her rose-branch.

"Happy?" said Felicia. "No; I am miserable."

"What makes you miserable?" James asked.

For a moment she had a mind to tell him; then her courage failed.

"I can't go back," she cried, evading the truth, with a sudden impetuous burst of emotion. "Oh, Jim, if you loved me you would help me; but you don't, and I hate you!" Then a minute after she was suddenly sorry for him for the first time that day, and as he stood silent and hurt, she put her hand on his arm. "You know I don't hate you, Jim," she said, piteously. "How silly you are to mind." And she dashed the rose-branch across her face to wipe away her tears.

Nobody noticed this little scene, except perhaps Aurelius, who had been standing near, and who walked away with little Lucy and began pulling down ivy-wreaths for the child.

I don't know how he knew, but at that minute Jim, in his turn looking from one to the other, seemed to understand it all. He left

Felicia for a minute, and then came back, wistfully.

"Can't you trust me, Felicia?" he said, in an odd, doubtful voice.

But poor Fay had not even trust to give him as yet. She did not understand, and stared with beautiful listless gray eyes. Then she went and flung herself down by the fire, and watched the flame crackling and drifting among the glowing twigs, and listened to her aunt talking on and on to Miss Flower, and to the sound of the river running by the bank, and washing against the leaves and the grasses. . . .

VIII.

THE tea-party was over—they were floating with the stream again, and travelling back at a rapid pace past the trim green rustic lawns at Wargrave towards Henley — past a desolate-looking island, where a barge was floating ; past banks of wild roses, flowering and hanging in fanciful garlands : golden flags were springing, and lilies opening their chalices, and stars, white and violet, were studding the banks of this lovely summer-world. Then they left it all, and passed into a dark cavernous dungeon of waters, shut in by great wooden doors. Felicia was not yet used to locks, and she and little Lucy grasped each other's hands as the boat began sinking into the depths, sinking to the roar of the weir and the mill, into slimy green profundities, hollowed and destroyed by the discolored tides. The little rose-cottage where the keeper lived went right up into the air—so did his little children, who had rushed out to help to open the sluices.

Down went the boat to the very depths: the great green dripping walls were covered with slime and weeds ; up above roses were flowering on the surface of the earth ; down here the sunlight scarcely touched the gloom, and dank dripping mould and creeping vegetation. Little waterfalls burst through the rotten gates and fell roaring and rushing into the dark waters.

"Oh, what a terrible place !" said Felicia.

Miss Marlow gave a little shriek as the boat bumped suddenly against the side of the lock.

"Are you frightened ?" said Baxter to Felicia.

"Yes," said Felicia ; and then she looked up and smiled. "I mean no," she said, "not if you—" Then, seeing that James was looking at her, she stopped short.

Jim, who was standing up with the boat-hook in his hand, turned away, and, stooping over the edge of the boat, looked at something deep down in the river. Perhaps a minute may have passed—it seemed a very long while to him. When he looked up again, Felicia was blushing still, the great gates were opening, the water was pouring through, and a glimpse of the sweet flowing river shone once more between the great

portals : it all looked more lovely if possible for the gloom in which they had been waiting.

Then Jim and Baxter pushed with their long boat-hooks, and the boat began to slide out from the dark jaws in which it had been inclosed. The gates creaked as they opened wide: the boat was almost between them—when something happened. I can not exactly tell how, a great barge that was waiting outside began to move, and struck against the gate. The lock-man had been called away, one of the two boys turning the pulley tripped and fell, the other boy's hand slipped ; the windlass began to untwist rapidly, and the great gates to close fast upon the little boat.

"Pull ! pull !" shouted Baxter, who was at the bow, to James, who had instinctively begun to back.

Their two contrary efforts delayed them for an instant ; James, seeing the danger, with a great effort caught at the gate with his boat-hook, and, with an impetus from his whole body, urged the boat through. It was just in time, the boat was safe, the barge was stopped ; but the boat-hook stuck in the wood, and before any one could help him, Jim was over and splashing in the water.

It was no very great matter : a punt close at hand came to his help, and the little boat's crew landed, and waited in the garden while the lock-keeper dried Jim's clothes. The man lent him some of his own while the others were drying, and Jim, coming out of the little rose-cottage in a fustian jacket, top-boots, and fur cap, found Miss Flower sitting on a little green wooden bench under a rose-tree. He saw old Miss Marlow's broad back as she stood placid, gazing at the river, and Aurelius and Felicia and little Lucy were wandering along the banks under the little row of willow-trees in the meadow, where the cows were crunching the buttercups. There was a bird singing somewhere, and a dog leaping in the grass, and a sweet flood of peaceful light.

Miss Marlow turned round from her contemplation of the river, hearing Jim's voice. She came up and took his arm, and leaning heavily, proposed that they should follow the others.

"Come, Miss Flower, you are not doing your duty," said the old lady, "allowing your cousin to flirt as he does with engaged young ladies."

But Emily said gravely, "No, thank you. I am tired, and I will wait for you here."

Felicia and Lucy had found great bunches of forget-me-nots growing down by the river. They were trying to tempt the cows to come and eat them.

It was about eight o'clock when they reached the station. Little Lucy was to go home immediately, and to bed. She and Emily Flower had come up for a two-days' visit to a friend. Miss Marlow, like an old goose, instead of saying good-bye, cordially invited Captain Baxter to come back to supper with them. Wouldn't Miss Flower come, too, if they dropped little

Lucy on their way? But again Miss Flower refused very decidedly.

"I think Lady Mary expected you, Aurelius," she said.

"Then I will go with you," said Aurelius.

"Oh, Miss Flower, our last night!" cried Miss Marlow, reproachfully.

And then poor Emily, who could not bear to seem grasping and unreasonable, said, blushing, that she could easily explain to Lady Mary, and she begged Aurelius to call a hansom for her and Lucy, and the two drove off to the house in Chesham Place, where they were staying. They were to go home the next morning.

Felicia and her aunt went off together in a brougham which had been waiting, and reached Queen Square some little time before the two gentlemen arrived. Felicia's first question was for her grandmother. The old butler said that Mrs. Marlow was in her room. She had been out that afternoon, and came home about four o'clock complaining of faintness. Felicia thought her looking ill, when she ran in, in the glad way that girls burst in after a pleasant day.

"Are you ill, dear grandmamma? We have had such a day!" said the girl. "Oh dear me, why is it over? I wish you had been with us. Oh, how I wish we were not going to-morrow! What has been the matter?"

"I don't know," said Mrs. Marlow a little strangely. "I have been ill and out of spirits. I could not have staid away longer from home, Felicia. I have suffered too much for your pleasure as it is."

Felicia flushed up, hurt. "My pleasure, dear grandmamma! I don't have so very much."

"You never think of any thing else," said Mrs. Marlow. "Girls are always thinking of their pleasure: they don't mind what pain they give others," the old lady went on, still in this strange excited way. "There is your grandfather alone; here am I quite ill and overdone. I shall be thankful when this marriage is over."

"You need not tell me that," cried the girl, indignant. "I know it."

"When a thing is settled and determined, the sooner it is done with the better," said Mrs. Marlow.

Fay's heart began to beat.

"Determined and settled, grandmamma!" she cried. "I think it is cruel the way in which you and grandpapa talk: you have settled every thing for us, and it is cruel, yes, cruel! I can do nothing, and no one will help me, and you care for nothing, so long as grandpapa has his own selfish way," said the girl.

"Hush!" said Mrs. Marlow, white and angry. "This is not the way for you to speak of your grandfather. I am frightened by your impertinence."

The poor lady was ill, nervous, thoroughly unstrung, almost for the first time since Felicia had known her. She had never before taken any of the girl's outbursts seriously. Fay, too, was excited, unreasonable. The idea of breaking off had never occurred to her till that day; she was in an agitated state of mind, impressionable, easily upset.

It all happened in a moment. Miss Marlow had barely time to pant up stairs to find the two in high controversy—Felicia in tears, Mrs. Marlow flushed and agitated.

"What is the matter? My dear Eliza, I am so sorry to hear of your indisposition. Fay, go and get ready for dinner," cried Miss Marlow.

It would have been better, far better for Felicia, if they had ended their little quarrel, fought it out, and made it up with tears. As it was, Miss Marlow separated them, and when the gong sounded, Felicia, still indignant, came into her grandmother's room.

"I am going down, grandmamma; are you ready?"

The old lady was busy packing in the hair-box.

"You had better go, Felicia," said Mrs. Marlow, without looking up. "I will follow. Pray remember never again to speak to me of your grandfather as you did just now. It is what I can not listen to."

She spoke so coldly, that once more Felicia felt a thrill of injured indignation; and she swept down stairs with a heart aching sorely, notwithstanding all the pleasures of the day.

IX.

It was in the evening. They had all finished dinner. Mrs. Marlow had gone up again to see to her packing; Miss Marlow had got up from table and come away into the after-dinner drawing-room, holding Felicia's hand in hers. Baxter—(Miss Marlow, as I have said, had insisted on his coming. I can not imagine how a woman of her sentimental experience can have been so silly. Is it possible that a thought of thwarting her brother may have added a little malice to her hospitality?)—Baxter, who had come back at the old lady's request to say good-bye, was sitting with James in the dining-room. The great windows were wide open upon the balcony, and the dusky park gloomed without, at once hot and cool and mysterious. Felicia, who had scarcely spoken all dinner-time, who was angry still, was summoning up her courage to speak now—to say what was in her heart—to implore Miss Marlow to help her. She loved Jim dearly, dearly. Some day, years and years hence, she would marry him if he wished it; but now, ah, no! it was impossible. She fell down upon her two knees by her aunt's low chair, then for a minute was silent, looking out across the gray evening, watching the distant lights, the bright stars shining clear in the faint summer sky. She thought of the river flowing on —of Jim and his faithful kindness, with more affection and remorse, I think, at this minute, than in all her life before; and then suddenly she burst out, in her childish, plaintive voice, seizing Miss Marlow's hand tight in her two eager little palms—"Oh, tell me what is to happen—what is to happen! Oh, Aunt Mary Anne, what shall I do?"

Aunt Mary Anne was a coward at heart. She turned round and stared at the imploring face upturned to her; she had not realized the edged tools with which she had been playing when she brought two impulsive young people together. There had been, as I have said, a little quiet spite in her doings; a little selfishness, for she liked the Captain's company; a little common-sense and good-will and a feeling that Felicia should see some other man in all the world beside Jim, before she retired with him forever to the solitudes of Harpington. But Miss Marlow had judged by her own vague and manifold sentimental experiences. Felicia's strange looks that afternoon, her sudden cry of pain, frightened the elder lady.

Miss Marlow felt for a moment afraid of poor eager Felicia, and started up all flustered. "Do just what you like, my dear," said the old lady, very nervously. "Nobody can force you to do any thing you don't like. I—I must go and see how your grandmother is getting on." And so saying the old maid trotted out of the room.

She was gone in a minute, and poor Fay was left frightened and disappointed—bitterly, bitterly disappointed. "What was the good of being old, of having lived all those years, if she had no help, no kind word to spare for a poor little thing in trouble?" thought Felicia. There was a something wild and self-reliant in the girl's nature that would not be daunted. She set her teeth. "I will make her hear me," she said to herself: she would speak again when this evening was over, when Aurelius was gone, and the last happy hour of her life ended forever. Presently, sitting there still, she found that Baxter had come in and was talking to her; she had hardly noticed him at first, so busy was she thinking about him. She jumped up confused, and then they both with the same impulse went out upon the terrace. "James is gone off for a smoke," the Captain was saying, as he followed her. "There he is under the trees." Felicia looked and saw that it was not James, but she did not speak.

A sort of sleepy apathy had come over Felicia after her day's excitement. She did not care what happened just at that minute. It was like one of her many visions, to be sitting there with Baxter, to hear him speak—to listen to his voice in the dusk. What was he saying? He had been praising Jim for the last five minutes. He felt as if by praising the poor boy he made amends somehow for the unowned treachery in his heart against him.

It was some such feeling which irritated Felicia; she was not going to sham and pretend what she did not feel. In all her life this faculty

had been hers of speaking the truth boldly. Some people have loved her for it; others have hated her. All this day the poor child had been driven to the very utmost end of her powers by inward assaults, and doubts, and terrors, born of the very excitements and happiness of the last few weeks. When Baxter spoke, she said quickly that "it was not Jim's goodness she cared about, and yet he was a hundred times too good for her."

"Too good for you!" Baxter said, speaking his thought inadvertently. "Ask him. He does not think so: why, it would break his heart to part from you."

"Do you think so?" cried Felicia, desperate. "Do you think people mind very much, when others break their hearts—when these sort of things are broken off? Don't you see how unhappy I am?" she went on.

Was she false to Jim, poor child, in being true? She trusted Baxter so utterly; she was so young, she felt so convinced that she might trust him; she had begun the talk just now with her aunt—it was but going on with it now, leaning forward with her piteous little face upturned, and waiting for an answer. But no answer came; no one would help her. Baxter was too loyal to want her confidence.

"Come and let us talk to Miss Marlow," he said, very gravely; "she will want you to come in."

"No one—no one will help!" cried Felicia, desperately. "She won't help me. You won't listen to me, you won't help me," she said, as he turned to go; it was all over, there was no hope anywhere.

"Poor child!" he said.

"Are you sorry for me?" said Felicia, simply. "Then I don't mind so much."

"Sorry!" cried poor Baxter, at an end of his courage. "Don't you see how it is, Felicia—that I am trying to be an honest man?"

"Oh, what am I to do? Tell me what I ought to do?" said Felicia, breaking into tears.

Poor little thing! Her heart beat, her tears flowed. She trembled so she could not stand, and she put out her hands wildly to grasp some support. She had no strong sense of duty. When had she ever seen duty practised in that dreary self-seeking household? She did not love Jim as she loved Aurelius. She could not understand that, loving and trusting him, she should not appeal to him.

"Oh, help me!" she said once more, wringing her hands. "Oh, I can not, can not go back!"

You blame him, and so do I, that he was weak; that he did not turn away and leave her; that he caught her two poor little outstretched hands.

"Oh, Felicia," he said again, "do you think it is you only who are unhappy? Don't you see that I—that some debts are almost more than we can pay."

And then he stopped short. What was he saying? What could he say or do that was not a treachery to his friend? And yet these two loved each other; and was it fair that their whole love and life should be marred so that one person should be made half happy, half content? Only, somehow, Aurelius could not reason thus.

"James trusts us; and he is right," said he, in an altered voice.

Poor Aurelius! If Felicia had been older, different, more able to decide; but, as it was, he felt that it was for him to take a part. Felicia, Heaven bless her! was ready to give up her faith, her word, if he had desired it. He had dropped her two hands. She stood crying still, and leaning against a chair.

"I will do what you think I ought," she said.

It was at that minute that a light from the room fell upon the two, and that some one came and stood in the window—some one with a pale face, who did not speak for a minute; then Miss Marlow, following quick and bustling out—

"Why, James, where have you been?" she said. "I have been looking for you. There is a telegram for you. Dear me! it is getting quite chilly, and they have not brought the tea. Would you ring, Captain Baxter?"

"I am afraid I must be going," said Baxter, in a steady voice. No one would have guessed from his voice that any thing unusual had happened, though his face might have told the story, had the light been upon it. He nodded to James, shook hands with Miss Marlow. Felicia never moved or looked up, nor did he look at her again. Aurelius went down the stairs and passed out by the narrow iron wicket into the Park, and then all his strength left him. He went and leant against the railings, resting his arm upon the iron, and covering his eyes with his hand. Shut eyes or open, he saw that trembling, wildly-appealing face. It was no use—it was in vain he had known Felicia. He would do his duty, heaven help them both. His part was clear for the present; he must go and see Felicia no more.

When Aurelius had said good-night to James, the young man had scarcely responded. Baxter did not know how long he had been standing in the window or how much he had heard of what had passed. Aurelius, sorry as he was, vexed, troubled, unhappy, could not but feel that he had acted as an honest man as far as James was concerned. Towards poor little Felicia his conduct had been less praiseworthy. Leaving her, he felt like a traitor, poor fellow; and yet what could he do but leave her? Where it was all to end, Aurelius could not tell. He was a man not greatly given to self-dissection and examination. His life had been too active for more than a sort of jour le jour conscience. He knew that on the whole he hoped to do his duty as a gentleman and a soldier: to wrong no man or woman, to speak the truth, to take a fair advantage of the enemy when he saw a chance. For all his thirty-five years there was a certain boyish rigidity about him; and having said that

black was blue, or discovered that he intended to leap a five-barred gate, or be in such a place by such a day, black was blue in his eyes, he leaped the gate, he went through any inconvenience to keep his word. I do not know that there is any particular advantage in playing this sort of game of skill with fate and inclination. But it is a way some people have, and they are honest people for the most part.

Aurelius, contrary to his wont, had allowed himself to drift a little along the stream in the pleasant company he had been keeping of late. Now he stopped short, and as he stood for a minute by the iron railing, he made up his mind. No; he would not go any more to the house. He would not say good-bye to Felicia. He would not meddle in the business. He could not help it if the girl was to be sacrificed. She was not the first or the last woman to make a mistaken marriage, and it was no affair of his. So Baxter walked away angry through the twilight of the summer's night, quick, straight, rigid, disappearing rapidly into the gloom. As he went along he saw Felicia's sad eyes appealing everywhere, through the glimmering twigs on the trees, shining from the stars, and once in the gas-lit windows of a shop-front. He did not care, he hardened himself and walked on quicker. Poor Aurelius! he thought it was a shame to leave her. He told himself again that it was a crime that two people should be sacrificed for so little cause. He knew James well enough—that scrupulous soul—to be sure that a word would set his conscience swaying and whirling, and secure Felicia's liberty. He knew all this, he knew it would be right. He felt that he was acting wrongly and cruelly, and inflicting unnecessary pain; and yet, somehow, right as it might be to interfere, he (Baxter) was determined that the deed should not be of his doing. He should not be the one to hand his friend the weapon with which to destroy his happiness, nor to suggest to Felicia the possibility of inflicting upon her lover a deadly wound. And so he walked away with brisk steps farther and farther from the dim balcony where the passionate cry had so nearly touched him, where the poor, pale, trembling little creature was still crouching in the dark.

Poor little Felicia! Baxter was gone, and the child, shrinking out of sight, sat down upon one of the low window-steps. James went to find his telegram. The tea-tray was brought up, then Miss Marlow came and called her, and went away. Fay gave no answer. She only wanted to be alone—to be left to hide herself there in the gray darkness and melancholy of the night. There was a black corner behind a little laurel-tree in a box. Felicia—poor little Daphne that she was—longed to creep into the narrow dark hole and stay there. Never come out again, never hear her own voice speak again, never ask people for help and be refused any more. No one helped—no one cared for her. She covered her face with her hands at the thought—abandoned and despised. Ah! if she could only be nowhere; but wherever she was, she cumbered the earth, thought poor little Fay in her despair. Would there be vast groves of laurel, I sometimes wonder, if men and women possessed the power of changing themselves at will into inanimate trees in moments of shame and bewilderment? What a terrible boon it would be to humanity! One can imagine the fatal wish granted—leaves springing from the slender finger-ends, the wreath of laurel creeping round their heads, the narrow choking bark inclosing them in its rapid growth. And then the faint aromatic breath of the prussic acid, and then the wind shivering among human leaves. Poor Fay would have wildly grasped at the power if it had been hers at that minute; but nowadays, little girls in trouble can only cry and sit with their faces hidden in their hands, instead of becoming stars and streams and plants. She had spoken in an impulse, and now that the impulse was over, what would she not give to have been silent—her life, her right hand, any thing, every thing. So the night wore on, the black leaves rustled close to her shining head, London was rolling itself asleep and quiet by degrees.

Felicia at last hearing some clock strike eleven across the house-tops, pulled herself wearily up, and came out of her hiding. Very pale she looked, with a black smudge upon her white muslin dress, and wild, sad eyes, with great pupils. She could not see, coming into the dazzle of the drawing-room lamps, but she heard voices calling her, "Felicia, Felicia!" They seemed to be everywhere; and then James, who had come into the room, rushed up to her. "Oh, Felicia," he said, "I have been looking for you. Go—go to grandmother—there is terrible news from home. . . ."

While Felicia had been absorbed in her own griefs and preoccupations the great laws of life and death and fate had not been suspended, and the news had come that the Squire was dead.

He had been seized with some fatal attack in a field, and carried to a cottage close by, where he died. He had been found by some laborers.

X.

JAMES and Felicia never forgot that terrible night. When the morning came, her despair of a few hours before seemed like a remembrance of some old tune played out and come to an end abruptly in the midst of its most passionate cadence. The tunes of life stop short just in the middle, and that is the most curious part of our history. Another music sounds, mighty, sudden, and unexpected, and we leave off our song to listen to it, and when it is over some of us have forgotten the song we were singing. Perhaps in another world it may come to us again.

This death-music was now sounding through the old house in Queen Square. The poor grandmother lay crushed and stunned by its

awful thunder; the old aunt, to whom it was familiar enough, came and went with a troubled and yet accustomed face.

"You had better not go to your grandmother, child," she said, looking into the room; "she is best alone."

Fay appealed to Jim, who looked distressed and took her hand in his, and to comfort her he said they would go together, when Aunt Mary Anne was below.

And so about midnight there was an opportunity, and the two went up stairs together. The unshuttered windows let in the gleam of a starry sky, for the vapors had drifted away. They came along the passage to the door of the dim front bedroom, where Felicia had left her angry grandmother a little while before, and where she was now lying stricken, cold, and motionless, and stretched at full length upon the great bed. There was a dim night-light in the room, and they seemed to feel the hard, stony grief as they came in; to meet it—a presence with a vague intangible form. Felicia, with a beating heart, stood by the bedside. Mrs. Marlow neither moved nor spoke. At last the girl knelt down, and softly and imploringly kissed the old brown hand. It was moved away. "Grandmamma, dear grandmamma!" sobbed Felicia; but her grandmother, in an odd, harsh, hissing voice said, "Is James there?" and when he came, said, still in this quick strange way, "I want to be alone, James. Take her away."

Poor Fay! she was trembling like a little aspen, and as she got up from her knees she held to the chair by the bedside. She was hurt and wounded almost beyond bearing. She put her hand to her heart: "Oh, grandmamma," she faltered, "I who love you so—"

But Mrs. Marlow never moved, or looked, or answered, and James, putting his arm round Felicia, brought her away gently and closed the door. Once outside in the passage, Felicia cried and cried as if her heart would break. Miss Marlow came up stairs, and finding Fay there, tried to scold her.

"You should not have gone to her when I told you not. She is not quite in her right mind," said the old lady; "and people in her state often turn against those they love best. You must be good and patient, and James shall come and fetch you. I think—Jim, don't you think—Fay had better stay here and pack up after we are gone, and then you can come back for her to-morrow?"

And poor Fay meekly assented, crying still, and utterly crushed and worn out. But she would not go to bed: nobody went to bed that night. There was an early morning train at six o'clock, by which the travellers were to go. A conveyance had to be found, preparations had to be made, packing done, and notes written. Felicia fluttered about, trying to help, utterly weary. Then at last she lay down, about two in the morning, on the golden sofa in the drawing-room, and slept till a cab driving up through the silence awoke her. She knew it was the cab which had come to take the others away, and she jumped up from the sofa and went out on the stairs: she was afraid to go to Mrs. Marlow's room.

Felicia stood with a wistful face waiting to see them off, but her grandmother passed her without a word or a look. The women came down together, followed by James, with bundles and cloaks upon his arm. Miss Marlow stopped to kiss Fay and bid her go to bed and try to sleep. Jim said with his kind face that he would come back; and then they were gone, haggard mourners, in the light of the clear early dawn. The cab-wheels rolled and echoed through the silent streets. Fay stood where they had left her, listening to the sound, but presently a kind housemaid came and begged her to come to bed, and helped Felicia to undress, and brought her a cup of tea, and sat by her bedside till she had fallen asleep.

When Felicia awoke it was ten o'clock, and a misty morning sun was streaming into the room. The housemaid had been opening and shutting the door and peeping in many times, and she now appeared to ask Miss Marlow if she would come down to breakfast, or if the butler should clear away.

Felicia said she would come down, and dressed in a hurry and ran down stairs, with an indefinite impression of a scolding from some one. But there was no scolding: only the teapot, *The Times* all to herself, a little dish of cold buttered toast, a new pot of strawberry jam sent up by the sympathizing housekeeper. Felicia liked the jam, but she had no great appetite, and presently she forgot to eat, and sat looking at her own reflection in the teapot, and conjuring up one last scene at home after another, and picturing the sad home-coming.

There was her grandfather standing before her, as she had seen him that last time, stooping to button the leather apron of the gig. She seemed to see him riding off on the white horse, with his gray wide-awake pulled tight over his gray head; or coming home and walking into the morning-room where she and her grandmother were sitting: then she saw him under the tree that sunshiny day busy over his accounts. Poor grandfather! he had mended her wheelbarrow for her when she was a little girl; and one delightful day she remembered he had taken her in the gig to a farm-house, and given her a cup of milk with his own hands. A crowd of thoughts and remembrances came, and were driven away by a crowd of fancies of what was now, of Harpington all gloomy and shut up. Felicia was so frightened at last that she rang the bell for old Matthew to clear away (Matthew was a portly and prosperous old butler, very different from the poor drudge at Harpington). Matthew stopped a long time, but at last Felicia saw him carry off the last plate and knife, and then she found herself alone once more with the bare dining-room table before her: the mahogany sideboard, the mahogany wine-cases, and

the print of Queen Adelaide over the chimney. She tried the drawing-room for a change. When animate things are away, inanimate things attain to a strange life and importance of their own. All the gold tables and couches seemed to spread themselves out to receive her. Felicia sank down in a corner of the sofa and took the first book that came to her hand; but somehow she could only see the legs of the chairs and the tables, the stuffed birds, and the bust of Miss Marlow in her youth nodding. When she had tried to read for ten minutes, she thought she had been sitting there for hours and hours, with Rogers's *Italy* open before her, and the prints of the mountains, and the reflection of the little boat sailing in the finely-etched lake. Was that horrible little boat never going to reach the shore? Felicia shut up the book and threw it down on the cushion beside her. She was accustomed to being alone; but alone was different at home, where she knew every corner of the house, with the garden, and the farm, and the village children to play with. This was hateful. How could Miss Marlow bear such a life, so strange and still, and crowded with chairs and tables? Felicia did not feel that she might run from the top of the house to the bottom, dive into outhouses and cupboards—as she did at home: here to gaze through glass-doors at the shells and Japanese gods, and through glass-windows at the silent old houses opposite in Queen Square was all that she dared to do. Felicia had taken a horror of the balcony. She went into the passage, and looked for a long while at the old brown house opposite, with the dim slit windows; at the statue of Queen Anne standing calm in all her ruffles and frills. It must be very dull to be a statue, Felicia thought. She wandered up to her own room, but the grandmother's door was open, and through that open door passed a troop of sad hobgoblins: all the grandmother's stern looks, all the miseries of the night before, coming with a rush, and surrounding her.

Felicia fled into the passage again. She looked at the pasteboard effigy, painted and glazed, of a little page in the corner. In one of the glass cupboards on the stairs was a plate which put her in mind of the old dish at Harpington. There was a garland and some scrollwork. But it was not the same, for the clasped hands were missing, nor was Sola written on the scroll. What a horrid thing it was to be alone. Sola—Sola meant alone as well as the only one. Fay made up a little story of some Portia asking her knights to choose off which of the two plates they would dine; and one knight said—"I will dine alone, lady, for I have a good appetite, and don't care to share my meal." And the other knight said he would never touch food again unless one only lady would consent to break bread with him. And then Felicia began to wonder what the lady would say, suppose she liked the greedy knight best. That was a difficult question to answer, and as she was debating it she heard a ring at the bell, and she leant over the banisters to see who it could be.

One of her two knights was at that minute standing outside the door, and she knew his voice when he asked if Miss Marlow was at home, and if Mrs. Marlow was gone back to Harpington.

Then Matthew began a long long story, and when finally he made way for Captain Baxter to come into the hall, it seemed to Felicia that it was like the stream of life rushing into the hushed house again, and that the door of the lock had opened, and that her boat was rising upon the rising waters; but she started away as usual, and ran and hid herself in the little dressing-room out of Miss Marlow's bedroom, where, after a long search, the housemaid found her.

XI.

MEANWHILE poor Baxter was waiting in the dining-room and looking forward with some perturbation to his interview. He had had two lines from James that morning begging him to call in Queen Square, and telling him what had happened. "If I can not get back to-morrow, I am going to ask you to bring Felicia to us," James wrote. Aurelius confounded James's stupidity. Why was Felicia left behind? Why was he, of all people in the world, chosen to escort her to Harpington?

Baxter could not pretend to any great personal regret for the old Squire, but for the poor widow he felt a great compassion, and as for Felicia, well, it would delay her marriage, poor little thing, and so far at least she was the gainer. It was not in human nature not to be glad of the excuse to see her again, although all the way Aurelius railed at his friend, and said to himself he deserved his fate for his dullness and want of comprehension.

Was Jim so dull? He knew Baxter better than Baxter knew himself, and by the light of his own honest heart he judged his friend. Baxter need not have been afraid of the meeting. The long sad night had come like a year between Fay and the indignant tears she had shed for herself the night before. They were wiped out. Baxter's first word brought other tears into her eyes, tears of regret and of feeling for others. Felicia was a whole year older in experience than she had been when he last saw her. As she came into the room with half flashing eyes, Baxter felt ashamed of his alarms, and met her quite humbly, saying something about the shock that they had had and his note from James. "I came to see if I could do any thing for you?" he said.

Felicia shook her head and sat down listlessly in the big chair by the empty fireplace.

"I am alone here," she answered, looking away. "There is nothing wanted. Poor grandmamma went away before six o'clock this morning. She could not bear to have me with her, and so they left me here to wait. I want nothing, thank you."

"Poor child!" Aurelius said. He was more sorry for Felicia, left alone for a day with these gloomy fancies, than for the whole life-agony of the widowed woman. He was, poor fellow, in a state of indescribable pity, vexation, that he could do nothing to help this poor little stricken creature. This time it was not Felicia who appealed to him; it was Baxter appealing to Felicia. "I wish you would let me do any thing for you," he said. Something in his sympathizing looks roused the girl's indignation. It was too late; she did not want his kindness now. For Felicia was used to be adored, and to command poor Jim, and to speak her mind plainly enough. Her almost childish admiration and confidence in Baxter had received a shock. She had discovered that their friendship meant very little after all; that to count upon people outside is of little use in home affairs. To think of her own feelings seemed a sort of sacrilege now at this time. Last night, when she asked him to help her, he left her; to-day, when she did not want him, he came with offers of help that meant nothing at all. There was a certain combativeness, a certain determination in Felicia's character—a horror of ridicule, a want of breadth and patience of nature, all of which feelings kindling suddenly brought a bright flush of angry color into her pale cheeks. "Jim will be here before long," she said. "He will take care of me. Now I want nothing from any one else."

"Good-bye," said Aurelius. "Please remember, however, that if you want me ever at any time anywhere I will come." He spoke so humbly that it was impossible to be angry. Felicia looked at him steadily with her curious gray eyes; her mouth quivered, the color died out of her cheeks.

Felicia's heart began to sink as soon as Baxter had left the room. She sat quite still, and the minutes became hours again, and time appeared interminable, and release so far, far off, that it seemed to this impatient little creature as if in that one instant she had waited for an eternity—an eternity with James at the end of it! Felicia had said good-bye, the door was closed, the parting was over, time had passed, and now, with a very simple impulse, she sprang up and ran out into the hall. Aurelius was still there, turning at the many complicated locks and chain-works that Miss Marlow considered necessary for her security and old Matthew's. They had done Felicia good service on this occasion.

Baxter turned, hearing his name called, and saw Fay in the doorway. "Will you do me a kindness now directly?" she said impetuously, "Will you take me home? I want to go. I can't bear to stay here any longer."

"Had not you better wait till you hear from Jim?" said Baxter, coming back, and not much surprised. "I am ready at any time, but he may be on his way."

"I have been thinking of it. He will not

come till to-morrow," said Felicia, sharply. "Will you do this for me or not? Please do," said the girl. "I do so want to get away. They must want me; they can't be so cruel as not to want me. Don't you think so?"

"They only want to spare you," said Baxter, but when she begged again he could not resist her any longer. "Will you like to go by the five o'clock train?" he asked.

"Yes," said Felicia, eagerly. "Is that the soonest? Please come and fetch me." And Baxter said he would come, and then went to put off half a dozen engagements. He thought the girl would be better off in a home, no matter how sad, than vexing and chafing in the solitudes of Queen Square.

And so it happened that Felicia came back to Harpington all of a sudden. She and Baxter scarcely spoke to each other during the three hours they were on the road. He had come to take care of her, and not to make himself agreeable; and he conscientiously read the paper in a corner of the railway carriage. Fay looked at him once or twice, surprised at first by this silence, and then she watched the fields flit by the telegraph-posts, the cows, the cottages with their smoking chimneys and all their inhabitants; and so they sped along from one county to another; here and there came a shining hamlet, now a gig passing a bridge, now a woman carrying a bundle. Felicia tried to follow some of the people with her mind, but another cow, another gig, another tree-stump, would come and drive out the remembrance of the last. Fay, as I have said, had almost put away the remembrance of the night before. She had thought she should never be able to look at Baxter again to speak to him, but now she felt that they might be friends once more. He was changed, but Felicia was too full of her own thoughts to perceive this. What a strange progression of new feelings and realizations had hold of her—visions of home—visions of London delights—visions of the sorrowful, terrible present, and of the happy past, and of the future of marriage, of loneliness, of doubtful hope.

And so, if Baxter was changed and silent, Felicia, too, was changed and silenced. There were some other people in the carriage who did not find out the two were travelling together. One old gentleman, interested by the pair of innocent, penetrating gray eyes that he caught scanning him, asked the young lady if she was travelling alone, and if there was any thing he could do for her. Then for the first time Baxter looked up from his paper, and said in his blackest and stiffest manner that the lady was under his care.

It was nearly eight o'clock when they got to the station. Baxter had telegraphed from London, and he expected to find Jim upon the platform; but there was no Jim, no sign, and the only thing to do was to walk to the inn and order a fly. They waited under the rose-grown porch in the twilight. Every thing seemed sweet, and still, and peaceful. A gardener belonging to the inn was pumping water for the pretty old garden flowers — lilies, and lupins, and marigolds, and white honeysuckles; the sky was sweet with sunset, and the air with perfume. A couple of dusky figures stood in the middle of the street talking quietly; an old woman came to the door of her cottage. This purple dusk was making every thing beautiful, and how fragrant the air was after the vapid London breath they had been living in!

They had a long, sweet, silent drive across the fields, and between dim horizons and wooded fringes. The evening star came and shone over the twilight silver and purple world before they got to their journey's end. Baxter was silently happy and so was Felicia, who, for a mile or two, had almost forgotten the sorrow to which she was travelling, in the peace and sweetness of the journey. But when the house appeared above the hedge at the turn of the road, her heart began to beat and every thing came back to her.

"The gates are closed," said the girl, startled, as they passed the front of the house.

The gates were closed for the first time since Felicia could remember, and the ivy and wild creepers had been crushed and torn in the process.

This one little incident, perhaps, brought all that happened more vividly to Felicia's mind than any thing else that had gone before. They stopped at the back door, the front gate being locked, and Aurelius desired the fly-man to wait, and came with Felicia to see her safe into the house before he drove away. They crossed the stable-yard and the end of the garden, and so reached the terrace along which were the windows, barred and fast, except one looking more black than the rest. And suddenly came a cruel minute for Felicia, in which all the pain of parting, all the sadness into which she was going, all the gloom of that great shut house and of her hopeless future, seemed realized and concentrated. Baxter, too, looked up at the gloomy walls behind which little Fay was about to disappear; there stood the hall, closed and black, and he thought of the poor raving widowed heart aching within, and with a pang he thought of the little white victim standing beside him.

"Good-bye," he said, putting out his hand quickly.

"Oh, I am frightened," said Felicia, not taking it, not looking, and trembling and standing irresolute. "Oh, what shall I do?"

"There is nothing to be afraid of," said Baxter, kindly. "I have seen a great many people die. It is a much more peaceful process than living. I don't think you need be afraid." Felicia sighed, but did not answer.

"Look, is not that study window open?" Baxter asked.

"Yes, but—but I could not go in there alone," said the girl, as with a shaking hand she tried to unfasten the door. "Don't go yet, please don't go," she said.

"I will wait here as long as you like," said

Baxter. "Perhaps James will see me for a minute. You can send me word."

"Yes," said Felicia. She had got the door **open at** last. Once more she said, "Please **wait,** please don't leave me yet. I will come back to you." She spoke in a shrill, nervous voice, and the words travelling through the silence, woke up James, who had fallen asleep on the study sofa, utterly worn out and tired after his journey, his sleepless day and night of agitation and excitement. Had he dreamt them? had he heard them? He did not know—he started from his sleep, from a vague dream of Baxter and Felicia in the garden outside. He **sat up and** listened—"Don't leave me yet! I **will come** back to you!" He heard her voice plainly ringing in his ears—was it to him she was speaking? Was it Felicia come to make him well and happy by her presence? or was it Felicia speaking to some one else? Felicia false, Felicia lost to him forever!

XII.

Poor Jim! It was when they were going down into the lock the day before that he had made up his mind to it, and told himself that cost what it might he must give up his darling. Felicia was not for such as him. She was too bright and brilliant a creature to mate with any but her own kind.

Little Jim was a hero in his way. His whole life had been a forlorn hope. He had made up his mind, but in this feverish dream from which he was waking, he had forgotten his calmer self-decision and courage—only the natural pain was there, the jealousy, the humiliation, the heart-burning. Aurelius's telegram had come, and he had meant to go and meet them, but as he was waiting, turning over papers in the study, till the time should come to start, he had fallen asleep. Miss Marlow was up stairs with her sister-in-law; the whole house was silent, and no one had come near the study, and Jim for the last hour or two had been lying in a fever, dreaming uneasy dreams and moaning in the deserted room. And now when he started wide awake from his sleep, he was wide awake, but dreaming still in a sort of way, forgetting all his resolutions, remembering only the fancies that had haunted his sleep. Felicia outside with Baxter! Ah false! ah faithless! As the door opened, and she came in, Jim had groped his way to the table, and struck a light.

"I knew you were there," he said, turning his haggard face to greet her. "Oh, Felicia, I was dreaming. Are you going to leave me, quick, tell me? How could I bear it? How can I bear it? It will kill me. I have little enough life; you will take it all if you go."

He looked so strange and so excited that his cousin was frightened.

"Going, Jim? What do you mean?"

"I heard you say so to some one outside," he went on, in his strange agitation.

"Dear Jim," said Felicia, trembling still, "be quiet. Hush! pray hush! See, lie down here. I—I won't leave you," she said; and a faint glow came into her pale cheeks. "Lie still. Don't be afraid. You have had some nightmare," faltered the girl, knowing full well that it had been no nightmare, but her own words, which he had overheard.

"I thought I heard you say you were **going,**" Jim said, still half distraught. "It was a **dream** then—I had fallen asleep. **Oh, thank heaven!** Oh, my Felicia!"

She soothed him, she quieted him with a hundred kind words and looks, and all the while her heart smote her. She was ashamed to meet his honest upturned loving glance.

"Poor boy!" said Felicia, passing her cool hand across his forehead. "Lie still, dear," she said. "I am going for one minute. I shall come back to you."

He sprang up with a frightened sort of cry.

"Ah! now I know it was true," he said. "Felicia, Felicia! You are going. I shall wait and wait, and you will never come back."

"I swear I will come back," said Felicia, earnestly, fixing her great gray eyes upon her cousin.

A minute after, as Baxter stood waiting, listening for the voices, Felicia appeared for one moment in the darkness of the doorway. "Good-night, good-bye, and thank you," she said. "I am not afraid **any** more, and I am thankful I came," and she gave him her hand and was gone.

"Did Baxter come back with you?" James asked, as Felicia came back to him. He seemed like himself again, calm and different, and with his own natural expression. "Have you sent him away? It was a pity," he said. "A pity, a pity," he repeated, thinking, poor fellow, of himself as he spoke. "Dear," he said. "I think I was half asleep just now. I don't know what nonsense I talked. Forgive me."

"You are quite tired and worn out," said Felicia. "You must go to bed, Jim, directly May I go to grandmamma?" But James begged her to wait, and he went and found Miss Marlow, and then he went to bed as he was bid.

Miss Marlow was surprised to see the girl, but welcomed her kindly. "So Captain Baxter brought you? Well, I am glad you are come," and then she told Felicia a long long history of their coming home.

The old lady was very gentle, and cried a little, and she came with the girl to her own little room, past the door of the state apartment where the poor old grandfather was lying. And Fay followed her about meekly, seeing all with her startled gray eyes. Aurelius was gone, but she did not mind. When every body else was so unhappy, Felicia accepted her own share with more resignation. Her grandmother would not see her—that was the thing which most troubled her. Jim was very ill—that was evident—she must do what she could to help him. And then, utterly wearied out, Felicia fell fast asleep, with all the trouble and doubt round about her, and the darkness and gloom of the night, and dreamt the hours peacefully away till the morning light came to awaken her.

XIII.

Two days more, and the closed gates were opened to let the old Squire's funeral pass through, travelling down the periwinkle walk, and followed by the steps of a few old neighbors. Baxter came to the church-yard, but did not come back to the house; and then the blinds were drawn up, and the business of life began once more; only Mrs. Marlow remained still in her room, and scarcely ever left it. The lawyers came to read the will. It was dated many years back. The house and the chief part of the estate had been left to Jim's father, and now consequently fell to the share of the young man himself. There was a jointure settled upon Mrs. Marlow, which (under a stringent clause) she was to forfeit if she married again. Felicia (whose mother had married an offending cousin) was only to have a hundred a year. Another later will had been prepared, but never signed; it was much to the same effect as the first, only that the jointure was increased, and more in proportion to the bulk of the old man's property. He had left nearly £6000 a year behind him, and Jim, who had never until now possessed a spare sovereign to do as he liked with, had money in stocks and land, and check-books, and credit without stint. . . .

James was closeted all day with different people, lawyers, and agents, and tenants; and one day a doctor came over from the neighboring town, and Jim declared next day that he had business in London. Little Lucy, who happened to meet Felicia that day, told her her papa had gone to town with Mr. Marlow.

James came back, and Felicia tried to think that he was the same, but she felt a difference. He was busy arranging, docketing, putting away. People come and went; Felicia scarcely spoke to him. She dined with him (Felicia was surprised to see that Jim could carve), but immediately after dinner James would go away into the study.

As for Aunt Mary Anne, being naturally of cheerful and gregarious disposition, she found it all very dull, and packed up at the end of a week and went off to Cheltenham for a change.

The day Miss Marlow left, Felicia begged her grandmother timidly to let her be with her a little more.

"No, no," said Mrs. Marlow, with a little shiver. "Pray don't ask it; go—you agitate me."

So Felicia went away, pained and forlorn, flitting about with a feeling of disgrace, and the strange uneasy sense of being some tamed animal that had lost its master and was suddenly set free.

One day—it was a little thing, but she took it foolishly to heart—her crystal bracelet, that she liked to wear, came unclasped and fell off her arm. She went roaming about a whole morning looking for it in the empty rabbit-house, in the kitchen-garden, on the terrace walk.

James, coming out of the study for a little turn on the terrace, was struck by Felicia's scared, woe-begone face.

She had been sitting on the step for half an hour in the sun.

"Fay, what is the matter?" said Marlow, in his old familiar voice, as he came up to her.

"Nothing," said Felicia, looking up.

Nothing! That was just the answer to his question. Nothing to hope, to fear, to love, to try for. She did not think that James loved her now: she knew her grandmother had taken a strange hatred and aversion to her presence.

"Nothing?" said James, looking gravely at her troubled face.

"I have lost my pretty bracelet," said Felicia; "but that is nothing, of course. And every thing is horrid, but it does not matter."

"But is every thing horrid?" said James, sighing. "You have lost a bracelet," he continued, absently, feeling in his pockets. "I picked up one this morning on the landing." And he pulled out Felicia's beloved gold and crystal ring.

She seized it with a little cry of delight. "Oh, how glad I am!" she said. "Thank you, James; how clever of you to find it." And she began fastening it on her slim wrist again.

"How clever of you to let it fall upon the landing," he said, smiling. "And now I want to talk to you, Fay," James went on, sitting down beside her on the step. Then he was silent for a little, then he began very nervously: "I have been thinking about a good many things these last few days," he said, "and happiness has been one of the things. Don't you think, dear, we must not care about it too much?"

"Not care!" his cousin said. "How can we not care when we do?"

James looked more and more nervous.

"'We bow to heaven that ruled it so,'" he said, hesitating, quoting from a lay preacher. "I saw Dr. —— when I was in London, and he told me that matters were more serious with me than I had imagined. I don't know how much more, or what may be in store for us; but, Fay, you and I—our two lives, I mean—belong to something greater than our own happiness, at least one hopes so; for one's own happiness seems a stupid thing to live for altogether, doesn't it, dear?"

Felicia's circling eyes were fixed upon his. She was twisting her gold bracelet round and round. Jim looked paler and paler as he spoke.

"I think," he said, "our duty in life, Felicia

—yours and mine—is not to think whether we are very happy or not, or satisfied"—and the poor fellow's voice ached a little as he spoke—"and, perhaps, the mistake we have both made has been that we have thought a little too much of ourselves and our own feelings, and not enough of something beyond them. . . ."

"Dear, dear James!" said Felicia, and her eyes filled up with tears.

James went on steadily, holding her hand in his,—

"And I have been thinking that we have both other things to do just now than marrying and giving in marriage. I must go away and try and get well, to live to do a few of these things; and you must—darling Fay, don't cry—take care of grandmother, and be patient with her, and wait here, and love me a little. And then," resolved to finish what he had to say, he went on hastily, "There is poor Baxter, who wants to come with me; and some day, if he comes back to you, Fay, I think you would be doing wisely to try and make him happy. Perhaps you may not like to think of it just now, but in a little time—" Jim's voice faltered—"One can not foretell the future—"

"Oh, Jim, what a hateful, hateful creature I am!" burst out Felicia, covering her face with her hands. "I have not deserved any thing, and you want me to have every thing; but I will never—never—"

"Hush, hush!" said Jim, gravely; "take care of grandmother, and don't make any vows, and—and—trust me a little, Felicia," he added, smiling a little sadly himself as he got up to go away.

And so Jim cut the knot that bound him—cut it, and all the difficulties that had beset him of late were vanquished. No one had guessed at the depth of his secret grief, and the pain of the parting—not Aurelius, not Felicia, looking up into his calm face, not Jim himself, who thought himself a foolish stupid fellow, but no hero; only it was all over now.

It was the last of the late summer days. As he stood, he heard the distant thrill of the birds, the drone of buzzing insects: the warm touch of the sun came falling upon them both. A feeling came to Jim as if he was looking at Fay, with her sweet upturned face, for the last time; and it was in truth their real parting, though he did not sail for some days later. And yet, of the two at that minute, it was not Jim who was most unhappy. The light of his true heart was shining in his eyes. Felicia never forgot his look: a man of gentle will, standing there, that summer's day, with a gift in his hand, priceless, a life's gift, a true heart's love. And Jim, as he left her, felt that he loved her as she ought to be loved. Loved her enough to leave her with a benediction. He was a sick, and dull, and stupid fellow; but he had played his part like an honest man. Felicia was the only woman he ever loved, hers the only hand he ever cared to grasp; but while he held it, he had held it by force, and when he loosened his hold, the fair hand fell away. And he was content that it should be so, and he wisely accepted the very pain as part of his love.

There is something in life which seems to tell us that no failures, no mistakes, no helplessnesses make failure; no successes, no triumphs make success. And so James walked away victorious, leaving the poor vanquished victress alone upon the sunny steps. Was it Felicia's wish to be the only one? It was granted, and she did not care for it. She was alone now, but free. She stood watching the young fellow as he walked away. Jim's heart was sad enough, but at rest. Felicia's was beating with passionate gratitude, with anger against herself, with a dim new hope for the future, and, at the same time, with a great new love and regret for the past, for the tie that was now broken forever. It was a pang that lasted her for all her life.

Later that day, as she was passing through the morning-room, she happened to catch sight of the old Sola plate through the glass of the china cupboard, and with one of her quick impulses, Felicia opened the glass-doors, took it quickly off the shelf, and flung it to the ground, where it lay broken in many pieces at her feet. . . . . Is this the end of the story? Does any story finish while the flame of life is alight, burning up, and reviving and changing from day to day. Fay's story was a blank for a time after Jim left her in charge at Harpington; a blank from all those things which had seemed to her so all-important. In after-life her love-story may have begun again. But that was when she was alone in the world; when those who loved her best were gone; and Baxter, coming back after years of absence, met her as of old—lonely, sad, glad, eager, and unchanged, flitting between the gray walls of the old Harpington House.

MORETTI'S CAMPANULA.

MORETTI'S CAMPANULA.[*]

* Moretti's Campanula is a flower that grows among the Alps on precipitous rocks.

> "That very time I saw (but thou couldst not),
> Flying between the cold moon and the earth,
> Cupid all arm'd: a certain aim he took
> At a fair vestal, throned by the west;
> And loos'd his love-shaft smartly from his bow,
> As it should pierce a hundred thousand hearts:
> But I might see young Cupid's fiery shaft
> Quench'd in the chaste beams of the wat'ry moon;
> And the imperial vot'ress passed on,
> In maiden meditation, fancy-free.
> Yet mark'd I where the bolt of Cupid fell:
> It fell upon a little western flower—
> Before, milk-white; now purple with love's wound—
> And maidens call it, love-in-idleness.
> Fetch me that flower. . . ."—*A Midsummer-Night's Dream.*

I.

IF you could see Dorchester House, age-worn, sun-burnt, and wind-beaten, with many wooden shutters flapping in the sun, with strange sweet southern tufts of weed springing along its cornices, and from one and another marble window-ledge, house-leeks with soft pink heads, delicate feathery grasses; here and there a trailing nasturtium hanging like a fringe and swinging against the wall, and in the court-yard an orange-tree and a cactus or two, and a mountain-ash with its burning flame of scarlet berries—you would see the palace of the family of Pavis, one of the oldest in South Tyrol. It stands in a little sun-baked town, half-way between Italy and Germany, among the Venetian Alps, and its many shutters open out upon a green and deserted-looking piazza, where a donkey feeds, and women spread their linen strips to bleach. . . . . There is a hotel upon the piazza, and a coppersmith's shop, from whence comes a monotonous sound from the blows of the great hammer; and then on the opposite side of the green stands a church, vast, and empty, and tawdry, as many of these North of Italy churches are, of which the silent dusty gloom and emptiness suggest a curious contrast to the fervor of North Tyrol. Here the vast wide open doors show fading deceptions of pasteboard and tinsel ornament, and admit a dazzle of dust-flickered light into the gloom. Worshippers are scarce now, but in the time of the father of the present Count de Pavis they were more numerous. The Countess and her daughters were often to be seen in their places. In these churches brazen plates are affixed to the benches with names engraved thereupon: those of Claudia, Irminia, Valeria de Pavis, are still to be deciphered upon the worn brass plate that marks the seat of the Pavis family, though Claudia, the mother, is long since dead, and Irminia and Valeria have married and left their old home in the mountain city. Another name, that of Saverio de Pavis, is also inscribed upon the family plate. He is the owner of the palazzo, but it is said that he does not keep up his mother's pious practices.

One day I wandered into the church: the only worshippers were two girls kneeling near a small open side-door. The light fell upon their youthful heads, upon an altar ornamented with cotton laces and pasteboard vases: outside the door was a bright white wall, a creeping pumpkin with great starry golden flower and pantomime-like fruit, and the lizards darting from stone to stone. The girls came away presently, passing out by this white wall to the piazza again, where they had tied up their donkey at the copperman's shop.

The coppersmith, with whom I had had some dealing, was a kind old fellow. He seemed to love his great saucepans, over which he might now see the two pretty girls' faces, and the donkey's head, and the Palazzo Pavis, and the mountain beyond; and he nodded a friendly greeting as we all passed together.

How delicately lovely the mountains looked, in fair ridges round about the little town: strange peaks of dolomite, crushed, shivered, splintered sharp, with a net-work of lines and modellings, of light and passing shadows: now a cleft, now a pinnacle standing out sharp, now a shadowy black veil hanging from some topmost point; and then see it melt away, and the shining crystallized peaks flash quivering and clear. . . . It was a wonderful fairy country through which we had been wandering for ten days past—among alps and rocky passes—wild fairies they surely are who inhabit them : mossy trunks hang over precipices ; thousands of flowers shine, sweet autumn cyclamen, starry parnassus ; above and below, the waters dash, filtering through rocky cups, and foaming crystal among the fringing leaves and mosses. Green alps, too, flow from rock to rock along the mountain side where the gray cows are feeding ; tranquil little villages perch along the wandering track, whence dark eyes watch you as you pass on your way to the smiling valley below. Strangers are strangers still, and not yet tourists on the road. The host greets you with friendly gladness ; the fresh straw beds are covered with the winter-spun linen. The fare is scant sometimes, but quaint and good. For the chamois hunters are out upon their raids, the valleys are spread with waving fields of Indian corn ; there are trout in the lakes and streams. Along the road the pumpkins are swelling in the sun, and the flax grows with its fringed plumes, or hangs drying in yellow bundles from the eaves of the cottages.

All this smiling land lies along the frontier between Austria and Italy. We had crossed the line a dozen times on our way to the little sun-baked town, which seemed to us dreary, and tattered, and saddening, after the prosperous villages. We were going on again that day to the neighborhood of the Marmolata, the noblest mountain of the Rhætian range, and thence home by Bötzen, where civilization begins.

I, for one, do not wish to cry out against it. The jolts and difficulties in the world of civilized life are mental, instead of physical. The problems are human. There are by-ways and bold ascents, precipices to skirt, deep and distracting as any of these. Opinions grow instead of crops of Indian corn ; sympathies and aspirations dazzle us and thrill us, in the loneliness of our souls, as do still mountain ranges or wide-spreading horizons. The music of civilized life is not in the song of birds, or the flow of streams, or the tinkling of flocks. Alas! it is a music sadder and more boisterous and more incomplete ; but it may be there is a deeper tone in it than in the calm self-satisfaction of pastoral completeness. Because the cries are loud, the instruments unequal to the tunes they should play, shall people decry it ? Is Nature divine ? Perhaps in the darkest London slum, where dirt and sorrow and filth are massed together, there may be a deeper divinity than in the widest, sweetest valley where sheep are browsing, evening lights shining on the hills, hamlets sprinkling in still nooks, crops ripening in their season, and wayside crosses casting their shade across the precipitous road.

II.

Under the dark entrance-porch of the hotel our luggage was piled, and H. and my nephew Tom were looking out for me. The carriage had not come, and all my Italian, such as it was, was wanted to urge the stout old padrona with the garnet necklace to wake up from a sort of trance, and send for it. "When we pleased ; when we pleased. Ah! we were going on to C——. The Count had ordered the carriage. It should come back for us. There was no hurry—no hurry." But here a tall, pale-faced young man, with spectacles, with a straw hat, and a green case for plants slung across his shoulders, came striding hastily into the hotel. He nearly tripped up over the strap of my nephew's knapsack : he flushed up impatiently, and kicked it away. "I have come to say I shall not want the carriage," he cried, in a harsh, quick voice. "Supper? No. I shall not sup here to-night."

"Then Beppo can conduct these gentry by the equipage," cried the old padrona, brightening up for a single moment to a gleam of intelligence. "Your servant, Signor Conte."

The young Count, still impatient, shrugged his shoulders ; then, recollecting himself, raised his straw hat to us, as if to make up for the shrug, and began striding off as quick as he could go, flying along with an odd, swinging walk.

"He is an original," said the hostess, speaking in her sleep. "He only thinks of herbs—always herbs—he studies them from one season's end to another. Ah, his father was not of that sort."

In a few minutes more a little old trembling conveyance, with swinging handles, bits of string and broken straps, and a youthful but incompetent driver, shivered and ambled up to the door. Our way led through a melancholy defile, where the white road wound in long zig-zags, overhanging the depths below ; while the peaks seemed to crowd higher and closer with a wild melancholy monotony, to which the moan of the torrent flowing in its white stony bed, and straggling between arid flats, seemed to respond. In the distance, far, far ahead of us, down in a dip of the valley, we could see a donkey and some one following, and at a turn of the road we met a little calf, driven along the pass by a peasant-woman. It looked at us and at the horse with lively and suspicious interest ; but the calf and the poor old horse were respectively urged on by their drivers, who nodded as they passed. The calf-woman was worn-faced, brown, and kind-eyed. She wore a bead necklace and took off her hat. I don't know why it all seemed so dreary to me, like a presentiment of impending ill. It was but a fancy, for no harm came, beyond a variety of bumps, and jerks, and lurches over into the abyss by which we were travelling, so numerous and alarming, that H. exclaimed in horror, and Tom, indignant, jumped down at last and led the horse down the steeper places; while the vivacious young driver amused himself by winding and unwinding the drag at the wrong minute, with **immense** energy and many exclamations.

Our advance was not very quick, but by degrees we gained upon the donkey, and as we got nearer we saw that there was a young soldier with the two girls, whom I recognized as those I had seen in the church. One girl was sitting on the donkey's back, the other walking ahead, with a free, striding peasant step. Both had their great fair plaits pinned round with many long pins like little arrows. The pedestrian wore **a conical hat** on the top of her plaits; she had **white sleeves, a** black bodice and a shirt, **and a** coral necklace, and her dress was a little above that of the peasants. As she walked she looked up and around in a free yet dreaming way. Her companion on the donkey had discarded the white country sleeves altogether. She was small and delicate-looking, with beautiful red hair and brown eyes; her dress was only black alpaca: she, too, wore a coral necklace. The young soldier spoke to her now and then, but she scarcely answered him: they were evidently brother and sister, from their likeness and **peculiar** red locks. The donkey tripped **along** lively and careful; every now and then the young people called it by name: "Hu, Bruno! Ehu, Bruno!" Bruno seemed to be an independent little fellow, with a very decided will of his own. At one place, in the descent, we all came together to a stream that flows across the road into the torrent below. Bruno and the soldier seemed to have some difference as to the place where it should be forded. The girl jumped off in a fright; the soldier tugged; Bruno pulled, and set his fore paws. Some one cried out from above; the soldier looked round; **Bruno** seized the moment, jerked the reins out **of his** leader's hand, and was over before his master **could come near** him. "Look, Mary," said my sister-in-law, "there is that young man from the Hotel." He was coming scrambling down the side of the pass, leaping with wonderful agility from one splintered rock to another. Every movement looked wild and clumsy and unpremeditated, and yet his progress was secure and unfailing. It seemed a horrid-looking place and impossible to get over; but there he was in a minute, safe on the road, and hurrying after the little party, with his swinging green canteen behind him.

"Well," said Tom, my nephew, "I couldn't **have done** that better myself." (Tom was a **sailor for some** years, but he came into a fortune **and is a** country gentleman now, and only exerts **himself once** in a hundred years or so, when my sister-in-law drags him abroad.)

The athlete joined the little party, and after walking with **them a** short way, suddenly left them, flying off **at a** sharp ridge of rock and disappearing by degrees. We had got to take an interest in them all by this time. Bruno completely won our hearts by a last sudden dash he made at a haystack that was coming walking

along on two blue worsted legs and brown knee-breeches: he overpowered his conductor and got a good bite of sweet dry hay before any one could prevent him. The hay was going to a little stony lodge on the wayside, from whence a raven and flamingo maiden stepped out to see us pass. Then we began to ascend, and left our fellow-travellers and Bruno behind us, conversing with the apparition; and the dismal gorge came to an end at last in fields of Indian corn, in a tattered village with falling balconies and blackened gables, and fences, and children **with** wistful faces swarming out to see us pass.

We all breathed more freely as the **road** climbed up again by the mountain-side into a wider, fresher world, while a lovely green valley opened, and high cliffs came rising from still green alps, with evening clouds like bubbles trembling along their ridges; and then, still passing on, we presently reached a terrible valley, where a hundred years ago the crest of a mountain thundered from its height, crushing houses and people and flocks in its fall—crashing up the river, and creating a calm blue lake. Great masses lie scattered as they fell, for who can raise prostrate mountains? But they are wreathed and pine-crowned, and their fierce edges are softened by the sweet-spreading green veil which hangs over all this Alpine country: **a veil which** only seems rent here and there **by the sharp** rocky points that burst through it.

III.

"Presently a maid
  Enters with the liquor,
(Half a pint of ale
  Frothing in a beaker).
Gads! I didn't know
  What my beating heart meant:
Hebe's self I thought
  Entered the apartment.
As she came she smiled,
  And the smile bewitching,
On my word and honor,
  Lighted all the kitchen!"

WE were only going a short day's journey to C——, at the other end of the blue lake, and it was still light when we reached the village. There was a cheerful sound of music as we came down into the street, and an echo of one of the Alpine chants that the young men catch up and troll out with great skill, spirit, and good tune, and presently we met a row of five young fellows walking arm-in-arm towards the town, with plumes and flowers in their Tyrolese hats, short sleeves, and long flowered waistcoats, loudly chanting their evening song. It was a feast-day, our driver told us, a feast-day as far as the bridge; (where, by the way, he sent us over, fortunately, in a place where the earth was heaped up to support the planks, so that the horse was able to pull us safe back again). All the white shirts had turned out in honor of St. Bartholomew, the little children had their best clean faces on, the mothers sat in their doorways resting from their heavy burdens, the fathers smoked silver-topped pipes, the young men walked about arm-in-arm, as I have said, and a grand game of *pallone* was going on in the village street. Our arrival distracted some triflers, but not so the real players of the game. The marker stood under an old arch with his two strange little wooden implements. The balls flew high over the house-tops, rolling down and dropping from the wide-eaved roofs, sometimes flying in at a window and violently thrown out again—the young men leaped after them, and the people shouted in excitement.

These Tyrolese houses are stables to enter by, with horses and carriages and cows stowed away; but as you mount the stairs each floor improves. The first floor is the kitchen and the public room, where you catch a glimpse of peaked hats, of gaiters, of bottles of wine and shirt-sleeves. The hostess comes out of her kitchen to greet you, and takes you up to the second floor, which is quieter, fresher, and with flowers in the balcony at the end of the passage, where you dine. At Signora Sarti's "Black Eagle," the flowers were brighter, the bedrooms lighter and more comfortable than any we had yet seen. The rooms were clean, great pots of carnation stood promiscuously on the stove, and in the corner and in the window of the sitting-room; we saw wooden benches against the wall, wooden floors, some odds and ends of poles, and then in the bedrooms huge beds, so high that you had to leap from ledge to ledge to reach them. A back-door from our bedrooms opened upon the outer wooden balcony running along the back of the house. The balcony looked out upon what they call the piazzetina—a little grimy back-yard sort of place, with six dozen arched doors and windows at all possible angles, looking over and under one another. Here, too, were more carnation-pots and dried wisps of flax under the roof hanging out to dry.

Before and behind us were casements with wide-open wooden shutters through which we could see into the lives of the people. Strange little framed pictures of unknown existences. How much can four feet by three of one's daily habits disclose? Not much, perhaps, in a world where every thing is changing and flitting; but here, where day by day the sun shines upon the same peaceful sights and customs, it may be enough to give a hint of them. There was the old tailor sitting on his bed on the second floor—there was a daily dinner laid at a certain window at twelve o'clock—there were the three washerwomen living on the first floor. They looked out of window, stretching their long brown necks with the bead necklaces, their wisps of hair were pinned up like the plaits we had admired on the road, with aureoles of silver pins. (As their brown necks were constantly stretching through the window, the aureoles beamed down not unfrequently upon the passers-by in the street below.) Now comes music again. An air out of the "Trovatore," an air out of the "Dame Blanche." The musicians are two soldiers in the Austrian uniform: they

are singing as they sit at a little table, and we see their glasses filling among the red and yellow cloves that are falling from the window-sill.

Clatter—clatter! "Here is the donkey," says Tom, looking out of window, and we heard a sound of little hoofs, exclamations, embraces, cheerful girls' voices, and presently the padrona comes in with flushed happy cheeks to ask us what we would have for our meal.

"I should have come sooner, but my son is just arrived," she said. My daughter Fortunata, and Joanna my servant, went into Agordo to meet him."

"Is he a soldier?" said H., smiling. "Was there a donkey?"

"Yes, yes," said the beaming signora. "The gentry must have passed them. It is two years since I had seen him; now he comes home because I —— on business." And here her face fell. "A mother's heart is in many places," says the padrona with a sort of little chronic sigh.

Tom, who was very hungry, and not so much interested as we were in these family details, now asked somewhat inconsequently if there was any fish to be had for dinner.

"Fish? No. The fisherman had to be told the day before, and then he went out at sunrise and caught it; but" (hesitating) "a friend had sent some wild partridges, and if we liked she would roast a couple. Would we choose white wine or black?"

With the white wine came our dinner:

1st. A rice soup with little sausages floating in it.

2d. Slices of a sort of fried plum-pudding.

3d. Biftek. This is a mince with a sweet garlicky batter, and polenta to eat with it.

4th. The partridges, with prunes.

5th. A sort of white cream-cheese eaten with cinnamon.

Tom complained that it was all puddings, but he eat them with good appetite; and then we went and drank our coffee in the window, watching the lights gleam away on the mountain-tops above the roofs. I could see some one down below also supping off wild partridges at a sort of little terrace where his table was set. From the number before him, and the way he eat them up, I guessed that he was the sportsman who had brought them down. It seemed to me that I knew the green box lying on the table, and I also recognized in the sportsman our wandering Count.

IV.

WE had, strange to say, an acquaintance living at C——, an old lady whom we had met a year before drinking the waters at a watering-place in the Alps, where H. had been sent by a German doctor. She was only a humble sort of companion, she told us, to another old lady, who owned the country-house in which they spent their summer months. She seemed to be loved and trusted by her employer; and able to do as she liked, and she had begged us to come and see her if we passed her way. She assured us that their garden was well worth a visit. We had taken a liking to the gentle, intelligent, somewhat melancholy woman, with her simple Italian ways and ready sympathies. Signora Elizabetta della Santa was tall, with many bones and wrinkles, and a few black and gray hairs. She spoke slowly in a deep guttural voice; she was dressed like an old wallflower, in dingy yellows and greens, for the most part. This evening, strolling out along the street, it occurred to me to look her up, and when I came back to the hotel I thought I would ask for news of my old acquaintance. I went up stairs in the twilight to the landing beneath ours; it lead to the terrace, where Fortunata and Joanna were both standing talking to the Count. He seemed to be emptying his vasculum of all sorts of plants, ferns, roots, and flowers, and I did not like to disturb them. Tonina, the padrona's eldest daughter, was very busy in the general room, coming and going from one table to another, with her leathern bag of office strapped to her waist. I looked into the kitchen to see if the mother was there. Yes, the padrona was standing in the last sunlit window with her son. I noticed that Mario, as they called him, was looking odd and flushed, and that his honest face was as red as his hair, but I put it all down to the evening glow, and asked my question without any thought of trouble.

"What does the Signora ask?" said the padrona, hastily. "Signora della Santa and the Marchesa are here; they live close by. Mario will—no, Fortunata will—you turn to the right by the bridge; you—" but here suddenly her voice failed, and the poor thing burst out crying. "It's nothing, nothing," she went on, volubly. "Don't ask; don't ask; and oh! do not tell the girls that I am troubled; they at least shall never know what a cruel—" Mario, who was hissing and spluttering between his teeth, stopped her with a kind impatience. "He is here," said the poor thing, recovering herself, and wiping her eyes. "He will take care of us, and all will be well now." And she laid her hand on her son's arm and looked at me, and then at his carrot-face, with wistful tender eyes.

I went away sorry to have come in, and left them in their window. There was a roar of laughter from the tap-room as I passed. The Count seemed to have done with his botanizing, and to be beginning a course of astronomy from the little terrace. Up stairs I found Tom with a pipe, and H., who was much interested when I told her of the padrona's unknown trouble. "I am afraid money matters must be wrong," said H. But there was no sign of any want of prosperity in the little household. Fresh piles of linen were carried in from the bleaching-field, cows came dragging stores of hay for the stable, bare-legged assistants brought fruit and corn and wine, like people in the Bible. The padrona

was walking about with a carpenter early next morning devising alterations, and I found Fortunata displaying a perfect store of ribbons and laces she had bought for Tonina in Agordo the day before. Tonina, the eldest daughter, wore a gold brooch and earrings, and two horns of black hair; she was engaged to be married, and was shortly to depart, earrings and all, for the town where her intended was employed. Tonina was a big handsome young woman, with a perfect passion for dress. I never heard her speak with interest on any other subject. She would waylay us, feel our gowns, settle our bonnet-strings; she was forever straggling into our rooms and trying on our clothes.

I did not care for Antonina at all, but little Fortunata, with her sweet, quick, gentle ways, was irresistible. She was spoiled by them all, and she seemed to me like a little brownie at work, sparing her mother, helping Joanna, and stirring about us with a kind energy. She could sing all sorts of songs, mountain catches, and opera tunes too. She had brown startled eyes and red hair, plaits upon plaits that Joanna used to put up with the silver pins in a sort of truelover's knot every morning. She used to be up quite late, till midnight and even later, and again at six in the morning this young woman was about—often at four if any early traveller was starting. "Tonina would never get up," Joanna said, shrugging her shoulders.

But the person who most interested me in the household was the padrona, with her dark sweet anxious face and her tender care for her children. The woman was a born lady, whatever her station in life might be. I liked to see her receiving her guests, with a gracious courtesy that was shyly returned by funny red-faced, blear-eyed men with knee-breeches and conical hats, coming to drink *vino nero*, and slouching young conscripts, half-shy, half-proud, with their flowers and numbers stuck into their caps. If there was any disturbance, the padrona would walk boldly in and quell it with instant measures. The gentle decision with which, on one occasion, Beppo was summoned to assist one of these young fellows out of the house amused me. It was a handsome, fair-haired boy, dressed in green, with a great bunch of pink roses, and neat, white knitted hose. With a sudden yell, he tore off his gay hat and flung it on the ground, trolling out something between a hymn and a drinking-song in a hoarse, tipsy voice. The padrona laid her hand on his shoulder. Her grave look seemed to steady him. "Angelo Soya," she said, "enough of this; go home, my boy." And Angelo actually got up and disappeared without a word.

Italians, if they trust you, will speak of themselves and their feelings with an openness that is touching to people of a more reserved habit. Very soon the signora spoke to me of impending anxiety, of Fortunata, and her eyes would fill with tears of love and care. Something was amiss in the little household; good and affectionate as they all were, and tenderly devoted as was the mother, she had not been able, even in that lonely mountain-inclosed village, to keep her young ones safe and away from harm and evil speaking. Joanna's indignant fealty, Mario's manly protection, what is of avail against spying eyes and spiteful tongues, and three long brown necks stretched out? I could have wrung them with pleasure when I knew the harm they had done. The rest of the household consisted of a wild undermaid called Jacoma, of Beppo the old man, and numberless assistants, with bare legs and short petticoats, appearing and disappearing, carrying tubs, gourds, great baskets of Indian corn, inflated pig-skins, and what not. Labor is cheap in these parts, and garments are dear. This was hard upon Tonina. In houses where every thing is made at home—soap, bread, wine, linen, cheese, etc., there is, of course, an infinity to see to. They had a farm from whence provisions came; they had granaries, fruit-stores. I could see sacks heaped and heaped in the store-rooms on the ground-floor, and often there, too, was Joanna at work among them with an assistant barelegs.

V.

JOANNA seemed to have a temper of her own. I was passing the open door of one of those ground store-rooms next morning on my way to join H. on the hill-side, when I heard Joanna rating her unlucky assistant at the pitch of her voice. Barelegs answered, tossing her head. Joanna, with a sort of shrill contemptuous whistling noise, orders barelegs off; and finally the poor creature slinks away with a basket full of polenta meal on her head, leaving Joanna triumphant.

"What was it?" said Mario, who had been standing in the door with his usual long weedy cigar in his mouth. "Joanna, don't scold poor Jacoma."

"Ah! you pity La Jacoma," said Joanna, sharply. "Now Mario has come back he is to set every thing right. Go and console her, and ask her if she does not deserve my indignation."

"What the devil is it all about?" says Mario.

"It is the work of devils," she repeated. "Something that she ought never to have listened to," cried Joanna, still in a fury. "I will not have her trouble the mistress. Do you hear?"

Mario's face changed; he seemed to understand her as he too marched off. Joanna, who was in a downright passion, went on violently tying and shaking the big sacks, but more than once she stopped to stamp off her fury, and to shake her conical hat in anger at some one outside in the street.

Joanna was a character—a loyal rebel belonging to the dynasty of Sarti. Fortunata seemed to be the object of her blind devotion, the others the victims of it. She was a handsome girl; her

teeth were like milk, her fair hair was pinned up like her mistress's, but she wore three or four little short sprays or frizzes over her forehead and cheeks, and I hardly ever saw her without her hat. There was a melancholy look in her blue eyes, which contrasted oddly with her broad smiles and childish gapes. She was curious and clumsy. She asked me endless questions about myself, my family. She would give a certain solemn shake of the head when she was puzzled, as if there were profundities unexplored into which she did not choose to inquire: such as the countries beyond Germany, the railways, the strangers who were beginning to come over the mountains to the valleys, where they came from, and their watches, what was to be done to procure them butcher's meat. Joanna looked stupid, but she was really full of cleverness. She could have thought and reasoned if she had chosen, and she had real flashes of genius at times when any thing came to stir her from her usual clumsy apathy. But as she was also extremely pig-headed and superstitious, her flashes of genius used to die out very often without making much impression upon herself or any one else.

"Ah!" said she, calming down at last, preparing to shoulder her sack, and wiping some tears out of her eyes, "it's a cruel world, that poisons the sweetest and dearest, that respects neither innocence nor youth."

There was a pathetic emotion in her voice that surprised and touched me.

"What is it?" I asked.

"Eh! who can tell?" said the girl. "There are three devils, three washerwomen, opposite, who say wicked things of us, and La Jacoma repeats them to me. But I think she will not dare to do so again," cried Joanna, "or to disquiet the padrona any more with her tales."

"But can't it be stopped?" said I.

"What can one say? what can one do?" cried Joanna. "I am only a servant. Mario, he is the master, he is. And he comes to put all right—Hé! I know that he will make it all wrong. But who is to keep clear of error? Not masters, any more than servants. Mine will not listen to reason, and they will sacrifice a dove to their pride."

Italian women are eloquent when they are excited. This girl whisked up the sacks, her blue eyes sparkled, then dimmed, and there, like enchantment, was a gaping, wide-mouthed stupid Joanna again standing before me with her load. I remember the look of the queer cellar-like place, with its bars, and the round iron scrolled windows, and green vine-stems outside.

Madama Sarti's voice was heard calling overhead, "Beppo! Beppo!"

"She wants him to stir the polenta," said Joanna. "It is no good to dwell upon evil. We know how to make good polenta in our house. Will you come and taste?"

VI.

Joanna walked carefully up stairs into the kitchen, where a great wood flame was leaping on the **high** stone hearth, and a comfortable incantation in a huge caldron already begun—**water** and Indian-corn meal, which the padrona **shook in,** while Beppo, in his **shirt-sleeves,** stood by with a wonderful serious **face. Then** he began working the mass round **and round with** a stick; then he got excited, and **worked** harder and harder as the difficulty increased; then he finally leapt on the fire-place, and stood above them all, pounding **and** pushing and poking away with all **his might.** At last, after some five minutes, when the steam has carried away the water and the mass is hardened enough, the fire begins to fail: just when Beppo seems exhausted, Joanna brings a great wooden platter, and on to this board they cleverly rolled out a polenta—an **avalanche—a huge** smoking, steaming mass. **Then** Tonina rushes forward and cuts the mass **into** two halves with a string, one for the servants—one for the master's table—and Beppo **wipes his** brow as he leaps down triumphantly from the stone hearth.

The widow still stood in the fire-place, making up the fire. Joanna was bearing off one of the great smoking hemispheres on its platter; and Jacoma, the maid, was yawning in a chair, and resting from her morning's labor. It was a common enough scene of family life. A woman peeping in through the doorway, with a great pile of flax upon her head; for color, take a blue gleam of sky, black beams and rafters, shining coppers, and white walls, against one of which stands the tall black crucifix; and just beside **it** Fortunata in her coral necklace and **auburn locks.** At this moment, as if he had been conjured up somewhere out of the great boiling **copper,** the Count's tall figure suddenly appeared. There was a hush and silence as he looked in.

"I shall want a room to-night," he said, abruptly, "and supper at eight. Here is some game; more than I shall want." Little Fortunata, with her face all alight, seemed to awake first, and she sprang forward and took it from him. "Thank you," said he, smiling, and then he was gone. He was running up stairs, four steps at a time. Madame Sarti had turned pale, and looked at her son. Antonina drew herself up very primly. Joanna flashed, and **gave** one quick glance at Fortunata. I began to guess the state of the case when, as I walked **out** into the street to join my sister-in-law, I saw the **three** heads nodding and straining from the opposite window.

In these **friendly** villages the people come crowding round the strangers, and staring with wondering brown eyes, like the little calves do on the mountains. H.—whom I had left alone safe installed in the shade of a hay **châlet,** with a penknife, a pencil, a church spire, a range of low mountains, india-rubber, and all the materials **for** a sketch—I now found surrounded by a large family, on its way to the fields after the midday meal: there was a bald, good-humored woman, with false plaits; a row of little boys and girls, pretty, as all the children are in these parts. Poor H. was finishing her sketch **to** the usual catechism. "Married? Where is the husband? How **many** boys and how many girls? Does our country please you?" (Pause for a compliment.) "Are you Germans or Italians? English? Under what rule is England?—Across the sea?"—a whistle. **Then** a hurried dialogue among one another. "**They** are not Christians." "No." "Yes: look at their rings." Then a kind smile, and a genuine friendly "Happy journey" at parting. The bald woman was unusually cheerful and talkative. She too was married, and these were five of her children. "Were we staying at the inn? So the soldier had returned? It was as well, perhaps. Eh? It is always well to have a man in a family; women are apt to be silly and indiscreet. Of course Madama Sarti and her daughters were far above her, but she loved them (our friend did); only there were enemies in the valley. Hé, they say terrible things. They say Fortunata looks too high, and are jealous, in short; but she is a pretty creature, and has no malice in her ways," says our informant, preparing to resume her trudge. "Deh! come along, little ones," **and off she goes, with** her brood scrambling after **her up the steep rocky pass.**

"**So that is the key to the poor** mother's **anxieties,**" said I. "**That dear** pretty little **creature—can** any one be so cruel **as** to talk **spitefully of her?** It is too sad, H."

"The padrona should be careful of appearances," said H., gravely, "for the girl's own sake."

Then, as we had already agreed, we walked on a little way to call upon our friend. It was a curious lovely old garden, at the back of the low white house in the village street, with great closed gates, and balconies, and little buttresses, and clothes hanging to dry upon the terrace. Here the two old ladies had lived for I don't know how many tranquil years. The grass was green, but long and straggling, and the paths were rough, so that, to our English eyes, there was a certain sadness about the place. But there was a real wealth of wonders; **and** precious plants and trees and shrubs for those like H. who know something of such things. Under a little wooden umbrella, darting up, green, and with delicate lace-work branches, was a slender Norfolk pine-tree; there an aloe in flower; here one or another learned fragrant shrubs, and great oleander-trees with the flames bursting through the green, and pumpkins, common enough, but always splendid, along the wall, and strange, deep-colored scentless flowers in close serried rows along the beds, and trees, with unknown fragrant blossoms tossing. It was under one of these that Signora della Santa met us with a friendly welcome. "Will you come in, or stay here?" she asked. "The

Marchesa desires her best compliments. She is not yet up, or she would have the pleasure of receiving you." Then, after our usual little talk of journey and recollections, etc., H. began to praise the garden, and exclaim in admiration at the treasures she had seen there.

"To tell the truth, we deserve small credit," said Signora della Santa, much gratified. Saverio de Pavis, who is a botanist, a nephew of my Marchesa, has the garden planted, and conspires with the gardener to carry out his experiments. He lives at Agordo, but often comes over to see his aunt and his trees here. He is away just now." (H. and I looked at each other.) "I am glad he is keeping away," the signora said: "for, to tell the truth, there has been some gossip in the town, and people said he was paying great attention to your hostess's little daughter. I happen to know that no such thought has ever crossed his mind; he thinks of his plants only, and doesn't live in the world around him."

Our friend was clever and reasonable, and I thought it better to confess that I had seen her hero that very morning.

"I am sorry to hear it," said she. "It was but the last time I saw him that he was complaining of the inn, the bad attendance, and indifferent cooking there. I regret that people should make remarks. The Sartis are too good and respectable to allow themselves to be attacked by evil tongues."

I could quite imagine her to be right. We had a little more talk, and from what she told us it seemed indeed as if the Count lived in a world different from that which we inhabited. A world in which there were changes, but they took thousands and thousands of years to effect; in which there were kingdoms, and dynasties, and conquests perhaps, but silent conquests undisputed. If one flower perished, another succeeded in its turn. Laws could not be broken in this tranquil realm, its state secrets might be disclosed without fear of ill. For this mystic silent existence Saverio had given up the cares and turmoils of quick daily life. At one time the philosopher had been ambitious and keen enough for the cause he loved, and had been heart and soul on the Italian side, although a captain in the Austrian army. This was in his youth, and he had been remarked and called to account. He had been taxed by the Austrians until his fortune was completely ruined, and now Saverio was a poor man. He had worked, waited, and hoped, but when the Italian rule was established, the recognition he had expected never came. And then it was that, indignant and disappointed, he turned his back upon Europe, upon kings, and court intrigue, and favor. He felt that he was by nature too hasty, too nervous a man to keep pace with the rest of the rout. And so he shut himself up in his old palace, and watched the growth of the dandelions, and speculated upon the formation of the rocks about his home (his theory was that they were coral rocks), and he wander-

ed from peak to peak and from pass to pass, and came home and wrote philosophical treatises. "His sisters are in despair, and think he has gone mad, to shut himself up with his books and avoid all human society," said the old companion, "but he is not mad. He is moderately happy in his own way."

VII.

WE did not think, when we left her waving farewells at the great gate, how soon matters were to come to a crisis. We were to go on the next day; and talking over our plans and schemes, we had almost forgotten the existence of the Sartis. I walked up by the back way. As I opened my door I found, as usual, some one in my room (the whole family used to invade it unscrupulously)—a pile of linen on the floor, two great copper pots full of water, Joanna standing by a huge open press, with her back turned. As I entered in there came from the sitting-room beyond a great burst of voices. The girl turned round quick, and then I saw that her face was all working, flushed and agitated.

"It is my fault, all my fault!" she said, wringing her hands in an agony of despair. "Ah, signora, go in. You may stop Mario. He is trying to make a quarrel with the Count."

Mario had most certainly succeeded in his endeavor. I opened the door. There they all stood round the table, where the well-known green vasculum was lying—Mario flaming, Tonina smoothing her apron, Fortunata crying bitterly.

"Why do you stay here to be insulted? Why don't you go?" cried Mario to his sisters. "What can you want with the Count's dried herbs? What does his Excellency mean by speaking to you in such an impatient and insolent fashion, and suspecting you honest girls of stealing them?" Then, turning round upon the Count again, who was looking very haughty and puzzled—"I tell you that my sisters are not the common drudges that you seem to imagine. My sisters are not to be spoken to as if they were servants. They were well born, and respected by all."

"Who ever doubted it?" said the Count, containing himself with difficulty, seizing his hat and his stick, and hastily crushing and doubling up a map, which he twisted round and round and stuffed into the vasculum. "I asked for a missing specimen and was vexed that it should have been destroyed. Who talks of stealing?"

"They are well born," persisted Mario, who was in a tremendous passion, and evidently anxious to impress the fact of a quarrel; "and I, too, although your Excellency may not choose to acknowledge it, am not of those who will endure the insults of the rich."

"I have never given your existence one moment's consideration," said his Excellency, now fairly in a passion too. Then seeing my door open, he hurried past me into the bedroom, where he stopped short with all his paraphernalia, while Joanna sprang forward.

"I—I only am to blame," she cried, and would have caught his arm.

"Silence," roared Mario from the next room, while the Count shook her off.

I thought it as well Saverio should not encounter the fierce champion Mario any more, and I silently pointed to the second door upon the balcony, which was open, and through which, with a haughty salutation, the Count strode away. I saw him marching down the village street, and disappearing in the distance—a gray-linen gray-hatted figure. The peasants saluted him respectfully as he went along, but he, flying by at his usual pace, paid no attention to any of their greetings: on he went past the wine-shop—past the black arched entrance to the old brown house. He was gone.

But the scene was not over yet. A cry from Tonina called us hastily into the next room. Poor little Fortunata had fallen back fainting into her sister's arms. Dead, pale, dishevelled, with the silver pins falling loose from her hair, Tonina had dragged her to the carnation window. Mario, looking at once sulky, sorry and pacified, was pouring himself out a glass of black wine. Joanna had run for one of the great copper pails of water, and with angry, blue glances at the corporal, for all his uniform and mustaches, began dashing the water with both hands into Fortunata's face. "Go and fetch mamma, Mario," said Tonina, severely; and then mamma came back, followed by the irrepressible Mario. He had evidently given his own version of the story. Poor mamma! troubled, puzzled, she alternated from the tenderest expressions of pity and sympathy to no less affectionate, but less sympathetic, maternal snubbings. "For shame, Fortunata! Here is the lady. They will all see you down the street. Would Tonina do such a thing as faint for a caprice? Mario is right. Let the Count go his way. He is an original; nobody can predict from one day to another what he may do or say. His Excellency's state is too high for us. Thou art not born to be a countess, my little Fortunata—my dearest." (Very sharp:) "Mario, go, for the love of heaven! It will vex her to see thee when she recovers herself."

Mario, doggedly, and calming down, with both hands up in the air and his fingers together —"I am her true friend, for all that; you women are ignorant, short-sighted, talkative, ambitious. You care not for the censure of the neighbors—for the insults that nobleman heaps upon the family of Sarti. But I—I tell you that I have saved you from the most imminent peril, and that you are ingrate all of you."

So saying, Mario marched off, opening wide his ten fingers, clanking down stairs, and the padrona, who was evidently struck by his eloquence, again snubbed little Fortunata, who had quietly come round with her head on her sister's shoulder, and who was staring through the window and between the straggling branches of the carnations, with a sad far-away look, inexpressibly sorrowful and affecting.

"Eh! it is a bad day's work," said Joanna, shrugging her shoulders. "Mario has made an uproar and sacrificed his sister's happiness. She might have been a countess but for his stupidity."

"I never thought he would have said so much," sighed Tonina.

"Be quiet," said Signora Sarti. "Joanna, go to thy linen. Mario is justified. The count has retired, and it would never do to allow the neighbors to talk with disrespect of Fortunata, and to look upon us with evil eyes. Mario says that the Count is sporting with the affections of an innocent. He is an original, and no one, not Mario nor any other, shall understand him."

Fortunata was led off by Tonina, who was very kind and, as I thought, compunctious. Joanna began storing away the linen in the great closet in my room, but her tears dribbled on the pillow-cases with the frills, and the folded linen. "To think it was all for that bit of grass, that little nasty flower," poor sobbing Joanna burst out at last. "To think that I—I, who would give my life for Fortunata, should have been the one to bring all this upon her. It was a little lilac flower of nothing at all. I have never seen any like it," said the girl. This plant, it seemed, the Count had brought out of his tin case and examined during supper the night before, and then Fortunata had come in and talked to him and asked him to tell her the names of the stars (for the Count could tell every thing by name—stars, flowers, animals, languages, medicines, printed books, it was all the same to him), and while they were out on the balcony, Joanna had cleared away the supper and found the flower lying on the lid of the green case. For a little joke, after the Count had gone to bed, she had given it to Fortunata, saying it was a flower of good-luck his Excellency had sent her. Fortunata teased Joanna half the night to know if this were true. It was a foolish joke, and when Joanna saw how deeply her young mistress took it to heart, she had confessed that it was but a joke. And then Fortunata, half laughing half weeping, said, all the same she should keep it, and next morning she showed Joanna a tiny crystal locket, into which she had put the lilac bell. It would not hold the leaves, so she had cut them away. And then came the Count, hunting everywhere and in a state of excitement about his lost flower, and Joanna, laughing, asked him if it was a magical charm, and said it was safe, and when he exclaimed eagerly, at last showed him the crystal locket shyly, not knowing if he would be angry. And then the Count said they had undone him, that he had picked it at the risk of his life, that there was no other like it. And while he was scolding, and Fortunata crying, Mario came in.

"He meant to quarrel," said Joanna, "at the first opportunity, and now they have quarrelled, and our poor Fortunata is the victim!"

"But, Joanna," I said, "the Count never has been serious in his intentions."

"That is it. They will not believe it; but Fortunata felt, and I, too, felt that at one time he meant to marry her, and she would have been his countess. He is hasty in temper, but true in heart. Now all is over. That flower has done it. I, too, am to blame. Who is not? Eh!"

A shake of the head—clink, clank—a great sob—exit Joanna, swinging her brazen pails.

VIII.

THE result of this painful little scene could not yet be known, as far as the Count was concerned. It seemed not unlikely that he would come no more. "Perbacco! That is exactly what I wish," said Mario. "If it were an honest fellow who loved our Nata, and wished to make her his wife, that would be another matter; but the Count only amuses himself, and the neighbors laugh in their sleeves."

"It is to be hoped he will come no more," said Tonina, placidly. "Fortunata will forget him. She is young, and has been silly. She must marry in her own station, to her credit, like me, and then she can continue the business of the inn."

II. said she felt inclined to box Tonina's ears, she spoke so complacently.

"Wait, wait, only wait," cried Joanna, with a sapient shrug. "Do you think our misfortunes are completed? No; Nata will die before long, and that will break my heart and the padrona's. She will die, I tell you, if the Count abandons her." (Then a shake of the hat, then a mysterious mutter.) "I think he might return when that blockhead of a Mario is gone. . ."

Mario, whose leave was almost up, seemed to have some notion of the sort. He decreed in his decided way that Nata was to depart immediately, the farther the better. There was their cousin Hofer who would receive her at R——, in German Tyrol, and he would pass that way and see her on his return to Innspruck, where his regiment was quartered. Mario was in the Austrian service. That young man was a born autocrat. He would allow no excuse, grant no delay. I think, perhaps, under the circumstances, he was right, for he heard more of the universal gossip of the place than the poor women had dreamt of. So Mario declared that Nata wanted no new clothes for her journey. Escort! Joanna could take her; or, if she cared for company, there were the English ladies going that very way.

"But, Mario, it is such a long way," said poor Signora Sarti, who was not herself without a lingering hope that all might yet come right.

"All the better," cries Mario, magniloquent.

"I myself will tell those who dare speak of us that she is gone. Then let them say what they choose. They will see that our family is uncompromising in its self-respect, and will allow no interference where its honor is concerned. I had rather you put a poniard into my heart than allowed my sister's name to be lightly spoken of."

"My poor little Nata," sighed the poor mother, taking the girl's hand and stroking it. "My poor, poor child!"

"If it were I," cried Joanna, cocking her hat fiercely, "do you think I would go? No, not for empires. Hi! you might offer me gold and diamonds in vain; if I loved truly, it is not I who would conceal my passion. Struggle not against thy nature, my Nata, or thou wilt die. I know thy delicacy and tenderness of heart. How can Mario, who has no more sentiment than an ox, understand?"

"Will you be silent, you girl of nothing at all?" in a shriek of indignation from Tonina.

"I have a heart impassioned, but noble and self-sacrificing," exclaims Mario, very angry, and looking as red as a turkey-cock. "Why am I accused? I am acting for mamma, and upholding her wishes. Is it not so?" cries the young man. And he turned round upon the poor padrona, who only began to cry, so worried and troubled was she.

Little Nata was kissing her mother's withered cheeks again and again. "Don't believe La Joanna. I am not going to die, my mamma," she said. "I suffer a little, but only a little. Mario is right. It is fitter that I should go, for how can I venture to believe the Count when he tells me he prefers me to all others? Yes, I will go, if it will stop people from blaming us." And then she ran out of the kitchen, and went and sat on her little low chair in the corner by the window, at the far end of the passage, with her face hidden in her hands. There she sat, poor little soul. Over her head the great brown carnations were hanging; outside all the busy voices were echoing; the squares of light were travelling along the wooden floor. She never moved till she heard her mother's step upon the stairs; then she pulled out her work from her pocket, and began to sing a little song as she stuck the stitches.

When dinner was over, H. and I, and Tom and his pipe, generally went out together for a sociable little quartet upon the bridge. That evening, seeing Nata in the doorway, I called her to come with us. I thought it as well she should be seen with us; we two followed, and H. walked slowly ahead, leaning upon her son's arm. We left the *pallone*-players beginning their game; we went along the narrow street. In every doorway the little white children were clustering on the step nibbling their suppers—lumps of polenta, little bowls of milk; the parents ate within, or stood leaning over the little balconies where the flax was hanging to dry. We caught glimpses of copper and wood and fire interiors; in the air was a tinkling of coming flocks, a murmuring chorus of voices, and then the thud of some late carding-pin, still falling upon the flax. Old women past other work were sitting spinning at the doors and nodding their white locks at us as we passed. The attention we generally excited was rather diverted on this occasion by the passage of two peddlers with huge green umbrellas slipped down into the little rings along the side of the packs. I saw a group as we passed standing round some drawers opened out to display the glittering tinsel treasures that dazzle the peasant-girls in wonder; and then, beyond the village, we came to the little bridge across the stream, and we sat down upon a log that happened to be felled and lying on the bank.

So Tom smoked his pipe in the glow of the evening; the stream washing by reflected yellow and crimson, and the emerald lights from the broad leaves of Indian corn, among which the country people were strolling. Presently another echo reached us, an Alpine chant, at once cheerful and melancholy; then came a hurried procession of little goats, followed by the deliberate steps of the gray cows coming down from the mountains; then more women plodding home with their loads of flax, and little children running bare-legged, and dragging implements of labor bigger than themselves, or carrying small heaps in little baskets fitted to their backs. Then came the cheerful company of gallant country youths, walking six of a row, shirt-sleeves gleaming, arm-in-arm, hats well cocked, like Joanna's; they struck up again with all their lungs as they entered the village. After a little while we saw another group of people advancing, with a hum of voices that sounded both softer and shriller than the peasants' queer falsettos. "It is all the gentry of the town," Nata said; "a great party went out this morning to camp in the woods."

The gentry seemed to have been enjoying their picnic thoroughly; they advanced in a long line, two and two, young men and pretty young women with dark heads all uncovered, except one, who, I think, wore a black veil flung over her white dress and glossy black locks. They, too, were walking arm-in-arm, laughing, and whispering, and talking gayly, and coming in a sort of step.

"That first lady is to be married on Monday," said Nata. "That is her 'sposo' she is walking with: he is engaged in the mines at Agordo." They swept by quite close, their garments touching ours as they passed. One young girl nodded gravely to Fortunata, the others were too happy or too absorbed to notice her. There was something almost bacchanalian in the little procession: the white dresses, the garlands and flowers they were bringing back, the subdued happy excitement as they swept on through the calm of the evening. As the last of the file went by, I saw Fortunata flush and start. There was the Count with a lady on his arm walking on with the rest. I thought he saw us, for he stopped, imperceptibly almost,

never looking, but he passed on without a sign, and disappeared with the rest down the village street.

A minute after, Nata quietly said she must go home and see to the supper; would I please not disturb myself to come with her? And she got up and walked very quickly, in a sort of zigzag way at first, but afterwards straightly as usual.

Later in the evening we also got up to go. Tom's pipe was smoked out. It was getting chilly, and H. was wrapping her Indian shawl more and more closely round her shoulders. On our way we met the padrona, standing with the little group that was still gazing at the peddler's wondrous wares.

"Why, Signora, have you been buying some of those little saints?" said Tom.

"These are silver pins for Nata," said the padrona, joining us, showing us her little parcel. "I ran after the peddler," she explained, coming along. "My little Nata came home so pale, so sad, that I thought I would try and give her one moment's pleasure. Mario is right. I have been foolish and ambitious; but Fortunata is so good, so dear, that is my excuse," said the poor proud mother. "I thought my child was deserving of any fate, or never would I have encouraged the Count; but oh! they must not dare to say things against her fair fame. It is as if one of these sharp pins was piercing my breast when I think of it all. But when she is gone, people will see that we are proud and will not suffer a breath against our honor." Then she began to tell me that "Cousin Hofer" was a lady like herself, a widow in German Tyrol, keeping, as she did, an inn partly for pleasure—for the advantage of society. The Hofer's house was only habitable in the summer. If we really intended crossing the Seisser Alp on our way to Bolsano, we should pass very near it, "and," said Signora Sarti, "I know not how to thank the gentry for their offer to look after the girls. I shall keep Mario three days longer, and it will be better," she said, "for us all; and Joanna will be a companion to Nata. The two are faithful friends."

Fortunata met us pale but smiling when we came in. She had laid out the supper, she had brought a lamp to light us. All that evening she was coming and going, nervously busy, and more than once I heard her laugh. It was a sad musical laugh, very near to tears, but not bitter. There was nothing bitter in her nature. My nephew, Tom, who had had a sentiment early crushed in the bud, he told us, was much interested when we spoke to him. He willingly agreed, at his mother's request, to the extra infliction of two more women to escort. "Four was no worse than two," Tom remarked: "and it was not for long."

IX.

THAT evening I went to bed to toss and turn, and hear voices and see lights and faces suddenly flashed upon the darkness. Long after midnight I heard the padrona silently creeping up stairs. I lay starting at the striking of shrill clocks, at the melancholy cry of the watchman. "The hour is one," he said; "The hour is two;" and his voice echoed all along the silent village. At last I got up, and putting on a dressing-gown, I opened the door upon the wooden gallery, and I saw that I was not alone to watch and wake; another figure was standing leaning against the banister. I guessed who it was when I saw the dark shade of a conical hat.

"Who is it?" whispered Joanna; "ah, the Signora frightened me!" Then for a minute we stood together looking at the burning sky above the black roofs of the houses. "Look at the stars how they shine! Is it not a beautiful silence?" said Joanna. "The Count can tell the name of every one, big and little. He is learned, too learned," said Joanna bitterly, with a shrug. "He has bewitched her. Ah, Signora! Fortunata is asleep at last! She restrains her complaints not to vex her mother; but when we are alone it is as if she would be broken by her sorrow. She has told me how he passed her without a look. I suffered so in her sorrow I could not rest, and I thought the stars would do me good."

Joanna had something of her great namesake's nature—a simple enthusiasm and courage, and deep-hearted devotion. To her, the kingdom to be conquered was Fortunata's happiness; her dear Fortunata who lay crying herself to sleep upon her straw mattress with all her gleaming hair twisted over the pillow, and her white beautiful face hidden. The padrona's white linen was not whiter than Fortunata's skin. A lady! she was sweet enough to be a lady all the rest of her life if it so pleased her, and sit with her hands before her for ever and ever. Tonina, so Joanna thought, was no better than herself, except in being the padrona's daughter and wearing an alpaca dress; but Nata! It was to Nata that all Joanna's gratitude and love for the shelter and home-love the widow had given her was bestowed. So she whispered on in the darkness. It was then, as she looked up over the housetops at the clear burning night, that she vowed a vow to the bright stars that if she could do any thing, any thing in the whole world to make Nata happy she would do it, and suddenly the thought came to her of replacing the flower. Nata's mother was asleep after her long day's work; for a time, poor soul, her anxieties were calmed. Nata's sister was dreaming warm and placid in her bed by the window.

What would I not have given afterwards to have been quietly asleep in my bed, instead of waking, and making cruel mischief by my thoughtless words! Is it an excuse that, at that minute, dreams seemed so vivid, commonplace, and realities so far away? "Signora," Joanna said to me in mysterious whispers, "shall I tell you what I think? I think the Count makes magic with his flowers, and that the purple bell-flower poor Nata destroyed was a magic herb, and has worked all this ill. He spoke strangely. He said that alone was wanting to complete his work, and he could find no other in its place. He was angry, so angry! Signora, do the English believe in magic?"

"No one believes in charms, Joanna," I said; "only poets, not practical people. My nephew burns a magic leaf, and a smoke rises and rises, and those who practise the incantation say that it cures ill-humor. And I, too, have a precious little herb in a tin box in my portmanteau. It looks brown and dry; but, if I pour water on it, a delicious fragrance comes, and if I am tired and sad it cheers me. Some people might call these wonderful things tea-leaves and tobacco, . . ."

"Eh!" says Joanna, "who can tell! If the Signora only knew of precious herbs that would bring honorable love as well as peace of mind, that would be well for all."

I thought she was laughing, that she understood me. It was so dark I could not see her face; but I make no excuses, for I was punished after, and blamed myself when it was too late.

"There was a great enchanter once in England, Joanna. His name was Gulielmo. He could summon fairies at his will, and once he sent his messengers flying, and bade them bring a purple flower, of which the juice divided lovers strangely, and made much mischief; and then, when all seemed hopeless," I said, getting sleepy by degrees, "the fairies flew at his command, and upon the wild thymy bank another flower was growing, and all was well again, and the lovers united. But that was hundreds of years ago, and the great enchanter is dead. Good-night, Joanna. It is time for you to go to sleep, instead of looking at the stars." And so I went back to peaceful dreams, all unconscious of the ill I had done.

X.

THE village turned out to see our start on the morning of our departure for C——. The Austrian soldiers lent a hand, knots were tied with immense exertion, chairs and steps placed in convenient positions for the ascent of gigantic mules. Windows were noisily opened, advice was given, pieces of string were freely distributed; an hour must have passed in tying and untying every part of the apparatus of four bags and a knapsack and three sheepskin saddles: the very tails of the mules seemed to me fastened on with string. At last we clattered off cheerfully through the village street with our heads over our shoulders responding to the signora's farewell wavings and blessings. I can see the slim anxious figure before me now standing by the fountain and watching us go. Mario cried out that he should follow on Monday, and flourished his cap. The three hateful washerwomen burst out into shrill laughter. Then we passed Signora della Santa's door; then the house of our talkative friend with all the children. Five or six of them rushed out frantic into the street. Tom trudged ahead with his great axe, then came Bruno, who had bustled to the front with his panniers full of hand-bags; then H. and I on our sheepskins highly perched; and Nata last with Joanna walking by the side of her mule. She was very pale and silent, and Joanna spoke not a word at starting. More than once I saw her looking back at the familiar sight. The ridges of the mountains, with the well-known dents and clefts, the piled roofs of the village, the steeple. There was Signora della Santa's gate, looking now quite small, like a doll's house; there was the chimney of the "Black Eagle," and the smoke from the kitchen where the pot was boiling. I could imagine how those lines and shadows must look to Joanna, like the lines and marks on a familiar face. Nata never turned her head, but rode on drooping and thoughtful all through the golden hours of that great day.

How can one write it down? A flowing melody of mountain, and valley, and rushing water, and green things drifting and creeping everywhere; flowers white, and gold, and violet, as it were, striking sweet notes. High and solemn ridges dominating green valleys, and limpid streams rippling with a sweet impetuous dash. Now we follow Bruno along a narrow gorge of dazzling shadow and solemn lights. They come flowing from the towering heights overhead. We ride through a dell of moss and of lawn folded against the rocks, and round the tall stems of the cedar-trees. They stand keeping watch like sentinels at the gate of the pass. Then higher still the open world shines round us, snow-peaks heave, the blue heaven comes down, the mules climb step by step, the sun begins to burn; we pass crosses casting a slender line of shade across the rocks that pave our way; we scale smooth fragrant alps, where the goats and cows come from over the horizon tinkling down to meet us, and to gaze at us with wild brown eyes. The people at work up in the faint green heights seem to look down at us too. Time passes: the lights grow more clear, the colors more light. We cross a wide green alp, where a few satyrs, and shepherds in goatskins, and brown-faced children are keeping the flocks; and then at last we stop in a scooped, green, silent valley, where the procession comes to a halt, and Bruno quietly begins to browse, and the mules, seeing Bruno stop, stop too, and Peter and Luigi, the mule-men, light their pipes afresh. We are at the summit of the pass.

Peter was a great big fellow, a German Tyrolese, with his constant pipe in his mouth (it was painted with a cottage and a rural view).

He seemed much taken by Joanna, and tried to make conversation all along the road. He now came to offer assistance; but she treated his advances in a very lofty fashion, and turning her back, began unpacking for herself the basket of provisions we had brought—ripe figs, hard eggs, and rolls, and a little wine. The guides went to a wooden châlet close by, and came back with a pail of milk. They were followed by some children, and a girl of about fifteen, and a calf that instantly trotted up to Bruno and moo'd. High up the father and mother were at work reaping the grass, and one little girl was toiling up the long burning slope with their midday meal. I was going to begin my lunch when H. called me.

"Come here for one minute," she said. She was standing on a little eminence. I hardly know now what we saw at that hour as we stood there together. Our hearts and eyes were opened suddenly, for the sky was so purple blue, the rocks at hand tinted, dented, modelled with tender inscrutable transitions, beautiful, tremulous, with blue and brown; the world beyond was snow and light and rocky ridge. The ice-bound Marmolata rose before us: we saw peak beyond peak, an infinity not too infinite. At our feet the soft brushwood all flowered and tangled with tendrils and leaves. There were great soft gray star-thistles, blue-bells, leaves tongue-shaped, streaked with red veins, argentine, and bronze, and silver. . . .

When we came back I was surprised to find Joanna talking very confidentially to the tall guide, Peter of the shirt-sleeves. Her haughty reserve seemed to have melted, and she was asking him questions, one after another, about the country, the ways, the guides, the travellers, and the rocks. Had he ever been up the Marmolata? What was it like up there? And the Schlern—that was where we were going: was it green? were there any flowers? was it very difficult to ascend?

"It was not easy for women," the guide said. "The Count de Pavis had been up last year, and this year again; but he had alert legs, they said."

"I should like to go," said Joanna, thoughtfully.

"Shall I take you?" said the guide, gallantly.

Joanna looked at me, and did not answer.

That night we slept at a little inn in a lonely, desolate place, with ragged, gentle people, wooden houses falling to decay, and foaming waters rushing through many streams and troughs. Fortunata dined with us in a great bedroom, where our dinner was served, by a crucifix. Joanna waited—nothing would induce her to sit down.

On the second day's journey we came to a desolate pass, where rocks, rounded and massed in strange unnatural shapes, were piled along the road. There was something *human*, and, to me, most horrible about them: they were not ragged, and rugged, and wild, like those we had passed before ; but they looked as if they had been modelled by some terrible hands, rounded, smoothed, and kneaded for some strange purpose, and poised one on the other in awful-looking heaps of lumps and balls and columns, upon which no flowers could spring, no green things could grow.

"There! Nata is crushed by a load like one of those," said Joanna ; " and I, too, have one upon my heart."

For some time past the clouds had been gathering, and a damp mist inclosed us closer and closer, parting to show black tossing waves of cloud beyond : there was an echo of thunder in the air.

Nata still rode on in her sad, listless way ; she did not seem to care whether storm or sunshine fell upon her head.

"There is a storm coming," said Tom cheerfully.

"Don't be afraid," cried the guide. "We are close to a shelter."

We pushed on, and, as he promised, we were able to reach a little lonely hut, standing at the edge of the great Scissor Alp, just before the storm broke. The old landlord came out to shake us by the hand and make us welcome. He was a strange old man, with leather-breeches and gray stockings, and a hook nose and a lean brown face. He brought us into his room, smoked-stained and wood-panelled, and bidding us be seated, he left us hastily, to hurry down and put the animals under shelter ; and then the shadowy armies came rolling across the mighty Alp, echoing, deafening, and breaking into falling streams of water.

"It will soon be over," the landlord said, coming up with the guides, and putting places for us all at his tripod table. "I have got bread," he said, "and cheese, and wine ; plenty to make merry with for married and single. Are you married?" he asked Fortunata, who blushed up and shook her head smiling.

"Then," said the old fellow, "you have no sorrows and no joys. The single have neither sorrows nor joys. Will you stay with me and be my sennerinn? You shall milk the cows, and learn to call my pigs by their names."

"That is more suitable for me," said Joanna, laughing. "I will stay and be your sennerinn."

So we sat breaking the hard wooden biscuits, and listening to the storms all trouping round the lonely châlet. Tom stood outside the door, on the wooden balcony, watching for a break in the clouds. The old fellow busied himself waiting on us, talking, and serving us. He made his own cheese, he told us, and his butter ; he did every thing himself, and lived alone, except when travellers came, like ourselves, to visit him. He had various ingenious devices for lessening his labors. I remember, among other things, noticing a wooden pipe for pigs'-wash from the balcony straight into the trough below. The tall guide, who was used to storms, sat with his two arms on the table, gaping at Joanna,

and philosophically smoking his great pipe. His companion went down to have a look at the beasts. Our old host, in his turn, produced a handsome silver pipe, with a top such as they use in those parts ; and when H. said, smiling, that it was pretty, he pulled it out of his mouth and begged her to smoke it for him. Tom went off into convulsive chuckles at the notion of his mother smoking a pipe. The old fellow laughed, seeing us laugh, and then skipped off quickly to see to some household arrangement.

"The last visitors I had," said he, clattering about among his pans, "were English, like yourselves—two ladies and two gentlemen. The gentlemen had been up the Schlern. One of them was a botanist, and he told me that there was no such place, not in all his country, for flowers and grasses. He had white and blue, and red and violet—a box full. See, he left me some edelweiss," said the old fellow, pointing to a great bunch stuck into his hat that was hanging on a peg.

"And this is the way to the Schlern ?" said Joanna.

"This is one of the ways," said the host. "You cross the Alp by the Horses' Teeth—oh, it is nothing ; and if I had my young legs—" here he slapped his leather gaiters. "People sometimes sleep here before they start ; look, I have a handsome guest-chamber." And as he spoke he opened a door and showed us a wooden chamber with three beds in it. "You ladies will be comfortable in there if you have to stay all night."

"Confound the weather !" said Tom, coming in from the gallery, and shaking himself.

There were three rooms to the châlet : the dairy, the kitchen, and the guest-chamber, all opening into one another ; underneath was the pigs' house and the hay-stable. In another stable, separate from the house, the mules were safely housed, dry and warm, out of the pouring rain. It was falling in sheets of water, and hail came, we could scarcely tell from whence, so thick were the clouds and the vapors rolling along the ground. But the guides went on predicting fine weather, and about three o'clock the clouds broke and the vapors drifted away ; a bright sun came out suddenly, a world was created out of the chaos, and once more we started on our journey. The old fellow bade us farewell, and then let us go our way. He stood in his gallery as we rode away ; he never looked after us. I can hear him now calling his pigs by their names. They were his real friends and companions in his lonely châlet in the midst of that great Alp.

XI.

THE baths of R—— lie deep hidden among cool green woods, where the waters ripple through mosses. From the crest of the opposite mountain we could see the shining summits of fir-trees and a golden gloom among their stems. An old ruined castle on the hill stood solitary and radiant. Some black rooks were floating over it in a crescent, but I could see no sign of a dwelling-place for human people. As we stumbled along we passed some peasants, who stared, and smiled, and marched on. One woman looked earnestly at Fortunata riding by, and suddenly emptied half the pears in her basket into the girl's lap. But it was Joanna who nodded "Thank you," and begun to crunch the ripe fruit. All day long she had come with even steps, never hurrying, rarely lagging behind; and yet she talked to every passer-by, told them with pride that we were travelling together, asked questions all along the road, shook hands freely, and made the holy sign by every wayside cross. As for Nata, she hardly looked up or spoke, but jogged on quietly, drooping a little with sad eyes that scarcely brightened. She did not care for the beauty of sights we passed. People in far worse trouble than Nata's can perhaps feel with living people and animate happiness, and find comfort in it; but it is in vain to ask them to be glad because we have taken them to a high pass, and because the sun is shining on a heap of earth and trees, and the flowers are luxuriant. It is only when the first bitterness of the spirit is past that the voice of Nature can reach sad ears. Her call is too still, too gentle, to be heard when a tumult is in the heart.

"This is now the last ascent," said the guide, as we reached the woods: "this path leads straight to the baths."

Where had we come to? Did gods bathe in the waters above? had they passed before us, leaving the radiance of their footsteps behind them? Now that we had entered the gloom we found it changed to a delight, a mystery, a shimmer. Golden twigs and stems, and creeping sprays hid the radiating sky: everywhere hung veils of moss, so wild, so soft, that it seemed as if they must have come gently blown by the wind; we passed a crystal pool reflecting these sweet wonders; there was a faint fragrant essence in the air, glistering pine-cones were piled along the grass, and flowers and wild strawberries sparkled like rubies. It was the last golden minute of this long day: suddenly the evening came upon us, and the enchantment was over.

We were not yet at our journey's end, for Peter lighted a fresh pipe. When we asked where the house could be, the men nodded and pointed, and strode on by the stumbling mules. We were utterly tired out, and the way seemed very long; but at last the path opened wider, and a woman came strolling along knitting in the twilight. She signed to the men and passed on; then we saw four people walking arm-in-arm, who stood to let us pass, but said nothing; and at last, at a turn, we came upon an open space, in the midst of which were two dusky wooden houses. Shadowy groups were standing round about in the twilight, and overhead

silent dusky figures were watching from a wooden gallery.

So here, in the very heart of this fairy land, the country people had built their little bath-house, and would come to drink the waters. They were big, gentle, ox-eyed people, with solemn ways and calm faces. Even the children played in a sober fashion in their little conical hats. Frau Hofer came half-way down the wooden stairs to meet us, and gravely kissed her cousin; she was followed by a sort of Audrey—a big peasant-woman—who strode before us along the gallery, and silently flung wide open the doors of our room. The gallery crossed one great window dimly lighted, and as I passed I saw that this was the altar window of a little chapel, and the lights were burning on the altar. At the end of the gallery was an open balcony, where two old men were sitting on a bench close to my door, smoking their silver-topped pipes and listening to the chorus coming from the dusk below. It was a quaint mystical place that we had come to. I thought of the woods through which we had passed rustling in the twilight, now that the tide of light had ebbed away; of sleeping birds, of torpid insects, and closed chalices of flowers, of the little snakes lying drowsy in the mossy rocks, and squirrels, and all the harmless woodland life, while here was this strange silent company, wakeful still, and assembled round the little chapel. Was it all fairy work? were these stately people courtiers in disguise? was Rosalind among them, and melancholy Jaques? or was this the wood in which poor Hermia wandered, and Titania hid her Indian boy? Had Shakspeare been here in a dream one night?

The bedrooms were little rooms with wooden doors and floors and windows, and little straw beds; Joanna and Nata had one together, and my room came next. "Come quick and rest, Nata," I heard the sturdy Joanna saying. She had speedily made friends with the landlady, and I presently met her hurrying along the passage carrying some supper for herself and Nata on a little tray: some fish, two glasses of sparkling water, and a piece of bread.

"She is tired, poor little thing! I am taking this to her," said Joanna. "The gentry are served in the dining-room—they will find the priest there and our guides."

There was a tall crucifix at the end of the long bare dining-room, where the priest was supping with his candle before him, and a table was set opposite with another that was lighted for us. Peter and the other man were also sitting drinking and munching the hard seed-biscuit of the country with their enormous mouths, a few peasants looked in at us and went away, the little waitress came and went, like Nata and her sister used to do, with her pouch of office hanging from her waist. In the middle of his supper the old priest rose from table, and stood with folded arms and reverently said a prayer, and then sat down again. Joanna, who had come in, crossed herself devoutly, and then went up and entered into conversation with him. He listened and ate, and responded with benevolent nods. Did many gentry come to the place? Not many, Joanna imagined; it was not to compare for furniture to their own "Black Eagle" at C——.

"But it is pretty here in the forest in summer-time," said the old priest.

"Eh! summer is better than winter," says Joanna; "every thing looks so green, and there is plenty of food for the cattle, and flowers grow by the cart-full."

The old priest told her, as he helped himself to prunes, that this was the country for flowers. "Collectors came from every part of Europe; up on the Schlern," he said, "there are many rare species I myself have gathered there." We left her still plying him with questions, to go and sit out in the dusk of the wooden gallery until it was time to go to bed. Fragrant and cool came the air blowing in our faces, softly shone the stars and the great crescent moon beyond the ruined castle. One or two of the people spoke to us, as they, too, stood admiring and leaning against the wooden balustrade. One funny little girl, called Urse, came up and sat upon the bench beside me, and asked as usual if we were married, and showed H. her silver ring that her father had given her, only it was too dark to see the little cross upon it and the letters beneath.

XII.

FORTUNATA came knocking at my door early next morning before I was quite ready. I had been listening for some time to the waking sounds, the voices in the chapel, the children calling to one another, the pump, the footsteps on the wooden gallery. I had heard little Urse chattering outside my door, and Fortunata and Madame Hofer calling Joanna once or twice.

"Is Joanna with you?" Fortunata said.

I answered through my door: "I have not seen her; tell them to prepare our breakfast with buttered eggs."

"Yes," said Fortunata, going away.

Our breakfast was ready spread in the long room. There were three glasses, very brightly polished, to drink the coffee, three dry twisted horns of bread, and a great dish of eggs broken up, and smoking and cooked with pepper. We felt a little ashamed of our luxurious habits when we saw the peasant-women coming shyly to ask for their modest glasses of fresh water and dry half horns of bread. I was pouring H.'s coffee into her glass when Fortunata came again.

"Had we all we wished? could she get us any thing?" "Signora?" Fortunata said, "I can not imagine where Joanna can be. She was gone when I awoke this morning; she has not been to mass; she has had no breakfast; I can not find her anywhere."

"She has gone off for a ramble this lovely morning," said H. "My dear, ask Madame Hofer for some more hot milk."

"Cousin Hofer says she may have gone up to the castle," Fortunata cried, coming back with the milk; and then H. proposed we should all go there after breakfast.

Many of the women were only now coming out of the chapel and crowding through the doorway. The old fellows, whose devotions were shorter—naturally, at their age, they could not have so much to pray for—were already established on their wooden benches, and stiffly stretching their kneebreeches along the gallery and in front of the baths; they gravely nodded good-mornings over their pipes. Urse and her little brother were standing swinging two great baskets on the green in front of the houses, and we asked them to come with us. But they said no, they were going to pick strawberries with Peter; he had desired them to wait.

Peter came up at this minute, and I asked him if he had seen nothing of Joanna. We had missed her, and were a little anxious. The giant chuckled, as if it was a capital joke. "Had she run away? She was a strong one, she had no timidity, and would come to no harm.' She wishes to outrun you all," Peter said. "There are plenty on the Alp to help her if she loses her way; besides, I told her many things as we came along; and now she will see the world for herself."

I could not help a disagreeable feeling that this great fellow knew more than he chose to tell. However, my suspicions were too vague to put into other people's heads. I watched him march off with swinging shirt-sleeves, and the two children scampering after with their baskets.

We had a charming stroll to the old castle, climbing step by step between the circling stems of the fir-trees, among gray stones and mosses, and under bright changing shadows. Fortunata cheered up a little, and told us a story on the way.

"Once," she said, "there was another castle belonging to a cruel knight, who ravaged all the country round, and when the owner of this castle had to go away for a long journey, he desired his lady if she loved him not to pass beyond the walls till his return, and he collected provisions for a year, and he left her with her maid to wait his return. And some time after he had left, a little baby was born to the lady, and she and the maid tended it and nursed it. But when the year was nearly at an end, the provisions began to fail.

"The knight did not return till a year and a day after he had left his home. Then he came hurrying up the hill, and he saw some one watching for him from the tower-window, and he spurred his horse and waved his hand. But when he entered the castle all was silent, and no one came to meet him. The lady was dead," said Nata; "she had died watching from the window, with her little baby in her arms. The provisions were all gone and they had starved to death; and the poor maid was dead, too," said Nata, and as she said it she turned a little pale and stumbled over a stone. "The villagers say the white lady sometimes watches still from the old tower-window with her infant in her arms," she added. "Look! was that any one? can Joanna be up there?"

We reached the mossy old castle, with its sweet wild woodland view, but we found no Joanna, only some goats browsing the grass among the ruins. I could see that Fortunata was getting very anxious, though she said little; she was weak and impressionable, and her languor seemed to have changed into a sort of fever; her cheeks burned. I scolded her for it and for being so silly as to be frightened, but in truth we too thought it strange when we got down to find no news of the girl. Our Audrey was cleaning her pails, and knew nothing of Joanna, except that she had not come back. And then Nata went away into the little chapel. I saw her kneeling there, poor little thing, with her face buried in her hands, as I passed the gallery window.

Joanna was a stout, hearty girl. Madame Hofer said, as Peter had done, that she had gone out for a walk and probably lost her way; but there were people at work on the Alps all about who would put her in the right road again. To quiet Fortunata, we determined to send round to the neighboring châlets and ask if she had been seen, and this being settled, Madame Hofer went on with her cooking. All the peasant people were very kind and reassuring; one or two of them volunteered to go off and look for her. The old fellows took their silver pipes out of their mouths to recount their own early exploits. "Perhaps she has gone up the Schlern," said one of the boys, open-mouthed; but he was peremptorily snubbed for the suggestion by his grandfather. "The Schlern was not for little boys or women." And so the time passed slowly as the shadows shifted, to the hum of the voices tranquilly discoursing, to the measured footsteps of the people crossing the little gallery. The old men, who seemed permanently established on the bench outside my door, made their jokes as the younger women passed by; the housemaid, followed by her tame goat, clumped from the well to the kitchen and back to the well again with her tubs. It was all sunny and warm and sweet, and would have been utterly peaceful to me if it had not been for the thought of poor little Nata with her burning cheeks. Seeing her flit past my window, I thought it best to lay hands upon her.

"Come in here, Nata," I said, "and keep still, my dear. You will flurry yourself into a fever if you come and go in the sun. We have sent some messengers to ask for news of Joanna. Madame Hofer will send us word when they return."

"Cousin Hofer only laughs," Fortunata said, trying not to cry. The troubles and agitations of the last few days had told upon her nerves.

I guessed that they had been strained to the uttermost before. For herself, the girl had plenty of spirit, and had done her best to bear the doubt, vexation, and wretchedness from which she had suffered so cruelly of late. She had been good, and uttered no word of complaint; but who can say what cruel pangs that poor little heart had endured. She had been foolish, perhaps, and romantic; but Nata's was a deep, sweet nature, and her heart beat truly; and though she could struggle for herself, she broke down in nervous terror for Joanna.

"Oh, Signora," she said, a little wildly, "all this time I have tried not to feel, and to-day I am all like one who is dead. I don't feel, and yet I know that I am suffering. Yesterday was a terrible day—so beautiful, and yet so sad; all I saw only seemed like beautiful pain, and Joanna walked beside me, saying, 'Courage, courage;' and now, if harm has come to her, if wild beasts—if—" Nata broke out into sobs.

"Listen, my dear," I said. "This is all nonsense; there are no wild beasts in these woods except little squirrels and rabbits, and when Joanna comes home we will give her the scolding she deserves for frightening us all. Now you must lie down and wait patiently till the messengers return. Don't, my child." She was kissing my hand just like a child. She did not lie down, but sat on the straw chair beside the bed, resting her aching head on the dark cotton counterpane. The tears and the silence soothed her, and now that she had ceased to struggle against her terrors they seemed to harass her less. At last she was quiet, and I, sitting in the window, took up a book and tried to read. It was a pretty story, but I could not fix my mind upon it. I looked at Madame Hofer standing in the gallery and resting after her morning's work, and then at the fir-trees, and at the bright azure beyond them; and then I watched little Urse and her brother running across the green. They ran straight towards a peasant-woman who was knitting a stocking in the sun. At first I thought they were at play, for they clung to her skirt and the woman bent over them. I fancied she might be their mother. She dropped her knitting and caught little Urse's hand. Something in her action disturbed me, and at the same time I saw Madame Hofer lean forward over the low wooden gallery. It might be a fancy, but my heart began to beat with a nervous apprehension as I put down my book and went out quickly. When I came out on the balcony I found that it was indeed no play that was going on: the children were sobbing, and their mother, with a scared face, was hurrying towards the house.

"Frau Hofer!" she said, "come you quick —here is something happened in the wood!" We ran down the steps together. I had left the door of my room open, and at the cry the woman gave Nata came running out too. She seemed to guess what had happened almost before the children spoke.

"Joanna was lying at the foot of the

Schlern," they said. "The gentleman found her, and he called Hans," sobbed little Urse, "when he was climbing for strawberries, and I called Peter, and when Peter came he told us to stop, and ran away, and he did not come back, and she was lying quite still in her hat."

"And there was blood upon it," said Hans, "and Urse said she was dead, and the gentleman got angry, and said, 'Why did no one come?' and I was frightened. And Urse came too."

"I could not stay alone with the stranger, he frightened me," sobbed little Urse.

"You heartless children, to leave her!" cried Frau Hofer, striking at Hans. Nata caught her hand. "It is well that they came to tell us; now we can go to her," she said, quite calmly, and in a faint shrill voice. "Hans will show the way. Will you tell some one to follow us, Cousin Hofer, with wine and a blanket to carry her home." Nata was the calmest and most collected of us all.

The children led the way along the winding path, under the trees; on our way we met Peter, the carter, flying through the brushwood. He had been, I don't know where, to leave a message for the doctor. "He is in these parts to-day," he said breathless; "he is curing Anton Burlis's mother of her fever. Courage," said he, kindly, "I guessed where she was gone. Joanna is not dead, don't fear. So I said to the man who found her, 'Ho! she will live. I gave myself just such another crack on the head, and I am none the worse.'" Madame Hofer shrugged her shoulders. "Your head!" she said, expressively.

"The stranger is gone," said Peter. "Here she is by this great rock."

She was not dead, poor dear child. She was lying senseless, alone, in her hat, as the children described her, in a still green nook, at the foot of the great Schlern mountain. Everywhere hung green veils of light, and of soft mosses spreading over every stone and pathway, and green misty depths showed beyond the stems of the fir-trees. Was this sweet silent valley the valley of the shadow of death? I wondered. Was this a death-bed?—this carpet, where gentians and harebells were shining, and white petals blown by the wind, and insects gathering sweet juices out of silver stars. Even from the rocks green creepers were hanging; those cruel massed rocks from which she must have fallen!

At the time I hardly saw any thing but her pale lips. Now the whole scene rises up before me in its intense sadness and beauty. That still green dell with the sound of the crickets whistling, Madame Hofer's scared face, the children hanging back behind their mother's skirt, and Nata, tender and passionate, kneeling by the poor senseless body, raising the pale head in her arms, gently loosening the hat from the clotted plaits to which it had been fastened. If Joanna lived, this absurd hat had probably saved her life. Dear honest Joanna! surely there was no life so precious among us all; so useful, so kindly, so cheerful and contented. Soon some of the good people came from the bath-house, bringing a hay-cloth to carry her home. They laid her gently down upon it; they were all subdued by that mystery of inanition, and spoke below their breaths. Only Peter talked out as usual, and described "his crack" to each new-comer.

XIII.

SOMETHING now happened which seemed to add to the strangeness and unreality of this sad moment. For some minutes past a murmuring sound had reached us from the heights above, and we now saw a quaint procession—men and women—passing along the edge of the cliff overhead, in conical hats like poor Joanna's; the men wore flapping waistcoats like Peter's; they all held rosaries in their hands, and were praying aloud as they went. They did not see us, nor did they hear Peter when he called; their prayers drowned his voice. It is not the first time that such a thing has happened. As he cried "Hola!" they walked on and disappeared, but another voice, nearer at hand, and from a different direction, answered, and in a minute more a figure came leaping from rock to rock with quick awkward haste, and hurried towards us. . . . Did I not recognize it? Those long loose limbs, that nervous haste, that green vasculum swinging from its strap! I looked once, and then again bewildered, and then at Nata, who was gazing with a changing face. . .

Yes, she too recognized him: it was the Count, he was unmistakable. "Ah, there he is come back," said Peter, in a satisfied tone. "He found her, but he did not know what to do till I came up." Even at this moment, to my shame I confess, a thought of what the future might have in store came to me. Dear honest Joanna herself, would she not have been the first to share it. The load seemed lightened. All must be well for Nata, since Count Saverio had come to her. All well! Of what was I thinking? Here was De l'avis trembling and scared, Nata crying, and our poor Joanna lying senseless, still in her bearer's arms, with her fair hair clotted with blood.

"Thank heaven you are here! I thought you were never coming," said the Count, coming straight towards us and not looking surprised to see us. "I had gone a little way to look for you. We must get her home. I found her by the strangest, saddest chance. Don't cry, Nata; she *must* get well." He was trembling. He seemed quite unnerved, and unlike himself; perhaps for the first time in his life he had come in contact with a real sorrow.

And so they carried her home, quickly and carefully, along the little winding paths, crossing the little brooks, stooping beneath the branches of the fir-trees. Peter was at Joanna's head, two stout peasant-women held the cloth at her feet, and Nata walked at her side. The first great burst of summer was over, and the life of this sylvan world seemed subdued to a gentler radiance. The year was ending in peaceful dissolution. But our Joanna's life was not yet at its end; nor had her warm heart ceased to beat forever for those she loved. Many of the peasants from the bath-house had joined us, and came quietly along. More than one of these compassionate people fell down on their knees by the wayside cross to pray for Joanna's life, as she was carried by, with that silent face, and the heavy hand hanging over the side of the cloth.

All the way back Saverio never spoke, nor did Nata seem to heed his presence: her whole wistful heart seemed given to Joanna. But as they walked along, I saw him looking at her with a humble pitiful look that touched me and made me like him better than I had ever done. She was so changed, so thin, so sad. Even his return could not bring back her bloom all in one moment. What a mystery it is that the happiness, the light of one life, should be so often in the gift of another's will! Which of us is there that does not hold chords that may vibrate from the very hearts of those about us? Let us pray that with reverent and loving care we may use our power, half-unconscious as it is. . . .

I hurried on before them to make ready a room, and I had hardly prepared every thing, with Audrey's help, when she said, looking from the gallery, "Here they come, and there is the doctor." The doctor came walking through the wood, and met the little procession as it reached the foot of the wooden stairs. Many brown hands were held out to greet him, and he nodded right and left as he followed Joanna's bearers up the creaking wooden flight. He was an old man with long white hair and a staff and silver pipe, which he gave me to hold while he helped to lay Joanna on the straw bed which had been made ready.

"There are too many here," he said, motioning the people gently out of the room. "She will soon revive."

"That is as I told you," said Peter, with a slap upon his knee. Then he jerked his chin. "What is that she is holding in her hand?" he said.

Madame Hofer gently unclasped the poor fingers and took a tuft of crushed purple flowers from between them. "It is only a flower!" she said.

"It is Moretti's Campanula," said the doctor, taking it into his own hand. "She must have caught it as she fell, poor child. It grows high up on the rock."

There was a moment's silence, then a sudden burst of new tears.

"Oh, my dear, my poor dear!" sobbed Nata, as she fell on her knees, and hiding her face in her hands, "The flower, the lilac flower! Oh, Signora, do you remember?"

Did I remember!—my foolish words and non-sense—talk of charms and magic, Joanna's wistful eyes and self-reproach that night upon the terrace. Only too well I remembered it all. Could it be that I had done all this mischief by my idle words? Ah me! the reproach was mine now, and I was too old to cry it away like Fortunata.

The Count seemed uneasy too; he turned very red, and I think he muttered something about the "Devil take that infernal flower!" as he left the room; but he came back wistfully the next instant to say, "Courage, Nata: don't cry!" And he put his arm round her and raised her up. She looked at him through her tears with a half-doubting trustful look, like some little wild animal that trembles yet knows no fear.

Then they all went away, and we undressed Joanna as well as we could. It seemed an age while the doctor examined her. She was cruelly bruised and cut and sprained on the side on which she had fallen; and there, besides, was the one deep cruel wound beneath her hair; but the skull was uninjured; the high hat had truly saved her life. Peter stood outside ready to go off again for medicine and bandages to the Alp where the doctor was staying; Nata's tears kept dropping—dropping on the counterpane, on the straw mattress, on the dear pale face. They were softer, happier tears, as Joanna's color revived a little beneath this gentle rain; light came into her dim eyes, she stirred and whispered, "Nata, here!" then she opened her soft lids wide and looked a little wildly from one to the other. The doctor nodded. "All goes well," he said; and then he wrote something against the wall, and he went to the door and gave it to Peter, who bounded down the gallery in two steps. There was a whisper outside amongst the peasants, while here inside Madame Hofer stood with a candle and a pair of scissors; and Nata was hanging over Joanna's bed silently, and yet with all her tenderest heart's signs and unspoken language welcoming her back to life after that awful journey from which she was returning.

"The Signora!" Joanna said, recognizing me; then she began feeling about the bedclothes and faltered something about a flower.

"Hush—hush! It is safe, you are safe; all, all is well," said Nata, clasping her hands. "Lie still while we thank God for your deliverance from peril."

Some minutes afterwards I saw the doctor looking about uneasily from one side to the other. "Is any thing amiss?" I asked anxiously. "I have mislaid my pipe," he said, and then I discovered that I had been holding the pipe all the while in my hand.

The doctor had done his work, and sat chattering with the old oracles down below. Joanna was unconscious again, but this time it was only a quiet sleep after the pain and fatigue of having her hurts dressed and attended to. H., with her kind face beaming with sympathy, came gently stirring the door-handle to call me to supper.

"This morning it was Joanna. Now it is Fortunata who is lost, just when supper is ready too," said Madame Hofer, meeting us, and speaking with some asperity.

XIV.

H. WAITED till she was gone, then she laid her hand on my arm and pointed to two dim figures on a seat beneath a tree. As we were looking at them they got up and came strolling towards the house. A minute or two after they came into the dining-room. They stood at the door, blinking their eyes in the dazzle of two candles and the soup-tureen. Perhaps I ought to have had more apprehensions, but somehow since Saverio's return I had felt none, and I went to meet them, saying, "Come, here is the soup. Joanna is asleep, and Urse's mother is with her, and we are only waiting for you."

"I am sorry to have detained you," said the Count, standing quite erect, with a look of such real happiness in his face that it was not difficult to foresee what was coming, while Nata took my hand and pressed it, with a long soft thrill that told me all I wanted to know. However, they said no more just then, and all supper-time the Count was much as usual. Nata ate nothing, but sat with innocent, happy eyes, looking as I had never seen her look before. I was struck, for the first time, by her extreme beauty and dazzling brilliancy of color. It was like sunlight shining after a cloud had passed away. During supper the Count told us that he had been busy of late completing a collection, and writing the last chapters of his work upon mountain campanulas. There are no less than sixty different species of these charming flowers, he informed us, of which forty are to be found in the Alps alone. "I wished to give my whole mind to my work," he said, with an odd look as he ate his chicken. "My book has given me a great deal of trouble, and taken a long time to write," he added.

Almost too long a time for his happiness, I thought. After supper I went out into the gallery again. Seeing me standing a little apart, Nata came up, flung her arms round me, and began whispering her happiness in the twilight.

"Oh, Signora, he loves me—he loves me—he is my betrothed!"

Afterwards I heard more, not from Nata nor from the Count, but from my old friend Della Santa; she it was who had warned him of the cruel gossip of the place. He was greatly disturbed and shocked, and very indignant. He had never faced the matter fairly until then. In spite of his aunt's horrified warnings he started at once to follow Nata, and only once (so he confessed long afterwards) did he hesitate at the thought of the storm he should bring about his head by such a marriage. This was a minute before chance, or Providence, brought him to the rock where poor Joanna was lying.

How sweet the evening fell after that long toilsome day! The full moon came sliding up from behind the roof, the lights gleamed, the dark figures passed, and very very far away the echo of an evening hymn reached us from one of the Alps. The doctor and the priest passed us smoking their pipes. "You may be quite at ease about your patient," said the doctor, nodding as he went by.

It seemed too much almost. "You will never be able to persuade Joanna that the purple flower is not a charm," said H.

"I will try," I said, feeling very much ashamed. "I shall tell her that charms are not the things themselves, but are signs of the facts they represent. When I put my hand in yours, it is a sign that I love you, that I am thinking of you. When people love each other truly, any thing, every thing becomes a charm; and flowers, and bits of hair, and old ribbons, and rings, and all sorts of rubbish, become priceless."

"I think I understand you," said H. smiling; "but I don't think Joanna will." And I am afraid H. was right.

MISCELLANIES.

LITTLE SCHOLARS.

YESTERDAY morning, as I was walking up a street in Pimlico, I came upon a crowd of little persons issuing from a narrow alley. Ever so many little people there were streaming through a wicket; running children, shouting children, loitering children, chattering children, and children spinning tops by the way, so that the whole street was awakened by the pleasant childish clatter. As I stand for an instant to see the procession go by, one little girl pops me an impromptu courtesy, at which another from a distant quarter, not behindhand in politeness, pops me another; and presently quite an irregular little volley of courtesyings goes off in every direction. Then I blandly inquire if school is over? and if there is any body left in the house? A little brown-eyes nods her head, and says, "There's a great many people left in the house." And so there are, sure enough, as I find when I get in.

Down a narrow yard, with the workshops on one side and the schools on the other, in at a little door which leads into a big room where there are rafters, maps hanging on the walls, and remarks in immense letters, such as, "COFFEE IS GOOD FOR MY BREAKFAST," and pictures of useful things, with the well-thumbed story underneath; a stove in the middle of the room; a paper hanging up on the door with the names of the teachers; and everywhere wooden benches and tables, made low and small for little legs and arms.

Well, the school-room is quite empty and silent now, and the little turmoil has poured eagerly out at the door. It is twelve o'clock, the sun is shining in the court, and something better than schooling is going on in the kitchen yonder. Who cares now where coffee comes from? or which are the chief cities in Europe? or in what year Stephen came to the throne? For is not twelve o'clock dinner-time with all sensible people? and what periods of history, what future aspirations, what distant events, are as important to us—grown-up folks, and children, too—as this pleasant daily recurring one?

The kind, motherly school-mistress who brought me in tells me that for a shilling half a dozen little boys and girls can be treated to a wholesome meal. I wonder if it smells as good to them as it does to me, when I pull my shilling out of my pocket. The food costs more than twopence, but there is a fund to which people subscribe, and, with its help, the kitchen cooks all through the winter months.

All the children seem very fond of the good Mrs. K——. As we leave the school-room, one little thing comes up crying, and clinging to her, "A boy has been and 'it me!" But when the mistress says, "Well, never mind, you shall have your dinner," the child is instantly consoled; "and you, and you, and you," she continues; but this selection is too heart-rending; and with the help of another lucky shilling nobody present is left out. I remember particularly a lank child, with great black eyes and fuzzy hair, and a pinched gray face, who stood leaning against a wall in the sun: once in the Pontine Marshes, years ago, I remember seeing such another figure. "That poor thing is seventeen," says Mrs. K——. "She sometimes loiters here all day long; she has no mother; and she often comes and tells me her father is so drunk she dare not go home. I always give her a dinner when I can. This is the kitchen."

The kitchen is a delightful little clean-scrubbed place, with rice pudding baking in the oven, and a young mistress and a big girl busy bringing in great caldrons full of the mutton broth I have been scenting all this time. It is a fresh, honest, hungry smell, quite different from that unwholesome compound of fry and sauce, and hot, pungent spice, and stew and mess, which comes steaming up, some seven hours later, into our dining-rooms, from the reeking kitchens below. Here a poor woman is waiting, with a jug, and a round-eyed baby. The mistress tells me the people in the neighborhood are too glad to buy what is left of the children's dinner. "Look what good stuff it is," says Mrs. K——, and she shows me a bowl full of the jelly to which it turns when cold. As the two girls come stepping through the sunny doorway, with the smoking jar between them, I think Mr. Millais might make a pretty picture of the little scene; but my attention is suddenly distracted by the round-eyed baby, who is peering down into the great soup-jug with such wide, wide open eyes, and little hands outstretched—such an eager happy face, that it almost made one laugh, and cry too, to see. The baby must be a favorite, for he is served, and goes off in his mother's arms, keeping vigilant watch over the jug, while four or five other jugs and women are waiting still in the next room. Then into rows of little yellow basins our mistress pours the broth, and we now go in to see the company in the dining-hall, waiting for its banquet. Ah me! but it is a pleasanter sight to see than any company in all the land. Somehow, as the children say grace, I feel as if there was indeed a blessing on the food: a blessing which brings color into these wan cheeks, and **strength and warmth into** these wasted little limbs. Meanwhile, **the** expectant company is growing rather **impatient,** and is battering the benches with its **spoons, and** tapping neighboring heads as well. There goes a little **guest,** scrambling from his place across the room and back again. So many are here to-day, that they have not all got seats. I see the wan girl still standing against the wall, and there is her brother—a sociable little fellow, all dressed in corduroys— who is making funny faces at me across the room, at which some other little boys burst out laughing. But the infants on the dolls' benches, at the other end, are the best fun. There they are—three, four, five years old—whispering, and chattering, and tumbling over one another. Sometimes **one infant** falls suddenly forward, **with** its nose upon the table, and stops there quite contentedly; sometimes another disappears entirely under the legs, and is tugged up by its neighbors. A certain number of the infants **have their dinner** every day, the mistress tells me. Mrs. —— has said so, and hers **is the** kind hand which has **provided for** all these young **ones;** while a same kind heart has schemed how to shelter, to feed, to clothe, to teach, the greatest number of these hungry and cold and neglected little children.

As I am replying to the advances of my young friend in the corduroys, I suddenly hear a cry of "Ooo! ooo! ooo!—noo spoons—noo spoons—ooo! ooo! ooo!" and all the little hands stretch out eagerly as one of the big girls goes by with a paper of shining metal spoons. By this time the basins of soup are travelling round, with hunches of home-made bread. "The infants are to have pudding first," says the mistress, coming forward; and, in a few minutes more, all the little birds are busy pecking at their bread and pudding, of which they take up very small mouthfuls, in very big spoons, and let a good deal slobber down over their pinafores.

One little curly-haired boy, with a very grave face, was eating pudding very slowly and solemnly, so I said to him:—

"Do you like pudding best?"

Little Boy. "Isss."

"And can you read?"

Little Boy. "Isss."

"And write?"

Little Boy. "Isss."

"And have you got a sister?"

Little Boy. "Isss."

"And does she wash your face so nicely?"

Little Boy, extra solemn. "No, see is wite a little girl; see is on'y four year old."

"And how old are you?"

Little Boy, with great dignity. "I am fi' year old."

Then he told me Mrs. Willis "wassed" his face, and he brought his sister to school.

"Where *is* your sister?" says the mistress, going by.

But four-years was not forthcoming.

"I s'pose see has walt home," says the child, and goes on with his pudding.

This little pair are **orphans out of** the workhouse, Mrs. K—— told me. But somebody pays Mrs. Willis for their keep.

There was another funny little **thing, very small,** sitting between two bigger boys, **to whom** I said:

"Are you a little boy or a little girl?"

"Little dirl," says this baby, quite confidently.

"No, you ain't," cries the left-hand neighbor, very much excited.

"Yes, she is," says right-hand neighbor.

And then three or four more join in, each taking a different view of the question. All this time corduroys is still grinning and making faces in his corner. I admire his brass buttons, upon which three or four more children instantly crowd round to look at them. One is a poor little deformed fellow, to whom buttons would be of very little use. He is in quite worn and ragged clothes; he looks as pale and thin almost as that poor girl I first noticed. He has no mother; he and his brother live alone with their father, who is out all day, and the children have to do every thing for themselves. The young ones here who have no mothers seem by far the worst off. This little deformed boy, poor as he is, finds something to give away. Presently I see him scrambling over the backs of the others, and feeding them with small shreds of meat, which he takes out of his soup with his grubby little fingers, and which one little boy, called Thompson, is eating with immense relish. Mrs. K—— here comes up, and says that those who are hungry are to have some more. Thompson has some more, and so does another rosy little fellow: but the others have hardly finished what was first given them, and the very little ones send off their pudding half eaten, and ask for soup. The mistresses here are quite touchingly kind and thoughtful. I did not hear a sharp tone. All the children seemed at home, and happy, and gently dealt with. However cruelly want and care and harshness haunt their own homes, here at least there are only kind words and comfort for these poor little pilgrims whose toil has begun so early. Mrs. —— told me once, that often in winter time these children come barefooted through the snow, and so cold and hungry that they have fallen off their seats half fainting. We may be sure that such little sufferers—thanks to these Good Samaritans—will be tenderly picked up and cared for. But, I wonder, must there always be children in the world hungry and deserted? and will there never, out of all the abundance of the earth, be enough to spare to content those who want so little to make them happy?

Mrs. —— came in while I was still at the school, and took me over the workshops where the elder boys learn to carpenter and carve.

Scores of drawing-rooms in Belgravia are bristling with the pretty little tables and ornaments
these young artificers design. A young man
with a scriptural name superintends the work;
the boys are paid for their labor, and send out
red velvet and twisted legs, and wood ornamented in a hundred devices. There is an industrial class for girls, too. The best and oldest are
taken in, and taught housework and kitchen-
work and sewing. Even the fathers and mothers come in for a share of the good things, and
are invited to tea sometimes, and amused in the
evening with magic lanterns, and conjurers, and
lecturings. I do not dwell at greater length
upon the industrial part of these schools, because
I want to speak of another very similar institution I went to see another day.

On my way thither I had occasion to go
through an old church-yard, full of graves and
sunshine; a quaint old suburban place, with
tree-tops and old brick houses all round about,
and ancient windows looking down upon the
quiet tombstones. Some children were playing
among the graves, and two rosy little girls in big
bonnets were sitting demurely on a stone, and
grasping two babies that were placidly basking
in the sun. The little girls look up and grin as
I go by. I would ask them the way, only I know
they won't answer, and so I go on, out at an old
iron gate, with a swinging lamp, up "Church
Walk" (so it is written), and along a trim little
terrace, to where a maid-of-all-work is scrubbing
at her steps. When I ask the damsel my way
to B—— Street, she says she "do-ant know
B—— Street, but there's Little Davis Street
round the corner;" and when I say I'm afraid
Little Davis Street is no good to me, she says,
"'Tain't Gunter's Row, is it?" So I go off in
despair, and after some minutes of brisk walking, find myself turning up the trim little terrace again, where the maid-of-all-work is still
busy at her steps. This time, as we have a sort
of acquaintance, I tell her that I am looking for
a house where girls are taken in, and educated,
and taught to be housemaids. At which confidence she brightens up, and says: "There's a
'ouse round the-ar with somethink wrote on the
door, jest where the little boy's a trundlin' of
his 'oop."

And so, sure enough, following the hoop, I
come to an old-fashioned house in a court-yard,
and ring at a wooden door on which "Girls'
Industrial Schools" is painted up in white letters.

A little industrious girl, in a lilac pinafore,
let me in, with a courtesy.

"May I come in and see the place?" say I.

"Please, yes," says she (another courtesy).
"Please, what name?—please, walk this way."

"This way" leads through the court, where
clothes are hanging on lines, into a little office-
room, where my guide leaves me, with yet another little courtesy. In a minute the mistress
comes out from the inner room. She is a kind
smiling young woman, with a fresh face and a
pleasant manner. She takes me in, and I see a

dozen more girls in lilac pinafores reading round
a deal table. They look mostly about thirteen
or fourteen years old. I ask if this is all the
school.

"No, not all," the mistress says, counting,
"some are in the laundry, and some are not at
home. When they are old enough, they go out
into the neighborhood to help to wash, or cook,
or what not. Go on, girls!" and the girls instantly begin to read again, and the mistress,
opening a door, brings us out into the passage.
"We have room for twenty-two," says the little
mistress; "and we dress them and feed them
and teach them as well as we can. On week
days they wear any thing we can find for them,
but they have very nice frocks on Sundays. I
never leave them; I sit with them, and sleep
among them, and walk with them; they are always friendly and affectionate to me and among
themselves, and are very good companions."

In answer to my questions, she said that most
of the children were put in by friends who paid
half a crown a week for them, sometimes the
parents themselves, but they could rarely afford
it. That besides this, and what the girls could
earn, £200 a year is required for the rent of the
house and expenses. "It has always been
made up," says the mistress, "but we can't
help being very anxious at times, as we have
nothing certain, nor any regular subscriptions.
Won't you see the laundry?" she adds, opening a door.

In the laundry is a steam, and a clatter, and
irons, and linen, and a little mangle, turned by
two little girls, while two or three more are
busy ironing under the superintendence of a
washerwoman with tucked-up sleeves; piles of
shirt-collars and handkerchiefs and linen are
lying on the shelves, shirts and clothes are
hanging on lines across the room. The little
girls don't stop, but go on busily.

"Where is Mary Anne?" says the mistress,
with a little conscious pride.

"There she is, mum," says the washerwoman, and Mary Anne steps out blushing from behind the mangle, with a hot iron in her hand,
and a hanging head.

"Mary Anne is our chief laundry-maid,"
says the mistress, as we come out into the hall
again. "For the first year I could make nothing of her; she was miserable in the kitchen,
she couldn't bear housework, she wouldn't learn
her lessons. In fact, I was quite unhappy about
her, till one day I set her to ironing; she took to
it instantly, and has been quite cheerful and busy
ever since."

So leaving Mary Anne to her vocation in
life, we went up stairs to the dormitories. The
first floor is let to a lady, and one of the girls is
chosen to wait upon her; the second floor is
where they sleep, in fresh light rooms with
open windows, and sweet spring breezes blowing in across gardens and court-yards. The
place was delightfully trim and fresh and peaceful; the little gray-coated beds stood in rows,
with a basket at the foot of each, and texts were

hanging up on the wall. In the next room stood a wardrobe full of the girls' Sunday clothes, of which one of them keeps the key; after this came the mistress's own room, as fresh and light and well-kept as the rest.

These little maidens scrub and cook and wash and sew. They make broth for the poor, and puddings. They are taught to read and write and count, and they learn geography and history as well. Many of them come from dark unwholesome alleys in the neighborhood—from a dreary country of dirt and crime and foul talk. In this little convent all is fresh and pure, and the sunshine pours in at every window. I don't know that the life is very exciting there, or that the days spent at the mangle, or round the deal table, can be very stirring ones. But surely they are well spent, learning useful arts, and order and modesty and cleanliness. Think of the cellars and slums from which these children come, and of the quiet little haven where they are fitted for the struggle of life, and are taught to be good and industrious and sober and honest. It is only for a year or two, and then they will go out into the world again; into a world indeed of which we know but little —a world of cooks and kitchen-maids and general servants. I dare say these little industrious girls, sitting round that table and spelling out the Gospel of St. John this sunny afternoon, are longing and wistfully thinking about that wondrous coming time. Meanwhile the quiet hour goes by. I say farewell to the kind, smiling mistress; Mary Anne is still busy among her irons; I hear the mangle click as I pass, and the wooden door opens to let me out.

In another old house, standing in a deserted old square near the City, there is a school which interested me as much as any of those I have come across—a school for little Jewish boys and girls. We find a tranquil, roomy old house with light windows, looking out into the quiet square with its ancient garden; a carved staircase; a little hall paved with black and white mosaic, whence two doors lead respectively to the Boys' and Girls' schools.

Presently a little girl unlocks one of these doors, and runs up before us into the schoolroom—a long, well-lighted room full of other little girls busy at their desks: little Hebrew maidens with Oriental faces, who look up at us as we come in. This is always rather an alarming moment; but Dr. ——, who knows the children, comes kindly to our help, and begins to tell us about the school. "It is an experiment," he says, "and one which has answered admirably well. Any children are admitted, Christians as well as Jews; and none come without paying something every week, twopence or threepence, as they can afford, for many of them belong to the very poorest of the Jewish community. They receive a very high class of education." (When I presently see what they are doing, and hear the questions they can answer, I begin to feel a very great respect for these little bits of girls in pinafores,

and for the people who are experimenting on them.) "But the chief aim of the school is to teach them to help themselves, and to inculcate an honest self-dependence and independence." And indeed, as I look at them, I can not but be struck with a certain air of respectability and uprightness among these little creatures, as they sit there, so self-possessed, keen-eyed, well-mannered. "Could you give them a parsing lesson?" the doctor asks the school-mistress, who shakes her head, and says it is their day for arithmetic, and she may not interrupt the order of their studies; but that they may answer any questions the doctor likes to put to them.

Quite little things, with their hair in curls, can tell you about tons and hundredweights, and how many horses it would take to draw a ton, and how many little girls to draw two-thirds of a ton, if so many little girls went to a horse; and if a horse were added, or a horse taken away, or two-eighths of the little girls, or three-fourths of the horse, or one-sixth of the ton—until the room begins to spin breathlessly round and round, and I am left ever so far behindhand.

"Is *avoirdupois* an English word?" Up goes a little hand, with fingers working eagerly, and a pretty little creature with long black hair and a necklace cries out that it is French, and means, *have weight*.

Then the doctor asks about early English history, and the hands still go up, and they know all about it; and so they do about civilization, and despotism, and charters, and Picts and Scots, and dynasties, and early lawgivers, and colonization, and reformation.

"Who was Martin Luther? Why did he leave the Catholic Church? What were indulgences?"

"You gave the Pope lots of money, sir, and he gave you dispensations." This was from our little portress.

There was another little shrimp of a thing, with wonderful, long-slit, flashing eyes, who could answer any thing almost, and whom the other little girls accordingly brought forward in triumph from a back row.

"Give me an instance of a free country?" asks the tired questioner.

"England, sir!" cry the little girls in a shout.

"And now of a country which is not free."

"America!" cry two little voices; and then one adds, "because there are slaves, sir." "And France," says a third; "and we have seen the emperor in the picture-shops."

As I listen to them, I can not help wishing that many of our little Christians were taught to be as independent and self-respecting in their dealings with the grown-up people who come to look at them. One would fancy that servility was a sacred institution, we cling to it so fondly. We seem to expect an absurd amount of respect from our inferiors; we are ready to pay back just as much to those above us in station; and hence I think, notwithstanding all the kindness of heart, all the well-meant and well-spent exertion we see in the world, there is often too great an inequality between those who teach and those who would learn, those who give and those whose harder part it is to receive.

We were quite sorry at last when the doctor made a little bow, and said, " Good-morning, young ladies," quite politely, to his pupils. It was too late to stop and talk to the little boys down below, but we went for a minute into an inner room out of the large boys' school-room, and there we found half a dozen little men, with their hats on their heads, sitting on their benches, reading the *Psalms* in Hebrew ; and so we stood, for this minute before we came away, listening to David's words spoken in David's tongue, and ringing rather sadly in the boys' touching childish voice.

But this is not by any means the principal school which the Jews have established in London. Deep in the heart of the City—beyond St. Paul's—beyond the Cattle Market, with its countless pens—beyond Finsbury Square, and the narrow Barbican, travelling on through a dirty, close, thickly-peopled region, you come to Bell Lane, in Spitalfields. And here you may step in at a door and suddenly find yourself in a wonderful country, in the midst of an unknown people, in a great hall sounding with the voices of hundreds of Jewish children. I know not if it is always so, or if this great assemblage is only temporary, during the preparation for the Passover, but all along the sides of this great room were curtained divisions, and classes sitting divided, busy at their tasks, and children upon children as far as you could see ; and somehow as you look you almost see, not these children only, but their forefathers, the Children of Israel, camping in their tents, as they camped at Succoth, when they fled out of the land of Egypt and the house of bondage. Some of these here present to-day are still flying from the house of bondage ; many of them are the children of Poles, and Russians, and Hungarians, who have escaped over here to avoid conscription, and who arrive destitute and in great misery. But to be friendless, and in want, and poverty-stricken, is the best recommendation for admission to this noble charity. And here, as elsewhere, any one who comes to the door is taken in, Christian as well as Jew.

I have before me now the Report for the year 5619 (1858), during which 1800 children have come to these schools daily. Ten thousand in all have been admitted since the foundation of the school. The working alone of the establishment—salaries, repairs, books, laundresses, etc.—amounts to more than £2000 a year. Of this a very considerable portion goes in salaries to its officers, of whom I count more than fifty in the first page of the pamphlet. " £12 to a man for washing boys," is surely well-spent money ; " £3 to a beadle ; £14 for brooms and brushes ; £1 19s. 6d. for repair of clocks," are among the items. The annual subscriptions are under £500, and the very existence of the place (so says the Report) depends on voluntary offerings at the anniversary. That some of these gifts come in with splendid generosity, I need scarcely say. Clothing for the whole school arrives at Easter once a year, and I saw great bales of boots for the boys waiting to be unpacked in their school-room. Tailors and shoemakers come and take measurings beforehand, so that every body gets his own. To-day these artists having retired, carpenters and bricklayers are at work all about the place, and the great boys' school, which is larger still than the girls', is necessarily empty—except that a group of teachers and monitors are standing in one corner talking and whispering together. The head-master, with a black beard, comes down from a high desk in an inner room, and tells us about the place—about the cleverness of the children, and the scholarship lately founded ; how well many of the boys turn out in after life, and for what good positions they are fitted by the education they are able to receive here ;—" though Jews," he said, " are debarred by their religious requirements from two-thirds of the employments which Christians are able to fill. Masters can not afford to employ workmen who can only give their time from Monday to Friday afternoon. There are, therefore, only a very limited number of occupations open to us. Some of our boys rise to be ministers, and many become teachers here, in which case Government allows them a certain portion of their salary."

The head-mistress in the girls' school was not less kind and ready to answer our questions. During the winter mornings, hot bread-and-milk is given out to any girl who chooses to ask for it, but only about a hundred come forward, of the very hungriest and poorest. When we came away from —— Square a day before, we had begun to think that all poor Jews were well and warmly clad, and had had time to curl their hair, and to look clean and prosperous and respectable, but here, alas! comes the old story of want and sorrow and neglect. What are these brown, lean, wan little figures, in loose gowns falling from their shoulders—black eyes, fuzzy, unkempt hair, strange bead necklaces round their throats, and ear-rings in their ears? I fancied these must be the Poles and Russians, but when I spoke to one of them she smiled and answered very nicely in perfectly good English, and told me she liked writing best of all, and showed me a copy very neat, even, and legible.

Whole classes seemed busy sewing at lilac pinafores, which are, I suppose, a great national institution ; others were ciphering and calling out the figures as the mistress chalked the sum upon a slate. Hebrew alphabets and sentences were hanging up upon the walls. All these little Hebrew maidens learn the language of their nation.

In the infant-school, a very fat little pouting baby, with dark eyes, and a little hook-nose and curly locks, and a blue necklace and funny earrings in her little rosy ears, came forward, grasping one of the mistresses' fingers.

"This is a good little girl," said that lady, "who knows her alphabet in Hebrew and in English."

And the little girl looks up very solemn, as children do, to whom every thing is of vast importance, and each little incident a great new fact. The infant-schools do not make part of the Bell Lane Establishment, though they are connected with it, and the children, as they grow up, and are infants no longer, draft off into the great free-school.

The infant-school is a light new building close by, with arcaded play-grounds, and plenty of light and air and freshness, though it stands in this dreary, grimy region. As we come into the school-rooms we find, piled up on steps at either end, great living heaps of little infants, swaying, kicking, shouting for their dinner, beating aimlessly about with little legs and arms. Little Jew babies are uncommonly like little Christians; just as funny, as hungry, as helpless, and happy now that the bowls of food come steaming in. One, two, three, four, five little cook-boys, in white jackets and caps and aprons, appear in a line, with trays upon their heads, like the processions out of the Arabian Nights; and as each cook-boy appears, the children cheer, and the potatoes steam hotter and hotter, and the mistresses begin to ladle them out.

Rice and browned potatoes is the manna given twice a week to these hungry little Israelites. I rather wish for the soup and pudding certain small Christians are gobbling up just about this time in another corner of London; but this is but a halfpenny-worth, while the other meal costs a penny. You may count by hundreds here instead of by tens; and I don't think there would be so much shouting at the little cook-boys if these hungry little beaks were not eager for their food. I was introduced to one little boy here, who seemed to be very much looked up to by his companions because he had one long curl right along the top of his head. As we were busy talking to him, a number of little things sitting on the floor were busy stroking and feeling with little gentle fingers the soft edges of a coat one of us had on, and the silk dress of a lady who was present.

The lady who takes chief charge of these 400 babies told us how the mothers as well as the children got assistance here in many ways, sometimes coming for advice, sometimes for small loans of money, which they always faithfully repay. She also showed us letters from some of the boys who have left and prospered in life. One from a youth who has lately been elected alderman in some distant colony. She took us into a class-room and gave a lesson to some twenty little creatures, while, as it seemed to me, all the 380 others were tapping at the door, and begging to be let in. It was an object and then a Scripture lesson, and given with the help of old familiar pictures. There was Abraham with his beard, and Isaac and the ram, hanging up against the wall; there was Moses, and the Egyptians, and Joseph, and the sack and the brethren, somewhat out of drawing. All these old friends gave one quite a homely feeling, and seemed to hold out friendly hands to us strangers and Philistines, standing within the gates of the chosen people.

Before we came away the mistress opened a door and showed us one of the prettiest and most touching sights I have ever seen. It was the arcaded playground full of happy, shouting, tumbling, scrambling little creatures : little tumbled-down ones kicking and shouting on the ground, absurd toddling races going on, whole files of little things wandering up and down with their arms round one another's necks; a happy, friendly little multitude indeed : a sight good for sore eyes.

And so I suppose people of all nations and religions love and tend their little ones, and watch and yearn over them. I have seen little Catholics cared for by kind nuns with wistful tenderness, as the young ones came clinging to their black veils and playing with their chaplets ;—little high-church maidens growing up rosy and happy amid crosses and mediæval texts, and chants, and dinners of fish, and kind and melancholy ladies in close caps and loose-cut dresses ;—little low-church children smiling and dropping courtesies as they see the Rev. Mr. Faith-in-grace coming up the lane with tracts in his big pockets about pious negroes and broken vessels and devouring worms, and I dare say pennies and sugar-plums as well.

Who has not seen and noted these things, and blessed with a thankful, humble heart that fatherly Providence which has sent this pure and tender religion of little children to all creeds and to all the world?

TOILERS AND SPINSTERS.

I confess that I have very little sympathy for those unmarried ladies whose wail has of late been so constantly dinning in the ears of the public, and who, with every comfort and necessary of life provided, are supposed to be pining away in lonely gloom and helplessness. There are a score of books with which they doubtless while away their monotonous hours. Old maids, spinsters, the solitary, heart-broken women of England, have quite a little literature of their own, which can not certainly be cheering to these forlorn spirits. It demands a degree of public sympathy for this particular class which would be insulting almost in individual cases, except, indeed, that there are no individual cases, and very few, who, while desiring such commiseration for others, would not quite decline to present themselves as its deserving objects. To come forward, for instance, and say, "Oh alas! alas! what a sad, dull, solitary, useless, unhappy, unoccupied life is mine! I can only see a tombstone at the end of my path, and willows and cypresses on either side, and flowers, all dead and faded, crumbling beneath my feet: and my only companions are memories, and hair ornaments, and ghosts, prosy, stupid old ghosts, who go on saying the same things over and over and over again, and twaddling about all the years that are gone away forever." This is no exaggeration. This is what the "thoughtful" spinster is supposed to say in her reflective moments. There are Sunsets of spinster life, Moans of old maids, Words to the wasted, Lives for the lonely, without number, all sympathizing with these fancied griefs, urging the despondents to hide them away in their own hearts, to show no sigh, to gulp their bitter draught, to cheer, tend, console others in their need, although unspeakably gloomy themselves. One book, I remember, after describing a life passed in abstract study, in nursing sick people, in visiting unhappy ones, in relieving the needy, exclaims (or something very like it): "But, ah! what at best is such a life as this, whose chief pleasures and consolations are to be found in the cares and the sorrows of others? Married life, indeed, has its troubles," these single but impartial critics generally go on to state; "but then there is companionship, sympathy, protection"—one knows the sentence by heart. "Not so is it with those whose lonely course we should be glad to think that we had cheered by the few foregoing remarks, whose sad destiny has been pointed out by a not unfeeling hand. Who knows but that there may be compensation in a lot of which the blank monotony is at least untroubled by the anxieties and fears and hopes of the married?" These are not the exact words, but very much the substance, of many of the volumes, as any body who chooses may see. Where there really seems to be so much kindness and gentle-heartedness, one is the more impatient of a certain melancholy, desponding spirit, which seems to prevail so often.

"Perhaps I shall be told," says one lady, "that while professing to remove some prejudices against it, I have, in reality, taken too gloomy a view of single life. My observations will cause a good deal of laughter among happy spinsters, a good deal of animadversion among proud ones. Those who laugh most will be those who have most thoroughly tried the state I describe, and learned that, happy or unhappy, it is their portion for life, and that, as such, both wisdom and propriety of feeling require them to make the best of it. There are many such; let them laugh with full contentment. . . . . But I appeal from such well-fortified spirits to women of weaker mould, whose tenderness of heart is uncured by time. . . . . What woman is there among such as these who does not mournfully acknowledge the loneliness of her life, and the frequent need of some one to lift her up when borne down by all the sorrows which oppress her? . . . ."

Here is a melancholy climax! But what has the poor lady, thus acknowledging her need, been about all these years? Who has forced her to live alone? Is there nobody to come forward and give her a lift? What possible reason can there be to prevent unmarried, any more than married, people from being happy (or unhappy), according to their circumstances—from enjoying other pleasures more lively than the griefs and sufferings of their neighbors? Are unmarried people shut out from all theatres, concerts, picture-galleries, parks, and gardens? May not they walk out on every day of the week? Are they locked up all the summer time, and only let out when an east wind is blowing? Are they forced to live in one particular quarter of the town? Does Mudie refuse their subscriptions? Are they prevented from taking in The Times, from going out to dinner, from match-making, visiting, gossiping, drinking tea, talking, and playing the piano? If a lady has had three husbands, could she do more? May not spinsters, as well as bachelors, give their opinions on every subject, no matter how ignorant they may be; travel about anywhere, in any costume, however convenient; climb up craters, publish their experiences, tame horses, wear pork-pie hats, write articles in the *Saturday Review?* They have gone out to battle in topboots, danced on the tight-rope, taken up the Italian cause, and harangued the multitudes. They have gone to prison for distributing tracts; they have ascended Mont Blanc, and come down again. They have been doctors, lawyers, clergywomen, squires—as men have been milliners, dressmakers, ballet-dancers, ladies' hairdressers. They have worn waistcoats, shirt-collars, white neckcloths, wideawakes, parted their hair on one side—and, oddly enough, it is strong-minded women who take this curious method of announcing that they are single: they have tried a hundred wild schemes, pranks, fancies; they have made themselves ridiculous, respected, particular, foolish, agreeable; and small blame to them if they have played their part honestly, cheerfully, and sincerely. I know of no especial ordinance of nature to prevent men, or women either, from being ridiculous at times; and we should hate people a great deal more than we do, if we might not laugh at them now and then. To go back to our spinsters, they have crossed the seas in shoals, been brave as men when their courage came to be tried; they have farmed land, kept accounts, opened shops, inherited fortunes, played a part in the world, been presented at Court. What is it that is to render life to them only one long regret? Can not a single woman know tenderest love, faithful affection, sincerest friendship? And if Miss A. considers herself less fortunate than Mrs. B., who has an adoring husband always at home, and £10,000 a year, she certainly does not envy poor Mrs. C., who has to fly to Sir Cresswell Cresswell to get rid of a "life companion," who beats her with his umbrella, spends her money, and knocks her down, instead of "lifting her up."

With all this it is dismally true that single women may have, and many of them have, a real trouble to complain of, and that when the barest necessaries are provided, life can only be to them one long privation from books, from amusement, from friendly intercourse, from the pleasure of giving, and from that social equality which is almost impossible without a certain amount of means; but then surely it is the want of money, and not of husbands, which brings them to this pass. Husbands, the statistics tell us, it is impossible to provide; money, however, is more easily obtained, and above all by those who already own a little store. Somebody says somewhere, that it is better a thousand times to earn a penny than to save one. I have just been learning how, in a few cases, this penny may be earned. Other means, ways, pennies, there are without number, and might be more and more.

There are—to give the first instance which comes to me—Schools of Art all over the kingdom, where young men and young women are taught the same things by the same masters.

It is a fact that the women generally take higher places than the men in the examinations; and when they leave, a person in authority has assured me that he did not know of one single instance where they had failed to make their way. They can earn generally from one hundred to two hundred a year. This would be by teaching privately or in government schools, and by designing for manufacturers. One girl I have heard of was engaged at two hundred a year to invent patterns for table-cloths all day long for some great Manchester firm. I think the melancholy books themselves nearly all most sensibly urge upon parents their duty either to make some provision for their daughters or to help them early in life to help themselves. For troubles come—sad times—and it is hard to look out for a livelihood with eyes blinded by tears.

For mere sentimental griefs for persons whose comforts are assured, and whose chief trouble is that they do not like the life they lead, that they have aspirations and want sympathy, I think fewer books of consolation might suffice. One friendly little volume, which came out the other day, gives such wise and kindly hints to these sufferers, that I can not help mentioning it here.[*] Instead of vague longings after sympathy and protection, might they not themselves give such good things to others whose need is, perhaps, more urgent, and so find work and occupation too?

And the best and the most grateful surely. No one can witness the first-fruits of such good labor without coming away, for a little time at least, more Christian and gentle-hearted.

But it can only be by long patience and trouble that such work can be achieved. For to sympathize I suppose people must know sorrow in some measure, to help they must take pains, to give they must deny themselves, to know how to help others best they must learn themselves.

And the knowledge of good and of evil, as it is taught to us by our lives, is a hard lesson indeed; learnt through failure, through trouble, through shame and humiliation, forgotten, perhaps neglected, broken off, taken up again and again. This lesson taught with such great pains has been sent to all mankind—not excepting old maids, as some people would almost have it; such persons as would make life one long sentimental penance, during which single women should be constantly occupied, dissecting, inspecting, regretting, examining themselves, living among useless little pricks and self-inflicted smarts, and wasting willfully, and turning away from the busy business of life, and still more from that gracious bounty of happiness and content and gratitude which all the clouds of heaven rain down upon us.

When one sees what some good women can do with great hearts and small means, how bravely they can work for others and for themselves, how many good chances there are for those who have patience to seek and courage to

---

hold, how much there is to be done—and I do not mean in works of charity only, but in industry and application and determination—how every woman in raising herself may carry along a score of others with her—when one sees all this, one is ashamed and angry to think of the melancholy, moping spirit which, out of sheer dullness and indolence, would complain of lost chances, go hankering after husbands, and more prosperous ways and means, and waste hours of daylight in gloomy sentiment and inertness. I do not mean that this is the spirit of the self-denying and self-concentrated persons of whom I have just been speaking, for honest and persistent efforts must make themselves respected in any form. I suppose I am addressing that vague but useful scapegoat whom all clergymen, advertisers, advice-givers, speech-makers, and article-writers attack, and who misbehaves in every convenient manner in order to give the wrath-pots of eloquence an opportunity of pouring out.

Statistics are very much the fashion nowadays, and we can not take up a newspaper or a pamphlet without seeing in round numbers that so many people will do so and so in the course of the year; so many commit murder, so many be taken up for drunkenness, so many subscribe to the *London Journal*, so many die, so many marry, so many quarrel after, so many remain single to the end of their lives, of whom so many will be old maids in the course of time. This last number is such an alarming one, that I am afraid to write it down; but it is natural to suppose that out of these latter thousands a certain number must be in want of some place where they can have lunch or tea more quietly, and cheaply and comfortably served than at a pastry-cook's shop. Good tea and bread and butter for sixpence, and dinner off a joint, with potatoes, for ninepence, must, I should think, be a boon to a good many who are perhaps out and about all day, earning their sixpences and ninepences. By subscribing, we are told, to the Ladies' Reading-Room, No. 19 Langham Place, they may not only partake of all these and other delicacies, and join in intellectual conversation, but go up stairs and read *The Times*, and the *Englishwoman's Journal*, and the *Cornhill Magazine*, etc., etc., and write their letters on neatly stamped paper, when the meal is over.

The governesses and hard-working ladies, however, do not seem to frequent this strong-minded little refreshment-room as much as might have been expected; a few country ladies, coming up to town to shop and to see governesses, seem to patronize it more, as well as some of the members of a society which has come to live in the same house. Their labors over, they may, if they like, indulge in tea at five o'clock in the quiet little coffee-room. There are tables, neatly spread, awaiting them, a waitress ready to attend to their wants, windows looking out upon a broad and cheerful street, and on the wall a list of prices, all of the most moderate dimensions.

It is now about two years since this society was started. It is called the "SOCIETY FOR PROMOTING THE EMPLOYMENT OF WOMEN," and Lord Shaftesbury, strange to say, is the president.

"Miss Boucherett and a few ladies," says the report, "feeling deeply the helpless and necessitous condition of the great number of women obliged to resort to non-domestic industry as a means of subsistence, consulted together as to the best way in which they might bring social position and influence to their aid. . . . . They resolved on the formation of a new society, which should have for its object the opening of new employments to women, and their more extensive admission into those branches of employment already open to them." The report goes on to describe briefly enough some of the difficulties which at once occurred to them. Among others, where they should begin their experiment. "For highly educated women, we could for a time do nothing; women of no education could do nothing for us. That is to say, we could open no new channels for the labor of the former, and our experiments would have failed, owing to the inefficiency of the latter. But we felt convinced that in whatever direction we made an opening, the pressure upon all ranks of working-women would be lessened."

This well-intentioned society has only been in existence for a little time; it lives, as I have said, at 19 Langham Place. It is busy apprenticing girls to hair-dressing, printing, law-copying, dial-painting. It is making inquiries in other directions, but it finds many obstacles in its way. Their means are small, apprenticeship is expensive, very few of the girls who come to them can give the time to learn a new trade. They almost all want immediate work and payment, and something to do which needs no learning nor apprenticeship. Can one wonder how it is that women earn so little and starve so much? I have seen a dismal list belonging to the secretary of the society, which tells of certain troubles in a very brief and business-like way. Here is:—

"Miss A., aged 30, daughter of a West Indian merchant, reduced to poverty by his failure: highly educated, but not trained to any thing. Just out of hospital. Wants situation as nurse-maid, without salary.

"Miss B., aged 30. Father speculated, and ruined the family, which is now dependent on her. He is now old, and she has a sister dying.

"Miss C., aged 50. Willing to do *any* thing.

"Miss D., aged 80. Obliged by adverse circumstances to seek employment: unsuited for teaching.

"Mrs. E., widow, with four daughters, aged from 14 to 23. Not trained to any thing, imperfectly educated, lost large property by a lawsuit.

"Mrs. F., husband in America, appears to have deserted her. Wants immediate employment.

"Mrs. G., aged 55; husband, a clergyman's son, ill and helpless. Would do any thing. Go out as charwoman. Orderly and methodical in her habits. Applied at St. Mary's Hospital, refused as being too old.

"Miss H., aged 30, clergyman's daughter, governess **seven** years. Dislikes teaching, is suffering in consequence of overwork."

One has no training, no resources; another poor thing says she is neither well educated nor clever at any thing; she had a little money of her own, but lent it to her brother, and lost it.

"Miss I., energetic, willing to do any thing.

"J., middle-aged woman, not trained to any thing in particular; tried to live by needlework, and failed."

Here we are only at J, and there are yet alphabets and alphabets of poor souls all ready to tell the same story, more or less, whom this friendly society is endeavoring to help.

It has already opened two little establishments, which are making their way in the world with every chance of prosperity and success. One is the law-copying office in Portugal Street, and the other the printing-press in Great Coram Street, which is better known, and where twice as many hands are employed.

To this printing-house in Great Coram Street we went, my friend A. and I; A. telling me, as we drove along, of all the thought and pains and money the house had cost. The money it is already giving back; the kind thought and trouble will be paid in a different coin.

One of the best hands in the office, A. said, is a poor printer's daughter from Ireland, who learnt the business there at her father's press. After his death, she fell into great poverty and trouble, and could find no work nor way of living, when one day she happened to pick up an old torn newspaper, in which she read some little account of the Victoria Press. She set off immediately, begged her way all the way to London, and arrived one day covered with grime and rags, to ask Miss Faithfull to take her in. There was another printress whom I saw diligently at work, a little deaf and dumb girl, who had been trained in the office. I scarcely know if I may say so here, but I know that the printers in this office are trained to better things still than printing.

The workwomen are paid by the piece at the same rate as men are paid. The money is well-earned money, for the work is hard; but not so hard—and, I think, some of these very women could tell us so—as working button-holes fourteen hours a day at five farthings an hour, and selling life and spirit, and flesh and blood, in order not to die. Here are eighteen and twenty shillings to be made a week between nine and six o'clock, except, of course, when some sudden press of business obliges them to work on late into the night.

On the ground floor there is an office, a press-room, a store-room; down below, a dining-room, where the women cook their dinners if they like, and rest for an hour in the middle of the day. On the first floor are work-rooms. The front one is filled up with wooden desks like pews,

running from the windows, and each holding three or four young women. At right angles with the pews run tables, loaded with iron frames and black sheets of type, which are being manipulated by two or three men in dirty-white paper caps. There are also men to print off, and do all the heavy work, which no woman's strength would be equal to.

It is a very busy, silent colony; a table of rules is hanging up on the wall, and I see NO TALKING ALLOWED printed up in fiery letters. All the tongues are silent, but the hands go waving, crossing, recrossing. What enchantresses, I wonder, weaving mystic signs in the air, ever worked to such good purpose! Backward, forward, up and down, there goes a word for a thousand people to read; hi, presto! and the GUINEA BASSINET is announced in letters of iron.

Besides all the enchantresses, there is a little printer's devil, who haunts the place, and seems to have a very pleasant time there, and to be made a great deal of by all the womankind. He has a pair of very rosy cheeks; he wears a very smart little cap, with "Victoria Press" embroidered upon it, and he goes and waits in the halls, and sends up for the ladies' manuscript, just like any other printer's devil one has ever heard of.

"The Society for the Employment of Women apprenticed five girls to me," says Miss Faithfull, describing their start, "at premiums of £10 each. Others were apprenticed by relations and friends, and we soon found ourselves in the thick of the struggle. . . . . When you remember that there was not one skilled compositor in the office, you will readily understand the nature of the difficulties we had to encounter. Work came in immediately from the earliest day. In April we commenced our first book."

Every body, I think, must wish this gallant little venture good speed and all the success it deserves. Here is one more extract about the way in which the printers themselves look at it :—

"The introduction of women into the trade has been contemplated by many printers. Intelligent workmen do not view this movement with distrust. They feel very strongly that woman's cause is man's, and they anxiously look for some opening for the employment of those otherwise solely dependent upon them." And I feel bound to add that I have seen exactly a contrary statement in another little pamphlet, written by another member of the society.

The other place to which I went was a law stationer's in Portugal Street, Lincoln's Inn, where are a series of offices and shops in which lawyers' clerks, I believe, go and buy all those red tapes, blue bags, foolscap papers, plain or over-written, in stiff, upright, legible handwriting—all of which seem to play such an important part in the legislature of the country. Blue paper, white paper, of a dozen tints, ruled, unruled, abbreviations, erasures, ordered, permitted, forbidden—all these things are decreed by certain laws, which are as much the laws of the land as 3 Vict. or 18 Geo. III., which one reads about in the newspapers. All this was good-naturedly explained to us by the manager of this copying-office, into which we were invited to enter by an elaborate hand hanging up on the wall and pointing with a pen which was ornamented by many beautiful flourishes. I was rather disappointed to find the place perfectly light and clean, without any of the conventional dust and spiders'-webs about. The manager sitting in a comfortable little room, the clerks busy at their desks in another —very busy, scarcely looking up as we go in, and working away sedulously with steel pens. I am told that the very first thing they learn when they come in is to stick their pens behind their ears.

There were about ten of them, I think. The manager told us that they were paid, like the printers, by the piece, and could earn from fifteen to twenty-four shillings a week; receiving three halfpence a folio, or twopence a folio, according to the difficulty of the work. They go on from ten till about six. This business, however, can not be counted on with any certainty; sometimes there is a press of work which must be done, and then the poor clerks sit up nearly all night, scratching with wearied pens, and arrive in the morning with blear eyes and pale faces, and fit for very little. Then, again, there is comparatively nothing going on; and they sit waiting in the office, working and embroidering, to pass the time. The idea of clerks embroidering in their office, and of young women with pens behind their ears bending over titledeeds and parchments, seemed rather an incongruous one; but young women must live somehow, and earn their daily bread; and a great many of these had tried and failed very often, before they drifted into Miss Rye's little office.

It was opened some ten months ago, she told us, by the society, and was transferred to her in November, and already begins to pay its own expenses. It was very up-hill work at first. The copyists were new to their work; the solicitors chary of reading it. Many of their clerks, too, seemed averse to the poor ladies. Others, however, were very kind; and one, in particular, came to see Miss Rye of his own accord, to tell her of some mistakes which had been made, and gave her many useful hints at the same time. Without such help, she said, they never could have got on at all. Now the drudgery is overcome; the little office is flourishing; the steel pens find plenty of work to do.

One of the copyists is a widow, and supports two children; another is a Quaker lady, who writes the most beautiful hand imaginable. Applicants come every day to be taken in, and Miss Rye says that if they seem at all promising she is only too glad to engage them; but

many and many of them lose courage, cry off at the last moment, find the occupation too severe, the distance too great, would like to come sometimes of an afternoon, and so go off to begin their search anew after that slender livelihood that seems so hard to win—so hard in some cases, that it is death as well as life that poor creatures are earning, as they toil on day by day, almost contented, almost cheerful.

In these two places I have seen in what way ladies have tried to help—not ladies, but women of a higher class than needlewomen and shopwomen and servants. Ladies—those unlucky individuals whose feelings have been trained up to that sensitive pitch which seems the result of education and cultivation, and which makes the performance of the common offices of life a pain and a penalty to them—might perhaps at a pinch find a livelihood in either of these offices, or add enough to their store to enable them at least to live up to their cultivated feelings. At any rate, it must be less annoying and degrading to be occupied with work, however humble, than to contemplate narrower and narrower stintings and economies every day—economies which are incompatible with the very existence of cultivation and refinement. Scarcely any work that is honest and productive can be degrading. If a lady could earn £60 a year as a cook, it seems to me more dignified to cook than to starve on a pittance of £30 or £20, as so many must do.

There are now two other places I want to speak of, which concern a class of women a little lower in the social grade: I mean shopwomen and needlewomen. The shopwomen we have all of us seen a hundred times, dressed in black silk and vast crinolines, and gliding in and out of the "Mantle and Millinery Department" at Messrs. Swangroves and Snellonbigs. Three shopwomen are advertised for in some great establishment, perhaps, and fifty or sixty go and apply for the places; out of these, three of the best-looking are picked out—so these poor things have told a certain good friend they have. They are well paid for the time; they are put into black silks, and into their "departments." They earn, perhaps, 25s. or 30s. a week, or even more; their business is to be well-dressed and good-looking, and to persuade or frighten people into buying. They have hard work; they must live well and comfortably. They are country girls, perhaps; they have no friends in London, nobody to give them a word of advice, except indeed plenty of bad and foolish advice. The houses at which they board and lodge ask them exorbitant prices—a guinea a week, I believe, is the general charge—and they live there apart in lonely little rooms, away from home, from all good influence, good teaching, good sympathy. This goes on for three or four busy months, and then suddenly it all comes to an end. Every body goes away; the mad dance breaks off in the middle, all the busy figures coming and going disappear somehow; nobody wants new dresses; breakfasts, dinners, teas are all over, or at least partaken of at home in less brilliant costume. The ladies' season is over, and they all go away to the country quite wearied out, and the poor milliners' season has come to an end too, and where are they to turn to? They have not been able to save any money, living at a guinea a week—how was that possible? They can only make and sell flounces, they know no other trade. People don't want gauzes and flounces in October and November, and so the dressmakers and the great shops don't want them any longer, and they tell them so. One day last year thirty young women were turned out into the street from one great house, without friends or means of any kind, or hope of work, and literally not knowing where to turn to.

I spoke just now of a certain good friend they have, from whom I heard all this. Because of this, and for other reasons, this friend and a few other people have tried to help these young women by opening a house in Welbeck Street, where they may lodge at a much cheaper rate than in those other places spoken of, and where they will be safe and well cared for as long as they remain. There is a sort of kindness and goodness and homeliness and comfort about the place, which a loving spirit seems to give somehow to four walls. It is a spacious old house, of which the upper rooms are divided and subdivided into little wooden bed-rooms; there are little high-church pictures, and cleanliness and airiness everywhere. It is only a lodging-house. It does not pretend to be a charity. Young women are free to go and come as they like. They dine together down below, and those ladies who live in the house dine and breakfast at the same time. "We know them all," said their good friend, in speaking of them, "and there is not one among them we do not care for and take deep interest in." These ladies live with them in order to be their friends really. They look after them when they are gone. I don't think any girl living in such a home as this, and with such kind hands stretched out to help her, need ever be in lonely grief or trouble, however unprotected and solitary she may find herself here in London town.

There is a little chapel attached to the house, which was opened and dedicated by the Bishop of London some short time ago. Here are prayers morning and evening, to which they may come or not, as they like; for most of the girls in the house are dissenters, and have been bred up in other forms. One can not help wishing this place were better known, and that young women coming up to town, instead of getting into debt and difficulties elsewhere, would come off here straightway to the shelter of this kindly roof.

At present there are many vacancies; and the first starting off is found difficult. "It has been so very expensive fitting up this house," writes the kind lady who let us in, to a friend, "and the rent is so high. We want to take a room for others, for classes outside; also, we

are in need of books of a good tendency, as well as entertaining. These young people will not read directly religious books; and the novels they get hold of are generally of the worst kind, and to them specially dangerous. . . . We should never get on at all if the ladies did not pay high (for their board), as well as give their work." These ladies, who pay high for their narrow little sleeping-rooms in order to live and dine and breakfast with all those young milliners, are willing to receive subscriptions if any people care to send small sums to help them on in their good work. The house is No. 47 A, Welbeck Street, and here is a list of the prices :—

LODGINGS.

Second-floor bedrooms, with all meals on Sunday., 4s. 6d.
Third-floor bedrooms, with all meals on Sunday.. 3 6

MEALS, BY THE WEEK.

Breakfasts, with tea or coffee, bread and butter.... 2 0
Dinners, without beer............................ 2 6
Teas... 1 6
Suppers, bread and cheese, or butter, and coffee... 1 0

The Needlewomen's Home is in Lamb's Conduit Street. Here, in big front rooms, furnished with long, narrow benches and tables, are women seated in rows, wan, haggard, untidy, pale with watching, bent with sewing, stupefied by a long, sad life of labor. It was tea-time as we got there, and from a door on the landing issued a file of gray women, with soiled clothes and weary, pinched faces. They passed me, and went down, one by one, to the kitchens below—dull, old, for the most part careless—tired out, so it seemed to me. A lady who had come to see the house made some little joke to one disheveled old woman decked out with some black and ghastly finery. The old creature brightened up in an instant, and went down stairs laughing, and one or two other poor ghosts laughed a little too. This was no hard-task shop in which we were. We had not come to be made melancholy, but to see how much help, comfort, assistance was to be found in this gloomy old house of call for needlewomen; only, somehow, what these poor women prized so greatly seemed to us so scant a measure—their privileges such sad ones, so it seemed to us—that I am afraid we came away thinking more of their ill than of their good fortune.

Only a few workers were left in the room out of which the dismal little procession had filed. One deformed woman I saw stitching still, but stopping every now and then to rub her eyes. Another old woman was at work upon a shirt-front. I asked her how much she earned in a day, but she would not answer—said she didn't know. I asked her if she earned less before she came; but she still shook her head, and said she could not tell me, and folded up her shirt and went away. Another brisk old lady was much more communicative; she took off her spectacles, put down some fine stitching, and quite good-naturedly told us any thing we wanted to know.

"Bless you," says she, "I have not been used to this all my life; I've had a house and servants of my own in my time. So has Mrs. Gunter. Oh, she is gone to her tea; but she sits the third from the window there. I earn a good bit; and so I did before I came here, but I worked harder."

"At what time used you to begin?" asked my friend.

"At six, mum," says the old lady, quite cheerful. "By going on regular from six in the morning till eleven at night, I could earn about two shillings; and so I can here."

"But you know you are one of our very best hands, Mrs. ——," says the matron.

Mrs. —— looks quite pleased, and assents.

"This is very comfortable," she goes on. "We only work from nine to eight; we get plenty of light and fire, and a little company to cheer one up a bit."

"Does not the fine working make your eyes ache?" asks the lady.

"Dear me, no," cries Mrs. ——. "Why, that old lady there in the corner, she is past seventy, and never wore spectacles. I should just like you to see some of her stitching."

"Mrs. Gunter, would you kindly let us see your work?" asks the good-natured matron.

"I'm not Mrs. Gunter," says the old woman, very tartly, and looks up suddenly, with a pair of bright brown twinkling eyes. Just to think of their twinkling so brightly through seventy toilsome years!

"I'm sure I beg your pardon," said the matron, kindly; and then turning to us, adds, "This good lady not only keeps herself by her work, but supports a bed-ridden sister. Is it not so, ma'am?"

"Well, I do, perhaps, partly," said the old woman. "She can't help herself much, poor thing! she is crippled in the hands; some of her fingers are drawed together like." The fact being that the good, bright-eyed old creature did support her sister, but did not care to get the credit of it.

Our first acquaintance had gone to tea by this time, and now the friendly matron began to tell us about the place. It was opened by Miss Barlee some time ago; I can not quite remember how many hundred needle-women have worked there since. There were about fifty in the house the day we went; some of them up stairs sewing at government shirts and jackets, for which Miss Barlee has obtained a contract; others busy at lady's work, and the shirt-makers down below. By coming to this house, the women get constant and certain employment, thread, needles, light, firing, and tea, for which they pay a penny in the shilling; bread and sugar they have to find themselves. They earn from one shilling to two shillings for their ten or eleven hours, and I need not count up the advantages of light, spacious work-rooms, and company, instead of cold, darkness, and solitude. My friend was telling me of a girl who was found working in a garret by the light of a piece of twisted paper, as she had no money to buy a candle; and of another who came to this place to beg for

work, and when it was given to her, asked if she might be allowed a penny in advance to buy some bread, as she was so weak for want of food that she could not hold her needle. The ladies here do not only give work and money, they go to the women at their own homes; and if they miss them from the house, look after them, and give them help if they want it. They also distribute coal-tickets and soup-tickets in the winter and at Christmas. This year a great dinner was given, with speeches, and plum-pudding and roast-beef, to which scores of guests sat down—guests to whom at last a holiday had come in all the years.

The matron, whom we made friends with, who is a most kind and cheerful person, told us, also, how much better paid the women are here than in shops, where all the work goes through the hands of contractors. They would never have time, she said, to give out one half-dozen handkerchiefs here, another there, or pillow-cases, or whatever it may be; to look after so many stray women, and make sure that none of their goods are pawned, or stolen, or made away with. That is why they engage contractors who do all this, and give good security.

"And these are the wretches who grind and screw the poor creatures," cries sentimental indignation.

"Why, the fact is, I was a contractor," says the kind matron. "Of course I had to live. I was very, very sorry for the poor things. I hired a room for them, where I had twenty or thirty at work; I helped them as much as I could, but it made my heart ache often. At last one of my workers came to me and told me of this place, and heard of it from a missionary, and so, finally, I came to be matron, and look after them all."

She also told us that where they earn ten or twelve shillings here, they could only get eight or nine elsewhere, out of which they have to find their thread. "They are sad rovers, though," she added; "they think they have heard of something better, and off they go." Perhaps it is a shilling a day making up net cuffs for some shop in Oxford Street; but the net is worked up in a week, the shop does not want them any more, and they are glad enough to come back to the quiet old house again.

It seems the most practical, the most useful and friendly of places, a thoroughly work-a-day usable tool for helping the greatest number most effectually, and at the least cost. If funds are forthcoming, Miss Barlee is prepared to establish twelve branches in different parts of London. This house is at No. 26 Lamb's Conduit Street. Persons wanting work done, and wanting to help the workers, have only got to send it here; and I do not know why these persons should not be shopkeepers as well as buyers, and why the one and the other should not be sorry for, and eager to help, women seeking so wearily their scanty portion of the bread of life.

They seek it wearily, but it is to be found. By roadsides, in arid places, springing up among the thorns and stones. Patient eyes can see it, honest hands may gather; good measure, now and then pressed down and overflowing. Only poor women's hands are bruised by the stones sometimes, and torn by the thorns.

I seem to have been wandering all about London, in and out by Coram Street, Lamb's Conduit Street, Lincoln's Inn, and to have drifted away ever so far from the spinsters in whose company I began my paper. But is it so? I think it is they who have been chiefly at work, and taking us along with them all this time; I think it is mostly to their kindly sympathy and honest endeavors that these places owe their existence—these, only a few among a hundred which are springing up in every direction :— springing up, helpful, forbearing, kindly of deed, of word, gentle of ministration, in the midst of a roaring, troublous city. Somehow grief and shame and pain seem to bring down at times consolation, pity, love, as a sort of consequence.

THE END OF A LONG DAY'S WORK.

To many of those who but a few weeks ago were sitting in the shady garden at the back of Mr. Senior's house at Kensington, it must have seemed as if his last words of welcome were almost sounding yet, his kindly greeting still their own, when they heard that their old friend was gone from amongst them.

Mr. Senior had been ill for some little time, and was scarcely able to go beyond his garden ; but every day, besides the members of his own family, some of his friends and acquaintances would come and see him, and sit with him talking over the topics of the day. The last time the writer saw him, Mr. Senior was as usual sitting out on his lawn, shaded from the sunshine by the trees which he had himself planted when he laid out the garden and built the house in which he was to live for so many years. A rug was wrapped around his knees, a table with papers stood beside him, and one or two of his friends were coming across the grass. It was not much to see, and yet we remember the pleasant impression which came to us as we witnessed the little scene. Sunshine — early summer green—the distant hum of sounds— the gathering of friends—the host seated in his chair, and welcoming each of the new-comers with kind courtesy. As they enter, it is to leave the haste and the noise and the dusty glare of the world without, and to come into a green and tranquil garden, where a man, after long years of labor, is peacefully resting and enjoying his last spring days.

Nassau William Senior was born at Compton, near Uffingham, in Berkshire, in 1790. He was the eldest son of the Rev. John Senior, a man of great ability, who chose to be his son's sole instructor for some years before he sent him to Eton and to Oxford. At Eton, Mr. Senior has said he learned nothing, though he dearly loved the place, and liked to speak of it in after days ; but from his father he learned a very great deal. Nevertheless he was plucked at Oxford, when he went up for an ordinary degree. The examiners asked him some question out of the catechism, to which he replied by giving the sense, but not the exact words of the answer. When this was remarked upon, he said that if he had been asked some years before, when he was a child in the nursery, he might have been able to satisfy them. This excuse did not mend matters, and the young man was sent back. But he was not used to fail in what he undertook, and determined that he would take honors. His sister, nearly twenty years younger than himself, writes (speaking of those bygone days): " Almost the first thing I can remember of my brother is his reading hard in a summer-house at the end of my grandmother's garden. To the best of my early recollection, he seems to have *lived* a long time in that summer-house surrounded by books."

Mr. Senior's reading in the summer-house was to some good end, for he went up to Oxford a second time, and took a first class in classics. He was elected a Fellow of Magdalen College in 1811, and in 1818 was called to the bar. Long before this, when he was quite a young man, he had commenced journal-keeping. He used to say that he found it cleared his brain to hammer out his thoughts on other people.

The letter already quoted goes on to say that, in all his boyish and youthful years, he was a great lover of poetry ; wrote addresses to the nymphs of Tenby—Latin verses, etc. These old MSS. are in existence still, and must have been treasured up by his mother and by an elder sister, to whom he was tenderly devoted, and who died of consumption at five-and-twenty. The same letter speaks of his coming down to see her, and drawing her about the garden in a chair. " I well remember," the writer says, " the joy that his coming home used to cause, and the tone in which he was always spoken of, as ever dearly loved and thoroughly trusted."

It seems likely enough that the early death of his beloved sister, and perhaps other causes for sorrow at the same time, may have been the secret springs of Mr. Senior's activity in the service of his country.

It would be curious to trace how much of public good is owing to the individual troubles and pangs of this man or the other ; what battles and victories are won, desert lands reclaimed and cultivated, hungry folks fed, and weary folks comforted ; what noble thoughts are given utterance to in noble words; what good work of every sort is achieved by the smarting pang of regret, the sickness of disappointment, the aching certainty of enduring sorrow. To give and to take appears to be the inevitable law, and it would almost seem as if those who had suffered most were indeed those who had given most to us in our sore human craving for help and for sympathy.

"When I was about five-and-twenty," Mr. Senior said, one day—perhaps nearly half a century later—to his daughter, "I determined that I would reform the condition of the poor in England."

In his father's parish, for many years, Mr. Senior had been accustomed to hear a great deal and to see a great deal of the suffering of poor people in their own homes, and he had constantly occupied himself with the means of effectually relieving some of the misery which he witnessed daily. Now, after a lifetime almost, he might well look back and remember his early aspirations, for the half-century which had elapsed was full of hard work accomplished, of determinations loyally carried out. Each man travels his own way ; and it seems sometimes strange that so much sympathy should exist for those kindly philanthropists who labor with their hands, and actually distribute the loaves to the half-dozen hungry mouths, while there is so very little shown for others who, without making any particular pretension to charity, work with their heads as well as their hearts, in the cause of the needy, and distribute *their* loaves to the unknown multitudes, who could not even tell the names of their benefactors.

A very able article in the *Economist* gives an excellent *résumé* of Mr. Senior's political economy. In the *Examiner* (as well as in quotations given from another paper for June 11th, 1864), we read of a professorship of Political Economy at Oxford in 1825, and again in 1847; of a Poor-Law Commission of Inquiry into the distribution of the poor-rates ; of the abolition of the law of parochial settlement; of the inquiry into the relief of hand-loom weavers throughout the country ; and of his latest and most conspicuous service in improving the elementary education of the children of the working-classes. And so, while the planes and mulberry-trees which he had planted were growing up tall and shady, the other seed which Mr. Senior had sown was fallen in good ground, and had been taking root, and spreading in all its branches, and long after this generation has passed away, will be still growing and fructifying, year by year.

Mr. Senior was seventy-three years of age when he died. Although long ago he had given up public life, yet his interest in the events of the time remained keen and lively to the very last. His power of application had always been remarkable. Only a few months ago, he was to be seen at his desk apparently quite un-

disturbed, while his family were assembling in the room, and the servants were preparing the table for breakfast ;—he himself had been up and at his writing for several hours. His desire for information and power of work never left him. He sometimes has said that "he should never live long enough to have read all the books he should like to read." His journals fill many volumes, the interest and value of which will only increase as time goes on. Of his important works on political economy and of his political career another pen will be better able to write : these few words are meant to concern "the man rather than his works," the kindly friend, the hospitable host of many a year.

Among his chief friends were Archbishop Whately, who had been his tutor at Oxford ; Sydney Smith, Lord Lansdowne, Sir James Stephen, M. de Tocqueville, Dr. Copleston, the late Bishop of Llandaff, Sir George Cornewall Lewis. Many an honored name might be added to the list of those whom Mr. Senior has welcomed under his roof. He has rejoined his old friends ; and now, as one looks back, it seems as if the guests of his lifetime would almost comprise the history of the last half-century. Here and in France he has held relations with almost every body of name and of mark.

In Mr. Thackeray's paper, entitled *De Juventute*, there is mention made of one young member of Mr. Senior's family, under the name of Walter Juvenis, who goes twice in one day to the exhibition at the Horse Riders' Circus, and comes away "with eyes looking longingly towards the ring as we retreated out of the booth. We were scarcely clear of the place, when we heard *God save the King* played by the equestrian band, the signal that all was over. Our companion entertained us with scraps of dialogue on our way home—precious crumbs of wit which he had brought away from that feast. He laughed over them again as we walked home under the stars." . . . .

Some of this boyish enjoyment and cheerfulness Mr. Senior retained all his life. His disposition was singularly bright and placid ; there was constant kindness, great sweetness of temper, and although great reserve and little expression of feeling, there was a deep and unfailing affection and fidelity toward those whom he loved best. Painful subjects, unavoidable misfortunes, he would never allow to be dwelt upon. He has often said, even quite lately, that he would gladly live a hundred years longer, and that life was to him a constant happiness and interest and occupation.

> Till many years over thy head return :
> So mayest thou live, till like ripe fruit thou drop
> Into thy mother's lap, or be with ease
> Gathered, not harshly plucked, for death mature.
> *Paradise Lost*, book xi.

Does the task which is set to each one of us last as long as life itself? Do some only live to complete it ? Do others outlive their lives ? At times we all try to imagine the great work progressing through generations of men. The strong laborer works with his might all through the heat of the day. At the eleventh hour comes, perhaps, the feeble and failing workman, and he also accomplishes his task; both of them laboring together toward the great completion; both alike receiving their penny. But it is all the same a comforting sight to see now and then a complete picture, as it were, spread out before our eyes; to listen to the end of the story. It would seem somehow as if this were the case when we hear of a life which can be best counted by long years of usefulness and conscientious labor; of kindness, simplicity, contentment; of early endeavors and aspirations, matured and executed in later days; of success well and hardly earned, and interest enduring to the last. Then, when it is a little tired, perhaps, but in a cheerful and contented and humble spirit still, the life which has done so much good and willing service comes to an end.

Shall we quote once more from the paper *De Juventute?* The last words seem fitly to apply to the end of this long day's work :—

"It is night now; and here is home. Gathered under the quiet roof elders and children lie alike at rest. In the midst of a great peace and calm the stars look out from the heavens. The silence is peopled with the past; sorrowful remorses for sins and short-comings; memories of passionate joys and griefs rise out of their graves, both now alike calm and sad. . . . . . The town and the fair landscape sleep under the starlight, wreathed in the autumn mists. Twinkling among the houses, a light keeps watch here and there in what may be a sick-chamber or two. The clock tolls sweetly in the silent air. Here is night and rest." . . . .

HEROINES AND THEIR GRANDMOTHERS.

WHY do women nowadays write such melancholy novels? Are authoresses more miserable than they used to be a hundred years ago? Miss Austen's heroines came tripping into the room, bright-eyed, rosy-cheeked, arch, and good-humored. Evelina and Cecilia would have thoroughly enjoyed their visits to the opera, and their expeditions to the masquerades, if it had not been for their vulgar relations. Valancourt's Emily was a little upset, to be sure, when she found herself all alone in the ghostly and mouldy castle in the south of France, but she, too, was naturally a lively girl, and on the whole showed a great deal of courage and presence of mind. Miss Edgeworth's heroines were pleasant and easily pleased, and to these may be added a blooming rose-garden of wild Irish girls, of good-humored and cheerful young ladies, who consented to make the devoted young hero happy at the end of the third volume, without any very intricate self-examinations, and who certainly were much more appreciated by the heroes of those days than our modern heroines, with all their workings and deep feelings and unrequited affections, are now by the noblemen and gentlemen to whom they happen to be attached.

If one could imagine the ladies of whom we have been speaking coming to life again, and witnessing all the vagaries and agonizing experiences and deadly calm and irrepressible emotion of their granddaughters, the heroines of the present day, what a bewildering scene it would be! Evelina and Cecilia ought to faint with horror! Madame Duval's most shocking expressions were never so alarming as the remarks they might now hear on all sides. Elizabeth Bennett would certainly burst out laughing, Emma might lose her temper, and Fanny Price would turn scarlet and stop her little ears. Perhaps Emily of Udolpho, more accustomed than the others to the horrors of sensation, and having once faced those long and terrible passages, might be able to hold her own against such a great-granddaughter as Aurora Floyd or Lady Audley. But how would she deal with the soul-workings and heart-troubles of Miss Kavanagh's Adèle, or our old favorite Ethel May in the *Daisy Chain*, or Cousin Phillis, or Margaret Hale, or Jane Eyre, or Lucy Snowe, or Dinah, or Maggie Tulliver's distractions, or poor noble Romola's perplexities? Emily would probably prefer any amount of tortuous mysteries, winding staircases and passages, or groans and groans, and yards and yards of faded curtains, to the task of mastering these modern intricacies of feeling and doubting and sentiment.

Are the former heroines women as they were, or as they were supposed to be in those days? Are the women of whom women write now, women as they are, or women as they are supposed to be? Does the modern taste demand a certain sensation feeling, sensation sentiment, only because it is actually experienced?

This is a question to be answered on some other occasion, but, in the mean time, it would seem as if all the good humors and good spirits of former generations had certainly deserted our own heart-broken ladies. Instead of cheerful endurance, the very worst is made of every passing discomfort. Their laughter is forced, even their happiness is only calm content, for they can not so readily recover from the two first volumes. They no longer smile and trip through country-dances hand in hand with their adorers, but waltz with heavy hearts and dizzy brains, while the hero who scorns them looks on. Open the second volume, you will see that, instead of sitting in the drawing-room or pluck-ing roses in the bower, or looking pretty and pleasant, they are lying on their beds with ag-onizing headaches, walking desperately along the streets they know not whither, or staring out of window in blank despair. It would be curious to ascertain in how great a degree lan-guage measures feeling. People nowadays, with the help of the penny-post and the tele-graph, and the endless means of communication and of coming and going, are certainly able to care for a greater number of persons than they could have done a hundred years ago; perhaps they are also able to care more for, and to be more devotedly attached to, those whom they already love; they certainly say more about it, and, perhaps, with its greater abundance and opportunity, expression may have depreciated in value. And this may possibly account for some of the difference between the reserved and measured language of a Jane Bennett and the tempestuous confidences of an Elizabeth Gil-mour. Much that is written now is written with a certain exaggeration and an earnestness which was undreamt of in the placid days when, according to Miss Austen, a few assembly balls and morning visits, a due amount of vexation reasonably surmounted, or at most "smiles reined in, and spirits dancing in private rap-ture," a journey to Bath, an attempt at private theatricals, or a thick packet of explanations hurriedly signed with the hero's initials, were the events, the emotions, the aspirations of a lifetime. They had their faults and their ac-complishments: witness Emma's very mild per-formances in the way of portrait-taking; but as for tracking murderers, agonies of mystery, and disappointed affections, flinging themselves at gentlemen's heads, marrying two husbands at once, flashing with irrepressible emotion, or only betraying the deadly conflict going on within by a slight quiver of the pale lip—such ideas never entered their pretty little heads. They fainted a good deal, we must confess, and wrote long and tedious letters to aged clergymen residing in the country. They exclaimed "La!" when any thing surprised them, and were, we believe, dreadfully afraid of cows, notwithstanding their country connection. But they were certainly a more amiable race than their successors. It is a fact that people do not usually feel the same affection for phenomenons, however curious, that they do for perfectly commonplace human creatures. And yet at the same time we con-fess that it does seem somewhat ungrateful to complain of these living and adventurous hero-ines to whom, with all their vagaries, one has owed such long and happy hours of amusement and entertainment and comfort, and who have gone through so much for our edification.

Still one can not but wonder how Miss Aus-ten would have written if she had lived to-day instead of yesterday. It has been often said that novels might be divided into two great di-visions—the objective and the subjective: al-most all men's novels belong to the former; al-

most all women's, nowadays, to the latter defi-nition. Analysis of emotion instead of analysis of character, the history of feeling instead of the history of events, seems to be the method of the majority of penwomen. The novels that we have in hand to review now are examples of this mode of treatment, and the truth is, that except in the case of the highest art and most consummate skill, there is no comparison be-tween the interest excited by facts and general characteristics, as compared with the interest of feeling and emotion told with only the same amount of perception and ability.

Few people, for instance, could read the story of the poor lady who lived too much alone with-out being touched by the simple earnestness with which her sorrows are written of, although in the bare details of her life there might not be much worth recording. But this is the history of poor Mrs. Storn's feelings more than that of her life—of feelings very sad and earnest and passionate, full of struggle for right, with truth to help and untruth to bewilder her; with pow-er and depth and reality in her struggles, which end at last in a sad sort of twilight that seems to haunt one as one shuts up the book. In *George Geith*, of which we will speak more presently, there is the same sadness and minor key ringing all through the composition. In-deed, all this author's tunes are very melan-choly—so melancholy that it would seem al-most like a defect if they were not at the same time very sweet as well as very sad. *Too Much Alone* is a young woman who marries a very si-lent, upright, and industrious chemical experi-mentalist. He has well-cut features, honorable feelings, a genius for discovering cheap ways of producing acids and chemicals, as well as ideas about cyanosium, which combined with his per-fect trust in and neglect of his wife, very nearly bring about the destruction of all their domes-tic happiness. She is a pale, sentimental young woman, with raven-black hair, clever, and long-ing for sympathy—a *femme incomprise*, it must be confessed, but certainly much more charm-ing and pleasant and pathetic than such people usually are. Days go by, lonely alike for her without occupation or friendship or interest; she can not consort with the dull and vulgar people about her; she has her little son, but he is not a companion. Her husband is absorbed in his work. She has no one to talk to, noth-ing to do or think of. She lives all alone in the great noisy life-full city, sad and pining and wist-ful and weary. Here is a little sketch of her:

"Lina was sitting, thinking about the fact that she had been married many months more than three years, and that on the especial Sun-day morning in question she was just of age. It was still early, for Mr. Storn, according to the fashion of most London folks, borrowed hours from both ends of the day, and his wife was sitting there until it should be time for her to get ready and to go to church alone. Her chair was placed by the open window, and though the city was London, and the locality either the ward of Eastcheap or that of Allhallows, Barking (I am not quite sure which), fragrant odors came wafted to her senses through the casement, for in this as in all other things save one, Maurice had considered her nurture and her tastes, and covered the roof of the counting-house with flowers. But for the distant roll of the carriages, she might just as well have been miles away from London. . . . She was dressed in a pink morning-dress, with her dark hair plainly braided upon her pale fair cheek, and she had a staid sober look upon her face, that somehow made her appear handsomer than in the days of old before she married. . . . ."

This very Sunday Lina meets a dangerous fascinating man of the world, who is a friendly well-meaning creature withal, and who can understand and sympathize with her sadness and solitude only too well for her peace of mind, and for his own: again and again she appeals to her **husband**: "I will find pleasure in the dryest employment if you will only let me be with you, and not leave me alone." She only asks for justice, for confidence—not the confidence of utter desertion and trust and neglect, but the daily confidence and communion which is a necessity to some women, the permission to share in the common interests and efforts of her husband's life; to be allowed to sympathize, and to live, and to understand, instead of being left to pine away lonely, unhappy, half asleep, and utterly weary and disappointed. Unfortunately Mr. Storn thinks it is all childish nonsense, and repulses her in the most affectionate manner; poor unhappy Lina behaves as well as ever she can, and devotes herself to her little boy, only her hair grows blacker, and her face turns paler and paler, day by day; she is very good and struggles to be contented, and will not allow herself to think too much of Herbert, and so things go on in the old way for a long, long time. At last a crisis comes—troubles thicken—Maurice Storn is always away when he is most wanted, little Geordie, the son, gets hold of some of his father's chemicals, which have caused Lina already so much happiness and confidence, and the poor little boy poisons himself with something sweet out of a little bottle. All the description which follows is very powerfully and pathetically told—Maurice Storn's silence and misery, Lina's desperation and sudden change of feeling. After all her long struggles and efforts she suddenly breaks down, all her courage leaves her, and her desperate longings for right and clinging to truth.

"She said in her soul: 'I have lost the power either to bear or to resist. I have tried to face my misfortune, and I feel I am incapable of doing it . . . . why should I struggle or fear any more? I know the worst that life can bring me, I have buried my heart and my hopes with my boy. Why should I strive or struggle any more?' And Lina had got to such a pass that she forgot to answer for herself, Because it is right. Right and wrong, she had lost sight of them both."

And so poor Mrs. Storn almost makes up her mind to leave her home, unconscious that already people are beginning to talk of her, first one and then another. Nobody seems very bad. Every body is going wrong. Maurice abstracted over his work, Lina in a frenzy of wretchedness; home-fires are extinct, outside the cold winds blow, and the snow lies half melted on the ground. The man of the world is waiting in the cold, very miserable too; their best impulses and chances seem failing them, all about there seems to be only pain, and night, and trouble, and sorrow for every one. But at last the morning dawns, and Lina is saved.

Every thing is then satisfactorily arranged, and Maurice is ruined, and Lina's old affection for him returns. The man of the world is also ruined, and determines to emigrate to some distant colony. Mr. and Mrs. Storn retire to an old-fashioned gabled house at Enfield, where they have no secrets from each other, and it is here that Maurice one day tells Lina that he has brought an old friend to say good-bye to her, and then poor Herbert Clyne, the late man of the world, comes across the lawn, and says farewell forever to both his friends in a very pathetic and touching scene.

Lina Storn is finally disposed of in *Too Much Alone*, but Maurice Storn reappears in disguise, and under various assumed names, in almost all the author's subsequent novels. Although we have never yet been able to realize this stern cat personage as satisfactorily as we should have liked to do, yet we must confess to a partiality for him, and a respect for his astounding powers of application, and we are not sorry to meet him over and over again. Whether he turns his attention to chemistry, to engineering, to figures, to theology, the amount of business he gets through is almost bewildering, at the same time something invariably goes wrong, over which he has no control, notwithstanding all his industry and ability, and he has to acknowledge the weakness of humanity, and the insufficiency of the sternest determination to order and arrange the events of life to its own will and fancy. To the woman or women depending upon him he is invariably kind, provokingly reserved, and faithfully devoted. He is of good family and extremely proud, and he is obliged for various reasons to live in the city. All through the stories one seems to hear a suggestive accompanying roll of cart-wheels and carriages. Poor Lina's loneliness seems all the more lonely for the contrast of the busy movement all round about her own silent, sad life. "At first it seemed to give a sort of stimulus to her own existence, hearing the carts roll by, the cabs rattle past, the shout and hum of human voices break on her ear almost before she was awake of a morning. . . . . But wear takes the gloss off all things, even off the sensation of being perplexed and amused by the whirl of life."

In *City and Suburb*, this din of London life, and the way in which city people live and strive, is capitally described; the heroine is no less a person than a Lady Mayoress, a certain Ruby Ruthven, a beauty, capricious and wayward and impetuous, and she is perhaps one of the best of Mrs. Trafford's creations. For old friendship's sake, we can not help giving the preference to *Too Much Alone;* but *City and Suburb* is in many respects an advance upon it, and *George Geith* is, in its way, better than either. The *Moors and the Fens* did not seem to us equal in power to either of the preceding works.

It seems strange, as one thinks of it, that before these books came out no one had ever thought of writing about city life : there is certainly an interest and a charm about old London, its crowded busy streets, its ancient churches and buildings, and narrow lanes and passages with quaint names, of which dwellers in the stucco suburbs have no conception. There is the river with its wondrous freight, and the busy docks, where stores of strange goods are lying, that bewilder one as one gazes. Vast horizons of barrels waiting to be carted, forests of cinnamon-trees and spices, of canes, of ivory, thousands and thousands of great elephant tusks, sorted and stored away, workmen, sailors of every country, a great unknown strange life and bustle. Or if you come away, you find silence, old courts, iron gateways, ancient squares where the sunshine falls quietly, a glint of the past, as it were, a feeling of what has been, and what still lingers among the old worn stones and bricks, and traditions of the city. Even the Mansion House, with its kindly old customs and welcome and hospitality, has a charm and romance of its own, from the golden postillion to the mutton-pies, which are the same as they were hundreds and hundreds of years ago. All this queer sentiment belonging to old London the author feels and describes with great cleverness and appreciation.

George Geith is the latest and the most popular of Mrs. Trafford's novels, and it deserves its popularity, for although *Too Much Alone* is more successfully constructed as a story, this is far better and more powerfully written than any of her former stories. It is the history of the man whose name it bears—a man " to work so long as he has a breath left to draw, who would die in his harness rather than give up, who would fight against opposing circumstances whilst he had a drop of blood in his veins, whose greatest virtues are untiring industry and indomitable courage, and who is worth half a dozen ordinary men, if only because of his iron frame and unconquerable spirit." Here is a description of the place in which he lived, on the second floor of the house which stands next but one to the old gateway on the Fenchurch Street side :—

" If quietness was what he wanted, he had it ; except in the summer evenings when the children of the Fenchurch Street housekeepers brought their marbles through the passage, and fought over them on the pavement in front of the office door, there was little noise of life in the old church-yard. The sparrows in the trees or the footfall of some one entering or quitting the court alone disturbed the silence. The roar of Fenchurch Street on the one side, and of Leadenhall Street on the other, sounded in Fen Court but as a distant murmur, and to a man whose life was spent among figures, and who wanted to devote his undivided attention to his work, this silence was a blessing not to be properly estimated save by those who have passed through that maddening ordeal which precedes being able to abstract the mind from external influence. . . . For the historical recollections associated with the locality he had chosen, George Geith did not care a rush."

George Geith lives with his figures, " climbing Alps on Alps on the other with silent patience, great mountains of arithmetic with gold lying on their summits for him to grasp ;" he works for eighteen hours a day. People come up his stairs to ask for his help :—

" Bankrupts, men who were good enough, men who were doubtful, and men who were (speaking commercially) bad, had all alike occasion to seek the accountant's advice and assistance ; retailers, who kept clerks for their sold books, but not for their bought ; wholesale dealers who did not want to let their clerks see their books at all ; shrewd men of business, who yet could not balance a ledger ; ill-educated traders, who, though they could make money, would have been ashamed to show their ill-written and worse-spelled journals to a stranger ; unhappy wretches, shivering on the brink of insolvency ; creditors who did not think much of the cooking of some dishonest debtors' accounts—all these came and sat in George Geith's office, and waited their turn to see him."

And among these comes a country gentleman, a M. Molozane, who is on the brink of ruin, and who has three daughters at home at the Dower House, near Wattisbridge.

There is a secret in George Geith's life and a reason for which he toils : and although early in the story he makes a discovery which relieves him from part of his anxiety and need for money, he still works on from habit, and one day he receives a letter from this M. Molozane, begging him to come to his assistance, and stating that he is ill and can not come to town. George thinks he would like a breath of country air and determines to go. The description of Wattisbridge and the road thither is delightful ; lambs, cool grass, shaded ponds and cattle, trailing branches, brambles, roses, here a house, there a farm-yard, gently sloping hills crowned with clumps of trees, distant purple haze, a calm blue sky and fleecy clouds, and close at hand a grassy glade with cathedral branches, a young lady, a black retriever, and a white poodle, all of which George Geith notices as he walks along the path, " through the glade, under the shadow of the arching trees, straight as he can go to meet his destiny."

Beryl Molozane, with the dear sweet kindly brown eyes, that seemed to be always laughing and loving, is as charming a destiny as any hero could wish to meet upon a summer's day, as she stands with the sunshine streaming on her nut-brown, red golden hair. She should indeed be capable of converting the most rabid of review-ers to the modern ideal of what a heroine should be, with her April moods, and her tenderness and laughter, her frankness, her cleverness, her gay innocent chatter, her out-spoken youth and brightness. It is she who manages for the whole household, who works for her father, who pro-tects her younger sister, who schemes and plans and thinks and loves for all. No wonder that George loses his heart to her; even in the very be-ginning we are told, when he first sees her, that he would have "taken the sunshine out of his own life to save the clouds from darkening down on hers. He would have left her dear face to smile on still, the guileless heart to throb calm-ly. He would have left his day without a noon to prevent night from closing over hers. He would have known that it was possible for him to love so well that he should become unself-ish. . . . ."

One can not help wondering that the author could have had the heart to treat poor pretty Beryl so harshly, when her very creation, the stern and selfish George himself, would have suffered any pain to spare her if it were possi-ble. It is not our object here to tell a story at length, which is interesting enough to be read for itself, and touching enough to be remember-ed long after the last of the three volumes is closed—to be remembered, but so sadly, that one can not but ask one's self for what reason are such stories written. Is it to make one sad with sorrows which never happened, but which are told with so much truth and pathos that they almost seem for a minute as if they were one's own ? Is it to fill one's eyes with tears for griefs which might be but which have not been, and for troubles that are not, except in a fancy, for the sad, sad fate of a sweet and tender woman, who might have been made happy to gladden all who were interested in her story; or are they written to cheer one in dull hours, to soothe, to interest, and to distract from weary thoughts, from which it is at times a blessing to es-cape ?

A lady, putting down this book the other day, suddenly burst into tears, and said, "Why did they give me this to read?" Why, indeed! Beryl might have been more happy, and no one need have been the worse. She and her George might have been made comfortable together for a little while, and we might have learnt to know her all the same. Does sorrow come like this, in wave upon wave, through long sad years, without one gleam of light to play upon the wa-ters ? Sunshine is sunshine, and warms and vivifies and brightens, though the clouds are coming too, sooner or later, and in nature no warning voices spoil the happiest hours of our lives by useless threats and terrifying hints of what the future may bring forth. Happiness remembered is happiness always; but where

would past happiness be if there was some one always standing by, as in this book, to point with a sigh to future troubles long before they come, and to sadden and spoil all the pleasant spring-time and all the sport and youth by dreary fore-bodings of old age, of autumn, and winter snow, and bitter winds that have not yet begun to blow. "So smile the heavens upon that holy act," says the Friar, "that after sorrow chide us not." "Amen, amen," says Romeo; "but come what sorrow can, it can not countervail the exchange of joy that one short minute gives me in her sight." And we wish that George Geith had been more of Romeo's way of thinking.

A sad ending is very touching at the time, and moves many a sympathy, but in prose—for poetry is to be criticised from a different standard —who ever reads a melancholy story over and over and over, as some stories are read ? The more touching and earnestly the tale is told, the less disposed one is to revert to it; and the more deeply one feels for the fictitious friends whom one can not help loving at times, almost as if they were real ones, the less heart one has to listen to the history of their pains and fears, and sufferings—knowing, as one does, that there is only sorrow in store for them, no relief com-ing, no help anywhere, no salvation at hand. Mr. Thackeray used to say that a bad ending to a book was a great mistake, and he never would make one of his own finish badly. What was the use of it? Nobody ever cared to read a book a second time when it ended unhappily.

There is a great excuse in the case of the writer of *George Geith*, who possesses in no com-mon degree sad powers of pathos. Take, for in-stance, the parting between George and Beryl. She says that it is no use talking about what is past and gone; that they must part and he knows it.

"Then for a moment George misunderstood her. The agony of her own heart, the intense bitterness of the draught she was called upon to drink, the awful hopelessness of her case, and the terrible longing she felt to be permitted to live and love once more, sharpened her voice and gave it a tone she never intended.

"'Have you grown to doubt me?' he asked. 'Do you not know I would marry you to-mor-row if I could ? Do you think that throughout all the years to come, be they many or be they few, I could change to you ? O Beryl, do you not believe that through time and through eter-nity I shall love you and none other?'

"'I do not doubt; I believe,' and her tears fell faster and her sobs became more uncontrol-lable. . . . .

"What was she to him at that moment ? More than wife; more than all the earth; more than heaven; more than life. She was some-thing more, far more, than any poor words we know can express. What he felt for her was be-yond love; the future he saw stretching away for himself without her, without a hope of her, was in its blank weariness so terrible as to be beyond despair. Had the soul been taken out of his body, life could not have been more valueless. Take away the belief of immortality, and what has mortality left to live for?

" At the moment George Geith knew, in a stupid, dull kind of way, that to him Beryl had been an earthly immortality; that to have her again for his own had been the one hope of his weary life, which had made the days and the hours endurable unto him.

" Oh! woe for the great waste of love which there is in this world below; to think how it is filling some hearts to bursting, whilst others are striving for the lack thereof; to think how those who may never be man and wife, those who are about to be parted by death, those whose love can never be any thing but a sorrow and trial, merge their own identity in that of one another, whilst the lawful hands of respectable households wrangle and quarrel, and honest widows order their mourning with decorous resignation, and disconsolate husbands look out for second wives.

" Why is it that the ewe-lamb is always that selected for sacrifice? Why is it that the creature upon which man sets his heart shall be the one snatched from him? Why is it that the thing we prize perishes? That as the flower fades and the grass withereth, so the object of man's love, the delight of his eyes and the desire of his soul, passeth away to leave him desolate?

" On George Geith the blow fell with such force that he groped darkly about, trying to grasp his trouble; trying to meet some tangible foe with whom to grapple. Life without Beryl; days without sun; winter without a hope of summer; nights that could never know a dawn. My reader, have patience, have patience with the despairing grief of this strong man, who had at length met with a sorrow that crushed him.

" Have patience whilst I try to tell of the end that came to his business and to his pleasure; to the years he had spent in toil; to the hours in which he had tasted enjoyment! To the struggles there had come success; to the hopes, fruition; but with success and with fruition there had come likewise death.

" Every thing for him was ended in existence. Living, he was as one dead. Wealth could not console him; success could not comfort him; for him, for this hard, fierce worker, for the man who had so longed for rest, for physical repose, for domestic pleasures, the flowers were to have no more perfume, home no more happiness, the earth no more loveliness. The first spring blossoms, the summer glory on the trees and fields, the fruit and flowers and thousand-tinted leaves of autumn, and the snows and frosts of winter, were never to touch his heart, nor stir his senses in the future.

" Never the home he pictured might be his, never, ah, never! He had built his dream-house on the sands, and behold, the winds blew and the waves beat, and he saw it all disappear, leaving naught but dust and ashes, but death and despair! Madly he fought with his sorrow, as though it were a living thing that he could grasp and conquer; he turned on it constantly, and strove to trample it down."

No comment is needed to point out the power and pathos of this long extract. The early story of George Geith is in many respects the same as the story of Warrington in *Pendennis*, but the end is far more sad and disastrous, and, as it has been shown, pretty bright Beryl dies of her cruel tortures, and it is, in truth, difficult to forgive the author for putting her through so much unnecessary pain and misery.

One peculiarity which strikes one in all these books is, that the feelings are stronger and more vividly alive than the people who are made to experience them. Even Beryl herself is more like a sweet and tender idea of a woman than a living woman with substance and stuff, and bone and flesh, though her passion and devotion are all before us as we read, and seem so alive and so true, that they touch us and master us by their intensity and vividness.

The sympathy between the writer and the reader of a book is a very subtle and strange one, and there is something curious in the necessity for expression on both sides; the writer pouring out the experience and feelings of years, and the reader, relieved and strengthened in certain moods to find that others have experienced and can speak of certain feelings, have passed through phases with which he himself is acquainted. The imaginary Public is a most sympathizing friend; he will listen to the author's sad story; he does not interrupt or rebuff him, or weary with impatient platitudes, until he has had his say and uttered all that was within him. The author perhaps writes on all the sad experience of years, good and ill, successes, hopes, disappointments, or happier memories, of unexpected reprieves, of unhoped-for good fortunes, of old friendships, long-tried love, faithful sympathies enduring to the end. All this, not in the words and descriptions of the events which really happened, but in a language of which he or she alone holds the key, or of which, perhaps, the full significance is scarcely known even to the writer. Only in the great unknown world which he addresses there surely is the kindred spirit somewhere, the kind heart, the friend of friends who will understand him. Novel-writing must be like tears to some women, the vent and the relief of many a chafing spirit. People say, why are so many novels written? and the answer is, because there are so many people feeling, thinking, and enduring, and longing to give voice and expression to the silence of the life in the midst of which they are struggling. The necessity for expression is a great law of nature, one for which there is surely some good and wise reason, as there must be for that natural desire for sympathy which is common to so many. There seems to be something wrong and incomplete in those natures which do not need it, something inhuman in those who are incapable of understanding the great and tender bond by which all humanity is joined and bound together—a bond of common pain and pleasure, of common fear and hope and love and weakness.

Poets tell us that not only human creatures, but the whole universe, is thrilling with sympathy and expression, speaking, entreating, uttering, in plaints of praise, or in a wonder of love and admiration. What do the **sounds** of a bright spring day **mean?** Cocks crow in the farm-yards and valleys below; high up in the clear heavens the lark is pouring out **its** sweet passionate trills; shriller and sweeter, and more complete as the tiny speck soars higher and higher still, "flow the profuse strains of unpremeditated art." The sheep baa and browse, and shake their meek heads; children shout for the very pleasure of making a sound in the sunshine. Nature is bursting with new green, brightening, changing into a thousand lovely shades. Seas washing and sparkling against the shores, streaks of faint light in distant horizons, soft winds blowing about the landscape; what is all this but an appeal for sympathy, a great natural expression of happiness and emotion?

And perhaps, after all, the real secret of our complaint against modern heroines is not so much that they are natural and speak out what is in them, and tell us of deeper and more passionate feeling than ever stirred the even tenor of their grandmothers' narratives, but that they are morbid, constantly occupied with themselves, one-sided, and ungrateful to the wonders and blessings of a world which is not less beautiful now than it was a hundred years ago, where perhaps there is a less amount of sorrows, and a less amount of pain most certainly, than at the time when Miss Austen and Miss Ferrier said their say. Jane Austen's own story was

more sad and more pathetic than that of many and many of the heroines whom we have been passing in review **and** complaining of, and who complain to us so **loudly;** but in her, knowledge of good and evil, **and** of sorrow and anxiety and disappointment, evinced itself, not in impotent railings against the world, and impatient paragraphs and monotonous complaints, but in a delicate sympathy with **the** smallest events of life, a charming appreciation **of** its common aspects, a playful wisdom and kindly humor, which charm us to this day.

Many of the heroines of to-day are dear and tried old friends, and would be sorely missed out of our lives, and leave irreparable blanks on our book-shelves; numbers of them are married and happily settled down in various country-houses and parsonages in England and Wales; but for the sake of their children who are growing up round about them, and who will be the heroes and heroines of the next generation or two, we would appeal to their own sense of what is right and judicious, and ask them if they would not desire to see their daughters brought up in a simpler, less spasmodic, less introspective and morbid way than they themselves have been? Are they not sometimes haunted by the consciousness that their own experiences may have suggested a strained and affected view of life to some of their younger readers, instead of encouraging them to cheerfulness, to content, to a moderate estimate of their own infallibility, a charity for others, and a not too absorbing contemplation of themselves, their own virtues and shortcomings? "Avant tout, le temps est *poseur*," says George Sand, "et toi qui fais avec d'esprit la guerre à ce travers, tu en es pénétré de la tête aux pieds."

A SAD HOUR.

This little introduction is to open the door of a home that was once in a house in a pleasant green square in London — a comfortable family house, with airy and light and snug corners, and writing-tables, and with pictures hanging from the walls of the drawing-room, where the tall windows looked out upon the trees, and of the study up stairs where the father sat at his work.

Here were books and china pots and silver inkstands, and a hundred familiar things all about the house, which the young people had been used to for so long that they had by degrees come to life for them with that individual life with which inanimate things live for the young. Sometimes in the comfortable flicker of the twilight fire, the place would seem all astir in the dance of the bright fires which burned in that hearth—fires which then seemed

to be, perhaps, only charred coal and wood and ashes, but whose rays still warm and cheer those who were gathered round the home hearth so many years ago.

On one side of the fire-place hung a picture which had been painted by Miss Edgar, and which represented a pretty pale lady, with her head on one side. The artist had christened her Laura. On the chimney-piece, behind the old red pots, the little Dresden china figures, the gilt and loudly-ticking clock, stood the picture of a kind old family friend, with a friendly yet troubled expression in his countenance; and then, against a panel, hung a little water-color painted by Hunt, and representing the sweet little heroine of this short history. Opposite to her for a while was a vacant space, until one summer, in Italy, the father happened to buy the portrait of a little Dauphin or Neapolitan Prince, with a broad ribbon and order, and soft fair hair; and when the little Prince had come back from Italy and from a visit to Messrs. Colnaghi's, he was nailed up in his beautiful new frame on the opposite panel to the little peasant girl. There had been some discussion as to where he was to be placed, and one night he was carried up into the study, where he was measured with another little partner, but the little peasant girl matched him best, although the other was a charming and high-born little girl. Only a short time before Messrs. Colnaghi had sent her home, in a gilt and reeded frame, a lovely little print of one of Sir Joshua's pictures. She lived up above in the study, and was christened Lady Marjory by the young people, who did not know the little lady's real name. And it happened that, one night in this long ago of which I am writing, one of these young folks, sitting basking in the comfortable warmth of the fire, dreamt out a little history of the pictures they were lighting up in the firelight, and nodding and smiling at her as pictures do. It was a revelation which she wrote down at the time, and which she firmly believed in when she wrote it; and perhaps this short explanation will be enough to make the little history intelligible as it was written, without any other change.

There was once a funny little peasant maiden in a big Normandy cap and blue stockings, and a bright-colored kerchief, who sat upon a bank, painted all over with heather and flowers, with her basket at her feet, and who looked out at the world with two blue eyes and a sweet, artless little smile which touched and softened quite gruff old ladies and gentlemen who happened to see her hanging up against the parlor wall.

Opposite to the little peasant maiden was a lady of much greater pretensions. No other than Petrarch's Laura, indeed, in a pea-green gown, with a lackadaisical expression and her head on one side. But it was in vain she languished and gave herself airs;—every body went up first to the grinning little peasant maid and cried, "Oh, what a dear little girl!"

At first the child, who, you know, was a little French child, did not understand what they were saying, and would beg Mrs. Laura to translate their remarks. This lady had brought up a large family (so she explained to the old gentleman over the chimney-piece), and did not think it right to turn little girls' heads with silly flattery; and so, instead of translating rightly, she would tell the little maiden that they were laughing at her big cap or blue stockings.

"Let them laugh," says the little maid, sturdily; "I am sure they look very good-natured, and don't mean any harm," and so she smiled in their faces as sweetly as ever. And quite soon she learnt enough to understand for herself.

Although Laura was so sentimental she was not utterly heartless, and she rather liked the child; and sometimes when she was in a good temper would tell her great long stories about her youth, and the south, and the gentlemen who were in love with her—and that one in particular who wrote such heaps and heaps of poetry; and go on about troubadours and the belle-passion, while the little girl wondered and listened, and respected Laura more and more every day.

"How can you talk such nonsense to the child!" said the old gentleman over the chimney.

"Ah! that is a man's speech," said the lady in green, plaintively. "Nonsense!—yes, silent devotion. Yes, a heart bleeding inwardly—breaking without one outward sign; that is, indeed, the nonsense of a faithful woman's love! There are some things no man can understand—no man!"

"I am surprised to hear you say so," said the old gentleman, politely.

"Are you alluding to that creature Petrarch?" cried Laura. "He became quite a nuisance at last. Always groaning and sighing, and sending me scrawls of sonnets to decipher, and causing dissension between me and my dear husband. The man disgraced himself in the end by taking up with some low, vulgar minx or other. That is what you will find," she continued, addressing the little girl—"men are false; the truth is not in them. It is our sad privilege to be faithful—to die breathing the name beloved; heigh-ho!" and though she spoke to the little girl, she looked at the old gentleman over the chimney-piece.

"I hear every day of a new arrival expected among us," said he, feeling uncomfortable, and wishing to change the subject; "a little Prince in a blue coat all covered over with diamonds."

"A Prince!" cried Laura, brightening up—"delightful! You are, perhaps, aware that I have been accustomed to such society before this?"

"This one is but a child," said the old gentleman; "but they say he is a very pretty little fellow."

"Oh, I wonder—I wonder if he is the little Prince I dreamt of," thought the little girl. "Oh, how they are all talking about him!"

"Of course they will put him in here," said Laura. "I want to have news of the dear court."

"They were talking of it," said the old gentleman. "And the other night in the study they said he would make a nice pendant for our little friend here."

When the little peasant maiden heard this, her heart began to beat, so that the room seemed to swim round and round, and if she had not held on by the purple bank she would certainly have slipped down on to the carpet.

"I have never been into the study," said Laura, fractiously; "pray, who did you meet there when they carried you up the other night to examine the marks on your back?"

"A very delightful circle," said the old gentleman; "several old friends, and some very distinguished people — Mr. Washington, Dr. Johnson, the Duke, Sir Joshua; and a most charming little lady, a friend of his, and all his R. A.'s in a group. Our host's great-grand-father is also there, and Major André, in whom I am sure all gentle ladies must take an interest."

"I never heard of one of them," said Laura, tossing her head. "And the little girl, pray who is she?"

"A very charming little person, with round eyes, and a muff, and a big bonnet. Our dear young friend here would make her a nice little maid."

The little peasant child's heart died within her. "A maid! Yes, yes; that is my station. Ah, what a little simpleton I am! Who am I, that the Prince should look at me? What was **I thinking about? Ah, what a silly child I am!**"

And so, when night came, she went to sleep very sad, and very much ashamed of herself, upon her purple bank. All night long she dreamed wild dreams. She saw the little Prince coming and going in his blue velvet coat, and his long fair hair, and sometimes he looked at her scornfully.

"You low-born, wretched little peasant child," said he, "do you expect that I, a prince, am going to notice you?"

But sometimes he looked kind; and once he held out his hand; and the little girl fell down **on her** knees, in her dreams, and was just going to clasp it, when there came a tremendous clap of thunder and a great flash of lightning, and, waking up with a start, she heard the door bang as some one left the room with a candle, and a clock struck eleven, and some voices seemed dying away, and then all was quite dark and quiet again.

But when morning came, and the little girl opened her eyes, what was, do you think, the first thing she saw leaning up against the back of a chair? Any body who has ever been in **love**, or ever read a novel, will guess that it was **the little** Prince, in his blue coat, with all his beautiful orders on, and his long fair hair, and his blue eyes already wide open and fixed upon the little maid.

"Ah, madam," said he, in French, "at last we meet. I have known you for years past. When I was in the old palace in Italy, I used to dream of you night after night. There was a marble terrace outside the window, with statues standing in the sun, and orange-trees blooming year by year. There was a painted ceiling to the room, with flying figures flitting round a circle. There was a great blue sky without, and deep shadows came striking across the marble floor day after day at noon. And I was so weary, oh! so weary, until one night I saw you in my dreams, and you seemed to say, 'Courage, little Prince, courage. I, too, am waiting for you. Courage, dear little Prince.' And now, at last, we meet, madam," he **cried,**

clasping his hands. "Ah! do not condemn me to despair."

The little peasant maiden felt as if she could die of happiness.

"Oh Prince, Prince," she sobbed, "Oh, what shall I say? Oh, I am not worthy of you. Oh, you are too good and great for such a little wretch as I. There is a young lady up stairs who will suit you a thousand times better; and I will be your little maid, **and** brush your beautiful coat."

But the Prince laughed away her scruples and terrors, and vowed she was fit to be a princess any day in all the year; and, indeed, the little girl, though she thought so humbly of herself, could not but see how well he thought of her. And so, all that long happy day, the children talked and chattered from morning to night, rather to the disgust of Laura, who would have preferred holding forth herself. But the old gentleman over the chimney looked on with a gentle smile on his kind red face, and nodded his head encouragingly at them every now and then.

All that day the little peasant maiden was perfectly happy, and, when evening fell, went to sleep as usual upon her flowery bank, looking so sweet and so innocent that the little Prince vowed and swore to himself that all his life should be devoted to her, for he had never seen her like, and that she should have a beautiful crown and a velvet gown, and be happy for ever and ever.

Poor little maiden! When the next morning came, and she opened her sweet blue eyes, alas, it was in vain, in vain—in vain to this poor little loving heart. There stood the arm-chair, but the Prince was gone. The shutters were open, the sunshine was streaming in with the fresh morning air; but the room was dark and dreary and empty to her. The little Prince was no longer there, and, if she thought she could die of happiness the day before, to-day it seemed as if she must live forever, her grief was so keen, the pang so cruel, that it could never end.

Quite cold and shivering, she turned to Laura, to ask if she knew any thing; but Laura could only inform her that she had always said so—men were false—silent devotion, hearts breaking without one sign, were a woman's privilege, etc. But, indeed, the little peasant girl hardly heard what she was saying.

"The housemaid carried him off into the study, my dear," said the old gentleman, very kindly, "this morning before you were awake. But never mind, for she sneezed three times before she left the room."

"Oh, what is that to me?" moaned the little peasant maiden.

"Don't you know?" said the old gentleman, mysteriously. "Three sneezes on a Friday break the enchantment which keeps us all here, and to-night at twelve o'clock we will go and pay your little Prince a visit."

The clock was striking twelve when the little

peasant girl, waking from an uneasy dream, felt herself tapped on the shoulder.

"Come, my dear, jump," said the old gentleman, holding out his hand, and leaving the indignant Laura to scramble down by herself as best she could.

This she did, showing two long thin legs, cased in blue silk stockings, and reached the ground at last, naturally very sulky, and greatly offended by this want of attention.

"Is this the way I am to be treated?" said she, shaking out her train, and brushing past them into the passage.

There she met several ladies and gentlemen hurrying up from the dining-room, and the little Prince, in the blue coat, rushing towards the drawing-room door.

"You will find your love quite taken up with the gentleman from the chimney-piece," said Laura, stopping him spitefully. "Don't you see them coming hand in hand? He seems quite to have consoled her for your absence."

And alas! at that instant the poor little maiden, in an impulse of gratitude, had flung her arms round her kind old protector. "Will you really take me to him?" she cried; "Oh how good, how noble you are!"

"Didn't I tell you so?" said Laura, with a laugh.

The fiery little Prince flashed up with rage and jealousy. He dashed his hand to his forehead, and then, when the little peasant maid came up suddenly, all trembling with shy happiness, he made her a very low and sarcastic bow and turned upon his heel.

Ah me! Here was a tragedy. The poor little girl sank down in a heap on the stairs all insensible. The little Prince, never looking once behind, walked up very stately straight into the study again, where he began to make love to Sir Joshua's little lady with the big bonnet and the big round eyes.

There was quite a hum of conversation going on in the room. Figures coming and going and saluting one another in a courtly old-fashioned way. Sir Joshua, with his trumpet, was walking up and down arm-in-arm with Dr. Johnson; the doctor scowling every now and then over his shoulder at Mr. Washington's bust, who took not the slightest notice. "Ha! ten minutes past midnight," observed the General, looking at the clock. "It is, I believe, well ascertained that there exists some considerable difference between the hour here and in America. I know not exactly what that difference is. If I did I could calculate the time at home."

"Sir," said Dr. Johnson, "any fool could do as much."

The bust met this sally with a blank and haughty stare, and went on talking to the French lady who was leaning against the cabinet.

In the mean time the members of the Royal Academy had all come clambering down from their places, leaving the model alone in the lamp-lighted hall where they had been assembled. He remained to put on his clothes and to extinguish the lights which had now been burning for some hundred years. At night, when we were all lying stretched out on our beds, how rarely we think of the companies gathering and awakening in our darkened rooms below! Mr. H. C. Andersen was one of the first to note these midnight assemblies, and to call our attention to them. In a very wise and interesting book called *The Nutcracker of Nuremberg* (written by some learned German many years ago) there is a curious account of one of these meetings, witnessed by a little wakeful girl. On this night, alas, no one was waking; the house was dim with silence and obscurity, and the sad story of my little peasant maiden told on with no lucky interruption. Poor, poor little maiden! There she lay, a little soft round heap upon the stairs. The people coming and going scarcely noticed her, so busy were they making the most of their brief hour of life and liberty. The kind old gentleman from over the chimney-piece stood rubbing her little cold hands in his, and supporting her drooping head upon his knee. Through the window the black night trees shivered and the moon rose in the drifting sky. The church-steeple struck the half-hour, and the people hurried faster and faster.

"Tira, lira, lira," sung a strange little figure dressed in motley clothes, suddenly stopping on its way. "What have we here? What have we here? A little peasant maid fainting in the moonlight—an old gentleman trying to bring her to! Is she your daughter, friend? Is she dead or sick or shamming? Why do you waste your precious moments? Chuck her out of window, Toby. Throw the babby out of window. I am Mr. Punch off the inkstand;" and with another horrible chuckle the little figure seemed to be skipping away.

"Stop, sir," said the old gentleman, very sternly. "Listen to what I have to tell you. If you see a little Prince up stairs in a blue velvet coat, tell him for me that he is a villain and a false heart; and if this young lady dies of grief it is he who has killed her; she was seeking him when he spurned her. Tell him this, if you please, and ask him when and where he will be pleased to meet me, and what weapons he will choose."

"I'll tell him," said Mr. Punch, and he was off in a minute. Presently he came back (somewhat to the old gentleman's surprise). "I have seen your little Prince," said he, "and given him your message; but I did not wait for an answer. 'Twere a pity to kill him, you cruel-hearted old gentleman. What would the little girl say when she came to life?" And Punchinello, who was really kind-hearted, although flighty at first and odd in manner, knelt down and took the little pale girl into his arms. Her head fell heavily on his shoulder. "Oh dear! What is to be done with her?" sighed the old gentleman, helplessly wringing his hands and looking at her with pitiful eyes; and all the while the moon streamed full upon the fantastic little group.

*   *   *   *   *   *

Meantime the little Prince up stairs had been strutting up and down hand in hand with the English beauty, little Lady Marjory, of the round brown eyes. To be sure he was wondering and longing after his little peasant maiden all the while, and wistfully glancing at the door. But not the less did he talk and make gallant speeches to her little ladyship, who only smiled and took it all as a matter of course, for she was a young lady of the world and accustomed to such attentions from gentlemen. It naturally followed, however, that the Prince, who was thinking of other things, did not shine as usual in conversation.

Laura had made friends with the great-grand-father, who was an elegant scholar and could speak the most perfect Italian. "See what a pretty little pair," said he; "how well matched they are!"

"A couple of silly little chits," said she, "what can they know of love and passion?" and she cast up a great quavering glance with her weak blue eyes. "Ah! believe me, sir," said she, "it is only at a later age that women learn to feel that agonizing emotion, that they fade and pine away in silence. Ah-ha! What a tale would it be to tell, that untold story of woman's wrongs and un—unrequited love!"

"Ookedookedoo, there's a treat in store for you, young man," said Mr. Punch, skipping by. "Will you have my ruffles to dry your tears? Go it, old girl." And away he went, leaving Laura speechless from indignation. He went on to where the Prince was standing, and tapped him on the shoulder.

"Where do you come from, you strange little man?" said Lady Marjory.

"There are many strange things to be seen to-night," said Punch, mysteriously hissing out his words. "There's a little peasant girl fainting and dying in the moonlight; she was coming to find her love, and he spurned her; and there is an old gentleman trying to bring her to life. Her heart is breaking, and he wants blood to anoint it, he says—princely blood—shed in the moonlight, drop by drop from a false heart, and it is for you to choose the time and the place. This lady will have to find another cavalier, and will she like him, Prince, with fool's cap and bells, and a hump before and behind? In that case," says Mr. Punch, with a caper, "I am her very humble servant."

Lady Marjory did not answer, but looked very haughty, as fashionable young ladies do, and Mr. Punch vanished in an instant.

"I hope I shall never see that person again," said she. "The forwardness of common people is really unbearable. Of course he was talking nonsense. Little Prince, would you kindly hold my muff while I tie my bonnet-strings more securely."

The Prince took the muff without speaking, and then dropped it on the floor unconsciously. Now at last he saw clearly, in an instant it was all plain to him; he was half distracted with shame and remorse. There was a vision before his eyes of his little peasant maiden—loved so fondly, and, alas! wantonly abandoned and cruelly deserted—cold and pale, dying down below in the moonlight. He could not bear the thought; he caught Lady Marjory by the hand.

"Come," said he, "oh, come! I am a wretch, a wretch! Oh, I thought she had deceived me. Oh, come, come! Oh, my little peasant maiden! Oh, how I loved her!"

Lady Marjory drew herself up. "You may go, Prince, wherever you may wish," she said, looking at him with her great round eyes, "but pray go alone; I do not choose to meet that man again. I will wait for you here, and you can tell me your story when you come back." Lady Marjory, generous and kind-hearted as she was, could not but be hurt at the way in which, as it seemed, she too had been deceived, nor was she used to being thrown over for little peasant maidens. The little Prince with a scared face looked round the room for some one with whom to leave her, but no one showed at that instant, and so, half bewildered still and dreaming, he rushed away.

Only a minute before the old gentleman had said to Punchinello, "Let us carry the little girl out upon the balcony, the fresh air may revive her." And so it happened that the poor little Prince came to the very landing where they had waited so long, and found no signs of those for whom he was looking.

He ran about desperately, everywhere asking for news, but no one had any to give him. Who ever has? He passed the window a dozen times without thinking of looking out. Blind, deaf, insensible, are we not all to our dearest friend outside a door? to the familiar voice which is calling for us across a street? to the kind heart which is longing for us behind a plaster wall, maybe. Blind, insensible indeed, and alone; oh, how alone! He first asked two ladies who came tottering up stairs helplessly on little feet, with large open parasols, though it was in the middle of the night. One of them was smelling at a great flower with a straight stalk, the other fanning herself with a dried lotus-leaf; but they shook their heads idiotically, and answered something in their own language, —one of those sentences on the tea-caddies, most likely. These were Chinese ladies from the great jar in the drawing-room. Then he met a beautiful little group of Dresden china children, pelting each other with flowers off the chintz chairs and sofas, but they laughed and danced on, and did not even stop to answer his questions. Then came a long procession of persons all dressed in black and white walking sedately, running, sliding up the banisters, riding donkeys, on horses, in carriages, pony-chaises, omnibuses, bathing-machines; old ladies with bundles, huge umbrellas, and bandboxes; old gentlemen with big waistcoats; red-nosed gentlemen; bald gentlemen, muddled, puzzled, bewildered, perplexed, indignant; young ladies, dark-eyed, smiling, tripping and dancing in hats and feathers, curls blowing in the wind, in ball-dresses, in pretty morning costumes; school-boys with apple cheeks; little girls, babies, pretty servant-maids; gigantic footmen (marching in a corps); pages walking on their heads after their mistresses, chasing Scotch terriers, smashing, crashing, larking, covered with buttons.

"What is this crowd of phantoms, the ghosts of yesterday and last week?"

"We are all the people out of Mr. Leech's picture-books," says an old gentleman in a plaid shooting-costume; "my own name is Briggs, sir; I am sorry I can give you no further information."

Any other time and the little Prince must have been amused to see them go by, but to-night he rushes on despairingly; he only sees the little girl's pale face and dying eyes gleaming through the darkness. More Dresden, more Chinese; strange birds whir past, a partridge scrambles by with her little ones. Gilt figures climb about the cornices and furniture; the bookcases are swarming with busy little people; the little gold Cupid comes down off the clock, and looks at himself in the looking-glass. A hundred minor personages pass by, dancing, whirling in bewildering circles. On the walls the papering turns into a fragrant bower of creeping flowers; all the water-color landscapes come to life. Rain beats, showers fall, clouds drift, light warms and streams, water deepens, wavelets swell and plash tranquilly on the shores. Ships begin to sail, sails fill, and away they go gliding across the lake-like waters so beautifully that I can not help describing it, though all this, I know, is of quite common occurrence and has been often written about before. The little Prince, indeed, paid no attention to all that was going on, but went and threw himself down before the purple bank, and vowed with despair in his heart he would wait there until his little peasant maiden should come again.

There Laura saw him sitting on a stool, with his fair hair all dishevelled, and his arms hanging wearily. She had come back to look for one of her pearl ear-rings, and when she had discovered it, thought it would be but friendly to cheer the Prince up a bit, and, accordingly, tapped him facetiously on the shoulder, and declared she should tell Lady Marjory of him. "Waiting there for the little peasant child; oh you naughty fickle creature!" said she, playfully.

"You have made mischief enough for one night. Go!" said the Prince, looking her full in the face with his wan wild eyes, so that Laura shrank away a little abashed, and then he turned his back upon her, and hid his face in his hands.

So the sprightly Laura, finding that there was no one to talk to her, frisked up into the study again, and, descrying Lady Marjory standing all by herself, instantly joined her.

This is certainly a lachrymose history. Here was Lady Marjory sobbing and crying too! Her great brown eyes were glistening with tears, and

the drops were falling—pat—pat upon her muff, and the big bonnet had tumbled off on her shoulders, and the poor little lady looked the picture of grief and melancholy.

"Well, I never!" said Mrs. De Sade. "More tears. What a set of silly children you are! Here is your ladyship, there his little highness, not to mention that absurd peasant child, who is coming up stairs and looking as white as a sheet, and who fainted away again when I told her that the Prince's intended was here, but not the Prince. As for her—I never had any pa...."

"His Highness? The Prince, do you mean, —is he safe then?" said Lady Marjory, suddenly stopping short in her sobs. "Tell me immediately when, where, how, did you see him?"

"The naughty creature, I gave him warning," said Laura, holding up one finger, "and so I may tell your ladyship without any compunction. Heigh-ho, I feel for your ladyship. I can remember past times;—woman is doomed—doomed to lonely memories! Men are false, the truth is not...."

"Has he fought a duel—is he wounded?" Oh, why did I let him go!" cried Lady Marjory, impetuously.

"He is wounded," said Laura, looking very knowing; "but men recover from such injuries. It is us poor women who die of them without a g-g-groan." Here she looked up to see if the bust of General Washington was listening.

Lady Marjory seized her arm with an impatient little grip. "Why don't you speak out, instead of standing there maundering!" she cried.

"Hi-i-i," squeaked the green woman. "Well, then, he likes the peasant girl better than your ladyship, and it is his h-heart which is wounded. It would be a very undesirable match," she continued confidentially, recovering her temper. "As a friend of the family, I feel it my duty to do every thing in my power to prevent it. Indeed, it was I who broke the affair off in the first instance. Painful but necessary. Who cares for a little shrimp of a peasant—at least—I am rather sorry for the child. But it can't be helped, and nobody will miss her, if she does die of grief."

"Die of grief!" said Lady Marjory, wonderingly.

"La, my dear, it's the commonest thing in the world," remarked Laura.

"Die of grief," repeated Lady Marjory; and just as she was speaking, in came through the door, slowly, silently stopping every now and then to rest, and then advancing once again, the old gentleman and Punchinello, bearing between them the lifeless form of the little peasant maiden. They came straight on to where Lady Marjory was standing: they laid the child gently down upon the ground.

"We brought her here," said the old gentleman, gloomily, "to see if the Prince, who has killed her, could not bring her to life again."

"Oh dear! oh dear!" sighed Punchinello, almost crying.

"Poor little thing! dear little thing!" This was from Lady Marjory, suddenly falling on her knees beside her, rubbing her hands, kissing her pale face, sprinkling her with the contents of her smelling-bottle. "She can't, and shan't, and mustn't die, if the Prince or if I can save her. He is heart-broken. You, madam," she cried, turning to Laura, "go down, do you hear, and bring him instantly, do you understand me, or you will repent it all your life." And her eyes flashed at her so that Laura, looking quite limp somehow, went away, followed by Punchinello. In a minute the Prince came rushing in and fell on his knees beside Lady Marjory.

And so it happened that the little peasant maiden, lying insensible in Lady Marjory's arms, opened her sad eyes as the Prince seized her hand. His presence had done more for her than all the tender care of the two old fellows. For one instant her face lighted up with life and happiness, but then looking up into Lady Marjory's face, she sank back with a piteous, shuddering sigh.

The old gentleman was furious. "Have you come to insult her?" he said to the Prince. "To parade your base infidelity, to wound and to strike this poor little thing whom you have already stricken so sorely? You shall answer for this with your blood, sir, and on the spot, I say."

"Hold your stupid old tongue, you silly old gentleman!" said Mr. Punch. "See how pale the little Prince looks, and how his eyes are dimly flashing! He has not come hither to triumph, but to weep and sing dirges. Is it not so, little Prince?"

"Weep, yes, and sing dirges for his own funeral," cried the old gentleman, more and more excited. "Draw, sir, and defend yourself if you are a gentleman."

But Lady Marjory, turning from one to the other, exclaimed—

"Prince, dear Prince, you will not fight this good gentleman, who has taken such tender care of your little peasant maiden. Sir," to the old gentleman, "it would be you who would break her heart, were you to do him harm."

"And why should you want to do him harm?" said the little peasant, rousing herself and looking up, with a very sweet imploring look in her blue eyes, and clasping her hands. "He has done me none. It is the pride and happiness of my life to think that he should ever have deigned to notice me. It would not have been fit, indeed, that he, a Prince, should have married a little low-born peasant like myself."

The Prince, scarce knowing what he did, beat his forehead, dashed hot burning tears from his eyes.

"Sir," said he to the old gentleman, "kill me on the spot; it is the only fate I deserve, it will be well to rid the earth of such a monster. Farewell, little maiden; farewell, Lady Marjory. You will comfort her when I am gone. And do not regret me; remember only that I was unworthy of your love or of hers." And he tore open his blue velvet coat, and presented his breast for the old gentleman to pierce through and through.

Now Lady Marjory began to smile, instead of looking as frightened and melancholy as every body else.

"Button up your coat, dear little Prince," said she. "You will have to wait long for that sword-thrust you ask for. Meantime you must console the little peasant girl, not I; for it is I, who bid you farewell."

"Ah, gracious lady," cried the poor little monster, covering her hand with kisses, "it is too late, too late! a man who has broken her heart, who has trifled with yours so basely, deserves only to die—only to die."

"Let me make a confession," said Lady Marjory, speaking with a tender sprightliness, while a soft gleam shone in her eyes. "Our English hearts are cold, dear Prince, and slow to kindle. It is only now I learn what people feel when they are in love; and my heart is whole," she added, with a blush.

Such kind words and smiles could not but do good work. The little Prince almost left off sobbing, and began to dry his eyes. Meanwhile, Lady Marjory turned to the little peasant maiden.

"You must not listen to him when he talks such nonsense, and is so tragic and sentimental," she said. "He thought you had deceived him, and cared for some one else. He sobbed it in my ear when he went away to find you."

"Hey-de-dy-diddle!" cried Punchinello, capering about for joy: "and I know who told him—the woman in green, to be sure. I heard her. Oh, the languishing creature! Oh, the pining wild-cat! Oh, what tender hearts have women! Oh, what feelings—what gushing sentiment!"

"You hold your tongue, you stupid Mr. Punch," said the old gentleman, who had put up his sword, and quite forgiven the little Prince.

"And so good-bye, dear friends," said Lady Marjory, sadly indeed, but with a face still beaming and smiling. "See, the moon is setting; our hour is ended. Farewell, farewell," and she seemed to glide away.

"Ah, farewell!" echoed the others, stretching out their hands.

The last rays were streaming from behind the housetops. With them the charm was ending. The Prince and the peasant girl stood hand in hand in the last lingering beams.

"Good-night," said Punchinello, skipping away.

"Farewell," said the old gentleman.

"Goodness! make haste!" said Laura, rushing down stairs two steps at a time. . . . .

It seemed like a dream to the little peasant child, still standing bewildered. One by one the phantoms melted away, the moon set, and darkness fell. She still seemed to feel the clasp of the little Prince's hand in hers, she still heard the tones of his voice ringing in her ears, when she found herself once more on her bank of wild-flowers, and alone. . . . .

OUT OF THE SILENCE.

There is a certain crescent in a distant part of London—a part distant, that is, from clubs and parks and the splendors of Rotten Row—where a great many good works and good intentions carried out have taken refuge. House-rent is cheap, the place is wide and silent and airy; there are even a few trees to be seen opposite the windows of the houses, although we may have come for near an hour rattling through the streets of a neighborhood dark and dreary in looks, and closely packed with people and children, and wants and pains and trouble of every tangible form for the kind colonists of Burton Crescent to minister to.

We pass by the Deaconesses' Home: it is not with them that we have to do to-day; and we tell the carriage to stop at the door of one of the houses, where a brass-plate is set up with an inscription setting forth what manner of inmates there are within, and we get out, send the carriage away, and ring the bell for admission.

One of the inmates peeped out from a door-way at us as we came into the broad old-fashioned passage. This was the little invalid of the establishment, we were afterwards told; she had hurt her finger, and was allowed to sit down below with the matron, instead of doing her lessons with the other children up stairs.

How curious and satisfactory these lessons are, any one who likes may see and judge by making a similar pilgrimage to the one which F. and I undertook that wintry afternoon. The little establishment is a sort of short English translation of a great Continental experiment of which an interesting account was given some months ago in the Cornhill Magazine under the title of *Dumb Men's Speech*. Many of my friends were interested in it, and one day I received a note on the subject.

"Dumb men *do* speak in England," wrote a lady who had been giving her help and countenance to a similar experiment over here; and from her I learned that this attempt to carry out the system so patiently taught by Brother Cyril was now being made, and that children were being shown how to utter their wants, not by signs, but by speech, and in English, at the Jewish Home for Deaf and Dumb Children in Burton Crescent.

The great difference in this German system as opposed to the French is that signs are as much as possible discarded after the beginning, and that the pupils are taught to read upon the lips of others, and to speak in words, what under the other system would be expressed in writing or by signs. The well-known Abbé de l'Epée approved, they say, of this method, and wrote a treatise on the subject, and his successor, the Abbé Sicard, says (I am quoting from a quotation), "Le sourd-muet n'est donc totalement rendu à la société que lorsqu'on lui a appris à s'exprimer de vive voix et de lire la parole dans les mouvements des lèvres." This following very qualified sentence of his is also quoted in a report which has been sent me: "Prenez garde, que je n'ai point dit que le sourd-muet ne peut pas parler, mais ne sait pas parler. Il est possible que Mapaiz apprit à parler si j'avais le temps de le lui apprendre."

Time, hours after hours of patience, good-will, are given freely to this work by the good people who direct the various establishments in the Netherlands where the deaf and dumb are now instructed.

How numerous and carefully organized these institutions are may be gathered from a little pamphlet written by the great Director Hirsch of Rotterdam, who first introduced this system into the schools, and who has lately made a little journey from school to school, to note the progress of the undertaking he has so much at heart. Brussels and Ghent and Antwerp and Bruges, he visited all these and other outlying establishments, and was received everywhere with open arms by the good brothers who have undertaken to teach the system he advocates. Dr. Hirsch is delighted with every thing he sees until he comes to Bruges, where he says that he is struck by the painful contrast which its scholars present as compared to the others he had visited on his way. "They looked less gay (moins enjoué) than any of those he had seen." But this is explained to him by the fact that in this school the French method is still partly taught, and he leaves after a little exhortation to the Director, and a warning that public opinion will be against him if he continues the ancient system as opposed to the newer and more intelligible one. It is slower in the beginning, says the worthy Doctor; it makes greater demands upon our patience, our time, our money, but it carries the pupil on far more rapidly and satisfactorily after the early steps are first mastered, until, when at last the faculty of hearing with the eyes has been once acquired, isolation exists no longer, the sufferer is given back to the world, and every one he meets is a new teacher to help to bring his study to perfection.

The Jewish Home for Deaf and Dumb Children in Burton Crescent has only been started for a few months. The lady who wrote to me guaranteed the rent and various expenses for a year, after which the experiment is to stand upon its own merits. Since the opening of the home I believe that great modifications have taken place in its arrangements, and that it is now to be enlarged and thrown open to any little dumb Christians who, as well as the little Jews, may like to come as day scholars there, to be taught with much labor and infinite patience and pains what others learn almost unconsciously and without an effort.

F. and I have been going up stairs all this time, and come into a back-room or board-room, opening with folding-doors into the school-room, where the children are taught. As we went in, the kind young master, M. von Praagh (he is a pupil, I believe, of Dr. Hirsch's), came forward to receive us, and welcomed us in the most friendly way. The children all looked up at us with bright flashing eyes—little boys and little girls in brown pinafores, with cheery little smiling faces peeping and laughing at us along their benches. In the room itself there is the usual apparatus—the bit of chalk, the great slate for the master to write upon, the little ones for the pupils, the wooden forms, the pinafores, the pictures hanging from the walls, and, what was touching to me, the usual little games and frolics and understandings going on in distant corners, and even under the master's good-natured eye. He is there to bring out, and not to repress, and the children's very confidence in his kindness and sympathy seems to be one of the conditions of their education and cure.

He clapped his hands, and a little class came and stood round the big slate—a big girl, a little one, two little boys. "Attention!" says the teacher, and he begins naming different objects, such as fish, bread, chamois, coal-scuttle. All these words the children read off his lips by watching the movement of his mouth. As he says each word the children brighten, seize the idea, rush to the pictures that are hanging on the wall, discover the object he has named, and bring it in breathless triumph. "Tomb," said the master, after naming a variety of things, and a big girl, with a beaming face, pointed to the ground and nodded her head emphatically, grinning from ear to ear. But signs are not approved of in this establishment, and, as I have said, the great object is to get them to talk. And it must be remembered that they are only beginners, and that the home has only been opened a few months. One little thing, scarcely more than a baby, who had only lately come in, had spoken for the first time that very day— "â, â, â," cried the little creature. She was so much delighted with her newly gotten power that nothing would induce her to leave off exercising it. She literally shouted out her plaintive little "â." It was like the note of a little lamb, for of course, being deaf, she had not yet learned how to modulate her voice, and she had to be carried off into a distant corner by a big-

ger girl, who tried to amuse her and keep her still.

"It is an immense thing for the children," said Mr. von Praagh, "to feel that they are not cut off hopelessly and markedly from communication with their fellow-creatures; the organs of speech being developed, their lungs are strengthened, their health improves. You can see a change in the very expression of their faces, they delight in using their newly-acquired power, and won't use the finger-alphabet even among themselves." And, as if to corroborate what he was saying, there came a cheery vociferous outbreak of "â's" from the corner where the little girl had been installed with some toys, and all the other children laughed.

I do not know whether little Jew boys and girls are on an average cleverer than little Christians, or whether, notwithstanding their infirmity, the care and culture bestowed upon them has borne this extra fruit; but these little creatures were certainly brighter and more lively than any dozen Sunday school children taken at hazard. Their eyes danced, their faces worked with interest and attention, they seemed to catch light from their master's face, from one another's, from ours as we spoke; their eagerness, their cheerfulness and childish glee, were really remarkable; they laughed to one another much like any other children, peeped over their slates, answered together when they were called up. It was difficult to remember that they were deaf, though, when they spoke, a great slowness, indistinctness, and peculiarity was of course very noticeable. But these are only the pupils of a month or two, be it remembered. A child with all its faculties is nearly two years learning to talk.

One little fellow with a charming expressive face, and eyes like two brown stars, came forward, and ciphered and read to us, and showed us his copy-book. He is beginning Hebrew as well as English. His voice is pleasant, melancholy, but quite melodious, and, to my surprise, he addressed me by my name, a long name with many letters in it. Mr. von Praagh had said it to him on his lips, for of course it is not necessary for the master to use his voice, and the motion of the lips is enough to make them understand. The name of my companion, although a short one, is written with four difficult consonants, and only one vowel to bind them together, and it gave the children more trouble than mine had done; but after one or two efforts the little boy hit upon the right way of saying it, and a gleam of satisfaction came into his face as well as his master's. Mr. von Praagh takes the greatest possible pains with, and interest in, every effort and syllable. He holds the children's hands and accentuates the words by raising or letting them fall; he feels their throats and makes them feel his own. It would be hard indeed if so much patience and enthusiasm produced no results to reward it.

"What o'clock is it?" Mr. von Praagh asked.

"Foor o'clock," said the little boy, without looking up.

"How do you know?" asked the master.

"Miss —— is come," said the little fellow, laughing. This was a lady who came to give the girls their sewing-lesson so many times a week.

I need not describe the little rooms up stairs, with the little beds in rows, and the baths, the play-room—the kind arrangements everywhere for the children's comfort and happiness. If the school is still deaf and dumb for most practical purposes, yet the light is shining in; the children are happy, and understand what is wanted of them, and are evidently in the right way. For the short time he has been at work as yet, Mr. von Praagh has worked wonders.

Babies, as I have just said, with all their faculties, are about two years learning to speak. There is a curious crisis, which any one who has had any thing to do with children must have noticed, a sort of fever of impatience and vexation which attacks them when they first begin to understand that people do not understand what they say. I have seen a little girl burst into passionate tears of vexation and impatience because she could not make herself immediately understood. I suppose the pretty croonings and chatterings which go before speech are a sort of natural exercise by which babies accustom themselves to words, and which they mistake at first for real talking. Real words come here and there in the midst of the baby-language—detaching themselves by degrees out of the wonderful labyrinth of sound—real words out of the language which they are accustomed to hear all about them, and something in this way, to these poor little deaf folks, the truth must dawn out of the confusion of sights and sounds surrounding them.

This marvellous instinctive study goes on in secret in the children's minds. After their first few attempts at talking they seem to mistrust their own efforts. They find out that their pretty prattle is no good: they listen, they turn over words in their minds, and whisper them to themselves as they are lying in their little cribs, and then one day the crisis comes, and a miracle is worked, and the child can speak.

When children feel that their first attempts are understood, they suddenly regain their good temper and wait for a further inspiration. They have generally mastered the great necessaries of life in this very beginning of their efforts: "pooty," "toos," "ben butta," "papa," "mama," "nana" for "nurse," and "dolly," and they are content. Often a long time passes without any further apparent advance, and then comes perhaps a second attack of indignation. I know of one little babe who had hardly spoken before, and who had been very cross and angry for some days past, who horrified its relations by suddenly standing up in its crib one day, rosy and round-eyed, and saying *Bess my soul*, exactly like an old charwoman who had come into the nursery.

A friend of mine to whom I was speaking quite bore out my remarks. He said his own children had all passed through this phase, which comes after the child has learned to think and before he is able to speak. One's heart aches as one thinks of those whose life is doomed to be a life of utter silence in the full stream of the mighty flow of words in which our lives are set, to whom no crisis of relief may come, who have for generations come and gone silent and alone, and set apart by a mysterious dispensation from its very own best blessings and tenderest gifts.

I was thinking of this yesterday as we went walking across the downs in the pleasant Eastertide. I could hardly tell whether it was sight or sound that delighted us most as we went along upon the turf; the sound of life in the bay at the foot of the downs, the flowing of the waves just washing over the low-ridged rocks with which our coast is set; the gentle triumphant music overhead of the larks soaring and singing in the sunshine. The sea and the shingle were all sparkling, while great bands like moonlight in daylight lay white and brilliant on the horizon of the waters. The very stones seemed to cry out with a lovely Easter hymn of praise; and sound and sight to be so mingled that one could scarcely tell where one began or the other ended.

If by this new system the patient teachers can not give every thing to their pupils, the ripple of the sea, the song of the lark, yet they can do very much towards it, by leading the children's minds to receive the great gifts of nature through the hearts and sympathy of others, and give them above all that best and dearest gift of all in daily life, without which nature itself fails to comfort and to charm—the companionship of their fellow-creatures and of intelligences answering and responding to their own.

A CITY OF REFUGE.

To be well, to be ill, to be sad, to be cross; to feel jars that shake, pains that tear and burn, and weary nerves that shrink and flutter, or that respond so strangely and dully to the will that it seems almost as if we were scarcely ourselves, at times, when, longing to feel and to sympathize with the emotions of others we are only conscious of a numb cold acquiescence in their gladness or pain—all this is in the experience of us all, of the most happy as well as of the least happy alike, of the softest and hardest hearted. Only with some it is the experience of an instant and with others of a lifetime.

The range of this mysterious gamut teaches us, perhaps, something of the secret of what others are feeling; and in the same way that the sick and unhappy may imagine what vigor, hope, love, the fervor of life and youth, mean, to some, by its help, the fortunate may guess now and then at the sorrows of years, understand the hopelessness, the patience, the disappointment of a lifetime—guess at it for an instant as they stand by a sick-bed or see the poor wayfarer lying by their path. There is a group I have now in my mind that many of us may have noticed of late—some tired people resting on the road-side, a sunset marsh beyond; they have lighted a fire of which the smoke is drifting in the still air, and the tired eye looks out at the spectator and beyond him in the unconscious simplicity of suffering. We all understand it, though we have perhaps never in all our lives rested for the night, wearied, by a ditch-side. It is so true to life that we who are alive instinctively recognize its truth and uncomplaining complaint.

The persons of whom I am going to write just now are most wise in the sadder secrets of life, which they have learnt by long years of apprenticeship. Poor souls! We have all come across them at one time or another. Sometimes we listen to their complaint, sometimes we don't; sometimes we put out a helping hand to pull them along, sometimes we get weary and let them go. It would almost seem as if the range of the pity that we feel for others, for the same troubles at different times, were as wide and as changeful as the very experience from which sympathies most often spring. But although it is easy enough to help our brothers and sisters seven times—more easy than to forgive them—it is difficult enough for us individually to help them seventy times seven times; and in this must lie the great superiority of institutions over individual effort, of whom the

kindness is left to chance and to good-natured impulse, instead of being part of a rule that works on in all tempers and at all times.

It seemed to me the other day that it was real help that was being given to some afflicted persons whom I was taken to see, at the Incurable Hospital on Putney Common, a few of the afflicted out of all those that are stricken and in trouble, and in numbers so great that, for the most part, we might pass on in despair if it were not for the good hope of present and future help such places afford.

We crossed Putney Bridge one bright spring day, and drove up through the quaint old Putney High Street. The lilacs were beginning to flower in the gardens and behind the mossy old walls. When we had climbed the hill we came out upon a great yellow gorsy common, where all the air was sweet with the peach-scent of the blossom. Its lovely yellow flame was bursting from one bush and from another, and blazing against the dull purple green of the furze. We had not very far to go. The carriage turned down a green lane of which the trees and hedges did not hide glimpses of other lights and other blossoming commons in the distance; and when we stopped it was at a white lodge, of which the gate was hospitably open, and from whence a shady green sweep led us to a noble and stately house, which was once Melrose Hall, but which is now the Hospital for Incurables.

A little phalanx of bath-chairs was drawn up round the entrance, and in each a patient was sitting basking in this first pleasant shining of summer sun. The birds were chirping in the tall trees overhead, the little winds were puffing in our faces, and those of the worn, wan, tired creatures, who had been dragged out to benefit by the comforting freshness of the day. Some of them looked up—not all—as we drove to the door.

M. sent a small boy with a card to ask for admission for some friends of Mr. H.'s, and we waited for a few minutes until the answer came. All the time that we were waiting, an eager, afflicted young fellow was trying hard to make himself intelligible to the sick man in the bath-chair next to his own. The poor boy could only make anxious uncouth sounds; the sick man to whom he was speaking listened for a while, and then shook his head and turned wearily away. So it wasn't all sunshine even in the sunshine in the lovely tree-shaded garden, with the chirruping birds and lilac-buds coming out. There were some attendants coming and going from chair to chair. There were other little carriages slowly progressing along the distant winding paths of the garden, and presently the message came that we might be admitted. The matron was away, but the head-nurse said she would show us over the place; and she led the way across the vestibule with its pretty classical ornamentation, opening the tall doors and bringing us into the stately rooms where a different company had once assembled, and yet it was not so very different after all, for pain and ill health are no excessive respecters of persons. The Duke of Argyll, who was chairman at the last anniversary dinner, spoke of some of the persons who used to meet in these very rooms once upon a time, before they were turned to their present uses—among the rest Sir Walter Scott and Lockhart, and Sir Humphry Davy. I could almost fancy the kind and familiar face of Sir Walter looking on with gentle interest and compassion at the pathetic company which is now waiting in the big drawing-room of Melrose Hall, with the stately terrace and lofty windows that let in the light so bountifully—lame, blind, halt, and maimed, from London highways, and the distant country by-ways. They sit in groups round the tables and windows, busy, somewhat silent. At the end of the room there is a golden-piped organ, the gift of the treasurer. A governess, who is one of the patients, often plays to the others upon it, and so do the ladies who visit the place. Once when I was there some one opened the instrument and began to play. As the music filled the room we all listened, beating a sort of time together. It seemed like a promise of better things to those who were listening, for themselves and for others. The sitting-room is a lofty, stately place, as I have said, with columns and mouldings. All about there are comfortable chairs and tables, and spring sofas for aching spines that can not sit upright, tables for work over which all these patient creatures are bending. They have still tranquil faces for the most part, quiet and pale, and resting for a time in the refuge into which they have escaped out of the weary struggle and crowd of life. The privilege is sad enough, Heaven knows, and the price they have paid for it is a heavy one.

The head-nurse went from one to another, and the faces all seemed to light up to meet hers. It is a very simple and infallible sign of love and of confidence. "It would not do for me to pity them too much," the kind nurse said; "I always try to speak cheerfully to them." We who only come to look on may pity and utter the commonplaces of compassion and curiosity. How tired the poor things must be of the stupid reiteration of adjectives and exclamations! There was one old woman, so nice and with such sweet eyes, that I could not help sitting down by her and saying some one of those platitudes that one has recourse to. She didn't answer, but only looked at me with an odd long look.

D D

"She can not speak," the nurse whispered, beckoning me away.

A few of the patients were reading, but only a few. *Good Words* seemed to be popular, and the story in it is particularly liked, they told me. Some of the patients do plain work, and as I was speaking to one of them the door opened, and a good-natured-looking man came in.

"Any of the ladies like to go out for a drive to-day?" he said, in a brisk business-like tone.

Two or three voices answered, "Only Miss ——," and then Miss —— began beckoning and waving her hand from the other end of the room, and was rolled off accordingly for her drive in the garden-chair.

It was not my first visit to the hospital; but though a year had passed, there were many of the faces as I remembered them, sitting in the same corners, stitching and hooking, blind women knitting, the clever, patient fingers weaving an interest into their lives with threads of cotton and wool; one gentle-looking old lady, in a frill cap, was working a pair of slippers, dull red with bright green spots. She had but two fingers to work with, and only, I think, this one painful crippled hand; but she was working away on a frame to which her canvas was fixed.

"I can not like your colors this time, Mrs. ——," the nurse said; "your last slippers were so pretty, and your work is so beautiful, that it is quite a pity you should not have pretty-colored wools to set it off."

The old lady shook her head; she wouldn't be convinced. "These are lovely wools, my dear," she said. "I shall certainly go on with them. It's all your want of taste, that is what I think." And she nodded her head and laughed, and stitched on with fresh interest.

As we went up stairs we were shown lifts and pulleys and all sorts of comfortable appliances for the use of the patients. I could not help admiring the extreme order and neatness of all the arrangements, and the freshness and ventilation of all the places we went into.

In one of the rooms up stairs was a funny old fellow, in a tall nightcap, was stitching away at his torn shirt-sleeves. He was sitting quite by himself in a big ward, with many empty beds in it. He laughed when he saw us, winked, waved his nightcap with an air, and then informed us he was the oldest patient, and was doing a bit of work; he didn't like to trust his shirt to others—not he—he was a poor old bachelor, he had to sew his own buttons on—and he was then very mysterious and confidential about a shirt which had been lost at the wash a year ago. Dark suspicions evidently were still haunting him on the subject, but he cheered up, winked, laughed, waved his nightcap again to us when we went away out of the room. "She is my greatest joy and comfort," he said, with a bow to the nurse, who could not help laughing. The men have much more courage than the women, they keep about until the last, this lady told us; women would be in bed and refuse to get up, when the men crawl down stairs day after day, and insist upon making the effort.

And yet in the men's sitting-room there is a much sadder, duller, and more helpless community than in the women's. The numbers are fewer, and in most cases the brain seems more hopelessly affected. One boy was making paper fly-catchers, but I don't think any of the others were doing any thing. I have a vision of an old man sitting at a table, while we were there, trying to take up a broken piece of bread. His hand passed beyond it again and again; it was by a sort of chance that he feebly clutched it at last and carried it to his mouth.

It didn't seem much to be able to walk away, to look back, to remember what we had seen; and yet how is it that we are not on our knees in gratitude and thankfulness for every active motion of the body, every word we speak, every intelligent experience and interest that passes through our minds?

There was a great scampering of children's feet in one of the passages as we came up the wooden stairs, and some bright eyes peeped at us, and three little girls in the short kilts and plaid ribbons of middle-class London retreated into a room of which the door was wide open, and fled to a bedside, where they all stood shyly in a row until we could come up. Our guide led the way and we followed her in, and there from the bed a pair of big bright brown eyes, not unlike the children's, were turned upon us, and a handsome young girl, lying flat on her back, greeted us with a good-humored smile. "Aunt Mary" the children called her. Big and handsome and strong though she looked, this poor bright-looking Aunt Mary, she was completely paralyzed as far as the head: she could not move hand or foot; it was a dead body with this bright bonny living face to it. She did not look more than six or seven and twenty; she had nice thick brown hair and even white teeth. With these this brave girl had imagined for herself that with practice she should be able to hold a pencil and guide it, tracing the words against a little desk that was so contrived as to swing across her bed when wanted. She was perfectly enchanted with the contrivance, and said it was the greatest delight to her to be able to write for herself. The doctor, she told me, not without pride, had been quite surprised to receive a letter from her one day, and could not imagine how she had written it for herself.

Leaving her, we crossed a passage and came to a room not far off, where two women were lying: one of them had got something in her bed that she was caressing and talking to in a plaintive pitying voice, patting as if it was some animal or living thing. M., wondering what it could be, went up to see; she found that it was a watch of which the glass was broken. In the other bed a gentle-faced, very old woman was lying, afflicted with palsy. Her poor body shook and trembled painfully as I stood beside the bed, and her hands, in attempting to meet, crossed

and passed each other again and again. I said to her that I could not think how she bore her affliction so patiently, for the head nurse had told me that her sweetness was quite touching, she never complained, never said an impatient word.

"When I am not well," I said, "I grumble and complain to every body, even for little trifling ailments. You make me feel ashamed."

"Ah," the old woman answered gently, "'tis good to be still."

She said it so simply and quietly that it came home to me then and there, the gentle remonstrance coming from the weary bed where so many long hopeless hours had passed for her, where she lay patiently enduring while we walked away. The other woman was still talking to her watch, and did not notice us as we passed.

The room, which was formerly the library, makes a delightful room for one or two of the patients. It has tall windows, opening upon a broad terrace-like balcony, and beyond are the same elm-trees and glimpses of sky and common that we see from the big room down below. There is one great sufferer here who does not often get down. She can not sit up, from spine disease, and when I saw her last she was lying by the window, with a face wrapped in cotton-wool, poor soul, for she had been suffering tortures from neuralgia; and though the dentist had come and taken out two of her teeth, she was still in pain. The head-nurse pitied her, and recommended a little blister to draw away the inflammation. The patient shrunk and laughed and shook her head. She couldn't bear any more pain, she whispered imploringly; she wanted so to get down for a change. A little belladonna plaster where nobody would see it, under her cap, so that it shouldn't show, and look ugly, and where nobody would see it, please. There were two good-sized baskets standing on a table near this patient. They were literally piled and packed with tracts. "We get a great many," she said, seeing me look at them; "more than we can read." Poor soul! I hope her belladonna plaster has done her good. As we came away, the nurse stopped for a moment to speak to quite an elegant old lady, who was sitting up, extremely nicely dressed, in a chair, with a grand cap and ribbons, and a knitted lace shawl.

It was getting late, and we began to pass blue-garbed under-nurses carrying little trays with teas. The patients who are well enough to get down have their meals in the big dining-room; but these little trays looked very nice and appetizing; the whole order of the place is perfectly appointed. Some of the rooms up stairs were like little bowers, with pots flowering round the windows, bird-cages hanging up, pictures on the walls of the friends of the sick people. One pale face looked at us as we passed a white bed. Her room was like a little chapel, with light streaming in from through the flowers and bird-cages and the climbing greens upon the casement, and the poor martyr, alas! lying on her rack.

There was another pale face that looked out, too, as we passed; but as we were going in, the nurse stopped us, and said she feared the patient was dying; and so we moved away. I asked to be taken to a sick woman I remembered a year before, a kind, merry person, who had gone through a terrible operation. She was in bed still in the same room, still looking the same, bright, friendly, with smart little curls, and a friend gossiping by her bedside.

To see such a place as this as it is, to be sorry enough and tender enough to continue to sympathize with all its suffering, would need, I think, a mind scarcely human in its powers. The whole subject is so vast, so mysterious, and utterly beyond our comprehension, that it is easier to dwell upon the comforting kindness, the helps to endurance and courage, that are to be found here more than in any place I ever saw. There was one poor girl who had been lying for seven years upon her side. All the lines of those seven years seemed to me in her white wan face. She did not complain, though her eyes complained for her; but she said she had a nice water-bed—that was a great comfort; and her cup of milk and toast for tea were beside her, so nicely served and prepared that it was a pleasure to see the little meal: and there was a great bunch of spring lilac-buds in a glass, that another patient had brought to her out of the garden—the first of the year.

Up stairs, higher still, there is a room which is not generally shown, where a strange weird party of poor little deformities are assembled. Little women with huge heads, so sad, so grotesque and horrible that one's very pity is scarcely pity, but wonder. They were sitting round a little tea-table, which they were preparing for themselves; one of them was boiling the kettle. They seemed quite happy and busy. It was like some pantomime of nature; like some strange people out of another planet, sitting together and staring at us with those huge weird-like faces, supported by living bodies. And yet with all its endless combination of pain and of sorrow, this hospital does not send us away sad and rebellious at heart, as so many refuges for sorrow and trouble: for instance, a work-house ward, where there are cases often enough that might be admitted here if there was room for them; or a sick close room, in a narrow street, where the healthy and unhealthy are shut up together for days and for nights. Here where there is such great suffering, there is also great comfort and tender nursing and companionship; there are trees, and grasses, and sweet lilac, and gorse-blown winds, close at hand. There is a certain liberality in all the arranging and economy of the place, that seems to disprove the practical notion of Charity being a grinding, snubbing sort of personage, who would like to get the scales into her own hand if she could, and to weigh out her kindness by the ounce. Such a plan as this would defeat its own object

if the inmates were not well and generously tended. Perhaps I should in fairness confess to having heard of the bitter complaints of one of the patients, who had a fancy for lobsters every day, and who was denied this delicacy; but she is not the first to long for the unattainable, and certainly, to some of us grumbling is almost as great a privilege as eating lobsters every day.

It seems fitting and seemly that in a great country like ours there should be munificent charities, comforting and liberal in their dealings; one only longs that their doors should be set open more widely, if possible, to the crowds that are waiting about them for admission. Here is a paper before me, it is two years old, and I know not how many have succeeded in their efforts; but looking at it, it would indeed appear as if the wayfarers were lying all along the road, and the Samaritan passing by has only one ass to carry them away upon.

These biographies are not very long in writing, and I may quote one or two that I have copied off the list:—

Paralysis, Loss of Speech..........	Captain of a Steam-vessel.
Disease of the Brain and Debility....	Governess.
Disease of the Spine and Joints,	Governess.
Paralysis......................	
Paralysis.......................	Captain of a Mail Steamer.
Disease of Spine and Throat........	Schoolmistress.
Injury to Spine...................	Working Engineer.
Paralysis and Asthma.............	Master Tailor.

These are seven out of 160—a whole sad life of labor and suffering told in a few words. There are laundry-women, servants, journeymen, dressmakers. It is a comfort to turn back to those who are safely within reach of kind hands, helpful appliances, and friendly words such as those which I heard the head-nurse speaking to her patients as I followed her about from one room to another.

It has been proposed lately to establish a hospital on somewhat similar principles for children, with this one comforting proviso, that the children are to be cured if possible. A doctor of very great experience and reputation, who once superintended a children's hospital in Paris, and for whose opinion his friends have a great and just regard, was speaking on the subject to a friend, and saying that there are many chronic cases in childhood deemed incurable, which are in reality perfectly curable, but which require a doctoring of fresh air, of regular diet, of cleanliness, etc., that it is impossible they should receive at home. I believe it was in this way the idea originated, and now the hospital really seems in a fair way to being established. Four or five people have each promised a hundred a year towards it of their own accord, without solicitation. When a thousand is assured, the hospital will be begun. A big garden is the first thing wanted for the children to play in and to exercise their limbs. The children's hospitals, admirable as they are, can not keep the little things always, and are obliged to change their patients constantly. Any body who has seen the piteous crowd waiting at the doors in Great Ormond Street will understand the necessity there is for more and more such help and assistance to the good work which is done there.

Only yesterday there was a little patient who had been discharged almost cured from what seemed a hopeless and chronic illness, after only two months of care in the children's hospital, who was begging and praying to go back from his home in the back kitchen with the mangle. One patient! A hundred—a thousand, to-morrow, if one searched for them, and know what to do with them when one had found them or where to send them. This incurable children's hospital has, however, good friends among people who love their own children, and who are willing to come forward with generous hearts and great sums to assist it, and there is great hope of its speedy establishment.

But one of the greatest difficulties that have to be contended against at present in the management of any thing of the sort is the extraordinary system which has grown up all about us, and which seems to be almost impossible to contend with.

I have the reports before me now of two hospitals, conducted by different people, each doing a great and important work. How much the help might be extended if the machinery were more simple and the manner of administering aid less complicated and costly, it would be hard to say. A great country like ours should have noble charities; niggardliness seems to me a far more deprecable fault than excess of generosity in the help afforded. But what people complain of, and with reason, I think, is that part of the money they subscribe, instead of going to the objects of their charity—the attendance, the food, the comfort of the patients—is by the mere fashion and necessity of the day put to strange and vexing purposes: to printing little books that nobody reads, to sending circulars that go straight into the fire, to arranging an elaborate machinery of admission that in no way benefits the patients. The postage and advertising and printing of two hospitals comes to £1300 in the course of a year; of which £100 a year for the postage of each hospital represents something like, say, 240,000 letters. I don't know how many hard days' work 240,000 letters would mean, and how many of them are mere circulars, or how many might be spared; but it seems as if so much of our energy went into advertising and crying our good intentions, that in time there will be no strength or time left for any thing else.

An experiment has been partially tried at an institution where no canvassing is allowed, and no public election. The votes—so a friend to whom I had spoken on the subject writes—are quietly "counted at the office, and the result is announced." He, however, goes on to say that this plan is not successful in a pecuniary point of view; and a charity in which all the power was vested in a committee would have still less

chance of success. I had spoken to him on the subject of this incurable hospital, and asked why the most pressing cases were not elected by a competent board instead of those people having the best chance who had most friends, and whose friends were most active in their behalf. "You do not know," he said, "all the outcry and discontent that such a proceeding would give rise to. We should be accused of unfairness, of partiality. We ourselves dislike the system as much as you do, but we can not help ourselves; we are obliged to give in to the common cry and common weakness of human nature, and to take the good and the bad as they come together." And so it is, and we must be content to accept things as they are, but with the bad and the good there is certainly given to each one of us an instinct for better things, and is it quite impossible that any effort should ever be made to disembarrass good and noble things from the cumber of selfish-interest patronage which weight them so heavily? Is there no divine indignation left among us strong enough to overturn the tables of the money-changers, to chase away those that sell doves in the temple?

What a horrible complication it seems, looking at it honestly with unbiased eyes! Is it possible that we are sunk so low that we can not give freely and with generous, tender, and grateful hearts, without this hideous system of patronage, of rules, of complimentary clapping, of bad dinners and wines, of subscription-lists and names affixed to little miserable scraps of crumbs from our table that should make us ashamed instead of complacent, as we turn to B or A, or whatever our initial may be, and see our honest name set down with a shabby price to it, like the cheap rubbish in a huckster's shop?

I think Mr. Froude, in his essay on *Representative Men*, has put words to a difficulty which a great many have felt, but which few people have put words to before. It is a difficulty of words in itself: and concerns the constant cry of the age, the advice of the preacher, which comes to us from every side, calling and urging us to be good, and bidding us be noble, crying that to us is intrusted a mission of love and of charity. "Go forth," so they say, "go forth and fulfill it." And then the difficulty occurs to some of us, where are we to go forth? how are we to be good? when are we to be noble? Passive charity is useless without a practical use for it, and so the teachers acknowledge. But have you no neighbors to tend? they cry, no sufferers to comfort by the way? Are there no wayfarers who have fallen by the road-side? And all this is true enough—too true, alas!—for the wounded wayfarers may be counted by thousands.

And yet, as I write I feel that the preacher is right in the main, though his talk is satire, and he has not sufficiently applied the science of the truth he instinctively feels to the daily facts of life. Life, I suppose, must for most of us be a rule of thumb—if I may be allowed so to speak; and to go forth must mean to take a cab and call upon a dull friend, or to protest, when we see occasion, against wrong-doing of any sort, or to take trouble about things that do not interest or concern us very much. There are some noble and honest natures to whom instinctively the impulse comes for action, and for right and great action too—some lives whose love and example are benedictions to those who are about them—one noble tender heart leavening the dough by its unconscious generous tenderness and example. These people need ask no questions, for theirs are the voices that answer, not in preaching, but by their simpleness, their truth, their tender impulse. As a rule, we who ask are not the people who work and achieve.

A woman died not long ago who had lived some twenty-six or twenty-seven years one of those lives that do not question for themselves, but that seem like answers to the vague aspirations of others. I do not know if I may write her name, but those who have loved this lady will know how it is that I quote her as one of the examples of this bright and resolute devotion, that shines like a beacon in the storm to those who are wandering about in search of a way. She was the head-nurse of the hospital at Lincoln, where in time a terrible mortality and illness overtaxed her strength, and, her strength of life being gone, she died. And as I write these words, there comes the news of the passing away of a man whose kindness and true Christian strength of heart and of mind spoke better than any words what a life can be—a blessing, a kindness, a help in trouble, to all those who have lived round about it.

I have drifted away from the incurables a little; any one who likes to go and see the place is welcome, and no one can go without coming away touched and humbled, and perhaps a little the better for the visit.

The privilege is a sad one, Heaven knows, that belongs to all these poor people; but sad as it is, when one looks at these gentle and tranquil faces, it is hard to think of those still outside, in a world that looks peaceful enough, and pleasant and green to-day from these open windows, but which is a weary illimitable place for those who, with paralyzed limbs and racked bodies, are hopelessly and helplessly trying to escape from the overwhelming tramp of the legions by which they are overwhelmed—legions that advance upon them as one has sometimes dreamed in dreams, by every road, by every turn of life. I can imagine poor wearied, hunted souls trying to fly from want, from anguish, from loneliness, from neglect and cruel words, but their limbs will not carry them; they can not work, they are too weak even to beg, friends weary, subsistence fails, their own hearts fail. The Duke of Argyll says that nearly 6000 people annually leave the London hospitals suffering from incurable disease. Of these how many must there be in miserable condition! One's own heart might indeed fail at the thought of such tremendous calamity; but for 6000 incurables, how many hundreds of thousands are there not among us who are well and strong, and who have enough to live and enough to give to others, and asses and pennies to spare for others in their need?

CHIRPING CRICKETS.

I WENT the other night to see a play called *Dot*, in which a beneficent cricket, chirping on the hearth, brings a kindly warmth to the very hearts of the people assembled around it. The poor, ill-used husband, sitting all night staring at the empty grate, softens and kindles under the influence of this beneficent cricket. The skeptical young sailor tears off his disguise; the narrow-minded taskmaster, after a short experience of the chirpings of this friendly insect, becomes generous, charitable, and begins to pay the most marked attentions to the poor toy-maker's daughter. Then, lo, and behold! the fire-place opens, and a glowing apparition comes down the chimney, and the beaming spirit of the hearth is revealed to the spectators, who laugh kindly and clap applause.

As we all know, it is not only at the play the spirits of the hearth appear. In the darkness of these long winter evenings their lights gleam, and their voices echo cheerfully through the old houses. Newport Refuge (my text for to-day) is alight; other hearths are kindling. There is an old house near the river with red wings,

and a stately roof, and diamond panes, where I saw a real spirit on the hearth the other night; only it was more beautiful and shining even than the crowned lady at the play—a tall spirit in robes of green, lighted by stars, twinkling crimson and golden; a spirit Briareus-like, with outstretched arms, and beautiful gifts hanging from them, and glittering flags and wreaths. All round about it stood a crowd of wistful little babies, with big round eyes, in which this wonderful shining was reflected. Only one night in all the year does this lovely wonderful spirit appear to the little patients at Gough House Hospital—poor, tiny, aching creatures, with wounds, and pains, and plagues innumerable. Their little pale faces may be seen peeping out of the narrow windows of the old house—at the people passing by, at the men at work in the wood-yard, at the boats sailing along the river hard by. Other little children who are well come, nod to them, and play upon the old steps leading up to the ancient door-way, over which "Victoria Hospital for Children" is written up in big letters for those who run to read.

In this community, which the lady in charge kindly gave me leave to explore for myself, there are about thirty little children. The first room into which I wandered belonged to eight babies, who are put to bed about six o'clock in cradles all round the room. In each cradle lies **a silent**, abstracted, blinking heap; one nurse and a little helpful patient are tucking them all busily away. There was not a dissentient voice among them. Home babies shout, kick, shake the house with their indignant voices. But these infants were all good, all going to sleep, clutching their prizes and tiny dolls and clenched fists behind their little chintz curtains.

*   *   *   *   *   *   *

In the older wards the children were gathered round the tall fender in the fire-light, chattering to one another, the little blind boy lying flat on the floor, the little white wan girl in her night-cap sitting in a tiny wicker-chair, so still, so touchingly tranquil, that it gave one a pang to **see**. A sweet-faced rosy little maiden, with great brown eyes, is lying paralyzed on her back in her crib.

"I don't want to go home," said one little fellow who had come from his back-kitchen home to be cured and dipped in these healing waters. "I likes being here best."

"I'm going home," said the little blind boy, kicking on the floor. "I'm going home to-morrow, I am."

"He is always saying that," laughed the other children.

"I have been here—oh, a very long time," said a tall boy called Georgy: "oh, a long time; **but I don't remember. I have** been here six **weeks, I think."**

"He has been here the longest," said the little children, wagging their heads; "longer nor any one."

"Do you like this better than school, David?" I asked one of them.

David nods and nods. "Ye-es, ma'am," says he. All the little children laugh.

"He don't want to go home," says a little girl, sitting up in her crib.

They are very happy, poor little souls! and it is not while they are in the hospital that one is sorry for them. The lady who has charge of them all says the hardest part is sending them away; but others are waiting, and they must go in turn. She amused me by describing their bewilderment sometimes when they come, at the sight of the baths and the water provided. They have never even heard of such things at home, and can not make them out. Their complaints are, many of them, caused by sheer neglect and want of cleanliness; and yet, how can it be helped? A man came to the hospital the other day; he had eight children, no work, a wife sick in a hospital, and one child very ill at home. David is one of the seven in a dark kitchen, where he lives with a mangle, a sick father, a thriftless mother. What chance have the poor little children? The mangle can not do every **thing.** It is only a mangle, and it could not

feed and clothe nine people, though it went on of its own accord turning from one year's end to another.

"It is not only that the children are generally cured when they come here," said Miss S——, "but they learn things which they never forget. They are taught little prayers; they get notions of order and cleanliness. One little girl said she should go home and teach the others all she had learned. She came from a miserable place, poor little thing. One would be glad to think that any good influences might follow the children after they have left us."

For the first time they hear of something besides the squalid commonplaces of their daily lives. This hospital is doing true and good work in its district: one can only hope that others in their places may rise up, and that there may be more and more kind teaching and comfort in store for all poor little children, and more and more kind hands to succor them, and friendly roofs to shelter them from the blast.

The ladies who superintend the children's hospital are trying an experiment just now. They want to establish a fever cottage somewhere in the country, to which they may send the poor little patients who can not of necessity be let into their wards.

Every one knows the Great Parent Hospital in Ormond Street. Yesterday I heard some one speaking of a little offshoot in Queen's Square, founded by two ladies who take in children afflicted with hip disease—an illness so tedious and so long that the other hospitals are obliged to refuse them admittance. In town and country villages and seaside places people are at work, and sisters of charity of one sort or another (for it is not the quilled cap which makes the difference) are nursing and tending their little patients, stirred by the same gentle, natural impulse which makes real mothers love their little ones with an anxious pain and love and fear, in which some women find the greatest happiness which this world can bestow. At Brighton there is more than one little home for sick children. One specially in Montpellier Road, for little convalescents, where the care is so wise and tender, that people who like myself go to see, come away with a real friendship and love for the little place.

If some mighty spirit were to give us the gift of seeing into the lives of the people who are passing like ourselves through the slush and mud and dim vapors of a London winter, we might well be scared, we middle, respectable classes, hurrying along from one comfortable fire-lit world to another—worlds closed in by curtains and shutters, warmed by fires and carpets, steaming with the flavor of good things. We go out into the streets, and hurry back again to our snug paradises, where white-robed houris are singing and playing upon grand pianos with golden strings, where ministering butlers and waiters and parlor-maids are pouring claret into thin glasses that sparkle, where tables are spread à la Russe with fruit and with flowers, and the faithful are feasting in companies of six, eight, and ten at this season of the year. As they feast they are reclining upon seats of mahogany and rosewood, and discoursing of past and future deeds. Shining is the broadcloth, spotless the white linen; veils and crowns are set on the heads of the matrons, and wreaths lie on the maidens' heavy tresses that are platted and stained to gold; and soft words are uttered, and smoking viands pass round between the pauses of the conversation. But speaking seriously, it seems almost impossible to some of us living in a certain fashion to realize the state of mind in which certain other people alongside are existing — people whose chief possessions are a few rags perhaps, a body to hunger and weary with, aching feet to tramp along the pavement, the fierce winds blowing at the corners, the gusts of rain, and the piled-up mud in the streets. The wet railings to lean against are theirs too, a curb-stone perhaps to rest upon, and the bitter fruits of the knowledge of hunger, of patience, of utter weariness, of the length of the night.

"I dare say you don't know what it is to walk about all night long," a woman said to me one day not long ago; and her eyes filled up with tears as she spoke quietly in a sort of whisper. "I walked about three nights this week," she said, "till a person I met took pity on me, and let me into her room. She was only a poor woman; not a lady," the woman said. "She told me to come here." "Here" was the women's ward in the Newport Market Refuge, a long room, with slender iron pillars, and a double row of narrow beds on either side of the middle passage. The beds were wooden frames stretched with sacking, and fastened to the wall. By each bed a woman was standing, waiting while some one at the far end of the room was busily preparing bowls of hot coffee and dividing hunches of white bread. One or two of the women looked scared and sad, but not all. Till this person spoke to me, I should never have guessed how the week had passed for her, nor what straits she was in. I had even wondered to see her there, for her appearance was decent and respectable, and her face looked quiet and cheerful; only, when she answered me, her eyes filled with tears, and her voice failed. This was the only woman to whom I spoke; but I suppose there were some thirty of them in the long room, who had just been let in out of the rain.

I had come a long way, and the horse had struggled and stumbled through the black, twinkling mud, for it was dark and wet with rain, this London winter's evening; dim crowds were flitting and hurrying along shadowy pavements that all the flaming gas-becks in the shop-fronts were not enough to lighten; no sky overhead, no tops to the houses, but a dense Christmas vapor dripping upon the heads of the passers-by. We turned from gas to utter blackness out of the long street which had put me in mind of some foreign street for odd

stores, tobacco, bird-cages, jewelry-shops; and then we jolted into dark and lonely places where no lights were shining, and no one passed. The cab stopped, and the man asked me which was the way to go. A small shrill ghost appearing in a door-way, and hearing us talk of the Newport Refuge, screamed out to us to "go ba-ack, turn to the roight, and then to the lef' agin;" and then, in another gloom, the stumbling horse stopped once more, and the driver opened the door of the cab. The rain was beginning to cease, but the drops still dripped as I stood in the middle of a muddy sheet to which I could see no shore. As well as I could make out, we were in a narrow sort of court-passage opening into a wider court, with tall tenements inclosing it. One or two people were standing round about something that looked like a big barn-door half open. "In there, missus," said a man with a pipe; and so out of the darkness I stumbled through the barn-door.

I was a little bewildered after my long drive by what seemed at first a dazzle of light, a din of voices, a sudden strumming of distant music. . . . . I think I went up some steps. I saw a staircase, a passage, in which was a lighted window, and a man's face looking out over some books. A woman was standing at the window, a great round clock was ticking, and its hands were pointing to ten minutes past five. I asked the porter if this was the Refuge, and if the people were all in for the night? Yes, they were all come, some sixty of them, out of the street. "We let them in early to-night," said the man at the window, "because of the rain."

I myself was glad enough to get under shelter. I don't know how I should have felt if I had been walking about all day and all the night before, and all the day before that, and the night before that again, in the slough without, as some of the people had done who were just admitted. If I had come to ask for a night's lodging, the man at the window would have asked me my name, what I worked at, where I slept the night before. The other woman standing beside me said she made envelopes, had been turned off some weeks, meant to go to this place and that in the morning to ask for work; had tried all day long, and all the shops, and didn't know what she should do.

"There is no reason why you should not find employment," said the man at the window. "People write as many letters in winter as in summer. You should ask at the manufactories instead of going to the shops. There is a man here to-night who had given up asking in despair. I sent him to Messrs. ——, and he got work immediately. You can go up."

One of the committee, who had come in with a dripping umbrella, asked if the woman had ever been there before?

"No," she said, anxiously. "Mrs. So-and-so in the court had took her in last night, and the neighbors told her to come."

The porter nodded, and at this sign of Watchful's the poor Christiana, nothing loath, trudged up to her supper by the wooden stairs that led to the women's dormitories. It was a very simple affair, soon settled, and the man shut up his book for the night, for the people were all in. There they were, two long lines of names all the way down the page.

I followed Mr. C. through the men's ward, which was on the ground-floor. It was like the women's ward, more beds, more suppers preparing, and more weary folks waiting to eat, and rest a little while, before they started again on their rounds. I followed my friend quickly down this middle passage, for the many eyes fixed upon us made us glad to escape. I was surprised by the respectable self-respecting look of most of the refugees. They did not look like people often look in work-houses, with that peculiar half-hopeless, half-cunning face, which is so miserable to see. There were some work-men and others, shabbily dressed, but still respectable, and looking like shopmen or clerks or servants out of place. One boy, I remember, glanced up with a bright handsome Lord Byron face as we passed, and I also carried away the vision of a melancholy old man with a ragged beard, sitting staring before him, with his hands on his knees. After we left the ward, Mr. C. began telling me something of the people who came to it. They were of all trades and callings: clergymen, officers, schoolmasters, a well-known radical reformer, a billiard-marker, a surgeon. In last year's list I see fifty-one tailors and sixteen waiters were admitted. They come in for a night or two, or stay on longer if there seems any reason for it, or chance of employment. To some of us it may seem sad to read that no less than sixty-five soldiers took refuge in the ward last year, and that no other calling has sent so many applicants for relief. "Of all who come," said Watchful, "they are the most difficult to provide for. We got one a situation in a county jail the other day; but it is not always that we can help them." Men of war, mulcted of their arms, discharged before they have served their time, knowing no trade, sick, helpless. It seems a hard fate enough. I heard of some poor invalided fellows coming back from India the other day, discharged, in high spirits at the prospect of getting away and seeing their friends and homes again. "Good-bye, you Asiatics!" one of them shouted, waving his cap, as the train set off. The farewells are cheerful, perhaps, but the welcomes awaiting these poor men at their journeys' end are not cheering to contemplate. Some of these soldiers are discharged for bad conduct, but others have sad stories to tell. I could not help wondering the other night, as I talked to my guide, who there was among the men of peace ready to fight their battles.

Here, in the Newport Refuge, many got helped, one way and another. Trouble and time are given ungrudgingly by the committee, by the people upon the establishment, and by the kindest of sisters, in her nice gray dress and white cap. This lady is in charge of the women's department. She sits in her quaint dark room, leading out of the women's sleeping-ward, with its glass doors opening every instant to admit one or other person — application, complaint, inquiry, petition. The women come, the boys come, the committee comes, and its wives and stray outsiders like myself; but there is a method in all these comings and goings, a meaning and an unaffected kindness and good fellowship that impress one irresistibly. The sister told me to go and see the boys' refuge, and the kitchen, where all the suppers were preparing. It was a large kitchen on the ground-floor, with cocoa-nut matting and generous-looking pans and coppers, and a white cook watching the coffee-pots that were just beginning to boil.

The Newport Refuge not only takes in people to sleep for the night and cooks their supper for them, but there are also some small folks whom it keeps altogether—certain homeless boys, who live in the old house, and who are taught and fed, and finally started in life from this curious busy hive of a home. We went wandering among the dark passages of this ancient high-roofed barn, this foggy, flaring, winter's night. A painter dealing in lights and sudden glooms might have found more than one subject for his art. Through an open door I caught sight of a little group of tailors at work. They were in a long low play-room, where I have been amused to see the boys darting about in the twilight like imps at play, shouting, galloping, gambolling. Now the little imps were hard at work in a bright corner of the dark room, squatting cross-legged in a circle on the floor, round a tall lamp, and demurely stitching at the rents and patches in their various garments. Gray walls, gray boys, with their little brown faces, a black master; strongly marked shadows and lights, a red handkerchief tied round a boy's neck—it does not take much to make up a harmonious picture. The little fellows were unconscious of pictorial effect as they sat cobbling and mending a few of the tears and tatters that exist in this seam-ripped world. The triumph of the tailors was a grand pair of trousers that one of the little fellows had achieved, with all the buttons gleaming brass. The conqueror himself, I believe, was dispatched to fetch the garment, which was displayed before us—the banner of the industrious little phalanx at our feet. The master-tailor and the committee-man had a little talk together, while I watched the boys' youthful fingers sticking in stitches with much application, but some uncertainty. So-and-so was to be apprenticed, such an one had sent a good account of himself, another wanted to give up tailoring altogether; and when the little consultation was over we left the tailors, and climbed a winding stair. It seemed to lead us into the kingdom of boys. A cheerful jingle of sounds, scrapings, boyish voices, met us from above, from below; small clumping steps and echoes; boys flying up and down, disappearing through doors. In one room by the light of a blazing fire, a number of little fellows were trolling out a Christmas hymn, at the pitch of their childish voices. In the intervals of this hymn came a brilliant accompaniment from above of I don't know what trumpets, trombones, flutes, executing some martial measure. The two strains went on quite independently of each other, and making noise enough, each in its own place, to deafen the auditors and drown every other sound.

One of the choristers was pointed to by the umbrella, and beckoned off to come and show us the sleeping-ward, where the boys each possess a box, a suit of Sunday-clothes, a bed, a gray blanket and a red one, and a nice little pair of sheets, all doubled up like a roly-poly pudding, neatly cut through the middle.

The young chorister proceeded to make his bed very nicely and expeditiously. While he was accomplishing this little task, I saw the grand pair of trowsers being carefully put away in the box of their fortunate possessor.

Up stairs, in a sort of loft, where the bandsmen were practising, while the master beat time energetically, the little musicians puffed and blew at enormous instruments, by the music on the stands before them. The little fellows seemed to me like all the champions of Christendom manfully struggling with vomiting monsters and yawning dragons. One boy was solemnly puffing away at an ophicleide quite as big as he was, with an enormous proboscis that seemed ready to gobble him up each time it advanced; others gallantly grasped writhing brass serpents; a rosy-cheeked infant was playing on the flute, a boy on a bench was reading a song-book, a charwoman was scrubbing the floor. The sister, in her quaint gray gown, came up the stairs, and stood smiling at the overflowing music, and beckoning to us: for we could not hear her speak in the din of their youthful lungs and violent trumpets and trombones. The sister wanted us to come to the shoemakers, before they left off work.

So we left the musicians, playing their triumphant march. Well may they play it, fortunate little musicians, rescued from the darkness without, where no stars are shining, and monsters, not harmless and tamable like these, are wandering ready to make a prey of children and weakness and helpless things, vainly struggling against the dark and deadly powers of ignorance and want.

The little shoemakers were finishing for the day. They lived at the other end of the building in a cell all to themselves. There was a kind, eager young master to direct them; there were more gas-becks, more lights and shadows, brown-faced boys, drills and lasts, very thick little boots on the floor, with nails, drills, and shapes, and abundant energy. The sister laughed, seeing the little fellows' desperate efforts. "Look at Carter," she said, "how hard he is working!" Carter grinned, but did not look up, and tugged away at his leather thongs more vigorously than ever. They offered to make me a pair of shoes. They had made some for the sister already. This very day a friend has consented to be measured for a pair of hobnailed boots. As we were finding our way down stairs back to the sister's room again, we began to meet trays of food, like trays in a pantomime, coming up apparently of their own accord. "Go down, trays," cried the sister, and the slices of bread, the mugs, etc., began slowly to descend again.

The sister told me that the little bandsman I had seen with the flute was the son of a soldier at the Cape, who had brought him to the Home before he left, and who regularly paid for him out of his earnings, and wished that he should be brought up a bandsman. Some children are drafted on to other institutions; some are apprenticed. Grown-up people are helped one way and another. I heard of a cook who had no clothes, but who knew of work. This man was given clothes, and allowed to live there long enough to save a few shillings out of his wages, so as to redeem his things and set up in a lodging for himself. The report tells of newspaper editors and musicians helped on to work. Servants come in great straits, and they, too, are assisted.

I have not space to set down all the ways and means, and people, and wants, and supplies, that are brought together here.

It is pleasant to come away from these refuges and hospitals with a remembrance of children's laughter in the twilight, and voices at play, of troubles quieted, of the sick and wounded made whole, of a divine light of hope and love shining upon the arid and blighted vineyard, and the weary or failing laborers at work among the vines.

THE END.